# THE KNIGHTS OF ECHOES COVE BOXSET

---

BOOKS 1-4

PLUS REBEL HEART & BONUS SCENES

LILY WILDHART

Published by Bright Lights Publishing Ltd



Editor: Encompass Press, LLC
Proofreader: Sassi's Editing Services
Interior Design: Wild Elegance Formatting

The Knights of Echoes Cove Boxset - 1st ed

# SERIES PLAYLIST

Most Girls - Hailee Steinfeld
Hailey - WRENN
Better Than Revenge - Taylor Swift
All the Fucking Time - Loote
Skin - Sabrina Carpenter
Fuck You - Don Vedda
STAY - The Kid LAROI & Justin Bieber
Hoodie - Hey Violet
Sex With Me - TRAMP STAMPS
Beautiful Way - You Me At Six
Good 4 u - Olivia Rodrigo
Last Night's Mascara - Brynn Cartelli
Fuck Being Sober - Annika Wells
She's So Gone - Naomi Scott
Karma - MOD SUN
Queen - Loren Gray
You Don't Own Me - SAY GRACE & G-Eazy
Say Your Prayer - Blithe
Don't Need A Man - Liv Grace Blue
Survivor - 2WEI & Edda Hayes
X Gon' Give It To Ya - DMX
Boss Bitch - Doja Cat
I Am Defiant - The Seige
I'd Rather Die - TRAMP STAMPS
Sociopath - Olivia O'Brien
Future Ex - Abigail Barlow & Ariza
Deal with it - Ashnikko & Kellis

S.L.U.T - Bea Miller
Kiss or Kill - Stela Cole
Intimidate You - Bloom Line & Brooke Alexx
Bitchcraft - Jax
Lost Without You - Freya Ridings
Unthinkable - Cloudy June
Only Be Mine - Arrows in Action
Never Ending Nightmare - Citizen Soldier & Kellin Quinn
PSYCHOLOGICAL WAR - RORY
What the Stars See - Cassadee Pope
again&again - Against The Current
Just My Type - Taylor Bickett
You Oughta Know - Gabbie Hanna
Murder Party - NOT THE MAIN CHARACTERS
Playing with Fire - Sam Tinnesz
This Little Girl - Cady Groves
Cravin' - Stileto
Fake - The Tech Thieves
Serial Killer - Moncrieff
Back to You - Taylor Acorn
Middle Finger - Bohnes
Panic Room - Au/Ra
Control - Halsey
Uncomfortably Numb - Arrors in Action & Taylor Acorn
Prom Queen - Molly Kate Kestner
Partners in Crime - Set It Off
Saints - Echo
Dance in the Dark - Au/Ra
Who Am I - Besomorph
I Love You's - Hailee Steinfeld
I Fall Apart - Living in Fiction
The Diary of Jane - Breaking Benjamin
Wildest Dreams - Taylor Swift
Back to You - Taylor Acorn
Burn It All Down - PVRIS
Favourite Place - All Time Low
Strangers - Yours Truly
Heavenly - Broadside
Orchestra - Drew Ryn
That Way - Tate McRae
Foolish Believer - Broadside
When The Sky Falls Down - Yours Truly
Stitch Me Up - Point North
Nothing Left to Lose - Point North
CWJBHN - Jake Scott
I Wanted You - McKenna Breinholt

When You're Around - Jutes
Figure You Out - VOILA
Someone Else - Loveless
Lock Me Up - Paloma
Left You Instead - Taylor Acorn
Teardrops - Bring Me The Horizon
Can You Feel My Heart - Bring Me The Horizon
Me Against Myself - Wage War
Dark Can Be Beautiful - Alec Chambers
Legends Never Die - Against the Current
Carry On - Falling In Reverse
Going Ghost - Jeris Johnson
Crash and Burn - Maggie Lindemann
Blink-182&u - Cali Rodi
Fall to Pieces - Pale Waves
Only Place I Call Home - Every Avenue
My Happy Ending - Avril Lavigne
Bring Me to Life - Evanescence
Welcome to the Black Parade - My Chemical Romance
Face Down - The Red Jumpsuit Apparatus
Miss Murder - AFI
Bite Me - Avril Lavigne
Street Lightning - The Summer Set
Lately - Future Palace
Dangerous Woman - Ariana Grande
As You Leave - Canaan Cox
Take on the World - You Me at Six
Hell and Back - Self Deception
I'll Be - Edwin McCain
Shivers - Ed Sheeran
Stay - Justin Bieber and The Kid Laroi

# CONTENT WARNING

This book is a **dark**, high school, bully, why choose romance.
It contains scenes and references of abuse/sexual assault, assault and suicide that some readers may find triggering, along with graphic sex scenes, cursing and violence.

*Please note: The other book worlds referred to within this series were done so with permission from the authors. Those references are - The Allstars - from Toxic Creek by KC Kean, and Happily Adams After - from Banner Hill by Cassie James. There are no other crossovers from other authors, though this world* does link with *The Saints of Serenity Falls & The Secrets We Keep by Lily Wildhart.*

# TORMENTED ROYAL

THE KNIGHTS OF ECHOES COVE

LILY WILDHART

*I don't need you to light up my world.*
*Just sit with me in the dark.*

UNKNOWN

# CHAPTER ONE

"Rise and shine, princess." The snicker makes me stir, but it's the icy water raining down on me that wakes me right the hell up.

"What the fuck?!" My shout comes out half choked as I struggle to breathe against the stream of freezing cold water raining down on my face.

"Welcome back to Echoes Cove, Octavia. You may be the nation's Princess to the rest of the world, but here, I'm the Queen. You better not forget it." My vapid bitch cousin, Blair, flicks her long, blonde hair over her shoulder before spinning and leaving the pool house I'm currently calling home.

I lie back down on the wet sheets, in a pool of icy water, and curse my dad for being so fucking selfish once again. Thanks to him, I'm trapped in Echoes Cove for senior year, and I am obviously not wanted around here, by anyone. Unfortunately for everyone involved, I'm trapped in this hellhole for at least ten more months until I graduate. My eighteenth birthday cannot get here fast enough, at least then I can move out of this house of horrors.

Taking a deep breath, I push myself up and out of bed, not caring about my wet hair or pajamas, and strip the bed. I know my aunt and uncle have staff for this sort of thing, but one, it's so not cool to leave this kind of mess for someone else; and two, I want the mattress to actually be dry when I go to sleep tonight. Luckily, the bed is in the middle of the room, so if I keep the curtains open it should heat up plenty and dry everything out.

The pool house, where I've been shoved like a toy no one wants to play with, is deceptively big. I have my own kitchenette—not that I can cook to save my life, but I keep the mini fridge stocked with peach iced tea, and all the things I need to bake red velvet cupcakes in the cupboards, should the urge hit me. The headboard of the bed sits against the counter, which is convenient when I want water but can't be bothered to get out of bed, and there's a small sofa to the left of it where there is a small living space. Two of the walls are basically just giant panes of glass, so it looks bigger than it is. Luckily, the curtains in here are all blackout, so I can get some half decent sleep.

Once I've wrestled the sheets into the hamper, I take a deep breath and repeat the mantra that has gotten me through the past few weeks.

*I can get through this. It's just under a year. I can survive this.*

I pull my wet, chestnut-brown hair into a messy bun, pull on some dry yoga pants, pocket my earpods, and trudge over to the main house, wet t-shirt and all. I don't have any fucks left to give about what the people in there might think of me. Thankfully, the blistering summer heat means I won't be cold or wet for long.

"Good morning, Miss Royal. How are you this morning?" Pattie, my aunt and uncle's cook, cleaner, and well, general caretaker, smiles at me warmly as I enter the kitchen from the back of the house. Her smile drops when she takes in my appearance, but I shake my head.

"I'm fine." I give her a tight smile, and hope the shake of my head is enough to keep her from peppering me with questions as she has done every morning since I arrived. My father's death was originally ruled as suspicious, and everyone seems to have their own opinions on that. Despite my requests not to talk about it, everyone wants to tell me their theories, even though that ruling was overturned. It took two weeks before they deemed it a suicide, during which I stayed with Mac and the rest of the team. My found family. But after the cremation, and reading of the Will, child services dragged me here despite my protests.

Out of everyone in this place, Pattie's been the nicest since I arrived two weeks ago, though the bar here has been set pretty low. But she, at least, has treated me like an actual human being.

"If you're sure." She frowns as she looks me up and down again, but then forces a smile as I shift from foot to foot and try to look anywhere but directly at her friendly face. "Food is on the table in the breakfast room. If you need anything else, please let me know."

"Thank you, Pattie." I turn and head toward the breakfast room, trying not to laugh. Who the fuck has a room just for breakfast anyway? This McMansion is beyond insane, and for the umpteenth time, I can't help but be kind of glad I'm in the pool house. At least I can't get lost out there.

"Good morning, Octavia." My aunt's shrill voice makes me wince. Fuck ever having a hangover around her. Her voice is squeakier than a fucking dog toy. "I assume from your current state, you fell into the pool on your way to the house?"

Blair snickers from her chair, hiding it terribly as a cough, but my aunt and uncle are too busy scowling at me to notice. Though my aunt has had so much work done, it's hard to tell if she's frowning at me or if that's just how she looks now. Almost everything about her is devoid of life and emotion. Even her platinum hair hangs straight and dead.

My uncle brings his newspaper back in front of his potbelly and rounded face, his disapproval very much evident from the narrow-eyed look he gave me. Though his sparse hair doesn't exactly help the thinning look, his dark combover just makes me laugh. "In the future, I expect you to be dressed before you come for breakfast. I don't care how you lived when you were with your father. While you're living in our house, you'll follow our rules."

"Sure thing, Uncle Nate." I sigh as I slip into the spare chair opposite Blair. Her smug look is almost enough to make me lose my appetite, but I'm not about to give up the joy of food because of her.

"You need to go to the office when you get to the school," Aunt Vivienne starts, and I clench my jaw in preparation for the deluge of bullshit that's getting ready to spew from her lips. "The office administrator will have your schedule and locker designation for you. Your uniform is hanging in your closet, Pattie collected it for you on Friday… And before I forget, you haven't sent over your rent payment. I suggest speaking to your bank and having a regular payment set up so we don't have any issues while you're staying here."

"Yes, Aunt Vivienne," I grind out. Paying them rent is my penance for my father leaving everything he had to me, with no limitation and no guardian to watch my money until I turn eighteen. Well, so long as I graduate ECP with a 4.0 GPA, but that's beside the point. Hell, the only reason I'm staying here is because of the clause in my father's Will, stating I must actually reside with my guardian until I come of legal age. Stupid fucking clause if you ask me, since I'm financially independent, but what's a girl to do? "I thought I'd have to meet with the guidance counselor to pick my classes?"

She looks down her nose at me and tuts. "If you'd paid any attention to the brochures I put in the pool house, you'd know that isn't how things work at Echoes Cove Prep. Your classes are picked in advance so they can build the schedule. You were a late enrollment, so you should be thankful you have a spot there at all."

I nod and take a deep breath, pushing down all the spiteful comments that threaten to rise. I reach for a bagel, and Vivienne clucks, looking down her nose at me with a quirked eyebrow. Got to love the disapproval coming from her in waves.

"Carbs will do horrible things to your hips, Octavia," she scolds, and I roll my eyes, slathering the bagel in cream cheese and taking a bite anyway. I'll be damned if I'm letting these assholes dictate any more of my life to me than they already have power to. I'll eat whatever the hell I want.

"She's a lost cause, Mother. I mean, just look at her. She's not going to fit in at school at all. I don't understand why she's coming to the prep anyway. I'm sure Octavia would feel much more comfortable at public school," Blair whines. She makes it out like she's doing me a favor, but if her little show this morning is anything to go by, she doesn't want me anywhere near her school. I have no idea why, though. The last thing on Earth I want is her perceived crown. She can keep it. Popularity contests don't interest me in the slightest. I'd rather have a small group of true friends than the masses kissing my feet just because they feel like they should. Life with my dad on the road taught me that much. Fake friends are not the way forward.

I finish my bagel, drowning out their inane drivel by slipping one of my ear pods from my pocket into my ear. If nothing else, I will always be a child of music. Music is my higher power—my soul needs it to survive. Once I finish my food, I push away from the table, not saying a word since no one is paying attention to their newest inconvenience anyway, and head back to the pool house to find my uniform. Maybe Echoes Cove Prep won't be worse than being here with a group of people who couldn't feel any less like a functional, loving family.

I snort. *Yeah right.* Here, at the house, there's only Blair. At school, there will be an entire fucking herd of mini-Blairs. Once upon a time, I went to school with most of these people, but that's before my mom split and my dad hit the big time with his music. Both of their families were richer than God, though after my mom left, they disowned us both. Thankfully Dad had his own money, so life wasn't turned upside down anymore than it already had been. When we went on the road, he had huge arguments with my grandparents, but I was never close to them. They died not long after we left… It feels like a lifetime ago now.

I'm not the same person I was back then, and I don't expect anyone else to be either. Life on the road, with my dad, his band, the roadies… They are my people. They helped shape me into the person I am today, and I'm glad. I think if I'd grown up here, I'd be just like Blair, and the thought alone makes me want to yeet myself through a plate glass window.

After going back to the pool house, I lock the doors from the inside, double checking them since I'm pretty sure I locked them last night and Blair still got in. Once I know it's secure, I head toward the shower. The bathroom is one of the only redeemable qualities about being forced to live here. The shower is legit becoming my fortress of solitude. I never want to leave. After living in hotels and on a tour bus for years, a good shower is something I've learned to appreciate.

I don't rush. It's just fucking school, and I've never really been a high maintenance kind of girl, so why be in a hurry? I smother my hair in my honey and vanilla shampoo that I discovered when I was in the UK, and I refuse to ever go back. When I put the conditioner on, I use my honey soap that I ship in from Marseille. It's to die for, and I just adore the smell. I enjoy the solace of my morning, knowing that once I leave here, my peace isn't likely to last.

I blow out my dark hair, which falls dead straight down to my waist, though the only real attention I pay styling is to my bangs. My hair is pretty thick, so it requires a little wrangling to make my bangs look awesome. Once my hair is done, I head to the closet, but I don't find the uniform Pattie supposedly left for me. I swear to God, if Blair took it to fuck with me, I'm not afraid of punching her right in her new nose.

I close the empty closet door and open the door next to it—another fucking closet—and find the uniforms. Five of them. At least that's one for each day I guess. Who needs this much space for clothes? I'm used to living out of a suitcase… Tour life isn't as glamorous as people think. I'm not sure I've ever had or needed enough clothes to fill one of these closets, let alone two. Pulling the protective, plastic bag from the hanger, I take in the uniform.

The skirt is black and white plaid, which comes with thigh high socks and a starched white shirt. Along with them is a black and white neckerchief thing and a fitted black blazer, both embroidered with the school crest which has accents of a teal green… Someone fucking save me. There's a note taped to the hanger that catches my eye.

*Shoe choice is optional.*

*However, I suggest a pair of Mary Janes or something equally as sophisticated.*

My aunt can choke on a dick.

If I have to wear this get up, and the shoe choice is optional, I'm wearing my Chucks. I pull on the excuse of a uniform and groan as I take in my reflection. I knew it was going to be bad, but holy fuck. I spin around and face-palm. My ass is practically on show with how short this stupid skirt is, like I know I have curves, and I've always loved them, but damn. I look like something out of a fucking porn movie.

Please let this be the worst part of my day…

---

Whispers follow me as I walk from my rental car toward the main doors of Echoes Cove Prep. At this point in my life, rumors and gossip are nothing new. Being the daughter of Stone Royal means this stuff has followed me for almost my entire life. He was the nation's King, and I was their Princess. Whispers were part of the territory.

Except these whispers… They have nothing to do with my old life. These whispers have everything to do with me being back here at Echoes Cove Prep for my senior year. It's not hard to overhear everyone talking about me. Most of it isn't true, so the whispers of whore and slut don't bother me so much. It's the whispers about my dad that sting. I should've known that Echoes Cove would have more gossip than Page Six.

It's obvious from the sneers and lewd glances that these people don't want me here any more than I want to be here. I wonder once again why my dad thought that this would be a good idea, what it was that made him put that stipulation in his Will. There are better schools in the world than ECP, so why send me back to this pit of despair?

The whispers of why I'm back just add to my want to be anywhere but here. The jealousy from having full access to my inheritance seems to be another thing that fuels the rumor mill.

*"I heard she fucked her lawyer to get him to change her dad's Will and forge the signature."*

*"I heard she offed her dad just for the money."*

*"Well, Becky heard her dad didn't even commit suicide. It was a murder cover up. I bet she did it."*

I roll my eyes. The things people say blow my mind, but I know the truth, so I try not to let it get to me. They might not want me here, and honestly? I would have much rather spent the year homeschooling and continuing to travel, so the feeling is more than mutual. Plus, I'm a little worried about how well I'm going to fare in traditional schooling compared to homeschooling as it is.

I know I'm not like a lot of the trust fund babies here, thanks to my dad. While most of them will have limits to what they can access in their trust funds, I don't… And I'll never, ever have to worry about money again, so long as I stick to the stipulations in the Will, and I fully intend on doing that. All that money is one hell of a point of contention with my aunt and uncle. Apparently, despite the mansion on Ballers' Row and the fact that they're both from what Aunt Vivienne likes to call 'old money,' plus the fact that Uncle Nate is a hugely successful investment banker, I'm still an incredible drain on their resources.

Yeah, that was a fun conversation. The one where they told me I'd have to pay my way because they couldn't possibly take me in, out of the goodness of their hearts. It doesn't really bother me, though. Money isn't everything… I'd much rather have one last day with Dad, doing all of our favorite things. Granted, if I said that out loud around here, I'd probably be shot.

I shake my head to clear the thought and focus on the front of the school as I approach. It looks like the type of school you see on TV with the pale stone arch around the large main entry doors. The year the school was founded along with the school crest—a shield with a horse and swords, topped with a crown, surrounded by flora—is engraved at the apex of the arch, just the way I remember it. The red brick exterior is still covered with ivy, and it screams money as much now as it did the last time I walked these halls. It might only be a three-story building, but it's so fucking imposing. It all feels like a lie. This isn't a place where dreams come to thrive. It's where they go to die.

I watch the people around me and wish I was anywhere but here. Everyone around here is so fake, and despite how I grew up—or maybe because of it—fake is everything I despise.

These people… Well, they were my people once upon a time, but everything I've seen in the few weeks I've been back in Echoes Cove tells me that either I'm not the same person I was when I left, or they aren't. My cousin, who was once practically my sister, is nothing short of a vapid bitch from hell, and my once three best girlfriends… Well, from what I've heard from Blair, they're her friends now and every bit like her.

That's before I even think about the boys who were once my rocks… my saviors. If they're anything like Blair has said, then everything about being back here is going to suck. I haven't heard from any of them since I got back into town, and Blair made it clear to me that I was *persona-non-grata* to them. I hate that she might be right, but if they're anything like I've heard, then maybe it's for the best. It seems I'm not the only one who's changed in the last five years.

Thankfully, I've been able to hide out in the pool house since coming back to Echoes Cove. I've been able to avoid the truth of my new reality, but today there's no escaping the facts of it all. Now I'm here, ass deep in it and wishing I was anywhere else.

I try to pull down the skirt of this stupid-ass uniform while I walk, ignoring everyone, and head to the office to pick up my schedule and locker assignment. How this skirt, along with the thigh high socks, can be considered a demure school uniform is completely beyond me. My best guess is that the principal is a perv. That or whoever is pulling his strings likes this ridiculous outfit… and is also a perv. My shirt is almost too tight around the girls, and I'm pretty sure the outline of my bra is on full show, and the blazer is definitely a slim fit too. I look fucking ridiculous. I would kill for my jeans, band tees, and leather jacket back.

I push open the door to the office to find an older, gray-haired woman sitting behind a desk in an excessively lush office. You'd think the wood paneling would be enough, but no. There are gold accents on everything, and a mass of plants that makes me feel like I've stepped into an alternate world entirely. Maybe I'm in the wrong place.

"Hello, dear, can I help you?" She looks me up and down, her bright and sparkly voice at odds with the resting bitch face she looks at me with.

"My name is Octavia Royal. I just started here and was told this is where I should come for my class schedule and locker assignment."

"Oh yes, I should have known. We don't get new students very often at all. Please take a seat, and I'll get your things." I glance over my shoulder as she points, spotting a shiny, black leather sofa. Taking a seat, I try not to wince at the chill of the leather on the back of my thighs. *Stupid fucking skirt.*

She gets up and heads into one of what I'm assuming are smaller offices just as the door to the principal's office opens. My stomach drops. I swear to fuck, I didn't think my day could get any worse, and yet here we are. I knew I'd see one of them at some point, the school isn't big enough for me to avoid them for long, but to see him before my day even starts? It feels like a bad omen.

Maverick Riley walks out of the door, flicking his messy brown hair out of his eyes, swagger on point like he's walking a fucking runway. If it wasn't for the twisted grin on his face, I'd think he was actually in trouble; but when the principal shows his sweaty face, I know that's far from the truth. "It was good doing business with you, teach. Just remember the rules, and this year will go just fine."

That's when he sees me, and his twisted grin turns to nothing. His dark brown eyes look at me as if he can see all the way through to my very soul. If my icy wake up call this morning hadn't already chilled me to the bone, his look would freeze my black little heart. "You're back."

I roll my eyes because, well done, Sherlock Holmes. "Obviously."

"I didn't think you'd be brave enough to actually do it. Not after the way you ran away," he says, his empty voice giving me goosebumps as he looks me over. I try not to react to the boy who was my best friend once upon a time. Well… one of my best friends. Especially when I have no idea what he's going on about. "Guess I'll be seeing you, princess."

His dismissal stings as he saunters out of the office. His tall, lean form shouldn't be so fluid and graceful, yet somehow he pulls it off with an insane amount of swagger.

I didn't expect things to go back to how they were, but to be treated like we have no history? Yeah, that cuts deep.

The office door closes behind him just as the older woman returns to her desk. I brush off the interaction, instead taking note of the principal retreating back into his office. That only holds my attention for a second because I can't get Maverick off of my mind. Why was he so cold in the short period of time we were in the office together? And what did he mean that I ran away? None of it makes any sense to me. I guess being friends with the guys is off the table, but that's fine. I don't plan on sticking around in Echoes Cove long enough for it to matter too much.

*I hope*.

My phone buzzes, so I slide it out of my pocket as the office lady shuffles through some papers.

**Unknown: Welcome back to Echoes Cove, Miss Royal. We look forward to seeing you soon.**

Yeah, because that isn't weird at all. Nope.

I delete the message with a decisive shake of my head. It's probably just an automated prep school message or some shit. No one really knows that I'm here, especially not anyone who has this number anyway. Though knowing my delightful family, I'm sure Blair probably has it. And considering her feelings toward me, anyone here at Echoes Cove Prep could have it too.

Fuck my life.

"Here you go, dear," the woman finally says, offering me the stack of papers she's been shuffling around on the desk. "Your schedule is as was pre-approved with your guardian. As you know you were a late enrollment, so your guardian picked your classes with the guidance counselor—I know that your old house manager was consulted about your prior education since no one else seemed to have any answers. It's all locked in now, so let's hope it's all okay." She smiles at me softly, but it doesn't bring me joy. I look down at my schedule and roll my eyes. AP English, Business, AP Music, Stats, French, and Gym. This structured schooling thing is going to *hurt*. I can feel it already. But at least Gym is at the end of the day, I guess. "Your locker combination and a map of the school are there too, along with the Code of Conduct, and a few other things. Just have a quick read, sign them, and drop them back here before the end of the day. I've also included your login for ReachMe, it's the school's social media site. Students aren't permitted to use wider social media without permission from a parent or guardian while attending the school, for your safety and the safety of the other students. You will just need to reset your password once you log in. If you don't have any questions, hurry along. You don't want to be late for your first class."

"Thank you." I smile at her, standing with a wince as my skin pulls against the cold leather, and grab the papers before leaving the office. She couldn't be more wrong. I'd love to be late for my first class and every class after that too. Hell, I'd like to just leave and never come back. If it wasn't for my dad's insane demands via his Will, I'd be out of here in a heartbeat, but the thought of giving up my dreams keeps my ass in this school. There's nothing quite like the possibility of my dreams going up in smoke to keep me on track.

I head to my locker. Thankfully, it isn't too far from the office, but unfortunately it is in the main freaking hall as you enter the school. I shove my bag inside before checking my schedule.

"Well, well, well, the princess really is back to grace us with her presence."

I groan into my locker, stomach jumping at the sound of *that* particular voice behind me. I am so not ready to deal with this bullshit right now, but I guess if I get it all out the way now, the rest of my year should be clear. Right?

I turn around to find Maverick standing with Lincoln Saint and Finley Knight.

The three guys who were once the closest people in the world to me are now glaring at me like they would prefer it if I'd died along with my dad—and I have no idea why.

"Do you guys have something important to say? I have to get to class," I huff, refusing to show them just how rattled I really am that they sought me out, especially like this.

After Blair's cruel taunts and my run-in with Maverick earlier, I didn't exactly expect a warm welcome from them, but at least when I left here, we were friends. Sure, it's been a minute, but the icy chill coming from them feels like a little much, though it does match the theme of the day.

Despite the chilly reception, I can't help but give them a quick once over. Lincoln still looks just as dark and broody as he did as a kid. All the way from his jet black hair down to his dark gray eyes, he still looks like a permanent storm cloud. His smile never quite reaches his eyes. And Finley… well, he bulked out more than I would've imagined from when I knew him before. He must live at the gym in his spare time. His blond hair falls into his icy blue eyes as he stares at me, and the wave of chilly energy coming off of them makes the hair on the back of my neck stand on end.

They don't say anything. I expect it from Finley; he's always been the quiet one. Lincoln, though, he's always been the leader of their little Three Musketeers boyband. He sneers at me as Blair and her merry band of bitches appear to stand with the guys. I guess this is the royal court of Echoes Cove Prep.

"Little Miss thinks she's better than all of us. I mean, really, look at those shoes. Maybe her having access to her inheritance is a lie. Who would wear those ratty excuses for shoes? Maybe she's just a gold digger here to snatch up a rich husband." Emma—one of my old friends, now seemingly attached at the hip with Blair—taunts, but I turn back to my locker and sort out my books that were already waiting for me. Got to love private school, I guess.

"I think whoever ordered her uniform thought she was skinnier, look how fat her ass is. It's practically hanging from her skirt. What a whore." I don't know which of them said it this time, but I grit my teeth, trying to ignore the comments and the giggling.

I turn back around to face the three boys who were once my whole world, standing among the snarling girls who look like they'd happily smother me in my sleep just for returning.

The guys still don't say anything, and their silence almost stings more than I imagine their words could. Once upon a time, they would have never iced me out like this or let others speak to me this way. Once upon a time is starting to feel like a lifetime ago. So I slam my locker closed and head toward my first class, feeling their stares burn into the back of my head the entire way.

Stares don't bother me. Those I'm used to, so I shut it all out and keep my head held high.

This is just another day in the life of Octavia Royal.

# CHAPTER TWO

After wandering the halls trying to get my bearings again, I walk into English class, which is mostly full already, to see Blair and one of her vapid besties drooling over two football players. The resulting eye roll is so hard that I worry I won't be able to undo it. I glance around the rest of the room before heading straight for the back corner where there's a seat near the window, next to a girl with the brightest purple hair I've ever seen… And, considering the groupies I've met, that's a feat in itself.

She smiles at me as I slide into the chair, but the teacher walks in the room as I go to say hi, so I shut my mouth and give her an awkward little wave. Her smile only grows in response, and there's just something about her that tells me she and I are going to be friends.

That, or I'm projecting because she's the first person not to treat me like a pariah since I showed up this morning. But I guess there's still time for that to change.

"Morning, ladies and gents, welcome to the start of your senior year. You don't know me, and I don't know you, so let's fix that. I am Ms. Summers, and I'll be your English teacher for the year. Yes I'm new here, but don't think that I'm a pushover. I don't care what you did over the summer, it's done. Right now, we're going to focus on how I can get you out of this classroom and off to the college of your dreams. If I see your phone, it will be confiscated. I am not afraid of detentions, and bribes will not be accepted. Now that that's clear, let's start with your reading list, shall we?"

Oh my God. She's English. My English teacher is English. Brilliant.

*I wonder if she gets hung up on her 'u's?*

The girl next to me snorts, and I bite down on my lip to stop from laughing too. I don't know who this teacher is, but she just became my hands down favorite. I'm also glad I'm not the only new person here so I can avoid the whole new girl introduction thing. I make sure my phone is on silent in my pocket, because I really don't want it to be confiscated by my new favorite teacher, and turn to focus on what she's saying.

Ms. Summers passes around a piece of paper detailing the reading list in full, and I grin as I scan it. I've covered half of these with my tutors already. I knew I was ahead, but I didn't realize just how ahead I was. Maybe, just maybe, this structured schooling thing won't be as bad as I've been worrying about.

"I've highlighted the texts we'll be focusing on, but I suggest reading the others because this is AP English, and you're here for a reason. You'll be doing the first assignment in pairs. Pick wisely because you'll be stuck with each other for the rest of the year."

I guess I'll do some re-reads to refresh my mind on them, but some of my favorites are on this list. Plus, *Wuthering Heights* is highlighted, which only makes my smile widen. I've always been an avid reader, so the thought of re-reads just excites me.

Purple Hair glances over at me, pointing at me then back to herself, and I nod. She might be godawful at English for all I know, but she's a decent human, and that's all I give a fuck about.

"Pick your favorite book on the list and discuss with your partner why you believe it's the best one there. Try to convince them that your book should be at the top of the list." She waves at us to begin before sitting behind her desk, and the room becomes a hive of movement as people shift to sit in their pairs.

"I'm Indi," Purple Hair says, turning to face me, and the first thing I notice is that her big green eyes shine like seas of emerald. She literally looks like a living, alternative pixie. The ring in her nose and lip, plus metal studs all the way up her ears shock me. I'm surprised she gets away with them with the dress code. "And you're Octavia Royal."

Normally someone knowing who I am in this sort of situation would make me uncomfortable, but there's something about her that makes me feel at ease. Maybe it's her laid-back demeanor, or maybe it's that she very obviously doesn't look like one of the ECP drones, but I like her already.

"I swear I'm not like a crazy, psychopath stalker or whatever… Though I will say I listened to your dad somewhat obsessively in my tween years, *but* I'm past that little obsession. Sorry about him by the way. Also, I have really bad verbal diarrhea when I'm nervous, so sorry about the babbling. Oh my God, I need to stop." She covers her mouth with her hands, and I just can't. I laugh quietly at her, feeling my eyes crinkle at the edges as I do.

"Dude, you're fine. Take a breath."

"Sorry, yeah okay. Right, let's start again, shall we? I'm Indi, it's nice to meet you." She puts her hand out for me to shake, looking more than a little awkward, so I take it to make that lost puppy look on her face disappear.

"Octavia, though a lot of my friends just call me V."

"I like that." She grins and scoots her desk closer to mine. It's then I notice the pattern beneath her shirt.

"Midnight Blue?" I ask, and her grin grows.

"I am more than a little obsessed with them. And the lead singer… I swear I'm not into girls, but Jenna B gives me such a lady boner. I can't even."

"Yeah, she's pretty cool." I laugh, relaxing in her presence. She just radiates warmth and joy, and it puts me at ease despite myself. "And they put on an epic show."

"Oh my God, have you met her? I'm going to hyperventilate. You know Jenna B?" She's practically fangirling, and I have to say it's pretty refreshing to find someone in Echoes Cove who isn't so up their own ass that they care about shit like this.

"I've met her a couple times, yeah," I tell her, downplaying how close I am with her. Some people get weird when they know the people I'm friends with. "They were on one of Dad's tours in their early days. They only did about seven shows, but they were amazing even then."

"I am officially going to die. I dub thee my new bestie." She cackles, and Ms. Summers looks over at us, narrowing her eyes at us in a way I do not like. Especially on my first day here.

"Done. Now… let's talk about *Wuthering Heights*." I bring our conversation back to the class because I don't want to fail before I even start. I grin at her, and she shakes her head, feigning a look of betrayal as she lays a dramatic hand over her heart.

"Oh no, you're one of those. I take it back," she scoffs before shaking the list in my face. "How can you pick Catherine over Jane Eyre?"

"Ah, the great sister debate… This is going to be the start of a beautiful friendship."

---

I leave Indi behind and head to Business. I'm early, so I snag a seat in the back corner again and watch as the sea of new and old faces filter into the room. There are more than enough whispers and side glances in my direction for me to know that my return isn't a small thing. I knew it wouldn't be, and that's exactly why I didn't want to come back. Despite the fact that the people I grew up with in Echoes Cove have grown while I've been away, nothing much changes in a town like this. It's still just as judgmental and gossipy as it was when I was a kid.

It's not even that shocking that my mom ran off when she did. While I hate her for abandoning me, I'd like to run the fuck away from here right now too, so a small part of me almost understands her actions.

I sigh at the thought of my mom and pull my phone out, only to see a video waiting for me from Mac, the head of security and a general pillar of my dad's touring team. He basically helped raise me on tour. I find the video along with a few messages from the roadie group chat about how much I'm missed and wishing me luck. My heart pangs with sadness. This group of people are my real family, the people who always had my back no matter what. It may not have been a long time since I've been away from my found family, but fuck I miss them. I send them a message back, telling them just how much I miss them and wish I was back with them before a shadow washes over me.

"You're in my seat." I look up to see Lincoln staring down at me as he towers above. Why the fuck does he have to be so freaking tall?

"There's plenty of others." I jut out my chin, the action practically begging him to fight me over it. I don't know where the defensiveness is coming from, but after my run in with him and the others earlier, it isn't hard to see that we aren't going back to the way things were before I left.

"Mr. Saint, please take a seat, any one will do," the teacher says as he breezes into the room, dropping a ton of textbooks on the table.

Lincoln glares at me before dropping into the seat beside me. Maverick and Finley finish out the back row.

Well, this is going to be fun.

I listen to the teacher drone on, introducing himself and the curriculum for the semester, trying to remember why I picked Business as an elective in homeschooling. I know I'll never start my own label without it, and yeah, I plan on pursuing a Business degree eventually, but fuck. Could this guy's voice be any more monotone? The guy's rocking a monobrow too. I bet his name *is* Mono. Mono fucking Peters.

I look around the room, and spot Brittany, Blair's best bitch, leaning back to talk to Maverick. She flicks her blonde hair at him, and her shirt is undone so far that I can see her bra from here. I roll my eyes when he throws a pen between her tits and she starts to giggle.

I turn my focus back to Mr. Peters and try to pay attention to what he's talking about, but something about his voice just makes me tune out. Maybe I got my hopes up too early. Passing this class is essential. Not just to my GPA, but for my college applications too. I bite my lower lip, trying to pay attention again. I knew structured school was going to be an adjustment, but shit. If the teachers here are all like him, I'm fucked.

"What's wrong, princess? Too good to be here with the rest of us?" Lincoln's voice startles me. The question is quiet enough that I'm pretty sure Mr. Peters didn't hear, but the snickering from the row in front of us tells me that they definitely heard.

I try to ignore him, but I can feel his stare burning into the side of my head. Why the fuck is he being such an asshole? "I just prefer different company."

"Oh, I bet you do. I heard you enjoyed slumming it on the road." His sneer, along with the obvious insinuation, pisses me off more. He doesn't know one fucking thing about me.

"And here I was thinking Lincoln Saint wouldn't ever lower himself to reading tabloids."

I don't deny his statement because there's no point. If I deny it, it only makes it more true in their minds. If I say he's right, I become a dirty slut. You've got to love the politics of Echoes Cove.

He doesn't get a chance to respond as the teacher draws the class to a close. Shit. I didn't take any notes. I couldn't even tell you what he talked about. Fuck my life. I need to ask someone to help me with some notes.

As soon as the bell rings, I grab my bag and try to haul ass from the room but find myself cornered anyway.

"You shouldn't have come back, princess," Maverick snarls. "You're not wanted here."

I roll my eyes at him and try to push past him, but he's a wall of immovable muscle. "Trust me, no one wants me to be here any less than I do. It's just this year, and then I'm gone. How about you stay out of my way, and I'll stay out of yours?"

"Look at baby Royal trying to tell us what to do like she runs this place." Lincoln barks out a laugh, and other laughter rings out. That's when I realize the only person who left the room was the teacher.

Fuck, I hate private school.

"I'm not trying to tell you anything," I insist, standing taller as I try to leave again, only for Finley to block my path. He's always been a guy of few words, but when he says something, he always makes it count. I've known him to make people cry with less than a handful of words.

He still doesn't say anything, though. He may be quiet, but he's loyal as they come. He won't move until Lincoln says so. It's always been like this with them, but now I'm learning what it's like to be on the other side of their team.

"I suggest you get with the program, princess. This is our school now. And you? You're nothing but a minnow. Piss me off and see what that gets you."

I narrow my eyes at Lincoln, hating the gauntlet he just threw down. I am not some weak-ass bitch. My dad might have come to a bitter end, but he raised me to be a boss-ass queen. "You already seem pissed off to me, so what's the worst that could happen?"

The grin on my face only seeks to add fuel to the fire my words have ignited.

Lincoln's eyes turn icy, and he curls his lip. The wicked smile on his face doesn't quite meet his eyes as his gaze roams over me from head to toe. The stare causes an icy drop of dread to run down my spine, but I try to keep my face impassive. "Sad, sad lost little princess. Nobody wants you, nobody loves you, and well… Let's just say that when you're gone, nobody will miss you either. You have no idea of the game you're playing. Don't say I didn't warn you."

"What the fuck is that supposed to mean?"

The absolute quiet that follows me challenging him is enough to charge the air and make my hair stand on end.

"That means, Nobody, that you shouldn't be here. This school doesn't cater to the weak and pathetic. You're not wanted here. You should have stayed gone with your coward daddy." His sneer pricks at my heart, but I refuse to let myself be beaten on day one, and I'm becoming very aware that this really is going to be day one of what, I'm sure, is sure to be a nightmare of a year at ECP.

"But even your coward daddy couldn't stand the sight of you, could he? Did you enjoy finding his cold dead body? His note to you telling you how you weren't enough to make him stay in this world? You'll never be good enough, Octavia Royal. Not for him, not for this school, not for any of it."

Rage pulses through my veins, but I refuse to cry in front of these assholes. I hate how he's airing out shit that I didn't think anyone in the general population knew about. Things like the note from my dad, or the fact that I'm the one who found him. We kept all of that from the press. I stand, trying to compose myself, but all of the eyes crawling over me, looking for cracks in my armor, make me want to vomit. I shove it all back, trying to piece myself back together while he just smiles that dead smile of his back at me.

"You are nothing, Octavia, and while you might like to pretend you're more, you never will be. The longer you resist, the more it's going to hurt. You made yourself free game by coming back here. It won't ever stop, not until you leave."

Maverick steps toward me, leaning forward before pulling a face. "I guess they forgot to take the trash out."

He turns and leaves with the other two close on his heels, but everyone else simply watches as I stand here trying to piece my armor back together.

"Fuck this." I leave the room, determined not to let them get to me, but fearing it might be a losing battle.

---

The morning passes in a blur, but for the most part, I'm left alone after Business. Mostly because the guys, Blair, and her friends aren't in my Music or Statistics classes. That doesn't mean that more of the same bullshit whispers and taunts haven't followed me, though. I always thought I had a thick skin, but apparently something about being back in Echoes Cove has me feeling a bit more sensitive. It's only been half a day, and I'm already exhausted by it all. The whispers, the structure, the classes. Thankfully my Music and Stats teachers were better than Mr. Peters, and the classes were engaging enough to hold my partial attention. I'm used to chaos breaks between my lessons, so four in a row has my brain all kinds of numb. I'm seriously starting to question if a 4.0 GPA is actually doable. I might need to hire a tutor if I want to meet the terms of the Will because I can't seem to get my brain to play ball.

After I leave Statistics, I head to the cafeteria, which of course is on the other side of the freaking building. At least the walk gives me a chance to decompress a little, as I try to shove down the rising panic about passing my classes along with surviving this cesspit of a school for the rest of the year.

I spot Indi waiting for me at the doors, and my anxiety goes down by about three levels. I might be Stone Royal's daughter, used to paparazzi and crazy fangirls, but I'm still a seventeen-year-old girl on her first day at a new high school. This is a whole different ball game. Knowing that Blair and her bitch squad will be behind those doors makes me want to grab lunch off campus.

"Hey! Rough morning?" she asks as I approach, and my mood lightens with each step. There's something about her that's just all sunshine and rainbows. Even with the whole alt/emo thing she apparently has going on at heart.

"My morning has been filled with Blair and her vapid bitch squad as well as a delightful run in with Lincoln and his merry band of jerks, so yeah, you could say that." I groan, and she tucks her arm through mine.

"Oh no, not the Saint Squad." She sighs dramatically, and I can't help but laugh. "I don't know where these assholes get their sense of power from, but they know this is just high school, right?" I let her drag me through the doors, my stomach tightening as I get my first look at the cafeteria. The people are no less cliquey now than they were the last time I was here. The popular kids occupy the rectangular tables near the center of the room, with everyone else taking the space around them.

"You're not from around here, are you?" I ask, and she shakes her head.

"Nah, I grew up back East, but my dad is a tech genius and landed a job in the Valley, so now I'm here… With all of the California sunshine and vapid assholes I can handle." She laughs as we walk to the lunch line, and I can't help but roll my eyes when I see what's on the menu for the day. At least there are still burgers and pizza. Fuck the salad bar. I don't do a rabbit food diet. I tried it once, and it was the most miserable and cranky two hours of my life.

"Well, what you've probably learned is that the Saints basically own this town. Maverick and Finley have been his best friends since we were all kids. Even when we were younger, everyone just gravitated toward them. I have no idea why. Back then, I was too young to notice it, but I guess the power is something they were born into." I shrug as we make our way to an empty table by the windows. We pass the jock table and the table filled with Lincoln, Blair, and all of their pseudo-sycophants. "Table in the corner?"

"Sounds perfect, away from all the crazy."

"There's a spot here without crazy?" I pull a face of faked shock, and she laughs as we head toward the table and slide into the empty seats.

"Back to the power system… I've noticed it. It's just really different from the public school I was at before I came here last year. But hey, now you're here and I'm not the new kid anymore, so thanks for that." She tips her can of soda toward me, and I laugh.

"You're welcome, I guess?" I take a bite of the cheese pizza I slapped on my plate and groan at how good it is. I mean, it's not as good as Denny's in New York, but for high school cafeteria pizza, it's the fucking shit. "So you only came here last year?"

"Yeah." She nods before taking a bite from her burger. She chews thoughtfully before she picks up a fry, points it at me, and continues, "And you better believe my alt loving, purple hair rocking personality wasn't exactly par for the course around here. I mean, my hair was blue when I started, but I'm pretty sure the change to purple hasn't made a difference."

"Dude, I love your hair," I tell her with a shrug.

"V, you love Midnight Blue, lived life on a tour bus, and love my hair. I knew I was making the right decision having you as my bestie."

I grin at her because I obviously think she made an awesome decision; and while I might not be here for long, surviving this year with a friend like her will make it much easier. We eat in a comfortable quiet, and I download the social media app for the school onto my phone while Indi scrolls through the reality news on hers, showing me random articles about shit I've never heard about. I nod and smile regardless.

I sign in to the app, change my password, then close it down. Social media always seemed a bit icky to me, but if this is how stuff works here, then I'm willing to give it a go. I slide my phone away as I finish eating and look up at Indi. "Want to go catch some sunshine before lunch is over?"

She stands, nodding, and I follow suit. We dump our trays in the trash cans, and I turn in time to walk straight into Blair, her lunch spilling straight down the front of my uniform. "Watch where you're going, you stupid bitch."

The way she smiles at me tells me this wasn't an accident, not that I ever actually thought it was. Granted, the spaghetti making its way down my shirt only serves to confirm how unaccidental this fucking run-in was. This bitch doesn't eat carbs.

"Here, let me help with that stain." Brittany cackles before throwing her drink over me, the sticky liquid staining my uniform further. The entire cafeteria is silent until Maverick starts laughing, and then the rest of the students join in. Fury and embarrassment burns in my veins, and it takes every ounce of control that I have to not lay this bitch out.

I clench my fists and remember that Mac taught me never to hit someone first. Finish the fight, but never start it. Even with this crazy bitch.

"Blair, that shit is out of order." I look up and see some of the football team heading in our direction. I look over to Lincoln who is scowling over at us, but he just sits there, watching it play out and not bothering to intervene. If he's pissed off, he could've stopped Blair himself, but fuck him because we both know he started all of this.

"Come on, let's go get you a new uniform," Indi says, trying to pull me away from them when Blair leans in.

"I told you this was my school, Octavia. You should leave because this isn't going to get any better for you. If anything, it's only going to get that much worse. Don't say I didn't warn you because this is the only warning you'll get."

"That's enough, Blair," a male voice shouts across the cafeteria, but Blair pays no fucking attention.

I shrug out of Indi's hold and lean in closer, making sure she can see the fire in my eyes. "Blair, you have no fucking idea what I've lived through. A vapid little bitch like you isn't going to scare me."

She laughs loudly, like I've told her some hysterical fucking joke, before turning and flicking her hair in my face and walking away. Brittany's at her side like a perfect little lap dog.

Fuck this shit. I walk out of the cafeteria with my head held high. I won't give them the satisfaction of my tears. They're just angry tears, but they won't fucking know that, and they wouldn't believe it anyway. I refuse to let them see me cry.

"Are you okay?" the blond football player asks, pulling me to a stop before I get past the doors, and I try my best to smile up at him though really, I'd just like to get cleaned up.

"I'm fine, this uniform sucks anyway." He offers me a megawatt smile, and I think Indi nearly drops dead beside me. I think she's actually holding her breath, her hands shake at her sides before she sucks in a breath and clasps her hands together, looking at him all googly-eyed. It's like she's star struck.

"It does, but you rock it. Even with the additions." He shoves his hands in the pockets of his slim fit pants, and his megawatt smile only brightens as he says, "I'm Raleigh."

"Octavia." I smile back, not wanting to be rude since this is the only guy who stood up for me. I glance around him into the cafeteria. I don't want to be dismissive, but I really want to get the hell out of here.

"I have a spare uniform in my locker, come on." Indi swoops in and saves the day, like a fucking superstar. I wave at Raleigh as she loops her arm through mine, pulling me into the hallway.

"Definitely didn't think you'd be into the jock type," I joke as she leads me in the opposite direction of the cafeteria.

"I'm so not, well usually anyway, but dude, that smile. Exceptions can always be made." She fans herself, making me laugh as she leads me to a bathroom. I strip out of my shirt as she disappears and do the best I can to get the soda out of my hair. I tip my head under the hand dryer, but it's a useless effort, so I focus on drying my bangs and put the rest up into a ponytail.

It doesn't take long for her to get back, handing me a shirt as she leans against the wall. "This isn't the first time this shit has happened, so I tend to keep at least three spares in my locker at all times."

I'm pretty sure my jaw just about hits the floor, but she only shrugs in response. "Like I said, I know what it's like being the new kid."

I'm not sure if I'm more pissed off for her or for me at this point, but I make a vow to myself right then.

I am not letting these assholes win. Not now, not ever.

# CHAPTER THREE

Indi meets me at the door after I finish my AP French class, and we head to the locker rooms for Gym. We're the last ones to arrive, and I groan internally at all of the bitchiness I can already sense swirling around in here. It's just a fucking gym class, not the Olympics, of course we all look like shit. I tune everyone but Indi out as we get changed, and since we were the last ones in, we're the last ones to head to the gym. I'm so glad this is the last period of the day. It feels like I've been here for twelve hours.

As I push the door open to the gym, I hear, "Is that you, V?"

*No fucking way.*

I look up and find Easton Saint grinning at me. His startling gray eyes light up as he watches me. I take in a grown up East, raking my eyes over his mouth-watering… everything. Tall, broad, and ripped as fuck. His once long and floppy dark hair is now short on the sides, and longer on top, and I can tell from looking at it that he's been running his fingers through it all day. He has that mussed, just woke up, I don't give a fuck, look going on.

I head straight for him and practically jump on him. He catches me and spins me around before putting my feet firmly back on the ground. "East, what the fuck are you doing in this hell hole?"

He belts out a laugh before taking a step back. That's when I notice the whispers, the phones pointed in our direction… and what he's wearing. "Picked up a job till Linc is out of here. Just something temporary, and the school board was desperate after Coach White quit suddenly just before the semester started."

"You're my freaking Gym teacher?" I groan, and he nods, the glint in his eye dimming a bit. "So, I guess wrapping myself around you like that is going to really help with these assholes all calling me a whore."

He leans in, glaring over my shoulder before whispering. "Fuck them, V. You know who you are, and you always have." He pulls back, his megawatt grin firmly back in place. "Now line up, it's track day."

The round of groans around me makes me smile real hard. I don't know if he did it for me, or if it was already his plan, but I've always loved running. It's never been a secret among my friends. I follow everyone outside and line up on the track. East winks at me, and I get the feeling we probably weren't meant to be out here, but fuck yes.

"You're enjoying this, aren't you?" Indi moans, and I nod.

"Hell yes, there is nothing quite like running on a clear track."

She rolls her eyes at me, and I laugh softly. "This is the peppiest I've seen you all day, so I'm not going to rain on your parade. Move up front, Running Barbie. Leave my slow 'I don't wanna' ass back here. Might as well get some joy out of the day."

"You're officially my favorite person." I beam at her and move through the crowd to the front, where some of Blair's bitch squad are all simping over East. Damn, these girls need to pick one guy and stick to him. They call me a whore, and yet they're drooling fucking everywhere they go.

"Ready!" East shouts before he blows his whistle, and I shoot off, ignoring the entire fucking world except the track beneath my feet. I run, not paying any attention to one damn thing until the whistle sounds again. It's not until I stop that I realize the cheer team, which includes Blair and the rest of her bitch squad, and the football team are all out here too. Who knew cheer was a replacement for Gym?

By the time I make it back to where East is standing, pretty much everyone else has already headed back to the locker room. "I see you still like to run."

The look on his face is a total contradiction to his cheery, laid-back tone. He sounds light and breezy, but he looks at me like he's haunted. "Running soothes my soul. Usually it's music, but I haven't been able to play since…" I trail off, and I hate the pity I see in his eyes. But I can't play right now, I've tried picking up my guitar a dozen times over, and I just can't do it. Even in Music today I just mumbled my way through. Music has always been the thing I did with my dad.

"I guess that explains a lot. You did good today, though I didn't realize you were back. Honestly, I didn't think you'd ever come back here."

"I didn't have much of a choice. I'm only here for the year," I tell him, trying not to focus on just how much even hinting about my dad hurts. It's like a stab straight through the heart—the sting of a thousand cuts. It's fucking unbearable, and I can barely breathe.

"Yeah, I heard about your dad. I'm sorry, V. That sucks. Where are you staying?"

"With Blair." I sigh, rolling my eyes. "I'm in the pool house at least. Their McMansion is just weird. It's like a fucking museum."

"Yeah, that place has always been creepy," he laughs, running a hand through his hair. "Okay, you better head to the showers, otherwise you'll be late. We should catch up sometime, though."

"I'd like that." I smile at him. "Drop me a text, and we'll sort something out."

I give him my number before heading to the locker rooms. Indi is the only one hanging around, clearly waiting for me, so I haul ass in the shower. I leave my hair up because I can't make myself care enough to wash it just to go home.

"You want to grab milkshakes before heading home?" Indi asks when I reappear in nothing but my underwear. I've never been particularly shy about my body, especially since growing up on a tour bus meant that privacy wasn't exactly something there was an abundance of.

"Sure, as long as there are burgers. I'm fucking starving."

"After leaving us all in your dust out there, I'm not surprised. Though why Coach Saint let you just keep running rather than doing sprints like the rest of us was unusual." Her observation isn't much of a surprise. My hello with East wasn't exactly discreet, but then, I didn't realize he was our Gym teacher. I have to admit that hearing him called Coach Saint is pretty fucking hilarious.

"East and I go way back, actually. Let me finish getting dressed, and I'll explain everything over food." I grin widely as I shimmy back into this ridiculous uniform. She just nods and swings her car keys around on her finger.

"Sounds good, you need a ride?"

"No, I have my rental, but if you want to follow me home, we can ride there together. I don't have my own car yet. It's just another thing on my never ending to do list."

"Then that sounds like a perfect way to spend our weekend," she says with her infectious smile. She nods on a pause, like she's confirming a car shopping trip on her mental to-do list. After a moment of what I'm guessing is unusual quiet for her, she says, "But yes, that absolutely sounds like a plan. No need to take both cars."

I nod along as I stuff my gym gear into my bag, pulling my blazer on as I turn to face her. "I am so here for that. But first, let's eat!"

I pull my phone from my bag as an afterthought and groan at the ton of messages flashing at me from unknown numbers. Oh awesome, I guess this is going to be a thing now. I flick through a couple of them—the vitriol reflecting back at me isn't anything I haven't already seen on social media—and just delete all of them before looking back up at Indi and smiling. A few hateful remarks are not about to ruin my day.

We head out to the parking lot, and she heads to the pale blue, old-school Jeep Wrangler sitting in the lot. "This is yours?"

"Look, my obsession with Stiles is real, and if you tell me you don't know who that is, I'm going to have to rethink this entire friendship," she deadpans, and I start laughing so hard.

"Girl, he is a beautiful man. I watch everything he's in. Of course I know who Stiles is. Teen Wolf is an obsession of mine too."

She grins at me as she unlocks the doors. "Good, then we won't have any issues here."

---

We pull up at Penny's in Indi's Wrangler after dropping off my rental, and I'm not even surprised that it's absolutely packed. Penny's has always been the spot to hang since the food is to die for. It might just be burgers and shakes, but when I tell you they're the best burgers and shakes you'll experience in your life, I'm not messing around.

"Hey, Octavia." I look up and see Raleigh sitting with a few guys from the football team at one of the booths. I wave as we pass by him and weave through the masses to a booth in the back, sliding in opposite each other. I pick up a menu and grin. This place hasn't changed at all. I mean, sure, it's been updated inside a little, but it still looks like a sixties diner, all bright pink and white with splashes of orange. It absolutely shouldn't fit in here in Echoes Cove, but it somehow does.

"You know what you want?" Indi asks as a server heads in our direction on skates. Man, I really do love this place. I nod at her, and she drops her menu just as the server comes to a stop by the booth.

"What can I get you girls today?" the blonde woman asks with the warmest smile I think I've ever seen in Echoes Cove.

"I'll have the double bacon cheeseburger with a chocolate shake and extra fries, please," I say, grinning at her while Indi snickers at the look on the poor woman's face. I may be reasonably small, but I like to eat.

"I'll have the same."

The server nods before skating away, and Indi looks at me like an evil genius, wagging her eyebrows at me. "So… you and Coach Saint?"

"And here I was thinking that I'd at least get a bite in before the inquisition commenced."

"Oh, I am definitely not a sit around and wait for something to happen for me kind of girl." She grins. "Now spill the freaking tea."

I roll my eyes and let out a deep breath. "Okay, so I already told you I lived here when I was a kid. Back in the day, Linc, Mav, Finley, and East were a fearsome foursome. They were tight as tight could be, and nobody fucked with them. Back then, when my mom was still around, I lived in the house next door to East and Linc, so we were pretty friendly, I just wasn't one of them. But then one of the bigger kids at school thought it would be fun to push me off the swing set when I was like five, I think? East, who didn't take shit even back then, basically made the kid eat dirt and took me under his wing. The other three accepted me into their circle, and we were inseparable.

"I don't think I'd have gotten through my mom disappearing the next year if it wasn't for those guys. I remember feeling so lost, but between the four of them, I was literally never alone. I remember Linc sneaking over and climbing the tree next to my window. He'd sneak in my bedroom and stay with me overnight just so I didn't have to be alone."

She just leans back in the booth, staring at me with wide eyes. "Are you sure we're talking about the same people? Because I'm not going to lie, that doesn't sound like the guys I've seen jackassing around here at all."

"We were all crazy close until Dad hit it big and took me on tour with him just before my twelfth birthday. It wasn't as easy to stay in touch then, cell phones were a thing, but not like they are now, and my dad wasn't a fan of me having one. He was weird about technology. We lost touch, and by the time I had a cell, we hadn't spoken in so long that it didn't feel right getting back in touch with them. I have no idea what happened while I was gone, but the icy reception I got when I came back isn't exactly what I expected. But I can't hold it against them, not really."

"Hell yes you can. You left with your dad—it's not like you had a choice. They have zero reason to be the giant bags of dicks they were today."

"I mean, they didn't really do anything…" I trail off just as our shakes are brought over. I take a sip, groaning at how good it tastes when my taste buds come alive. So thick and chocolatey. I would happily go into a food coma after having this.

"No, but they didn't stop Blair from being a catty bitch either. You and I both know, even if you have been away, that they could have stopped her if they wanted to." She's not wrong, and now that I think about it, I realize they could also be behind the wave of messages coming through to my phone. I can't prove any of it, so I just shrug.

"I can handle Blair and her bitch squad. They can give me their worst, and it still won't top some of the shit I've been through before."

She scowls over my shoulder as I finish my mini-rant, so I turn in time to see the guys, Blair, and her bitch squad walking in. Awesome.

They don't immediately spot us in the corner as they take up one of the bigger booths on the other side of the diner. As if hearing my thoughts, though, Linc glances in our direction, his frown deepening when he sees me. I really wish I knew what I did to piss those three off, especially since East was so chill with me.

"Well, at least Coach still seems to be on Team V," Indi says, pulling my attention away from the guys and bringing my focus back to her.

"East was always the most laid-back of them all. Linc was the protector, Finley was the quiet one, Mav was the psycho, and East was the glue that held them all together."

"Not much has changed there then," Indi laughs, and I join in.

"It doesn't seem like it."

Our food arrives, and I grin at the size of the portions. Seriously, salads are for the birds. "Oh man, this is going to be so worth the extra laps I'll have to do in the pool tonight."

"You're going to swim even after all the running? Girl, you're crazy. I work out as much as they force me to, and that's it. I'm not going to feel even a little bit of guilt over it either. I'm going to spend my night in a food coma, and maybe, just maybe, I'll pick up my sketch book at some point. I'm not going to stress if I don't, though."

I grin at her and take a bite of the burger, and I swear I come a little in my panties. "Goddamn, this just became my new favorite thing in the world."

She nods, agreeing as she sinks her teeth into her own.

"So come on, it's your turn. Catch me up on the hierarchy around here. Obviously the boys are at the top of the food chain still, but how the fuck did Blair attach herself to them?"

She swallows her mouthful and takes a slurp of her shake before she starts to speak. "I have no idea how she attached herself to them. By the time I got here last year, this is how it was already. I had the unfortunate pleasure of being Blair's target last year, so as much as I hate that it's on you now, thank you." I laugh at her, and she shrugs, chomping down a few fries before continuing, "After the bitch squad, you have the jocks and the cheer team. Though Blair and some of her squad are on the cheer team, so maybe that's how that works. Then it's the rest of us, though being the new kid and outcast definitely put me at the bottom of the pile."

"That's so shit."

"It is what it is, and I'm pretty chill about it. I'm good with being left alone." She shrugs like she doesn't care, but I can see that she does really. No one in high school wants to be the kid with no friends. No matter how okay you are on your own.

"So Linc and the guys, Blair and the bitch squad, then Raleigh and the team. Who are the party people these days?"

She snorts a laugh. "Oh that's easy. Raleigh's best friend, also the wide receiver on the team, Jackson Jones—there's a back to school thing at his place this weekend. He started here the year before I did and by the sounds of it, he's a freaking NFL guy, which in football speak basically means he's something of a superstar." She blushes a little talking about him, so I nudge her foot with mine.

"You like the superstar?"

"He's a jock, and I'm, well… me. Pretty sure he doesn't even know I exist." She dips one of her fries in her shake, looking down at the table like she's embarrassed by what she admitted to me. I might have only just met this girl, but there is something about her that calls out to my goddamn soul. If she wants an intro to the superstar, I'm going to figure out how to make it happen. Even if I hate the idea of partying with these people.

I glance over at the jock table and catch Raleigh looking over at me, so I smile at him. "Maybe we should get ourselves invited to that party."

"Good luck with that," she snorts, and I grin wider.

"Oh, Indi, I know you've been here a while, but you've only just met me. They might be treating me like the new kid, but I can guarantee that I can get us invites to that party." I sound conceited as fuck, but I don't care because the grin on her face makes it worth it.

"Then hell yes, let's get us an invite to that party."

I turn back around and wave Raleigh over. A puppyish smile crosses his face as he jumps up from his booth and saunters toward us before slipping into the booth next to me. "Hey, how was your first day?"

"It was like being chum in a fucking shark tank outside of meeting my girl Indi here and my run-in with you. Indi tells me there's a party this weekend?" I smile at him as his arm goes over the back of the booth. He doesn't quite have it wrapped around me, but it's pretty damn close. This QB is smooth, I'll give him that. He also seems like a genuinely nice guy, so I'm not opposed to the closeness.

"There is, and my boy Jackson is throwing it. He's only like three houses down from you, so you could just walk down the beach if you guys want to come." He gives me that megawatt smile of his, and I smile back at him before glancing over at Indi.

"We could probably do that," I say, and Indi nods in agreement. "Are you going to be there?"

"Of course, I wouldn't miss it. Especially if you guys are coming. You probably know a lot of people here already, but I'm sure I can introduce you to some of the half-decent humans at Echoes Cove Prep." I can't help but laugh. It seems I was right. He actually is a nice guy.

"You weren't here before I left the Cove, right?"

He shakes his head, the smile of his still in place as he gets comfortable beside me. "Nope, I came here freshman year. I've been dominating the field since. It's been my only focus because man, some of the people here fucking suck."

"Yes, yes they fucking do," Indi snorts. I offer my plate to Raleigh, who takes a handful of fries as I take a bite of my burger. I sit and listen while he and Indi talk up a storm about people I don't know, but I'm glad that she seems so chill with him too. Maybe it won't be so bad making some friends before I ditch this place at the end of the year.

"I better get back to the guys, but I'll catch you both tomorrow."

"See ya." I grin as he drags himself out of our booth and makes his way back to his friends. I wait until he's gone to say, "See, easy as pie."

My skin prickles and I look up, feeling someone's eyes on me. I find Linc glaring at me from his booth. His jaw clenches as he looks from me and over to the table where Raleigh is sitting before saying something to Maverick. He turns his dark-eyed glare in my direction too.

Fuck both of them.

If they don't want to be my friend these days, that's fine. But they don't get to pick who I *am* friends with either. I turn back to Indi who looks happier than I've seen her all day, even with her evil genius smile on.

"You, Octavia Royal, are my new favorite person in the entire world." I cackle at her words and take a sip of my milkshake.

"Right back at you."

We sit, chatting about the other politics of Echoes Cove. It's the standard bullshit that's probably worth knowing before attempting day two at prep, considering just how bad day one went. Our phones buzz in sync on the table, pulling our attention away from our conversation.

Indi grabs hers, swiping on the notification, and all of the blood drains from her face.

"What's wrong?" I ask, picking up my phone. The notification is from the ReachMe app. I swipe across on it, and the app opens to a picture of me wrapped around East from gym class today with the caption 'School slut screws the Coach.'

It's been up for less than a minute and already has over fifty comments. I scroll through them, and the hatred and degradation is beyond disgusting. These people don't even know me.

Blair laughs across the diner, and I clench my hands around the edge of the table.

"I'm sorry. This is so shit. I've reported the picture already, which means it will be taken down—" Indi starts, but I shake my head, cutting her off.

"The damage is already done." I sigh, shaking my head again. I almost feel bad for East because this isn't going to be good for him either. He could lose his job. My skin crawls as people's eyes rake over me all around the diner. "Can we go?"

Indi shoves the last of the burger in her mouth as she stands up. "Sure."

I grab my bag, and hightail it across the space. Leers and catcalls follow me as I go, along with laughter and calls of 'whore.'

Just as we reach the door, Lincoln's voice reaches me, almost cutting me deeper than everything else. "Don't be stupid, no one will believe this. East would never stoop so low as to fuck a disease-ridden whore. You all saw how she grew up; she's probably ridden more dicks than we have at the school. East thinks way too much of himself to slum it with her."

"You're right," Blair's shrill voice follows his demeaning vitriol. "We're going to have to burn her sheets rather than just wash them. Nothing else will get out the smell of cheap perfume and desperation."

Maverick's laughter booms around me, like the last nail in today's coffin, and Finley looks at me, his lip curled up in disgust. I thought I could come back and live a quiet life for a year before escaping.

How fucking wrong was I?

# CHAPTER FOUR

I ask Indi to drop me off at my childhood home after everything that happened at Penny's rather than at my aunt and uncle's stupid-ass mansion. I don't want to be near my cousin or anything else relating to the other people in Echoes Cove. I just want the sanctuary that my old home brings. Technically, this is still my house since, you know, I own it now. I just can't live here because of the stupid term in my dad's Will stating I must live with my legal guardians, which is complete and utter bullshit if you ask me.

I use the code to open the gates, making sure to re-lock them behind me, and make the long walk up to the house.

It looks exactly how I remember it. It's like something from a haunted house movie, but I love it. The house itself is a tall dark stone building, with the windows and door arched in a paler stone. Finished with dark gray window frames and a matching door. I'm pretty sure my parents had a 'we want to be scary' vibe going on when they picked this place. If I remember correctly, even the back balconies are black wrought iron and a bit pointy on top. Dad used to joke it was to keep the boys away from my room.

If he only knew.

The door opens before I even reach it. I pause, wondering who the fuck is in my house already. Once it's open fully, Smithy steps out and grins down at me. "Miss Octavia, it's so lovely to see you. Welcome home! I've been wondering if I'd be seeing you."

I run up to him and hug him tight. He's much older than I remember, but I guess being away from here for five years coupled with a child's memory will do that. Smithy was the house manager when I was younger, but he was also like a surrogate parent. He was there for me when my mom left, when my dad drank too much… even just when I fell and needed patching up. He might have been the house manager, but to me, he was so much more.

"I had no idea you were still here, otherwise I'd have come to see you sooner," I tell him as he squashes me against his chest. Just over two weeks I've been in this godforsaken town. Seeing him would've made it feel more like home. I could kick myself for being too chicken to check the house out before now.

"Of course I'm still here. Who else was going to keep this place in working order and ready for your return?" He grins down at me before ushering me inside. I follow him to the kitchen, which looks exactly as I remember it—all black and white marble tops and white cabinets with silver handles. It's maybe a little more updated, appliance wise, and I don't remember the espresso machine, but I'm not sad about it. As I'm taking everything in, he pours me a glass of peach iced tea with extra lemon slices. I love that he remembers my favorite drink. I sit on a stool at the center island, and he sits opposite me.

"If I'd known you were here, I'd have fought harder about living with Vivienne and Nate. I'd much rather be here with you."

"I thought your father put me down as your guardian in his Will. I assumed you chose to be with your family after going through such an ordeal." He smiles sadly at me, and I nearly spray tea out of my nose with the derisive snort I let loose.

"Those people are not my family. I'm going to call the lawyer to see what he says. If I can be back here, I'll be here before the end of the week."

He smiles widely and claps his hands together. "Nothing would make me happier, Miss Octavia." The genuine happiness in his tone hits me a little harder than it might have before, and I fight the urge to rub the place on my chest just over my heart. Damn. I didn't know how much I missed being wanted. "Now then, have you eaten? I can whip you up some mac and cheese. I assume that's still your favorite."

I groan at the memory of his mac and cheese and find myself wishing I hadn't already eaten. "I had a burger at Penny's with a new friend, but now that I know you're here, I'm definitely coming back to eat tomorrow. If that's okay?"

"This is your home, Miss Octavia. You're always welcome here. Feel free to bring your friend with you." His smile reaches his eyes, and it warms my heart. I missed him more than I ever thought possible. I freaking adore him.

"That I can totally do. Am I okay to go have a look around?" I know this is technically my house, but if he's been here the last five years, it feels wrong to just stomp about the place.

"Of course, this is your home. Do as you like. I packed your father's things away. I didn't want you to have to do it, but I've put the boxes in his old study. I left your room alone, but if you're coming back here, we can update it or even move you to the master."

I hadn't actually considered any of this, and it's enough to make my mind reel with the possibility. But I'm glad he's packed away my dad's things. I still haven't been through the stuff that he had on tour with us. I imagine that was all brought back here too. I definitely don't have it in me to go through the boxes. Picking at that wound isn't something I'm strong enough to face yet.

"I'll speak to the lawyer and make sure that it's okay that I do move back here.

I don't want to lose access to anything. If he says I'm good to go, I'll sit down and think about where to go from there."

"Sounds perfect," he says as he stands, taking my empty glass and putting it in the sink. "It will be nice to have some life around the place again."

"It'll be good to be home." I smile up at him before heading upstairs. The thought of being able to move back here, away from Blair, makes me happier than I've felt since I found out I had to come back to Echoes Cove. I might actually be able to relax in my own space rather than being on edge twenty-four fucking seven.

I head straight to my room and cringe as I step inside. Yep, this room definitely isn't suitable for me any more. There's a single bed with a white canopy, and the entire room has a pink and white theme… None of this is even close to the person I am now. I smile at the blossoming tree still outside my window, then frown from the memories this room pulls to the forefront about Lincoln and the others.

This definitely isn't my room anymore. And those are not memories I need haunting me, especially when it's clear the guys have no intention of even being civil toward me.

I pull my phone from my pocket and send an email over to the lawyer who's been in charge of my inheritance and my father's estate, asking him to give me a call as soon as he can. Hope blossoms in my chest, and I do what I can to quash it. Hope can be a dangerous thing.

I head toward the master suite on the other side of the house. My heart aches in an echo of the emptiness on this side of the house. There isn't even any furniture in here. I don't remember Dad having much in here before anyway, but this still seems extra barren. He rarely spent time here because of his insomnia, but my heart still pangs a little from being here in the room that was once his. I'm pretty sure I've cried every tear I have in my body for him, and so I find myself flickering between anger and sadness. I suppose if I give myself a moment to really consider everything, I'm overall just kind of sad.

I know some people might find it weird to move into a room like this considering the circumstances, but it feels right to me. I don't really remember ever seeing my dad in here, so it's not like there are *that* many memories to dredge up in this room. Plus, he left the house to me—he'd definitely want me to make use of it. I pad over the cream carpet to the wall of glass that looks out over the backyard and open the door that leads to the balcony.

If I lean just the right way, I can see the tree that stands by my old bedroom window. I push away thoughts of the guys that threaten to rise and focus on the rest of the view of the yard. The pool sits covered and undisturbed in the middle of the expanse of yard, and the loungers dot the edge. The outdoor kitchen still gleams. Smithy really did keep this place spick and span, and I can't help but smile. I'm glad that someone had some love left to give to this place.

My phone chimes, pulling my attention away from my slow perusal of the property. I glance down, and my stomach clenches at the sight of an email from my lawyer confirming he'll call me in half an hour.

Awesome.

I lock the balcony door back up and head back downstairs, making sure to say goodbye to Smithy before heading down the drive so I can walk back to my aunt's place. It's not too far from here, and while their house might be on the beach, I'd rather be up here looking over the cove than right on the beach anyway. Fingers crossed my lawyer confirms what I want him to, so I can move up here.

Just as I'm locking up the gate, a black Porsche Cayenne stops on the road in front of me. The window rolls down, and I try to hide my shock as Lincoln's face comes into view. "What are you doing here?" he spits, eyes narrowed as he all but sets me on fire with his eyes.

I cross my arms, refusing to let him get to me. "I was just checking in. Problem?"

"You shouldn't be here, Octavia. You should crawl back in the hole you came from."

I roll my eyes and sigh. For the life of me, I truly cannot work out exactly why he's in asshole mode. "It's my house, Lincoln."

"I meant in Echoes Cove. You left this place behind and never looked back. Why the fuck would you come back now? You're not wanted here. And don't think cozying up to my brother is going to make things easier for you. He wouldn't touch you if you paid him." The bite in his tone hurts me more than it should, but I refuse to let it show.

"I didn't exactly plan on coming back here. My dad fucking killed himself—I didn't have a choice. Now if you'll excuse me, I have places to be." I turn quickly on my heel and walk away from him, not giving him a chance to answer. I don't dare to breathe those first few steps, listening with bated breath for him to throw his car in reverse and come back to tear me down some more. What a fucking asshole.

I quickly swipe at the tear that falls down my cheek. I hate that I'm crying because I'm angry… Angry at Lincoln. Angry at my dad. Angry at myself for letting it all get to me. I'd really like to go back three months and try and get my dad the help he needed. But I didn't know, and now I have to live with that.

---

I slide the door closed on the pool house just as my phone starts to ring. I kick off my boots as I see the lawyer's company name on my caller ID. "Hello?"

"Octavia? It's Derek. You asked me to call, so I thought I'd check in. Is everything okay?"

"Hey, Derek," I say, putting as much of a sunshiney tone into my voice as I can muster. Considering that I cried most of the walk back here, it's not actually much. "I'm fine, I just had an interesting conversation with my estate manager, Smithy—sorry, James Smith—so I wanted to clear something up with you."

"Oh," he mutters, and even without being face-to-face with him, I know he's pulling the collar of his shirt. During the few meetings I had with him, I noticed that he did it when he was uncomfortable. "How can I help?"

"I was just told that my aunt and uncle *aren't really* my legal guardians, so I'm just curious as to why I was told I was required to stay with them until I graduated."

"Oh, well. You see…" he trails off, and I sigh as I drop down onto the sofa. I don't know whether I should be relieved or pissed off. I settle somewhere in the middle of the two.

"Spit it out, Derek."

"They thought it would be best if you came to stay with them even though they weren't named your sole guardians, so they approached me about ensuring you would be with them." I cackle at his words, but of course they did. This explains the exorbitant rent they demanded. They wanted my father's money. "I figured since they were actually related to you and wanted you with them, that it was probably for the best."

"What are the *actual* stipulations of my inheritance, Derek?" I try not to be a total bitch, but I've been in this fucking house for weeks now, absolutely miserable. I was dragged here by child services from my hotel room where I was staying with Mac after my dad died. I was told I needed to stay with my aunt and uncle which has been miserable, so yeah, I'm in full bitch mode.

"The only stipulations your father made for your inheritance remaining in your control were that should you be under the age of eighteen in the event of his death, you would be required to graduate from Echoes Cove Prep with a 4.0 GPA and remain in the care of your guardian or guardians. Failure to do either of these things would result in you not having access to any of the inheritance until your twenty-fifth birthday."

"Thank you, Derek." I smile, and for once, I don't have to force it. I might not *want* to be in Echoes Cove, but at least now I know I don't have to stay with my shitty aunt and uncle and their demon spawn.

"Was there anything else, Octavia?" he practically stammers, giving away just how nervous he is. The first thing I'm going to have Smithy do for me once I sort out the house is find me a new goddamn lawyer. I want a shark, not a fucking minnow. I hang up the phone, but my grin only grows as I stare up at the ceiling.

I have to make a checklist of everything I need to buy for the house before I can move in. I'm pretty sure Smithy will handle everything for me if I shop online and get shit delivered. I bounce off of the sofa, practically skipping up to the main house.

Aunt Vivienne is in the formal dining room with Uncle Nate and Blair, finishing their dinner. Blair was just at Penny's. Her mocking still rings in my ears. I guess she couldn't possibly eat in front of her friends. Vivienne sneers at me as I enter the room, and I practically laugh. The sheer audacity of this woman trying to make me feel like a burden when she demanded I be here is astounding. "Octavia, you're late. You'll need to sort something out for yourself."

Goddamn, her voice is so fucking shrill. Just a few more days, and I'm out of here. "No problem, I already ate. I was just coming to find you to let you know I spoke to my lawyer. I'll be moving out of the pool house this weekend and moving back into my house. I'll make sure to pay you in full for the time I stayed here, though, don't worry. But you won't be seeing another penny of my father's money beyond that. I'd say I appreciate you letting me stay here, but since you manufactured it that way and then made me feel like a burden, I'll just say fuck all of you."

I spin on my heel, not giving any of them the chance to respond. I walk from the dining room, leaving Nate spluttering, Vivienne uttering strangled curses under her breath, and Blair glaring.

All things considered, this might just be the best night ever.

---

*Today was a bad day. I spent the day with Linc and East because Dad was so angry. I don't know what I did, but he just kept yelling at me to leave too. So I ran away next door and spent the day with my friends. By the time I got home, Dad wasn't mad anymore. He was just sad. All he does since Mom left is write songs with his guitar and drink that brown stuff that makes him smell funny. Smithy said he'd look after him and that I should get to bed, but I just can't fall asleep.*

*My sadness is too big.*

*I cry into my pillow, trying to keep my sobs quiet. Dad doesn't like it when I cry because it makes him sad too. He's been so sad since Mom went away, and I don't know how to make it better. I still don't know where she went or why she left us, but I really wish she'd just come back. It's been nearly a whole year since she left, and I still miss her every day.*

*I go still when I hear a tap against my window. After a moment I turn over to find Linc standing in the tree branches, trying to open my window. I rush from the bed and open it for him. He grins as he climbs in. "What are you doing here?" I whisper. He's going to get in so much trouble if his mom finds out he's not in bed.*

*"I knew you were sad; and I didn't want you to be alone, so I'm here. Now get back into bed before your dad hears us." He closes the window, and that's when I notice he's in his pajamas. I crawl back beneath my sheets, and he slides in beside me, lying so he's facing me. "You don't need to cry anymore. I'm here now."*

*I smile at him as a tear runs down my face. He smiles back, a little sad too, and wipes it away.*

*"But if you need to cry, that's okay too," he says as my tears come faster again. He hugs me tight and whispers, "I've got you. I'll always be here."*

*I cry into his shirt until I can't cry anymore. "Won't you get in trouble for being here?" I finally manage to ask.*

*"Nah, East knows I'm here. He'll cover with Mom." Lincoln seems so grown up sometimes, and I just feel like a cry baby. He's only nine months older than me, but sometimes he's more of a grown-up than East is.*

*"I'm okay now. You can go home if you want to," I tell him through my sniffles.*

*"Don't be silly. I'm not going anywhere. Now go to sleep. We have a pop quiz in the morning."*

*"Linc..." he cuts me off by putting his hand over my mouth. I lick it, and he narrows his eyes at me, making me giggle.*

*"Go to sleep, V," he whispers before wiping his hand on the sheets and closing his eyes. I smile and close my own, happy that he's here. He always makes me smile, even when I cry.*

*I believe him when he says he's not going anywhere, so I drift off to sleep feeling happier and safer than I have since Mom disappeared.*

# CHAPTER FIVE

Feeling much lighter than I did last night, I practically bounce out of the pool house and over to the main house for breakfast. Nothing will bring down my mood this morning. Not even my dream about Lincoln. I'm marking that down in the 'going back to the old house and shaking up my memories of a time lost to the past' column and leaving it there.

I smile at Pattie as I skip through the kitchen, beyond happy to find I'm the first one here for breakfast. I pile up my plate with all of the breakfast goodness I can manage and dive in. Pattie and her cooking skills are pretty much the only good things that came from being at the McMansion.

I eat happily until my phone buzzes. I pull it out of my pocket, smiling when I see Indi's name popping up in the notifications.

**Indi: Need a ride? I can swing by and grab you.**

**Me: That would be amazing. I'm at the house of horrors rather than where you dropped me yesterday though.**

**Indi: LOL! That's fine, I know where that is. I'll swing by in 15?**

**Me: Sounds good. I'll be ready**

**Indi: See you soon!**

I take a bite of my toast and slam back the last of my coffee before jumping up from the table and escaping the McMansion without a run-in with my so-called family. Thank God. I change out of my pajamas and into my uniform, and despite hating this ridiculous outfit, it doesn't put a damper on my day.

I pull my hair back into a high ponytail. It's a little messy, with tendrils of hair surrounding my face, but I kinda like it, so I leave it as it is. I finish my look with eyeliner and a swipe of mascara, then slip on a pair of black Louboutin heels. I might usually be a Chucks kind of girl, but today feels like the kind of day where I'm going to need the boost these shoes give me. I grab my bag and dash out the front in time to see Indi pulling up the drive.

"Morningggg!" Indi grins at me like the alt sunshine child that she is as I jump into the Wrangler. She turns down the Midnight Blue blasting through her speakers as I buckle up, and she peels away from the McMansion like zombies are chasing us. I can't help but laugh at her, and she chuckles along next to me. She slows once we reach the main intersection before looking over at me. "Coffee?"

"Hell yes. There could never be enough coffee in my system to deal with going back to this hellhole of a school." She laughs, turning away from the direction of school and swinging into the drive-thru at the closest Starbucks.

"How was visiting your old place last night?" she asks, and I grin so freaking wide.

"Well, it turns out my old place is my new place. Long story short, my family are assholes and wanted access to my dad's money, which is the only reason I was apparently ever with them."

"Wait, don't they have enough of their own?" she interrupts, eyes wide, and I shrug.

"I thought so, but there's no such thing as too much with people like them. Either way, it turns out my house manager, Smithy, was also in my dad's will as a legal guardian, so this bitch is escaping the house of horrors and going home. Also, before I forget, you're invited over for dinner tonight—Smithy insisted. He'll be serving up some mac and cheese goodness."

She goes to answer when the speaker box crackles outside her window. "Good morning! Thank you for choosing Starbucks; what can I get started for you?"

"Peppermint Mocha Frappe with extra cookie crumble, extra whip cream, and mocha drizzle," she says into the box, before turning back to me and laughing when she sees the look on my face. "Don't knock it till you've tried it. What do you want?"

"I'll just take a cold brew with mocha and almond milk," I tell her, reeling off the floofiest drink on my personal coffee menu. It's too goddamn warm for hot coffee right now, and I know if I have her sugary drink, I'll crash before lunch.

Once we get our drinks, she cranks up the latest Midnight Blue release and we sing at the top of our lungs until we pull into the parking lot at school. I smile when I see Raleigh and his friends standing near the steps up to the school, and we head straight for them.

"Octavia, hey!" Raleigh calls out, and I smile at him. I loop my arm through Indi's, practically dragging her along with me.

"Hey, guys," I offer with a smile, and Indi gives them all a small awkward wave. Oh my God, she's the cutest. I love her so much, and it's only been a day.

"I hear you guys are coming to my party this Friday?" one of the guys says, beaming at us with a classic puppy dog smile.

"If you're Jackson, then you'd be right."

He clasps his chest, acting like a swooning heroine from some fifties movie. "The girl doesn't even know who I am, my poor little heart."

I can't help but laugh at him as Indi giggles at my side. The girl fucking *giggles.* She must be downright smitten.

Raleigh drops an arm around my shoulder and puffs out his chest. "She doesn't need to know your name, bro, she already knows mine."

Jackson pulls a face, and Raleigh removes his arm from my shoulder before lunging at him. They start wrestling and laughing, so we say our goodbyes and head inside to our lockers. I drop off most of my books, only keeping what I need for English, and groaning at the thought of repeating the day I had yesterday. The monotonous schedule is one thing I didn't miss about traditional schooling. On the road, my tutor would change up what we did each day, because ya know, variety is the spice of life. The thought of having the same lessons at the same time every single day makes my little black heart shrivel some more. I'm just hoping that today I can focus enough to take notes at least. Hopefully I'll actually even learn something. The only classes that I feel confident about are English and French, because languages have always come easy to me. Music would usually be on that list, but right now, the thought of playing or singing makes me want to die a little.

"You ready for another bright and sunny day at Echoes Cove Prep?" Indi asks, shoving her head in her locker like she's trying to disappear into it.

"Oh yeah, it should be joyous," I quip, wishing I could disappear too. If she has a portal to Narnia in there, she better not be fucking keeping it from me.

"Whore," one guy coughs as he passes, and I flip him the bird as his friends laugh like he's just told the world's funniest joke. It's good to see that the delights of yesterday are going to continue today.

I need way more coffee than I've already had this morning if I'm expected to actually deal with this shit. If I make it through the day without being arrested, it'll be a good day.

---

English was a breeze. A debate with Ms. Summers about which main character from all of the books on our list fit best into the stereotype of a Byronic hero got my day off to a stellar start. Obviously I chose Heathcliff because well… duh. It's freaking Heathcliff.

I didn't even have time to care about Blair and her bitch squad being catty the entire class. Though, knowing I'll be moving out of her house at the end of the week is definitely keeping my mood nice and breezy.

My entire day is going great until I find myself sitting in Business class, the not-so-proud co-owner of a project with Lincoln fucking Saint… A project that's going to last the entire fucking semester and make up nearly half of our grade.

Fuck my actual life.

The lesson draws to a close, and I escape to Music without incident. I might need to work with Lincoln on the project, but I'm just stubborn enough that I'm positive I can do it without actually speaking to him.

I slide into the back of the music room, just the same as yesterday. This lesson is a refuge as much as it's a waking nightmare. None of the assholes haunting my life are in this class. In fact, the only person I know here is Raleigh. The problem is that everything about this lesson reminds me of my dad.

Miss Celine flounces into the room, her scarf waving behind her as she flourishes her arms to bring the chatter to an end. "Morning, everyone, I hope you're ready for the day! I've done some thinking after we finished the vocal seating assignment yesterday, and I couldn't help but reflect on the skill level of this group in particular. I want to challenge you, so I've decided that a solo will be required from each of you. The solos will be performed at the end of the semester, and I'd like it to be an original piece. You are permitted to work with another on the composition if you don't have the skill to play an instrument yourself, but you will each be required to perform a solo performance."

I fight the simultaneous urges to groan and pull out my hair. There goes my refuge. This class was meant to be easy. I mean, it's not like I got a choice with the class since my schedule was picked by my guardian. I know Smithy didn't mean anything by it, so I can't hold it against him… But *fuck*.

It's not that the project will be hard. I literally spent as much time composing music as I did studying when I was growing up. The problem is that I haven't been able to play, or even really sing, since my dad died.

I got through the last class by the skin of my teeth. I only had to sing one solo line and mumbled through the rest, and I handled that okay. It's just that I totally hid in the bathroom for ten minutes after that, trying to pull myself out of the dark hole that threatened to consume me from the inside out.

Everyone says that senior year is meant to be one of the best years of your life. I dare those fuckers, whoever they are, to live through the past few months of my life and tell me it's the best time ever.

"The music rooms will be open to you before the day begins, during lunch, and for an hour and a half once the school day is over. Use your time wisely. Now, let's warm up!" She turns on the music system, and I can't help but grin at the song that blasts through—"She's So Gone" by Naomi Scott. I'd be totally lying if I said this song didn't feature heavily in my early teen years.

Miss Celine blushes a little before shrugging. "You guys probably know the words, so let's do this."

The words wash over me in a wave, and I remember the time I sang this with Dad's band before one of his shows. It was my first arena performance, and I was hyped for weeks after it. I've never been one for performing publicly, but that performance was what solidified my desire to work in the music business. I just wanted it to be in a different way from my dad.

Music has always been a higher power of sorts for me. There's something about a song that can say more with a few words than I could ever manage in an essay.

I take a deep breath when the song reaches the chorus, singing along quietly. It's not really a quiet kind of song, but I don't have it in me to belt it like it deserves. As sad as I am, the song is still too fun to not get lost in it, so I manage to lose myself just a little. When the music wraps up, Miss Celine splits us into groups. I end up paired with Raleigh, and he saunters over to the back corner where I've been hiding all class long.

"I did not expect the QB to be a singer," I tease as he takes the seat beside me.

He grins at me before twisting his chair so he can face me with ease. "There's a lot more to me than being a QB."

"I have no doubt. You seem like the white knight type," I say with an easy laugh, and he brushes off the backhanded compliment, completely unfazed.

"I might have something of a hero complex, but only when it's needed. I'm all about independent women owning their shit." His grin widens, and I can't help but laugh at him. He really is something else. "As for singing, my grandma was a singer. She used to have me singing blues with her as a kid, and I've loved it ever since. This was a just-for-fun class for me this year. I don't need the art credits or anything."

"An overachiever too, I see."

"I do like to excel at everything I do." He flexes his arms as he talks, wagging his eyebrows in an over exaggerated sort of way, making me laugh once more. "Speaking of, you should come to our first game. We're playing the Asheville Allstars. The guys there can be total douchebags, but I have a feeling we're going to fucking annihilate them this year."

"When's the game?"

"Next week."

"I'll be there! I'm sure Indi will come with me, and I hope like hell she has a better understanding of football than me. Otherwise, we're going to end up cheering for the wrong team. Either way, we'll definitely be there!" He looks horrified at the thought, which only makes it that much more comical.

"Don't worry," he says, nodding sagely as he pats my arm, "I'll make sure to give you an idiot's guide at the party this weekend."

"You usually spend time at parties explaining football to girls?" I ask, an eyebrow raised.

His shit-eating smile is back as he pretends to dust off his shoulders. "Nah, I don't usually have to flex that hard."

"You're such a jock!" I tease, throwing my pen at him.

"I'll show you how much of a jock I'm not. Come on," he says as he stands, offering me his hand. This is the most fun I've had inside these walls, so I place my hand in his and let him lead me from the room. He pulls me inside one of the other music rooms a few doors down, and I crane my neck while I look around. The ceiling is ridiculously high and one of the walls is fully glass, looking out over the field at the side of the school. A lone piano sits in the corner of the room near the windows, and he takes a seat, clearing his throat before placing his fingers on the ivory.

A lump threatens to choke me as he starts to play a haunting melody, and then… it hits me. It's a remix of one of Dad's songs. I go to stop him, but he opens his mouth, and I'm struck fucking stupid.

The boy can sing.

How does he get to look and sound like sin?

He sings the entire song, with so much passion and emotion that I feel a tear trickle down my cheek—I've not listened to any of Dad's songs since his death, and I can't lock my emotions down. I swipe it away quickly, not wanting him to see just how affected I am. "That was amazing."

My voice is scratchy as fuck, and it's instantly obvious that I didn't hide my sadness well because he jumps up and rushes over to wrap me in the biggest hug I've had in months. "I didn't mean to make you cry."

"It's okay, it's all just kind of… raw still," I murmur, enjoying the feeling of being wrapped in his arms. It's rare that I take comfort from people I don't really know, but there's just something about him that tears down all of my carefully constructed walls.

"This looks cozy." My spine goes rigid at the voice, and dread pools in my stomach with his presence. I pull back from Raleigh at the words and turn to find Maverick standing in the open doorway.

"What is it to you, Riley?" Raleigh snaps at him, keeping his arm hooked over my shoulder.

Maverick's dark hair falls into his brown eyes as he smirks at Raleigh in that ruthless, malicious way he has. It's like every super villain's smile you see on the TV. He somehow seems fucking lethal with just a goddamn smile. "She's off-limits."

"What the fuck does that mean?" Raleigh says, maneuvering himself so he's standing just in front of me. Maverick saunters forward until he's toe-to-toe with Raleigh, crazy-bastard vibes rolling from him.

"You should leave now, quarterback, or I'll end your promising career before it begins." He stays in Raleigh's space, and I watch as Raleigh pales. Maverick pushes him, hard enough to make him shrink just a little, so Maverick turns his focus to me. He steps toward me, and I hate that I falter, that I take a step back. The smile on his face grows until he has me pushed against a wall.

"You won't get away with this," Raleigh hisses.

"Oh really? Who's going to do anything about it? You?" Mav taunts him without taking his eyes from me, and I shrink under his intense gaze.

"Yeah, I am," Raleigh says, but what he thinks he's going to achieve other than pissing Maverick off is beyond me.

Mav grins that ruthless smile down at me, ignoring Raleigh entirely.

"You can't do this," I stammer, looking around for Raleigh, but I can't see him. I hope to God he's gone to get a teacher.

"Can't do what, princess? Talk to you? Get in your space? Declare you off-limits?"

"Any of it!" The words fall from my lips in a rush, and I clench my fists, digging my nails into my palms in a desperate attempt to center myself. I hate how easily he can make me feel so small. He puts one hand on the wall just by my head, and reaches behind him with the other. When he brings it back, he has a knife in his hand.

A fucking knife.

He presses the blade against my throat, and I swear my heart stops. I can't even breathe with the cold, sharp metal pressing into my skin.

"Your pupils dilate so pretty," he murmurs as he pushes the blade harder, and I wince at the bite against my skin.

"You can't do this," I say again, my voice shaking despite my paralyzed state.

"Are you going to stop me? Are you going to fight me? Poor lost little princess. Sad little princess. Everyone would believe it was you if I slit your wrists and walked away, wouldn't they? The apple never falls far from the tree."

I look up into his eyes, and the delight in them as he stares down at me makes my blood run cold. "Please, Maverick."

I hate that I'm begging him, but I don't know just how far he's willing to push this. I've only been this scared a few times before in my entire life, and each time, I froze.

"That's it, beg me like the pathetic dog that you are." He sneers at me as he drags the knife down from my neck to my chest, cutting the skin as he goes. I can't help but hiss at the sting of the blade as it makes the shallow cut. "You sure make pretty sounds for me, little slut. Make some more."

I cry out as he cuts through my shirt, drawing blood as he goes, until the blade is at my navel. He removes it, and I almost sigh in relief until he places it against my thigh and draws it higher until it's at my panties. He breathes in deeply with his nose against my neck before rolling his tongue over the skin he cut.

"I bet you're wet aren't you, whore? I bet being fucked by my knife wouldn't even be the most fucked up thing you've done. I'd put money on you enjoying it too. I bet I could get you off with just my knife, couldn't I? Look at how hard your nipples are. Pebbling under my touch like a whore begging for more. I bet if I pushed my fingers past your panties you'd be wet, wouldn't you? Fucking pathetic. You're nothing but trash."

"N…n…no."

"You really think you get to tell me no?" He quirks his brow and pushes the cold metal harder against my skin, and I squeak again. I hate how small he makes me feel. I flinch as he brings his face close to mine, almost nose to nose. I turn my face to the side, closing my eyes, praying he got what he came here for because I'm not sure I can take much more.

"Off. Fucking. Limits, Octavia. You've been warned."

He pushes off the wall and walks away without another word. My misery is burned away by my fiery fucking rage. My hands shake, and I feel warm from the flush on my face. How dare he do that shit, say that like he owns me? Shame, embarrassment, and anger flood my veins. He has no fucking right, and no reason either. I haven't done anything to him.

The boy I once knew is definitely no more, in his place is a psychotic savage of a man. I already know there will be no reasoning with him. He's become the honed weapon his father always seemed to want him to be.

*I'll give him fucking off-limits.*

I clutch my shirt to my chest and send Indi a message with an SOS for yet another shirt. I need to clean up this blood too. Fucking Maverick Riley.

I curse myself for not finding this rage when he was here. Next time, I promise myself I'll be stronger.

Next time… because I already know that this won't be the end of it.

---

My rage stays with me all fucking day, like a close friend keeping me warm, with that cold, slimy shame lying just beneath it. Raleigh did eventually come back with a teacher but Maverick was long gone, and Indi had already saved the day with a new shirt, thankfully I managed to clean up the majority of the blood with the neckerchief.

I scurried off with Indi after reassuring them both I was okay. She didn't ask questions, just helped me out, and I'm glad. Because reliving what happened isn't something I want to do. The shame of enjoying what happened, having him pressed up against me, that his words sparked something primal in me, is still too raw.

Raleigh didn't seem to put much stock in Maverick's words, but I know that those three assholes hold more power here than people let on. They rule this fucking place with an iron fist.

That much has been drilled into me time and again.

It was more than apparent at lunch that Maverick's decree had been heard when even Jackson refused to meet my eyes. Apparently *off-limits* means being my friend puts you on a hit list, and no one wants to be on the wrong side of Lincoln and his faithful followers.

Though considering what happened with Maverick, I don't blame Jackson and the others. But if Lincoln and his two besties think they can actually control my life, they have another thing coming. I've had just about e-fucking-nough of that lately, thank you very much. I just need to find my rage sooner when they're around. Thankfully this shirt covers all of the marks he left on my skin, and the cuts weren't deep enough to scar.

To top it all off, it seems like we're back to our regularly scheduled programming in Gym class. Rather than taking us out to the track to run laps and practice sprints, East has us working circuits. Thirty minutes of the intense routine isn't even enough to burn away my rage.

At the end of class, he sends us to run suicide drills. I throw myself into them wholeheartedly, running until my heart feels like it's going to burst out of my chest.

The bell rings, and East blows his whistle, calling the drill to an end. Everyone leaves the gym while I stand, bent over, trying to catch my breath. I'm seriously considering continuing to run until I'm too numb to do anything else.

"V, what's going on with you?" East calls once the gym is clear. His footsteps echo in my direction when I don't answer right away, but I keep my mouth firmly closed so I don't flay him with all of the vitriol bubbling up inside of me. "Hey, V."

I stand to face him, and his eyes go wide. I guess my fury is written all over my face. I'm usually pretty good at hiding my emotions, but I'm beyond all that today. This whole fucking town is toxic.

"What's wrong?"

I take a deep breath, trying my damnedest to tamp down some of the boiling rage, because I know I'm going to have to answer him. I just don't want to piss him off.

"Your fucking brother and his crazy-ass friends," I say, my jaw still clenched.

"What did those little dicked, sons of bitches do now?" His question actually makes me laugh for the first time since Maverick's little declaration earlier. Fuck, I needed that.

"I assume you saw the crap on ReachMe?"

He rubs the back of his neck, his discomfort obvious. "Yeah, I did, but don't worry. No one will believe that it's true."

His words sting, echoing Lincoln's yesterday.

"If you say so." I shrug, trying not to let the sting of his words show. I refuse to believe that he shares the same views about me that his brother does. "But between that and the three of them casting me out publicly—I'm untouchable, and being my friend will make you an outcast. Being anything more than that is, well… social suicide. You know as well as I do that that'll extend beyond school."

"Those boys are fucking idiots," he grumbles, rubbing a hand down his face. "Let me see if I can't talk some sense into those assholes."

"No, don't bother. We both know that'll just make it worse. I've got this. You know me, I never start a fight, but I will sure as hell finish it." He barks out a throaty laugh before pulling me in for a hug, and I just hope I find the strength to see my words through.

"Damn, I missed you, V. You show those assholes what you've got. Maybe they'll pull their heads out of their asses." He squeezes me tight again before releasing me and looking back down at me with a soft smile on his way too pretty face. "How are you settling back into the Cove?"

"It's been pretty shit, honestly. Though, I did find out yesterday that I don't have to stay with Vivienne and Nate, so I'm heading back home this weekend."

His eyes go wide as I tell him my plans, and then he grins. "I guess it'll be just like old times, well, kind of. I'm still at the house with Linc. Since Mom fucked off not long after you guys left and Dad is always gone with work, it's like we have the place to ourselves."

"Your mom left?" I ask, shocked as hell. I had no fucking idea, I know I haven't been here, but that seems like the sort of thing I'd have heard before now.

"Yeah, I figured Linc told you after you left." He scratches the back of his neck and shifts from one foot to the other. He offers an off-kilter smile before shrugging. "I guess not, though. That's all in the past now anyway. But it'll be good to have you back around. Smithy still makes me a birthday cake every year, so now I'll have an excuse to come back around more often."

"You're welcome whenever." I smile, then notice the time. "Shit, I better go get changed. Indi is going to kill me if I keep her here too late."

"Sure, go. I'll talk to you later." He hugs me again quickly before I run to the locker rooms and jump in the shower. When I head back into the main part of the locker room, the place is empty. I open my locker, pull out my phone, and see a message from Indi.

**Indi: Got to grab a book from the library. I'll meet you by the car.**

**Me: Sorry! I didn't mean to take so long. I'll be out in a minute.**

**Indi: No rush, the parking lot is still practically full so I can't get out yet anyway.**

Weird. Most people would usually be gone by now.

I throw my phone back into my bag, slipping out of my gym clothes and pull out my uniform. It takes me all of a second to notice the giant holes cut into my shirt.

Fucking bitchy asshole girls.

I check out my skirt to find it in tatters too.

I fucking hate this school.

Fuck this, I could leave in my gym clothes, but fuck them all.

I throw the shirt and skirt in my bag, slipping on my untouched underwear and blazer. I let my hair down from its ponytail and fluff it up. If these assholes think I'm going to cower just because they fucked with my clothes, they have no idea who they're fucking with. I have bikinis that show more skin than this.

I pick up my bag, slip on my heels, and check out my reflection. At least I picked pretty black lace underwear today. I look like something out of a fucking Victoria's Secret ad. It's so fucking stupid, but you can bet your ass I'm going to rock this shit. I refuse to be beaten twice in one day. These assholes have no idea who I am, and the girls at this school don't scare me.

I hiss as I apply a little foundation over the red line down my skin to hide the mark Maverick made earlier before sliding on some lip gloss. I head out of the locker room in nothing more than my underwear and blazer.

The comments are almost instantaneous. I guess news of what the bitches in my gym class did spread around the school, which explains Indi's message about the parking lot. I hold my head high and strut through the halls, owning my shit like a badass bitch. I find Blair and her bitch squad all giggling by my locker, phones out and taking pictures. They stop laughing when they see the look on my face. I know I'll see those pictures online later, but what's one more at this point?

"I look fucking awesome, right?" I ask with a small wave as I pass them by. If they thought this would break me, they can think again. I've survived worse than their attempted humiliation.

I get to the end of the hall just to come face to face with Lincoln, Maverick, and Finley. Linc's jaw ticks as he takes in my appearance. Maverick's heated gaze on my chest where the cut on my skin is hidden almost makes me want to cower. But not again, not today.

"Not so off limits after all, am I?" I wink at him, and I swear to God Finley smirks as I push between him and Linc.

The catcalls and shouts I get as I pass the football field to where Indi is parked just make me shake my head. I can't help but laugh when I hear Raleigh tell them to shut their mouths before yelling, "You look like fire!"

I finally reach Indi, and she gawks at me as I climb in the car. "Don't even ask."

"Bitch, you just owned that. Whoever did this to you fucked up. There's no way in hell you look as good as you do right now and don't get half the school simping over you by tomorrow morning."

I bark out a laugh as she throws the car in drive and peels out of the parking lot. I knew I loved her for a reason.

# CHAPTER SIX

I survived.

Kind of.

Well, my first week anyway. It's been pretty fucking hellish. Between Lincoln, Maverick, and Finley terrorizing me daily, plus the general taunts and social media hate from the rest of the student body, I'm worn thin.

A girl can put on a brave face, but on the inside, I'm crumbling a little. Bullying isn't something I've ever dealt with before, not like this anyway. The online stuff I can handle, I'm used to tabloid bullshit, but my dad was there to shield me from most of it. Now I'm alone, and I'm not so sure I can handle it. I've questioned more than once this week if my inheritance is worth staying here. Between that and the struggle I'm already having trouble focusing in some of my classes, I'm not sure I'm going to meet the requirements of the Will anyway.

I'm just glad I made a few good friends who haven't even blinked at the social bullshit that seems to come with being associated with me. Indi is my fucking rock, and Raleigh has all but ignored the *off-limits* warning. We've sat with the jocks everyday at lunch since then, which meant that at least at lunch, I've felt somewhat safe. Some of the players still won't talk to me, but Jackson seems to have gotten over his aversion to eye contact, at least. He mostly spends time talking to Indi rather than me, but that, at least, makes me happy. Jackson chatting up Indi was always my endgame anyway. Becoming friends with Raleigh along the way is just an added bonus.

Throughout the week, I've managed to get lost inside my own head and packed up my meager belongings in the pool house. I also returned my rental in fear of it being fucked with because I wouldn't put it past the animals I go to school with to do something like that. Surprisingly, my aunt and uncle haven't put up much of a fight, though that could have something to do with the money I've already transferred to them for my 'rent'.

The few boxes of my dad's records are stacked in the corner along with the three duffel bags full of my clothes.

My new furniture has been delivered to the house throughout the week, and according to my regular updates from Smithy, everything is coming along nicely. Indi is going to help me drive the few things I have here over to the house in the morning, and then I never have to grace this house of horrors with my presence again.

It's almost enough to make me let out a whoop of joy. I focus on getting ready for Jackson's party instead. I'll save the celebrating for tonight.

I finish the final touches on the waves of my hair and add a batwing of eyeliner to each eye before adding a swipe of mascara. It's simple, but that's all I've ever done anyway. I'm not a cake-it-on kind of girl. I have mad respect for those who can, but contouring my face is basically the same as asking me to contort my body… It's just not going to happen. I'm hopeless.

I'm just glad that the cut Maverick made has mostly healed and what's left can be hidden with makeup. I sure as fuck don't want to spend my night explaining that away.

Indi sashays out of my bathroom, and I can't help but grin. She looks like an emo princess. "Damn girl, you are fire!"

"Why thank you." She blushes, taking a curtsy in her tutu, and I laugh. I'm not sure many people could pull off a black tutu dress with a leather jacket and flip-flops. "I don't want to get sand in my boots, so I figured I'd make this work."

"Dude, you look amazing! You're totally making it work."

"Are you ready to go?" she asks as I shrug on a kimono over my white tank top. I glance at the storage box of my shoes and ultimately decide to go shoeless. It's on the beach anyway, so fuck it.

I look outside at the pitch black sky and grin. I mean, who turns up to a party on time anyway? "Yeah, let's hit it."

I pull my phone out of the pocket of my cutoffs and send a message to Raleigh.

**Me: You still there? We're heading down now.**

**Raleigh: You know I got you. I'll meet you at the bottom of the stairs.**

I shove my phone back into the safe in my closet before we head down the stairs from the McMansion down to the sand below. I'm not going to need it tonight, but I learned long ago not to be stupid enough to just leave it lying around.

It's impossible not to see or hear the party from here, but it's nice of Raleigh to come get us anyway.

I think he might be one of the nicest guys I've ever met.

Indi's phone goes off, and she squeals a protest when she looks at the screen.

"What happened? Is everything okay?"

"*Adams Ever After* was canceled. Goddammit!" she exclaims, stomping her foot. I want to go on whatever journey this is with her, but I literally have no fucking idea what she's talking about. "Like, I know Ken died, but dammit, I was so freaking invested! I need to know what happens next. Natalie just went back to Banner-Hill. For fuck's sake."

"What on earth are you going on about?" She looks at me like I just kicked her puppy and took away her eyeliner stash all at once.

"You don't know what *Adams Ever After* is?" I wince at her screech as we reach the bottom of the stairs. Luckily, Raleigh is there waiting for us to save me from whatever this mini-tantrum is. I bounce across the sand toward him while Indi stops to take off her shoes.

"I've never heard of it," I yell back to her before turning to Raleigh. "Hey!"

"You and I have a trashy TV marathon coming up, V. This is an atrocity!"

"What is she yelling about?" Raleigh asks, laughing as she stomps across the sand toward us.

"*Adams Ever After*? I don't know." I shrug just as Indi catches up, waving her flip-flops at me.

"You mean the TV show?" he asks, and Indi grins wide at him.

"See, he knows! Natalie just went back into Banner-Hill. I need to know what happens. I know I'm whining, but you don't understand! I've watched this show for years! I know they haven't finished airing all of this season, so I still have a little more, but this is bad, bad news. What am I supposed to do on Thursday evenings now?"

I can't help but laugh at her dramatics. TV has never really been my thing, but if she's this invested… "I've honestly never heard of it, but for you, I'll give it a go."

She does a weird little dance in the sand, and Raleigh shakes his head before leaning down and saying, "You're going to regret that."

He's right, I might, but she's happy. I can live with it.

It doesn't take long for us to reach the outskirts of the beach party, and everyone says hello to Raleigh as we pass. The school might be for rich kids, but they seem to love football as much as any other town with a half-decent football team. I might as well be fucking invisible, though.

Raleigh leads us to where Jackson and a bunch of the jocks are sitting around the fire, beer in hand. Music thumps loudly all around us, but not quite so loudly that I can't hear myself think. It also doesn't quite drown out the squeals of girls being dunked. It's not like other parties I've been to, but then, technically this is my first high-school party.

Indi gravitates toward Jackson, while I chat with Raleigh and some of the other guys on the team. Apparently after my whole strut through the school half naked thing, everyone's just straight up ignoring Maverick's decree because I'm too hot to ignore, at least according to Raleigh.

I'm pretty sure that's the most backhanded compliment I've ever gotten in my life, but fuck it.

I drink a little, not so much that I'm going to feel it tomorrow, but enough that I can feel a buzz and loosen up a little. I can't believe it's only been a week since I started back at Echoes Cove Prep. It feels like a fucking lifetime with the amount of shit I've already dealt with.

So I decide I'm going to have a little fun tonight.

What's the worst that could happen?

---

Tonight has been way more fun than I expected it to be. Raleigh told me that the only reason Blair is here is because the cheer team is always invited, but they've basically left me alone. In fact, I haven't seen them around for a while. I'm not exactly sad about that either.

I lean into Raleigh, who's had his arm around my shoulder most of the night. He's so warm compared to the cool breeze, so I haven't complained about it, even if it does feel a little possessive. He's so chill, I'm sure that's not his intention. I'm new at this whole 'being around people my age all the time' thing, though, so who knows?

Man, I miss the roadies.

My attention is pulled back to the group when a roar of laughter goes up across the fire. I go on high alert when I notice Indi gasp. Her eyes go wide as she looks over my shoulder.

I look behind me and groan when I see what has her so on edge. Lincoln, Maverick, and Finley. I should've known that I couldn't have one fucking night of peace. After a week of shit, of course they have to show up at a party I know they weren't invited to. Even if it is on the beach.

Fuck my life.

"It seems the party started without us, boys," Maverick snarks as they approach, the firelight glinting on the bar in his eyebrow. Somehow the lighting makes him seem more menacing than normal. How an eighteen-year-old guy can look so menacing in a muscle tank and a pair of ripped jeans is beyond me, but he manages it. It also reveals the ink I hadn't realized he had. All of it is normally hidden by his uniform, but tonight his colorfully painted skin is fully on show.

"I didn't realize you guys were coming," Jackson says, pulling Indi closer to him. "You know you're always welcome."

Raleigh throws a sharp glance over at him, and Jackson just shrugs. I get it. Those three run the school. Just because Raleigh dislikes them on my behalf doesn't mean Jackson can afford to as well. I elbow Raleigh softly, bringing his gaze to me, and smile at him before looking over to Jackson to let him know I'm good.

"Of course we're welcome. This is our beach just like ECP is our school," Maverick says before grabbing a beer and heading toward the gaggle of squawking girls by the water, crashing into my shoulder as he does.

Jackass.

"Surprised you showed your face, Royal," Lincoln says, his tone biting as he grabs two beers from the cooler. He offers one to Finley who refuses it. The refusal doesn't surprise me. His mom always had substance abuse issues, and he definitely seems like the straight edge type.

"Why wouldn't I? My friends are throwing a party—of course I'm here." I raise an eyebrow in challenge but bite back any other response. I couldn't be anymore fucking annoyed with myself for responding to him, but prodding probably isn't going to make my life easier either. I haven't spoken to him since he saw me in my underwear as I left school the other day, and it isn't like he's made any effort to talk to me either. He's just watched as his loyal sycophants have terrorized me all week.

He stares at me, his expression blank, before walking away to another group as Finley drops onto the sand and gets comfortable.

Of course he fucking does.

I try not to let their appearance fuck with me and turn my attention back to Raleigh and the guys, but it feels like the whole tone of the party has changed. The music is lower, and everyone's mood seems a bit more subdued. It's almost like a parent just crashed the party. My buzz sure as shit took a hike when they appeared. I let out a sigh and untangle myself from Raleigh. "I think I'm going to call it a night. I have a big day tomorrow."

"You sure?" He frowns down at me as I take a step back.

"Yeah, I'm sure."

"Okay, you want me to make sure Indi gets home okay? I've only had one." I look over at her, and she looks so happy I don't want to rain on her parade.

"That would be awesome if you don't mind?"

"Nah, it's good. I'll make sure she's safe."

"Thank you." I smile at him before heading over to Indi. "I'm heading home. Are you still cool to go car shopping with me tomorrow?"

"You know I am." She grins at me, and I can tell from the faraway look in her glassy eyes that she's quite a bit more buzzed than I am, and I bite my lip.

"You okay staying? Do you want me to get you home?"

"I'm good," she giggles. "I haven't drunk that much, and I'm sure Raleigh the Protector will make sure nothing nefarious happens."

"He did say he'd get you home for me," I tell her, and she giggles again.

"See, I'll be fine. I'll pick you up bright and early in the morning!" She moves from Jackson and wraps her arms around me, holding me tight for a second before letting go.

"Have fun." I grin and wink at her before turning and heading back up the beach toward the pool house. I definitely have a lot going on this weekend. Between moving, car shopping, and homework, I'm sure I'll barely have time to breathe. And I'll bet there's probably more that I've forgotten about, but I mean… I need a car, and I need to get out of the McMansion. Stat.

I rub my hands up and down my arms as I trek down the beach. It's definitely cooler than I thought it would be. I lose myself to thoughts of the rolling to-do list in my head, but the sound of sand shifting behind puts me on high alert. My heart rate spikes as I look over my shoulder, but it's so fucking dark out here, there could be someone there and I wouldn't know it.

I pause for a moment, but I don't hear anything else, so I pick up my pace. I practically run up the steps to the house, but freeze when I take in the backyard.

The doors to the pool house are all open, and my clothes are in pieces and scattered across the yard. Fuck. Some of them are in the pool too.

I decide to leave them and head into the pool house. There's no point trying to collect the clothes outside. They're in shreds. I just hope whoever did this didn't find my band tees. Dad and I collected those from his shows, as well as some others that we went to together. They're more than just t-shirts.

I flick on the lights and stop dead in my tracks.

*No.*

My dad's records… They're in pieces around the room.

This cannot be happening.

I fall to the ground, my knees crashing against the wood flooring with a bang. I can't breathe.

This is like losing him all over again.

This is all I had left of him. All that really mattered anyway.

All I can see is the destruction around the room. Of my memories.

Of my dad.

I think I might officially be losing the tenuous grip I've been holding over everything since Dad died.

This? This might be the thing that actually breaks me.

I didn't have much that mattered left in this life, just the contents of these boxes. And now everything's gone. Destroyed. In a matter of hours.

I don't even have to think twice about who did this. I knew there was a reason the bitch squad disappeared from the party. I just hadn't considered that even Blair would be this hateful. What did I ever do to her?

"Lookie what we found here, boys… You know, you really shouldn't spend so much time alone, whore." I spin around at the voice and see four guys I don't know. I recognize their faces from school, but I couldn't name them even with a gun to my head.

"What do you want?" My voice sounds as broken as I feel. I climb to my feet, tired of all of this already. All I want to do is tidy up and then drown myself into oblivion, preferably with tequila. Because this week has been fucking awful.

They press closer into my space, and the hair on the back of my neck goes up. It didn't occur to me to be afraid of anyone that wasn't Lincoln, Maverick, and Finley, but the smiles these four give me tells me that was stupid. "We just want to have some fun. You're already putting out for Coach. Why not us too?"

"I didn't put out for anyone," I argue, folding my arms over my chest to hide the shake of my hands. I don't even have my phone to signal for help, it's locked in my goddamn safe.

The leader of the pack steps even closer to me, so close I can feel his breath on my skin. "That's not what we heard. What's wrong? Are we too good for you?"

"I said scare, not play." I look up over the guy's shoulder and see Lincoln, Maverick, and Finley, all leaning against the glass wall that makes up the front of my pool house.

Of course this was them.

"You heard him," one of the other four guys says, and they rush me. I kick and shout, trying to get them off of me, but they hold me while tearing at my clothes. Pawing at me in the process. I call out until my throat is raw, but it's no use. No one is going to help me but me.

They have me down to my underwear, and I thrash harder. They are not getting me naked. Not a fucking chance. I throw out a fist, catching one of the guys in the face, but I don't have time to take any happiness from my victory when he clasps me around the throat. "Stupid bitch."

"That's enough!" Lincoln's voice booms around the room. "Leave."

At his decree, the four of them pull away from me, grumbling under their breath as they leave the pool house. They each look like they'd like to complain, but they don't actually speak up. Who would dare complain to the King?

I clutch my arms around my body, trying to cover myself up as humiliation burns through me. "What the fuck do you want?"

My voice is harsh, but it doesn't affect them. Not at all. They close in on me, and I stumble backward until my back is pressed against the wall. I might not have had the sense to be afraid before, but I know for sure that these three have zero hesitation in regards to hurting me. Maverick already proved that. And money talks in this town, so even if I went to the police, nothing would be done. Nothing is ever done with people like this.

"You came back." Lincoln shrugs, like that should explain everything. Tears well in my eyes, but I blink them back. I refuse to let them see me cry.

With a slight nod from Lincoln, the other two step forward. Finley grasps my wrists, and despite my attempts to break his grip, he lifts them and pins them above my head on the wall. I'm usually all for consensual restraint, but this is different, despite the shudder of excitement that runs through me. I struggle against him, but Maverick pulls that knife of his again. "Please, don't."

"You don't make the rules here, Octavia. We do. The moment you set foot back in our town, we owned you. You want control? Leave," Lincoln says as he smirks at me. "But don't worry. You'll enjoy this."

He drops to his knees at my feet, and I lock my ankles together. "What the hell are you doing?"

He glances up at me before his gaze moves to Maverick. The sinister grin on his face as he steps toward me makes me fight Finley's hold even harder. He is not putting that knife near me again.

"Stop. Wait. Fine," I say because really, what other choice do I have? I uncross my ankles, and Mav steps back, watching me like a bird of prey. I am most definitely the mouse in this situation.

Lincoln reaches forward, his fingers brushing softly against my skin as he pulls my panties down my legs. Goosebumps erupt all over my skin at his touch, and I hate that my body reacts to him like it does. He smiles up at me knowingly, so I can't help but taunt him. "This is the only way you'll ever be able to touch me. Pathetic."

The light dances in his thunderstorm eyes as he chuckles softly. "By the time I'm done with you, Octavia, you'll be begging for me to touch you again."

"You think this is a game?" I pull against Finley's grip again, but it's futile.

"Princess, the sooner you figure out that life is a game, the sooner you'll understand." Lincoln throws that bit of fucked up philosophy my way right before his tongue does a leisurely swipe of my pussy that has my entire body shaking with need.

"I hate you!" My words are harsh, but my delivery of them is weak as hell. My traitorous body has abandoned me, leaving me alone with my thoughts.

"That's okay," I hear Finley whisper in my ear, his erection rubbing against my hip as he keeps a steel hold on my wrists above my head. "We hate you too."

I turn to face him, and the fire in his eyes is enough to shock me to silence. It takes a second for me to remember that I want to answer his retort, but Lincoln swiftly grabs my thighs and throws them over his shoulders—giving him open access to my pussy to do with it as he wishes—stealing my attention away from Finley's hurtful words.

The first full contact of Linc's mouth on my body sends shivers down every inch of my skin in slow fucking motion. How is this even possible? Why am I reacting this way?

Rustling sheets to my left catch my attention, and when I turn to see what's happening, I see Maverick leaning back on one arm as he sits back on my bed, his other hand gripping his eye-wateringly big cock like he lives here. Like this is his room, his bed.

Like I'm his to admire.

Narrowing my eyes at the sight before me, I try to growl at him, but it all comes out in a moan like I'm the star of an orgy video. None of them miss the sound, the smirks on each of their faces telling they heard it loud and clear.

"Nice. I might just come in my pants if you do that again," Finley whispers, lips tickling the shell of my ear.

"Fuck you!" I hiss, and Lincoln pulls back from me to look into my eyes. You'd think him being on his knees would give me some form of power, but it's glaringly obvious to all involved that I am not the one with power here.

"Maybe one day, but first, I want to see how fast I can make you come," Lincoln taunts, which only pisses me off more.

"You're delusional if you think you can force me to come," I spit at Lincoln just as his mouth latches back onto my pussy. Finley's cock rubs up against my naked skin as he grips my chin, turning my head toward Maverick who's jacking himself off, eyes fixed on where Linc's mouth is fucking my pussy like he owns it.

"There's nothing more powerful than owning a cunt's orgasms. And trust me, Octavia, while you stay in Echoes Cove, we own you."

I can smell my arousal, hear the wet sounds coming from Linc's mouth, and the slapping of Maverick's cock as he increases the rhythm of his strokes. I squeeze my eyes closed to try to shut out everything else. I am trying really fucking hard not to enjoy any of this.

What kind of fucked up person am I that I have to force myself not to enjoy being taken by three guys I hate?

I'm going to Hell. Yeah, scratch that.

I'm already in Hell.

Finley's grip on my chin tightens before his hand moves down to hold my throat, and he squeezes. "Open your eyes, whore. Watch him."

All of my good intentions go flying out the window as Lincoln pushes two fingers inside my pussy and curls them just right, hitting some sort of magic button deep inside me that no-one before him has managed to find.

"So tight for a dirty little whore." Lincoln grins up at me before letting out a dry laugh.

"Fuck you," I pant, wishing I didn't sound as turned on as I do, and I grit my teeth at his degradation yet again. If only he knew the truth of it.

He thrusts his fingers inside of me again and I see fucking stars. A shudder runs down my spine, and the sound that comes out of my mouth isn't normal. It's animal-like. Something uncontrollable and unwanted.

Maverick grins from where he's splayed out on my bed. "There it is. Keep going, Linc, I think she's enjoying herself."

Fucking Finley and his dirty whispers.

Pressing my head back against the wall, I make the mistake of looking down. What I see undoes me completely.

Lincoln is eating my pussy like it's his last supper, two fingers pumping in and out of me as his lips latch onto my clit and squeeze hard enough to make me groan in pleasure. I'm almost resolved to just letting it happen, but then I look at Maverick, and the smug expression on his face gives me the strength to keep fighting them. Until Lincoln hits that spot again, and every thought but their touches and stares leaves me.

"Stop! Oh God, right there! No, yes! Yes!"

I don't know what the fuck is spewing from my mouth, but the sight of Maverick's forearm tensing with every stroke, veins popping with the effort, the sound of Linc's mouth and fingers fucking my pussy like he owns it, and the feel of Finn's body rubbing up against my naked skin as he squeezes my throat, not letting me take a full breath… It's making my brain melt.

Fuck it, I can't control my body's needs, so I just let it happen.

As I make that decision, I relax my body and feel my juices trickling down my inner thighs, eliciting a moan from Linc. It's the first time I've realized his enjoyment, and I get a small feeling of empowerment from that. Because they may be using my body against me, but my body is making them lose control just as well.

With a small grin on my face, I bask in the knowledge that I might be having the same effect on them that they're having on me, and it feels like a small victory.

I open my eyes once more, focusing on Maverick's face and notice he's about to come. His dick is a deep, angry red, ready to explode and that, too, gives me a sense of power.

It's only when I feel another breach of my body that I lose all self-control.

Gathering my juices on his finger, Lincoln pushes one then two fingers inside my ass, and that brief moment of pain is like fuel to an already blazing fire.

The sound that escapes my body is probably loud enough for the entire town to hear, but in that moment, I don't give a shit.

In that moment, all I want is bliss.

So, I let it happen. I even rub my pussy in Linc's face, making sure he'll be tasting me for hours to come, smelling me on his breath long after he's gone.

I writhe and groan, watching as the first spurts of Maverick's cum splashes on his chest. I watch him as my body, my pussy, makes him lose his own control. His cum coats his entire hand before he smears it on my bed, smirking at me as he does. Oh, how the tables have turned.

Linc doubles down on fucking me with his mouth like it's his only mission in life. He's all lips, tongue, and teeth. His fingers move in sync, fucking my pussy and my ass, and I'm a goner. Beside me, Finn whispers filthy words that only add to my orgasm as it hits me like a Mac truck.

*"You're our dirty little whore."*

*"That's right, that tight little cunt of yours is begging for us."*

*"I can't wait to bury my dick inside your pretty little pussy."*

*"Next time, you'll be sucking my cock."*

My senses can't take it anymore, and my entire body erupts with an orgasm so powerful I think I actually pass out for half a second.

When it all ends and I come back to the reality of my situation, I hate myself almost as much as I hate them. My brief feeling of empowerment is stolen by the shame coursing through my veins. Looking down at Lincoln as he takes one last leisurely swipe of his tongue across my soaked pussy lips, I glare at him.

They won, and I hate them for it.

He must read my thoughts because his next words are like a bucket of ice spilled over my naked body.

"I told you, Octavia. We control everything. Even things as primal as this. The only way to be free is to leave." Lincoln glares at me as Finley finally releases my wrists and Mav tucks his dick back in his pants.

"Leave," I somehow manage to say around the painful lump in my throat. I swallow and clear my throat, but my voice still comes out scratchy as all of my emotions hit me at once. "Get out."

They just stand there watching me, and I hate how I gave in to them. No matter how much I enjoyed it. I slide down the wall until I'm sitting on the floor, knees pulled against my chest, protecting myself from them the only way I can.

"Get out. All of you. Just get the fuck out." They don't move, and my anger burns hot and ugly in my gut. I slam my fists on the hardwood floor as I yell, "Leave!"

Lincoln steps toward me, a glare on his face, but Finley puts a hand on his shoulder, stopping him. They all turn and leave without a backward glance.

I swipe furiously at the tears that stream down my face and shut down the hurricane of emotions that are swirling around inside of me.

Tonight was too much. I lost too much.

The second I know they're gone, I break.

And I'm not sure I can be put back together the same.

# CHAPTER SEVEN

I wake up, feeling bleary-eyed and stiff, and sit up from where I lie curled on the rug. I blink through grainy eyes and take in the destruction from the night before. The stiffness in my body is a stark reminder of last night, of just how much I've lost in the past month.

Once I showered, trying to scrub away the feel of them on me, denying how much I enjoyed their touch, I managed to get everything in one pile and even salvaged a few records. My band tees were completely unscathed, though I have no idea how. I found the duffel under my bed, so either someone knocked them under there by accident, or I shoved them under there and forgot I put them under here. Everything else is gone.

I literally have nothing but the clothes on my back.

They destroyed everything else.

I cannot wait to get the fuck out of here. I'm tempted to set fire to the fucking pool house with everything in it on my way out, so I don't have to see what they did to me anymore.

I stretch out my stiff limbs and climb to my feet before packing the few things that I salvaged in my duffel with my band tees. It doesn't take long, and as soon as I'm finished, my phone buzzes away in my pocket.

**Indi: Morning! I'm on my way. I'm bringing coffee, because shit.**

**Me: I'll wait for you out front**

**Indi: Sure thing. I'm going to get you a floofy coffee, prepare yourself.**

I can't help but smile at her and her floofy coffee. At least something can still make me smile. Maybe I'm not beyond help after all. Something inside of me definitely broke all the way last night, though, and there's no coming back. I am so done with these Echoes Cove assholes. But I decide to keep what happened with the guys to myself. Indi doesn't need to know my shame. Telling her that I didn't hate it, even admitting it to myself… I just can't.

I'm keeping my head down and getting the fuck out of here the second I can. It's not hard to see why both of my parents left this hellhole the second they got the chance. My phone buzzes just as I reach the gate at the side of the house.

**Indi: Here!**

**Me: 2 secs**

I don't even bother going through the house. If I see Blair, I might smash her face in, and while she deserves the beating, my aunt and uncle would definitely press charges. No question. That's just not something I want to deal with on top of everything else right now.

I jump into her Wrangler, throwing my one lonely duffel bag in the back. She looks at me, and I can tell the questions are on the tip of her tongue, so I shake my head and ask, "Coffee?"

"I got you the Java Chip Frappuccino. Not too floofy, considering you usually like a Mocha, but it is life."

I laugh at her, shaking my head before buckling myself in. She peels out of the drive, whipping through the neighborhood. We drive in silence for a few minutes, but I can tell her curiosity is eating her up from the inside. She taps her fingers against the steering wheel and glances at me every few seconds. I sigh with a roll of my eyes but incline my head in her direction. I'll have to tell her eventually, about some of it anyway.

Her silent questions are damn near suffocating. I take one long, deep breath before answering, "Blair and her bitch squad destroyed most of my shit, so that bag is all I have left." The car swerves as she jerks her head in my direction, jaw slack.

She focuses back on the road quickly and straightens out, but her knuckles are white on the steering wheel. "Those fucking cunts," she all but growls, and I can feel my eyebrow inching upward on its own accord. "Sorry, bitch just isn't cutting it. Who the fuck even are they? Entitled little twats."

"What the fuck is a twat?" I laugh.

"Girl, you and I need to watch Green Street. Charlie Hunnam, with a British accent, calling people a twat is a whole experience," she gushes, and I can't help but laugh at her. "A twat is basically a British insult that covers most things, and just sounds good. But at least now you're smiling."

I finish telling her about my evening and then realize I'm being a terrible friend. I shove down all of my misery and vow to be at least a little happy—I'm still getting out of my aunt and uncle's house after all. I refuse to bring her down just because my shit is all kinds of fucked up at the moment. "Wait, screw my shitstorm of a night! How did your night go with Jackson?"

She grins, and I swear I can spot a sparkle in her eyes. Damn. Must've been good. "It was fun, nothing really happened, but it was fun to hang out. Him and Raleigh made sure I got home safe, and he was a perfect gentleman the entire time."

"Uh-huh, if you say so." I grin, and she sticks her tongue out at me before pulling into the Jaguar dealership. "So, we start here?"

I take a look at the cars on the lot and shake my head. "No way, this place just screams evil villain. I want something a little more me." I pull up one of the car ads I found online and show it to her. "I'm thinking something more like this."

She grins at me and nods, putting the car back in drive. "I know exactly where to go."

She pulls out of the lot and jumps on the highway. We sing and dance around like idiots to "You Me at Six", and I feel a little more like myself. This girl is literally the embodiment of sunshine and joy. I swear to God if anyone tries to take that from her, I'll flay them alive.

She pulls off the highway, and it's not long before she pulls to a stop in front of a showroom full of vintage cars.

Now this is what I'm talking about.

I look across the lot, and within seconds, I see the car I'm leaving with. It's fucking beautiful. A black 1967 Chevrolet Impala gleams in the sunlight, and I want it. No, I need it.

It doesn't take long for me to convince the salesman that I want what I want, and he's not going to sell me on anything else. Less than thirty minutes later, after a swipe of my pretty little plastic and a call to Smithy to confirm the sale, I leave with the keys to my newest joy. Got to love the way that money makes everything go faster in Echoes Cove.

"I'm gonna call her Izzy the Impala." I grin at Indi who laughs at me. "You want to follow me back to my house, and then I can show you the place properly since you ditched me earlier in the week?" I pout at her, and she rolls her eyes.

"Oh please, I ditched you to have dinner because my aunt came into town as a surprise. We both know I'd rather have been eating mac and cheese with you."

"Oh I know, it's just fun to poke."

"Yeah, yeah, Royal." She rolls her eyes and spins her keys on her finger. "Now get your pretty little butt in your car so I can follow you home in your beautiful new Impala."

I grin at her and practically skip over to my new car. Once I'm in, I take in the fact I just bought my first car. I refuse to dwell on the fact that Dad and I talked about this day way too many times for this not to hurt a little, but I already hurt so much that I just can't think about it properly.

I start the car up, practically quivering over the pure American muscle growl that it makes. I peel out of the lot, heading back toward Echoes Cove. The car drives like a dream, and I almost wish the journey was longer.

By the time we pull up to the gates of the house, I'm grinning from ear to ear, having played more than a little to see what the little beauty is capable of. I lean out of the window and hit the buzzer, smiling into the camera lens. It buzzes again, and the gate starts to open. I head up the drive, with Indi following behind me in the Wrangler. Our cars so do not fit into the whole uptown rich bitch vibe of Echoes Cove, but I kind of love that.

I jump out, before grabbing my duffel from the backseat of the Wrangler, and head to the door with Indi on my heels.

"Miss Octavia, welcome home." Smithy greets me with a huge smile as he opens the door. "You must be Miss Indi. Welcome."

"Oh, I like him. Where can I get one?" Indi snickers, and Smithy laughs in that deep, throaty way he does.

"You are welcome here at any time, Miss Indi." He waves us in the house, and I swear, a weight I hadn't realized I'd been carrying lifts from my shoulders. Even with the bullshit of everything that's happened in the last twenty-four hours, I'm finally home, and I almost feel content. "I've had the bedroom put together as per your directions, and all of the deliveries are arranged in the room for you too. I'll start putting together something for lunch. Will you both be eating?"

"Thank you so much, Smithy." I hug him tight, and he squeezes me just as tightly back. "We'll both be here for lunch and maybe dinner too. And thank you for handling everything, really. I appreciate it."

"That's what family is for, Miss Octavia. Now then, head upstairs! Do you need me to get the rest of your things?"

I twist my lips instantly, still a little pissed off about everything, and he frowns in response. "This is everything I have left. Blair and her friends destroyed everything else."

"That girl… I swear…"

"It's fine," I say, waving him off. If I go down this path again today, I'm never going to pull myself out of the pit of despair that's always lurking just beneath the surface and threatening to pull me under. "You said you packed most of Dad's stuff up in the basement, right? And all the other stuff that was sent back from the tour bus is there too? I'm sure I'll find some more momentos in that stuff, so no worries."

"Yes, of course, if you say so." He twists his lips like he disapproves but shakes his head before smiling at me again. "Now you girls head on upstairs. If anything isn't to your liking, just let me know, and I'll get it all sorted out for you."

"Thank you, Smithy," I say before turning to Indi. "Ready?"

"As a church goer on a Sunday." We head up the stairs, and I show her my childhood room, which gives her more than a few laughs. The pink really needs to be sorted out. Maybe I'll have Smithy arrange for the room to be painted and turned into a spare room or a music room. Anything but this pink nightmare.

We leave the pink disaster behind and head to the master suite. I can't help but grin as I take in what Smithy did to the room. He didn't just do what I asked—he decked the room out to the extreme. There are guitars hanging on one wall with a keyboard sitting just beneath them, regardless of the fact that we have a baby grand downstairs. The carpet is a cream colored blanket of thick, plush luxury, and the walls are dark gray. All of the furniture is a shabby white, and it's just… perfect. I smile as my eyes catch the accents of teal peppered throughout the room.

"Dude, can Smithy be my interior designer? This room looks amazing."

"Right? He nailed it." I walk in further and notice a ton of bags from what looks like clothes stores lined up beside the bed. Then I notice the envelope sitting on the pillow with my name on. "What the…"

I pick it up and take the note out.

*To replace what was damaged at my behest.*
*Linc*

"You have got to be fucking kidding me," I practically spit, seething with the anger burning deep in my gut.

"What?" Indi asks, and I pass her the note. She reads it, and her eyes go wide as I clench and unclench my fists. What the actual fuck? "Oh boy, did he actually just buy you a new wardrobe?"

I reach for one of the bags, recognizing the lingerie brand and my anger ratchets up another thousand degrees or so. "He bought me fucking everything, including underwear."

"Is he crazy? Why would he do this?"

"Because Lincoln Saint is a control freak, and he always has been. Apparently that's one thing around here that hasn't changed." If he thinks I'm accepting this bullshit, he has another thing coming. This isn't an act of kindness. This is just another reminder of his words last night. Money means nothing to him. This is just another show of control."

"I mean, some of this is nice, though," she jokes, spinning a lacy black thong around in the air, and I can't help but laugh. "Maybe after seeing how hot you looked earlier in the week, he was inspired."

"He can shove his inspiration up his ass." I start snatching up the bags, and Indi joins in, grinning even though she's out of the loop of my plan.

"What are we doing?"

"We're going next door."

"Next door?"

"To the Saints' house." I grin, and her eyes go wide.

"Wait, they still live next door too? This is so delicious. Girl, I can't even." She's practically giddy as she follows me out of the house and down the drive. I buzz on the Saints' gate and wait, trying not to sigh as I bounce from foot to foot. My hands clench around the handles of the bags as fury pierces through me. I still can't quite believe Lincoln had the nerve to do this, and yet, I don't know why I'm really that shocked.

"V? Is that you?" East's voice comes through the system, and I smile. Better him than his brother. I can't help but wonder if he knows what Lincoln and the others did to me over the weekend? I can't help but wonder if East would have joined them. Would he have pinned me and whispered dirty words to me like Finley did? Or watched me like Mav? Or would he have touched me like his brother did? Shame floods me at the thought, and I push it back the best I can.

"Yeah, it's me. Can I come in? I'll only be a minute."

"Er, yeah sure," he says, and buzzes me in, sounding more than a little confused. Indi follows me up their drive, and I ignore the onslaught of memories that threaten when the house comes into view. We find East standing in the open front door, eyes wide when he takes in the sight of us with all of the bags. "V, what is that?"

"This is all for Lincoln. You can tell him to shove his so-called gift up his ass."

East drags a hand down his face as I drop the bags at his feet and groans. "What the fuck did he do now?"

I give him a quick run down of some of the shit I've been going through, leaving out the more… graphic parts… and the look on his face tells me he has had no idea about anything that's been going on beyond what I told him that first day in Gym.

His rage over everything is obvious. His hands shake as he clenches his jaw, looking more like Lincoln than normal, though they could be twins on a bad day. "My little brother needs to get a fucking clue. I'm sorry, V."

"You don't have anything to be sorry for," I tell him before giving him a quick hug.

He frowns at me and says, "I'm still sorry, V. If there's anything I can do to help, you know I will. I can't believe they trashed your dad's stuff. I'm going to have words with that little fuck head."

"There's no use, we both know that it won't stop anything. It might just make him worse. I just wish I knew what I did." He frowns at my words as I wrap my arms around myself. He steps forward and hugs me tight, and for a moment I let myself relax into his arms. Taking comfort that he, at least, is still my friend. "I'll see you soon?"

"You know it," he says before Indi and I head back home.

"Actually, fuck going home, do you want to go shopping? I do need a new wardrobe after all." I smile at her, and she squeals happily.

"Hell yes!" We head inside and grab my keys before heading back out. Shopping has never been something I massively enjoy, but then I've never had a girlfriend like Indi to shop with.

I chew on my lip as I climb in the car, trying not to get lost in my own head as Indi gets in. I thought coming home would solve all my issues, but I have a feeling being next door to the Saint boys again is going to bring a whole host of new issues.

At least life won't be dull, I guess.

# CHAPTER EIGHT

"You think he was pissed?"

I glance over at Indi sitting in my passenger seat, chewing on her lip. She's been fidgety ever since I picked her up for school this morning. Gone is the badass that helped me dump clothes on Lincoln's doorstep, and in her place is the sunshine child who doesn't want to hurt anyone.

"I mean, probably, but he was pissed at me anyway. This won't have made much of a difference. Plus, I don't give a shit if he's pissed. After everything they've done to me this last week, they deserve to be pissed off." I smile at her, trying to reassure her, but she wrings her hands in her lap. I haven't even told her everything that's happened, and right now I'm glad for that. I'm not sure her sunshine persona could handle the avalanche of bullshit I've been buried under. "Don't worry, even if he is, I won't let anything happen to you. You did your time with the bitch squad already. I won't let being my friend drag you down harder."

Her eyes go wide, and she shakes her head. "Oh please, that isn't what I meant at all. I just mean like, the bitch squad are the ones who have been messing with you so far. What if the boys step up their assholeness? I'm not worried for me, just for you. You've only been back at FCP a week, and look at what you've already dealt with."

My heart swells at her words. Total sunshine child. She is literally the embodiment of joy in a dark little alternative shell. For the first time in a long time, it's nice knowing that I have someone who is one hundred percent on my side and has my best interests at heart. "Don't worry about me. I grew up here, playing these games is practically a part of my blood. Blair and her little minions already took the last few things that were precious to me. There isn't anything more they can do to truly hurt me."

My mind flashes over everything they've already done. I'm not really sure that it can get worse than it has.

"I don't know, you have some pretty banging hair, and I've seen the Saint Squad do some pretty shitty things."

I shrug as I pull into a space in the student lot. "It's just hair, it'll grow back. But trust me, they won't go after my hair. I swear, Blair's hair is her greatest treasure, so she wouldn't want me to retaliate that way. She might seem like a dumb bitch, but she's calculating as hell."

"Okay," she starts but cuts off with a squeak as Raleigh jumps in front of the hood.

He lets out a whistle before walking around and opening my door for me as I grab my bag from behind Indi's seat. I look up and see Jackson at her door, and she's blushing like crazy. I wink at her, which just makes the red on her cheeks deepen closer to maroon as he opens her door.

"Good weekend?" I ask Raleigh as I lock the car.

"Yeah, not so bad, just chilled and slayed Jackson on Apex and all that. It was a pretty chill weekend. You?" We circle toward the back of the car, reaching the other two as he asks, and Indi's eyes widen comically, looking like a deer in headlights. I give her a small shake of my head.

"It was fine," I tell him, the lies like ash in my mouth. No need to dump my baggage everywhere since it won't help me anyway. "We went car shopping, obviously, and I moved back into my old house. It was a pretty chill one too."

"That is one sweet-ass ride," Jackson says with a whistle as he slings an arm over Indi's shoulder. "I mean, compared to the others in the lot, she stands out. She's got that old school beauty."

"Yes, yes she does." I beam, glancing back at my car before climbing the steps to the school. "I need to hit the library quickly before I head to class, so I'll see you guys later."

"Oh, I'll come with you, I need to ask Mrs. Smith to source a book for me," Indi exclaims, ducking out of Jackson's hold. He protests weakly, and her blush goes damn near as purple as her hair as we walk away with a wave.

"Well, that looked cozy," I tease, bumping her shoulder with mine.

She grips her books against her chest and glances at me from the side of her eyes. "I have no idea what that was."

"That was the start of *something*." I grin and then hum the High School Musical song at her until she pushes me away laughing.

"You are such a dork."

"I know, but I totally rock the dork thing." I grin as we reach our lockers. My smile drops when I notice the new 'art' engraved into my locker door.

*Slut.*

How original.

"People are such assholes," Indi hisses, her anger worse than mine.

I shrug and open my locker. "Fuck them and their opinions. Words can't hurt me if I don't let them." I smile over my shoulder at her, but she doesn't look like she agrees. "Let me just throw my stuff in my locker, then we can hit the library on the way to English."

"Sounds good to me, I'll do the same." She huffs, and I hope she'll just ignore the latest attempt at tearing me down. I need her to treat it the same way I am. As nothing but pathetic. She ditches her stuff while I unload mine and is back before I'm even done.

"Octavia, we should talk." I groan at the sound of Lincoln's voice.

"Will you run to the library for me, get your thing, and then check out *Jane Eyre* for me? There's something about the feel of a real book when you're reading the classics, you know?"

"Are you sure?" Indi asks quietly, her gaze bouncing over my shoulder to Lincoln. I don't need to actually see his face to know how annoyed he is that I haven't actually addressed him. I can already picture his face, which is exactly why I'm still facing her instead of him.

"I'm sure. I won't be long." I smile at her, trying to reassure her, and she nods before scurrying away. I love that she's willing to go against Lincoln, Maverick, and Finley on my behalf, but I also totally understand her fear of them after surviving a year at this school alone.

I take a deep breath and shut my locker before turning to face the guy in question, with a saccharine smile on my face. "Lincoln, what can I do for you?"

"You can take back the things I bought for you. I told you, you have no control until you leave. Don't make me force the matter again." He leans against the locker, like he's as casual as casual gets, but the tightness of his shoulders and the tic in his jaw tells me just how tense he is, really. I can feel the eyes of people in the halls on us, but I'm determined not to make a scene. I've had enough of that already.

Then it hits me what he means, and I feel a blush creep up my chest. I know he notices because his jaw relaxes, and he has that smug-ass smile of his back for a moment. He's too close right now, but I don't want to take a step back. I don't want him to know that he's getting to me as much as he is, so I take a deep breath and tough it out.

"I don't want the things you bought, Lincoln, so no, I will not take them back. I already went shopping for myself. Return them, burn them, donate them—I don't care… That's a lie, I'd totally rather you donated them, but still. I won't take them. What was taken from me was irreplaceable—control or not."

"Why do you always have to be so obstinate?" he growls through clenched teeth.

"Pot, meet kettle," I say, flicking my hair over my shoulder, pulling on the rage from everything that's happened so far as I face him down. I'm sure this moment of stupid bravery is going to be short lived and something he'll make me regret later. But for now, I'm going to cling to it like it's my last lifeline. "Now if that's everything, I have to get to class."

He doesn't say a word, just narrows his eyes and glares at me. I know I've poked the bear. And I know I might possibly regret it later, but dammit, I don't want to be the weak damsel he and his friends keep turning me into.

---

Compared to last week, this morning has been a breeze. My classes have been easy enough, and even Music didn't send me into a spiraling melt down. I'm calling it a good morning.

Even Blair didn't bother to acknowledge my existence, and I for one, am thankful for it. Because if she tries me today, I'm likely to lose my shit. I've been just about keeping myself together, like a reasonable human being, but if she mentions Friday night, I will not be held responsible for my actions.

I walk into the cafeteria, arm in arm with Indi, and I wave over at Raleigh when he calls my name. We grab a tray each and slide into the line, but then the room goes so quiet you could hear a pin drop. I'm immediately on alert in the seconds before I feel heat at my back. Indi turns to face me and startles. I don't have to question who's behind me.

I paint a smile on my face as I turn to find Maverick standing way too close behind me. "Can I help you?"

He smirks back at me before leaning into my personal space and whispering, "I can think of a lot of ways you can help me, V."

I jolt back, hating that I'm giving him the power yet again, but I don't want him that close, or even in my space at all. Shoving him backward would only start something I'm not willing to finish here in the cafeteria.

"Pretty sure you can help yourself with that," I sneer before turning my back on him and facing Indi again. I grab my tray from the counter and encourage Indi to move forward. She still doesn't know what happened, and I'm not ready for Maverick to out me. I've helped him plenty already.

When nothing happens to satisfy the needs of the drama-seeking student body, the noise in the cafeteria starts back up, and we make our way to the table we claimed as ours last week, waving at the football guys as we pass them.

"That was weird," Indi says as she slides into the chair opposite me.

"Maverick has always enjoyed games," I tell her, trying to breeze past it and dig into the chicken and broccoli Alfredo I picked for my lunch, groaning at how good it tastes. I swear the food in this place is the only redeeming feature of the entire school. I mean, the teachers are okay for the most part, minus the whole 'being afraid of the students' thing. I can *almost* understand that, though. They're just here to get a paycheck, and these kids could ruin their lives in a heartbeat; but shit, it's frustrating.

"He definitely seems like the crazy one of the three," she says, cracking open her soda and taking a sip. She has no fucking idea.

"Who's crazy?"

I groan as Maverick slides into the seat beside me, and Indi about chokes on her drink, spluttering over the maniac of a boy sitting next to me.

"Why are you here?" I ask, glaring at him.

"It's lunchtime, where else would I be?" His eyes dance with delight, and I want to nut punch him, just to wipe the stupid smile from his face.

"Why are you sitting here, Maverick?" The words come out through a tightly clenched jaw. I hate how much they affect me without even really trying.

He clasps at his chest, a look of mocking disbelief on his face. "Why, Octavia, are you saying I'm not welcome here? And here was me thinking we could be friends."

"Maverick Riley, you made it all too clear that we are not friends. So fuck off and sit with your actual friends." I try to put a brave face on, letting my anger lead me, and point over to where Lincoln and Finley are watching us. Their matching frowns almost make me want to laugh, but I clamp it down in favor of maintaining the stern look I'm giving Maverick.

"I don't remember doing any such thing." He's so fucking nonchalant as he reaches over and takes one of Indi's fries. I slap his hand so he drops the fry while Indi just watches us. Her panic is clear. She has no clue what to do right now, so I smile at her.

"Leave her fucking food alone, you heathen." I swear his grin grows, and I just want to roll my eyes at him.

He turns his gaze on her, and I swear she blanches. "She doesn't mind, do you, Indigo?"

"Don't be such a dick, Maverick." I sigh, leaning back in my chair. "Of course she minds. If she wanted you to have her lunch, she'd have offered it, and she didn't."

"Fine, fine. I see I'm not wanted." He brushes his hands together as he stands, but leans down to whisper in my ear again. "But don't think that I'm done, V. I told you you were off-limits, and you bucked against it. You'll see what happens when you defy me if you keep this up."

An icy drop of dread runs down my spine, making my entire body shiver, but I keep the bored look on my face as he pulls back. There's no way in hell I'm letting him think he's actually managing to intimidate me. Not again. I don't know what his little show today has been about, but I'm going to work it out. How can they possibly think that what they've already done isn't enough?

Those three are frustrating as fuck, and I am already so over it.

He saunters back toward his usual table, and Indi's color comes back to her face more and more with each step away from us he takes.

"Sorry," I sigh at her, but she shakes her head.

"No, I'm sorry. I need to grow a backbone when it comes to those three. I can face off against Blair and the bitch squad without really thinking twice, but there is just something dark about those three that makes my blood turn to ice."

I shrug before picking at my lunch again. "I get it. Something's definitely changed with them since I left, I just wish I knew what their game was."

"With the rumors I've heard around this place, it could range from just some bored fun to something fucking deadly. Please be careful." My eyebrows raise at her comment. What the actual fuck does she mean *deadly*? Apparently I've been away from here for way too long, but if they've set their sights on me, I'm not about to back down.

Deadly or not.

---

We make it through the rest of lunch without any drama, and I leave Indi to head to her class as I meander toward my locker. I have French next, and considering the amount of time I've spent in France, it's not really a class I'm worried about passing. I speak six different languages, all fluently, thanks to my badass tour tutors.

"Octavia!" I groan at the sound of my name on Lincoln's lips again. What is it with him and Maverick trying to steal the small moments of peace I find?

"Yes, Lincoln?" I turn to face him, crossing my arms. It might be a small barrier between us, but I'll take any barriers I can get until I work out what the fuck he's playing at. I don't think he'd attack me in the hall, but I wouldn't put anything past him at this point.

"I want you to reconsider the gifts." He frowns at me, and it's more than apparent that he's not used to people telling him no. Despite their father not being around much, the Saints basically own this town, so I'm sure no one has ever really told him no in his life.

I sigh and pinch the bridge of my nose. "I don't want the clothes, Lincoln."

"Why not?"

"Because they weren't a gift. I'm not a willing participant in this game you're playing. You can try to intimidate me all you like, but I'm not budging on this. You already took enough from me."

His frown deepens, and his shoulders tense. "You always could see me like no other."

His muttering makes absolutely no sense to me, so I just raise an eyebrow and wait for him to get on with whatever it is he has to say.

He takes a step forward, so close I can feel the heat of his skin as his warm, earthy scent assaults me. I refuse to step back and give him the space I did Maverick in the cafeteria. I can feel that he's a different kind of dangerous, and I just need to work out exactly how. "A lot has changed since you left. You'd have been better off not coming back here."

"Oh awesome, we're back to this again. You're a broken record, Lincoln. I already told you, I didn't have a choice."

His entire demeanor changes, turning icy cold. He narrows his eyes, and his calculating stare makes me hold my breath. Something just changed, and I have no idea what or why.

He grips my arms, so tightly I think I might bruise, before leaning down until we're eye to eye. "Don't get me started on things you don't have a choice in, Octavia. You should've stayed away. But you're here now, and that means you need to get the fuck in line before you get hurt."

"The only thing hurting me right now, Lincoln, is you." I try to pull away, but his grip is ironclad.

"You can't imagine the things that could hurt you here. Everything so far... that's just a small taste. Your dad might have taken the easy way out, but at least he got out. He left you here to fend for yourself in his stead like a fucking coward." His biting tone has nothing on the pain piercing my heart.

"You don't get to talk about my dad like you knew him," I hiss, pushing him away from me. "You have no idea what he went through or why he did what he did." Tears threaten to fall at the thought, but I won't let them fall here. Not in front of him. Not like this.

"You have no idea what I know," he growls before standing up straight and smoothing down his blazer. I have no idea what the fuck he's talking about, but I don't have a chance to ask him before he turns on his heel and stalks away from me.

My emotions roar inside of me like a storm I can't outrun.

Anger.

Confusion.

Devastation.

The emotions build to a roaring pitch inside of me as I watch him walk away. I'm startled by the bell followed by the principal's voice through the intercom. "An assembly has been called in place of your next class. Please make your way to the auditorium. Attendance is mandatory."

The halls fill with noise and bodies in an instant as kids spill out of their classrooms. It's damn near suffocating, and I struggle to breathe as they force their way past me in the halls to get to the auditorium. This is all way too fucking much.

"Fuck this," I mutter, and walk in the opposite direction of the auditorium. I need a refuge right now, and there is only one place I can think of to go.

---

I sit down on the piano bench, my fingers touching the cool ivory. It feels like it's been forever since I played. The quiet of the room soothes me. I know that no one else is on this side of the school, at least no one that truly matters, not when everyone else is in the auditorium. My chest aches with thoughts of the last time I played, messing around with my dad on his stage before his show, just playing because we loved it. It was our thing. Before every show, he'd clear everyone out except for Mac, and we'd just play the songs we loved the most. Him on his guitar, me on the keys.

I start to play, the soft chords fill the room as silent tears fall down my face. I know the reason I haven't played in forever is the exact reason I'm playing right now. It makes me feel. Too much. Everything. I just need to let this raging storm of me out. Just a bit of it though, otherwise I'm going to break so catastrophically that I might not come back from it.

I fall into the music, playing out every swirling emotion that's been rotting inside of me since he died.

Every single thing I've dealt with since I came back to Echoes Cove pours out of me, and I start to sing my old favorite song for any kind of heartbreak. I put every piece of myself into the music, like cutting myself open and letting myself bleed over everything, while ignoring the tears that track down my face, instead focusing on feeling every fucking thing I've been avoiding. I never usually let myself cry, despite being pushed to it by others so far this year, but just this once, I let go of the walls I've kept around myself since everything happened with my dad.

The song draws to a close, the soft tinkling of the ivory echoing in the room, eventually giving way to absolute silence beyond my own breaths.

"Octavia…" I spin on the bench and find Finley standing in the doorway, his voice barely more than a whisper. Just like the dark knight that he is, watching me in the shadows. The emotion on his face isn't anything I've seen before. At least not from him, but I don't care. Not anymore. Not after everything that's happened recently. I stand, clutching my arms against myself. I have no idea how long he's been there, and even though I'm fully clothed, I've never felt more exposed in my entire life.

I rush past him, tears still streaming down my face. I do not have the emotional capacity to deal with Finley Knight right now. I hear his heavy footsteps behind me, and he reaches me before I make it to the end of the hall. He grabs me from behind, pulling me back until my body is flush to his chest, and just holds me against him. I cave and lean into him, pretending the comfort is coming from anyone but him. He turns me around once he realizes I'm not going to struggle, and wraps me in his arms as I war with myself over taking comfort from someone who is one of the main reasons I need it.

He holds me until my tears slow, pulling back to wipe them from my face after a couple of minutes. He cups my face gently. "Octavia…"

His voice is like a bucket of cold water.

This isn't right.

I untangle from his arms, despite his protests, and turn and walk away from him.

Finley Knight is not the guy who comforts you. He's the guy that makes you cry. Something I'm all too fucking aware of. He's still the guy who iced me out the second I got back here, and I'm not stupid enough to think this means something now. He might have caught me at my weakest, but I'd be an idiot to think this changes anything.

We're still not friends, and we're definitely not what we used to be.

I doubt we ever will be again.

# CHAPTER NINE

## FINLEY

Octavia fucking Royal makes my world spin off axis.

Always has.

Always will.

Ever since she came back, my entire life has been upside down and ass backward. Something about that girl pulls all of my attention, and everything else just goes to shit.

Which is exactly why I hoped she'd never come back.

It was safer with her gone. For us, and for her.

# CHAPTER TEN

## OCTAVIA

"Where did you disappear to earlier?" I look up from my locker to see Indi leaning against the one next to mine.

"I went to the music rooms, which was a huge mistake. I should've just gone to the stupid assembly. Did I miss much?" I ask as I pull my books from the locker into my bag and slam it shut. Apparently, I'm still not over my run-in with Finley earlier.

"Just Principal Evans droning on about his expectations for the year and some new rules being introduced after the summer of war between us and ECH." I lift my eyebrows in question, and she continues. "Echoes Cove High… a guy called Ryker Donovan and his boys practically run the place, and to say the rivalry between this school and theirs is epic is an understatement. One guy ended up in critical condition after a fight over the summer apparently."

"Well shit, I think I remember Ryker… He's a twin right?" I ask, as we start heading down the hall to escape this living nightmare of a school.

"Yeah, that's him. Ellis is his twin. They have an older brother, Diego, and a younger sister, Scout," she says, nodding as she opens the door. She freezes on the threshold before peeking over her shoulder at me. "Uhm… Octavia…"

She grimaces as she turns back to me all the way. I look over her shoulder, and rage floods my system. Most of the school is out front with their phones out, pointed in our direction. Waiting. My eyes flick from my brand new car, which now has bright yellow paint poured all over it, to the smirk on Blair's face. My eyes slide to Lincoln, Finley, and Maverick, who are watching me, straight-faced.

I take a deep breath and paint a smile on my face. These assholes would love a video of the nation's princess losing her fucking shit to go viral online. I'm not about to give that to them.

"Do you want me to give you a ride home? The garage dropped my car off at lunch," she asks, but I shake my head.

"No, I'm good. Come on, let's go face my adoring audience." My sarcasm is thick, but she looks as devastated about the state of my car as I feel. Fucking assholes, the lot of them.

I'm not sure what they think any of this is going to achieve, but I'm not going anywhere. My only stipulation in the Will was a 4.0 GPA from this school and staying with my guardian, so even if they burn my shit to the ground, I'm here to stay.

Indi steps fully out of the door, and I follow her out, pulling my aviators from my bag and sliding them onto my face. I finger wave at those with their cameras out, smiling like I couldn't give a fuck about the state of my car. Lincoln and company watch me as I head to my car before they climb into Lincoln's 4x4 and head out of the lot.

Fuck them all.

Fuck every single asshole here that thinks making my life hard is funny.

I get in the car and hook up my phone before blasting "Fuck You" by Don Vedda. I hit the wipers, smearing the paint just enough that I can actually fucking see and peel out of the lot. I clutch the steering wheel so tight my knuckles go white. Yellow paint spills down the rear window as I drive, fueling my rage. Angry tears fall down my face, which just pisses me off more.

I end up stuck in a row of traffic, and the stares from people when they see the car just prickles me further. The car can be fixed, but it's the sheer fucking audacity of it all. What gives these pricks the right to fuck with me just because I came back to this hellhole?

If they're not careful, they're going to push me too far, and they're not going to like it when I fight back. I don't fight like these prissy rich bitches. I'm all about getting my hands dirty. Be it blood or actual dirt, I'm not afraid of throwing hands. The one thing about growing up with roadies and a security team… My life was different from all of the people here. Their petty bullshit is just that.

It takes way too long to get home, and just as I'm pulling up to the house, I spot Lincoln leaving his house. Finley and Maverick are with him, and both of them look surprised to see me pulling into my drive. I guess the details of my move hadn't made it to them yet.

*Interesting.*

I hit the clicker on my keys, and the gates swing open. It doesn't take a minute to reach the front of the house, but the yellow paint is dripping all over the drive. I fucking hate people. It's official.

I need to run. It's the only way I'm going to destress. Usually I'd use music, but after this fucking day, there isn't a chance I'm touching an instrument again any time soon.

I grab my bag and head inside, finding Smithy in the kitchen. "Good day, Miss Octavia?"

"Not exactly," I sigh, and jump up onto one of the stools at the island.

"This calls for a milkshake," he says, frowning. I'm not sure how he always knows the perfect thing to aid my calm, but in less than three minutes, the thickest, chocolatiest milkshake is in front of me, and he smiles sadly. "Drink up, then tell me all about it."

I take a sip of the shake. It's like a mouthful of happy and ecstasy, and the flavors burst over my tongue. I tell him about my car, though I leave out some of the other, more delightful, parts of my day. I'd have hidden the car thing from him if I thought it was possible—he's already done more than enough for me, he shouldn't have to deal with shit like this too. But there's no way he would have missed the damage to the car. He's not blind.

"I have a man who can fix your car, let me handle that. It might take about a week, but I'm sure we can sort you out a lease in the meantime." He pats my shoulder gently before getting up and pulling his phone from his pocket. "I'll call him now. You head upstairs and take a nice long, relaxing bubble bath."

"I'm thinking about going for a run, but that sounds perfect. I'll do that later. Thanks, Smithy, you're the best."

"It's no trouble at all, Miss Octavia, and I think a call to Mr. Evans to remind him exactly who funded that new football field is in order. Your father was very generous to that school, and it's appalling that Mr. Evans forgets who was good to him when he needed it."

"You don't need to do that. It'll just make things worse," I tell him with a sigh before taking another sip of the heavenly milkshake.

He frowns at me and shakes his head. "Let me go and make a call about your car, the rest we can discuss later." He leaves the room before I can respond, leaving me alone with my thoughts, which is possibly the worst place I could be.

Fuck this shit, I'm going to run.

---

My run through town takes the edge off of the burning anger, but it's still a fiery pit inside of me. Mac thought I should see a therapist after Dad's death, but I've never really been the kind to sit and talk to a stranger about how I'm feeling. Usually I'd write it out and put it into a song. Dad always said every experience in life is just another plot line, but considering the fact that every time I try to play I end up crying, that isn't an option right now.

So I run, and I keep running, until I can't anymore… Then I go a little further. Except this godforsaken town just won't let me have any peace. If it's not someone from school staring and pointing, it's the paparazzi who think I can't see them, trying to get a picture of me being anything other than the picture of perfection they've always made me out to be.

You'd think the death of my dad would excuse me from the paparazzi chaos I've experienced since I went on tour with him, but apparently not. I managed to get some privacy when I first came here, but I guess more than one video or photo of the shit from school told the vultures where I ended up.

Wonderful.

By the time I reach the shoreline, my chest burns, but my anger hasn't subsided in the slightest. If anything, it's grown. So I push myself onto the sand and keep running. The summer sun beats down on me, and sweat trickles down my back as I run. The burn in my legs intensifies, but I push through.

I run until the beach is desolate and I'm beyond all of the houses that back up onto the beach. Until I can pretend I'm the only person in existence and the rest of the world isn't trying to beat me for a reason I haven't worked out yet.

I come to a stop, lifting my hands to the back of my head, and suck in lungfuls of air before downing water like it's going out of fashion.

Echoes Cove, in a lot of ways, is the same as I remember, but something definitely changed while I was gone, and I have no fucking idea what it is. I don't remember the people here being so… secretive. So sadistic and twisted.

My mind wanders back to the four boys who were once my saviors. I wonder what happened to them to make them so twisted. I get that the parents in Echoes Cove aren't the most attentive… The greed here makes me sick, but the sadistic streak in Maverick is worse than I ever remember it being, and Lincoln was always dark and broody, but the anger that seems to fuel him is insane. I can't quite get a read on Finley, but something definitely isn't right there either. The only one who seems reasonably unscathed is East… And none of it makes any sense.

Not that I expect it to, but Indi's comment about deadly secrets has been swirling around in the back of my mind since she said it. Part of me wants to just put it down to the rivalry she mentioned… But another part of me tells me not to be so dismissive.

Echoes Cove has always been a web of lies and deceit.

*"I can't stay here with all of this, Stone, we need to get out. Now. Before they come for Octavia." My mom screams at my daddy, and I rock back and forth in the pantry with my hands over my ears. All my parents seem to do now is argue and shout. I wish I could make it stop.*

*"There is no way out of this, Emily. What part of that don't you get? The best thing we can do for V is to just do what we need to do." My dad's voice gets quieter. He sounds so sad.*

*A glass smashes, and my mom shrieks again. "Why do you have to be such a fucking doormat? I didn't sign up for this, Stone. I'm taking our daughter, and I'm getting as far away from this cesspit as possible."*

*"If you run, they will chase you. It's what they do."*

*"We can't just let them dictate our lives like this. I'll suffocate if I stay."*

*"You think they'll let you live if you leave… if it's not on their terms? What about that is safe for her, Cami?"*

*I don't understand any of what they're talking about, so I stay quiet. No one knows I'm here, and I don't want them to yell at me too. Mom yells all the time now. Ever since they went to that party I wasn't allowed to go to. I wish I'd never made such a fuss. Maybe then they wouldn't fight anymore.*

*"Have either of you seen Miss Octavia?" Smithy's voice interrupts them, and I scurry into the back corner. If they find me here, I'm going to be in trouble. I push harder on my ears and close my eyes, counting my numbers like Daddy asked.*

*I wish they wouldn't fight about me all the time. Maybe if I was better they wouldn't fight. Maybe if I could just learn my numbers, the yelling will stop.*

I drop to my knees as the memory hits me, the ache in my chest growing. I don't have that many memories of my mom from before she left me… or so I thought.

What even was that?

I take a deep breath and close my eyes, racking my brain for more of the memory. What on earth would my parents have been trying to run from?

I shake my head, trying to clear the memories. Before who comes for me? Surely my dad wouldn't have sent me back here if it wasn't safe? All he ever tried to do was keep me safe.

That's why he took me on tour, he wanted me with him after Mom left. It was our big adventure, a way to keep us together. I was safer with him on tour than here in the Cove on my own.

None of this makes sense, and I only have a fragment of the puzzle. It's probably nothing, just my stressed out brain trying to manifest my trauma or some bullshit.

My phone buzzes in my arm strap, so I slide it out. Any distraction is better than this.

**Indi: You doing okay? Did you get the car sorted out?**

**Me: I'm fine, just out for a run. Smithy is getting the car taken care of, but it's going to take at least a week. FML.**

**Indi: Want a ride in the morning? I don't mind playing taxi for a week if you need me.**

**Me: You are a lifesaver, floofy coffees are entirely on me the whole week.**

**Indi: See this is why we're going to be BFFL. You understand me on a baser level.**

I can't help but laugh at her. Coffee is definitely one way to this girl's heart. That, reality TV shows, and good music. I can get down for most of that. The train of thought gives me an idea.

**Me: Exactly… speaking of BFFL, when is your birthday? A good bestie requires this information.**

**Indi: Uhm… it's actually in a few weeks. I don't usually do much, birthdays aren't a big deal in my family.**

**Me: Are you shitting me? You turn 18… this requires celebration!**

**Indi: If that comes in the form of eating so much I pass out, that's a celebration I can get down with. Beyond that, just nope.**

**Me: Deal!**

This totally gives me an idea for her birthday, and I smile wider than I have in a week. I am going to rock this bestie thing.

**Indi: *eye roll emoji* If you say so. You sure you're okay? Running doesn't sound fun.**

**Me: Running is awesome. I promise I'm good, just burning off some anger rather than going to jail. This seemed like a better option. Orange isn't my color.**

**Indi: *cowboy emoji* You slay me. Okay, if you're good, I'm going to get started on my Econ assignment. Enjoy your run. *shudders***

**Me: Have fun with that. *middle finger emoji***

I laugh a little and slide my phone back into the strap before finishing my water. Maybe the Cove is the cesspit my mom thought it was, but with people like Indi bringing the sunshine, I'm pretty sure I can survive the chaos.

I'm Octavia fucking Royal… How bad can one year be?

---

I get home from my run, exhausted but feeling lighter than I was when I left. The thought of the bubble bath Smithy suggested puts an extra bounce in my step as I finish running up the driveway.

I flick through the mail on the entry hall table as I kick off my sneakers. Bills, junk mail… and a black envelope with my name embossed on it.

Different.

I flick it over to open it and notice it's sealed with red wax and stamped with a symbol I've never seen before. I peel it back and pull the card from inside.

***Octavia Royal***
***You are cordially invited to the Echoes Cove Orphan Society fundraiser ball.***

***Date: December 5th***
***Location: The Nesthood Hall***

***Dress Code: Black Tie***

***Please RSVP by August 20th with note of any additional guests.***

***Yours***
***TKS***

Apparently charity gala invites got bougie. Who would've thought? And the

Nesthood Hall? Not on your life. I've avoided that place my entire life. The building creeps me the fuck out, so I don't think so.

I drop it back onto the pile with zero intention of going. Balls have never been my thing, and Dad stopped taking me to red carpet shit after the first one we did. It was horrendous. I don't have a pretentious bone in my body, and my whole 'speak your mind' attitude didn't exactly go down well. I know my place, and charity balls are not one of them.

"Did you enjoy your run, Miss Octavia?" Smithy appears, startling me, but the smile on his face brings me joy.

"It was amazing, thank you."

"What would you like for dinner this evening?" I think it over, craving tacos way more than I should… But it's been a hot minute since I actually ate a vegetable, so I know I need to make some good decisions, shitty as they are.

"Chicken and veggies?" I say, biting my lip, and he pulls a face at me.

"I know you're not that uncreative, Miss Octavia," he scoffs, and I stifle the laugh that threatens. "I have a perfect idea. Give me an hour."

"Sure thing, Smithy. As long as you join me. Eating alone isn't so much fun."

He softens a little and smiles at me. "It would be my pleasure."

"Awesome, I'm going to grab a shower, then I'll be down." I jog up the stairs, the bubble bath can wait for the minute. My stomach growls at the realization that food is far higher up the priority list right now.

It doesn't take long to shower and wash my hair, though blowing out my waist length hair takes longer than I'd like. I'd cut it, but well… My hair is the only thing I'm really fussy about when it comes to my looks. It's weird, but it is what it is. I'm allowed to be vain about one thing.

I throw on a pair of leggings and a hoodie, pulling my hair up into a messy bun before making my way back down to the kitchen. I find Smithy humming along to the music he has funneling through the speakers in here, almost dancing as he's standing at the chopping board. If I wasn't hungry before, the smells coming from this room would have me ravenous.

"Anything I can help with?" I ask as I enter the room, and he shakes his head as the gate buzzer sounds.

"Expecting anyone?" he asks, frowning.

I shake my head. "Not that I know of. I'll go see who it is, don't let me interrupt you. Whatever you're cooking smells delicious."

Smithy offers a noncommittal grunt in return, so I turn on my heel and go to the monitor in the small room just by the front door. I peer into the monitor, but I don't see anyone at the gates. I push the button to the microphone while frowning. "Hello?"

No one responds, and the monitor flickers to another one of the cameras we have set up, and I catch sight of something leaning against the gate.

Flowers?

That's weird as fuck.

"Who is it?" Smithy calls out as I leave the security room.

"Looks like a flower delivery, but they left them at the gate. I'm just going to go get them." I slip my sneakers back on, giving zero fucks that I look like a hot mess, grab my keys, and jog down to the gate. I use the clicker to open the gates, standing back and waiting to see if anyone jumps out. Apparently the assholes at school have me a little on edge. I've seen too many movies where the mean girls cover the girl in honey and feathers, or worse… If they fuck with me like that, I'll do far worse to them than has already been done to me. I've not really retaliated at this point but that doesn't mean I won't.

When I'm confident there's no one there, I rush forward and grab the flowers, hitting the clicker for the gates as soon as I'm clear.

It doesn't take me long to get back to the house, and I drop my keys back into the bowl next to the mail and take the flowers to the kitchen.

"Oh tulips, how lovely," Smithy says as I lay the flowers down on the counter. "I'll grab a vase as soon as I slide this into the oven."

I look at the veggie lasagna he's layering and practically drool. "Smithy, you are a culinary wonder."

He ignores my compliment in favor of studying the flowers for a moment. "Who are the flowers from? Yellow tulips aren't a usual gifting flower." He moves across the kitchen and grabs a vase from fuck knows where and fills it with water.

I pull the card from the flowers, but there is no inscription on the envelope. It's sealed with red wax, a horse inside of a rose. Weird. I break the seal and find a black card inside, embossed with the same image on the seal. "No idea who they're from. There's nothing on the card."

I show him the card, and I swear I see fear flicker behind his eyes, but it's gone as soon as it appears, so I question if I even saw it at all. "Well, a mysterious suitor. How quaint."

He takes the flowers and arranges them in the vase, placing them on the windowsill. Smithy admires them for a short moment before turning back to me and asking, "Now, are we eating in here or with a movie, Miss Octavia?"

"Serial killer TV?" I ask hopefully, knowing he won't really tell me no.

He shakes his head, smiling softly. "Why not? Maybe we'll learn a thing or two."

I grin at him and clap my hands. "That's the spirit, Smithy. Every girl should know how to hide a body."

My phone buzzes on the counter, and I see a notification from the ReachMe app. Dread pools in my stomach. The last time I used the app was when the picture of East and I was on there. I haven't opened it since. I don't need to see the vitriol being hurled at me from every angle reflected on the school's shitty app.

Smithy turns his focus back to cooking, so I leave the room quietly and curl up on one of the sofas in the main room. Curiosity bites at me. Maybe the notification isn't about me.

My phone buzzes again, though, and I glance at it to see a message from Indi.

**Indi: I'm sorry, they're such assholes. Just ignore it. I've reported this too, so it should be gone soon.**

Butterflies kick up in my stomach at her message. My curiosity gets the better of me, and I open the stupid closed network app. My notifications are insane.

Apparently pictures and videos of me on here are rife. I'm tagged in so much shit, each caption more hateful than the next.

I clear the history of notifications, going to the most recent tag. *"Royal really is just this pathetic. Who cries to the guy who hates her? Just how fucked up is she? Maybe she's as fucked up as her dad. It takes a special kind of fucked up to off yourself the way he did."* I click on the attachment, and the sounds of my crying fill my ears.

No.

Someone recorded my breakdown on Finley. Someone took that moment of weakness and decided to use it against me. What the fuck is wrong with the people around here?

Tears prick my eyes, falling down my cheeks, and I wipe them away angrily.

How much longer can I do this? I don't know if I'm strong enough to survive another month here, let alone a whole fucking year. I've tried to be strong, but there's only so much a girl can fake. I thought I was doing so well hiding my shit. I thought if I put on a brave face, they'd get bored and back off but I'm getting the feeling that isn't going to happen.

Echoes Cove Prep isn't just where dreams go to die… it's become my waking nightmare.

# CHAPTER ELEVEN

After a sunshiney start to my day with Indi, literally bouncing our way into school with Midnight Blue blaring through the speakers, my day actually hasn't been that bad.

The repercussions of the video haven't been exactly fun, and people around the school have been anything but nice about it. Not that I expected them to be, the entire Cove is full of shrivel-hearted assholes. The fake love notes in my locker 'from Finley' have been the highlight for me. Declarations of love for a slut who throws herself at the guy who hates her.

It's been awesome.

I should've ignored it, pushed it down with all of the other shit that's been bothering me, but I couldn't help torturing myself by watching it a few times over. Every time I watch it, I can't help but focus on Finley. He seemed so sincere in the moment, and he even looks it in the video, but I know better than most how good those guys are at wearing a mask.

All things considered, today could have been significantly worse, that much I'm sure of. As much as I'd like to become a wallflower while the boys keep up the tirade of terror, encouraging everyone else to be giant assholes along with them… Well, I know that isn't going to happen.

Everyone used to assume—and I guess they still do—that I wanted attention, being the daughter of 'The King.' I was blasted across the tabloids, and people think that life is all fun and games when you're in the spotlight like that… Until you get your period without notice and have to hide from the world because you had a moment of actually being *human*.

I've always preferred to fade into the background, which is why I want to open my own record label and just write music. I'd get to do what I love with music without having to be the face that everyone wants to see. I'm very aware of the chaos that comes with fame. Having had more than a little taste of it, I'm beyond over it.

So after a relatively quiet morning when I slide into what I've dubbed our table in the cafeteria, and Maverick drops into the seat opposite of me, I am overwhelmingly not prepared.

"Sitting alone, princess?" He reaches over to grab for the garlic bread on my plate, and I slap his hand, making him grin. "Maybe if you were a little nicer to people, you'd have more friends."

"Maybe if you weren't such a psychopath, you wouldn't think that," I bite back, making his grin widen. "You're in Indi's seat."

At that exact moment, Indi sidles up to the table, eyes wide as Maverick leans over so that he is very much in my space. "We have unfinished business, V. You'll be seeing me around."

I roll my eyes. Of course I'm going to see him around. Echoes Cove isn't big enough for me to avoid him, or I'd have already made that my number one mission.

"You don't get to call me V," I tell him as he stands, and an evil glint appears in his eyes, a malicious smile on his face.

He circles to my side of the table, standing behind me and caging me in as he leans over me to whisper into my ear, "You don't get to tell me what to do. You have no power here, princess. You'd do well to remember that."

I look up to find a wide-eyed Indi, who stands watching us, fidgeting like she doesn't know what to say or do. I smile up at her to let her know it's fine, despite his proximity.

He pulls back and saunters away from me, all eyes on him as the whispers start again.

Indi slides into the chair he vacated and drops her tray onto the table. "Do I even want to ask?"

"Probably not." I take a bite of my pasta, hoping the joy of carbs can take me back to the happy place I was *almost* in ten minutes ago. I make myself smile up at her because I'm not going to ruin her day too. "How's your day been?"

"I can't complain. I saw Blair trip and faceplant into her locker, so that was fun." She grins wide, and I can't help but laugh. "I just wish I'd been able to record it so we could bask in the bliss of it together."

"I'd have paid good money to see that."

"To see what?" Raleigh asks as he drops into the seat beside me.

"Blair faceplant into her locker," Indi tells him, practically bouncing in her seat as she takes a bite from her burger. He bursts out laughing, which only makes my smile widen.

"Yup, I'd have paid good money to see that too." Jackson and some of the other guys on the team join our table, and lunch break passes in the blink of an eye.

When the bell rings, I can't stop my frown. I am so not ready to go back to class, French might not be one of the classes I'm having issues with, but I'm starting to panic at how behind I'm getting in Business and Statistics. Focusing on those lessons is beyond hard. Paying attention for four lessons in a row isn't a strong suit of mine. I really do miss my chaos breaks.

"I'll see you after school?" Indi asks, and I nod.

"Sure thing. You still good to give me a ride?"

"You know it!" She blows me a kiss before scurrying out of the lunchroom and off to class. If I had my car, I might just head out to the beach by my damn self and skip the rest of the day. You know, if that 4.0 GPA wasn't hanging over my head. I let out a deep breath and grab my bag.

"I'll walk you to French," Raleigh says as he waves off his boys. I can't help but smile. I don't think I've ever met someone as sweet, yet as cocky, as him.

"You totally don't have to."

He scoffs and drops his arm around my shoulders. "It's on my way, and I wanted to talk to you about Friday."

"About the game?" I ask as we head out of the cafeteria. I can't help but catch Finley's eye as we're walking, and his stare is like a brand on my back as I leave with Raleigh. A part of me wants to shrug off Raleigh's arm because I don't want those three going after him too, but I don't want to cower from them any more than I already have. I hate feeling so weak, especially where they're concerned.

"Kind of. I was wondering if you wanted to hang out after. Just the two of us..." he trails off as we hit my locker, and I swap my books over.

"You mean like a date?" Color me fucking shocked. I mean, I know he's been a little tactile, but I figured that was just his way.

"Yeah, I mean like a date." He hits me with that megawatt smile of his, and I find myself nodding, despite my reservations about going on a date with him. This probably isn't a good idea, I don't think him and I will ever work, but one date can't hurt, right? Maybe I'll be wrong, and it won't be so bad.

I can't help but think this is likely going to piss off the guys even more, but fuck it. That's their problem, not mine.

"Awesome." His excitement is contagious, and I find myself smiling up at him before letting him walk me to class.

He kisses my head when he leaves me at the door to French before running off toward his own class when the warning bell sounds. Maybe this isn't a bad thing... Except I've never actually been on a date. The guys I dated before now were all roadies or people I met out on tour, and we hung out on tour, so actual dates weren't really a thing.

Nerves hit me as I take my seat at the back of the room. This totally isn't what I had on the cards for this year. It's just one date, what harm could it do?

---

My phone buzzes in my pocket, so I sneak a peek at it while the teacher isn't looking.

**Indi: I am so sorry, but my mom called an SOS. She had a fender bender and needs me to pick her up from the garage. I had to leave early.**

**Me: Dude, no sweat. I hope your mom is okay, I can get myself home.**

**Indi: Thank you, I hate letting you down.**

**Me: You're not, I have legs and if all else fails, there's Uber.**

**Indi: Sorry! I'll make it up to you.**

I can't help but laugh at her. Not giving me a ride isn't the end of the world, but her sunshine heart really is just that big. While the thought of walking home doesn't exactly fill me with joy, things could be much worse.

Then I realize she's not going to be around for Gym.

Fuck my life.

I groan as the bell rings, knowing I'm going to have to face the bitch squad alone. Here's hoping that my weirdly quiet day continues. The only hiccup in my whole day was lunch when Maverick joined me uninvited, and I'm hoping that this new turn of events continues.

I pack my shit away and head to the locker room, grabbing my gym uniform on the way.

It's only once I get to the locker room, and the stares intensify, that I really even notice them. I head to my locker, keeping my head held high. Being the nation's princess for the majority of my existence taught me a few things, and keeping your head up despite the bullshit is one of them.

I change in silence, double checking the lock on my locker once I'm done before heading out to the gym. I'm practically the first one out of the door, despite being one of the last in.

*What the fuck's happened now?*

I head to where East is already talking to a few people and start stretching out. Circuits are killer, but doing this shit is going to get me in better shape than I've ever been in before. Mac would be proud.

Thinking of him, I realize I should probably find a self-defense class around here somewhere to keep up on the training I was doing with him before. He'd be so disappointed if he found out I'm slacking, and that is more of a dagger to the gut than I need. He was basically my second dad on tour, disappointing him totally isn't something I want to do.

I really need to text him back later too.

East blows his whistle, calling my attention back to him, and I stop my stretching. His sadistic grin inspires a little bit of fear to spear through my gut. Circuits are already a bitch without that smile.

"Ladies, since you all enjoyed them so much, we're going to start today with suicide drills and learn not to fuck with other people's shit. Am I clear?" He glances over to me. Goddamn, why does he have to be so pretty when he's going all white knight on me? Those gray eyes of his practically fucking sparkle. I smile down at my shoes as everyone groans.

Serves those assholes right for what they did to my clothes and my car.

I'm not surprised he knows, though I am surprised he's doing anything about it. Not one other faculty member has even mentioned what happened to me. Though considering Maverick seems to have the principal wrapped around his little finger, I'm not that surprised. That and the sheer amount of money floating around this school is enough to keep any teacher under their thumb.

East blows his whistle again and starts the drills. Personally, I have zero issue with them. I mean they fuck my shit up, but I like running, so it's not exactly a hardship. The other circuit shit is worse for me.

He keeps running us until half the class looks like they're going to pass out. I can't even laugh because I'm so freaking out of breath, but it's such a good feeling seeing the others so fucked up that I'm not sad about it. Not even a little.

East blows that fucking whistle of his again, his sadistic grin still in place. "Get your asses up off the floor, we're not done yet. Start your circuits; and if I see anyone slacking, I'll keep you extra long!"

I laugh under my breath and head toward one of the empty circuit points, smiling at East as I do. My foot suddenly catches on someone else's ankle, and I trip and fall, barely managing to catch myself without smashing my face on the hard, wood floor. I may have saved my face, but my knees are fucked.

I turn to see one of the bitch squad, whose name I literally haven't cared to learn, snickering as she skips away from me like she didn't just trip me. "You stupid bitch!"

I push myself to my feet and go to charge her, finally seeing red because today was a good day, goddammit. An arm wraps around my waist, and I'm literally lifted off of my feet. "Calm down, V. She's not worth it." East plants me back on the floor, pointing in the other direction. "Serena, detention tonight."

"Sounds fun, sir," she flirts, fluttering her lashes, and I almost want to be sick when East smiles back at her.

"I didn't say it was with me, did I? Detention tonight is with Mr. Avery. Have fun with that."

I burst out laughing because Mr. Avery has some serious hygiene issues and is more than a little bit of a creep. Obviously he wouldn't do anything to her, but just the thought of detention with him is enough to make her almost cry. She stomps her foot as East turns his back on her before blowing his whistle again. "Circuits!"

This time when he yells the word, I don't even care. I'll do all the circuits in the world if it means she has to suffer.

---

I practically bounce through the halls after class. Gym wasn't exactly fun, but seeing someone in this school finally getting punished for being a giant bag of ass has me all kinds of gleeful.

Even the fact that I have to walk home doesn't get me down. The sun is shining, the sky is clear, and today might just have been the best day I've had since being forced back to this horror show town.

I make my way through the parking lot, slipping my aviators on, when a white Mustang pulls up beside me, the roof retracting. "Need a ride, V?"

I smile at East, who looks way less like a teacher right now with his backward cap and his sunglasses. He's rocking that whole hot as fuck college frat boy vibe with his music blaring from the car. "I'm not going to say no if you're heading straight home?"

I can practically feel eyes on me as I walk around his car, dropping my bags on the back seat before climbing in. Maybe I should feel a little more wary of him, considering how his brother has treated me since I got here, but I'm not about to hold him accountable for Lincoln. That would just be a shitty thing to do.

"Yeah, I'm heading straight home. Buckle up." I do as he says while he grins wide at me, and as soon as I'm secure, he peels from the lot so fast that my head shoots back against the headrest. A laugh rips from me at the exhilaration that comes from the speed. He drives like he's a street racer, but he seems so confident and at ease that I don't panic at all.

I enjoy the thrill as he drives through the town, the disapproving glances bounce off him like water off a duck's back, and it is so refreshing. I'm almost disappointed when we pull up to the gates in front of my house. "Thanks for the ride."

"A gentleman doesn't drop a lady at the gates," he says, wagging his eyebrows. "Drop the code in. I need to see Smithy about some cake anyway."

"You and your cake," I say, shaking my head as I have to almost crawl over his lap so I can key the code to the gate. I can feel his breath on my neck as I reach out to the box, realizing I should have just given him the stupid code. The tension ramps up by about three thousand degrees when I realize just how close my hand is to his dick as I lean on his thigh.

I shift back, accidentally brushing my hand against it and gasp, looking up at him with wide eyes as my heart races. Part of me wants to lean in and kiss him, but the other part, the part who doesn't want to be rejected by him, freezes. His eyes are hooded as he stares down at me, and I can't breathe. His face is so close to mine, and he leans in further just as the gate groans open.

The noise seems to pull him back to reality, and he jerks back. The moment is shattered, and I hurry back to my seat. Heat creeps up my chest as I blush. East might have featured heavily in my fantasies for as long as I can remember, but I've never considered that he'd feel like that too. And well… I wasn't imagining the fact that he nearly kissed me just then.

Was I?

When we reach the house, Smithy is already at the door waiting for us.

"Good afternoon, Miss Octavia. Master Saint, it is wonderful to see you again." I beam at him as I jump out of the car. East struts around to my side, grabbing my bags before I get a chance to.

"Smithy, my man! How are you doing?" East hugs Smithy, who looks almost relieved to see my old friend.

"Fine, thank you, Master Saint. Are you joining us for dinner this evening?" Smithy looks so hopeful that when East glances back at me, I just shrug. Who am I to say no? East has been nothing but my white knight since I got back. I have zero issues with him. If he wants to stay for dinner, it doesn't bother me at all. We head inside, and East finally gives my bags back to me.

"Sounds good to me, Smithy! Now… let's talk about cake." I laugh as Smithy leads East to the kitchen as I head to the laundry to dump my gym stuff. I wait for the light to flicker on, trying not to shudder at the thought of entering the small dark room.

You'd think life on a tour bus would've forced me to get over my issues with small dark spaces, but even the small bunk couldn't cure me. After being trapped in my closet for almost a whole day when I was younger, the fear manifested, and I've never really gotten over it. Dad felt so bad when he finally found me. He was at work when there was a smaller earthquake and my dresser fell in front of the doors after I hid.

It was the first time I experienced an earthquake, and they still make me almost shit my pants. Though not quite as much as small dark spaces. I shudder just thinking about it. No thank you.

I empty my gym clothes into the hamper and then head upstairs to change. It doesn't take me too long. I don't ever really obsess about how I look, so leggings and a hoodie with messy hair is absolutely my go-to. By the time I get back downstairs, Smithy already has a milkshake for me on the counter, and East is halfway through the one in his hand. "Making yourself at home, I see."

He grins over at me before taking another sip of his milkshake. "If Smithy makes you these every day, I might never leave."

I climb onto a stool at the counter, and somehow he still towers over me. What the fuck are they feeding people here, super grow Wheaties? "I mean, you're only next door. It's not like you're exactly far away, is it?"

"This is very true. Smithy, one of these days I'll convince you to jump the fence and come live with us." Smithy scoffs at his words and shakes his head.

"Very unlikely, Master Saint. Then who would look out for Miss Octavia?" He smiles warmly at me as I take a sip of my milkshake. "But, as long as you treat her well, you will always find a milkshake here for you. Now then, if you two want to go get comfortable, I'll start dinner."

"What are we eating?" I ask as I jump from my seat.

"My main man Smithy is making homemade pizza," East says with a grin as Smithy shoos us from the kitchen, and I blow the old man a kiss. My love for pizza knows no bounds. I could literally eat it every day and not get tired of it.

I head into the lounge with East and drop onto one one of the sofas. "Movie?"

He sits on the sofa with me and makes himself comfortable. "Sounds good to me. Anything in mind?"

"There's that new one out about fighting a war in the future…" I offer with a small shrug. Why does this feel awkward all of a sudden?

"Action movie. Girl after my own heart. Glad to see that much hasn't changed." His smile is sad, and I get the feeling that I'm missing something. I have no fucking clue what, though, so I put the movie on and settle in.

The uncomfortable feeling leaves once we get into the movie. I'd almost forgotten how alike East and I can be. While Linc was always my savior in the shadows, the dark protector, East was the sunshine on a cloudy day. It's funny to me that East is the older of the two when Linc has always acted like the eldest.

Smithy joins us once he brings the pizzas in, and it warms my heart to have him back in my life so much. I missed him when I was gone, even if I did have Mac and Dad. There's no one quite like Smithy.

Time passes in a blur as we eat and watch the movie, and once it's over, Smithy makes his excuses to disappear. Not that I blame him, he has his own life to be getting on with, rather than spending all of his time with me. I hope he does anyway. The thought that he's putting his life on pause for me doesn't exactly fill me with joy.

"I should probably head back before the world implodes," East says once Smithy has left. He stands and his t-shirt rides up, giving me a glimpse of his abs and that freaking 'V' making me want to groan. Goddamn. "Do you need a ride in the morning?"

"No, I should be good. Indi will be back to playing chauffeur tomorrow. She just had to go rescue her mom tonight, but thank you." I stand and stretch out as I yawn. Apparently, I'm more tired than I thought.

I walk him out, and as he stoops to slide his shoes back on, he picks up the black envelope on the mail table. "What's this?"

"Just some stupid charity gala invite. I'm surprised you guys didn't get one too." I shrug and lean on the wall as he drops it back on the table and turns his attention back to his shoes.

"You going?" he asks, eyebrows raised as he slips the shoes on and leans down to tie them.

"What do you think?" My sarcasm is on fire, and he just starts laughing.

"Fair point. Octavia Royal and charity galas don't go hand in hand. I'll see you tomorrow?"

I roll my eyes at him as I usher him out of the door. "You'll see me in Gym, unless you plan on quitting anytime soon. You having that job still seems so weird to me."

A look of guilt flashes across his face, and he runs his hand through his hair. Weird. "Nope, no quitting till Linc can escape."

He jogs down the steps and jumps back into his car, driving off with a wave before I shut the door. This has been the strangest fucking day, but I'm too tired to try and dissect it. I call out a good night to Smithy before heading upstairs.

The door to the balcony is open, which is unusual, but I guess Smithy has been in here cleaning. I shut the room up and climb into bed, shutting off the light. The moon shines in from the windows, still lighting the room enough that the darkness doesn't make my heart race. Thinking about being trapped always puts me on edge in the dark.

I close my eyes and try to unwind, and just as I start to drift sleep I hear soft music coming from outside. It's one of my dad's songs. Just like that, my good mood disappears, and I drift to sleep with tears slipping down my face.

# CHAPTER TWELVE

I went out for a run first thing this morning, trying to burn off the funk last night left me in. Things have been too quiet, and that's making me almost as jumpy as when I was being attacked almost daily.

Quiet usually means the calm before the storm, but after everything the guys and Blair have pulled so far, I can't imagine it getting much worse. Even with Lincoln's sideways warnings.

I get back to the house to find the gate open, and my stomach drops.

The gate should *not* be open.

I run up the drive, spotting the open front door. Fear trickles down my spine, and I curse myself for thinking things couldn't get worse.

Moving as silently as I can, I enter the house, my heart beating so fast I'm scared it'll be heard.

The place is trashed. The artwork is slashed and the knick-knacks and decor smashed, but I can't think about any of that because Smithy was here.

If they hurt him, I swear to God...

I creep through the rooms, trying not to make a sound while hoping like fuck whoever broke in isn't still here. The squeak of my shoes on the floors seems so loud that I pull to a stop, holding my breath so I can hear if anyone else is in here.

I try to keep a hold on the panic threatening to take over my entire body, but I need to find Smithy before I do anything else. That one thought is the only thing holding me together.

I stumble over one of the smashed statues, falling and cutting my palms as I do. I curse under my breath for being so loud.

Fuck it. If anyone else is here, they already know I am at this point.

"Smithy!" My shout echoes in the giant space, but when there's no response, my heart thunders in my chest. I hurry through the rooms and head for the kitchen, hoping Smithy is in the panic room under the island.

I find Smithy in the kitchen, face down on the floor, blood spilling from a wound on his head. "Shit!"

I rush toward him, trying to wake him. I shout at him as I shake him, but it's no use, so I do what any reasonable person would do. I call the police, while trying not to sob and freak out that he won't wake up.

When I hang up, I take a deep breath, trying to calm myself and roll Smithy onto his side, moving his arms and legs into the recovery position, making sure his airways are clear and that he's still actually breathing.

Who the fuck would do this? And why would they hurt Smithy? He hasn't done anything to anyone.

I look up and see a piece of paper stuck to the refrigerator.

*No one you love is safe while you stay here. Don't say you weren't warned.*

Those fucking assholes. This can't have been them, right? They wouldn't have hurt Smithy. Would they? I see red, snatching the paper from the fridge and crumpling it in my hand. If the police see this, I'll never hear the end of it. All I want is an ambulance for Smithy.

He has to be okay.

He can't be seriously hurt because of me.

When the buzzer at the gate sounds, I make sure it's open wide as one cruiser and an ambulance come up the drive. The paramedics come in first, and I direct them to the kitchen. The officer pulls me to the side and asks a ton of questions I don't have the answers to.

"Is he going to be okay?" I ask as the paramedics wheel Smithy's unmoving body out of the house.

"He has a contusion to the head and has lost quite a lot of blood. They'll be able to assess him better at the hospital. Will you be following?"

I nod, and the paramedic rushes out to join his partner. The officer asks me a question, but I don't hear it as the sirens start up.

I can't believe they hurt him.

Guilt churns in my stomach, more powerful than any rage I can feel. This is my fault. I should've listened to them. I could have stopped this.

"Miss Royal?" The officer calls my name, and I shake my head, pulling myself from my thoughts.

"Sorry, Officer, this is a lot."

"Sure, I can imagine. Do you know if anything was taken?"

I shake my head again, clasping my arms around my waist, holding myself tight. "I'm sorry, I have no idea. I went straight into the kitchen and found Smithy… sorry, James."

Just saying the words makes me feel cold. How is this my life?

"That's understandable, are you okay to walk through with me quickly before you leave for the hospital?"

I find myself nodding before I start walking him through the house. The main floor is completely destroyed. Anything that wasn't bolted down has been thrown or smashed. The contents of the kitchen are spilled over the counters and floors.

We head down the stairs to the basement, and I choke back a sob when I see the music room.

The place that was my dad's sanctuary, it's… almost unsalvageable. The smell of urine makes me gag, and I leave, unable to look at it anymore.

Finally, we head upstairs, and I find much of the same. More destruction. My clothes aren't shredded this time, but they are strewn across the room. The only things left alone are my dad's guitars hanging on my wall.

I nearly fall to my knees as relief floods me in waves.

"Everything seems to be accounted for, but I can go through more thoroughly later once I've been to the hospital. Is that okay?" I say to the officer, my voice thick with emotion. This has been one hell of a day, and it's not even eight in the morning yet.

---

My week has been a clusterfuck, but I refuse not to let today be a good day. Smithy was released from the hospital last night. He had a slight concussion, but other than that, the cut was his only wound. Though if you ask him, his pride was wounded more. The doctors wanted him to stay overnight, but the man is stubborn as a mule. So I ended up bringing him home.

While we were waiting for the doctors to finish their tests, I called in a cleaning company to sort out what could be salvaged from the house and throw away anything that couldn't. It's just stuff. It can be replaced, and besides, I didn't want Smithy going home to that madness.

When I asked him who attacked him, he said there were five thugs but that he didn't recognize them because they were wearing masks and gloves. Which I guess makes sense, but it doesn't explain why my wall of guitars was left untouched or why nothing was actually taken.

It hurts my head just to try and make sense of it all. I can't help but hope it wasn't Lincoln and the others. Surely they wouldn't hurt Smithy. But who else would leave that note?

I pushed him a little harder on the drive home, but he didn't have anything else to say. I get it, he was tired, and he'd answered all the police's questions as well as mine, but he doesn't seem… angry enough about it? Maybe that's just my response to everything these days.

Then this morning, he demanded that I go to school despite everything that happened, so I made him promise to take it easy. It took some doing, but I threatened to have Pattie come and check on him if he didn't behave. I'm not entirely sure why those two hate each other so much, but it worked, so I'm going to take the win.

Lincoln, Maverick, and Finley are suspiciously absent from school, which has the gossip mill all aflutter. Luckily, it means I've actually been able to relax—the thought of confronting them about what happened to Smithy fills me with anger and fear at the same time. I hate that the fear is there, especially when I've never been the kind of girl to cower, but something about those three and what they're capable of… It puts me on edge. Catty pettiness from Blair and her girls I can cope with, but the boys… They know me so much better than anyone else here.

They know the real ways to hurt me if they want to.

And for some reason, they seem to want to.

So a day without them here is a good day, and I haven't let it go to waste. Even circuits in Gym isn't getting me down. Though that could be because Indi, the sunshine child extraordinaire, has done nothing but bitch and whine as we've worked the course together, and it gives me such life.

"If I do another squat, my thighs are going to explode," she complains, and I can't help but grin as I finish my round of burpees before sitting cross-legged on the floor.

"Want to swap? I will happily do your squat set if you want my burpees."

"Not on your fucking life, my friend," she practically hisses, and it makes me laugh out loud. She looks like she's ready to collapse by the time East blows his whistle, calling an end to the lesson before the bell actually goes off.

"Thank fucking Christ for that. I hate Gym. Exercise is not for everybody. This body of mine was made for coffee, chips, and pizza. Not exercise." She leans against the wall while I climb to my feet.

"I so feel that."

"You have much going on tonight?"

I groan in answer. "I have to finish dealing with the house shit. I'm trying to work out what we need to replace to take some of the pressure from Smithy. At the same time, I have *so much* homework to catch up on. How can we only be like two weeks in, and I'm this behind already?"

"Same! It's like the teachers want to torture us or something. Want to have a study date? I could use a few hours where Mom isn't trying to talk to me every two minutes so I can work. Plus, I can help with the house stuff. Or try at least."

"Sounds good, I'll let Smithy know you're coming over. Just remember the house is a disaster. I mean, the cleaners came in, and I'm sure Smithy didn't rest today, but still." I shrug a little, and once I reach my locker, I drop the man in question a quick message to let him know my plans. I get a smile emoji back, which, considering he didn't text before I showed him how to last night, is a definite win.

I go to drop my phone back in my bag before I head to the showers. It buzzes before I put it away, and it's like a surround sound of pings goes off. My stomach drops. Everyone getting the same notification from ReachMe is never a good thing.

Indi's eyes go wide as she looks at her phone before looking back up at me. Her discomfort is instantly obvious as she bites down on her lower lip.

"What?" I ask, and she shakes her head, so I pick up my phone and open the app. The post just has a link in it. So I click on it, and immediately really wish I fucking hadn't.

My screen fills with something from a porn movie… Except that's my face… And my voice—did they record me in the pool house?

I close my eyes as the breathy sounds fill the locker room.

This can not be happening.

I know I've sure as shit never fucked the guy in this video, and I sure as hell never videoed myself having sex… That would require me having had sex, which I haven't. Fuck my actual life. Whoever made this is a fucking pro.

Even though I know that it isn't me in the video, shame and humiliation floods my system, and I want to fucking cry. My hands shake as I shut down my phone, shoving it into my pocket. I can usually keep my head held high, but despair filters through me. I haven't even been here three fucking weeks. How is this my life?

"What a whore."

"Nice tits, Octavia. Why don't you show us since you don't seem to mind baring all to the world."

"Of course she made a sex tape. She's nothing but trash."

Their words hit their mark, and I struggle to breathe around the pressure that's sitting squarely in the center of my chest. Why is this happening to me? There's a buzzing in my ears, and my blood runs cold as my skin goes prickly. I need to get out of here. "Let's shower at my house?"

Indi nods, bundling her shit into her bag almost as quickly as I am. I'm not usually one to run from bullshit, but this… This is too much. "Let's go." She wraps her arm around me, squeezing me quickly once, while everyone around us laughs and watches the stupid clip on repeat. I try to keep my head high as we rush from the school.

"Want to ride on me, Octavia?" someone leers, and Indi flips them the bird as she tries to get me out of here as quickly as she can. The taunts and jibes follow us all the way through the school, each one like another dagger to the heart.

These people don't know me. If they did, they'd know I'd never do anything like that; but that doesn't matter to them. It doesn't make their words hurt or fill me with shame any less.

We leave the building and head toward Indi's car. The shouts and catcalls follow us the entire way. I nearly manage to keep my tears at bay, until I catch Finley's eye as he stands by his car. He wasn't at school today, so why is he even here?

The smug look on his face tells me everything I need to know.

*He did this.*

I bite down on my lower lip to stop myself from crying harder. Why would he do this? Indi has her car unlocked before we even reach it. I climb in, blinking back my tears. She starts the car up and peels away from the school. We're out of the parking lot before the first one falls.

*What did I ever do to deserve any of this?*

Indi says nothing the entire drive back to my house, and I whisper the code to her so she can go straight to the house. Once she pulls to a stop out front, her hands clench around the steering wheel. She takes a few deep breaths before turning to face me. "Do you know who made that bullshit video?"

"You don't think it's real?" I ask, shock coloring my voice. I might not be answering her question, but the fact that she didn't even ask me if it was me has me shook.

She shakes her head and squeezes my hand. "I may not have known you long,

V, but I'm pretty sure you're not the type of girl who fucks on camera, even with the wild rockstar shit that happens. So no, I don't think it's you in the video."

"I think… No, I know… It was Finley," I say quietly, picking at the skin beside my thumbnail. I swallow what little of my pride I have left and finally tell her what happened with the three of them. Telling her every little thing that I've been withholding. It's like a weight has been lifted from my shoulders, but she looks horrified.

"What a fucking dick stain! The fucking lot of them. I am so sorry, V. About all of this, I wish there was something I could do… say… to make it better for you."

"You're here, and you're my friend, in spite of everything. That's what I need."

"Then I've got you." She clasps my hand and squeezes before she climbs from the car. I follow suit, finding a worried looking Smithy waiting for us.

He twists his hands in front of him, and I can't tell if he's worried about me or about what it is he's waiting to tell me. I take a deep breath and try to prepare myself for whatever it is. He ushers us inside, and I know it's bad when he pulls out the teapot, one of the few things that apparently survived the break in.

I slide onto one of the stools, and Indi does the same as we wait for him to pour us both a cup. I pull my phone out of my bag and turn it back on before placing it down on the counter as Smithy turns and looks at me, frowning. "I heard what happened, Miss Octavia. The lawyers are already working on getting it pulled down… but I'm afraid that it's already online—more than just your school network. And that stupid gossip rag TV show, Celebrity Time, are threatening to pick it up for their news cycle. Obviously they can't run the video, but they *can* run the story."

"Of course they are," I sigh, putting my head in my hands. "I wonder who leaked it? I mean, being on the school network is bad enough, but to go wide…"

"I've been speaking with a friend in the police to get this shut down. She believes she already has the source of who leaked it wide, and they're working on finding out how it was posted to the school network too. Someone will be punished for this. I've also arranged for personal security too, just until we get this under control."

"I don't want that. I'll hide out in here if I need to, but I don't want someone following my every move ever again." He nods, taking my wishes into consideration, even though I can tell from his frown that he disagrees with me.

Indi sits, practically shaking with rage, on the stool next to me. "This is such horseshit. Can they even play or print it? You're still a minor!"

"The tabloids don't care about that. They won't play it… but the 'nation's princess' in a sex tape scandal, even if it's fake one, is hot news," I explain, and she curses enough to make a sailor blush.

"My sentiments exactly, Miss Indi."

My phone starts blowing up and I groan, covering my face with my hands. "What a fucking mess." I look back up at Smithy, seeing the concern in his eyes and let out a sigh. "You know that isn't me right?"

"Of course, Miss Octavia. I would never believe such things." My heart warms at his words. His unwavering faith in me is fucking everything. Though my guilt over him dealing with this when he should be resting makes me feel sick.

I nod and look over at Indi, loving that she never thought it was me either. "I'm going to fucking murder someone. How fucking dare they!" My sunshine girl is gone, but I'm so grateful to have somebody this fucking angry on my behalf.

I shrug, hating how resigned I am to the fact that this is my life now. "This is going to be absolute fucking chaos."

# CHAPTER THIRTEEN

I wake up bleary-eyed, dreading the day. I shut my phone off almost as soon as I turned it back on last night. I couldn't bring myself to look at it, so Indi and I hid in my room, binging reruns of Gossip Girl, trying to convince myself that it could be worse.

My lawyers called to advise that lawsuits had been drawn up against the publications who said they were going to run the story, which should stop it from ending up on the actual news, but that doesn't mean it hasn't already gone viral.

I cover my face with a pillow and scream into it. I want nothing more than to roll over and go back to sleep, to ignore the world for a week, a month, hell, even a year. But I'm not letting these assholes fuck with my GPA, and missing any school means getting even further behind than I already am. Needless to say, I did not get my study date last night.

Fuck this shit. They don't get to win. Not now, not ever. I'm not the type to tuck tail and run.

They can go fuck themselves up the ass with no lube.

I'll face the day the way my dad always rode out a storm. By looking and feeling fucking fierce. I mean, he didn't tend to do it sober, but that's not exactly an option for me—I don't have that choice. If I did… well, fuck being sober.

I kick off my blankets and stomp into the shower. Today, I'm going to look like a bomb-ass bitch because I need the armor. It's the only way I'm going to either stay out of jail or not break down to a puddle of nothingness.

I turn my phone on, flicking quickly over to airplane mode before linking it up to the sound system, and blast "Queen" by Loren Gray. There's nothing like music to help reset your mindset. I put it on repeat because this song is absolutely fucking life right now. It's like they wrote it just for me.

I take my time scrubbing, shaving, and preening every inch of my fucking body till I almost shine. I let the music wash over me, sinking into my pores to help build up the mental walls I need for today. This is the one part of being my father's daughter that I hate. The paparazzi, the media storms, the inability to have much privacy at all. If I was anyone else, this wouldn't be a potential national news story.

There have already been some paps here, but this... This will reveal to everyone where I am, which only makes Echoes Cove have the potential to become even more of a nightmare for me than it's been already. I wish my dad had thought through the stipulations of his Will. Why would he make me come back here?

When we left here, we never looked back. Or, at least, I didn't think so. I guess since Dad kept Smithy on, he had more intention of coming back here than I ever realized.

I lose myself in the monotony of getting myself ready for the day. Once I've picked out the most badass underwear I have, I sit down to do my hair and makeup. I pay special attention as I blow my hair out, letting it cascade down my back in dark, shiny waves. I finish the look with thick winged liner and a lipstick called *Bitchcraft.* It's a deep purple and makes my eyes pop in contrast.

It's not lost on me that I have to practice my smile in the mirror to make sure it's somewhat convincing today. But if this is what I have to do to show them that they won't break me, then this is what I'll do. I just wish I knew why.

What did I do to inspire such venom from the people who I was once closest to in the world?

I shake off the thought. Focusing on that shit isn't going to help me today.

Today, I need to keep my head high and rise above.

Fuck being a princess, today I'm going to be a goddamn queen.

I finish dressing by slipping my feet into a pair of black Louboutins to complete the look. I check out my reflection in the full-length mirror in the closet and feel almost prepared to face the day. After grabbing my bag, I head downstairs to find Smithy in the kitchen making pancakes.

My stomach revolts at the thought of even trying to eat anything. I take a deep breath as my mouth fills with acid. There is no way I'm going to vomit right now. No fucking way. "Smithy, I adore you, but I can't eat."

He startles a little as I put my bag on the stool and head to the coffee machine. The sweet nectar of the gods is going to be absolutely necessary today. I can feel it already. "Oh, Miss Octavia, you really should eat."

"And you should really call me V. Or at the very least, Octavia," I tease.

He scoffs at me, waving the spatula in my direction, looking highly offended. I'd worry if he wasn't smiling with his eyes. "That, Miss Octavia, is never going to happen. Now, please sit and try to eat something. There were some developments overnight. I've already called Miss Indi. She won't be able to get you this morning thanks to the vultures camped at the gates."

My stomach drops at his words, and I drop onto the closest stool with a heavy sigh. Why is this my life? "Well, I guess school really is out of the question today then."

He frowns at me and shakes his head, piquing my interest at what he could possibly have up his sleeve this early in the day. "I've already been on the phone with the school this morning. They've put more security measures in place. It's not the first time they've needed to keep the media away. They are also aware that if we find out someone at the school created and leaked that video, we will be pressing charges, and including the school in the lawsuit if any of their equipment was used."

"Thank you, Smithy." Relief floods my system at not having to face school with people trying to take my picture all day. I mean, they will definitely try, but if there's extra security in place, it's unlikely any will be too successful.

He moves behind me to the refrigerator and pours a glass of juice before placing it in front of me. He pats my shoulder before saying, "Drink your juice, Miss Octavia. Only having coffee won't be a good start to the day."

I pick the juice up and take a sip as he raises an eyebrow, watching me to make sure I actually drink it before he moves back to the stove. He plates up a few pancakes for me, topping them with blueberries and whipped cream, before sliding it in front of me. "Now then, I've also arranged for you to ride into school with Master Saint. You can use the gate between the yards so that you don't have to go out the front. Then they won't know for some time that you've left."

Relief floods my body at the thought of not having to go out the front of this house. The thought of facing it all before I even really start my day is enough to make me want to crawl back into bed. Bad bitch persona or not. "You're the best, Smithy."

"Just doing what I can, Miss Octavia." I jump up and hug him tight. It takes him a second to react, but then he holds me just as tight.

I feel safer now than I have in a while. I guess I have more pseudo-dads than I realized. "Thank you, Smithy."

He nods before motioning to the plate on the counter before me. "Anything for you, Miss Octavia. Now eat up, you don't want to keep Master Saint waiting."

I take a few bites of the pancakes, since my stomach is basically the home of nothing but butterflies right now. Enough to make him happy, but not so much that I feel sick. I love that Smithy arranged for East to take me in. Maybe going for a spin in his car will be a good start to the day.

I hop down and grab my bag, planting a kiss on Smithy's cheek. "See you later!"

"Have a good day, Miss Octavia."

I feel a little lighter as I cross the yard to the hidden gate between our property and the Saints'. It wasn't there originally, but once I became such good friends with East and Lincoln when we were younger, Dad installed the gate for us.

I cross over onto the Saint property, and a shudder runs down my spine. It almost feels like I'm in enemy territory, but I just need to find East and haul ass out of here. I walk around the property, and it feels like I've gone back in time. Nothing over here has changed. This far back in the yard, it's like I'm in a secret garden, protected from the rest of the world.

Walking around to the front of the house, I'm assaulted by memories of my childhood, which are not welcome considering everything that's happened since I got back here.

I reach the front of the house and freeze, an icy drop of dread runs down my spine when I see the black Porsche sitting in the drive. Smithy wouldn't have done this to me, right?

Then Lincoln walks out of the house and glares at me.

*Fuck my life.*

"Nope."

I pop my 'p' and turn the fuck around. I'll just take extra credit for my GPA.

"Octavia, stop being a brat and get in the fucking car." The growl in his voice causes goosebumps to erupt over every inch of my skin.

I spin back and glare at him, my anger like a writhing beast beneath my skin, just to find him leaning against his car. "You don't get to call me a brat when this is your fucking fault."

When he rolls his eyes, I swear my blood ignites. My rage grows to natural disaster levels.

Fuck this. He doesn't get to win, and his total lack of denial is staggering. I strut back to the car, stopping before him and mirroring his pose. I fold my arms over my chest, stand tall, and jut out my chin. He raises an eyebrow before he stands up properly. I almost feel small standing before him. He's easily a head taller than me, but I don't give up any ground.

He moves and opens the door for me, I keep the smile from my face at the small win. "Get in the fucking car, Octavia. I won't say it again."

I climb into the car without another word and sink into the soft leather seats. I'm not usually one for foreign cars, but this one is a wet fucking dream. Not that I'm going to tell him that. He slams the door closed and stalks around the car before climbing in himself as I buckle in. He doesn't say a word as he starts the engine. The throaty sound does things to me that it definitely shouldn't.

And it definitely isn't linked to being in such a small space with all of his growly big dick energy.

Nope.

He puts the car in gear and heads toward the gate. I hold my breath, hoping that the crazy people stalking me and trying to get through my gates don't notice me.

"They can't see you, the windows are tinted enough that they won't have a clue." I look over at him, wondering why he cares enough to reassure me. Not that I take his words as gospel. It's not until we're past the savage masses of paparazzi that I relax even a little. Not that I can relax fully, I'm still in a moving vehicle with someone who very obviously doesn't want me around. The only reason I know I'm safe is because Lincoln has always had too much ego to off himself.

We ride the rest of the way to school in total silence. The worst part about it is that it's not even uncomfortable. Other than the fact that I can't stop glancing over at him. Why does the asshole have to be so pretty to look at? And since when are forearms a thing that are so goddamn hot? I can't help but steal glances at him. He's changed a lot since we were kids, and I haven't exactly had a chance to watch him without care before this point. His thunderstorm colored eyes are focused on the road, and his dark hair is just a smidge longer than I imagine someone as controlled as him likes since it's long enough to fall into his eyes. His blazer looks fit to burst around his broad frame, which is almost enough to make me bite my lip, but I refrain as his strong jaw stiffens.

I think I might have been caught checking him out. Oops.

His hands clench around the steering wheel when he looks over. He definitely catches me looking, so I stare back at him with a raised eyebrow, almost begging him to say something. He stays silent.

I can't help the smirk that plays on my lips as we continue the ride in silence. Finally, he's the one on the back foot and uncomfortable. This might not last long, so I'm going to enjoy it while it does. I slide my phone from my pocket and pull up the thread with Indi.

**Me: You will never guess who my ride is this morning.**

**Indi: Smithy said it was Coach???**

**Me: I thought that too… turns out it was the **other** Saint.**

**Indi: Fuck your life.**

**Me: My sentiments exactly.**

**Indi: How is it?**

**Me: Other than choking on my own resentment and his big dick energy? It's totally fine. Most quiet I've had in days.**

**Indi: **cowboy emoji** Well, there are worse ways to start the day? Maybe? You're not dead at least…**

**Me: Definitely… the madness at my gates was beyond insane.**

**Indi: I'm sorry. Did Smithy get the legal shit sorted out?**

**Me: Yeah, I'll explain everything when we're at school.**

**Indi: I'm already here, floofy coffee in hand. I'll meet you in the library.**

**Me: Indigo Montoya you are a freaking goddess.**

**Indi: I know, see you soon **heart emoji****

It doesn't take long for us to pull into the student parking lot, and he drives straight up to the front of the lot nearest the doors. Of course his spot is just left empty. He pulls in between a white Lamborghini that Finley climbs out of and a Ducati Panigale V4. That's when I notice Maverick sitting on the steps of the school, helmet on the ground between his legs.

Why am I not even surprised he's the one with that deathtrap of a bike?

I look at Lincoln, and he pauses before unlocking the doors. "Was it you? That attacked Smithy? That leaked that tape of me?"

He watches me, not saying a word but quirking his eyebrow in a way that makes me feel ridiculous for asking. As if he'd stoop so low as to bother. But he and I both know he's been on a mission to get me to leave, so it's not that ridiculous if you ask me. Except now I feel kind of stupid for even mentioning it.

I move to open the door, but Finley is there already opening it for me. I guess Lincoln warned them that he was bringing me in today. I slide from the car once the door is fully open before turning back to Lincoln. I hate thanking him for anything, especially when I know this mess is his fault, but manners don't cost a goddamn thing, and I'm not that bitch.

"Thank you." He glances over at me and just nods, effectively dismissing me as he climbs from the car. The other two just watch me, as silent as Lincoln has been all morning. I huff and head toward the school to meet Indi in the library.

I've had enough big dick energy today already. I can't deal with the three of them right now. More so because I know that the current chaos in my life is entirely their doing. As much as I'd like to confront them about it, I know I won't get anything from it. They won't be sorry, they won't apologize, and they can't take it back.

Pandora's box is officially open.

Just as I reach the doors, I hear Blair's screeching voice yelling my name across the lot.

Fuck my whole life today.

I contemplate pretending I don't hear her as my hand finds the handle and twists. But she screeches again, and this time she's closer, so it's louder.

*Delightful.*

I take a deep breath and prepare myself for more emotional warfare. I turn and find Blair at the bottom of the steps, practically foaming at the mouth. "What do you want, Blair?"

Her eyes go wide at the blatant lack of fucks in my tone. Her hands clench at her sides, and I can't help but wonder what's gotten her so worked up. It's not like it was her fake sex tape everyone was watching yesterday. "Why the fuck did you ride in with him?"

You have got to be fucking kidding me. "That's seriously why you were screeching my name like a banshee? Because I got a ride to school with Lincoln?"

She climbs the steps so that she's face-to-face with me. I'm glad I put my heels on today otherwise she'd be looking down at me. Fuck that.

"Answer the fucking question." She practically spits the words at me. "I warned you before the year started, he's mine."

I burst out laughing because I just can't help myself, and she slaps me across the face, shocking the shit out of me. "Don't fucking laugh at me."

She practically vibrates with anger, and her eyes are wild. Apparently laughing at the self-appointed queen of ECP isn't something that happens around here. A crowd gathers around us, but the last thing I need is another video of me circulating. I take a deep breath and try to calm myself down so I don't retaliate, because breaking her new nose isn't going to help me right now. "I needed a ride to school because my house is a circus right now."

"That better be all it is. Next time, call the pathetic, depressive dirty emo puppy you've adopted to save you." My sight bleeds red at her words, and I shove down all of my good intentions and punch her square in the face. The crunch of her nose, followed by her scream and the gush of blood, makes me feel better for about two seconds until the reality of the situation seeps in.

*Never start the fucking fight, Octavia.*

I turn on my heel and walk into the school while she wails on the front steps. Her bitch squad fawns over her and leads her away from the school. Her nose probably isn't broken, right?

I close my eyes and take a deep breath—I *can* survive this day. And maybe if I do actually survive the day, I can survive the year.

I open my eyes and head to my locker. My stomach bottoms out when I catch sight of them… Dozens of stills from that fucking video are taped all over the walls and lockers.

You have got to be fucking kidding me. Could this day get any worse?

I start tearing them down before anyone else heads inside, but I'm sure if they're here, they're everywhere. I throw a ton of them in the trash before realizing that it's a waste of my time. The video is already out there. The pictures are just another taunt.

Fuck it, I'm not wasting any more time on this bullshit.

I drop my stuff off at my locker before going to find Indi. *Please fucking Christ let this day get better.* I don't think one fucking good day is too much to ask for.

I strut into the library to find Indi waiting at the table for me with the biggest Frappuccino possible topped with *so much* whipped cream that all of my bad mood disappears. Well, at least for the moment.

She hands it to me, her grin matching mine. "There is nothing that whipped cream can't fix."

I take a sip of the sugary goodness, wondering how I ever came around to this drink, and sigh. I think she might be right.

I look up from the drink after a quiet moment, and my eyes catch on a trashcan stuffed to the brim, realizing after a moment that it's full of pictures from the sex tape. Indi blushes a little and shrugs when she notices me looking at it. "I took down as many as I could on the way here and then all of the ones that were taped up in here too. I know I couldn't get them all, but I figured the more I got the less there were for you and everyone else to see."

I hug her tight, and she squeaks a little. I fucking love this girl. She has my back without me even needing to say a word. "It's official, you are my ride or die, bitch."

She grins at me enthusiastically and nods when I let her go. "You had me at ride or die."

---

English with Ms. Summers is always a dream, but there's a rock in my stomach as I walk to Business. I need this class so badly, but I literally can never focus. Mr. Peters' voice is so dreary and monotone. And after having already focused for a whole lesson, it feels like my brain just won't engage during this time period.

It sucks.

I sit in my seat next to Lincoln, groaning when he glares at me. What a joy.

"Ladies and gents, as per the email last week, your first proposals are due at the end of the lesson," Mr. Peters says as he drops down into the chair at his desk.

I look at Lincoln, who looks smug as fuck. I didn't get any damn email, and I'd put money on him being the reason why. "Why didn't you say anything?"

"I didn't realize I was your keeper." He rolls his eyes, and just once, I wish I was brave enough to fuck him up a little. I've fought bigger guys than him, but there's something almost feral underneath that calm surface of his that gives me pause everytime I think about lashing out.

"Of course you're not." I sigh, exasperated. Why does he take everything I say the wrong way? "But we're supposed to work on this together."

Mr. Peters draws my attention back to him as he drones on about plentiful returns and profit margins, and it takes everything I have not to zone out and panic about the project I'm meant to be doing with Lincoln. After most of the class has passed, Mr. Peters tells us to finish up our first proposals before handing them in.

The first part of our project is to write a proposal for a business venture with full-scale profit projections. Apparently, Lincoln has taken it upon himself to decide what the business venture is. I look over at him and he's got a smug smile on his face as he watches my panic ensue. "Are you going to show me what you've worked on at least?"

"Why would I do that?" he asks, smug smile firmly in place.

I let out a deep sigh and rub at my temples. "Just this once, don't be an ass, Lincoln. Please?"

Here I am, begging again. I'm starting to despise Lincoln Saint and his web of bullshit.

"Fine," he says, dropping the file onto my desk before leaning in close. "But only because I like the way my name falls off your lips when you beg."

The bell rings before I have a chance to even read the first page. Fuck. Fuck. Fuck.

He takes the file from my hand, nodding once before stalking to the front of the room, dropping the proposal he wrote up on Mr. Peters desk. "I did this myself. Octavia felt she was above the task, so I completed it on both our behalf."

Mr. Peters looks over to me with an eyebrow raised. "Miss Royal, if you'll please stay behind."

I groan and drop my head onto the table, waiting for the rest of the class to filter out, the snickers following as they go. When the last person has left and closed the door, I grab my bag and head to his desk. "Mr. Peters, I wasn't aware that our proposals were due today, and Lincoln hasn't exactly been open to being my partner—today was the first time I knew he'd even been working on it. If you give me an extension, I can make notes on his proposal and expand on the presentation."

He leans back on his chair, and the look of indignation on his face tells me just how much he believes me. I could fucking kill Lincoln. Does he have any idea how much I need to pass this class?

"Miss Royal, it's obvious from your work and lack of attention that you are not dedicated to this class." He stands, moving closer to me before perching on the edge of the desk. "At this point, with what you've done so far, you are looking at a failing grade on this project."

The blood drains from my face, and I feel a little woozy. I can't fail this class.

I just can't.

"Please, Mr. Peters, if there is anything I can do, I'll do it. I need to pass this class." I hate that I'm begging. I hate what Lincoln has reduced me to yet again.

The lewd smile that crosses his pasty face makes me feel sick. He stands up and brushes back my hair behind my ear, and I shudder. "I'm sure we can think of some way for you to earn extra credit."

"Mr. Peters, that isn't exactly what I was intending." I take a step toward the door, and he follows again, reaching for his zipper.

"I hear things, you know. No one would have to know, not that they'd believe you if you said anything. I'm a respected teacher and well… I saw that video. A few times."

My stomach rolls as he pulls his dick from his pants, and I look anywhere but at him.

"No, Mr. Peters. I won't do it."

"A little whore like you must be very good at sucking dick. Imagine how easy that A would be. I'm sure you're a girl of many talents." He walks closer toward me until my back slams against the door. This can't be happening to me right now. "Be a good girl and get on your knees."

"No!" I shout, pushing him away from me. "You're a fucking pervert. I'm not going to do anything for you."

His face turns red as he tucks his dick away. "You'll regret that. And you'll fail this class no matter what you do. No one would think twice about a girl like you failing this class."

Angry tears prick at my eyes, and I blink them back.

"Fuck you, Mr. Peters."

"I did offer," he says, with the creepiest smile I've ever seen. I tear the door open and storm from the class, feeling dirtier than I ever have. But he's right, who is going to believe me after everything that's happened since I came back here?

Why is this year not over yet?

---

My morning has not gone the way I hoped it would, but the sugar rush definitely carried me through it. The bell for lunch rings just as my sugar crash hits, and I groan. At least I can eat and recaffeinate. Caffeine is absolutely necessary to ensure no more fists are thrown.

I haven't seen or heard anything of Blair since this morning, but most of her bitch squad have been MIA too. I'm taking it as a blessing, because the whispers and looks have already been so insane today, that, despite my armor and the sugar, I feel like I'm bleeding out.

I pack my things up into my bag and head for the cafeteria, not paying attention to anyone around me. I guarantee I've taken nothing in during any of my lessons today, so I'm definitely going to have to beg someone for their notes at some point.

I meet Indi by the doors for lunch, and the grimace on her face tells me that she has bad news. "Blair is back… and she is pissed."

"Of course she is," I groan. I mean, she definitely deserved at least a bitch slap, but I definitely saw red earlier. You can fling shit at me, and I'll let it go, but you do *not* insult or fuck with my friends. All reason disappears when you cross that line.

"Apparently her nose isn't broken, though." She shrugs and links her arm with mine. I love her show of loyalty, even if it is a subconscious thing. "So ya know, she has no real reason to be pissed."

"I'm almost disappointed that it's not broken," I joke, and she snickers.

"The day isn't over yet."

We walk into the cafeteria laughing, and it goes so quiet you could hear a fucking pin drop. *Just awesome.*

Indi stills at my side, and I love how fierce she looks right now. There's a nasty sneer on her face like she'd happily throw hands if anyone says one goddamn thing.

I jut out my chin and glance around the room. I don't see Blair here yet, but I catch the eyes of at least half of the room as I go. My eyes dare them to be brave enough to say something to my face rather than whispering about me behind my back. No one says a fucking thing or even moves until I lock eyes with Lincoln. He raises an eyebrow at me, but I refuse to look away first. Finley leans over and says something to him, drawing his attention from me, and I smirk.

Once he looks away from me, conversation starts again, and Indi leads us toward the line to actually get some food. I grab a cheeseburger, fries, and a soda despite the fact that eating feels like that last thing I want to actually be doing.

As we head to our usual table, coughs of 'slut' and 'whore' follow me across the room. "Fuck you all, like you're the virgin fucking Mary," Indi snaps at someone who I don't remember having ever seen before.

"Not worth it," I tell her, pulling her to our table and letting the words slide off of me like water from a duck's back.

She slams her tray down, and her hands shake as she sits, her face red with anger. "People are such fucking dicks. Not one of them would call you out on shit to your face. Cowards, all of them."

"They are." I shrug. "But they're not worth your rage for exactly that reason."

She shakes her head and jams a fry in her mouth. Apparently, her hangry is showing. "I don't know how you do it. I'd have already broken under the pressure of everything you've been through the last few weeks."

"Nah," I say, shaking my head as I unwrap my burger. "You're stronger than you think. You survived last year here on your own."

"Let's agree to disagree."

We sit and eat in a comfortable silence until Raleigh and some of his friends join us. No one says a thing about the video, Blair, or my outburst this morning. They just talk about the upcoming game this week, and it's just so fucking normal. I love it.

"Are you okay?" Raleigh asks when everyone else is distracted with another conversation about the Asheville Allstars.

I think about his question for a quiet, contemplative moment. Am I okay? I feel okay considering everything that's happened, so I nod and smile. "I could be worse."

He frowns a little, the lines on his forehead deepening as he does. "How come you didn't call me for a ride today if you needed one?"

I swear it takes everything in me not to roll my eyes. I don't get why me coming in with Lincoln is so out there. I mean, yes, he hates me. That much is obvious, but still. I bite back my frustration at being called out, especially since it's really not any of his business. Yeah, he's been a good friend, and he asked me out on a date, but that doesn't give him the right to question me.

Despite all of the mild resentment swimming in my head, I answer him, trying to sound as rational and as calm as I can. "Smithy, my guardian, arranged it. I thought I was coming in with Indi, but with the amount of press at the house, it wasn't possible. Lincoln is my neighbor, and it was easy for me to get to his house undetected, so I could actually get to school."

He frowns again, but nods. "Okay."

That's all he says. Like I needed his permission. I grit my teeth together and take a deep breath. I'm on edge today, so I'm not going to snap at him. This could be me fully taking it the wrong way. He's been nothing but nice until now, so this has to just be me.

Just as I find my zen, Blair enters the room and glares at me. Her nose isn't strapped up, so it obviously wasn't broken. Though even from here, I can see the extra concealer on her face, so I guess there's some bruising.

*Shame.*

She stalks toward me, pissy as hell, but Finley steps in front of her and diverts her attention to Lincoln. I don't know why that pisses me off more, but when she smiles smugly at me, I clench my fists under the table.

The bell rings, and Indi glances over at me. "Want to skip?"

I love her so fucking much.

I shake my head and grab my bag and tray. "Not a fucking chance. Then they'll think they've won, and they need to learn that I'm not going anywhere."

"Damn, you are slaying this badass bitch vibe today," she says, smiling wide. We say our goodbyes to the table and hurry out of the cafeteria to my locker.

They're going to learn that I'm not just another one of their lowly subjects. This bitch doesn't take it lying down.

# CHAPTER FOURTEEN

I'm woken by my phone pinging like crazy on the nightstand. Groaning as I roll over, I look at the messages.

**Indi: I need you.**

**Indi: I was carjacked.**

**Indi: I don't know what to do.**

**Indi: Help.**

I blink down at the screen in horror.

What the actual fuck? I dial her immediately, my heart racing at all of the possibilities of what could have happened to her. My panic flips to anger as I wait for the line to connect. I swear to God, if she's hurt…

She answers on the first ring and her sobs echo across the line. "Where are you?"

"V… I…" she stammers like she can't get her words out around her panic. "I'm just past the railroad tracks on the other side of town. I'm hiding down an alley right now. But, V, they took my car, they hit me…" her words taper off as her sobs pick up again.

"I'll be there in a few, okay. Just stay on the line."

I rack my brain, trying to think of how the hell I can get to her when my car is still in the shop. I run down the stairs and head for the security room where Smithy keeps the keys for my dad's cars that are locked in the garage. I haven't touched anything in the garage since I got back to Echoes Cove. My dad's things were his, but right now, I need one of his cars. I grab the closest keys to me and run to the garage. When I push the button, the lights on the black SUV flash.

I don't hesitate, I just climb in and start the engine. The tires screech as I pull down the drive, smashing the gate clicker so it opens. "I'm on my way. I'm in the black Range Rover."

"Okay." I push the button on the dash so my phone connects to the bluetooth, keeping the connection to her open, her sniffles filling the car.

"Did you call the police?" I ask, but I'm pretty sure I already know the answer.

"No," she hiccups. "I panicked. I ran. I just texted you. I don't know what to do. They hurt me, and I'm so fucking scared they're going to come back." Her sobs start up again, and I grip the steering wheel tighter as I fly through the city toward the less savory part of Echoes Cove. I can't help but wonder why she was over there in the first place. That's a question for later.

I scan the roads as quickly as I can. Once I cross the tracks, I slow the car. "I'm nearly there, can you come out to the street side so I can see you?"

"Okay." Her voice is so small, and I hate that someone did this to her. She's possibly the nicest person that I've ever met. She didn't deserve this.

I see her appear on the right. I jerk the wheel in her direction, screeching to a stop before jumping from the car. A bruise is already forming on her cheekbone, and she's bleeding from a cut above her eyebrow.

"Oh, Indi," I sigh and wrap her in my arms. Her knees give way and I take her weight, lowering us to the ground, holding her while she sobs. Her entire body shakes as she buries her face into my neck, clinging to me for dear life like I can save her, and my anger blazes again that someone would do this to her.

We're in the middle of some residential buildings, and it doesn't look like there are even any businesses here where she could've gone for help. This entire place looks sketchy as hell. "We should get you to the hospital to get checked out and then call the police."

She shudders in my arms before pulling away and wiping at her tears, wincing as she touches her cheek. "My mom is going to be so mad."

"Your mom will be happy you're okay, I promise."

I usher her into the car before taking her to the hospital, calling her mom on the way. It doesn't take long to reach the hospital, and thankfully we don't wait long before someone comes to tend to her since it's so early in the day, but I'm instructed to stay in the waiting room. Her mom breezes through the waiting room and heads straight for me, looking fucking terrified. "She's okay, she's just in with the nurses."

"Thank you, Octavia." she says, taking a deep breath before she heads into the room. I can't imagine how she feels; that's her daughter in there. Though her helplessness and rage are written all over her face. And after everything I've been through the last few months, I get it.

I move to actually sit in the waiting room and stare up at the tiled ceiling, searching for some answers. I drop a message to Smithy to let him know I'm going to miss school today, and he confirms he'll let the school know. It isn't like Thursdays are a typical skip day, and while I might be worried about my grades and getting behind, I'm more worried about my friend.

My phone buzzes again, and my heart stops when I see the message.

**Unknown: We told you nobody you loved was safe. When will you listen?**

This is my fault.

Holy shit.

I can't breathe.

I put my head between my knees as I try to stave off the panic attack that threatens. My heart thumps in my chest and my hands shake; my temperature rises as everything around me becomes overwhelming. The noises in here sound like I'm underwater as I struggle to focus on my breathing.

This can't be my fault. It has to be a coincidence. They wouldn't do that.

Right?

---

Friday morning at school is like nothing I've ever experienced. The hype for tonight's game is *out of this world.* School spirit's at an all time high, and it's like everything else that happened this week is long forgotten. It feels like I'm not here, as if everyone's forgotten to make my life a living hell, and I'm so fucking here for it.

Indi's excitement is palpable. The cut on her head was small enough to not need stitches, and makeup covers the bruising on her cheek. I showed her the message I got when the nurses finally let me in her room, but she refused to put any of the blame on me. She said the guys that stole her car were older, so that it was likely someone heard about what happened and was trying to use it against me.

I hate to hope that it's true, but she's been adamant about it, and despite everything, she's still my sunshine friend. When she appeared at my gates this morning in her Wrangler, I was beyond shocked. Apparently it was found not an hour after we reported it stolen, without a single scratch on it.

That alone makes me think she's wrong about it being a coincidence. She won't hear any of it, so I keep my thoughts about it to myself.

As I walk through the halls with Indi, I can't help but be amazed once more about the complete change in the whole mood and demeanor of the entire fucking student body. "This is weird, right? It's just a high school football game."

Indi looks at me with wide eyes full of fear, which is sobering but makes me want to laugh at the same time. "Please, sweet baby Jesus, do not let anyone hear you saying those words. Football is basically a religion here. Why do you think that Raleigh and the guys are basically untouchable? Even Lincoln and his merry band of assholes don't tend to fuck with the team. *Religion.*"

"It's still weird," I say with a shrug as we reach my locker. I open it and put my bag inside, grabbing my phone and sliding it into my pocket before locking it up.

"Oh, it's absolutely fucking nuts, but is that even a surprise about this place at this point? Everything about Echoes Cove is fucking weird. The sheer amount of money that gets funneled into the team is staggering. If there isn't some shady shit going on with that, I'd be amazed." She pops her bubblegum when she finishes speaking, and I consider her words. She's not wrong. Echoes Cove is a web of lies and secrets. There's no way there's this many rich people in such a small place without there being something shady going down.

I'm just glad I've managed to keep out of that shit.

She shoves her stuff in her locker and we head to the cafeteria in time for a mass exodus. The cheers and chanting leave me at a loss as the loudspeaker sounds with the principal's voice. "Today's pep rally will start in thirty minutes. Please start making your way to the gym."

Indi groans beside me, rolling her eyes. "I totally forgot they wipe the whole fucking afternoon for this bullshit."

My stomach growls at her words. "Okay, well, if I have to deal with this much school spirit and not kill people, I need food."

"Same, girl. Same," she says as she heads into the near empty cafeteria. I follow her, stoked to see that the one advantage of the insane pep rally is that there's no one in line for food. Some of the tables still hold kids, the ones who are obviously choosing to study instead of going to the pep rally.

Maybe they have the right idea.

I grab a couple slices of pepperoni pizza and a bag of chips before heading to a table with Indi, who carries her own pizza and a brownie. "Maybe we should skip and study? We never had our study date."

She pauses, her slice of pizza halfway to her mouth before shaking her head. "If I wasn't a football fiend, I would usually say yes… Except for the fact that Jackson asked if I'd be there, and I already told him yes."

"Ooh, how's that whole thing going?" I ask, wagging my eyebrows, and she blushes.

"It's going." She takes a bite of her pizza and groans. I won't push her for details if she isn't comfortable giving them. I get it. "I also heard that you have a date after the game tonight."

"I totally would've said something, but well…"

She interrupts me by putting up her hand and shaking her head. "You've had shit going on, and I'm not worked up about it. I was a little shocked since he doesn't seem like your type."

I can't help but laugh at that. "I have a type?"

She shrugs as the bell rings again, letting us know the pep rally is about to begin. I grab my pizza and chips, ditching my tray. There's no way I'm leaving my food behind. Indi follows suit and we start heading to the gym. "I mean, I've never seen you date anyone, but a typical high maintenance, golden boy quarterback doesn't really seem to scream *Octavia Royal's type.* But I mean, what do I know?"

"I've never dated a sports type, but Raleigh's nice. Plus, it's only one date, even if I'm not all that confident about it. Who knows what will happen? I have bigger worries before my date tonight," I quip and she looks at me, eyebrows raised in question. "What the fuck happens at a pep rally? It can't be like what I've seen on TV, right?"

She bursts out laughing at me, her shoulders fully shaking, and she pauses walking as she pulls herself together. "Oh man, I'm not even going to explain. This is too good."

I mean that doesn't exactly fill me with joy, but I follow the swarm of people to the gym with her. We take a seat toward the back of the bleachers, and I already know that I'm going to hate whatever this is. The hype in the room is enough to choke a girl, and while I might like that sort of thing, this is totally not the place for it.

The principal walks up to the podium in front of the bleachers and lifts his arms. A roar of shouts and applause echoes around the room as the entire fucking school loses their shit.

*This is fucking insane.*

He lowers his arms, and the room goes quiet. "Are we ready for tonight, Raiders?"

The response is almost fucking deafening as people stomp their feet and shout. Indi leans over, grinning at the look of horror on my face. "Oh girl, this is only the beginning. Just wait for the dancing, the glitter, and the streamer rockets."

My eyes widen at the very thought of it. I barely have time to question it as the dance team struts onto the hardwood floor in shiny shorts and bandeaus made of sequins. Fucking sequins.

Music blares through the PA, and everyone goes crazy again. I glance around and even the three boys who have made my life hell seem to be enjoying themselves. I think I'm more shocked to see them actually smiling. I hate that despite everything else that's happened, I still seek them out in a crowd. Not that they're hard to miss. There's a ring of empty seats around them, as if everyone else is afraid to get too close. The girls who would usually, are all on the dance or cheer teams who are going crazy on the floor below us.

This level of hype should be reserved for concerts, not high school football games.

"Do you think anyone would notice if I escaped to the Music rooms?" I ask Indi, having to lean into her to be heard over the chaos. I have to give props to the dance team because they're fucking slaying their routine to AWOLNATION's "Sail", but still… This amount of pep is kind of gross.

Indi points as the football team breaks through a banner and runs into the room, joining the dance team as the crowd screams and cheers. "Pretty sure your boy would notice."

Fuck my life.

*Someone please fucking save me.*

---

Tonight's game has been bad.

I don't know much about football, but the triple threat of players from the Allstars—according to Indi—is fucking lethal. I literally only know the names Xavier, Hunter, and Tobias because she's cussed them out so hard all night. I'm assuming they're the other team since I don't recognize the names, but who knows at this point?

All of the student body's pep and cheer from earlier in the day is officially dead. The score is 35-14 to the Allstars, and apparently there's no coming back from that with the amount of time left on the clock. I have zero idea what's happening on the field, except for the fact that these guys spend more time taking breaks than they do running plays.

The mood's grim as the game ends, which doesn't exactly leave me hopeful for tonight. I accepted the date without really thinking it through, and I've regretted it ever since. Indi was right, I'm not the one to date a sports type… I'm also not looking to date. Having Raleigh as a friend is one thing, but anything else… I'm just hesitant. Dating was not on my radar this year, and I don't want the tentative friendship we've built to be ruined by him thinking this could be more.

Blair and her bitch squad look so salty about the loss that I almost want to throw them a bottle of tequila.

*Almost.*

The team heads for the fieldhouse after the clock runs out, and the stands start to empty. Indi drops into her seat and folds her arms across her chest, looking equally as pissed off as the cheer team. "Well, that was a fucking shit show. I know the Allstars are good, but fucking hell. Our defense was fucking useless tonight." I sit down beside her, feeling bad for her and our friends, but I don't really get the whole 'football is a religion' thing. "Those Allstars fucking annihilated us."

"I'm sorry?" I say, unsure if there's anything else I *can* say.

She shakes her head, shrugging. "It's just a bad start to the season. If we have too many losses, the chances of a championship slip away."

"Dude, you're totally a football nerd, aren't you?" I tease her, and she blushes a little. I never would have pegged her for a secret football lover but here we are.

She nods and tucks a strand of her freshly colored purple hair behind her ear. "I totally am. It's all Dad's fault. He's a fucking football freakazoid. He didn't have a son to share his love for the NFL with, so he shared it with me, and now I'm somehow hooked."

I smile, thinking of all the things my dad shared with me. There really isn't anything quite like the bond between daddy and daughter. "Hey, no shame. I get it. My dad shared music with me."

"Am I ever going to hear you play, by the way?" she asks, and I shrug. The thought of playing in front of people still makes me want to be sick.

We wait in comfortable silence until the stands are empty and head toward the back of the fieldhouse. With a loss like this, apparently the coach will be bitching them out for a while, so I prepare myself for Raleigh to cancel on me. I wish that made me more upset, but it doesn't, which isn't a great omen. I'm almost sad about not being sad.

"What are your plans for the rest of the night?" I ask her while we wait, and she blushes.

She fidgets a bit as she looks down at her feet. "I'm heading to a party over at ECH with Jackson."

I grin at her and nudge her with my shoulder. "Look at you go. Are you excited?"

"A little," she nods. "I'm more nervous than anything, though. He's a football god, and I'm… well, me." Her self-deprecation is not okay with me. Not even a little.

I grab her by the shoulders and force her to look at me. "Indi, you are a fucking amazing human, and he's the lucky one here. Football gods come and go, but you are literally the nicest human I've ever met in my life. Your sunshine sparkle mixed with your sassy as fuck snark gives me life. If Jackson can't appreciate that, then fuck him. You are a goddamn goddess."

She blushes in response to my words and starts to laugh softly. "Dude, you are so freaking fierce. I know you hate that you had to come back here, but I'm so glad you did."

I hug her tight. I know she's deflecting, but I totally understand. Compliments are hard to handle when they're not something you're used to. I let her go as the doors behind us open and the team filters out. The unwavering pep from earlier is noticeably absent. I guess the party at ECH is going to end up being a commiseration rather than a celebration. "Be careful tonight. If any shit goes down, call me, and I'll be there in a heartbeat."

"Awh, look! You do warm and fuzzy too," she teases, and I roll my eyes. "But yeah, I'll be careful. I know the rivalry is real, but things are usually pretty okay at parties. Everyone just wants to get fucked up." She looks over my shoulder, and her smile widens. I glance over my shoulder and see Jackson heading toward us.

"Have fun," I whisper in the moment right before Jackson reaches us and slings his arm over her shoulders.

"You ready?" he asks her, and she nods. "Awesome. We'll see you later, V."

I salute him as he leads her toward the parking lot before turning back to the locker room door. Most of the team has already left, but there's no way in hell I'm heading in there. Especially with the bellowing voice from the football coach filtering under the door. Not on your life.

I sit on the grassy mound behind the fieldhouse and play a game on my phone while I wait, ignoring the world around me.

"Sorry that I took so long." I look up and find Raleigh standing above me.

I smile and climb to my feet, dusting off my ass as I do. I'm only in denim cutoffs and a tank with a shirt over my shoulders. I wish I felt more excited, but maybe that will come later. "You're good. Are you ready?"

He nods and takes my hand. It feels a little weird, but I go with it and follow him to his car. "Where are we heading?"

"That's a surprise," he says with a wink as he opens the truck door for me. I slide into his pickup, and he closes the door before slipping around and climbing in the driver's side.

I'm not really a fan of surprises, but I'm not about to tell him that and ruin whatever he has planned. Though if anyone actually jumps out at me and yells surprise, I won't be held responsible for my actions.

He drives us through town and pulls up outside a Mexican place that I haven't seen before. "Indi said you were a sucker for tacos, so I figured my family restaurant was the perfect place to eat."

My eyes go wide, and I get a flutter of panic as my heart starts to race. His family restaurant means his family is in there, and that feels like way too much for a first date. Even if the food is some of my favorite. "Oh, uhm, yeah, I love Mexican food. I didn't know your family had a restaurant."

He puts his hand on the handle of the door before winking at me. "There's a lot you don't know about me."

---

The night ends, and I'm more than a little underwhelmed. I mean the food was fucking amazing. I've never had Mexican food that good, and I'm definitely not mentioning that to Smithy, but I'm never going to be able to eat there again.

His mom and older sister were there, and they fawned over us like he was literally their little golden prince and I his prize. That was turn off number one. I wasn't even that pampered out on tour with my dad. It was kind of sickening.

Then there was how he totally changed once we were out. He was so controlling, and like, not in a good way. At first, I thought he was being a gentleman. Opening doors, pulling out my chair… until he commented on my clothes and how he thought I should've dressed better for him. Then he ordered for me without even handing me a menu, talked down to me about the amount of food on my plate, even about ordering a soda. All massive red flags to me. Some girls like the controlling thing, but I am not one of them. Not like that.

Don't get me wrong, he's the nicest guy usually, but as anything more than friends… It's never going to work with us. Of that much, I'm already pretty sure. He pulls up to the front gates, and turns off the engine.

This doesn't feel weird for me or anything. No, not at all. Fuck my life. I grasp the door handle quickly, wanting to escape before this gets any more awkward. I'm preparing myself to say goodnight before I close the door, but he gets out of the car too.

He stalks round to my side, golden boy grin on his face, with his hands shoved in his pockets. "Tonight was fun."

"It was, your family's restaurant was great, and the food—"

His grin widens, and he nods, interrupting me. "Yeah, my mom knows how to cook."

I twiddle with my thumbs, wishing I was better at this. He's been nothing but nice since the day I met him, which is why I don't want to lead him on. I don't want to crush his feelings either, though after tonight, I'm not entirely sure that'll be an issue.

The sound of metal cogs whirring fills the silence as the gate to the Saint household opens, and I spot Finley's pearly white Lamborghini rolling through it. He and Maverick look over in our direction as the car rolls forward, windows down, and Raleigh moves closer to me.

He wraps his arms around my waist and pulls me against him. My hands press on his chest; but before I can say another word, his lips are on mine. Shock has me paralyzed for a moment before I pull away. He looks over his shoulder, grinning at Finley and Maverick, who glare in our direction. Maverick says something to Finley that I can't hear despite how close they are, and Finley shakes his head once, his knuckles turning white on the steering wheel before the car speeds away from us.

Did he actually just try to claim me in front of them? With the world's most underwhelming, no fireworks kiss at that? That's not exactly how I pictured my first kiss with him going, though I hadn't pictured kissing him at all. That should probably have been my first warning sign. I pull myself out of his grasp, and he frowns as I quickly dash through the gate and close it.

"We should do this again," he calls out, and I try not to grimace.

How the fuck am I going to do this right? "Yeah, maybe. I'm tired, so I'm going to head to bed."

"Yeah okay." He grins at me like he can't tell how grossed out I am by him right now.

I turn to head up the driveway, calling out a 'night' when I realize he's still standing there, watching me.

"Night," he shouts back, and I hear the slam of his door before the engine starts and he drives off into the night.

I run a hand down my face and pull my phone from my pocket, clicking on the message thread with Indi.

**Me: I'm home, alive and well… Just wanted to check in with you. Hope you're having a good night with J.**

**Indi: I will require all of the details, but yes, having an awesome night.**

I smile at her message, glad that one of us is having a successful night, and repocket my phone before entering the house. I need a shower to wash the night off of me.

If this is how actual dating works, I'm not sure I'm a fan.

---

I groan as I roll over in bed and stare up at the ceiling. Last night was… Well, it wasn't great.

I tossed and turned most of the night trying to decide what to do, but I'm convinced that Raleigh's going to go strictly into the friend zone. The more I think about that kiss, the more disappointed I am.

There were no fireworks, it was underwhelming, and the whole claiming thing skeeved me out.

It was a weird fucking night. I was extra glad that the press wasn't camped out at the house again. I guess Smithy's legal threats finally hit home with people. At least that's one less thing to worry about now.

My phone buzzes on the bedside table, so I grab it and groan when I see Raleigh's name on my screen.

**Raleigh: Morning beautiful. Last night was great, we should do it again. You have anything planned for the weekend?**

Apparently the eager beaver thought last night went much better than I did. Now I have to work out how to walk us back to being friends because this isn't going to work for me. I should have trusted my instincts and cancelled the date.

**Me: Hey, I've got some shit to do this weekend, but I'll see you at school on Monday?**

My phone buzzes again almost as soon as the message is sent.

**Raleigh: Well that sucks, but it's cool. Yeah, I'll see you Monday. Have a good weekend.**

The sulkiness that comes through with his message is unreal, and I groan again as I run a hand down my face. This was a mistake, a huge one. I hope he takes the 'let's be just friends' talk okay.

I take a deep breath and decide to start the day off with a run. It's been too long, and I swear my blood feels itchy under my skin with the need to pound pavement and escape the world. I pull up my thread to Indi and smile at the picture of her and Jackson down at the beach that she sent me last night.

They're so stinking cute together.

**Me: You look like you had a good night.**

**Indi: You could say that **laugh emoji****

**Me: I feel like I need details. Want to come on my run with me?**

**Indi: You and your run can fuck right off.**

I burst out laughing at her response. Coming back to Echoes Cove has fucking sucked, but I can't be too mad about it since it gave me her.

**Me: **pouty face** but running is good for the soul.**

**Indi: Running is the devil's work. Burgers… now they're the work of the gods. We can grab lunch if you want to?**

**Me: Grease sounds perfect**

**Indi: I'll swing by and grab you, just let me know when you're back from your run.**

**Me: Will do**

I jump up and get dressed, pulling my hair into a high ponytail and sliding on my arm strap. I absolutely need this run today, even if only to process how I'm going to talk to Raleigh. I bounce downstairs and find Smithy waiting for me in the kitchen. "Miss Octavia, good morning."

"Morning, Smithy. You have a good night?" I ask as I head to the fridge and pour myself a glass of juice. I grab a bottle of water for my run when I put the juice back.

He smiles at me as he motions for me to sit down. "It was fine, thank you. The repairs to the house were finally completed yesterday, so it was nice to not have to think about that anymore. I'm glad all of that nonsense is done with. Now then, I was wondering if you have anything planned for Labor Day weekend?"

"Nothing at all yet, why's that?" I ask as he slides a plate of Eggs Benedict in front of me.

"My sister informed me that she's hosting something of a family get together back east, so I'm thinking about going, but if you're going to be home…" he trails off, and I shake my head.

"Go. Absolutely go!" I tell him, excited for him. I didn't even know he had a sister! "I'll find a way to keep myself busy and alive. You deserve a weekend off."

"Well, I don't know about that," he utters as he sits opposite me with a plate of french toast. *Gross*. Syrup on eggy bread is just a no from me.

"You have to go. I'll be so sad if you miss out on seeing your family because of me." I have to practically beg him to go before he agrees to it. Silly man. I have no blood relatives left—I'm not counting my runaway mother—and I'd do a lot to have some time with my dad again.

Suddenly the itch to run is replaced with an urge to play, and I haven't felt like this since Dad died. I can't help but smile. I've missed music so fucking much.

I finish my breakfast with a smile on my face as we discuss his plans to go away, and I confirm he managed to secure my birthday present for Indi. Happy that everything's in order, I put my dishes in the sink. "I'm having lunch with Indi today, so you don't need to worry about me. I'm going to go and chill in the music room for the rest of the day."

He motions to my outfit and frowns at me. "I thought you were running."

"I don't feel like I need to run right now. There's a song burning under my skin. I might not have played much since I got back, but there's no way to ignore a song like that. Plus now that the repairs are done, I want to play. I might reschedule with Indi too…" He nods at me, and I grin before I practically skip upstairs and then head to the music room in the basement that sits in a soundproofed space, along with a small recording studio.

This is my happy place.

I changed a few things with the repairs to make it more my own space now. The chairs are comfier and the colors a little warmer. I'm glad they managed to erase all evidence of what happened here. If I didn't have this space, I'm not sure how I'd stay sane.

I drop a quick message to Indi to reschedule until tomorrow, because God only knows how long I'll be in here, and her relief is real at not having to get out of bed. I laugh softly at her insanity before locking myself in the music room.

I sit at the baby grand piano and close my eyes, feeling the music inside of me before placing my fingers on the keys. I can hear it before I even press a single note.

This is what I needed. So I start to play, and nothing can take this from me.

And if anyone tries… well… there will be blood.

# CHAPTER FIFTEEN

A knock at the door has me pausing the movie in the theatre room and hopping over to the door. I open it to find Smithy smiling at me on the other side.

"Miss Octavia, I have a surprise for you!" He's so excited that I can't even bring myself to remind him how much I dislike surprises. He turns and heads down the hall, so I turn off the projector, pull down the sleeves of my hoodie, and follow him. This might be interrupting my Sunday chill, but it's Smithy, so I don't mind. The man is a freaking saint.

He heads outside, and I follow, beyond curious at this point. He's like a kid in a candy store. I step outside to see what has him so excited.

"They just delivered it." His grin matches mine as I take in the sight before me. My beautiful Impala, in better condition than she was in when I bought her. Not one spec of that hideous yellow paint is on her.

I clap my hands together as joy swells in my chest, and I practically squeal as Smithy holds out the keys for me. I grab the keys and hug him tight. "Thank you, Smithy!"

He pats me on the back, finally getting used to my random hugging. "Anything for you, Miss Octavia."

I pull away and slide my phone from my pocket, snapping a picture and sending it over to Indi.

**Indi: Holy shit, she looks good as new!**

**Me: Right, want to go out?**

I'm suddenly over my Sunday chill, imagine that.

**Indi: Sure thing! Give me 10 so I don't look half dead. **Skull emoji****

**Me: I look half dead, but I don't care. I'll be there soon, send me your address **heart emoji****

**Indi: **middle finger emoji** #attachment**

I can't help but laugh at her as I slide into the car, joy pulsing through my veins. I bring up the pin drop she sent me, feeling a little bad that I've never been to her house before. "Thank you, Smithy! I'll be back soon."

He waves as I start the car, and I head down the drive and out of the gates. I use the clicker to make sure they're shut behind me before driving toward Indi's. It thankfully doesn't take me long to find her house. I pull up out front, and she's already sitting on the steps waiting for me. She jumps up when I pull to a stop and skips down the path toward me.

I unlock the door, and she climbs in, grinning at me like a crazy person. "You look happy."

"I spent yesterday with Jackson again, *and* you have your beautiful baby back. What's not to be happy about? Oh, and I forgot to ask yesterday 'cause I was so wrapped up in myself, but how did Friday go?" I groan and bang my forehead on the steering wheel, which makes her laugh. "That bad?"

"Don't even get me started," I say before restarting the car and heading out to the Pacific Coast Highway to coast around in my pretty, not so little, car. I tell her everything about Friday night as we drive around, and she pulls as many faces as I wanted to on the night in question. By the time we end up back in Echoes Cove, she's as confused about his behavior as I was.

"It doesn't make any sense. Maybe it was because they lost the game?" She shrugs, trying to offer an explanation.

It doesn't really make a difference to my decision though, and I tell her as much.

"Makes sense, if it's not right, then it's not right. I'm sure it'll be fine. He's pretty chill," she says as I pull the car to a stop in the lot by the pier.

"Here's hoping. You want to fuck around on the pier? It's been ages since I rode the rides and did all the fun shit." I unbuckle and turn to her, finding her eagerly nodding.

"Hell fucking yes I do. I love that shit."

We climb from the car, and I strip off my hoodie, leaving it in the car. The sun's beaming down, so I grab my cardholder and phone, stashing them in my pockets before I slide my aviators on. It's such a beautiful day and spending it on the pier sounds like the best idea.

"To the games," Indi yells, pointing toward the pier before linking her arm with mine, and I can't help but laugh at her.

"To the games!"

---

Indi left the pier after a call from her mom, who picked her up, so I sit at the edge of the pier looking out over the water. It's so beautiful, so vast, and so fucking terrifying. I've always had a love-hate relationship with the water.

When we were younger, one of the girls in our class was swept out to sea and was never found. Ever since, I've had an issue with the ocean. It took years for me to even dip my toes in again. Swimming pools are fine, but natural bodies of water? No thanks.

All that being said, I do still love the sound of waves crashing in the surf. It's possibly the most soothing noise of nature there is.

I find myself humming along to the songs being played by the booth closest to me as I watch the sun begin to set. I hadn't even realized the time.

I stand when I hear my dad's voice, and my heart stops. I close my eyes, and for a second, it's like he's back here with me. I smile for just a moment before that hope slips away. I clutch the railing of the pier as his laugh sounds on the speakers, and a lump forms in my throat.

This is why I don't listen to the radio.

I can't move as the interview plays; and when they start playing one of his more popular songs, I break. Tears stream down my face as my heart shatters in my chest. Without even thinking about it, my feet move, and I'm running down the pier. I keep running onto the sand and down the beach, trying to escape the pain.

It feels like I can't breathe. Like the pain of hearing his voice is going to be the thing that finally sends me over the edge. Hearing him sing hurts so bad, but hearing him talking and laughing like that hurts even worse. For a second, just one, it was like he was here again. Like my life wasn't a fucking mess. It was as if my mind forgot he was gone and felt peace before having all of my safety barriers torn away once more.

I run until there's no one else in sight and fall to my knees in the sand, letting out a scream filled with so much pain that it makes me cry harder.

My dad was my safe haven. He was the person that didn't leave. He was always there.

Always.

And now he's gone, and it's like I can't breathe properly anymore. My whole world crumbled once he died, and I feel so lost.

I've tried to find myself ever since I lost him… Since he left me… And I've done so well at pretending like I didn't lose myself at the same time.

I shift in the sand and clutch my knees to my chest as I sob, hoping that the tears dry themselves out. I've tried to be strong, but I'm so crushed without him here. The pain of not having him with me is so devastating, especially after the second of mindlessness on the pier where I almost convinced myself that he was here with me again. The legacy that he left behind for me, his music, was meant to be his gift to me, but it haunts me instead, and I'm raw.

Placing my forehead on my knees, I cry until I feel hollow. Even then, I can't stop. It feels like losing him all over again.

I hear footsteps coming toward me, and look up to find Finley staring over at me before heading in my direction. I let out a deep breath and wipe away the still falling tears. "I can't deal with you today, Finley. Please."

My voice cracks on the last word, and he hesitates as if he's fighting an internal battle of his own. He shakes his head and finishes stomping over to me, dropping down beside me in the sand. He doesn't say a word. Instead sits, staring out over the water with me while I try to stop the flow of tears.

Another wave of grief crashes over me, and my shoulders shake as I struggle to control the sobs. I hate being this weak, especially with him here. This is the second time he's seen me lose it.

"Fuck it," he growls, standing and lifting me out of the sand. He sits with me in his lap and holds me. I don't want to be here, but I'd be lying if I said being in his arms didn't make me feel less alone. So I allow myself the weakness of leaning into him once more, vowing that this will be the last time.

But for now, I let myself crumble as I mourn losing my dad all over again.

By the time I lift my head, darkness has blanketed us, and the moon in the sky is the only source of light. My heart feels empty and broken, but I push myself out of Finley's arms and stand.

"Octavia," he starts, and I glare down at him.

"Did you make that video?" I don't have to say anything else or even wait for his response. His guilt's written all over his face.

He stands, brushing himself off, the wet patch on his white t-shirt obvious despite the dark night. "Let me explain."

"There isn't anything to explain," I hiss. "You don't get to keep comforting me when you have no issues with making me cry. I am not a toy you can pick up and put down."

"Please—" he starts, and I cut him off with a wave of my hand.

"No. Thank you, for this, but no. This doesn't make up for anything else, Finley. We were friends once, and I have no idea what I did to incur your wrath so badly that you'd do something as horrific as you did." His face falls, and he looks as defeated as I feel.

"I..." he starts but trails off, shaking his head. He puts his hands in his pockets, that stoic, passive glare back in place. "You're right. We were friends once, and we're not anymore. This was a mistake."

He walks away from me without another word, leaving me speechless.

How the fuck did he cut me and make me bleed with only his words when I thought I was already broken beyond repair?

---

Mondays fucking suck. After last night at the beach, I decided to skip my run today. I had to talk myself into it, but I decided to swim laps instead. Swimming a mile isn't too hard. I used to be able to do it in forty minutes, but it's been a minute since I swam.

I'm about halfway through my mile when I spot a shadow at the end of the pool. I finish my lap and come up for air to see who it is. I take a deep breath and lift my hands to wipe the water from my eyes, but I find myself plunged back under the water. A hand grips my hair, keeping me beneath the surface. Panic sets in.

I claw at the hand, but I can't focus. My entire body is freaking the fuck out.

I never thought to worry this morning about drowning in my own pool.

I never considered how deep it is.

As I try to push up for air, I see a flash of my dad's face and a dark thought hits me.

*Would it be so bad if I didn't fight?*

But then I see a flash of my Smithy's face, and I think of Indi. I see all the people who would be disappointed in me if I just gave up, and I start fighting again.

My lungs burn as I struggle not to draw in a breath.

My limbs start to feel heavy as I continue to fight, but the lack of oxygen slows me down.

The thought of that girl being lost at sea hits me; and I vow that if I survive this, I'm never getting in the water ever a-fucking-gain.

As quickly as it appeared, the hand leaves my hair. I sink a little before pushing up from the bottom, gasping as I clutch the side of the pool. I wipe the water from my eyes, but I don't see anyone around.

*How is that even possible?*

I stay where I am until my eyes focus again and my hands stop shaking before pulling myself from the pool.

I look around the lawn, but there aren't even footprints in the dirt thanks to the dry summer.

I grab my towel and wrap it around me, trying to get a hold of myself before I go inside. My entire body starts to shake as the adrenaline quickly wears off, and I sink to the ground as my knees give out. I suck in a breath as my emotions get the better of me and hold it, trying to stop the noise in my head. I cling to the towel, hoping the pressure helps stave off the panic, as I curl up as small as I can.

Hot tears slip down my face, and I don't bother trying to wipe them away. Why does this shit keep happening to me?

I let myself break, before trying to piece myself back together. Once I can breathe normally again, and my heartbeat doesn't sound like thunder, I splash myself with cold water to try and hide my red, puffy cheeks. It takes a minute before I'm sure my legs will hold me, but I climb to my feet before hurrying into the house. My only thought is finding out who did this. I don't think we have security cameras out back, but I'm sure as hell going to check them if we do.

Whoever it was obviously wanted to scare me—I just wish I knew why.

That's when I see the note taped to my back door. It says *'Leave. It will only get worse from here.'*

I leave the note exactly where it is and head off to find Smithy. I don't know who the fuck did this, but I'm done.

I find Smithy and tell him what happened. He has his phone in his hand, dialing the police in less than five seconds. "No, I don't want the police involved. We both know they're just as corrupt as the rest of this town."

He knows as well as I do that this town is run by those who have money…

Except my dad left and pissed off a ton of people before he did, so I don't get the same privileges that others do. I've only heard whispers of the shit storm my dad left behind, but I've heard enough to know that in this situation, the police won't be of use to me. He hangs up and drops his phone on the counter. I shake where I stand, wrapped in a towel, in the middle of the kitchen. "We can't just let this go, Miss Octavia."

"And we won't. I still have to get ready for school, but can you check the security feed? And if we don't have footage, we need to increase the security on the property." He nods at my words, and I can see his guilt, clear as day in the set of his jaw. "This is not your fault."

"I'm supposed to be looking after you." He frowns. "I'm letting you down. I'm letting your father down."

My heart sinks at his words. "You're not letting anyone down. None of this is your fault, and I won't hear another word about it. Can we increase the security some more?"

He nods, looking a little less defeated than he did a minute ago. "Yes, I'll get it sorted as fast as we can."

I feel a little better, taking care of the situation, or at least preventing the chances of it happening again. It could have been anyone. It doesn't seem like a Lincoln move, but I wouldn't put it past Blair or one of her little cronies. "Perfect, thank you. I'm going to go and wash up, get ready for school, and try to forget this morning ever happened."

I climb the stairs to my room and shudder at the thought of going back under the water, but I need to wash the chlorine off of me.

*You've got this, Octavia, there's no one else but Smithy in the house. You are safe.*

It takes a minute after my pep talk to actually get my ass in the shower, and I rush through my usual routine; but once I'm out, I feel a lot better.

Though if this is an example of how this day is going to go, I'm not even going to bother to hope for a good day.

---

I make it through the morning without issue, and Indi's been almost glued to my side since I told her about what happened this morning.

Whoever did it didn't hide their reasoning behind it. The note was crystal fucking clear, but I'm not going anywhere. I do want to know why someone wants me gone so badly, though.

None of it makes any sense.

I'm here for my diploma, and I'll happily leave once I have it.

Indi meets me after Music, like she has after every lesson so far today. She's like a snapping turtle, losing it at anyone who so much as looks sideways at me. I love this badass sunshine version of her almost as much as the dancing in the rainbows side.

"Do you mind if I talk to Raleigh for a minute? I'll meet you in the cafeteria." I feel bad because I should've said something when she got me from

Statistics, but I spent my entire period pep talking myself to have this conversation with Raleigh. I hadn't intended on doing it till after school, but he was overly touchy in class, and I can't go through the rest of the day without saying something.

She eyes me, making sure I'm okay before nodding. "Sure thing. I'll grab you a tray so you don't end up with the dredges of what's left."

"You're the best."

She squeezes my arm before heading down the hall while I wait for Raleigh to finish talking to Miss Celine. It doesn't take long, and the slimy smile he gives me when he sees me waiting for him, sends shivers down my spine confirming that I'm making the right decision.

"You waited." He beams at me and slings his arm over my shoulder.

I pause, extracting myself from his embrace, and he frowns. "We should talk." I wince a little hearing the words fall from my lips because well, cliché much.

"That doesn't sound great." He folds his arms across his chest and leans against the wall. And it occurs to me just how alone we are… how empty the halls are.

I know it's just my paranoia from this morning rearing its head, so I shake it off. I'm not having this conversation with people around. I won't do that to him or to myself. "It's not… I really like you, Raleigh. You're an awesome guy—"

"But you just want to be friends." He laughs haughtily after cutting me off. "Of course you do."

He scrubs a hand down his face, and I shift from one foot to the other. This could go either way, and I really hope it doesn't go badly. I don't need another enemy at this school, and he has been a good friend to me. We're just not a good match otherwise.

"Yeah, pretty much. I wasn't really feeling it," I tell him, trying to be as honest as I can.

He shrugs, stuffing his hands in his pockets. "I get it. I don't like it, but I get it."

I smile up at him sadly. "I totally don't want to say it because it's awful, but I'm really hoping we can still be friends."

He belts out a laugh, and I wince again. This morning really has left me on edge. "You're right, that was awful. But yes, we can still be friends. What's one date between friends? It isn't like we fucked or I declared my love for you."

My eyes go wide at his words, making him laugh harder.

"Chill, I don't love you." I let out a breath of relief at the clarification. "Now let's head to lunch, I'm starving."

---

I make it through the rest of the day without issue. In fact, everything was looking up until I started the drive home.

Stupid me didn't think to check my car after school.

That was my first mistake.

So when I need to stop the car at a traffic light, and my brakes fail, I smash into the car already sitting there. Thankfully there *was* a car there, otherwise I'd have hit the kids crossing the road. But fuck my life.

So now I'm sitting in the back of an ambulance getting checked over while the police look over the road.

What an awesome way to finish this day.

My neck's so fucking stiff, and a bruise is already blooming on my chest from the seatbelt. The pain relievers the paramedic gave me aren't helping much, but I don't want to take anything stronger. A police officer approaches the ambulance, and I spot Lincoln's Porsche pull to a stop behind the cop car.

"Miss, are you okay to answer some questions?" I nod and stand, only a little dizzy from where I hit my head in the crash. I'm pretty sure I look worse than I feel. I'm glad no one was hurt too badly, but I am beyond pissed that my car is fucked up yet again.

"Can you please tell me what happened here, in your own words?"

I sigh at the question. I know it looked like I just plowed straight into the back of that woman, but they're not going to believe me until they check out the car. I explain everything that happened about my brakes not working.

His look of skepticism isn't lost on me. "Who would want to mess with your brakes?"

I look over at Lincoln, and he smirks at me as he leans against his car, arms crossed over his chest. Jackass. I don't know why he's here, but we both know that if he backed me up right now, this cop would believe me without hesitation.

Of course, we're not friends anymore, so I don't expect his help. But it's likely he knows who did this if he didn't do it himself. Though this seems too blue collar for Linc. He knows his way around an engine—he's always had a fascination with how things work—but I doubt that even if it was his idea that he did the damage himself.

"I don't know, Officer. All I know is that they didn't work. I never said that someone messed with them." The officer's cheeks go red as he splutters an apology. "Is there anything else?"

"No, miss. We've called a tow truck for your car pending investigation for your insurance company, but once everything's cleared up, someone will contact you."

I nod at him, wishing I hadn't because pain rips through my skull. Well, that's a fun little side effect, awesome. "Thank you, Officer."

He heads back toward his car, and the paramedics pack up, leaving me with my smashed up car to wait for the tow truck. The woman I hit scowls at me, and I smile apologetically. I don't know how many more times I can say sorry to her. Thankfully, her car isn't too damaged, so she climbs in and drives away, leaving me with my undrivable Impala.

Lincoln saunters over to me, smirk firmly in place. "I do not have the time or patience for your bullshit today."

"And here I am, a nice bystander, waiting to offer you a ride home." I scoff at his words. There is no way he's here just to be nice.

I roll my eyes at him, beyond exasperated and so done with this day. "Yeah, right, I totally believe you." My smile conveys every ounce of snark I have building up inside of me. "Besides, I already called Indi, she's on her way."

"She isn't. I was at the library too when she got your call. I told her I'd come and get you since I was heading home anyway."

I let out a growl of frustration. "Of course you fucking did. If you're being so helpful, why not help me with the cop?"

He laughs at me and crosses his arms, watching me like a hunter watches his prey. "Why would I help you with that?"

I roll my eyes again, but it makes my head pound. I wince, grasping my head. God, he's such an asshole. We're interrupted as the tow truck arrives, asking me to sign a dozen different forms before he hooks up my poor car and takes it away.

"Do you want a ride home or not?" He's so fucking shitty about it. I almost want to say no, but the world starts spinning. I groan internally because I don't think I'll manage it if I try to walk home.

"Yes, please." I grind out the words through a clenched jaw, and he grabs my bag from the ground.

"After you," he says, waving to his shiny black SUV. I start walking, and my stomach flips. I really hope I don't vomit. Though the thought of fucking with his impeccably spotless car does give me a sadistic sort of satisfaction.

He opens the door for me and closes it once I'm buckled in, striding round to his side before climbing in. His gaze runs over me—almost as if checking for injury, but I know better than to think that—as my stomach rolls, and I practically feel the blood run from my face. "If you vomit in my car, I'll make you clean it."

I flip him the finger and open the window, taking deep breaths.

At least that wouldn't be the worst part of my day.

# CHAPTER SIXTEEN

"HAPPY BIRTHDAY!!!!" I practically jump on Indi when I meet her at school. The last couple of weeks since my car crash have been pretty shit, but she's the sunshine in my life, and it's her birthday. I've been planning her gift for what feels like forever.

I grin at her when I release her from my hug, and she looks all sassy and beautiful. Her long hair is now a cascade of rainbow colors, and I fucking adore it. "Here. This is for you!"

Not bouncing up and down in excitement about her gift is fucking hard as she opens the envelope.

She gawks down at the tickets in her hands, blinking. I think I might've broken her.

It only takes a second or so before she comes back to life, and her squeal is so high-pitched, I think dogs on the other side of town can hear her. "Oh my God! You absolute fucking rockstar! Are these real?"

She waves the All Access Passes I got her for the Midnight Blue gig in San Diego in my face; and when I nod, she squeals again before jumping on me and hugging me so hard I almost fall over. I'm glad the bruising on my chest is gone, otherwise I'd be fucked right now.

"You're coming with me right?" she asks.

"Yup!" I say with a nod, popping my p. "I have a hotel sorted out for us already, and it's only a few hours drive away, so *road trip!* We just need to make it through to lunch because Smithy and your mom have already let the school know we won't be around this afternoon." I might need a 4.0 GPA but bringing her this joy is so worth missing class. Plus, I already spoke to East directly, and he's not going to penalize us for missing one class. I'm caught up on everything else, having gotten straight As on all of my assignments so far. Except for the project I have with Lincoln. That class I'm worried about, especially considering Mr. Peters being a grade A pervert, but I'm hoping I can work on Lincoln to actually work with me since I'm pretty sure he doesn't want a bad grade either. I can afford to skip a little, because Business is going to hang in the balance either way.

"I'm so fucking excited. Oh my God. I'm going to meet Jenna B. What if I fangirl too hard and make a total ass out of myself? Oh shit, that's definitely going to happen. This is going to be so good and so terrible, and I don't even care. I'm too excited." The babble continues to fall from her lips, and I can't help but laugh a little. It brings me so much joy seeing how happy she is.

"You'll be fine, she's excited to hang out too. I spoke to one of my friends earlier, since he's on her team now. Jenna basically hired my dad's entire road team and I love her for that, so we have All Access Passes for the entire thing."

She stills and blinks at me for a second before whispering, "You spoke with Jenna B?"

I nod, and she covers her mouth with her hands. "Holy. Fucking. Shit."

"Are you okay?" I ask, a little worried about her. I don't care about everyone watching us, they can fuck right off. This is Indi's day, and if she wants to be crazy and loud, then so be it.

She nods, looking back down at the tickets with wide eyes. "My bestie just got me the best present ever and told me she talks to my ultimate girl crush on the regular. I'm just having a moment."

She grins up at me, and I burst out laughing. "I love you."

"I love you too," she says, linking her arm with mine, practically skipping as we head toward the main entrance of the school. "So where are we staying?"

I run through the details with her as we hit our lockers before heading to English.

The day passes quickly, with Raleigh finally back to being his usual laid-back, cheerful self during Music. He's been understandably distant the last few weeks, but it's nice having him back to how he was before the world's most unfortunate date.

By the time the bell rings to signal lunch, I'm beyond excited to get out on the road with Indi for the gig tonight. Her squeal reaches me before she does as I head down the hall toward her. I grab my shit from my locker, and then we head straight out to the parking lot. "Head home, pack yourself a bag, and I'll be there in less than an hour to get you."

"Holy shit, I'm too excited, my heart is racing." She grins and hugs me. "Okay, I'll see you soon."

I head over to my newly repaired Impala, checking to make sure every inch is safe before I jump in and drive home. I already packed my overnight bag, but I still need to get ready for tonight. I say a quick hello to Smithy as I climb the stairs to my room to shower and get my shit together.

Opening the door to my room, I freeze. The balcony door is open again and there's a note lying on my bed. Fuck, that's so creepy.

I pick the thick cream paper up, taking a deep breath before opening it.

*I told you to leave. You didn't listen. You're going to regret that.*

Fuck this, I'm not letting whoever this is ruin my weekend. I should probably be a little more concerned after the car crash and everything else that's happened, especially when the note is on my bed; but today is Indi's birthday, and I refuse to be rattled. I drop the note back onto the bed and head for my bathroom. I'll let Smithy know about it before I leave and ask him to look into it, since we're still waiting on his security guy.

I take extra care getting ready and pep talk myself into not breaking down on Indi's birthday. Going back to the stadium I was at last with my dad has me all kinds of fucked up. Tonight isn't about me, though, so I'm shoving all of my bullshit in a box to deal with another day.

Once I'm ready, I grab my bag and head down to find Smithy. He's waiting for me in the kitchen. "Oh good, Miss Octavia, I'm glad I caught you. I got a call while you were upstairs. My sister is in the hospital. Since I know you're away tonight, I was wondering if you would mind terribly if I flew home to be with my family?"

"Smithy, of course not! Go, family comes first, always!" Fuck the note, we can deal with that when his sister isn't in the fucking hospital.

"Thank you, Miss Octavia. I've made a call to a friend at the security company, he's going to come and check on the house a few times while we're gone to ensure nothing untoward happens in our absence. He'll also be upgrading the system to a new state of the art system, so I'll ask him to leave instructions for you."

"You don't need to thank me, Smithy, she's your family. Can I have your friend's details? Just so I can let him know when I'm home. That way I won't get freaked out by people I don't know being in the house when I'm back."

"Yes of course. I'll send the contact over to you. I need to organize a flight, and then I'll sort it out."

"Take the jet," I tell him, and his eyes go wide.

"I couldn't."

"You could. It's just sitting there doing nothing, and it's way better than flying commercially. It's not like I need it." I shrug because I'm not wrong. Why pay for a drop hat staff if you don't use it?

"If you're sure," he says, looking uneasy, so I smile and nod.

"Beyond sure. I don't need it, and you do. It'll get you there faster too. Then you can come back whenever you're ready without having to worry about flights."

"Thank you, Miss Octavia. Enjoy your trip away. I'll keep you up-to-date with the details of when I'm coming home as soon as I know exactly what's going on."

"There's no rush, honestly. If you need to stay there, do it. I can ask the security guy to be here if I need to." I'd rather not, but considering the note, it might be a good idea. Smithy almost looks uncomfortable at the thought but nods anyway.

He thanks me once more, so I hug him and tell him goodbye before heading out to the car to go grab Indi. Excitement bubbles in my chest at the thought of how much fun this weekend is going to be.

I slide my aviators into place and start the car.

San Diego, here we come.

---

"Please don't pass out," Indi murmurs to herself as we walk toward the doors of the stadium, and I can't help but laugh softly under my breath. I take her hand and squeeze it, just to find that she's shaking like crazy.

I nudge her shoulder with mine to grab her attention from where she's staring at her feet. She looks all kinds of amazing in her knee-high rainbow Converse, little shorts, and band tee coupled with her rainbow hair. "You okay?"

"I'm good," she says quietly. "Trying not to freak out. You'd think I'd be more chill than this. But I've never been to a concert before, and you did all of this for me. I'm a little overwhelmed."

I pull her to a stop before moving us out of the crowd of people heading toward the stadium. "If this is too much, we can wait out here before going in. Or we don't have to go in at all."

She takes a deep breath and looks up to the sky. "There's no way in hell we're not going in. I tend to avoid big crowds because they make me anxious as fuck. I thought I'd be okay, but apparently my brain is working against me. I just need a minute, and I'll be fine. Sorry."

"Dude, you have *nothing* to apologize for. You do whatever you need to. I'm chill." We move to sit on a bench, and I give her the space she needs to get herself together. My phone buzzes in my pocket, so I slip it out and take a quick look.

**Panda: Are you here yet?**

I can't help but grin. I've missed his face so goddamn much. I've been away from tour life for too long.

**Me: Yup! Just outside, shouldn't be too long. I'll find you as soon as we're in.**

**Panda: I'll hang around near the back doors, so just head this way, don't worry about going through the front.**

**Me: You rock, P! See you soon**

I drop a message to the security guy too, so he has my number should anything happen, before tucking my phone away and focusing on Indi. Her eyes are closed and she's breathing deeply, as if she's meditating, but her smile grows. That's all I really give a fuck about anyway. An anxiety attack definitely wasn't part of the plan today, but I've been there, so I totally get it.

She opens her eyes and bounces to her feet, practically vibrating positivity. "Let's do this!"

I grin at her, glad to see her back to her usual self, and get to my feet. "Hell yes! Panda messaged me, and he's waiting for us round the back. We can head to the crew entrance, so we don't need to deal with the crowds and lines out front."

"You freaking rock. Sorry for freaking out just then. Also, who the fuck is Panda?"

"You have nothing to be sorry about, and you don't need to explain. If I said I'd never had a panic attack, I'd be flat out lying. And Panda is… well, Panda. He's one of my dad's old roadies. He isn't much older than us, and he's a fucking legend." I shrug and link my arm with hers. "Now let's go enjoy the rest of your birthday, shall we?"

"Lead the way, oh wise one!" she jokes, and I laugh. It doesn't take long to get to the back, and I drop Panda a message when we're close.

"V baby!" I look up and see the metal door opening, and I squeal. I run toward him and leap into his giant fucking arms. The guy's a fucking tree, catching me easily before spinning me around. "I missed you!"

"I missed you too, P!" I squeeze him before he puts me down. Indi reaches us, and I smile at her sheepishly as she checks my friend out. "Sorry, P, this is my girl Indi. Indi, this is Panda."

"That's one hell of a name." She gives him a wicked grin, and he groans.

"You wear eyeliner one time and end up with a name like Panda. I swear to fuck, it's going to follow me for a lifetime. My name is Evan, it's nice to meet you! You must be the birthday girl. Welcome to the Psycho Girl tour." He shakes her hand, and her excitement goes up a few notches as she bounces on the balls of her feet. If I wasn't convinced she's head over heels for Jackson, I'd swear she was crushing. P has that charm about him that puts you instantly at ease. He also looks like a golden fucking Adonis, so I get it. I'd be lying if I said I hadn't rocked a major crush on him before now.

"I mean, was it questionable eyeliner?" she asks, and he grins. I laugh, thinking about that night.

"He forgot he had it on, rubbed his eyes, and well… It was really hot in Atlanta. It smudged a lot, so he became Panda." He grabs me by the waist and lifts me, tickling me while Indi laughs.

"What the fuck's going on out here?" a shout comes from inside the stadium halls. Indi's eyes go wide with fear, but I smile wider as P puts me down.

"Mac!" I basically attack him as he walks into view, and his anger disappears as soon as he sees me.

"V, is that really you?" He blinks down at me for a second before hugging me back, and P moves to stand by Indi, making her feel included. I love him for that. This is her birthday, and I'm sucking all the fun up.

"Hey, Mac," I say quietly, squeezing him before I let go. "Indi, this is Mac. Mac, this is Indi, my bestie from back home."

"It's good to meet you, Indi. I didn't realize you were coming tonight." He almost looks sad to see me, but I know that's because of the last time we were here together. I feel the pain in my very fucking soul, but I refuse to let all of my baggage ruin this day for Indi.

"P helped me keep it a secret so I could surprise you guys. It's Indi's birthday, and she's a huge Midnight Blue fan," I explain, and he nods.

He moves over to Indi and talks to her quietly for a minute before hugging her. "Thank you for looking after my girl."

I swear I get all misty, and I look up to the sky to stop the tears that threaten to spill over. Tonight is not about me, and I'm not ruining this eyeliner.

"Now, that's enough of this mushy shit. Let's go find Jenna and the girls, shall we?" Mac coughs and bangs his fist against his chest, going hyper macho. I can't help but giggle a little.

"Let's do it," I say, grabbing Indi's shaking hand. "Tonight is going to be fucking awesome."

"You're in for a treat tonight too. They're unveiling the new single live tonight," P tells us as we enter the stadium and the chaos that is the backstage area before a show. Indi huddles closer to me. I'd almost forgotten how nuts it can get backstage, but at P's words, her excitement overtakes her. She practically bounces next to me, eyes wide.

"Best. Birthday. Ever!"

---

We head to the green room to meet the girls before the gig, and Indi is so nervous. She keeps shaking out her hands before clenching her fists, over and over again. It's like she's literally fizzing.

I adore her so freaking much.

It's the only reason I'm clinging to the happy she's putting out. Because inside, I feel like I'm dying a little. Walking these halls is crushing. The last time I walked them, I found my dad. He just looked like he was asleep, and then I saw the pill bottles, the bottles of whiskey, and the tinge of blue on his lips. I'll never forget that moment. Sometimes I see it when I close my eyes, and I hate that it's my last memory of him.

I still don't believe he was trying to kill himself. They ruled it as a suicide, but I think it was accidental.

Mac squeezes my shoulder as we close in on the green room, and I guess he's remembering the same thing I am.

At least we're not heading to the dressing room. I'm pretty sure that that would break me fully, and that's the last thing I want tonight.

"You ready?" I ask Indi, forcing as much excitement and happiness into my voice as I can. Hopefully she can't see the strain in my smile through her nerves.

"I am *so* ready."

She's like a kid at Christmas, and it's adorable.

"Please don't let me word vomit on them?" she asks, clutching my arm, and I giggle a little.

"I swear I will stop you if that should happen."

She nods and hugs me, just outside the green room door. "This is why I love you the most."

Panda grins at me, his hand on the door handle before opening it a little and popping his head through the space.

"Get out of the way, Panda! Where's my girl?" Jenna's low, husky voice reaches me seconds before her beautiful face appears around the door frame. "There she is!"

She rushes me and hugs me, jumping with excitement. It's been a minute since I saw her last, but she's one of the few people who was there for me throughout all of the stuff with Dad. Indi's eyes go wide as she leans against the wall, and I pull out of the hug. "It's so good to see your face."

"Yours too, bitch, don't hide from us for so long next time. Selena's been like a nagging mom, totally on my ass about getting you out to see us." I can't help but laugh at her dramatics as she flicks her long pink hair over her shoulder. Truthfully, though, Selena, who's the drummer of Midnight Blue, is totally the mom of the group.

"I'll try not to get dragged, kicking and screaming, to a hellhole the next time I can't be on tour." I stick my tongue out at her, and she rolls her eyes like I'm the drama queen here. "J, I want to introduce to you my girl, Indi. She's literally been my saving grace since I went back to the Cove. She's something of a fan."

"Hi," Indi squeaks, waving awkwardly at her, and I half want to die on her behalf as red spills across her cheeks. Jenna's a pro and takes it in her stride, though.

"Thank you for watching out for our girl. Come on, I'll introduce you to the others." She slings an arm over Indi's shoulders like they've been friends forever and drags her inside the green room.

I move to follow them, but Mac stops me with a hand on the shoulder. I turn to face him, and he looks me over like the over protective papa bear he is. He watches me closely while I stand for inspection, cocking an eyebrow at him. "Are you going to be okay being here tonight?"

I nod at him, acting like there isn't an open wound in my chest and I'm not bleeding out all over the floor. "Yes. Tonight isn't about me. I'll be fine."

He gets my hint and nods wordlessly. I'm glad. I don't want him to prod because it won't take much to bring down the carefully constructed walls I put into place to deal with being here tonight. He lets me go into the green room, and Indi is grinning like a cat who got the cream as P snaps pictures of her with the girls. I lean against the doorframe, letting her have her moment with them before they spot me.

She looks so fucking happy, and I'm not going to take that from her. Then Jenna grabs her acoustic and starts playing a ballad version of one of their most popular songs. Indi drops onto the sofa with P, absolutely rapt. It's kind of adorable.

Selena heads over to me and pulls me into her arms wordlessly. To look at her, you'd never think she was the mom of the group. She's absolutely covered head to toe in ink, her eyeliner's thick as fuck, and her blunt black bangs frames her face in a way that almost makes her look like an intimidating badass. But she's one of the softest, cuddliest humans I've ever met in my life.

She lets me go, asking me with a look if I'm good, so I nod and sway with her as Jenna sings. Indi doesn't take her eyes from Jenna as she plays. The song comes to close as a girl I don't recognize enters the room, clipboard in hand. "Time to go, ladies!"

"Let's do this!" Emmy, the bassist shouts, and a whoop goes up around the room. "You going to come hang with us later?"

I look at Indi, who looks fully starstruck, so I answer Emmy myself. "You bet your ass we are."

"Yes, bitch!" Jenna high fives me as she passes me. "Enjoy the show, Indi!"

They leave us with P, and Mac follows them, ever on guard. "You ready to go watch?"

"I don't think my legs are working," Indi says, the awe in her voice evident.

"Want to watch from backstage?" P asks, and I love him a little more in that moment. Watching without the crush of the crowd is absolutely my favorite way to gig, but I look to Indi because this is up to her.

She nods, and she finally jumps to her feet. "Lead the way, maestro!"

# CHAPTER SEVENTEEN

"Morning, sunshine!" Indi bounces onto my bed, and I groan, rolling over. The sun spills into the room through the open windows, and I pull the duvet over my head. We stayed out way later last night than I've stayed out in forever, and I definitely forgot how much roadies drink. I never used to partake; but when Jenna and the girls invited us out with them, and the crew came too, I decided to let loose. Indi was there with me, shot for shot, so I have no idea how she's exuding her usual dose of sunshine like she is, but I am so not ready for it right now.

"Oh come on, grump. The sun is shining, the views are beautiful, and yesterday was possibly the best day of my life!" She literally bounces on the bed, singing her words. It's a little bit annoying, but it still draws a smile out of me. I peek out from the sheets to find her grinning down at me. "I have coffee coming."

"Thank fuck," I groan as I squint through the blazing sunlight. My head pounds, and I almost want to just crawl under the covers again. "I'm glad you had so much fun."

"Are you kidding me? After my little meltdown over meeting the girls, I thought I was toast. But everyone was so nice, and watching the show from backstage was fucking epic! Then going out after and being treated like a freaking goddess… What about that isn't something I'd love? Best. Night. Ever!" Her joy is infectious, and my hangover ebbs a little.

I climb out of the sheets and sit up in bed, basking in her joy as she scrambles over me and jumps under the covers beside me. She rests her head on my shoulder, and I lean my head against hers, resting with narrowed eyes until a knock on the door jolts us into action. I climb from the bed in my tank and boy shorts, sorting out the tray of room service she ordered for us. I groan as I lift the plate lids and piles of bacon and eggs stare up at me. She walks into the main room of the suite and grins while I drool over the food and coffee. "You are a goddess."

"I know." She grins before coming to sit with me at the small dining table. We spread the plates out and pick at the food in a comfortable silence as music plays softly in the background. It doesn't take us long to inhale the food and coffee, and once we're done, I feel like I could sleep for an eternity again, but I don't want to waste the time we have on our trip.

"What do you want to do today before we head home?" I ask, and she almost looks shocked.

"We're not going straight home?" she asks, and I shake my head, finishing the dregs of my coffee.

"No, I figured we could chill here for most of the day and head home later, but if you want to go straight home, we can. It's your birthday, and the world is your oyster."

She claps her hands together and does a little dance in her chair, and I can't help but grin at the sheer amount of joy bottled inside of one very small human. "Zoo! I want to go to the zoo so bad, and then maybe we can go snorkeling at La Jolla? Can we do both? Do we have time?"

"We can do whatever you want." I grin, basking in the glow of joy she's emitting. "So if you wanna do both, we can totally do both."

"Yes!" She jumps to her feet and continues her wiggling happy dance. "I'm going to get ready. I am too excited."

She bounces all the way to the bathroom, and I laugh, pouring myself another cup of coffee. Pulling up the San Diego zoo website on my phone, I buy us two all inclusive passes before looking for a snorkeling company in La Jolla. My dad always made a big deal out of birthdays, and it's the one tradition I'm determined to continue.

By the time she's done in the shower, I have everything booked that she asked for, and then jump in the bathroom to get ready myself. I wash off the grime from last night. As much fun as gigs are, they're totally gross. I hate myself a little for not showering before I passed out last night.

It takes a little longer than I'd like to get myself ready for the day, the sluggishness from last night slowing me down. By the time I'm washed and dressed, Indi has our bags packed and the room straightened up.

She's like the goddamn Energizer bunny.

I wouldn't have her any other way, though. "Ready to go?" My question is a little redundant, but her eyes flash with mirth as she nods and grabs her bag.

"I am so ready. Let's do this, San Diego!"

---

Our day in San Diego was fucking amazing. I don't remember the last time I went to the zoo or went snorkeling. Or even just had a fun, almost regular day. It's been so fucking refreshing and clarifying. It woke my soul up a little.

The drive home has me exhausted after the last forty-eight hours, so as I pull up out the front of Indi's house, relief floods me. Reds, purples, and pinks paint the sky as dusk hits, and my bed is calling my name. I texted the security guy before we left and confirmed the new cameras and sensors were in place, but he said he'd be gone by the time I got home, and also confirmed that whoever got in before was a tech wizard, because the tapes were cut, but there was no trace of the hack into the system at all. Not scary at all. Nope.

He also sent me some lengthy instructions on how to set the new system but I'll check that out later.

"Thank you so much for the best birthday ever," Indi says, wrapping an arm around my neck and hugging me tight.

"It was my pleasure. Thank you for being the best friend ever."

"You're going to make me cry if you keep being this nice to me," she says as she pulls back, her eyes already a little watery.

I smile and shake my head at her, the little softie. "Then prepare to cry, my friend, because I'm not going to stop. You're a beautiful human, and if I can do things to bring the joy to you that you give me, then I'm going to."

She laughs as a tear runs down her face. She wipes it away with a shaky sigh before saying, "See, look what you did. I'm going to go now, before I start ugly crying."

"Go on," I laugh. "I'll see you tomorrow?"

She shakes her head, looking a little sad. "Tomorrow is family day for my birthday, I have aunts and uncles and all sorts coming in for a big dinner. I'd invite you, but my family is weird as fuck. Plus, one of my cousins is weirdly obsessed with you."

I bark out a laugh. There are absolutely zero interesting things about me to be obsessed with. "You're fine. I should probably get some decent sleep and down time. I'll see you on Monday then."

"You will," she says before climbing out of the car and grabbing her bag from the back. "I love you, and thank you again for the best birthday ever. Drive safe and let me know when you're home."

"I absolutely will. Have a good sleep. I'll speak to you soon."

She closes the door, and I wait until she's in the house before I pull away and head home. I swear my eyes hurt—I'm that freaking tired, but it was so worth it. The drive home doesn't take long, but as I get closer, the thumping sound of loud bass shakes the car and I groan.

Of course Lincoln's having a party. The one night I want to sleep, there's going to be so much noise that sleep is going to be a long time coming. I can't complain too much. It isn't even that late, but damn. All I want to do is crawl into bed.

I put in the new code for the gate that the security guy sent over and head up the drive. I should put the car in the garage, but I really can't be fucked. One night out front won't hurt, I groan at myself and decide to move it into the garage, especially with the party next door. Knowing my luck, some asshole will discover the gate and egg my car or some shit, and this car has been through enough in its short time with me.

Once the car's secure, I trudge into the house, shutting off the alarm. It's so eerie when it's this empty and dark. It's way too big for one person really. I have no idea how Smithy survived years in this place alone, but it's home, so I doubt I'm going to change it any time soon.

I drop my bag in the entry hall. The bass from next door isn't so bad in here, but I swear I can feel the low thump inside of my chest, almost in time with my heartbeat. I head to the kitchen and put on the coffee pot, and the smell is freaking divine as it brews. I figure if I'm not getting any sleep for a while with the noise anyway, why not?

I finally go through the new security details, happy that this new system has a room by room system, meaning I can have the ground floor protected but still keep the door in my room open to let in some fresh air. I don't like to sleep with the air conditioning on if I can help it.

A crash out front draws my attention, and I groan. If their party overspills here, I'm going to be pissed. The Saint house is plenty big enough—there's no reason for people to sneak over here.

Fuck my life.

I slip my Chucks back on, glad I left my hoodie on, and check the monitors before I head out front. I can't really see anything on the monitors, though, and sigh. Of course I can't. That would make my life too simple. The new alarm system might be awesome, but maybe I need to call him back and upgrade the cameras.

I find a group of drunk assholes literally starting an orgy around the side of the house. "How the fuck did y'all get over here?"

My shout seems to startle them, like they hadn't even considered there would be someone home. The girl giggles as she does the buttons on her shirt up and one of the guys groans. "We didn't think there would be anyone here. The lights were all off."

"Well there is, but you didn't answer my question." I fold my arms over my chest. I'm aware I don't look even remotely intimidating, but fuck it.

"There's a break in the fence, through the trees. It isn't easy to find, and we came across it by accident," one of the other guys says as he zips up his jeans.

Of course there fucking is. Fuck my life.

"Show me?" I ask, and the guy nods. They lead me over to the hidden entry, and I curse under my breath. It isn't big—they had to have squeezed through—but it's big enough. I mean, it wouldn't be the end of the world usually; but with Lincoln having a party, it's a problem. They head through the gap, and I follow them through, coming face-to-face with the man in question.

"What are you doing?" he sneers as I come through the trees with the disheveled group. They scurry away at the sound of his voice, leaving me alone with him. Cowards.

"Coming to find you. I found them up against the house, starting a private party of their own. They showed me a weak spot between the properties," I explain, and I can tell he doesn't believe me from the sneer on his face. "I'll get it sorted out, but if you can keep your drunken rabble of friends away from here, that'd be awesome."

"Where were you? The house was dark. It's never dark," he asks, completely ignoring my request. I don't know why I'm shocked, but I can't tell if I'm more shocked that he ignored me or that he noticed I was gone.

"Not that it's any of your business, but I was away with Indi for her birthday."

"The girl with rainbow hair?" he asks, and I nod. "Where's Smithy?"

I sigh, exasperated. "With his family, there was an emergency. Can you keep people away from here, or do I need to call someone out tonight to sort it out?"

"I'll keep people off your property." He scans the front of his house. The party is in full swing and spills out here. There are people everywhere, so good luck to him with that.

"Thanks," I say before turning my back on him and heading home through the gap in the fence. He doesn't say anything else, and I don't expect him to.

I pull out my phone and set a reminder to call someone about the fence tomorrow, then remember to text Indi as I head back into the kitchen. I make sure all the doors are locked and the alarm is set on my way.

**Me: I'm home, party next door. All the fun**

**Indi: Assholes. Earplugs?**

**Me: Nah, I'm going to fuck around in the music room for a bit, just exhaust myself so I don't care about the noise.**

**Indi: Sounds like a plan. I'm going to pass out. Good luck with the noise!**

I pour a mug of coffee and pad downstairs to the music room. The quiet is such joy after an intense few days. I sit down at the piano, flicking through the sheet music I started writing when I was down here last.

I twinkle my fingers on the ivory, falling back into the place of utter peace at the feel of it at my fingertips. Emotion swells in my chest as everything I shoved down last night wells up. Being back there, with the people who loved my dad almost as much as I did, hurt me. But they're the only people who seem to miss him like I do. Nobody else knew him like we did, not really. They didn't see the highs and lows that came with tour life, with the success and the fame, or with the crazy fans and people who only seemed to want things from him.

I won't lie and say it was easy, but his love for music made it all worth it to him. I can't say that I agree with those decisions, but they weren't mine to make for him. Even if I think the toll of it all is part of why he isn't with me anymore.

I let my emotions flow out through my fingertips and onto the ivory as tears stream down my face. I find myself playing the song I wrote with him at the beginning of summer, and I sing through my tears. My voice breaks as I sing, but I keep going. Music's the best therapy I'm going to get. I play and cry until my shoulders shake and until my tears blur my vision so much that I can't see anymore. I close the lid on the piano and fall apart in the one place that I can feel my dad in this entire house.

I curl up in a ball in the corner, my heart in a million pieces in my chest, until the tears won't come any more. I miss him more than I can express, but music makes me feel so close to him. Being at that stadium last night with everyone made everything so raw.

Once I've gotten a hold of myself, I trudge up the stairs to my room, too broken to care about the noise anymore. I crawl into bed still in my hoodie and leggings. I close my eyes and let sleep take me to a place of peace that I can't seem to find when I'm awake.

---

Something startles me awake. The room is still dark and silent, but it feels wrong somehow. An icy drop of dread runs down my spine and my hair stands on end as I spot something moving in the darkness of my room. My heart races, and I can hear the blood rushing through my veins, like white noise in my ears as I become hyperaware of my surroundings.

Someone is in here with me. I don't know how I know, but I just do.

I move to try to grab my phone from the bedside table, but a hand clasps around my ankle and pulls. I scream, and another hand clamps over my mouth.

Everything Mac ever taught me about self-defense goes right out the window as I try to fight off my attacker. More hands cover me, and I suddenly realize there isn't one person here.

There are at least three.

Fear floods my system with icy dread, and my blood feels like it's on fire as I try to kick and wriggle out of their hold as I'm ripped from my bed.

They don't say a word as they manhandle me. I lash out with my hands when one of them captures my wrists in one hand, and it would be silent if not for my grunts of protest.

I try to bite the one who has their hand on my mouth. I just barely manage it, and the attacker lets go, hissing. The top half of my body starts to fall, and I think I might have a chance, so I flail. They drop me, and the breath leaves my body as I crash to the floor.

I can't move for a second. It's like my soul is ripped from my body for a minute, and then everything whooshes back to me. I scramble onto my hands and knees as I try to crawl away. I can't see shit—it's too dark—but there's a pressure on my back, and I'm forced to the floor, face down. One of them is on top of me, grappling with me until they have my hands bound in theirs behind my back. I scream out again, and someone pushes my face harder into the carpeted floor to smother the sound.

I suck in a breath, but my mouth's covered again as I'm lifted.

I hear the door open before they start walking with me, but we don't go far before I'm thrown. I smash against a wall. A door slams closed, and what little light there was completely disappears. I move to stand and get stuck.

That's when I realize where I am.

The half closet in the hall.

*No, no, no.*

This can't be happening. I can't even stand up in here, it's so small.

I bang on the door, screaming at the top of my lungs when I can't get it open.

Please, God, no.

"Please! Please let me out," I beg, my voice breaking as fear grips me round the throat. "Please."

I feel a pressure against the door, and I know someone's out there, leaning against it.

"You don't have to do this. Please. You can take whatever you want, but please don't keep me in here."

I push against the door with everything I have and scream until my throat is hoarse.

I can't be trapped in here.

Not again.

Panic swells in my throat, and it feels like I can't breathe.

*I need to get out.*

So I bang, kick, and push against the door until my hands bleed. I scream until no more sound comes from my ravaged throat. Tears stream hotly down my face.

I hear movement outside the door as someone walks away from the cupboard. I push against the door in hope, but I'm crushed, realizing that the door is locked. I'm trapped.

I fall to the floor, spent, curling in a ball and rocking.

I can get through this.

Someone will come for me.

Someone will find me in here.

*Right?*

# CHAPTER EIGHTEEN

## EAST

I've messaged Octavia five times since she was due home, and she hasn't responded to one of them. Usually I wouldn't worry, but Smithy isn't at the house, and he asked me to check in on her. That's hard to do when she won't answer the goddamn phone. I've paced around my room for the last half hour trying to convince myself not to go over there.

She could still be sleeping. She had a big weekend. But it's nearly lunchtime, and she's usually an early riser.

I could be worrying about nothing. Considering the threats that hang over us all—especially her, though she doesn't know it yet—I'm feeling overly paranoid.

I know Lincoln has a plan to get her to leave, but it doesn't seem to be working. I don't want her to leave, which is why I've kept myself removed from it all. Do I want her to be safe? Yes. But I'm the only one who seems to think I can keep her safe by keeping her close.

My brother doesn't agree with me, but from what I've seen, he doesn't seem to be able to stay away from her either.

When she first left, the four of us moped around for about a year. We might have been young, but every single one of us was in love with her. Sure, we might not have realized it back then, but seeing her again was like a punch in the gut. I thought I'd gotten over the puppy love, but I obviously haven't.

I can't say the same for the others—they're all so coveted these days—but I wouldn't be surprised if they felt it too. There's something about Octavia Royal that is completely undeniable.

I look down at my phone again and growl. "Fuck this."

Grabbing my hoodie, I head out through the back of the house and through the hidden gate that joins the two properties. Stone Royal installed it when we were kids.

All of the lights are still off, which isn't unusual, and I can't shake the feeling that something's wrong.

I grab the spare key that Smithy left me for emergencies and let myself in.

*The alarm isn't on.*

My heart rate spikes. There's no way she wouldn't have set it, right? She wouldn't have been in this giant house alone without the alarm on.

"Octavia!" I yell out, not giving a fuck if she's asleep. My blood feels like it's on fire, and I'm frantic to figure out what the fuck is going on. I move through the house, yelling her name, before I hear a whimper coming from upstairs.

I swear to fucking Christ, if they got to her, I'll burn down their world and bathe in their blood.

"Help me, please," she yells, sounding so fucking broken as I run up the stairs and crash into her room. She's not here, but there was clearly a struggle.

There's a faint tapping down the hall, so I follow it, trying not to panic. It gets closer before disappearing again.

"Octavia!" I shout, hoping she calls out again.

"East…" her voice is scratchy as fuck, but I realize she's in the cupboard at the top of the stairs. What the fuck happened here? She would never crawl in there on her own. She hates small spaces. I try to open the door, but it's locked.

Fuck this shit.

"V, sweetheart," I say as softly as I can while rage pulses through me. I know she needs a sense of calm right now, so that's what I'm going to be for her. "I need you to cover your face so you don't get hurt when I get this door open, okay? Move as far away from the door as you can for me."

She whimpers a soft, "Okay," and anger floods me again.

I take a deep breath before punching a hole in the door to the left of the handle and ripping my way through it.

My heart breaks when I see her.

She's curled up on the floor, her fingernails bleeding, looking completely broken. I lean down and slide my hands under her, lifting her and cradling her against my chest. "I got you, V."

I murmur and coo comforts to her as I walk her down the hall to the bathroom. She needs to be cleaned up, but the way she grips my shirt makes me want to commit fucking murder.

I sit her on the counter in the bathroom and start the taps on the clawfoot tub, all while keeping contact with her. Once the taps are running, and I've poured in some bubble bath, I focus all of my attention on her. The way her hair's ruffled and her tear-stained cheeks. Then there's the fact that she won't look up. Instead, she stares at the floor like she's still afraid. The dried blood from where she tried to escape, or maybe even fight back, coats her skin. I clench my hands at my sides because getting angry won't help her. I tuck a finger beneath her chin and lift her head so that she's looking at me. My heart breaks for her, and I declare war in my mind on whoever did this to her. "What happened, V?"

My voice is gentle, trying to coax her to talk; but when she tries, there's barely a noise. It's as if she screamed herself silent, and I hate that I didn't hear her screams and get to her sooner. I'm furious that I wasn't here to protect her so she didn't have to scream at all.

"It's okay. You can tell me later. Let's get you in the bath, yeah?" Her eyes go wide, and she shakes her head frantically. Her fingers dig into my forearms, like if she lets me go, I'll leave her alone again. "I'm not going anywhere, okay? I've got you. We just need to clean you up a bit."

I try to get her out of her clothes, but she's shaking so badly, it's almost impossible. She won't let me go, so I quit trying to make her.

Fuck it.

I shut off the taps and kick off my shoes before lifting her into my arms. She's still shaking, even when I hold her, and it pisses me off. I take a deep breath, shoving my rage down to deal with once I know she's okay. After that, I'll gladly lose my shit.

I step into the tub fully clothed with her against my chest and sit with her. I try to clean the blood from her arms, hands, and legs as much as I can, but it's difficult since she's still mostly dressed. "V, can you take off the hoodie so I can make sure there's no more injuries?"

She nods, but it's barely a movement as she curls up on my chest. I strip the hoodie from her and drop the sopping wet bundle on the floor. I don't give a fuck about the mess, that's a problem for later. I scour her with my eyes, but it doesn't look like she has any other physical injuries. No, whoever did this knew it would hurt her in a much deeper way than that.

Then it hits me.

Those fucking little assholes.

I clench my jaw and take a deep breath. I'll deal with them as soon as I have her settled. I help her wash, stripping her down as we go, then wash and rinse her hair. "We need to get out now, okay?"

She nods, and I lift her from the bath, grabbing a towel and wrapping it around her. Doing this fully clothed wasn't the greatest idea, but there's no way I was stripping down and climbing into a bath with her naked when she's like this. Once I pat her hair dry and drop her robe around her shoulders, I climb out of my clothes and quickly wrap a towel around my waist. "I'll be back in two seconds, okay?"

She looks up at me with those big brown eyes of hers and just blinks.

I run to the spare room, which I know probably still has some of Stone's old shit in it, and grab a pair of sweats. I throw them on and rush back to her, finding her sitting where I left her, staring down at her cut up hands.

I contemplate whether I should ask her to walk but think better of it and pick her back up in my arms and carry her to her room. "Let's get you dressed and back into bed."

She blinks at me as I sit her on the stool by her dresser before I rush into her closet, grabbing a pair of leggings and a tank for her. I don't bother with underwear. She needs to sleep, and sleeping in a bra doesn't sound like a good time.

I finish getting her dry and help her into the clothes, but she's still shaking like a leaf.

Blood will be spilled today.

"Let's get you into bed, okay?" Her eyes go wide, and she shakes her head, clinging to me like I'm her only lifeline. Right now, I just might be.

It suddenly hits me that she was probably asleep when they dragged her from the room. Fucking hell.

"I have another idea, okay?" She calms a little and sags against me. "Can you walk?"

She blinks up at me again, still fully mute, and I swear to God I see fucking red.

"It's okay. I've got you."

I gather her into my arms and walk through the house, not bothering to lock it up. I'll deal with that later. Right now, my sole priority is her. I walk barefoot and half dressed across her yard with her lying against my chest. Crossing onto my property, I see Maverick leaving the house. My eyes narrow at him as shock registers on his face.

I'll deal with that twisted little asshole later. I keep her held against my chest as I pad into the house, up the stairs, and to my room. "You can sleep here today, okay? You're safe in here."

She nods, and I tuck her into my bed, drawing the curtains closed to shroud the room in darkness. I leave a sliver of sunlight so she doesn't freak out after being locked in that fucking closet all night.

"Cold." The one word is all her scratchy voice manages, so I root through one of the drawers in my dresser and find her my old college hoodie. If the situation were different, seeing her in my hoodie would do things to me, but right now, I just want to look after her.

I pull it over her head, helping her slip her arms into it, and tuck her back in once she's basically drowning in the sweater.

"Thank you," she sighs as she closes her eyes. "Don't leave."

There's no way on this fucking earth I'm going to deny her a damn thing, so I climb on top of the sheets on the other side of the bed, giving her space. But then she rolls over and tucks herself into my chest and closes her eyes again. It doesn't take long for her breathing to slow, and I'm sure she's so exhausted she has no option but to sleep. I don't know how long she'll actually manage to rest after what happened last night, so I settle in for the long haul, stroking her hair.

I'll deal with those little fuckers later.

---

I leave Octavia sleeping in my room. Her sleep has been anything but restful, and my rage has done nothing but simmer and grow all day in response. By the time I manage to slip away, darkness is falling. I find Linc in the game room. I grab the nearest thing I can find and launch it at the TV. I'd rather it be his head, but I'd also prefer to make him bleed with my own fists than the random trophy I launched.

"What the actual fuck?" he roars, jumping to his feet and turning, finding me standing behind him. I don't even care that the TV is busted up and he looks spitting mad. His anger has nothing on my pulsing rage.

"What the fuck? What the fuck? You have got to be shitting me, Linc. I know you're not asking me what the fuck I just did because *what the actual fuck did you do?*" I'm practically foaming at the mouth, shaking where I stand. I stay where I'm standing because I know if I move toward him, I'll beat his idiotic face in.

The cold persona that he uses on everyone else washes over him, and he transforms from my little brother into Lincoln Saint, the boy genius who isn't afraid of getting his hands dirty. The kid that makes fully grown men piss themselves. "I have no idea what you're talking about."

I pick up the closest thing to hand, a glass vase, and launch that at him too. He ducks quickly enough that it doesn't hit him, but it still smashes to shards on the wall behind him. "Don't feed me your bullshit company line, Linc. I know you had a plan to get her to leave. I know you did this. You've gone too fucking far. She's broken!"

Emotion flickers in his eyes, and I can see the doubt creep in. Despite my rage, there's still a part of me that knows he's trying to save her in his own way, but this is too fucking much. "You said you didn't want to be a part of this. You don't get to storm in now and tell me what I've done is wrong. Anyway I haven't done anything to her for weeks. At least if she's broken, she'll leave. Better broken and alive…"

He trails off and pinches the bridge of his nose. His words deflate me and my rage entirely. The alternative doesn't bear thinking about, and I'm still not convinced I believe him about not being the one who fucked with her last night. Who else could know the significance of locking her in a closet? But I don't want him to lie to me, and I know just how ruthless Linc is when it comes to her and her safety. I won't ask him outright because we don't lie to each other, and I don't want him to have to, but I am done with all of this.

"We can't put her through this. If she doesn't leave, you need to find another way. *We* need to find another way. I want her safe, happy, and out of their clutches."

He laughs haughtily, watching me with those hawk-like eyes of his. "You still love her, don't you?"

"Are you trying to tell me you don't?" I ask, quirking an eyebrow. He shakes his head and drops down into the leather chair beside him.

He sighs and leans his head back, looking up at the ceiling. "Even if I did, nothing could ever come of it. She isn't safe here. Plus, the other two… When it comes to Octavia Royal, everything is always way too complicated."

No truer words have ever been spoken.

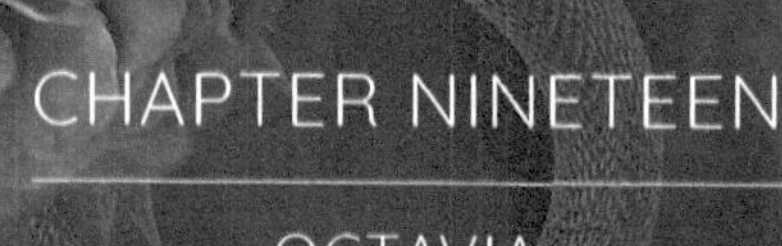

# CHAPTER NINETEEN

## OCTAVIA

Spending the last day and night in East's bed isn't exactly how I pictured my weekend ending. He walked me back to the house this morning so I could get ready for school, and only left after my insistence that I'd be okay. I'd set the alarm and locked the door as he'd watched from the back patio.

I'm not going to lie, walking back into my house alone might be one of the hardest things I've done these last few months. However, I refuse to let whoever it was that did that to me win. I've already survived too much to let this be the thing that breaks me.

Well, fully break me. I'm definitely partially broken.

Who would have thought that it would only take four weeks to break me?

Except, I'm also my father's daughter, and there's too much fight left in me to tuck tail and run. I have very little doubt it was someone from school. I'm also fairly certain it was the three people who knew exactly how much locking me in a small space would fuck me up, but I have no proof.

Even if I did, what could I do?

Absolutely fuck all, that's what.

So I'm going to go to school and pretend like nothing happened. Letting them see how fucked up I am about it all gives them more power than I'm willing to relinquish.

So I pad up the stairs, still wrapped up in East's hoodie. I've been wearing it since he found me yesterday morning, but it smells like him, and right now, he's my safe harbor in these shark infested waters.

As I reach my bedroom door, I freeze, my hands shaking at my sides. I close my eyes and clench my fists. I hate feeling so fucking weak. I hate that they found a way to make me crumble, but what I mostly hate is how much rage I feel toward my dad for putting me in this position in the first place.

If he hadn't left me, I wouldn't be here. I wouldn't be going through this. I'd still be safely out on tour, living my life the way I always have. I wouldn't be subject to the webs of lies and torture that is Echoes Cove.

If I don't get my dad's inheritance, it goes back into my trust. If that happens, my guardians might get access to it. I'm not convinced that isn't why people want me to leave. Considering how close Blair and Lincoln seem to be, it wouldn't surprise me if she asked him for help. She must have a magical pussy to get him to bend to her will like that, though.

I hate how fucked up the thought makes me feel. Him fucking her. Him being on her side. That she really has replaced me when it comes to those three. I can't help but wonder if he crawls into her bed and holds her the way he used to hold me.

I shake the thoughts off and cross the threshold to my room, taking deep breaths as I undress before changing into my uniform. I take extra care doing my hair and makeup, making sure no one can tell I've slept like shit the last two nights. I don't want to look affected by the nightmare that plays on a loop when I close my eyes.

A shudder runs down my spine as I think about it again, and tears prick my eyes. I blink them back. I fucking *refuse* to cry over it anymore. They don't deserve any more of my tears.

I find my phone on the nightstand where I left it and grab the charger before heading down to the kitchen. East called Smithy for me yesterday to let him know why I was MIA but told him to stay with his family as long as he needed. His sister is in a bad way, and I don't want to be the reason he isn't there for her.

I plug my phone into the charger once I'm in the kitchen and start the coffee pot. Looking through the refrigerator, my stomach flips at the sight of all the food, so I grab the cream cheese, then put a bagel in the toaster. I get lost in my own head while I'm waiting, staring out into the yard. When my bagel pops up, I let out a little scream.

Fuck my actual life.

*Get a grip, Octavia.*

I shake myself off and sort out my bagel and coffee before putting the TV on so there's at least some background noise. I don't need the creaking of the house to freak me out entirely. My phone starts to buzz like crazy as it comes back to life, and I groan.

Twenty text messages and ten missed calls from Indi.

*Shit.*

Just as I go to open the thread of the messages, my phone rings with a video call. I answer, not bothering to put on a smile. Indi's the one person I won't hide my pain from. She's a true friend, I don't need or want to hide from her.

"Thank fuck you're alive! Where the actual fuck have you been?" she screeches over the line, her eyes crazed.

I run a hand through my hair and sigh raggedly. She stills, her expression changing from angry to concerned at the sound. "Sorry, some shit went down after I texted you Saturday night, and I didn't have my phone until this morning."

"Are you okay? What happened?" Her concern is almost enough to make me cry again. I've never been much of a crier before this fucking year. "Fuck it, I'm coming over. I'll drive us to school, and then you can explain."

"You don't have to—"

"Shut up." She cuts me off, and I can't help but laugh dryly. "I'm already grabbing my shit and heading to the car. I'll be there soon."

The line disconnects, and I stare at the phone. I guess that's that.

My little sunshine friend seems to be finding her confidence, and I couldn't feel prouder.

Now, if only I could find where I put mine.

---

School's been surreal today. No one spoke to me with disdain. No one spoke about me, or at least not that I heard, and no one tried to fuck with me. Well, except for Blair and her merry little band of bitches, but having them leave me alone would be a goddamn miracle at this point. I don't know what happened between Saturday night and today, but it's like I've become a wallflower, and I'm so here for it.

The football team still sat with us at lunch. Though Indi sat beside me rather than opposite me like normal with me sitting at the end of the table. That way none of them could get too close to me, and I love her for it. To say Indi went nuclear when I explained what happened and why it fucked me up so much is the understatement of the century. I've never heard her cuss quite like that. She was like a stabby little viper spitting venom.

It was crazy and kind of awesome.

She's barely left my side all day. And I genuinely thought she was going to rip into one of my teachers when he tried to hurry her away from my desk. She isn't even in the class with me. Apparently, my little ball of sunshine is also a vicious little ball of fire.

So we're relaxing poolside at my house, sipping on the iced tea I found in the fridge, and sunning ourselves. It isn't normally something I do, but I think after everything that's happened, some decompression time is good.

"Octavia." I sit up, sighing at the sound of Lincoln's unexpected voice. I pull my aviators down so they cover my eyes and I can actually see. Indi looks just about ready to fight him if he starts fucking with us. I can't blame her. She fully agreed with me that they're the most likely culprits for what happened Saturday night.

The only thing that has my guard coming down is that when I look over toward him, I find him flanked by Finley, Maverick, and East.

I know that East won't hurt me. He never has, and there isn't one thing about him that makes me think he ever would.

"What do you want?" Indi snaps, and I can't help but smirk. Lincoln's face mirrors mine, which only makes me more suspicious. He never reacts well to people calling him out, or at least, he never used to.

"Calm down, little miss warrior. We come in peace," Maverick jabs at her, and she flips him the bird before settling back down on her lounger.

"If you say so, asshole." She lifts her book to cover her face, nodding at me. I know if shit goes sideways, she'll absolutely throw hands for me. Not that I'm sure either of us could fight them physically if we need to. I've trained in some self-defense, but there's four of them, and none of them are small. Plus the last few attacks I've suffered, I've frozen. So I'm pretty sure I'd be royally screwed if they were here to attack us.

"Can we talk?" Lincoln asks, ever the mouthpiece for the band of them. Thick as thieves. I eye them, and while East looks a little uneasy, the rest of them are pretty much unreadable.

Shocker.

I'm not going to give them even an inch. Every instinct tells me that those three are the three who locked me in that fucking closet, so I won't relax around them or forgive them, unless I'm somehow proved wrong. "I guess that depends on what you want to talk about."

Finley steps forward, hands stuffed in the front pockets of his jeans, and I hate him a little for looking so good. He literally looks like some kind of dark and brooding god. It isn't fair that all four of them are so droolworthy when three of them are such giant assholes. "We want to apologize and call a truce of sorts."

I cock an eyebrow, folding my arms over my chest. "A truce? I don't remember declaring war."

"You declared war by coming back here," Lincoln huffs, and Finley turns to face him, glaring.

"You are not helping. Shut up," he growls, and East clips his brother around the back of the head.

It's amusing to see the dynamics changing so much. Finley has never stepped out on Lincoln before. He's always been their unofficial leader. There's obviously a 50/50 split here with this truce, but if this means they're going to leave me alone, I'll take it. All I ever wanted was to keep my head down and get through this year. I want to graduate as per my dad's wishes, and then do what I need to at college to start my record label.

That's all I've ever wanted.

"What brought on the change of heart?" I'm beyond curious. I have a feeling this all came from East. He did such a great job of looking after me over the weekend; and if he, like me, thinks these assholes were behind it, I wouldn't put it past him to call them out on their shit.

Finley looks back toward me, while Lincoln scowls, and Maverick fidgets. I'm not surprised Maverick leaves the talking to the others. He's always been the kind to fix things with his fists and leave diplomacy to everyone else. Even when we were kids, things were the same.

It's Lincoln who steps forward to answer my question, and his *cold prince* demeanor he wears so well is back. "We have more important things to worry about. If you want to be back here, so be it; but don't come running to us when your world's crumbling."

"She doesn't need to run to you assholes," Indi chirps up, and I can't help but laugh.

"What she said. But whatever," I say with a shrug, lying back on the lounger. "I'll accept the truce. I didn't start this mess anyway. Make sure to call off your bloodhound. If you think Blair is going to take your new declaration lying down, you've got another thing coming."

"We can handle Blair," Lincoln grinds out.

His jaw is clenched, and his shoulders are stiff, showing me just how pissed off my words have him. I'm glad. I don't want to let them see that I'm a mess inside. That I'm afraid to go back into my house after this weekend. If he's angry, he won't see it. They don't need to see or know any of that. "Then we have a deal."

---

Indi didn't go home until after we ate dinner. When she left, I locked all the doors and set the alarms; and I've hid out in the theatre room ever since. This house is too goddamn big to be in alone. Especially when I jump at every little noise. Indi did offer to stay the night, but honestly, I hate putting that on her.

I don't want to be afraid.

So it's time to sit up and get on with it.

I take a deep breath before I leave the room, making sure all the lights are off.

Do I run through the dark house to the next lit room? You bet your fucking ass I do. I repeat my ridiculous routine until I'm in the kitchen and all that's left to do is reset the alarm and go upstairs.

I take another deep breath, trying to calm my racing heart. My hands shake as I set the alarm for overnight and prepare myself to race to my room. I left the light on up there earlier. I know it's bad for the environment, but dammit, so is my car. It makes me feel safer knowing the light's on, and right now, I need that feeling.

I flip the switch for the light in the kitchen and haul ass through the entrance hall and up the stairs. I'm practically panting by the time I reach my room and slam the door behind me. Leaning against my door, I suck in air until my heartbeat slows.

This is ridiculous. But fuck it. No one's here to watch it.

*At least, I hope.*

I check the room, the closet, the ensuite, and even under the fucking bed to make sure I'm alone before making sure the balcony door's locked; and then I lock my bedroom door, completing my barrier from the rest of the house. The only thing getting me out of here is a fucking fire.

*Please, fucking Jesus, do not jinx me.*

Once I'm positive the room's secure, I finally get ready for bed. I can't help but wonder what exactly brought on the white flag that was waved earlier today, but I'm not going to question it. Well, not too hard anyway.

I slide between the sheets and turn off the light before trying to lie down and close my eyes, but every time I do, I see the inside of the cupboard.

I put a podcast on, murder and makeup probably isn't the best thing to fall asleep to, but it's what I have, so it's what's happening; and I can't help but wish someone else was here with me. But at least now, maybe with their truce, I'll finally have a good week.

A girl can dream.

# CHAPTER TWENTY

I slept like absolute fucking shit. Nightmares plagued me all night, so to say there are bags beneath my eyes might be the understatement of the century. If I managed even an hour of sleep, I'd be amazed.

I pull up at school with Indi in the Wrangler almost holding my breath. Despite the white flag that was waved yesterday, there's a part of me that doesn't trust it, even though East was there. It's not like he was in on the bullshit that came before, so why would they listen to him now?

The whole Finley stepping out on Lincoln to agree with East thing has me off kilter too.

None of it quite makes sense to me, but if the truce means the rest of this year is going to be easier, I'll grab onto it with both hands.

Now, if I can just get past my own trauma to actually sleep properly again, life will be great.

"I still can't believe you passed on sugary goodness for espresso." Indi shakes her head at me as she pulls into a parking spot. "There's nothing good about pure espresso."

I can't help but bark out a laugh. Despite my extreme tiredness, she's managed to keep me smiling and laughing ever since she picked me up this morning. "Tell that to any Italian and see how far you get. Espresso and pasta are basically a religion. At least to the Italians I've met."

I remember when I went to Rome on my dad's world tour. I snapped the spaghetti to make it fit in the pan, and the horror on the face of the Italian tour manager was enough to make me cry with laughter. Apparently that shit's practically illegal there.

I sip on my espresso, exaggerating my gasp of joy as the bitter beautifulness hits my taste buds, and she scrunches up her face in disgust. "Just no," she hisses, taking a sip of the whipped cream topped iced coffee she clutches in her hands. "Now this shit is good."

She starts to laugh, and I join in, feeling grateful again that she came into my life when she did. The laughter is the most catharsis I've felt over the past twelve or so hours.

I try to fight the yawn that overwhelms me and makes my eyes water, but I lose.

"Will you be okay today?" Indi's concern is heartwarming. She frowns at me again, the same way she did when she arrived at my place and saw my disheveled state. "I can stay till Smithy gets back. Or you can come and stay with me?"

I shake my head, smiling softly before yawning again. "I appreciate it, but no. I'm not going to get over this if I let everyone coddle me. I'll be okay. Nightmares can't hurt me. I just need to push through it."

I pull out my phone, shooting a message to Smithy to check in with him like I promised I would.

"Surviving ECP on so little sleep might not be safe," she snorts, before climbing out of the car. I follow suit, shaking my head because she isn't entirely wrong.

We head into the school, arms linked and smiling. When we reach my locker, I start swapping out my books that I need for the morning. "So, I keep meaning to ask, but forget with all of my bullshit. What's going on with you and Jackson?"

She's uncharacteristically silent. Once I have what I need, I close my locker and look at her. A blush spills across her cheeks, and she wrings out her hands. "We're okay. I thought it might get a little weird after you brushed off Raleigh, but it didn't. He's a lot sweeter than I expected him to be, but we're taking things slow."

"I'm happy for you." I smile down at her, genuinely overjoyed that it's working out for her. She brings so much joy to me, I'm glad I helped her take the leap she needed in that regard.

We head to her locker, while she fills me in on her family stuff. I'm the terrible friend who hadn't asked because I'd been drowning in my own drama, but I can listen. "You didn't miss much. Though when Ella found out we were friends, she went a little crazy. I managed to ice her out, but it was weird as fuck. I'm glad my cousins live on the other side of the country. They all have way too much hype for me. I was exhausted by the time they left. They sapped my well of joy and positivity dry with all of their mania."

"I'm sorry I wasn't around to help," I say sadly.

"I mean, you were literally indisposed, you're fine. I wouldn't put them on you anyway. Families are weird."

It's almost like her words summoned my crazy-ass family. Because once she's finished speaking, Blair stalks past us, bitch squad firmly attached to her ass. She flicks her hair over her shoulder as she passes me, and I can't help but roll my eyes when she glares at me. I guess the muzzle Lincoln put on her isn't one she was happy with.

I shudder at the thought of the two of them together. I refuse to think my feelings are anything beyond disgust. There's a small pang in my heart, but that's just a young girl's crush dying. Once upon a time, Lincoln, Finley, Maverick, and East each owned a piece of my heart. As an almost grown-ass woman, I'm aware that I can't have all of them. Hell, I can't have any of them. But that young girl's crush still exists inside of me somewhere whenever I get a glimpse past all of their bullshit and hate.

Maybe even in spite of it all.

But a young girl's wishes are nothing but that. Reality isn't even close to aligned with those wishes, and I don't know that I'm all that sad about it. Especially considering everything they've done since I got back here.

Especially with what I'm positive they did to me over the weekend.

Except for East—he might be the only one of them who hasn't completely changed. The others, though… Let's just say there are some things a girl can't get over. And there's no reason that I can think of for them to have done that to me.

So I tuck that small girl's crushes deep in the back of my compartmentalized heart and take a deep breath.

Indi's eyes go wide as she looks at me. "Did you remember to do your assignment?"

*Well, fuck.*

---

After spending last night cramming with Indi and catching up on every assignment and piece of homework that I've left floating, and forgotten about, it occurred to me while we were working that Lincoln and I are still pretty behind on our Business project. Despite the threats of a fail from the creep that is Mr. Peters, I haven't gotten an F yet. That wasn't something I was going to deal with last night, though. So as I head to my Business class, I steel myself against seeing Mr. Peters and talking to Lincoln to catch up on everything.

I didn't sleep much again last night, the nightmares that haunt me when I slip away into sleep are fucking awful, and I woke up hoarse from screaming again this morning. To say I'm tired is an understatement, and the thought of dealing with Lincoln today doesn't exactly fill me with joy.

Lincoln wasn't an ass to me yesterday, but he wasn't exactly warm and fuzzy either. I'm not sure Lincoln Saint *has* a warm and fuzzy side. It's as if he let East take all of the laid-back and chill vibes as they grew up, and he took on the responsibility that comes with being a Saint in Echoes Cove, growing icier as he did it. I can't say for certain about any of it since I wasn't here, but it's sad to see how much he's changed since I left.

I slide into my seat as the final bell rings and Mr. Peters strolls into the room. A shudder crawls down my spine even just seeing him, the same way it has every time since his disgusting proposal. It would seem the fates are on my side today, though, because he sits down and looks around the room, seeming about as awake as I feel. After a moment, he says, "Buddy up with your partners and discuss your project. I expect your second proposal after Labor Day weekend."

I look over and see Lincoln scowling at me. Awesome.

"What are you looking at?" he snaps, and I roll my eyes at him.

The guy is as mercurial as a thunderstorm. It's freaking exhausting. "Well, you are my partner." I sigh. "I was trying to work out how the fuck we're going to catch up."

"We don't have anything to catch up on," he snarls before reaching into his bag and dropping a folder onto my desk. "All you need to do is read up and write your half of the proposal."

"Not this again." I huff. As if what happened last time he pulled this wasn't bad enough. I can't help but frown at him before flicking through the file. An icy rage fills my veins. "I don't expect you to do all of the work, Lincoln. I'm fully capable of doing my part. After last time, I started my own goddamn proposal. Let me read yours, and I'll work out how to merge them."

"I will not risk my GPA, or my chance to escape this place, on some little rock princess who has no idea how the real world works."

I lean back in my chair, blinking at him. I have no idea where this animosity is coming from, but he looks as tired as I feel. I take a deep breath and decide to take the high road. Snapping at him won't get us anywhere. He also doesn't need to know how much I need my GPA to be on track either. "So much for our truce," I mutter. "I'll take a look at what you've done, and I'll give you my feedback before the weekend so we can finish our proposal before it's due in."

He responds with a grunt before pulling an identical file from his bag and opening it. "There isn't anything that needs feedback. The work is solid."

"I'm sure it is." I sigh, exasperated. Why does he take everything I say the wrong way? I decide the truce is on a very thin layer of ice, so rather than pushing, I turn to the work he's already done and start reading. I slide him over the work I've done too, since I'm not risking another chance at a fail or another proposition from our slimebag teacher. There's no way in hell I'm getting on my knees for him.

The first part of our project was to write a proposal for a business venture, with basic scaling and projections. The second part is to rework it based on feedback with full-scale profit projections. I worked blind, considering I didn't have feedback on the first part; and as I read through Lincoln's work, I kind of hate how solid the project is that he's put together.

There are definitely tweaks to be made and other profit streams that could be explored but considering he went at this alone, he's done a fucking lot of work in a short space of time. I am loath to admit that to him though. Especially when he already has a smug asshole way about him. If he was the Lincoln I used to know, I'd have zero issues letting him know how good of a job he did.

But that isn't the situation we're in, so I use the time to sit and scribble notes on the pages while the other groups in the class discuss their projects. The silence wouldn't bother me if I couldn't feel his eyes on me. I look up, watching him practically twitch as I make notes on his well thought out pages. But I refuse to let him do all of the work alone. He might think I'm a useless princess now, but he should know better than that. I haven't done anything to give him that impression of me. I take a deep breath and smile softly at him. "It's a solid plan, but I think there are a few tweaks we could make to widen revenue streams and increase the profit margins."

He looks a little shocked as he leans back in his seat, nodding stiffly before turning to his version of the file. I do a mental fist pump at shocking him into not snarling at me and take the win. Maybe at some point, he'll realize he actually has no clue about the girl I grew up to be and clue in to the fact that I'm far more competent than he wants to give me credit for.

I go through and add notes, waiting until the bell rings before handing him the file. "Have a look, see what you think. If you agree with what I've done, we can merge our two plans, since they aren't worlds away, then write up the final proposal *together.*"

He takes the file from my hand, nodding once before stalking from the room. I can't quite tell if this was a total win, but I head to my next class feeling way lighter than I did before I came to this one.

---

"Do you have plans for next weekend?"

I glance over my shoulder at Indi who's sitting on the counter of the island in my kitchen. Rooting through the fridge trying to find something to eat is a disappointing endeavor, so I sigh and shut it before turning my attention back to her. I sit down at the island as I consider her question.

I squash down the ripple of sadness that runs through me. Dad and I always used to just get away from everything on Labor Day weekend. We'd escape the insanity that his lifestyle brought and find a remote cabin somewhere. I'm not really one for nature, but staying in a log cabin with beautiful water views and making S'mores at night over an open fire was always a really nice escape. It won't happen this year, and I'm trying not to focus on just how much that thought hurts. "For the long weekend? No, I was just going to curl up in the theatre room in my pajamas and pretend the world doesn't exist. Why?"

She shrugs before jumping down and sliding into the chair next to mine. "I was thinking maybe we could get away for the weekend. You could definitely use some time away from here. I was thinking of a spa weekend. Ultimate relaxation and all the sleep rolled into one weekend."

I smile wide. That actually sounds kind of perfect. It might not be what I've always done, but it might give me a chance to escape the ever-haunting memories of this house. Both of my dad and what happened recently. I might actually get some sleep. "Yes, let's do it. That sounds amazing."

Grinning wide, she pulls her phone out of her pocket, and after tapping at her screen, she shows me the site of a mountain spa. "I was thinking we could go to this place."

I almost can't contain my excitement as I take in the images from the website. It looks so fucking zen, I can't even handle it. It looks perfect. "Yes, let's book it. Right now. I need this way too much."

I grab my purse from my bag while she puts all of the details of our stay in. "You don't need to pay, I can cover my half." She shoves her hands at me as I go to hand her my card, but I shake my head and refuse to take it.

"Hush, what's the point in having money if I can't spend it on the people I love?" I shrug and hand her my card anyway. Money hasn't ever been an issue, and I know I'm lucky that I can say that. I mean it, though, I know she has plenty of her own money; but I couldn't spend what my dad made in three lifetimes, so if I can do this, I'm going to.

She books it in my name and grins at me, showing me the confirmation. "Thank you, I mean you totally paid for my birthday weekend away, so I feel like I'm taking advantage—"

"Hush!" I cut her off, laughing. "No one is taking advantage."

Her phone buzzes, pulling her attention away from the topic at hand, and I see Jackson's name on the screen before she takes it back from me. She smiles down at her phone, and my heart soars for her. I love how happy she is, but I swear to God; if he hurts her, I will literally pop his nut sack. Pop it.

"Do you mind if I jet?" she asks, biting at her lip.

I shake my head. I don't want to be alone, but I could totally try to head to bed early. I might not get much sleep, but I figure the earlier I start trying, the more I might get in overall. "You're good. And don't worry about getting me in the morning either. I can drive in."

"Are you sure?" she asks, conflict written all over her face.

I grab her bag and push it at her, laughing. "Of course I'm sure, go on, get. Go enjoy that boy of yours. I'll see you tomorrow."

She grins, taking her bag from my hands and slides her books from the counter into it. "Thank you. You absolutely will. I'll grab coffee and meet you in the parking lot."

"Sounds perfect," I say as I walk her to the front door. I disable the alarm and open the door to let her out. "Have fun."

She practically skips to her car, waving once she's buckled in. I open the gate from the remote system as she reaches it and wait for the lock to engage before resetting the alarm. Some might call the level of security I have here overkill, but all things considered, I don't think even Fort Knox would be overkill at this point. I've been attacked in my home twice, and Smithy was attacked once. That's three times too many, and I'm not willing to take chances anymore.

After making sure all of the doors and windows are shut, I manage not to run up the stairs tonight, and I mark that down as progress. At this point, I'll literally claim any win I can. I head straight to my bathroom as I put my hair up in a messy bun and jump in the shower to wash the day off. It's been unseasonably warm today, and I feel kind of gross.

I pad my way into my room in my towel, grabbing a pair of boy shorts and a tank from my dresser along the way. It's way too warm for full pajamas, and I open the balcony to let some of the cool night air into the room. The smell of the flowers from the trellis filters in, and I smile. Wild roses are some of my absolute favorites.

It doesn't take me long to brush out my hair, then shut my balcony door before climbing into bed. I feel so fucking tired after the last few days that it doesn't take long for sleep to pull me under.

I wake up screaming less than forty minutes later and bury my face into my pillow. All I want is one night of sleep—just one—so I set up my podcasts again and try to calm myself enough to sleep. When I see that it's two in the morning on the screen of my phone, I groan.

As sleep finally starts to pull me under once more, I hear noises outside and freeze. I want to move, to run away, but I'm paralyzed by fear. My fight or flight response is, apparently, just die. Awesome.

The balcony door creaks, and I manage to get control of myself. I flip over, sitting up to face the door, and see Lincoln stalking toward me in nothing more than a pair of sweatpants. "What the fuck are you doing here?"

He glares at me and climbs right into my fucking bed.

"What are you doing?" I screech, my fear and anger mashing together.

I grab the sheets, fully ready to kick his ass out when he lies down, grumbling, "I can hear you screaming from my room. Now lie down and sleep, I'm not going anywhere."

I scoff. *The audacity of this guy.* But as he pulls me onto the bed, I can't deny how much safer I feel with him here. Which is ridiculous considering I'm pretty sure he's the cause of my nightmares, but I never claimed I made sense.

I turn my back to him and close my eyes, feeling him move closer to me as he tucks me against his chest, his arm draped over me. Sleep is already dragging me under, so I don't bother complaining. I'm not sure it'd make a difference anyway. As I start to slip away, I hear him murmur, "You don't need to cry anymore. I'm here now."

---

When I wake up, Lincoln's long gone, and for a minute, I think I dreamed of him being here. Until I roll over and catch his scent on the pillow.

So fucking weird.

Him being here was not what I expected when I heard someone climbing the trellis.

Lincoln Saint doesn't seem like the type to sneak in my window anymore. I didn't think he cared enough to even notice my screams.

But apparently, I am Jon Snow because I appear to know nothing.

I play it all over again in my head, trying desperately to work out why he would come over here. I eventually decide that I'm not going to figure out the enigma that is Lincoln Saint without coffee, if I can even work him out at all.

I try to push it from my mind and get ready for the day. I shoot Smithy a message to check in on him and his sister. They're a few hours behind me, so hopefully I don't wake him. Once I roll out of bed, I head to the shower, trying to clear my mind a little. I slept like the fucking dead after Lincoln came over, and I still feel dazed.

The shower helps a bit, but after I'm dressed, I still stumble down to the coffee pot like it holds all of the answers to life. As I'm waiting for it to brew, my phone buzzes, and I smile when I see Smithy's name.

**Smithy: Good Morning, Miss Octavia **smiley face emoji** My sister has taken a turn for the better and things are looking up. I can be home in a few**

**weeks, I hope. Just need to get her back home and settled with a nursing team.**

**Me: I'm so glad! You don't have to rush, things are all quiet here now. Take care of your sister, I'm absolutely fine.**

**Smithy: If you say so. I did, however, arrange for a grocery delivery. It will be put away before you're back from school. I asked Mrs. Potts, who looks after the Saint household, to sort it out for you. Master Saint will ensure the alarm system is sorted out.**

**Me: Smithy, you rock.**

I open the refrigerator and wince. I probably should have thought to go shopping myself considering how bare it is in there.

**Smithy: I know. I've asked her to prepare you some meals so you don't live off of take out too.**

The guy's a total fucking sweetheart. I miss him so much, and it's hard to remember how I survived without him. I send him a quick thanks before realizing I need to forage food before school. I grab my bag from the counter, making sure I have my purse and keys, and head out to the garage. This morning calls for a breakfast burrito, *STAT*.

I jump in the car and head toward the only place in town that does them. It doesn't take long for me to weave through the early morning traffic and hit up Raleigh's family restaurant, smiling at his sister as I enter. The food smells beyond amazing once I have the take-out bag in hand, so I take it out to my car and basically inhale it before heading to school. I pull into the space beside Indi to find her waving at me like a kid on a sugar high. I guess she had a good night.

Climbing from the car, I hear her door slam, and then there's a chocolatey, whipped cream delight of a coffee floating in front of my face. I grin, taking it from her as she sips on hers and bounces on the spot. "Morning, angel face!"

I laugh at how peppy she is this morning. "Morning, cupcake?"

"You seem cheerier than you have been," she comments as she links arms with me, and I decide to keep the Lincoln thing to myself for now. I don't understand it, and I don't trust it. The last thing I want is her to think it was something I instigated. She's starting to see the truth of who he is and likes it about as much as I do, which is to say, not at all. I'm not going to poke the mama bear.

"I slept better. And I had a breakfast burrito. What's not to be peppy about?"

She beams at me as we enter the school. "You mean other than these unhallowed halls? Absolutely nothing."

---

The week has been strangely quiet, and since Indi's heading off campus for lunch with her mom, I decided to spend my break in the Music rooms. The longer I spend being back here in Echoes Cove, the more I want to be around music.

After my dad died, I was a little worried I'd never play again, and while I've played piano, I haven't picked up a guitar yet.

Today, that's going to change.

I pick up the acoustic that sits on a stand in the corner of the room and drop onto one of the stools with it in my hands. The smooth of the wood and the rough of the strings transports me to a different time entirely. I go all the way back to the time my dad first gave me a guitar. I revisit learning different chords from him. To the first time he asked me to play a track with him for one of the songs on his album… The first time in a studio. So many memories flash behind my eyes, and I smile despite the tear that rolls down my cheek.

I pick at the strings. The sounds of the first song I wrote with him echo around the room, and I close my eyes, going back to a time before I felt broken. A time when I wasn't so sad. A time before…

I let the music take me away to another place, the sting of the metal strings a comfort I'd forgotten. The acoustics in this room remind me of some of the places we've played before. It's like I'm back there, with him, and with my eyes closed, I can pretend that's exactly where I am.

I lose myself to the feelings, the music, and the memories. It isn't until the bell rings that I open my eyes and see that Finley is standing there, silently watching me, and I startle.

How wrapped up was I to not notice his presence that almost chokes me now? He stalks up to me, and the stool I'm sitting on puts me almost eye to eye with him. He clasps my cheek in his hand, shocking the hell out of me as he rests his forehead on mine.

I close my eyes at the feeling of him this close, and my heart races. I have no idea what this is or why I'm so calm about it, but there's something so serene about the look in his eyes that makes me sit here with him.

It only lasts a few seconds before he pulls back, stepping away and looking torn.

"I'm sorry," is all he says before he stalks away, leaving me so far beyond confused my world spins.

There are too many things he could be sorry for at this point, but that sorry felt different.

Like goodbye.

# CHAPTER TWENTY-ONE

"Girls' trip, baby!" Indi practically sings as she slides in her socks across the hardwood of the entry hall. Thank God Smithy isn't here to see her nearly slam into the artwork on the walls. He'd have a conniption. It's officially Labor Day weekend. I'm a little sad he still isn't back yet, but I understand that he's looking after his family.

This past week has been one of the strangest in my life. There hasn't been any bullying, no comments have been made behind my back, and somehow the deep fake sex tape has been wiped from existence. And Lincoln has spent every night in my bed, sneaking in through the window each night and disappearing before I wake.

Some nights I went to sleep without him there, and the only way I knew he was there was his scent on my pillow the next day.

Stranger yet, the three of them haven't said a word to me all week long. It's as if they're pretending I don't exist. It's not much different from when I arrived, just minus the bullshit from the rest of the student body.

Indi dances around in the doorway like an absolute loon, but she brings me so much joy. I laugh at her antics and excitement. "Three whole days of no school, no Echoes Cove, and nothing but utter relaxation. What's not to be excited about?"

"Absolutely nothing!" She slips her feet into her Chucks before spinning to face me. "Let's go!"

I grab my weekend bag, keys, and phone before double checking that the doors are all locked up. Once I'm sure everything's good to go, I grab my handbag, enable the alarm, and haul ass out of the house before locking the front door too.

We jump into her Wrangler, set up our road trip playlist, and prepare ourselves for the couple hour drive inland to the resort.

As we drive out of Echoes Cove, I can't help but feel like we're being followed. There's a prickling on the back of my neck as if I'm being watched, but when I check the mirrors, I can't see anyone there. It's creepy as fuck, but I shrug it off and put it down to paranoia. Despite my nightmares quieting with Lincoln's presence, I'm still not over the whole being jumped in the middle of the night thing.

Which isn't really that surprising considering the trauma from the experience, but this weekend is about getting away from all of that, relaxing, and being at one with myself. I'm totally sure I can do that.

Not.

I finally relax as Echoes Cove disappears in the rearview and sing along to the playlist with Indi, getting into the road trip spirit.

The time passes quickly, and before I know it, the navigation system announces we've arrived at our destination. We turn off onto the entry road, the giant wooden arch welcoming us to Mountain View Spa Resort, and I swear I'm already feeling more relaxed than I have in months. Indi drives us through the green expanses, and it feels like the world falls away as the mountains come into view before us. Tucked away to the left, behind a giant fountain, is the resort.

"Holy shit, this looks better than it did in the pictures!" Indi exclaims, bouncing in her seat as we pull into the valet bay. My door's opened in an instant, and the valet smiles at me warmly.

"Welcome to Mountain View, Miss Royal. Please let us get your bags. If you'd like to head inside with your friend and get checked in, we'll take your luggage straight up to your suite." He offers me a hand and helps me down from the car, and Indi shrugs at me as she reaches me.

"I figured if I put it in your name, we'd get better service, but this is something else."

I shake my head, not caring that she used my name. There are definite perks to being my father's daughter. "Fine by me, let's head inside."

She links her arm with mine, and we head inside. I lift my aviators as we cross the threshold into the building, and the house manager greets us. "Miss Royal, it's good to have you with us. We've already checked you in. If you follow me, I'll show you to your suite. We upgraded you for your stay. There is a private spa space in your suite that you can use as well as the facilities here."

"Thank you," I say, as Indi nudges me like an excited kid. Her joy is officially overspilling. We follow the manager up to the suite on the top floor of the resort.

She opens all of the rooms and shows us the spa menu that's available. She's finishing the tour as our bags are delivered to the room. Indi looks like she's almost a little freaked out by the service, so I try to take charge of the situation, tipping the bell boys before they disappear. Their grins are wide as they thank me before scurrying away.

A knock sounds at the door, and the house manager moves to open it. "Delivery for Miss Royal."

*What the fuck?*

She takes the delivery and closes the door before turning back to face me with a bouquet of yellow tulips. "For you."

She hands them to me, and I tamp down the freak out that's threatening. What the actual fuck?

I paste a smile on my face as I pull the same envelope sealed with red wax from this bunch as there has been on the others. It felt fine at first, but for whoever's sending them knowing where I am is a little creepy. I check the envelope and again, just a plain black card, embossed with the same image as the wax seal. I quickly put them in a vase and push the thought to the back of my mind. This weekend is about relaxing with my bestie, not focusing on creepozoids.

I turn my focus back to the house manager, who's smiling warmly at me as she asks, "Is there anything else I can help you with?"

"No, this is all wonderful. Thank you."

"Perfect, well, if you need anything, dial '0' on your in-room line. You'll come directly through to me."

"That's great, thank you." I usher her out of the room after tipping her too. I close the door behind her then lean back on it, taking a breath.

I look over at Indi, who still looks pretty overwhelmed from her spot on the sofa, staring at me. "Dude, is this what your life was like before? People tripping all over themselves to be around you?"

"Pretty much," I say with a shrug before moving into the suite and dropping down next to her. "Not everywhere, and not always, but yeah. It can be a little much."

"It's totally out of this world. I'm sorry if putting it in your name was out of line."

"Dude, you're fine," I say, swatting her with a cushion and making her chuckle. "What do you want to do first?"

She picks up the menu, handing me the second one, and grins. "Let's try everything!" Her excitement is contagious, and I'm not about to stomp on it.

I grin at her, happy as hell that she pushed me to get away this weekend. "Sounds perfect."

---

After two days of total relaxation and treatments, I think I might be tapped out. There are only so many ways a girl can be poked and prodded before she needs some space.

Indi bounces into the bedroom, her excitement at full capacity as ever, before dropping down onto the bed beside me. She shoves her phone under my nose, and I pull away so I can actually focus on the screen. "I found this low-key music bar in the next town over. Restaurant by day, bar by night. Do you want to check it out?"

"Sure, why not?"

"And it's called Midnight Blues! What are the chances?"

"That's kind of brilliant. We can head there in a bit?" I ask with a smile, seeing the open mic night announcement on the website seconds after the agreement leaves my mouth.

Devious little shit. "I'm not singing, though."

"But, V," she draws out the letter, practically singing it. "You're so good! You should share your gift with the world, rather than just me and your shower head!"

I burst out laughing as she wags her eyebrows at me. "My 'gift,'" I say, making air quotes with my fingers, "is a curse. I saw what it did to my dad. I'd rather stay behind the scenes, thank you."

She sighs and flings herself backward dramatically, lying down as she stares up at me. "But it's just a small place, I'm sure there'll be hardly anyone there."

I raise an eyebrow at her and she huffs. "Fine, fine. No singing, but it looks like they do banging chicken wings, and I'm so down for that right now."

"What the fuck is a banging chicken wing?" I ask, completely bewildered.

She sits up and huffs, crossing her arms across her chest. "I really need to get you to watch more British TV. Their language is so much more imaginative. They have such a way with words. Banging means really good. So, banging chicken wings."

"And you couldn't have just said good wings?" I laugh, and she shakes her head violently.

"It just doesn't have that same feeling. The same… pizzazz."

Her pouting makes me laugh harder until she's laughing along with me. "Okay, so no singing but great wings. Sounds good."

It doesn't take us long to get ready and request the car back from the valet. Before long, we're in the Wrangler and heading to the next town.

We pull into the lot of Midnight Blues to find that it's already crazy busy, and I immediately wonder whether we should've booked a table. We can at least see how bad the wait's going to be, I guess. My internal worries are reflected on Indi's face as we climb from the car.

We walk in, and even though it's pretty busy, the hostess greets us straight away. Her eyes go wide when she sees me, and I instantly regret the decision to come here. She visibly gulps before smiling again. "Good evening, just the two of you?"

"Please," Indi says, moving to stand slightly in front of me. It's a bit over protective, but my heart swells anyway.

The girl nods and grabs two menus before motioning for us to follow. "Follow me, please." She weaves us through the tables to the back corner, and offers us a small smile before saying, "I thought you might like some privacy."

This girl is awesome. "Thank you, I appreciate it."

"Of course," she nods, and Indi and I slide into the booth. "I'll give you a few minutes to go through the menu, and then I'll check back in with you."

She disappears without another word, and Indi picks up the menu. "Isn't it strange for the hostess to be our server?"

I shrug as I pick up the other menu and glance over it. "People have always been weird when I go to new places. It's frustrating, but you just kind of get used to it after a while. Plus, she was reasonably chill. Someone else might not be so laid-back."

She clamps her lips together and looks almost guilty. It isn't her fault people are weird. "I didn't ever really think about this side of your life. Not properly anyway. It doesn't seem like much fun."

We chill out and enjoy our food once it arrives. The ambience in this place is so chill, that time slips away without us noticing. When the open mic starts, Indi looks over at me with those big puppy-like eyes of hers. "You sure you don't want to get up there?"

My heart pangs with the memory of doing small nights like this with Dad when we went to places like Nashville. It was always so much fun. I guess it could be again, but I doubt it would be the same. "Not entirely."

"Yes!" She jumps to her feet and scrambles toward the stage before I can say another word. I drop my head into my hands, wondering what the fuck I just agreed to. I'm equal parts anxious as fuck and excited about the prospect of being on a stage again. Even if just for a few minutes.

Indi skips back to the table, sliding into the booth beaming with joy. "They had a spot for you."

She practically sings the words and a flutter of excitement builds in my chest. We watch four acts, and then they call my name and gasps sound around the place.

*This might have been a bad idea, but fuck it. I'm here now.*

I reach the stage and take the guitar from the sound guy up here. I lift the strap over my shoulder and perch on the stool in front of the mic. As soon as I sit down, I know exactly what I'm going to sing. The song Dad and I wrote together. I lean forward to the mic, the heat of the lights blasting down at me as I try not to squint out at the crowd. "Evening, everybody, it's great to be out here with you all. My name's Octavia Royal, and this is 'Raindrop.'"

---

I wake up Sunday morning to Indi shaking me. "What's wrong?"

"Uhm, so… I know you shut your phone off when we got here so you could escape everything, but you should maybe turn it on." She wrings out her hands as she speaks to me, shifting from foot to foot, nervous as fuck.

"What happened?" I ask, scrambling to grab my phone from the nightstand.

She shuffles around so she's sitting cross-legged, looking like she might cry. "I'm so sorry, I didn't think this would happen, but apparently someone recorded you singing last night. And uh… It's kind of gone viral."

I let out a deep breath. The way she was going on, I thought someone had died. "Is that all?"

"You're not mad?"

I laugh softly as she deflates in front of me. "Why would I be mad?"

"Well I basically made you get up on stage."

I put my hand on hers and squeeze. "Indi, you didn't make the video or post it. Plus, this isn't the first tape I've had go viral, even just this month. I'd much rather this one than the deep fake. Honestly, it's fine."

I push the button on my phone, powering it up as she flops backward on the bed. It's barely seconds before it's buzzing out of control in my hand.

I push through most of the junk, deleting all the crazy shit, when I find a text from Raleigh. I haven't really spoken to him properly since we decided to just be friends.

**Raleigh: You were amazing, V.**

**Raleigh: I miss you**

**Raleigh: I really wish things could have worked out between us.**

**Raleigh: Why are you ignoring me?**

**Raleigh: Oh I see, you go viral and suddenly you're too good to talk to me. I see how it is.**

**Raleigh: Well fuck you too**

I let out a deep breath and flop back to lie beside Indi. "Why are boys so gross?"

"What happened?"

I pass her my phone because showing is easier than telling. She sits up, red in the face. "What a fucker. He's been a little weird about you since the whole thing happened, but I figured it was simply a bruised ego. He has no right to talk to you like this."

I shrug my shoulders, resigned to the fact that boys are not worth the hassle. "Privileged football players aren't used to hearing the word no, I guess. Not all of them of course, some of them are beautiful humans, like Jackson. But there's something about quarterbacks. And this is precisely why I don't usually date sports types. The egos are way too fragile."

"I'm sorry, V. What a dick."

I sit up and smile. "Fuck it. It is what it is. Now what are we doing with our last day here before we go back to normalcy?"

"Massages?" she suggests, and I can't help but grin.

I wonder if there's a Dylan O'Brien look alike around here.

# CHAPTER TWENTY-TWO

When I got home yesterday, I was glad to see that there weren't any media stalkers at my gates. That's the upside to the video having been taken not in my hometown, I guess. I might have to take Smithy up on the personal security thing if it gets bad again, though.

Lincoln didn't appear last night either, and I hate that I'm conflicted about whether or not I'm happy about that fact.

So much for wanting a normal year.

I head to school, swinging by the drive through to grab coffee for Indi and I, all while losing myself in today's song of the day, "I Am Defiant" by The Seige. The beat of the song has me all kinds of hyped up, which is definitely new for a Tuesday morning. The beat makes my heart race as my blood pounds through my veins. I'm a strong believer that the right song in the morning can set up your entire day properly.

I pull into the parking lot, swinging into the space next to Indi with the music blaring. As I bop along to the end of the song, Indi jumps along to the bass outside of my car.

Fuck, I love her.

I lean over and grab the coffees from the passenger seat before shouldering my bag and sliding out of the car.

"Thank you," she practically sings as I hand her the drink.

"You whore!"

I turn around at the screech and let out a sigh as Blair storms toward me, her hands clenched at her sides as her hair blows around her face in the breeze. She looks pissed.

I glance up at Indi, who looks ready to bitch slap Blair already. She's been too quiet lately. I sigh. I knew it couldn't last. "I wonder what I've done now."

Blair closes in on us, her blonde hair a wild mess as her rage makes her shake. What the actual fuck?

I hand Indi my drink before stepping around the front of the car to meet my cousin, placing my bag on the hood. She reaches me and pulls away before slapping me across the face so fucking hard I swear my brain rattles.

"What the fuck is wrong with you?" My voice is quiet and calm despite the rage pulsing in my veins. I'm not the screeching type, but if she thinks I'm going to take this lying down, she has another thing coming.

Her eyes are wild as she comes at me again, trying to claw at my face. "You just had to come back and ruin everything, didn't you? You couldn't be happy with what you had. You had to take what was mine too." Her words come out in pants as she tries to attack me. I try to hold her off, but her fingernails rake down my cheek, and I hiss as she breaks the skin. You'd think with the amount of self-defense classes I've taken, I'd be better at fending off bullshit attacks like this. I really am rusty. I reach up and touch my cheek. The warm, wet of the blood on my fingertips makes me see red.

Fuck this shit. I push her backward and punch her in her already delicate nose. She should've learned last time.

Her wail is enough to pierce my eardrum as she falls flat on her ass, clutching her nose. Her eyes narrow at me, and she actually fucking smiles. She's a fucking psycho. "You'll pay for this, you little bitch."

Blair gets up and stalks away, leaving me wondering what the fuck just happened. I reach up, hissing as I touch my stinging cheek. My fingers touch the blood that trickles down my face, and my rage pulses inside of me again. I turn back to Indi, who is sucking down her coffee like she's watching a movie, and I can't help but laugh. "Enjoy the show?"

"Like you wouldn't believe," she grins. "Watching her fall flat on her ass with a potentially broken nose, again, brings me way more joy than it should."

"Any idea what any of that was about?" I ask as I grab my bag, and she hands me my mostly melted iced coffee.

She shakes her head and pulls a wet wipe from her bag, handing it to me. "For your face. And no, I have no fucking idea. She's a legit psychopath, though, so it could be anything."

I take a sip of my drink and take the wet wipe compact she offers me so I can clean up my face. I swear cuts like this sting way more than a deep wound. I'm generally fine with pain, my threshold is pretty high, but fuck, that stings. "Well, that was a fun start to the day. I wonder what other joys this day will hold."

"At least life is never boring?" Indi offers as she tucks the compact into her bag.

I shrug and let out a sigh. "A little bit of boring might be a nice change of pace, though."

I finally turn back to head into school and notice the large crowd of people watching us. Of course there were people here. That's probably why she did it. And I reacted. What a *dick.* I should know better by now.

*Do not react to the crazy people.*

I keep my head held high, ignoring the whispers that follow me into the building about being an unhinged whore. Because despite no one being in my face about it, and the fact that all traces of the sex tape are gone from the internet, I know some of these assholes still have it. They still talk about it and call me a slut or a skank. But these people don't mean anything to me, and that's what I have to keep reminding myself of.

The world has written lies about me and my family almost my entire life. This is just another one to add to the list. The people who know me know the truth.

At least, I hold onto the hope that they do.

I take a breath and steel myself against this day. It can't get any worse than this, right?

---

Yesterday morning was such a shit show that Indi and I chose to have lunch off campus at Joe's. There was no way I was heading into the cafeteria for more bullshit. First Blair, then the whispers, and then in Music, Raleigh acted like he didn't even send those messages while we were at the spa, trying to be my friend again.

I can't even deal with this place this week. Lucky for me, I have the world's greatest bestie.

So today, as we head into the school I cross my fingers and hope for a better day. We pass Lincoln, Maverick, and Finley standing on the steps like a group of dark gods surveying their subjects. My gaze is pulled to them as we climb the stairs. I can't help but take in the way they command respect from those around them, even in silence. Each of them drips with the type of confidence you can only be born with. Everything about them screams power, attitude, and raw fucking sex appeal. I almost hate how undeniably hot they all are, my mind drifting to exactly what they could each be capable of. I try to shake the images from my brain.

Nope, I'm not going there.

As we get closer, I realize the only thing they're actually watching is me, like I'm their possession and their enemy all at once. Even Lincoln, who's acting like he hasn't spent every night until last curled around me in my bed.

"Octavia," Lincoln starts, and I swear to fuck I nearly trip up the goddamn stairs. Why am I such a mess around these guys? "You have a minute?"

I look at Indi, who shrugs and crosses her arms. I swear this entire place has me just trying to catch up. I don't get why everything has to be so complicated. "Uhm, sure."

Lincoln pulls me to the bottom of the stairs and back toward my car so we have a little privacy. I'm positive that the other two know exactly what he's talking to me about, and I'm definitely going to tell Indi, so it seems a bit much, but fuck it.

He scowls at a group of kids walking toward us. They squeak and walk around the cars rather than passing us directly. "You don't have to be so cruel, you know." I sigh, and he turns his glare on me before rolling his eyes.

He rubs his fingers against his temples before looking back at me. "You've been gone too long. You have no idea how this place works."

Now who's being dramatic? I know this place is shady as shit, but he could leave as easily as I did if he wanted to. "What did you want to talk to me about?"

His eyes flash, and I watch conflict play out on his face. I have no idea what that's about or why he's giving me a peek behind the mask he wears like a second skin, but I see when he changes his mind about whatever it is he was thinking about before he starts to speak. "The video from the weekend. I know a guy, so if you want it taken down, I can handle it."

My eyes go wide at his offer. This definitely isn't what I was expecting him to say. "Why are you being nice to me?"

I can't help but be suspicious, truce or not.

He glares at me again. I swear his face is going to get stuck that way if he isn't careful.

"We called a truce, remember? Plus, if East mopes around much more, I'll have to make him move out. He's still being pissy with me, and it's fucking with my chill."

And now it all makes sense. He's thick as thieves with Finley and Maverick, but he and East have always been weirdly close. Their bond's the kind that nothing could ever break.

"Well, thank you, but unless shit turns dark, it's not the end of the world. I don't have the media banging down my door this time, so this is the kind of viral I can handle."

He nods at my comment, like he expected as much. I'm pretty sure I wouldn't accept his help, truce or not. After everything that's happened since I came back, I don't see me ever going to him for anything. Whether he's helped with my nightmares or not. I'm still not convinced he wasn't the one responsible for causing them. "Okay, if you need help, you know where to find me."

"Was that it?" I ask, at a loss as to why he'd pull me aside for that. His eyes rake over me, and the conflict from before is back. I'm beyond curious what's going on inside his head. There was a time not too long ago when he couldn't hide anything from me.

Things were so much simpler back then.

Unfortunately, I don't have a crystal ball or a time machine. Either would be useful these days, but I don't live in a fantasy universe. I mean, I wouldn't pass up the opportunity for a mind reading superpower either. That might make my life simpler too.

His jaw sets, and I know he's made up his mind. "Yeah, that was everything. Have a good day." He walks away from me, leaving me slack-jawed staring after him. Nothing about Lincoln Saint makes sense to me anymore.

I walk toward Indi, and we head inside. "What was that about?"

"Absolutely nothing." I run her over the whole encounter, and she looks as baffled as I feel.

She shakes her head as we walk down the hall. "The people here make absolutely no sense to me."

We head to my locker so I can sort out my books, and the main door slams closed. I look up and see Raleigh stalking toward us.

"Incoming," Indi murmurs, moving so she's standing just in front of me. I really do love her, and it's been so much fun watching her come into her own.

"Morning," she practically sings at him, making herself an obstacle before he can get to me. He straight up ignores her and stares daggers at me instead.

He folds his arms across his chest, practically vibrating with rage. I do not understand this guy at all. I thought I was good at reading people, but apparently I misjudged him a lot. "Why were you talking to Saint? I thought you hated him."

Indi rolls her eyes before chirping up. "Hi, Indi, how are you doing? Yeah, I'm great, thanks, did you have a good weekend?"

He glances over at her before pinning me with his stare again. I have exactly zero desire to justify myself to him, so I don't bother. "Whatever this is about, Raleigh, it's a you problem." The bell rings, saving me from this entire situation. "I need to get to class. When you have your shit together, come find me."

He clenches his fists, but I spin to shut my locker then head down the hall with Indi toward English.

Could this day possibly get any weirder?

---

My afternoon breezes by pretty easily. Lincoln was almost nice in Business, and it shocked the shit out of me. Not to mention, Blair was noticeably absent after our run-in earlier today. It would've been nice if her bitch squad wasn't in hyper mode about what happened while we were in Gym, but East shut them down so beautifully I almost wept.

There's nothing better than seeing bitches put in their place by the guy they simp over so much.

"V, you got a minute?" East asks as we're heading to the lockers after Gym finishes, and I can't help but laugh at how alike he and Lincoln are. I say a quick goodbye to Indi before turning and heading back to East.

I haven't really seen him much outside of class since the whole *him saving me and making the others call a truce* thing. I should probably thank him for what he did, but the time I spent in his bed after being locked away made things feel weird and tense between us. I'm at a bit of a loss about what to even say to him now that we're alone. "What's up?"

He looks more than a little conflicted when he looks down at me. "How are you doing? With everything?"

I tuck my hair behind my ear where it's escaped my ponytail, wishing this didn't feel so freaking awkward. "I'm okay. The nightmares have almost stopped now. So I'm actually mostly good."

He clenches his jaw and uncurls his fists. "Nightmares?"

My eyes go wide because I figured if Lincoln heard my screams, he would've too. "Yeah, I thought you knew. Lincoln said he could hear my screams when he…" I shake my head, trying not to trip over my words or let it slip that Lincoln snuck in my room and stayed more than a few times when I definitely shouldn't have let him.

"When Lincoln what?"

"Nothing, it isn't important. I'm sorry I haven't been around much since that weekend. I still haven't thanked you properly." I wring out my hands, trying to think of a way to make it up to him. "You want to hang out soon? Maybe have a pizza and Xbox night or something?"

He beams at me in a way that makes my heart race. "Yeah, that sounds like fun. Let me know when."

"I'm free tomorrow if you want to chill?" I swear I feel like a girl who's never hung out with a guy before. East literally bathed and dressed me when I was catatonic, and now I'm a blushing mess over a night of pizza and Xbox? God, I'm so lame.

He grins and runs a hand through his light brown tresses, and butterflies erupt in my stomach. "Sounds good. I'll text you later?"

"Okay." I nod before turning and heading toward the locker room. I can't help but glance at him as I walk away and catch him checking me out. He has the decency to blush, and I laugh, shaking my head as I leave the room.

Most people have already left by the time I hit the locker rooms, and Indi's sitting on the bench flicking through her phone when I reach her. "You don't have to wait. I'm going to shower and then head home. Tonight is totally a study night for me."

She smiles up at me and slides her phone into her pocket. "Okay, sweet cheeks. I'm going to go catch Jackson. But don't book Friday night up. I have plans for us." She winks at me as she stands, and I laugh a little.

"How mysterious."

"Jackson told me about a fight night that's happening. Sweaty hotties, all kinds of adrenaline… It's just yummy." Her grin is so devious, I love it.

A thought hits me and puts a damper on it. "Is Jackson going?" I don't tag on Raleigh's name, but it's more than implied.

"Nope," she says, popping her p. "He was complaining that he couldn't go because of the game."

My grin is firmly in place as I grab my crap from my locker. "Perfect! I'm there."

"Fabulous. I'll see you in the morning." She waves before floating out of the locker room, and I realize I actually have plans like a normal teenager, like, twice this week.

Who would've thought?

I hurry through my shower, not washing my hair, and change into my uniform before heading out. East is leaving the gym as I reach the hall, and he grins at me. "You're running late."

"I wonder why." I stick my tongue out at him, and he bumps his shoulder against mine. We walk through the halls, keeping a reasonable distance. Despite the fact that he's only four years older than me, and we've been friends our entire lives, he's still my teacher, and people are weird as shit about stuff like that. Especially the petty jealous bitches around here who simp over him and wouldn't think twice about trying to fuck me over.

I can't help but wonder what it would be like to date East. It's not only that he's beautiful and has a body that would make the gods weep. The protective side of him both drives me nuts and makes me gooey all at the same time. He's just so fucking nice, which doesn't sound like the compliment I mean it to be, but that doesn't make it any less true either.

He opens the main door for me, and I walk through, smiling at him. But then he looks over my shoulder and his smile drops. He looks fucking terrified.

What the hell?

I look around and find Lincoln, Maverick, and Finley facing off with a guy who makes Maverick look like an upstanding citizen. His black hair musses in the wind, and his ebony eyes are fixated on the boys until he looks up and sees me. His angry look shifts to a maniacal grin.

East moves to stand in front of me, blocking me from the view of whoever is standing with the others. "What do you want, Ryker?"

It takes a second, but it hits me who he is. Ryker Donovan. The Kingpin of ECH. Holy shit, he looks different from how I remember him. He grew up a *lot.* He's easily as tall as Lincoln, with the same fighters build as Maverick, but every inch of skin I can see below his chin is covered in tattoos.

"I came to pay a visit to your brother and to remind him of a few things. Though, I see why he's been so distracted now." His gravelly voice turns my blood cold.

Is he talking about me?

I refuse to cower behind East, so I step beside him and cross my arms.

Belatedly, I notice the gun in Ryker's hand.

*How the fuck is this happening?*

Ryker raises the pistol, and Maverick saunters toward him like he gives absolutely zero fucks that the guy has a gun pointed at him. My heart leaps to my throat, and the world slows to almost a stop as Mav leans forward and puts his forehead against the end of the gun, grinning like the crazy son of a bitch that he is. "Don't raise a gun at me unless you're willing to pull the trigger, Donovan."

I swear I can't fucking breathe. What the fuck is he doing?

Ryker lowers the gun and tucks it in the back of his jeans, and I feel like I can finally breathe again before Ryker looks over at Finley and Lincoln. East is a fucking statue at my side, and I have no idea what we've stumbled into. Whatever it is, I want no fucking part of it.

Ryker crosses his arms over his chest, and Maverick laughs. Ryker gives him the bird and looks over at East and I before looking back to Lincoln and Finley. "Tell the Knights to back off. I'm not bowing down."

Without waiting for anyone to say anything, he climbs into the idling car behind him and peels out of the lot.

The Knights? Finley's family?

I'm so confused.

Lincoln looks over at me before glancing at East. He looks more afraid than I've ever seen him.

*What the fuck are they mixed up in?*

# CHAPTER TWENTY-THREE

## MAVERICK

Well, that couldn't have gone worse. I mean, people could've been shot, so I guess it actually could've; but of course Octavia showed up. And of course Ryker had to see her. I swear, every time we think we have shit figured out, she does something that blows it all to pieces.

It doesn't matter how hard I try to keep a distance from her, it's like I end up gravitating toward her. Like she's the sun at the center of my universe, and it pisses me off like nothing I've ever experienced.

"What the fuck was that?" I look up at the sky, sucking in a breath, ready to do anything I can to distract her from what Donovan just said. Her knowing what he meant could ruin everything. We've worked too hard to have this blow up in our faces now.

I turn to face her while Linc and Finn do what they do best and plot. East looks at a loss for words, leaving this fully in my lap. I smile the most sadistic smile I can muster and stalk toward her as East moves to talk to the others. We might have called a truce, but that doesn't mean I'm not still convinced that leaving's the best thing for her.

Once I'm in her personal space, crowding her so she can't see the others, I lean down until my nose almost touches her. "What's wrong, princess? A little bit of real life too much for you?"

She rears back, and I can see how much my words hurt as the fire in her eyes dims a little. As much as I hate hurting her, if it'll keep her safe, then I'll do it until I'm so broken there's no coming back. I'm no stranger to pain.

Her eyes go wide, and my dick twitches at how innocent she looks right now. Her soulful brown eyes are like windows to who she really is. Even when she tries to hide, I can see her.

I've always seen her.

"You're such an asshole, Maverick," she hisses, and she clenches her fists.

Fuck, I'd love to see her unleash the fiery rage I know lives deep inside her. The thought of her repressed rage makes me hotter than how innocent she looks. This girl has always been my weak spot—the one person with the power to truly ruin me. Not that I'll ever let her know that.

So I smirk at her again and get in her space, tucking a lock of her dark hair behind her ear. "Oh, princess, you have no idea." I walk her backward until her back connects with the wall. I lift one arm and place my hand on the brick over her head, boxing her in. "But if you ask real nice, I could show you."

She scoffs at my words, realizing belatedly that I've pinned her in. She slams her hands against my chest pushing me off, and hot damn, that fire is out for all to see today. Her chest heaves as she sucks in a breath, and I can practically see her trying to pull in her rage. I wish she'd let it all out instead.

"What's up, princess, things not so fun outside of your ivory tower?" The taunts roll from my razor sharp tongue so easily. Mostly because I pretend I'm not speaking to her. It's easier that way. I've been in love with Octavia Royal my entire life, but I agreed with Linc when we were all inducted. Keeping her safe is the most important thing, and if that means I have to deny myself from having her, then that's what it takes.

"Fuck you." Her breathy words give away how affected by me she is, and it makes the hunter inside of me excited. I do love to taunt and chase my prey.

"Oh, sweetheart, you're practically begging for it, aren't you? I saw how much you wanted it when Finn had you pinned against the wall in the pool house. I saw everything, including how much you enjoyed it when Lincoln was between your thighs."

Her eyes flash with a mix of lust and anger, my favorite mix.

"I saw how much you enjoyed me watching you too," I murmur, and she rolls her eyes, pushing me even further away from her. I'm kind of impressed. I'm not exactly an easy guy to move. On one hand, I like knowing that she could probably fight off anyone who was trying to fuck with her, and I know she can throw a punch. Her cousin's broken nose is proof enough of that. On the other hand, all her fight does is make me want to push her harder, to see how much it would take to snap the controlled restraint she has.

My eyes flare at the thought of it. She pushes past me, slamming me with her shoulder as she does, and heads toward her car. My eyes stalk after her as I watch her leave. "That's it, V, run away. You've always been good at that."

She flips me the bird as she climbs into her car. Only once she's in with the door closed, do I head over to my boys to find out what's been going on while I handled the girl we've all been so fucked up over.

When I reach the group, East glares at me. "You look like you enjoyed that way too much."

"Just taking one for the team." I shrug, and his eyes narrow at me, telling me that I'm pissing him off even more. "What did I miss?"

Unsurprisingly, Linc's the one who answers me. "I'm catching East up on the conversation we were having with Ryker before he showed up with Octavia."

"We really need to deal with him and his little gun toting buddies. He can't just show up here with a fucking weapon like that," I growl, and Finn nods his agreement. "This little rivalry is becoming too much of an issue, and we have bigger things to worry about."

I bounce on the balls of my feet. All this anxious energy makes me wish Ryker had pushed me a little harder. Given me a reason to end this stupid rivalry with my fists.

"The rivalry was started by the football teams even if it escalated way beyond that. I'll deal with it," East pipes up, glancing over to V. Of course he's trying to play it down since she's here, in case she hears, but she's not stupid. She'll see through it. I wish it was just a football rivalry still. The minute the Knights set their sights on Ryker, Ellis, and their brother's business, it became more. He huffs before turning to his brother. "We still need to find out who broke into V's house and locked her up like that. Since you three insist it wasn't you."

I grind my teeth at the reminder. I saw her when he carried her to his house the morning he found her. My shock at seeing her in his arms was all too real. Doing that to her is one of my biggest regrets, and I hate myself for it but we thought it would make her leave, and well… Let's just say my fights in the cage have been extra bloody ever since.

The noise of her engine starting makes everyone pause. I don't take my eyes off her until she's out of the lot and I'm sure she's not coming back.

"We need to reassess. What started as a simple year and a reasonably clear chessboard has turned into a fucking riotous mess." Lincoln sighs, pinching the bridge of his nose. "I need to think. The Knights have us bent over a fucking barrel, and I don't like it. If we're not making Octavia leave, we need to think of another way to keep her safe, all while dealing with Ryker and his little band of wannabe bangers. Not to mention we have to figure out whoever the hell it is that seems to be hunting Octavia."

A growl passes my lips at the thought. The only person that should be hunting her is me. "I think I can get some answers at The Nest this weekend."

"I'll come with you. Divide and conquer," Finn adds, and I nod. I'm never against having a wingman with me in that place. I might have gotten into the underground fights as a way to hone my skills before I'm old enough to fight officially, but it's turned into a treasure trove of secrets from the scum that live in the snake pit that is Echoes Cove. Plus, Finn's quiet demeanor scares the shit out of people. Quiet but deadly is his entire persona.

Except for when it comes to V.

Though sometimes, especially when it comes to her.

"We're not going to figure everything out tonight. Let's get out of here before we try to work anything else out. I'm meeting with David about the security at Octavia's since Smithy's still out of town," East says quietly. "I'm going to see if there's any clear footage that captures the faces of whoever broke in. So speak up now if it was you fuckers."

Finn spears him with a look that would have him bleeding out if looks could kill. "It wasn't us."

His ice cold tone is enough to send a shiver down even my spine. I mean, I can see why East would think it was us, and usually we wouldn't lie to him, especially when it comes to her. After our usual go-to guys got way too carried away the last few times we used them, there was no way Linc was outsourcing that particular taunt. But I think the other two regret it as much as I do. What he doesn't know is that there's no way our faces are on any of those tapes. Finley's a tech fucking genius; he already made sure of it.

"Fine," East says with a nod. "You three need to work out your shit with the board. If this keeps getting out of hand, we're going to have to do what they want, no matter how much we hate it."

Lincoln practically vibrates with rage. I don't blame him. East was happy to step back and let Lincoln shoulder all the responsibility that came with the bullshit legacy our families handed down to us. Now he's trying to tell us what to do, all because V's back. It rankles even me.

"Any more leads on who keeps sending her those fucking packages?" Finn asks, looking at Linc who shakes his head.

"That's another fucking unanswered question. I know it's not the board since it isn't their style. Way too creepy. I think I've managed to intercept all of the packages so far. Today's gift was an envelope of pictures. Whoever it is has been stalking our girl hard."

"How do we not know who it is yet? And how are there this many people after her? It's like she's a magnet for psychopaths," East grinds out, his fists clenching, and I can't help but laugh. I'm the only psychopath she needs in her life. I'll eliminate the others through any means necessary.

"I'm on it," Linc snaps, and East nods as he turns to leave. "We'll continue this at my place," Lincoln growls through his teeths before he stalks to his Porsche looking like he's angry enough to kill someone. If only that's the first time this year he's done that.

I look at Finn and clap a hand on his shoulder. "Come on, we better head out. You know he'll pitch a fit if we keep him waiting when he's in this mood." Linc speeds out of the parking lot, almost as if proving my point.

"You want burgers?" he asks, shrugging out of his blazer before unlocking his Lamborghini. I grab my helmet and leather jacket from the passenger seat and grin at him.

"You know I do."

"I'll swing by and grab some on the way and then meet you there."

I move over to my Ducati and swing my leg over so the powerful machine is between my legs. I shrug into my jacket and grasp my helmet in my hand as I start the bike. "Sounds good to me."

He shakes his head at me as I rev the engine. The purr of his car has nothing on the roar of my bike, but he loves that car like nothing else. I suppose if I'd sacrificed what he had for it, I'd love it like that too. I'm pretty sure the only thing he loves more than his car is Octavia. She hung the moon for him from the first moment she arrived in our class all those years ago.

We all have our own shit to handle, but we agreed when we were inducted that we'd keep her out of it for as long as we could, whatever it took.

I slide my helmet over my head and walk the bike back as it rumbles between my legs.

Octavia might hate us right now, but we'll do whatever it takes to protect her. Even if that means spilling more blood than anyone's ever seen.

---

This fucking week has been enough to push a saint to kill. So my sinning, pitch black soul's shit out of luck. It's why I grin so hard as blood drips from my knuckles and splatters across my chest.

The tall, scrawny guy in the cage with me is one of the assholes we think has been sending the creepy as shit gifts to V. Whether she knows about them or not, I'm going to get answers out of this dick. I'd really rather she never find out about any of this.

The guy staggers toward me, barely able to stay on his feet. I catch a flash of brown hair behind him, and it distracts me enough for him to land a punch on my jaw.

*Focus, Mav.*

I shake my head to clear it. There's no way V knows about this place. I swear I see her fucking everywhere.

I shake off the hit and bounce around this dickhead, jabbing him so much he groans as he falls to his knees.

I bark out a laugh at how easy this fight was. I really need to make sure my other opponents for the night are more of a challenge, otherwise the rampant rage burning in my veins won't find the outlet it so desperately needs.

I finish him with an Achilles style punch to the temple, and his eyes roll back in his head as he slumps. He's face down on the ground as the bell sounds and cheers go up around the warehouse.

The ref comes in and lifts my arm, officially declaring me the winner before making sure my opponent isn't actually dead. I pause for a second until he confirms it, looking out into the crowd. I catch sight of the flash of brown hair again and narrow my eyes until I can see that it's actually her moving through the crowd.

I run a bloody hand down my face and groan.

*What the fuck is she doing here?*

I jump down from the cage and search through the crowd for her. Once I find her, my eyes narrow in her direction. We've done everything to try and keep her safe, and she strolls into this vipers' nest like nothing fucking matters.

Adrenaline rushes through my veins, and I'm high on the win of my fight as I stalk toward her. I know she sees me because her eyes go wide as she sucks in a breath. The way her chest heaves does things to me it definitely shouldn't, but I'm over denying myself of Octavia Royal. She spins on her heel and walks away, trying to escape me, which makes me grin.

*Oh how I love to hunt my prey.*

It doesn't take me long to reach her as the crowd parts like the Red Sea before me. These people know not to fuck with me.

I grab her arm and spin her around forcibly. She rips herself out of my grasp, eyes narrowed.

Fuck, I love her fire.

The high of the chase, of catching her, and her retaliating struggle… All she's doing is making my dick harder than it's ever been. She came here for me, to watch me fight. I know it. Her being here tells me all I need to know.

There are a lot less people down this hall of the pit, so I let myself be the animal I know I am. I want her. She wants me. I can see it in the flush of her skin. In the way her eyes go wide as she looks up at me. I grab her chin, my large hand spanning across her cheek and neck, and shove her against the wall. Her gasp rocks me, making me impossibly harder as her eyes dilate.

She wants this as much as I do. I watch as she ghosts her tongue along her bottom lip, and it's like a red flag to a bull.

I push my body against hers, and her eyes flash when she feels how hard I am. "You shouldn't run from me, V."

That fire returns to her as she pushes on my chest, but she isn't going to move me. Not when I'm finally where I've wanted to be since she came back. "Fuck you."

My grin widens as she struggles in my grasp. Fuck, I love the fight in her. Stoking that fire in her is going to be so fucking sweet, I can almost taste it. Taste her.

I crush my lips against hers, stroking my tongue against her lip like I just watched her do, unable to resist any longer. I tighten my hold on her throat. She resists me a little more, pushing against me; and I almost stop, but I've waited long enough to claim her.

The second I feel her soft, plump lips part, I know what I've always known. She's mine to claim.

*Mine.*

# CHAPTER TWENTY-FOUR

## OCTAVIA

Maverick fucking Riley has me trapped against a wall, devouring me. As much as I hate it, I can't help but love it too.

If I said I hadn't thought about what being with him would be like, I'd be lying. Fighting against him is a token resistance. Fighting's in my nature. If I wanted him off me, I wouldn't crave him as much as I do.

His lips are brutal, taking and claiming, and my mouth falls open slightly on its own accord. I'm almost putty in his hands.

*Almost.*

I slam my palms against his chest and push, breaking his kiss so I can breathe. I'm beyond dizzy right now. It doesn't matter how much I might want him. I'll never forgive him for what he's done to me. I can't.

"Get off me, you fucking asshole!" I try to put as much fire and spit into my insult, but even I can't escape the breathy edge to my words. His sheer presence, boxing me in like this, makes me wet. His lips turn up into a devilish grin. I have zero doubts that he knows exactly how wet I am. He all but confirms it with the way he looks down at my half exposed tits in my low-cut tank. He licks his swollen lips.

That, however, is no reason to give in.

Never.

"The lady doth protest too much—" He tightens his hold on my throat, his fingers digging into the flesh to the point I'm afraid I might actually pass out. He trails his nose up my cheek, and my body betrays me as a shiver runs down my spine.

Fuck, the move turns me on, but I can't let him know. His entire upper body bends just enough for his nose to blaze a trail of fire across the skin of my neck, inhaling like a fucking animal before its attack. "—her pussy doth beg to be fucked, way too fucking much."

"Shakespeare was a poet, not a pig like you." I can barely hear my words with his fingers locked so tightly around my neck. I clench my hands at my sides.

"What can I say, V, I like it dirty."

Then his mouth crashes back on mine, his tongue breaching the space between my lips without waiting for any kind of verbal consent. My mind screams at me to run, but my body's primed for the attack. Wanting this. Waiting for it, like I've waited for him my whole life.

For a second, I let the fantasy take over. I enjoy the reprieve of this intimate moment. For a brief second, I forget that this guy's the reason for the literal hell I've lived through since coming home. I forget that he hates me, and that I *want* to hate him. Truce or not.

Our tongues battle for control, stroking against each other like silk, even though we both know he holds the control in the palm of his hand. A hand that's hellishly close to choking the life out of me. I can't explain it, but I fucking love it.

Rubbing my thighs together and trying like hell to ignore the fire between my legs, I wonder if something is seriously wrong with me. Why is this turning me on? Why the fuck do I love this so much?

Maverick groans into my mouth. His body is a punishing weight, caging me in so that no one can see us—see me—and that movement reminds me of where we are. That people can see us. And then like a film reel going backward in time, all the shit he's put me through flashes through my mind. Reminding me of all the reasons this is an incredibly stupid and bad idea.

My hands that pushed him away earlier, press against his sweaty, deliciously inked skin now. My nails curl around his pecs, digging into his flesh and hopefully drawing blood. He deserves the kiss of pain, even if I'm almost sure he gets off on it.

Good sense slams into me, and I'm able to push him away enough to break the kiss once more.

"Get off me!"

"Oh, baby, I thought you'd never ask."

*What?*

In an instant, his free hand is at my ass, two fingers slipping inside my super short cutoffs, pushing past the thong and making me gasp into his waiting mouth as he returns to his kiss.

An unexpected moan slips from my lips as Maverick thrusts his fingers inside of me. I can feel him smile against me when he feels how fucking wet I am. In an instant, I'm a slave to what my body desires. I can't help but groan at how good it feels. He fucks my pussy with his fingers like he owns it, all the while thousands of people are milling around us like nothing out of the usual is going on.

I slam my eyes shut, refusing to let everything else filter in as I stand here at his mercy.

I freak out a little at the fact that anyone could see us. Anyone could catch us, and after everything I've already experienced these last few months, having this caught on video is the last thing I want. The thought gives me pause as I try to push him away again, but my movements are weak, and I feel his grin against my skin as he kisses me harder. He's treating this like a simple game of push and pull to him.

The span of his large hand is across the lower end of my ass, while two of his fingers are pumping inside me. It makes it really fucking hard to concentrate on anything other than the pending orgasm that I do not want him to witness. I don't want any of these people to witness what's going on here. Yet something about the thrill of getting caught almost makes me hotter, and I feel goosebumps burst over my skin.

Almost is the key word here.

I don't want him to know he has an effect on me, which is ridiculous since he can feel my reaction to him as it coats his fingers.

Maverick pulls back slightly from our kiss, his teeth pressing together with my bottom lip trapped between them as he slams his fingers so deep I nearly buckle under the ecstasy of it all. To anyone passing by, we're a couple making out against a wall, kissing like teenagers often do. They probably wouldn't even notice us with the amount of debauchery that's normal in this place, but it's still enough of a thought to give me pause.

Meanwhile, he's getting me off without even asking me what I want. Like he already knows and doesn't need my input. As his teeth free my lip, I take the opportunity to bite down on his lip. Hard. Hard enough to taste the tanginess of blood as I cut him open in the process. I hate that this motherfucker seems to know my body better than I do.

I thought he'd be pissed and storm off, but as I open my eyes, I see his lighting up. His tongue leisurely swipes at his lip, collecting the blood, and then he licks mine like he's coating them with lipstick.

At that exact moment, it occurs to me that he's an actual fucking psychopath. He adds another finger to my pussy, stretching me to a point I've never experienced, and it makes my knees weak.

Fuck, he knows what he's doing.

He presses even closer against me and rubs his hard cock against the seam of my shorts, hitting my clit like he knows exactly where it is.

My breath catches, and I can feel my eyes widen at the knowledge that I'm about to explode in a public space with thousands of adrenaline-pumped assholes roaming around. The gleam in Maverick's eyes tells me that our location's a huge fucking turn-on for him. I'm pretty sure no one can see what he's doing, but the risk is there, and he's loving every second of it.

It's when he pulls me away from the wall and turns me around like a rag doll that I understand how much control he really has over me. With one hand in my hair, pulling it toward him so he can tower over me and force me to watch his face, now my body faces the wall he uses his other hand to push my shorts down far enough that he can slide his impossibly hard cock between my thighs.

"What the fuck are you doing?" I wish I was screaming at him, but my voice comes out breathy and horny.

"Whatever I fucking want and right now, I want to feel your dripping wet cunt all over my dick."

Without giving me the time to register his next move, he buries his cock deep inside me, filling me to the point of madness. It doesn't hurt like I thought it might, and any sting of pain is lost in the amount of ecstasy I'm drowning in.

I can feel his entire body huddled around me as he bends and thrusts inside me like an animal, like a beast taken over by his baser instincts.

Feral.

Brutal.

Savage.

All of the fucking above, and I'm the prey that's about to come all over his cock. Apparently, I've lost my fucking mind because being treated like a fuck toy is my jam.

I hate him.

I hate this.

But I also can't stop loving it.

I want it. I want more. I want it harder.

To my horror, I say those last words out loud, and the sound that comes from Maverick's throat reminds me of a lion grunting while it fucks its lioness into submission.

Because that's what this is. Maverick's punishing me by fucking the fight out of me, and I'm the crazy bitch loving every second of it.

"You're so fucking wet, don't try to deny that you love this fucked up shit." I don't deny it, not because I don't want to lie, but because speaking is impossible. All I can do is feel.

Feel his velvety dick slam through the walls of my pussy.

Feel the head of his cock ram into my cervix.

Feel his balls slapping against me every time he thrusts impossibly deeper and then deeper still.

"Get the fuck out of here, or I'll slit your throat from ear to ear, motherfucker."

My body freezes at the growl of Maverick's words.

Is he talking to me?

My silent question is answered when I hear a faint, "Sorry, man, my bad."

Fuck. Someone saw me.

I want to care, but when Maverick goes back to pistoning his hips, all other thoughts evaporate.

"Christ, you're even wetter than before. You like that, don't you, you little fucking slut? You like it when total strangers watch you get fucked from behind? Maybe I should fuck your ass. You want that?"

My traitorous body shivers at his words.

My ass?

Hell no.

Yet…

"Oh yeah, you fucking whore. You want me to take your ass, don't you? I bet it's a virgin ass, isn't it?"

To my horror, Maverick slides out of my pussy and glides his wet dick between my ass cheeks making a show of his head circling my asshole.

Oh God.

No. No, no, no.

But curiosity begs me to open up for him, giving him what he would take anyway.

"Yeah, that's what I thought. Good whores like it in the ass."

But he doesn't go through with it. He slams into my pussy and fucks me like he owns me, one hand still pulling my hair, my face angled straight at his face where I can see a sheen of sweat making an appearance on his forehead.

Simultaneously, his free hand reaches around for my clit as his mouth slants over mine and his tongue demands entrance. I fight him on it. Our mouths battle like a war is on the line. A sudden scream escapes me, but no one hears because Maverick's mouth swallows every one of my sounds. He's devouring me, eating up all of my pleasure as he fucks my mouth as thoroughly as his dick fucks my pussy.

I'm shaking in his grasp as the orgasm takes over my entire body, and my legs are unable to hold my weight as the waves crash through me again and again. The power shuts down every one of my synapses. All the while, Maverick owns me, gorging on me like I'm the last drop of water in an endless sea of sand. I feel him freeze behind me, his breaths feeding me as his dick swells inside me. He suddenly pulls out and comes all over my ass, spreading my cheeks to make sure he coats me all over my asshole. It's hot—a psychopath's wet dream.

It's only once the pleasure's gone that I remember he's the enemy and I hate him. He took my moans, but he doesn't get to take my fucking pride with him.

"I told you to get off me, you fucker!"

"My bad, I thought you asked me to get you off."

"You're an asshole." I spit the words at him for effect, hoping I'm as feral as I feel.

After dipping three fingers in my still soaked pussy like he's collecting honey from a beehive, he puts them in his mouth and sucks on them like a damn lollipop. "Your wish is my command. Next time, I'll just fuck your ass."

I pull my shorts back up over my ass, the remnants of my orgasm ghosting my skin as he trails his fingers over my hips. I look up and he has the fucking audacity to give me a good little boy grin like he's the preacher's son.

*Fuck that.*

"You can dream, I guess. This isn't happening again." He takes advantage of my open lips and pushes his wet fingers into my gaping mouth.

I can taste myself and him all mixed together, and it does something to me. My tongue slips against his callous tips without thought, and I lose myself to him again. It stirs up things inside of me that shouldn't be there. I shouldn't be feeling any of this. I don't want it.

This has to stay as something he will never know I feel.

*Ever.*

"Screw you!" I cry out once I free myself of him and his spell, pushing everything rising up inside of me down, before ducking out from under his huge, sweaty arm. The cords of his triceps pull tight as he strains against the wall.

He grabs my arm, looking as menacing as he did in the cage earlier, and my body tenses. "Go home, V. And fucking stay there. Nobody wants you here."

"He did what?" Indi screeches as we climb into my car. To say I hauled ass out of that warehouse after escaping Maverick's clutches is an understatement. The guy is giving me severe whiplash.

"He, uhm… well… we fucked." I shrug, glazing over the whole I just lost my virginity thing, because I don't put much stock in the whole virginity thing.

I start the engine as she squeaks beside me, fully losing her shit. "How exactly did this happen?"

I pull the car out of the space and head out of the run-down, old industrial area of Echoes Cove, trying to find the words to explain this properly. "He, uhm, grabbed me, and well, shoved me against a wall."

Indi slams her hand against the dash and curses. "He forced himself on you? Fuck me, I'll kill him. Who gives a fuck about jail. I'll saw his dick off."

"He didn't force himself… exactly. There were mixed wires, and while my brain was in two minds about it all, my body was definitely on board. I could have stopped it if I'd wanted to. Maverick Riley is a lot of things, but he isn't a rapist."

She grumbles incoherently under her breath as I cross the train tracks and the buildings begin gradually turning back into the picture of wealth that Echoes Cove likes to portray itself as. "Was it good at least?"

I bark out a laugh. Of course that's her next question once she knows I'm okay. "It was possibly the best orgasm I've ever had."

She whistles before grinning over at me with a shit-eating grin. "Hot damn. Why are the psychos always the best in bed?"

"I don't know, but uh… How would you know?" I poke at her, and she blushes, shaking her head, so I leave it for now. I'm sure she'll share when she's ready. "Anyway, it won't be happening again, no matter how good it was. This was a blip. A lapse in judgement. It absolutely can't happen again."

She scoffs and crosses her arms, moving in her seat so she's facing out the windshield. "We'll see. 'Cause, girl, they might act like they hate you, but I've seen how all three… no wait, how all four of them look at you when they think no one's watching. Now that's a party I'd insert myself into. No offense."

"None taken. But that plan's not in the cards. I'm here to graduate—to get the grades I need to finalize the terms of my dad's Will—and get into college. There's a whole world out there, and I have plans. The four of them don't factor into them, no matter how pretty they are. They made that choice when I arrived." I clutch the steering wheel, hating how the words taste like lies on my tongue, despite the fact that I absolutely intend on them being true.

"Girl," she drags out the word, and I can't help but laugh. "If you say so."

We spend the rest of the short drive to her place in a comfortable silence, with just the sounds of Brynn Cartelli's "Last Night's Mascara" playing through the sound system. I pull to a stop in front of her house, the brakes squeaking a little as I do.

"Thank you for coming with me tonight," she says, leaning over and hugging me. "Even if it ended up being more fun for you than it was for me." She winks at me, and I flip her off as she climbs out of the car, laughing softly. Leaning down, she looks at me solemnly. “Drive safe, and please tell me once you’re home. Any news on when Smithy is coming back yet?”

“He’s due home on Monday,” I tell her, beaming. I'm so ready for him to be back now.

“Good. I don’t like you being there alone, not after everything that’s happened. Are you sure you don’t want to stay here tonight?”

I shake my head, my heart swelling at her obvious worry for me. “No, I’ll be fine, I swear. Go to bed already. You have a big weekend ahead of you.”

She rolls her eyes at me, but I know she’s excited really. “Fucking camping in the middle of nowhere and likely no cell service.”

“It’s romantic,” I tease, and she scoffs.

“If you say so. Right, I’m going. Night. Love you.”

“Love you too,” I call out as she closes the door, waving at me once she reaches her porch. Once she’s inside, I put the car in gear and start the drive home.

The drive passes in the blink of an eye; but when I pull up to the gate and see police cars sitting there with lights flashing, dread floods my system.

What the fuck happened now?

I pull in through the gate, and one of the cars follows me up the drive. My heart sinks as ice cold fear squeezes my heart.

*Please let Smithy be okay.*

I put the car in the garage, making sure it’s safely tucked away before hauling ass outside to the waiting police. “Evening, Officers, how can I help? What’s wrong?”

“Miss Octavia Royal?” one of them asks, stepping forward.

I nod, clutching my arms around myself, praying to God this isn’t as bad as my mind tells me it is.

“Miss Royal, you are under arrest for the assault and battery of Miss Blair Royal.”

My jaw drops to the fucking floor at his words. “You have got to be kidding me.”

The officer moves toward me, grabs me, and spins me around, pulling my wrists behind my back. The cold metal of the cuffs stings my skin, and once he secures them, they’re way too fucking tight. “You have the right to remain silent. Anything you say can and will be used against you in a court of law. You have the right to an attorney. If you cannot afford an attorney, one will be provided for you. Do you understand the rights I have read to you? With these rights in mind, do you wish to speak to me?”

“What the fuck is going on here?” Lincoln appears, roaring at the officers as he storms across the front yard. The officer that has a hold of me manhandles me into the back of his police car while I watch another officer try to handle Lincoln.

I lean my head back on the headrest as the door slams on the car before the officer climbs in and starts the engine.

Just when I thought things couldn’t get worse, my cousin fucking ups the stakes.

Fuck my actual life.

---

I sit in this holding cell for what feels like hours before an officer arrives to walk me to an interrogation room.

My shock must show on my face when the door opens and I find Lincoln standing inside waiting for me. The officer laughs under his breath. He walks me over to the chair and undoes the cuffs.

"Good luck, kid," is all he says before he walks away, leaving me in the room with Lincoln.

"What are you doing here?" I ask, looking nervously around the room. I've never been arrested before, and this is scary as fucking shit. I haven't even had my phone call yet. I have zero fucking idea what's going on or how the hell I get out of this.

He sits in the chair on the opposite side of the table, watching me closely. I can't tell which Lincoln Saint sits opposite me. The guy who crept through my window to help keep my nightmares at bay or the one who declared open war on me when I returned here. "I'm here to get you out."

"Then why am I still locked in here?" I fold my arms across my chest, trying to create some heat. The entire station is fucking freezing, and I'm in nothing more than my little denim cutoffs and tank top that I wore to fight night. I'm definitely regretting the outfit, given the circumstances. I likely still look like I was fucked within an inch of my life. Since I didn't get a chance to clean up, there's no way he can't tell.

Lincoln frowns at me before steepling his fingers beneath his chin. "There are stipulations."

I bark out a laugh at him and sit in the chair. "Of course there fucking are. Go on then."

"You need to leave Echoes Cove. Within twenty-four hours of your release. You can not have any contact with anyone here, and you can't ever return."

I laugh incredulously, but his expression hasn't changed. "You can't be serious?"

I watch his face as he waits for my answer, and I realize he really is serious. This is fucking insane. So much for our truce.

"I'm not leaving, Lincoln. You might have your reasons for wanting me gone, but I have reasons keeping me here too. Yours are no more valid than mine." I huff and run a hand through my hair. What an asshole he is, using this against me. It occurs to me that the truce was a lie. That he could be working with Blair to manipulate me into this position, making it impossible for me not to accept his help.

"I won't ask you a third time, Octavia. Agree to leave, and I'll have you out of here in the next five minutes." He folds his arms over his chest, looking like the arrogant fuck that he is. He thinks he has me, that he's won. But he doesn't know me. Not anymore. Not really.

"Fuck you, Lincoln. I'll get myself out of here without your help." I let out a deep sigh, wondering if that's actually even possible, but I'll be fucked if I'm agreeing to his terms.

His hands shake as his jaw clenches, his rage on show for anyone to see. Except I'm the only one here to witness him unraveling. He stands to attention, the metal chair flying backward with the force of his movement, and he slams his hands down on the table, making me jump. "You're a fucking fool, Octavia."

"Better a fool than a puppet."

I quirk an eyebrow at him, and he growls before spinning and leaving the room. I guess he really isn't here to help me.

That's fine. I can totally save myself.

I think.

# CHAPTER TWENTY-FIVE

To say a night in a holding cell is uncomfortable might be the understatement of my entire life. The upside is that I'm probably safer here than I've been at home since Smithy left town. No one can terrorize me in a jail cell.

Well, other than the officers, and they've been okay, despite still not allowing me to make a phone call.

Lying down and staring at the discolored ceiling while shivering is basically how I spent the night. I'm officially living the dream.

"Miss Royal, you are free to go." I look up and find an officer unlocking the door to the cell with a really fucking angry East looming over him. "The charges have been dropped."

I sit up, eyes wide as shock floods my system. I have no idea how that's possible, considering my cousin's the biggest asshole in the world, but I won't question it. At least not until I'm alone with East.

I stretch out before standing and exiting the small, cold cell. East wraps his jacket around my shoulders, all while wordlessly glaring at the officer. "Let's get you home."

I look up at him as he puts an arm over my shoulder and tucks me against his side. "Thank you."

The words are little more than a whisper, but he squeezes me tighter before leading me out of the station to his waiting car. He opens the door for me and helps me in before running around the front of the car.

I try to wait until he's in with the engine running to question him, but he beats me to it. "What happened?"

His knuckles turn white as he grips the steering wheel, his cheek twitching as he clamps his jaw shut.

I pick at the skin beside my thumbnail, hating how small I feel having been saved by him yet again. I never saw myself as the damsel in distress type, but I seem to keep ending up in situations where I need rescuing. Shame floods me at the thought as my stomach twists, making me feel like I might be sick. "I have no idea. I got home last night, and the cops were waiting for me. They said Blair had pressed charges for assault and then carted me away. Lincoln came and basically told me he wouldn't help me. So I figured I was on my own, but they wouldn't give me my phone call after he left."

"He's such a fucking asshole." His words are clipped, his rage obvious in the set of his shoulders as he maneuvers the car toward our homes. "He was supposed to get you out, not leave you in there. He told me it was handled, otherwise I'd have been here sooner."

He takes a deep breath as my eyes go wide. Here I was thinking Lincoln and I were making progress. I guess I was wrong. "So, how'd you get me out?"

He glances over at me, his gray eyes like a raging storm. The eyes are the one thing he and Lincoln have in common as far as looks go. Their eyes are the same liquid steel, and they're like an endless pool to get lost in. "I pulled a few strings. Let's just say that your family shouldn't be a problem again."

I gasp, my eyes wide. "Do I even want to know what that means?"

He shakes his head once, and I look down at my feet. I didn't think I'd end up caught in the web of crazy that is Echoes Cove while I was back here. It's only one year, but it feels like each day I stay here, the more entangled I get in the inner workings. Though, it feels like I have no idea what's actually going on around this place.

We spend the rest of the drive in silence, with the sound of his radio filling the space along with the black cloud of his rage. I mean, I'm the one who spent the night in a cell, but he's definitely more worked up about this than I am.

Am I pissed at Blair? Absolutely. But am I shocked that she did it? Absolutely not. I knew the second I hit her again that I'd regret it at some point. I hadn't considered this to exactly be *how* it would blow up in my face, but I knew something would happen. She's too spiteful and petty to just let shit go. Though I still have no idea why she attacked me in the first place.

I really should start working through all the bullshit swirling around me. Maybe I need a journal or a whiteboard or something. Just to try and work shit out.

That's a future me problem. For now, I'd like to get home, shower, and sleep for a few hours. Maybe then I can try to figure out what actually happened last night. With Maverick and with Blair.

I thought my life was a rollercoaster when I was out on tour with my dad. That shit has nothing on Echoes Cove. East puts in the code to the gate and drives up to my house. I jump out of the car and head for the front door, finding yellow tulips waiting for me again, with another blank envelope, red wax seal and embossed black card.

Yet another thing to add to the ever-growing list of mine.

East slams the door and stalks over to where I'm standing, flowers in hand. "What is that?"

"Flowers, they arrive here every now and then," I say with a shrug. He plucks the card from my fingers, and the blood drains from his face. My heart races because I'd put money on him understanding this more than I do. "What?"

"Do they always come with this card?"

He takes the flowers from me as I unlock the door and disable the alarm. Once we're inside, I put the flowers in a vase with some water, and he seems to be taking note of how many vases of flowers there are now. "What does the card mean? I figured it was a fan of Dad's, and since I love yellow tulips, I've kept them."

"I'm not sure what it means." His eyes flicker down to his feet, and I swallow down the disappointment I feel. I know he's lying to me.

What is it with these guys constantly lying to me?

I shrug and move to the refrigerator, pulling out one of the meals Mrs. Potts put together for me, shoving it in the microwave to heat since I haven't eaten since lunch yesterday. Lasagna for breakfast would probably send Smithy into a conniption fit, but he isn't here right now. "Fair enough. Well if that's all, I'm going to eat, shower, and head to bed. Thank you for dealing with Blair."

He opens and closes his mouth a few times before shaking his head. "Yeah, okay. I'll be at home if you need anything."

He comes over and kisses my forehead before turning and leaving out the back door, despite his car being on my driveway. I thought we'd come leaps and bounds, especially after our not-quite-date night earlier this week, but now I feel like we've taken about ten steps back.

One day I'll figure out what the fuck's going on around here, but today's not that day. Today calls for sleep, food, and not leaving my bed.

Absolute perfection.

---

I wake up to someone pounding on the front door, and I scramble from my bed, half asleep still. My feet clap against the hard wood of the stairs as I rush downstairs. My brain is hazy, but I have enough wits about me to wonder what the fuck is going on. I try to not care about my somewhat feral appearance as I catch a glimpse of my reflection in the window as I rush to the door.

I open the door ready to yell, and I find a stoney-faced Mac standing in front of me. Thank God I showered before I slept. "Uhm, hi?"

I blink a couple of times, and he stands there, silent, with his arms folded across his chest.

"What are you doing here?"

"Let me in, Octavia." His voice is low and rumbly, and I don't think I've ever heard my dad's old head of security sound so mad. I step aside without question and wave him in. That's when I notice a few paparazzi camped out by the gates.

Fucking awesome. This is just what I wanted.

I groan as I move to shut the door. I'm super tempted to flip them all the bird. A picture of me looking like this and acting like that, would be worth more money than I want any of them to have. So I resist the urge and lock the door once Mac's in the house.

"What the hell's going on around here, V?" Mac's voice booms through the entry hall, and I wince at the volume of his apparent anger. "Five years you were under my watch, and not once did anything like this happen. Less than three months away, and you've been in the media more times than I care to count. The latest being pictures of your arrest."

"Okay, look, I can see that you're mad, but how about you tone it down a little, and I'll explain. Coffee?" I walk toward the kitchen without waiting for a response from him. If I'm going to get a dressing down from a disappointed Mac, I need coffee to make it through. I pour myself a mug from the pot I brewed before my nap and pour him one too before sitting down and waiting for him to catch up.

What is it with all of the men in my life generating their big dick energy in my direction? I'm tired of being everyone's go-to to be pissed at.

"You had better start explaining, Octavia, otherwise I'm either pulling you from this place or moving in. Because something isn't working." He leans against the wall, arms folded, and I sigh. I don't technically owe him an explanation, and he doesn't have the power to make me leave; but he helped raise me, so I understand some of his frustration.

I walk him through everything that's happened since I got home, and I wish I could say that it abates his anger, but at least it's redirected for the time being.

"These boys need to be taught a thing or two," he growls before finally sitting down and drinking the tepid coffee.

I bark out a laugh at the thought of him dealing with the four of them. "I'm not sure you'd do anything but give yourself high blood pressure and a potential heart attack. The four of them aren't really big on the whole authority figure thing."

He huffs a dry laugh and leans forward on the counter. "That sounds like they need a swift kick up the ass. But since I'm here, what can I do to help with this mess?"

"Honestly, I'm not sure there's much to do besides ride it out. Smithy's had the security increased on this place, and you're welcome to have a look around to make sure it's up to your liking. But beyond that, I'm kind of keeping myself on the down low as much as I can." I smile sadly at him and clutch the coffee cup in both my hands, hating how helpless it all sounds. I always thought I was a bad bitch, but being back in Echoes Cove is testing every single thing I ever thought to be true.

He stands, circling the island to wrap me up in those giant arms of his, making me feel like a little girl again. The fatherly comfort that radiates from him nearly makes me cry, and it hits me once again how alone I've really been without my dad around. There's nothing like being an orphan with literally no family left in the world—and my mom doesn't count because she left. She's never coming back, and I've made my peace with that.

"Let me take a look at your security system, and if anything's lacking, I'll sort it out. I wish there was more that I could do."

I squeeze him a little tighter before letting go. "You're here. That counts. But you have other people that need your special brand of protection now. I'm a big girl, and I have big walls here. I'll survive. It's not like I have a few thousand fans trying to break into my tour bus." I laugh at the memory of Mac trying to wrestle the door to the bus shut as a bunch of teenage girls tried to get to my dad. In the moment, it was terrifying, but looking back, it was kind of funny too.

He shakes his head, chuckling a little as he rubs a hand down his face. "Teenage girls are way more feral than anyone gives them credit for."

---

Mac left after checking my security. He upgraded the software so the cameras start recording ten seconds before the buzzer is pushed. He also installed an app on my phone so I can interact with people at my gate wherever I am out in the world. I had to give him more reassurances than I've ever given to anyone in my life that I'm okay. That was a few hours ago, and I've basked in the peace and quiet of the theatre room since.

I drop Indi a text to let her know I'm okay before I start the next movie, even though she has no cell service since she's camping. I can already tell she's going to be spitting feathers when she gets back to civilization and realizes what happened while she was gone.

I'm halfway through the action movie when my phone buzzes, telling me someone's at the gate. I pull up the app and see a guy who can't be much older than I am, standing with a giant box. "Hello?"

"Delivery for Octavia Royal," is all he says. I check out the van behind him, which looks legit enough, so I buzz him in.

I pause the movie and pad out to the front door, ready to meet him. It's a little late in the day for deliveries, but what do I know? I reach the entry hall as the knock echoes around the entryway, making everything seem far more sinister than it is.

Get a grip, Octavia. It's just a delivery.

I hope.

After the last few months, anything's fucking possible at this point.

I open the door and find the acne-ridden guy holding the box out to me. "Octavia Royal?"

"That's me. Who sent this?" I ask, skeptical as hell as I take the box from his outstretched hands. The black rectangular box is heavier than it looks, and I sag a little as I take its weight in my arms. Apparently I need to work out more.

He shrugs and thrusts his gadget thing in my face. "I have no idea, I just make the deliveries. I don't ask questions. Sign here, please."

I take the stylus from him and squiggle on the screen. He takes the gadget back with a nod before loping back to his van and driving down the lane to the still open gate. I wait until he's gone and close the gate, securing it once more before taking the box to the kitchen.

I contemplate calling East before opening it, but that seems way too dramatic. It's only a box. From an unknown source. With unknown contents.

Fun times.

I take a deep breath and undo the black ribbon that secures the lid, practically holding my breath as my heart races like I'm waiting for a bomb to go off or something.

I really need to watch fewer thrillers. My mind is in hyperdrive right now.

As I pull the ribbons of the bow, a card falls to my feet.

It's the same black card that always comes with the flowers. Except this time, there's red lettering on the back.

***For the Gala,***
***With Compliments***
***TKS***

Well, that isn't creepy at all. I'm kind of glad I made the decision to not go to the gala.

I lift the lid and find black tissue paper inside.

*Whoever this is needs a new color scheme.*

I work my way through the tissue paper and gasp when I finally uncover the contents. I lift the soft material from the box, eyes going wide when I realize what it is.

The floor-length gown is breathtaking. The creamy champagne material is covered in white lace, and the neckline plunges down to the navel. It has a choker design with a high back and capped sleeves.

It really is stunning.

Creepy, but stunning.

I lay it over one of the barstools and rummage through the rest of the tissue paper, but there isn't anything else in the box. No extra notes or anything.

I bite down on my bottom lip, trying to decide whether or not I should maybe tell someone about the dress when my back door swings open, and I find East standing there with Lincoln, Finley, and Maverick.

What a way to make this day better.

The alarm sounds, and East ducks to the keypad to turn it off. I keep forgetting he got the codes from Smithy.

"What is that?" Lincoln asks as he pushes past East into my kitchen.

I roll my eyes as they all enter the room, Finley closing the door behind them. "Hi, guys, yes, come on in why don't you. Make yourselves at home."

My sarcasm is met with mixed reactions.

Mav saunters over to the fridge behind me, grabbing a soda and slapping my ass as he does, making me yelp. Of course since we've fucked, he's overly touchy now, even if he was an asshole to me afterward. The tension as he looks at me is suffocating, so I glare at him, and he winks as he slides onto one of the stools at the counter. I wonder if the others know. Surely not. Finley leans against the wall with his arms crossed over his chest. East heads for the coffee pot, and Lincoln inspects the dress. Surely they'd say something if they knew. Lincoln huffs, and I turn my attention back to him and his earlier question.

"It was a gift," I say, finally answering him. I point toward the card, and he picks it up, scowling as he does before passing it around to the others, despite my frown. East is the only one who reacts, the same way he did when he saw the flowers.

East scowls at me, which seems to be his current default setting. I'm getting kind of sick of it. I don't know what's going on with him, but I'd like my chill, laid-back friend back. "I thought you weren't going to the gala."

I drop onto the stool as Lincoln folds the dress back into the box and sigh. "I'm not, not that it's any of your business. Can you stop looking at me like you hate me? I've had a day already, the last thing I need is all of this big dick energy pulling me down."

Maverick barks out a laugh, but East looks a little horrified.

"We wanted to stop by and make sure you were okay after yesterday," Finley finally pipes up, watching me intently. Maybe he does know, but if they're not outright saying it, I'm sure as hell not either.

I hold my hands out to my sides, lifting them in a sort of mock surrender. "Well, as you can see, I'm fine. So if that was all…"

"That was all," Lincoln says abruptly, pocketing the note that came with my dress. I'm too tired to argue with him about it. I'm officially learning to pick my battles when it comes to these guys.

I jump from the stool and glance at each of them in turn. It's hard to pinpoint exactly when I became more comfortable around them, considering everything that's happened since I returned to Echoes Cove. It's strange, but having them in my space doesn't make me want to light them on fire, so I guess we're making progress compared to just a few weeks ago. Maybe it's some weird Stockholm Syndrome type thing where I don't hate them despite all the shit they've put me through.

"I'm tired. If that's all, you guys can leave so I can sleep."

Mav jumps down so he's standing behind me, closely enough that I can feel his hard dick rub against my ass. "Sure you don't want me to stay?" he purrs in my ear, quietly enough that I'm sure no one else can hear. "I can make sure you have a real good time again."

A shiver runs down my back, but I shake my head. Last night was a mistake. I have no intention of repeating it. Even if the orgasm was so good my brain melted. His hands circle my waist, and it feels like an electric current passes through the room. I need to stop this before the others notice. Because if they don't know yet, it won't be long until they figure it out if he keeps this up.

"I'm sure," I say firmly, making Finley laugh while Mav looks a little disgruntled. That is firmly a *him* problem.

Lincoln's gaze zeroes in on me, and the heat of it is enough to scorch before his eyes land on Maverick. He definitely didn't know, but I'd put money on him knowing now. He's way too astute to miss Maverick being extra handsy with me.

"Am I missing something?" East pipes up, noticing the new tension in the room, and I step even further away from Maverick.

"Nope, not at all," I say, popping my p. "It's officially time for you all to go."

I usher them out of the house, despite their objections, and close the door behind them. I lean against the door once they're gone, finally feeling like I can breathe again.

All I wanted was a nice, simple year back in Echoes Cove.

I should really know better by now.

# CHAPTER TWENTY-SIX

It's been two weeks since the arrest, and life is somewhat back to normal.

Well, my version of normal anyway. After all of the bullshit with the guys and the media, I decided to put my head down and refocus my life. I've caught up on everything for school and managed to get ahead in most of my classes where I can.

I've become a model student and an upstanding citizen. I've also managed to avoid all four of the guys who have made my world tilt on its axis over the past couple of months.

I don't know what to think or feel when I'm around them anymore, so I've decided that avoidance is the key to keeping sanity firmly in place.

I grab my keys and phone from the counter and make my way to the garage. Thank fuck this week's nearly over. Tomorrow is my dad's birthday, and to say I'm dreading it is an understatement.

Smithy ended up not coming back when we thought because his sister took a turn for the worse again. I can't be angry that he's looking after her when she's suffering so much, but I'm kind of sad that I'm going to be on my own for an unknown amount of time. Even if Mrs. Potts is looking after the basics. It's just not the same.

I shake my petulant pity party off and climb into the car. The dread I'd started to feel when heading to the unhallowed halls of ECP doesn't exist anymore. Even Blair has left me the fuck alone lately. I don't know what East did or said to my family when he got them to drop the charges, but I even got an apology note from my aunt about the 'misunderstanding.' It's been a very surreal few weeks.

I pull into what I've come to see as 'my spot' next to where Indi's already parked in the Wrangler. I grin up at her when she bounces around to my car door, two coffees in hand. I double check my hair in the mirror before climbing out of the car and taking the coffee she thrusts in my direction. "You, sweet cheeks, are a goddess."

"I know," she says with a weird little curtsy that makes us both laugh. We link arms and head into the school. I give Maverick a little finger wave as I pass by him, basically scaring the snot out of a freshman. He grins at me, and I shake my head as he drops the kid, who runs off the first chance he gets. "How are things going with the guys?"

I look at Indi, who has the audacity to look sweet and innocent, like she didn't just imply some sordid shit. "We've come to a mutual agreement of avoidance, I think."

"So no more public fuckery then?" She laughs, wagging her eyebrows, and I feel a blush coloring my cheeks.

"No, nothing like that. I told you, I'm not here for anything like that. I don't have time or the want for a guy in my life. Let alone multiples."

She pouts as she leans up against the locker beside me. "Spoilsport. How are we meant to do double dates if you won't date?"

"You think any of them would do a double date?" I bark out a laugh, and she shrugs. "Even if I was to date someone, it wouldn't be any of them. They've been so hot and cold that I have no idea where I stand with any of them anyway."

She rolls her eyes at me, and I sigh like we haven't had this conversation a few times over already. "I'm telling you, all four of them are chasing your kitty cat. They would all definitely do terrible things for a peek at the meow. Just sayin'."

I close my eyes, trying not to laugh at her absurdity. Who the fuck says shit like that? "Indi, it is a good thing I love you. Anyway, you don't need the comfort of double dates, right? I thought things were okay with you and Jackson."

She shrugs and clutches her books closer to her chest. I can't help but frown, apparently I've missed something. I've been so wrapped up in my own shit that I haven't noticed what's been going on with her. "Things have started fizzling out after the camping trip."

"Please tell me you didn't put out and now he's ghosting you. If you tell me that, I'll murder him. I'll have a straight up murder party and dance on his grave."

"I wasn't really ready to take that step with him; but he seemed so into it, I didn't know how to say anything since we were out in the middle of nowhere just the two of us." She shrugs, looking down at the floor, and I see red. That fucking asshole. I'm going to rip his dick off and then see how he feels. A tear slips down her cheek, and she wipes it away quickly. "I'm sure it's not that. Maybe I wasn't any good and that's why."

Her voice is so small, and I hate him for doing this to her, and I hate myself for not noticing something was off with her. I pull her into my arms and hug her tightly. "I'm going to kill him."

I let her go and look up and down the halls, searching for the jacked-up jock. And here I was thinking he was a half decent guy. I'll gut the motherfucker.

All of the weird emotions I've felt about my own shit, mixed with the looming sadness of tomorrow, are pushed into my well of rage toward Jackson.

Finley walks toward us, and his eyes go wide when he sees me. I'm seething, and I can't control how hard I'm shaking. "Who pissed in your Wheaties?"

"Uhm…" Indi starts to talk, but I spot the jock in question. She reaches for my arm, but I shake her off.

"You!" I hiss, moving toward the asshat that broke my friend's heart.

Finley doesn't even ask questions. He hauls Jackson up against the lockers, lifting him from his feet by his throat.

"What did you do?" he hisses, and Jackson coughs and splutters where he holds him.

The football player claws at Finley's hand, and Indi taps on my shoulder. "Please don't hurt him. Not here."

I look at Finley and nod. He drops Jackson, who crumples to the floor in a pile. Finley crouches down and talks to him so quietly that I almost miss the words that spill from his lips. "We are not done here, Jones. I'll be waiting."

He stands and nods at me before heading down the hall toward his class like nothing just happened. I turn to Indi, who's watching Jackson as he catches his breath. I move closer and press my foot against his balls, applying pressure before I lean forward to talk to him myself. "If I hear that you've done something like this before, you can expect to lose these." I push a little harder, and he squeaks like a pathetic fucking loser.

I lift my foot and turn to Indi, linking her arm in mine before dragging her down the hall.

"Thank you. No one has ever stood up for me like that before."

I give her a side hug, squeezing her as tightly as I can. "Ride or die, bitch. There isn't anything I wouldn't do for you."

She gives me a watery smile, and I want to turn around and step on Jackson's balls so hard they actually pop. I'll deal with him later. For now, my friend needs me, and that's all I'm going to focus on.

---

I wake up bleary-eyed from having cried myself to sleep last night. The room is shrouded in darkness, and I'm glad. Nothing about today makes it a happy or light day.

It's my dad's birthday.

The first since he died.

And I feel fucking hollow.

I wish I could say I cried myself out last night, but every time I woke up throughout the night, the tears started again. I look down at my phone and see that it's already ten in the morning.

I guess I'm skipping school. Honestly? Fuck everything today.

I keep my eyes open long enough to shoot off a message to Indi to let her know I won't be in and to not panic before putting my phone on silent and laying it face down.

The whole world can suck it today.

I curl up into a ball, trying to stop from feeling like my heart's bleeding out of my chest. Memories assault me of how we spent his birthday last year. We were half a world away from here, in London, doing all of the stupid things that made

Dad happy. Like visiting the Queen's Guard and making fun of their unwavering stature. Wondering how many cake places we could hit up before someone was sick. Doing all the cheesy touristy stuff like riding the London Eye and visiting Big Ben.

And now… Now he's gone, and we'll never do any of that again.

I remember complaining about all the stupid stuff last year, taking for granted that it was just another birthday because we'd have plenty more of them together.

Sobs rack my body as the memories flood my mind, and there isn't anything I can do to stop them.

I miss him so fucking much.

I startle when the balcony door opens, and Lincoln walks in, his school shirt partially open. "What are you doing here?"

He kicks off his shoes and drops his blazer onto my dresser before climbing into my bed. "I remembered what day today is, and I didn't want you to be alone. You weren't at school, so here I am."

I try to wipe my face as he pulls me closer, until I'm lying on his chest. "Remember that one time, when we thought it would be fun to try to make a treehouse. Your dad ended up helping, but managed to nail-gun his shirt to the wall?"

I'm somewhere in the middle of laughing and crying at the visual. That day was so much fun. It was my eighth birthday, and the guys and I thought it would be a great idea if we could build the treehouse we'd been talking about for weeks. My dad was very much not a handy guy, but he loved me and wanted to help.

I sob on Lincoln's chest, and he strokes my hair, not saying a word about my tears staining his shirt or the fact that I've barely spoken to him in weeks.

He's here for me, exactly when I need him. Just like he was when we were kids. "Thank you," I murmur to him when my tears finally subside enough that I can form words.

He rests his chin on top of my head as he runs his hand up and down my spine. "You don't need to thank me, Octavia."

It occurs to me that he's the only one of them that hasn't called me 'V' since I returned. Not that I wanted them to call me the nickname, but it's like he's always known that we'll never be what we once were. Something about that realization hurts me more than it should, especially since he's right here, looking after me the way he did when my mom left.

Maybe it has something to do with me.

All my life, I thought it was everyone else, but maybe there's something wrong with me. My mom left. My dad killed himself. Even these four… They didn't want me around once I came back, so they left me in a roundabout sort of way too.

I let out a shuddery breath and pull away from Lincoln, refusing to get too caught up in the comfort of his embrace. I won't survive it if I get attached and he leaves me too.

I have to remember that.

People always leave.

---

"We should do something tonight," Indi says as we finish changing after Gym. "We haven't done anything in weeks, and it's Halloween. I freaking *love* Halloween."

I cannot believe it's Halloween already. This used to be my favorite holiday, but this year isn't the same. With that in mind, I realize that I desperately need to reclaim some joy. I've burrowed myself away, doing nothing but studying and starting my plans for the recording studio.

I've also written more songs than I have in my entire life.

It's been a weird few weeks.

I finish buttoning up my shirt and slide my blazer on before looking back at her. "Did you have anything in mind?"

She smiles up at me, her eyes full of hope. I haven't been able to say no to her since the whole Jackson thing. The sniveling little asshole hasn't said a word to her since that day either. I fucking hate cowards like that. "There's the house of horrors on the other side of town?"

I groan as I grab my bag and slide my feet into my Chucks. "Fine, fine. We can do it."

"Yes!" she exclaims, jumping to her feet. "At least we don't have to wear costumes, right?"

"I'll take the win."

She does a little jig on the spot, making me laugh. "You should because I was going to make us be Pippy Longstocking twins."

I laugh even harder at her as she grins. We head out of the school, ignoring everyone we pass, arm in arm, to where the cars are parked. "I'll pick you up at eight?"

I nod as I head to the driver's side of my car. "Sounds perfect. I'll dress comfortably."

"Whoop! I'll see you in a bit." She bounces into her car, and I shake my head as I get my shit sorted out before starting the engine.

I feel eyes on me, so I look up and see the three boys who haven't been that far from me since my dad's birthday all watching me. They're kings surveying their kingdom, yet I'm their only focus. It's almost a heady feeling.

I shake it off because their attention isn't what I need right now. Or maybe even ever. I might have forgiven them for being assholes and taken refuge in each of them at one point or another since I returned to Echoes Cove, but we're not anything more than people who used to be friends.

I put the car in reverse and pull out of my spot, the weight of their gazes burning into me.

Sometimes I wish we'd never left here. I can't help but wonder how different life would be if I hadn't left with my dad all those years ago. But I can't really wish that I didn't have that time with Dad.

I drive home, unable to think about anything but the four boys who've had me twisted up in knots since I returned to Echoes Cove. One way or another, everything always seems to lead back to them.

I pull the car into the garage, spotting another delivery of yellow tulips on the steps.

I can't help but frown. No one should be able to get this close to the house without me letting them in unless they're coming in via the Saints' property. I'm pretty positive the flowers aren't from Lincoln or East, and it's starting to feel a little creepy. Especially after how they both reacted to the cards that come along with them. So I leave the flowers where they are, spotting the plain white envelope and decide to head inside to get ready for tonight's house of horrors.

Fall is officially here, so I dig out a pair of jeans and the hoodie East wrapped me in the day he rescued me before grabbing a quick shower. He's definitely not getting the hoodie back, like, ever

It doesn't take me long to get ready, and I reheat some of the shrimp linguine Mrs. Potts prepared while I flick through the series I keep meaning to start on Netflix. I have way too many TV subscriptions for the amount of TV I don't watch, but fuck it.

I flick through the videos on the 'for me' page on my latest addiction of an app, glad that despite the shit I've dealt with, very few people even know about the account I have on here. The pictures of the football team preparing for their game make me scowl. What a fucking let down those guys ended up being. Indi has bounced back from the Jackson thing pretty well, but it's impossible to miss how she freezes up when he's near us at school.

I know she hasn't been to any games since their camping trip too, which fucking sucks because she loves football.

Boys are so stupid. Who even needs them?

My phone buzzes in my hand, and I pull up the message thread.

**Indi: On my way**

I put my dishes away in the dishwasher and pull my hair up into a messy bun. Screw hot girl summer, this is comfy girl fall.

I lock everywhere up and head down to the gate to wait for her, finding another bunch of tulips leaning against the railing.

This is getting to be a little much now, so I pull up my phone and snap a picture. I shoot a message to someone I totally didn't envision messaging anytime soon.

**Me: Is this you? Because two bunches in one day is a lot *laughing emoji* also, if it's not you, can you check your security to see if someone's using your place to access mine because one set was left against my front door.**

**Lincoln: Wasn't me. I'll look into it**

I check the post box while I'm waiting for Indi to arrive and flick through the junk mail. I find a manila envelope stashed in here. It has my name on it but no address, so it was hand delivered.

Weird.

I open it and the contents fall out.

There are so many photos of me in here. Photos of me with the guys, with Indi—all of their faces scratched out.

I think I'm going to be sick.

Then I see the note.

*One day we'll be together. You won't have to be alone anymore. You won't have to run to them when you're sad.*

*One day isn't too far away.*

This can not be happening.

# CHAPTER TWENTY-SEVEN

After reporting the pictures to Smithy's friend at the FBI and actually having a meeting face-to-face with the guy Smithy sorted my security out with, I feel a bit better.

Needless to say, Halloween was fucked up, and I felt so bad for Indi. Which is exactly why I'm about to cave to her yet again.

"*Please*." She gives me those puppy dog eyes of hers, and I about die.

I hate telling her no, especially after how shit these last few weeks have been, but I can't help but want to hide away in my house and never leave again. "This probably isn't a good idea. Not if I have a weird stalker out there."

"There's no way your stalker would dare to do anything to you at Ryker Donovan's party. The stalker seems like a total creep, but Ryker Donovan's a legitimate psychopath."

I swear, she almost sounds wistful when she talks about him like that. "I think I've had enough of psychopaths lately."

She bursts out laughing like I'm a fucking comedy genius, and I can't help but shake my head at her.

"Come on, we deserve some fun. We've been so good, and this is our senior year. One party won't hurt. We won't even drink if you're worried. I just want to dance and have fun. We could both use a night of that. I'm friends with Ryker's little sister, Scout, too, so if we hang out with her, Ryker will keep an eye on us anyway. Plus I have, uh… history with the twins. But that's a story for another day."

"Don't think we're not going to revisit that little tidbit." I bite my lip, indecision eating me. It would be really good to let loose for a night and live my life like an actual fucking teenager, but I can't help feel uneasy about it. Between the flowers, the dress, and the creepy-ass pictures, I want to hide in a hole somewhere that no one can find me.

We head to my locker so I can pick up my books before heading home for the weekend, and I consider going to the party. It's the moment I have all of my books gathered in my arms that I hear my name called.

"Octavia."

I look up to see Lincoln stalking toward me, looking just about ready to commit murder.

*What the fuck did I do now?*

Indi winces as he comes to a stop before us, and I put on my cheeriest smile. "Hey, what's up?"

"The flowers. Have you gotten any others?"

Ah yes, I almost forgot I asked him to look into that. The creepy stalker thing took over my every thought, and it only just occurred to me that the flowers could be from whoever that is too.

"A few different bunches since I came home, yeah. Some were also delivered when we were away on our spa trip… And there's the dress too, I guess." I pause, contemplating telling him about the photos. I ultimately decide it's probably better to tell him since he offered his help once already. "I, uh… also had to call the police last week because I seem to have a stalker."

He clenches his jaw and quirks an eyebrow at me, like he's waiting for me to continue. "Someone sent me a manila envelope full of pictures of me with Indi and you guys. Everyone else's faces were scratched out, and there was a creepy-ass note too."

"Why are you only just telling me about this now?" he asks, his fists clenching and unclenching at his sides.

I bite my lip, not afraid of him, but definitely afraid of how he'll react. "Honestly, I didn't even think about it. I only just called the police. It's the first envelope like this I've gotten."

His eyes flash, but he locks down his features in a heartbeat. "If you get any more shit, call me first."

That's all he says before he stalks off, joining Finley and Maverick where they're waiting for him at the main doors. I huff, trying to keep calm about him giving me orders, while trying not to overthink the weird protective thing he has going on. I let out a deep breath because I know Lincoln's like a dog with a bone. He'll find something out. He has ways of doing stuff that I don't. I'm not willing to ask what they are, or look at it too deeply; but if he can stop the flowers from showing up, I'd appreciate it.

"Dude, I'll never figure those guys out," Indi says, almost dreamily. "They're like your black knights or something. Can't call them white knights, but they're definitely always there watching out for you."

"Because that isn't creepy at all." I laugh. "Okay, let's hit this party, why the fuck not?"

She does a little dance as she bounces down the hall. "Hell yes!"

"Do you want me to drive, so you can have some fun at least?" I ask as we head out of the school.

She grins at me as we reach the cars and clasps her hands together in front of her. "Why don't we grab a cab? That way neither of us has to worry. Besides, I'm sure Ellis can give us a ride home if we need it."

"Ellis?"

She smiles dreamily, and I can't help but laugh. Okay, there's definitely some history there that she has to tell me about, pronto. "Ryker's twin brother."

"Of course," I say, rolling my eyes. "I'm good with whatever as long as we don't end up stranded or dead in a ditch somewhere."

"Deal! I'll text you when I'm on the way to your place."

I nod before climbing into the car. I'm almost looking forward to tonight if I'm being honest. Though there is a part of me that's dreading getting home to the possibility of more flowers or weird envelopes. My mood's a wash, I guess.

I cross my fingers and send up a thought to anyone who might be listening to let me have one night of normal, teenage fun.

That's all I want.

---

When Indi said these guys are the life of the party, she grossly downplayed how hard the ECH crowd likes to party. I've spoken to a few people I used to be friendly with, but for the most part, I keep to myself and dance the night away.

I'm not even sure whose house we're in, but the bodies are packed in here pretty tight. There have been more than a few wandering hands, but I've been able to fend off most of them and enjoy myself.

Indi has been whisked away into the arms of Ellis Donovan, and I get the feeling I'm missing a big chunk of their story. I'm not about to interrupt them to get more details. She deserves to be happy, and well… She definitely looks happy right now.

I push my way through the crowd. I desperately need some water and some fresh air. When I reach the kitchen, I freeze.

What the fuck is the ECP football team doing here? I thought there was some ridiculous school rivalry stemming from the two teams?

"Octavia!" Raleigh cheers my name like he hasn't been a giant asshat for the last month or so. He says it like I'm his favorite person in the world. He's obviously had more than a few too many beers.

I smile tightly at him and grab a bottle of water. "Come sit with us. Talk!"

"I'm good, thanks." I try to be as polite as I can considering no one knows where I am. Plus, he and his friends are all way stronger than I am, beer or not, and I do not want to have to throat punch anyone today.

I try to move past them, to escape out the back door and into the cold night air, but he loops his arms around my waist and yanks me back against him. He takes the water from my hands and puts it on the counter before spinning me round so the others can't see us as well. "I know you miss me. You were meant to be mine," he murmurs into my ear, and an icy shiver of dread runs down my spine. He sounds *way* too much like the creepy stalker's note.

It can't be him, right?

I shake off the thought and push at his hands until I manage to worm my way free of him. I grab my water from the counter and duck out before anyone can say anything else or grab me again. It's only seconds before I push out the back door and stumble onto the much less occupied patio out back, relieved to get some space for a moment.

This might be the 'bad' side of Echoes Cove, but the Donovans clearly aren't doing badly. I've heard a few rumors about them, but I'm not one to judge people based solely on rumors. I mean, that would definitely be the pot calling the kettle black.

I suck in lungfuls of the cool night air and chug the water back. It tastes weird, but it's been a minute since I had carbonated water. The cold liquid feels too good going down, so I sink the bottle and move to sit on one of the loungers out here.

I stare up at the dark night sky, and the scattered stars call to me, so I stay where I am, enjoying the quiet as the noises around me begin fading out.

"There you are." I look up, my head heavier than I remember it being, and see Raleigh stalking toward me. "Did you miss me? Look at you finding us some privacy."

I try to sit up, but it feels like my body won't respond. He crouches beside me and brushes my hair away from my face. I try to speak, but my words come out slurred. My eyes dart around the space, but everything is fuzzy. Panic creeps in as the world seems to slow down.

What the hell is going on right now?

I try to sit up, but the world spins.

My heart races in my chest and I can't think straight, despite a thousand things racing through my mind. I try to suck in a breath, but it's like my body won't work right.

"Where are you going? This is our time." He pushes me against the lounger before he starts kissing my neck. My blood turns to ice in my veins as I try to push my hands against his chest but my arms are like jelly.

What is happening to me? Why can't I move properly?

Fuck.

My skin feels like I'm rolling on a bed of needles, the pricking so bad it steals most of my attention.

I try to push him off, to tell him no as tears slip down my face. "You like that, baby? I knew you wanted me."

My eyes flutter closed, and when the world focuses again, my tank top is gone, and I don't know how. His lips move down my chest, and I scream out in my mind. No noise comes out of my mouth as he pulls the cups of my bra down, exposing me, before his tongue licks one nipple and then he sucks on the other.

*I'm going to be sick.*

I manage to lift my hands and place them on his chest as he lowers himself on top of me. "That's it, baby, fight me. I love it when they fight."

*This can not be happening to me right now.*

"No," I manage to murmur, but it seems to excite him, even as more tears slip down my cheeks.

His hand plunges into my jeans, and I manage a garbled scream as his fingers brush against my lace-covered pussy.

*Please God, no.*

"You motherfucker!" I hear Lincoln's voice in the seconds before Raleigh's body is ripped away from me. Indi's face appears in front of mine, and the sound of flesh against flesh fills the quiet space around us.

"V, are you okay?" Indi asks, tears running down her own face. She looks more angry than anything. She helps me sit up and grabs my tank top from the ground by my feet, helping me back into it so I'm no longer exposed. I look up and watch as Lincoln rains blow after blow down on Raleigh as a sob rips out of me.

I can't say anything as I rock in her arms.

"Ellis called Lincoln for me as soon as I saw you. They were already here. I didn't know what else to do. Let's get you out of here," she says, trying to help me stand, but my legs won't work. I can barely keep myself sitting up. Everything just feels wrong.

"Lincoln!" she yells, but he's lost to his rage. Seconds later, Finley and Maverick appear. Mav glances over at us, and then nods at Finley before heading straight for Lincoln, each of them practically vibrating with rage. Finley comes straight over to us, a sense of calm visibly washing over him despite his rage moments ago, and I swear I want to cry all over again.

I feel so fucking dirty.

I can still feel him on me.

God, I want to vomit.

"I got you," Finley murmurs quietly, lifting me into his arms like a rag doll. I hate being so compromised, but I know that while they're here, nothing else will happen to me. Even after everything we've been through, I know they'd never try to hurt me like that. Try to rape me.

I start to cry again just thinking about it.

Lincoln and Maverick appear before us, and Lincoln looks fucking feral as he growls at Finley. "Give her to me."

"Have you got yourself under control?" Finley asks him, and he nods once.

"Good, now I can show him what happens when he touches things that aren't his," Finley says quietly as he hands me over to Lincoln.

Maverick smiles softly down at me as he runs a finger down my face. "Don't worry, princess. You won't need to worry about him ever again."

I close my eyes at his touch, and Lincoln adjusts me on his chest so my face is tucked into his neck. "I'm going to get her home. Call me if you need any help with him."

"Oh, we won't need any help," Maverick says almost wistfully.

"I'm coming with you," Indi speaks up, and I see Ellis standing beside her.

Lincoln shakes his head. "You stay here, I've got her now. She's safe." His menacing growl is enough for Ellis to place a protective hand on Indi's waist and pull her against him.

She looks at me and nods. "You better have her, I'm not afraid of you, Lincoln Saint." Just then, Ryker joins her and his twin, looking just as protective as Ellis does.

He chuckles, his chest shaking where he holds me. "I don't think you are, and that makes you either very brave or very stupid. Thanks for the call, Ellis. We'll be seeing you both soon."

He starts to move, and my eyes flutter closed.

The next time they open, he's belting me into his car, being more gentle with me than he's possibly ever been. "Sleep, V. I got you."

---

Linc pulls me from the car and against his chest. I'm not sure what Raleigh drugged me with, but I'm starting to get control of my extremities back, and my brain doesn't feel quite as foggy as it did before. "I can walk," I murmur, but Lincoln holds me tighter.

"I'm sure you can, but I already told you I've got you."

"What the fuck happened?" East's voice reaches us, and Lincoln sighs. He gives him a brief rundown of the night's events, but that only seems to piss him off more. "Why didn't you call me?"

"You weren't with us. Would you have preferred we left her to be raped because we were busy getting you instead?" Lincoln argues, and a shiver runs down my spine.

"Let me down, please?" I ask him quietly, but his arms tighten around me. I place a hand on his cheek and bring his gaze back down to me. "Please?"

He watches me intently, but I see the moment in his eyes that he relents before nodding. He lets me down, catching me as I stumble while struggling to find my footing. "Thank you."

I *really* need to fucking shower.

I walk toward the front door slowly but pause when I see it.

A note on the doorstep.

I brace myself on the door to pick up the note, my heart racing as I do. I pull the black card it from the envelope and my heart fucking stops.

*You're out of time, Miss Royal.*
*We're coming for you.*
*Ready or not.*

# CHAPTER TWENTY-EIGHT

## LINCOLN

## THEN

"What the fuck do you mean she's coming home?" Fear runs down my spine unlike any I've ever known.

She was supposed to be safe. That was the deal he made. Lose one, keep one. No matter how hard the decision was.

"Her dad's dead." Finley's words pack a punch, practically sitting me on my ass.

"How?" This can't be right. We did everything right.

"Suicide, apparently," Maverick grunts as he hits the punching bag in the corner of the room.

East drops onto the sofa and throws back his glass of whiskey. "You really think Stone Royal would commit suicide?"

*This can't be fucking happening.*

"You and I both know there's no way it was fucking suicide," I growl as I pull at my hair. "Stone Royal would have hung the fucking moon for Octavia. He would never have left her defenseless against them like that."

"You really think they'd do that?" Maverick asks, stilling the punching bag.

"You really think they wouldn't?" Finley asks, while I rack my brain trying to come up with a way to keep her safe and far, far away from here. "The real question is why? What could they possibly gain from his death and her submission?"

It hits me in an instant, of course. We've been blocking what they want for too long, and they know us too well. They know our weak spot.

It's always been her.

"Us… They fucking get us."

# ACKNOWLEDGMENTS

This book has taken a village. I know everyone says it but it's true. That being said, I'm going to try and keep this short!

First, I need to say a huge thank you to my besties who kept me on track when I have spiraling and doing the rewrites for this book. If it wasn't for you, I never would've had my ass in my chair long enough to get this book finished. And to the one who doesn't want to be named for creating my beautiful cover. It's so freaking stunning.

To my alpha team & wolf pack - I know this one was a little different, but thank you all for the feedback.

Steph & Elisabeth - we all know this wouldn't be happening without your help. Thank you for the translations, keeping my shit in line, and well, everything.

To Sarah, Sam & Christine for making my word baby sparkle. You guys work so hard, and I really do appreciate it.

To all of the bloggers, instagrammers, booktokers who have been so nice to me on this journey. You didn't have to, but it was so lovely to feel the warmth of the indie community.

Finally, to you guys for picking this book up and giving it a chance. I know the book will be marmite, but I hope you fall on the 'love it' side.

# 29

## BONUS SCENE

### INDI

This year is going to *suck*. After the worst summer in the history of summer's, there is no way it's not going to suck.

Even the sight of Jackson, aka my personal football God, isn't enough to perk me up. All of my pep apparently stayed in bed when I crawled out of it this morning.

I absolutely do not approve of the thundercloud following me around today.

Dodging the Saint Squad, I rush to my locker and ditch my books, glad to be rid of the weight on my shoulder, grab what I need for English and haul ass toward class.

Told You So by The Band Camino plays in my ear, and I hate that it reminds me of the twins. Damn them for ruining good music for me. Still, I refuse to turn it off. I like this song dammit.

I slide into the classroom and head for the back of the room, it's safer back here. No one can throw stuff at my back or try to cut my hair from behind. Let's just say I learned my lesson last year on how to be strategic about where I'm sitting this year.

It also happens to give me a great view of Jackson and that tight end ass of his. It should be illegal for people to look that hot. He's sitting next to his bestie, Raleigh, the QB, on the opposite side of the room.

Blair Royal and the rest of the Saint Squad, aka the mean girl bitches that made my life a living hell last year, walk in and take a seat on the guys' desks, their giggles, hair twirling and obvious stupid girl routine makes me want to vomit.

I open my notebook and start to doodle, when the whispers catch my attention.

Holy shit.

Octavia. Motherfucking. Royal.

The princess herself is standing in the doorway to my English class and I hold my breath to stop the fangirl squeal.

I heard whispers that she was going to be back in the Cove after what happened with her dad, but I didn't think it was actually real. I totally feel for her, what happened with her dad was awful, and the vultures of the media have been as delightful as you'd expect.

The last thing she needs is me losing my shit because she's here.

*Deep Breaths, Indi.*

She glances around the room, rolling her eyes at Blair and co and I press my lips together so I don't start laughing and keep my gaze firmly on my notebook. She doesn't need me gawking at her either.

*God I'm so freaking lame. Get yourself together, Indi.*

I just about manage until I see her standing in front of my desk, and then she slides into the open seat between me and the window. I smile at her as she takes a seat but then chastise myself for the likely psycho stalker smile I just flashed at her.

She looks like she's going to talk to me, and I swear my heart is like a freaking murder of crows in my chest trying to get free, except the teacher walks into the room and stops anything she might have said.

*Freaking teachers. Don't they understand? God.*

Instead, she gives me a little wave and I feel my smile grow in response.

Looking away from her before I can make a fool of myself, I turn to pay attention to our new English teacher.

"Morning, ladies and gents, welcome to the start of your senior year. You don't know me, and I don't know you, so let's fix that. I am Ms. Summers, and I'll be your English teacher for the year. Yes, I'm new here, but don't think that I'm a pushover. I don't care what you did over the summer, it's done. Right now, we're going to focus on how I can get you out of this classroom and off to the college of your dreams. If I see your phone, it will be confiscated. I am not afraid of detentions, and bribes will not be accepted. Now that that's clear, let's start with your reading list, shall we?"

*Oh my God. She's English. My English teacher is English. Brilliant.*

I snort a laugh, and then want to die, until I notice Octavia's shoulder shaking as she bites down on her lip like she's trying not to laugh too.

Huh, maybe we could even be friends. She's just the new girl here, and lord knows I know all about being the new girl in Echoes Cove.

The teacher keeps talking and I make sure my phone is shut off because detention isn't on my to do list.

Ms. Summers passes around a piece of paper detailing the reading list in full, and I groan as I scan it. I already know this is going to suck. I've only read a few of these, and some of them were *work,* but my girl Jane Eyre is on the list, so I'm onto a winner there at least.

"I've highlighted the texts we'll be focusing on, but I suggest reading the others because this is AP English, and you're here for a reason. You'll be doing the first assignment in pairs. Pick wisely because you'll be stuck with each other for the rest of the year."

I glance over at Octavia, and find her looking at me, so I suck up the fangirling and decide to treat her like anyone else. If I'd been through what she has, I imagine that's all I'd want. So I point at her then back to myself and she nods.

Win.

She might be terrible at English, but I'm not exactly getting A's across the board here.

"Pick your favorite book on the list and discuss with your partner why you believe it's the best one there. Try to convince them that your book should be at the top of the list." She waves at us to begin before sitting behind her desk, and the room becomes a flurry of movement as people shift to sit in their pairs.

"I'm Indi," I say as I turn to face her, resisting the urge to fidget and play with my lip ring. It's a weird nervous habit I've picked up so I practically sit on my hands to keep still. "And you're Octavia Royal."

*Andddd there goes my weird verbal vomit.* She probably thinks I'm a total freak now. Panic swamps me and I start to babble, wishing desperately that I could, just. Stop. Talking. "I swear I'm not like a crazy, psychopath stalker or whatever… Though I will say I listened to your dad somewhat obsessively in my tween years, *but* I'm past that little obsession. Sorry about him by the way. Also, I have really bad verbal diarrhea when I'm nervous, so sorry about the babbling. Oh my God, I need to stop."

I cover my mouth with my hands because I don't think there's any other way it's going to stop. She laughs softly, and her eyes crinkle when she does. "Dude, you're fine. Take a breath."

"Sorry, yeah okay. Right, let's start again, shall we? I'm Indi, it's nice to meet you." I push my hand toward her for her to shake, looking like an absolute moron and feeling more than a little awkward, but she shakes my hand and I feel like less of a dork.

"Octavia, though a lot of my friends just call me V."

"I like that." I grin and scoot my desk closer to hers, trying not to feel hyper conscious of her studying me.

"Midnight Blue?" she asks, and I realize she saw my t-shirt under my shirt and I smile wide at her.

"I am more than a little obsessed with them. And the lead singer… I swear I'm not into girls, but Jenna B gives me such a lady boner. I can't even."

*Oh god, there goes my mouth again.*

"Yeah, she's pretty cool," she says with a laugh as she leans back in her chair. "And they put on an epic show."

My eyes go wide and I try my hardest not to squeal and fangirl. Don't get me wrong, this is Octavia Motherfucking Royal, but Jenna B? I'd crawl over broken glass to get to her. "Oh my God, have you met her? I'm going to hyperventilate. You know Jenna B?"

"I've met her a couple times, yeah," she says so blasé that I want to pass out. "They were on one of Dad's tours in their early days. They only did about seven shows, but they were amazing even then."

"I am officially going to die. I dub thee my new bestie." I cackle, and Ms.

Summers looks over at us, narrowing her eyes. Ugh stupid teachers ruining my fun.

"Done. Now… let's talk about *Wuthering Heights*," Octavia says having seen Ms Summers' glare too. She grins at me and I shake my head, feigning a look of betrayal as I lay a dramatic hand over my heart at her pick of books.

"Oh no, you're one of those. I take it back," I scoff before picking up the reading list and shaking it in her face. "How can you pick Catherine over Jane Eyre?"

She grins wickedly, her eyes sparkling and it takes everything in me not to cackle at her. "Ah, the great sister debate… This is going to be the start of a beautiful friendship."

# LOST ROYAL

THE KNIGHTS OF ECHOES COVE

LILY WILDHART

*Courage is grace under pressure*

ERNEST HEMMINGWAY

# CHAPTER ONE

## FINLEY

Some monsters live in the shadows. Some live in the depths of your soul. But mine… I keep mine close to the surface, just in case I need them.

For times like now.

The pounding from the body in my trunk sounds in time with my heartbeat.

I clench my hands on the steering wheel, my knuckles white as I try to calm myself down. Maverick just slips into that cold quiet he has.

It's a trait we share.

The killing quiet.

And this son of a bitch will be lucky if we kill him after what he tried to do to Octavia. When Maverick declared her off-limits, he was being a dick, but he was also trying to protect her. Even if it was in that twisted way of his.

No one touches her but us.

No one.

Raleigh has been left to his own devices for too long. The Knights rarely go after their own, but I don't care if we're punished for this. He isn't a Knight, not yet. And he deserves to scream.

The same way he wanted to make her scream.

Luckily, I've never been the squeamish type. Probably not so lucky for him.

"Where are we heading?" Mav asks, piercing the silence. The dark of the night shrouds us, the perfect time for monsters to come out and play.

I glance over at him as he cracks his knuckles, the anger in his eyes reflected in the set of his shoulders and the tic in his jaw. "The Cage."

My lips curl at the edges just thinking about it, and he barks out a laugh. "Nothing less than what he deserves."

We drive through Echoes Cove, over the railroad tracks and into the vast wasteland of desert outside the city. Then I keep going. Way beyond the Kings' territory and into what I like to call the barren lands: stretches of open road with not a soul in sight for miles.

Nothing.

Except for the ruins that cover what is just one of many bases for the Knights.

This one in particular is a nice little hellscape they dreamed up. A headquarters of sorts with a nightmare basement. The Cage. It's usually reserved for initiation, but I'm pretty sure they won't mind us going off book.

Not that I'd give a fuck if they did.

The pounding in the trunk stops, and I let out a dry, sharp laugh.

Of course he gave up already.

If he thinks that will save him, he has another thing coming.

We already warned him. He thought that the Knights wanting his mom's connections would keep him safe.

I guess he's about to learn that here, you only get one warning.

I pull off the main road onto the dirt backroad, our dust a thick cloud as we make our way across the bumpy terrain. Shouts of pain from the trunk make Mav laugh, low and dangerous, as we drive the eight miles down the dirt road that brings the crumbling building into view.

I look over to Mav as I pull the car to a stop and turn off the engine. "Do not kill him."

"You spoil all my fun." He sighs before climbing from the car, practically skipping to the trunk. I meet him there. He's rubbing his hands together, the look of glee on his face like a kid at Christmas. He might be more than a little unhinged, but I'd trust him with my life.

I push the button to unlock the trunk of the sedan, stepping back as it pops open. Raleigh's bound body comes into view, his eyes wide as he tries to shout around the gag in his mouth. I step forward and rip it away, letting him scream into the night.

Mav laughs beside me, his eyes dancing with excitement as he leans forward to speak to the piece of shit. "You can scream as much as you like. No one can hear you out here."

And just like that, the screams die out. "You guys can't do this."

"Watch us." I grab him by the hair and drag him from the trunk, dropping him face down in the dirt.

Raleigh scrambles on the ground, rolling himself over so he's looking up at us. He looks so afraid I think he might actually piss himself. Whatever buzz he was riding before has well and truly gone. One eye is already swollen shut and his lip is still bleeding from where Lincoln laid hands on him.

"What are you going to do to me?" His voice wobbles and I roll my eyes. Why is it that the entitled assholes who don't know how to take no for an answer are the first ones to crumble?

Mav reaches down and yanks him to his feet by the throat. "Oh, QB. I warned you once already about touching Octavia. What do you think I'm going to do to you for what you did?"

Raleigh pales as his eyes go wide, the reality of his situation sinking in. "You can't. My mom won't join. Not if something happens to me. The Knights need those connections."

"You think you're the only one with connections?" I ask, letting the silence of the night fill the space once I'm finished speaking. I learned long ago that there is power in silence. Words have more power when you use them less often. People fear noise, but there's something unsettling in silence that most can't handle; something that resonates with the darkest parts of our souls and brings them forward, reminding us that we *all* have those secret parts of ourselves that we try to hide away from the world.

"Please, you guys, I'll do whatever you want," he begs, and Mav grips his throat tighter until his breaths come in strangled, rattling gasps.

"Pathetic. If I wanted you to beg, I'd *tell* you to beg." He releases him, letting him drop to his knees before pulling his knife from its sheath at the small of his back. Raleigh whimpers in the dirt like a fucking coward as Mav crouches down. He cuts the rope at Raleigh's ankles before straightening and kicking him square in the chest.

Raleigh crumples to the ground, wheezing.

I look down at him, a sneer on my face, making sure to catch his gaze before speaking. "Get up. And if you even think about running, I'll slit your throat myself."

He whimpers and I turn my back on him, looking over at Mav who grins sadistically down at our toy. "He said get up!"

I head into the ruins, ignoring the wildlife that scatters as my footsteps echo through the cement and stone entry. Footsteps behind me let me know that Mav and Raleigh aren't far behind. I descend the crumbling spiral staircase, using the flashlight on my phone to illuminate the way down.

As I reach the lower floor, the lights flicker on, the lone hall illuminated in a sickly shade of yellow, leading to the only door down here.

The elevator.

The lights flicker in and out, buzzing like a fucking mosquito in my ear. I'm halfway down the hall when Raleigh stumbles onto the cement. I turn in time to see him faceplant and I'm not sure if he tripped or if Mav pushed him. Either way, I don't care. He whimpers. Once I reach the elevator, I push the button to call the car and try to shove away the memories of the first time I came here. It's hard to believe that it was nearly five years ago.

It was the day that changed my life and took away every hope and dream I ever had.

This is the place where dreams come to die.

The place where innocence is stripped and any semblance of freedom you thought you had is caged up and put on display as a mocking reminder of a life you once lived.

The weight of the guns in the shoulder holster under my jacket are yet another reminder of just how far I've come since I learned these tortured halls existed.

The ding of the elevator echoes in the space as the two of them finally catch up. I step into the car, turning to face them once I'm in. Raleigh has a bloody nose to add to his collection of minor lacerations and contusions, and the blood on

Maverick's knuckles tells the rest of the story. I say nothing as I lean against the metal wall, waiting for them to join me.

"What is this place?" Raleigh stammers as Mav pushes him into the car without a word. He steps in and stands beside me, his arms at his sides, hands clenched as he bounces on the balls of his feet.

Mav was made for this world long before we ever knew about it. I've never figured out if his dad was intentionally merciful in never letting him know a life outside of this, or just a twisted sadist.

There's a reason we tried to keep Octavia from The Cove.

This place is just one of the many reasons we tried to protect her from this world, but I think we might be swimming out of our depths in trying to save her.

She was always our light, but even the brightest of lights fades in the depth of this darkness.

That's what the last five years have taught me.

Taught us all.

Raleigh's whimpers fill the silence as the elevator descends into the depths of hell. Six basement levels of pure nightmares.

But we're going to the base level, where I know no one will be, not at this time of night.

When the elevator stops and the doors open, Raleigh pushes past us, trying to run, and Maverick barks out a laugh. "I love it when they run."

His eyes light up as he stalks after our prey. I stroll casually from the car, knowing that Raleigh isn't getting far. Even if I did doubt that Mav would catch him, there's no way out of here except the way we just came in.

The lights along the walls of the circular room flicker on, starting at the doors as they close behind us and slowly making their way to the opposite end of the expanse.

A strangled scream fills the room, followed by the crunch of bone, just as the last of the lights flicker on, illuminating Maverick standing over Raleigh's quivering body.

I move toward the single metal chair in the middle of the room, nodding to Mav who drags Raleigh toward it by an ankle that juts at an unnatural angle. I move to the left of the room, running my hand over the hidden panels in the wall to open the cubbies I want access to, and grab cable ties and lighter fluid before closing them.

Between the two of us, we have everything else we need already.

By the time I get back to them, Raleigh is trembling with his ass firmly planted in the chair. I throw the cable ties to Mav, who catches the pack in one hand, his sadistic smile widening. "Move again, and I'll cut you open and play with your insides while you watch."

I don't doubt Maverick would do it either. A smile plays on my lips at the squeak Raleigh lets out as Mav binds him to the chair. Mav steps back, admiring his handy work before nodding. There's no way Raleigh is leaving here without us.

"It's not so fun being the one with no control, is it?"

I tilt my head as I ask the question, letting him see the monster I keep caged inside of me. He gulps audibly and I smile.

"I wasn't going to—"

"Ah, ah. Do not lie to us," Maverick says, waving the tip of his blade in Raleigh's face. "Digging for the truth is one of my favorite things to do."

He cuts through the QB's t-shirt until he's sitting topless, then does the same to his jeans so he's sitting bared to us.

That'll teach him to go commando.

Mav bounces giddily once he throws the cut up clothing across the room.

"What are you going to do to me?"

I move across the room to lean on the wall, letting Mav have his fun. I won't let it go too far. While the Knights might overlook us maiming him a little, I'm pretty sure the punishment for killing him is more than either of us are willing to pay.

"Nothing less than a rapist deserves," Mav replies, dragging his blade from the hollow of the worm's throat, down to the bottom of his abdomen, laughing as Raleigh roars in pain. "What's wrong? Don't like being defiled? Made to bleed? I told you she was off-limits, you should have listened."

I watch as Mav works his blade like a master. There really isn't much worse than death by a thousand cuts. Raleigh's skin peels open like butter under the knife, and blood runs from his wounds like a gloriously macabre waterfall, mixing with the pool of piss beneath the chair.

Some of these scars will fade, but not all of them. Maverick avoids his face—the Knights don't usually like it when you mess up the pretty faces that belong to them.

"Should I peel your dick like a banana? I bet my knife would enjoy that real good," Mav taunts before I tune him out and ignore the scene playing out before me. I don't enjoy this shit like he does, but I'm not about to hide from it either after what this asshole tried to do to V.

After a while, the screams Mav tears from him don't even really register. Except for when he pours on the lighter fluid and they get even more high-pitched. But when Raleigh falls silent and looks like he's going to pass out, I step in. "Enough."

Mav steps back, covered in almost as much blood as Raleigh. "I was barely getting into it." I quirk a brow at him and he barks out a laugh before shrugging. "At least let me finish what I started?"

He motions to the cuts on Raleigh's crotch, and I look, trying not to laugh. "Go on." I wave, encouraging him, and Raleigh cries out as Mav finishes carving the T of rapist into his skin.

Ink can be removed. Scars are forever if you cut deep enough.

When Mav is done, I pull one of the guns from the holster and point it at Raleigh's head. I smile as his screams turn hysterical. "You said you couldn't kill me. I heard you from the trunk. You said *he* couldn't kill me!"

"I guess I did, didn't I? Though I didn't say I couldn't kill you." I tilt my head and laugh before lowering the gun, levelling it at his dick and letting off a round. "That won't kill you at least."

His screams echo violently off the distant walls, almost matched in volume with Maverick's laughter.

"Next time you're warned… Pay fucking attention. Do not touch things that aren't yours. Especially when they're ours." I holster the gun as his head lolls to one side, his eyes unfocused and glassy, before heading back to the elevator with Maverick on my heels. When the car arrives, we climb in and I hit the number three.

We reach the third level and find Eleanor behind the front desk of the office-style space that's housed on this floor. There is someone here twenty-four seven, either Eleanor or Elisabeth. The Knights always have someone available.

Her lips twist when we step from the elevator toward her desk. "Finley, Maverick. What brings you here?"

"Clean up in the basement. He'll need a medic pretty quick so he doesn't bleed out." I grab a towel from the pile on a cart near her desk and throw it at Mav. "Clean up before we head out."

He nods and saunters down the hall to one of the many rooms at our disposal, and I lean against the desk. I don't bother with the cleanup—I didn't get any blood on me—whereas Mav looks like he took a blood shower.

"Who is it?" Eleanor asks with the phone to her ear.

"Raleigh Rittenhouse." Her eyes go wide before she looks down at the desk and calls for a medic. It doesn't take long for two of the doctors on the floor to rush past me to the elevator, not even sparing a glance in my direction.

"We'll need a car too. The one we arrived in was borrowed."

Maverick appears, freshly showered in clean jeans and t-shirt, a few minutes later. "We good?"

"I think so." I cut my eyes to Eleanor who nods. "Perfect. Let's head back."

We ride the elevator in silence to the first floor and when the doors open, Jerry —yet another cog in the machine that is The Knights Society—greets us with a set of keys hanging from his fingers. "Where to, gentlemen?"

My phone buzzes in my pocket as cell service returns and I see the message from Linc.

**Linc:**
At V's. East is here.

I show Mav the message before pocketing the phone and turning to Jerry. He doesn't need to know where we're going and, right now, I've never been more grateful that Octavia moved back home. "To the Saints'."

---

Jerry drops us off at the gates to the Saint mansion, waiting until we're on the grounds with the gates shut before he drives off. I have no doubt that the Knights are watching us closely with V back in town.

Especially since I'm convinced they're the reason she's here at all. I'd put money on Stone's suicide being a cover up. The Knights specialize in fixing their problems. Even if the problems are of their own making.

I walk up the drive and head straight to the hidden gate between this property and V's. Maverick is hot on my heels. Neither of us has said a word since we left the base.

"Shit," I hiss, halting abruptly.

"What?" Mav asks, perplexed.

I tap my ear, then motion to his clothes. It only takes him a second to clue in to what I mean and he starts to strip out of the Knights-issued clothing. Bugs and trackers are implanted in pretty much everything they have. He grins as he stands in front of me, butt-ass naked, then walks the clothes to the trash cans before heading into the Saints' house. A few minutes later he reappears in another jeans and t-shirt combo, but this is one of his own.

Once he's ready, we make our way to the Royal house, heading in through the back doors to the kitchen where the lights are already on, illuminating the backyard. The alarm beeps as I open the door and I disable it. Mav closes the door then re-arms it. I'm pretty sure V doesn't know we have the codes, but in this instance, what she doesn't know won't hurt her.

We keep quiet as we remove our boots and pad through to the living room, where we find Octavia asleep on the couch, wrapped in a blanket, while Linc and East murmur quietly between them. Linc sees us hovering in the doorway and stands. East looks over his shoulder then follows his brother toward us and we head into the kitchen.

"How is she?" are the first words to fall from my lips. The rest of the world might think we hate her, but there are few secrets between the four of us.

Lincoln drops onto a stool at the island while Mav grabs us all sodas from the fridge. "As good as can be expected. She's sleeping off whatever he gave her. Is he dealt with?"

"He won't be raping anyone else." Mav grins as he hands out the drinks. "Finn shot his dick off."

I roll my eyes at the exaggeration and accept the drink, dropping into the stool opposite Linc. "I shot him in the dick after you carved rapist into his crotch, but yes, he's dealt with, we took him to The Cage, so the Knights are cleaning up."

"This was by the door when we got here," East says, dropping the black card onto the table.

*You're out of time, Miss Royal.*
*We're coming for you.*
*Ready or not.*

"Motherfuckers," Maverick hisses as he slams a fist on the table.

"Keep your fucking voice down. Do you have any idea how long it took for her to fall asleep?" Linc glares at him, that commanding tone of his biting. It's rare that we bicker between us, but when we do, it's usually because of her.

She has always been our weak spot.

"So what do we do?" I ask, looking to the brothers.

Lincoln always has a plan. He runs his hand through his dark hair and sighs. "I don't know. She won't leave, that much is obvious. Even after this, I don't know that we could drag her away with a herd of wild horses, so we need a new plan."

"I've been saying that for weeks," East grumbles as he gets up and walks back to the doorway to check on her. I turn my attention back to Lincoln, who glares at his brother.

The resentment that East is still here when he could've escaped is real, and while I have my own suspicions about the whole situation, I keep my mouth shut. They have their issues, but the bond between them is ironclad.

"As I was saying, we need a new plan of attack. She won't leave, and what we've been doing isn't working."

I lean back in the chair, watching him closely. "So what do you propose?"

A scream cuts through the air and I move without even thinking. My heart pounds in my chest until my eyes are on her. Tears stream down her face as she claws at her throat. I stride across the room, and lift her from the couch. I sit, placing her on my lap and hold her so she can't hurt herself anymore than she already has. "You're safe, V. I got you."

I murmur the same phrase to her until she calms, rocking her softly until she falls asleep again. The others are all standing around the room, just watching us.

I have zero doubt in my mind that any chance of us giving her up, of getting her out, went out the window when Raleigh attacked her.

That means we need to do the opposite of what we *were* doing.

"We need to keep her close. It's the only way to protect her now." My words aren't meant for anyone in particular, but Lincoln nods.

"He's right. We tried pushing her away, but the only way to keep her safe now is to keep her as close to us as possible."

East runs a hand through his hair and pulls his phone from his pocket. "I'm going to call Smithy. He needs to know what's happened." He leaves the room and I hold my breath as V shifts in my lap, clinging to me even in her sleep.

I'm not surprised Smithy has some clue of what's going on. You don't work for the Royals and not know about the Knights—they go hand-in-hand. The downside of being involved with a legacy—something I know all too much about. I'm not sure how much he knows about the finer details though.

As if reading my mind, Linc speaks up. "He can help us keep her safe. We just need to bring him into the fold."

Mav shifts from foot to foot before crossing his arms over his chest. "This stuff isn't my strong suit. You point me in a direction and I'll make people bleed—to get them out of the way, or to keep her safe. I'm not the guy with the plan, but I'll do what needs to be done to keep her."

He doesn't give himself enough credit, but I nod anyway and Lincoln does the same.

"Now all we have to do is convince her that this is either the right plan of attack or the only option." I sigh.

Lincoln barks out a dry laugh before leveling me with a scowl. "Yeah, because she's not going to be stubborn about that at all."

"Can you blame her? Especially after these last few months. We just have to be more stubborn than she is. She'll come around eventually."

"If you say so," he murmurs, eyes fixed back on the girl in my arms. The girl we've all been in love with our entire lives. "You make it sound so easy."

I lean back, shifting to cover her with the blanket again. "Nothing has ever been easy when it comes to her."

He huffs and drops down into the armchair across from the couch. "Maybe, but I'd do it all over again if I thought it would save her."

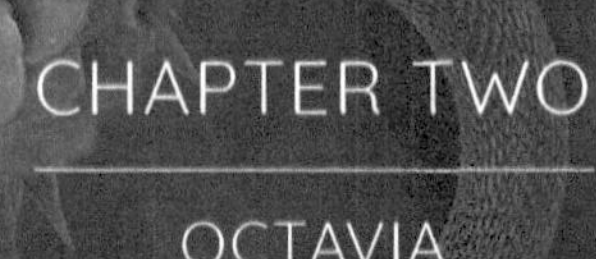

# CHAPTER TWO

## OCTAVIA

A scream rips from my throat, the remnant of a nightmare that clings to me as I struggle against the hold someone has on me.

"You're safe, V. You're safe."

East's voice soothes me a little. My heart hammers against my ribs, even as his grip loosens a bit, helping me to relax some more. I open my eyes and squint against the brightness. The sun is just starting to rise, and the light is filtering in through the windows.

For one moment, I feel a little peace before icy dread runs down my spine as broken memories of last night hit me. The fractured flashes make my stomach churn. "I'm going to be sick."

I scramble off of the couch to the downstairs bathroom, just managing to get my head over the bowl before the feeble contents of my stomach show themselves. My head pounds as memories of Raleigh continue to assault me, the images making the room spin. The back of my neck heats, so I look at the doorway, seeing Maverick standing there, watching me. I groan before my stomach churns again. He moves quickly, pulling back my hair and rubbing my back until the somersaults my insides are doing calm for a moment.

I lean my head on my forearm, trying to remember exactly what happened. How far Raleigh went. How the fuck I got back here, and why the hell East and Maverick are here.

My head pounds like my heart is in my fucking skull. I close my eyes, wishing the room wasn't so goddamn bright. The feel of a cold washcloth on the back of my neck makes me jump, but I groan in appreciation as the water trickles down my spine.

I should not be taking comfort in anything Maverick Riley does or says, but the world is spinning backward, my stomach is a rollercoaster, and I don't have the strength to tell him to get the fuck away from me. He waits with me until the puking and the dry heaving stops.

I take a few deep breaths, hoping that they'll help my stomach to stop flipping. When I'm fairly confident I have a handle on my upchuck reflex, I stand up and brush my teeth, ignoring the fact that Maverick is still in here with me. I'm still not entirely sure why he's here at all.

Once my mouth doesn't taste like a trash can, I splash cold water on my face to try and clear some of the cobwebs from my mind. I try not to panic about the black holes in my memory from last night; what I do remember is enough to make me not sleep for a week.

Last time something like this happened… well, I got justice. Kind of.

This time… this time I'm not really sure what happened. I know I'm going to have to ask them, even though I wish I didn't have to. I don't want to feel like I owe them anything. They've been such assholes to me the last few months, the last thing I want is to be indebted to them.

I glance at Maverick in the mirror. He's standing with his arms folded across his chest, watching me as he leans against the doorframe. His gaze is like a red-hot laser on my skin—it's so intense—his broody look as menacing as ever.

So much for the softer side of him I thought I might see.

"Are you done?" he asks, the softness of his voice a complete contrast to his demeanor.

I turn to face him and scrub a hand down my face, exhaustion sweeping through me despite the fact I *just* woke up. "I'm done. You can leave now."

"I'm not going anywhere." He pushes off the frame with his shoulders and opens it, ushering me out of the bathroom.

He stays on my tail as I head back toward the living room; where I find East still on the couch and Lincoln sitting in the arm chair, watching me as I come to a halt in the archway. Mav stops at my side and leans against the wall.

The sound of sizzling and a shout of "Fuck!"—which sounds very much like Finley—comes from the kitchen, drawing my attention. "You're all here?"

"Where else would we be?" Lincoln snaps, and I wrap my arms around myself.

Mav straightens up and moves closer to me. "Don't be an ass, Linc."

"Who's being an ass?" Finley asks as he appears in the doorway from the kitchen, a plate in each hand.

"You have to ask?" East sighs and stands, moving toward Finley. "I'll get the other plates."

Finley glares at Lincoln while I shift from foot to foot, wondering what fucking twilight zone I stepped into when I woke up this morning.

"What the hell is going on?" I don't ask anyone in particular, but Finley looks over at me before putting the two plates he's holding on the table in the far corner of the room. Lincoln rolls his eyes before standing and moving to the table. Mav follows suit, leaving me standing alone as Finley approaches me.

"Come and eat, you probably need something to line your stomach."

I twist my lips, stepping back as he reaches out to touch me. I don't want to be touched right now. What I really want is a shower and more sleep. "I'm not hungry."

"I'm sure you're not, but that doesn't mean you shouldn't eat."

I let out a sigh and run a hand through my hair. "Why are you here, Finley?"

His hand drops to his side and he smiles sadly at me. "Like Linc said, where else would we be? After what happened to you last night…"

He trails off, like he doesn't want to trigger me, but these guys being in my space is enough to do just that.

"What *did* happen tonight… last night?" I ask, pulling at the hem of my top.

All of them look at me, a mix of surprise and discomfort on their faces. "I mean… I remember some of it, but my memory is a little patchy." I swallow down the emotion that threatens to rise. I remember enough to know I'm going to roundhouse Raleigh's head off his shoulders if I ever see him again, but I *need* the holes filled in. I can't let the blank spots in my memory fester.

*I survived this before, I can survive again.*

I repeat the mantra in my head. Maybe if I say it enough, it'll be true.

"V," Finley starts, moving closer to me again. He raises a hand toward me, but seems to think better of it and lowers it again. "You eat first, then we can tell you whatever you're missing."

I move toward the table. I have zero intention of eating, but maybe if I play along they'll just tell me what I want to know and leave. I sit at the end of the table, opposite Lincoln, and next to Maverick. Finley takes the seat on my other side as East reappears with the last of the plates. There is silence for a minute as East sits between Finley and Lincoln, and they all just stare at me.

It's so fucking suffocating.

I look down at my plate, the smell of the freshly baked croissants is beautiful, but my stomach protests. I know I should eat something, but the thought of it… just nope. Picking at the skin beside my thumb nail, feeling more vulnerable than I have since I got back to The Cove—which in itself speaks volumes—I try not to spin out about everything that's happened.

The silence hanging in the air is so fucking loud it's practically deafening.

"V," East starts, but doesn't say any more. I look up to find Linc glaring at him before he turns his stare to me.

"Raleigh drugged you and attempted to assault you. We stopped him, and brought you home."

I glare at him. Way to play it down. Here's me going through the worst possible scenarios and that's all he gives me. "I'm going to need more details than that."

His eyes harden, staring me down. "What else is there to know? He tried, we stopped him."

For just a moment, the darkness inside me is burned away by fiery rage. "What else is there to know? You're kidding me right? It's my fucking body. I'm the one who was violated. You want me to just sit and imagine what happened? Wait for the memories to come back and knock the breath from my lungs? Tell me what the fuck happened."

"V—" East starts but I shut him down.

"No, I'm sick of whatever all of this is that you guys have been doing. So either tell me or get the hell out." I fold my arms across my chest, glancing between all of them, waiting for someone to speak.

"Ellis called me," Lincoln starts, and I sit in silence, waiting for him to continue. "He said you looked out of it, and that Raleigh was following you around like a bloodhound. Since he's known for being, well, a rapey asshole, we found you. When we did, you were telling him no, but you were topless and I'm pretty sure his hand was down your pants while he was slobbering all over you. I couldn't really make out for certain, because I was too busy getting him off of you. Is that what you want to hear? That he had his hands all over you?" Anger simmers just beneath the surface of every word, and I can't tell if that anger is directed at me or elsewhere, but whoever it's meant for, it's bleeding all over me.

"Of course it fucking isn't, but you know what's worse than knowing? Fucking imagining what happened!"

"He didn't do any more than that," Maverick adds, looking at me like I might break.

I don't want him to look at me like that, because then I might actually curl up and shatter rather than stuff it down and put it on a shelf like I've been doing since my dad died and I came back here. I've just been trying to survive this place so I could escape it. I'm pretty sure if I opened up the mental closet with all of my trauma, my mind would splinter.

Instead, I nod once and look down at my plate again. "Thank you for telling me."

The sounds of silverware against flatware fills the space and no one says another damn word. I don't even pretend to eat. I just sit and wait for them to leave, trying not to let everything swirling inside of me spill over.

*Not much longer.*

Once they're finished eating, I finally stand, my legs still shaking a little. "I'd like you all to leave now."

My voice comes out shaky but I jut out my chin, trying to feel a little like my usual self, and catch everyone's gaze one at a time.

East looks like he's going to object, but Linc interrupts him by standing from the table with a glare tossed in my direction, making me wince.

"Fine," he spits and heads out of the room toward the door.

Finley looks up at me with sad eyes. "V—"

I cut him off with a shake of my head. "I'd really just like to be alone. *Please.*" I stress the last word and it's only then, when my desperation to be alone so I can break comes through, that the three of them stand.

"You know where we are if you need us," East says before leaving. Maverick just looks at me like he wants to object more, but Finley shakes his head. At the move, Maverick follows East, leaving me alone with Finley.

He watches me closely in that assessing way that he has. "Are you sure you're going to be okay alone? What happened tonight… last night… I'm happy to stay."

I clutch my arms tighter around my stomach and step back, giving me some more space from him. While I'd probably feel safer with him here—which I'm aware is fucking moronic, all things considered—if he stays, he'll keep looking at me like he is now, and I can't cope with that. My dad raised me to deal with stuff on my own, so asking people for help isn't exactly the easiest thing for me. "I'd really just rather be alone."

He frowns, and I'm aware he doesn't agree, but why he thinks I'd feel safe with the four of them baffles me. East, I could understand, but him, Maverick, and Linc? Other than last night, they've not done one thing that tells me I can trust them. And I sure as hell am not about to forgive them just because they did what any decent human should have done.

Finley watches me closely and I guess that, despite me trying to keep my face passive, he can see everything I've tried to hide, because he just nods. "Okay. I'll be next door if you need anything."

He gathers the dishes and leaves the room. I stay where I am, staring out into the back yard until I hear the alarm arm and the door slam shut. Only then do I let the emotion out. Only then do I fall to the floor and clutch my knees to my chest, crying tears of violation, of devastation for everything that happened at that party last night.

This is the only time I'll let Raleigh Rittenhouse break me, after this, I'll put my armor against the world back on, but right now… right now I need to be broken.

I just hope I can put myself back together after.

---

After spending most of the morning breaking and drowning in the despair I try not to feel; showering to try and wash off the violation of everything and failing; then trying to sleep and failing; spiraling in my shame, I find myself down in the music room.

Composing was part of my healing process the last time something like this happened. The crazed fan that thought I was in love with him… I shudder as the memory assaults me.

*I survived this before, I can survive it again.*

I'd never been so scared in my entire life as when he grabbed me in that hall and I felt the needle plunge into my neck.

My memory of that night is all too vivid from when I came around, tied to a bed, with him standing over me, watching me. If it wasn't for Panda… no… it isn't worth thinking about. I shake my head, trying to chase away the memory, the pain, so I don't sink further.

My therapist encouraged music to help me heal, and it did. So while I might not have all my memories of last night like I did before, I'm pretty sure that it's still the best way for me to deal with everything that's whirring inside of me like a hurricane.

I sit down at the baby grand, but I can't bring myself to put my fingers on the ivory. I still feel dirty, and I don't want to taint the pureness of the keys. A shudder runs through me as I close my eyes, the feel of Raleigh's hands still on my skin.

It occurs to me that I should probably call the police. That I should do something. But I also wonder what the point would be. The police in this town have never done anything against people like him. His dad owns a Fortune 500 company, not to mention his mom's restaurant—fucking power couples—so even if the police did anything, his dad would just pay to get it swept away.

The corruption in the system, especially in The Cove, is disgusting.

Still, I wonder if it would stop him from doing it to someone else.

Or if I'm the only person he's done this to, did I do something to deserve it? Did I lead him on?

I close my eyes and tip my head back, trying to take deep breaths.

While, logically, I know that I don't deserve what he tried to do, the fact that this isn't the first time it's happened to me… it makes me question if I didn't bring this on myself? Was this my fault? What is it about me that makes people think something like that is okay?

I need to call the police.

Report what happened.

*Do something.*

Even if it's fruitless, at least I tried, and then maybe he won't try it with anyone else.

I stand, fixed in my decision, when I realize I haven't seen my phone since I woke up this morning. Heading back upstairs, I search everywhere for it and come up empty.

*What the actual fuck?*

I find my clothes from last night and go through the pockets, still nothing.

*Where the fuck is my phone?*

Trying to cast my mind back, I can't think of where I had it last, so I do the only thing I can think of.

I put on my hoodie and head next door.

It doesn't take more than a minute to head through the gate in the back yard to bang on the Saints' front door. Not thirty seconds later, it's ripped open and I find a half-naked Lincoln looking back at me. His jeans aren't even zipped up.

Who the fuck opens the door like that?

"Do you have my phone?" I ask before he can say a word, because my fragile state can not handle him being this new, cold version of Lincoln I've known since coming back. Right now, I'd give just about anything to have my old friends back.

Which reminds me to call Indi as soon as I've spoken to the police.

God, I'm such a bad friend sometimes.

Lincoln just stares at me, and jams his hands in his pockets.

"Well?" I take a deep breath, trying not to get frustrated.

He nods and walks away from me, the muscles in his back flexing as he goes. I shift from foot to foot while I wait for him to return, trying not to look as awkward as I feel. The seconds seem to drag out and it feels like it's been at least an hour when he returns, though I know it was likely just a few minutes. At least he's done up his jeans now, even if he is still topless.

He hands me my phone and when I tap the screen, nothing happens. Of course it's dead, why wouldn't it be?

"Thanks," I say, smiling stiffly before turning and heading back the way I came.

"Octavia." I turn as he barks my name, and realize he's only a few steps behind me, barefoot on the paved ground. "Are you okay?"

A glimpse of the boy I used to know shines through for a moment, but I'm not foolish enough to think that the ghost I see is who Lincoln still is. Maybe, deep, deep down, my friend still exists, but I don't have the energy or the time to go hunting for him. Not right now.

I shrug at him and play with the cuffs of my hoodie. "I'll be fine. I've survived worse."

He looks confused for a minute but doesn't say anything else, so I turn back around and walk away from him. As I reach the gate between our properties, I find him still watching after me. I give him a tight smile and head home, determined to make a stand.

Once I'm back in my own space, I set the alarm before finding my charger to plug my phone in. The silence in this empty house is deafening, I hate it. I hit the tablet on the wall and start a playlist of low, classical music, just to fill the silence.

As I stare into nothingness, flashes of last night replay over and over in my mind until the buzzing of my phone brings me back to the present. I look down at my screen and see dozens of messages from Indi. I swipe them off the screen for the time being, determined to call the police without further distraction. I open up the phone app and my phone starts ringing in my hand. I don't know the number so I hesitate, just a few seconds, before answering anyway.

"Hello?"

"V?" I relax at Finley's voice. "I've been trying you on and off all day, I was starting to worry."

"What do you want, Finley?"

The line is silent for a moment and butterflies take flight in my stomach. "I need you to not call the police."

I practically hold my breath, wondering how he could've known and why he'd even ask that. "How? How did you know?"

"Because despite what you might think, I know you, Octavia Royal. Always have, always will. Which is why I know you've wrestled with the decision of what to do, and you think this will help stop it from happening to anyone else. I need you to trust that it's been handled. There isn't anything the police can do that hasn't already been done."

My heart thumps in my chest at his words. "What does that even mean?"

"I'll tell you one day, when you're ready to know. Just know that it was handled."

I suck in a breath as I clutch the counter. My knees shake as I try to calm myself. None of this makes any sense to me. None of it.

"He won't hurt you ever again. No one will. He won't hurt anyone else either. I know you don't trust me, you have no reason to, but that will change. I promise you that much. Call me if you need anything." He pauses, and I'm stunned to silence. "I mean it, V. *Anything.*"

The line drops, and I stare down at my phone wondering exactly what just happened. I'm still tempted to call the police, but something in his voice makes me pause. I've nearly chewed through my lip, grappling internally with the decision before me, when my phone rings again and Indi's face fills my screen. The phone is barely to my ear when I hear her screech. "About fucking time!"

---

It didn't take long for Indi to ditch whatever she was doing once she realized I was conscious and home alone. Less than forty minutes later, she blasts through my front door like a hurricane on the warpath.

"Are you okay? That's a stupid question. Goddamn, I am still so angry I could murder!" She practically vibrates with rage the way she radiates negative energy.

I smile a little, for the first time since I woke up, and laugh softly at her. "I'm okay. Kind of. I *will* be okay, and that's what matters. What happened to you last night? The guys just said they got me home."

"Yeah, it was kind of hectic after everything happened. The party shut down pretty fast when Maverick and Finley hauled Raleigh out of there after Lincoln got you out." My eyes go wide at her words, and my earlier conversation with Finley rings out in my head.

*What did he do?*

She watches me closely with narrowed eyes. "They didn't tell you that bit I'm guessing?"

"No, no they definitely didn't. They just told me that Raleigh drugged me, and attempted to… yeah… that they stopped him, and brought me home. I was out cold and I still don't remember anything. All I know is that the four of them were here when I woke up this morning."

She huffs out a laugh. "That's definitely the condensed version. I tried to get you home myself, but Lincoln refused to let anyone else near you. Hell, he parted the crowd at that party like Moses parted the freaking sea."

"Enough about me, and all of that. I can't yet. I need some time to process. What happened with you last night? The last thing I remember properly, you were with Ellis Donovan?" I wag my eyebrows at her, feigning the excitement I want to have, because fake it till you make it, right?

A blush spills across her cheeks at his name and I smile a little wider. Apparently music therapy isn't the only thing to get me through the bad times. Especially when I have friends like Indi in my life.

"Spill!"

"Are you sure? I don't want to, like, sweep what happened to you under the rug. We should be outraged, angry, and all of the fucking things about what happened to you." That fire in her flares bright once again and my heart pangs that she cares for me so much.

"I'm sure. The last thing I want to do is focus on what happened. Finley told me it was handled. I have no reason to trust him fully, but I trust that much at least," I tell her with a shrug.

She goes a little pale and nods. "Girl, I would. You should have seen his face as he and Maverick hauled Raleigh out of there last night. I don't think I've ever seen him that angry. I would not want to be Raleigh."

I get comfortable on the couch and she joins me. "Moving on… Ellis Donovan."

She blushes again, and I laugh softly. She throws a cushion at me and I grin harder.

"Ellis Donovan… is a long story. I told you I knew the brothers before, that I was friends with Scout…" She trails off while I sit, butterflies taking flight in my stomach. My excitement for her is the exact distraction I needed from my own freak show of a life. I curl up, pulling the cushion against my chest and hugging it while she spills the tea. "Well, I actually dated Ellis last year. And Ryker… and their friend Dylan."

My eyes go wide at her confession. "Holy shit, you've totally been holding out on me!"

She looks down at her hands, wringing them uncomfortably. "Yeah, not everyone is too open-minded about a girl dating three guys."

"Dude, I am so not that girl. Date seven of them if you want. Power to you! So, you and the three of them… what happened?"

She shrugs before looking back up at me. "I'm not really sure. We got halfway through the summer, and they told me it wasn't working anymore. That it was too dangerous for me to be with them."

I roll my eyes and lean back on the arm of the couch. "Ugh, boys fucking suck sometimes. Why do they get to judge that shit?"

"Well, I mean, their brother runs The Kings… they're basically his seconds. Shit can get dangerous real quick in their world."

"The Kings?" I ask, beyond confused.

Her eyes go wide as she realizes I have no idea what she's on about. "I…I thought you knew. That's literally the rivalry between the Donovans and Lincoln and co." She blinks at me, squirming, while I sit waiting for her to continue. "I don't know everything, but I'll tell you what I do know."

She takes a deep breath, pausing as if trying to find the right words. "I'm not sure exactly what Lincoln and those guys are mixed up in, but I know that Ryker and Ellis got dragged into something last summer that they were a part of, and that's why the rivalry between the schools seemingly escalated."

"That explains the gun…" I trail off and she looks at me, jaw slack.

"Gun?"

"Yeah, Ryker was at the school one day a few weeks ago, talking with the guys, and pulled a gun on them."

"He did what?!" she shrieks, outraged, before taking a deep breath. "I swear to God, they might have been right. Their world is not anything I've ever experienced before. They kept me out of most of it, so I don't really know that much. All I know is that if something nefarious is happening in their side of The Cove, they probably know about it. Though, they didn't know about my car getting jacked. When they found out, they were pissed…" She trails off, blushing again.

"So are you back with them? Or just Ellis? Or?"

"Honestly? I have no fucking idea." She shrugs and I laugh softly again. "How did we end up dating—or not dating in your case—but still smack in the middle of the two biggest rivals in this not so big town?"

"That, my friend, is my luck. My curse. Whatever you want to call it." I sigh, trying to get comfortable. "All I've ever wanted is zero drama, yet that shit chases me like I'm its favorite main course."

"You don't have *that* much drama," she says, wincing a little, and I bark out a laugh.

"No, no, not that much. Just my dad turning my world upside down, putting me in the public eye, then making it so I have to come back here after he kills himself… only to find out that the people I thought were once my closest friends basically hate my guts. Let's not forget my only family in the world *also* hates my guts. And well, I mean, you've been around since I got back. You know the rest. Being stuck in the middle of their… what? Turf war? That doesn't feel like that much of a stretch at this point."

She stares at me, eyes wide, and starts laughing so hard she cries. "Man, and I thought I was the drama queen." She wipes at her eyes, trying to take a deep breath but just ends up laughing harder. I get caught up in it and end up laughing until I cry too.

What the fuck even is my life?

"But for reals, if the guys are willing to aim fucking guns at each other, we might have issues," I say, chewing on my lip.

"Boys are idiots. Way too much testosterone," she says with a shrug. "They can hate each other all they like, it's not going to fuck with us."

I nod, because well, I've never had a bestie before. I'd lay down my life for her at this point.

She grins at me, looking freaking devious as fuck. "Maybe they'll learn to love us enough that they can love each other."

I burst out laughing. "The chance of those four falling in love with me is pretty slim. Let's just hope for a truce?"

"Girl, you are straight up blind sometimes, but you didn't see their faces at that party either. They love you, whether any of you admit it or not." She spares me a sad smile for a moment before changing the subject. "Fuck boys… not literally, either. Crazy assholes. How does pizza and a movie sound?"

My stomach gurgles at her words and she giggles. I realize I haven't eaten since yesterday morning. That might explain the spaciness I've felt today. "That sounds like heaven."

She grins and fist pumps. "Perfect, you order the food, I'll pick the movie."

I grin back at her, glad that, even while everything else in my world feels up in the air, my bestie is my rock and my safe space. I might not have wanted any friends when I came back here, but I'm not sure I'd have survived here this long without her. I'm just thankful I won't have to find out.

The buzzer for the gate sounds and I grab my phone to check the security feed, my stomach twisting when I see what's waiting for me at the gate.

Yellow tulips. Dozens of them sprawled across my entire driveway.

That's when I remember the note from the night before, and fear flushes through me.

*You're out of time, Miss Royal.*
*We're coming for you.*
*Ready or not.*

Out of time for what?

# CHAPTER THREE

## OCTAVIA

A night with Indi was exactly what I needed. I ignored the flowers, and by the time the pizza arrived, they were gone. Which is a-okay with me. I do not want to know what is going on. I just want a quiet life, dammit. I knew coming back to Echoes Cove was going to be insane, but everything that's happened thus far is *so* beyond that.

By the time she left, after me practically forcing her out of the door, I'd learned even more about the Kings, and what sort of stuff they do. I'm more than a little shook by it all, but more really by the fact that she kept it from me; this huge part of her life.

On the one hand, I understand it, but on the other… I don't know. I guess I thought we were closer than that. Hell, I told her everything that has happened to me since I arrived here. *Everything.* I'm trying real hard not to be butt hurt about it.

Trying and not succeeding. I'm aware I'm likely hyper focusing on that to distract from the clusterfuck that has been my life this weekend, but still… it doesn't stop my illogical emotions running riot.

In my attempts to distract myself from the insanity playing on a loop in my mind, I'm trying to just live life as normally as freaking possible. I messaged Smithy when I woke up to check in with him, casually leaving out the events of my weekend, because I don't want him to worry. Now I'm attempting to cook breakfast.

Cooking has never really been my strong suit but I've got to earn points for trying.

Right?

I put the English muffins in the oven and decide to head outside to the mailbox. I haven't been out there for a few days, so lord only knows what's going to be in there. The fresh air of the morning is so cold that goosebumps rise on my arms as I step out of the house. I scurry down the drive and grab the various envelopes and magazines from the mailbox before practically running back into the house. I should've put on a hoodie today apparently.

I'm aware that it's November, but still, this is California. It shouldn't be this damn cold.

Once I'm back inside, I drop the mail on the counter in the kitchen so I can go through it while I eat. I grab my hoodie and slide it over my head before I grab the eggs and bacon from the fridge. This cooking thing can't be *that* hard, right?

Wrong.

After butchering my attempt at simple meal preparation, I sit down at the counter to try and eat some of what I cooked. If I liked my eggs rubbery and my bacon charred, I'd have this cooking thing nailed. The only thing I managed to get right were the English muffins, and that's because they only had to go in the oven for ten minutes and I set a timer.

I give up on trying to eat the charred remains and pop a bagel in the toaster. That's got to be simpler… I grab the cream cheese from the fridge, smearing it over the bottom part of the bagel once it's done, then go about opening the mail. Bills and junk mail freaking galore. If it's not that, it's people wanting me to buy stuff.

I get toward the bottom of the pile and spot a manilla envelope. Just the sight of it makes my pulse race. I gingerly pick it up, my hands shaking as my mind flicks back to the last envelope like this I got. This is not how my morning was intended to go. I wanted a slice of normal, dammit.

I open the envelope and tip it up on the counter. A ton of photos cascade over the surface and my stomach turns.

They're from Friday night.

Pictures of me alone.

Ones with Raleigh. A red cross through his face.

Ones of Lincoln beating the crap out of Raleigh.

Of him putting me in his car.

Of Finley and Maverick putting Raleigh in the trunk of a car.

Others of just them with their faces scratched out, some of me just puttering around the house and in the yard. It's so fucking gross. Underneath them all, I find a note.

*They can't keep you safe. Not like I can.*
*You'll see.*

What the *fuck* is my life?

I grab my phone and dial the number Finley called me from yesterday. I'm aware I could just go next door to Lincoln or East, but I feel so exposed that I don't want to go back outside. I put the phone to my ear and Finley picks up on the first ring.

"V, what's wrong?"

I suck in a breath that that's his first assumption, hammering home that my life really has gone to hell in a hand basket since I came back here, but I might actually need to rely on them for help with this and not just sweep it under the rug, or put it on a shelf with the rest of the shit I don't want to deal with. It's not like I have the security team with me twenty-four seven anymore, and this isn't just bullies or paparazzi. I'm going to have to be the girl my dad raised me to be. The headstrong, smart and capable girl I was before I came back to The Cove. Something about coming back here, whether my grief or not, had me putting my head in the sand, but the time for that is done.

The problem with that is I don't have the resources I used to, which means I need to rely on someone, and they're all I have right now whether I like it or not. And if I need their help, he needs to see these pictures. They all do. "More pictures turned up in my mailbox." I know I don't need to say any more than that for him to understand what I mean. Lincoln took the last set of photos that arrived, but there's no way he didn't share the news. My voice shakes more than I'd like as I speak, but considering this weekend has been a living fucking nightmare, I'm cutting myself some slack for being a little weak.

My life shouldn't be this insane. I don't know what I did to deserve it all but if I could repent, I would. I take a deep breath and realize he hasn't said a word but I can hear him moving around whatever room he's in.

"I'll be there in less than ten. Stay on the line with me till then."

"I don't have to—"

"Just humor me. Please?" Something in the way he says please makes me relent. I put the call on speakerphone and place it on the counter before going around and closing all the blinds and curtains. My skin crawls at the thought that someone has been watching me inside my house. It was bad enough when the last set arrived and they were me out and about, but I'm used to that, because, well, paparazzi. This is a little different.

I've dealt with a fully fledged stalker once before, and that's all I can assume this is. Except last time… last time I had round-the-clock security. Mac and Panda barely left my side. My dad might've wanted me to be capable and independent, but he also made sure I was safe… most of the time anyway. Last time, my dad and Mac kept most of it from me—which still pisses me off but I can't change the past—and it wasn't until I was taken that I had any idea there was something wrong.

The purr of the Lamborghini sounds down the line, and I let out a small breath of relief. I should not be relieved that he's on his way here, not after everything, but better the devil you know and all that.

"I texted the others. Everyone's on the way." Finley's voice is tight, and I let out a shriek when there's a bang on the back door. I spin to find Lincoln and East trying to get in the back door.

"What's wrong?" Finley's voice is urgent, and it takes me a second to speak as I try to calm my racing heart.

"Lincoln and East are here. They scared the shit out of me."

I move to let them in. I forgot I'd moved the spare key to the back door, but all things considered, it seems to be a good thing that I did. The door opens just as Finley responds.

"Okay, I'll hang up since they're there. I'll be two minutes. Open the gates for me."

I end the call and open the gates from the app on my phone. East locks the door once he's in and disables the beeping alarm. I really need to work out just how many people have the code to that freaking thing. That, or figure out how to change them myself since these four all seem to have it.

Lincoln doesn't say a word as he moves to the counter and starts going through the pictures. East moves toward me, wrapping me up in his arms, and I sink into him. He's been one of the few shining lights I've had since I got back, so I take his offered comfort. "Are you okay?" he murmurs, squeezing me tighter before letting go.

"Not really. It's been a long few days, but I'll survive," I say, shrugging, just as the front door opens and slams closed. Seconds later, Finley and Maverick are in the kitchen with us.

Mav glances at me, like he's trying to work out just how unstable I am, before moving toward the counter with Lincoln. Finley assesses me quietly too, before stepping toward me. "We should reset the alarm, just in case. You secure the gates, and I'll do the house alarm."

I nod and do as he says, wishing my brain would function properly for a minute. That should have been a no-brainer. I look down at my phone and bring up the app to make sure the gate is locked and closed.

"Is this everything?" Lincoln asks, his voice harsh. My head snaps up to look at him and I find his face practically blank. Just his usual cold stare looking back at me. I nod, frozen on the inside from his chilly demeanor. It's the only thing that keeps my anger toward his dickhead behaviour in check.

Finley glares at him before ushering me onto a stool at the counter. He and East sit on either side of me, as if protecting me. Which is the funniest thing considering the hurt Finley has helped to cause the last few months.

"Yeah, that's everything that was in the envelope." I sigh, and sag a little. This is all too much. I don't understand any of it. I'm not usually the type to tuck tail and run—at least I never used to be, I used to face my shit head on—but that's all I want to do right now. Just to escape the madness surrounding me. "Is this linked to the note that was on my door when we got back here Friday night?"

They all glance at one another, and that gets my back up. What the fuck?

"What note?" Maverick asks, leaning back on the far counter and folding his arms across his chest.

"The note that was on the door when Lincoln got me home from the party," I deadpan, because what sort of question is that?

"There wasn't any note, Octavia," Lincoln finally says.

I pinch the bridge of my nose, trying not to be exasperated. Why would they lie about something like that? They obviously know something, and I don't understand why they're withholding details. Getting information from them is like trying to get blood from a fucking stone. "Enough with the gaslighting! Of course there was a note! I remember seeing it. It said I was out of time."

"There wasn't any note, Octavia. Maybe you dreamt it up. A lot happened that night." Lincoln shrugs and turns his attention back to the photos.

I close my eyes, trying to tamp down the anger that rises. "I don't know why I even bothered calling. You're not going to help me. I'm just going to call the police. There's nothing any of you can do. Just leave. I'll handle this alone. Like I've done with everything else."

"Octavia, don't be so fucking ridiculous. I already have a PI looking into the last pictures you gave me, I'll give him these too. Just leave it to us," Lincoln chastises, and I see red.

I have had enough.

"Don't be so ridiculous? Are you fucking kidding me? You come over here, chastise me, give me no information, and expect me to just what? Accept that shit? I don't know who the fuck you think I am, Lincoln, but I am not that girl. I was wrong to call you guys for help. I should've known better. Just fucking leave. I'll figure it all out on my own. And give me the other pictures back." I jump down from the stool and move to the back door to emphasize my point, but none of them move.

I take a deep breath but my anger is spinning out. I am so sick and tired of them treating me like this. Helping me on Friday does *not* make up for everything they've put me through up to this point. I'm sick of being this girl, I've let too much slide, and I am done. Shit is going to change. Starting right the fuck now. I hit the app on my phone, disabling the alarm before ripping the door open, refusing to have them in my space any longer than they already have been. "I said get the fuck out!"

---

This entire weekend has been too much. I've survived so much, powered through, stayed strong, but everything that's happened these last few days, the things I've learned… I thought I had a handle on it all until this morning. This stalker thing might just be what pushes me over the edge to the place I can't come back from.

I wish it was just the Raleigh thing. I've survived that before. I know I can do it again, but that on top of everything else? I don't think I can handle it all at once, but I don't have any other option. Nobody else is going to do it for me. I have to save myself.

My world is spinning off axis, and I feel so fucking alone. Not for the first time, my anger at my dad rears its head for leaving me to this cesspit. He might have raised me to deal with shit on my own, but maybe, just maybe I don't want to. I tried to deal with him spiraling alone and look where that got me. Back here, acting like someone I don't recognize. It's like losing him turned me back into that useless little girl I was before we left.

Sitting around in the dark probably isn't helping me deal with anything, but that's what I'm doing anyway. I thought coming to the theater room and putting on a movie might help me compartmentalize; I usually do it so well. But today… it's as if that part of my brain has just fully shut the hell down. The absolute nothing I got from the boys this morning just has everything turned upside down. Telling them to get the fuck out was only the smallest part of what I wanted to do.

I can't tell if I'm angry, disappointed, or just so fucking sad.

I guess the only person I can really rely on is myself.

My phone beeps, the new security system letting me know one of the doors has opened. Got to love that nifty little upgrade. I flick to the cameras and see Finley walking through my entrance hall. What the hell is he doing back here?

He pauses, tilting his head as if trying to work out where I am, and then a small smile plays on his lips as he looks directly up at the camera. *'Found you'* he says to the camera, then disappears off screen. It's not long before the door to the theater room opens and his frame casts an imposing silhouette in the light spilling through the doorway.

I should probably feel angry that he's here, scared even after everything that's happened, but I just feel numb. "What do you want, Finn?"

His old nickname slips from my lips but I'm too tired to care. This man staring down at me is so far from the boy I used to call my friend. "I wanted to talk. Just the two of us."

"I'm not sure what there is to say." I sigh, tucking my knees up against my chest inside my oversized hoodie.

He shakes his head and steps forward, the door closing softly behind him as he approaches with his hands up in surrender. "This morning was a colossal fuckup. I didn't say much of anything, but what I should have said was, I'm sorry."

"You're sorry?" I let out a dry laugh, quirking a brow at him as he sits down next to me, turned so I can see his face clearly.

He nods, and as much as I hate to admit it, I can see just how sorry he is in his eyes. It's hard to describe, but it's just there for me to see. The guy who opens up to no one, showing me a part of himself. Just like he used to. "What exactly are you sorry for?"

"I'm sorry for hurting you. I know it won't make any sense to you, but I was trying to keep you safe. There's more going on here than you know but I can't tell you yet, and I'm sorry for that too." He takes a deep breath, scrubbing a hand down his face.

My heart pounds in my chest at that small bit of information. I knew there was something else going on. I knew I wasn't hallucinating. I cling to that tiny shred of information like it's a lifeline. "But why can't you tell me? If it affects me, I deserve to know what the hell is going on."

I'm sick of being left in the dark. If I'm really going to start taking charge of my own shit. I need to know what's happening around me.

"V, I wish I could tell you, but I can't."

I sigh, exasperated. What the fuck does that even mean? "That's a bullshit non-answer, Finley. I deserve to know what's happening. Especially when I'm supposedly the one in danger. You say you're trying to keep me safe, but I'd be safer if I knew what the hell is going on, and if you guys weren't such giant jackholes to me."

"I'm sorry for being an asshole, I am. If there was any other way… but I won't apologize for trying to keep you safe. I will never be sorry for that, but I'm sorry for the way we went about it. For the pain it caused you. I never wanted to hurt you… Not really. " He drops his head so he's looking at his clenched hands in his lap. I hate that I hurt for him, that he's obviously been through a lot, but I don't know how to move past this. "I'm mostly sorry for not getting to you sooner on Friday."

I let out a deep sigh and tuck my chin under the neckline of my hoodie too. "Friday wasn't your fault. You guys got me out of there before anything really happened. That much I should probably thank you for… but the rest of it? How am I supposed to believe that everything has changed between us? You won't tell me anything, you treated me like shit, attacked the people I love, hell, you nearly broke me… Keeping me in the dark isn't exactly the way to go about fixing things. I felt so alone after my dad died… the only bearable thing about being sent back here after that was that I might get to see you guys again, and honestly… you guys crushed me. If I didn't have other shit to keep me going…"

He swallows, his throat bobbing, and I know my words hit home. "I'm sorry—"

"Sorry doesn't fix everything, Finley," I snap, tired of the empty apology.

"I know," he says, nodding, "and you have no reason to trust me, but I'm still going to ask you to trust me on this one thing. I'm going to do everything I can to earn your trust back, V. Whatever it takes."

Biting the inside of my cheek, I consider his words. He seems genuine, and he's letting me see past his walls, but I still don't know what to do. That little voice inside my head tells me not to trust him, but my heart, my intuition, tells me he's on my side.

And holy fuck could I use someone on my side.

"Okay," I nod, "but earning my trust isn't going to be easy, Finn. You guys put me through *hell* these last few months. I'm not ready to forgive you yet, either, but we can have an actual truce or something."

"I'll take whatever you give me. But, V, I'm not going anywhere. I'm in this. I lost you once already, I tried to push you away and that didn't work, so you had better prepare yourself for having me in your life, because I'm not going anywhere ever again."

His declaration makes my heart race and I nod, because there isn't anything more I can do. I want to ask more questions, find out what is happening, but he already shut me down once.

"What are you watching?" He shifts around on the couch, getting comfortable.

I bite down on my lower lip, glancing up at the black screen. Maybe a distraction from all of this heavy shit will be good for me. "I was just watching musicals."

He grins at me, the first real grin I think I've seen on him since I returned back to The Cove. "You always did have a weak spot for them. Come on, get comfy with me and we'll put another one on."

I eye him skeptically as he pats the couch beside him.

"Come on, I don't bite. Not unless you ask nicely." He says it with such a serious look that I can't help but laugh a little, relaxing almost instantly.

I roll my eyes and untangle myself from my hoodie, scooting over beside him. I flick through the other musicals available and flick on *Wicked*. He doesn't say a word, just settles in and watches the screen with me.

You'd think, after everything, I'd be tense. On edge. Yet something inside of me never wanted to believe they hated me. That little girl who loved these boys more than almost anything is dancing a little bop inside of me as I start to relax.

I lose myself to the joy of love and friendship, of power and betrayal, and how much a person can sacrifice for their dreams before they're not themselves anymore. Not trying too hard to hide that I'm basically singing along, and trying not to smirk when I hear him humming beside me. I *might* have watched this more than a few times with him when we were younger. By the time we're halfway through the movie I start to relax a little more, leaning into his warmth. It's insane that I feel safer with him here, especially considering how they've treated me, but I try not to overthink it.

"You okay?" he murmurs into my ear, a shiver running down my spine at the feel of his breath on my skin. I turn to face him and his face is so close to mine that it causes my heart rate to spike. His gaze drops to my lips and before I can think anything of it his lips are on mine.

He kisses me like this might be the only chance he gets and it's filled with heat. Want. Need. Pulling me onto his lap, I'm helpless, lost in the pull of him. The logical part of my mind tells me I shouldn't be doing this. That this is absolutely not a path I should be going down, but my body is louder.

I place my hand on his shoulder and he stiffens a little before pulling back from the kiss.

"What's wrong?" I ask, confused, wondering yet again if this is all just a game.

He shakes his head and takes my hands in his. "Nothing. I just don't want to push you."

I can't help but frown at him. They've all been pushing me; just look at what happened in the pool house. He had no issues pushing me then. But I guess that was before…

"I'm sorry," I say, feeling weirdly ashamed as I start to climb off his lap.

He grabs my chin and forces me to look at him. "Hey, none of that. I didn't say I was done with you, just that I didn't want to push you. I'm not here for that." My eyes go wide at his words, and I feel more confused than ever. He grabs my hips, lifting me with ease, turns me around, and pulls me back onto his lap so my back is flush with his chest. "Let me look after you."

A shiver runs down my spine as his lips touch my neck. The screen before us goes dark, and music starts playing softly in the room. I stiffen a little at the move and he pauses, putting his hand in my hair, gripping firmly until I can see him. "Relax, V. I'm not going to hurt you or do anything you don't want to."

"Okay." The word comes out breathy and he releases my hair. In the next second, he has my hoodie up over my head and tosses it across the room, leaving me in my tank and leggings. His lips caress my shoulder as one hand wraps around my throat.

I suck in a breath and feel him smile against my skin as my heart rate increases. "I won't ever hurt you again, V. Do you trust me?"

I nod, trying to relax as his hand slips beneath my leggings and panties.

Inching down at a snail's pace, I barely register what's happening when the pad of his middle finger reaches my clit and he applies just enough pressure to make a shudder run down my spine. Contrary to before, this time my body's reaction is one of pleasure, not fear, and for that I'm grateful.

Finn scoots down just enough to spread his legs wider—opening my thighs to give him better access—then follows a path down to my slit. I can hear just how wet I am as his fingers slide up and down, in and out.

This is insane. I should be hating him and pushing him away, but I don't. I can't. Something inside of me wants this, even though I know I shouldn't. When two of his fingers push in deep, I melt into his touch, feeling oddly secure—safe even—with his other hand firmly on my throat and pinning me down against his shoulder.

"Relax. I got you."

Easy for him to say.

His fingers at my throat tighten as he brings my cheek to his mouth, the warmth of his breath like a drug.

His tongue burns a path of lust from my jaw to the slope of my nose. It's so dirty and primal. It's filthy and animalistic. It's everything I should hate but don't.

In fact, I fucking love it. That simple act of dominance gets me even wetter and by the low chuckle he lets escape, I'm guessing he's figured it out too.

"Hmm, I licked you and now you're mine." I try not to laugh, because now is *so* not the time, but who says that? Feeling bold, I reach back to hold his head in my hand, but as quick as a snake, he's got my wrist trapped in his fingers before he brings it to his mouth and kisses the inside of my wrist softly.

In the following second, every bit of my attention hones in on just how obvious it is that I want him.

"Mmm," is all I'm capable of saying as he finger-fucks me like it's a punishment. Except the harder he goes, the more I want.

*I am definitely more than a little fucked up.*

Just when I think I'm about to come, when I feel like I'm going to fall off that cliff of ecstasy, he stops everything.

"What the fuck, Finley?" I untangle myself from him and stand so I can face him and give him a piece of my mind. Quickly realizing Finn has other—more twisted—plans when he grabs me.

I do end up facing him but instead of standing, Finn tugs at me, twisting around our positions so I'm somehow lying facedown on the couch, his big frame kneeling on the floor behind me. It's a good fucking thing this double decked couch is fucking huge or else my face would be smashed against the back of the couch.

"Give me your hands." I don't even hesitate—which, again, is fucked up—but I'm intrigued. Finley takes both of my wrists and places them behind my back, right where my ass begins.

I can't see what he's doing behind me but I hear the tell-tale sound of a belt sliding through the loops of his jeans right before I feel the leather strap imprisoning my forearms. "Is that okay?"

I think it over for a minute, all things considered I should probably be panicking right now, especially after everything that's happened recently, but weirdly, I'm okay. So I nod, and he starts to move again. He places his big hands on my thighs, guiding me to kneel with my ass up and out and at the perfect height for his mouth but—

"Holy shit." The words come out as a whisper when I realize what he's planning, except my legging are on so—

The slashing sound that breaks the silence and the sudden breeze of cool air at the apex of my thighs tells me my leggings are a thing of the past.

*RIP leggings.*

"What the fuck, Finn?" When I twist my neck just right to see what's going on, though, I'm even more pissed off. "A knife? You destroyed my fucking leggings and panties with a fucking knife? You could have hurt—"

My words and my anger dissipate in the seconds that follow when Finn lies beneath me, his shoulders keeping my legs spread and his mouth latches onto my pussy and all I can think about is how fucking good that feels.

Holy fucking shit.

With both of his hands on my thighs, spreading them impossibly wider, I forget about ripped leggings and knives at my pussy and just enjoy his very skilled tongue.

From clit to slit, he feasts on me like he's a man starved. He's never been one to express his feelings or… much of anything, really, but his moans and the occasional growl when his tongue intrudes inside me is enough to tell me he's enjoying this as much as I am.

My shoulders are tightly pinned back, so movement on my part is difficult, which makes the whole experience even hotter. All I can hear is the sound of Finn's mouth drinking up everything I have to give him. My heart pounds in my chest and I feel almost dizzy from it all.

I push back, seeking more—needing more—wanting to feel everything from his lips to his tongue to his cock.

It's like he can read my mind and in the next second, he's pushing two fingers inside me, curling them just right and reaching that perfect spot.

My entire body jolts up off the couch at the sensation. Fucking hell, he knows what he's doing.

I kind of hate that he does, it means he's got a whole hell of a lot of experience. That simple thought brings about a pang of jealousy that I'm not ready to analyze quite yet.

He curls his fingers once more, causing me to jolt again. His response is almost primal as he pulls me impossibly closer to his mouth, giving him a whole new level of access to my throbbing clit.

As his fingers relentlessly fuck me, his tongue fixates on my swollen nub. My blood begins to thrum, running through my body like uncontrollable fire, and I know I'm about to lose my mind with this orgasm.

With his free hand, Finn grabs the strap of the belt and pulls enough for my upper body to lift. My head tilts back, my hair spilling over my arms and ass. Finn is relentless. He fucks me with fingers and tongue, driving me toward the brink

I'm almost there. I can feel it taking over but it still feels just out of reach.

Then he curls his fingers and massages that sweet spot just as his teeth bite into my clit, and I'm a goner.

I don't recognize the sound that escapes me. It's both a cry for more and a scream to stop. It would be scary if it weren't for the intense pleasure burning through my veins. I can't breathe, I can't move. I'm frozen with the power of this tsunami of ecstasy that I don't know how to handle.

Finley doesn't let up. He laps up every fucking drop of my orgasm until I come again, the filthy sounds of his mouth another detonator to a smaller but equally intense orgasm.

It's only when he lets me fall back down on the couch that he gives me a single soft, lingering kiss on my clit before releasing my arms and unbuckling his belt.

I'm panting, trying to catch my breath to no avail, when he turns me back around, pulls my body closer to his, and bends down to lightly touch my lips with his.

I can taste myself on him, and that light kiss turns into a battle of lips and tongues. Just when I'm about to reach up to wrap my arms around his neck, he's gone. In the blink of an eye he's standing at the foot of the couch, looking down on me with longing in eyes and my orgasm on his mouth.

I want to think he doesn't regret what just happened, not while I'm lying here half naked and blissed out, but why else would he practically run from me? "Fin—"

I'm cut off by the ringing of his phone. He looks down and goes pale. "I have to go. I'm sorry." He looks torn as his gaze bounces between me and his screen. I just nod at him, open-mouthed, and he disappears from the room, looking back once before the door closes behind him. I watch him leave the house via the feed on my phone, hating how twisted up I feel about everything.

I flop down onto the couch, staring up at the ceiling. When will I learn?

He might say he won't hurt me and maybe he didn't mean to, but I should know better than to trust a damn thing any of them say.

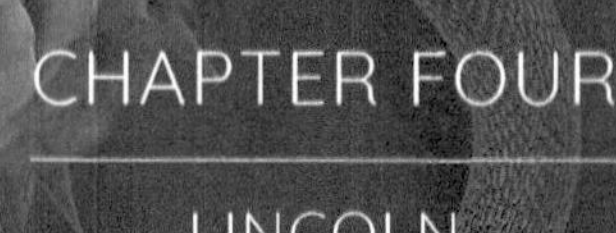

# CHAPTER FOUR

## LINCOLN

I barely slept last night, tossing and turning over the tangled web we've found ourselves in. With each move we make to save Octavia, we end up deeper in the murky waters. At one point, my greatest hope was to escape the Knights… but it has become painfully clear that my fate is written. With each job they have me do, the monster inside of me grows. He feeds on the darkness that spills across my soul with every person I destroy. With every life I end.

I stare into the darkness, having given up on sleep shortly after three a.m.. Though I have no idea what time it is right now, the blackout everything—walls, shutters, tightly sealed doors—makes this room almost like a sensory deprivation chamber. Yet… I still can't find sleep.

The only time I've known peace and actual sleep recently, is when I slept with Octavia. I don't know what it is about her that soothes the demons writhing inside me, but I'm past questioning it.

I already know I can't have her, and I sure as fuck can't keep her, so I can't get attached.

None of us can.

I can see my brothers slipping under her spell, that glow of light that she radiates captivating them all and there's nothing I can do to stop it. The more I push, the harder they'll pull.

East might be my brother in DNA, and I can read *him* like a book, but the other two are my brothers in blood and we don't have many secrets from each other.

We all survived initiation, just barely, and we survived it together.

I'm not sure we'd have made it alone. Not all of us.

Memories from those weeks still haunt me, and I'll do anything I can to save Octavia from it. Even if it means sacrificing everything I thought I wanted and needed in life.

Stone tried to save her, he sacrificed more than most would, but in the end even that wasn't enough.

I'm still convinced they killed him. I just don't know why. Even Finley, the quiet genius that he is, hasn't been able to find any information from hacking into their files.

I just wish I knew what their end game was with all of this. I know we started the ball rolling by voting against the trafficking being brought into town. They tried to justify it by claiming that tourists get lost every year, so no one would notice, but still, Echoes Cove isn't that big. Not really. Even with the number of people on their take, someone somewhere would have eventually worked it out.

My phone buzzes on the bedside table for the third time in what's probably the last half hour, and I give up pretending I'm going back to sleep. I roll over and flip my phone, the screen illuminating the room, and groan when I see my father's name.

It stops buzzing while I'm trying to decide if it's worth the headache to answer, saving me from making the decision. The last thing I need right now is my father wading in. He is all about the Saint way of life. Loyalty to the Knights is basically his life blood. He doesn't even see how broken his belief system is. He doesn't care who he hurts, or what he breaks, as long as it benefits him.

Benefits the Knights.

The phone starts buzzing again and I groan, scrubbing a hand down my face, trying to mentally prepare myself for this conversation. "Harrison, what can I do for you this morning?"

I can practically hear his frown at the use of his name, but he lost the right to be called Dad when I was thirteen. "Lincoln, you and your friends have been making a mess, and it's becoming something of a headache, all this nonsense with the Rittenhouse boy. His father has been pitching a fit, and his mother is thinking about taking her cartel connections elsewhere."

"He tried to rape Octavia." I don't say anything else, because I don't need to justify myself to him, and I'd do what we did all over again if needed.

Harrison scoffs down the line, like rape is nothing, and I suppose to a guy like him, it isn't. It could be worse.

"Regardless of what he did, it's causing me a headache. It needs to be dealt with."

His impatient tone makes me grind my teeth. This fucking guy. "What exactly is it that you want me to do?"

"I'm going to handle it, but you're going to owe me a favor." I take a deep breath as I pinch the bridge of my nose, trying to rein in my anger. Owing my father a favor is never a good thing. Never. I've tried to avoid it at all costs. The last time… well the last time wasn't pretty.

"I can handle it," I say, and I swear to fuck I can hear his smile stretch across his face.

"No, no, Son. I've got it covered." He laughs softly, and I can just picture him checking his watch, looking out over the skyline of whichever city he's in, lording over the population he rules, and they don't even know he exists. He's everything

I fucking hate, and I despise that I'm destined to become him. "You'll just owe me."

"Fine," I grind out, because I don't want to prolong his joy. "Was there anything else?"

"There was. You and the boys are needed later today. Prepare yourselves and be ready for instruction." I grip my phone so hard I'm a little worried it'll smash in my grasp, but take a deep breath and try to push past it.

I fucking hate The Knights Society.

"Anything else, Harrison?"

"I'll be home for Christmas. Make sure the house isn't trashed when I get back." The line goes dead. He has what he wants, so there's no need for him to stick around. That has been the story of my life.

I remember, once upon a time, I thought my dad hung the fucking moon. Then I got the slap of reality and I've never looked at him the same since.

I drop my phone and flop backward onto my pillows.

I wish this was the shittiest start to a day I've ever had, but compared to some, this is sunshine and fucking rainbows. Gritting my teeth against the urge to scream out at the injustice of this entire fucking thing, I fist my hands into the comforter and count back from ten.

*My father won't break me.*

I repeat the mantra that has kept me going for the last five years and focus on one thing: Doing what needs to be done to keep Octavia safe.

---

I've spent this entire godforsaken afternoon in my basement gym trying to work out my frustration; yet, it doesn't matter how hard I run, how much weight I lift, or how hard I hit the bag, my anger only grows.

I wish I could tell her the truth, but if she knew… it would just put her in more danger. There is also no way she would believe me. Hell, I wouldn't believe me if I were her. It all sounds like something out of a movie.

I wish it was a fucking movie, at least then there would be a happy ending, but there is no happy ending in this. Not for me anyway.

This is exactly why I wanted her gone from here. This place is toxic. Twisted. It will eat you alive if you let it.

Fuck knows it tainted all of us.

My phone pings on the floor, so I step back from the punching bag, wishing my wrapped hands were the only pain I felt anymore. I pick up my phone and shut off the music when I see the message.

**Unknown:**
You're up. Mission details will meet you at the drop.

Fuck my fucking life. Could this day get any fucking worse?

I pull up the thread with Finn and Mav, sending a message of my own.

**Me:**
You get the message?

**Mav:**
Yep. You driving?

**Me:**
Sure. Be here in ten.

We've always been sent on these missions together. They tried sending us separately to begin with, but we all went together no matter what, so eventually the Board decided this was easier for them. One small tick in our column of wins.

I wait for Finn to respond, frowning when it doesn't come through. It doesn't usually take him more than a few seconds when we get hit up by the Knights.

**Finn:**
Yeah. Be there in a few.

I grab my towel from the weight bench and dry off before putting my tank back on and heading upstairs. I snatch a bottle of water from the fridge in the kitchen and drop onto the couch to wait for the others.

East has no idea how lucky he is that he's not a part of this fucking shit. I still don't know why Harrison chose me instead of him, but sometimes, it's hard not to resent him for it. Especially when he chooses to stay here when he could go anywhere in the world. He is free from their clutches. Well, as free as anyone can be. He isn't a slave to them.

Not like we are.

I'm pulled from the spiraling darkness by Finley walking through the front door. He looks about as happy as I feel. Most people wouldn't be able to see the nuances, he doesn't really show much emotion, but the set of his jaw, the tightness of his shoulders… let's just say when you've been through what we have together, you notice the small things. He nods at me and heads straight for the bathroom. I turn back on the couch just as the door opens again and Mav strolls in, rubbing his hands together.

The guy is twisted.

We all are, really.

"Any idea what this is about?" Mav asks as he jumps the back of the couch and drops onto the seat beside me.

I finish my bottle of water, just as Finn reappears. "Not a fucking clue, but where's the surprise there?"

Finley takes a seat in the arm chair opposite the couch and runs a hand through his hair. Something isn't right with him. "What's wrong?"

He looks at me, his stare cold, almost calculating. "We need to tell V about the Knights."

"We've had this conversation, her not knowing is the best way to keep her safe." I sigh, wishing that our lives were different. That this wasn't our reality, and that we didn't have to shoulder everything we do. But the more she knows, the more danger she's in. I don't understand why they haven't realized that. I know her, and she's like a dog with a bone. If we give her even a little, she'll dig until she gets to the heart of it, and then it'll be too late. Then there will be no saving her, and I couldn't live with myself if she became like the rest of them.

"I don't agree. Not anymore. You saw that note, they're going to come for her. She'll be better prepared if we tell her. Even if we just tell her a little."

I sit up straight and pin him with a look while Mav just glances between us. The three of us have never argued, not since initiation. But since V came back, things have been different. "You think she'd believe us? You think she'd think it was anything more than another ploy to run her out of town? If we tell her now, she'll brush it off, and that'll probably just put her in more danger. We need her to trust us first. So we keep her safe. We do what we can to keep her with us, to build back what we once had, and then we can tell her."

"She'll think we betrayed her," he counters, and I run a hand through my hair.

"Maybe, but she's also not stupid enough to not see that we did it to keep her safe." I lean back on the couch and look up at the ceiling. "The hardest part is going to be getting her to trust us first. Finding out who the fuck is stalking her and dealing with them will help, but we did a lot of damage in the last few months."

My phone buzzes in my pocket, and theirs ping at the same time.

**Unknown:**
Be at the drop in twenty minutes.

"We need to table this for now and deal with whatever bullshit they're throwing at us today."

Finn looks torn and I don't blame him. He hates the chokehold we're in as much as I do. "What if we didn't?"

"Then they'll use her against us. That was their plan all along. Now she's here, and we know they can get to her easily, they already know we'll do what we have to in order to keep her safe."

"This is bullshit. I still don't get why they wouldn't just accept Blair and Nate to take over the Royal seats. Then Octavia would still be blissfully ignorant, a world away from here." He hisses and stands. "Let's get this shit done. Where is East? Someone needs to be with V while Smithy is still away."

"I have no fucking clue." I drop him a message to let him know we're heading out and ask him to keep an eye on V before grabbing my keys. "Let's head out. The quicker we get going, the quicker we get back."

"If only that were true." Mav laughs. "Remember that one time a job took us out for three fucking days? Let's hope that's not the case tonight. I like 'em quick and dirty."

I clap his shoulder and belt a laugh. "Oh, we know, buddy."

He shoves me, grinning. "Asshole."

We head into the garage and pile into my Cayenne. I hit the clicker to open the garage door, half hoping we get another text cancelling this little outing, but I know it's not going to happen. Most of my hope has been beaten out of me at this point. It's only the thought that we can keep Octavia safe that keeps my head above water.

I drive on autopilot toward the drop. I hate that my body remembers the way because I've driven it so many times. I'm not stupid, I know that they send us on more missions than the others because of our reluctance, our free will, the unwillingness to buckle under their thumb, but I'll be fucked if they ever take that fight from me.

The difference between us and those who submit easily is we have something else, *someone* else, that we're fighting for. Even when she wasn't here, when Stone had her away from us, when he did what he could to keep her from this, we fought for her. Even if she didn't know it.

I hope she never has to.

We drive through the pitch black of night, no moon in sight, and a shiver runs through my body. It feels like the darkness is an omen of what is to come. The Knights have made us do some fucked up shit, do things I never thought I'd be able to do to another human, but when it comes to survival, I'm always going to pick me and mine.

I pull up in front of the office building on Main Street and idle at the curb while Finn jumps from the car and enters the dark building. He's only gone for a few seconds before he returns with the envelope and three bags. Once he's back in the car, he opens the envelope and shows it to Mav and I.

*Dominic Taylor*
*3465 Crest Crescent*
*Sand Bay*

*A debt unpaid. Bring him to the Snake Pit.*

"He must owe Diesel money," Mav pipes up from the back, putting voice to my thoughts. "But if he hasn't paid Diesel, tonight is going to be bloody."

Finn hands Mav and I a bag each. Black clothes, boots, untraceable guns. The usual kit. All of which will be bugged to the high heavens.

*Fuck, I hate this shit.*

"Let's hope we're just the delivery system this time," I say, shoving my bag in the back and settling back into my seat while Finn puts the address in the GPS. A glance at the screen tells me tonight is going to be a long night. This address is two cities over.

*How the fuck did this guy get on Diesel's bad side?*

Diesel, one of the Knights, runs the Snake Pit. A den of underground fighting, and so much worse. Things that, despite everything I've done, still make my skin crawl. Things I will never condone.

Since we have legacy votes, we've managed to oppose some newer things—which is exactly what brought Octavia to the attention of the Knights in the first place—but some shit was already established and getting that stomped out will take more juice than the three of us have alone.

Money and blood make the world go round, and we're drowning in both.

We head around the building and enter through the back door after I punch in the code and change into the contents of the bags. I feel like one of the fucking X-Men in this get up. So fucking ridiculous.

It doesn't take long and I stash my clothes back in the bag before we head back out to the car. We throw the bags in the trunk. I already know we're going to need the back seat for transport, so this is just efficient for later.

Once we're all sorted, I climb in and start the engine, taking a small piece of joy from the purr of the car. Just one moment, one sliver of a speck of light in the dark, before I throw myself into the oblivion of what's to come.

Mav and Finn talk quietly for most of the drive, and I sit in silence, mentally preparing myself for whatever we're about to walk into. I'd like to hope he'll come quietly, but they never do. Mav's favorite thing is when they run. He really does run the gauntlet of psychopathy, though really he's just a product of his father's twisted ways.

The same could be said for us all.

They groomed us from a young age to be ready for when the Knights would come calling, but it was done in such a subtle way we never saw it coming.

I shake my head to clear out the memories. That is not a dark hole I need to go down. Not now. Not ever.

I focus back on the road, the dark of the night split only by the headlights of the car. Before I realize just how much time has passed, the GPS has me pulling into a fairly upscale suburb in Sand Bay. We come to a stop in front of a two-story house with a white picket fence.

The children's toys in the front yard make my stomach churn.

I don't hurt kids. None of us do.

It's a hard and fast rule.

"Fuck," Mav mutters when he sees what I do. "What do we do?"

I swallow against the lump in my throat as they both look to me for direction. I hate that I have to be the shot caller, but it's always been this way. "We do this quietly. We don't wake the wife or the kids. We get in, we grab him, we get out."

They both nod and we climb from the car, blending into the shadows. Finn heads up front, the guy can get past any lock or alarm system. He's a goddamn magician. He pulls the small tablet he never leaves home without from his back pocket before nodding back to us. The door is open and he heads straight for the alarm.

In less than a minute he reappears in the doorway. "We're in."

We move through the house quietly, making sure not to stand on, or trip over, any of the toys strewn across the floor. I'm just thankful that the stairs don't creak as we climb them.

"Linc," I pause, turning to see Finn at the bottom of the stairs, staring at the photos that line the wall there. "I think he's a single dad."

Fuck.

"Call Ellie, she's the closest person we have to this place," I tell him and head back up the stairs as he heads outside to make the call. This changes everything. Thankfully, we've had some time to build our own network of people outside of the Knights, so we have contingencies for shit like this. I grit my teeth, trying to swallow down my frustration as I head down the hall. I pause at the kid's room—obvious from the rainbow wood letters on the door spelling out 'Sofie'—hating that if this goes wrong we're going to rip away her innocence the same way ours was.

I fucking hate this bullshit.

But if I have to sacrifice this kid to keep the Knights' sights away from Octavia… It's not a competition.

I continue toward the master, opening the other doors as I go to make sure there isn't anyone else here.

Mav is on my heels as I enter the master and find Dominic fast asleep. I grab the guy's phone from the dresser and pocket it. Best way to avoid any accidental texts or calls. Mav pulls his gun and points it at Dominic's head as he covers the guy's mouth with his free hand.

"Dominic," I bark out, and his eyes open instantly. They go wide with fear as he takes in the gun and Mav hovering over him. "You've been summoned by the Knights to the Snake Pit. If you shout, or try to evade us, we'll have to kill you. I'd really rather not, especially with Sofie down the hall. So let's do this like men, shall we?"

I hate using the girl against him, but this will go better for us all if it happens quietly.

Dominic nods once and Mav releases his mouth. "I already asked for an extension, Diesel granted it. Why are you doing this?"

"We're following orders. Now get out of bed, slowly. My friend is a little trigger happy," I say, as Mav smiles maniacally at him. The shiver that racks Dominic's body is almost audible, it's so visceral. He climbs out slowly, in his pajama pants and tank top. At least he's dressed.

That makes this easier.

We head out of the room, Dominic first with Mav behind him, gun pointed at his back, and I follow them out.

When we reach the ground floor, Finn joins us and ties Dominic's hands and feet with zip ties before gagging him. I look at Mav who nods, holsters his gun, and fireman-carries the guy out to the car, leaving me with Finn.

"Ellie is on her way."

"Good," I say, nodding. "You stay here till she arrives. I'll take him to the pit and stay to make sure he leaves alive, even if not in one piece. The less that little girl knows about all of this the better. Meet us there when Ellie arrives. Use her car, we know that it doesn't have a tracker."

He nods once and I turn, knowing he'll handle things here while I deal with whatever horrors await us at the Snake Pit.

I just hope I can live up to my word and keep this guy alive for that little girl. No kid deserves to grow up without their parents, and I'm going to try my damnedest to ensure she doesn't end up an orphan.

---

My alarm goes off and I groan as I hit the screen of my phone, bleary-eyed. I take in the time and groan again. I barely got an hour of sleep after last night's activities.

While I'm pissed I barely slept, I'm glad I managed to ensure that the guy got home to his kid, even if he was more than a little bloody. Diesel isn't a guy you want to cross, and apparently Dominic tried to extend one too many times. I get the feeling if I hadn't insisted on staying, he'd probably be in a shallow grave somewhere this morning. The advantages of being a legacy and not just a pawn piece.

I roll out of bed and into the shower in my ensuite. I keep the spray ice cold, trying to shock myself into some semblance of consciousness, and run a hand over my face in an effort to wipe away the last of the sleep before turning the temperature up. I stand under the hot spray and try to wash away the stains last night left on my soul.

I already know I'm beyond saving, I lost hope of that a long time ago, but I try to counter the dark shit with things like looking after that little girl as much as I can. The world is too broken. I know I can't fix it all, but if I can keep some people from the darkness that's overtaken my life, then I will.

After spending too long in the shower, I rush through my morning routine and head to school. By the time I pull into my space in the lot, I'm exhausted and caffeine deprived.

Today is not going to be a good day.

Mav pulls in on his bike as I'm climbing from my Porsche, and Finn is already waiting, leaning against the door of his Aventador. At least some things never change.

They meet me at the hood of my car, each of them looking as exhausted as I feel. Not that anyone here would dare say a word.

"Lincoln!" I wince at the screech of my name, turning to see Blair practically skipping in our direction. I hate that we tried to make a deal with her—not that she knows it was all to help Octavia—especially now that she thinks we're friends. Maybe once upon a time, but the person she's become just isn't someone I want to associate with. Her thirst for what the Knights can offer her and her family tells me all I need to know, and it's enough to know that she isn't my kind of people.

"What do you want, Blair?" I snap, too tired to deal with her bullshit today.

She flinches, her step faltering a little, but only for a second before shaking it off and squaring her shoulders as she stops in front of us. "I want to know what your next steps are? I heard about Friday. This is the perfect thing to get her gone."

"We're done, Blair. Plan's changed." I don't mean to be a giant asshole, but it's a switch that got stuck on a long time ago and just won't turn off anymore. "Back off of Octavia."

She jolts back, looking like I just hit her. "But we had a deal. I need this, Lincoln. You can't just change your mind!" She stomps her foot and I roll my eyes. She looks like a toddler having a tantrum. The quiver of her lip doesn't escape me, but she's deluded if she thinks that's going to work.

"Shit happens." I shrug and lean back against my car, folding my arms across my chest.

It takes her a moment as her gaze bounces from me to Finn to Mav to realize that I'm being serious. Once she does, that cold, calculating bitch stare washes over her features. There's the Blair I know she is deep down. She really would have done well with the Knights.

I just wish I knew why they rejected the suggestion of her and Nate replacing Octavia. There has to be more to it than just keeping us three in line. "You're going to regret this."

She flicks her hair before turning and stomping away from us. Mav starts to laugh beside me while Finn shakes his head. "We should head inside; I need coffee."

"Sounds good," Finn says, grabbing his bag from his car.

"Can I throw my shit in your trunk?" Mav asks. I nod, unlocking the car with the key fob. He puts his jacket, helmet, and boots in my car, changing into the shoes in his bag before throwing that in there too. "Let's do this."

I lead the way up the stairs with both of them flanking me, and the sheep part like they'll shrivel up and die if they get too close to us. Almost no one here knows about the Knights, but everyone still seems to be able to sense the danger that rolls off us in waves.

Even Blair's friends don't know what she was trying to get wrapped up in.

If only she knew the true cost, I'm not sure she'd be so eager to join the sect.

We head to my locker, banners everywhere for the upcoming Homecoming dance, and I roll my eyes. I am so done with this dance bullshit already. Listening to the girls in this school titter on about it for the last few weeks, about who will be homecoming queen… I'm so over it. As I close my locker, having grabbed my books for the morning, I notice Indi, Octavia's new friend, saunter past us and head to her locker. I look around, but Octavia isn't anywhere to be seen. "Either of you know where Octavia is?"

Mav shakes his head. "No, I haven't seen her since she kicked us out of her place over the weekend."

Finn shakes his head once and glances down at his phone. I feel like I'm missing something with him, but I'm sure it won't be long until he spills whatever's on his mind. I move across the hall to where Indi stands at her locker and lean against the one beside hers.

She sees me standing there and turns to face me, crossing her arms over her chest. "You were supposed to look after her after Friday. Not piss her off more."

I guess they really do share everything.

"Wasn't my intention, Octavia just has a way of getting under my skin," I tell her honestly. No point in hiding from her, especially if she's dating the twins again. Chances are, she knows more than she's meant to. Between them and Octavia, she probably knows more than most.

"Well try harder," she says, slamming her locker shut. "Was there something you wanted?"

"Where is Octavia?"

She quirks a brow at me before barking out a laugh. Apparently Octavia really is rubbing off on her new friend. Awesome. "She's staying home today. After Friday she didn't care to face the student body. Especially since Raleigh was posting over social media that he'd be back in today. I guess whatever your boys did to him wasn't enough to keep him down for long."

I glance over my shoulder at Finley and Mav, who look about as shocked as I feel at the news. They worked him over pretty well, so the fact that he'll be back today… not something I expected.

"Thank you for telling me."

She nods once before heading down the hall toward her class. The other two join me as I let out a deep sigh. "Apparently, she's staying home today."

Mav claps his hands together, smiling. "So we're skipping too? With everything going on, it's not safe for her to be home alone all day. Not with all four of us here."

I nod, because there's no way in hell I'm leaving her vulnerable like that. Finn looks like he's going to say something, but thinks better of it, "We should grab coffee and breakfast on the way."

"Sounds good to me. You get breakfast, I'll get coffee?" He nods. "Awesome. Mav, you head straight to her place. The less time she's alone the better."

He grins like a Cheshire fucking cat at the command. "Oh goodie. Octavia in the morning is fun to play with."

# CHAPTER FIVE

## OCTAVIA

I swear I ache worse today than I have all weekend. It could be a delayed reaction from Friday, or it could be that I beat myself stupid in the gym yesterday as penance for succumbing to Finley's pretty words.

I should know better by now that actions speak louder than words. And his actions are hot and cold as fuck. I'm not beating myself up about messing around with him—a girl has needs—and he *is* a talented motherfucker with his hands and tongue. Even if I did fuck around with Mav a few weeks ago. No one is about to shame me for what I do with my body. I am not about that life.

Am I more fucked up about the fact that I did that with Finley so soon after what happened with Raleigh? Yes, that bit I'm a little conflicted over, but we all deal with trauma in our own way, so I'm not about to beat myself up over that either.

What I *am* going to beat myself up over is believing his words to me and then saying nothing when he disappeared. I haven't heard a peep from him since either.

Like I said, actions over words.

I flop down onto the couch, having resigned myself to taking a few days from school. While I might be able to compartmentalize my trauma pretty well, the thought of facing Raleigh today while dealing with Blair and her bitch squad too, just no. I might be strong, but I know when to give myself a minute.

So I pull the blanket off the back of the couch and turn on the TV. A couch day is exactly what I need in my life. A couch day *alone.* That is the key part here. A day alone, dealing with my thoughts so I can steel myself and prepare to face the masses. It might be worse because I skipped a few days, but fuck it. I'm not letting the opinions of a bunch of virtual strangers rule my life. I never have before. I'm not about to start today.

It's only a few weeks until break. I'm sure I can survive till then. I just don't really want to see Raleigh if I can help it. I hate what he did to me, and I need enough space to build some emotional walls before I can handle seeing him again. Plus I need to deal with the anger I have building toward him, otherwise I'm going to land my ass back in jail on assault charges again.

I flick through the channels on the TV and settle on some mindless comedy show to pass the time. Something I can get lost in and not have to think too hard about . Usually I'd use the day to watch my true crime documentaries, but I'm not sure watching about how to get away with murder would be great for my mental health at present.

I snuggle beneath the blankets, preparing for a long day of absolutely nothing, when the buzzer on my gate sounds. Picking up my phone, I check the camera and see Maverick sitting on his bike. He pushes the buzzer again and doesn't let up.

God, he knows how to literally push my buttons.

"I know you're in there, V. Let me in." His voice comes through the speaker and I groan, hitting the button on my app to respond to him.

"No."

"Come on, V. I just want to talk."

"Are you going to answer some of my questions about shit that's going on?" I ask and am met with silence. "Exactly. So no."

"Don't make me come in the side gate. We both know I can."

I hit the button to speak, my rage flooding back. "Why are you such a fucking asshole?"

"I'll tell you if you open the gate."

I scream into a cushion, relenting because he's going to get in here one way or another. As much as I don't want to deal with him right now, at least this is kind of on my terms. Plus it's easier to hear him out and get him to leave than to try and ignore him. Maverick is the kind of guy who will sit there all day with his finger on that goddamn buzzer just to piss me off.

I hear the roar of his bike as he pulls up in front of the house, and laugh when he tries to walk in and I hear the *bang* as he walks into the door with the full force of his body weight behind him.

Smooth. So smooth.

I cackle to myself as I walk across the room and unlock the door, opening it a fraction before moving back to my spot on the couch. I don't know why he's here, but if he thinks I'm giving up my spot he has another thing coming.

He closes the front door before kicking off his boots. He puts his helmet on the table by the door and hangs his jacket up, like he's almost a civilized human. He wags his brows at me, smiling as he asks, "Want company under that blanket?"

I roll my eyes as I snuggle down. "Get your own damn blanket."

He takes me literally and jumps the back of the couch, grabbing the blanket draped there as he does, and settles in opposite me.

"What are you doing here?" I stare over at him and wait for his response. Sometimes I wish I could fight him and the others as hard as they've fought me since I got back here, but a piece of me still belongs to them, even though I've denied it since my return.

The bond between us might be frazzled and frayed, but it's still very much there. No matter how much I might not want it to be.

I don't think I'm alone in feeling it though. Not if I look at their actions over the last few weeks. Even with them being assholes, there have been small glimpses of the boys I used to know.

"You weren't at school," he says, finally answering my question.

"No shit, Sherlock. That doesn't explain why you're here." I sigh, rolling my eyes again.

"Of course it does." He shrugs and steals the remote from the table, flipping over to some football game replay that's on from last night. I pick up my phone, realizing I didn't close the gate, just to see Finley's Lamborghini pulling up the drive as Lincoln's Porsche slides in behind him.

Awesome, the whole gang is here. Well, almost. I guess being a teacher makes skipping a little harder.

I hit the button on my app to close the gate once their cars are clear, accepting my fate and preparing myself for a day with the boys, whether I want them here or not. Better to resign myself to it and get them out of here as soon as possible than fight it. I get the feeling that fighting them isn't the best way to get the information I want from them. This way, at least I can find out what they want without draining myself emotionally. I don't have much reserve left to fight them, so I'm hoping they're not here to argue with me.

Seconds later, Finley and Lincoln enter the house, the smells of coffee and food hitting me almost instantly. My stomach grumbles at the smell and I realize I've barely eaten all weekend.

Oops.

Usually food isn't far from me, but I'm a terrible cook and I'm out of pretty much everything. I've also been a little preoccupied.

Finley looks over at me, and I don't know how, but just like I know Lincoln hasn't shared that he's been hopping in and out of my bed at night, I know that Finley hasn't shared what happened over the weekend. The same way I'm pretty sure Maverick never divulged what happened between us.

These boys hurt my fucking head.

"We brought breakfast," Lincoln says, holding up a tray of coffees in his hand as he strolls past me into the kitchen. Finley follows him with a brown bag that smells like heaven while Maverick just seems to wait for me to move.

I follow quickly. I'm hungry and it smells too freaking good to pass up. I'm going to have to learn to pick my battles with them eventually and now seems as good a time as any. If they want to feed me, who am I to deny them that? Totally not a battle I mind forgoing.

Heading into the kitchen with Maverick hot on my heels, I grab plates for everyone as Finley unpacks the bags. "I got some of everything. Pancakes, eggs, breakfast burritos—"

"Dibs on the burrito!" I interrupt as I jump onto the stool at the island where the rest of them are standing. They all just stare at me as I grab the burrito and do a little jig in my seat. Mav barks out a laugh while a small smile plays on Finn's lips. I let out a groan as I take my first bite, because goddamn that shit is good.

Thanks to breakfasty goodness, I can almost forgive them for barging in on my morning.

"So, other than feeding me, why are you guys here?" I ask once I'm done having my happy dance, then swiftly take another bite, groaning all over again.

Mav coughs and just watches me. "V, you keep making those noises, we're going to have another moment."

"Moment? Are you referring to taking my virginity, Maverick Riley? Because that was definitely some moment. However my happy groans about food should probably not take your mind to the same place." He pales, and Lincoln's hands turn to fists on the counter.

"Virginity? But there was no blood…" Mav's eyes go wide, gulping as he sits. "V, I didn't… I didn't know. Why didn't you say something?"

I just shrug and take another bite. "It was a good orgasm, why should me being a virgin get in the way of that?"

"Mav, do you maybe want to explain what the fuck she's talking about?" Lincoln practically growls. Not going to lie, it makes my kitty flutter a little, but I mentally tell her to calm the fuck down. We're playing happy times with too many of these assholes as it is, we do not need to add another one to the mix.

Mav just looks from me to Linc, looking like I just junk punched him. Not my problem he didn't tell them we fucked. Him not knowing about the virginity thing might be my fault, but since it's not a big deal to me, it shouldn't be to him either.

"Calm down your growliness." I grin up at Lincoln after swallowing my last bite and grabbing another one, because apparently I am hungry as hell. "We fucked. We're both grown-ups. No harm, no foul." I shrug, but let out a squeak when Lincoln flies across the counter and hits Maverick.

Well shit.

Did not see that coming.

Nope.

I look at Finley who is just watching the two of them beat the shit out of each other as they roll across the fucking room. "Will you do something?"

He looks at me a little worried before glancing back at them.

"Mav took my virginity, and Finn ate me out in my theater room!" I shout, and the fighting on the floor stops momentarily. "Boom, all three of you had a peek at my kitty; it's really no big deal. Now can we stop with your macho bullshit please?"

Apparently Indi's sassy bullshit is rubbing off on me, but that was too much fun to shout at them. "The food is going cold."

Personally, I don't get the fighting. It's not like Linc didn't eat me out all those weeks ago in the pool house.

God, that seems like a fucking lifetime ago.

They get up off the floor and Lincoln brushes himself off before taking the seat opposite me. They all glare at each other as the other two sit down and start eating in silence, too.

*Well this is fun.*

I finish my second burrito, refusing to let their stupid boy bullshit fuck with my little slice of happy. Once I'm finished, I rinse off my plate and put it in the dishwasher before sitting back at the island. "Which coffee is which?"

"Yours has your name on it," Finley says softly, passing me a cup. I take a sip, black and sweet. Freaking heaven. It might not be the floofy goodness Indi has taught me to love, but I love it like this just as much. I sigh happily into the bitter liquid gold that makes me feel more human and Maverick looks at me again before dropping his head into his hands.

"Okay, so, does anyone want to enlighten me as to why you crashed my morning? There I was, all set up for my pity party for one, and now you're here when a few weeks ago you'd have rather been anywhere but here." I lean back in the chair, sipping at my coffee as I look between them.

"Why didn't you tell us you were a virgin at the pool house?" Maverick asks, and I level him with a look.

"Would it have made a difference? You guys had those strangers manhandle me, and watched while they did it. You didn't give a shit about what they were doing to me, what you all did after, virgin or not."

He looks down his lap like he's almost ashamed, and good. They were assholes. Not that I didn't enjoy Lincoln going down on me while Mav watched and Finn whispered dirty nothings to me, but still. That kind of isn't the point. Not right now anyway.

I look to Lincoln who just stares at me. "Would it have stopped you from telling Mr. Peters that I didn't do our assignment? Do you know what he tried to do to me when he kept me back?" I pause, looking at each of them, waiting for an answer that I know I won't get. "Did you know he'd ask me to suck his dick to pass his class? Did you know he'd get his dick out, right there in class, and threaten me with it, telling me how no one would believe a word I said because of that sex tape? Did you even care?"

"He did what?" Mav roars, his emotions doing a full one-eighty. Shame replaced by blazing anger.

"It's done," I tell him with a shrug. I've moved past it and put it in the column of things I can't change, so I'm letting go. I just wish there wasn't so much in that column lately.

"We need to tell her," Finley says, looking at Lincoln. "She needs to know why."

"Does why even matter?" I sigh, gulping down the last dregs of my coffee. "What could you possibly say to excuse it? What could *possibly* be a good enough explanation for anything you did to me? I know you guys did me a solid on Friday with Raleigh, and you looked after me, but I'm not ready to forgive any of you. I have absolutely no reason to. And you still haven't told me why you're here."

"I told you I was sorry," Finn says quietly. "If I'd have known…"

"It probably wouldn't have changed a thing." I shrug and let out a deep sigh. "Now what is it you need to tell me? I have TV to watch, and I'd rather be alone to do it."

"Octavia…" Lincoln starts, scrubbing a hand down his face. "I don't even know where to begin. Or even how, but everything we did was to try and keep you safe. I won't apologize for that."

I roll my eyes, because of course that's his answer. "Wow, such a way with words. You gave me so much insight there. Bravo."

Finley's eyes narrow as he looks toward Lincoln, and I swear to fuck, if they start brawling in my house, too, I'm going somewhere fucking else.

"There's so much you don't know," Lincoln says, almost resigned. "And plenty more you won't believe."

I lean forward and rest my elbows on the counter, resting my chin in my hands. "Why don't you just try me?"

"We did what we did to make you leave," he starts, and I bark out a laugh.

"No shit, Sherlock. I caught onto that bit. But you're still not answering any of my goddamn questions. If you're not going to let me in on what's going on, you might as well go back to school."

He glares at me and I roll my eyes. If he's going to be Captain Obvious, then I'm going to give him shit for it.

"Well, what you obviously didn't catch on to was just how much danger you're in by being here in Echoes Cove. Which is exactly why we wanted you gone."

My eyes go wide at that little tidbit. "You want me to believe you were doing all of this *for* me? Give me a fucking break. That would require you giving a fuck, which you have very clearly shown you don't. Doing this shit for me because I'm in danger. I mean, fucking really?" I scoff.

"I told you she wouldn't believe me. What's the point?" Lincoln huffs and stands, looking back at me. "You're obviously not going anywhere, so we're changing tactics. You won't believe me about the rest, and I don't want to waste my breath trying to force you to hear me, so just don't expect a whole lot of privacy anytime soon. You're in danger, we can help. *That's* why we're here."

He grabs his coffee and leaves the room, putting his phone to his ear. I'm more surprised he didn't have something more to say about all three of them having got me off in one way or another, especially after his outburst earlier, but I shrug it off.

I don't claim to know anything about him anymore. He's confusing as fuck.

I look back at the other two who look conflicted as hell. "Do either of you have anything to add to his sparkling insight as to why you've all been such giant assholes since I returned? Or has the king spoken?"

My challenge hangs in the air, met with nothing but silence. Of course they're not going to tell me shit if Lincoln doesn't sign off on it.

"I figured as much. You should all just leave. You talk about keeping me safe, but the only thing I can see that I need protecting from is you three."

And maybe a stalker, but who's counting?

---

After successfully clearing my house of those who seem to love to hate me, I decide my mental health can take the backseat and get lost in a documentary on cults and killers—the blood and gore is a welcome change from the jumpy shit I've been dreaming up—which is perfect to distract me from the insanity of my own life. I might have made everything worse by letting it slide the last few months, and that has to stop, but I'm going to give myself today to ignore it all.

Well, kind of anyway.

My phone pings with an alert from my security app, and I groan, wondering which of those fuckheads is coming back to mess with my zen some more. It's only when the door opens and I see Smithy that my mood lifts. I jump from the couch, letting out a squeal as I run across the room.

Wrapping my arms around the old man, who I've missed way too much, he chuckles as he drops his bags and hugs me back. "Good morning to you, Miss Octavia. I didn't expect you to be home."

"I didn't expect you home today! I'd have made a cake or something!" I gush, happier than I thought I would be to have him back.

"Miss Octavia, I wouldn't wish that fate on my kitchen," he chuckles. "But I appreciate the sentiment. Now, why are you not at school?"

I pull back as he frowns down at me, though a small smile still plays on his lips. "It was a rough weekend. I needed an extra day."

His frown deepens, but he shakes it off. "Well, okay. Just this once it won't hurt, I suppose. What are your plans for today?"

"Honestly?" I say and pull at the bottom of my hoodie. "TV day."

I grin up at him and he shakes his head, smiling softly. "But of course. Well, how about I get these unpacked, then make us both a milkshake, and you can introduce me to whatever it is that has you so fascinated you can watch it for a whole day."

"Sounds perfect! Do you want some help?"

"No, no, Miss Octavia." He pats my shoulder gently. "You go get comfortable. I won't be long. Will Miss Indi or Master Saint be joining us this evening?"

"The Saints most definitely are *not* joining us, but Indi might. I'll drop her a text now."

He nods and grabs his bags before heading down the hall to his room. I feel lighter than I have in weeks as I bounce back over to the couch, get comfy, and find the crime documentary we started watching together a few weeks ago. Picking up my phone, I check in with Indi.

**Me:**
How is your day going, sunshine?

**Indi:**
It's weird. You missed it, Raleigh's schedule has been changed and he blew up first thing this morning about it. He's on crutches though. The football team is raging. Blair seems to be on the warpath again too. So… Typical day at ECP.

**Me:**
I'm sorry you're out there alone. I'll be back tomorrow.

**Indi:**
You sure you've taken enough time?

**Me:**

I'm not going to know if I stay hidden away. Smithy just got home. He asked if you were coming for dinner?

**Indi:**
Is he cooking mac and cheese?

I grin down at my phone. I tried to warn her before she ate it the first time that it was addictive.

**Me:**
I can ask.

**Indi:**
I am soooo there. We both know that adorable man won't deny you a thing.

**Me:**
Awesome, I'll see you in a few hours. Good luck and may the odds be ever in your favor.

**Indi:**
I love you, ya big nerd. See you in a bit.

I laugh at her message just as Smithy appears in the kitchen and starts making milkshakes.

"So how is your sister doing, anyway? Everything okay back home?"

He stops as he pulls the ice cream from the freezer and smiles at me. "She's doing much better, thank you, Miss Octavia. Now that she's situated everything is much better. We managed to arrange for some home care for her until she's fully back on her feet too."

Guilt spikes my stomach, knowing that he came back here for me, rather than looking after her. "You could've stayed longer if you'd needed to. I would've been okay." I chew my lip because I'm not sure how true that statement actually is, but I hate that I'm the reason he had to leave her.

"Nonsense, Miss Octavia. I was going a little stir crazy there. There is only so long a person can be around their family before they need to be with the people who are truly their family." He winks at me before starting the blender for the milkshakes. He pours chocolate sauce on the inside of the milkshake glasses before adding more chocolate chips to the blender.

My mouth waters at the thought of how good that's going to taste.

He brings the two glasses over and gets comfortable on the other side of the couch. "So what did I miss while I was gone?"

I take a sip of thick, chocolaty goodness to give me a second to think of how to answer that question, groaning as the sweetness hits my tastebuds. There's no way I can tell him everything that's going on, but a small part of me wonders if he knows more about what's happening here than I do. He's lived in The Cove while I've been gone. He obviously kept an eye on the Saints, surely he wouldn't keep secrets from me if they put me in danger, right? So I decide to counter his question with one of my own. "Do you know why the boys want me out of Echoes Cove?"

His eyes go wide quickly, and he turns to face me, putting his milkshake down on the table. "Not exactly."

My heart sinks. He does know something, and he kept it from me. I thought I could trust him.

"I knew they weren't all happy about your return, but I didn't know they wanted you out of here. I hope they haven't been too persistent." He frowns, guilt shining in his eyes, but I say nothing. If he isn't aware of what I've been going through, I'm not about to add to his obvious guilt. "I've worked for your family for a long time. For your grandfather before your father. You don't work with a Royal for as long as I have and not know that everything isn't what it seems. I know enough to keep myself out of what they were wrapped up in, enough to know that the boys are likely trying to keep you safe. The same way I am. As for the exact details, I don't know much. I'm sorry I didn't tell you this before, but I assumed your father would have passed the details on. You are his legacy after all." He pauses, and I wait for him to continue as my heart pounds in my chest. "What I do know is that your family has been wrapped up in the darkness that beats under the surface of Echoes Cove since the beginning. They were a founding family here, the same as the Saints, the Knights, and the Rileys, and it wasn't long before they became tangled up in the web of The Knights Society."

"The Knights Society?" I blink, trying to take it all in. So much information—and so little—all at once. And it still sounds so unbelievable. I don't think he'd lie to me, but how can any of this be real?

He nods before glancing around the room. "They are more dangerous than you can imagine, Miss Octavia. There's a darkness prowling just beneath the surface of Echoes Cove. Sometimes The Knights are there to fight it back, but more often than not, they're the ones ushering it to the surface. From what I understand, it's been that way for close to two hundred years. I've kept my head down and stayed off their radar. I don't know for certain exactly what they are, but I know that nothing good can come from being tangled up with them.

"They had their claws in your father at one point, but I assumed he broke free when he left this place, though it was never confirmed, not to me at least. He took you from here for a reason, and I'd lay my life down to say it was to get you away from the Knights. And if I had to make a bet, I'd say the boys were trying to protect you from it all too. The same way they protected you when you were younger. "

My brain about implodes with that little nugget and I lean back in my chair, taking in his words. I'd put money on this being what Lincoln thought I wouldn't believe. What Finley wanted to tell me. My mind works overtime going over everything that's happened since I arrived back here.

The only thing I know for sure anymore is that nothing is what I thought it was.

# CHAPTER SIX

## OCTAVIA

I've been stewing over what Smithy said to me all week, and in the end, I decided to take most of the week off. When I woke up this morning, I knew that today was the day I'd bite the bullet and head back into school. It's a Friday, so it's only one day to suffer through before the weekend.

I can totally do this.

I just need to work out how to face the guys without asking them a million questions. I know them better than they realize. Going in for the kill isn't the way to get the answers I want. I tried to ask Smithy more, but with the amount of fear he seemed to have about it all, I dialed it back. Giving him a heart attack really isn't on my to-do list.

Even if I'm still not really over the fact that he withheld information from me.

On the one hand, I get it. If this is a legacy thing, my dad really should've said something. I can't help but wonder if this is why I had to come back here. If that's why he killed himself; to be free of them. But if that's the case, why would he leave me at their mercy?

I put on my last swipe of mascara and fluff up my hair, shaking off the thoughts. I've been lost to this train of thought way too much the last few days, but without more information I'm just going around in circles. I really need to get some fucking answers, I just haven't worked out the best way to go about it yet. Finley and Maverick obviously won't say anything if Lincoln doesn't approve, and Lincoln is a tight-lipped motherfucker. So I need to think of something to get them to open up a bit. East might be an option, but I'm not even sure how much he'll say without Lincoln.

My phone pings on my dresser and I smile when I see Indi's name on the screen. My one silver lining in all of this is that I'm pretty sure Indi isn't in on this Knight bullshit. She's new to the city, and she already told me about Ryker and Ellis. I'd like to think if she knew about any of this, she'd have told me then.

I hope, anyway.

**Indi:**
Yes bitch! You're back. I'll have coffee waiting for you on the steps!

Me:
You're the best. See you soon!

Butterflies kick up in my stomach, more than just nerves about seeing Raleigh again. I'm a little nervous about seeing the guys. Including East. He is the biggest enigma to me so far, because if Lincoln knows about all of this shit, then surely East does. So if he wanted me gone too, why be so nice to me?

I pinch the bridge of my nose, my head aching from the swirling thoughts, all of the questions that I don't have answers to. I intend to get some answers, and soon.

I head downstairs and find the four of them waiting for me in the foyer. I eye them suspiciously as I reach the bottom of the staircase. "What are you guys doing here?"

East steps forward, smiling sadly at me. "Smithy called me last night. Said you'd had questions that maybe we were better off answering."

*Oh he did, did he?* Old man is suspiciously absent, too. So much for my plans to get answers my own way. Once I reach the ground floor, I walk past them into the kitchen and grab a bottle of water from the refrigerator. "So, talk."

Lincoln eyes me, like he doesn't want to say a goddamn thing, which is exactly what I expected. No one else says a word.

*Of course they fucking don't.*

"We have to tell her," Finley says, and I quirk a brow. Finally, some movement.

Lincoln shakes his head and folds his arms over his chest.

"If you don't tell her, I will," Finley argues, and Lincoln levels him with a look.

"Seriously?"

"I told you Lincoln, I won't hurt her again. Keeping all of this from her is going to get her hurt." Finley stares Lincoln down until Lincoln runs a hand through his hair.

"Fine. Fuck." He glances over at me, as icy as ever. "Sit down. We have a lot to talk through."

I move back to the counter and take a seat, waiting for someone to start talking.

"Was I right? Is this about the photos?"

Lincoln takes a seat as Maverick opens the fridge, grabbing water for the rest of them before joining us. "Okay, so let's start with the photos. No, the photos have nothing to do with everything else as far as we know. They're a problem all on their own. This is obviously a stalker of some sort. I already told you I have someone looking into it, so I'll give them this information, too, but currently we're coming up empty. If you have any ideas about who would be stalking you, anyone who seemed overly interested, anything suspicious, let me know."

I nod at him, letting the words sink in. Of course I have a stalker. Awesome. "The only one who's been overly interested is Raleigh, and considering the photos, I'm going to say it's not him."

East squeezes my thigh and Lincoln nods at me.

"Okay, well I'll keep digging."

I look around at each of them, waiting for someone to start talking, but I'm met with deafening silence. "What about the note?"

"The note…" Lincoln starts, before looking up to the ceiling as if looking for the right words. I knew there was a fucking note! I knew it. Asshole. "The note, the flowers, the dress… They're all from the same people."

I think back to all of the things I've received with the black cards. "Right? But that doesn't explain much. Why am I out of time? Out of time for what? I feel like I'm missing a huge chunk of information here."

"The people who sent you all those things are part of the same organization. They want you to join their ranks. You're a legacy, and legacies don't escape them." He looks me directly in the eye and I see a glimpse of the boy I once knew, but then the shutters come down. In a blink he's back to this new version of himself. "They are the reason we tried to make you leave. The reason we did everything we've done since you arrived. You're not safe here. Stalker or not. The Knights Society is the bigger threat to you right now."

"The Knights Society?" I laugh, glancing around at their somber faces. That's what Smithy called them too, and as much as I want to believe him, believe them, it still all just sounds made up. Like something out of a movie. "Are you fucking with me right now? Trying to get me to forget, or figure, that you've all been giant assholes the last few months with a made up what? Secret society? I'm a lot of things, Lincoln, but stupid isn't one of them."

He looks from me to East and then Finley. "This is why I said there was no point in telling her." He pushes back his stool and paces the floor. "The Knights Society is very real. I wish for all our sakes this was some elaborate ruse, that I was making it up, that it was all a ploy to fuck with you some more, but it's not. You should be thankful Stone made the deal he did before you left. It's the only thing that's bought you this much time."

It's like the room sucks in a breath at his words. "My dad? What are you talking about, Lincoln?"

He pauses to stand and stare at me for a minute before clenching his hands into fists at his sides. "Your dad was a part of TKS. So was your mom. Just like all of our parents. We're all legacies. Three other families in The Cove make up the board for the sect here, but their reach spans, at least, nationwide. They are the chess players behind everything that happens. They are the real monsters in your closet, the demons that live under your bed, and even though you think you're free, I promise you… they've had more control over your life than you can ever think possible. They are everywhere, and once they have their claws in you, you can never escape."

I clasp my throat, trying to take what he's saying seriously. He certainly believes what he's saying, and from the looks around the room, so do the others. There's no way my dad would have been wrapped up in something like this.

This can't be real, right? Secret societies or whatever this is are just crazy things you read about in books.

"Okay, so what do I do?" I ask, trying to work out what it is they're not saying.

Lincoln looks me dead in the eye and puts his hands in his pockets. "You do what we've been trying to make you do all along. You leave."

I throw my hands up in the air, exasperated. This all ties into what Smithy said, but it's just so hard to believe. "And this, right here, is exactly why I don't believe what you're saying. You've wanted me gone since I got back here, this is just another ploy."

"Why else would we want you gone?" Lincoln yells, and I startle.

"Lincoln, enough," East says, touching my arm as if trying to soothe me.

Lincoln turns his cold look on his brother and narrows his eyes. "You don't get to say when it's enough. You're already out. You chose that, remember?"

I'm obviously missing something, because Lincoln's rage seems to grow as East deflates next to me. "You're not a Knight?"

"No," he says, and it looks like it hurts him to say it, so I decide not to ask any more questions on that for right now. I look over to Maverick. He's still standing in the same position he was in earlier, watching everything play out, ready to throw hands if it's needed. But he seems happy enough to sit back and observe.

Finley on the other hand, looks like he's close to breaking point. I don't think I've ever seen him look like that.

"Let's just dial it back a little, shall we?" Finley says to Lincoln who throws his hands in the air and leaves the room. Mav follows him after a nod from Finley, leaving me with just him and East.

"This is just madness." I drop my head into my hands, trying to work out which way is up. How everything got so twisted. How exactly it is that my life ended up at this crux.

"Octavia, I know it's hard to believe," East says softly. "But Lincoln is telling you the truth."

I look up at him, and I wish I saw something that made me think he was lying, but East hasn't lied to me yet. Not that I know of. "None of this makes any sense, let alone sounds believable. Surely if they were this all-knowing, all-powerful, terrifying whatever it is they are, they'd just do what they want?"

"The Knights live by a code. It might be a fucked-up code, but it's still a code. To break it is to betray the Society," Finley says quietly. "That is why they do what they do, the way they do it. We still don't know exactly what they want from you, but trust me, it's better to be out and not know."

He clenches his fist as he stops speaking, and an icy drop of dread runs down my spine. They all seem so… scared. Which isn't something I'd have thought I'd ever use to describe any of them.

"My dad really knew about all of this?"

East nods in response to my question, and my heart breaks a little more. I didn't realize that was possible. "These knuckleheads have been trying to get you to leave to keep you safe."

A quiet rage pools in my stomach at his words as a realization comes to me. "You knew what they were doing?"

His eyes go wide and he leans back, pulling away from me. "I mean… not exactly. I didn't want any part of it, but yes, I knew they were going to try to do something to keep you safe. To make you leave."

"You have got to be fucking kidding me," I hiss and start pacing back and forth. Just when I thought I could trust him, that he wouldn't lie to me."This is so fucked up. And while we're just laying out the truth bombs, I'm just going to be straight with you guys—which is more decency than any of you have shown me, I might add—I can't leave," I grind out through clenched teeth, trying not to hulk out over that little revelation.

Finley turns to me and I take a deep breath to try and focus my thoughts.

"Why not?"

I debate telling him the truth, whether they'll just use it against me later, but at this point, what more could go wrong? "My father's will states that in order to have access to my inheritance, I must graduate from ECP with at least a 4.0 GPA. That, and stay living with one of my guardians until I'm of age."

"Those motherfuckers," Finley hisses before slamming a hand down on the table as Lincoln and Mav re-enter the room. Finley looks up at them, a quiet rage washing over him. "They brought her here. I'd put money on it."

"It's what we thought," Lincoln says with a shrug. "They had a hand to play, a pawn on the board to move, so they did. The question is, what do we do about it now?"

"Wait! Will you all just wait a freaking minute?" I stand up to put some distance between us. This is all getting too much, and I've had about as much of their cryptic bullshit as I can take.

"You tormented me, bullied me, rallied the whole fucking student body against me. My car was trashed, my home was broken into. *Smithy was put in the fucking hospital.*" I suck in a breath, trying not to go nuclear and failing. "My best friend had her car hijacked, YOU MADE A FUCKING DEEPFAKE SEX TAPE, and you're trying to tell me you did all of that shit, and more, *to keep me safe?* From a supposed secret society. And then you talk about it like it's nothing more than another breezy Monday morning. You have got to be fucking kidding me."

They all just stare at me, not saying a word. Not trying to deny a thing. I look at East, and rage fills me further. "And you did nothing to stop them! You're as bad as they are!"

"V…" East starts, standing to move toward me. I put my arm out in front of me to stop him.

"No. Don't you 'V' me. My dad fucking died. I came here to get the resolution I needed so I can get on with my life, and you made these last few months *hell.* Do you have any idea what I've been going through? Then, on top of that, I have some fucking psycho stalker, and someone I thought was my friend tried to rape me. I am so done. You all need to leave." I pull at my hair and turn my back on them. "Fucking secret society," I mutter. "What a bunch of horse shit."

I spin back around when nothing but silence greets me. "I said get the fuck out!"

They stand in unison and leave without a word, leaving me with more questions than answers.

What a fucking joke.

---

This morning was a mess, and by the time I pull up to school, my anger hasn't really subsided. What an absolute mind fuck of a few days. Hell, my entire time since I came back has been a shit storm. So I make a pact with myself to buck the fuck up. I need to shake some of my grief off and start thinking clearly.

Letting stuff happen around me, *to me*, isn't helping anything and it's become very apparent that if I don't demand answers, or look into stuff myself, I'm never going to get anywhere. Everything I've discovered so far is about as useful as trying to travel on a paper airplane.

Indi bounces down the steps to the front of my car as I take a deep breath. She doesn't deserve bitchy me. She's done nothing but be my friend. I just wish I wasn't so jaded. I was convinced she had no idea, but everything in my life is tipped upside down.

I grab my bag and climb from the car, painting on a smile as I come face-to-face with my new bestie. She thrusts the ice-cold coffee topped with cream and chocolate sauce in my face. "I know fall is here, but I'm holding onto my iced coffee like it's a lifeline. We can move over to hot coffee next week."

My smile widens genuinely. I could kick myself for doubting her. She's too good, too genuine, to have known and not said anything. "Thank you," I say, linking my arm through hers. "Now, let's go and survive this day, shall we?"

"We've so got this." She grins and we head up the steps into the school. I pretend like everyone isn't looking at me like a lion at the zoo. I flick my hair over my shoulder and walk through the hall with Indi, heading to my locker.

"So what did I miss?" I ask as I empty the contents of my bag into my locker and grab my book for English. "Anything juicy?"

"Not really. Raleigh is off the football team. Well, benched anyway. He broke his ankle Friday night." Her eyes dart across the hall to where Maverick is leaning against the lockers, watching us.

Not creepy at all. Nope.

I roll my eyes and bring my attention back to her. "Wannabe rapists get what they deserve."

She nods reverently. "Yes, yes they do. Also, that creepy hall on the far side of town burned down. It's been all over the news."

"Nestwood?"

"That's the one. Place gives me the creeps everytime I drive past."

I bark out a laugh. "Dude, *same.*" I make a mental note that that means I'm totally free and clear of that stupid gala invite and do a mental fist pump.

We head over to her locker, dodging Maverick as we go, as she fills me in on all of the other drama that has filled the school this week. "And the best one yet, which I'm not sure anyone has told you about… but er… you've been nominated for homecoming queen."

"I've been what?!" I screech. I groan and bury my face in my hands.

She just laughs that twinkly laugh of hers as she closes her locker. "Yeah I knew you'd be happy about it. The dance is next week, later than usual, but something to do with vandalism. At least now we have an excuse to go shopping again?"

"You want to go to the dance?" I ask, shocked, as the bell rings.

She shrugs as we head toward English. "I've never been to a dance before. I figure you haven't either, what with homeschooling. It could be fun, right?"

I suck in a breath before letting it out slowly. "Sure, why not get all dressed up to spend more time with people who hate me?"

"Yes!" She does a fist pump, twirling as she enters the classroom for English. "I knew you'd be on board. We could head up to Santa Monica tomorrow, do some shopping, hang out on the pier. Do normal teenage girl shit."

"You're not hanging with the twins?" I ask as I slide into my desk, wagging my brows at her.

She rolls her eyes at me as she takes her seat. "No, I am not. I have zero idea what's going on with them right now. I've barely heard from them all week, so fuck them. I'm not going to do the chasing thing. Especially after the whole thing with Jackson. I am done running around after boys. If they want to speak to me, they know where to find me."

I smile softly, feeling a little proud of her. "Good, you deserve better than chasing around after boys who don't know what they want."

"Speaking of boys who don't know what they want." I look up at her words, and find three of the four of them watching me from outside the class. "Any idea what's going on with them and their total turn around since Friday?"

I open my mouth to speak, having no idea how to even begin to tell her about what happened, as Miss Summers breezes into the room, closing the door behind her. I've never been more glad for not having to answer a question. "Good morning, all. Let's finish this week with a bang, shall we? I declare today debate day!"

A groan sounds across the room and I smile.

Maybe this day will turn around after all.

---

I somehow managed to evade everyone I didn't want to see yesterday. No Raleigh, no Blair, even the guys kept their distance—though that could've been them trying to avoid any more of my questions. It was a nice change and a pretty easy day to settle back in with. Admittedly, we went off campus for lunch, heading back to Penny's. It's hard to believe it's already been three months since we set foot in there.

The day is unusually hot for November, apparently we're getting a last minute dash of summer sunshine, and I'm totally not opposed to it. I pull on my cutoffs, pair them with my knee-high Chucks and a crop top, finishing the look with my leather jacket. My waves cascade down my back and I check my face once more in the mirror before I head to pick up Indi.

I still can't get over this whole homecoming thing. Not going to lie, I've been completely oblivious to all of the posters lining the walls of the school, but it's not like I didn't have enough going on to distract me. Apparently I've been oblivious to a lot since I got back to The Cove.

I grab my keys, phone, and purse before I head downstairs, calling out a goodbye to Smithy before skipping out to my car. Sliding on my aviators, I connect my phone to the sound system, blasting *This Little Girl* by Cady Groves as I drive out of the gate and through the center of town. I can't help but smile at the lyrics of the song because they're so freaking true.

I pull up in front of Indi's house just as she skips down the front sidewalk. "Morningggg!" she sings as she slides into the car and buckles in.

"New hair?" I ask, taking in the vivid violet, somehow darker yet brighter than the purple she had when I first met her. I have no idea how she always makes it so bright and shiny, or how she suits every freaking color, but I love it.

"I fancied a change again. The rainbow is fun for a minute, but the root touch up is murder. Plus, how awesome are these extensions?" She grins as she steals my phone, flicking through the playlists.

"They are all kinds of beautiful, I'd never know it wasn't your hair." The curls wave down her petite frame to just below her boobs, the perfect compliment to her thickly lined eyes and deep purple lipstick.

"My hair woman is a freaking genius with extensions. Now then, are we ready for all of the shopping?"

I grin at her, shaking my head as I pull away from the curb. "Not even a little. Homecoming dresses aren't exactly my usual repertoire."

"I mean, mine either, but it's got to be fun right? It's a 007 Casino theme. We can be Pussy Galore."

I burst out laughing while she just grins at me, trying not to laugh, "You, my friend, definitely know how to cheer a girl up."

"That's what besties are for. You know I'm here if you want to talk it out." I grin over at her before looking back at the road. As much as I'd like to unburden myself, I don't really know much yet. And the last thing I want to do is drag her into this bullshit. If she's free and clear, I'd like to keep it that way.

"Thank you." I pull out onto the PCH and head up toward Santa Monica. We spend most of the journey singing at the top of our lungs.

It's so nice, just driving with the windows down, wind in our hair, singing, acting like the seventeen-year-olds we are. Everything going on in my life makes it easy to forget I'm still allowed to be a teenager sometimes.

I pull into the parking lot at the pier once we reach Santa Monica and turn to face Indi once I'm parked. "So, are you going to tell me more about the twins and… Dylan, was it?"

She lets out a deep breath, blowing her hair out of her face. "What do you want to know?"

"How did you guys all meet?" She looks a little shocked, like she thought I was going to go for the jugular, but that's not my style. Plus, I adore her, I'm not going to judge her for a goddamn thing.

She smiles softly as she looks out at the water. "It was the first summer I moved here. I had no idea who the hell anyone was, so I just kind of did my own thing. I met some people at the beach that invited me to a party. The party was at the Donovans'. I actually met Scout first. She accepted me instantly, the twins were such giant assholes—mostly Ryker, but Ellis stands by his brother in pretty much everything—but Scout and I got along really well. I hung out with her a lot at the start of the summer, but then… I still don't know exactly what happened, but it was like Scout couldn't go anywhere without one of her brothers or Dylan present. So I got to know them all slowly too."

"That's kind of adorable," I tell her, and she sticks her tongue out at me, making me laugh.

She climbs from the car and I follow suit, double checking I have everything, before locking it up and dropping my keys in my purse.

"It was. Ellis was attentive, Ryker was a little dangerous, and Dylan… well, he was their perfect balance. They were so freaking loyal, but that was part of the problem. The Kings came first. And I get it. Kind of. But being second priority, or even fourth, because of their dedication to each other… it just got to be too much. I tried to ride it out, and it was harder with me coming to Prep and them going to High, but we were doing okay. Then, at the end of the summer this year—after an entire year, I might add—they dropped me like a hot freaking penny, telling me it was for my own safety. Boys." She rolls her eyes and loops her arm through mine.

Her words trigger a memory… Ryker out in front of the school, talking to the guys, mentioning the Knights. My eyes go wide as my heart pounds in my chest. Maybe they really were trying to keep her safe. I keep it to myself and shove the emotion down. That's another question for Lincoln and the others, when I can finally pry open the treasure trove of information I know they have. Today is about having a day with my bestie and shaking off this week. I can deal with the other bullshit later.

Assuming it doesn't catch up with me first.

# CHAPTER SEVEN

## EAST

This week has been fucking torture. Between arguing with Lincoln, dealing with my goddamn father, trying to look into this stalker with the PI Linc and I hired, and kind of coming clean with V then her icing me out… I'm beyond ready for it to be done.

I also need to try and find a way to apologize to V. I'm not sure she wants to see me. She iced me during class yesterday, only speaking when absolutely necessary, and I haven't heard from her otherwise.

Not that I blame her; I'd be pissed if I was her too. I might not have played a part in what sounds like the torture those little fuckers put her through, but I knew they were trying to make her leave, and I didn't do anything to try and stop them.

I'd like to say that I was just trying to keep her safe—that because I'm not a Knight, I wasn't as involved—but that's just a bullshit cop-out. I might not be a Knight, but that doesn't mean I don't know almost as much about them as Linc and the others. It also doesn't mean that I couldn't have fought the others harder when they came up with their little plan.

I hate my father for having put us in this position, for making me keep even more fucking secrets. I hate this place and everything it stands for. But mostly, I hate that I don't think I'm going to be able to get Lincoln, or any of them, free and clear from the grasps of those controlling them.

That was my plan once upon a time; once I discovered I wouldn't be taking the Saint seat at the table, when I learned there might be a way out, I wanted to get us all out.

Then Stone took Octavia away, and I thought I could really do it. I thought if he could find a way, so could I.

And then the boys were taken.

That's when I knew I was too late.

The Knights already had them. By the time they came home two weeks later, none of them were the same. I knew they never would be again.

None of them ever spoke about what happened while they were gone, but I knew it was the Knights.

I stare back down at the mountains of pictures that have been delivered to V, trying to work out if there's anything that could give away who is stalking her. There are so many more than she's seen because Linc started intercepting them before she could.

I know at first he took them because he thought he was fucking with her. But when he saw what was inside the envelope he took, he pulled me in on it and we called Lucas, a PI we discovered that has zero ties to the Knights. Not the easiest person to find, especially with their reach being as wide as it is, but there are some advantages to me not being a member. This was one of them. I'm not watched. Well, not as closely as Linc is anyway.

Fuck this. I'm not getting anywhere just staring at these pictures.

I need to speak to Smithy. I need to know if he's seen anything, but I don't want to bring him in any further than he already is. The last thing I want is anything else happening to him. Her house being broken into and Smithy ending up in the hospital wasn't the boys, that much I know, which means it was the Knights. Likely a warning for him to remember his place.

I wouldn't be surprised if they were the reason for his sister being in the hospital either. Their reach is wide, and crossing them isn't typically a wise move. I'm not sure what Smithy did to end up on their radar the way he did, but maybe he saw something that connects to this and he hasn't said anything just in case.

God, that sounded convoluted even in my own head.

I head over to the Royals' house, half hoping I'll get the chance to speak to V, but also not holding my breath. She's nothing if not stubborn. Not that I blame her, but how can I make it better if she won't let me explain?

That is a problem for later. Right now, I need to focus on dealing with the sicko hunting her. She has enough psychopaths in her life already, she doesn't need any more.

I head through the back gate between the properties and find Smithy in the garden, tending to the flower beds by the kitchen. "Smithy, my man! Good to see you."

"Master Saint!" he exclaims, squinting up at me as the sun beats down on my back in the late afternoon. He stands, brushing himself off. "What brings you here?"

"I wondered if you had a few minutes to talk about Octavia."

He frowns at me, and I swear I feel like a kid again, being scolded by him for touching the cookies when they were still cooling. "I'm afraid, Master Saint, that she is rather displeased with you. Well, all of you, really. She's out with Miss Indi today."

My smile falters, but I put it back on. I might not be a Knight, but I'm still a Saint, and I'm all too familiar with wearing a mask of emotion. "That's fine. I need to speak to you about her anyway. It's probably best she isn't here for this."

"Okay then, let's head inside and I'll sort some refreshments. Iced tea?"

I nod, my smile a little more genuine this time. "Sounds great."

Following him inside, I close the door, enjoying the cool air from the a/c as it washes over me. I lean on the counter while he pours the drinks, trying to sort out everything in my mind. Do I just tell him all about the stalker, ensure that he's as aware as we are, or keep him safe and just ask questions?

The bigger question is, which option will keep V safest? Because as much as I love Smithy, she is my priority. Even if she doesn't know it yet.

---

The guys all pile into the kitchen this morning as Mrs. Potts is serving up breakfast. "Don't forget I'm not around much this week. I've put dinners in the fridge for you for the week, but other than that and breakfast tomorrow before school, you'll need to fend for yourselves."

"We got this, Mrs. P." Mav grins cheekily as he drops a kiss into her hairline, taking the plates from her hands and sitting down at the table with me. She mothers over him, clucking as he charms the socks off of her—the little psychopath—before disappearing into the laundry room.

I dig into my eggs as they all sit down. "You guys got in late last night."

"Don't we know it," Linc grumbles. "We were out on an errand that ran long."

Well, that explains it. They don't talk much to me about what it is they do for the Knights, but I know Lincoln doesn't sleep much anymore. Though, from what I've managed to piece together about the Knights, I'm not sure I would either.

Guilt slams into me once more over him being the one carrying the mantle. Not that I had much choice about it—a secret I am prepared to take to my grave, even if he resents me for it. It's better than him knowing the truth.

"Something big happened though. Not sure what's going on, but all recruitment has been paused," Linc adds, and my eyes go wide. "Means V should be safe for a little longer, but Dad was flipping his shit last night. Apparently being the head honcho of our sect isn't all roses right now."

"Serves him right for being a giant fucking cunt." Mav shrugs before plowing into his food—you'd think he'd never eaten before, Jesus fucking Christ. He isn't wrong though.

"Well, I'm not going to be sad about it. If things stay down for long enough, maybe you guys will catch a break." I look around at them, each of them nodding while they eat.

Lincoln stays quiet while Mav snorts. "Gives me time to dream something up for Mr. Peters."

I groan. "What does that mean?"

"He got his dick out in front of V. Told her he'd pass her if she would play with him."

My jaw drops seconds before the burning anger takes root in the pit of my stomach. "He did fucking what?"

Mav shrugs while Linc fills me in. "It's our own fault. Everything we did to get her to leave. The tape, the attacks. Everything. But we tidy up our messes."

"Attacks?" I ask, raising an eyebrow. "I think maybe it's time you guys fill me in on just what you've been doing so there are no more surprises."

Sitting back, I fold my arms, my gaze bouncing between them. Finn and Mav look to Linc, unsurprising really, but this means there's likely something I'm going to be pissed about. We don't usually keep secrets, but these last few months, I've known less and less of what they've been doing. Both with the Knights and V. I get it. I'm not one of them, but we've always been close. I hate that there's so much I don't know now, things I can't help them with.

Lincoln starts talking, and I clench my fists as I try not to blow up. I manage to keep my cool through most of it. The car jacking, the sex tape, Mav's threats—but when he finally admits to locking her in the closet, I lose my shit.

"Are you out of your goddamn minds?! Why would you do that to her? I know you were trying to protect her, but fuck! That shit was too far. Did you see what you did to her? How broken she was? Fuck you all." I seethe quietly, trying to calm myself, while they all sit there looking thoroughly guilty.

"I hadn't thought it was so bad till it was listed out like that," Mav says sheepishly, rubbing the back of his neck. "No wonder she won't forgive any of us."

I pinch the bridge of my nose. Sometimes it's easy to forget that he's only seventeen. That Linc and Finn are only eighteen. Hell, that I'm barely twenty-two. Our lives are so fucked up. I take a deep breath, trying to remember everything V has told me about so far this year, when something pings in my mind. "What about the break-in at her house? The attack on Smithy. You didn't mention that. Was that you?"

Linc shakes his head. "No. I think that was the Knights. She was ignoring them. That, or Smithy learned something he shouldn't."

"I'd had the same thought," I say, nodding. "We really need to work out what it is they want from her. I know I'm not officially a Knight, but I don't think keeping secrets is going to help anyone. I don't give a shit if something happens to me. We just need to keep her safe."

"Agreed." Finn nods. "Her safety comes first."

"Any luck with the stalker shit?" Linc asks, and I shake my head, hating that the answer is no.

"I haven't heard from Lucas yet either. It's on my list of calls to make today."

"Okay, well you do that. We didn't get much sleep last night, so I'm heading back to bed. Any idea what V is doing today?" Lincoln asks, glancing around the team.

"I volunteer as tribute!" Mav grins as he drops his fork on the table, "Maybe I can get her to forgive me for the whole taking her virginity thing."

"I'm sorry, what?" I growl. The punches just keep rolling today.

Mav shrugs, standing before moving to the counter to grab his crap. "Shit happens. We all know any one of us would be happy to carry that ticket. Don't be pissed 'cause it was me. I just need to get her to forgive me so I can do it again. I like that no one else has had her."

He leaves out the back, leaving me gawking after him, wondering what the fuck just happened.

---

After a somewhat friendlier gym class today than I was expecting, I call out Octavia's name as everyone else leaves the gym. I watch her hesitate for a second before saying goodbye to Indi. I know they came in together today, not that I'm stalking her or whatever, I just happened to see Indi pick her up as I was heading to my car this morning.

*Yeah right, stalker.*

She turns and struts toward me, looking hotter than anyone should, especially in that outfit.

*Down boy, now is not the time.*

She juts her hip out as she stops to face me, arms folded across her chest. "Yes?"

"I'm sorry." The words fall from my lips, and she deflates a little. "I never meant to hurt you, and I know that not telling you things, and letting Linc and the others do what they thought was right, was the wrong thing to do but I didn't know what else to do. There's still a lot you don't know, but I'm basically powerless. I just wanted to keep you safe, and I went about it in the wrong way."

She runs a hand through her long, dark hair and lets out a sigh. "East, I just… I feel betrayed, ya know? I thought you were the one person who hadn't changed. Who was still on my side."

"But I was on your side! I *am* on your side, V. I might have gone about it the wrong way, but I will always be on your side. Just let me make it up to you." I don't even care that I sound like I'm begging. I wish I could say I haven't loved her my entire life, but I'd be straight up lying.

"I guess."

"Let me drive you home, we can talk some more?"

She looks over her shoulder, like she's expecting to see someone, but turns back and smiles sadly at me. "Sure, why not? I came in with Indi today, but this will save her going out of her way to take me home."

"Thank you."

She nods before scurrying out of the gym, and I take a few deep breaths to calm myself.

*You're not forgiven yet. Don't get ahead of yourself.*

I tear through my office, getting everything I need as quickly as I can so I don't keep her waiting.

Heading out through the back, I jump in my car and pull it around to the front of the school just in time to watch her coming out of the front doors with Indi. She waves goodbye to her friend and heads for the car, a wary smile on her face.

This is progress, I just need to remember that. Baby steps, East. If we rush this, we're going to fuck it up.

Once she's in, she buckles up and I cruise out of the lot slowly. No need to draw more attention to us than necessary. I'm just a guy giving a girl a ride home. It can't be any more than that right now, even if I want it to be. The thought of being blackmailed, and having that hurt her in the long run… a shiver runs down my spine at the thought of it.

I won't be another bad guy in her story, and I refuse to be the reason she ends up pushed into a corner.

I'm pretty sure that at twenty-two, being blackmailed isn't supposed to be the thing I'm thinking about when the girl I've loved my entire life is in my car, but here we are. Echoes Cove warps fucking everything.

She connects her phone to the bluetooth and starts playing *Who Am I* by Besomorph, and I frown a little. "You doing okay, V?"

Her brown eyes look more than a little lost when she looks over at me. "I'm fine. I'm just tired of everything already, and I get the feeling that this is just the beginning."

"I'm sorry. I wish there was something I could do to help you."

"Is there any way out?"

I clench the steering wheel until my knuckles turn white, trying to find the words.

"You managed it, right?"

I glance over at her, at how hopeful she looks, and hate that I'm going to be the one to crush that hope in her. "Yes and no. I didn't have a choice. It was my father's choice, but trust me, just because I'm not in, doesn't mean I'm out."

"Do any of you ever not speak in riddles?" She sighs as she flops back in the seat just as we pull onto our street.

I consider her words. "We do, it's just something of a minefield with all of this. Things with you are so different than usual. Nobody knows exactly what the Knights want with you. It could be something to do with Stone, it could be something entirely different. It's more about not saying the wrong thing."

Trying to be as honest as I can while not putting my foot in anything is harder than I imagined it would be.

"How about we spend the night just hanging out, and forget about all of this bullshit. One night of normal?" The suggestion is mostly for her, but I'd really like to have just a little bit of normal with her.

A smile plays on her lips as we pull through her gate and up to the front door. "Sure thing. It's been a while since I kicked your ass on the Xbox."

"Those be fighting words."

She laughs softly and climbs from the car as I shut off the engine before moving to follow her out, but I pause as I try not to stare at her ass in that skirt. I don't even notice the uniform on anyone else, but Octavia Royal is undeniable.

I close my eyes, taking a deep breath, trying to picture things that aren't her in that skirt so my dick isn't obvious as I walk into her house. She's already through the front door before I even climb from the car. If nothing else, tonight will test my strength of will.

I head inside, closing the door and kicking off my shoes.

"Smithy isn't here. He's shopping," she calls from the kitchen, so I head in that direction. I find her with her head in the fridge, ass cheeks hanging out of her skirt.

Being her teacher never felt like such a bad idea, even if I am just the gym teacher.

"Water?" she asks, pulling a bottle from the fridge, and I nod, catching the bottle she throws at me.

"Stop delaying the inevitable." I grin, trying to push back any nefarious thoughts. "I promised you an ass kicking."

"Bring it on." She laughs as she sashays past me, flicking her hair over her shoulder. Following her into the living room, I drop onto the couch beside her, taking the offered controller. I'm looking forward to this more than I should be. It's been a hot minute since I had just a normal evening.

We settle into playing Apex, and surprise, surprise, she kicks my ass, just like she did last time. I'm not really sad about it though. Seeing her relax and let go, just enjoy herself, has been reward enough.

God, I'm turning into a sappy shit.

She throws her hands in the air and starts a dance that takes her to her feet as she celebrates winning. I can't help but laugh at her. Right up until she trips. I rush to stop her from face-planting the floor, catching her in my arms, her face barely an inch from mine.

She looks up at me, like I'm the guy that can save her.

Then she looks at my lips and everything changes. I know I shouldn't be doing this.

Despite knowing it, I find myself leaning forward and brushing my lips against hers. Her fingers tighten in my hair as she takes the kiss deeper.

Groaning, I pull back. I make sure she's steady on her feet before I let go of her and drop back onto the couch.

She sits down beside me, looking down at her hands. I don't want her to feel like I don't want her, but I'm pretty sure this isn't a line we should cross. She has enough going on in her life that she doesn't need any more complications.

I sit, white-knuckled, on the couch as she inches closer and closer to me. I've just about managed to restrain myself tonight, other than that one slip, but denying myself isn't really in my nature. That doesn't stop me being aware of the fact that she's seventeen, and technically she's my student. That's what I need to keep reminding myself.

But putting her off-limits just makes me want her even more, and I didn't think that was possible.

I take a deep breath, trying to calm myself down, but she stands back up and turns to look at me. Her skirt flares a little as she spins, and sweet baby Jesus, that skirt. She puts her hands on her hips as she looks down at me.

"Really?"

I swallow, blinking up at her. "What?"

She rolls her eyes and faster than I can object, she steps forward and literally drops onto my lap. Straddling me, looking down at me from where she's seated. I try to count back from ten, to focus on anything but the fact that she's right there, her hands on my chest, looking at me like I'm the only thing in the world she wants.

If someone found out about this…

My cock strains against my sweatpants as she wiggles on my lap. If she keeps that up, I'm going to turn into a goddamn teenage boy and come right in my fucking pants. I grasp her hips to keep her still, and she smiles at me.

"Vixen."

She grins again and grinds against me.

Leaning forward until she's pressed against me, she touches her lips to mine and my resistance snaps.

My arms band around her, pulling her closer against me, and I kiss her like she's all I need to breathe.

I'm acutely aware of everything about her. Her scent—sweet vanilla and honey—creeps up my nose and weakens my already precarious control. Her hands are on the back of the couch just inches from my head, and her tits press against me, but I restrain myself, making sure to keep my hands clasped around her waist.

Mostly, it's the heat coming from what I'm imagining is a seriously wet fucking pussy. I can't think of a better way to die than this, but fuck my life, I don't want to until I've at least had a taste of her. As delicious as her mouth is right now, I want to know what her pussy tastes like. I want to bury my tongue deep inside her and kiss her there just as I'm kissing her mouth.

My fingers curl tighter around her waist and without consciously thinking about it, I pull her closer, kiss her deeper, and moan a little louder from the feel of her all around me.

Faster and faster, V rubs against me like a cat needing release, and I'm the only asshole in this place with a conscience who refuses to touch her.

My dick hurts from how hard I am, from the friction of her all over me, from the need I won't allow myself to indulge. It all hurts. This fucking situation, this reality we have to live in, every fucking thing about this life sucks ass, and not in a good way.

Fuck, now I'm thinking about her ass and this is not good. Not fucking good at all.

"East, please."

Christ, how am I supposed to deny her? Her lips are gliding from one corner of my mouth to the other, her begging words a mere whisper across my kiss-swollen lips.

"I can't, V. I want to, but I can't."

If I thought she'd back off, maybe give me a little breathing room so I don't fucking come in my sweats, I was dead wrong. Instead, this little minx doesn't relent and rubs even harder, her resolve a clear message.

She wants me to make her come.

Fine.

Just because I refuse to take advantage of her, doesn't mean she can't have pleasure, right?

*Right?*

With one hand at her waist holding her down and close to my aching cock, I bury my other in her hair, fisting her long, dark locks right at her nape. She's trapped in my grasp, my prisoner in this very precarious moment. Yet her breathing kicks up, her thighs squeeze mine, and her breaths against my mouth are shallow and quick.

All the signs are there—she wants me as much as I need her—but I will not be a selfish asshole, not for this.

Our mouths slam back together, our tongues fighting out our baser instincts. We are just lust and chemistry, our bodies calling one to the other while my mind tries to slam on the brakes to no avail.

"Please, East. I want you so bad."

Fuck my fucking life.

"I can't, V. I just… I can't." Jesus Christ, how did I get myself into this mess? This perfect, irresistible mess.

Instead of hearing my silent pleas, the universe decides to up the ante. Octavia fucking Royal doubles down and starts grinding my already painful cock like she's trying to get off on that alone.

My head is leaning against the back of the couch, her mouth no longer on mine, and when I open my eyes, the sight before me is nothing short of spectacular. The hand at her nape falls to her waist, and I watch in utter awe as she transforms into a full-blown woman with carnal needs.

Head thrown back—her throat deliciously exposed—her face bathed in pleasure as her clothed pussy rubs freely around the hard ridge of my dick. She looks every inch the queen I've always known she would become.

My resolve is holding on by a thin, frayed thread that could snap any second, but instead of doing the right thing and pushing her off of me, I lift my hips just a tiny bit and give her the pressure she needs. This is fine, right? I'm not technically doing anything wrong. She's getting herself off, I'm just the means to her own end.

Until, that is, she snaps her head back up, fists her hand in my black t-shirt, and rests her forehead on mine before she says the words that nearly break me.

"With or without your help, I'm gonna come very soon. Please, East, make me feel good."

Fuck. This. Shit.

V is every man's dirty little fantasy. My ultimate fantasy, wearing a schoolgirl uniform and begging to be fucked. How I'm resisting her is beyond my comprehension.

Sliding one hand down her pleated skirt and up her silky thigh, I expect to find cotton underwear, something that acts as some kind of barrier, helping me to backtrack from what I'm about to do.

I should have known better because what my fingers feel is a whole new temptation.

Satin.

Smooth, hot, and wet. She's been doing such a good job using my covered dick as her own personal toy that she's soaked her silk panties.

Fucking soaked.

Christ, I'm not going to survive this.

Using one finger to pull aside her panties, I allow myself to slide my index finger along the smooth lips of her pussy, gathering her wetness and using it to rub her clit around and around.

Fuck, I can smell her. Her need and her want. I'm doing this to her, and it gives me a sense of power I've never felt before.

"Yes, East. God yes."

This is for her. It's all for her.

V keeps grinding up against my cock while I rub even circles around her clit, watching her breathing grow shallow, her chest rising and falling with every intake and exhalation of air. Her eyes fluttering closed as her lashes caress her cheeks.

Her mouth, her fucking mouth—with swollen lips from my fucking kisses—parts just enough for me to imagine my dick sliding inside and coming right down her throat.

"Fuck!" My dick hurts in all the best ways.

"Yes!" That one word breathing out from between her lips is like a fucking detonator.

"Don't stop, East, please don't..." As V accelerates her movements over the hard length of my cock, she chants out my name over and over again until I can feel the tingling in my lower stomach that tells me I'm about to fucking lose it.

But I resist. I'm no thirteen-year-old watching porn for the first time, I can control myself.

That is until she grabs my hand and pushes two of my fingers and one of hers inside her pussy, fucking our joint hands like she's about to lose her ever loving mind.

Which is exactly what I do when I feel her walls constrict around my fingers and her juices coating my skin.

I gasp as my hips instinctively thrust up like I'm fucking her, my fingers doing the job my dick would much rather be doing.

As her moans turn into a cry of ecstasy, I feel my own wetness coat my dick.

So much for control.

It would seem that when it comes to Octavia fucking Royal, I have none.

# CHAPTER EIGHT

## OCTAVIA

This week, so far, has been strangely quiet. I still haven't seen Blair or Raleigh, and happy as I am about it, I'm suspicious as fuck. I swear I keep ducking around corners, waiting for someone to jump out at me and attack.

I don't know if the guys finally managed to call Blair and the bitch squad off, or if Blair just isn't around this week, but considering it's homecoming week, I can't imagine she'd miss it. Especially since I was nominated for Queen.

I'm half expecting her to tar and feather me, if I'm being honest. Even if I can't think of anything worse than being crowned homecoming queen, being the center of attention like that… just nope. I've had enough attention to span a few lifetimes. I'm done with it. I'd happily fade into the background for the rest of time, please and thank you.

I head to my locker after my Stats class and find Indi waiting there for me. I smile as I open it, sliding my books in before grabbing my purse. "Cafeteria or Penny's?"

She grins at me. "I would love to say Penny's, but I need to hit the library. I have a test after lunch, so swing by the cafeteria then study?"

"Sounds good to me. God knows I've got plenty to catch up on." I bite my lip, mentally going over what I need to hand in before Thanksgiving break in a couple weeks. Fuck my life. I'm basically going to do nothing but study between now and then.

It could be worse, I guess.

I just wish I didn't have everything else crowding my mind. Focusing on school and keeping my grades up is proving hard enough as it is. We head to the cafeteria as Indi tells me about her morning. She opens the door and steps inside before pausing. I almost run into the back of her. About to ask her why she stopped, I look up and realize why.

The cafeteria is in full homecoming mode.

"As you all know, the court will be present at the football game on Friday night, remember to get your votes in for your King and Queen. This might just be the most important decision you make all year."

I snort a laugh at the declaration and everyone turns to stare at us. Apparently laughing when it's this quiet was a bad idea. Mikayla glares at me from the makeshift stage she has set up in here. Apparently the bitch squad *is* at school. I've just missed them.

Definitely not sad about that.

I nudge Indi forward, looping my arm through hers as I drag her to the line so we can grab food and escape as quickly as possible. Everyone stares at us until Mikayla starts droning on about the dance again.

"Remind me why we thought going to homecoming with these assholes would be fun."

"You're going to homecoming?" I jump at the sound of Maverick's voice, groaning when I turn and see the grin on his face.

I turn back to get food as quickly as I can, and Indi follows suit.

"Don't make me ask again, princess," Mav growls slowly as he moves into my space, his front flush with my back. I can hardly breathe, and I don't even have to look around to know that every set of eyes in the room is on us. I can fucking feel them.

"I don't have to answer your questions. You sure as hell never answer any of mine." I say it quietly enough that I know he heard it, but it's unlikely anyone else did. He growls in my ear and grips my arm, but I tear it free.

"Yes, we, as in Indi and I, are going to homecoming." I sigh, deciding this isn't worth the attention it's garnering as I pay for my sandwich, chips, and soda before moving out of the line to wait for Indi.

Maverick steps back from me, the room still so quiet you could hear a pin drop, as he drops to his knees. "Octavia Royal, will you go with me to homecoming?"

That cheeky glint in his eye matched with his smile makes me want to laugh. Especially after everything we spoke about over the weekend. There's no way he can be serious.

"Not a chance in hell. I told you, I already have a date."

At my rejection, the whispers start in the room and Maverick almost looks sad. I didn't know psychopaths could feel sadness. I link arms with Indi and head out of the cafeteria as she giggles beside me, looking back over our shoulders.

"Well, that was definitely something."

I look behind us and see him still on his knees, grinning at me sadistically. "It was, though I might have just poked the bear."

I smile internally, because maybe this is the way to get answers? Play them at their own game? I'm clutching at straws, so it's probably a terrible idea, but I tuck it away as an unlikely maybe.

We stop by our lockers before heading to the library and I fill her in on my Sunday morning with Mav, lazing around the pool enjoying the last of the summer sun that the weekend brought, even though the grounds guy was around cleaning the pool and stuff. I definitely took advantage of him offering to do my lotion and parading around half naked. Even if it did look like he'd had only about an hour's sleep.

Funnily, I feel closer to him than I do the others. Maybe it's 'cause we messed around, just hung out like I'd thought we would when I came back, but there was something just… different about him. He seemed lighter, and I felt safe around him.

Not something I thought I would say a few months ago. Especially not after the whole knife incident. With everything else going on, I'm leaning toward just letting some stuff go. Lord knows my plate is piling high enough without holding onto anger. Yes he did some bad shit and I still want answers, but it was fun to just hang out with him and not have a million things hanging over us. Forgiveness has never come easy to me, but it's time to put my big girl panties on and just get on with shit.

"He made it more than obvious he's not opposed to jumping into bed together again, too." I laugh as we sit at our usual table in the library.

Indi exhales a drawn out "Oooh," as she sits and I laugh.

"Well, I mean, you did say it was the best orgasm ever." She grins as a smile dances on my lips.

She's not wrong. I did say that. Though, after sampling what the others had to offer too…

I get lost in my own mind, letting that dumb horny bitch part of my brain take over and only return to the real world when she snaps her fingers in my face.

"You've been holding out on me haven't you? That was the face of a well-pleased woman."

I shush her as I feel a blush spill across my cheeks. "Maybe."

"Girl, you had better spill."

"We're supposed to be studying," I say, trying to wave her off as the librarian glares at us from across the room. "Later," I mouth to her, and she gives me a look that says that's a conversation she isn't going to let slide.

I pull my Business text book from my bag and drop it on the table with a thud. Might as well take the time to catch up while I can. Especially with that F still looming over my head.

Mr. Peters can eat his own dick, 'cause I'm sure as hell not going to.

---

I cannot believe it's Saturday already and that tonight is homecoming. This week has been a whirlwind. I swear it was only Monday yesterday. I honestly don't know where the days have gone.

Indi is due over any minute. We have a full day of full-scale pamper treatments planned. Smithy is cooking as we speak, he has sparkling apple juice for us because, bless his heart, he didn't think champagne was suitable. He is just too precious. I booked someone to come and do mani-pedis for us, hair and makeup. The whole nine yards.

I might not be that bothered about this whole homecoming thing, but Indi has practically bounced with excitement all week. I still can't quite believe she's never been to a dance before.

What I do know is that there's no way I won't be seeing Raleigh or Blair tonight. They're both also in the homecoming court which, considering he tried to rape me, is a fucking joke. But I guess that's just Echoes Cove Prep tied up in a bow, really.

I bounce down the stairs in my robe, only shorts and a tank beneath the fluffy goodness, and head into the kitchen where Smithy is in full chef mode.

"Morning, Smithy!"

"Good morning, Miss Octavia. How are we feeling today?"

"We are bright and sunshiny. Ready to spend the day with Indi getting our girl on."

He chuckles at me, shaking his head, "You do say some of the darndest things, Miss Octavia. I also spoke to Master Saint, who asked me to let you know that your ride to the dance tonight is sorted."

That motherfucker.

I don't let my smile drop though; Smithy wasn't to know and I refuse to let those boys rain on my parade today. "Which Saint?"

The words are practically dripping with saccharine sweetness as I flutter my lashes up at him. He gets a little flustered and heads back to the stove. "Master Lincoln."

"Thank you for letting me know."

"Of course, I'm just glad that you seem to have made up with them all. It's not good for a girl to be alone so much and an old man like me isn't the best of company."

I move to stand beside him, nudging his arm with my shoulder.

"Best old man I know." I smile up at him and he blushes a little. "Oh! I knew I had to ask you something. Do you have plans for Thanksgiving?"

"Not yet, Miss Octavia, though I suppose I should start thinking about it since it's only just under a week away!" He seems flustered all over again, which definitely wasn't my intention.

"Well, if you're going to be home, I was wondering if you'd mind if I invited some friends over. People from the tour. People who knew Dad. I thought it would be a nice way to celebrate this year."

He gazes down at me warmly before wrapping an arm around my shoulders and hugging me tightly. "That sounds perfect. Just let me know numbers, and I'll begin the preparations."

"You're the best, Smithy. Thank you."

"Anything for you, Miss Octavia. How long until Miss Indi arrives? The bagel boats are nearly done."

I practically drool at the sound of that. I don't know what a bagel boat is, but I am here for it. I check my phone and see a message from Indi.

**Indi:**
On my way! Driving in pj's is weird AF!

I laugh at the message and see it was sent a few minutes ago. "She'll be here any second," I tell him, and he smiles, nodding as he pulls the bagels from the oven.

My God, they smell divine.

The bagel bread is squished to the sides to make a little river inside, filled with egg, cheese, bacon, green onion and then topped with more cheese, baked until they're gooey breakfast beautifulness.

I really am so very lucky to have him in my life, and not just because of the amazing food he keeps feeding me. Without him, I'd still be stuck with my aunt and uncle. I can't think of a fate much worse.

The buzzer at the gate goes off, and I hit the button on my app to let Indi in. I do a little dance as I skip to the door.

"It's dance day, bitches!" she squeals as she bounds up the stairs, her dress bag in hand. She hugs me tight before bouncing into the foyer.

"If you want to hang your dress in there," I say, pointing to the security room, "Smithy is just serving up breakfast."

"Smithy is a *GOD!* Is that what smells so good?"

"Yes, yes it is." I grin and she drops her dress in the security room and runs past me into the kitchen. I hear her squeal again as she says hello to him and laugh softly as I hit the button to close the gate before following her.

We enjoy breakfast and the sparkling apple juice just in time for the mani-pedi girls to arrive. The morning of pampering is divine and I adore just how much Indi is loving it. She is my little ball of happiness, and I am here for it all.

When our mani-pedis are done, Smithy reappears. "Afternoon tea, anyone?"

He holds two cake tiers full of tiny cakes and sandwiches. It's freaking adorable.

"You are my favorite person ever!" Indi beams at him as he brings the tiers in and places them on the coffee table. He disappears and returns with a tray of tea cups, a teapot, sugar cubes, and a little jug of cream.

"You didn't have to do this!" I exclaim, though I am not so secretly loving it.

He just waves me off. "This is just an easy lunch. Enjoy, girls, let me know if you need me."

"You can join us if you like," I offer but he shakes his head.

"I've got a few errands to run, but I'm just at the end of the phone. I'll be back before you leave for the dance." He waves before heading back into the kitchen and we dig in.

"Dude, these tiny sandwiches are so soft." Indi grins as she shoves another one in her mouth and I start laughing.

"I wouldn't know. These tiny white chocolate and raspberry blondies are freaking divine and I don't plan on sampling your adult food. Give me dessert or give me death." I stuff another one in my mouth to prove my point. "You sure you wanna go to this thing tonight? I'm pretty sure Smithy will feed us all day long if we really want."

"Hush," she says, waving me off. "We are going to that dance, dammit. We are going to be the belles of the ball, and you are going to be queen."

I groan at the thought, "Please do not tempt fate."

"I can feel it in the air. Octavia Royal, Queen of Echoes Cove Prep." She grins as I groan again.

Someone please save me.

---

The day passes in a blur of happiness. Of stupid antics and laughter. By the time I'm slipping into my dark-green dress, I find myself wondering where the day has gone. I walk out of my bathroom and find Indi struggling with the strings of the corset on her dress. "Want a hand?"

She spins and gasps when she sees me. "Girl, you are *fire*!"

I laugh at her assessment and motion for her to turn around so I can do her up. "You're not exactly the pumpkin of this ball, yourself."

She grins at me in the mirror as I help her and do the strings on her corset-topped tutu dress. "Oh yeah, we'd totally get it."

I burst out laughing at her assessment, though she isn't wrong. When we went shopping for these dresses, I was just having fun with it, but we definitely made some choices that brought out the best in us. Her vivid locks are a shocking contrast to her pale skin and dark dress. Put together with a vampy eye and dark purple lipstick, she's rocking that emo chic look most girls would kill to pull off.

"What shoes are you wearing?" I ask as I smooth down the front of my emerald satin dress. I check my hair once more. The front is pinned away from my face and the rest of my dark locks cascade down my spine in curls, brushing against the bare skin of my back. This dress makes me thankful for tit tape, because without it I'd never pull it off.

"Docs, of course." She grins and I turn my attention back to her, barking out a laugh. "A girl needs some comfort."

"Yes, yes she does." I pull out a pair of Choos from my closet. They're not so high that I'll break my neck, and they're so freaking pretty. I grab a black clutch to match the shoes before turning back to Indi. "Okay, I'm ready. You good?"

"Hell yes I am, let's get our dance on!" She throws her hands in the air and does a little jig on the spot before leading us from the room. She dances all the way down the hall but pauses at the top of the stairs. "Umm… V?"

I come to stand beside her and see why she stopped.

Four very delicious, and mostly unwanted, guys stand in the foyer of the house fully suited and booted.

Well *shit*.

All eyes are on me as I descend the stairs, trying not to scowl at the four of them. I turn to Mav first. "I thought I told you no."

I fold my arms over my chest, quirking a brow at him, just as Indi lands beside me.

"You did. I chose not to listen." He grins at me. "And damn am I glad I did. You look good enough to eat, princess."

I glance from him to Finn who smiles softly, to East who looks more than a little sheepish, then to Linc who just looks bored.

"Are you ready to go? The car is waiting," Linc says, his tone as bored as his countenance.

I roll my eyes at him and turn to Indi. "You good riding with them? If not, I'll just drive like we planned."

"No, no. I'm good." She grins, so I bend down and slip my shoes on. The boys head outside and Indi grabs my arm to hold me back. "If they don't want a peek of your kitty cat in that dress, I'll eat my own damn kitty cat."

I burst out laughing at her and the guys turn to face us, making her blush.

"Well, they can just keep wanting," I say, winking at her. "Let's go!"

I take her hand and yell out a goodbye to Smithy before heading out. Finley offers me a hand to help me step into the limo, kissing the inside of my wrist as I take it. His lips are a scorching heat on my skin.

I slide into the car and Indi climbs in behind me, followed by the guys.

They talk quietly amongst themselves during the drive. If they were going to ignore us, why even bother asking us to ride with them? They seem to be arguing, so I turn the music up and have a mini party in the backseat with Indi instead. Tonight is not about them or the chaos we seem to be tangled up in. Tonight is about a night with my bestie.

When we pull up at the school, it's like there's been a freaking transformation outside of the gym. The trees that line the back steps up to the entryway are wrapped with twinkle lights and music spills through the doors. Indi practically vibrates in her chair as someone opens the door and she slides out.

"Thanks for the ride." I wink at Mav and follow Indi out, taking her hand once I'm standing straight again. "Let's go rock this, shall we?"

We strut inside, and it really is a full transformation. There's a makeshift stage that holds a few guitars, a drum set, a keyboard, and a couple of horns, while a DJ plays from his decks. There are all sorts of tables in here, living up to the 007 casino theme. There's poker, blackjack, craps, and a ton of other stuff I don't recognize.

"Dance or gamble?" I ask Indi. She stares longingly at the dance floor. "Dance it is!"

---

After dancing until my feet feel like they're going to fall off, I tap Indi's shoulder and prepare to slink over to a free table. These shoes might be beautiful, but they are not built for dancing, that much is for sure.

I start to move away from Indi just as a hush settles across the room, despite the music. Looking over to the main doors, my jaw drops.

"Umm, Indi?" I grab her and turn her so she can see what I see: the three drop dead gorgeous bad boys dressed up in suits that just crashed our dance. "Isn't that…"

She nods, gulping. "Yes, yes it is."

I look at her, my eyes wide. "Well, I guess the message about you not doing the chasing was fully received."

She smiles at me, blushing a little.

"And fuck anyone who says a thing. Trust me on this, whoever says shit is just jealous as fuck." I push her in their direction just a little. She glances over her shoulder at me and I motion for her to go to them as they walk toward us. Ryker leads them, Ellis and, who I assume is Dylan, flanking him on either side.

If she wasn't my bestie, I might almost be jealous. Instead, I am just insanely happy for her.

I drop into one of the chairs at my recently claimed table as the song changes and everyone loses their minds as the bass drops. I kick off my shoes and discreetly rub one of my feet under the table.

"You having fun?" I look up as East slides into the chair beside me.

"Should you be seen talking to me?" I tease. He frowns.

"I'm technically a chaperone. I can talk to whoever I want. Just like I talk to you in class."

I roll my eyes at him. I get he's on edge about what we did, but it's not like I'm going to tell anyone. I just wish he wasn't acting like he regretted it. He's barely spoken to me all week, even in class. "I was joking. You know, giving you shit?"

I get up and head to the drinks table where Maverick finds me. "I wouldn't touch the punch if I were you." He smiles down at me, wrapping an arm over my shoulders. "Want to get out of here?"

"Maverick Riley, what on earth makes you think I want to leave this dance, and with you of all people?" His grin widens at my words.

He stoops down to whisper in my ear, "Oh I can think of a lot of reasons, princess."

I blush a little at his insinuation.

"Did I tell you yet that you look good enough to eat?"

I cough, trying not to laugh at just how cheesy he is. "Yes, you did. But all women like to be told they're pretty, so thank you."

His hand brushes across the bottom of my back, skimming just above where the material of my dress sits above my ass, sending a shiver down my spine.

Nope. Not today, Satan.

And definitely not here.

I remove myself from his grasp and take a step back. "What are you doing?"

"Being friendly," he says, wagging his eyebrows at me.

I roll my eyes at him, because despite the good day we had over the weekend… I'm still not ready to forgive him. "We're not friends, Maverick. You made sure of that."

"We could be friends though. You're going to forgive me one day."

"Maybe." I shrug. "But today is not that day and I am not that bitch. And until you guys start answering my questions, or even just fucking respecting me, that isn't going to change."

I walk away from him and head to the bathroom, catching a glimpse of Indi dancing like a loon on the dance floor as I leave.

The bathroom is empty when I enter, so I close the door to the stall and just lean back against it, trying to catch my breath. These boys are going to give me whiplash if they keep going back and forth like they are.

Lincoln might drive me to insanity, but at least he's mostly consistent with his iceman routine. He's even stopped sneaking into my bed since that night with Raleigh. I don't pretend to know what's going on in that head of his.

When I came back, I wanted nothing more than to reconnect with them. But too much has happened now, and I'm not sure that's what I want anymore. Beyond the occasional mind-blowing orgasm anyway.

How does a girl get over the things they've done?

I don't even know for sure exactly which bits were them and which bits weren't. But the bits I know for certain are already enough for me to have reservations about ever forgiving them. No matter how much I might want to at times.

I hate how back and forth I am about this; I need to just make a fucking decision and stick to it.

The door to the bathroom opens and the click of heels echoes throughout the room.

Time to head back out I guess.

I'm trying not to regret coming tonight, because Indi is having so much fun, but I was right. School dances really aren't my thing. Taking a deep breath, I head out of the stall and come face to face with Blair, Mikayla, Serena, and Emma.

Oh awesome. Just what I needed to make this night better. If I had to guess, I'll find Brittany outside the door. I try to move past them, but they block the way to the door. "What do you want?"

"I warned you, Octavia. I warned you on your first day of school. Do you remember what I said?" Blair's shrill voice fills the silence of the room, and I wince at just how hysterical she sounds.

I resist rolling my eyes at her, and let out a sigh. "No, Blair, I don't remember what you said. It was a hot minute ago."

Despite the truth of my words, they just seem to anger her further. She clenches her fists at her sides, practically vibrating with rage. "I told you that this was my school. That I was queen, and that you had better remember it."

"Oh that." I sigh, "I don't want your school or your crown, Blair. You can have them. Now if I can just leave, please. I'll get out of your hair."

She smiles at me, looking almost possessed and maniacal as her eyes go wide. "I have a better idea in mind."

The four of them rush at me and we all go down in a tangle of limbs. I try to fight them off, but apparently being cheer barbie gives you more muscles than my pathetic attempts at working out recently.

"Get the fuck off me!" I shout, and Blair just laughs again as she basically sits on my chest while the others hold my arms and legs.

This is fucking insane.

"I'll teach you to take what is mine. It was all meant to be mine. *They* were meant to be mine but you just ruined everything! And now I'm going to ruin you!" She pulls a pair of scissors from her clutch, and my eyes go wide before I struggle against them even harder.

She cackles before grabbing a handful of my hair and starts snipping. I scream until my throat is hoarse, but no one comes to help me. I don't give a fucking inch though.

"You're going to regret this, Blair," I shout as she makes her last cut.

She laughs dryly as she drops the scissors and pulls a Sharpie from her purse. "There isn't anything left that you can do to me. I already lost everything."

She grabs my cheeks and uses the Sharpie to write on my forehead before slapping me on the face twice.

"Suck on that, homecoming queen."

They clamber off of me and I scream, jumping up and lunging after them, but they yell and run from the room. I growl in frustration as they reach the gym and enter as if nothing happened. I storm back to the bathroom to grab my bag so I can get my phone, and I get a look at the damage they've done. I lock the door before turning to face the mirror, not wanting to be interrupted while I bathe in my shame.

My long, dark locks hang in uneven lengths around my shoulders, the word 'Slut' smeared across my forehead. I blink back tears of anger because I refuse to cry.

There is no way they will see me fucking cry.

I try to call Indi, but it goes to voicemail so I send her a text instead. I hate pulling her from her guys right now, but selfishly, I need my bestie.

**Me:**

SOS. Bitch Squad got me. I need to head home.

I try to scrub the marker from my forehead but it won't come off. I bark out a dry laugh. Of course it won't. My phone pings on the counter and Indi's name flashes on the screen.

"Where are you?" she asks the second I answer.

"In the bathroom."

I hear her footsteps down the line as she walks through the empty halls. "Let me in," she says as a knock sounds on the door.

I end the call and open the door. She gasps when she sees me, covering her mouth with her hand. "Oh, V."

"I know. I just… I need to go home," I say, my throat thick with emotion, still trying not to cry because it seems ridiculous that this is the thing to push me over the edge. So I do what I vowed I wouldn't and shove it down for the time being.

She wraps me in a hug, but I shake her off. If I let her hug me, I'll cry. "Okay, come on. Let's go. I swear to fucking God, I'm going to burn those bitches to the ground."

I try to smile, because I love how feisty she gets when she's mad, but I just feel beaten.

"I'm sorry, I don't want to ruin your night…" I trail off and she pulls me to a stop making me face her.

"V, boys will come and go, but best bitches are for life. You have nothing to be sorry for. I'm sorry I wasn't here to help you."

A lump forms in my throat as I shake my head, trying to tell her that she has nothing to be sorry for, but words don't come. I managed to stay strong through so much. I thought I could survive it all, but I was wrong. I thought I'd finally made it past everything. I was beginning to have hope, and now…

I open the door and come face to face with Lincoln, whose gaze scours me from head to toe.

That's when a tear slips down my cheek. I wipe it away quickly, not wanting him to see me cry, but when his eyes narrow, I know I wasn't fast enough.

"Who?"

The one world fills the space between us, but I don't have to say a word. I see it on his face when it comes to him.

Another tear falls and he reaches forward to wipe it away, caressing my cheek. Without another word, he turns on his heel and walks away from me, shoulders rigid as he heads back toward the gym.

Maybe one day Blair will get what's coming to her, but I doubt today will be that day. Regardless, she's officially pushed me over the edge. A war is coming, and whether she thinks she has nothing to lose or not…

I'm going to show her that there is always something more to lose.

# CHAPTER NINE

## OCTAVIA

I take a deep breath as I stare at my reflection in my bathroom mirror. Gracie—Indi's hair woman—is a fucking magician. You can't even really tell I was butchered at the dance. If anything, the extensions just make it look like I had a few layers put into my hair.

Looking the same doesn't stop my simmering rage though. I'm not even sure exactly what I did for Blair to hate me so much; we used to be so close. Our history doesn't stop me from wanting to watch her world crumble. Not at this point.

I am so done being the victim in her story. She started this, but I'm sure as fuck going to end it. I just need to bide my time and work out what is going to hurt her the most.

I finish getting ready for school and head downstairs. As I go to open the fridge, I notice a note from Smithy, telling me he's gone grocery shopping and he'll see me later. Inside, I find a smoothie along with a berry box waiting for me.

He is too good to me.

I notice the time and practically inhale my breakfast before rushing out of the house. I drive like a crazy person to make sure I get to school on time, finding Indi standing beside her Wrangler in her usual spot. I pull into my space, practically jumping from the car, flustered. Not exactly how I wanted to start the day.

*Just three days until Thanksgiving break. We've got this.*

She beams at me and hands me my coffee. "Your hair looks fucking amazing. I'm so glad that Gracie did such a good job for you."

"Me too." I smile before taking a sip of the hot mocha goodness. "I never put myself down as a vain person, but apparently I was wrong."

We head into school and come face to face with Blair and her bitch squad. I put on my fiercest smile, enjoying the shock on their faces when I'm not the hot mess they expected me to be this morning. We breeze past them and I give them a little finger wave while Indi giggles beside me.

Okay, so that might not be the revenge I'm craving, but it definitely felt good. I don't even care if it's petty as fuck. "Do you have any plans tonight?"

She looks up at me from her phone and shakes her head, "No, I saw the guys yesterday while you were with Gracie, so my night is free and clear. What did you have in mind?"

"We are one hundred percent coming back to you and the guys in a moment, don't think you're getting off the hook with that, missy," I tease, and she blushes a little, "but I was thinking of an all night homework and cram session to prepare for all the things we have to hand in this week before break. I'm so freaking behind. I swear, next semester, drama or not, I *need* to put my school work first."

She nods as I grab my books. "Sounds good. I've got a ton to do, too."

"Perfection."

We make our way down the hall to her locker so she can grab her things before heading to English, where Miss Summers is already waiting for us.

"Morning, girls!" She beams at us as we enter the room.

We head to the back of the room and take our seats. The bell hasn't rung yet, so I take the opportunity to interrogate her. "So. Boys. Weekend. Spill the tea."

She blushes again, hiding her face behind her hair. "Well, after they showed up at the dance and basically begged my forgiveness, we decided to just hang out on Sunday. It was weird being their main focus again. I forgot how intense they can be."

I fan my face and she laughs. "Yeah, but the best kind of intense I bet."

"You could say that." She sighs happily, and I smile.

"Hey, as long as you're happy, I'm happy. But if they hurt you, I'll bring the shovels. I know how to get rid of a body or three."

She bursts out laughing just as the bell sounds and we turn our attention to Miss Summers, who starts talking about our exam coming up before Christmas break next month. Groans chorus around the room and I try to calm the spike of anxiety that makes my heart pound in my chest.

I've fallen so behind with all of my school work thanks to everything that's been going on. Despite my stubbornness that I wasn't going to let any of it mess with me… it already has. I try to focus on Miss Summers as she talks about what's going to be covered on the exam, but my mind goes down the rabbit hole of just how much shit I have to get done to not just pass my classes, but also meet the terms of my dad's will.

Usually the money thing wouldn't bother me too much, but the thought of losing the house, of Smithy being without, of potentially no college—nothing—until I turn twenty-five is enough to have me spinning out. When I first heard the terms of the will, I wasn't too deterred. I've never had a problem with my grades. But with everything that's happened, alongside adjusting to freaking mainstream schooling, it hasn't been great.

I'm so fucked.

I spiral for so long that the bell rings before I realize the class is even over.

Fuck my life.

"Please tell me you took notes," I hiss to Indi, who nods, looking more than a little concerned. "Awesome. Time to go face Mr. Peters."

"I still think you should report him." She frowns as I shudder, thinking about his gross proposal.

"There's no point, who would believe me?" I shrug, hating that he'll get away with it. That he might do it to someone else. But he hadn't been wrong about that part: no one would believe me.

She looks like she wants to say more, but as we leave the class, I almost run straight into Lincoln, Maverick, and Finley.

"I'll see you at lunch?" I say to Indi, who nods, her gaze bouncing between me and them. I smile at her, trying to reassure her that I'll be okay. She turns and heads down the hall in the opposite direction I need to go. "Can I help you?"

I move out of the doorway and head toward Business when none of them respond. They trail behind me like guard dogs and everyone scurries out of our path as we make our way to the class. It's not even unnerving.

God, the sarcasm in my own head needs to come down a notch.

I enter the classroom for Business and come face-to-face with Mr. Peters. I've managed to avoid being alone with him, or even in close contact, since that day. This is the closest I've been to him since he practically waved his dick at me like a flag.

"Miss Royal," he says, his eyes raking over my body, making me feel as dirty as I would if I'd bathed in blood and dirt.

I feel the heat at my back as the guys catch up with me. Mr. Peters' eyes go wide and he takes a step back, as if he's flustered. I don't even care that he did that purely because of their arrival, there has to be some upsides of these assholes hovering around me. I take advantage of the situation and scurry over to my desk. Once I'm seated, I look up and find Mr. Peters is caught in a battle of wills with Lincoln and they're staring each other down.

Mr. Peters looks away first, and I smile as I look down at my text book. I hate that Lincoln is a giant asshole ninety-nine percent of the time, but just this once, I kind of love it.

The bell rings again and they finally move, allowing the rest of our class to filter into the room once they take their seats.

I guess someone did believe me after all.

---

I pull up at home, grinning wide. Last night was a whirlwind of catching up and essay writing, and today has been a day of avoiding the guys, Blair, and… well, everyone that isn't Indi, as much as possible.

Now school is almost done for the week and we have a long weekend to look forward to, I just need to survive tomorrow, then I'm free for four whole days.

I am too excited to see everyone. Jenna messaged me yesterday to confirm that the whole gang is definitely still coming. Smithy has been rushing around like a crazy person to get everything ready, even though I offered to have it catered.

He looked like I stomped on his puppy at the suggestion, so I didn't bring it up again.

It might only be Tuesday, but the thought of having all of my found family together under my roof is too exciting. Indi even managed to persuade her mom to let her stay here over the next few days, rather than heading back east with them to see their family.

I just need to finish setting up the guest room for her.

I bounce into the house, excited butterflies taking flight in my stomach. "I'm home!"

"In the kitchen," Smithy hollers back, and I grin as I head in the direction of his voice. With how much time the man spends in here, I'm beginning to think he sleeps under the table.

I find him arm deep in pie crust, with five pie dishes already lined with pastry. "Do we have enough pie?"

"Well, I thought I'd do pecan, but nut allergies, so I did key lime, which led me to pumpkin. Then I remembered lemon meringue is your favorite, so I added that too, and well… I added a lemon tart and a chocolate and raspberry torte to the menu too. Because why not?" He grins at me like this is truly his happy place. Who am I to stop a man keeping me stocked in pie?

"I'm sure it'll be amazing. Do you need me to do anything?"

He shakes his head. "Not a thing. My kitchen doesn't need that sort of punishment," he teases and I laugh. "Plus, I might have invited the Saint boys over since Mrs. Potts is away for the long weekend and their father… well, let's not discuss him, shall we? Mrs. Potts is going to help me prep some more dishes tomorrow before she leaves. I hope you don't mind."

"No, it's fine," I say, my heart sinking just a little. I suck it up though, because he doesn't ask for much, and despite my topsy turvy feelings toward the brothers, it'll be nice to have a full house. "Indi will be heading over Thursday morning and she'll be with us until Sunday night."

"Sounds perfect, Miss Octavia. Do you have many plans for tonight?"

"Just finishing up some more school work, so I'll be around if you need me." I smile at him and take my bag to the living room. I take a quick detour to my room to change before settling in on the floor and spreading my books out over the coffee table.

I work for about an hour until the smells get so distracting that I'm practically drooling over my Business textbook.

The buzzer for the gate sounds, officially pulling me from my studies. "I'll get it!" I yell to Smithy and grab my phone. I frown when I open the app and an empty drive appears on the screen.

Weird.

Getting up, I pad over to the front door and open it to see if there's just something wrong with the camera, but there's still no one at the gate.

Probably just kids fucking around.

Stepping back to close the door, something catches my eye and I freeze. There, at the bottom of the steps, is a small parcel wrapped in manilla paper with my name written on the top.

My stomach churns as my heart pounds. Everything else that comes in that shade of package has been from that creepy stalker fuck, but this isn't an envelope.

My hand shakes as I rush down the steps and reach for the box. I stop before I pick it up, an icy drop of fear running down my spine.

What if it's something that could hurt me?

I take a deep breath and do something I really don't want to do.

I call Lincoln.

He picks up on the third ring, sounding out of breath. I'm too freaked out to think about why. "Lincoln. I'm sorry, I didn't want to call…"

"What's wrong?"

"There's a box on my steps. I don't suppose you guys are playing another weird-ass prank or something are you? 'Cause if not, someone got through my gates. Again."

"I'll be there in two minutes."

The line disconnects and I bounce from one foot to the other, wishing I was wearing something on my feet. I use the cold ground to try to distract myself from whatever could be in the box.

Less than a minute later, he's jogging toward me with the other three hot on his heels. All of them in various states of workout gear or half naked, and I'll be damned if I don't find myself suddenly *very* distracted.

Definitely not the time to ogle them, but it's better that than focusing on the stupid box.

Finn heads straight to me and wraps me up in his arms. "You okay, V?"

"I'm fine, just a little freaked out. Plus Smithy is inside, and I haven't told him about any of this. I didn't want him wrapped up in it all. But I don't know what's in there, and I'm spiraling a little."

He nods before stepping away from me and crouching down to look at the box. Mav hands him a knife which he uses to cut the brown string on the box and the manilla paper falls away, revealing a nondescript white postage box. He cuts through the tape and opens the box.

The lid falls away and I gasp at the contents.

A bloody knife inside a plastic bag, and a note. I reach past Finley to pick up the paper and regret it immediately.

*They can't keep you safe. Not like I can.*
*You'll see*
*x*

I think I'm going to be sick.

"Whose blood could that be?" Lincoln asks, and I shake my head.

"I have no idea. I have no fucking clue about any of this." I hand him the note and wrap my arms around my waist.

Lincoln turns to East and they murmur between the two of them while Mav strides over to me and runs his hands up and down my arms. "We'll find whoever this sicko is and deal with it. I swear."

I nod, because what else can I do? "I feel like I should be doing something to help find out who it is, rather than sitting around waiting for something to happen."

"I get it, feeling helpless fucking sucks. I'm right there with you, princess, but for now, Lincoln is on it. You know he's like a dog with a bone when it comes to a mystery. He won't let it evade him for long."

I chew on my lip as I consider his words. Maybe I really should go to the police? Or speak to Smithy. He has friends in all sorts of weird and wonderful places.

But what if that makes him a target too?

Lincoln turns and motions to Finley, who picks up the box and heads over to the brothers.

"Come on, let's get you inside. These guys will deal with it. I'll stay with you for a bit."

This might be the softest side to Mav I've seen since I got back, but there's still a hardness behind it, like he's just trying to protect me, and that sets me off balance all on its own.

"We'll be in touch soon," Lincoln says as Mav starts to usher me inside, and I nod, feeling more than a little numb.

Maybe one day my life will be normal, but at this point, I think that's nothing but a dream.

---

After Smithy's delight at having Maverick around for the evening, we ate, and the two of them chatted up a storm like two friends who had been separated for years. I left them to it and grabbed a shower, throwing on a pair of cutoffs and a hoodie, because comfort is key right now.

I make my way back to my room and find Maverick sprawled out on my bed, grinning wickedly at me.

I definitely shouldn't be thinking about how good he looks, but right now he looks like the perfect kind of escape. He's taken so much from me at this point that I don't even feel bad about taking something for myself.

Especially when I want to feel something other than fear.

I know I shouldn't want him, and I know I definitely shouldn't forgive him, but there is something about Maverick Riley that makes me weak. He makes me feel brazen, like I can take on the world and come out swinging on the other side.

Having him lie there, on my bed, in my space, makes me bold.

I might not have completely forgiven him yet, but that doesn't mean we can't have fun. I only just lost my virginity, and while I put absolutely zero stock in the whole virgin thing, maybe I shouldn't be messing around with three different guys? I've never had any issues with women owning their sexuality, but I can't help but second guess myself. Especially when it's *these* guys I'm messing around with. Pretty sure I should be avoiding them at all costs. Or at least put up more of a fight. Retaliate against everything they've done… make them work a little harder, or at least give me some of what I want.

"Get out of your head, princess. I know what you're thinking, and trust me everyone is okay with sharing as long as we get to have you. Now, crawl up on this bed with me." The devilish smirk on his face promises even more than the fantasies his words trigger in my mind, and it sparks a fire in me. The challenge in his eyes emboldens me.

Fuck overthinking it.

I sashay across the room, compartmentalizing the events of the evening as I go, and crawl up the bed like he instructed until he's caged in beneath me. Not that I'm taking that for granted. Caging Maverick Riley is like caging a tiger—dangerous as fuck.

He captures my lips with his, pulling me down on top of him until our bodies are flush. "Tell me what you want, princess."

I bite the inside of my lip, considering his words.

"I want to suck your dick."

His eyes go wide at my words, and then he grins that signature smirk of his. "If you think I'm going to turn that down, you are out of your damn mind."

The next thing I know, Mav has deftly swapped our positions and *I'm* now caged beneath *him*, his eyes burning with what I can only describe as dangerous lust. Unhinged desire. A beast cornering his prey, playing with them, before going in for the kill.

It's exhilarating.

Maybe something is wrong with me. Maybe my fight or flight instinct really is broken. But that look in his eye has me so fucking excited that butterflies take flight in my stomach.

"Just remember, princess, you asked for it."

It's my turn to grin up at him, because fuck it. "Bring it on."

There's a moment, no more than a heartbeat, where I'm almost afraid I've gotten myself into a heap of trouble. Then he leans in and captures my mouth like I'm the last piece of his complicated puzzle. Our tongues battle, each of us fighting for dominance, but it takes less than a second for me to know it's a fight I'm not going to win. He's leading the charge. He's got a plan and it's all I can do to stay caught up. My hands fly up to his black t-shirt and fist the fabric like it'll be able to keep me on solid ground as Mav kisses the breath out of me. His hands hold me so tightly I know he'll leave behind the imprint of his fingers before long. While I know I shouldn't like it, a sharp thrill runs through me at the thought.

When he's done kissing me to the brink of unconsciousness, he doesn't just stop. No, that would be too normal. Instead, he traps my bottom lip between his teeth and slowly, like time is on his clock, sinks his teeth deep into my flesh until I can taste the iron of my own blood.

It's when he sucks and licks my blood that I admit to myself that Maverick Riley is a man apart from all others.

Maybe my vampire fantasies and all the Anne Rice books I read on the road have finally caught up to me.

As I'm contemplating the situation at hand, I feel Mav's hand gliding beneath the leg of one of my cutoffs before he grabs a handful of ass cheek and winks. Not a flirty wink, though. This one is more of a promise that I might end up regretting what I wished for.

He leans over me and kisses my throat, discarding my shirt as he works his way down, biting, licking, and kissing my flesh, marking me further as he goes. When he pulls back and sees the still-faint line from the cut he made on my chest, his eyes go wide and his pupils dilate.

He likes seeing his marks on my skin.

Goosebumps break out over my entire body under the heat of his blazing stare. "Lie sideways on the bed."

That's it. Those are his only instructions before he's off the bed and standing with one hand at the button of his jeans, his muscles contracting beneath the layers of ink across his skin.

I turn sideways, my feet hanging off the side and my head turned toward the end of the bed, following him as he makes his way to me, unzipping and grinning like he knows a secret and won't tell until the timing is perfect.

His fly is open, revealing *just* enough of his thick cock begging to come out and play.

My mouth waters at the thought and I wonder how he'll taste. Salty or tangy. Will he make me swallow? Would I even consider it?

Mav leans over me, both of his hands on either side of my head, and kisses me upside down. It's strange and different and nothing fits the way it's supposed to. Then again, when it comes to Maverick, nothing ever has.

With one long, lingering swipe of his tongue across my lips, he puts both of his hands on my waist and hauls me up closer until my head is hanging off the side of the bed.

Well, this is weird. And a little uncomfortable, if I'm honest.

"When I fuck your mouth, I want to see my dick in your throat."

Oh.

Maybe I should have thought this through a little more.

"Don't be afraid, princess. You'll love it, I'll make sure of it."

I relax a little. Despite his unhinged tendencies, for some reason, I trust Maverick when it comes to this. Which says more about my state of mind than it does about his.

"Okay."

"Hmm, now open up and show me how much you want my cock." God, I love his filthy mouth.

With my hair touching the bedroom floor and my fists clenching the bed, I watch Mav from my position as he meticulously takes out his cock then rubs the head across my parted lips.

"Such a pretty, dirty mouth you have." He's watching himself paint my lips with his precum, going round and round like the sight mesmerizes him. "A dirty, filthy mouth fit for a princess. Now, open nice and wide while I fuck the filth right out of it."

I do as I'm told and he slowly—almost delicately—pushes his dick into my mouth. At first he dips in and out in shallow pumps, but I want more.

More of him, of this power that I feel as I watch his eyes turn molten with undeniable fire. The sight of me with my mouth full of his cock is turning him on like nothing else I've seen.

He humors me by pushing a little bit more and staying in a little bit longer.

My gag reflex is starting to work, and I'm afraid I won't be able to go as far as he'd like.

"Breathe through your nose and open up your throat for me, princess."

I try to follow his instructions and soon enough, I've got tears streaming into my hairline. Mav picks one up with his thumb and brings it to his mouth, making a whole production of licking it up.

"Hmm, even your tears are delicious. Now, be a good girl and swallow my dick." Without further warning, he presses the rest of the way forward. Just when I think I'm going to tap out, he places his open palm over my throat and squeezes, practically choking me.

I should be afraid—I should be freaking the fuck out—instead, I'm strangely comforted by his dominance. Like he knows what's best and if I don't fight him, I'll be okay.

We'll be okay.

When he pulls back out of my mouth, his hand squeezes just a little bit tighter around my throat, making my pussy clench with need.

"You like that, don't you? You're fucking soaked for me."

I don't answer, I'm not sure there's even anything to say to that because he's one hundred percent correct.

"The next time I'm fucking your throat, I want you to play with your clit."

"But I don't know if I can—"

"Don't talk back, princess. Do what I tell you."

He's back to circling my lips with his cock just as he leans in to unbutton my shorts and lower the zipper.

"Off."

I shimmy my shorts off and take my underwear with them so that I'm bare when he moves back into position.

The feeling of the blood rushing to my head is making me even hornier, a tingling sensation overtaking my entire bloodstream.

Mav taps the head of his cock on my lips, and I take that as my cue to open up.

Next thing I know, I'm reaching for my clit as Mav's dick is slowly pushed in and down, his hand back at my throat, squeezing even harder.

I concentrate on my breathing, getting used to the feeling of being completely full.

And then he starts to fuck my mouth.

Like, seriously. I can feel everything. Every inch of him as he slides down, the pressure of his palm when he reaches as far as he can go. His balls slapping my face. His scent. Holy shit, his scent is everywhere.

My fingers are frantically working over my clit and my orgasm is about to fucking explode like a furious volcano.

"Goddamn, your fucking mouth. I knew it'd be good, but fucking hell, V."

I can't talk, I can't nod, I can't fucking think.

"I'm gonna come, V. You better fucking swallow every goddamn drop."

My hips fly off the bed at his words, my climax taking over my entire body just as he comes straight down my throat.

I think I'm choking when he pulls his cock out, one hand pumping the last remnants of his cum onto my chin, the other holding me down by the throat.

My body is trembling and my hands fall to my sides as my eyes drift shut, heavy from the effort my orgasm demanded of me.

I swallow everything down as I was instructed, and although I was afraid of this moment, I enjoy every single second of it. So much so that I hungrily swirl my tongue around his thumb when he brushes it across my chin and presses it into my mouth, ensuring I don't waste a single drop.

He's salty and thick and all fucking male.

Breathing heavily like I've just run a marathon, I take a second to get my heart rate down.

Without bothering to tuck himself in, Mav picks me up and cradles me in his arms as he makes his way to the middle of my bed.

After being the beast in my dirtiest fantasies, he becomes the prince who protects me from himself.

Resting my head against his chest as we lie there in silence, I wonder what other parts of himself he's hiding from me.

# CHAPTER TEN

## MAVERICK

I wake up bleary-eyed, having slept deeper than I ever remember doing. I usually only manage about three hours a night, at best, and they're broken as fuck. Blinking against the light spilling into the room as the sun rises, I try to orient myself. I'm so fucking warm I'm practically sweating. I blink a couple more times and realize why as the haze finally lifts from my mind.

V is curled up on my chest, snoring softly. She sounds like a fucking kitten. Except her claws are much sharper than that.

I try not to take too much pride in the marks on her skin. Proof that she is mine. Just seeing it reminds me of the first time I marked her. Dragging my knife between her tits. Just thinking about it makes me hard again.

Extracting myself from her hold is easier than I thought it would be, but leaving her isn't. I don't know what sick motherfucker is messing with her like this, but when I get my hands on him, he's going to regret every decision he's ever made to this point. And if he doesn't, I'll make him bleed until he does.

I glance back at her once as I slip my sneakers back on and head out of the room before jogging through the house. Smithy is sitting in the kitchen sipping a cup of tea as I walk in. He looks up at me over his newspaper, an eyebrow raised. "Master Riley."

"Morning, Smithy," I say, raising a hand and smiling sheepishly. I'm not used to getting caught making a great escape, though usually I don't sleep over. "I'll just, uhm, see myself out."

He grumbles quietly, before looking back down at his paper. I take the opportunity to duck out of the back door. Thankfully the alarm is already disabled. Jogging through the back yard over to Linc's only takes a minute and I check my phone as I let myself in through his kitchen door. I didn't look at it once after I left them to chill with V last night. There's just one message from Linc waiting for me.

**Linc:**
Knife handed over to Lucas. I'll update you when you're back.

Oops.

I shrug and slide the phone back in my pocket as I grab the orange juice from the refrigerator.

"You better not drink that from the carton." East's sleep-filled voice breaks through the silence of the room, and I grin as I lift it to my lips and take a swig. "You're a fucking heathen."

I swallow the juice and replace the lid before putting it back in the fridge. "Tell me something I don't know."

I jump up on the counter as he grabs the eggs from the fridge and pulls a pan from the hooks on the wall. "How was V?"

"Satisfied and sleeping when I left." I grin as he glares at me. "Hey, I know you went there too. We already vowed we'd be open about everything when it comes to her."

"You really think last night was the time?" he scolds, waving a spatula in my direction. He hands me the bread and I drop a few slices in the toaster as he cracks the eggs into the pan and starts to scramble them.

"She seemed to think so. I'm done with trying to think I know what's best for her. I'll leave that to the rest of you."

He mumbles in response, but I'm not surprised. I'm not wrong and he knows it.

"Where's Mrs. Potts? Why are you trying to kill us off with your cooking?"

He glares at me again. "She's sleeping in. She's helping Smithy with Thanksgiving prep today before she leaves for the weekend."

Ahhh Thanksgiving. The one holiday when my parents try to pretend we're a big happy family. "What are you guys doing for the day? Feel free to come crash Happy Days at my house."

"We're going to V's." My jaw drops at his response.

*The fuck they are.*

I guess my parents are going to be real pissed off this year, because that isn't a day I'm missing. "Count me in, sounds like fun."

"That wasn't an invitation," he growls, just as Linc and Finn enter the room.

"What wasn't?" Finn asks as he sits down at the table.

"These fuckers are spending Thanksgiving with Smithy and V, so I invited myself along." I jump down from the counter as Linc rolls his eyes at me.

"I guess we'll let Smithy know to add two more," Linc says, turning to Finn. "I assume you'll be coming too?"

Finn pauses for a second as if, like me, he's wondering just how much shit he'll get for not being home. But, his parents are worse than mine. Though they don't usually try to pretend like mine do. "Yeah, count me in."

"Awesome." I grin as I drop down next to him at the table. "Now what did I miss last night?"

Linc starts the coffee brewing before he speaks. I swear his veins hold caffeine not blood. Though, he usually sleeps about as much as I do, so it's not surprising. Once he's holding a mug of coffee in his hands, he turns back to face us. "Lucas has the knife; he's running it for prints and DNA to see if this asshole left any traces behind. He's also running the blood to see if we know who that belongs to."

"It's probably pig's blood," I offer. "That's what I'd do if I wanted to freak someone out."

"Maybe," Linc says, nodding, "But for now, we need to play our cards close to our chest. How was she last night?"

East cuts his eyes to me at the question, so I shoot him a shit eating grin before turning back to the others. "She was shook up, but that's to be expected. She's tougher than we give her credit for though. She handled it with more grace than most people we know would."

Lincoln sits at the table as East plates up the eggs. He brings them and the toast over to the table, and I dig in. Linc looks at the food like it offends him. I went without food often enough that I learned to eat when food is there. Whether the eggs taste like rubber or not.

"That's good. Hopefully it's not just a trauma response from something we don't know about. She seems to compartmentalize like a pro," East offers, and Finley frowns at him.

"Do you know something we don't?"

"No, we said we'd be open and transparent about everything to do with her going forward. You know what I do," East says with a sigh. Getting over the secrets we kept from each other these last few months is taking a minute. Everyone's so goddamn possessive and protective when it comes to V, which makes it difficult.

"She knows we all know by the way," I chime in, and they look at me. "She was feeling squirrely about fucking around with all of us." I look at Linc and grin. "Well, most of us. So I told her we were all chill about it. Do *not* make me a liar."

"And what if one of us wants her to ourselves?" East asks, an eyebrow raised.

"We don't make her make that decision," Lincoln adds. "If you're not okay with sharing her, then you don't get her. Unless she makes the decision on her own."

"Dude, you're not even trying with her. Who says you make the rules?" I challenge. I mean, Linc usually makes the rules, but with V, everything is different.

"I never said I was trying with her," he says gruffly, "I said that no one puts that pressure on her. None of us get to keep her anyway."

"I'm chill with that. I mean, I'd like her to myself, but I'd rather have her and share than not at all," Finley agrees before getting up and pouring himself a glass of milk.

"Fine," East says, basically pouting. Sucks to be him, but that's what happens when you hand the mantle of power down to your little brother, I guess. You lose the power that should've been yours. "I'm going to go and get ready. Are you assholes going to school today?"

"Yeah, we'll see you there," Linc says, and it's my turn to frown. I am very much looking forward to never having to go to school ever again. Though I do have one thing on my agenda today. I feel a sadistic smile stretch out across my face.

A day with blood on my hands is always better than one without.

---

I follow my prey out of the school parking lot on my Ducati when the school day ends, excitement making my heart race. I spent the entire day dreaming up ways to punish this motherfucker for what he did to Octavia.

You could say that others have done worse shit to her, me included, but I'm working on ways to make up for that. Plus, I did what I did *for* her. This asshole crossed a line purely for himself, taking advantage of her situation and exploiting it.

I'm going to make sure he knows he fucked up… and that he can never do it again. To V, or to anyone.

I follow him to his home, glad that he lives his pathetic existence alone, because that's going to make my life easier. Even better that he lives outside of town in the middle of nowhere. The joys of living on a teacher's wage, I guess.

I ride past his house as he pulls in the drive, and circle back around. There aren't many places to tuck myself out of the way, but I want to wait until the sun sets before I enter his house. Just to make sure there isn't anyone else in there.

Shutting off the engine, I take off my helmet and place it at my feet before shrugging my backpack off. I went home at lunch just to make sure I had everything I needed to deal with this scumbag. Dad just smiled when he saw me getting my collection.

I'm not sure what it says about me that he seemed proud. I guess it's why people think I'm such a psycho. Clinically speaking, I might not be a psychopath, but it's easy enough for me to slip into that state of mind where emotion doesn't exist that I'm probably toeing a line or two. My dad made sure of that from a young age.

I shudder at the memory before shutting it away and going to that quiet part of my mind. The part that lets me enjoy the pain I inflict. The part that stops me feeling even one drop of remorse for my actions.

I watch the house for hours until the sun sets, and once I'm confident there's no one but Mr. Peters in the house, I make my approach. The silence of the night makes me grin. Everyone likes to believe it's the things that go bump in the night that they're afraid of, but in reality, it's the oppressive silence that gets to most people. If you can find a home in the shadows and silence, that's when you know you can truly claim the title of monster.

Unfortunately for Mr. Peters, I embraced the monster inside of me a long time ago.

I drop a text to Eric before I creep in through the back door of the small house. He was more than on board for tonight. Pedophiles are his favorite type of victim. The sounds of the TV filter through the house and his laughter at whatever drivel is showing grates on me like nails on a chalkboard. I palm my knives, one in each hand.

The others prefer guns, but I like to be up close with the pain I inflict. There's just something more personal about drawing blood with a blade than with a bullet.

This way, I can coat myself in their blood as I revel in their screams.

I have some special humiliation planned for Mr. Peters. I just want to have some fun with him on my own first.

Try and humiliate my girl and you'll regret it.

I slink into the living room and find him in the lone recliner in front of the TV. Moving silently up behind him, I place my blade at his throat. "Surprise."

He squeaks, jumping at the word and causing the steel to split flesh where the two meet, widening my smile. I move around the chair, keeping the blade at his throat.

"M…M…Maverick? What are you doing here?" he splutters, beads of sweat rolling down his face.

I grin at him and crouch, adrenaline rushing through me, the thrill of having prey at my mercy making my heart pound. "Did you really think your predatory ways would go unnoticed? In our school? Did you not understand that *we* are the apex predators?"

His eyes go wider and I genuinely think he might piss his pants. Fucking pathetic.

"I didn't… I don't… Nothing happened."

My grin widens. At least he didn't try to lie to me. Not about this time anyway. There is no way that this is the first time it's happened, and while it wouldn't be on my radar if it weren't for V, like I told him… *we* are the apex predators.

We bathed in blood and walked through fire to claim that right.

Literally.

"What are you going to do?" he whines, his sweaty skin turning the color of a tomato.

My grin widens at his question. "What do you think I should do?"

He sputters, trying to answer, and jumps when my phone dings, scoring another bloody mark across his throat in the process. I pull it from my pocket with my free hand and glance down at the screen.

**Eric:**
Be there soon.

"Oh, Mikey boy, you really should've kept your hands and cock to yourself." I laugh harshly, and he starts to cry a little.

"I wouldn't do that if I were you. Tears aren't exactly a deterrent. Not to me, and especially not to my friend. He really likes tears." I tilt my head a little before standing. "Get up."

I walk him to the lone chair at the dining table and zip tie him to it.

"It's not so fun being the powerless one, is it?" I use my blades to slice through his clothes, making sure to nick his skin as I go. His small squeaks just make my heart pound harder.

If he thinks being weak will make me stop, he's sorely mistaken. I appreciate strength. Even a quiet strength. Weakness just disgusts me.

I drag my knife from his throat down to his exposed tiny fucking dick. "Should I just cut it off? You'll survive it, plenty do. Then you couldn't try to use it as a weapon against people, could you?"

He starts to cry harder, and I roll my eyes.

"Cry some more and I'll cut it off just because you're being a fucking pussy, so you may as well have one of your own."

He sucks in a breath, trying to stop the tears, but the pathetic fucking weasel just continues to whimper. "Don't say I didn't warn you."

I push my knife into the soft flesh between his dick and his thigh, reveling in the scream he lets out. I mirror the cut on the opposite side, and sobs rack his body.

If he thinks this is the worst part of his night, he has no idea what's in store for him. I'm just the warm-up act.

The thought makes me grin.

I take my time, carving into his skin. I have a thing for branding people with their sins. Which is exactly why I use my blade to carve the word *pedo* into the skin on his chest, basking in his screams as his blood flows like a waterfall, coating my own skin as I go.

Headlights break through the darkness, and I see the hope in his eyes. Like someone is coming to rescue him. Butterflies take flight in my stomach, because watching that light go out in his eyes is going to be too much fun.

I continue drawing screams from his lips as his blood begins to pool at our feet. I haven't really got started with punishing him as much as I'd like to, but also, killing him isn't a part of my plan. If I lose myself to the bloodlust, to the anger of what he tried with V, then that's exactly what's going to happen.

The light in his eyes grows as his gaze continues to dart to the front door. Like he's waiting for someone to save him.

I almost laugh, but manage to refrain.

Seconds later, when his front door bursts open, my desire to watch the hope in his eyes die is fulfilled. I watch as relief briefly washes over him as his would-be rescuer steps through the doorway, his eyes lighting up like his prayers to a deaf God have been answered. Then his brain processes the behemoth of a man that is Eric.

"Jesus, kid, I thought you were going to hold back until I got here."

I bark out a laugh, watching as panic floods Michael Peters and he tries to fight against his bindings. "This *is* me going easy," I tell him with a shrug, and he shakes his head.

"I guess it's no less than he deserves." Eric's grin is almost as sadistic as mine when he laughs. "So this fuck likes to shove his dick at little girls and make them choke on it?" He looks Michael up and down and laughs again. "Well, choke on it might be a stretch."

I snicker as the pathetic lump of skin that is my teacher freaks the fuck out in the chair.

"I'll show you how to choke on a dick." Eric smiles. "Maybe then you'll be more hesitant in the future. You got your camera, kid?"

I don't even bristle at being called kid—it's just part of who Eric is. I pull my phone from my pocket and wave it at him.

"Oh, good," he says as he unzips his jeans. I step back, giving him the space he needs to deal with Mr. Peters. I hadn't quite planned this bit, but who am I to stop him meting out his own form of justice. After what happened to his daughter, after she took her own life because of it, Eric has always held a special place for pedo rapists. Wannabes or not. It's almost hilarious that he's one of the Knights, considering the other… proclivities of some of the other Knights, my father included. But I guess that's just life. A total double standard of a mind fuck.

"Ready to choke on a real dick?" Eric asks Mr. Peters, who starts crying in earnest. I disassociate myself from it, just turning on the video function on my phone. Our own insurance that Mr. Peters won't say a word to anyone. Not that it would do him any good. Unfortunately for him, the police in this town are as corrupt as they come.

It's only when Eric comes over Mr. Peters' face, laughing at him and calling him a scumbag, that I shut the camera off. "You're good to leave, kid. I'll make sure that he knows the game."

I nod, pocketing my phone and grabbing my kit. I'll clean my blades once I get home. Mr. Peters sits quietly in the chair he's tied to, the cum mixing with the blood as it runs down his chest.

"I'll see you in class after the holiday," I say, saluting the room before heading back to my bike.

Maybe next time he'll think twice about fucking with people at my school.

---

I wake up Thanksgiving morning, groaning as I roll over. The music blasting through the house makes me want to crack heads. I had the delightful conversation with my mother yesterday about missing dinner today—which went about as well as expected—but after sharing the details of my little detour on the way home last night, Dad was too proud to say no.

I'm not sure who's more twisted: him or me. Either way, there's no denying I am definitely a product of my father.

I jump in the shower and let my mind wander to the last time I saw V. I swear every time I think about her, I end up with a raging fucking hard-on. I palm my dick, because I might as well start the day off right. I picture those firm-as-fuck tits of hers, the way she gasps when I squeeze her throat just a little too tight, the way her pulse races under my touch, the way her skin bruises in my grasp.

Everything about her makes me like a fucking prepubescent boy and I come way too fast for my own liking. Fuck it, maybe I can convince her to fuck me again later.

I finish up my shower and throw on sweats and a t-shirt before heading downstairs to see what sort of masochism my mom has dreamt up for the day. I might not be sticking around, but that doesn't mean this house won't be the usual fanfare of dinner followed by the worst kinds of debauchery.

"There he is," my mom coos as I enter the kitchen. From the outside she looks like your typical, overbearing PTA mom-ager type. Don't let that fool you though. She'd gut you like a fish and giggle about it if you knocked over one of her vases.

I learned that the hard way, and I have the scars to prove it. Not that you can see many of them anymore; they hide beneath my ink the same way she hides behind her mask.

"What time are you heading out? Do you want breakfast?" she practically sings. I'm going to guess she was with one of her toys last night. That's the only time she's this cheery.

"I'm good, I'm heading out in a few, just came down to say hello before I leave."

"Okay, sweetheart." She grins at me, and that's when I notice the speckles of blood on her throat. Yep, she was with one of her toys last night. She blows me a kiss and I head back upstairs, practically jogging in anticipation of escape.

While I might be basically immune to my parents' brand of dysfunction these days, that doesn't mean I want to be here any more than I need to be. There's a reason my father is one of the top members of the sect of the Knights in The Cove. He's ruthless and has almost no limits. You do not fuck with Edward Riley. While he's happy with me right now, his moods are mercurial as fuck and I do not want to be here when the switch flips.

I get to the top of the stairs and head for my room, when the roar sounds. I wince on reflex.

I knew Mom was too happy. The morning was going too well.

I hurry into my room, but I know there's no real escape from his anger. Even if he's not pissed at me.

His shouts echo through the house, the walls shaking as he slams doors. The smash of glass reaches me as I lean against my bedroom door.

Shit.

This right here is why I need out of Echoes Cove. I might revel in the shadows, playing with my monster, but my monster is a creature of necessity. One born of fear to help me survive the horrors my parents put me through.

I close my eyes and take a deep breath. I can face almost any other monster and not think twice about it. Hell, I won't even break a sweat, but my father…

He's a whole other type of darkness.

I grab my phone and drop Finn an SOS. He and Lincoln are the only two people who know the truth of my father and his… extra curriculars.

Finn lives closer.

While I'm not confident of my chances to escape here on my own, two against one ups the odds. They're still not odds I like though.

Usually I wouldn't even think about including the boys in my shit, but I need to tell them about yesterday, and I'm pretty sure that turning up to Thanksgiving at V's half dead might be questioned.

My phone buzzes in my hand and I see Finn's name, letting out a small breath of relief.

**Finn:**
On way.

No more than those two words are needed. Hell, even if he just distracts my dad long enough for me to sneak out of my window, I'll owe him one.

Shit.

I hate feeling this weak. Like that scared little twelve-year-old boy again.

Finley and Lincoln were right there with me when we were taken for initiation. My father's playground. Just thinking about it makes my mouth water like I'm going to vomit.

My mother screams like a banshee and it breaks something in me.

They hurt each other all the time, but not like this.

Fuck.

I can't listen to that.

I take a deep breath before leaving the sanctuary of my room and charging down the stairs, trying to amp myself up to take on the biggest monster in my world.

I find them in the kitchen, him holding her against the wall by her fucking throat.

Fuck my life.

I look around the room and grab the first thing I see.

A goddamn rolling pin. Not my usual weapon of choice, but it's all I've got. I swing it as hard as I can at the back of his head. The crack it makes on impact reverberates down my arm, and I jump back, preparing for his attack. He drops my mom, who crumples in a pile on the floor, and turns to me, practically foaming at the mouth.

He lifts a hand to the back of his head, his fingers come away red, and his look of anger turns into a twisted smile.

Shit. Shit. Shit.

"There he is. The little boy who thinks he's a big man. Want to come and play with the grown-ups do we? You're nothing but a pathetic little worm." He steps toward me and it takes every ounce of strength I have to stay in place, even if my hands do shake a little. "You think you can go up against me and win? Because you dealt with a pathetic fuck last night? You, boy, are about to learn a fucking lesson."

He unbuckles his belt and steps toward me again, but still I hold my position. I've cowered from him my entire fucking life. I am sick of it.

My dad pauses, and for a second, I think it's because of me. But his gaze goes over my shoulder and his eyes widen quickly as he smiles. "Now, that is how you deal with a problem."

I turn and find Finley standing behind me with a gun leveled at my dad's head.

I don't say a word. There's no point. Instead I move to stand shoulder to shoulder with Finn who walks backwards as we leave the house, never lowering the gun. I don't want to leave my mom behind, but I've tried to get her to leave him before. There's no use. She's as bad as he is, and I think that she feeds on the pain he puts her through. Hopefully he got his anger out on me, and she won't suffer any more of his bullshit.

Once the front door is closed, we run down the drive and jump in his Aventador, which is parked on the street. "Thanks, man."

He nods, no other words needing to pass between us. This isn't the first time, and I doubt it'll be the last.

Hopefully the rest of our day is less eventful.

# CHAPTER ELEVEN

## OCTAVIA

I wake up in a thunderstorm of a mood. I've been so excited about everyone being here, that it was easy to push away the fact that this will be my first Thanksgiving without my dad. But now that it's here, I wish I hadn't arranged anything. Even with learning more of the truth of who he was and what he was mixed up in, none of that takes away from the fact that he was a fucking awesome dad, and that I miss him.

You don't have to be a great person to be a great dad. Though I find it almost impossible to merge the version of him that the guys have with the man I knew.

All I want to do is sit in the bottom of the shower, cry, and eat ice cream until my chest doesn't hurt anymore, but I promised myself that I wouldn't bury my head in the sand anymore. I've done enough of that. While I don't want to see anyone, especially those people who are going to remind me of my dad—it's going to be so much more obvious that he isn't here with them all around—I know that seeing them is exactly what I need to heal.

I've been tossing and turning since the ass crack of dawn, toying with the idea of pretending to be sick, but the thought of letting everyone down when they've come all this way to spend the day here makes me feel even worse.

It's going to be one of those "Suck it up, buttercup" kind of days.

My phone pings on the nightstand for the eleven millionth time so I roll over and pick it up.

**Indi:**
I'll be over soon, do you need me to bring anything?

**Indi:**
V?

**Indi:**
Helllloooooo

**Indi:**
Did you die? I swear TG if you died and you don't haunt me, imma be pissed.

**Indi:**
Worrying just a little. Are you okay?

The corners of my mouth tug up. Thank God for my little ball of joy.

**Me:**
I'm here, sorry, slept in. We don't need you to bring anything but you. Just jumping in the shower now.

Smiling at just how lucky I am to have her in my life, I send her another message with the code for the gate so she can get in if I'm in the shower or Smithy is busy then climb out of bed. I glance over at the Saints' house through the glass doors in my room, wondering what today will bring. I know Smithy said they were both coming, but where two of those boys are, the others will surely be.

They're like a pack of wolves in that they rarely travel alone.

Closing my eyes, I take a deep breath and head into the bathroom, trying to psych myself up for this day. I don't want to be the storm cloud that rains on everyone's parade.

Turning on the shower, I step under the hot spray and try to wash off the funk that I woke up in.

I hurry through my usual routine, knowing that Indi will be here soon, and quickly sort my hair and dress once I'm done.

Smithy already has the house in full freaking swing by the time I make it downstairs. There are decorations everywhere and my mood lifts a little. This season is my favorite, and he has not forgotten, apparently.

A smile tugs at my lips as I follow the delightful smells coming from the kitchen and find Smithy working away. "Good morning, Miss Octavia! Happy Thanksgiving!"

"Happy Thanksgiving! This all smells amazing already. What can I do to help?"

He looks at me in horror. "Oh no you don't. You don't need to do anything at all. I already told you about this poor kitchen."

I laugh at him because I can tell he's deadly serious. "Okay, if you're sure. What's the plan for the day?"

"Well, once everyone arrives, I have light appetizers prepped for everyone while dinner finishes cooking. I'm hoping we'll sit down at two. You're sure nobody has any allergies or dietary requirements?"

"Nope," I say, popping my *p*. "For a bunch of roadies and rockstars, everyone is really chill apparently."

"Good, good," he mumbles and goes back to whatever it was he was doing before I came down. I pour myself a glass of orange juice, skipping breakfast to save space for later. Hell, I even wore stretchy jeans in preparation for *all* of the food goodness.

The front door bursts open, making me jump. "I'm here, bitches!" Indi yells and I laugh, the last remnant of my funk lifting. She's like a walking, talking happy pill.

She bounces into the room and wraps me up in a hug as she does. "Morning, pumpkin, are we ready for today?" I laugh as she pulls on the waistband of her leggings.

*Great minds think alike.*

"I think so." I smile, hoping it comes across as genuine.

She bounds toward Smithy, who hands her a cookie.

"Where's *my* goddamn cookie?" I ask in fake outrage.

Indi sticks her tongue out at me before taking a bite. "*Mmmm,* so good."

"Miss Indi requested snickerdoodles, and since I made you your pie, I made her snickerdoodles," Smithy says as he laughs softly. "Now out of here, both of you. I have a lot to get done."

He hands me a cookie and I grin wide. "Thank youuuuu."

Indi and I head into the living room and drop onto the couch. I haven't told her about the stalker thing yet, and I don't intend on bringing down the mood, so I decide I'll fill her in tomorrow.

"We're putting the game on today, right?" she asks hopefully, looking up at me with those big green eyes of hers.

I just laugh softly, because while I won't tar all football players with the Raleigh-is-a-douchecanoe brush, I totally hadn't thought about it. "Sure, why not? I'm sure you won't be the only one who wants to watch since Smithy invited the Saints over."

"He did what?" she asks, eyes wide.

"You heard me. Mrs. Potts is going out of town, and their dad isn't around."

"Oh," she says, like her heart hurts for the sad, poor, lost puppies that they most definitely aren't. "I mean, you've started to forgive them, right? Kind of? It won't be so bad, maybe?"

"No, sometimes I think I've started to forgive them and then they do something to fuck it up, so I've not forgiven them. Not really. In fact, I had an idea that I could use your help with." I feel a little devious even suggesting it, and I know the look on my face is as devious as I feel because she shakes her head at me.

"Oh, Lord. Save us all. Tell me everything."

"Not yet, tomorrow, when everyone is gone. People should be arriving soon, and well… this will take time to plan." I laugh a little, the idea born from a dream I had a few nights ago. At first it seemed silly—maybe even a little petty—but the more I think about it, the easier it becomes for me to convince myself that it isn't petty at all. Who knows, I might change my mind a dozen times between now and tomorrow.

"Are you okay?" she asks, and I realize I totally spaced.

"I'm good, just missing my dad," I tell her with a small smile.

"I get that," she says, squeezing me with a one-armed hug. "It's okay to miss him, just don't miss out on the joy still around you."

Indi manages to keep me plenty distracted from spiraling thoughts of my dad with her uniquely magical ways until everyone else starts arriving.

It's not long before the house is a hive of activity. Mac, Panda, and a ton of the other crew arrive with Jenna B and the other Midnight Blue girls. The guys are inside watching the football game while Smithy cooks, since he banned us all from the kitchen. I'm outside, sitting beside the pool with the girls and Panda, drinking mimosas and laughing as we talk about shit from tours of the past.

It's only when the gate to the Saints' house opens that the jovial conversation comes to a halt. Lincoln leads the pack in his black shirt and suit pants, followed by East, Finn, and Mav all in various states of formal shirt and pants.

Jenna looks back at me and winks. "You're drooling," she whispers, trying not to laugh. I stick my tongue out at her before turning back to the boys.

"Afternoon," I call out, lifting my glass. "Drinks?"

They head toward us, and it's only then that I notice Panda's change in demeanor. His shoulders are stiff, his eyes glued to Lincoln as he approaches.

"Everything okay?" I ask him, nudging him with my shoulder.

He looks at me, conflicted, before glancing back at the boys. "I'm sorry," is all he says.

"What does that mean?" I ask, wondering what the fuck else it is I'm missing. And how the fuck does he know Lincoln? He doesn't get a chance to speak again before Lincoln and the others are standing before us.

"Happy Thanksgiving, V," East says, and I stand to give him a hug, being passed from him to Finley, before Maverick lifts me from my feet, spinning me around before putting me back down. I give Lincoln an awkward wave, because hugging just isn't a thing we do.

"You guys, this is Lincoln, Maverick, Finley, and Easton," I tell the others, making all of the introductions needed. When Lincoln moves toward Panda I'm still unsure what is going on.

"Evan, it's been a while."

My stomach flips as my heart races. I lean in to Maverick and ask, "How the fuck does Lincoln know Panda?"

Panda stands, offering his hand to Lincoln who looks at it before shaking. P looks at me quickly before settling his gaze back on Lincoln and nodding. "It has."

"What am I missing here?" I ask the two of them, and Indi jumps to her feet beside me.

"Drinks, anyone? Let's go harass Smithy for more, shall we?" She ushers everyone else inside, leaving me with the five guys who all look as guilty as the next.

Once everyone else is inside and the doors close, I fold my arms over my chest, waiting for someone to explain whatever the fuck is going on.

"V… I'm sorry. I should've said something before now," Panda starts, and Mav begins to laugh.

"Said something about what?" I huff, already tired of the lack of fucking answers yet again.

"You didn't tell her? Oh man." Mav drops into one of the just vacated chairs and kicks back like he's watching a goddamn show.

Panda's eyes go wide as his gaze bounces from Mav to me. "I didn't know how—"

"Tell me what, exactly?" I demand, and Linc's smile turns dark, his eyes glinting with something sinister, reminding me of how he looked at me a few months ago.

"Evan here," Linc says, turning to face me, "is a Knight."

He is?

They've got to be fucking with me. I know Panda. He isn't anything like them. He's fun and laid-back. He's had my back more times than I can count.

"No he isn't. He's a roadie." I try to deny it, and it sounds stupid even as I say it but the way P looks at me tells me I'm only lying to myself.

"I was sent on tour to make sure nothing happened to you," he confesses, stepping toward me as I step backward, away from him. I clasp my throat as I shake my head.

This can't be happening.

*Why does everyone lie?*

Panda steps closer to me, and Finn shoulder checks him, putting himself between us. "V, I'm sorry. Will you let me explain?"

"What is there to explain?" I utter, shock making me stupid, but it does occur to me that maybe he will answer some of my questions. I open my mouth to speak but Lincoln beats me to it.

"Were you spying on her or Stone?" Lincoln asks, and I'm shook stupid again. I didn't even consider that. This Knight shit is so out of this goddamn world. I was still half convinced—half hoping—that it was some bullshit, but everything seems to lead back to this shit. "Are you responsible for Stone's death?"

I suck in a breath and the world tilts. My knees feel like they're about to give out as ice fills my veins, and I grab Finn's arm to keep myself upright

As much as I want answers, this is too much. I was having enough issues getting through today without wondering if my friend killed my dad. I can't go down that rabbit hole right now. If I ask and he tells me something I don't want to hear, I'm going to spin out.

"I didn't!" His eyes go wide in panic, and he tries to move toward me, but Lincoln stops him. "You have to believe me. V, you know me! You have to know I wouldn't do that."

"Do I? I can't do this right now, but, P, you and I are apparently due for a conversation. This isn't over." Leaving them to get the answers they're obviously seeking, I step back into the house. Leaning back on the door, I take a deep breath. I want answers, hell, I crave them, but am I really strong enough to hear the answer to that question?

I find the game on in the living room, which is where everyone moved to while we were outside talking. Indi glances over to me, looking a little worried, but I shake my head, and give her a watery smile. Now is so not the time. I take another deep breath, deciding to join everyone when I see that Smithy has the formal tables all pulled together in here too.

Then I notice the tablecloth.

My throat thickens as tears prick my eyes. This is too much right now. This entire day is too fucking much. I rub the heel of my palm against my chest, trying to ease some of the pain that tears through me, praying for the strength to get through today without breaking.

Smithy enters the room, looking more than a little concerned when he sees me. "Miss Octavia, what's wrong?"

"The tablecloth…you remembered?"

He smiles softly before moving toward me and hugging me. "Of course I did. It's tradition. I figured we'd keep it up, especially with so many of your friends here."

He rubs my back up and down before releasing me. I move toward the table, barely able to stop the tears from falling as I take it all in.

The messages from my dad from the last Thanksgiving we spent at home. It was a silly tradition my nana started when I was young. Each year at Thanksgiving, we'd write what we were thankful for on the table cloth and sign our name with the year until that cloth was full, and then we'd start another.

Trailing my fingers against my father's spider-like writing makes the tears fall down my face.

*I am thankful to be surrounded by the people I love. To be graced with a daughter as talented as she is graceful, and a wife who loves us both so much.*

I wipe the tears from my face as I feel someone at my back.

"Are you okay?" Finley asks, and I lean back on him, just for a second while I compose myself, stealing some of his quiet strength.

"I'll be fine," I whisper, taking a deep breath just as Smithy announces that the food is ready.

As I take my seat, Finley moves to sit in the chair to my right as my found family take their places around the table. I know that, despite everything, I have a lot to be thankful for. Selfishly, I just wish for more.

Indi sits to my left and clasps my hand, squeezing tight. She has no idea what's wrong, but I know she's there for me no matter what.

Smithy, East, and Mav appear, carrying dishes to start loading up the table and laughter sounds at the other end where Mac and some of the other roadies are sitting. The corners of my mouth lift in a watery smile and I close my eyes, thanking my dad for giving me these people, even if he can't be here with me.

Life might not always be sunshine and rainbows, but today, I'm going to be thankful for all of the grace in my life. Starting with these people.

Even the ones that lied to me.

---

After the emotional whirlwind of a day on Thursday, Indi and I relaxed for the rest of the long weekend. At least until her parents came home a day early. I swear all we've done is eat the entire time she's been here. I'm going to need to run every day this week just to recover from it. I'm not opposed to some extra curve on my ass, but damn, eating this much pie and not running is going to ruin me.

Indi left here yesterday afternoon, giving me my Sunday to myself. Which is exactly why I'm still in my pj's, curled on the couch under blankets with Smithy, watching crime documentaries. What else is to be done over the weekend but chill after eating my own weight in turkey and all the trimmings? That and putting off calling P. Stupid move I know, but I need to process the shit that Thanksgiving brought back to the surface before I dive into that cesspit. That and the thought of him not answering my questions or lying to me again isn't something I'm sure I can handle right now with my grief gripping me just beneath the surface.

I'm not ready to discover if our entire friendship was one giant lie. Not yet.

A knock at the back door has me pausing the TV and Smithy gets up to see who's there. Since it's the back door, I can only imagine it's one of four people. Everyone else is civilized and uses the front.

I take a deep breath and prepare myself to deal with whichever one of them it is. I haven't spoken to any of them since Thursday.

"Master Saint! What brings you by?" Smithy's voice carries through, making me turn on the couch, just as a sweater-and-jean-clad Lincoln enters my house.

What the fuck have these boys been eating, and why do they look edible in fucking everything?

Why are the assholes always so pretty?

And why does my kooch seem louder than logic sometimes?

"I was hoping Octavia would be free. I was going to head to the range, and I figured with everything going on, she could probably use the extra practice."

Goddamn, why does he have to be so well-mannered to Smithy. Manners cost nothing and are fucking hot, too.

"She's just in the living room. We were, as you youngsters call it, binging television." His footsteps echo on the wooden flooring as he walks toward me, and I pull my blanket up a little higher. He might *think* I can use a refresher. Little does he know that going to the range is something my dad and Mac insisted we do weekly.

He steps into the room, hands in his pockets, and stares at me. I smile at him, batting my lashes while trying not to laugh. He rolls his eyes at me before speaking. "Well?"

"Well what?"

"Do you want to come to the range?"

Usually, spending any time with just him would make me want to be a little sick, but the thought of going to the gun range makes butterflies take flight in my stomach. It's been too long since I went, and Dad would be super disappointed in me for not keeping it up. Much like all of my defense stuff.

I make a promise to myself to start up my training again in the new year before jumping up from the couch. "Give me ten to get dressed, then sure."

He nods in response and I practically skip up the stairs. I am not a gun nut, but there is something about holding a firearm that makes a girl feel powerful. And after everything that's gone on since I've been back here, I could use a little dose of that. Plus, this might be the perfect opportunity to pepper him with questions.

I grab a pair of jeans, a tank, slip on a V-neck sweater, and pull on my boots. I flip my head upside down and gather my hair in a messy ponytail, trying to make sure my extensions aren't too visible before heading back downstairs, where I find Lincoln watching my crime show with Smithy.

I smirk to myself. I knew the old man was secretly loving this show.

"Ready," I call out before I hit the bottom stair and bounce into the room. I grab my leather jacket from the security room where I left it and head back through to the living room where Lincoln is waiting.

He looks me up and down and nods when he apparently decides I meet his standards.

Asshole.

"I'll catch you later, Smithy." I lean down and kiss the old man's cheek as I grab my phone and keys from the coffee table.

"Have fun, both of you. Let me know if you'll be out late, please."

I grin at just how paternal he can be sometimes. "Sure thing. Have fun!"

I give him a finger wave before following Lincoln out the back of the house and through the gate to where his Porsche sits in his drive.

He might be a douchebag, but I still love his car.

I slide into the passenger side once he unlocks it, sinking into the cloud-like seat, just as soft and comfortable as I remember it being.

He starts the car without saying a word and we make the drive in silence. I stare out of the windows as he drives me out past the other side of town and just keeps driving. "Should I be worried that you're driving me out into the middle of nowhere to kill me without a trace?"

He looks over at me and smirks. "You've been watching too many crime documentaries. Anyway, if I was going to kill you, I'd have done it before now. And Smithy wouldn't know you were with me either."

"Reassuring, Lincoln, really reassuring." I sigh, shaking my head. "So where are we going?"

"A private shooting range that a friend owns."

I quirk a brow. What is it with him and just giving a little bit of the information but never really answering the question? "A Knight friend?"

"So you're finally starting to believe the Knights are real, rather than a ploy then?"

"Did you really just answer a question with a question?" I counter, and he barks out a laugh, relaxing a little.

Point one for me I guess. Ice man finally melts a little.

He shakes his head, glancing at me before answering, gripping the steering wheel a little tighter. "No, the friend isn't a Knight. I wouldn't take you to a Knight freehold unless there was a gun to your head."

I ruminate on his words and decide to answer his question too. "Yes, I'm starting to believe it, even though it's entirely *un*believable. I mean, I believe they're real, but I don't think I believe that I'm in any danger from them. A few bouquets of flowers and a dress don't exactly scream danger."

"The most dangerous of things are usually unsuspecting."

I mean, he's not wrong. Silent but deadly isn't a phrase for no reason.

Deciding this is as good a time as any, I deliberate where to start. "Will you tell me more about the Knights? About what's going on with you guys? It's hard to just trust blindly, you know?"

"Octavia," he groans. "Really?"

"Yes really. You guys haven't told me much of anything, and I'm tired of being in the dark. I'm tired of reacting rather than actually being proactive. I'm aware I've walked around in a bit of a daze since my dad died, but that's not who I am."

He nods, and I feel a glimmer of hope. "You get three questions."

Hell yes! I mentally do a fist pump, and try to decide which questions to ask since I only get three.

Holy shit this is harder than I thought it would be.

"Okay," I start. "Three questions. First one… Who is in control of the Knights?"

He side-eyes me, letting out a deep breath. "I don't know."

"Oh for fuck's sake!" I shout, throwing my hands in the air. "I should've known you wouldn't have answered my questions. What is the point in asking me to trust you when it obviously doesn't go both ways?"

His knuckles go white as he clenches the steering wheel. "It's not that I don't trust you, Octavia. It's that I really don't know. I'm just a junior, that means my knowledge, while vast, is still limited. I can tell you that the sect in Echoes Cove is run by the seven senior members of the Conclave. But the Conclave is overseen by the Regent. My father."

My eyes go wide. I was not expecting that. Not even a little. Holy shit.

"Okay, so what does that mean for you? What do they make you guys do?" I pick at the skin by my thumbnail while I wait for him to answer. His jaw clenches, and that vein in his neck pulses as the silence grows thicker.

"That's two questions," he huffs. "But I'll give you them as one. For me, it means my entire life is mapped out, whether I want it to be or not. I'm the Regent Heir, and as such, in charge of the junior Conclave. Not that I have any real power, Harrison wouldn't allow that. As for what they make us do… It depends."

I try not to get excited about the fact that he's actually giving me information. My heart wars in my chest between glee at finding some answers and pain for him. But knowing Harrison could be the key to all of this could help. I don't know how yet, but every little bit has to help. "On what?"

"That's another question," he says, quirking his brow. "But it depends on what they need. Sometimes we're errand boys, collecting people, goods, and basically acting like mules for them. Others, it can be getting information…other times, it's wiping a board clean while drowning it in blood."

"Killing people?"

"Killing, maiming, torturing. All the things in life we really want for you."

I look down at my hands folded in my lap, trying to process everything he's told me, even with the sarcasm dripping from his last words. It's good, getting information, it means I'm no longer walking around in the dark completely blindfolded, but I know this is just scratching the surface. But I'm going to take the win, because with Linc, this is a big win.

I contemplate a million different questions running through my mind, aware that I've had my three, but trying again anyway. "Are all legacies bound to them?"

"Yes. Usually." He hits the blinker, taking the turn when the lights on the road allow before continuing. "I haven't heard of any legacy getting out. Not until the deal your father made to get you free, and before you ask, I don't know all the details of the deal either. All I know is that he made a deal, gave up his place, and in exchange, you were supposed to be out."

I sit quietly, going over all of that in my head. What exactly did my dad do, give up, for me to be free? Just another question to add to my ever-growing list.

"Thank you," I say quietly and he nods, not speaking any further.

We continue the drive in a weird but comfortable silence. I flick the stereo on, the radio helping to pass the time. It's only when we pull into Sand Bay and head further into the city, that I relax a little. We weave our way through the city and finally, on the other side, he drives down a dirt road. A few minutes later, I see the building come into view and relax even further.

He pulls to a stop out front, silence filling the space between us.

"Come on, let's go see if you're any good with a gun, shall we?" He smirks again, like he thinks I'm going to be useless. I just nod, not bothering to tell him otherwise. Following him inside, I gaze around the front; it's basically a gun store with a range out back.

"Will, good to see you," Linc calls out, doing that weird guy chin-tilt nod thing to the guy behind the counter.

"It's been a while, Linc, my man. And who is this pretty little thing?" His southern drawl makes my insides go funny. Damn, I love me a southern accent.

Lincoln looks back at me before scowling at his friend. "That is Octavia Royal, and no, you can't play with her."

"Says who?" I challenge, quirking a brow.

"Oh I like her." Will grins, looking me up and down before turning back to Lincoln. "You need anything?"

"No, I've got everything in my locker. I'll yell if I need you."

He motions with his head for me to follow him before going through a door in the back of the room that has a sign reading 'Range' above it.

I follow him out back to his locker, which is basically a giant metal trunk. He unlocks the padlock on it and lifts the lid, showcasing enough guns to equip a small army, I'm sure. "We'll start you with something small since, you know, you're small, and see how you get on."

"Sure thing." I smirk at him, letting him go through the motions, taking the ear muffs when he hands them over before leading me to the very empty shooting range.

He walks me through my stance and how to hold the gun he hands me. I have to admit, Lincoln is a very good teacher. He has more patience than I'd have expected. I follow his instruction without question, and as he wraps his arms around me to help me bring the gun level with the target, I almost hold my breath. "Relax, aim, and shoot."

He releases me, but my entire body feels like it's on fire. I shake my head, trying to shake off the feeling, and pull the trigger, the kickback reverberating up my arms.

"Good," is all he says before moving to the target beside me. He moves into position and empties the clip of his gun into the target.

"Show off." I grin as he turns to look at me with an eyebrow raised.

"You'll get there."

I laugh. "Oh I know." I raise my arm at my target, gun in hand, while keeping my eyes locked on his before letting off three rounds.

His eyes go wide as he takes in the target, and I bark out a laugh. Turning to my paper target, I grin. Apparently I haven't gone rusty.

Head.

Chest.

Dick.

Just like Dad taught me.

---

"Thank God this semester is over! You have much planned for Christmas?" Indi asks as we head out of school. The last few weeks since Thanksgiving have been a whirlwind of exams, handing in papers, and trying like fuck to catch up with all the work I had fallen behind on. I think I might have just got everything done by the skin of my teeth.

The sub in place of Mr. Peters in Business even offered me a make-up paper for what I missed at the beginning of the year. Things might finally be looking up for me. Especially if Mr. Peters' sudden trip away stays permanent.

"No, we're keeping it low key this year," I tell her with a smile as we reach my Impala. I open the trunk and grab the gift bag I stored there. "But this, my friend, is for you. Merry Christmas."

She grins wide as she takes the bag, bouncing on the balls of her feet. "You totally didn't have to, but thank you! I'd rip it open right now if I didn't think my mom would withhold Christmas dinner for breaking tradition."

"As she should." I laugh. "It's not Christmas for three more days."

"But I love gifts. Speaking of…" She pauses before bounding to her Wrangler and opening the back door. "This is for you."

She almost falls over as she pulls a giant-ass box from the back, decorated with ribbons, bows, and so much more. I rush over to give her a hand, wondering how the hell she got it in her car. "What on earth is in there?"

I lean back and open the passenger door to the Impala and help her slide the box in. "You'll find out Christmas morning," she says, sticking her tongue out. I close the door and she hugs me tight. "We're hanging out on New Year's, right?"

"You know it." I grin at her and wave before climbing in the car. The last few weeks have been quiet. Too quiet. And I still haven't seen Raleigh. The school isn't that big, so I have no idea how. I almost want to just get it out of the way, but since school is done for two weeks now, I don't have to worry about it too much.

I start up the car, hooking my phone up and playing *Prom Queen* by Molly

Kate Kestner, my latest song obsession. Just as I go to buckle up, I see Finley jogging toward my car.

Since the shooting range, those three have been strangely MIA, too. In fact, other than for gym, I've barely seen East either.

Of course, the second I start to accept that we might be becoming friends, that this whole Knight thing is real and I might want some more answers, they all pretty much drop off the face of the Earth. I've gone from not being able to get rid of them when I didn't want to see them, to them never being around. Finley didn't even respond to the text I sent him.

Weird as fuck, but I'm not sure why I expected anything different. These guys are never what I expect.

I roll down the window and Finley leans forward, his arms on top of the car. "I was hoping I'd catch you."

I bite down on my lip, waiting for him to speak.

"How are you doing?" he asks, almost awkwardly.

Letting out a dry laugh I look up at him. "I'm fine. What do you want, Finley?"

He lets out a deep sigh and stands, rubbing the back of his neck. "Do you have some time to talk?"

"So now you want to talk?" I quirk a brow at him, and he at least has the decency to look sorry.

"I know, I'm sorry. We've had some shit to deal with. Mav…" He shakes his head. "It doesn't matter, not my story to tell. Do you have some time?"

I consider his words. I'd noticed that Maverick wasn't really himself on Thanksgiving, even though he put on a good show. He's been oddly quiet around school since then, too. Eventually, I nod. "Yeah, I have time."

I shut the engine off and go to unbuckle, but he leans back down. "I'll follow you home."

"Okay." I nod, starting the car back up again. He moves back and heads over to his car. I can't see Maverick's bike in the lot, but Lincoln's Porsche is gone, too, so I might have just missed them I guess. I drop Smithy a quick message to let him know that Finley is heading back with me, and he responds almost instantly to let me know he's out shopping this evening.

Little sneak.

I remind him we said no gifts, knowing full well I have at least five for him tucked away, before pulling out of the lot and driving home through the very festively decorated streets of Echoes Cove. The world would probably come to an end if it snowed in southern California, but apparently no one here cares. It's fake snow galore.

Finley follows me the entire way and enters the gate behind me as I pull onto the drive.

Jumping out of the car, I head to the passenger side to grab the box from Indi, but Finley catches up to me and lugs it out instead. "What the hell is in this thing?"

"I asked the same thing." I laugh as I open the front door, pausing when I take in what Smithy has obviously been up to while I was at school today. The giant tree in the living room, decorations freaking galore.

I guess my quiet Christmas plan isn't what he had in mind. Hell, I was even going to skip the big tree thing. "I'll put this under the tree."

"Okay, thanks. Do you want a drink?" I ask as he heads across the room before placing the giant box beneath the tree where there are already more gifts than I care to count.

"Sure." He smiles softly at me and follows me to the kitchen.

*Why does this feel so awkward?*

"So what did you want to talk about?" I ask as I stick my head in the fridge, grabbing a couple of sodas before handing one to him.

He sits at the counter, taking a swig of his drink before looking at me. If I didn't know better, I'd think he was stalling.

"About the Knights." I nod and take a seat across from him, waiting for him to continue. "Lincoln told us that you were finally starting to believe us, that he gave you some answers when you went to the range. And I know your friend being one of us was something of a shock. Plus, we haven't been around much."

I take a sip of my drink, waiting for him to get to the point. I hate it when they talk in circles. Finley isn't usually one to use this many words so I know he's a little uncomfortable, which is exactly why I don't interrupt him.

"I wanted to know if you had any more questions. I can't promise you answers to all of them, but if I can answer, I will."

My eyes go wide at his words. He's really going to give me information.

Well, color me shocked.

Except, of course now that the opportunity is here, the thousand questions I've had on the tip of my tongue jumble up inside my brain and tie my tongue in knots. Why are you guys so interested in saving me from these people? How come I've never heard about this before if I'm supposed to be a legacy? What's so special about the society and why is it such a big secret? If the Knights are such a big deal, why did my dad run and what do they want with me after all these years of being away? Are there benefits to me being involved with them?

But when I try to speak the words, they turn to ash and I have nothing.

"You asked Panda about my dad's death. Why would you guys ask him that? What did he say after I left?" The question spills from my mouth even though I'm not sure I want the answer to it. I've still been too scared to ask Panda myself, mostly because I can't take him lying to me any more.

"He said again and again that he had nothing to do with it. That he was put on the tour to look after you. It had nothing to do with your dad." He looks me in the eye as he answers, and it's the only reason I believe him. "And we asked him, because he's a Knight and we thought he could be linked to it. We told you we don't think your dad committed suicide, but Evan didn't have any other answers for us either."

"That doesn't make any sense. I don't understand any of this." I sigh, dropping my chin into my hand. "Does it make sense to you?"

"No, it doesn't, but we're trying to find out as much as we can. We've just had a few… obstacles pop up the last few weeks."

"The Maverick thing?" I ask, and he nods, "Is there anything I can do?"

He smiles softly but shakes his head. "No, but thank you. Just do me a favor?"

I raise an eyebrow but stay quiet and wait for him to continue. "Something big is happening with the Knights and I don't know if it's good or bad, but please, don't go anywhere alone for a while."

My stomach drops at the thought of being in more danger. Just what I wanted for Christmas.

"I'll try my best," I offer, because that's all I've got right now. "Do we have any information on my stalker?"

He grins wide at me. "Now that… that I have good news about." His phone chimes in his hand, and his smile drops. "Except I'm going to have to come back to it. I have to run. I'm sorry, V."

"You have got to be kidding me." I sigh, throwing my hands up in frustration. This hot and cold, push and pull bullshit is getting old.

He steps forward and kisses me, like it's an everyday occurrence. I hold onto his waist as he kisses me like he needs me to breathe. He pulls back, resting his forehead on mine. "I'll come back. I swear. Just… be patient with us. Please."

It's the "please" that gets me, and I nod before he pulls back and jogs out of my house.

I have no idea which way is up, but I do know that I'm getting a little tired of everyone picking me up and putting me down like a doll. These people need to learn that I am more capable than they realize.

# CHAPTER TWELVE

## OCTAVIA

Christmas with my dad was always a giant affair. Even on the years when we were traveling the world, he made a huge deal of it. Going through all of these firsts without him is more painful than I could've ever imagined.

More pain than I'd wish on anyone.

That's why I spent the last few weeks just focusing on school, on my friends, rather than on Christmas itself.

I also didn't want to be Scrooge McDuck because well…who wants that?

Before this year, I had always loved Christmas. The joy of being around the people who loved you, making the day entirely about family. Yes, we did the same on Thanksgiving, but that was always extended family and just *all* of the people. Christmas was about the people we loved the most.

I remember Christmases as a kid-- we'd have giant dinners at our house: the Saints, the Rileys, the Knights. Every year we'd be in each other's pockets. I'm not sure if my friendship with the boys came first, or if our parents' friendships did. All I remember is that's how it was.

For a while anyway.

Until Mom left.

I never knew why things went sideways after that. Dad still made a big deal of Christmas even though she wasn't here, but we didn't spend it with the others. I don't remember asking why, or being told why, but after she left my whole world was upside down, so I guess I never really questioned it.

This Christmas reminds me of the first one that Mom wasn't here. Except it hurts more. I was never as close to her as I was my dad.

A knock sounds at the door, pulling me from the dreary thoughts keeping me company under my comforter. "Miss Octavia, are you awake? Your guests are arriving."

Did he just say guests?

I throw the sheets off and scurry to the door, opening it a fraction. "What guests?"

"Miss Octavia, you're not even dressed! It's nearly ten in the morning. The Saint boys are already here; I have breakfast in the warmer. Master Riley and Master Knight will be here soon according to them. I assumed you had something planned with them."

I grind my teeth, leaning my head against the side of the door. "No, no I did not."

"Well, now then, we can't be rude. It's Christmas after all. You get dressed and I'll start serving breakfast. It almost feels like the Christmases of old." He smiles so wide, joy practically radiating from him, and I don't have the heart to tell him I don't want to human today. Instead, I nod and close the door, groaning as I lean against it.

Just what I wanted for Christmas… those four idiots.

Fuck it. Smithy seemed happy, so I'm going to suck it up, push down the dark and twisties haunting me, and put on a smile all damn day if that's what it takes.

I refuse to ruin his Christmas. Even if I would rather just climb back into bed.

I head to my closet, grabbing a pair of jeggings, a tank, and a hoodie. No one said I couldn't be comfortable, even if we do have company. I finish grabbing everything I need and get ready for the day quickly, thankful I washed my hair the night before.

I plod downstairs in my thick, fluffy socks, hearing laughter coming from the kitchen.

Is that… Lincoln Saint laughing? Be still my heart. I didn't think that was even possible these days. I pause on the stairs, sitting down to listen to them laughing and joking. Because I know the moment I go in there, it'll stop. Something about me seems to put him on edge, and it's Christmas. I don't want to ruin his joy. Not today anyway.

The front door opens, and I'm caught red-handed, very obviously eavesdropping, by Finley and Maverick. "Fancy seeing you here." Maverick smirks up at me. I let out a sigh and stand, heading down to them.

"Merry Christmas," Maverick says as he sweeps me up in his arms and spins me around. I can't help but laugh, squealing as he continues to spin me. "Not too mad we're here?" he whispers into my ear when he stills.

"I suppose not," I breathe back as he lowers me down, holding me tight so I feel every part of him on my descent. He tucks my hair behind my ear before capturing my lips in a kiss so hot it makes my toes curl. I lose myself to the feel of him, curling my fingers in his hair, enjoying every second of the surprise.

It's only when he pulls back and I spot Finley watching us over his shoulder that I blush. Mav sees the red on my cheeks and grins before releasing me. "I'll go find the others." He moves past me, slapping my ass as he goes, making me squeak again as his laughs echo around the giant space.

Turning to face Finley, my blush deepens. The heat in his eyes does things to me that it definitely shouldn't. Especially when I was just locking lips with his bestie. "Merry Christmas." It comes out more as a question as he stalks toward me, until he's less than a hair's distance from me.

"Merry Christmas, V." He runs a finger down my face, until he cups my chin. I stand frozen, unsure of where this is going right now. The last time I saw him, he kissed me, and then bolted at Lincoln's beckoning. I've not heard from him since then and I'm still kind of pissed about it, but I don't want to cause a scene at Christmas. Mostly for Smithy's sake. But I can't help but get caught up in him and the way he looks at me.

"There you are!" East's voice shatters the moment, and Finley takes a step back, putting distance between us. He turns to face East, a small smile on his face, before heading in the direction the voice came from.

I have no idea why these boys are here, but I have a feeling today is going to be a very long day. Heading through to the kitchen, I find Lincoln, East, and Maverick sitting at a table I've never seen before with Finley as Smithy hums Christmas carols while he cooks.

I hate how the smile on Lincoln's face fades with my approach. Mostly because I don't understand it. I don't know what it is I could have possibly done to make him continuously react to me like this.

I thought after our day at the range that things might turn around for us. I've seen glimpses of the boy I used to know since I got back. The one with a slightly softer side. I say slightly because he's never really been soft, though he was at least compassionate… empathetic… Whoever it is he grew up to be doesn't seem to like being that person anymore. I'm beginning to wonder if I'll ever know this version of him at all.

"Miss Octavia, please, sit, breakfast is just being served, and then we get to do my favorite part of the day." Smithy's eyes sparkle as he speaks. "Gifts!"

It occurs to me that there are four people here I hadn't planned on seeing today. Even though I may or may not have picked up something for each of them during my shopping trip with Indi because I have *zero* impulse control and couldn't stop myself. What they don't know, and I'll likely never admit, is that I have gifts for them for every Christmas we were apart.

As much as I've tried to convince myself otherwise, these boys have been a part of me for as long as I remember. I doubt that will ever change.

Even if they do try to push me away.

I take a seat at the table between Finley and the empty space, which I'm hoping Smithy will take. The man in question drops plates in front of the boys loaded with stacks upon stacks of pancakes with bacon and syrup. I look up at Lincoln, the corners of his mouth tilted up a little.

This always was his favorite.

I don't know what's going on with him, but apparently Smithy noticed the sadness about him too. He always made Lincoln pancakes when he'd come here seeking refuge from the chaos at home. Smithy takes his seat beside me as he hands me my plate, no syrup and bacon for me. Chocolate chips with whipped cream and berries. Just how I like them.

"Thank you." I grin up at him.

He claps his hands together, smiling at the people at the table. "It's been quite some time since we did Christmas here, so dig in, please."

Guilt pangs in my stomach at the thought of how lonely it must've been here for Smithy while Dad and I were away.

"Eat," he says, looking at me pointedly, so I chow down, staying quiet as the five of them talk about the football game that's on today. I swear, I don't remember football being such a big thing here before I left, but I guess a lot changed while I was gone. That or I was more oblivious that I realized.

"Are you okay?" Finley asks quietly while the others debate back and forth about who's going to win today's game.

"I'm okay. Just another big day without Dad." I shrug a little and he nudges me with his shoulder. "I'll be fine."

"You will, that's exactly why we're here," he says quietly. "And we have a few more surprises in store too."

He pulls back from me, leaving me hanging, and rejoins the conversation with the others.

What the fuck does he mean surprises?

I shake it off and try to join in on the conversation even though I have zero clue about football. It quickly becomes painfully obvious I'm out of my depth.

"I'll clear the table," East says, standing once everyone is done. He quirks a brow at Smithy when he tries to object, and it's amusing seeing him told. Smithy leads the others into the living room, literally as happy as I remember seeing him, while I help East clear the table and load the dishwasher.

We work in silence, which is weird and awkward as fuck, but it's been a minute since we've even spoke, let alone had a private moment together.

I close the door to the dishwasher, making sure I haven't missed anything before pressing the start button.

"V…"

I look up at East, who looks at me with those puppy dog eyes, and I just know he's about to take a wrecking ball to what's left of the wall I put up between us.

"I'm sorry," he says softly. "I'm sorry I've been so MIA and so fucking weird since the Raleigh thing. I didn't want to push, and then… shit happened, plus homecoming… and then it'd been a minute since we'd spoke just the two of us. I hadn't heard from you, and I know that's not an excuse, I just… I didn't know what to do. If you wanted space, if you wanted me around--especially since things are better with the others."

He pauses, like he didn't mean to word vomit all over me, and I let out a sigh. "Honestly, I get it. I haven't exactly been present since Halloween. And with everything after homecoming too… I retreated. I swear there's been so much going on lately, I feel like I've barely been able to catch my breath. Some days I don't even recognize myself. So it's fine, I get it. But even if things are getting better with those knuckleheads, that doesn't mean that I don't want you around."

He smiles at me, the joy reaching his eyes, and it's like a little weight I hadn't realized was there lifts from my shoulders. He wraps me in a hug, squeezing me tight, and I relax against him. Here was me thinking that after fooling around he had second thoughts about everything, even if I hadn't put voice to those thoughts. He rubs his hand up and down my back, and I relax into him, more than I've relaxed in weeks. "Come on, let's go join the others. But first…"

He lets go of me and pulls a long, thin box from his back pocket. "This is for you."

I open the black velvet box, and inside is a charm bracelet, with just one charm. A music note. "East… this is…"

"To be completed. I figured I can add to it, as I intend on being around for a long fucking time. V, I lost you once, I don't want to ever lose you again." He cups my cheek and kisses me softly. "Want a hand putting it on?"

I nod, still unable to speak properly from the emotion cloying my throat. It's so fucking thoughtful. No one has ever bought me jewelry before. He takes the box and lifts the silver chain out, joining the clasp around my wrist. "It's perfect."

He grins down at me and kisses my hand. "I'm glad you like it. Now we should probably head in there before Smithy gets impatient about gifts. You know how he gets."

I laugh because he's not wrong. Maybe this Christmas won't be as dark and twisty as I thought it would be. We find the others all sitting around the base of the tree where there are way too many presents. "Did you guys move your entire Christmas here?"

"They did." Smithy grins. "And I, for one, am more than happy about it. Now come on over and take your seat so I can play Santa. Do you know how long it's been since I got to play Santa?" His joy is infectious, and I sit down with East close beside me.

"Oh wait!" I say, scrambling back to my feet. I run upstairs and head to my closet. I grab the gift bags that I stashed back here. I figured these would just go on the pile of other gifts that I bought and never actually gave to them, but I guess this year is going to be different. I chew my lip, considering whether or not this is a good idea. I get that they've been helping me, and that, well… other than Linc, I've gotten a lot closer to them again, but I'm also aware that I haven't exactly forgiven them yet. Fuck it. It's Christmas. Today, we can put it all aside and just enjoy the day.

I head downstairs, bags in hand, and slip them under the tree. I already put the ones for Smithy under there. Plonking myself back down where I was, Smithy starts handing out the gifts, and the shock on his face makes me laugh every time he grabs a gift for himself.

I watch the boys open their gifts from their families and I can't help but wonder why they're not with them today. Not that I'd take this joy from Smithy, but I'd give pretty much anything to be with my dad today.

I laugh as I unwrap the ridiculously big box from Indi, to discover it contains another box. I continue to unwrap them and when I get to the final one, I blush furiously, trying to hide the gift. I pull out the gift tag in the box.

*For you to explore with your guys. Love you, boo.*
*Merry fucking Christmas - see what I did there? Ha!*

I cannot believe she got me sex toys and fucking restraints. And didn't warn me not to open it with company. I move the box to one side, trying to keep my composure, but Maverick winks at me and I know he saw my fluster.

Dammit.

Well, they have their secrets, this can be one of mine.

I move to open one of the boxes in front of me and feel the burning intensity of Linc's stare as I look at the tag. It's from him.

Undoing the gray ribbon from the flat black box, a weird sensation of anticipation and dread fills me. Please don't let him use this as another way to hurt me. I lift the lid and find a leather-bound notebook sitting inside.

It's freaking beautiful.

I lift it from the box, and open it, admiring the handwriting on the first page.

*V,*

*Sometimes it's hard to say the right things, but putting it on paper makes the darkness not so bleak.*

*Maybe this can be your light in the dark.*

*L*

I blink back the tears. How does he always know the best ways to break me? This might not have been meant to break me, but it did.

For once, being broken doesn't seem so bad.

---

After an emotional Christmas and several days of even more emotional down time as the black hole I've been running from finally caught up with me, today, I decided to get out of bed. I missed New Year's Eve, but Indi was super chill about it. I'm kind of glad she has her boys back, because as much as I love her, I really needed those days to wallow.

Today though, I'm washing off my funk. I'm starting this new year right, and dammit, something has to go better than it has the last six months.

I finish putting on my sports bra and leggings, tying the laces on my sneakers and putting my hair up in a ponytail. Glancing out of the doors to my balcony, I contemplate taking my jacket. I decide against it and pull on the armband for my phone, picking up my AirPods before heading downstairs.

"I'm heading out for a run!" I call out to Smithy as I slide one pod in.

"Be careful, Miss Octavia! I'll have breakfast ready for your return." I smile and slip the other pod in, hitting play on my running playlist. I stretch out a little before jogging down to the gate, enjoying the brisk morning air.

There's nothing quite like the icy bite of winter air filling your lungs to start the day. I hadn't realized how much I missed starting my day like this, but now I'm here, I promise myself that I won't lose my routine again. No matter how much crazy shit I have going on. This helps me physically and mentally.

I can't stay afloat through all the crazy if I'm already drowning in my own.

I hit the pavement, the sounds of *Partners in Crime* by Set It Off blasting through my pods. A grin spreads across my face as my lungs start to burn in the most delicious way. I lose focus on everything but the wind on my face, the beat in my ears, and the ache in my muscles from not having run in so long.

It's only when I reach the pier and take a few seconds to suck in lungfuls of air that I spot Lincoln about fifty yards away, jogging in shorts and a sleeveless t-shirt.

I head to the stall selling drinks at the edge of the pier and grab two bottles of water. Thank God for contactless. When Lincoln catches up, I wave the water bottle at him and he comes toward me as I take a drink from my own.

He takes the bottle and drinks half of it in one go, splashing some on his face when he's done. I try my hardest not to smile, but fail. Without even trying, he's like something off a goddamn commercial. His golden skin glistens, even in the winter sun, the water merely emphasizing it.

"Were you following me?" I ask, and he looks at me like I'm ridiculous. And I might be, but I'm pretty certain I've never seen him out running.

He finishes his water before answering. "Maybe. But I mean, who goes out running alone when they have a stalker?" He raises his brow and I bite my lip. Sometimes I wonder if I have any sense of self-preservation at all, because I definitely hadn't considered that when I decided to run today.

"Right. That… Thanks."

He shakes his head, muttering something under his breath I can't make out. "Are you heading back?"

I check the tracker on my phone. It's only about half of my usual distance. "Yeah, we can head back."

He quirks a brow at me, crossing his arms. "Were you done?"

"No, but it's fine. I should've thought. I'll just hit the treadmill later or something."

"Octavia, I swear…" He trails off, pinching the bridge of his nose. I try not to feel like a scolded little girl and tamper the sass that rises in response. "Just run your normal route. I'll be fine, this was barely a warm-up."

I bite the inside of my cheek, wondering if he's just being polite or if his ire is from something else. I shrug, deciding that he's big enough to make his own decisions and if he says we can still run, then I'm going to keep running. I might as well start my new routine properly if I want to keep it up.

"Okay, then let's go." I slip my AirPod back in, the music starting up automatically as I finish my water and drop the bottle in the recycling bin before taking off up the promenade. I only ran this route a few times before Halloween, but it's the perfect loop. And at this time of day it's beautiful, the sunrise spilling orange and pink over the horizon. There's something hopeful about it that makes me feel better about my day.

I take off at a steady pace, trying not to go too fast in case Lincoln was exaggerating, but after another half mile I get restless and pick up the pace.

There's something freeing about the burn of running.

After another half mile, Lincoln runs basically beside me, looking bored, like this really isn't a challenge for him. I have no idea why that riles me, but it does.

*Keep up with this, buddy.*

It's another four miles back home but I pick up my pace, pushing as hard as I can. It's stupid, foolish, and childish, but I grin inside through the pain. I know I'm going to regret pushing this hard on day one back out, but I can't help myself.

When we're about a mile from home, I look behind me to find Lincoln keeping back, maybe two strides behind me. The asshole grins at me. He fucking grins. Like my lungs aren't burning to the point where I think I might combust.

Then the asshole has the sheer audacity to increase his pace, so that he's running ahead of me. The sight might not be a bad one, but it gripes me nonetheless, and I push harder so we're running shoulder to shoulder.

When we finally reach the gates to the house, I hit the code, and basically crumple on the lawn on the other side.

"That was fun. Nice warm up before I hit the gym." He grins down at me, and I flip him the bird from where I'm lying face down on the lawn.

*Asshole.*

---

I take a deep breath as we pull into the parking lot at school, clutching Indi's coffee as she pulls into my usual space. My Impala isn't loving the cold snap we seem to be having, but I have the world's greatest bestie because she rescued me from having to come in with Lincoln.

"Are you okay?" she asks, glancing at me with a furrowed brow once she's parked.

I bite my lip, trying to think of how to explain it. "There's just this pit in my stomach, like something bad is going to happen today. Usually I'd ignore it, put it down to weird dreams or some shit… but with everything that happened here last semester, I can't help but wonder if my intuition is kicking in or something."

She pinches her lips together, like she's thinking over my words real hard. "I mean, you called a truce with Lincoln and the others… and you're definitely reaping the rewards of that, right?"

I nod, trying not to roll my eyes. As unconventional as it might be dating more than one person, my bestie is rocking it and she's all for me playing the field with these guys. "Yeah, well not with Linc, but yeah."

"Okay, well then they're clear from the board at least."

"Yeah." I sigh. "That just leaves the rest of the student body. Awesome."

She squeezes my hand, trying to reassure me. "Most of them will back off now that the Saint Squad have pulled back. That just leaves Blair and her bitch squad."

"And Raleigh," I tag on. I swear, I had no idea it was possible to avoid someone in this school for as long as it's been since I've seen him, but whatever Finley and Maverick did to him, he's avoided me like the plague since.

Somehow that's made it worse. The anticipation and anxiety of seeing him has built up into this big thing. Because I know I'll see him again. Except now I've had the time to dream up a million different variations of what that looks like.

It might sound silly, but if I could stop it, I would. My brain isn't always the kindest to me.

"We got this. I will stick to you like glue all day if it helps." I shake my head at her offer, sweet as it is.

"Thank you, I love you for offering. I just need to pull up my Bridget Jones and get on with it." I take a sip from my mocha as she grabs her bag and nods.

We climb from the car just as Maverick and Finley pull into the lot, one after the other. They park in the spaces beside us, leaving one between them for Lincoln. I pull down the beanie on my head, my curls flowing down my back beneath it as I huddle into my coat. I swear it almost feels as cold as the winter I spent in London right now.

I can happily say I've adjusted back to California weather, and this cold is so not appreciated. Especially when I still have to wear this goddamn skirt. Even if the socks are cute and warm.

"Morning." Mav grins at me as he pulls off his helmet, his dark hair flicking back as he climbs from his bike.

I smile back, waving at him and Finn before scurrying inside with Indi. I haven't seen either of them much since Christmas, but Maverick does at least seem back to his usual self. On the outside anyway. I know as well as most that a mask is easily worn.

We head into the main hall, moving toward my locker, when we're stopped by Blair and her bitch squad.

I let out a sigh, moving myself just a little in front of Indi, because I'll be fucked if they mess with her too. "What do you want now, Blair?"

I feel heat at my back moments before hearing, "Yes, Blair. What do you want?"

I bite back my grin at Maverick's voice. Looking back, I see the three of them flanking Indi and I. Not going to lie, having that power at my back feels good. It feels like coming home. Almost like I have my friends back, even if I'm still not fully convinced they're entirely in my corner.

Her eyes go wide as she takes them in behind me and, I swear to God, actually stomps her foot. "I'd heard you were all slumming with the whore, but I figured it was just a rumor. I guess spreading your legs finally got you somewhere, Octavia. I hope you boys wrapped up, because she's nothing but a dirty skank."

"You listen here, you two-bit trash," Indi starts, jumping in front of me like she's about to throw down. Mav grabs her around the waist and pulls her back.

"Calm down, Cujo. We got this." He winks down at her, and I swear my ice heart melts a little more for him.

"Blair, just because I wouldn't put my dick in your shriveled-up bucket, doesn't mean I'm fucking your cousin," Linc says so bitingly even I wince a little. "Even if I did, it would have absolutely fuck all to do with you. So I'll ask again, slowly this time so you can comprehend. What the fuck do you want?"

He steps closer so I'm practically leaning against his chest, Finn on my other side, while Mav stays with Indi.

"I came to tell this skank that some of her shit was delivered to the house over the weekend if you must know. I didn't realize that she had guard dogs watching her every move. At least now I'll know for future reference."

"I'd keep an eye on that future of yours, Blair. We both know how much hangs in the balance. It would be so easy for everything to fall down around you," Lincoln says, and she pales. I have no idea what the fuck he's going on about but whatever it is, he obviously hit a nerve.

She lets out a humph and spins on her heel, storming away, her little band of bitches scurrying along behind her. I turn to face the guys, trying not to smile too wide. "Thank you, you totally didn't need to come to my rescue, but I appreciate it."

"We always had your back before," Mav says, making Indi snort. "Well, not before, but before before. And we told you over break that things would change. We meant it."

Lincoln nods, just as the bell rings. "We'll see you later."

He and Finley head up the hall as Mav kisses my cheek before he bounces along behind them.

"Well. That's a weird new kind of normal." Indi laughs as we rush to my locker.

"Tell me about it." I throw my stuff in my locker before we dive to hers.

"I get the feeling I missed out on some stuff that happened over break, so this weekend you and I are having a catch up date."

I grin at her, because I am so down for that. "It's totally a date."

---

I walk into the cafeteria with Indi at my side and freeze when I hear his laugh. My blood turns to ice in my veins as I turn and see Raleigh laughing and joking with the football team at their table. Blair and her bitch squad flitting around them like a hive of bitch bees.

"Oh look, it's the girl who cried rape!" Blair's voice echoes around me, and I feel like I've been plunged under an ice cold wave. The laughter that sounds around the room makes me want to be sick.

"Come on, we don't need to be here," Indi says, tugging at my arm, but it's like my feet are made of lead and I can't move. I thought his timetable changed; he wasn't meant to have lunch with us anymore.

Raleigh saunters toward me, with Blair clinging to his side. Now is so not the time to freeze, but I can't make my fucking body respond, despite my mind screaming at me to get the fuck out of here.

"You didn't really think I wanted you, did you, new girl? I guess points for not giving it up as easily as your friend did to my boy. But crying rape when you were just a little tipsy is a bit much, don't you think?"

Indi sucks in a breath, and I see the tears fill her eyes. Anger rushes through me and I clench my fists, turning to face Raleigh when a blur moves past me. The crack as Maverick's fist connects with Raleigh's jaw is enough to turn my stomach. He rails on him as Blair starts squawking. She turns to me, practically spitting, "Call off your fucking guard dog!"

I take two steps toward her, and despite what happened last time, I slap her petty fucking face, making sure to curl my fingers so I scratch down her cheek. It's not even close to what I want to do to her after everything, but for now, it's all I can do.

I smirk, and she screams as blood trickles down her cheek. "You bitch!"

"I'm the bitch? Blair, you've done nothing but be an absolute asshole since I got back here and I have no idea why." She charges at me, looking almost fucking possessed. She tackles me to the ground, screaming like a banshee, and it's all I can do to stop her blows from landing.

She's fucking insane.

I get the feeling insane is the only way I'm going to get out of this, so I go limp for a second and then headbutt her as hard as I can. My head spins but damn it feels good, and her scream is like music to my fucking ears.

She's lifted from me, and I notice Finn carting her away as Lincoln pulls Mav from Raleigh's fucked-up form on the ground before turning back to Indi, who looks frozen stiff with watery eyes.

"Come on," I tell her, mouthing a thank you to Finley as he deals with the mess I leave behind.

"I think I'm going to bail," Indi says, her voice shaking. I swear I want to go back and nut stomp Raleigh for announcing her business the way he just did. How I ever thought he was a good guy is baffling. She pulls her phone from her pocket, tapping on the screen. I feel useless and furious.

"Is there anything I can do?"

She shakes her head, wiping at her face as we reach her locker. "No, it's fine. I think I'm just going to go and chill with Ryker and Ellis. They're not back at school till tomorrow anyway."

"Okay, I'm sorry my shit keeps spilling over onto you."

She looks at me, more fierce than I think I've ever seen her. "Don't you dare. None of this is on you. He's just a giant fucking asshole, and I hope Maverick cuts off his fucking dick."

I laugh because, well, that'd be hilarious. But also, I'm not convinced he wouldn't do it.

"I love you. I'll see you tomorrow," I say as I hug her.

"Thank you, I'm sorry for leaving you stranded."

I wave her off, because hell no is she going to worry about me right now. "I'll find my way, we're good. You go chill with the guys and I'll see you in the morning?"

"You will," she says, squeezing me once more before grabbing her stuff from her locker and bolting for the doors.

I head for my own locker, my stomach rumbling despite the chaos. Times like this I wish I still stashed granola bars everywhere.

"You want to get out of here?"

I turn and find a bloody-knuckled Maverick grinning at me.

"I am definitely not opposed to the idea," I say, smiling back at him. My GPA is pretty healthy right now. I can totally cut the afternoon. Especially after what just happened. I'd rather be anywhere but here.

"Awesome, let's go grab some food and chill." He puts an arm out and I grab my jacket, bag, and beanie from my locker before sidling up beside him.

"Thank you for that. You didn't have to."

He tucks me under his arm and leads me outside. Thankfully, the sun is back and it's no longer bitingly cold out here anymore. "You don't have to thank me, princess. He hurt you, and what he said about Rainbow… shit's out of line." I smile at his apparent nickname for Indi. It does suit her though. "Plus, I have a lot to make up to you. I'm not the guy to fix things with fancy words, or give you the answers I know you crave. But I am the guy that can make your enemies bleed and wish they were never born."

A shiver runs down my spine when he smiles at me. His version of romance is drenched in blood and brutality, but with everything I've learned lately, I can't be too surprised. Plus it's kind of sweet in a Maverick kind of way.

He heads to Lincoln's Porsche and opens it with a fob on his keys, grabbing his jacket and two helmets from the back. "I keep a spare back here just in case." He winks, handing it to me. I look longingly at the bike, then down at my skirt.

Fuck it.

I pull my jacket on, slinging my bag across my body before pulling my beanie on and putting the helmet on over the top. He gazes at me, groaning. "You shouldn't look that good in a fucking helmet," he grumbles, and I laugh.

He climbs onto the bike and I swing my leg over, sliding in behind him on what might be the tiniest seat I've seen in my life. "Hold on tight, princess. I'll take you for a ride."

I can't help but laugh at his teasing tone as I wrap my arms around him. This isn't exactly how I saw my day going, but I'm not sad about it.

The bike vibrates beneath me when he starts it up, and my grin widens. I shouldn't feel this good right now, but I'm not going to question it. We head out of the parking lot and he opens her up, pulling a squeal from my lips as he does. His torso shakes, telling me he heard the squeal, too.

I am having too much fun, so when Mav steers the bike away from home, I don't bother to object. I hold on tight, literally just along for the ride. I lose track of time, enjoying the escape. I know I've forgiven him—even if I probably shouldn't—even though he hasn't apologized yet.

There is just something about him that calls to me.

Like calls to like I guess. It just means we're both more broken than I ever realized.

We ride to the other side of town before he heads into one of the parks around The Cove. He pulls the bike to a stop at the side of the lake and takes his helmet off. "I thought you might want to decompress a little before you go home."

I take my helmet off and climb from the bike to set it on the ground. I take Mav's and place it next to mine, trying not to smile. I guess he does have a softer side after all. He doesn't step from the bike, so I raise a hand above my eyes to see him properly, to take a guess at what's going through his mind.

I take a step forward and he grabs me by the hips, lifting me with ease, and puts me on his lap, facing him. My heart races as I cling to him and the asshole just smirks. "Isn't this a little dangerous?"

"You telling me you don't like a little danger, princess?"

His hands run up my bare thighs and under my skirt. I squirm under his touch. "Someone could be here, anywhere. They could see."

"If you didn't catch it last time, that doesn't exactly faze me. If anything…" He trails off as I roll my eyes at him. His fingers toy with my pussy through the lace of my panties, and I bite the inside of my cheek to stop from groaning. "But if you don't want to play…"

Without a word, I slap my hand on his wandering one and press it hard against my thigh, encouraging him to inch forward. The tank behind me isn't exactly comfortable but I balance myself on him, not wanting him to stop.

Leaning in, his lips brush up against mine with a tenderness so shocking it takes my breath away. It's only when he sinks his teeth into my flesh that I remember who I'm dealing with.

Mav swallows my gasp like that bite of pain is his own personal oxygen.

"Why do you do that?" I lick my bottom lip, sampling the coppery taste it leaves behind. Meanwhile, he's staring at my mouth, his chest rising and falling with each breath and his dick getting impossibly harder by the second.

"Do what, princess?"

I roll my eyes at him and his devilish smile. I'm not opposed to a little pain with my pleasure, but I can't help but wonder about him making me bleed. "Bite me until I bleed."

Slowly, the corners of his mouth rise into a sinister, albeit sexy as fuck, grin and his eyes drag up from my mouth to my eyes.

"Because I can." As if to accentuate his words, he pushes one long finger into my pussy and curls it up to a place that makes me jump closer to him.

The strength he must have in his thigh muscles impresses me as he keeps his Ducati stable, even though I'm writhing from his touch.

Dragging his finger out, he brings it to my mouth, coats it from side to side, pushes it between my lips, and says, "Suck."

With zero hesitation, I do as I'm told and feel an electric satisfaction at the pleased look in his eyes.

But it's when he brings his finger to his own mouth that I feel myself getting exponentially wetter.

"I'm going to fuck you, princess, and this bike's not gonna work for the things I have planned."

In seconds, he flicks down the kickstand and lifts me as he swings off the bike. I wrap myself around him, trying not to fall as he moves. He grins at me as he walks us to a small patch of soft grass. The hard length of his cock is pushing against my aching pussy and every step he takes makes me rub against him.

I suck in a breath when he lowers me to the ground. Anyone could see us.

Fear spikes through me at the thought. I look up at him and he grins. He gets off on this shit. The risk. The power. Being watched.

"Mav," I start, and he stops my words with his lips.

"I'm about to show you just how much fun it can be, taking risks." He winks at me as he kneels between my spread thighs. He grabs his cock through his jeans and gives me a lascivious grin. I can't help but laugh outright at him.

"Shut up and do something or I'm walking home."

His expression goes from lighthearted to feral in half a second.

Leaning down, he rips open my button-down shirt and sinks his teeth into the smooth skin right above my nipple. "You're not going any-fucking-where."

My hips jolt off the ground at the sting of his teeth, moaning out loud at the pain as my pussy gets slicker.

Apparently my appreciation for pain with pleasure goes deeper than I thought.

I lick my lips, wondering exactly where this is going as he looks at me with a heated gaze.

He trails his tongue around my nipple, licking his way up to my neck before he unzips his jeans enough to get his dick out just as he reaches the soft space right beneath my ear.

"Every bite I take is me claiming you, princess. And you best believe that's exactly what you are. Mine." Just as he promised, he first sucks on my tender skin and then bites hard enough to make me whimper.

Fuck.

That's going to leave a mark.

Another one.

When he pulls away, I watch him as he stares at what I'm guessing is the red patch on my throat. The look on his face is fucking priceless and without conscious thought, my thighs spread even wider, a silent invitation.

Flipping up my skirt, he pushes my panties aside and in one determined thrust, pushes his dick inside me to the hilt.

We both groan, the fullness a stark reminder of just how big he is; how perfectly he stretches me. He pauses for just a moment, barely a breath of time, before he lifts my legs, my ankles resting on his shoulders and one hand at his favorite place: my throat. With his free hand holding the weight of his body, he pulls out slowly and then slams right back inside me.

Again.

And again.

And fucking again.

Each time he buries himself inside me, the force of it pushes the air right out of my lungs. Every time he pulls out, he squeezes my neck hard enough that I worry he might cut off my oxygen but I relax when I realize he's obviously not a beginner at this and I can breathe just fine. I bet he'll leave a mark there, though.

I'm a little fuck toy to this man. This animal that gets off on the control he wields. This savage who gets off on my pain. This lover who probably doesn't even know what love feels like.

It's when he turns his head—all the while keeping his intense stare on me—and sinks his teeth into my calf that I realize just how true my thoughts are. He's the predator and even though he's got his prey right where he wants it, he's not done. He wants to keep playing with me before going for the kill.

With every thrust of his hips, my body slides on the ground. If not for the tight hold of his hand wrapped around my neck—one finger gently caressing the new bite mark—I would be moving all over the place.

He angles his body just a little differently—positioning his groin to rub perfectly against my clit—and my entire body lights up with my building orgasm.

"That's it, princess. You're about to come all over me, aren't you? You like it when I hurt you? When I squeeze my fingers enough to cut off your oxygen? When I make you bleed?" He squeezes my throat harder, and it's like my entire world lights up.

I fall over the edge as he pushes me into oblivion. I cry out, no longer caring who might see or hear us, but almost no sound comes out around his grasp.

My eyes roll back and my fingers dig into the grass, trying to keep myself grounded because I feel like I might fly off somewhere into the ether. Everything is heightened. The sound of the water, the smell of a California winter creeping up on us, the feel of him overpowering me. It's too much.

Pinning me down and basically choking the air out of me, he slams one last time inside me, biting my other calf as he comes.

We don't move for what feels like an eternity. I'm trying to gasp but he's still cutting off my air. My chest is rising and falling, fighting for breath, and it's only when I reach up and claw at his wrist that he opens his eyes back up—giving me his signature crazy-as-fuck grin—and releases my throat.

"You fucker! You almost killed me."

“Nah, I know what I’m doing. You had plenty of time left,” he says, winking at me. Fucking winking. “Fuck, V. That orgasm was fucking intense."

Then he kisses me, like I’m his only tether to the earth, and any frustration I had melts away.

He might infuriate me, but Maverick Riley is worming his way back underneath my skin, and I’m not sure I have the desire—or power—to stop him.

# CHAPTER THIRTEEN

## FINLEY

*I hide in my closet as my father's roars shake the house. I know I shouldn't hide from him. I know he'll make me play like he always does. But I don't want to play tonight. Every time his special friends come over…*

*I don't want to play.*

*I never want to play.*

*But they always make me.*

*One day, when I'm bigger, stronger, they won't be able to make me play.*

*If I can just hide until then, maybe I'll be okay.*

*Mom always says this time will be the last, but it's never the last. She just laughs as she breathes in the white powder, telling me it will be okay.*

*But it's not okay.*

*And I can't even tell anyone. Dad told me he'd make it hurt more if I told.*

*I don't want it to hurt anymore.*

*Maybe if I run to Lincoln's house or Octavia's house, I won't have to play tonight.*

*Holding my breath so I don't make any noise, I push the door of my closet open a little. He's not in here yet. I creep from my hiding spot, crawling across the room.*

*I make it to the window, trying to push it up, but it squeaks so loud as it moves. Fear spikes through my heart as it pounds in my chest, hammering against my ribs, and my vision goes funny from holding my breath.*

*He's going to find me.*

*I dive under the bed, hoping that gives me enough time to hide from him, that he looks somewhere else.*

*I scream as I'm dragged from under the bed by my ankle, trying to grab onto the floor to stop him from getting me.*

*"You little shit!" Dad screams as he pulls me to my feet. I ball my hands into fists, trying not to cry.*

*"I'm sorry," I say, my voice wobbling. We don't cry in this house. Knights don't cry. If I cry, he'll make it hurt worse.*

*"You will be sorry if you ruin this for me. I'll make your mother pay for it too. Do you understand?" He spits in my face, and I shake so hard as I nod. "Get fucking dressed. Our guest will be here in ten minutes. Do not disappoint me. You know what happens when you disappoint me."*

*He storms from the room, and I run to my bathroom and throw up.*

*My mom used to read me fairy tales and tell me about princes and saving people, but I don't think anyone is coming to save me.*

---

I wake up from the nightmare in a cold sweat. Those nightmares haven't haunted me for a long time, but considering what today is, I'm not exactly surprised they've unburied themselves from my subconscious.

I've visited my mom in her 'wellness center' this weekend every year since I committed her. It's the only time I visit her, and even then it's more out of guilt than anything else. I'm aware that she is a terrible human, and the worst kind of mom, but she is still my mom and we both suffered at my father's whims.

The only reason I still stay in this house of fucking horrors is because my father is all too aware that he doesn't own me any longer. This is not my home and my father uses the place as his own fucking pleasure den these days. He runs all sorts of shit from here, and on those nights I make sure I'm anywhere else.

His lessons taught me many things: that using words beyond reason will get you nowhere, that actions mean far more than words ever could, that being the smartest guy in the room is vital, and that listening to what people are *actually* saying when they talk is the smartest thing you can do.

Nothing is ever black and white. We live within the shades of gray.

The difference between my father and I, is that my monster has limits, and his… his does not. If it's for the bigger picture—whatever the fuck he convinces himself *that* looks like at the time—it's justified. No matter what.

I will never be the man—or the monster—my father wants me to be, and I am perfectly fine with that. The only thing that will see me truly happy is when he's six feet under by my own hand. Anything else will feel like it was stolen from me.

One day I'll taste my revenge in the form of his blood. Until then, I will bide my time, clinging to the small hope that the one true light in my life can be saved.

Another reason for today's visit.

We need some answers and my mom is likely the only person able to give them. Assuming she's actually coherent. Turns out, years of drugs and physical abuse fucks a person up to the point that they just check out of real life.

Committing her on my sixteenth birthday was a real hoot. Especially after I found her trying to slice open her wrists after one of my dad's bouts.

Happy fucking birthday to me.

I roll out of bed and head straight for my bathroom. I need a shower to wash off the haunted remains of my nightmares. I crank the shower to a glacial temperature and step beneath the icy spray, gritting my teeth against the sting as it jets onto my skin.

Once I'm fully awake and free of the lingering memories of my personal hell, I turn the temperature up and rush through the rest of my shower. Do I want to go and visit my mom today? Absolutely not. Am I going to? Yes, because despite the lifetime of trauma, I'd walk through the fires of hell for V if that's what she needed from me. Even if she has no clue where my mom is—or that I'm even going, for that matter.

I finish getting ready for the day, dressing as I'd be expected to at the center: slacks, button-down, and polished, scuff-free shoes. It's a fucking care facility, but God forbid I tarnish the Knight name by turning up in jeans and sneakers. I learned early on that it's easier to pick my battles, and dress-code isn't one worth fighting.

Heading downstairs as quietly as I can so as not to draw the attention of my father, I grab a granola bar and a bottle of water before heading out to my car.

Why he thought that buying me a car would make up for the fact that I was forced to commit my own mother on my birthday, I will never fucking know. Given the fact that he's lorded it over me every day since then, I could never forget it even if I wanted to. To this day he's still bitter that I cracked the careful façade he'd worked so hard to build over the ugliest parts of our family.

If only the world knew the reality of what happens behind the closed doors of this house.

I mean, my father's closest friends know, but to everybody else, he's just a well-respected businessman. No depravity or filth on his gleaming record.

I'm not sure how many outside of his inner circle know the true depths of what he's capable of, but it doesn't matter. It's exactly why the Knights keep him around. That and the whole legacy thing. God forbid anyone ever be free of them.

Yet, I still cling to the hope that we can get Octavia clear of it all.

I jump in my Aventador, the purr of the engine soothing me when I start it up. Driving well above the speed limit, I head down the freeway toward the inner-city center my mom is still at. She moved here over the summer from the stricter facility I had originally put her in. On paper, it's because she's doing so much better. In reality, it's that the new facility is owned by the Knights and they can keep her under their thumb here.

Gripping the steering wheel tight, I remind myself why I'm making the trip today.

My mom has answers. She has to. She lived through everything, even if it was in a haze.

In less than an hour, I pull up to the front of the gleaming white stone building that's way too fucking bright in the winter sun. I take a deep breath before parking in the open space opposite the main entrance.

Gritting my teeth, I paste a smile on my face, the mask too easy to slip into, and head inside the building. "Namaste, Mr. Knight. It's so lovely to have you back with us. Your mom will be so pleased to see you."

I glance at the blonde's name tag. Candy. Of course.

"Thank you. Is she in her room?" I ask, acting the part of the polite, dutiful son that I'm expected to be.

"I believe she's actually in the yoga center. If you'd like to have a seat, I'll check for you."

I nod, taking a seat, before grabbing my phone. I scroll mindlessly through my social media apps to pass the time. I haven't heard anything back from Mav or Linc yet, and as much as I want to message V, I don't want to get distracted, which is exactly what would happen.

Instead, I slip my phone back into my pocket and lean my head against the wall. This charming persona is draining as fuck. I am so not this guy--the guy who works the room. I leave that to Lincoln. He's the people person. Me, I revel in being the strong silent type. Or… well, just the one people don't talk to.

I'm much happier when it's that way.

"Mr. Knight, your mother is this way, please." The peppy voice pulls me from the darkness of my musings and back to this way-too-bright space, the contrast between the two stark to the point of painful.

I follow her through the halls lined with floor-to-ceiling windows, the winter sun filtering through down to the visitors' room.

The yellow space has big gray couches scattered throughout, a few tables surrounded by stylish, uncomfortable chairs, and a lone TV on the wall.

"There he is, my beautiful boy." I turn toward the sound of my mother's voice, and she strides across the room toward me. Dressed in all white, her blonde hair shining, she wraps her arms around me and I stiffen. This woman lost the right to this sort of greeting a while back, but I grit my teeth and briefly embrace her. Fuck knows who is watching.

"Mother. You're looking well."

We move to sit at a table in the far corner of the room, away from the few other people in here. There isn't much privacy, but if she thinks this is a good place to talk, then I'll have to trust her. I grab my phone as we sit, putting it on silent, and turning on the jammer app I installed the moment I got it. If I can protect this conversation, then I'm going to.

She sits opposite me, her eyes glassy and her gaze somewhere far beyond the walls of her cage, and smiles absently until she tries to grasp my hand and I pull it away from her. "What brings you here? It's been so long since I've seen you."

"Octavia is back." I keep my words to a minimum. She doesn't need more than that to know why I'm here. She might be off her fucking rocker, but even *she* has to realize I'm here for answers.

Her eyes go wide, and she leans back in the chair. "Oh."

"I need to know how Lincoln's mom got out. How Octavia's mom got out." A small grin plays on her lips and a sadistic glint briefly flashes in her eyes before she turns back into the new-and-improved Stepford version of herself. For just a moment, I got to see the woman who raised me, the funhouse reflection of herself that my father warped her into. Hell, maybe she was always that person, and my dad just brought out the worst in her. Fucked if I know.

"They didn't get out, Finley dear." Her voice lilts at the end, like I made a joke. Gritting my teeth, I take a deep breath.

"Don't fuck with me. I need answers and I know you have them." Her eyes glaze over, like whatever drugs she's on have taken hold. "Mom!"

She blinks, turning her attention back to me, but it's like she's an entirely different person. This is the mother who would hear my screams and laugh. She rolls her eyes, before leaning forward, resting her forearms on the table. "You always were besotted with the Royal girl. Following her around like a sad, lost little puppy. You and the other two. It was like she was the flame and you the moth. She was always going to be your demise and, mark my words, she will be if you keep chasing her the way you seem to be. The fact that you're even here tells me that you're already on the road to your own destruction."

I roll my eyes and let out a sigh. "You always were one for dramatics. This was a waste of my time. I don't know why I even bothered."

She blinks again, her eyes glassy. "Oh Finley, no. Don't leave. Please."

I pinch the bridge of my nose, trying not to lose my shit. I'm getting whiplash from her multiple personalities. "I need information, Mom. Can you help me?"

She pats my hand, looking at me like a doting mother. "I can try, but the Knights… well, it's not something you can fight against. My poor little boy, all grown up. Fighting them is like swimming against the tide. You're likely to get tired and slip up. But there was that one time… she skitted away like a butterfly, beautiful and never seen again… she might help. Though his dad always did have an obsession with her, he might be willing to help."

I sigh as she smiles at me, looking at me like I'm a freaking unicorn. "I don't know what any of that means, Mom."

"It means, sweet boy, that if you grow wings, you can fly away too. You just need to become so powerful that they can't clip them."

This trip was a waste of time. I'd really hoped that she would've been able to help. But I have no idea what she's talking about.

"You should speak to his guard dog, maybe he got her out. Though he might've clipped her wings too."

"Speak to who?"

She looks almost afraid and shakes her head, covering her mouth like she just said something that might get her killed.

"No, no… nothing, sweet boy. Nothing at all. It's Christmas soon, right? Will you come and see me? I have something to give you." She pats my cheek, her finger tracing the faded scar that's there. She fixates on it, but I pull out of her grip.

That isn't a memory lane I want to walk down.

"Why don't you give it to me now, Mom?"

She shakes her head, looking all around as if we're being watched. I should really speak to someone about whatever it is she's on. Though they're probably keeping her on a concoction so she can't speak out about shit. "No, no. Not yet. It isn't time yet. If they knew you had the key… no. The King kept it safe, and now it's yours. She has the key too. Pretty little thing. But it's yours, really. Maybe then your wings will grow."

"This isn't helping me find a way out, Mom."

I sigh and move to stand but she grabs my wrist, her nails digging in hard enough that I feel my skin break beneath them. "Don't you get it?" Her eyes are clear and sharp, glinting with the all-too-familiar malice I had grown up with. "Once you're in, you're in. There is no escape. The only way out is if they don't want you in to begin with, and if you were already in, the only way out is in a box."

"But they got out!" I hiss as I rip my wrist from her grasp, blood trickling down onto my hand. Fucking crazy.

She laughs, the sound cold and hard. "If you think that, then you're a fool." Her voice softens and she lazily picks at an invisible spot on the table. "No one makes it out of this alive."

---

I wait with Lincoln and Maverick in the corner of the room, hands in my pockets. My visit with my mom was a bust and tonight isn't going to make this day any better.

The quarterly dick measuring meeting held by The Knights Society. It's not just for the inner sanctum or those of us who have a ruling vote. No, tonight is for a wider audience. For those in the second and third rings of hell. The Bishops. Those with enough skin in the game that they're important enough to rub shoulders with the Conclave. In our case, the Conclave are the seven founding families of The Cove.

Along with the prospects: a.k.a. the Rooks: people who want in, who believe they have something to offer. Though, just by being here they're already one foot in the grave. If it wasn't damn-near to a guarantee they'd be in, they wouldn't have set foot on the property. Taking care of people who see more than they should has proven time and time again to be too much of a hassle to accept the risk. It's just easier to run a tight ship and keep our circles small.

The military-grade security outfit also helps.

There's everyone here from drug and human traffickers to gun runners. From politicians to presidential candidates. Cartel bosses to CEOs of household-name brands. And that's just people in this sect.

I'm just glad I'm not deemed important enough to have to show my face when the senior members of the Conclave get together.

Not yet anyway.

For now, I'll take my junior status and run the fuck with it. The less I have to do with this fucking hellscape the better.

"So your mom had no details?" Lincoln asks, picking at the lint on his jacket, looking as nonchalant as expected.

I shake my head and swig back the whiskey in my glass—the only upside of these bullshit meetings. "Not a thing. She said no one gets out alive."

"Which is bullshit, because Fiona is currently sunning herself in the Caribbean with a beach boy." Lincoln rolls his eyes, referring to his mother. "There is very little chance my father would just let that happen if she wasn't out and completely unattached."

Maverick laughs dryly, just before a shadow appears over my shoulder. I turn and find Harrison, Lincoln's dad, standing just behind me. "Boys. Being sociable as usual I see."

I step sideways, not wanting him at my back. I make a habit of not letting anyone I don't trust be there.

Not anymore.

"Harrison." Lincoln smirks at his father. "What's on the schedule for tonight's display of debauchery?"

Harrison laughs, though it doesn't quite reach his eyes. "You'll see. I have a feeling that tonight's piece is going to be something that the three of you might finally pay attention to. After the fire at Nestwood before Christmas, we put together a plan of attack on certain holdings of the Conclave. Tonight… well, you'll see."

An icy drop of dread runs down my spine, but I don't let it show on my face. The key to survival here is to be entirely devoid of any emotion. Anything that can be used against you will be. It's partially why we were such assholes to Octavia when she arrived; we had hoped that the sect's Conclave would think she couldn't be used against us.

Unfortunately for her—and us—that plan didn't exactly prove successful. In fact, it was so *un*successful they even dropped their plans to start trafficking drugs through The Cove. It's all just a little too suspect if you ask me. It puts me on edge.

Harrison leaves us alone after dropping his little breadcrumb of what the night holds and goes back to his guests. And they are *his* guests since he's the head of the Board for our sect, making him a Regent: one of the few with a seat at the round table that makes up the inner sanctum of The Knights Society.

The night drags on, rubbing elbows with people whose names and faces I store for future use, just in case. As of right now, they mean absolutely nothing to me. But this place is a pit of vipers, and only the strongest and smartest survive. So I stay on edge, making sure I'm aware of our surroundings, the three of us never separating. We learned a long time ago that there's safety in numbers.

I get pulled in a dozen different directions, never too far from the boys, but I swear I've never been so fucking bored and on edge at the same time. Everyone in here is drenched in whatever fragrance they deem to be the one that makes them seem the wealthiest. No one in here is in anything less than designer, dripping with jewels and it's more than a little obscene. The only reason I'm in this monkey suit is because I'd bleed if I wasn't.

I tune back into the conversation between some of the Bishops, showboating because I'm a legacy. "Did you hear about the shipment of girls we sold to the Russians last month? Made an absolute fortune. Got at least twice what they were worth. Dirty, homeless bitches all hopped up on whichever drug was cheapest at the time. Thirty mil for six girls. Got to love how much they go for when they're young."

It takes a lot to keep the sneer from my face as the others laugh at this nameless idiot's boasting.

"Well, I was shocked to see Erica here, especially after that scandal. Twenty pounds of cocaine in her daughter's car. I mean really, who would be so sloppy."

"I heard that Michael swept it under the rug for her."

"He's out of prison?"

"Yes, good behaviour. Twenty-five years for one little explosion was a bit over the top if you ask me."

God, I might go to prison if it means escaping this fucking conversation.

"Well he did kill, what was it, five people?"

"Yes, but I was his lawyer. Here's my card if you need me." Their snooty laughter grates on my nerve endings, but I keep my stony mask in place as they pat my shoulder, and smile at me like I hold the cards to the rest of their lives.

Just when I think I can't take it any more, that I might just massacre the entire room to escape this posturing bullshit, the lights dim, and Harrison's voice booms around the room. "Members of the sect, welcome to tonight's quarterly get-together. It has been a pleasure to speak to you all." He pauses for applause which, of course, he is given. The sycophants here want a piece of him. Some would rather that piece be his head on a platter, but all must kneel before the King. "Tonight, as promised, we are unveiling things to come. Things that we know you want to be a part of, and for the Rooks of the room, a little taster of what is to come should we allow you to join us."

I stifle a yawn, because a beating from my father isn't on my agenda for the night, especially with school on Monday. Bruises don't fade in a day, unfortunately for most people in this room. I drown out Harrison's drivel, trying to work out more about what these assholes could want with Octavia.

We're all pretty certain her dad didn't commit suicide, which means either the Knights took him out, or someone wanting a seat in the Conclave did. Except, why leave Octavia alive if that's the case? My first suspect was Nate, especially with the way Blair came sniffing around us like a bloodhound. She wanted that seat at the table real bad. Too bad for her, the senior members shot that down.

Pretty much everyone in this room is a suspect. Not a soul in attendance is innocent. Every one of them has done something that lands them on the wrong side of the moral scale. You don't get in this room by having clean hands.

"Fuck," Lincoln hisses, bringing my attention back to the room, applause sounding again.

"What? What did I miss?" I ask, looking between the two of them, each looking as angry as the other.

I turn back to where Harrison was standing when neither of them respond and I get my answer.

*Fuck.*

# CHAPTER FOURTEEN

## OCTAVIA

Pulling up to school on a Monday morning is never any fun. But pulling up *this* Monday morning sucks on a whole new level.

I find Blair hanging off of Raleigh on the steps of the school, along with most of the football team and cheer squad, plus the rest of their cronies. All of them watch me as I pull into my space.

That I could cope with. Being watched isn't anything new to me.

It's the taunts as I climb from my car that piss me off. If I thought Blair teamed up with Lincoln was bad… well, let's just say things can *always* get worse.

I can deal with the usual shouts.

*Whore.*

*Slut.*

*Skank.*

Words like that are water.

It's the "girl who cried rape" and "liar" that cuts me.

Keeping my head held high, I try to push through the crowd because there's no way around them. I climb the steps, but its so fucking claustrophobic as I try to reach the doors. People surround me on all sides, pushing in around me as they yell their taunts.

It's only when I reach the top step, coming face to face with Blair that it lets up and I can breathe. I try to shoulder past my cousin, but with Raleigh behind her, she's immovable. She laughs in my face as both of her palms connect with my chest and I fall backwards. Shock envelops me as I fall down the stairs, but the noise stops and before I hit the hard ground, a pair of massive arms catch me.

"We've got to stop meeting like this, princess." I blink up into Maverick's easy smile. He helps me back to my feet and the smile falls from his face as he looks at the congregation on the steps. "Did you all enjoy that? I warned you once, you were put on notice. Octavia Royal is ours. That means our protection. Consider this your last warning, and thank her for even getting a warning, because we all know if it was up to me, this would be dealt with here and now. Do *not* make me come for you. You know I won't come alone."

Without another word, everyone but Raleigh and Blair disperses as Lincoln and Finley arrive and flank me on each side.

Blair sneers at me before leaning into Raleigh. "Come on, babe, we don't need to waste any more of our morning on this trash." She looks back at us, gazing over my shoulder to Lincoln. "You picked the wrong Royal. You'll see."

"Blair, your desperation is showing," Lincoln says dryly.

Stifling my laugh at the look on her face, I turn toward the sound of laughter as Indi approaches us, hearing the end of what feels like a way-too-long morning already. Blair flicks her blonde locks over her shoulder and practically drags Raleigh into the building. His gaze cuts to me before he goes, the scorching hatred shining in his eyes is enough to steal my breath.

He has fuck-all reason to hate me. Anything that may or may not have happened to him is fully a consequence of his own actions. Nobody forced him to try and drug me, to try and rape me. I'm just lucky that Lincoln and the others arrived when they did.

I'm all kinds of confused about how I exactly feel about them all. I don't feel like I've forgiven them, yet there are moments when that's exactly what it feels like. Then, the next second I'm so spitting mad at them, I don't think I could ever forgive them. It's giving me fucking whiplash trying to keep up with it all.

But now is not the time to examine my emotions too closely. I apparently have no respite from my cousin this semester, which means that even with the guys having backed off, this place is still likely to be a fucking nightmare.

Awesome.

"What did I miss?" Indi asks as she reaches my side, bumping Lincoln out of the way to loop her arm through mine as she hands me a cup of sweet nectar. I mouth a thank you before taking a sip. I sigh as the caffeine goodness hits my tongue. *Hello, liquid gold.*

"Just Blair's latest attempt to show me how much she hates me. Oh, and she's apparently simping over Raleigh now." I roll my eyes as I speak, only laughing a little as her jaw drops open.

"She is a crazy son of a bitch."

I lift my coffee in a salute. "That she is, my friend." Turning back to the boys who are all whispering between themselves, I quirk a brow. "Thank you for the save."

Mav grins at me before strutting forward and capturing my lips with his. I lose my mind at the heat of the kiss, curling my free hand into the lapel of his blazer as he overwhelms me entirely. "All in a day's work, princess. What else are dark knights for?" He winks at me before heading into school and the other two look at me with so much fire in their eyes that I feel like I'm going to combust on the spot before they follow behind him without a word.

"So that happened…" Indi says, laughing as I blink at her. That's when I notice the sheer number of people standing out here just watching us, and a blush creeps up my neck. "I guess it must be official now."

Looping her arm back through mine, she pulls me from the stairs and into the school.

"Nothing is official. Fucking Maverick. He might have an almost-magical dick, but he'll be lucky if I don't cut it off if he doesn't quit his shit."

She laughs loudly as we head toward my locker. "Dude, we don't maim magical dick unless it's absolutely vital to our survival. Maim other, less important, body parts."

I grumble under my breath as I sort the combination on my lock and open the door. "Yeah, yeah."

"So are things any better between you guys?" she asks, and I realize we still haven't had a chance to have a proper catch up. Life is totally kicking my ass at the minute. It feels like I've barely had a chance to catch my breath, let alone catch up with my bestie.

I shake my head as I sort out my books and slide my jacket into my locker. "Kind of but not really. They're starting to open up, and they've told me some stuff, but I still feel like I know basically nothing. Like I wish I could just lock them in a room with me until they tell me everything I want to know. That being said, I need some boy-free time. Want to hang out this weekend? I could use some bestie time. I feel like I've barely seen you since Thanksgiving."

"Hell yes. Life has been chaos. With Ryker and the others stealing so much of my time, I know exactly what you mean. I need me some bestie time. What did you have in mind?"

"Sleep over, pj's, ice cream, the whole nine yards." I grin and she returns it with one just as wide.

"You had me at pj's." I close my locker and follow her over to hers. "I'll tell the guys that I'm MIA this weekend. I am too excited. I'm not even that far behind on school work, so if we have a study night this week too, I'm clear."

"Perfect. I've got a paper due for French and another for Statistics by Friday, so unless I get something else this week, I'm good too. Study night Wednesday?"

She nods as she grabs her books. "Perfection. Now let's just hope Miss Summers doesn't pile a ton of shit on today."

I loop my arm back through hers and finish the coffee she brought me, dropping the cup in the trash can just before we enter the class. It's still empty since the bell hasn't rung yet, so we head to our corner in the back.

"How are things going with *your* guys?" I ask, flashing her a knowing grin.

She blushes furiously as she slides into her chair. "They're definitely going. Apparently them deciding I was better off without them is a thing of the past and they're… erm… making up for lost time."

"Good for you!" I grin, wagging my brows at her. "I'm just glad you're happy, but if they don't treat you well this time, I'm not afraid of them. I will break them all."

"I have no doubt, but I think we're good. Something's changed since they broke it off. I don't know what yet, they don't talk much about that stuff with me, but there's definitely something."

I chew on my lip, wondering just how tied up they are in this Knight bullshit. I really need to pin Lincoln down and ask some actual questions. I know I'm not likely to get much from the other three: East, because I'm not sure how much he knows, and the other two because… well, Lincoln is the answers guy.

"Are we still going to work on your list?" Indi asks quietly as a few other people start to filter in the room. "Because I had a few ideas."

She smiles darkly and, well, color me intrigued. "I don't know, but I think so. I think they deserve to feel a little pain after everything. I'm just not sure how far I want to take it. Especially with things being so up in the air with them as they are at the minute. That reminds me, I need to tell you—" The bell interrupts my words, and Miss Summers floats into the room.

"Later," she whispers, and I nod. It's nothing that won't keep.

"Good morning, ladies and gents. I hope you shrugged off those back-to-school blues last week, because today we ramp it up. How does everyone feel about Shakespeare?"

Groans sound throughout the room, including one of my own. I am all for the classics, but Shakespeare has always been a bit much for me. Give me a remake any day of the week. Sacrilegious words to some, I know, but there's something about modern retellings that's absurdly enjoyable to me.

"Glad to hear you're all so enthusiastic this Monday, but I guess it sucks to be you guys, doesn't it? Let's get this going, shall we?"

The days this week are passing slowly, but I'm not too sad about it. There has been minimal drama, minimal crazy, and I am here for it. I never did get any information from Finley about the knife that was delivered to my house, but it's on my list of questions to pepper Lincoln with when I manage to pin him down again.

Literally, if need be this time. I'm still convinced he only gave me those questions because he had nowhere else to escape to.

East's whistle blows and I finish my circuits, sucking in lungfuls of air. My morning runs with Lincoln have become a thing, and it's been so nice working out regularly again, but there is something about circuits that fucks me up every time. I can run for miles, but ask me to do aerobics and I crumble.

Indi dramatically wilts to the floor beside me and I laugh at her as she puts the back of her palm to her forehead as if she's a damsel from a fifties movie. She flips me the bird, making me laugh again before East shouts, stealing my attention.

He's been more than a little distant at school lately. I get it. He's my teacher, but it still stings a bit. He certainly didn't mind getting up close and personal with me at home and it's only since then that he's been so off. I thought we'd worked shit out over the holidays, but I guess not. Just because I get it, doesn't mean it hurts less when he barely so much as glances at me during school hours now.

I've hardly spent any time with him alone since then. It's like he's gone from being my pillar of reliable strength to full-scale ghosting me unless the others are around.

"We're changing it up as of next week, ladies, so enjoy the circuits while they last. Next week won't be so easy. That's it for today. Get out of here." He blows his whistle again and people start to filter from the room.

Indi groans from where she's still lying on the floor. "Want a hand?" I offer her one, which she takes, and pull her to her feet.

"We still studying tonight?" she asks as she bends in half, hands on her knees.

"You know it. Smithy already promised milkshakes when we get in. He made you more cookies, too." Her grin is instantaneous, and it's like she is renewed.

"That man is a goddamn *saint.*"

I nod, because he absolutely is. "Come on, let's get changed and get you to the sugary heaven that awaits."

"V, do you have a minute?" East calls just as we start to head toward the locker room. I pause, biting down on my lip and glancing at Indi. She nods and heads out, leaving me alone with him in the gym.

"What's up?" I ask, sounding far lighter than I feel. I'm not sure when things got so weird and tense between us, but I'm putting that fully on him and his ghosting tactics.

He rubs the back of his neck, those stormy eyes of his seeming darker than usual. "I wanted to apologize…" He trails off as I stand awkwardly in front of him.

"Right?"

"I mean… damn… I don't want what happened between us to change shit. I don't want to rush you, or push you… and I'm your teacher, you're so much younger and despite how I feel about you… I just… I'm sorry." He looks so sad, so lost, that all of the weirdness I've felt about everything with him, all of the not-quite resentment, just melts away.

I move toward him, and wrap my arms around him, holding him tight, not giving a fuck who might see. "You have nothing to be sorry about. I'm sorry I've been a shitty friend. You've been there for me since I got back here and I hadn't even considered the sort of position all of this put you in. I'm the one who should be sorry."

He bands his arms around me and lets out a deep sigh as I melt against him. There is something about being in his arms that just feels safe. Like coming home after being out in a storm. He is solid, and reliable, and everything I need.

We stay like that for a few minutes, his face buried in my hair as I rest against him, until the bell rings again, breaking the moment between us. I untangle myself from him and tuck the loose strands of my hair behind my ear. "I should probably go and change, but we should talk soon. Just the two of us."

He nods, looking a little less sad but still just as lost. I wonder what's going on with him that I don't know, because it can't just be whatever this is between us that has him looking like that. My heart hurts for him. "I'm here if you want to talk."

"Thanks, V." The corners of his lips turn up as I grab the handle to the door. I want to say more but I'm not sure what I *can* say that will make any difference.

Another thing to add to my list of things to work out.

I head out to the locker room, changing without showering. I can do that once I'm home.

"Is it cool if I swing by home and then head over?" Indi asks as I finish changing.

I nod with a smile. "Sounds good. I need to shower anyway."

"Okay. All okay with that?" she asks, motioning in the direction of the gym with her head.

I shrug, wishing I had a better answer. "I think so?"

"Okay, we'll talk more in a bit," she says and I nod, conscious of the number of other people still in here with us. She heads out as I finish putting my gym clothes in my bag and generally sorting my shit out. By the time I'm done, the locker room has mostly emptied out and I head to my car with no issues.

I drive home with *Uncomfortably Numb* by Arrows in Action blasting through my speakers. It speaks to me way more than it probably should, but I lose myself to the lyrics and the melody, letting out some of the emotions I've been stuffing down lately. There is something about singing at the top of your lungs when you're on your own in the car that is so fucking therapeutic. I have yet to find anything else in the world that feels as good as belting out your feelings to a windshield.

I pull into the garage, glad that hump day is basically over and looking forward to my study night with Indi. Trying not to focus on the half-conversation I had with East, I climb from the car and head into the house, going straight up to my room. I take longer than I probably should in the shower, cranking the music up again and singing at the top of my lungs once more.

There are probably healthier ways to process emotion, but this works for me so I'm not going to question it. Music has always been an emotional outlet for me and I'm not about to change the habit of a lifetime.

By the time I'm done, dressed, and make my way downstairs, I find Indi sitting at the counter in the kitchen with Smithy, slurping on her milkshake, a plate of snickerdoodles in front of her.

"There you are, Miss Octavia. I was about to send out a search party," Smithy teases as I slide into the stool next to Indi. "Milkshake?"

"Sorry, I got a little lost in my own world." I give him a small smile. "I'd love one, please."

My stomach rumbles as I finish speaking and he quirks a brow at me. "Dinner will be ready shortly, too. I do hope you're eating properly at school."

"Me eating isn't something you need to worry about. I eat plenty," I tell him, trying to reassure him. Because yeah, food isn't something I torture myself with. I make sure I work out plenty, but I am firmly in the camp of team food.

"As long as you are." He eyes both of us before sliding a milkshake in front of me. "I've got some things to get sorted, but I'll let you know when dinner is ready. Will you be joining us, Miss Indi?"

"I'd love to." She beams at him.

"Good, I'm making chicken parmigiana, so there will be more than enough." She groans at his words and rubs her stomach.

"Smithy, you keep talking dirty like that and I'll never leave."

"Indeed, Miss Indi," he says, shaking his head as he leaves the room, and she bursts out laughing.

"Dude, I think I just talked dirty to Smithy."

I shake my head, grinning at her before taking a sip of my shake. "Yeah, I think you did."

"God, I'm such an idiot when I open my mouth sometimes." She facepalms, and I snicker lightly. "We should probably just start studying so that I get something out of tonight other than just making an idiot of myself."

"You can be you here, there's zero judgement from anyone. We love you just the way you are, goofy words and all." I wink at her, and she buries her face in her hands.

"I love you, too. Now, let's study before I die of mortification."

The night passes in a blur of working out standard deviations and interpreting the results for my presentation on Friday, and my French homework for tomorrow, while Indi groans about her upcoming Calculus test.

By the time she leaves, my eyes feel like they're going to fall out of my head. Not to mention we were so busy focusing that we had almost no time to actually catch up. Our only respite was dinner and I'm pretty sure Smithy didn't want to hear all of our dick talk over his delicious parma.

"I'm going to bed, do you need anything before I go, Miss Octavia?" Smithy asks, standing by the counter in the kitchen in his silk pj's and nightgown.

The old guy is freaking adorable. "I'm good thanks, just going to finish up this homework and then I'll be heading to bed too."

"Okay. Have a good night."

I smile up at him before jumping to my feet and giving him a hug. "Night, Smithy. Thank you for everything. I don't think I say that enough. Love you."

He squeezes me back, and gives me a croaky, "I love you too, Miss Octavia." He kisses the top of my head before padding out the other door in the kitchen toward the part of the house that has always been his. I've never even crossed that threshold.

I head back to my spot at the coffee table and drop down to the floor to finish my French homework, the words practically swimming on the page. I know people say that school is easy compared to 'real life' but honestly, I think adults just fully forget how hard shit can be at school.

My phone buzzes on the table while I finish writing my paper on music theory in French. Thankfully, French is probably the most fluent of the five languages I speak outside of English.

When it buzzes for the fourth or fifth time, I pick it up, sighing as I rub my eyes.

**East:**
I was thinking we could maybe continue our conversation from earlier.

**East:**
Can I come over if you're still awake?

**East:**
V?

I smile a little at the messages, a wicked thought bubbling to the surface.

**Me:**
Want to go for a swim?

I bite my lip in anticipation. Maybe the best way to get him over the whole weirdness is to push a few more of his buttons. Plus, Maverick told me they're all aware of everything, so if they're good with us all messing around, why shouldn't I be? I'm not about being put into a box with a label.

**East:**
A swim?

**Me:**
Sure. We can talk in the pool right?

**East:**
You're aware it's January?

**Me:**
I'm aware. Want to swim or not?

Sometimes his logic drives me insane, but I guess he is a Saint after all. Logic defies all, even in the face of emotion. Always has, always will. Harrison Saint was always that way when we were younger, too. Fiona had always been the emotional one in their house.

**East:**
That isn't something I'm going to say no to.

I grin and hurry upstairs to change into my bathing suit, grabbing towels for us both, and thanking God that my pool is heated, otherwise this would've just been a really stupid idea. From the kitchen, I hit the control to remove the covering from the pool and take a deep breath, preparing myself for the cold hit I'm about to take.

It's fucking freezing when I step outside in just my black bikini, so I scurry across the flagstones and drop my phone and the towels onto one of the chairs. Once they're safe, I hurry into the warm water, ducking my head under the surface, and let out a deep breath once I come up.

I hear the clink of the gate between here and the Saints' and wait for East to appear from the shadows. He's in sweatpants and a hoodie, looking every inch the Adonis, even dressed like a hobo. He grins wordlessly at me when he spots me, kicking off his sneakers and stripping down to his boxers. I'm held captive by every delicious inch of him. He steps forward and dives into the water, staying under until he reaches me on the other side of the pool. Surfacing, he cages me between him and the side of the pool. "Late night swims are definitely a good idea."

His eyes heat as he speaks. His gaze, bouncing down before trailing back up to meet mine, leaves a scorching path where he looks at me. Releasing the side of the pool, I wrap my arms around his neck as he presses me back against the wall. "I thought we were going to talk."

"We could talk," I say before pressing my lips against his gently. "Or we could do this." I move to kiss him again, but he grabs the back of my neck, stopping my advance.

"You know I want you. I've made that clear. But if we start this, and I mean properly, not this half-assed whatever it is we've had going on, then I am all in. I know you have something going on with the others, and while I'd rather have you to myself, I won't make you choose. But I don't want you to think that I don't want you as mine."

His words stoke the embers inside of me and a fully fledged inferno takes their place.

"We'll need to be careful until your birthday in the spring, and even after, until the school year ends. But even though I can't show you in public, just know that I'm in this, with every piece of me. I have loved you, Octavia Royal, for possibly my entire life, and I don't see that changing." He captures my lips with his as he presses me further into the wall, his dick pressing against me as I wrap my legs around his hips.

I have no words to say to him, I've never been one for pretty words, so instead I show him everything I don't know how to say.

I tell him how good he feels with each moan that falls from my lips. I make sure he knows how much I want him every time I press my almost-bare pussy against his cock. I plead with him to give me more with the tightening of my fist in his hair.

I may not have the words, but this… showing him what I want… this I excel at.

His big frame protects me from the chill in the air. The pool may be heated and California may not be anywhere near the North Pole, but the January temperatures are enough to make anyone think twice about being out here too long.

"You have no idea how long I've waited for this, Octavia. So fucking long."

His voice is deep in my ear, the tenor sending a trembling need down my spine and straight to my clit. "If you're not ready for this, really ready, I can keep waiting. I'd wait forever for you."

My heart pounds in my chest. He always seems to know exactly what to say to make me feel like I'm the only other person in his world.

I shake my head. "No more waiting."

Kissing him again, I try to show him just how much I mean what I say and he moans beneath my touch.

"You make me weak, Octavia Royal."

"More show, less tell." My words come out breathy and needy. I know he hears the pleading in my voice because I swear to fuck his cock grows even thicker than before as he pushes it against me.

He slides one hand down the column of my neck, across my collar bone, and down the length of my arm before he brings my own hand to my clit.

"Rub yourself nice and slick. Show me that you can be a good girl. I need you ready before I can fuck you exactly the way I've always fantasized."

His words make me shiver with unprecedented need.

I do as he says.

While obeying a Saint is never an easy feat, in this case it's an easy win-win.

With one hand still fisted in his hair, I keep the other alternating between my opening and my clit, his hand moving with mine as I keep myself nice and slick while the water tries to wash it all away.

No one ever told me that fucking in water was so goddamn counterproductive. Yet here we are, defying the odds and slaying it.

East showers me with kisses and licks and bites that turn me on even more. He's sexy and attentive. While the others might make my blood boil to warm me up, he has a whole different way about him. He is all man and I never knew being called a good girl by him would make butterflies take flight in my stomach, but I guess you learn something new every day, right?

When his hot mouth surrounds the hard peak of my nipple, my head falls back against the side of the pool as I enjoy each one of his torturous licks and sucks. It's like an electrified wire is linked from my nipple to my clit and every time he bites down just hard enough, I feel an orgasm begging to break through.

My ankles lock at the small of his back and my hips search out his cock all on their own. I don't even have to think about it. My pussy knows what she wants and it's got a Saint's name all over it.

It's when his hand takes over for mine that the pleasure amplifies to a level I never thought imaginable. Guiding my middle finger, he pushes inside me until both of our palms are rubbing over my clit as, together, we finger fuck my pussy. It's erotic in a way I didn't think was possible. I should probably be ashamed or some shit, but not even close. I'm practically breathless with the need to come.

"Can't wait much longer, V. If you're having second thoughts, now's the time to push me away." I almost laugh at the almost-gentlemanly undertones of his words but we both know I'm not going to push him away.

I slam my lips to his, slipping my tongue into his mouth and taking what I need

But when I release my grip on his hair and slide my hand down his chest and around his hip to push down his shorts, I feel the true girth of his cock as it's freed from its confines.

Fucking hell, I've landed myself the mother of all monster dicks.

"If you don't fuck me right now, East, I'm going to have to finish the job myself."

With a cocky grin I'm sure is responsible for many a spontaneous orgasm, East aligns the head of his dick at my entrance and whispers over my swollen lips, "I'm not going to lie, this might hurt."

A shiver of anticipation runs down my spine at his words, but I don't have time to respond because he pushes into me and I suck in a deep breath at the sweet sting.

East swallows every one of my cries, kisses the pain away as he pushes in and out, each time a little deeper.

"You feel so good, beautiful. So fucking good, like I always knew you would."

I almost laugh at his unintended rhyme but then the head of his cock is right there. Right fucking there and my entire body is shaking from the teasing of my g-spot.

"God, you're shaking. Are you cold?"

This time, I do laugh. A throaty, sexy sound I didn't know I had in me.

"If I were any hotter, I'd set this pool on fire."

He smirks at my words, and it's as if my words light something inside of him. He pushes me harder against the side of the pool, water splashing all around us with every thrust of his hips, East plants his big hands on each of my ass cheeks and squeezes hard enough to earn him a squeak from me.

The noise is like the strike of a match igniting the fuse within him and he fucks me like I'm all he'll ever need. Building my orgasm from a red-hot ember to a roaring flame of destruction.

His lips never leave me. He kisses me like he needs me to survive.

"Fuck, V," he groans into the crook of my neck before kissing me there too, biting on the lobe of my ear, pulling noises from me I've never made before.

He slows his rhythm, like he wants this to last forever.

"You're so fucking beautiful," he whispers against my lips before he loses control again, slamming his dick to the hilt and fucking me like he owns me while still worshiping me like I'm his queen.

"I'm close," I stutter, my nails digging into the flesh of his back. He sinks his teeth into the flesh of my collar bone in response, and just as he buries himself as deep as he can go, I lose every single piece of my control.

My nails dig further into his skin, I can feel it break under their violence, but it doesn't slow him down. He slams into me as I crest higher until a feral sound rips from him and he stills inside of me. Dropping his forehead onto my shoulder, I can feel the heat of his panting on my neck as we slowly come back down to earth.

"That was…" I trail off, and he laughs softly as he sorts himself out and pulls me back into his arms.

"It was." He shifts so he can carry me with an arm under my knees and walks us out of the pool. He puts me on my feet and wraps a towel around me before putting one around his own shoulders. "We should probably head inside, get you warmed up."

I nod, my teeth chattering from the cold air, and head inside with him close behind me. I put my finger to my lips when we enter the house—aware that it's probably a bit late to be worried about Smithy hearing—and re-arm the alarm before leading him upstairs. "Shower?"

"Sounds good." He smiles, almost bashfully. There is no way that he feels bashful after fucking me like that. Just no.

I take his hand and lead him into my bathroom, stripping out of my bikini, his eyes heating before he looks up to the ceiling. "You really are testing my self-restraint tonight, aren't you?"

I smirk at him, and he glances down in time to see as I drop my panties to the ground. "No one said you had to be restrained."

---

This week has been such a rollercoaster already and I didn't think it could get any more up and down. Boy was I wrong.

After Maverick kissing me on the steps on Monday and his general attention all week, the gossip has run riot like a freaking wildfire. So when Indi and I sit down for lunch on Thursday and everyone is staring at us, I think nothing of it.

"So, we're still on for tomorrow night, right? I so need some girl time, minus all of the homework." She grins at me before taking a bite of her chicken and avocado burger.

"Tomorrow night? What's tomorrow night?" Maverick asks as he slides into the chair beside her.

I look over at him, look him dead in the eyes, and say, "Nope. You don't sit here. Go back to your own table."

As I finish speaking, Finley and Lincoln drop into the seats on either side of me. "No, this isn't happening. Why are you three sitting here?"

Indi smirks at me from across the table and mouths 'kitty cat' at me, making me laugh, totally ruining my hard-ass façade that I need against the three of them.

"Didn't you hear, princess? You and I are hot tamales out here. We are officially the new 'it' couple, and your bitch of a cousin is spitting mad about it." Mav winks at me and I roll my eyes.

I look around at the others and no one else is smiling. "You're not kidding are you?"

He leans forward and steals a fry from my plate, grinning wide. "Why would I kid? They're not wrong are they? You and me baby, we're hot shit."

Indi giggles quietly as he wags his brows at me. "So, you two are cool with this?" she asks, her gaze bouncing between Lincoln and Finley before taking another bite of her burger. I grab my slice of pizza and take a mouthful because I am so done with this conversation already.

"Who cares what the sheep think?" Lincoln answers dryly. Except it's not really an answer at all. Unsurprisingly, Finley doesn't say a word, but I can feel the heat of his gaze on the side of my head, while I try to pretend that this isn't my life.

Sometimes I really miss tour life.

This is so… high school.

Sighing, I resign myself to the fact that this is, indeed, happening and say fuck it. Enough people saw Mav kiss me on Monday, there have been enough rumors flying around that I'm fucking them all—technically, that's just Mav as far as these guys know, too—so fuck it.

"Back to what we were saying earlier," I say to Indi, ignoring the other three despite the fact that Mav keeps stealing my fries, "Yes, I am so down for tomorrow night."

"What's tomorrow night?" Lincoln asks, and Indi smirks at him.

"Penis free, that's what it is."

I clamp my lips together trying not to smile. It's fun watching her slowly blossom into the badass I know she is deep down.

"I asked the same question, and got about the same response," Mav says with a shrug. "So if tomorrow night is penis free, then what are you doing Saturday?"

"Washing my hair," I deadpan, and Finley snickers beside me.

"You were asking for that one, man." He leans over and kisses my cheek before whispering in my ear. "Save Saturday night for us?"

A shiver runs down my spine and goosebumps erupt on my arms at his warm breath on my skin. I turn to face him and smile a little, then nod before leaning in and kissing him. If everyone's going to call me a whore, I have zero reason to try to hide whatever it is that's going on between us all. He tangles a hand in my hair, taking over the kiss, and I forget where we are as he burns through me.

"God damn," Indi says as I pull back, and she fans herself. "I think I need a smoke after that, and I don't even smoke."

Finley rewards her with a rare grin while I try to calm myself. The eyes in the room are all fixated on our table, but my fucks have officially disappeared.

I turn to Lincoln who raises an eyebrow at me, almost in challenge, and it riles me. But considering he has barely touched me since that night in the pool house, outside of rescuing me from Raleigh, I'm not about to push him. If he doesn't want to be anything but friends, I'm going to respect that.

The bell rings, ending my stare off with him, so I stand and look over to Indi, who looks like she's about to combust with laughter. "Walk with me to class?"

She stands, moving to grab her tray, but Finley puts his hand on it, along with mine. "I got it."

Indi looks up at me and shrugs. "I guess chivalry isn't completely dead."

Finley just looks at her and shakes his head. "Sweetheart, if you think that's chivalrous, you've been hanging with the wrong people."

# CHAPTER FIFTEEN

## OCTAVIA

I drop onto the couch in the theater room with a giant bowl of popcorn, putting it between Indi and me as she snuggles under the blankets we piled in here earlier. "Have I mentioned how much I love this room?"

"Once or twice," I say with a grin, and she sticks her tongue out at me.

Taking a handful of popcorn, she turns to me as I cross my legs on the giant couch. "So… boys… stop holding out on me and spill the goddamn tea."

I can't help but laugh at her as she flails her hands around.

"Okay. Tea… so uhm. I don't even know where to start."

"Maybe start with why Mav thought it was okay to kiss you at school on Monday and how you batted it back by making out with Finley yesterday?" Her grin widens as a blush spreads across my chest. "Also, zero judgement from the girl with three boyfriends, so tell me all the things."

And so I do. All about Lincoln staying pretty icy toward me despite Halloween, and Christmas. I tell her all about Christmas and the gifts from the guys, about Mav saving me after my first run-in with Raleigh, making out with Finn in here, and finally about East in the pool.

By the time I'm done catching her up her jaw is practically on the floor, so I flick a piece of popcorn at her.

"Dude, was it good? East totally looks like he can show a girl a good time."

I clamp my lips together, but a smile still pulls at the edges. "I mean, you could totally say that."

"God damn." She fans her face dramatically, making me laugh. "And you just know that Finley is going to be a scorcher too. All that tall and broody has to go somewhere."

"You are a little bananas. You know that, right?"

She grins at me and nods. "Oh I do, but Finley reminds me a lot of Dylan. He's quiet, but man that man's tongue is like nothing I've ever known. I mean, his dick is bomb, but his tongue…" She raises her hands like she's praising and I can't help but laugh, shaking my head at her.

"You still haven't told me much about them. They're Kings, right?"

She nods. "Yep… and yours are Knights."

"You know about the Knights?"

She bites down on her lip and nods. "Kind of. I mean, not really. Ellis told me some stuff. I know that they exist, that your guys are Knights. That most Knights are bad news."

I try to laugh, but it falls flat. "I don't know tons yet either, but yeah. That sums it up from what I've learnt. So you're with the Kings, and they're kinda like enemies with my guys? How did we manage that?"

She laughs before her smile drops a little again. "Yeah, I mean, Diego, their older brother, started the Kings. I don't know why, but it fucking terrifies me that they're so intertwined. If he goes to jail… well, let's not think about it. I don't know much about the thing between them and the Knights, but whatever it is, it's not good. Do you think Lincoln or any of them will tell you what's going on with it?"

I bark out a laugh, and then apologize. "Sorry, but Lincoln tells me jack squat. Though I have a plan to fix that, because I need some answers. They still haven't told me shit about my stalker either."

Her eyes go wide, and I realize I've not let her in on that little nugget yet either.

"Stalker?!" she squawks, "What fucking stalker?"

I tell her everything, the photos, the letters, that the guys have confirmed that it's not anything to do with the Knights. About the knife and the blood. Everything I hadn't realized I'd been keeping from her.

"Holy fucking shit, V. You need like a bodyguard or something. Can't Mac spare someone? Panda or one of the guys that you trust to keep you safe."

I frown, realizing I left out one last piece of that puzzle for her. "Panda is a Knight."

"*What the actual fuck?*"

"I know," I say with a sad shrug. "Nothing quite like finding out everyone's been lying to you your entire life."

"Girl, I swear now, I will never lie to you. Ride or die." She puts her pinky out to me and I wrap mine with it. It might be a little childish, but it makes me feel better regardless. "Just promise me that no matter what goes on with the guys, enemies, frenemies, or whatever they become, it doesn't fuck with us."

"I swear it. They'll just have to suck it up and deal. Ride or die."

She practically leaps across the couch and hugs me, and I try not to get all emotional. I've never had a bestie before, but I think she might be the best bestie in existence.

"So," I say, wagging my brows at her once she's seated back on the couch. "Tell me about *your* boys."

She blushes furiously and stuffs a handful of popcorn in her mouth. "They're boys," she says around it, and I laugh. "Movie time, right? Yeah, totally. You don't want to hear about the three-ways, and the er… other stuff, right?"

"Three-ways. As if you're holding out on me like that." I feign outrage and she looks at me with those big green eyes of hers, all puppyish, and I let it go. If she's not ready to share the details, I'm chill.

"I'll tell you one thing though," she says as she grabs the remote, "That twin intuition thing… definitely a thing. Oh boy, is it a thing."

"Any crossing of swords?" I ask, wagging my brows, and she blushes furiously again.

"Uhmmmm, I plead the fifth?"

"Yuh-huh." I grin. "One day you'll tell me, and then we'll both be living our best multi-peen lives."

"You think your thing with the guys could be serious?"

I shrug, and take another bite of the popcorn. "Not really. I think it's just some fun and I have no issue with that. East… well, he seems serious, but he's also chill with sharing. So for now, it is what it is."

"Do you *want* it to be serious?"

"I have no idea. These last six months have been a little insane. For now, I'm just going to enjoy myself and see where it goes. Are you and your guys serious?"

She nods. "As a heart attack. I was a little dubious at first, especially after they ended it over summer, but they seem to be all-in this time. I'm not sure what that means for any of us. Especially with them being Kings, with college, all of it, but that is a future me problem. For now, I'm going to enjoy being entirely loved up, and try not to stress about what the next few months hold."

I grab my can of soda and raise it. "Amen to that."

---

"You running with me today?" I ask Indi as I exit the bathroom and she groans, flopping back down onto my bed.

"Fuck you and your runs. What time is it even? The sun isn't even up." She flips me the bird and I bark out a laugh.

"Okay, drama. It's like six twenty-five, don't pretend you're not usually up at this time."

"Yeah, when I have school. It's a Saturday; this shit should be illegal."

I chuckle softly at her, drama and all, I wouldn't have her any other way. "Well, you can stay here and sleep, Smithy will fix you some breakfast if you want, but I have this weird anxious energy I need to burn off."

She flips over and sits up. "Are you okay?"

"I think so." I shrug. "Just feeling antsy. Running usually helps when it gets to be too much."

"You go run. I can chill with my man Smithy until you get back, then we can do breakfast before I head out. You're with the guys tonight right?"

"Finley asked me to keep tonight free for them, so I'm assuming so. I haven't really spoken to them much since then beyond Maverick hanging off me like a goddamn accessory on Friday."

She grins at me. "Yeah, I did notice that."

"It was hard to miss." I roll my eyes and drop down onto the bed with her before checking the time on my phone. Lincoln has been meeting me at the gate at six thirty to run, so I need to haul ass if I'm going to stretch out before I go. Asshole has been outpacing me ever since he started running with me two weeks ago, and I'm determined to sort my shit out so that I can put a stop to it. "I better go. Lincoln will be waiting."

"Wait! Lincoln runs with you? All that fine iceman man meat out there sweating with you, why on earth would you invite me to that? And now I'm considering my objections to running." She wags her eyebrows at me, so I reach back and swat her with my pillow.

"Iceman is about right. Egotistical asshole who is way too in shape is another apt description. If you're coming, you better haul ass, cause he's a stickler about being on time."

She leaps from the bed and runs into my closet. We're not super close in size, but fit wear is pretty universal. "Bottom shelf on the left," I tell her and less than two minutes later, she appears in my navy blue leggings and sports bra.

"Let's do this."

I shake my head because she's never this enthused about running. "We usually do about eight miles."

Her smile drops and I burst out laughing. "Eight fucking miles? Masochists, the pair of you. Come on, let's go before I change my mind. Maybe if we both pepper him with questions, he'll actually give us some answers."

"Don't bet on it." I grab my spare arm strap and hand it over to her. She slips it on, before rummaging through her bag and grabbing her headphones before we head downstairs. I call out a "good morning" to Smithy before we head outside.

We find Lincoln already waiting for us at the gate. He quirks a brow at Indi but doesn't say a word. Just taps his phone and motions for us to run ahead of him, same as he always does.

I know a lot of people might consider it strange that I trust him to have my six after everything that happened when I came back here, but I'm trying to take him at his word. He might not be sorry, but he was trying to protect me. In his own very fucked-up way.

I can't say if I was put in the same situation that I'd have done any different. I might have gone about it a little differently, but if my dad had been in danger… I can't say how far I would've gone to keep him safe.

I take off at a run, keeping my pace down for Indi because I know running isn't exactly her favorite pastime. We run the usual route, pausing at the pier for a water break like normal.

"You two are fucking insane. Are we done?" Indi pants and I smile, shaking my head.

"Do you want to tell her we're only halfway?" I say to Lincoln, the corners of his lips tugging up, he doesn't say a word as she flops down to the ground.

"Half way? Fuck you both all the way off. Stick a fork in me cause I am done." She pants on the ground, and I can't help but laugh at her.

"Come on, you've totally got this. I'll even make Lincoln run up front so you have incentive to chase," I tease and she flips me the bird. Lincoln just raises his brows at me before looking back down at his phone. "I'll have Smithy make chicken and waffles when we get back…"

"Now *that* is the best kind of bribe," she says, heaving herself from the ground, "Let's do this!"

I look over at Lincoln who nods, wordlessly, and puts his headphones back in. "Are you okay?"

"Just stuff with my dad. I'm good." In those few words, he gives me more insight into him than he's given since I got back. So I run the risk of stepping up to him and wrapping my arms around him. He stiffens under my touch, but I squeeze him anyway before stepping back. He looks at me like I've lost my mind, but his eyes just look sad, and I wonder when the last time someone actually hugged him was.

"You're welcome to join us for breakfast if you want," I offer, but he shakes his head.

"I've got an errand to run this morning, but if Smithy wants to make lasagne tonight, I'm not going to say no."

I grin at him, thankful that he is a little bit human after all. "I'm sure he can do that."

He looks at his watch and puts his AirPods back in. "Come on, ladies. We're running behind."

I roll my eyes and turn back to Indi, who is looking down at her phone, giving us a minute. "Come on, we don't want to make him late."

"Awesome. Let's do this. Come on chicken and waffles."

I laugh as I put in my AirPods, and take off on the way home, trying to slow down a little for Indi, but the antsy feeling keeps ramping up because I'm not pushing myself.

I look back at Lincoln, silently questioning if he'll stay with her, and he nods as if he knows exactly what it is I need. So I pick up my pace until my muscles and lungs burn in that beautiful way they do, and the chaos and noise inside of me quiets a little.

Once the feeling starts to subside, I slow back down a little. It doesn't take long for the two of them to catch up and we stick together until we reach the gates.

Lincoln waves as he heads toward his own gates. "I'll see you tonight."

"I'll be here." I smile and open my mailbox before tapping in the code to the gate. I pull out the handful of letters and magazines in there, and as I do, a black envelope falls to the ground at my feet.

Lincoln sees it and grabs it before I do. The red seal is there, like always.

"What does it say?"

He opens it and scans it, a frown wrinkling his forehead. "It's the new date for the gala, along with a new venue." He turns the card and shows it to me, my stomach sinking.

"Gala? What gala?" Indi asks as she sucks in lungfuls of air beside me.

"The Knights," I tell her, and Lincoln looks at her questioningly.

His eyes turn stormy as his gaze bounces between us before he focuses back on her. "Do not say a word to anyone about anything you know."

I take the invitation from his hand, frustrated. "She's not going to say a thing. Don't be such an ass."

"It's for her own safety as much as yours," he counters and I roll my eyes.

She puts her hands up in the air, as if in surrender. "I'm not going to do anything to jeopardize V, my guys, or you and yours. You can chill."

He nods once before heading inside his own gates and storming up the drive.

"Sorry," I say to her on his behalf. "He's such an ass sometimes."

"He is, but I genuinely think he loves you and is just scared shitless. Sometimes you can see it in his eyes. The scared little boy who has already lost too much."

I gaze at his back as he opens his front door and ponder her words.

Why on earth would he think he would lose me when I'm not his to start with?

---

I head downstairs in my leggings and sweater, my big fluffy socks like a hug for my feet. I have no idea what the plans are for tonight, but comfortable and warm are on my to-do list. The smell of the lasagne from the kitchen makes my stomach grumble as I hit the bottom step.

Smithy sings in the kitchen as he cooks and I can't stop the smile that breaks out over my face. "Someone seems extra happy tonight."

He jumps when he hears me and blushes a little at getting caught. "Miss Octavia. Sometimes you are quieter than a mouse."

"I didn't mean to scare you. You should've gone into music," I wink at him with a smile as I slip onto a stool at the counter.

"Oh no, Miss Octavia. My life suits me perfectly well, thank you." He waves me off and turns his attention back to the stove as he builds the layers of the pasta goodness. "Now then, this is done, all you will need to do is heat it when you and your friends are ready to eat. I prepped some cheesy garlic French bread to go with it, which is in the refrigerator. Can you promise not to destroy my kitchen when you do that? I've left written instructions on the refrigerator door for you."

I belt out a laugh. "No, but I can promise to let East or Finley do the cooking. Taking a well-deserved night off?"

He turns to face me, looking more than a little bashful, yet excited at the same time. "I, Miss Octavia, have a date."

"A date?" I raise my brows and fold my arms. "And who, kind sir, is the lucky participant of your date?"

"You wouldn't know them, I'm sure," he stutters, and I smile.

"Fine, keep your secrets, old man. But I hope you have a wonderful evening."

He shakes his fist at me in that hilariously endearing way. "I'll give you old man." I can't help but laugh at him and wave as he heads down to his room, I assume to prepare for his big night.

Who would've thought?

I check my phone and shoot off a message to Indi, just to tell her I love her, before heading into the living room and getting comfy on the couch. It's been full radio silence from all of the guys since my run with Lincoln earlier, so I have no idea what time they're planning on coming over or if they're even still planning to show up at all. But I'm not going to build my night around them.

My night is all synced up for some hot-ass Dylan O'Brien on my TV, because his new film dropped today and this girl here is *so* ready for it. Grabbing the blanket from the back of the couch, I lose myself in it, waving goodbye to Smithy when he leaves looking dapper as hell in his suit and wingtips, and fully lose track of time.

It's only when my stomach starts to rumble that I check my phone and realize it's nine.

Oops.

I bite the inside of my cheek, thinking about heating some of the lasagne that Smithy made earlier before remembering my promise to him that I wouldn't destroy his kitchen.

Still no word from the guys.

I head into the kitchen, chewing the inside of my cheek as I fret over breaking my promise, though I'm sure he'll be more furious if I just don't eat, so I turn the oven on and let it heat.

Snapping a picture of the lasagne, I create a group message with the four of them.

**Me:**

<image> I guess you guys miss out. More for me.

Passive aggressive? Hell yes. Do I care? Not even a little. I waited, got stood up essentially, so they can suck it. Here was me thinking that things were getting better, that we were moving forward, and now that stupid-ass nagging voice in the back of my head reappears, bitching about how this was all a ploy to lull me into a false sense of security. That I let them get too close after they were all—minus East—absolute fucking monsters to me. That I should've never let them in.

Once the oven reaches temperature, I pop the lasagne in and set a timer on my phone so I know when to put the garlic bread in.

I can't fuck it up if I stick to the times Smithy wrote down, right?

I put some music on, belting out the lyrics to *Burn It All Down* by PVRIS, realizing just how apt these lyrics are to my life sometimes. Burning it all down and walking away from the embers with just the few people and things I hold precious sounds like perfection.

Except… Could I really leave behind so much all over again?

The flames between me and the guys are there, flickering, and if I really looked inside my heart rather than ruling with my head, I know that I'm past everything. Except my brain is stuck on stubborn dumb bitch mode.

Problem is, she wants to have her cake and eat it too—personally the phrase never made much sense to me because who doesn't want to eat their cake—keeping them at arm's length *and* fucking around with them isn't going to work. Tonight being the perfect case in point. I try desperately not to be disappointed at the absolute lack of communication I've had from any of them. You'd think the least they could do is shoot me a text letting me know plans changed.

Though maybe it's a good thing, making me face exactly what it is going on inside of me when it comes to them. Introspection isn't something I've exactly made time for lately.

The timer on my phone pulls me from my thoughts and I pop the garlic bread in the oven, resetting the alarm so I don't burn everything to a crisp. The smell of the lasagne is enough to make my mouth water.

Instead of getting in my own head again, I grab my phone and do the only thing I can think of: Talk to someone with more sense than me.

**Me:**
Do you have ten minutes for me to ramble at you?

**Indi:**
Bitch, always. What's up?

Instead of texting back, I hit dial, and it doesn't even make it through the first ring before she answers. There's loud music, voices, and then a door closing, providing a sudden and impressive amount of silence. "What's wrong?"

I smile at her words. "Nothing is wrong. Well, not really. And did I mention today that I adore the freaking socks off of you?"

"Aww, I love you lots like gum drops too. Now what's wrong?" I can hear her smirk down the line as I lean back against the counter.

"Am I being a stick-up-the-ass, button-stuck-on-stupid bitch when it comes to the guys?"

She bursts out laughing, and I shake my head. Apparently she's not the only drama queen out here. "What, exactly, has you going down this particular path in your head?"

"Too much time to think and being stood up, probably."

"Those assholes stood you up? I swear to fucking Jesus, they make my job so hard sometimes." She pauses and confusion fills me as I wait for her to continue. "Back to your earlier statement. A little. Obviously I know what you've told me, and assuming that's everything, then yes, a little. I mean, Lincoln is the iceman, it's going to take him longer to thaw than the others, and it's not like they don't have some serious shit going on. But the others… they're trying—real hard—and as much as I love you, your walls are higher than *the* wall."

I let out a sigh. "See this is why I needed to speak to someone other than the voices in my head."

She laughs softly at me. "Hey, you've been through a lot. It's understandable that you'd be cautious, but the best things in life come with a risk. The greater the risk, the greater the reward right? So why not just try. Let them in the way you let me in. If you get your heart broken, I'll help you burn their worlds to ash."

"You're the best." I smile into the receiver. "I'm sorry for interrupting your night."

"You never have to apologize to me, V. Ride or die, remember? Anyway, this party sucks. The guys are too busy trying to find their asshole brother."

"Diego?"

“Yeah, he went on a bender last weekend, and nobody has seen or heard from him since. Chaos would be an understatement.” I can hear the worry in her voice, and my stomach tightens.

“If there’s anything I can do… anything you need…”

She sighs deeply and it makes me want to find Diego just to crack him in the nuts for making her worry so much. “Yeah, I know. I’ll call. But for now, it’s a waiting game. It’s not the first time he’s disappeared for a few weeks then reappeared as if nothing happened.”

“I hope for their sake, and yours, that’s all it is.” But there’s a niggle in the back of my mind that tells me something isn’t quite what it seems.

“Me too. I should head back before they think I’ve disappeared too.”

“Okay, I’ll talk to you later.” She says goodbye and ends the call just as the alarm on my phone goes off.

I rush around trying to get everything out of the oven before it burns, and I’m rewarded with the bubbling, gooey, cheesy pasta goodness. I drool a little, just watching it as it cools off a bit so I don’t basically eat lava.

Once I’ve served myself a plate and plopped down on the couch, I take stock of Indi’s words. Maybe I do have my walls too high and I really should just take the guys at face value. Forgive, even if I can’t forget yet. They’ve been upfront with me for the most part, so maybe it’s time I pulled up my big girl pants and did the same thing.

---

I wake up as sunlight filters through the windows, blinking against the harshness of it. I groan as I move, realizing I fell asleep on the couch. I’m too young to feel this achy from a single night of uncomfortable sleep. Fucking hell.

I stretch out, sounding like Velcro as I do. I run a hand through my hair, realizing it’s come out of the braid I put it in last night, before checking my phone.

**Smithy:**
Had car issues in the city. Getting a hotel for the night. I will be back in the morning.

**Me:**
Sorry, I fell asleep. Hope you’re okay!

I try not to be disappointed that the guys didn’t reach out.

I know Indi thinks I should drop my walls, but they’re making it really difficult. Just when I think I can trust them, that they won’t let me down… they do something like this and I wonder if they can’t do something so simple as communicate clearly, then how the fuck do we do the rest of this?

I let out a sigh, jumping when the house creaks. The house is quiet—too quiet—here on my own again.

I put my hair up in a messy bun and head into the kitchen, flicking on the coffee pot. The sound of the front door opening makes me pause, realizing I obviously didn't set the alarm last night after Smithy left.

Voices filter through and I realize who it is.

Hell no.

I lean against the counter with folded arms, an eyebrow raised as the four of them filter into the kitchen.

East at least looks a little sheepish as he comes to a stop in the archway. Maverick just grins at me while Lincoln heads toward the coffee pot like it's going to save his life, frowning when he realizes it's not ready, and Finley leans against the wall wordlessly.

"Hey, V," East says, rubbing the back of his neck.

"Hi." My voice clearly expresses just how unamused I am.

Maverick saunters toward me, smiling that cheeky as fuck grin of his at me. "Don't be like that, princess. We didn't mean to leave you hanging."

I blink at him. "You didn't mean to—"

"What he means," Lincoln says, ice dripping from his words, "is that something came up with the Knights and we didn't have time to speak to you."

I look up at East, wondering what his excuse is, since he's apparently not one of them.

"He was with us," Finley says as Maverick reaches me and puts his finger under my chin so I'm looking up at him.

"You're hot when you're mad, but just this once, please don't be mad?" What is it about them saying please that turns me into such a weak asshole? Maybe it's because I know they sure as hell don't say it to anyone else? Fuck knows. It's like he senses my weakness and kisses me right there in front of them all, again. His lips are soft as he tries to devour my anger with his kiss, stealing my breath right along with it. He smiles at me when he pulls back, like he knows I've already softened.

"So what was so important that not one of you could even send me a text?"

Mav grips my hips and lifts me onto the counter before standing between my legs. "I can think of far better things to do than talk about that."

It's then, when he's close to my eye level, that I notice the blood spatter on his neck. Just a fine dusting. I can't help but run my finger across it. "Do I want to know whose blood this is?"

He freezes and then grins again before walking out of the room. The slam of a door tells me he's gone to the downstairs bathroom.

My question hangs in the room until the front door opens and closes again. "Miss Octavia? Are you awake?"

Smithy's voice makes me smile, and I jump down from the counter. "I'm up. In the kitchen." He reaches the room before I'm even finished speaking.

"I am so sorry I was gone, Miss Octavia. Something to do with the spark plugs apparently. But we're all sorted now. Good morning to you all. Let me just get changed and I'll get breakfast started," he says in a flurry as he rushes through the room, dropping the mail on the counter.

"You really don't have to—" He cuts me off with a glare, and I close my mouth. Apparently he's dealing with breakfast. "I guess you guys better get comfortable."

I take a seat at the counter, picking up the stack of envelopes since none of them are explaining last night to me and, apparently, I'm just supposed to be okay with that.

Sucking in a deep breath, I remind myself of Indi's words and make a conscious effort to drop my walls. They've already made it very clear that they think they're protecting me from this 'big bad' of theirs, so if the secrets make them feel better, they can have them.

Flicking through the letters, dismissing most of them as bills or junk, I notice a handwritten one to me.

I roll my eyes, whoever this is really needs to be more original.

Much as I don't want to see what the latest terror my stalker wants to inflict on me is, I tear it open and pull out the note.

*They think they can keep you safe.*
*They're wrong.*
*No one can keep you safe but me.*

I look down at the hair taped to the bottom and my stomach churns.

Is that my hair?

"Octavia, what's wrong?" Lincoln's voice pulls me from the horror settling itself into the pit of my stomach and threatening to lose last night's lasagne. I look up at him and can't know what he sees on my face, but he stands and comes around the counter to my side, gently taking the letter from me.

Panic and disgust war for a place in my stomach as I pull my hair from its ponytail. My trembling fingers slide through the strands, searching blindly for the piece of me that has been taken until I find it. I stare at the square chunk missing from the ends of my extensions for several seconds, numb and overwhelmed, before I launch myself from the chair and run for the bathroom, shoving past Maverick as he leaves it.

I only just reach the bowl when the contents of my stomach make an appearance. I retch until tears stream down my face.

Why is this my fucking life?

Once I've thrown up everything but my memories, I take a minute to compose myself, brushing my teeth, putting my hair back up in a bun, and splashing some water on my face before heading back out to the kitchen. I find the four of them staring down at the counter. Once I get closer I see the pictures of me from last night, asleep on the couch.

I feel violated in a way that makes my skin feel like it's on fire.

"Why is someone doing this to me?" My voice comes out small, croaky and weak. I hate how weak I sound, but I'm not sure how much more of this I can take before I break. Finley doesn't say a word before heading past me toward the security room.

East moves to my side, and I let him usher me back into my seat. "I don't know, but it's obvious whoever it is knew you were alone last night. Did anyone know?"

I shake my head. "Just you guys, and Indi. Though no one knew Smithy was gone. Hell I didn't know until I woke up."

"He hacked the servers and left us a present." Finley steps back into the kitchen and sets a laptop on the counter, hitting a button before spinning it around so the rest of us can see the screen.

The front door cracks open and a figure enters, clad in black from the mask over his face to the boots on his feet, and stares up at the camera for a moment. Then the bastard cracks a smile and waves, like he knows the guys would be here watching with me. "He's taunting us," I whisper, my voice so soft I don't know if anyone else hears me. The camera shifts from the entryway to the living room, and I gasp as the figure drops into a crouch in front of my sleeping body. The hair at the back of my neck stands on end and a shiver runs down my spine as I watch him run a hand down my cheek, brushing hair from my face before snapping the photo that now sits on my countertop, mostly forgotten.

"I think I'm going to be sick again." They all look at me, and Finley pauses the video. "I can stop it. You don't have to watch."

"No, I have to. I need to know. I'm tired of being in the dark with everything."

I jump as the door behind me opens and Smithy walks into the kitchen. "Is everything okay?" His gaze bounces around us all until it lands on the screen. "What is going on?"

He looks up at East, his eyes steely. "Is this the trouble you told me about? I thought it was being handled." His voice is harsh, and he sounds more pissed off than I've ever heard him.

"You knew?" I ask before looking to East. "You told him?"

"Of course I knew. I'm your guardian. I can't keep you safe if I don't know." He looks at me like a disapproving father, and I look down at my hands in my lap. "Now then, I thought you boys told me this was handled. Obviously, that is not the case."

"We've got someone looking into it. A PI," East says, the others remaining suspiciously silent on the topic. Lincoln rarely lets someone else speak for him, so I glance up at him and find all of his attention on me.

East ushers Smithy into the other room, I assume to walk him through whatever they've already done and calm him down a little, leaving me with the others.

"You can't be left alone," Finley says so matter-of-factly that if I didn't know his voice, I'd think it was Lincoln that had spoken.

"I'm rarely alone. Lincoln already hammered that one home. Last night was a blip," I counter, because I really don't feel like having a bodyguard—let alone an entire squad of them. "A blip, I might add, that is entirely *your* fault. I wasn't *supposed* to be alone, remember?"

It was a low blow but, judging by the looks on their faces, it struck home.

*Good. Fuckers.*

"We can take shifts crashing here. One night each, on rotation," Maverick offers, and I roll my eyes.

"Or not."

"It's not a bad idea. That way one of us is here at all times. To protect you *and* Smithy, should it be needed," Lincoln says as East re-enters the room.

"Is this just a ploy so that you can get back in my bed?" I ask, my arms folded and an eyebrow raised. I'm more than a little shaken about all of this, so my defense mechanisms are kicking into place and deflection has always been my go-to. From the looks on their faces, it worked.

Finn's gaze bounces between us and he opens his mouth to speak but Mav cuts him off. "I'm sorry, what the fuck did you just say?"

"Is that seriously what you guys are focusing on right now?" East roars, and the room stills. I guess he doesn't lose his shit often, but he looks mad enough to burn the world down right now. "Some fucking psychopath got into her house and took some of her hair, and you're focused on who has been sleeping in her fucking bed? Someone give me some goddamn strength to stop me from strangling the pair of you."

"You could try," Mav huffs, the challenge in his eyes is real.

"How about we dial this back a bit, gentlemen?" Smithy soothes as he enters the room, "Calmer heads make for better strategists. Let me sort breakfast, then we'll work out a plan to keep Miss Octavia as safe as we can. *With* her input. This is not the fifties."

I swear I could kiss that man. The others don't look exactly impressed, but they nod regardless and Smithy heads to the stove.

One argument down, Lord knows how many more to go. Maybe one of these pointless dick swinging contests will actually help us discover who this stalker is and my life can have some semblance of normal back.

I laugh out loud at myself.

Normalcy feels more like a fantasy with each passing day.

# CHAPTER SIXTEEN

## LINCOLN

Octavia Royal is going to be the death of me. There isn't a length I wouldn't go to, no trauma I wouldn't endure, no bullet I wouldn't take if it meant she got to come out the other side happy and healthy. Laying down my life to ensure she has hers isn't something I take issue with, because I'd gladly give her everything.

But this stalker of hers might be my kryptonite.

No one knows who he is. He leaves no DNA, no fingerprints. Not a fucking trace.

Finn can't even trace his hacker coding.

I don't know that I can survive this crushing sense of helplessness that has settled over the four of us.

At the very least, I'm going to need new teeth from all of the grinding they've been put through the last few months.

I slam my fist into the punching bag again and again until my arms feel like jelly.

This morning went about as well as Pompeii. Except Octavia lands more direct hits than Vesuvius did. I get that she doesn't want us with her all the time. After everything she's gone through, I can't blame her. But I'll be goddamned if I won't do everything in my power to keep this sick fuck, and the Knights, away from her.

I've loved the girl since the day I laid eyes on her and it almost fucking killed me when she left us. I cannot, *will not*, lose her again. Even if that means I keep my distance and give all of my focus to keeping her safe instead of keeping her happy. I've watched the others make their way back into her good graces. Let *them* worry about her happiness.

They can play Happy Homemaker if that's what they want. I'll do what I have to do to keep her alive and free.

Hopefully doing what I have to do involves finding this stalker and putting a fist through his chest.

Mother.

Fucker.

"If you hit that thing any harder it's going to split." I swing at the bag once more before turning to find Finley sitting on the stairs that lead down to my basement. I flip him the bird and grab my bottle of water. Sucking down the cold liquid like it might fix all my fucking problems. "Still pissed you haven't heard from Lucas?"

I glare at him. "No, of course not. I'm just chilling, kicking back. Can't you tell?"

He lets out a rare laugh and stands while I undo the wraps on my hands. "Have you talked to V?"

"No, why?"

He shrugs before leaning back against the wall. "You're the only one not trying with her. I know what you said, about not wanting to get close to her, but I think you're doing more harm than good."

"What the fuck does that mean?"

He rolls his eyes as I drop down onto the bench. "It means that you were apparently sleeping in her bed, you're looking into the stalker, trying to protect her from the Knights, yet you ice her out like you do everyone else. It's got to be confusing as fuck for her."

"She's a big girl." I shrug and head up the stairs. "Coming?"

He follows behind silently, but his words weigh on me. Octavia has enough on her plate, especially after this morning. She doesn't need me wading in and further complicating everything for her. It's better for everyone if I keep her at arm's length. *She's* better off without me getting too close.

I head straight for the kitchen and find East making lunch. "Sandwich?" He holds a plate out to me but I shake my head, so he offers it to Finn. After breakfast from Smithy, I've eaten plenty, and my stomach hasn't stopped churning over what could have happened to her. All because the Knights kept us busy chasing our fucking tails on their little errand.

I clench my fists at the thought.

We should've known it was a bullshit errand, but it's basically impossible to say no to them. They have all of us clutched in their death grip. Except for East, but even he happened to be with us, which meant he had to play by the rules too.

"Should we tell her about Diego?" Finley asks as he sits at the table. "Indi's probably already told her he's missing and you know as well as I do that she'll try to help."

I shake my head. "For now, Diego is safe. If she starts sniffing around, then we'll tell her what's absolutely necessary to keep her from getting any more involved. For now, the Donovans probably think he's just disappeared on one of his benders. I say we let them continue to think that. If we can't get him out safely, and we need more hands, then we speak to Ryker. If we can keep Octavia out of it, we do so at all costs."

He nods, taking a bite out of the sandwich East handed him just as East takes a seat.

"Where is Maverick?"

East snorts before answering. "He volunteered to stay with Octavia. You missed that part after storming out, all holier-than-thou earlier."

"I was not holier-than-thou," I snarl. "We were done talking, so I left."

"Keep telling yourself that, bro." I glare at my brother before closing my eyes and taking a deep breath. Snapping at everyone isn't going to make me feel better.

Making some heads roll might. Especially if one of them belongs to whoever this stalker is.

"Hey, don't shoot the messenger." East holds his hands up in surrender. "You're the one who said you were done and stormed out. Just because you weren't the one calling the shots for a change, no need to get your panties in a bunch."

I try to smile at his teasing, but there's a part of me that very much needs that control he's ribbing me about. I zen out for a second, reminding myself that I might not be able to control my emotions, but I can control how I respond to them.

"Officially unbunched," I say through clenched teeth. "What else did I miss?"

"Not much," East offers while Finn finishes his food. "Just running through the basics of what we'd talked about before. Smithy confirmed he'd speak to his FBI friends to see if someone can take an official look into the stalker thing."

"His buddy is a Knight. I thought we wanted to keep them out of this."

"We do." Finn shrugs. "But there's only so much we can do alone. Since this is Smithy reaching out, it's not an official request, just a friendly one. It's as limited as we're going to get, especially if we want more eyes on her. She mentioned your morning runs too. You didn't mention you'd been running with her."

I shrug at them, not caring for the accusation in his eyes. "It's just a morning run. I go anyway and this way she's not out there alone."

"Are you sure that's all it is?" East asks, cutting his eyes to me.

"What else would it be?" I ask him, an eyebrow quirked.

He laughs, shaking his head. "You could've asked any one of us to go with her instead."

"Not all of us are just looking to get our dicks wet."

"Fuck you. You know it's more than that," he says, clenching the butter knife in his hand. Usually I'd laugh at the absurdity of the idea of him hurting me, but everything has been twisted since Octavia returned. I don't know how to get our dynamic back. Any of it.

"You run with her if you want. Why the fuck should I care?" I shrug and pull my phone from my pocket.

Two missed calls from Harrison. Fun.

"Of course it is," is all I can muster in response before I put my phone back in my pocket. "I'll catch you guys later. I need to shower and apparently Harrison wants my attention."

"You should talk to V," Finn says again before I leave the room, but I don't respond or react. He already knows it's futile. We've had the same conversation a dozen times since Halloween. If the rest of them want to chase what we know we can't keep, then I'm not going to stand in their way. But we vowed to keep her safe, and safe means out. Which means far the fuck away from here.

Far the fuck away from *us*.

---

I finish my shower and stalk across my bedroom, towel around my hips, as my phone rings on the nightstand. I pick it up, groaning when I see Harrison's name flashing on the screen.

"Harrison," is all I say when I answer, because I might not be able to beat my father in many ways, but I know it pisses him off when I call him by his given name. Petty maybe, but I'll take every jab I can get. Fuck knows he's gotten enough over the years—I have the scars to prove it. Mentally and physically.

"Lincoln, you know I hate it when you call me that. After I took care of your mess, too. You really should have more respect." I can hear his disapproval loud and clear for anyone to hear and roll my eyes. The days of me caring about his approval, or really much of anything, are long past.

I wait silently for him to speak again. He does the same. Except he called me, so if he expects me to buckle in this little game of his, he's got another thing coming. He taught me some shit too well and has no one but himself to blame.

He sighs as I drop down onto my bed, and I know he's going to give in. "It's time for you to repay that favor."

"What, exactly, does that mean?"

He huffs as if explaining himself to me is beneath him, especially when I owe him, but he obviously wants whatever it is enough to have been nice to this point. Well, nice for him. "It means you're coming to dinner with me tonight. We'll be dining with the LaFontaines. William and his daughter are prospects for the Knights and we want them in. William wants a suitor for his daughter, Georgia. Someone of high ranking to establish their footing."

I bark out a laugh. He has got to be fucking kidding me. "So you're my pimp now?"

"Lincoln, you owe the favor. I could think of worse ways for you to repay it." His threat sends a shiver down my spine. "I will send you the details. Do not be late."

"How long am I supposed to maintain this charade? Are you sure East wouldn't be a better fit?" I sigh and hate that I can practically hear his smile at my submission to his will. It rankles me to give in, but I refuse to regret what happened to Raleigh. Not after what he tried to do. If this is the price, so be it. But of the two sons he has, East is more likely to woo some girl. I am not exactly the warm and friendly one.

"East is not a Knight," he hisses back at me before ending the call.

Awesome.

My phone buzzes seconds later with the name of a restaurant in the big city. I guess I had better get my shit together, because that's a few hours' drive and the reservation is at eight.

What a fucking awesome way to spend my Sunday evening: being some hooker for my father. I'll play along, but if he thinks I'm going to lean into his charade he has another thing coming. I might not be getting close to Octavia, but I have zero interest in anyone but her. Some whimpering daddy's girl is the last thing I want.

And isn't *that* just a kick in the nuts? Here I am, presented with the perfect opportunity to distract myself with some piece of strange, and the only thing I can think about is Octavia fucking Royal. She's so deep in my head I can't even entertain the idea of spending an evening with another woman, but I can't bring myself to spend a night with *her* either.

Fucking ridiculous.

I pick up my phone and pull up my group thread with Maverick and Finn.

**Me:**
Tonight I pay the debt to Harrison. He wants me to woo some chick so her dad will join the Knights.

**Mav:**
Could be worse ways to spend your night.

**Finn:**
Guess it's a good thing you've kept your distance from V. Could you imagine trying to explain that?

**Me:**
I could, and it wouldn't be pretty. Not that any of this means anything.

**Mav:**
Yeah, and I'm sure she'd totally believe that. Where are you going?

**Me:**
Chateau Pierre in the city. Reservation at eight. Keep yourselves out of trouble for one night?

**Mav:**
Oh I intend to get into plenty of trouble. I'm still at V's. ;)

**Finn:**
Let us know if you need anything. And fuck you, Mav.

**Mav:**
Not you, buddy, but I'll sure let V ride me.

**Me:**
I'll catch you boys later. Keep your phones on.

I drop my phone onto the bed beside me and flop backward on the comforter. What a fucking shit show this is going to be.

A knock is the only warning I get before the door opens and East enters my room. "You know I was only fucking with you earlier, man. We can't let this shit come between us. Not now. We need to stay focused. Get V free, then get you free."

He drops onto the bed on the opposite side and I sit up, turning to face him. "I'm the one staying focused. It's the rest of you who got distracted."

"Don't give me that shit. You might not have waded into the pool with her like I did, pun not intended, but you're just as in with her as the rest of us." He scoffs and I storm over to my closet to start getting dressed for this nightmarish evening.

"You can say what you want, but I'm focused. As focused as it gets. Octavia isn't clouding my vision. We get her free and the rest comes after," I tell him, not wanting to break it to him that me getting free is probably only going to happen when I die. When we made the pact I was much younger and way more naive than I am now.

Now… the Knights have shown me my place and, while I might fight it, I'm accepting that once you're in, you're *in*.

The only reason I'm hopeful for Octavia is that, technically, she's not in yet. She hasn't been through initiation. She can still get free.

I just need to figure out how.

But first, I need to deal with Harrison. I dress in my gray suit pants and a black shirt. Pairing it with a pair of black shoes, and my Breitling Navitimer. My hair is already dry, so I just run my fingers through it. It sits naturally and I decide that this is officially as much effort as I'm willing to go through. Showing up should be more than enough to please Harrison.

At least I hope so.

"Where are you off to?" East asks when I exit the closet.

"Harrison called. He wants me to join him at dinner with the LaFontaines. The daughter apparently needs wooing. I tried to tell him that I'm not the guy for the job, but apparently that doesn't matter." His lips twist at my words as he frowns, and I shrug. Not like there's anything either of us can do about it.

"Fuck him and his requests. Why are you even bothering?"

I cut my gaze to him, trying not to glare. It's not his fault I'm pissed off. "Because he called in his favor. This is the payment for dealing with the Raleigh mess. So essentially, it's for Octavia."

He nods, because we both know that's all the reason I need to do much of anything. Even if she has no idea the lengths I'd go to for her.

I grab my phone and drop the boys a message to let them know I'm heading out, then pocket it along with my wallet. Snatching up my keys, I take a deep breath.

I can do this. I have to do this.

"Let me know if you need a bailout," East calls as I exit my room. I nod, but we both know I won't take it.

If doing this means eyes off Octavia for a little longer, then I'm going to suck it up and do what needs to be done.

No matter how much I hate it.

---

I pull up to the front of the restaurant wishing I was pretty much anywhere but here. Handing over my keys to the valet, I head inside and the maître d' welcomes me. He ushers me to a table in the back corner, the best table in the house, and brings me a glass of whiskey without even asking.

Upside of Harrison owning the place, I guess. I might only be eighteen, but considering no one here is going to jail for serving me, there are perks.

I'm glad that I'm the first one here. It gives me a chance to prepare myself. The whiskey helps, too. It'll be the only one I have. I'm going to need to keep my wits about me tonight, plus I'm driving home.

The drive here wasn't enough to loosen me up. Even driving like my life means nothing, the adrenaline hit was minimal. It says something when nearly dying is pretty much the only thing to get the blood pounding. I guess it's easy to see why so many Knights fall into the depravity of life. Trying to find a new way to feel alive when you become numb to the more standard highs life has to offer.

Sipping the whiskey, I watch the people in the room, mostly to pass the time.

At eight on the dot, Harrison walks in, his booming laugh overpowering the room as he strides toward me with, I'm assuming, William LaFontaine. The redhead that trails behind them must be Georgia. She's beautiful, in that model sort of way, but she looks like she lives with a stick up her ass. The resting bitch face she has on doesn't help. She kind of reminds me of Blair. All show, no substance. At least not until you dig real deep, and I'm just not willing to put in that sort of investment here.

I stand as they reach the table, lifting the corners of my lips just enough that my father stops glaring at me.

He turns his fake charming smile back to his guests, and I resist the urge to roll my eyes. "William, I'd like to introduce you to Lincoln. Lincoln, this is William LaFontaine and his daughter, Georgia."

I hold out my hand to William, who shakes it, before pulling back the chair beside me for Georgia. "Charmed, I'm sure."

She just glances up and down, taking in everything before her face transforms into a sultry smile. "I'm quite sure the pleasure is all mine." Her southern accent purrs in what I'm sure she thinks is a sexy way, it just does nothing to me. I smile tightly at her, waving for her to sit. Once she does, I push her chair in before taking my own seat once more.

"So, Lincoln. Tell me a little about yourself." She flutters her lashes, and all I want to do is laugh in her face. Does this shit really work for her usually?

Still, I keep my manners and give her my full attention, just as the favor calls for. I spend our time while we wait for the server to return to take our order ensuring she's entertained. She's older than me, but only just, and that doesn't seem to be an issue for her.

Apparently the allure of the Saint name is enough to keep her interested.

She's also way too fucking handsy for my liking, but I try to keep it as polite as I can in my rebuffing. Especially since Harrison has demanded I woo her.

Unfortunately for him, I'm not his fucking whore.

My dick, my choice.

"If you'll please excuse me a moment," I say to Georgia and escape to the bathroom for a minute of reprieve.

I splash my face with water and take a long look at myself in the mirror.

This isn't who I want to be.

Or where I want to be.

The door to the bathroom slams open and Harrison storms in, all of his charming façade long gone. "If you fuck this up, boy, I'll come for that pretty bitch of yours harder than I have been. And I won't stop until she's as broken as you are. Do you hear me? You make that girl believe you're in love with her. I don't care what the fuck it takes, what you have to do, fucking do it. If we lose the LaFontaines because of you, I'll make you regret ever looking at the Royal bitch."

His spit hits my cheek as he rants and I wipe it away with disgust, but I don't say one fucking word. He must really want the LaFontaines on board if he's willing to threaten me this hard. He's mostly refrained from acknowledging that Octavia Royal is my soft spot, but if he's poking at it that means he's desperate. I tuck that little bit of knowledge away for later and just nod at him. He spins on his heel and smooths back his hair before leaving the bathroom, back behind the mask of the man he wants everyone to think he is.

I'll work out exactly what is so special about the LaFontaines later, but for now, I need to be someone I'm not. I've always said I'll do anything for Octavia, so I guess we're about to see just how far I'll really go.

# CHAPTER SEVENTEEN

## OCTAVIA

I leave behind my Statistics class and head toward the cafeteria. This Monday morning can suck it. I am done. I know everyone complains about Mondays, but this is the Mondayest Monday in existence.

First, my car wouldn't start, then the garage gave me the news that despite all the repairs they've done on the Impala, it's, effectively, a dud, and I need a new car. Then we had a pop quiz in English, which I'm pretty sure I bombed, and Mr. Peters is back in Business after his sudden disappearance after Thanksgiving. Everyone was beginning to think he wasn't coming back, especially since no one knew why he was gone. I was starting to have hope that I wouldn't have to see his face ever again, but apparently I'm not that lucky this time.

Don't even get me started on Stats. I need some carbs, pronto. Preferably some chocolate too. It must nearly be that time of the month, because I've had an outbreak as well. I might not bleed thanks to my birth control, but that doesn't mean I don't suffer the rest of it. Bloating and cramps suck. Right along with the mood swings and bottomless pit of hunger that I become. I'm just feeling done.

I head into the cafeteria, spotting Indi already sitting at our table. I muster a smile and wave at her before stepping into the line for food. Mikayla shoulder checks me on her way out of the room, the rest of the bitch squad trailing behind her. Except for Blair. I close my eyes and take a deep breath, reminding myself that orange really isn't my color and those bitches are not worth going to jail for.

I grab an iced mocha from the machine and a tray. Piling it high and resisting the urge to do a dance when I grab the last chocolate torte, I pay and head over to where Indi is waiting for me.

I've just unloaded my tray onto the table and moved to sit when I feel the shove in my back.

Today is not the fucking day.

"Skank," Blair's voice snarks, and I see red. I grab the cleared tray and spin with it raised over my shoulder, ready to smack her with it, when someone catches my wrist.

I look up and find a smiling Maverick. "Woah there, killer," he says, stealing my tray, and turns to Blair. "What the fuck do you want?"

Usually I'd argue that I can fight my own goddamn battles, plus I could really use hitting something—the writhing rage inside of me is winning today. Instead, I drop into my seat and smile at Indi before taking a bite out of my chocolate torte.

"Bad day?" she asks with a sad smile, and I nod before tuning back into Maverick and Blair, who is stomping her foot in front of him. God, I'd laugh if I wasn't so pissed. Who the fuck even stomps their foot like that?

"You don't control me, Maverick Riley. I'll do what the hell I like. She ruined my family, so I'll see her ruined," Blair screeches and, while I have no idea what the fuck she's bitching about, I'm more than a little intrigued.

"How, exactly, did I ruin your family, Blair? 'Cause I'd really like to know why you hate me so much. All I did was come home and give your parents way too much of my fucking money." I sigh, leaning my head on my hand, looking far more relaxed than I feel.

"Don't act like a pretentious little bitch, like you don't know." She flicks her hair over her shoulder before narrowing her eyes at me. "I'll make you pay for it. Mark my words."

I roll my eyes, because apparently she's not going to tell me what it is I've supposedly done. "If you say so, Blair."

She squawks in frustration and spins around, stomping out of the cafeteria like a toddler having a tantrum.

"Well, it seems drama just follows you around, princess," Mav says as he drops onto the seat beside me. Leaning over and wrapping his arm around my waist, he pulls me into his lap. I squeak at the jolt of movement, but don't protest too much when he holds me tight.

Who would've thought the guy who held a knife to my throat would hug so well?

"She doesn't invite the drama, you know. You guys totally painted the target on her back. It just hasn't turned off yet," Indi says, and I can hear how pissed off she is, so I smile over at her while taking refuge in the hug.

He loosens his hold on me and pulls back so he can look at me properly. "People still haven't backed off?"

I shrug and Indi barks out a laugh. "Of course they haven't. You guys started something and you let it get out of control. Your hold is slipping. Blair keeps ignoring you all without consequence. No one knows if Raleigh was punished. People see them getting away with all of this with no retaliation from the kings of the school. So yeah… the order you guys once held is slipping."

As she finishes speaking, Lincoln and Finley arrive at the table. Lincoln looks exhausted. I thought as much earlier, but we didn't speak. He seemed to be in about as good a mood as I am. They sit without a word before he looks at me in Mav's arms then back at Indi. "What did you say?"

She repeats what she said, almost word for word, as I slip back into my own chair, despite Maverick's protests.

"We'll fix it," Lincoln says, before starting to eat. He spends the rest of lunch in a broody silence, but Maverick and Indi chat up a storm, more than filling the quiet created by the rest of us. I eat through my gargantuan lunch, feeling exactly zero shame at giving my body what it needs, and once some of the hangry slips away, I don't feel quite like I'm going to murder the entire student body anymore.

The bell rings and I groan, because how has time passed this quickly? The guys get up, Finn and Mav each kissing me on the cheek before they leave with Lincoln. I look over to Indi and smile apologetically. "Sorry, I totally spaced. Today is kicking my ass."

"You're good. Maverick was just telling me about his fight this weekend. We should totally go. It was fun last time, and if I remember correctly, you had a real good time after." She wags her brows at me and I bark out a laugh as we stand, clearing our food.

"Yes, yes I did. I'm totally down for that. You should invite your boys. Maybe we can make them all play nice." I grin and she nods.

"Yes, that sounds like a plan." She grabs her phone and shoots off a text before looping her arm through mine. "So long as they find Diego beforehand, it should be a good night."

"They still haven't heard from him?"

She shakes her head, biting down on her lip as we reach my locker. "No, not yet, which isn't exactly unusual, but it's starting to get more than a little tense with the Kings right now. Especially with the Knights sniffing around."

"Do you want me to ask the guys if they know anything?" Relief floods her face, and it hits me she's wanted to ask and just hasn't.

"Would that be okay? I don't like to ask—" I wave her off mid sentence as I swap over my shit in my locker.

"Don't even, it's fine. I'll ask. If I'd been thinking clearly, I already would've offered. Sorry, I'm such a shitty friend sometimes."

"You are not!" She swats at me until I smile at her. We head to her locker and then haul ass toward class. "I'll meet you outside French and we can head to Gym together?"

"Sounds good to me. Enjoy Spanish!"

"Oh yeah, it's a riot." She rolls her eyes and peels off down the hall while I laugh and head into French. I'm not sure what I did to deserve a friend like her, but I'll fight tooth and nail to keep her.

---

After a lousy start to the week, I'm finally smiling wide. It could be Maverick in his fight shorts, or the fact that I'm in the cage with him, but whatever it is, I'm not going to question it. When he offered to pick up my defense lessons so that I can actually defend myself if the occasion arises, I was not about to say no.

Especially not after seeing him fight already.

I had no idea that he owned a gym, but apparently he does. And when he kicked everyone out after someone wolf whistled at me, I just laughed.

Apparently Mav can share, just not with anyone who isn't inner-circle.

After one guy looked at my tits too long, I thought he was going to lose an eye with the vein that almost popped in Maverick's forehead.

So I'm here in my workout gear—which he groaned out his appreciation for already—in the octagon with him, pretending not to ogle his colorful chest and actually pay attention to what he's trying to teach me.

"Are you even listening to me, princess?" he asks, a smirk on his face as his gaze runs down my body.

"Not really. Focus is a little off," I say, poking my tongue out at him.

His eyes darken as his gaze narrows at me. "Do that again, and see where it gets you."

My heart rate spikes at the quiet words and I shake my head. This is not the place to be getting hot and bothered. I mean, it is, just not like that.

Instead, I bring up my hands like I've been shown a dozen times before, clenching my wrapped hands into fists, and prepare myself for what is likely going to be a shameful takedown if I don't focus and do what I need to.

"Okay, let's do this," he says, holding up the pads on his hands.

I work my way through the punching combinations he was showing me beforehand. They're simple enough, but my arms are burning by the time we go through them a couple of times. Apparently running isn't enough to keep me in tip top shape.

"Sweaty looks good on you, princess," he teases. I stick my tongue out at him again, a thrill running through me as his gaze darkens.

"I can think of better ways to get sweaty."

He closes his eyes and takes a deep breath. It's kind of fun being the one to push his buttons for a change.

"You shouldn't have let the others go. It'd be good to see if I can still fight off multiple offenders." My smile widens as his jaw tics. I shouldn't be getting off on this, but I definitely am.

The smile he gives me is nothing less than predatory, and a shiver runs down my spine in anticipation. "If you want more than my hands on you, princess, all you have to do is ask. I can get Finley here in a heartbeat."

"Promises, promises," I tease right back and lift my arms to protect my face again, except he shakes his head.

"Oh no, princess. I think you've graduated from the pads. I'm going to come at you, and you need to fight me off. I need to see just how skilled you are if I'm going to train you." His voice is a low purr, yet, it's impossible not to hear the threat in his tone. He lives for this game.

I tilt my head and jut out my chin in challenge. "Show me your worst."

His eyes flash and in a blink he's on me. He's got me in a lock from behind, his arm around my neck in a choke hold. I pull at his arm, but he's way stronger than I am. I claw at him, but that just seems to encourage him to hold tighter. "Come on, princess, I know you've got better skills than that," he whispers into my ear, and the threat to my oxygen intake almost makes me panic, which is ridiculous all things considered, but I never said I made any sense.

I need to focus, so I take as much of a breath as I can to try and clear my head, and think back to my training. Elbow, knee, balls.

So I thrust my elbow back into his gut.

As he hefts out a whoosh of breath I tilt the opposite direction, bringing my leg back and kicking at the back of his knee to topple him. Once he's on the ground, I hover my foot over his dick—rather than stomping it like I was taught—and smile down at him while I rub my neck.

"That was hot as fuck." He grins up at me and I laugh. Only he would think me taking him out would be hot. I offer him a hand up and he takes it, but instead of standing, he pulls me down and I fall on top of him. "I got you."

He rolls us over, caging me beneath him, and smiles again before capturing my lips with his. "You fighting me off really is hot as fuck," he says as he grinds his hard dick into me.

I can't help but smirk. "Apparently so, but aren't we supposed to be fighting, not fucking?"

He groans as I lift my hips and grind back against him. "You play dirty, princess, but yes, fighting not fucking."

I tangle my hands in the back of his hair and tug a little, bringing back that predatory smile. "Fucking does sound more fun though… except there's no one around. Can you keep it up when there's no risk of getting caught?"

Fire dances in his eyes at the challenge. "Oh, princess, you have no idea what I'm capable of when there's no one else around."

My heart thuds in my chest in anticipation of what's to come. This isn't how I saw my evening going, but I'm not exactly upset about it.

Just to fuck with him, I stretch my neck up to him so my lips are almost touching his and whisper loud enough for him hear me loud and clear.

"Oh yeah? Why don't you show me, tough guy?"

I barely have time to finish my last word when I find myself sprawled out on my stomach with a very heavy and very hard Maverick pressing down on my back. His mouth is at my ear, and I can almost hear the violence in his voice. That edge of danger that lives inside him is begging to escape and I practically give it the key.

"Do you know what happens to little girls who play with fire?" He grinds his hard dick into the crease of my ass cheek, almost like he's trying to get himself off.

"Orgasms?" I answer, my sass out for all to hear.

"Burns." I want to say he's joking or using some kind of metaphor, but Maverick is just this side of crazy to actually mean it. A thrill rushes through my veins at the prospect. What would it be like to feel that danger? The adrenalin from the fight, the attempt at flight?

*I guess we're about to find out.*

I poke the bear because I, too, am on just this side of insane, it would seem. Grinding my ass back so his dick is getting a good amount of friction, I hear his groan right down to my clit.

"Well, then, Mav. Let's see how hot you get me." I push my ass back again, in an attempt to get him off me but he's like a fucking wall, his weight a lead trap. It's as if he was expecting me to fight back. Then he lets up, giving me just an inch of leeway, and I pounce back with a good elbow to the gut. He doesn't whoosh air out this time, he seems to have my moves all figured out, but he does roll us over so that I'm lying back on his stomach. It's awkward for me this way but I still attempt to wriggle my way out of his hold.

My attempts are futile as he wraps his legs around mine and pins them down, immobilizing me at the same time his arm goes around my neck and I'm officially trapped. My hands immediately latch onto his arm, my instincts telling me to scratch him.

So I do. I go into fight mode but just as I'm drawing blood from his forearm, I feel his free hand pushing my leggings down right along with my panties.

"What are you doing?" My breath is coming out in pants, and my blood is boiling with adrenalin.

"I'm going to fuck you, just like this, while you fight for your next breath."

If he thinks I'm going to give in so easily, he has another thing coming. And this is too much fun to quit just yet.

As I buck my hips to give him a solid ball busting, he shifts his weight and has me back flat on my stomach, my head turned to the side and my hair trapped in his fist.

"When will you learn, princess, that I get what I want when I fucking want it?"

"Never," I hiss. I'm not going to lie, feeling how hard he is, seeing how much he's enjoying the push and pull, spurs me on.

"Is this your fantasy, V? Getting fucked while begging me to stop? You want me to be your monster? You want me to make you come while you're screaming at me to leave you alone?"

That's not what I want. Is it?

With my face turned to the side I watch as the excitement flares in his eyes. Not just sexual, though. He's geared up for a fight. He's also geared up for more.

And I'm about to give him exactly what he wants.

Bucking back, I try to crawl away from him. I try to break free of his hold.

"Stone." That one word makes me freeze. My dad's name from his lips at that moment is unfathomable.

"What?" My words are barely audible, the shock is so great.

"That's your safeword."

Again. "What?"

"Unless you say the word 'Stone', I won't stop."

Why the fuck did that one phrase get me even wetter? It doesn't matter because there is no fucking way I'm saying my father's name while Maverick is fucking me.

Why would he—

"You did that on purpose, didn't you? You know damn well I won't—" My words are cut off when I feel his hand push my leggings even further down than they were before. My ass is bared to him, but I refuse to let him win this easily.

I claw at the mat, using the little grip in my toes to push myself away from him but all I feel is his fist gripping tighter at my skull, the pressure pushing me further into the mat. There's just a second of rest before the pressure is right back.

"Don't fucking move, princess." I know we're role playing but, holy fuck, that tone he just used sounds really fucking real.

The smooth blunt head of his dick is now at my entrance. I want to just sink myself onto him, but at the same time I do not want to give up like this. Not so fucking easily.

With one last attempt to slink away from his monster dick, I heft myself up and try to gain an inch.

"Stop! Let me go!" The words rush out of me but not because I want to stop, I really fucking do not. Those words hurdle out of my mouth because this game is exciting me just as much as it is him. I can practically feel him vibrating with excitement. This whole thing is insane, and I fucking love it.

"You want my dick in your pussy, princess? You want me to make you cry?"

Now, the normal response to this type of question is "Fuck no" so I'm shocked when I hear the word "Yes" leave me in a breathy moan.

"That's what I thought, you dirty little whore. Now stop moving and give it to me. Give me that tight little pussy."

I don't stop moving. In fact, I fight even more until his dick slams inside my pussy and his weight pins me impossibly harder to the mat. My scalp stings from his tight grip and my legs are practically numb from the weight of him.

You'd think it would be fucking awful, but it's fucking amazing. His grunts fuel my fire. The friction of his pelvis against my ass is pushing me down and creating a delicious steady rubbing of my clit against the rough mat beneath us.

I'm already so close and he's barely been inside me for a minute.

Then I remember I'm supposed to be fighting him off, so I blurt out a weak, "Stop," but all it does is make him chuckle in my ear.

"If you come, I promise to stop."

Of course this makes me want to defy him, so I do what I can to fight back my swelling orgasm.

Maverick's free hand snakes beneath me and scoops up some of my wetness and like the little slut that I am, I rub up against him, taking advantage of his touch.

"Hmm, my little princess is a good little whore, isn't she?"

I want to cry out that yes, I am in fact a dirty little whore, but with his power of suggestion, all I can think of now is coming.

I need this fucking orgasm.

Like, right fucking now.

It's like he knows me better than I know myself.

Moments before my entire world explodes into tiny little pieces, Maverick motherfucking Riley pushes his slick, coated finger into my asshole and grunts in my ear.

"Time to fucking come, princess."

With my clit rubbing on the mat, his cock in my pussy, and his finger pushing deep inside my ass, I legit black out from the orgasm that hits me like a Mac truck.

My entire body convulses, I'm shaking and gasping and reaching for something to grab onto.

"That's it, baby, give it to me." That's when I feel the sting on my shoulder. The blunt ends of his teeth sinking into the flesh where my neck meets my shoulder.

I cry out, pushing my ass back into him as he fucks me even harder, rubbing my clit so he can get every last drop of this orgasm out of me.

Mav stills, pushing inside me one more time before everything around us disappears and I fall over the cliff once more.

There's no light.

No sound.

No pain.

Just the bliss of his dick buried inside my pussy, his finger deep inside my ass, and his tongue soothing what I'm guessing will be a very visible mark in the shape of his teeth.

He rolls off of me and pulls me onto his heaving chest. "Fuck, V, that was…"

"It was." My voice is a breathy mess.

"Are you okay?" he asks, tipping my face up to look at him. "Be honest with me. There's no room for anything else when we play like this."

"I'm more than okay," I tell him with a small smile. He kisses my forehead and just holds me on the floor of the octagon. I can't help but smile wider.

Maverick really does have a sweet side, even if he hides it from the rest of the world. I'm just glad I get to see all sides of him.

---

"Are you sure you're okay to give me a ride home?" I ask Finley as we head out of the school and make our way toward his car. Not having one of my own is a pain in the fucking ass.

He cuts his gaze to me and he rolls his eyes. "How many times do I have to say yes before you believe me?"

"A few more? It's on the opposite side of town from your place."

"It is, but Lincoln is busy and it's too fucking cold for you to go on Mav's bike. So you're stuck with me." He hits the fob on his keys and opens the passenger door of his Aventador for me.

"That isn't what I meant." I sigh as I climb in.

"I know," is all he says before he closes the door. He rounds the car and climbs in in silence. "Do you want to go straight home?"

"Did you have something in mind?"

He just stares at me, saying nothing. Typical Finley, but I'm not exactly ready for my day to be over, so why not? "Sure, let's do something."

He nods and starts the engine. The roar of the car sends a tingle through my body, and I grin as I buckle in. He peels out of the parking lot, and I cackle as he floors it. There is something about fast cars that just makes me feel alive.

He drives out to the beach and pulls up by the pier. "Wanna go on some rides? Like old times?"

I look over at him, and he looks at me so earnestly that I find myself nodding. I haven't done rides like this since we were kids. Theme parks were kinda off-limits when touring. Too many people, too many variables. I find myself grinning as he gets out of the car; this could actually be fun. I mean, the pier is reasonably limited, but there's still plenty of stuff to get the heart racing.

He opens the door and offers me his hand, which I take, because climbing out of this car, in this skirt, requires a 'degree in how to be a lady' if you don't want to flash the world. "Where to first?"

My stomach growls in response to his question, and the corners of his lips turn up just a little. "Soft pretzel? Or ice cream?"

"Both?" I shrug and he laughs softly before taking my hand and weaving his fingers through mine. It's a small thing, sure, but it's a small thing that makes my heart pound. Finley is an actions kind of guy, so this—all of this—means something. It's one of the things I adore about him. It's hard to misjudge him because he's as upfront as they come. If you know how to read him anyway.

We head to the ice cream stand and he gets a mint chocolate chip scoop, while I get a big ol' scoop of cherry with dark chocolate shavings and whipped cream. We walk the length of the pier in a comfortable silence eating the ice cream, and it's just… nice. It's calm, and I'm not sure the last time I had a moment of just feeling safe and calm, so I enjoy it for what it is.

A moment in time where we can just be.

I lean against the rail and stare out over the choppy water. "Do you ever wonder what life would have been like if I hadn't left?"

He drops onto the railing beside me, offering me a spoonful of his mint chocolate chip, and shakes his head. "No, I know what it would've been like. And as much as it hurt for you to go, for us to have basically no idea that you'd ever come back, I wouldn't change it. Because then you'd be broken too."

"We're all a little broken," I tell him, but the sadness in his eyes is almost my undoing. "You can tell me, you know? I'm not going anywhere this time. Even if I leave here, I'm not leaving you guys."

"You don't need to know my monsters, V. If we don't get you free, you'll have plenty of your own to keep you company." He lets out a deep sigh and looks back out over the ocean. "I went to see my mom over the weekend. I don't want that future for you."

"Your mom?" I ask softly, not wanting to poke too much. This is the first time he's really opened up since I got back, and the last thing I want to do is make him close back up.

"Yeah, she's in the city. At a care facility. I checked her in on my sixteenth birthday after I found her with her wrists in ribbons, lying in a bathtub.

"Oh, Finley," I gasp, reaching out to touch his arm, but he barely even reacts. "I'm so sorry."

"Don't be, it wasn't your fault. It was my father's. And the Knights'. This world is not made for the kindhearted. Anything good that comes here withers and dies. I'm not sure that my mom was ever good, she was with my father after all and that takes a special kind of person, but it got to even her. I don't want that for you. You've always been the light to our shadows. Between mine and Mav's parents, Lincoln's dad… it was never a real surprise that Stone ran with you when he got the chance." He takes a pause, turning to look down at me properly and cupping my cheek with his free hand.

"Do you know why he ran? I mean, if the Knights are such a big deal, why run?"

He laughs softly, shaking his head. "I thought you'd have figured that one out. Stone might have been a shitty person, but he was always a good dad. He left, or ran as you put it, for you. He knew initiation was coming, and he didn't want that for you." He pauses, and I open my mouth to ask what the hell initiation is when he starts speaking again. "You always had this way about you, a strength, and your dad didn't want the Knights to have you. To break you. He made a deal with them to keep you free. I don't know what the terms of that deal were, if I knew I'd tell you, but I know that the last thing he wanted was to pass his legacy over to you. So if you get the chance, V, you run, and you never look back."

"I'm not going anywhere. My dad killed himself, Finn. I don't know why, maybe I never will, but whatever it was, he couldn't have wanted me gone from here so bad if he made it a part of his will that I return here upon his death." I sound bitter, and I kind of am, but that's for a different time and a slew of therapy bills that I'll rack up one day.

"I don't think that was ever his plan. I think that was maybe a part of the Knights contingency. Part of their deal. I get the feeling they never really let him leave, just gave the illusion of it. It's something they'd do."

"I know you guys want to save me from whatever this is, but did you ever think that maybe I'm strong enough to handle whatever it is the Knights want from me?"

"Of course we did. But we've also lived this hell for five years."

"Five years?" I ask, my eyes going wide.

He huffs out a laugh and drops his hand from my cheek, running it through his hair. "Yeah, Stone got you out just in time. The rest of us weren't so lucky."

"What happened to you, Finn?"

"They took us for two weeks. All three of us. We went through initiation. That's what they call it when they break you to see if they can remold you into what they want you to be. When they make you kill, and record it so you can never break free. And that… that is just the tip of the iceberg. So don't tell me you're strong enough to survive it, because no matter how strong you think you are, no one survives initiation. Not really."

My stomach drops and I feel sick. They were thirteen. "How… I…"

I have no idea what to say.

For the first time in my life I might actually be speechless, while my heart breaks for the three of them.

"Yeah," is all he says before picking up my dropped ice cream cup and putting it in the trash. "This isn't exactly what I had in mind when I brought you out here."

"I'm glad I know," I tell him quietly, still not able to look at him properly as guilt consumes me. Maybe if Dad hadn't saved me, it wouldn't have been so bad for them. Were they punished because I was freed?

"But now you think I'm a monster. That we're all monsters. I don't blame you. We are."

I look up, a fire blazing in my chest and grab his chin. "You listen to me, Finley Knight. You are not a monster. You are loyal, and love fiercely with every single part of you. You might hide those softer parts of you from most of the world, but those of us lucky enough to see who you really are know the truth. You're no more a monster than I am. None of you are."

He drops his forehead to mine, his eyes closed, and wraps his arms around me. "Thank you," he says so quietly that I almost miss it, and my heart breaks for him, for all of them, all over again. It's no wonder they were so fucked up about how they went about trying to get me out of here. Especially if that's what they think is waiting for me if I stay.

And just like that, any remnants of anger I was holding onto disappear. How can I not forgive them when this is what they were trying to save me from?

# CHAPTER EIGHTEEN

## OCTAVIA

Staring up at the ceiling, I try to pull myself out of the rabbit hole I've been in since I got home from school. For once, this week was pretty reasonable, and after my time with the guys I'm feeling more grounded than I have since I returned. But talking to Finley about his parents has had thoughts of my mom in the back of my mind since I got home last night. No matter how much I try to shut that voice down, it still plagues me.

Where is she?

How did she get out?

Why did she never come for me?

Do the Knights have her?

Is she even still alive?

And 'round and 'round on the carousel I go. It doesn't matter that I know nothing good is going to come from pulling on that particular thread, I can't help but pull at it.

I've just about managed not to look too much closer at my dad's death since I found out all of this Knight bullshit, mostly because I don't think I'll be able to handle it if it was anything but what I know it to be.

All this being said, I don't have the first idea how to find my mom. I know Lincoln has a PI who's helping look into the stalker, but I don't really want to let anyone know that I'm looking for her. Especially if she did manage to escape the clutches of the Knights somehow, impossible as it seems.

Maybe she has the answers Finley's mom didn't. Or maybe at least answers she's willing to give that the others aren't.

I don't remember much about her, really. And Lord knows I was beyond oblivious to the shit going on around me. I was too young to really notice any of it, but it makes me question how much I missed. How much more there is that I don't know because I was too oblivious—too naive—to notice.

A lead weight in the base of my stomach tells me that there's a lot I still don't know, but I'm not sure how much of it I *want* to know. I've only just started to scratch the surface of what the guys have been through, and it already makes me so angry, so sad, that I just want to run away with them and never look back.

But Echoes Cove has its claws in me, and there's too much here that I couldn't leave behind now. Not to the point I could just disappear without a trace.

I can't help but wonder if Dad knew this would happen when he sent me back here. If this was what he had in mind.

I shake my head and sit up, trying to pull myself from the dark and twisty spiral that lies at the end of that train of thought.

None of this is productive, so I head downstairs and find the house empty. A note from Smithy on the fridge tells me he's out for the evening again, and a smile creeps over my face. I guess his date went well last week after all.

Pulling my phone from my pocket, I dial someone I know has zero connection to any of this crazy, but is likely to be able to help me.

I put the phone to my ear, and Jenna's cheery voice comes down the line. "Summertime Starlight! There you are! I was beginning to wonder when I'd hear from you again." I laugh at the eons-old nickname she calls me. I haven't heard that in years.

"Going back through old notebooks are we?" I laugh and she joins in.

"Maybeeeee. How you doing, girl?"

I let out a sigh, the last thing I want to do is kill her hobby with my bullshit. "Same old, same old."

"Are those boys of yours looking after you? I have to say, I never considered the poly thing, but damn, if I had four guys that looked like that chasing my tail, I'd play that game too, girl. Those boys are fire." She bursts out laughing, and I wonder if she's been drinking. She always gets super chatty when she's had tequila.

"They're not my boys. Not really. I don't think."

"Girl, if you say so. I saw the way they watched you. It was like you pushed and they pulled. I'm pretty sure if you told them to jump, they'd all ask how high."

I shake my head, envisioning me telling Lincoln to jump and him doing anything but glaring at me. "I have a favor to ask."

The music in the background turns down, and I hear the rustle of sheets. "Shoot, girl. What do you need?"

"Do you know any PIs? Good, but like, uber discreet?" I bite my lower lip as I ask, chewing at it while I wait for her to answer.

"Are you in trouble?" she asks, sounding as sober as I feel.

I can't help but smile. Jenna might not be Indi, but she's been a good friend of mine for a long-ass time. "No trouble, not yet anyway. I just need to find someone."

"Say no more. I got you, my friend. I'll shoot you Bentley's details. He isn't cheap, but he's good, and *very* good at discreet." She pauses and I feel my phone buzz. I check it and see the contact file on my screen. "If you need a place to hide out, or just somewhere to feel safe, you can always go to—"

"I know, thank you. You fucking rock. I love you."

"I love you too. Call me if you need anything, okay?"

"I will. Go back to your good time. I can't wait to come see you guys play again soon."

"We're actually not far from you tomorrow night. I'll send you the details."

"You're amazing. Love you. Talk soon."

"Love you too. Peace out."

She ends the call and I smile down at my phone, at what a beautiful human she is. Seconds later, details of the gig tomorrow are in my inbox. Pretty sure Indi will be down for a last minute road trip.

But first… I pull up Bentley's details and save them, trying to decide if this is really a good idea. The thought of not knowing is what spurs me on, because what if I could've had the answers all along, and I had my dumb bitch button stuck in the on position again and did nothing?

That alone is enough to spur me on to text the number Jenna sent me.

**Me:**

Hi, Jenna B gave me your number. I'm in need of some help. Do you have any time to meet to go through it?

I drop my phone on the counter, not expecting a response straight away, so I jump when it buzzes.

**Maverick:**

I have a fight tonight. You coming?

Shit!

I was supposed to be going with Indi. I scramble up the stairs and jump in the shower to freshen up. I rush through drying my hair, putting it up in a messy ponytail before looking at my closet. Fuck it. I dial Indi, and she picks up on the second ring.

"You almost ready? I'm leaving in ten."

"I'm currently staring at my closet, naked, trying to decide what to wear." She bursts out laughing and I grin. There's a lot to be said about not having to have a filter when it comes to your bestie.

"Considering the way your last fight night went, well, I guess it depends how you want the evening to end." I bite my lip at her words trying not to groan. My libido needs to calm the fuck down. She's been getting plenty, and yet, there's something about Maverick—about all of them—that makes me insatiable. I can't help but wonder what would've happened if Mav had called Finn earlier in the week when we were in the octagon. Or what it would be like to be at Lincoln's mercy, even though he hasn't shown any signs of wanting that.

What it would be like with both of the Saint brothers.

With all four of them.

"V? You there?" Indi's voice pulls me from my train of thought, and she laughs like she knows exactly what had me so distracted.

"I'm here, sorry, daydreaming. You make a good point, I think I know what I'm going to wear."

"Okay bish, I'll be there soon."

"See you soon!" I say just before she ends the call and I bounce into my wardrobe, pulling on some black lace and mesh undies before digging through my drawers for what I'm after.

When I find it all, I grin. This is one way to encourage Mav to win tonight, I guess.

I slide into the fishnets, cutoff shorts, pink tank, and mesh long sleeve top, finishing it off with knee-high Chucks. Sitting at my dresser, I do my makeup, reasonably subtle, except for the neon pink liner that highlights my eyes, framed with black. I pull a pink ribbon from my drawer and braid my hair with it.

Indi breezes into my room and whistles. "Damn girl, you sure know how to make those boys drool. You look hot as fuck."

I grin at her and take in her skater dress, with a tutu under the skirt, and Docs. "Girl, same!" She blushes, waving me off, but I love that she's embracing herself and sticking to exactly who she is, even with her guys chasing her again. "Did you pierce the other side of your nose?"

She nods, showing me each side of her face, the small gold hoops in each nostril.

"It looks cute as hell."

"Thanks. You good to go?" she asks, looking down at her phone. "Did I tell you Ryker and Ellis are coming tonight?"

I raise my eyebrows. "No, you did not, but I'm looking forward to officially meeting two of the boys coveting your heart."

"I'd tell you to play nice, but fuck it. They can sweat." She grins at me and I laugh.

"Damn straight they can." I snap a picture of myself and send it over to Maverick, finally responding to his message.

**Me:**

I am. See you soon.

**Maverick:**

Fucking hell. Fighting with a hard-on isn't the easiest, but that's my reality tonight.

I laugh at his response and pocket my phone, slipping my wallet and keys in too before looking up at Indi. "Let's rock it."

---

It doesn't take us too long to find the warehouse again, but parking is a nightmare. We end up in the butt-fuck middle of nowhere, and it's dark as fuck.

"Ryker told me to stay in the car till he gets here," Indi says, biting her lower lip like she's trying not to laugh.

"Wow, he really is all kinds of protective, huh?"

She blushes and nods. "Yeah, just a bit. You cool just waiting a minute?"

"Yeah, I'm good. I can't imagine Maverick would be thrilled about me being out there in this darkness considering no one has a clue who my stalker is yet."

She pales at the reminder. "Yeah, that's true." She hits a button on the dash and the doors all lock. I try not to laugh. "Better safe than sorry."

It only takes a few minutes before her phone buzzes again. "He's here. Didn't want to scare me."

"Aww, that's kind of adorable."

She unlocks the car and the door opens instantly as the tattooed wonder that is Ryker Donovan appears beside her. "Hey, baby." He grins at her like she is his entire world.

"Hey," she breathes before he kisses her, and I swear to fuck the entire car steams up with the heat of their kiss. I look down at my phone, giving them as much privacy as I can. "Ryker, you know V, right?"

"We knew each other once upon a time," he says, eyeing me suspiciously. I don't take it personally, he's a King. I'm meant to be a Knight. And while I don't know everything that's going on there, I know enough that he's not going to be my best friend.

"That we did. Time changes people though. Treat my girl right, and we're good."

"My girl," he growls, "and I could say the same to you."

I grin at them, while Indi rolls her eyes at him. "You're good. I'm never going to hurt her, and I never have." I quirk a brow at him and he nods.

"Touché."

"Let's get this show on the road, shall we?" Indi says, diffusing the tension. I drop Maverick a message to let him know I'm here, and that Ryker is walking us from Indi's car. Since we're in the middle of nowhere, I share my location with him at the same time. My stalker is still out there somewhere, and Ryker is about as likely to help me as he is to stick a knife in his eye.

I climb from the car, and we head toward the warehouse. The noise of the start of fight night reaches us, even all the way over here. I try to give them their privacy while not straying too far from them, but when a figure steps out of the darkness, I can't help but squeak. Ryker spins, gun out and aimed in my direction in a heartbeat.

"You better lower that gun before you find a bullet between your eyes, Donovan." Lincoln appears from the shadows, a gun of his own in hand.

"Lower the testosterone, boys. I'm a jumpy mess. No need for anyone to get shot," I say while Indi looks at me wide-eyed like she's about to freak the fuck out.

Lincoln doesn't move until Ryker lowers his gun, raising his hands in surrender. "No harm, no foul, Saint."

Lincoln nods at him before holstering his gun and pulling down his hoodie to cover it. It's only then, when the guns go away, that I take the time to take in the deliciousness that is a dressed-down Lincoln. Jeans, boots, and a hoodie topped with a leather jacket. Not exactly his usual attire, but hot fucking damn. I think my ovaries just went boom again.

"I'll see you inside, V," Indi says as Ryker steers her away from us, and I nod, giving her a little wave. I should probably try and smooth shit out with Ryker, just to make Indi's life easier, but I'll work on that later. Right now, I have an unexpected turn to my night.

"I didn't realize you were here tonight," I say to Lincoln, who motions for me to follow behind Indi and Ryker. He drops into step beside me, his hands in his pockets.

"I don't usually miss Maverick's fights, no matter how stupid they are. It's better for him to get his bloodlust out here than another way."

I nod at his words. I might not have Maverick all figured out yet, but it's impossible not to see that he enjoys dancing in the shadows a little more than the others. Not that that scares me. If anything, it intrigues me.

We continue in silence, the tension building between us with each step. "Thank you for coming to find me."

"I wasn't about to leave you out here with him. He'd probably leave you for dead if it meant Indi was safe."

I nod, because yeah. I'm at least sure enough that if I was in trouble, any of them would take the time to make sure Indi was safe too, purely because of how much she means to me.

Brownie points for each of them, I guess.

"Can I ask you a question?" I look over at him, blending into the shadows, but I catch the nod in the dim moonlight. "Why save me? You keep saying you were all trying to save me from the Knights, but if they're so vast, so powerful, why even try?" I don't really expect an answer, he doesn't exactly seem in the talking mood, but I figure it's worth a try.

He pauses and looks at me. "Some things in life are worth the sacrifice."

"You know that answer isn't an answer right?" I deadpan, and he just shrugs. Frustration builds up, but I let it out with a deep breath. Tonight is not the time, but at least I tried.

We head inside the warehouse without another word passing between us. He leads me over to where Finley and East are waiting with Maverick, who bounces on the balls of his feet in nothing more than his fight shorts.

I smirk at him when I see him, my gaze bouncing from his shorts back up to his eyes, and his grin matches mine. I know he's thinking about earlier in the week, just like I am. He pulls me into his arms, away from Lincoln's side, and kisses me until I'm breathless. My hands glide over his sweaty torso until my fingers tangle in his hair. He lifts me from my feet when Lincoln's voice snaps through our happy bubble. "Put her the fuck down, Maverick."

Maverick pulls back from me, putting me down and flips Lincoln the bird. "Don't be a jealous asshole. You could kiss her if you wanted to."

I suck in a breath at Maverick's challenge and catch Finley's eye over Maverick's shoulder, not daring to look back at Lincoln. Finley takes my hand and pulls me toward him, saving me from the testosterone showdown happening between the two of them. "Hey, you."

"Hey." I smile up at him as East moves to lean against the wall beside him.

"You two should leave the fighting for the ring," East says to the other two while I nuzzle into Finn's chest. Enjoying the warmth of him.

"You look beautiful, in a rave, party girl kind of way," Finn whispers in my ear, and I smile.

"Thanks." I pull back and East smiles at me. I don't get butthurt about the lack of affection from him. I'm very aware that crossing boundaries in private with him is one thing, but in public… well, I don't want him to go to freaking jail for getting handsy. He's here and that's what's important. "Do you guys know where Indi is?"

"She's with the Donovans," Finn says, pointing across the room.

"Thank you. I'm going to go get a drink and talk to her for a minute. What time is your fight, Mav?"

The guy in question grins at me like a crazy person.

"You called me Mav. I knew you were softening to me, princess." He winks and I bark out a laugh. "My fight is in thirty; you've got time. Just make sure you're back here to kiss me good luck."

I sashay over to him and stretch up on tiptoe to whisper in his ear. "I've got something better than luck for you. Win, and you can stay at my house tonight."

I drop back down and the wolfish grin he gives me is enough to send a shiver down my spine. "Oh, I was going to win anyway, princess, but that is way too good of a prize to let go."

I head to the bar and grab a bottle of water before elbowing my way through the crowd to where Indi is standing with her guys. Someone grabs my ass and I use the technique Maverick showed me to twist his arm, so if he moves too much his wrist will snap. "Do not fucking touch what isn't yours."

The asshole whimpers, nodding, and I release him, pushing him back into the crowd. Another point for Maverick tonight, 'cause he ran through that hold with me so many times I thought I was going to scream. I hear a whoop from across the room, and find Maverick looking in my direction, laughing hard. "That's my girl!"

I laugh, shaking my head before continuing through the crowd until I stumble into Indi. "There you are!" she exclaims. "I was going to try and rescue you from that jack hole, but I saw you had it covered, and these idiots wouldn't let me go anywhere." She points over her shoulder, and I find Ryker glaring at me while Ellis smiles.

"Is that Dylan?" I ask her, motioning to the other guy standing with the twins, and she giggles, nodding.

"That's him," she confirms, and I hug her.

"Damn, girl, Ryker might be a bit of a jerk, but they are fire. You deserve no less. I stick by my earlier words though. I'm happy to remove certain appendages if they fuck you over again." She giggles at me again and squeezes me tight.

"Oh, I'd let you, too, but I think we're good now. Is Mav ready for his fight?" she asks, and I look over my shoulder to where I know he's watching. She waves at him and he nods. Just like that, her guys are at her back. "Will you guys chill? They're not going to do anything to me. They all want V's kitty cat too much for that."

I burst out laughing at her, but I'm inclined to agree. Except for Lincoln. But he won't hurt her anyway. He might not want me like the others do, but I know he wouldn't hurt me like that.

"They already had your car jacked," Ryker growls, and as much as I hate to agree with him, he isn't wrong.

"They won't hurt her again. You have my word on that. No one will touch her because of me," I tell him, holding his gaze. I'm not sure how many people dare take on Ryker Donovan in a battle of wills, but I'm not about to back down. He might be dangerous as fuck, but I'd lay down my life for my girl, Indi. That includes going up against her guys if that's what's needed.

"Oh, I like this chick," Dylan says, distracting Ryker, and I smile over at him. He's taller than the twins, his floppy blond hair falls into his green eyes, and his t-shirt shows off every single muscle he's sporting. I stand by my earlier assessment. Hot fucking damn.

"Nice to meet you," I say to him with a grin.

He steps forward and bundles me into his arms. "Oh, girlie, we don't say hello like that. Not 'round these parts. And don't worry about Ryker, his bark is worse than his bite." He winks at me before releasing me. Indi's eyes go wide, and I let out a sigh as soon as I feel their heat at my back.

"Calm down. He was saying hello," I say to Mav, whose eyes flare as he steps up behind me, all territorial.

"Nice to see you again, Dylan," Finn says, sounding calmer than Mav looks.

"You too, man." Dylan smiles, and I look at Indi. Two down, the rest to go. "Good luck with your fight tonight, Maverick. That asshole deserves a beatdown. Did you hear what he did to the Erikkson sisters?"

Mav shakes his head and the three of them break off to talk about whatever that is, leaving Indi and I with the Donovans and the Saints. Not even a battle of wills going on here or anything. Here was me thinking after Halloween, that there might be a tentative peace, but apparently I was wrong.

"Well, this isn't awkward at all. Will you guys dial back the testosterone please?" Indi sighs, looking at the Donovans, while I look at East and Lincoln.

"What she said."

"Do you know where Diego is?" Ryker asks, ignoring us both and looking straight at Lincoln.

Lincoln puts his hands in his pockets and shakes his head. "No idea. Should I?"

Most people would miss it, but I see the tic in his jaw. He's lying. I don't say anything, but he's got another thing coming if he thinks I'm going to leave that alone. I won't do it here in front of the twins and Indi, but I know how worried she's been, so there's no way in hell I'm going to let that lie.

"If you say so," Ryker snarls while Ellis pulls Indi back so her back is flush with his chest. She sighs, relaxing into him.

"We should go. Mav's fight starts soon," Finley interrupts as the three of them rejoin us.

"Sure thing. I'll see you in a bit?" I say to Indi who nods and mouths a 'sorry.' I shake my head, she has nothing to apologize for, but if the guys want anything more than a quick fuck from me, they're going to have to get on board with the Donovans. I don't care what their history is; I won't consider one damn thing if it's going to fuck with our friendship.

Not a fucking one.

I let Finley lead me back over to where they were standing before, Maverick, Lincoln and East following behind. I wait until we're standing back by the wall before I turn to Lincoln. "You were lying. You know where he is."

His eyes go wide before he locks down his features. "I was not lying."

He turns his back on me and heads to the bar, and I try to swallow my frustration down as East follows him.

"Fight time!" Mav announces, bouncing in front of me. "Kiss me good luck, princess."

I step forward and kiss him, pouring every ounce of heat and frustration into it, while I try to lose myself in him. He pulls back grinning. "Don't think I forgot my reward for winning, either."

"I didn't imagine you would." I smirk. "Now go get him, killer. Make him bleed for me." I wink and he groans.

"Just you sounding all bloodthirsty is enough to make me want to forfeit and just take you to my bed instead."

"Blood first, fuckery later," I tease, and he stalks toward the ring.

"Thank you," Finley says as he pulls me back against his chest. "For not pushing Lincoln, and for being here for Mav. He'll never admit it, but he focuses better with you here. He keeps his head a bit more. You're good for him, so thank you."

"You don't have to thank me," I tell him as I lean my head back on his shoulder, and he slips his hands in the front pockets of my shorts. "I wanted to be here. Lincoln, however..."

I trail off and he kisses the side of my neck. "Be patient. He struggles."

"I wasn't asking much," I counter, and I feel him smirk against my skin.

"You were asking more than you think," he says, and I relax a little further. "He's coming around, but... well, he's Lincoln."

"Don't I know it." I sigh as the bell rings, announcing the start of the fight, and I turn my attention to Maverick and the fucking behemoth of a man in the ring with him. "Umm, should Mav be fighting that guy?"

"You doubt he can win?" Finn asks, his chest vibrating against my back as he chuckles. I like this side of him. I wish he relaxed like this more often.

"I mean, have you seen that other guy?"

"Have a little faith," is all he says before Mav flies through the air, fist raised as he bounces from the ground, and smashes his fist into the guy's cheekbone as he comes down.

Holy shit. It's like something out of a fucking movie. I grin as the crowd cheers, and Maverick winks over at me momentarily before focusing back on the guy in the ring.

I guess I'm not sleeping alone tonight.

When I get back from my run with Lincoln, who didn't say a word on the entire route, Maverick is still sleeping in my bed. I grin as I stand in my doorway, the white sheet tangled around him, bunched down at his hips, leaving the rest of him bare for my eyes to feast on.

"I can feel you watching me, princess," he murmurs, half asleep, lifting his arm to cover his eyes. Of them all, I definitely didn't expect Maverick to be the one that I warmed to the fastest, to get to this point with first, but there's just something reckless about him that makes me want to join him in his abandon.

"I can still feel you inside of me, so that makes us even," I counter and he groans. I grin at the sound as he grabs his dick through the sheet.

"You coming back to bed?" he asks as I start to undress. I glance over at him and catch his predatory stare following my movements.

"I need to shower. And then I need to speak to Indi about a gig tonight in the city," I tell him as I shoot Indi a message to see if she's around today.

"I could always join you in the shower," he grins at me, an odd mix of lascivious and dangerous, ripping a sharp laugh right out of me.

"You could, but I have a feeling, Maverick Riley, that if I let you do that, the rest of my plans for the day are going to get derailed."

He feigns indignation, scoffing at me. "Why, princess, must you always think the worst of me? I was merely offering to wash your back." I stick my tongue out at him, and his eyes darken as he sits up.

"Sure you were." He grins at me wickedly.

"You know me so well, princess, because by washing your back, I totally meant your ass… with my dick." I roll my eyes at him, trying not to laugh at how he goes from playful to Maverick in zero-point-two seconds.

"Exactly."

Sliding out of my leggings, I put them in my laundry hamper before padding into the bathroom and starting up the shower. "If you let me shower quickly, we can have breakfast before I need to head out."

"I can make it go faster if you let me have breakfast in the shower," he says as he enters my bathroom, stark fucking naked, dick standing to attention, wagging his brows.

I finish undressing and let down my ponytail. "Well, I guess it would be rude of me to make you starve like that…"

His eyes drag down my body, stopping on each and every mark he left on me last night. From the bruises on my hips to the teeth marks on my tits, amongst the various others scattered across my skin. "You look good wearing me," he growls as he steps toward me. I swear that growl alone is enough to make me fucking wet. "Ass on the counter. Now."

"But I just went running," I whine. "I should shower."

He quirks a brow at me and folds his arms across his chest. "Do I look like I give a fuck? Ass on the counter. Now, princess."

I let out a breathy moan but do as I'm told as he sinks to his knees, pushing my thighs apart. He bites the inside of my thigh and I jolt forward a little, but that just makes him grin harder against my skin. His tongue laves over the stinging flesh as his fingers dig into my thighs. That's going to leave yet another bruise and I'm totally good with that.

"I didn't think you were such a tease," I groan in challenge, and his eyes flash as his gaze meets mine, need and determination written all over them.

I cry out as he thrusts two fingers inside of me, circling my clit with his tongue, teasing every nerve ending inside me. There's a steady, mind-blowing rhythm to his actions and my entire body reacts to it all at once.

With every push and curl of his fingers, his tongue flicks my clit. Over and over again until my brain can't take it anymore. I'm a panting, writhing mess with one hand clutching the side of the counter while the other fists in his hair, encouraging him to send me over the edge.

His movements slow and I whimper.

"You wanted me to be a tease." He winks at me like this is a game and I'm his personal puppet, but the moan that escapes from my lips tells us both that I'm loving every second of his torturous ways.

"No, no I didn't," I pant as his fingers move in and out slower, curling to hit that magical spot inside me, pushing hard when he hits it, sending shivers through my entire body. "Please, Mav."

He pulls back and stands, looking down at me as his fingers continue their slow torture.

"Oh, I like it when you beg, princess. It's almost as good as when you fight me."

His words spur me on and instead of begging I change up my tactics. I want him to drive me wild and make my world spin. So, I raise my hand and slap him across the face. He grins down at me sadistically, catching my wrist in his free hand. "Oh, princess, you want to wake the beast?" A shiver runs straight up my spine and I'm not sure if it's from a tiny bit of fear or a whole lot of thrill.

Probably both.

He withdraws his fingers, watching me intently as he licks them clean. Pulling me from the counter, he pushes me into the shower and presses me up against the cold tile. I hiss as the chill hits my skin, but I'm trapped and barely able to breathe as he uses his entire body to keep me pinned. He takes my wrists and binds them in one of his large hands above my head. "You remember your safe word?"

I nod, barely able to make the movement, crying out as he thrusts into me and bites down on my shoulder. I welcome that sting of pain, crave it, even. With his dick fully seated inside me, I'm whole again. Needing everything he has to give to me.

Mav's dick is a relentless piston fucking me without abandon. In and out, he owns my body and has no qualms showing me exactly who's in charge. His body shields me from the hard sting of the shower water—muting its sound—and all I hear is the musical rhythm of skin slapping against skin. It's raw and carnal. It's crude, but it's us. It's everything I never knew I needed.

One hand snakes around my waist and slides down my lower belly until his middle finger flicks at my clit. A hoarse cry rips out from my throat at the bittersweet sting of pain, but he doesn't stop. He doesn't let up or even acknowledge my reaction as my orgasm flashes through me without warning. "That's it, princess, come all over my dick."

He fucks me until I wilt then pulls his still very hard dick out before turning me to face him. "Kneel."

I do as I'm told, his hand fisting my hair until it stings, the warm spray on my back.

"You're going to look so pretty with me painted all over you," he says, stroking his dick so hard the veins on his forearm pop out deliciously. It's when he taps the head of his cock against my lips that I take my cue and push my tongue out, earning me a groan so hot it makes me wet all over again. "Fuck, princess."

That's all the warning I get as he sprays his cum all over my lips, my cheeks, my throat. I keep my mouth open until he's done, licking up and swallowing down what little ends up on my lips.

"You really do look hot as fuck with me on your face." He smirks at his cheeky remark and it makes me laugh despite the intense moment we've just experienced. Tilting my head back, I close my eyes as the spray from the shower washes away all remnants of his cum from my face. I don't even bother trying to stand, my legs probably can't hold me up anyway.

"I suppose I really should scrub your back for you now, huh?"

I laugh as he lifts me to my feet and kisses me until my toes curl. "Probably should, yeah. I'm going to need to wash my hair now, too. You don't have to stick around for all of that."

"Pssh," he hisses and grabs my shampoo from the rack. "Turn around, princess, I got this."

I smile up at him, kissing his chest before doing as I'm told. He's so gentle with me after he fucks me. He washes my hair, massaging my scalp as he does, putting in the conditioner before scrubbing me head to toe with my loofah. Once he's done, he washes himself quickly before jumping out and grabbing towels. He wraps himself up before turning off the water and wrapping my hair in one towel and my body in another, carrying me through to my bed when he's done.

"Thank you," I say quietly when he crouches in front of me. "You didn't need to do any of that."

"I don't need to do anything," he says, capturing my chin in his thumb and forefinger. "But I wanted to look after you. Now let's get dressed and get that breakfast, shall we?"

My stomach rumbles in response and he chuckles at me.

"Come on, princess. Can't let you go hungry now, can I?" He winks at me as he starts to dry off, and I go through the motions of getting ready for my day. This wasn't exactly how I saw my day starting, but I am far from mad about it.

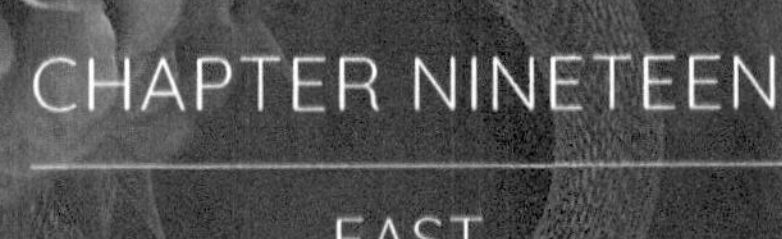

# CHAPTER NINETEEN

## EAST

“Linc—”

The slam of the door cuts me off and I let out a sigh. Good to see his mood has improved a ton since last night. I knew going there with V was a bad idea, but trying to stop any of them when they had something in mind is like herding fucking cats. He's been a grumpy fucking asshole ever since she called him out last night. Pretty sure Maverick spending the night over there didn't help either.

She might be safer with him there, and Lincoln might still be resisting being close to her, but I know my little brother. There are very few things in life that can fuck him up like this, but every single thing about Octavia Royal has him tied in knots.

Denying himself of her isn't helping either, but I don't know how to break through that thick skull of his and convince him that he won't lose her. Not if we all work together to keep her safe, Knights or not. Between the four of us we can shield her from the worst of it. Even if I'm not a Knight. Maybe even *because* I'm not a Knight.

I head downstairs and find Betty in the kitchen. Our housekeeper hates it when I call her Mrs. Potts, so I try to respect her wishes as much as I can. Especially since she's been more of a mother to Lincoln and I than Fiona has ever been.

Hell, Fiona hasn't even tried to contact us for nearly five years. She left not long after Stone and V did. I'm not sure if Lincoln even knows why she finally left, but I was older. It wasn't hard to see the way she looked at Stone; to see how depressed she became once he left. I'm pretty sure it's one of the reasons my dad hates V as much as he does.

In fact I'm pretty sure it's one of the reasons he allowed Stone to leave with her in the first place, to get her out. Because at least then he wasn't being humiliated by his wife fucking around with the guy next door. Someone who was, once upon a time, higher up on the Knights' food chain than he was, what with Stone having been the Regent before he stepped away.

"Morning, Easton. Would you like some breakfast?" Betty asks as I sit at the table, "Eggs? Pancakes?"

"Morning, Betty. Yes please. Whichever is easiest for you," I tell her with a smile. Really, I'm old enough and capable enough to make myself breakfast, but she'd chase me with a fucking spatula if I told her as much.

"Blueberry pancakes it is, I know how much you like those. I got some fresh berries from the market this morning too. Will Sir Grumps-a-lot be joining us?"

I chuckle at her description of Lincoln. To say he struggles with the whole affection thing is an understatement. Our parents really did a number on him, and it shows. "I doubt it, but I'll text him and let him know what you're making. He might come down."

I shoot off the text to Lincoln, giving him the option to ignore it if he wants to. He's already spent hours in the gym in the basement this morning, apparently that wasn't enough to sort out his funk. And that was *before* he went on his morning run with V.

My phone buzzes on the table, and instead of seeing Lincoln's name, I see my dad's.

"I'll just take this outside," I say to Betty and head out the back. No one else needs to bear witness to the joy that is me speaking to him.

"Father," I say as I answer the phone, more to piss him off. Lincoln refuses to give him the title and it infuriates him, but he wishes I wouldn't. "What can I do for you today?"

"What the fuck are you and your brother up to?" he hisses down the line, and I let out a deep sigh.

"I don't know what you're talking about."

"I'm not fucking stupid, Easton. This is all about the Royal girl isn't it? Of course you'd both fawn over the Royal bitch."

"Harrison—" I start, but he cuts me off.

"Don't take me for a fool, Easton. I will kill her and be done with it if you make things difficult."

I swallow the lump that rises in my throat. I have no doubt he would, too.

"What can I do for you?" I ask, trying to remain non-combative. He already holds too many of the strings to my life in his hands.

"You can fucking disappear, that's what you can do. Stop filling Lincoln's head with ideas that he'll ever be anything like you. You and I both know you're fucking nothing. I never should've let you stay at the house with him."

I grind my teeth together. How much he enjoys poking at me… but I refuse to stoop to his level. Unfortunately, I have to live with the grace of his mercurial mood. "We had a deal."

"That deal isn't working for me so much anymore." He pauses and I hold my breath. I don't want to beg him, but if that's what it takes to protect Lincoln, even in such a limited capacity as I am currently capable, then I will.

"What do you want?" I ask again, trying to sound as pliant as possible.

"I want Lincoln to be focused on the LaFontaine girl. Not Octavia. I don't care how you do it, but get it done. Otherwise this little deal of ours is done and you'll be out of that house, and out of The Cove, so fast your fucking head will spin."

How the fuck am I supposed to do that?

I take a deep breath, pinching the bridge of my nose. "I'll do what I can."

"You do that. You might have the protection of the Knights as per our deal, but that can easily be pulled, and all of those advantages you've existed on will quickly disappear. Including that little side job of yours." I hear a voice in the distance and he barks something out to them before speaking again. "I have to go. Do not fuck this up, Easton. You're living on borrowed time."

"Yes, sir." I sigh, resigned to the fact that, despite everything, he still has more control over me than I ever wanted. The sacrifices I've made to keep my brother safe aren't something I'll ever regret, but sometimes I wish I would have just run with him when I found out the truth.

Kidnapping a minor wasn't exactly something I wanted on my rap sheet though, even if I was still a minor at the time too, Harrison still would've locked me up and thrown away the fucking key.

I wait until he ends the call and lean back against the wall. Fuck my life.

I've been trying to push Lincoln toward V. I know that's where he'll find his happiness, and now Harrison is shitting all over my plans. That's not really anything new, but fuck.

Maybe I should just tell Lincoln the truth. Maybe then he wouldn't resent me so much for the position he's in. I've let him, and I haven't held it against him. It was part of the deal I made with Harrison. I thought it would be easier for him not to know… but I'm beginning to think I was wrong.

Fuck this is way too much for a Saturday fucking morning.

I head back into the kitchen and find Lincoln sitting at the table while Betty fusses over him. I can't help but smile. He might be a grumpy asshole, but he's our grumpy asshole. And even though he can't stand the fussing, he still lets her do it because he also understands that she's the closest thing to a real mother we've ever had.

"All okay?" she asks, looking up as I take a seat again. I just nod, and she heads back to the stove where the griddle is heating for the pancakes.

"You okay?" I ask Lincoln, who is focused on his phone. He drops it onto the table and sighs. The bags under his eyes make me worry. He never sleeps enough. There were a few weeks where he slept okay, and now I know that that's when he was sneaking next door and sleeping with V.

This is exactly why my father's wishes are so hard to follow. Octavia is good for him, even if he won't admit it himself. There is something about her that settles the storm that lives inside of him. All I want, all I've *ever* wanted, is for him to be happy. As much as I love V, if I knew it would make them both happier for me to step back, then I would.

"Just Harrison. He wants me to take Georgia—the LaFontaine girl—to the gala." He looks so fucking sad, it guts me. It's also how I know he's so fucking tired. He wouldn't usually show this much emotion. Even here. Even to me. "Except… I think Octavia is going."

"I didn't think she was going to go…" I'm shocked. Balls aren't exactly her thing.

He shakes his head before running a hand through his hair as the smell of the blueberry pancakes fills the air. "I'm not sure she has much of a choice. We've been distracting them from her as much as we can, but whatever the shitstorm was that they were dealing with over Christmas is finally clearing up. They're focusing again. I just wish I knew what they wanted from her. They don't usually go back on a deal, so for them to try and get her back, after freeing her in the deal with Stone… it has me all kinds of fucked up."

"We'll keep her safe."

He slams his hand on the table and hisses. "I can't keep her safe if I have to keep my attention on this Georgia chick. And you're not even invited."

"V has a plus one though, right? I can go with her, then she doesn't need to be officially linked as attending with any of you. And the three of us can keep her safe while you do what you need to do." I try to reason, and when he nods, I try not to let my shock show. He really must be tired if he's agreeing with me. My brother is a lot of things, but agreeable is not one of them.

Betty places the pancakes in front of us both, a smiley face on them made from extra berries and whipped cream. I can't help but laugh and even Linc smirks a little. "Eat up. You boys don't eat enough."

"Yes ma'am." I grin at her as I pick up my fork before looking back to Linc. "We'll get it all sorted out, and I'll help you where I can."

He nods, the sadness flickering back into his eyes. "Thank you."

He doesn't say anything else. My brother, the guy who usually has all of the words, reduced to two words that I know don't come easy for him. I don't focus on it anymore, but I make a mental note to speak to Finley, and to V.

We need to help him, and if I can do that, I will. Even if Harrison does renege on our deal. Some things are more important than his dirty little secret.

A secret that happens to be an entire human being.

A secret that happens to be his eldest son…

A secret that happens to be… me.

---

*I stride into the house, having just dropped Lincoln and the others off at football practice. It might be my sixteenth birthday, but some things never change. Including the argument my parents are having in the family room. I'm glad Lincoln isn't here. He might turn thirteen in a few months, but he's still too young to listen to this shit.*

*I've protected him from it most of his life, but that's what big brothers are for. I wasn't able to protect him when V left without a trace, but this? This I can protect him from.*

*I try to tiptoe past the doorway, but pause when I hear my father.*

*"There he is. The waste of space in question. Get your freeloading ass in here, oh son of mine."*

*Awesome, I guess he's been hitting the whiskey already.*

*"Harrison!" my mother shouts at him as I enter the room.*

*"What, he's old enough to know now, don't you think?" he says, staggering a little as he drops onto the couch.*

*"To know what?" I ask, even though I'm pretty sure I don't want to know.*

*"The reason that you weren't my legacy. I know you had to have had questions," he slurs as he sloshes his drink in his glass. I look at Mom, but she looks about as sober as he is. Though I'm not sure she's been sober since Stone left. Just another thing I probably shouldn't know, but do.*

*"The Knights?" I ask. Yet another thing I probably shouldn't know but do.*

*Harrison barks out a laugh. "You're astute, I'll give you that. Yes, the Knights."*

*"I didn't realize I wasn't your legacy," I say with a shrug, trying not to feed his drunken delusions.*

*He throws back the contents of his drink before throwing his glass at the wall. I duck and it just misses my head. Some people think being a Saint is everything in life. That we want for nothing. Little do they know what goes on behind closed doors.*

*"Oh you, bastard of mine, will never be my legacy. Happy fucking birthday to you and surprise."*

*I look between him and my mom, who cries softly as she sits in a mess on the floor.*

*"Bastard?" Shock runs through me. He can't be serious.*

*"Yes, your cheating whore of a mother got knocked up just after we got married, but it wasn't mine. You didn't think* Stone *was her first dalliance. I know you pay far more attention than that. You might not be mine in blood, but I taught you better than that." He says it like he's proud, but his words are at odds with his tone.*

*I take a deep breath, trying to process all of this. Happy fucking birthday to me, indeed.*

*"Who is my father if it's not you?" He just laughs and I look down at my mother, realizing she's not going to be any use. "What does this all mean?"*

*"It means that you will never be a Knight. That mantle will go to your brother, who is actually mine. And it means, that you can get the fuck out of my house."*

*I stagger back and slide down the wall. "No. You can't do that to him. I know what happens… initiation. You can't put him through that."*

*"You're too fucking weak for it anyway," he spits at me. "You don't get a fucking choice in it."*

*"I'm not leaving. You can't make me. The last thing you want is everyone to know you raised a bastard son," I argue, trying to stuff down the emotions raging inside of me. I can't leave Lincoln here alone with them. They'll ruin him.*

*"You won't breathe a word of this to any-fucking-one," Harrison shouts, lumbering toward me. Sucks to be him right now, 'cause he's fucked up and I'm not. He might be intimidating, but I've spent my entire life learning how to defend myself against him.*

*"Try me," I argue, and his face turns beet red. I guess he wasn't expecting an argument. "You try to get rid of me, kick me out, separate me from my brother, I'll*

*tell the fucking world that the Saints aren't the picture-perfect family that everyone thinks they are. Or I stay, I keep my mouth shut, and no one ever has to know."*

*What I don't say, is that I'd love to get the fuck away from here, but I'm not leaving, not without Lincoln. And there's no way Harrison will give up his one true heir. I could run off with him, but I don't want to rip him away from everything he's ever known when he's still reeling from V leaving.*

*But if we stay... and he goes through initiation... I don't know that I could ever forgive myself for not saving him from that.*

*"And Lincoln doesn't go through initiation," I say, trying to save him the only way I know how.*

*Harrison just laughs at me. "Oh boy, you've got some big balls, I'll give you that. But you don't get to say shit when it comes to the Knights. You know I could just kill you and be done with it?" My mother screeches at his words, and while they make me think twice about speaking out, I'm not that shocked. "If it wasn't for your brother, I probably would. Except he's going to be a Knight, and the last thing I need is him focused on you disappearing, or using resources to find you. I'll think over your terms. We'll finish this discussion tomorrow, but you don't breathe a word of this to anyone. Not even your brother. If he finds out, no deal." He waves his hand, dismissing me from the room. I head straight to my bedroom on autopilot. Once I lock the door and lean back against it, I try to suck in a breath. A lump builds in my throat as I try to process all of the emotions running through me.*

*He's not my dad.*

*I should be relieved.*

*I should be free.*

*I should be so many things, but instead I'm devastated. More for my little brother. Harrison not being my dad doesn't mean much. He's never been much of a dad anyway. But the fact that this means Lincoln will be inducted... that I can't spare him that.*

*Fuck.*

*A sob works through my chest, and I bite down on my fist to try and stop it from escaping.*

*This can't be happening. I was prepared. I've been prepared since I was thirteen. I know that's when initiation usually happens. Harrison was right about one thing: I do pay attention. I know far more than I should. But I was ready to face the horrors that come with initiation.*

*I should've known something was off. But there's been so much going on over the last few years, and my dad—Harrison—has been drinking more and more... I just chalked it up to that. That was why my initiation was delayed.*

*I never wanted to be a Knight, I just wanted for Linc not to have to be.*

*There has to be a way around this.*

*I can't help but wonder who my father is. If he's a Knight too. If he has more power than Harrison. Maybe he can save Lincoln. There has to be a way. Stone took V away, she's not being initiated. I heard my dad talking to Mr. Riley about it last week. It was the only upside to her leaving.*

*There has to be something I can do.*

*I slam my head back against the door before sinking to the floor.*
*Happy fucking birthday to me.*

---

After breakfast, I tell Betty I'll deal with the dishes and she heads back home to her family. It's the weekend, and I am more than capable of looking after Lincoln and myself. I hate that she spends so much of her time here rather than with her grandkids. Harrison might not care, but then, he doesn't give a fuck about much of anything outside of the Knights anymore.

Not since Mom left.

Lincoln retreated back to his room after he finished eating. He didn't say anything about my call with Harrison, but I know he called Lincoln during breakfast too. Lincoln ignored it, but it was impossible to miss how tense he got watching the call ring out.

This is everything I wanted to save him from, and I failed.

Now all I can do is run as much interference as I can and just be here for him. Even if he resents me for not taking the mantle with the Knights. Even if he blames me for the shit he goes through. I'm not going anywhere when he needs me.

The thing is, he needs V. And as much as I know he's in love with her, has been his entire life, he's a stubborn pain in the ass.

But I have to try.

If he would just speak to her—God knows he won't speak to the rest of us—then maybe, just *maybe*, some of that weight that he carries can be shared. Lincoln is the leader of their little group, and while I sit on the outskirts, I'm still a part of them. Always have been, always will be.

I weigh going to speak to him and suffering his wrath against letting him spiral some more and decide that him being pissed at me is worth it. Especially if it helps him.

It doesn't hurt that it will help V too, but I'm trying not to factor that into my decision. As much as I love her, Lincoln has to stay my priority. Even when he's up to shit I don't agree with, my end goal is still getting him free. Even if it means the end of me. Saving her, saving him. It's all likely to end the same way.

Climbing the stairs, I rack my brain, trying to find the right words, but when I hear the smash in his room, I pick up my pace and burst through his door. He's seated on the opposite side of the room on the floor, back against the wall. His phone is in pieces on the ground by my feet.

"Bad call?" I ask, trying to make light of it and he gives me the finger.

At least he's still him I guess.

"Harrison wants me to step up my game with Georgia. Apparently just taking her to the gala isn't going to cut it. I swear, he'll make me marry this girl if it suits his needs." His fists clench at his sides, and I hate what this is doing to him.

He's eighteen. His biggest worries are supposed to be girls, exams, and college applications.

Not this bullshit.

I head over to sit beside him, sliding down the wall as I do. "I'm sorry, Linc. What can I do?"

"There isn't anything anyone can do. I'm the heir, remember?" I take a deep breath, the venom in his words twisting the knife, but that's nothing new. "Will you ever tell me why you left the legacy to me?"

The vulnerability in his voice guts me.

"When I can," is all I say.

He barks out a dry laugh, void of any actual happiness. "What does that even mean?"

"It means exactly what I say. When I can tell you, I will."

"You didn't pick this did you?" he asks, and I just shake my head. Technically I'm not saying a word, so my deal with Harrison is still in play. He sighs and runs a hand through his hair. "It's so fucked up. I wouldn't really wish this on you anyway. Just sometimes…"

"Sometimes you wish it wasn't you," I finish for him and he nods. "You should speak to someone, Linc. Someone who isn't me, or the guys. Someone you can just be you with."

"You want me to speak to Octavia, don't you?" He sounds like such a broken kid when he says the words.

"Yeah, I do. She gets you, she always has. You never had to pretend with her. I don't know why you've been pretending with her since you decided not to run her out of town. The only people you're hurting are you and her."

He drops his chin onto his folded arms balanced on his knees. "I don't get to keep her. I'll never be free, and I wouldn't wish this world on her. It's the last thing I want for her."

"Did you ever think that maybe, just maybe, you could both get free? Or that if we can't get her free, that life might just be easier with her in it?" I counter, and it takes him a second, but he nods.

"I've thought of little else since I realized that she's stronger than all of us. That she'll probably survive this world without breaking as bad as the rest of us have." He takes a deep breath and looks over at me. "But how do I tell her that I'd rather wade through the cesspit of life with her at my side, so that she can save me, rather than let her be free?"

# CHAPTER TWENTY

## OCTAVIA

After Maverick left, I got another delivery from the Knights Society. Apparently my attendance at the gala next weekend is not optional. I'm going to have to speak to the guys, because I have no fucking idea what's in store for me when I get there, or how any of this shit works. I really hate being dictated to, but I'm almost more pissed that I have to fucking dress up.

I finish my laps in the pool, the air not quite as cold today, so I figured why the fuck not. My run this morning with Linc wasn't enough to get the antsy feeling out of my system. Since I can't run alone, and I haven't sorted out a proper gym at the house yet, the pool is all I have.

It takes a few minutes to psych myself up to get out of the warm water, but once I do, I haul ass, grab my towel, and run inside. It might be warmer outside than it has been, but it's still fucking January.

Rushing through another shower, I decide to spend the rest of my day relaxing with a movie since Indi can't hit up the gig with me tonight. I know I could go alone, but I'm trying to be smart about the whole stalker situation, so that's a real big no. I slip on a pair of leggings, a tank, and my hoodie before going back downstairs.

"Miss Octavia!" Smithy exclaims as I slide across the tiles in my thick socks, and I grin up at him.

"YOLO?"

"Indeed. I am going out for the evening again, do you require anything before I leave?"

"Smithy, you old dog, you. Are you on date number three?" I ask and he stammers a little so I hug him. "I hope you're happy."

"Thank you, Miss Octavia. It is making me very happy."

"Do I get to know who it is you're dating?" I ask hopefully, and he blushes a little.

"Maybe in time. Now is there anything you need?"

I shake my head and pull back. "No, I'm good. I *do* look forward to finally learning who this secret suitor of yours is, though. You have a good time. Will you be back tonight?"

"We're heading into the city, so I got a hotel room so I don't need to rush back. Please set the alarm when I leave."

I hold up three fingers and grin at him. "Scout's honor."

He shakes his head, laughing. "Very well. I'll let you know when I'm leaving."

"Okay, I'm going to make some popcorn and head to the theater room."

"I'll sort your popcorn, just please make sure to eat something more substantial for your dinner. I have a lasagne in the oven, all you need to do is heat it. I figured since you didn't burn the house down doing that last time, it was a good idea." He grins at me and I stick out my tongue.

I mean, he's not wrong, I did manage not to burn the place down, and it was some real good lasagne. "Thank you, I appreciate it. You sure you can manage the popcorn? I totally don't mind."

"Go," he says, shooing me toward the theater room. I laugh and pad my way down there, trying to decide what movie to watch, or if I'm just going to hardcore binge some TV. It's not usually something I do, beyond crime documentaries, but I have the urge to watch something mindless and full of drama. A bit of a distraction from the anxiety about next weekend.

This fucking gala is going to suck.

Especially since I have zero idea what I'm walking into. It's done up as a charity fundraiser, but after everything I've been told, I'm pretty sure that it's a way for the Knights to feel me out. With what little insight I have into how it all works, I can't help but be a little nervous.

On the upside, I might finally learn what it is they want from me.

It could be nothing, and the boys have been freaking out for no reason.

A girl can dream anyway.

I decide to watch the new Battle Royale TV show Indi has been going on about for the last few weeks, and get it all lined up. The door opens and I turn to thank Smithy. I find Lincoln standing in the doorway, holding a giant bowl of popcorn instead. "Smithy asked me to bring this to you and told me to tell you he's leaving."

"Oh, umm. Thanks," I say, shuffling around on the couch to make room for him among the piles of blankets. "Did you want something?"

Why the fuck does this feel so awkward?

He pads forward, and I try not to smile when I see he's in sweats and a hoodie. Another first for me, seeing him like this. He seems wound too tight for such chill clothes.

"I wondered if you had a minute or ten to talk…" He trails off, noticing the screen. "But if you're busy, it can wait."

"Don't be silly, come sit." There is no way I'm passing up on him actually talking to me. Getting anything from him these days is like getting blood from a stone.

He takes a seat, handing me the giant bowl of popcorn. I pop some of the buttery kernels in my mouth to stop myself from speaking. He's here to talk, so I'm not going to push. Lincoln Saint wanting to talk to me, willingly, about anything, is basically unheard of. So I'mma shut my mouth until he starts.

"I wanted to talk to you about next weekend…" he starts, running a hand through his hair. "The gala. I know we haven't talked much lately, but I wanted to try and prepare you a little better. The only upside of my dad being who he is is that sometimes I have extra information. Except that when it comes to you… he doesn't tell me a goddamn thing."

"It's okay, Lincoln. I don't expect you to have all the answers. I don't expect you to save me or whatever grand notion it is you have. Whatever it is that they want from me, I can take it."

He looks at me like I've lost my goddamn mind. "I thought Finley explained to you—"

"He did. A little anyway, but the fact is that I've been through a ton of shit and come out the other side. This isn't going to be any different. Except for the fact that I'll have you guys with me this time." I try to be as open and as raw with him as I can, because I can see how much it's fucking with him that he can't save me from the clutches of the Knights. "Who knows? Maybe the deal my dad made still stands, and they don't actually want anything."

"Maybe," he says quietly. We sit in silence, the previews for the show playing lowly in the background while I give him a minute. He's obviously not finished yet, but I'm not about to rush him. This might be the most vulnerable I've ever seen him. "They initiated us when I was thirteen. They held us for two weeks… and every single day I didn't think I would survive. But I pretended. I faked it, because Maverick and Finley were just as fucking scared out of their minds. All of our deepest and darkest secrets were laid out for each other to see."

I practically hold my breath, not wanting to interrupt him. He sounds so broken, yet so removed from whatever it was that happened. I know Finley told me some of this already, but if he needs to talk, then I'm not about to stop him. Even if my heart is breaking for him.

"Handing three thirteen-year-olds guns, and telling them that one person isn't leaving the room. That we had to decide between us who wasn't leaving…"

Oh my fucking God. I want to crawl across the couch and hug him, but he keeps talking and I know if I do, he'll stop.

"Do you know how long it took me to decide to put the gun to my head and pull the trigger to save them?" He looks at me, his eyes glassy as I swallow against the lump in my throat for the boy before me who will literally take on the world for the people he loves. "Thirty seconds. I thought it would be better for them if I just made the decision. If I didn't make them pick. Thirty seconds to decide that their lives were more important than mine. After I found out everything else they'd already suffered through, at thirteen, I decided it was my turn to take the hit."

"Linc—" I start, but he talks over me.

"The gun was filled with blanks. They all were. It was then that the Knights realized the bond between us wasn't going to be broken by them. That each of us would sacrifice for the other. That's when they changed their tactics. We went through hell for two weeks, and then they told us that you were going to be killed if we didn't kill the three men they put us in a room with. Do you know how long it took each of us to lift the guns we were given? Seconds. We didn't hesitate. Not when you were at risk. Maverick was twelve and he didn't even blink when the guy's brain splattered across his face. Twelve."

He takes a deep breath and finally looks me in the eye. "Do not think that you can beat them, because there is no winning. You are either free because they don't want you with them, and trust me, they *do* want you, or you're dead."

I take a deep breath and try to push down all of the warring emotions inside of me and fail. My heart pounds so loud that I can practically hear the blood whooshing in my ears. Panic seizes me at the thought. I get that he's being honest, and trying to scare me at the same time, which he is fully fucking succeeding at, but if I just lie down and cower in a corner, what use am I to anyone?

"There's really no way out?" I ask, and he shakes his head. I hate how beaten he looks. I've never seen him look like this. Lincoln is a force of nature, an oncoming hurricane that tears through everything in his path. He was always the strong one, the cunning one, the vicious one even, so the rest of us didn't necessarily have to be, but I'm beginning to think I'm going to have to become all of those things if I want to survive, despite my words of bravado.

"Maybe, if we work together, we could find a way out. For all of us. My dad did it, right?"

He laughs at me, straight up laughs. "Your father must have had something they wanted. And still, look at how that ended up."

My eyes water from the sting of his words. I'm still trying to wrap my head around the fact that my father was one of these people. That he made young boys do such awful things in the name of what? Power? My father wasn't that guy… was he?

"There's still a chance, right? That's why you've tried so hard to protect me."

"There could be. The sky could also be pink." I roll my eyes at him and get comfortable. At least he can still laugh, I guess. We sit together in silence while I try to process it all and after a while, he tips his head back and stares at the ceiling "My dad wants me to woo some girl, to convince her dad to join the Knights."

My eyes go wide in horror. The punches just keep coming and I'm at my limit of 'stuff it all down and put it on a shelf'. "He's pimping you out?"

"Fucked up, right?" He shrugs his shoulders. "Just another day in the life, I guess. Everything about the Knights is fucked up. The worst part… I'll do it, even though I hate it. Even though the thought of touching her gives me hives. Because while he's focused on them… he's not focusing on you."

"Linc…" I start, scooting toward him. I don't even know what to say.

"Don't. I don't deserve you. If you knew all of the things I've done, you wouldn't look at me like that, say my name like that."

My heart breaks all over again for him, because how could he ever think something like that? "Is that why you've kept your distance? Because you thought you didn't deserve me?"

He just clenches his jaw as he balls his hands into fists. I put the bowl of popcorn on the table and move to straddle him. I have exactly zero right sitting on him like that, but I'm pretty sure, despite the fact he is always the one with the right words, nothing but action is going to show him the truth of anything right now. I grip his jaw in my hands and make him look at me. "We all have monsters inside of us, but those monsters help us survive. I would never judge you for your monster. Never."

"You can't say that—" he starts but I cut him off, kissing him and pouring every piece of myself into it. I already knew he wouldn't believe my words, but despite the fact that he's kept himself withdrawn, I know he understands just how hard it is for me to lie with my body. His hands glide up my back before he pulls my hair out of my ponytails and his hands tangle in my hair.

He matches my fire with his own, and I'd happily burn with him like this forever.

When I run out of air, I pull back, and rest my forehead on his. "Don't tell me what I can and can't do."

He pulls on my hair, tipping me back as he leans forward, so I have to look up at him. "You can't save me, V. All you're going to do is drown alongside me if we start this. Because if I'm in, then I'm in, and I'm never going to let go. I can't lose you again."

My chest heaves as I try to breathe around everything he's telling me. "You can't lose me if you don't have me, Lincoln. But if you're in this, then I'll happily drown alongside you. Just don't underestimate my ability to keep my head above water."

---

I move to stretch out in bed but pause when I feel the heat of Lincoln wrapped around me. For a minute I thought last night had been a dream, but apparently it was very real. He's sound asleep, so I lie still and let him sleep. The bags under his eyes yesterday were more than a little prominent, and while I'm sure he wouldn't exactly appreciate me saying anything, or attempting to take care of him by lying here and letting him sleep, that's exactly what I'm going to do.

Lincoln spends all of his time looking after everyone else, but I'm not sure he's ever really let anyone look after him. God knows Fiona was never really a great mom, and Harrison is a giant bag of ass. He definitely isn't winning any father of the year awards.

With everything I've heard about all of their dads, I'd happily light the three of them on fire and dance as they burn for the way they've treated their sons. And I'm sure I've just started to scratch the surface.

Hearing what they did to the three of them in initiation… I just… I can't even begin to fathom how much that fucked with all of them. It makes everything they've done make a lot more sense. I wouldn't want someone I cared about going through anything like that. It also explains why they were so fucking extreme. They live life so far in the extreme with the Knights that their scale of what's, ya know, *normal,* is totally fucked.

"You think really loud," he murmurs, his arms tightening around me. "Are you okay?"

I glance at the time on my phone then snuggle back against him. "I'm good, go back to sleep. It's still early."

"Are we running today?" he asks, kissing the top of my head, burying his face in my hair.

"No, we don't have to. Sleep. You're tired."

He lets out a deep breath before kissing my head again. "Okay, let's sleep. We'll run when we wake up."

He falls back asleep almost instantly, so I close my eyes and enjoy the heat of him. The fact that he's trying. I know what he said yesterday, but a part of me half expected him to run the minute the sun came up. For yesterday to have been a blip. That we'd go back to the way it was before.

Some would call me greedy, selfish even, to be with all four of them and still hope that they only want me. Hell, it sounds conceited even in my own head, but it is what it is. As long as they're all as okay with this as they've made out.

I end up dozing back off, waking when Lincoln extracts himself from the bed and heads to the bathroom. I stretch out, groaning as I do. Nothing feels quite as good as that early morning stretch. I open my eyes and find Lincoln smiling at me from where he's leaning against the door frame in nothing but his boxers. It's really not fair that he gets to look like that first thing in the morning, and then there's me, likely looking like I got dragged backward through a bush with epic morning breath.

"Morning."

"Morning," I say with a small smile. Is it weird that I feel a little like a kid with a crush right now? 'Cause that's exactly what happens when he looks at me like that. Butterflies take flight in my stomach and my heart races. "You sleep okay?"

"Better than I have in weeks." He moves toward me and sits beside me on the bed. "You want to run?"

I think about it for a moment and nod. I really should. Though, the thought of just getting back under the covers with him is sorely tempting.

"Okay, I'll slip back home and get changed then meet you back here in half an hour?"

I smile up at him and nod again. "Sounds good to me."

He leans forward and kisses me gently before putting his sweats and hoodie back on. "I won't be long."

He jogs out of the room, and my phone buzzes a minute later as he disables the alarm. I climb out of bed and watch like a creeper as he jogs across the backyard to the gate then disappears onto his side of the fence.

I pad over to my closet and get dressed for the run, going with the black and navy leggings and sports bra combo, grabbing the matching jacket before putting my hair into a ponytail and making my way downstairs. Smithy isn't back yet, but it's only like nine in the morning, so I'm not overly surprised.

I head to the kitchen and grab a granola bar and a bottle of water before turning the dishwasher on to clean the mess from my dinner with Linc last night.

My phone buzzes on the counter, and I smile when I see Indi's name.

**Indi:**
Hey bish, I hope you had an awesome night in the end. Sorry I couldn't make the gig.

**Me:**
My night definitely took a surprising turn for the better, so no sweat. I hope you had fun with your boys.

**Indi:**
Oh I did. We went paintballing. I have paint in places it has no business being.

I burst out laughing. I love her way too much.

**Me:**
That sounds like fun for sure.

**Indi:**
Wait, why was your night surprising?

**Me:**
Lincoln.

I don't say anything else, I'm pretty sure I don't have to. She gets it better than most.

**Indi:**
I expect more info on this tomorrow, but Ryker is er… demanding my attention.

**Me:**
Go enjoy the D. Talk soon

I laugh as I drop my phone back onto the counter just as the back door opens and Linc strolls into the kitchen.

"Ready to go?" is all he says.

It still amazes me that a guy who exudes so much charm can sometimes be so short, but that's just a part of who he is.

I nod before finishing the water and taking the last bite of my granola bar. "Let's do it."

We run our usual route and he pushes harder today, so I push too. We might be… well, whatever the fuck we are, but I'm still not about to lose to him.

When we get back to my place, I'm laughing because he runs like an absolute dork, arms pinwheeling, his legs flailing, being a total goof for the last hundred feet and *still* beats me back. It's nice to see him a little lighter, a little more carefree. Apparently a good night's sleep does wonders for him. Who would've guessed? I grab the mail from the box as we head inside, and once we reach the kitchen, I drop it on the counter and flip on the coffee pot.

"Octavia…" Lincoln says, and I turn to find him holding a manilla envelope that has my name scrawled on it in Sharpie. That's new. "Do you want me to open it? You don't have to see this shit."

"No, I can see it. You don't need to protect me from everything." I smile at him and he nods, handing me the envelope even though I can tell he doesn't really want to.

Taking a deep breath, I open it and pour the contents onto the counter. A ton of photos spill out, except this time, they're not just me.

It's the guys.

It's Indi.

It's her guys.

All with a crosshair over their heads.

*I think I'm going to be sick.*

Lincoln picks up the note and reads it before turning it to me.

*They can't keep you safe. I told you.*
*You're mine.*
*Not theirs.*
*Don't make me prove it to you.*

"This is out of fucking control," I say, gripping the edge of the counter. "I wish I had even a fucking hint of a clue as to who this is."

"Smithy hasn't had any luck with his fed contacts?" he asks, and I shake my head.

"Not as far as I know. I'm not sure that a stalker who hasn't actually done anything is that high up on a priority list though," I tell him, biting the inside of my cheek. Why is this my fucking life?

"I'll get Lucas to link up with Smithy's contacts, and if it wipes my entire trust fund to find him, I don't give a shit. I'm tired of this sick fuck messing with you."

---

Riding into school with Lincoln now that he's all in is definitely something. I really should buy a new car, but finding the time hasn't exactly been the easiest.

I glance over at him and open my mouth before closing it and looking away. I don't know that I want to ruin whatever this is between us right now by asking questions, but if I don't I'm going to feel like a shitty friend.

"Just ask your question, Octavia. Your nervous energy is making me edgy." He doesn't even take his eyes from the road, but I should've known he would pick up on it. Lincoln is nothing if not astute.

I wring out my hands, but decide to bite the bullet. "Do you know where Diego is?"

His jaw ticks as his knuckles go white from the death grip he now has on the steering wheel. A few beats pass in silence before he glances over at me. "I can't tell you."

"So you do know, you just can't tell me where. Or you can't tell me whether or not you know?" He nods and I sigh in frustration. "I thought we were past the whole keeping me in the dark thing, Linc."

He lets out a deep breath and glances at me again, his body seeming to relax. "Compromise?"

I nod and wait for him to continue.

"I know where he is, but I can't tell you where he is. But he's alive, and while he might not be well, he's not close to death either."

It's not much, but it's something, and I'm going to take it. I might prod for more again later but for now, I'm going to take the win. I lean over the center console and kiss his cheek. "Thank you."

We ride the rest of the way in silence, the tension in the car as his palm is splayed across my thigh is so thick I could cut it with a fucking knife, but that has nothing on when we pull into the lot.

He comes around to open the door for me, pulls me from the car, his hands on my waist, and holds me against the door, kissing me like it's all he's wanted to do his entire life.

"It's about goddamn time, bro," Mav calls out as Linc pulls back from the kiss so hot that my panties now definitely need replacing. Mav claps his hand on Linc's shoulder, despite the fact he's still pressed up against me, having basically just claimed me publicly.

"You have got to be fucking kidding me!" I wince at the screech. Ah Blair, always with her perfect timing. She storms over to where we're standing as Linc lets me down to my feet and I push my skirt back down. "You're seriously all fucking her? What the hell is wrong with you?"

"I thought you were with Raleigh?" I say, feigning boredom. Sometimes I think that's the best way with her. "Why would you care who I'm fucking if you have him?"

"Shut up, you stupid fucking skank whore."

"Blair, speak to her like that again, and see where it gets you," Lincoln growls, stepping in front of me, while Maverick barks out a laugh. "Do not fucking test me. Not with her. You, more than anyone, should know fucking better."

I peek around him, and Blair looks like she's going to cry. I have no idea why. What could I have possibly done to make her hate me this much?

She stomps her foot and flicks her straight blonde hair over her shoulder. "This isn't how this was meant to go, Lincoln. We had a deal. You know what's at stake for me."

Her voice cracks, and I go to move in front of Lincoln, but Maverick weaves his arms around my waist and pulls me back. "Not yet, princess. She needs to get with the program."

"Blair, I don't give a fuck. I told you to back off and you didn't. I told you I'd still help you, but you just kept pushing and that's on you. You're on your own. I won't help you anymore, and that's not on Octavia. That's on you for being a desperate bitch. And just so you know, he really did try to rape her. He would have, too, if we hadn't shown up. So maybe you should think twice about just how much the fact that your world is about to crumble around you is your own fault."

"Please," she whimpers, a tear slipping down her cheek before she swipes it away. "I can't… I don't have any other options."

"I said no, Blair. You made your bed, now go fucking lie in it."

She glares at me over Lincoln's shoulder before turning and storming away, just as Finley pulls into the space beside us, followed closely by Indi in her Wrangler.

"What did I miss?" Finley asks as he climbs from his car and Blair screams at some unfortunate soul who dared get between her and the front doors of the school.

"I have no idea," I tell him, before he looks at Lincoln.

He shrugs and just says, "I called it a day." Like that explains everything.

"What he's not telling you is how he claimed our girl right here for all to see," Maverick says, laughing as Indi rounds the car, eyes wide.

"He did what?" she asks, handing me a cup of coffee.

I wrangle myself from Maverick's hold and smile at him before linking arms with Indi. "Girl, we have a lot to talk about," I murmur to her before taking a sip of the nectar. "I'll see you guys in a bit." I blow them a kiss and leave them standing there, watching me go, making sure to put an extra sway in my hips, just for giggles.

"You're telling me we have a lot to catch up on. I know you said Lincoln was your surprise, but I didn't think it would be quite *that* much of a surprise. Hot damn. Did you and your kitty cat have fun?"

"He didn't come near my kitty cat," I tell her, laughing. "But we had a nice time regardless." I fill her in on my weekend as we sort all our crap out before heading to English.

"Hot damn, I turn down one concert, and all the puzzle pieces fall into place for you." She laughs as we slip into our desks.

"Did you have a good weekend?" I ask, wagging my eyebrows.

"You could say that. I swear, I still have paint stuck in places. It's like fucking glue." She groans before sipping on her drink. "But they definitely made it up to me. Around searching for Diego, anyway."

"He's still not back?" I ask, biting the inside of my cheek, cringing on the inside. I totally spaced on asking Lincoln more about it, but I move it to the top of my list. I hate how worried she looks. It's not like I can tell her Diego is alive, because then I have to explain it, and we want the guys to get on, not start a goddamn war.

She shakes her head. "Not yet, and if he doesn't come back, or is in jail or something, Ryker has to step up as his second. It's totally fucked. I'm kinda head over heels for him, but I'm not sure I fit in their world."

My heart breaks for her a little. "I'm sorry. But maybe love can conquer all?"

She shrugs, turning to face the front of the room as the bell rings and Miss Summers floats into the room. "One can hope?"

# CHAPTER TWENTY-ONE

## OCTAVIA

I stare at myself in the mirror, and I almost don't recognize myself. I look way older than usual. My dark, smokey eyes, my long hair a cascade of curls with tendrils pinned back from my face.

And this dress.

The sweetheart neckline, snowy white, with a halter that buckles behind my neck, so light, it feels like it might not be there at all. I step forward, the thigh slit revealing my entire golden leg, extra bronze from the shimmer spray Indi insisted I add, and my white stilettos that ribbon halfway up my calves.

It's almost Grecian, and so freaking beautiful, but so far from what I'd ever usually wear.

Yet another delivery from the Knights.

Apparently the first dress wasn't suitable for tonight. I move back over to my bed and pull the lace mask from the box that arrived this morning.

A masquerade ball.

The white mask is beautifully intricate. The lace inlaid with pearls and what I'm really hoping are just little crystals. It shimmers in the light of the room, captivating.

For an organization that's supposed to be terrifying, they sure have good taste. I wonder, not for the first time, how they had my measurements. How this dress could fit so perfectly. How the shoes feel as if they were made just for my feet.

It's uncanny.

I grab the only white clutch I own, putting my lipgloss and eyeliner in it because you never know when you'll need a touch up. My phone buzzes on the bed, and I take a deep breath when I see Lincoln's name.

**Lincoln:**
Are you ready?

**Me:**
As ready as I'm going to be.

**Lincoln:**
Good. I'm heading over. We need to finish our conversation from before.

I can't help but chew on my lip. There was me thinking that we wouldn't have to discuss this again, but considering everything that's happened in the last week, how he has very much claimed me… I'd been wondering how tonight would go. Especially with everything Harrison expects of him.

Smithy is away for the weekend with his new beau, and I couldn't be happier for him. I'm also secretly glad that he's away because if anything goes wrong, at least he isn't here to suffer the consequences.

Not that I'm expecting anything to go wrong, but everything the guys have told me has me on edge.

I make my way down the stairs, glad that I've worn heels often enough that the slight tremors running through my hands and knees aren't making me worry about staying upright.

The front door opens as I glide down the stairs and I pause, taking in the sight that is Lincoln. Black suit, black shirt, black tie… the mask in his hand is different from mine: a solid half face mask, also black.

"You look…" he looks at me, eyes wide, and shakes his head as if he's unable to speak.

"Thanks," I say, a blush spreading across my chest. "You too."

I reach the bottom of the stairs and he holds out a hand for me, which I take, and gasp as he sharply pulls me into him. "Honestly, you look fucking exquisite."

"I mean, you don't clean up so bad yourself. Is the car here already?"

He shakes his head and takes a step back. "No. We've got some time. I just… I know that you're aware of Harrison's manipulations, but tonight, I don't get to be myself. Tonight I am nothing more than his puppet. Which means I will be with Georgia for the evening."

That destructive, nagging self doubt rears its head inside of me again. Was this last week just more of his games?

It can't have been right?

No, of course not. He wouldn't do that.

Would he?

He must see it all written all over my face, because he steps toward me and cups my cheek with his hand. "You know I don't want her, but I have to do this tonight. If I don't… well, it isn't worth thinking about. This thing between us, it can't—"

I sigh at his explanation, and while none of it makes complete sense to me, mostly because I still have a ton of things I need to know, my heart hurts a little at the thought of him attending tonight with someone else. You'd think having the other three with me would be enough, but no. "You don't need to explain yourself to me, Lincoln. You already told me what your dad wants of you. I get it. You have to be who they want you to be, and that means that whatever this thing between us is… was… it doesn't get to be more than it has been. I just wish you'd trust me enough, respect me enough, to let me help you."

"Octavia, must you really always be so obtuse." I quirk a brow at him. He really is just full of compliments tonight.

"What is that supposed to mean?"

"It means that you are infuriating and exasperating, and still, you're the only thing I want." I suck in a breath, trying to process what he's saying. His eyes blaze as he looks at me, like a thunderstorm that's about to unleash havoc on the world.

"The only person I've wanted in my entire life is you, but I am no good for you. So I keep my distance. You don't need my mess raining down on you. So for you, I stay away. It isn't about me trusting you, or respecting you, it's about what is best for you. Except that sometimes… Sometimes I can't help myself. Like when I'd hear your screams in the middle of the night, and I'd come to you. I am only human, and sometimes, even I break."

"Is that why you had those other guys paw at me in the pool house? Because I'm the only girl you've ever wanted. Your words are pretty, Lincoln, but actions speak louder." The words spill from my mouth, just the tip of the iceberg of the things we should've said to each other before now. I don't know if I can keep doing this with him. It hurts too much.

"Actions speak louder? Like me sending them away, because I couldn't stand to see anyone's hands on you but mine? Like when I dropped to my knees in front of you, because I wanted to replace their touch with my own? Like when I made you come on my face because the thought of anyone else making you come was like fire in my heart?"

I suck in a breath at his words, taking a step back with each declaration. He stalks toward me until my back hits the wall.

"Octavia Royal, there has only ever been you for me. No one besides my brothers gets to ever touch you again. The only person I truly belong to is you. And I'm going to prove it to you. It might be her body my hands are on at this farce, but it's you I'll be wearing." He drops to his knees in front of me, mirroring the movement he did so long ago, except this time he pauses, looking up at me, waiting for permission.

There is something heady about the power of having someone like Lincoln Saint on his knees before me. Waiting for my yes or no. I nod my head just once, untying the buckle behind my neck that holds the dress in place. It floats to the floor, nothing more than a puddle at my feet, leaving me in my white silk panties and white heels. I step out of the dress, lifting it while he watches in rapt silence. I drape it over the back of a chair and move back to stand in front of him.

That's all the permission he needs.

He traces his hands softly up my legs, until he reaches the white silk panties that barely cover me. Curling his index fingers, Linc slowly, to the point of torture, drags the thin fabric down my legs until the only thing between my pussy and his lips is thin air.

I don't touch him even though my hands are itching to sink into the mass of his perfectly combed hair.

Placing both of his large hands to the back of my thighs, he pulls me closer and closer, until my core meets his open mouth.

A shiver courses through my body at the first lick of his tongue. It's hot and warm and everything I need right now.

"Hmm," I moan as he repeats his languorous teasing. Sliding his hands from my thighs to my ass, he digs his nails into my flesh right before he circles his tongue around my clit, flicking it at irregular beats. Keeping me on my toes.

I choke out a mixture between a grunt and a moan, spreading my legs wider and leaning further against the wall to avoid falling flat on my face.

"Linc, God, yes."

His fingers slide from my ass to between my thighs and straight to my pussy where he opens the lips wider still to give himself more access.

My head falls back, my eyes fixed on the ceiling. I probably look like I'm praying. Maybe I am. To the gods of orgasms.

Linc's tongue stops teasing my clit, heading straight from my opening where it spears inside me and stays there until he does this curly thing at the tip and holy mother of God, it touches something in there that I didn't even know existed until this very moment.

Looking down, I see his entire face buried between my legs, his lips and tongue devouring every drop that I give him. His arms are wrapped around my thighs, his fingers contributing to my impending orgasm.

"What the fuck was that?"

He doesn't answer. He can't, what with being busy eating me out and all, but I can almost hear his smirk.

Smug bastard.

My legs shake with his every lick and suck. I'm barely able to stand at this point. Thank fuck for the wall.

Linc backs up just an inch and looks up at me with eyes so sincere I can't help but believe every word he said earlier was unfiltered truth.

He wants me.

He'll kill for me.

He *has* killed for me.

Without a second thought, I raise my leg and drape it over his shoulder, opening up for him even more. His slurps and moans are like a gift; I lock them up in my heart for future need, like when he's being a complete and total dickhead.

With the top half of my back still leaning on the wall, I thrust my hips at him, searching for more friction, more skin on skin, more… just more of him.

That's when he slams two fingers inside my pussy and rips a scream from my throat in the process. Steadily, he fucks me with his fingers while his mouth is sucking on my clit.

"Of fuck, don't stop, please do not fucking stop."

He doesn't. He just keeps building my orgasm up to its peak until I say fuck it and do exactly what I was trying to avoid all along.

I bury my fingers in his hair and push his face deeper into my pussy, grinding on him and spreading my juices all over his clean-shaven face.

I should be ashamed or some shit, but I'm not.

I'm fucking his face, completely out of control, pushing at his back with the heel of my foot. I need him closer, I need him deeper, I just *need* him.

Linc pulls back barely long enough to blow a gust of breath across my hypersensitive clit and I bite down on my lower lip hard enough to break the skin. I can taste the coppery tang of my blood but I don't have time to care because at that moment, Linc thrusts his fingers impossibly deeper inside me and rubs his entire face all over my wet-as-fuck pussy.

I am vindicated knowing that every time Lincoln is close to his date, she'll be able to smell where he's been.

All over me. That's where he's been. All the fuck over my wet pussy.

Linc may be prancing around with her, but he's mine.

*All fucking mine.*

That single thought and the slight bite of his teeth on my clit rip the climax right out of me like a lightning bolt through my bloodstream.

I rub myself all over him, making sure my scent is imprinted on his skin as he gives me one last lingering lick before he looks back up at me with a smirk that would disintegrate my panties right off. If I still had them on, of course.

"With any luck, my scent will be the perfect repellent," I tell him, rubbing my thumb over his bottom lip before bringing it to my own mouth and sucking on it.

Lincoln darts out his own tongue, licking my orgasm right off his mouth.

"Hmm, delicious." He pockets my panties but I steal them back from him, because hell no. Just as I slide them back into place and put my dress back on, the front door opens, and East is standing there, wearing the exact same thing as his brother.

"The cars are here," he says, smirking as he takes in the scene before him.

Linc climbs back to his feet and straightens his tie. "I'll see you both soon." He turns and leaves without a backward glance as East steps in, shutting the door behind him.

"You okay?" he asks and I nod, my heart rate just about going back to normal. "Okay. We should probably give him a minute and then go out to our car. Are you ready for tonight?"

"As ready as I'm going to be," I tell him, mentally steeling myself after the rollercoaster that has been the last twenty or so minutes.

He fixes his mask in place, and I do the same before he offers me his arm. "Then let's get this show on the road, shall we?"

I nod and loop my arm through his. "Let the games begin."

---

The car pulls to a stop in front of the mega mansion on the outskirts of the city, and I can't help but take in the beauty of it. The driveway, if you can call a three-mile road a driveway, has a long pond running down the center, evenly spaced fountains spraying delicate arcs of crystal-clear water into the night sky. The clean, white stone of the water features glistens warmly in the glow of the underwater lights, providing a welcoming sense of warmth and safety and *just* enough light to navigate the long, straight road to the house.

The giant building looms ahead of us, pure stately glamour. Stone columns rise from the top of a wide, stone stairway, illuminated in the same warm light as the fountains. Massive double doors stand in stark contrast to the white marble façade of the structure, dark and sturdy, prepared to stand the test of time and probably withstand a small militia. Every window visible from the front of the house is lit and glittering against the inky black sky as people slowly make their way up the front steps and slip through the doors.

I'm not normally one for obscene displays of wealth, but this place screams old money. "Whose house is this?" I ask, looking back to East, who has been pretty quiet the entire drive.

"This place belongs to Harrison's father. The old man keeps the place for occasions like this, but it usually sits empty, except for the staff."

Huh. Yet another thing on the long list of shit I didn't know but probably should have.

"Do you know everyone here tonight?" I ask, cursing myself for not peppering him with questions on the drive here. He seemed pretty nervous, so I didn't want to make it worse.

He nods, taking my hand as we wait for the car to pull to the front of the line. "Yeah, I've been around this world long enough to know most of the players. Though some are a mystery to all of us. Some people here aren't Knights at all, they're just rich enough to warrant an invite or they're actually nice people, here to help the fundraiser."

"It's an actual fundraiser? I thought that was just a stupid front."

He laughs at the shock on my face. "It's an actual fundraiser. How do you think they all uphold their ridiculous public façades of being decent humans? Every seedy underbelly has a shiny exterior to keep the darkness hidden from the masses. Despite the reach of the Knights, at its heart, it's still a secret society—one that's growing—but a lot of people don't even know they're dealing with the society. They just think it's rich assholes ruling their lives. Oh, to be so blissfully ignorant."

"So who do I need to be wary of?" I ask as butterflies take flight in my stomach.

"Everyone," he says somberly. "I'll do my best to point out who is who for you, and when Maverick or Finley can free themselves up, they'll likely do the same. Just keep your guard up unless there is more than one of us with you. Even then. This place might look beautiful, but the darkest of minds hide in the most beautiful of places."

I nod, and adjust my mask yet again, my hands shaking just a little at the prospect of stepping outside of this cocoon of safety.

"I've got you. You won't be alone at any time tonight, okay? No matter what happens, one of us will be with you at all times." He takes my hand and squeezes it just as the door beside him opens. He steps out and buttons his jacket before offering me his hand. I take it, because climbing out of this car in this dress while keeping my modesty… yeah, that requires assistance.

"Thank you," I say to the man who opened the car door. He's in a gray suit, with a gray mask. His eyes go wide behind the mask, like he didn't expect me to speak to him, let alone thank him. He closes the door to the car before scurrying to the next in line.

What is this place?

"He's a pawn," East explains, and weirdly that makes sense to me in this setting. Not that any of this makes sense complete to me, the whole pawn, prospect, rook, regent bullshit. Who thought a secret society named after a chessboard was a good idea?

It was definitely part of the penis parade.

So fucking pretentious. Then again, everything about the whole secret society thing is beyond pretentious, so at least it fits.

We climb the stone steps that seem to go on forever up to the ornately carved wooden double doors that wait for us. There are two security guards on the doors, so I pull my invitation from the clutch and hand it over. "Good evening, Miss Royal. Who is your guest?"

"Easton Saint." I quirk a brow, daring either of them to say a thing as they look at one another like they're unsure if he should be allowed to enter. I still don't understand the whole thing between Easton and his dad, and him not being a Knight, but I'm also not about to push him on it. If he wants to tell me, or it becomes need-to-know, he'll tell me. That much I trust.

They step aside and let us into a small room where four further guards are waiting. We wait for them to usher us forward. One of them takes my clutch, and before I get a chance to object, he says, "No phones."

"You have got to be kidding me." I look at East who is handing over his phone, which is put into a small plastic pouch with his name scribbled on it.

"Fine, fine." I take my keys from the purse along with the eyeliner and lipgloss, slipping them in East's pocket. "You might as well keep the damn thing. Saves me holding it."

The guy looks at me like I've lost my damn mind while East coughs to cover his laugh. What sort of stupid rule is no phones? Once they've waved their security wand things over us, they allow us entry into the actual gala.

I gasp when the doors open. This place might be a place of darkness where the depraved come out to play, but it sure does look pretty. Twinkle lights are strung up all over, the only actual source of light in the giant foyer. There's a bar set up to the right in front of the sweeping staircase, and there are way more people in here than I thought there would be.

"Drink?" A server asks as they pass us with a tray of what looks like champagne. I look at East and he declines the drink, so I do the same.

"Don't drink anything you can't see being opened," he warns and I nod. Good to know that the same rules apply here as at any high school party. His warning hits a little too close to home, though I learned my lesson well enough at Halloween.

We head through the foyer, and I try to see if I recognize anyone, but the masks make it pretty hard. All of the women are in white with lace masks like mine, the men in black with the solid half-face masks that East has on. All of the male servers in gray, with gray masks, and the females in red, I guess to show the difference of status, but who the fuck knows? It's a very fucking strange set up.

We go to move through the room when someone steps into our path. "Octavia, how nice of you to grace us with your presence."

It takes me a second, but when East stiffens at my side, I know instantly who it is. "Harrison. Good to see you."

"Indeed," he says, swallowing the champagne in his glass, the fake smile that graced his face no longer present as he looks at his son. "Easton, I see you wormed your way in here."

"You asked me to keep Lincoln focused, how better than this?" I look at him, a little shocked because I have no fucking clue what he's talking about.

Harrison barks out a laugh. "Well, at least you're good at following orders. Better than nothing, I guess." He looks down his nose at his son, and I want to kick him in the shins with my pointy shoes.

What a jackass.

"I'll come and find you later, Octavia. But next time we invite you to something, maybe bring better company." He saunters off into the crowd like he didn't just snub his oldest kid.

"Are you okay?" I ask East, who just nods once.

"Nothing I'm not used to."

I bite the inside of my cheek, not wanting to pry. I *do,* however, want to stab my stiletto into Harrison's eye for being such an ass. "Anything I can do to help?"

"It's fine. Let's see if we can find the others before the auctions begin," he says, taking my hand. I let him pull me into the masses, because despite Harrison's obvious distaste for East, he still knows this world and its players far better than I do.

I just hope I can learn the rules of the game fast enough that we can all survive it.

---

The night passes in a blur of faces, talking to people who very much know who I am, but I still have no idea who most of them are. East is the perfect escort, because he seems to know almost everyone.

We've danced so much that my feet are starting to hurt, and despite the circumstances, he's had me laughing so much that my cheeks ache.

Thus far, the Knights seem to have left me alone, and I even bid on a weekend retreat in the auction and won. I might have paid too much for it, but since the money is for orphans, I figured why not.

I've barely seen the rest of my guys tonight, and I know they warned me that would likely be the case, but I can't help but worry that something's happening while I stand here oblivious to it all.

My world could be crumbling and I'd have no idea.

The song finishes and East leans forward, whispering into my ear, "Water?"

"Sure," I nod and let him lead me across the room to the bar. While we're standing there waiting, a pair of arms wrap around my waist.

I stiffen until "Princess" is growled into my ear. I look back and find Maverick staring down at me. He looks like a man starved, and I'm the only food in sight. "You look good enough to fucking eat."

I turn in his arms, relaxing against him. "Hey, stranger. Busy night?"

"Frustrating night," he says when I notice the red on his collar.

"Bloody night?" I ask, and he grins.

"Nothing major, just someone getting a little too big for their britches. Nothing for you to worry about." He leans forward and kisses me chastely. "How has your evening been? East looking after you?"

"Yeah, he's been a perfect gentleman." I smile up at him, happy that he's okay.

Maverick looks up at East and grins that wolfish grin of his. "Lincoln was looking for you." He tilts his head, motioning across the room. "I've got our girl."

East looks at me and I nod. "I'll be fine, go see what he needs."

"Okay, I won't be long." He stoops to kiss my cheek before he leaves. I watch him cross the room and spot Lincoln, his arm around the waist of a redhead, whom I assume must be Georgia. A spike of jealousy runs through me at the smile he wears for her. Her hand rests on his chest.

He must feel me watching because he looks up and catches my gaze, holding it for just a second, his smile dropping before he puts his puppet mask back on and turns back to her.

"Don't worry, princess. It's all just a show," Maverick murmurs in my ear, "Now that I've got you alone, we should quit this party and have one of our own." He wags his brows at me, making me laugh.

"If only. I get the feeling leaving early isn't exactly an option," I say as I glance around the room at the shut doors, and the security standing in front of them.

He shrugs, pulling my attention back to him. "Maybe not, but I'm sure we could still have some fun."

"Maybe after, we can all head back to my place and relax?"

"Oh, princess, I like your style."

I laugh again, because that totally wasn't what I meant, but of course he went there. "Have you seen Finn?"

He nods, and points across the room. "He's with his dad."

I follow where he's pointing and find my blond, brooding god looking about as happy to be here as I've ever seen him. "Is he okay?"

"He's with his dad," is all Maverick says, like that holds all the answers. East returns in that moment and says something to Maverick.

"Best get back to the party, princess. I'll catch you in a bit." He quickly kisses me again before disappearing into the masses.

"Everything okay?" I ask East, who nods and takes my hand, leading me toward the stairs at the back of the room. "Where are we going?"

"You'll see," he answers as we begin the climb to the mezzanine level. It's quieter up here somehow. There are only a few people wandering around, and it's nice to be separate from it all. It's like I can breathe again without worrying about who is around us.

East jerks me into an alcove, and I come face to face with Lincoln.

This isn't where I saw this going when he dragged me away from the party.

"What—" I start, but Lincoln puts his finger against my lips to stop me from speaking. He pushes my mask up off my face and it flutters to the ground at my feet. East's chest pushes against my back until I'm flush against Linc, sandwiched between them. "I don't understand," I whisper, moments before Lincoln captures my lips with his.

I whimper under the heat of it. His lips on me as East's hands roam my body, teasing me in the most excruciating of ways.

"He needed to feel you," East whispers to me, his dick digging into my ass as Lincoln's presses against my stomach. Images of them both fucking me, both of them inside me, flash through my mind, sending shivers across my skin.

Holy shit, this is so fucking hot.

"So I brought you to him," East finishes, his hot breath dancing across my skin before his lips work down my neck, his tongue darting out and teasing. I clasp the lapels of Lincoln's blazer as his teeth latch onto one of my breasts through the fabric, his fingers slipping beneath the thigh slit of my dress, feeling just how fucking wet I am right now.

His groan reverberates across my skin as East unclips the buckle of my dress, letting the top fall down exposing my chest fully, while their bodies pressed against mine hold the rest of it in place.

"Does he make you feel good?" East asks, as he tweaks one nipple while Lincoln's mouth continues its magic on the other, biting down hard when I don't answer.

A breathy "Yes" escapes my lips before East captures them just as Lincoln's fingers slide inside of my pussy.

"We don't have too much time, so come nice and quick for him," East orders, all while Lincoln doesn't say a fucking word.

Forcing my head to turn to the side, East swallows my moans, his hand around my throat as Lincoln fucks me with his fingers while lavishing his attention on my tits.

"Quiet, V," East commands, and I whimper as Lincoln pushes me over the edge, flicking his thumb over my clit. The world bursts into color as I come for him for the second time tonight. He brings his head up and readjusts himself, before nodding to East. He kisses me once more, with so much need it makes my toes curl, then puts both of his masks back on and leaves without a word.

"What in the—" I start as East helps me reclip my dress into place.

"He's having a bad night. He needed you, so I offered some assistance," he says with a smirk, but I am not about to complain.

"Oh," is all I manage to say, and he chuckles before holding his arm out to me.

"We should probably head back," he says, a dark laughter lighting his gray eyes. "Mask back on, Miss Royal."

I pick my mask up from the floor where I dropped it and he ties it back into place for me. "Back into the depravity we go."

---

When my feet ache to the point that I don't want to stand any longer, East takes pity on me and we head out onto the balcony of the mezzanine level. It looks out over the expanse of land in front of the house. Beneath the starlight, lit up like it is, it's just breathtaking.

"We should be able to leave soon, right?" I ask him, and he checks his watch.

"Yeah, I'm not sure why they haven't opened the doors yet. The auctions and fundraisers are done. Dinner is done. It should be winding down by now."

An icy drop of dread runs down my spine at his words. If that's the case, why the fuck are we still here?

"It should be, but we wanted a word with Miss Royal." I turn at the voice and find myself basically pinned in by five men, all in the black on black suits, all with black masks, but set apart from the others by a navy-blue pocket square.

I don't recognize the voice. I try to place the face, but the mask makes it impossible. "And who," I ask, "is 'we'?"

"East, I suggest you give us five minutes with Miss Royal."

The words are more of a command than a request, but I take his hand and jut out my chin. "I think I'd rather he stayed."

One of the men laughs. "She's got balls, I'll give her that."

"No need to be so hostile, Miss Royal," the first voice says again, "This is merely a welcome chat, an invite, as it were, extended by the conclave to you, to join the Knights Society."

"An invite?" I ask, quirking a brow and trying not to laugh.

The man looks me in the eyes, his irises as dark as the night sky; the soulless eyes of a monster. A shiver runs through me as I hold his gaze. "Yes, an invite."

"Well, I'm flattered, but I think I'll decline. I'm very happy with my life as it is, thank you." I sound more confident than I feel and East squeezes my hand. I'm not sure if it's in encouragement or warning, but I'm just winging it and hoping for the best.

Lincoln said there's no escaping them, but if I don't become one of them, then they have no hold on me.

Right?

"You might want to rethink that," the man says, his voice low and menacing. The others stay quiet, watching and assessing my every move.

Nothing quite like feeling like I'm on show.

I take a step forward, keeping my fingers linked with East's. "If that was all, gents, I think I'll be heading home. It's been a long night."

I pause, waiting for them to let me pass, but the man who has been doing all of the talking grabs my upper arm and squeezes so tight, I know I'm going to have a bruise. "I will be seeing you again, Miss Royal, and next time, I might not be so nice."

I hold my ground and lift my gaze back up to his before trying to tear my arm from his grasp. "Maybe next time, I won't be so nice either."

I have no idea how my voice isn't shaking, because on the inside I'm a fucking mess. Each and every one of them looks at me like they want me dead. They probably do.

"Father, you should probably let her go." Maverick's voice rings out in the silence, and I suck in a breath. That's his dad?

How did I not recognize him?

I officially hate masquerade parties.

"Maverick, it's fine. We were just having a nice chat with your friend," Mr. Riley says as he releases me.

Maverick saunters over, standing at my side, flanking me with East. "I'm sure you were. But I'm also pretty sure she said she wanted to leave. I didn't realize tonight was a hostage situation."

"You should watch your words, boy," his father hisses, but Maverick barely flinches. If anything, he stands taller.

"Maybe you should keep your cool, old man. There're a lot of people here after all. God forbid you besmirch the Riley name," Maverick counters, and I swear I hold my breath, waiting to see how this goes down.

His father barks out a laugh and clasps Maverick's shoulder. "Indeed. Run along, children. I'll be seeing you soon, Miss Royal."

Maverick wraps his arm around my waist, my opposite hand still intertwined with East's, and we walk away from the Conclave.

I think I'm going to be sick.

"We should get out of here," Maverick says quietly, and East nods.

"I'll get the others and meet you by the cars," is all he says before he darts off, leaving me with Maverick.

I look up at him as he guides me down the stairs, into the safety of the crowd. "How much trouble am I in?"

He looks down at me, looking more somber than I've ever seen him. "I'm not sure, princess, but it's not good. The Conclave doesn't corner people like that. We need to get you out of here and speak to the others about it all."

My stomach rolls at his words, and the severity of the situation hits me.

I might just be royally fucked.

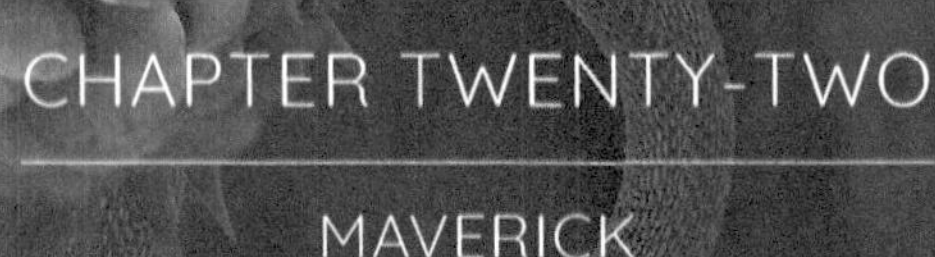

# CHAPTER TWENTY-TWO

## MAVERICK

After spending the night at V's, I kind of dread heading home. Last night did not go to plan, and we still have no fucking idea what the hell the Knights want with her, beyond them wanting her in their ranks.

The way they cornered her last night… it's just not usually how they do things, and it reeks of desperation. No matter how much I rack my brain, I can't think of a reason as to why they would want her so badly, other than her being a legacy.

Sure she has money, but that's not something the Knights are exactly short on. And if it was just about legacy, we already offered them Blair and Nate, which they refused.

Which means it has to be something about her specifically.

Something she has, or something she can give them.

We were up most of the night going over what it could possibly be. Not exactly how I pictured our first group sleepover going. Definitely not as fun as I'd hoped it would be either.

I tiptoe into the house, hoping that my dad is still asleep. Mother dearest wasn't at the event last night, so fuck knows where she was, but after the way it ended last night, I'm pretty sure my dad is going to try and beat my fucking ass.

Won't be the first time, but seeing his hands on V had me seeing red.

The stair creaks as I hit the first step and I curse internally, pausing in the hope no one is around.

"There you are, I wondered when you'd make it in." My dad looks down at me from the top of the stairs, before heading toward me. I take a step back, into the main foyer, and prepare myself for whatever is to come.

For V, I'll take whatever this asshole has to dish out.

"I spent the night with the guys."

He barks out a laugh as he passes me. "And with your little whore."

I clench my hands into fists and take a deep breath, that dark pit inside of me firing up. No one gets to call her that. Not even him.

"Don't look so angry, Maverick. I just call them as I see them." He pours himself a glass of scotch from the decanter, offering me one too, but I shake my head. "Your loss. It's the evening somewhere in the world."

He shrugs before coming to stand back in front of me, still in his suit, minus the blazer and tie. Glass in one hand, the other in his pocket. "I assume you all spoke about the Conclave last night?"

I don't make a move as he swigs back his drink, his dark eyes pits of nothingness as he watches me.

"You need to bring that little bitch to heel. And if you don't, it won't be just her that suffers. I can't, and won't, save you from the Conclave if you go against us," he says before turning his back on me, moving to where the decanter sits on the opposite side of the room. He pours himself another drink and takes a seat, calmer than I've seen him in a while.

He must've taken his anger out on some poor girl already.

"What do you want with her?" I ask, since he seems to be almost reasonable right now.

That was my first mistake. Thinking that the monster was dormant. He launches his glass at my head and I duck. It barely misses me before it shatters on the wall behind me. "That, you little fucker, is need-to-know. Don't think that I've forgotten you stood beside her instead of with me last night. It didn't go unnoticed. If I lose my seat because you're an ungrateful little shit… well, maybe I'll take that out on your little whore too."

I grind my teeth together, trying not to lose my shit. "Do not call her that."

"Well that's what she is. I assume she's fucking all of you. Just like her mother. Always up for a good time. I didn't say there was anything wrong with being a whore. Women aren't good for much else beyond what's between their legs." He shrugs and leans back on the couch while I practically vibrate with rage.

We stay frozen like this, a stalemate, for what feels like hours before he finally leans forward, watching me, and rests his elbows on his knees, almost taunting me. "What's wrong, boy? Angry? Think you can finally take me? I fucking dare you to try."

I take a deep breath, trying not to let the rage consume me.

"You're just like me. You might try to deny it. You might think you're better than me, but the apple doesn't fall far from the tree, does it?" His eyes flash with amusement while I stand there, unable to say a fucking thing. I hate how paralyzed he makes me. Give me any other monster, and I'll take them on without thought.

But him?

He'll always be the monster that hides in my closet.

The one that makes me tremble with fear.

Because he's more than just words and threats like Harrison. He enjoys it when you scream. He fucking gets off on it.

Maybe he's not wrong. The apple doesn't fall far from the tree.

But I'd never do to my kids what he's done.

He stands and strides toward me. He moves so quickly I almost don't get a chance to duck when he rears his fist back and swings at me. "I'll teach you to fucking defy me."

His fist grazes my cheek bone, as I manage to move just in time, but I don't see the follow up before it's too late, and he knocks the air from my lungs with a fist to the chest. I crumple to the floor, trying to suck in breath, but nothing comes.

His fists rain down on me in a flurry, until he gets bored and starts to kick me, stomp on me. By then, I'm too injured to move.

"Edward! What are you doing? You're going to kill him!" my mother screeches as she flies down the stairs. One of my eyes is basically swollen shut, but I can just about see her as she kneels in front of me.

"Little asshole deserves to die. He disrespected me last night, in front of fucking everyone. He's lucky I don't flay his little bitch and make him watch."

I groan, anger burning through me at the thought of V in his clutches. And he laughs. He fucking laughs before he spits on me. "He's nothing more than a dog; one who needs to be taught who his master is."

He kicks me once more while my mother screams at him, before walking away in the direction of the basement. I hear a scream as the door opens, but I can barely fucking move. Not that I've ever helped anyone in his basement. I've never gone down there, and I never will. That probably makes me a shitty human, but I have other things to worry about.

"Oh, Maverick, when will you learn?" My mother sighs. "Let me call an ambulance."

"No," I croak, "I'll just call Finn."

She pulls my phone from my pocket and dials, putting it on speaker.

"What's wrong?" is how he answers. I swear he's fucking psychic sometimes.

"Finley, it's Lenora. Maverick and his father… well, they had a bout. He won't let me call an ambulance."

I hear a car start and the line goes quiet. A door slams before he speaks again. "I'm on my way. And Mav? Pack a fucking bag."

The line disconnects and my mom looks down at me like she might cry. "He's right. You probably shouldn't stay here right now."

Usually I'd try to argue, but if this is the start of things to come, then I'm not about to stick around for it. My mother should leave too, but she's as bad as he is most of the time. She must be sober this morning. This is the most mothering she's done in a few years. I'm not expecting it to last.

She helps me stand up, and I grind my teeth so as not to cry out. My ribs are definitely bruised, if not broken.

Finley enters the house just as I manage to stand alone. "Fuck, man."

I nod, groaning as I grip the bannister to stay upright.

"You stay there, I'll go grab you a bag, and then we're out of here." I nod and he jogs past me, heading up the stairs. I should probably worry about the screams that came from the basement, or leaving my mom here with my dad, but I don't think about any of that.

All I think about is, if he's willing to do this to me, what the fuck would he do to V if he got his hands on her?

The thought alone is what keeps me standing until Finn reappears with a few duffels of my shit.

"Let's go," he says, putting an arm around me and helping me hobble from the place I've always called home.

I'm not sure when I'll be back here, and I'm not sure that I give a fuck.

---

After Finley takes me to visit his private doctor, we head to Lincoln's. My ribs are wrapped, I've got a full script of painkillers that I probably won't touch, and one of my eyes is entirely swollen shut. The worst part is the headache. Even just opening the one eye I'm able to hurts.

Doc said I probably have a concussion, but I'm not about to go to an actual hospital to get checked out further. The last thing I need is someone asking more questions.

I already told Finley about everything that happened with Dad and his insane interest in V. He's smarter than me, so maybe he'll figure out what the fuck it is they want with her, because God knows it's not likely to be me that pulls the rabbit from the hat.

We pull into the Saints' drive, the gate closing behind us with a loud clang that I swear has me seeing colors, and find Linc waiting for us when we pull up.

Finn hops out of the car, and I'm just glad he didn't bring the Aventador, 'cause fuck getting out of that right now. Lincoln opens the door and I slide down out of the Range Rover, groaning when my feet hit the ground.

"What the fuck happened?" Linc asks and I try to grin at him, but wince when the split in my lip pulls.

"My dad wasn't too thrilled about me taking V's side last night rather than standing with him."

He curses before slamming the car door closed. "This is bullshit!"

"It cool if I chill here for a few nights, till he's cooled down?"

Lincoln looks at me, and the bags in Finn's hands. "Usually, yes. But Harrison is home, and we both know he'll kick you out if Edward breathes a word to him."

"Well, fuck," I hiss, resigning myself to the fact that I'm heading back home to that nightmare.

"What in the fuck happened to you?" I look up at V's screech as she tears across the space between us.

I let out an *oomph* as she tries to hug me.

"Sorry, sorry. What happened?" She looks at the others when I don't say a word. "Someone better tell me what the fuck is going on and why he looks like he went ten rounds with Wilder."

Goddamn she's hot when she's pissed. "Just a little disagreement with dear old Dad, princess. Nothing for you to worry about."

"Your dad did this?" she asks, taking a step back, her eyes wide in horror. "Because of last night? Because you stood up for me."

Well, no one ever said she wasn't a smart cookie.

"It's all good. I'm still alive and kicking."

"Maverick Riley, don't you dare downplay this," she scolds. "I am so sorry."

I look to the other two for help, but they're whispering between themselves. "You've got nothing to be sorry for, V. This isn't your fault."

"Have you seen a doctor? Is there anything I can do?" she asks, tracing her fingers down my face.

"Well, you could let him crash with you for a few nights," Linc pipes up, and as much as I want to glare at him, also, hell yes. Unfiltered access to my girl? Not something I'm about to turn down.

She looks between Lincoln and I, a little shocked, but I watch as she makes the decision and it takes root. "Yeah, of course, whatever you need. Smithy will be happy to have more people in the house. Do you have everything you need? I'll go tell him you'll be staying. He was supposed to be away for the weekend, but came home early this morning."

She pulls away but I grab her hand, wincing at the sudden movement, and she looks at me, disapproving, but it melts away when she sees I'm in pain. "What's wrong?"

"Nothing, just didn't want you to go yet." I try to smirk at her, to hide just how fucking vulnerable I feel right now.

She wraps her arms around me gently and places her head on my chest. "You don't have to. Come on, let's get you settled in."

Pulling back, she glances at the others. "You coming too?"

They look at each other and nod. "Yep, we'll be over in a second. I'll bring his bags," Finn says. I have no idea what the two of them are up to, but I'm sure they'll fill me in soon enough.

V pulls on my hand gently and tugs me along behind her. We walk in silence over to her place, and Smithy is in the kitchen when we arrive.

"Oh, Master Riley! What in the… are you all right?" He clucks around me while V tries to explain that I'm okay, and that I'll be staying with them for a bit. "Yes, of course. I'll make up the guest room. Not a problem at all. You get comfortable on the couch. Do you need a doctor? I can call a friend of mine to take a look at you."

"Thanks, Smithy, but I already saw a doc. I'll be fine. Just need to take it easy for a few days."

He glances over me and his worry is obvious. "If you're sure."

"I swear it," I say to him, trying not to grimace at the ache in my ribs. He hurries out of the room, muttering about the Knights, but I don't quite catch what he says. "Can we sit?"

"God, yes, sorry!" V exclaims and helps me over to the couch, where I lie down. I groan with pleasure as I get off my feet. The ache in my ribs is still there, but nowhere near as bad as it was when I was standing. "Do you want a drink? Something to eat?"

"Stop fussing, I'm okay," I tell her playfully as she sits on the coffee table watching me.

"I've never seen someone look as fucked up as you do right now, so excuse me for fussing. I'm so sorry, Maverick. If I'd have just accepted their invitation…"

She trails off but I shake my head. "Then you'd be in as deep as we are, and

God knows what they'd have you do for initiation. Not gonna happen. My dad probably would've found another reason for this anyway. It's one of his favorite games. How far can he push before I die?"

She gasps, her eyes wide, and I realize what I said.

Fuck it. Can't take it back anyway. There's no point in lying to her about who my father is. If we can't find out what they want from her, she's going to find out at some point anyway.

"There are worse things in life than death, trust me," I tell her before getting comfortable on the couch. I'm saved from the questions in her eyes as Lincoln and Finley enter the room.

Thank fuck for that. Her puppy dog eyes slay me. I'd tell her every fucking secret I know if she hit me with them. Linc would probably kill me for it too.

"All sorted?" Finn asks as he drops my bags at the side of the couch. He steps forward and scoops V up in his arms, sitting in the chair with her in his lap.

Lucky bastard.

I might get to live here, but I'm severely out of action.

Though I'm pretty sure if she went on top, I could totally still get down with that.

"Yeah, Smithy is sorting him a room," she says as she snuggles into him. He smirks at me and I give him the finger. Asshole.

"I'm sure he'll work his way into your room soon enough," Linc snarks as he drops onto the couch by my feet, "But for now, this setup works. Shame you don't have room for Finn too."

"I mean, I do," she says with a shrug before looking up at the guy in question. "You can stay here if you need to."

He squeezes her tight before kissing her and I groan as she whimpers against him. I do love to watch, but fuck me. All I ever want to do with her is play.

"I might just take you up on that." He nips at her lip, and I look up at the ceiling. Only I could be this fucked up and still lie here with a fucking semi.

"Well, let me know," she says all breathy, and I swear I can fucking taste her.

"Please, for the love of my soon-to-be blue balls, take it down a notch," I plead, and Finn belts out a laugh.

"Fuck you, man. You deserve some blue balls."

I launch a cushion at him, gasping at the burning sensation that tears through my ribs and remembering at the last second that it's more likely to hit her than him, but he grabs it before it does.

He's about to tear me a new one when I'm saved by the Smithy.

"Your room is all made up, Master Riley. Please let me know if you need anything at all. Will you all be staying for dinner?"

V jumps off Finn's lap and hugs the old man while I give Finn a shit-eating grin, because I'm not the only one with a semi.

"Thank you, but you don't need to cook. We can just order pizza."

He scoffs at her in horror. "Wash out your mouth, Miss Octavia. I think not! We have guests. I'll make pizza if you would like pizza." He looks across at the rest of us, and I just try not to laugh. One: it totally won't be appreciated, and two: the idea of laughing right now makes my ribs scream, let alone actually doing it.

"Pizzas it is," he says, extracting himself from her and heading into the kitchen.

"Well, I guess you're all staying for dinner."

She smiles, leaning on the arm of the chair, when Finley pulls her back into his lap. He whispers in her ear and she laughs gently. "Nowhere else we'd rather be."

# CHAPTER TWENTY-THREE

## OCTAVIA

It's been almost a week of having Maverick in my space… and, oddly enough, it hasn't been weird at all. We seem to have just kind of fallen into a routine. Not that Maverick went to school for the start of the week, but I've driven in with Lincoln every morning, and either come home with him, Finn, or Indi.

Though, study night with Indi was definitely interesting with Maverick here too. They've developed this love-to-annoy-each-other thing, which was funny as fuck to watch, even if it was distracting as hell.

"You got much planned for this weekend?" Indi asks as we get changed after Gym.

I think over my plans and my eyes go wide. "Shit! It's Mav's birthday tomorrow."

"Oh hell," she groans. "You forgot?"

"I did, we've had so much going on that I totally spaced. I need to go shopping." I can't believe I forgot his birthday. His eighteenth.

Fuck.

"Maybe just go to like Six Flags or something? Or take him skydiving. He's the adrenaline junkie type, right? And he's on the mend, so why not? Or head out to the mountains for the weekend and go snowboarding. He seems the type."

"You, my friend, are a freaking genius." I swear I could kiss her. That's a great idea. Now to get the others on board, because there is no way I'm doing a weekend away with just Maverick. "And while I remember, I won a spa retreat weekend away for next weekend at the gala, if you're up for it."

She grins at me, nodding her head. "Massages, pampering, and time away from this place? Hell yes I'm in."

"Has everything been okay with you lately? I feel like a shitty friend. I've been so wrapped up in my bullshit that I feel like we've barely spent any time together since the start of the year."

She scoffs before closing her locker. "Girl, we've both been juggling, but you are far from a shitty friend. Plus, now we have next weekend. As for everything going on with me, it's fine. It's all Kings related. The time away from the insanity will be nice."

"Let's just hope the crazy doesn't follow us," I joke and then wince.

*Way to jinx yourself, V.*

"Fingers crossed. I've gotta jet; I've got a date with three very surly Kings. They have a meeting tomorrow, and if Diego isn't back… well, I have no idea what's going to happen. All I know is this stress is making me gray. Do you have any idea how many times I've had to touch up the roots of this purple? I'm honestly tempted to just go silver and save myself some time."

"I mean, you'd rock the silver. Why the fuck not?" I close my locker and head through the halls toward the parking lot with her.

Lincoln, Finley, Maverick, and Easton are all standing by the Porsche, which just happens to be next to Indi's Wrangler and has been all week.

"They're all a little protective, huh?" She smirks, nudging me with her shoulder.

I sigh, shaking my head. "I'd say you have no idea, but, well, I've met Ryker."

She bursts out laughing, drawing the attention of my guys. "Yes, yes you have. He's not usually so assholey, but this whole Diego thing has him on hyper alert. Plus, he really doesn't like the Saints."

"Yeah, I got that much. They'll come around, but we can worry about that later. I'll drop you the details of the retreat later?"

"Sounds good to me." She hugs me and breaks away to head to her Wrangler while I head toward the guys, who go suspiciously quiet as I approach.

"Talking about me?" I ask, an eyebrow quirked.

Maverick saunters over and wraps his arms around me, smirking at me in that cheeky way he has. "About you, princess? Us? Never. Do you really think so little of us?"

I plant my hands on his chest, swatting him a little, mindful of the bruises that still stain his inked skin. "Not at all, but if you think I'm not aware that you all still have a ton of secrets, you're kidding yourself."

His smirk grows to a fully fledged wolfish smile before he leans down and whispers, "Some secrets are better kept hidden." He pulls back a little before capturing my lips with his, biting my bottom lip as he ends the kiss.

"Do you have any plans for tonight?" Finley asks, and my cheeks heat a little as I turn to the rest of them. You'd think I'd be okay with it by now, but it's too easy to get wrapped up in each and every one of them.

"Not yet," I say cautiously. "Why?"

Maverick tightens his hold around my waist, dropping his chin onto my shoulder. "Well, you might have forgotten, but it's my birthday tomorrow."

"Had not forgotten," I tease. "What did you all have in mind?"

"Well, since he's still recovering, we were just thinking a movie night, the five of us. Smithy is still out tonight, right?" Lincoln asks and I nod.

"Yeah every Friday, like clockwork. He's nothing if not a man of routine," I confirm and East grins.

"Perfect. Then let's head to your place. I'm thinking tacos?"

I let out a whoop. "That, right there, is why you're one of my favorites."

"Hey," Mav whines. "It's my birthday. How come I'm not the favorite?"

I turn in his arms as the others pile into Lincoln's car. "I never said you weren't. I said favorites. The *S* is vital."

"Good." He nips at my lips again before Lincoln hollers at us from the car. "We should probably do as his Saintship requests."

I giggle at his nickname for Linc. "And here was me thinking you weren't one for following the rules," I tease, "But yeah, we probably shouldn't rile him up too much."

I take his hand and lead him to the car. He jumps in the front, riding shotgun thanks to his injuries. Finley is leaning against the side of the car, door open, waiting for me. "Thanks," I say as he takes my bag so I can climb in. I scoot over to sit in the middle since, despite all my curves, I'm still the smallest one of the five of us.

Finley splays his hand across my thigh as we drive back to my house, and I give Lincoln the code so he can just pull into my drive rather than go to his first.

We pile out of the car and into the house to find Smithy singing in the kitchen. It's so nice to see him so happy. He has definitely had a pep in his step since he starting dating whoever this mystery person is. I'm just excited to meet them. Though I wouldn't mind doing a deep dive into whoever it is' past, because, well, life in the Cove has made me more than a little cynical and untrusting.

"Afternoon all, having a night in?" he asks as we pile into the kitchen. "Milkshakes?"

"Smithy, you truly know the way to my heart." I sigh as I slip into one of the stools at the counter.

He grins at me, hand on his heart. "I try my best, Miss Octavia. I made some salted caramel earlier for a cheesecake, so how does salted caramel and dark chocolate sound?"

I salivate at the sound of it. "Yes, please." I nod and the others all agree.

"Don't worry, Master Lincoln. I've got strawberry in here for you too."

Lincoln smiles as he sits opposite me. "You're too good to us, Smithy."

Smithy's chest puffs out as he goes about making us milkshakes, and we talk about school shit until he's done. "Hot date again tonight?"

"Indeed, Miss Octavia. I'm heading out shortly. My cheesecake and I have plans." He winks. "Do you need anything before I leave?"

"Nope, I'm sure between the five of us we will survive."

He frowns at me. "Do not burn down my kitchen, Miss Octavia. I'll forgive you murder, just not murder of my kitchen."

The guys all start laughing. My lack of culinary genius is well documented at this point. "I promise not to touch a thing. Finley and East can both cook, even if the rest of us can't. If all else fails, I know there's still lasagne in the fridge."

He nods and heads back to his rooms, I assume to get ready. I turn to Maverick, who is slurping down his milkshake like someone might steal it. "So, since it's your birthday weekend, what are we watching?"

He grins while Linc and Finn groan. "Why don't you pick, princess? I'm sure I can get on board with whatever you choose."

"Maverick Riley, who knew you were such a cutie?" I laugh and his eyes darken.

"Just racking up favorite points."

I can't help but laugh at him. "No points needed. I don't pick a favorite anything. Them's the rules."

"Speaking of favorites…" Lincoln starts, stealing my attention. "We wanted to speak to you about this thing between us all."

I swear my heart stops in my chest. While I'm aware they've all spoken about it before, and Mav told me all casual that they're all good with it, we've not had 'the talk' and I am so not ready for it.

"Oh?" is all I manage to squeak out under his intense gaze. "What about it?"

"We wanted to lay down some… rules."

"Rules?"

"What Sainty is trying to say," Mav interjects, "is that we're all chill sharing you. As long as it's just us. No outsiders."

My eyes go wide. I hadn't even considered anyone else. The four of them are more than enough to juggle. "Okay…"

"And while it probably doesn't need saying." Lincoln pauses for a moment, sighing. "We aren't interested in anyone else. So it's just the five of us."

"What about Georgia?" I kind of hate myself as the words fall from my lips, but it's out there, so I hold my breath as he shakes his head.

"Georgia is nothing. I'm not interested in her. I'm doing what I must to repay Harrison for the favor I owe him. Nothing more, nothing less."

"But what happens if that favor means taking things further with her? You already told me your dad has zero lines that he won't cross for the Knights."

Lincoln leans back in his chair while the others just watch us both like we're the goddamn movie. "What exactly are you asking me, Octavia?"

"I'm asking if you're going to fuck her."

God, I sound so needy, and I hate it. It's selfish. I don't even know why he owes Harrison, but the thought of him touching her like that… it makes me sick and pissed off all at once.

He moves forward, leaning his forearms on the counter. His eyes darken as he narrows them at me. "The only person I intend on fucking anytime in the future is you, Octavia."

Sweet baby Jesus.

"Okay," I say, nodding, unable to tear my eyes from his.

"Well, now that's settled," East interjects, "Tacos anyone?"

I burst out laughing. Thank fuck for him. "Yes, please. I am so here for tacos."

"You, sweet girl, are on lettuce duty because Smithy won't forgive me if I let you near his stove." He kisses my cheek as he passes me on his way to the refrigerator.

Smithy appears seconds later dressed in jeans and a sweater, and I swear to fuck my jaw hits the floor. He owns something that isn't a suit? Well, damn.

"Smithy, my man, you look fly as hell." Mav grins at him.

"Why, thank you, Master Riley. Are you sure you don't need anything before I leave?"

East shakes his head. "Nah, I've got this. You've got taco boats in the pantry right?"

Smithy smiles and nods. "I run the house for Miss Octavia, of course I have taco boats."

I let out a cry of fake outrage and he laughs at me. "I will see you all on Sunday. Please try to behave."

"We'll be on our best behavior," Lincoln tells him, and Smithy gazes at me like he doesn't quite trust it, but turns to leave regardless.

"Have fun!" I call out as he leaves before focusing back on my guys. At least tonight should be fun, even with the conversation from earlier hanging between us. Well, for me at least. The rest of them start helping East prep tacos while I don't even end up with the goddamn lettuce.

Apparently I can handle a gun, but chopping food in the kitchen is too dangerous.

Not that I'm complaining. Watching the four of them be all domesticated is hot as shit.

Sometimes it's fun being me.

---

After the movie ended, Linc and East went back next door, but Finn decided to avoid home for the night, so he's crashing here with me and Mav.

"Someone needs to be able to protect you if your stalker comes knocking. Mav's still down for the count," Finn teases while Mav scoffs.

"I'm more than able to fight or fuck thank you very much."

I sit on my bed, more than a little amused as they bicker back and forth. Who would've thought that these two would be the ones that squabble like an old married couple.

"Prove it," I challenge, and they both still before turning to look at me. What can I say? I've thought about it enough, and since they all laid everything out on the table I'm feeling a little… bold.

They look at each other, a silent conversation happening in front of me, before they turn back to face me.

"Are you sure you're good with this?" Finn asks as I scoot further back on to the bed.

My gaze bounces between him and Maverick. This might not have been how I saw our evening going, but I am definitely not complaining. "What is there to not be good about?"

"That's my girl," Maverick says excitedly as his heated gaze roams over my body. I take off my blazer and push myself back against the pillows on my bed. I'd be lying if I said I hadn't thought about playing with more than one of them at once, but I haven't even fucked Finn yet.

"Are you good with this?" I ask Finn, because Mav is clearly fine with it all, and Finley just laughs.

“Yeah, V. If you’re good, I’m good.” I bite my lip from the heat in his stare. I’ve never done this before, so I’m hoping to God one of them is going to lead this thing, ‘cause if they’re waiting on me, it’s all going to go to shit.

Propping myself up on my elbows, I watch, in awe, as Maverick reaches back behind his head and pulls his t-shirt off in a move so fluid it's hypnotizing.

But when my eyes fall on his chest—with its array of colors and designs—my mouth waters at the sight of him, even with the extra bruises.

The sound of Finn's groan breaks my stare and I dart my eyes to him, my teeth trapping my bottom lip, sinking into my flesh.

Fuck, I wish I were biting something else… some*one* else.

"I told you she's fucking gorgeous when she wants to get fucked." Mav is being crude because he knows it turns me on.

"Don't be crass, asshole. But yeah, she's fucking perfect." Finn doesn't look at him when he speaks, he only has eyes for me and, damn, that makes me so wet just thinking about it.

With a scoff, Mav unbuckles his belt and unbuttons his jeans, slowly sliding the zipper down, one frustrating tooth at a time. "The dirtier the better, Finn. Trust me on that."

"You two need to stop talking about me like I'm not here." Cocky assholes.

Cocky—gorgeous, hot as fuck, and infuriating—assholes.

"Spread your legs, princess, show Finn just how wet your pussy gets when I talk to you like my favorite little whore." I almost wish he were wrong, but he's not and I have zero shame about just how hot he gets me.

Who needs shame when you can get orgasms?

As I spread my legs wide enough to give them a clear view, my skirt falls down my thighs until it rests at my waist. The only thing sitting between my pussy and Finn and Mav's view are my soaked panties. Judging by the impressive, if not scary as fuck hard-on Finn's sporting, he's definitely enjoying the view.

"See that? The perfect wet spot on perfect little silk panties covering a perfect little pussy.” My gaze goes back to Mav at his words and, with a purr in my voice, I give him what he craves. A fight.

"Maybe you're just the appetizer today, Mav. I think I'm hungry for more than you can give me." I grin at him, the defiance in my stare fueling his fire to dangerous levels.

"Hmm, princess wants to play." Not a question, a statement of fact.

Darting my gaze to Finn I drink him in as he pulls his monster dick out of his pants, palming it as he settles on the big chair by my dresser. I have them both in my sights, one behind the other, as I spread my thighs just a little bit further apart.

When Mav pulls his dick out too, all joking and playing are out the door.

He bends over and places both of his hands on the bed between my open legs—his dick bobbing against his bare stomach—as his gaze sweeps over my pussy and up my torso until he reaches my hungry eyes.

"You know what happens when you fight me, princess? I bite back." Without warning, he almost launches himself at me and in half a second his mouth is attacking mine with a kiss so hungry it short-circuits my brain a little. He's all tongue and teeth and punishing fingers digging into the flesh of my thigh.

And I fight right back. I fist his hair with my hand, clutching hard enough to make him growl and bite his lower lip as he tries to retreat.

Fuck that, I'm not done with him.

With eyes like lava rocks ready to incinerate me, Mav—slowly and methodically—swipes his thumb across his bleeding lip before he sucks on the digit with a snarl that should scare the fuck out of me.

It should, but instead… instead it lights a flame inside me that burns like nothing I've ever felt before.

"I told you, brother, she likes it hard and dirty. That's why she's perfect. For all of us," Mav tells Finn over his shoulder, all the while staring right at me with pride and danger written all over his face.

"Are we going to fuck or are you going to wax poetic all fucking night?" I'm having too much fun right now pushing all of Mav's alpha buttons, but I may want to dial it back a bit or else my body is going to be painted in bruises all over again.

Not that I'm complaining.

"Careful, princess." That's all he says before his mouth is on mine again.

When he moves his kisses down my neck, I look over his shoulder to see Finn stroking his dick. He looks at me, eyes blazing, and I cry out as Mav bites the side of my neck. The sound seems to encourage Finley on. Hot fucking damn.

This moment is so fucking hot. Feeling Mav all over my body while watching Finn rub his own cock and wishing he'd let me touch him instead.

The thought makes me moan and writhe under Mav's ministrations.

"You want him too, don't you, princess? You want to touch him and taste him while my dick is fucking you, don't you?"

Looking back at Mav's expectant gaze, I nod. I'm almost afraid of his reaction but then I remember who I'm speaking to, and I know it's fine. Mav is down with anything as long as he gets to have me.

Which he will.

Fuck yes, he will.

Maverick's mouth moves down my chest and with an ease that surprises me considering his injuries, his fingers latch onto both lapels of my shirt and pulls hard enough to send all my buttons flying across my bedroom.

Holy fucking shit, that was hot.

His eyes flash, and in a blink, his mouth is on my nipple, licking and sucking and biting until I can't form a coherent thought.

Instinctively, I grind up on him, silently begging for more.

When he reaches my stomach, Mav takes the zipper at the side of my school skirt and drags it down, exposing my skin to his hungry tongue once more.

I think he's going to take my skirt off, but he doesn't. He leaves it bunched up at my waist, making his way directly to my pussy.

"Please don't r—" The sound of tearing fills the room and I know I'm a second too late.

My panties no longer exist, Mav has ripped a hole right in the center and pulled it apart so that nothing stands in the way of him and my pussy.

"If you want to save your underwear, next time don't wear any." He kneels up, his hands gripping my waist, and pulls me further down the bed. Darting his gaze my way just long enough to smirk that delicious smirk of his, he turns his attention back to my bare pussy. Licking his way down my slit and across my clit in long, torturous strokes of his tongue until I gasp out his name. He murmurs something I can't hear but feels intimate nonetheless.

My view of Finn is now unhindered. His strokes slow down but he's still so fucking hot that I can't help but stare at him. Him and his giant cock. The girth alone should scare me but it just makes me want him more.

"I don't know what you were just thinking but fucking hell, V, think it again. I'm only just getting started."

"Mav?" I don't look at him as I speak, my eyes are fixated on Finn and every one of his calculated moves.

"Yeah, princess?"

"I want to suck Finn's dick."

The whole room freezes.

Mav's mouth is motionless, just hovering over my clit. Finn's closed fist is frozen midway up his cock as he stares right back at me. Me, I suck in a breath, afraid I've said the wrong thing.

The moment is broken with Mav's low chuckle and a long lick up my slit to my clit.

"You heard our girl. Give her something she can suck on, brother." Just as he finishes talking, he thrusts two digits deep enough inside me that I can feel the curl of his fingers. I buck against him, and he chuckles again, but not once have I let my gaze fall from Finn. I can practically see the wheels turning in his head before a calm washes over his features and he finally rises to his feet. His hand still on his cock, languorously moving up and down his shaft. With measured strides, he makes his way to us and stops at the side of bed where I'm sitting up against my pillows.

"You sure about this, V?" he asks again. His voice is low, almost a growl.

"Yes." It's one simple whimper, but it changes everything.

While Mav fucks me with his fingers, making me cry out as I buck into him, begging for more, Finley moves closer.

Placing a knee on the bed, I feel the weight of us shift. Mav comes up for air long enough to smirk at Finn as he scoots his way to the side of my face, his strokes long and even.

"Open your mouth, princess," Mav orders and I do as I'm told, no questions asked.

Obedient, I push my head back just enough to get comfortable and wait expectantly for Finn to give me what I want.

He doesn't move. Not even an inch. My gaze goes from Finn's dick to his face and frown.

"What's wrong?"

Mav stops eating me out right before he lets out an exasperated sigh. "Fucking hell, man. Really? I was nice and comfy all up in my girl's pussy."

Confused, my gaze bounces between the two of them.

What the fuck?

Mav rises to his knees and gently takes what's left of my panties off—leaving my skirt at waist—before turning me on my stomach with so little effort it takes me a minute to catch up. "He prefers it when you're on your hands and knees," Mav explains like it's the most natural thing in the world.

Okay then. I look up at him from all fours.

Finn's dick is just mere inches from my mouth, teasing me like an ice cream cone on a hot summer day. Mav's behind me, his dick gliding up and down the crease of my ass with shallow dips into my pussy.

"Open your mouth, princess." Again I do as I'm told, waiting to finally taste Finn's cock.

Finn's hand lands at the back of my head, fingers tight on my scalp, and he angles my head exactly as he wants it while Mav lines up the head of his cock at my pussy.

As if a silent command goes between them, they enter me at the same time and I whimper at the fullness of it.

Finn holds my head at the perfect angle for his cock to slide in and even though it stretches out my mouth to the point of pain, I don't pull away as Mav thrusts inside my pussy in a punishing rhythm.

I gag for a second as Finn pushes too far but instead of pulling back, he whispers, "Breathe through your nose."

I do as he says and little by little I accept the sheer size of him all the way to the back of my throat.

When I'm not sure I can take much more, Mav reaches forward and palms my throat. "Fuck." His groan fills the room and he fucks me even harder.

Finley grips my hair tighter, fucking my throat so slowly, I'm not sure how much longer I can keep it up.

"You. Are. So. Fucking. Hot." Each word Mav says is punctuated with a thrust that sends Finn's dick a little deeper inside my throat.

"There they are." I barely acknowledge Finn's words, I'm so concentrated on not gagging on his giant fucking dick.

"Fuck yeah. I love it when she cries."

He pulls out and I close my eyes as Mav removes his hand from my throat and moves it to my clit. Finn licks a hot path up my cheek with his tongue, and I realize that he's licking my tears away.

"That's it, do it again. She's digging it, brother. She's fucking soaked." The slapping of skin on skin behind me is hot. Mav's words are hot. Finn's dirty tongue and gentle touches are hot.

My entire body is on fucking fire, and I've never been more willing to burn.

"You wanna come, don't you, princess?" Mav pinches my clit with two fingers while his other hand digs into the flesh of my hip as he fucks me like a man possessed.

Finn is more controlled as he slides his dick back into my mouth, holding me down with one hand and fucking my mouth in careful, measured thrusts.

It's only when I look up at him and see the blazing fire in his eyes that I lose all semblance of control. Finn darts his eyes back to Mav and it's like an electric current flows through the three of us.

Finn growls as he comes down my throat, holding my head in place while I swallow him down. Mav thrusts one last time, burying himself inside me, the move tearing an orgasm from me so powerful I nearly choke on Finn's dick. He instantly pulls out just in time for me to cry out my ecstasy.

Mav follows closely behind me with a shout before we collapse onto my bed together. I close my eyes as I come down, hearing Finley as he pads across the room. "Gimme two seconds, princess," Maverick says as he untangles himself from me.

I can barely nod, feeling used in the best kind of way, and just lie in my bliss.

Mav reappears and helps me clean up before snuggling with me on the bed. "Where's Finn?" I ask, almost absentmindedly, but a little concerned too.

"He had to go, but he's okay."

I frown, but he holds me tighter. "Are you sure? Did he not want to—"

"Don't even think it, princess. It has nothing to do with you, I promise."

I nod and kiss his chest. "Are you okay?"

"I am more than okay." He chuckles softly as he holds me, and I start to give in to sleep.

"Happy Birthday, Mav," I murmur, and he kisses the top of my head.

"Best birthday ever."

# CHAPTER TWENTY-FOUR

## OCTAVIA

I wake up splayed across Maverick's chest, our legs tangled together, cocooned in his embrace. I really don't want to wake him up, but if I don't move, I'm going to have to do the pee dance, and that isn't exactly conducive to him sleeping either. So I kiss his chest in the hopes he stirs enough to release me, so I don't have to fully struggle-cuddle my way out of this.

He mumbles in his sleep, moving just enough that I manage to slip away and dash to the bathroom.

Once I'm done and freshened up, I grab my phone and pull up a group chat with the other three.

**Me:**
Morning, how does everyone feel about a night up in the mountains for Mav's birthday?

**Finley:**
He'd love that, but he already asked to have the day with just you.

I bite my lip because, well, that's adorable. I also can't help but wonder if that's why Finn split last night. I mean, I doubt it. Mav has never had issues sharing, but who the fuck knows?

**Lincoln:**
If he's changed his mind, we're up for whatever, we had the weekend cleared.

**East:**
I'm good with whatever he decides to do, just let me know. Surprised you fuckers are all awake already.

I laugh softly, because it is the ass crack of dawn still.

**Me:**
Okay, I'll speak to him and let you guys know.

I pull up my thread with Finley separately and drop him a quick message too, since I didn't get to speak to him last night after everything.

**Me:**
Mav said you had to leave. I hope you're okay, that I didn't push any boundaries.

**Finley:**
It wasn't you, pretty girl. Just some of my own shit. We're good. Let me know what the plans are for today, and if he's down for sharing you on his birthday, I'm in.

Staring at the screen, I can't help but wish I'd never left The Cove. Maybe then I'd have more of an idea what haunts each of them. But if I'd stayed, who knows what any of us would look like right now?

I shut off my screen and pad back to bed, dropping the phone on the nightstand before slipping in next to Mav.

"There you are, princess. Running away from the big bad wolf?" He smiles sleepily at me, and I brush some of the hair from his face.

"You're not the big bad wolf. You're the birthday boy."

"Hell yeah I am." His smile widens and he pulls me into his arms.

"What did you want to do today?" I ask, which feels a little like putting him on the spot, but if the mountains are out, I still really want to celebrate with him. Being the last one to turn eighteen sucks, but I love doing birthdays. I'm pretty sad I missed Linc and Finn's over the summer.

He smirks at me and wags his brows. "You."

I burst out laughing. "You're a cheesy fucker sometimes, you know that right?"

"Only with you, princess."

"Now that I believe." I sigh happily. "Now what do you really want to do for your birthday? Skydive? Snowboard? Theme park? The world is your oyster."

He shrugs, and sadness flickers in his eyes. "Birthdays haven't really meant much to me since you left."

My heart hurts for him. Initiation must have messed with him more than he lets on. I shouldn't be surprised, he was only twelve for fuck's sake.

My phone buzzes on the nightstand, but I ignore it until he picks it up and answers it. I look up and see it's a video call with Indi.

"Morning, assface. Where's my girl?" Indi says with a smirk, and I bury my face into his chest to stop the snort laugh that threatens.

"*My* girl is riding my dick," he answers, and her laugh makes mine worse.

"Must be a shitty dick if I can't even hear her," she retorts, and he flips her the finger. I pull his arm down and wave at her on the screen. "Oh, there she is, haiiiii bestie."

"Morning." I smile. "Everything okay?"

She nods and blows a bubble with her gum. "Yep, I just wondered if you guys had decided what you were doing with your day yet?"

"Not yet, why?"

I hear voices in the background, and Dylan appears on screen with her, kissing her cheek.

"We're heading paintballing and wondered if you guys wanted to come," Dylan says with a smirk. "Us versus you guys."

"A chance to shoot at Ryker's cranky ass and not get fucked up? I'm in!" Maverick whoops beneath me and I shake my head.

"I guess we're in. Drop me the details and I'll let the others know."

"Sounds good, sweet cheeks. We'll see you soon."

"You will, maybe this time you won't end up with paint in unspeakable places." I wink at her and she scoffs, sticking her tongue out before ending the call. "I guess we're paintballing for your birthday."

He grabs my hips and pulls me up to straddle him. "Hell yes we are. This is the most I've looked forward to a birthday in ages. But first, I'm hungry."

"Then let's get food."

He leans forward and kisses me until I'm breathless. "I didn't mean food, princess."

---

Getting geared up for paintball has been hilarious. I've never been, but it seems like a more painful version of laser tag. The body armor and mask I'm wearing definitely point to the whole painful thing, but fuck it. Maverick is so excited, a little pain is worth it.

Lincoln was not as excited as Mav at the prospect of shooting at the Donovans, but we're all here, and there seems to be a tenuous peace created by Dylan and one of the other Kings they brought with them, Thomas, and Finn and Mav. East and Linc haven't said a word to the Donovans yet, but the day is young.

"You think this might work? Getting them all to kiss and make up?" Indi whispers as we load our guns with the paintballs. She managed to convince the guy that she needed just purple balls for her and her guys, and we ended up with blue, which made Maverick laugh, because he definitely isn't suffering blue balls at the minute.

"It could. Maybe they just need to shoot at each other without, you know, killing each other, and get some of that testosterone out. Boys usually sort shit out by hitting each other, so it could work." I tighten the strap on my vest and grab my helmet.

"Why didn't we offer to be the stupid flags?" she squeaks. "I can deal with being taken by the opposing team and recaptured… being shot at is going to suck."

Dylan appears as she finishes speaking and lifts her over his shoulder. "Don't worry, shortstack. I got you. I won't let these assholes shoot my girl."

"Put me down, you big oaf!" She squeals and he slaps her ass in response.

"Don't worry, we chose the easy option for you girls. Just have to capture the flag, no having to return to your own base with it. To start with anyway. We'll go easy on you," he explains, still not putting her down, but it does make me feel a little better.

"See you out there, Octavia." He winks at me and walks off with Indi. She pounds his back, but he just laughs as he heads toward Ryker, Ellis, and Thomas. I head over to where my guys are huddled together.

"This looks very serious," I tease as I infiltrate their huddle. "Want to let me in on your super secret spy plans?"

Lincoln rolls his eyes at me, but that just widens my grin.

"Why so serious?" I quote and then burst out laughing, Mav along with me. "I'll stop, I'll stop. So seriously, what's the plan? Or is this just a free for all?"

Finn grins at me and Lincoln scoffs. "There is no way we're taking on the Donovans without a plan."

"You get that this is supposed to be fun, right?"

"Winning *is* fun," Linc responds, his eyes alight. "All you need to do is worry about not getting shot. Because you are our secret weapon. I've seen you shoot. They haven't."

I laugh, because of course that's his plan, but they all look so excited that I'm totally here for it. Even if the bruises are going to suck tomorrow.

I salute him, with a "sir, yes sir," which just makes him smirk again.

"That's more like it. Let's do this." They do a weird boy grunt thing and head out the same way Dylan carried Indi, and I trail behind them wondering if this is either genius on Indi's part or an absolute disaster waiting to happen.

We hike out into the wooded area where the purple flag is planted in the ground, and without even speaking, Finn and Mav break off from Lincoln, East, and me. It's like they're a well-oiled stealth machine.

Not going to lie, I'm kind of looking forward to seeing them Hulk out a little. Paintballing gear shouldn't be hot… but on these four… well hot damn. Apparently a guy with a gun and glorified football pads is hotter than I thought it would be.

Then again, these four could probably wear one of Indi's tutus and I'd still salivate.

"You'll be with us. You are going to capture their flag, and we'll cover you," Linc says as we crouch in front of our flag, waiting for the air horn.

"We're leaving the flag open?"

East chuckles under his breath. "You think he'd leave that to chance?"

My gaze bounces between the two of them and I shrug.

"Finn is currently climbing a tree to take the high ground, he'll act as cover for the flag." East whispers. "Maverick… well… he'll do what he does best."

"Just remember, we need them to think you're helpless until we're closer," Linc adds.

I nod as the air horn goes off, and the air gets real tense. Lincoln locks eyes with his brother and nods. They pull down their masks and stand in unison. It's freaking uncanny watching them move together like this. I make sure my gun safety is off, pull down my own mask, and follow behind them.

Their guns are raised, sweeping as we move through the bush, when I hear the *pop* of a gun in the distance.

Hopefully that's Maverick taking someone out, and not the other way round.

The two of them move through the woods like they've done this a thousand times, but considering East isn't a Knight, I'd be surprised if they have. I try to focus on where I'm going so as not to trip and become a liability, but this is all new to me.

Stealth and tactical advantages aren't exactly things I was schooled in on the road. I have no idea how East is so good at it, but Lincoln looks like he could wage wars single-handedly and come out unscathed. I might not be able to see his face beneath his mask, but he moves like this is second nature for him.

For all I know, it could be.

I see a flash of purple ahead, and tap East's shoulder, pointing in the direction I saw it. East peels off from us, as if to flank whoever it is ahead of us, and I stay with Lincoln.

"Their flag is going to be across the field, planted in the opposite wooded area. Unless they're carrying it."

"They might, Indi did say something about being the flag," I tell him and he nods.

"Let's do this."

He starts moving again and I raise my gun this time, trying to help if needed. We're near the edge of the tree line when I hear a squeal pierce through the air.

"Maverick, you ass hat! You shot me in the ass!" Indi cries, and I can't help but laugh.

East appears from the left and stands on my other side. "Ready?"

"Let's move," Lincoln says, and we haul ass, sprinting across the field, the two of them in front of me trying to protect me from any incoming fire. Maverick appears, bringing up the rear. Crazy asshole has his mask lifted and barks out a laugh as he runs.

He winks at me before he pulls it back down when the Donovan twins appear before us like fucking forest wraiths. Lincoln grabs me and spins me to the right, leaving East and Maverick to deal with the two of them. I want to see who wins, but I try and stay focused.

Who would've thought paintball would be enough to bring out my competitive side?

I see the flag in the distance and change direction, heading straight for it. It's only when I see Thomas I realize they laid their own trap.

Unfortunately for them, they don't know me.

I raise my gun and let off three rounds which hit him squarely in the chest, and I let out a whoop and keep running. I hear shots to the right where Lincoln was, but I don't let myself get distracted. I head straight for the flag and yank that sucker out of the ground when I reach it, setting off the alarm.

Lifting my mask, I do a little jig on the spot, because I feel like a fucking badass, even if this is only round one. Maverick appears and picks me up, spinning me around, before he starts dancing with me.

The others appear in the wooded area as we continue to dance, and Indi laughs at me. "You might've won the battle, but you haven't won the war." She cackles as Ryker steps up behind her.

He looks me square in the eye and smirks. Heart be still, the grump smiles! "We know your secret now, Royal. Game on."

We spend all fucking day running around, and I swear it's like I have a giant neon arrow above my head that says 'shoot here'.

The upside to the day is that Maverick is smiling wider than I've ever seen him and even Lincoln is smiling. Probably because we won.

The other upside is there seems to be an almost tenuous truce between the Donovans and my guys, which helps me breathe a little easier. Lincoln and Ellis are walking together as we head to the parking lot, while Maverick is talking shit with Ryker.

Me, I'm just hobbling along, enjoying the moments of peace and hoping they last.

We gather at the cars and I lean on East, laughing at Indi getting a piggy back from Dylan across the lot. "Today was actually more fun than I thought it would be."

East puts an arm around my shoulder, chest shaking as he chuckles. "Yeah, me too. Who would've thought the Donovans had a sense of humor."

"I heard that, Saint," Ellis shouts, pointing at us, but still has a smile on his face as he and Lincoln join us. "We're great fun when we're not surrounded by assholes."

"You know what they say about assholes," Indi chimes in. "Everyone's got one, some are just more full of shit."

Dylan's laugh booms around us, and even Ryker cracks a smile.

"Now if we just knew where Diego was, we could've had the full Donovan team," Ellis says, and while it's not with malice, the tension goes from sixty to one hundred in a heartbeat.

Indi sighs, tapping Dylan's shoulder to let her down. "I thought we spoke about this?"

"We did," Ryker answers for his twin, and my heart pounds a little faster at just how tense this feels. "Ellis isn't accusing anyone, are you?"

"I'm not. You asked us to play nice, so we're playing nice. Today has been fun. I just wish Diego was here too. That's all I meant."

I let out the breath I'm holding, especially because I know Lincoln knows where Diego is.

"We'd probably have lost harder if he was though," Dylan adds, laughing and breaking the tension. The guys keep up their smack talk, and Indi comes to lean on the car with me.

"That was close," she sighs, resting her head on my shoulder. "I thought all hell was going to break loose."

"Me too." I nod. "I'm glad it didn't. This was a good idea, thank you."

She grins and takes my hand, interlocking her fingers with mine. "It was, I'm glad we did it. And if they can start this without killing each other, maybe there's hope for them actually being friends."

---

Paintballing yesterday was fun, but fuck me, I am sore as fuck. I finish my run with Linc, trying not to whimper from the aches and bruises that cover my body.

We might've won yesterday, but it was close, and once the Kings knew I could shoot, they targeted me like a bunch of dick bags. I might be able to shoot, but tactical advantages really aren't my strong suit.

"You okay?" Linc calls out as I drop onto the lawn once I'm inside the gates. I put my hand up in the okay salute and try not to groan into the ground. He drops down next to me, and I roll onto my back. "What hurts?"

"Everything?" I say and he laughs softly.

Lincoln fucking Saint laughs.

Of course it's at my pain.

"I'd offer a massage, but bruises and massages probably aren't the greatest of ideas."

"I mean, I'm not about to turn down a massage, but you're probably right." I sigh. "At least today I have nothing on my to-do list but a long soak in a bubble bath."

He looks down at me and frowns. "Actually, I was going to see if you wanted to go car shopping. I know the Impala is down for the count, and you can ride with all of us, but I think it'll be safer if you have your own car."

"I can always use Dad's Range Rover if I need it," I tell him with a shrug. "You guys just didn't want me alone because of the whole stalker thing, so I figured riding with you was easier."

The lines on his forehead sink deeper as his frown grows. "We don't know who's had access to it. I'd rather we get you something new, something safe. Preferably bulletproof. Better safe than sorry."

"I'm pretty sure I don't need a tank, Lincoln," I say, rolling my eyes. "I have a stalker, not death threats."

"I don't know, those last round of images looked pretty much like death threats to me," he deadpans.

I sit up and shrug. "I mean, technically, they were against you guys. Not me."

"Octavia."

One word is all he needs to scold me, and I sigh. "Fine, fine. I was really looking forward to that bubble bath, you know."

"You can have your bubble bath after," he says with a shrug. "I'll be back here in thirty to grab you."

"Okay," I say as he stands.

He pulls me to my feet and I brush down my leggings before heading toward the house. "Oh, and Octavia?"

I turn at his words and he captures my waist, pulling me into him before wrapping my ponytail around his hand. "If you're good, you might even get rewarded."

A shiver runs down my spine at the growl in his voice before he leans down and kisses me. My fingers curl in his t-shirt as our tongues battle for dominance. I let out a whine as he tugs on my hair and wins the battle of wills. He pulls back, his eyes hooded as he looks down at me. "See? You do know how to behave."

He kisses me softly again before releasing me. "Thirty minutes. Don't keep me waiting."

I shake my head and haul ass inside. I mean, if that's what happens when I'm good, I'm looking forward to finding out what happens when I'm bad.

Shutting down the alarm, I run up the stairs and rush through a shower. Ugh, boys will never understand how long it takes to wash, condition, and dry hair as long as mine. I swear these extensions make it take even longer to dry too. Thankfully, they fall as wavy as my natural hair once they're dry.

Once I'm ready, I throw on a pair of jeans, my boots, a tank, and a blazer before heading back downstairs. I fire off a text to Smithy to let him know I'm out with Linc and grab my purse and keys before locking up. My phone buzzes and Bentley's name pops up on the screen.

**Bentley:**

Hello, Miss Royal. I'm sure I can help you out. I'm free Thursday evening if you want to meet and discuss your requirements.

I run a hand nervously through my hair, trying to decide if finding my mom is a good idea, then kick myself for going into dumb bitch mode. Again.

*It's better to know and not use it, Octavia.*

I drop him a response to let me know the date and time then head over to the Saints'.

I know he said he'd come over here, but somehow I have five minutes to spare. When I get there, the back door is open so I let myself in and find Mrs. Potts in the kitchen. "Oh, morning, Octavia dear. Lincoln is just upstairs, he mentioned he was popping out with you."

"Thank you, I'll just head up." I smile and make my way through the house. It's been a minute since I was over here, but it's exactly how I remember. I head up the stairs, going straight to Lincoln's bedroom, hoping he hasn't moved rooms.

I knock before I enter, but there's no answer so I let myself in. It's empty. That's when I hear the running water and notice the door to his bathroom is slightly ajar.

"Lincoln," I start, pushing the door open and find him in the shower, his hand wrapped around his dick. He locks eyes with me, but doesn't say a word or stop what he's doing. He strokes his dick, the look on his face almost daring me to look away, but I couldn't if I wanted to. Everything about him is fucking mouthwatering, and his dick… well fuck.

His eyes close as he leans his head against the glass, his cum coating his hand as he moans my name.

I lick my lips at the thought of wrapping them around his dick, having him at my mercy.

He clears his throat, drawing my attention back to him, and smirks. "I'll be out in a minute."

"Erm, yeah, sure, I'll just wait out here." I can feel my cheeks heating as I manage to stumble through my words. After everything I've already done with him, with the others, you'd think I'd have more composure at seeing him get himself off, but apparently not.

God, I'm an idiot sometimes.

I drop onto his bed, trying not to look as off-kilter as I feel. Car shopping with him after watching that is going to be… intense.

My mind wanders back to him in the shower until he appears in nothing but a towel, smirking at me. "I thought it'd take you longer than thirty minutes."

"So did I." I shrug. "Who knew I could get ready so quickly?"

"I'm just going to get dressed. Try not to let your curiosity get the better of you this time." He heads into his closet, and I give him the finger behind his back. Asshole. Taunting me like that is just asking for me to go in there, but I keep my ass where I'm seated and wait him out.

I can hear him laugh in the closet, but I just take a deep breath and pull my phone out, scrolling through the news, because well, how else am I supposed to kill time?

He reappears in a black t-shirt and jeans, grabbing the hoodie and leather jacket combo from fight night, and it's all I can do not to drool over him. "Ready?"

I tuck my phone away and smile at him like I didn't just see his dick. "As I'm going to be. Just promise me no tanks."

His eyes light up as he shakes his head. "Not going to make promises I can't keep."

I let out a deep sigh and stand. This is going to be interesting for sure.

# CHAPTER TWENTY-FIVE

## OCTAVIA

I try not to think back to the sight of Lincoln yesterday as he drives us to school in his Porsche, his hand on the bare skin of my thigh. Maverick stayed with Finn last night, he didn't give me a reason, but I'm also not his keeper, so I didn't question it. I know they're all still a little hesitant about telling me stuff to do with the Knights, so I let it go.

Car shopping with Linc was unsuccessful. I'm not that surprised as we don't exactly see eye to eye on a lot of stuff. He wanted safety, I wanted something not fucking hideous.

Not that I mind being without a car a little longer, because riding to school with him isn't exactly a hardship. Except for the fact that I kind of want to jump his bones. He's just so goddamn restrained, I know that I'm unlikely to push him over the brink before he chooses to take that leap himself.

Frustrating as hell, but I'm not about to push him. It's just not who I am.

We pull into the drive-thru to grab coffee, and I drop Indi a text to let her know I'll grab her one too.

Once we have the five drinks, we head to school, just the low sound of You Me at Six playing in the background. Definitely not what I pictured him listening to, but then, he could have just put it on for me. He's perceptive like that, and it's such a him thing to do.

It's also freaking adorable, but I'm not about to call him out on it either.

He sips on his coffee, handing it back to me as we pull into the parking lot. Indi is standing with the others and grins at me as Lincoln turns off the engine.

"I'll take them," he offers, taking the coffee trays from me once he's unbuckled.

"Okay, thanks." I hand them over and grab my bag, taking my cup back before jumping out of the car.

"My ass still hurts, assface." Indi nudges Maverick who barks out a laugh as I approach. "Good to see you all aren't as battered and bruised as I am."

"Speak for yourself," I huff. "Your boys got me good." Lifting my skirt I show her the purple spread on the top of my thigh, and Lincoln's eyes darken.

"You didn't tell me you had that."

I wave him off, because protector mode is not warranted. "It was paintball, and apparently I bruise easily there. It's fine."

He raises an eyebrow at me, but I just grab Indi's coffee, handing it to her before looping my arm through hers and heading into the school. "You have a fun Sunday?"

"Nope, my cousins flew in on Saturday, unbeknownst to me, and we had family freaking dinner. Dylan got invited in because he dropped me off at home. My family are a fucking nightmare, V. He basically got the Spanish Inquisition. Could you imagine if they knew I was dating three guys? Jesus fucking Christ, they'd lose their minds. Poor Dylan took it like a champ though."

"Well, that's good news at least. I bet he loved it, really. He seems like a people person," I say with a shudder. "Gross."

She barks out a laugh as I open my locker. "Yeah, he actually likes peopling. It's weird, but I love him just how he is."

"Aww, you're adorable. Were they bad losers about Saturday?" I ask as I sort my shit out before closing my locker.

"Nah, they took it okay. It was nice to see them all getting along, even if it was full of snark and jabby comments."

"It was. Maybe there's hope for them yet. Any news on Diego?" I ask, kicking myself for forgetting to prod Lincoln further still. I'm the fucking worst.

"Nothing. But they've put feelers out. They've officially given up on the theory he's out on a bender." She shrugs before opening her locker. "I just hope they find him alive."

"You think they might not?"

"Anything is possible. They work with some really fucked-up people."

I want to ask what they actually do, but the bell rings, stopping the words from forming. "Did you get your assignment done for Miss Summers?"

"Fuck, no. Fuck my life, how did I forget that?"

She grimaces as she closes her locker. "Because we didn't have an actual study night this week. It's fine, I'm sure she'll give you an extension. She's awesome like that."

"Ugh, I cannot let myself get behind again this semester. It was too stressful before Christmas. I have a study night with Lincoln tomorrow to finish up our Business project."

"Has Mr. Peters been gross again?" she asks as we walk to our seats at the back of the room.

I shake my head as I sit down. "No, thank God."

Blair and her bitch squad slide into the room as the second bell rings, all glaring at us. Shock. Horror. Thankfully they take their seats without saying a word. I guess whatever her and Lincoln talked about the other day has finally sunk in.

Maybe I should go over to her house. Try to work out exactly why she hates me so much, use the excuse of picking up the stuff she said I'd had delivered there. It's not that I want us to be besties, but I don't have much family left—she's pretty much it—and the fact that she hates my existence just for breathing, or so it seems, rankles me.

Miss Summers pulls me from my train of thought as she starts class, talking about the differences between the expectations of modern publications and those of classic literature in line with our next choices from the reading list. I'm not going to complain too much, this is by far my favorite class, so if I need to read and compare three texts in depth, and compare them to how I think they'd be perceived if they were released in today's market, then I can do that.

Text analysis is something I'm weirdly good at when it comes to literature.

The class passes in a blink, just like always, and before I know it the bell is ringing.

"Don't panic, leave your things where they are and head out to the fire evacuation point," Miss Summers shouts above the noise. It's only then I realize it's not the bell. It's the fire alarm.

I tap my pockets, making sure my keys and phone are on me. I don't mind leaving my books, but after everything I've been through lately, I'm not leaving my personal items lying around for anyone. We head outside to the evacuation point, everyone complaining around us. It's only when we're outside and I see the black smoke that I freak a little.

I can't see Lincoln, Maverick, East, or Finley.

I have a really bad fucking feeling, and my fingers start to tingle in anticipation as panic seizes me like a hand around the throat.

I scan the crowd as people pour from the building, trying not to freak the fuck out when I see them come around the corner of the building. My heart stops for a second as I acknowledge they're okay, and I try not to question why they're coming from that direction together.

What the hell is going on?

---

After the chaos at school, and basically getting no explanation from the guys, the day was cut short. Lincoln and Maverick had somewhere to go, and East had stuff to do with the school, so Finley offered me a ride home.

Except somehow, we ended up at his place instead.

It's been a long time since I've been in Finley's room, but it's entirely him. It's a different room from the one he had as a kid, and it's done in dark royal blues, white, and black. The giant bed is framed in dark wood, and light barely filters in through the thick curtains.

"So your dad is away?" I ask as I drop onto the bed.

He loosens the tie around his neck as he closes the door. "Yeah, he's gone all week. It's like a fucking vacation."

I can't help but smile. Knowing what I do about his dad, which is still very little, I'm sure that what he's saying is entirely true. "Why do you still live here?"

"Part of the deal. I might be eighteen, but my inheritance from my grandfather doesn't hit until I'm twenty-one. Same as my inheritance from my parents. I have basic access to funds, but nowhere near enough to survive without them. Just the way my father wants it." I bite my lip, contemplating what he told me, while he watches me with a predatory stare. "Is that really what you want to talk about?"

His eyes darken as his gaze roams over me sitting on his bed. My lips curve up, because no, I can think of much better things to do than talk right now. He's been so restrained with me until now, but I want to see him. All of him. All parts of that beast he keeps caged inside of him. I'm sure there's probably something wrong with me, that I want to see it. The thrill at the thought alone should be enough to set off red flags, yet… it changes nothing.

I watch intently as he starts to unbutton his shirt, but then he stops, as if realizing I'm in here too and lets his hands drop to his sides.

"Take it off, Finn. Show me."

His eyes dart to the side, the uncertainty clear in his eyes, but when he looks back at me it's like he's made a decision.

Pulling his tie from around his neck, he takes two steps closer to me and holds out his hand, waiting expectantly. I blink, unsure of what exactly he's asking of me.

"Give me your hands, V."

Our gazes lock and I hold out both of my wrists, watching, rapt by him, as he takes my arms and loops his tie around my wrists. It's mesmerizing watching him do it, almost as if it's instinctive, second nature for him because he never once looks at what he's doing.

He watches me the entire time instead, and being the target of his attention is almost heady. In those few seconds I become his prisoner, but as I study his features it feels like he's becoming mine too. I've never been more willing to be held captive.

"There are things you don't know," he says as he adjusts the tie. "Things I've told only my brothers." He tightens the knot and makes sure it's not stopping the blood flow to my fingers.

"You don't have to—" I start but he cuts me off with a shake of his head.

"I do." Those two little words hold so much weight, I can feel them on my chest and it's almost hard to breathe.

"Okay," I whisper with my hands out like an offering. I don't dare move for fear of breaking this moment. He doesn't speak much, so the chance of him finally opening up… I don't want it to disappear.

He looks around the room in a quick scan, moving to his dresser drawer and pulling out another one of his ties.

This one is a soft pink, almost the same shade as my lip gloss, which is fitting since he presses the largest end to my mouth then fastens it behind my head.

His outdoorsy scent surrounds me, his heat seeping into my flesh, overtaking my senses. He's everywhere without even touching me.

"No touching. No speaking. Those are the rules. If it gets too much, your safe word is kiwi. Nod if you understand."

A thrill runs through me, but I can't help but question his commands. I'm down for the big dick energy he has going on, but he never lets me touch him and I don't know why. Regardless, I nod and the relief on his face is palpable.

He moves me into a position of his liking, and I remain pliant. Straddling me, he scoots up to my chest and pulls my tied wrists up to his headboard. That's when I notice the hooks.

All along the top of his massive headboard, he's got evenly-placed hooks and he latches the tie to the one directly above my head.

It occurs to me that I'm not the first one he's had tied up here, but I push the thought away. We all have pasts. But I can't help but wonder if he's ever let *anyone* touch him.

Once he's satisfied with my position, he crawls back and admires me, eyes roaming me from head to pelvis.

The corners of his mouth tug up into a small smile, and I mewl under his intense gaze.

"There are things about me you don't know…" He reaches back for his shirt and slowly pulls it over his head, ruffling his gorgeous, thick hair.

"There are things no one needs to know." He keeps his shirt close to his chest long enough to bring his gaze back to mine.

"But you, V? You deserve it all. All of me for all of you."

When he discards his shirt to the side, somewhere on the floor, I see it.

I see them.

The scars. Dozens of them scattered haphazardly across his chest, his nipples, his stomach.

He's covered in past wounds inflicted on him throughout his lifetime. Years and years of suffering.

My muffled gasp doesn't surprise him. I try not to react, because he's finally showing me parts of himself that he's obviously self-conscious about, but the sight before me is shocking and cruel. It's abuse at the most profound depths of depravity. Burns, cuts, and things I can't decipher. A map of what he's survived, that led to who he is today.

Alone and closed off.

My shock dissipates and quickly turns into a burning rage. Who the fuck did this to him?

"Don't." One word and my focus is back on him. He's right, this isn't the time to get emotional about his past.

I push down the anger and settle back down onto the plush pillows, letting myself relax as Finn places both of his hands on the outside of my thighs. He runs them slowly up until he has palms full of my ass.

He hasn't taken any of my clothes off but I have a feeling he's taking his time with me. When he reaches the top of my skirt, he pulls the tab of my zipper down and with one expectant look, and a tap on my ass, he asks me to help him.

This is definitely a game I can play, so I raise my ass, a shiver running through me as he pulls it down my legs and tosses it across the room.

Once it's gone, he moves his focus to my shirt, unbuttoning it slowly, methodically, and my anticipation ratchets up.

I watch him intently, every move he makes is so precise and in a few moments my shirt is wide open, leaving me in just my underwear.

"You're stunning, you know that?" I can't answer. I'm pretty sure it's a rhetorical question anyway.

Curling his fingers around the lace cups of my bra, he pulls both down at the same time, exposing my tits, and places the fabric below them.

One thumb grazes my hard nipple, then the other. He's gentle, almost reverent, as he touches me exactly the way he wants to.

Bending down, he captures almost half my tit in his mouth and sucks hard enough to elicit a muffled moan from me.

He repeats the action with my other breast before he pulls back and gets up. I feel the cold where his heat had been just a second before.

Standing at the foot of the bed, Finn unbuckles his belt and pulls the leather strap from the loops before he lets it fall to the floor at his feet.

He undoes the zipper of his pants and my mouth waters. As they drop to the ground, I realize he doesn't have boxers on. He's been commando all fucking day. He bends down and places his pants neatly on the back of his desk chair. When he turns back to me, the fire in his eyes burns white hot and my heart pounds in my chest.

I want to lick my lips but this damn tie is holding my tongue hostage. I want to reach out and grab him, to feel the smooth skin of his cock, but again, I'm captive to his will.

With one hand stroking his cock, Finn places a knee on the bed and his free hand on my thigh.

"Open."

I obey, bending my knees and spreading my legs as wide as they'll go to allow for the sheer size of his body to nestle between my thighs.

He hasn't taken my panties off yet and I wonder if he's like Mav and believes they shouldn't exist, or if he prefers knowing there's an extra layer between me and the rest of the world.

Palming the back of my thighs, Finn places my legs over his shoulders and slides his hands to my ass cheeks before he bites into the lace fabric at my center, ripping it right off like a possessed animal.

It's hot as fuck and, judging by the satisfied grin on his face, I'm certain he knows it. But what is with these guys and ruining my fucking underwear. I'm going to need to go shopping again if this keeps up.

Using two fingers, Finn rips away the rest of my underwear until there's nothing left but two tiny strips at my waist. Then the heat of his mouth is on me and my hips buck against him. His tongue is fucking magical and he uses his fingers to open me up, curling upwards to push against my g-spot. I swear I almost see fucking stars.

He plays my body like an instrument he's mastered his entire life.

He builds me up slowly, biting gently on my clit as his fingers fuck me to a rhythm only he hears. It's the most exquisite kind of torture, and I want more. *Need* more. But this is his show and I'm just here for the ride.

Whimpers spill from me as he pushes me to the edge, and when he uses his other hand to pinch one of my nipples, it's like my entire body lights up as I fall over the edge. But he doesn't let up, pushing me through my orgasm like he's chasing a second.

And just when I think I can't take any more, I come all over his fingers again.

He pins me with his stare as I try to come back to earth and traces a hot path of gentle kisses up my stomach, my torso, each nipple. Reaching the hollow at my neck, he darts out his tongue and licks just enough to tease me.

That's when I feel the head of his cock at my entrance. My pussy is a greedy little bitch, because I'm practically panting for him. Thick and velvety, I yearn to have more—feel more—of him inside me.

He smiles at me, like he knows just how crazy he's making me and he loves it.

At a slow and torturous pace, Finn kisses his way up the column of my neck as his dick pushes inside me. I gasp at the size of him, but he takes his time, giving me a chance to adjust, because holy mother of monster dicks.

He continues to worship me with his kisses as he pushes in, the most delicious of stings ringing through my body as he does. I close my eyes as he pushes in further and feel his lips gently touch my lids, one, then the other, when his cock almost bottoms out.

It's only when I feel the blunt head hitting my most desperate spot deep inside me that Finn rips the tie from my mouth and slams his lips against mine, owning me with this desperate kiss like he can't hold back anymore. And I am more than here for it.

He lets his body tell me all the things he never has with words.

He fucks me like he's waited his entire life for me; hungry, and almost desperate as he drives me out of my goddamn mind. His dick slams in and out of my pussy with ardent fervor and his tongue lashes out all of his emotions, a fiery kiss filled with unspoken words.

Finn's body coils with every thrust, his muscles almost trembling above me when he bottoms out. The energy in the room is a living, breathing thing that burns me from the inside. What started out as calculated is now a series of hard, slamming thrusts and I'm convinced that Finn controls absolutely nothing right now.

Not a damn thing.

Except maybe his words.

He slows his thrusts and looks at me, like he's at war with himself. He leans back, removing my ankles from his shoulders before he unhooks my hands and releases them.

"Are you sure?" I ask, knowing, even though I don't understand why yet, that this is huge for him.

He nods. "I trust you."

I run my hands through his blond hair, stroking his cheeks, accepting this moment as a momentous one.

"I won't ever hurt you," I tell him, and his eyes close. He stills as I run the tips of my fingers gently down his shoulders and arms. He trembles beneath my touch, and I hate how much he seems to struggle with the touch, but love that he trusts me enough to allow me this moment with him.

I sit up and, without saying a word, he moves us so he's sitting where I was, and I'm straddling his lap.

"Are you sure?" I ask again, and he nods.

"With you, I'm sure."

I trace my fingers along his scars, following with my lips, wishing I could heal them, take them away, but I wouldn't change one part of him. Kissing him, I try to tell him all of this before sinking down onto his dick, his hands tightly gripping my hips as he trembles beneath my touch.

I bring my forehead to rest against his, our eyes fixed one on the other as our breaths dance with each of our gasps.

The thickness of him feels different, more meaningful maybe, in this position. I can feel every hard inch of his cock as I rise and sink onto him, his fingers digging deep into my flesh like an anchor to his aching soul.

"Fuck, Finley, you feel so good. So fucking good." I don't need to speak out loud, we're so close that my words travel in whispers from my mouth to his ear.

Releasing one hip, he brings his hand to the back of my neck and fists my hair at the nape, hard enough to elicit a sharp breath.

"More." He gives me one word and it lights up every fucking nerve ending in my body.

Suddenly, we're not moving slowly anymore. We're not making some kind of fucked-up love. With that one syllable, Finley went from loving to animalistic before I could even register the change.

Fucking me from underneath me, he slams his hips upward—hard—holding me against him by the hip and neck. I may be on top, but I'm no longer the one in control and I have exactly zero issues with it.

Our breaths become gasps, our moans become cries. Our foreheads no longer touch as Finn pulls my hair hard enough to give him access to my neck where he bites and licks and no doubt leaves marks of his own.

I'm okay with that. I want to look in the mirror tonight, or tomorrow, or the next day and see that he's been there.

Although, I'm sure my sore pussy will be all too happy to remind me.

With every bite, he bottoms out and with every lick, almost pulls me right off of him. Over and over again, he pummels my hungry pussy, taking everything he needs and giving me everything I've ever wanted.

He shifts his body a little lower, causing my already-sensitive clit to rub against his pelvic bone and I lose my shit.

The bolt of electricity that runs from my clit to every other nerve ending in my body makes my entire body shiver. The low growl that shakes his chest tells me he felt it and it makes him just as hungry as I am for this impending orgasm.

Speeding up his thrusts, Finn fucks me with abandon; not measuring his strength, just giving me pleasure like it's an Olympic sport.

His hand is back on my hip, allowing me to wrap my arms around his neck and meet him thrust for thrust. I'm breathless, chasing this massive climax that may ruin us both.

With his mouth at my ear he murmurs, "Give it to me, V. Give me everything you've got."

I break at his words. My body goes still, my breath locked in my throat. I squeeze him tight around his neck and let the blanket of pleasure envelop me with every rush of dopamine that invades my bloodstream.

Finn's hands slide up my back and latch onto my shoulders, pushing me down, as he halts his thrusts and spills deep inside me.

The only sound in the room is our breathing; rapid-fire bordering on wheezing.

I think he broke me.

I may have broken him, too.

Or maybe, just maybe, we mended each other.

I still for a minute, coming down from all of that and he adjusts us until I'm lying on his chest.

I could almost purr in satisfaction as I lie in his arms, trying to catch my breath as his fingers trace up and down my ribs. "You really aren't repulsed by the scars are you?"

I turn in his hold to look up at him. "Why would I ever be repulsed by any part of you?"

He takes a deep breath, tucking me back under his arm so I'm not watching his face. "Because you don't know how I got them."

"You don't have to tell me." A shudder runs through his body and my heart breaks for him, because whatever it is he has to tell me is obviously something difficult for him to talk about.

"This isn't exactly how I saw myself telling you, but I don't want to keep hiding from you. Until you know everything, it feels like there's this wall between us." He pauses, but I stay quiet. I'm not about to rush whatever this is. "I was eight the first time my dad brought his friends over and offered me to them. I didn't understand it, I just knew I didn't like it. That it hurt… but it didn't matter how much I cried or begged… the friends kept coming around."

I suck in a breath as I try not to cry for the horrors he's obviously endured.

"Each time I tried to hide or escape, my dad made sure I'd regret trying to stop it from happening the next time. When their tastes got more… bloodthirsty, the cutting and burning started. My mom… she just pretended it wasn't happening."

"Finn—" I start, but I feel him shake his head so I stop.

"I'm not telling you this for you to pity me, the last thing I want from you is pity. I just need you to understand that sometimes…sometimes I can't be touched. Sometimes I need that control over what's happening. Otherwise I just can't."

Anger burns through me and I vow to myself to make his dad and his friends suffer for every single mark. Those on his body, and his soul.

"This doesn't change anything," I tell him softly. "To me, you're still Finn. Scars or not. Past whatever it is. It's who you are that I care about, and despite the horrors, you are one of the kindest, most loyal people I know. You love fiercely, and you protect the people you consider family. I don't need to know anything else to know I love you."

He tilts my chin up, finally letting me see him. His eyes are glassy, and I kiss him softly, trying to show him just how much I mean what I say.

"I love you too," he breathes, holding me tightly against him, like he's scared I'm going to run away. But I'm not going anywhere. Not now, not ever.

I might've planned to escape The Cove when I returned here, but that was before I knew everything that was waiting for me, and the only way I'm leaving now is with all of them at my side.

---

After an intense few days, I'm more than ready for my girls' weekend away with Indi. But first, I have to pack… and I have my meeting with Bentley. I still haven't told the guys I'm searching for my mom. I'm not exactly sure why, but it seems like a fool's errand and I don't want to look like that pathetic little girl chasing the parent who didn't want her.

Regardless, I still want to know what happened to her. I need to know that she got out of this world in one piece. That Lincoln might be wrong and there is hope for us all to get free.

I'm not stupid enough to go alone, stalker alert and all that, so Indi coaxes Dylan into coming with us to the diner I'm meeting Bentley in. Which is exactly why I'm in the back of his car, butterflies running riot in my stomach, as we head out of The Cove.

"You sure this is a good idea?" he asks, glancing at me in the rearview mirror.

I shake my head and laugh dryly. "Not at all, but better to have all the information available, right?"

He quirks a brow at me and Indi pokes his ribs. "Don't judge her, mister. I thought you'd be the most chill one of you idiots to bring with us, especially since you don't hate her on principle."

"No judgement here, shortstack, but all things considered, from what you've both told me so far, this is a risky move."

I blow out a breath and nod again. "It is, which is why I'm not going alone. And as much as I know the guys want to protect me from everything, this is something I need to do. I have memories that don't quite make sense with everything I've learned since I came back here. My mom is probably one of the few people who has answers."

"Now that I understand. Don't worry, secret's safe with me. And if shit gets out of hand, I'll get you both out as safely as I can."

"I don't see it going that way. My friend gave me this guy's details; he should be solid. It's more the stalker thing." I shrug, like it doesn't totally skeeve me out. "Safety in numbers, right?"

He laughs. "Something like that, yeah."

He turns his focus back on the road, and Indi turns up the radio when a Midnight Blue song starts playing. She bounces around in the passenger seat to it while I try not to get lost in my thoughts.

It isn't long before we pull up to the diner in the next town over, and Dylan scouts the place out before coming back to the car. "Looks chill, like a little mom and pop diner. Smells fucking delicious, but no one looks too sketch. Let's do it."

He opens the door for Indi while I climb out of the car, trying not to let my nerves take over. I have no idea why I'm so fucking nervous, but I think this stalker thing is finally starting to hit me fully. It's also the first time I've been anywhere lately without one of my guys, and if anything happens they're going to be so pissed.

Rightfully so too, and I'm aware that this probably isn't the smartest idea I've had, but here I am. I did at least grab a gun from Dylan when he picked up Indi and me. It's small, a .22, but it doesn't need to have a big bang to do its job. My hands don't exactly work with a .44.

I head in with them, moving to a booth in the back, and they take one by the door like we agreed. The server comes to my table, an older lady who looks like everyone's favorite nana. "Afternoon, dear, what can I get you? I recommend the apple and blackberry pie, but I'm a little biased." She winks at me with a warm smile, and I instantly feel at ease.

"I'll take the pie." I smile back at her. "And a coffee please."

"Sure thing, sweetie. I'll get that right out for you." She wanders over to the counter, bringing my coffee and slice over before heading to the other tables. I take a bite, closing my eyes as the flavors burst across my tongue.

Pie is good enough to almost forget my nerves.

Almost.

I scarf it down. I hadn't realized how hungry I was, though it could be nervous hunger, then fidget with my coffee while I wait for Bentley to arrive.

It doesn't take too much longer before a man slips into the booth opposite me. "Miss Royal, it's good to meet you."

"Bentley, I assume?"

"The one and only. Jenna said you're good people, so I'll be straight with you. My fees aren't cheap, but I'm good at what I do and I don't rest until I find what I'm after."

My nerves settle a little. I like how to-the-point he is, I can do this.

"Good to know, and money isn't really an issue."

He nods as the server appears again, topping up my coffee and grabbing him a mug before disappearing. "So who is it that you want found?"

I take a sip of my coffee before meeting his brown eyes. "My mother. She left when I was younger, and I haven't seen or heard from her since."

"Is she definitely alive?" he asks, and I bite down on my lip.

"No idea. As far as I know, yes."

He nods, and I tell him everything I know about her, about when she left, but really I don't have that much information to give him.

"Okay, that's a good place for me to start. It might take me a week before I have anything even remotely worth mentioning for you, but I'll check in next weekend and let you know what I have, if anything." He slides me a card, tapping the top of it. "These are my account details. Transfer over the starting funds, and I'll get to work right away. We'll assess the fees as we go if money really isn't a problem."

"It's not," I confirm, and he smiles before standing.

"Well then, Miss Royal. I'll be seeing you." He leaves, and I let out a deep breath.

I'm not sure what I was so worried about, but I feel better already. Indi bounces across the diner to me, and sits in the spot he just vacated, Dylan not far behind her.

"All good?" she asks, sipping on the milkshake she brought with her.

"Yeah, I think so. Thank you guys for coming with me."

"Anytime." She grins around the straw of her shake. "Also, don't tell Smithy, but this cherry milkshake is the fucking bomb."

I bark out a laugh and mark a cross over my heart. "Secret's safe with me."

"Well, if we're done, I should get you guys back before anyone notices you're missing," Dylan says, draining his mug. I nod and do the same as Indi groans about having to sacrifice the last of her shake. He takes her glass over to the counter and the lady behind it pours it in a to-go cup.

"He's so good to me." She sighs as we slip out of the booth.

"He better be." I grin at her and loop my arm through hers as he ushers us out of the building. "You ready for tomorrow?"

"So freaking ready! Massages, hot tubs, and facials are calling to me."

"Still can't believe you won't let one of us come with you," Dylan grumbles. "Need an escort to a coffee shop, but not a freaking spa weekend."

"Don't pout," she teases. "It's a spa retreat, what's the worst that could happen?"

I groan at her words, because if she just jinxed our weekend…

No. I won't even think it.

It's going to be nothing but bliss.

Nothing but goddamn bliss, dammit.

# CHAPTER TWENTY-SIX

## OCTAVIA

I slide into the driver's seat of my dad's old Range Rover—which Lincoln insisted on having Finn check over before I was allowed to drive—as the valet loads our bags in the trunk. This weekend was everything I needed it to be. Relaxing, quiet, zero stress, and just happy times with my girl.

The early morning sun might be shining outside, but I'm kind of sad that it's over already. "We should do this more often… or go away over the summer."

"Yes!" She whoops as she buckles herself in. "I am so down for a summer vacation. The world is our oyster, right?"

"Hell yes it is." I pull on my aviators and grin at her. "Anywhere in the world, my jet can take us. You name the place, or places, and we're there. And if they behave, we can bring the guys too."

She giggles nodding. "Imagining all of them on your jet is too funny. The sheer amount of brooding would maybe be too much."

"You're not wrong." I grin as I start the engine. "They can get their own damn jet."

"Preach!" she exclaims as she sets up the playlist on my phone and I pull away from the retreat. "Just in future, let's not make travel plans where we have to get up at the ass crack of dawn. Please?" I laugh at her as we leave the resort and head onto the long winding roads. We're a few hours from home, but I don't even care about the long drive. I kept in touch with the guys all weekend, as promised, and had my location shared with them in case anything went wrong.

I'm beginning to think that all of this drama is just that. That maybe my stalker is harmless. That the Knights aren't after me.

A girl can dream, right?

We spend most of the drive singing at the top of our lungs, laughing about stupid shit the guys have said or done, and just enjoying the last of our bubble away before school and everything else comes crashing down around our ears.

I check the rearview and spot a black truck that's been behind us almost since we left the retreat. I bite my lip, trying not to be dramatic, because it can't be following us, right?

"What's up?" Indi asks, looking at me wide-eyed.

"I'm sure it's nothing," I tell her, checking the mirror again, changing lanes on the freeway just to see.

The car doesn't follow, so I let out a breath.

"I'm being a jumpy bitch. Ignore me," I tell her, and she glances out the back before turning back to face me.

"Are you sure?"

"Not entirely, but pretty sure," I admit, signaling for our exit. We're nearly home, so at least if I'm not being dramatic, help is close by. "Am I dropping you home?"

She shakes her head and smiles softly. "Nah, take me to the twins' if that's okay?"

"Course," I respond, taking the exit that will take us to that side of The Cove rather than toward home.

It doesn't take long to get to the twins' house, and I hug her tight. "Thank you for coming away with me."

"Always, bish. You're my favorite. Just don't tell Ryker." She laughs, winking at me.

"My lips are sealed." I make the zipper movement across my lips and she laughs.

"And that is exactly why you're my favorite. I'll see you at school in the morning. Do you need a ride or is Lincoln still happy giving you a ride?" She barks out a laugh at her punny before jumping from the car.

"I'm good, I can ride in with Linc. Saves you coming out of your way."

"Okay! I'll grab my shit and head in." She grins as Ryker appears at the front door. He stalks over to the car, motioning for me to open the trunk, so I hit the button and he heads straight to the back of the car. I wave to Indi as she closes the door and skips towards Ryker as he slams the trunk shut, banging the back of the car to let me know they're clear.

I pull away from the curb and decide to grab a coffee before heading home. I pull out of the drive-thru and spot the black truck again. So, rather than heading straight home, I detour toward the beach, just to see if I'm being a paranoid bitch, but when the truck follows me with every twist and turn, I realize I'm not.

So I do what I should've already done.

I call Lincoln.

The ring sounds through the sound system, each ring feeling like a lifetime, as my heart hammers in my chest.

"Hey, you almost home?" Lincoln sounds almost relaxed when he answers, and I feel bad dropping this in his lap.

"I am, but I think someone's following me. No, I know someone's following me."

"What do you mean?" His tone changes in an instant, fully alert.

"I thought I saw a black truck follow me back from the retreat, but then it didn't turn off to The Cove, so I thought I was imagining it. But the same truck is following me through town." I try to keep my hysterics to a minimum, but I am freaking the fuck out.

"Head straight home. The boys are here, we'll wait at the gate for you. But do not drop this line, Octavia."

"Okay." My voice shakes as I answer him, my eyes darting between the road before me and my rearview mirror.

"You can do this. Just try to drive like normal." His voice is calm, that soothes me a little, but I can hear him bark out to the others, and the sounds of movement come down the line.

"Do you think it's him?" I ask, my hands trembling as I clutch the steering wheel.

"It could be, but you're going to be okay." I know he's trying to reassure me, but holy fuck.

I pull onto my road, and I can see the four of them standing at the end of my drive, the gate already open. I try to drive like nothing's wrong and pull through the gate. It closes behind me once the guys are in.

The truck slows as it passes then speeds back up, disappearing. I end my call with Lincoln, and rest my forehead against the steering wheel, trying to take a few deep breaths to settle myself down. I've been in worse situations than this, so why the fuck is this messing with me so much?

Fuck my life.

The car door opens and I squeak, jumping at the movement.

"It's just me," Lincoln says as I turn to face him. "Are you okay?"

"Yes?" I try to smile, but I'm pretty sure all I manage is a grimace. Sometimes I feel like such a badass. Then shit like this happens and I become very aware that I am very much not a badass.

"Come on, let's head inside. Smithy isn't back yet, so Mav is just checking the house." He lifts me from the car and holds me against him until my hands stop shaking.

East grabs my bag from the trunk, handing it to Linc, and jumps in the car. "I'll put this away and meet you inside."

"Thank you." I smile at him just as Mav appears at the door.

"Coast is clear," he shouts, jogging down the few steps and stealing me from Lincoln's arms. "You okay, princess?"

"I'm better now," I tell him as I nuzzle against his chest. "Where did Finn go?"

"He got the plate; he's having Lucas run it to see if we can get an idea of who the fuck it was. Let's head inside and we'll run you through everything we've worked out so far," Lincoln says before heading through the front door. Mav leads me indoors and I spot Finn already in the living room on the phone. I close the door as East appears from the door to the garage.

"Hey, sweet girl. I'm sorry your weekend took a turn for the worse."

"Thanks." I shrug. "Just another day in my insane life, I guess?"

"We'll get it figured out. Nothing's going to happen to you while we're around." He steals me from Mav who grunts in response, but I've never felt more treasured than I do now being passed between them.

We head to the living room where Finley finishes up his call and curses. "It was a fucking rental. Lucas is looking into it now, but I think we were right: it's too neat and tidy."

"What do you mean?" I ask as Maverick pulls me into his lap on the couch.

"We're pretty sure your stalker is a Knight," Linc says as he paces back and forth in front of the TV. "It's the only thing that makes sense. We can usually find anyone. Trace them, get something. But there is *nothing.*"

My eyes go wide as his words filter through my chaotic mind.

"Do you have any idea who?"

"Not yet, but we're working on it. It explains why Lucas and Smithy's friends haven't been able to find anything. He can cover his tracks too easily. But I'm also not convinced he's working alone."

"Holy shit." I try to take a few breaths to keep from hyperventilating, but it doesn't work. I climb from Maverick's lap and start to pace.

"V, we're not going to leave your side. This twisted fuck isn't going to get to you," Maverick says vehemently and I pause, looking at them all, when it hits me.

"I'm not even worried about me, but what if whoever it is hurts you guys? Hurts Indi. Just to get to me? I couldn't live with myself if that happened."

"We've survived hell and come out the other side," Lincoln says, moving toward me while Finley stares at me intently. "We'll survive this too."

I take a deep breath just as the lights cut out. "What the—"

I don't manage to say anything else before all fucking hell breaks loose. I scream as the door bursts open behind me, followed by the smash of glass as people crash through the windows behind the guys. Gunfire pops around us and I try to move when an arm wraps around me from behind, and a cloth is placed over my face.

I try not to breathe in; I know that smell, and I do not want to pass out right now.

"Octavia!" I hear Lincoln cry as I'm dragged backward. I try to struggle against the giant body moving me backward, but my lungs burn in my chest from trying not to breathe and my vision starts to blur.

I see Lincoln try to run toward me, but more gunfire cracks across the room and East dives toward Lincoln.

I suck in a breath, unable not to anymore, and scream when I see the blood.

"No!" I kick and flail but it's no use. My arms grow heavy as my eyes start to flutter shut.

The last thing I see are the Saints on the ground in a pool of blood.

# CHAPTER TWENTY-SEVEN

## FINLEY

I don't even count how many bodies I drop as I try to get through them to get to V. Watching the door close as she's dragged out makes my blood run cold, so I fight harder.

The sound of screeching tires reaches me and the few bodies left standing do a fucking runner, except for the one Maverick's still fighting off. That's when I see Lincoln and East on the ground.

"Fuck!" I yell, pulling Maverick's attention. There's another *pop*. My attention swings to Maverick as the guy opposite him drops to the ground, the back of his head splattered on the wall.

Running to the brothers, I see the blood pouring from East's back. "Call an ambulance," I yell at Maverick as I try to move East off of Lincoln and put pressure on the wound.

He's still breathing so there's still hope.

This cannot be fucking happening.

Maverick has the phone to his ear as he drops to a crouch opposite me and checks Lincoln's vitals. "He's breathing, just a nasty gash to the head."

I nod, focusing back on East.

He can't fucking die.

"How the fuck did this happen?" I growl to no one in particular. Lincoln starts to stir, fighting off Mav who tries to keep him lying down. Lincoln is about as good at taking orders as his father. Which basically means he sucks.

"East!" Lincoln's voice is almost hollow as he takes in the picture before him. "Fuck!"

He runs a hand through his hair, blood dripping down his face as he rises to his knees. Putting his hands over mine, he sways a little. "I've got East. You two go get fucking Octavia."

I glance at Maverick, who is pacing the floor, and nod. "Okay, call us when you get to the hospital."

"This was the Knights. No one else would've coordinated an attack like that. We should've seen it coming. We were too distracted by her fucking stalker." Anger rushes through me at the thought but now is not the time.

"We'll head to The Cage. If they're going to initiate her, that's where they'll take her," I say, climbing to my feet and wiping my bloody hands on my jeans. Looking over at Maverick, I nod. "Let's go."

I move, almost on autopilot, out to her garage, grabbing the keys to her Range Rover and sliding into the driver's seat. I peel out of the garage and through her gates like my life depends on it.

Except it's worse, because *her* life might depend on it.

For once, Maverick is silent and tense beside me as the miles to The Cage speed past. I'm breaking every fucking speed limit that exists, but I'll be fucked if I'm going to let them just take her from us.

If she doesn't agree to their terms, they'll kill her. It's what they do.

Rage pools in my stomach, at war with the fear in my heart.

I can't lose her.

Not like this.

My phone rings and Maverick answers it, putting it on speaker phone.

"We're at the hospital, he fucking flatlined on the way in."

My heart sinks. If Lincoln loses East *and* V… he'll lose all of his humanity. I'm pretty sure East is the only thing that kept him human the last few years.

"Keep us up to date. We're nearly there."

"Let me know when you have her," he says before the call ends. I glance at Mav who looks as worried as I feel.

He has to fucking survive.

The car slides as I turn onto the dirt road, dust and stones kicking up all around us as we hurtle towards The Cage.

I slam on the brakes when we reach the entrance, making sure the safety is off of my gun. This might not be the smartest move, but it's all we've got. "You ready?"

"Let's get our girl back," is all he says in response as we climb from the car. I try to act normal, like we're just going to The Cage as if it's any normal day, but my heart beats so hard in my chest, I swear I can hear it like a fucking drum.

We enter the elevator and I push the button to take us all the way down. The ride feels like forever, and when the doors open, my heart sinks.

*She's not here.*

# CHAPTER TWENTY-EIGHT

## OCTAVIA

My entire body aches as feeling starts to come back to me. The brain fog is so fucking thick it's all I can do to remember to breathe—which has never fucking hurt so much before. It feels like someone sandblasted my esophagus. My fingers and toes prick with pins and needles as sensation returns and I whimper. It's as if someone turned every nerve ending in my body up to ten.

I drag in a few deep, painful breaths to try and clear the nausea and my eyes flutter open for a moment before slamming shut against the harsh, bright lights. My brain feels like it's moving through gelatin as I try to work out what the fuck is happening.

That's when it comes back to me.

Lincoln.

East.

The break-in.

Shit.

*Fuck.*

My breathing speeds up, and I try not to panic as darkness presses in at the edges of my vision.

"Oh good, you're awake."

I stop trying to breathe. I know that voice.

Pain lances through my body as I struggle against my bindings. I'm tied down to a table of some sort, but I'm vertical.

What the hell?

I open my eyes again, blinking as they fill with water in response to the harsh light and hope this is all a very fucked-up nightmare.

Then I see him.

This can't be happening.

The world swims as I take in my surroundings and fear claws its way up my throat, burning and acrid. I don't know if it's the pain of the bile tearing into my throat or the terror his words evoke, but my brain finally succumbs to the darkness and my vision goes dark. I hear him, but he sounds far away, distant and echoing. Even my barely conscious brain registers the threat of his breath on my cheek though.

"I told you they couldn't protect you. And now you're mine."

# ACKNOWLEDGMENTS

So… This is where we are… and I'm sorry.

Thats a lie. I'm not sorry at all LOL. But, I do want to say thank you for reading and sticking with me and V this far!

When I say this book took a village, I really freaking mean it.

Imma start with a HUGE thank you to my noodle loving besties. You know who you are and I wouldn't have finished this book without you… or at least without a mental breakdown without you. Who thought so many words could pour from these fingers!

The MVP of the book is by far Elisabeth Crowl, who without, this book wouldn't exist because my life would be chaos. She makes my squirrels into ducks and I adore her for it. So thank you Elisabeth, for fixing all the things, and a special shout of to Steph for plotting evil things with me, designing all my merch, and going off on tangents with me when Elisabeth wasn't looking muahaha.

To my alpha & beta teams, you guys are freaking rockstars. Lisa, Zoe, Megan, Kiera, Jeni, Lauren & Jessi. Thank you for your priceless feedback, and for loving these characters as much as I do.

To David, Sarah & Sam for making Octavia sparkle and shine. You guys pulled this one out of the bag, right down to the wire and you'll never know just how much I appreciate it.

Finally, to you the reader, thank you. For taking a chance on an author you've probably never heard of. For picking up a new book. For running the gauntlet with us. Just thank you.

Book 3 won't be long, so I guess I better go dive back into the book cave.

Peace out

Xoxo

# 29

## BONUS SCENE

### MAVERICK

*What the fuck is she doing here?*

The Pit is not a place for Octavia Royal, so why the hell is she here?

I jump down from the cage and search through the crowd for her. Once I find her, my eyes narrow in her direction. We've done everything to try and keep her safe, and she strolls into this vipers' nest like nothing fucking matters.

Adrenaline rushes through my veins, and I'm high on the win of my fight as I stalk toward her. I know she sees me because her eyes go wide as she sucks in a breath. The way her chest heaves does things to me it definitely shouldn't, but I'm over denying myself of Octavia Royal. She spins on her heel and walks away, trying to escape me, which makes me grin.

*Oh how I love to hunt my prey.*

It doesn't take me long to reach her as the crowd parts like the Red Sea before me. These people know not to fuck with me.

I grab her arm and spin her around forcibly. She rips herself out of my grasp, eyes narrowed.

Fuck, I love her fire.

The high of the chase, of catching her, and her retaliating struggle… All she's doing is making my dick harder than it's ever been. She came here for me, to watch me fight. I know it. Her being here tells me all I need to know.

There are a lot less people down this hall of the pit, so I let myself be the animal I know I am. I want her. She wants me. I can see it in the flush of her skin. In the way her eyes go wide as she looks up at me. I grab her chin, my large hand spanning across her cheek and neck, and shove her against the wall. Her gasp rocks me, making me impossibly harder as her eyes dilate.

She wants this as much as I do. I watch as she ghosts her tongue along her bottom lip, and it's like a red flag to a bull.

I push my body against hers, and her eyes flash when she feels how hard I am. "You shouldn't run from me, V."

That fire returns to her as she pushes on my chest, but she isn't going to move me. Not when I'm finally where I've wanted to be since she came back. "Fuck you."

My grin widens as she struggles in my grasp. Fuck, I love the fight in her. Stoking that fire in her is going to be so fucking sweet, I can almost taste it. Taste her.

I crush my lips against hers, stroking my tongue against her lip like I just watched her do, unable to resist any longer. I tighten my hold on her throat. She resists me a little more, pushing against me and I almost stop, but I've waited long enough to claim her.

The second I feel her soft, plump lips part, I know what I've always known. She's mine to claim.

*Mine.*

I've got her pressed against the wall, hard, as I attack her mouth with a vengeance. I can taste her sweetness, right there on her tongue. Her words say she hates me, but her kiss tells me the opposite.

She wants me. Bad.

She can fight me all she wants but we both know it's pointless. My girl is a fighter at heart. She never even considers backing down but that spark in her eyes and the sweep of her tongue in my mouth tells me she wants me to kiss her. That she wants to fuck me more than she wants to fight me.

And I intend to give her every damn thing she wants. Even when I know I shouldn't. I fight her back, giving her everything she doesn't dare ask for. With hard kisses that leave no room for confusion of just how much I need her.

I can almost feel the fight leave her muscles as her mouth falls open on instinct.

*Almost.*

Slamming her palms against my chest, she pushes hard enough to break our kiss and fuck me if that isn't the hottest goddamn thing she's done since she got here. Her chest heaves, her eyes narrow and that fire inside of her that I crave so much begins to burn in her irises.

Fuck do I want her to burn me.

Her hate for me takes over her lust and the fact that she has the strength to fight what she so obviously wants makes me even fucking harder.

This girl is going to be the best and worst thing that ever happened to me.

"Get off me, you fucking asshole!" She spits her words like a dragon spits fire but her body can't hide that breathy edge to her voice. Can't hide her need in each angry word she flings at me.

With my arms trapping her against the wall, I'm so close I can feel the heat coming from her. The monster inside me grins at her body's reaction. Allowing my gaze to slowly travel down her body, I zero in on her tits as they heave up and down with every heavy breath she tries to take. That low-cut tank does nothing to hide her half-exposed nipples. My lips are swollen, my mouth suddenly dry as the thought of me sucking on her hard nipples, tearing a moan or better yet, a scream from her throat.

When I look back up, she's still fucking fighting this. It's a waste of time, to be honest. This is fucking happening.

"The lady doth protest too much—"

My need to own her takes complete control of me as my fingers wrap around her neck and the pads tighten on her flesh slowly watching as her eyes begin to lose focus and pleasure fills her as the sensation of deprivation of oxygen hits her. I'm no fool, I know how to do this the right way. And I don't want her dead, not that she knows that.

I want her scent in my lungs, to smell her fear as I control the very essence of her life. Running my nose, oh so fucking slowly, from the line of her jaw, right up her cheek until I reach her temple, I finally feel her body speaking to me again as a shiver takes over her entire nervous system and I feel her skin raise beneath my touch. There may be fear in there but mostly, it's lust. I know because it smells a whole lot like her wet cunt calling out to me.

The monster chained inside of me battles to take her. To make her ours. But that monster is the darkest parts of me, and even if she wants me, I don't know that she's ready for that.

"—her pussy doth beg to be fucked, way too fucking much."

"Shakespeare was a poet, not a pig like you." My hand is squeezing her neck so tight, her words are barely a breath from between her lips. Fuck, it turns me on to know she's got little to no air and instead of begging for her life, she's still fighting me with her sharp tongue.

"What can I say, V, I like it dirty."

My need takes over, blinding me to everything and anything else around me as I crash my mouth to hers and invade the small space with my hungry tongue. I don't wait for that fire to leave her eyes, her pussy is howling with yesses and I can't wait for V's brain to shut the fuck off and allow her body to bend to her needs.

To bend to *me.*

For a brief moment, the hate between us is just a low hum somewhere in the back of my mind, and I ignore the plan the guys and I agreed to follow. Right now, the only thing that matters to me is her. Is this. The feel of her heated skin against my flesh. The smell of her lust filling me from the outside in.

My body may have complete control of this moment, my hand giving and taking the air she breathes but I'm not a fucking idiot. I know she's got all the power, she always has. And if she tells me to stop, I will.

*Fuck, I hope she doesn't tell me to stop.*

When her knees bump into my legs as she tries to alleviate the burning need I'm making her feel, I lose control of the monster inside of me.

Groaning in her mouth, I kiss her harder, push my tongue in deeper, owning more and more with every push of my hungry hips against her belly. I cage her, using my body to shield her from any prying eyes when I feel the shift in the air. Like she's shaking herself from the haze of lust and coming to her senses.

Though the thought of someone seeing us sends a thrill through me. She's mine, and people seeing that is hot as fuck. But also, they don't get to see her. I only share with my brothers, and they're not the ones walking past us.

Her hands press against my heaving chest, curling her nails around my pecs and digging the pads of her fingers into my flesh. I think she's drawing blood. but I can't bring myself to end the kiss. I can't imagine not having my tongue down her throat for the rest of my life. I wonder if she knows that the more she tries to hurt me, the harder my cock will get for her. Pain is fun for me and just heightens my pleasure and right now, I'm about to come from both.

I don't know where she gets her strength, but I allow her to push me away just enough for our mouths to break away.

"Get me off!" Her words filter through the haze in my mind. *Yeah, I'll get her off, all right.*

"Oh, baby, I thought you'd never ask."

She's cute when she's confused. Cute enough to devour.

My free hand is at her delicious ass, two fingers slipping inside her barely there shorts, pushing past a strip of fabric she calls underwear as I swallow the gasp of surprise that escapes her just as my mouth slams against hers once again.

I thrust my fingers up inside her pussy and I'm not sure what makes me harder, her sudden moan or the fact that she's soaking wet for me. Cum coats my fingers, dripping down onto my knuckles and feeding the beast inside me. I fuck her pussy with my fingers like I own it, thrusting in and out and wishing I could drop to my knees and suck on her clit until she comes all over my hungry tongue.

I don't give into my need because more than that, I can't stand the idea of any other motherfucker here seeing her with her head thrown back and her mouth hanging open from the pleasure I'm fucking giving her. I'd bet my life savings she's thinking the same thing… someone could see her. Fuck that. I'm not letting her go, in fact, I double down and bruise her lips with the harshness of my ravenous kisses.

She's close, so fucking close, yet she's still trying to keep that orgasm at bay. I can feel it in the trembling of her body and the deep rooted rumble of her moans.

I need to see her eyes, drown in the desire I know I'll find there as I fuck her pussy with abandon. Pulling back from my brutal kiss, my teeth trapping her swollen lips like I own her, I watch the internal debate play out across her features as her brows scrunch up and her breathing picks up.

But I don't stop. I give her exactly what she wants, what she needs right here and now, whether she knows it's what that is or not. I give her pleasure and danger and the chance of getting caught. I give her everything she can't bring herself to ask me for.

That's when she surprises me the most with her little tantrum. As I release the hold on her lip, it's her turn to bite down on mine.

*Hard.*

If she thinks this is going to turn me off, she knows fuck all about me. Tasting the blood from her little game almost makes me come in my fucking shorts like a preteen.

My tongue sweeps across my bottom lip, scooping up the red drop of blood before I lick her lips from bottom to top and around again. She looks so pretty decorated with my blood.

I grin, knowing full well I've got blood staining my teeth and lips and I probably look like a fucking psycho. That's okay because clinically, I probably fucking am. I add another finger to her soaking wet pussy and stretch her enough to get her ready for my cock. She almost loses her balance and I know… I know she wants me right now, psycho and all.

I press against her, unzipping my jeans and freeing my cock. I bend my knees up and down as I rub my steel dick against her plump, engorged clit. I want her to know what she's about to get, long for it, fear for it.

I see the exact moment she realizes I'm about to make her come in a public place where testosterone runs rampant and sex lingers in the air. These assholes around here will smell her cum like the sex crazed animals they are. Too bad she's with me and they won't be able to see a fucking thing. I love knowing that, knowing they can desire her but they can't fucking touch a hair on her.

I'm done playing. I pull her away from the wall and turn her around so her face is pressed against the hard surface.

Holding her by the hair, I pull her face to the side so she can still see me as I tower over her. Then I push her shorts down just enough for my dick to slide between her thighs. Fuck me, her juices are coating her inner legs and my cock is all but begging to slide on home.

"What the fuck are you doing?" Her words are venomous but her tone is as soft as a kitten's purr.

"Whatever I fucking want and right now, I want to feel your dripping wet cunt all over my dick."

To emphasize my words, I pull back just enough to line up my cock and then bury myself inside her in one, desperate, hard, thrust.

She tenses, her gasp stuck in her throat and I grin. She's mine and now she knows it.

Fuck me, she's so wet and so fucking tight I can barely contain myself, but I pause, letting her adjust for a moment.

Protecting her from wandering eyes, I wrap my entire body around her as I fuck her to within an inch of her conscious life. I thrust in and out, bury myself deep before pulling out and starting all over again. I can't think, I can't see, I can't feel anything but her wet, tight cunt milking me for everything I have.

I'm an animal right now. Reduced to my baser instincts and I'm okay with that.

"I want it. I want more. I want it harder." I don't even think she knows what she's saying, but I don't fucking care.

I groan like a beast as I fuck her harder. I bruise her from the inside out as my cock imprints with her pussy. I fuck the fight right out of her, teaching her a lesson about what she wants and I what I can take from her. I fuck her sass and her venom, telling her with every thrust that I own her and she has no say in the matter.

She never has.

"You're so fucking wet, don't try to deny that you love this fucked up shit." I don't fucking know what I'm saying, I'm just going on instinct as my body takes what it wants and gives her what she craves.

My dick hits her cervix every fucking time I bottom out, my balls slapping against her as I push inside her, deeper and deeper until it's impossible to know where I end and she begins.

I feel a presence, unwanted eyes watching me, watching V just as she's about to come all over my dick and that shit won't do. No one, no motherfucker except me and my boys are allowed to see her this vulnerable.

"Get the fuck out of here, or I'll slit your throat from ear to ear, motherfucker."

"Sorry, man, my bad." I ignore his feeble attempt at an apology. I'm too wrapped up in my girl to take the time to kill this fucker.

For a second, I'm afraid she'll stop it all, she'll wake up from her lusty haze and run away, but when her pussy gets impossibly wetter, I realize in this very moment that she is the other side of my psycho coin.

"Christ, you're even wetter than before. You like that, don't you, you little fucking slut? You like it when total strangers watch you get fucked from behind? Maybe I should fuck your ass. You want that?"

Jesus fucking Christ, her entire body shivers at my cruel words. Except they're not cruel, they're love letters to my soul mate. They may sound horrible to someone who doesn't understand me, but to her…she knows what they mean and it just makes me fuck her even harder.

"Oh yeah, you fucking whore. You want me to take your ass, don't you? I bet it's a virgin ass, isn't it?"

Fuck, she's so wet, so responsive. I pull out of her pussy and glide my soaking wet cock up and down between her ass cheeks making sure the head of my dick probes her tight little asshole. She flinches, but she pushes up against me. She wants to refuse me, but at the same time, she wants to feel my cock inside her luscious ass.

"Yeah, that's what I thought. Good whores like it in the ass."

Now is not the time for that, no matter how much I want to fuck her ass right here and now, I want to take my time a whole lot more. So, I slam right back inside her cunt and fuck her like I own her. Because I do. She's mine and she can't deny it. I pull her head back so I can see her face while I defile my little whore in the dirtiest place in town. I'm sweating from the effort of not coming, from the effort of not fucking her ass. I'm trying to be a fucking gentleman by only fucking her pussy and actually making her come. I should be getting some goddamn brownie points for that.

I reach around for her clit, my fingers finding it like I've known it my entire life just as I slam my lips back onto hers, my tongue devouring her mouth like a madman. She tries to fight, tries to battle me tongue for tongue but as her orgasm explodes, she screams right into my mouth and gushes her cum over my cock. I don't stop. I keep fucking her pussy and fucking her mouth as she loses control of her body.

I love how she shakes, how her knees give out and she has to rely on me to hold her up. I keep gorging on her, fucking her and kissing her until my own body gives out and I can't hold back any longer. I come, long and hard, deep inside her tight little pussy. She squeezes my cock and I can feel it up and down my spine. Then it hits me.

I own her.

I need to mark her.

And so I do.

I pull out of the warmth of her pussy and just as I'm about to come some more, I coat my seed all over her perfect little ass. Strand after strand of white cum lands on her creamy skin and I can't help but imagine myself eating her ass right now and gorging on her pussy.

It's going to have to wait for another time.

Because there will be a next time.

"I told you to get off me, you fucker!" Right, she actually believes that she meant those words.

"My bad, I thought you asked me to get you off."

"You're an asshole." She spits her words in my face and all I can think is… she's not wrong. But I am still hungry, so I do what I want. I dip my fingers inside her still soaked cunt and scoop up a little snack before sucking on my fingers like the mother of all lollipops.

"Your wish is my command. Next time, I'll just fuck your ass."

I'm fascinated by her movements, as she pulls her clothes back up and the remnants of her orgasm slide beyond the hem of her shorts. Fuck me, I want to taste her. I trail my fingers over her hips and flash her my best grin, let her think I can play the part of the good little boy.

"You can dream, I guess. This isn't happening again." Lies, every one of her words are lies, so I slam my wet fingers in her mouth and force her to taste the evidence of her lies.

I can see the exact moment her body understands the gravity of this moment. Her eyes widen, her tongue slips around my fingers and her lips suck at her own juices, tasting herself, tasting us.

"Screw you!" I have to give it to her, she gets an A for effort as she tries to escape me, but I'm faster and more determined.

I grab her arm and feel my lip curling up the way it does when I'm about to fuck someone's shit right up. "Go home, V. And fucking stay there. Nobody wants you here."

Now it's my turn to lie. But I can't let her know that.

# 30

## BONUS SCENE

### FINLEY

I stare at my phone, enraptured by the video I've seen at least a dozen times already while the others work out in the gym. I should be working out, helping Mav train, and yet here I sit, like some little fanboy, watching Octavia sing Raindrops for the umpteenth time.

She's supposed to be on a spa weekend with Indi, so I'm not sure exactly how they ended up at an open mic night or how the fuck Indi convinced her to sing—because I'm positive that's the only reason she was up on that stage—but I'm not mad about it.

Her voice is like a balm to my decimated soul and the pain in me is reflected back in her voice.

There's no other way to describe the way she brings me peace, she just *is* my peace.

A glove hits the top of my head and I fall back a little against the wall behind me. I pull out my headphones and look up to find Mav stalking toward me. "What the hell has you so distracted?"

It's only then I notice the pounding music in the gym has stopped.

Linc is only a step behind him. I turn my phone to show them, disconnecting my headphones and turning the volume up as I do.

"Evening, everybody, it's great to be out here with you all. My name's Octavia Royal and this is 'Raindrop.'" Her voice is raspy and I can hear the slight shake in it, but when she starts picking at the guitar strings, it's like all the fear disappears and she's exactly where she should be.

The video plays in full, and they stand totally still, as captivated by her as I am.

"Well fuck," Mav sighs, running a hand down his face. "I didn't think I could want her more, but I just got proven wrong."

Linc doesn't say a word, that stony mask of his still firmly in place like it always is when it comes to her, but I see his tells. The tic in his jaw, the slight frown, and the clenching of his fists.

He's just as affected as Mav and me.

"I thought she was at a spa?" He says, not really a question to either of us but I shrug in response anyway.

"So did I."

"How many views?" he asks, like he's calculating just how much this could affect everything we've been working toward, which is about right. Linc is that guy.

"Six million and counting. It's only been up a few hours."

"Shit," he hisses in response. "She's not meant to be drawing attention to herself. The Knights aren't going to let her go if she keeps showing them how useful she is to them. It's already a fucking problem."

"Yeah," Mav starts, running a hand over his head. "But it's not like she knows any of that. Maybe if we tell her—"

"Fuck no," Linc roars. "She doesn't need to know. We just need to work harder."

"Linc—" I start, but he cuts me off with a glare.

"We're in this, for better or worse." He storms from the gym, slamming the door once he reaches the main level of the house.

"Well, that could've gone better," Mav sighs as he drops onto the bench beside me.

"Could've gone worse," I say softly.

We sit in silence for a few minutes before I lean forward. "Want to get back to training?"

He nods, grabbing his glove on the floor by my feet. "Yeah, but first, play it for me again."

I hide the grin that wants to play out on my face and tap my screen to make the video start. Her voice fills the space, echoing off the walls as if she's here, singing just for us.

Maybe one day I'll convince her to do just that.

You know, after we save her from the wreckage of her life.

THE KNIGHTS OF ECHOES COVE

LILY WILDHART

*It doesn't interest me who you know*
*or how you came to be here.*
*I want to know if you will stand in the center of the fire with me and not shrink back.*

# CHAPTER ONE

## LINCOLN

"She's not here."

Three words is all it takes to shatter my already-spinning-out-of-control mind.

"Then where the fuck is she?" I growl down the line.

"I don't know, man. We're going back to her house to deal with that and check the security feed to see if there's anything on there we can use." Finley sounds like he's holding it together as well as I am.

Fuck.

I run a hand through my hair, tugging on it, hoping that the pain helps me ground myself. "Okay, keep me updated."

The sounds of doors slamming filter through the call, followed by an engine starting. I want to be with them, searching for her, but there's no way I can leave East.

I've never felt so torn in my entire fucking existence.

"Any updates on East?" Finn asks, sounding hollow as he puts me on loudspeaker.

"Not a fucking one. I'm just sitting here on my hands like a fucking idiot waiting for news."

I hate feeling this helpless. This isn't who I am. I'm the guy that fixes shit but this time as my world burns around me, I have nothing.

"Okay, let us know when you know anything, brother. And we'll keep you up to date too. They're both going to be okay."

I nod at his reassurances, even though he can't see me. "What if it wasn't the Knights that took her?"

"It doesn't matter who took her, we're going to get her back."

I can't help but wonder if this was her stalker. If whoever is behind all of that is involved with the Knights, then it makes sense that they'd have a team to call on. The Knights have made it more than clear that they want her in, so it's definitely the most obvious explanation.

"Check the bodies for the mark. Then we'll know where to start at least."

"Consider it done."

"I should call Harrison." I sigh, the idea about as appealing as pulling my own teeth.

The approaching squeak of sneakers on the shiny floor draws my gaze up. Seconds later, a nurse bustles through the door.

"I need to go."

I hang up, knowing he'll forgive it, and focus on the blonde nurse heading toward me. "What's wrong?"

"Nothing, Mr. Saint. I just wanted to let you know your brother has gone into surgery, and the surgeon will update you when we have any more news." She smiles tightly at me, and I drop back down into the chair I just vacated.

Twiddling my fucking thumbs like a useless asshole.

I knew we shouldn't have gotten close to her, that we should have just made her leave.

If I'd stayed strong, done what I fucking said I was going to, she'd be safe elsewhere and East wouldn't be fucking dying.

My self-loathing reaches a new all-time high.

I should've known better than to think I could grasp any kind of happiness. I don't deserve it, not with the amount of blood on my hands. It was foolish to think that just maybe, she could be the exception to all of the darkness.

I look down at the blood crusted on my hands and head to the bathroom. Scrubbing at my hands and my arms until the water runs clear. The guy staring back at me in the mirror is a fucking mess. I try to clean up as best I can, removing the blood from my face and neck, but there's nothing I can do about the blood crusted into my clothes.

It's not important enough to pull one of the guys away from looking into the shit with Octavia. Even if it does make my skin fucking crawl. I'm not a stranger to blood… but this is East's.

It's just fucking wrong.

I look at my phone, contemplating calling Harrison. East is his son, and he might die, but I'm not sure that Harrison will even care, and fuck me if that isn't depressing as hell. I have no idea what happened between the two of them, because neither of them will fucking tell me, but it's bullshit.

Harrison should be here.

Hell, Fiona should fucking be here.

Not leaving me to shoulder everything, like always.

I take a deep breath as I clench my hands into fists.

*Wallowing in self-pity isn't going to fix a fucking thing, Lincoln. Pull your head out of your ass.*

Sucking down the out-of-control feeling and shutting it away, I let the cold, killing calm take over. It's the only way I'm going to get through this and get Octavia back.

Right now, she needs my monster, not the man that controls it.

I can't do much of anything to help East beyond what I've already done. But her… I can do something about that. I might not be able to leave the hospital right now, but that doesn't make me powerless.

So I head back to the waiting room, scrolling through my contact list, and make a call. Calling in the last person I wanted to drag into this fucking mess.

"Lincoln, son, what's happening?" My uncle's voice is almost soothing, he's always been more like a dad than Harrison ever was, but the two of them are estranged so I haven't seen him in a long time. I'm just hoping he's actually in the country, not in a foxhole somewhere.

"I need your help, Uncle Luc."

"What's wrong?" His voice is somber but sharp. I can almost see him in my mind's eye, turning into the Lieutenant Colonel he's spent his life being.

"East is in the hospital, and I'm not sure he's going to make it. And Octavia… she's been taken."

"Well shit, kid, that's a lot to unpack. I didn't even realize she was back in town. Start from the beginning and I'll see what I can do."

I let out a deep breath, relieved to have someone I can trust to help. It's not often I'll go outside of the guys, but we might just be out of our depth.

So I briefly explain everything to him. From Stone's death, to Octavia coming back, and everything that's happened since then.

"Shit, kid. You should've called earlier. And you think this stalker is a Knight?"

"Pretty much. It's kind of why I didn't call sooner."

He barks out a laugh. "I get it. Your dad isn't exactly the helpful kind, and he likes me about as much as he likes your mom. Okay. I'm on my way. I'll be at the hospital in a few hours. Stay there, do not call your father yet."

"Sure thing, Uncle Luc."

"I'll see you soon, chin up." The line goes dead and I feel a little lighter. Lucas might not be part of the Conclave, but he's still a Knight. The difference between him and my dad, is that he doesn't really buy into the bullshit. He joined the forces as soon as he was old enough and dedicated his life to that instead. He's been in the special forces for as long as I can remember, so he's not really been around much. It's been occasionally useful to the Knights, but for some reason, they've left him to it for the most part.

He's really fucking good at what he does, so if there's anyone who can help me stop this ship from sinking, it's him.

I just hate dragging him into the center of it all when he has the luxury of living on the outskirts. No one should be pulled into this shit if they don't *need* to be, but I'm desperate.

Helpless isn't a good look on me.

Unable to sit still in the silence, with nothing more than the tick of the clock to keep me company, I end up pacing around in the small six by twelve room.

Time seems to stretch out forever, and each second feels like an hour.

Waiting for Uncle Luc to arrive might take more strength of will than I have.

My phone buzzes in my hand, and when I see a message from Octavia on the screen, my heart stutters in my chest. I swipe the message and a video starts playing.

The screen is so dark that I almost don't see her… strapped to a fucking table, bound at her ankles, wrists, and throat.

Rage tears through me as laughter crackles out of the speaker and the camera zooms in on her.

"I told you, you couldn't protect her."

---

"Is there a way to trace the video?"

I've tried to stay calm, listening to Finn tap away on his computer while I'm still stuck in this godforsaken waiting room, but my calm is in short supply and quickly running out.

"We knew this guy was good, but it's been bounced off a ton of proxy servers, which I didn't expect. Pretty sure she isn't in Novosibirsk. It also wasn't sent from her phone, despite coming from her number. A dozen apps can do that, so that's a dead end too, but I'm trying. Doesn't help that the voice was filtered. It doesn't give us much to go on."

I grip my phone tightly, staring up at the ceiling for a second before bringing it back to my ear. "Okay so what *do* we have?"

"We know that the bodies dropped here aren't branded. So either her stalker isn't a Knight, or he hired privately. We also have a plateless black SUV."

"So we have nothing," I hiss, "maybe Luc will think of something we haven't."

"Luc is coming? How much longer till he arrives?"

"Not sure. Few hours, he said."

I look up at the squeak of shoes on the floor and see the same blonde nurse from earlier, who looks at me like she's carrying a fucking IED. "I've got to go. I'll call when Lucas arrives."

"Laters."

For the second time today, I look at her and ask, "What's wrong?" She shifts from foot to foot, looking like I might slit her throat. I do not have the time or patience for this right now. "Spit it out."

"Your brother, he has a very rare blood type. We have some, but not enough. Are you willing to be tested to donate? As his brother, you could hopefully be a match."

I nod once. "Whatever he needs."

"Okay, please come with me." She turns on her heel and rushes down the hall. It's so empty that the click of my boots bounces off the walls and echoes down the empty space. Its only accompaniment the squeak of her sneakers.

I follow her into another room and sit on the bed, rolling up the sleeve of my shirt. I make a fist as she smiles at me, tightening the tourniquet before sliding the needle into my vein. It doesn't take her more than a few moments to collect the blood. "I'm going to put a rush on this, but to speed up the process, I'll hook you up for a donation now anyway, just in case."

"Yeah, whatever," I grumble and lie back on the bed at her instruction. I don't care if I'm treated like nothing more than a pincushion. I just need to know he's going to survive so I can start searching for Octavia.

The very blood she's taking feels like fire under my skin. Everything about this day is wildly out of my control, and it seems like nothing I do will put it back on track.

Except this. This I can do.

This is needed.

So I lie here, my blood draining from my arm, hoping it's enough to save my brother.

At least I can do something to save one of them.

I fucking hate being this whiny lost asshole. It's not who I am, but I'm barely holding my shit together right now.

I stare at the ceiling as another nurse monitors the blood donation, running through a checklist of questions longer than my arm to make sure I'm eligible to donate, which I'd laugh at if I had it in me right now, considering I'm already donating.

The blonde nurse reappears about thirty minutes later, looking fucking terrified again. "Mr. Saint, I'm, uhm, not quite sure how to tell you this but your blood type is A positive. Your brother is AB negative so we won't be able to use your donation for him, but we have a call in with all other nearby hospitals to see if they have any O negative available that they can send us."

I take a deep breath, trying not to let my rage overwhelm me. "I'll call my father."

Luc might've said not to bother, but I don't have any other choice.

"That might be wise, Mr. Saint. We've not been able to reach him."

I clench my fists, trying to rein in the anger. Of course they haven't. I let out a growl, and she squeaks before literally running away from me.

The other nurse removes the needle from my arm, and everything spins when I sit up too quickly. "Careful, Mr. Saint. You just lost a substantial amount of blood. Let me grab you some juice and a cookie."

I nod, grunting because that's about all I have right now as I fight off the dizziness.

This is such fucking bullshit.

I dial Harrison's number, but it rings out. Fucking asshole. So I try again. This time, he answers on the third ring.

"Two calls, Lincoln. It must be important."

I grind my teeth together at his haughty tone. "East was shot. He needs blood and I'm not a match. I need you to come down here."

I finish speaking and he laughs.

He fucking laughs.

"You really don't know, do you? I didn't think he'd actually keep it from you." He laughs again, and I hear the sound of a door closing before the background voices disappear. "I won't be a match either, Lincoln. I'm not his father. Call Fiona."

He ends the call and I blink down at the phone.

Say fucking what now?

---

This day can get fucked.

When I get my hands on whoever the fuck it is that took Octavia and shot East… I'm going to bathe in their fucking blood.

It's been a few hours since East went into surgery and I still haven't heard anything beyond they managed to source more blood. While that makes me feel a little better, it's not enough to erase my need to break things. People.

"Lincoln!" I look up as Uncle Luc saunters into the room and wraps his arms around me. I stiffen at the touch, and he backs up. "You doing okay?"

I deadpan, "I've been better."

"Yeah I guess you have. Do we know anything new?"

"Nothing yet, just a whole lot of waiting. Oh and finding out that East isn't Harrison's. And the fact that there is exactly zero anything leading us to whoever the fuck took my girlfriend. So yeah, fuck all."

He nods stoically, his brown eyes softening. "It'll be okay. I'll help where I can." He takes a seat next to the one I was just in. "Why don't you tell me everything you *do* know. This is one of your hospitals, right? So anything you say here is safe enough."

I let out a sigh, nodding as I sit. "Yeah, it's one of ours…" I trail off, trying to get everything lined up in my head after this fuck fest of a day and try to explain everything to him again, in more detail this time.

"Fucking hell, you definitely know how to wade into the really shitty waters, don't you, kid?" He scrubs a hand down his face as he processes.

"So your girl is wanted by the Knights, but we don't know why. We suspect they killed her dad and that's somehow tied into all of this. A secondary crazy has her held hostage somewhere, and we don't know why, and East is fighting for his life. That sum it up?"

"Yeah that's about it."

The squeak of sneakers on the floor echoes out again, and I stand, coming face-to-face with a woman I haven't seen before. "Mr. Saint?"

"Yes?"

"I'm Dr. Stanton. Your brother is out of surgery. It took longer than expected because they had to do a sternotomy in order to remove the bullet that damaged the right ventricle. Your brother had to be placed on bypass in order to repair the right ventricle."

Luc shakes his head as I try to work out what the fuck she just said. Pretty sure most doctors learn in med school not to use bullshit technical language when talking to civilians, but if the hatred she looks at me with is anything to go by, she knows exactly who I am and isn't a fan.

"What does that mean in normal people terms, lady?" Luc asks, and I roll my eyes but keep my mouth shut.

"Sorry, yes of course, Mr. Saint," she says, disdain dripping from the word Saint as she rolls her eyes at him. Fucking hell. "What I meant was the bullet entered the chest just below the fifth rib near the sternum and damaged part of the heart. We had to open his chest to fix it. In order to repair the right side of his heart, we had to put him on an ECMO machine since his heart stopped and his body continued to need oxygen. We were able to repair the hole in his heart and get it to start beating again. We then closed his chest. He's lost a lot of blood, so the next twenty-four to forty-eight hours are critical. If we can find the blood, he *might* make it through the next forty-eight hours. If he makes it through the next forty eight-hours, his chances of survival increase, but if we don't find a donor in the next couple of hours, he won't survive the night."

Pain rips through my chest at the thought of losing him. East not surviving isn't acceptable. "I don't care what it costs to do it, but you get that fucking blood."

She quirks a brow at me before she nods.

"Can I see him?"

She looks me over like I'm nothing more than a hindrance, and at any other time I'd want her head on a fucking pike, but East isn't out of the woods yet, so I need her alive for now. "He's still on a ventilator and in critical condition, so you're welcome in the room but…"

"I get it," I growl, and she leaves the room without another word.

I can't just do nothing. Uncle Luc claps a hand on my shoulder. "You head back to the house, kid, see what your friends have found out. Eat, shower, take care of yourself. I'll stay here with East."

I nod, thankful that I don't have to once again choose between the two of them, and head outside, dropping a message in our group chat to let them know I'm coming home. I stride through the hospital and everyone gets the fuck out of my way. One of the few upsides of my surname today. Though if I didn't have it, this wouldn't be my life and I wouldn't have been here in the first place.

I exit the front doors and take a deep breath, filling my lungs with the brisk air and taking a second to compose myself after this fucking day.

"Sainty!"

I look up and find a smirking Maverick behind the wheel of my Porsche.

"Need a ride?"

Usually I'd argue about being the one to drive, but today? Today I have other battles to fight, so I climb in the car and lean my head against the rest.

"We're going to find her, right?" he asks as he pulls away from the curb.

"We'll find her," I say. I just wish I knew for certain we'll find her in time.

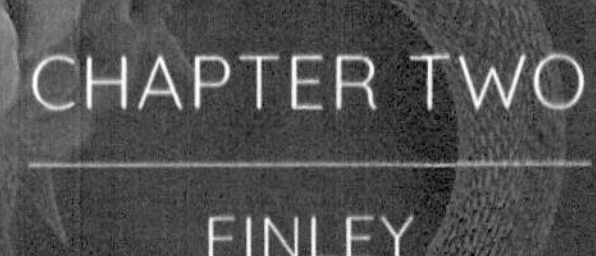

# CHAPTER TWO

## FINLEY

I don't know how this day went from bad to worse, but the punches just keep coming. The drive back from The Cage is tense and silent. Usually, I'm not one for being alone, but between the fury flooding my system and Mav's nervous energy… it's suffocating as fuck in this car.

My knuckles are white as I grip the steering wheel, trying to hold it together. Control is something I've craved most of my life. Lincoln and I are the same in that. He's one of the few people I feel comfortable enough with to trust him with shit, but this… spiral, it's too much. None of us are in control right now, and I feel so unfocused. Like there's an elephant sitting on my chest, and no matter what I do, I can't fucking move it.

Except, letting myself spiral isn't going to help anyone. And it sure as fuck isn't going to help V.

If she's hurt…

Nope, not the rabbit hole to go down. Not today. At least not right now.

We're going to find out who took her, who shot East, and then fucking deal with it.

Whoever it is might be a Knight, but we're the fucking legacy *and* junior Conclave. Never in my life did I think I'd be thankful for that, but right now… right now it means we have the might of the Knights at our fingertips if we decide to use it.

I know Lincoln will want to leave them out of it if we can, especially because we don't know who this sick fuck is, but I'm not averse to using the monsters we have in our closets if it means she's okay.

I'm willing to unleash hell on fucking Earth if it means we get her back unscathed.

The drive back takes too fucking long, even with my lead foot.

We need to clear the house, check the bodies, *dispose* of the fucking bodies, clean up as best we can, and see if there are any traces of whoever the fuck took her left behind.

Even just listing it out in my head slows my heart rate.

I have shit to do.

That's what I need to focus on.

That's what's going to bring her back.

I just keep seeing her face as he grabbed her. The way she tried to fight him off. The way he dragged her by her fucking hair after he drugged her.

I let out a deep breath, trying not to let my anger boil over and take control.

That's not going to end well for anyone, and I don't have time—V doesn't have time—for me to lose it.

By the time we pull back up at the house and get the gate closed, Maverick is so restless I think he's going to burst out of his goddamn skin.

"I need something to do, Finn. Someone to question, someone to bleed. I can't just keep sitting doing nothing." He looks at me, and all the raging emotions that simmer under my skin are written clear as day on his face. I'm envious of his ability to just feel everything and channel it, even if he does channel it into making people bleed.

"There will be plenty of time to make people bleed. We need to clean up the house, call Smithy, see if we know the bodies. I'll leave the heavy lifting to you. Maybe some manual labor will keep you distracted." I smirk and he punches my arm. Asshole. "Yeah, I probably deserved that, but still. We've got shit to do. Suck it up for now, and we'll make this dickhead bleed when we find him."

He nods, looking more than a little lost. It's almost unnerving. I haven't seen him look like this since the day Stone left with V. "Okay. You guys have a plan, right? How to find her?"

"We have a plan. We're going to get her back." I say it with way more bravado than I feel, but I have to believe the words as much as I need him to believe them. We can't all come undone at the seams, otherwise she is as good as dead.

Her stalker might've said that no one could protect her like him, but that doesn't mean she isn't in danger.

I climb from the car; the front door of the Royal home is still hanging from its hinges, and as I push it open, the metallic stench of blood and the heavy, putrid scent of death hits me. My stomach doesn't even roll anymore. It's just another smell, like grass after a rain or burning wood. It's just there—a normal part of my day.

Pretty sure that's really fucked up, but if I puked at every dead body I saw, I'd never fucking eat.

"We really made a mess," Mav comments as he pushes past me to the first body on the floor and rips off the guy's ski mask. "You recognize him?"

I shake my head, moving toward them. "We need to check them to see if they're branded." I absentmindedly rub the scar on my wrist, my own reminder that I'll never escape. Mav pulls up the guy's sleeves but there's no brand. "Nothing on show… but it could be somewhere else."

"Nah, the Knights are fucking ritualistic with that shit. It'd be in the same place as ours if he had one. Let's check the others just in case, but if this one isn't branded, I'd put money on the rest of them being clean. Which means they're private hires, and we have another fucking dead end."

"I'm going to check anyway. Are we calling in a cleanup?" he asks, looking at me like I have all the answers.

I scrub a hand down my face and stand back up. "No, this one's on us." I toss him my keys as I try to work shit out in my head. "Go grab the work truck from my place and bring it back here. We'll deal with it. I'll start looking at the security footage while you're gone. Bring me my laptop from the trunk before you take off."

"Sounds good, man. I won't be long."

He jogs back out of the house, and I feel a little better that he's busy at least. No fucking idea what we'll do with the bodies if we're not calling on the Knights, but I'll think of something. Or Lincoln will. We always figure it out in the end.

For now, I need to check the footage from V's security system and see if there's anything on there. I'm not that hopeful. Whoever this is has done a fantastic job of covering their tracks up to this point. I doubt they'd be stupid enough to leave us any breadcrumbs now, but I have to hope 'cause it's all I've fucking got.

"Laptop!" Mav calls out as he re-enters and slides my bag across to me. "I'll be back!"

He disappears again as I grab the sliding bag and pull my laptop from it. Once I'm in the security room, I get it connected and fire it up. The firewalls on this thing are a fucking joke; it's not a surprise someone hacked in. When we get V back, I'm going to personally revamp this bullshit.

First things first.

As I tap in, I notice a code path that leads to another server. Different. I set up a trace for all things tagged or mentioning Octavia or Stone then get back to the task at hand.

I run through the footage, and like I figured, there's fucking diddly-squat The guy, who is easily 6'4, throws V in the back of a plateless black SUV and peels off like a bat out of hell.

Just fucking awesome.

I hack into the local police surveillance, hoping beyond fucking hope, but there's nothing. Of course there isn't. I take a deep breath and go over the footage again. That's when I notice it's been looped.

How the fuck do people who are trained to find this shit *not* notice cams have been looped?

This is why the police force around here is in fucking shambles. I know the Knights prefer it that way, but fuck my actual life right now.

My phone pings with a message from Linc.

**Linc:**
<video>

What the fuck?

I press play and I swear to fucking God my heart stops. Indistinct shadows flicker on the screen for a few moments. Then I see her.

Clenching my fists, I take a deep breath and count back from ten, trying to keep my shit in check. I dial his number and he answers before the first ring even finishes.

"You saw it?"

"Of course I fucking saw it."

This day can go straight the fuck to hell.

I email the video to myself and start checking the tags on it. If I didn't hate this motherfucker, I'd be impressed with his skill set, but right now, all I want to do is gouge his eyes out with my fingers.

"Is there a way to trace the video?"

I sigh and try to track V's phone. Naturally, that's a dead end—because that'd be way too fucking simple—so I start a trace on the video.

"We knew this guy is good, but it's been bounced off a ton of proxy servers. Pretty sure she isn't in Novosibirsk. It also wasn't sent from her phone, despite coming from her number. A dozen apps can do that, so that's a dead end too, but I'm trying. Doesn't help that the voice was filtered. It doesn't give us much to go on."

Silence filters down the line, and I know Linc is as frustrated as I am. We're not used to running into so many brick walls. That said, we've never gone directly up against one of the Knights before. We've had no real reason to. This has to be someone high up the chain though. There's no way someone has this kind of skill and ability to fuck with stuff without being at the top of that particular food chain.

"Okay, so what *do* we have?"

"We know that the bodies dropped here aren't branded. So either her stalker isn't a Knight, or he hired privately. We also have a plateless black SUV."

"So we have nothing. Maybe Luc will think of something we haven't."

"Luc is coming? How much longer till he shows?" I ask, feeling a sliver of relief. Luc might be a Knight, but he's about as willing as we are. I know he hates that Linc effectively stepped into his shoes, but that's the way the Knights work. Seats on the Conclave are almost always passed down from father to son, so when one brother vacated his seat, the eldest son of the eldest brother filled the vacancy. Not that I think Luc hates his relative freedom from the Conclave… just that Linc had to step up into the position.

"Yeah, he said a few hours." He pauses and before I get the chance to ask him what he wants our next steps to be, he says, "I've got to go. I'll call when Lucas arrives."

He sounds fucked up, so I just say, "Laters," and rack my brain for another option. There has to be *something* on this video.

"Honey, I'm home!" Mav's voice echoes through the house. I poke my head around the security door and he's grinning as he drags a body out of the foyer. Only that crazy bastard could smile while moving dead bodies. I'm thankful for it though. If he's willing to take care of them, it means I don't have to and I can focus on the task at hand without worrying that he'll miss something. He might be a crazy sonofabitch but he's not stupid. He'll clean the house as well as any cleaning team would. Even if it's just because this is V's house.

"Fuck," I utter, remembering that Smithy is going to be home at some point soon. Pulling my phone from my pocket, I pull up a message thread with him.

**Me:**
It's not safe at the house, you should stay in the city. We're handling it.

I should probably tell him that V is missing, but I'm not sure what there is that he can do to help, and I don't want to be the reason the old guy's heart gives out. V will kick my ass from here to fucking Taiwan if anything happens to him.

My phone rings and I groan at Smithy's name on the screen.

This is going to go well.

Pasting a smile on my face, I answer the phone. "Smithy!"

"Don't you Smithy me, Master Knight. What in the blue blazes have you boys gotten yourselves into now?"

Officially dressed down in the politest way, I let out a sigh. "Octavia's been taken. We're working on it."

I wince at the shouting that comes through my phone, half of which I can't even make out.

"Smithy! We're handling it. We think her stalker is a Knight, which means he won't kill her."

"You better hope not," he chastises. "I left her in your care. You all promised me she would be okay. I'm coming back."

"There's nothing you can do here. Luc is coming into town to help. If we're forced to get the Conclave involved, I will let you know. But if you come back, it's just going to put a target on your back, so I'd really prefer it if you stayed put."

The image of him blustering at my words is crystal clear in my head. "You keep me updated, Master Knight. Because if any harm comes to her…"

"I know, I know."

"Do not let me down." His voice is more harsh than I've ever heard it. "More importantly, do not let her down."

---

By the time Maverick arrives with Lincoln in tow, we've managed to photograph and take prints from each of the bodies, clear the house, and take the bodies to the crematorium.

Thank God for friends in weird places.

The house still looks like something out of a horror movie, but the smell isn't quite so bad anymore. I send the pictures and prints to Smithy to forward to his friend with the feds to see if we can get a hit on any of them. They might be private hires, but if we know who they are, maybe that will help us. There's no way these guys aren't in the system somewhere.

My only worry is that if this guy is a Knight, then it's likely he's already wiped them from any database. He's always three steps ahead of us, and I am sick of chasing our fucking tails trying to catch up.

I'm in a thundercloud of a mood by the time I finally step away from my laptop, but if *my* mood is foul, Lincoln's is downright tempestuous.

"How is East?"

"In critical condition. They need blood, rare fucking blood. Luc is handling it," he snaps at me, but I don't hold it against him. Shit might be bad for us all right now, but he's carrying more than we are. "What do we have on Octavia?"

"We need help with this." I sigh, yet again. At least this might be the distraction he needs to bury himself in. "I know you don't want to involve the Knights, but we need help from someone. Luc has connections, but he doesn't have the pull that someone on the Conclave does."

"I will not ask my father for help. He's made his stance on East and Octavia quite clear," he grinds out. I can hear his teeth grinding together like gravel in a cement mixer.

"What does that even mean?" Mav asks as he sits on the sofa. He's about as tense as Lincoln is, and without East here to be the cool, calm, and collected one, that leaves me trying to be level-headed about it all.

Which is far easier said than done.

"It means," Lincoln starts, "that Harrison just told me East isn't his kid, and he couldn't give less of a fuck whether he lives or dies. And he's been telling me for months not to bother with Octavia."

"Holy shit, what?" I blink in shock at that little bombshell. "East isn't his? Well fuck. That explains a lot."

"No shit," he grunts. "I guess I need to apologize to him if he survives."

"So who is his dad?" Mav asks, brow furrowed.

"No fucking clue. I've called Fiona, but shocker: she's not answering." He pinches the bridge of his nose as he leans forward. "I was hoping Luc would have more information, but while he knew that East wasn't Harrison's, he doesn't know who his dad is either."

We sit in silence for a minute while I try to process this new information.

I wonder if his dad is a Knight?

More importantly: if he is, would he be willing to help us?

"But that doesn't help us find Octavia. I feel like we're just sitting here with our fucking dicks in our hands. We need to *do* something." Lincoln's frustration bleeds all over us all, while I rack my mind for options. Seeing him like this is jarring as fuck.

"We could talk to Ryker?" I offer. "The Kings have people on every corner of the city. Someone might have seen something."

He nods, even though I can see the conflict in his eyes over asking the Kings for help. "That means we'd owe them one…"

"We can give him Diego," Maverick offers, and I nod in agreement. "The Conclave are done with him. I heard my dad bragging about it."

For a guy who says he isn't the one to come up with a plan, he's full of good ideas today.

"I like it. Where is he?" I ask.

"He's in one of the cells at The Cage." Lincoln rubs a hand over his face before adding, "We don't have any other options, so let's do it. I can't sit around doing nothing anymore. We can stock up while we're there too. Whoever has her might not want to hurt her, but I'm sure as hell going to fuck him up anyway."

He stands, his face like thunder as he walks out of the house, dodging the drying pools of blood still dotting the floors. I grab my phone and send a message to a friend who is used to cleaning up after the Knights and call in a favor. The last thing I want is for the floor to stain and V be reminded of this day every time she sets foot in her living room.

"Let's go," I say, and Mav stands with me. "If we let him go alone, we'll probably end up with another war on our hands."

Mav just grins at me and shrugs. "I could use a fight."

"I think we've fought enough for one day." I shake my head as my phone buzzes with confirmation of the cleanup.

I just hope we get some answers, because the whole ghost routine this fucker has going on is getting on my last nerve. Just once, I'd like to get ahead.

Maybe then we'd feel closer to finding her.

---

Getting Diego from The Cage was the easy part. Getting him to shut the fuck up on the drive back to Echoes Cove was a whole other story. As we pull up at the Donovan residence, the tension in the car is thick enough to cut with a knife.

"You guys can't tell them where I was," Diego says, looking a little panicked. "They'll kill me if they know I made a deal…"

"They're your brothers. They won't kill you," Mav snorts.

"You don't know my brothers." He gulps, eyes wide. "But I was talking about the Kings as a whole."

"Fine by us. We'll say we tracked you down and in return, the Kings are going to help us," Lincoln commands, and Diego nods. I don't know what they did to him, or what deal was struck, but he looks fucking terrified.

At least he knows to be afraid of the Knights I guess.

I climb from the front of the car, opening the door for Diego and pulling him out. "If you betray us…"

"I won't," he squeaks, but I don't trust him. He's a fucking coward, and they always take the easy way out. Even if it means betraying the people closest to them.

And he doesn't give two fucks about us.

Lincoln walks toward the house and I push Diego to walk behind him while Mav takes my six. A very pissed off Ryker swings the front door open before we're even halfway up the walk.

"I fucking *knew* you had him."

"We didn't," Lincoln states, squaring off with him. "But we found him, and we're returning him."

They stare each other down, neither one of them willing to back down.

"He's telling the truth," Diego says quietly, and I can't help but wonder how this guy created the Kings. He's a fucking pussy. It's working in our favor for now, but fuck knows how long that will last. It might've been better for Ryker if his brother had stayed away

Ryker glares at his brother, not exactly the warm welcome I was expecting, but steps back to let us in. I follow Diego in and head down to the basement where Ellis, Dylan, and Indi are all sitting playing Xbox.

Indi's head whips around first, and her gasp draws the attention of the others.

"What's wrong?" she asks, her brow furrowed as she stands, her gaze bouncing between us all.

"They brought Diego back," Ryker says, pushing past me. "Nothing's wrong."

"Yes it is," she stresses. "Look at them. What is wrong?"

I'll be fucked if I know how she knows. Especially since reading any of us is usually impossible, but I guess she's hung around with V long enough to work some shit out.

"V was taken. East is in the hospital," Linc confirms, and her eyes go wide. He shifts his focus over to Ryker, and I can practically see how hard it is to say the next words that come out of his mouth. "We need your help."

Ryker smirks, letting out a sharp laugh before Indi elbows him in the stomach and he winces.

"What do you need?" she asks, and I am thankful once again that V found a friend like her. Fuck knows she deserves one.

"The guy who took her left in a black, plateless SUV. He put the surveillance on loop, so there's no trace of him," I start so Lincoln doesn't have to. He's having a shit enough day as it is. "We know you guys have people on every goddamn corner of the Cove, we just need to know if anyone saw the SUV so we can work out where she is."

"You mean it wasn't the Knights?" Ellis asks, scratching the back of his neck. "I thought that's who wanted her?"

"It is, and it's a long story. But it's not the Knights. Not as a whole, anyway."

"The stalker?" Dylan asks, and I nod.

"Yeah, except we think he is a Knight—he's just working unsanctioned."

"Well isn't this just a right fucking shit storm you boys have walked into," Ryker says with a smirk while Diego disappears into a different room. "I suppose since you brought Diego back, we can help."

"We will help because it's my best fucking friend," Indi snaps at him. The smile drops from his face and he nods.

"We'll help however we can." He looks at Dylan, who nods and takes his phone from his pocket, dialing as he leaves the room, motioning for Maverick to join him. "Why don't you tell us everything you've got so far and we'll see if there's anything we can do to help you guys out?"

Lincoln looks like he chewed a fucking wasp's nest, but this was a good idea. Whether he likes it or not. He knows it too, otherwise we wouldn't be here.

We sit with the three of them and lay out *almost* everything, leaving out some of the finer Knight-related details that aren't vital; Indi looks like she's going to have a freaking heart attack. "Why didn't she tell me it was this bad?"

"She probably didn't want to scare you," Ellis says softly, hugging her.

"That or she thought you guys would sort it before it got out of hand," Ryker snarls, and Lincoln clenches his fists so hard I wonder if I'm going to have to restrain him before we're done here.

It feels like hours pass as we wait in that fucking room. Linc makes a dozen calls trying to call in favors to help trace the car, Mav stays busy helping Dylan, while Indi flits around like her ass is on fire, trying to distract herself from the wait.

Me, I sit with my laptop trying to trawl through some of what I found while I was searching for Octavia. There isn't much more I can do to help with the hunt for the car right now, but if something is hidden in these files, something that might help her, then I'm going to fucking find it.

"We have a lead on the car," Dylan says as he and Mav enter the room. "And we think we have a potential location. You guys want help going in?"

Ryker looks like he might take Dylan's head off his shoulders, but I nod. Lincoln and Ryker might have a tenuous truce going on for the moment, but we need their help, and I'm not one to cut my nose off to spite my face. Especially when it comes to Octavia.

"We can use all the help we can get," I say, and he grins wide.

"I was hoping you'd say that."

My phone buzzes in my pocket as the Kings start to gear up. My eyes go wide when I see what my ping trace reports are showing. I flick to the document the trace has pulled up on my laptop and start to read.

Holy fucking fuck.

"Linc, I think I know how we can get her back and away from the Knights. For good."

# CHAPTER THREE

## OCTAVIA

I have no idea how much time has passed. The drugs he's giving me through the IV in my arm have me in and out so fucking much that I could've been here an hour or a week and I wouldn't know the fucking difference. My mind is so fuzzy, so patchy, it's all I can do to focus right now.

And I need to focus so I can get myself out of whatever this fucking is.

I blink against the blindfold that feels like silk against my skin. Confused, I frown. I wasn't wearing it earlier. Was I? Was that a drug fueled hallucination? Or just a dream?

The bindings around my neck, wrists, and ankles are icy cold, but there's a little bit of give to them. I think they're leather.

"Oh look, my little dove is awake. Are you feeling better? I gave you a drip to make sure you're not dehydrated, though you might still be a little woozy."

His voice makes my heart race, and by the sound of the beeping in the room, he knows it too.

Nope. Definitely wasn't a dream.

Fuck.

This is bad.

Never in a million fucking years would I have thought it would've been him.

*I trusted him.*

My heart aches at the betrayal as I try to wrap my head around my reality.

"No need to be afraid. I'm not going to hurt you, not unless you make me. I'm trying to protect you."

I gulp and my throat is so fucking dry, like I haven't drank anything for days. "Protect me from what?" My voice is scratchy and I jump when I feel the straw at my lips.

"It's just water."

I take a tentative sip. As soon as it's clear that ice-cold water is the only thing hitting my tongue, I take a few more. It might be stupid to accept anything from him, but he says he wants to protect me, so I'm hoping he isn't going to hurt me any more than he already has.

"There's a good girl, little dove." I flinch as he brushes back some of my hair and takes off the blindfold. I blink against the light, my eyes slow to adjust, but at least it's not as bright in here as it was before. Once my eyes focus, all I see is him.

This can't be happening.

"You need to sleep some more."

He lifts the syringe to the IV bag beside me, and I whimper as the drug burns through my veins before my vision blurs and fades to black once more.

"Sleep well."

# CHAPTER FOUR

## MAVERICK

The Kings' arms room is enough to make anyone smile. I get the feeling that Diego having been gone was good for them. Ryker is definitely the bigger, better beast. He has the same sort of smarts as Linc, which makes him a worthy rival. I'm just glad that he's on our side this time.

We need all the monsters we can get on our side to get V back.

Finley and Linc have been muttering in a corner for the last five minutes while I've been gearing up.

"You are not leaving me behind!" Indi argues with Ryker, and I'm not going to lie, as much as I bicker with her, it's almost as much fun to watch her argue with them. She's grown a lot since V blew back into town. Last year she took a lot of shit, and I feel massively guilty about it now. "She is my best friend. I'm not just going to sit on the fucking sidelines. I can help."

"Baby, I love you, but I'm not going to be the one to watch you march into whatever hell we're about to see."

She screams in frustration, and I smirk as I check over the gun Dylan gave me again.

"I'm going to get V to teach me how to shoot after all this, maybe then you'll stop treating me like I'm made of fucking glass. I can drive, so I'm driving. Whether with you or behind you. You pick." She juts out her chin, and I have to press my lips together to keep from laughing. Yeah, her and V are way too similar.

I leave Ryker to deal with his wildcat and head over to my boys. "So, what's the deal?"

They both look at me, and I know something's wrong. "What?"

"It doesn't matter until we get V back, but we worked out why the Knights haven't just inducted her. And if it is one of the Knights that has her, this changes *everything.*" Lincoln's words send a rush of adrenaline through me.

"Okay, we'll talk it out, but later. First, let's go get our fucking girl." I don't need to know the details and they know it as well as I do. I bounce on the balls of my feet, anticipation at the thought of getting her back—and fucking up whoever took her and put East in the hospital—has me all kinds of giddy.

I might not have started the fight for once, but I'm sure as fuck happy to finish it.

I crack my fingers and curl them into fists before stretching my neck from side to side in an effort to try and calm the raging inferno inside of me that just wants to burn it all down. Linc and Finn gear up quickly and we're heading out of the Donovans' basement to the cars in a matter of minutes.

I didn't even ask where we're going. The finer details are Linc's thing. Me? I'm ready to be pointed in a direction and go nuclear. She's only been gone a few hours, but that's a few hours too fucking long.

Ten seconds away from us with this sick fuck is too long.

Whoever it is, Knight or not, is about to discover that you don't fuck with what is mine. I am not a patient man with most things, but with punishment? I have all the patience in the world.

I jump in the back of Finn's Range Rover and triple check my knives. I've used them a lot already today, so I give them another wipe down, making sure they're the way I like them.

We convoy through town and pull up to a townhouse near the middle of the Cove.

"Well fuck," is all Lincoln says as we climb from the car. It's late enough that we're shrouded in darkness, but since this place is residential, it restricts some of what we can get away with. Even in *this* neighborhood.

"You take the back, we'll go in the front," Linc says to Ryker, who nods, glancing back to where Indi sits in the front of his car with Thomas, who looks about as happy to be sidelined as Indi does.

"Make sure she doesn't get hurt," Ryker grumbles at Thomas before heading to the back of the house with Ellis. I nod, even though he can't see it. If anyone is in here, they're not getting out with the ability to hurt anyone ever again.

That much I can promise.

"You really think she's here?" I ask Linc as we climb the stairs to the front door.

He glances at me, and I already know he doesn't. It's in the stoop of his shoulders. "Even if she's not, we might pick up a fresh trail here."

My stomach churns at the thought of her not being here. It was too easy. I should've known, but I take a deep breath and prepare myself for a fight anyway.

Finley moves up to the door and tests the handle. The door swings open without resistance. We're greeted by darkness and silence. Finn signals for us to go in quiet and start a sweep. He points to the stairs and I nod, my heart racing as I draw my gun and flick off the safety.

We move into the house as a single unit before we split up and I head to the stairs. Keeping my steps light, I climb them as quickly as I can while staying quiet. It's a typical townhouse, tall and narrow, and apparently not the biggest. I clear the first few rooms as Dylan approaches from the back. I nod when I see him. Nice to get an extra set of eyes. He helps me clear the rest of the level before we head back downstairs, finding the others holstering their firearms. "It's basically a shell. Not even a mattress on the floor."

"That's because whoever was here was set up down here," Ryker says as he appears from a door that I'm assuming leads to the basement. He flicks on a switch and heads back down, the rest of us following behind him.

I'm trying not to be too fucking twitchy about the fact that she isn't here; that I feel like we're failing her.

Again.

We were supposed to keep her safe. We're her Supermen and I'm sick of being bested by whoever the fuck this prick is.

My heart stutters in my chest as my feet touch the concrete floor of the basement. People might think I'm a little unhinged, but what in the actual fuck is this? The walls are papered with photos of V. The most recent of them was taken last night, hours before she was taken. The oldest, as far as I can tell, is from the day she arrived back in The Cove. There are even pictures of all of us and a few other Knights scattered throughout. Red string loops around push pins, drawing haphazard and mostly wildly inaccurate connections between us like a fucking crime board.

None of it makes any sense to me.

"What the fuck is this?"

"It's his nest," Lincoln growls, studying the walls. "He watched her, but there's obvious gaps. This was her at Nate's, I'd say before school started, but then there's nothing for a few weeks, because this was in September," he says pointing to a picture of him with V.

I lean in to study the photos more closely and realize he's right. There are gaps. Tons of them. Though fewer and fewer the last few months. It's almost like constant surveillance.

"Could all of this have been done by just one person?" I ask, fucking stunned stupid from the sheer number of photos.

"It could," Finn says, "but if he's a Knight like we think, he could've had help. Or just paid a private PI. It's easy enough to do."

"Whoever it is followed her on both trips she took with Indi," Ellis says from his spot on the far side of the room. "That picture over there is from the bar they went to when Octavia went viral for singing. Indi told me all about it… and this one is from the spa retreat they went on. I recognize the building." His finger taps one of the pictures in front of him.

"This is seriously fucked up. Who the fuck is after your girl?" Dylan mutters, and Lincoln glares at him.

If looks could kill, Dylan would be in a body bag already. "If we knew that, we wouldn't be standing here, dick in fucking hand, like idiots."

I rake a hand down my face. The last thing we need is for those two to start fighting. And coming from me, that's saying something. Because I really, really want to see someone bleed right now. My monster is scratching the inside of my skull, beating against the walls of his cage. Someone has what's ours and all he wants to do is make the streets run red until we have her back.

"We're going to need to go to the Conclave," Finn says, and Lincoln curses.

My heart races in my chest. Why the fuck would we ask them for anything? "With the information we have now, they'll help us. They won't want her hurt by a Knight. Your dad will have a fucking conniption and I don't want to ask them for help any more than you do, but we're in over our heads."

I guess whatever I need to catch up on is fucking vital if they think this is a good idea.

"If you need us, you know where to find us," Ryker says, nodding at Finn. "But our girl is sitting outside and we've been in here too long already."

"Thanks," Lincoln responds. "We should head out too. If we're going to ask the Conclave for help, we should leave this as it is for the sake of preserving evidence."

*Not our usual M.O., but okay...*

The fire in me burns red-hot as we leave the basement. How the fuck are we going to find her? This was our only lead. Even if the Conclave *does* help us, we have nowhere to even start.

"Fuck!" Ryker's shout has my feet moving faster as we run out of the house.

Holy shit.

Thomas is on the ground bleeding, both cars are fucked, and Indi is gone.

Ellis crouches down to assess his friend and lets out a sharp breath. "He's still breathing." Rolling him over, Thomas groans and I move to help Ellis while the others secure the rest of the area. Noticing the gaping wound in his gut, I apply pressure to try and stop the bleeding.

"Indi," Thomas coughs, blood trickling from his mouth. "Rebels."

He passes out again and Ellis curses before calling for his brother. "We need to get him to Doc, and quick. Rebels were here, they took Indi."

"Motherfuckers!" Ryker shouts, pulling his phone from his pocket. He yells at whoever picks up the other end, giving them our location. He finishes the call and curses again. A few lights go on in the house we're sitting in front of and the front door opens, but when the guy sees Ryker, he closes the door and turns the lights back off.

Clever man.

A car screeches to a stop in front of us and I help Ellis get Thomas in the back, Dylan taking over the application of pressure.

"Let us know if you need anything," Linc says to Ryker as he climbs into the front of the car. He just nods and slams the door shut before they tear the fuck away.

I stand there, the blood on my hands dripping onto the concrete, wondering how the fuck all of our worlds imploded in one fucking day.

"We should get back to the house," Lincoln says, pulling me from my thoughts. "It's nearly two in the morning. Much as I hate to say it, we're not going to find her tonight."

I grind my teeth together at the thought of trying to sleep while she's with this sick fuck. Much as I know I need sleep to function, and I can't find her if I can't function, I still hate it. But I nod regardless.

Finley checks over the Range Rover before deciding it's okay to get us home at least. We have to kick out the windshield to be able to actually see, but we get it done and make the drive back in silence.

I just have to tell myself we'll find her tomorrow, because nothing else is acceptable. I might have blood on my hands, but it isn't the blood I wanted and my monster isn't sated.

But he will be, and God help whoever has her, because no one else can save them from me.

---

The sound of my phone wakes me, and I groan groggily as the chiming just gets louder. I roll over and pull my phone from the nightstand, trying to shut off my alarm for school. I've barely slept an hour because my mind would not shut down and I felt antsy as fuck. After spending an hour in Linc's gym, I managed to wear myself down to a point where I could sleep, but by then, the sun was already coming up.

School can get fucked today. I'm not exactly a genius, but I have more important shit on my agenda today. Like finding V and checking in on East.

Linc called Luc on the drive back here last night to find out there's been no change with him, and he still hasn't woken up. I still have no idea what the fuck Finn found yesterday, because I wasn't in any mood to listen to more Knight bullshit last night, but today… today I want to know what the fuck is going on.

Throwing off the duvet, I climb to my feet and stagger into the bathroom. Switching on the shower and twisting the water to its coldest setting, I jump beneath the cold spray, the icy water pummeling my back as it helps me wake up and clears the fog from my mind.

Once I'm shivering, I turn the heat up and shower quickly. I don't want to waste any time fucking around when V is God knows fucking where, with this psychopath that has her. I'm the only psycho she needs in her life.

I'd sell my soul to the devil if I thought it'd help get her back… though I'm pretty sure that ship sailed a long time ago.

By the time I've sorted my shit out and get downstairs, Finley is already set up on the kitchen table, laptop out. "There're eggs if you want some. Or there are bagels."

"Thanks." I grab some eggs and put a slice of bread in the toaster. Culinary whizz I am not. Ramen and toast is about as far as my skills go. When it's done, I sit down opposite Finn and try to eat. "What's going on?"

"I've been trying to see if there's any footage on the cameras around the house we went to last night. I found the black SUV that took her pulling up and taking her into the house. The SUV leaves shortly after, but there's no sign of her or anyone else leaving." He turns the laptop around and shows me the sped up footage, right up until we arrived last night.

"How is that possible? You think they took her out the back?"

"Must have, but of course, that's a dead spot and there's absolutely zero fucking footage on the back street. Which is probably why he took her that way." He pinches the bridge of his nose and shakes his head. "This guy is a ghost. It confirms my suspicions that the people who came to get her were hired guns, rather than her stalker himself. Why risk being caught? Which means he's not stupid, even if he is fucking insane."

"Well fuck. Any way to trace the guy who actually took her?"

He nods, and for the first time since yesterday afternoon, I feel a glimmer of hope. "I've been running the details of the bodies we dropped. They all work for a private military company headquartered on the East Coast called *Dranas*. I'm hoping I can find out who hired them, or at least which of the team made it out alive. I've put a call in already, just waiting for someone to call me back."

"At fucking last." I look up and find Linc entering the room. "If you don't hear back in an hour, call them back and cause merry fucking hell."

"With pleasure." Finn grins. "What are the other plans for today? I hate feeling like we're doing nothing while she's gone."

Linc pours himself a cup of coffee and joins us at the table. "Since we're waiting on Dranas, I'm going to head to the hospital to see if there's been any change, and then I'm going to call a Conclave meeting. The two of you need to stay on Dranas. Any news on Thomas or Indi?"

"Nothing," Finn answers. "I dropped Dylan a message this morning, but he hasn't responded."

"Thomas said the Rebels took her," I tell them. "Either of you have any idea who they are?"

Linc frowns as he nods. "They're the Kings' rivals, but from the city. I didn't realize things had gotten that bad between the two gangs. If it was the Rebels… I'm going to make a call, because if something happens to Indi while V is gone, she's going to have our balls when we get her back."

He's not wrong. I'm just glad he knows who they are and that they're not someone we need to worry about. We've got too many balls in the air already at the moment, I'm not sure how much more we can juggle. At least not until we get V back and we know East is going to make it.

My phone buzzes in my pocket, and I pull it out, secretly hoping that it's Octavia's phone. That we can trace it. But my hopes are dashed when I see my mom's name on the screen instead. "Gimme two minutes," I say, and leave the kitchen before swiping the screen and answering the call.

"Maverick, I need you to come home." Her voice wobbles, and my heart sinks.

"What's wrong, Mom?"

She sniffles and I clench my free hand. I already know what's coming. "I need to go to the doctor."

"What did he do now?" I ask through clenched teeth.

"He didn't mean to… he just came home a little angry, he went down to the basement but that didn't make him feel any better and, well, I pushed his buttons."

"Don't make excuses for him, Mom," I growl. Taking a deep breath, I look up at the gray clouds in the sky. Fitting. "You need to leave."

"I can't do that, Mavvy. You know I can't." She sniffles again. I hate hearing her cry, but I'm not sure what else I can do. "I'm as trapped as you are."

"That's not true. Fiona got out, she's in the Caribbean. Erica is in rehab, though she probably doesn't need to be. You have options, Mom."

"Please just come help me. I can't drive. My eye…" she trails off, and it takes every ounce of patience and control I have not to launch my fucking phone.

"I'll head out now, but Mom, if you don't leave this time, I'm done helping." I hate saying the words, but I can't keep protecting her if she won't save herself. It breaks me every time, when she says she'll leave, and then just comes back for more of his bullshit.

"Thank you, Mavvy." I end the call and head back inside, dropping back into the seat I had vacated.

"Everything okay?" Finn asks as I shovel what's left of my cold breakfast into my mouth.

I shrug. "Need to take Mom to the hospital."

"Your dad?" Linc asks and I nod. "Well, I'm going to visit East, so I can drive if you want? Or you can take one of the cars in the garage."

"Thanks, man. She'll probably freak out if you're with me, so I'll just take one of the cars."

"Sure thing." He nods. "You know where the keys are. I'm going to go call Alexander, see if I can get some info on Indi and what's going on. Then I'm heading out. Let me know if you need anything, and I'll call once I've talked to Harrison."

"Alexander? As in, your cousin?"

He nods as he stands. "The one and only. He's affiliated with both the Rebels and the Knights. Go figure. Apparently my cousin likes to live dangerously."

I laugh, because only Alexander Saint would be crazy enough to play that game.

"I'll catch you in a bit," he says as he leaves, refilling his coffee cup on his way out.

"You sure you're good going on your own?" Finn asks as I finish eating.

"I don't think he's home. She probably wouldn't have called me if he was." I get up and rinse off my plate, putting it in the dishwasher before grabbing a bottle of water from the refrigerator. "If I need help, I'll call. Thanks."

It doesn't matter how many times we save each other, or how much we know about each other's shitty home situations, it doesn't stop the shame that crawls up my throat over the fact that I can't save my mom from my dad. It might just be my biggest failure… that I can't make her leave him. Not for me, not for her. Not for fucking anything.

I feel so fucking sick with the shame of it I can barely look at Finn. "I'll check in in a bit. Let me know if you get anything from Dranas."

"Will do," he calls out as I leave the room and grab the keys to one of the cars in Lincoln's garage. I don't pay attention to which ones, 'cause it doesn't matter. On autopilot, I slip on my boots, grab my hoodie, and head out to the garage.

I hit the button on the key fob, and the lights flash on the Mercedes. I slide behind the wheel of the midnight blue SUV and hit start along with the clicker for the garage door.

The drive over to my house doesn't take long, and as I suspected, my dad's car isn't here. I leave the Mercedes idling as I hop out and open the front door.

"Mom?" I call out, but realize I didn't need to, she's sitting on the stairs waiting for me.

"What the actual fuck?" I hiss when I take in the sight of her. It's not a surprise she couldn't drive, both her eyes are almost completely swollen shut, her nose looks broken, and her lip is split. God knows what's hidden beneath her clothes.

"Maverick, language," she scolds, and I roll my eyes.

"Fuck that, Mom. Look at you."

"I know perfectly well what I look like, now are you going to stand there and judge me, or are you going to help me into the car."

It hits me. She probably can't stand. Which means he beat the living fuck out of her.

I move forward and help her stand, practically carrying her out to the car. One day I'll free her. Free myself.

Even if it means killing him.

# CHAPTER FIVE

## LINCOLN

I wish I could say I didn't know when my life became so complicated, that I couldn't pin it down to the reappearance of a single human. Somehow it seems like that would make all of this feel less… chaotic. Chaos is not something I accept in my world. Not since initiation. I work fucking hard to ensure that my ducks stay in a row, that I have control of the shit in my life. But somehow, since Octavia came back into my life, my ducks have morphed into fucking rabid squirrels.

I have no idea what I'm going to do about my father pushing Georgia on me. He keeps hinting at me taking it further with her to secure his deal with her father. That's on top of the whole 'East isn't a Saint' bullshit, Octavia's stalker, and the documents Finley found. And because I need another fucking squirrel in this circus, Indi has been taken by the Rebels and if anything happens to her, Octavia will likely take my balls.

Which is how I find myself dialing Alexander's number before I do anything else this morning. I lean forward, resting my elbows on my desk, and pinch the bridge of my nose, hoping it helps the headache that's forming. It's too early in the day to feel this shitty.

"Lincoln! Cuz! How you doing? It's been a minute." Alex's cheery voice filters through and I smirk a little at how alike he and Indi are.

"I'd be better if my balls weren't about to be in a vise because your guys took my girl's ride or die."

His laughter on the other end of the phone is about the response I expected. Life has always been a game to Alex. He's a Knight, but he's not Conclave, so his initiation was substantially different from mine. Though I always thought he'd be better suited to life on the Conclave than I am. He lives for the darker side of life. Which is hilarious considering his sunshine demeanor.

"And here was me thinking I was the dramatic one in the family. I assume you're talking about the fiesty, purple-haired demon the boys brought in last night?"

"The one and only."

"Well shit, Linc." He pauses as voices sound in the background. He murmurs something to whoever it is before continuing. "What do you need?"

I roll my eyes, unsure how I can be more clear about what I need. "I need her back."

"That's not going to work. Wish it could, but the Donovans owe a debt and until we get what's owed, the girl is collateral." He actually does sound apologetic, but that doesn't help me right now. "But, since it's you… I can make sure nothing happens to her. She'll be treated as my guest rather than a prisoner."

I laugh dryly, because of course that's his offer. "Sounds like you've taken a few steps up the food chain."

"You could say that. The city is mine, Cousin."

I lean back, eyes wide. Well that could work in my favor at some point, I tuck the information away for later and get back to the task at hand. "Congratulations, I guess?"

"You know I'm a sucker for positions of power." I can practically hear his grin.

"That I do. So I have your word Indi will be okay and returned in the same condition you received her? Which, last I checked, was in one, *unharmed*, disturbingly sunshiney piece. I like my balls where they are and Octavia will take them if anything happens to her."

"Oh shit, V's back? And this is her best friend? Well, life just got a little more interesting. Unfortunately, she's not quite in one piece, but I'll make sure to patch her up."

I groan. What the fuck does that mean? With him, it could be anything from a skinned knee to missing digits…

Alexander always did like games.

Though he sounds far more interested in Octavia than I'd like. "Yes she is, and yes, that's her best friend. Don't fuck me over, Alexander. I'll owe you one."

"And I'll likely come calling. I'll keep you updated, gotta run." He hangs up the phone before I get a chance to say another word and I take a deep breath. This is either going to end really well, or really fucking badly.

Ryker *has* to know that Alex is my cousin. He's not stupid, it's not a secret, and that would definitely explain some of the extra hostility coming from him lately. As if the Knight bullshit wasn't enough.

Fuck my life.

Why is nothing ever simple?

I drop Luc a message to check in on East, letting him know I'll be there soon, before making my next bullshit call of the day.

Fiona.

What fun this should be. I press her name on the screen and put the call on loudspeaker. My headache can't take her usual screeching directly into my ear today. It goes through to voicemail, as usual, so I leave her a message telling her to call me and leave it at that.

Luc still hasn't responded, so I decide to just head to the hospital. There's no point in reaching out to Harrison to call a meeting with the Conclave this early in the day because he won't answer the phone. Instead, I wrestle my limbs out of my sweats and hoodie and grab a quick shower, trying not to think about the girl who haunts every waking—and sleeping—moment of my day.

She's the end game for me, so I need to get her back, and in one piece. Today is fucking Valentine's Day, and she's not even here. We had surprise plans for her last night and everything. That, quite literally, got shot to shit.

I've been trying not to focus on what could be happening to her, especially since I'm convinced that she's with a Knight and most of them are sick fucks. I've been going through everything in my head, trying to come up with a suspect list. While Edward Riley is near the top of that list, because he's had a weird obsession with her since she got back, I'm pretty sure he would've already boasted to Mav about having her. He's a twisted bastard who would derive a sick sense of pleasure just from taking her, but he'd tell Mav about it as a means of torture. He enjoys hurting people more than anyone I've ever met, but the amount of satisfaction he gets from fucking with his son is on a different level.

It's pretty much the only reason he isn't at the top of my list.

My other worry is that there are plenty of Knights I don't know. I'm just not sure how they could've come into contact with V. Especially in the time since she got back. I know she had a stalker before, but Evan dealt with him. The dead don't usually come back to stalk you again.

And while I don't *want* Evan to be on my list, he is. As is Mac. I'm not positive that guy is a Knight, but he seems like the perfect watch dog for my father. Especially knowing what we know now. Panda might've been there to keep an eye on V, but I have zero doubts someone else was there to keep an eye on Stone. Who better than his head of security? But it's not like the Knights keep a database of members that I can just have Finn sift through.

At least not that I know of.

There are limitations to being a junior.

My frustration only grows with each dead end I remind myself of, so I rush through the rest of my shower and dress quickly. I want to check on East and run my idea past Luc. He knows my dad better than anyone, he's probably the best person to help me hash it out before I make the call later.

I grab the keys to the Cayenne and head out to the garage. The guys know I'm going out, so I don't bother tracking them down again.

I need to zen my shit and realign my focus.

Chaos isn't going to get her back and I'm sick and tired of chasing my fucking tail.

---

By the time I make it to the hospital and park, there's still no response from Luc. That alone is enough to make me suspicious, but I head into the hospital anyway. He could've fallen asleep or put his phone on silent.

My brain continues to churn and lands on the fact that he didn't mention

Alex's new position with the Rebels. I know the two of them aren't exactly on the best terms and we had a lot going on, but that's the sort of shit he'd usually mention.

Unless he doesn't know.

There are too many balls in the air right now, and if I don't sort some stuff quickly, I'm going to drop everything. Which is not an option.

I am Lincoln Saint. Failure is unacceptable.

Especially where Octavia Royal is concerned.

Even if it means letting everything else burn down around me, I'm going to make sure she makes it out of this alive and unharmed. The only things keeping me reasonable right now are the knowledge it's been less than twenty-four hours, that her stalker claims to want to protect her, and that we have proof-of-life in the form of that damn video.

I cling to those threads of hope like my life depends on them.

But really, it's her life that depends on them, and that's worse. I'd happily sacrifice myself if it meant saving her.

If only that were an option.

The walk to East's room is quiet. The advantage of the small, Knight-owned hospital is that no one stops me and no one questions me. I pause at the door to his room, taking a deep breath to center myself. As far as I know, there haven't been any complications, and my brother—because he is still my brother, regardless of what Harrison might think—should still be alive, breathing and healing.

I'm not sure what I'll do if he doesn't pull through.

I step up to the door and before I put my hand on the handle, it swings open, bringing me face to face with Luc. "I was wondering how long you'd stand out there for."

"Just taking a minute." I enter the room, avoiding his judgmental look. The room is quiet except for the beep of the monitor and the whooshing of the ventilator. "How is he doing? I tried to text…"

"He's fine. No change since you left here last night, though you look like you've been through the wringer. Thought I told you to go rest." He quirks a brow at me as I drop into the chair beside East's bed.

"No rest for the wicked," I say with a shrug. "There's too much to do right now anyway."

"Lincoln, you're only eighteen. You shouldn't be this stressed." He frowns as his gaze roams over me.

"Yeah well, Knights don't tend to live that long. I guess stress is a part of it."

"You want to tell me what happened after you left here?"

I run a hand through my hair, wondering how much more to tell him. I need his help, but it's been a minute since he was around. I know I need him, but I can't help question how much help he'll be with anything beyond dealing with my dad.

Being this cynical and distrusting doesn't exactly make life easy, but when you've lived through and experienced what I have… it's kind of impossible to be any other way. Letting out a deep breath, I make the decision to just tell him everything. I called him here for a reason, I just have to hope he doesn't fuck me over to curry favor with Harrison.

I tell him everything that's happened since I left the hospital, trying to ignore the steady rhythm of the machines surrounding East. He doesn't interrupt or react, he just listens while I lay it all out. He speculates on a few points as I go but, for the most part, he just lets me work through it out loud.

The only information I keep to myself is what Finn found on Octavia's computer system.

I don't want anyone to know what we know until I get a meeting with the Conclave; an ace up my sleeve, as it were. God knows I need as many of those as I can get.

"So Alexander stepped up with the Rebels and had your girl's best friend kidnapped… on top of you thinking you found your girl, but instead of finding her you found that she was taken by a team from Dranas and delivered to whoever's been stalking her. Is that an accurate summary? Just so I know I'm not missing anything."

I nod as he leans back against the wall, folding his arms across his chest. "I know some of the Dranas boys. I can reach out to them, see if I can get any information on that for you. I might be able to get details Finley can't."

"Thank you."

Groans from East steal my attention, and when his eyes flutter open it's like the crushing weight around my chest loosens a little.

"I'm going to go get the doctor," Luc says before hightailing it from the room.

East raises a hand to the tube in his mouth, but I intercept and squeeze it. "Welcome back, Brother. Don't touch it, Luc's gone to get the doctor."

His eyes are a little glassy and unfocused, but he's awake. It's like I can almost take a full breath, and once we have Octavia back, I'll be able to breathe properly again.

It's not more than a minute before Luc returns with a nurse on his heels.

"Welcome back to the world of the living, Mr. Saint." She smiles at him before she shoos me out of the way so she can tend to him. "This is going to be a little uncomfortable."

I look away, because I know I wouldn't want anyone witnessing me like that, and I'm not about to steal any of my brother's dignity by not. When the nurse announces that she's done, and that the doctor will be by soon, I move back to East's side. His eyes are closed again, but they already told us to expect him to be in and out.

"He'll probably be thirsty, but we need to limit his intake for the time being. I'll go grab some ice chips for him," she says before she leaves the room.

I take my seat again and drop a text to Finley and Maverick to let them know he's awake.

Finn:
Glad to hear it. Still no call from Dranas, but I'll keep on it.

Me:
Luc knows some people at Dranas. I'll drop you his number so you can coordinate.

Finn:
Sounds good.

Mav:
Glad he's awake. Mom's getting seen now. I'll take her home and then come by to see him.

I put my phone away and focus back on East. The other monitors are still steady and his eyes flutter open again. He opens his mouth and rasps, "Octavia."

I smile, because of course it is, then grimace because he's going to be pissed. I shake my head, deciding not to tell him yet. "Once we've talked to the doctor, I'll catch you up."

The nurse reappears and helps him sit up properly, walking him through what he can and can't drink right now. He looks like he just chewed on a wasp, but he nods along as she goes through her spiel.

The doctor comes in just before she's finished. The same one I spoke to yesterday. She shakes East's hand before picking up his chart and looking over it as Luc slips back into the room. "You, Mr. Saint, are one very lucky man. I've seen injuries like yours before and the survival rate isn't great. Thanks to your brother acting quickly and getting you here as fast as he did, things went a lot better than expected." East looks at me, but I don't let on that I know about him and Harrison. "The bullet entered the chest just below your fifth rib near the sternum. We had to open your chest to repair the damage to the right side of your heart. In order to do that, we had to put you on a bypass machine. We were able to repair the hole in your heart and get it to start beating again, obviously. All of this to say you are very lucky, but the road to recovery is only just beginning."

"What does that mean?" I ask, a little tired of having to ask that in this place.

She looks over to me, arrogance coming from her in waves. I drop all emotion from my face, and she gulps. Fucking good. I am not in the mood to be fucked with right now.

"It means that your brother will be able to get out of bed in a few days and try to walk around. He'll be here a week, at least, so we can ensure there's no infection or complications before we discharge him." She looks back to East, who nods even though he still looks a little spaced out. "Then he'll be allowed to go home and will need to start cardiac rehabilitation as an outpatient."

"Cardiac Rehab?" Luc asks, and the doc jumps as if she forgot he was there.

"Yes. Basically, that is where they'll give him an exercise regime to help strengthen the heart after the damage it sustained both before and during surgery. He'll need to go twice a week to begin with, which may drop to once a week depending on how well he responds."

"And how do we arrange that?" I ask, thankful that it doesn't seem too restrictive.

"We'll have the referral put in and his first appointment will be scheduled before he's discharged," she says, nodding.

East croaks, drawing everyone's attention as he tries to speak. He looks like he's struggling, so I hand him my phone. "Type it out."

He takes the phone, his hands a little shaky. It takes him a minute, and he keeps blinking and shaking his head, but eventually hands the phone to the doctor, who laughs. "Mr. Saint, you're lucky to be alive. Sex can wait." I smirk and Luc barks out a laugh at the doc's words. She just glares at me before continuing. "You're looking at at least two months before your ribs and lungs are in good enough shape for that sort of activity. Anything like that before then could push your recovery back. You're officially on light duty until further notice. Five pounds, Mr. Saint. I assure you, you will regret lifting anything heavier than that."

East rolls his eyes as the doc hands me my phone back, and it takes everything I have not to laugh. Of course that was his first question. He doesn't even know about Octavia yet and that's what he asks. I guess the drugs really do have him feeling all the good things.

"If that's all…" the doctor says, and I nod. She leaves with Luc on her heels.

"V…" he croaks, and I sigh as I drop back into the chair beside his bed.

Shaking my head, I run a hand through my hair. "She's gone. We're still looking for her, but whoever took her is a fucking pro. We have leads we're working on, but I need you to focus on healing, because *when* I get her back she's going to kill us both if anything happens to you."

He laughs softly and nods before putting another ice chip in his mouth. "Not wrong."

"Oh I know." I scrub a hand down my face, his eyes flutter shut, and the pain meds drag him back to sleep.

I check my phone once he's fully out and decide it's time to call Harrison.

He's not going to be happy, but he can choke on a dick. I'm getting Octavia back, and if that means a deal with the devil, then so be it.

East stirs again, as if fighting the sedation. "I need to tell you something."

---

I straighten my tie, feeling all kinds of fucked up, but I pull on the monster inside of me and let that cold, stoic demeanor wash over me. I need my monster close to the surface when dealing with the Conclave. "You guys ready?"

"About as ready as I'm going to be." Mav laughs from the back seat, while Finn just nods beside me.

"Then let's get this show on the road shall we?" I climb out of the Porsche and look up at the office block the Conclave uses for meetings. I'm pretty impressed everyone convened as quickly as they did, but I've never called a meeting before and Harrison seemed pretty on edge.

Time to lay our cards on the table I guess.

We head into the building, the two of them flanking me. They wear suits as well, as expected by the Conclave. When you want to get shit done where they're concerned, there are some rules you play by no matter how trivial they may seem. Especially when you're about to fuck shit up in the way we are about to.

No one stops us as we walk through the lobby to the bank of elevators and head straight to the private one that requires a keycard to use. I swipe my card and push the button. It only takes a few seconds until it dings and the doors open. We enter the car and make the ride up to the forty-fifth floor in silence.

I gave Mav a quick breakdown on the way here so he doesn't look shocked when we get in there. He has one of the best poker faces I've seen, but still. Better to be safe than sorry.

When the car comes to a stop and the doors open, we walk into the reception area. This place looks like a swanky law office, but really, it's just a place for dealings and meetings with prospects and the Conclave. Or the Board, on the exceedingly rare occasion they deign to grace us with their presence.

The sound of our shoes on the marble floor echoes around the space as we head toward the main conference room. Voices filter down the hall and I'm pretty sure we're the last to arrive, which was the plan.

I push the door open and the room falls silent as we enter. Harrison sits at the head of the table, the other senior Conclave members flanking the seats to his left and right, so I head to stand opposite Harrison. Finn and Mav stay flanking me, and none of us bother to sit.

"Lincoln, good of you to finally grace us with your presence, considering you requested this meeting." My father glares at me as if we're late, but the clock literally just hit nine as we entered the room, which was the time he gave me.

"I like to be prompt," I tell him. "If you're ready, I'll begin."

A challenge flashes in his eyes at my defiant tone, but he nods while the rest of the Conclave remain silent. Except for Edward, who snorts a laugh, stifling it when Harrison glares at him.

"Perfect. So as I'm sure you are all aware, Octavia Royal is back in Echoes Cove after the… untimely death of our old Regent." I pull the folded document from my pocket and drop the copy on the table in front of me. "As I'm sure you're all also aware, Stone put several failsafes in place for Octavia, so that she remained free of the Knights. The document on the table is the contract he made with you all."

I push the paper across the table to Finn's dad, who opens the envelope and nods at Harrison after he confirms what I've said. If looks could kill, I'd be dead and cold on the ground from the look Harrison gives me.

"That contract clearly states that in the instance of his death, Octavia is to be protected by the Knights, but that her freedom is still granted. Her freedom is for life, and the rest of Stone's line will remain free but be granted the benefits of the Knights, unless they choose to join the Knights under their own volition *without* active influence from *any* member." I pause for effect, letting everything sink in before continuing. “It also states that, should Octavia be approached, hurt by, or initiated into the Knights, she instantly takes the Regency.”

Murmurs go up around the room and it occurs to me that maybe not everyone was privy to the details of the deal Stone made when he stepped down. And considering the fact that my father looks like he’s going to implode, I’m guessing he wasn’t aware either.

“What is the point here, Lincoln?” Harrison asks through clenched teeth, and it takes a lot of strength not to just laugh at him.

“My point, Father,” I spit, “is that Octavia has been taken, we think, by a Knight. It means that if any harm comes to her by his hand, she will be the rightful Regent of this Sect.”

# CHAPTER SIX

## OCTAVIA

My eyes flutter open for a moment, but my head pounds like a jackhammer with each heartbeat, forcing them closed again. My mouth is so dry I have to peel my tongue from the roof of my mouth. Everything feels so heavy.

Then I feel his breath on my skin and I flinch, opening my eyes again, the blindfold having slipped down enough that I can see a little, and find him watching me…

Standing way too fucking close.

I have to be imagining this. There's no way…

"Oh good, you're awake." His voice sends a shiver down my spine. It feels like he knows it when he smiles, looking crazier than I've ever seen him. He leans in closer, too close. His warm breath on my cheek makes my stomach flip-flop.

I try to speak, but my throat is so dry I can't form words. *How long was I out?* Where the hell am I?

What does he want from me?

This can't be happening to me right now. I close my eyes for a second, trying to calm the rising panic inside of me. How did I not see this? He wasn't even on the *second* list of people possibly stalking me. How did he get away from the tour?

*How is this real?*

I jump as something bangs, and I open my eyes again. I'm not sure what's worse. Seeing and knowing, or closing my eyes to this insanity.

He walks away from me, over to the darker side of the room. I realize the overhead lights are off, a dim lamp on a short table beside me the only source of light. I can't see much else, but my eyes are grateful for the break from the harsh glare of the fluorescent lights from earlier.

I need to be smart about this. I have no idea where the fuck I am, why I'm here, what time it is, or if my guys are still alive and on their way to save me. All I know is that it's cold and dark.

"Evan..."

He grins at me again, stroking a finger down my cheek and laughing when I flinch at his touch. "You should call me Panda. You always call me Panda."

I cringe at his touch. He looks at me like I'm his prize and it makes me feel sick. There's something sinister in his look that I've never seen there before.

"Why am I here?" I ask quietly, hoping not to push him too hard. He's never hurt me before… but I mean, he took me, drugged me… who knows what else he's capable of?

"Because those stupid boys don't deserve you. They just get in the way. You were always meant to be mine. I'm the only one who can protect you. Even your father knew it."

Bile rises in my throat at his words as they trigger my memories.

*Oh God.*

Lincoln.

East.

The vision of them lying in a pool of blood fills my mind, and I choke back a sob.

*Please let them be okay.*

"You don't get to speak about my father." The words come out as more of a croak than forceful, as intended. "You don't know anything about him."

His eyes narrow before his smile widens. "I think, little bird, you might be the one that didn't know him. Trust me. I knew your father pretty well…" His manic laughter causes bile to rise in my throat. "He promised you to me a long time ago, but he reneged on his deal, stole you away, and sent you here. Away from me and the protection *only I* can give you."

The sound of metal on metal screeches out, followed by a clatter. He leaves momentarily in the direction of the sound then moves back toward me. "I told you. I'm trying to protect you."

I blink up at him, trying to work this all out. "Protect me from what?"

"From them. From all of it. From me."

None of this makes any sense.

"You don't understand. Your father was a coward. He wasn't protecting you either. You were just left out in the cold. Clueless, defenseless. But you were meant for more. And the only way to *be* more, is if I help you."

I shake my head, more confused than I was when he started talking.

"Evan… Panda. P. None of this makes any sense. What do you mean more? And why am I tied up? I thought we were friends." I can't work out if I'm more angry or hurt right now.

He was supposed to be my friend.

He glares at me briefly then softens again, running a finger down my cheek.

"That's exactly why you're here. I need to deprogram you. They all made you believe their lies. I'm going to make everything better. Then you'll realize the truth. They infected you. Messed with your mind. It's the only reason why you'd let them do to you what they did; the only reason you'd forgive them. But I knew… when I saw you had forgiven them, I knew you'd forgive me too." He pauses and steps back, tilting his head as he looks at me. "You'll forgive me right, little dove? All I ever wanted to do was protect you. I saved you before, and that's all I'm doing now. Protecting you, mending your broken wings."

"The only one trying to break me is you," I hiss. This is such utter bullshit. "I will never forgive you, and I will never let you win. You can't keep me locked up here forever."

His smile turns into a glare and he stomps back toward me, moving so close his lips practically whisper against my skin. "You have no idea what I can do."

I take a deep breath and try to calm myself, because I think the only way I'm going to get myself out of this shit is if I play along with him. I'm not sure what happened to him. When did he stop being the guy I trusted and become this monster? Or has this always been him and I just didn't see it?

"My head is still a bit fuzzy, P," I say, forcing a smile on my face, wincing as my head pounds at the movement. "I just want to understand what you're protecting me from."

"The Knights," he hisses. "Don't you understand? No one else is trying to protect you, they're just preparing you to take over where your dad left off. It's all just a show, to lull you into a false sense of security."

"I want to believe you, P. But it's kind of hard to trust you when you have me tied up like this."

He frowns at me, then shakes his head as he mutters to himself. "You have to stay tied up for now. It's the only way. I'm doing this for you."

"P, are you okay?" He seems like he's lost his goddamn mind and when he looks at me, he almost looks like a lost little boy. "Maybe if you untie me, we can talk this all out?"

"I am not untying you! Stop trying to trick me!" he yells, and I startle. He starts to pace back and forth in front of me, tugging on his hair. Fear floods me, I've never seen him like this. "You're still under their influence. We need to break you free of it first."

I bite my lip, sad for my friend, because something is very obviously wrong with him. I can't help but wonder if this is because of his initiation, or if something else happened after I left the tour. He wasn't like this before. He was chill and stable, funny even. He was someone I could depend on, but the guy in front of me right now is a world away from the P I used to chill with.

I rack my mind, trying to think back to the Midnight Blue gig I took Indi to. He seemed okay then, just like the old P… had the flowers started arriving by then? Or was that trip what started his spiral?

He was quiet at Thanksgiving, sure, and I know he spoke to the guys, but he wasn't like this.

"What happened, P?" I ask, trying to keep my voice even and steady. I am very much at a disadvantage right now, but I don't think he wants to hurt me. Maybe if I can reach the guy I used to know, this won't end in tears. Or worse.

He looks at me, confused. "What do you mean?"

I take a deep breath and hope to fuck I can reach him. "I mean, what happened after I left the tour? Why did you think you needed to protect me?"

"I knew what would happen when you went back… I knew it. But I had to stay on tour. It was where they wanted me, and I didn't hate it. Then you came back, but we were there—at that venue—and I saw what it did to you. I knew I'd been right, that I was the only one that could protect you. I just need to put the final pieces in place. I think you should sleep some more."

He grabs a syringe and a knife from the metal table beside me, and fear spikes in my heart. "No, P. Please. I don't need to sleep."

I try to move, to get free of my binding, but the thick leather buckles don't move. He puts the knife against my throat to stop me from moving before using the drip already in my arm to administer whatever the fuck it is he's giving me, and the world spins.

"Sleep for now, V. We'll talk more when you wake up. Maybe then you'll be ready."

*Please, someone, find me.*

---

I wake up, my head pounding again, except this time there's no blindfold. Just darkness. I stay quiet, attempting to even my breathing despite my heart beating out of my chest. I can't hear anything but the rushing of my blood in my ears.

Trying to calm myself takes longer than I'd like, though that could be the brain fog.

I still can't believe it's him.

None of this makes any fucking sense to me. I've barely been in contact with him since Thanksgiving.

I shake my head, there's no way. But as I rack my mind, I can't think of what would push him to this. I have to focus on this, rather than the last thing I remember before coming here, because that was Lincoln and East in a pool of blood. If I focus on that, I'm never getting out of here. If either of them didn't make it… because of me…

I don't know what I'll do.

The overhead light flickers on and I blink against the harshness of the yellow light.

"You're awake," he says as he comes down the stairs, which is when I realize I'm in a basement. It's as if that knowledge turns my senses up, and I take in the stone walls and wrinkle my nose at the damp smell down here.

"Where are we?" I ask, my eyes watering against the harsh lighting.

"That doesn't matter. We won't be here long," he says, running a hand through his hair. "We need to get you away from them before they get you too."

"Before who gets me?" I ask softly, trying to remain calm. Pretty sure no one expected the guy who saved me from my last stalker to be the one to put me through this again, but I listen to my dad's voice in my memory, telling me to stay calm and collected, and it helps.

Only a little, but I cling to it like it's my only lifeline.

For all I know, it might be.

"The Knights." He spins to face me. "The Regent will send his guard dog for you. It's what he does. He came for everyone else in your line. He'll come for you too if I don't get you out."

My eyes go wide and my heart rate increases, but there's no beeping this time. I guess he took the monitor away. I shake my head, trying to clear the fog clouding my mind. It's useless, but I have to try.

"What does that even mean, P?"

"It means you're in danger, and I'm the only one who's trying to help you. Those four, the four you trust so willingly? They're in on it. Why else would they keep you so close? Covet you? They tricked you into thinking they wanted to keep you safe, but really, they want to gift you to the Knights." He pauses his pacing and scrubs a hand down his face, looking at me as if he's pleading with me to trust him. I've always trusted him, trusted him with my life… but he has to be wrong. There's no way they'd do that to me. "The final step of initiation. Losing something or someone you love. They just want power. I thought you'd be safe, but no. I've been watching. They don't want you to be safe. They want to sacrifice you for their own gain. The only potentially innocent one is East. He doesn't know everything, but they don't care. They'll sacrifice him too if that's what it takes to secure their seats in the Conclave."

I blink at him. He has to be wrong.

He has to be.

"They wouldn't do that to me, P," I spit. Listening to that voice in my head that says to remain calm and collected is a lot easier said than freaking done.

He glares at me, angry that I don't believe him. "Did they tell you about how your dad really died? 'Cause they know. They know the guard dog came for him."

I choke on the lump that forms in my throat. I try to swallow but it doesn't clear. He has to be lying. "I don't know what that means, P."

"It *means* that the Knights want you. I didn't tell your stupid boyfriends, because I didn't want them to know I knew anything. And I couldn't tell you. How could I? I knew the guard dog was coming and I didn't do anything. I didn't think he'd kill Stone. I didn't. And then you found him and I panicked. I don't want you to hate me, but I didn't want them to kill me."

"Who is the guard dog, Panda? Who killed my dad?"

He looks at me like I'm insane, like I should know.

"Riley… Riley is the guard dog."

My heart beats so fast I think I might have a heart attack. He can't mean Maverick. "Riley?"

"Yeah, Riley. Edward. The Regent's guard dog… he took your mom, then he came for your dad."

"My mom?" My mind spins, trying to filter through all of this. I'm half glad I'm strapped in, because I'm not sure I'd be able to stay standing right now. "Why?"

"I don't know. If I knew, I'd tell you. I swear it. I just know that he wants you now, and they're going to give you to him. So I had to get you away from them. Only I can protect you, V. You have to believe me."

A tear slips down my face and I try not to flinch as he wipes it away. "Don't cry, V. I didn't want to make you cry."

Rage bubbles up inside of me, and I snap. “You didn’t want to make me cry? Are you fucking kidding me? You stalk me, threaten me and my friends. My boyfriends. Then you fucking kidnap me, shoot at us they could be dead for all I fucking know—and now I’m tied up while you tell me that Maverick’s dad took my mom and killed my dad. What the fuck did you think I was going to do? Laugh? Thank you? This is fucked up, Evan.”

He steps back, looking like I slapped him when I called him Evan, but I’m all out of fucks right now.

This is so messed up.

I scream out into the nothingness as tears stream down my face and allow myself to break. There’s no point in trying to shove it down this time. It’s not going to save me.

Nothing is going to save me. Either I die here with Panda, or I die at the hands of the Knights apparently.

I’m not usually one for woe is me moments but right now, I’m going to woe the fuck out.

“V…”

“You don’t get to call me that,” I hiss. “My friends call me V, and you, Evan, are *not* my friend. Friends don’t kidnap each other and tie them up, or fucking shoot at each other. This is bullshit.” I struggle in my restraints, hoping that something comes loose. But even if it doesn’t, I get to at least *try* to do something.

He presses his lips into a thin line. It's like a switch inside of him flips and that darker side of him comes back to the surface.

He just laughs in response as he moves toward me. “I’m assuming you need to use the bathroom. Are you going to behave, or do I need my gun?”

As if triggered by his words, my bladder makes itself known. Apparently being hooked up to an IV will do that to you, and I’d really rather not pee myself. Though the thought of being even close to submissive to him raises my hackles.

I shake my head. “You don’t need your gun.”

He moves closer, unhooking the IV from my arm before releasing one of my ankles from its binding, but then shackles it to my other leg with a length of rope. He does the same to my wrists, binding them in front of me. “If you do anything stupid, I will teach you a lesson about disobeying me. Do you understand, little dove?”

I ignore him while trying to make sure I don’t fall. I have no idea how long I’ve been here, but my body is weak as fuck. As much as I’d love to fight him right now, I’m not sure my body could do it.

“Little dove?” The new nickname is gross. Like I’m something small and fragile to be protected and coveted. Fuck this, and fuck him.

I snap my gaze back up to meet his. “My name is Octavia.”

“There’s that fire. I’ll break you down soon enough, then you can rise. Like my very own phoenix from the ashes.”

I don’t respond, because it's useless and I need to save my energy to move. I also have no idea how to deal with this version of him. “Where is the bathroom?”

“Up the stairs.” He grins. I waddle toward the stairs as best as I can, but I’m out of breath and dizzy by the time I reach the bottom step. I try a few times to lift one foot up high enough to climb them, but the bindings make it impossible.

"I've got you, little dove," he says and steps up behind me, lifting me into his arms bridal style. He looks down at me with a twisted sort of affection in his eyes. My stomach rolls from being so close to him.

He buries his nose in my hair and sucks in a breath, and it's all I can do not to swing both hands up and hit him in the face.

Goddamn my body for betraying me, leaving me so weak.

He carries me up the stairs and across a dilapidated kitchen, down a hall, to a half bath. "Do you need help in there?"

"I'll be fine," I say through gritted teeth. There is no way I'm letting him in the bathroom with me. I'm all too aware that he could easily make me, but he seems to want to keep his façade of protector up, so I've just got to hope that stays in place. He puts me down, holding me until I'm steady. My skin crawls under his touch, but my head spins at the sudden movement, so I can't even pull away from him as quickly as I want to.

He hands me a fresh pair of pants and a tank. I consider ignoring them, the idea of accepting anything from him almost as disgusting as this imaginary relationship he seems to think we have, but I'm fucking gross right now.

As soon as I'm sure I'm not going to face-plant, I scoot toward the door and nearly fall on my face.

I turn back to face him, trying to look as broken as I can. "Can you untie me, please? I can't clean up if I'm tied up. I can barely walk."

He watches me closely, tapping the gun on his hip. "If you try to run, or do anything else just as stupid, I will use this."

My heart pounds in my chest at the possibility that he might actually untie me, but also the thought of getting shot. I really want to get out of here, but I really don't want to get shot. He steps forward and unties the bindings at my wrists before stepping back and pulling the gun. "Untie your ankles and head inside."

I do as he says, trying not to freak out about the gun pointed at my head. Usually I wouldn't think he'd pull the trigger, but he's a little unhinged right now. I pull at the bindings on my ankles, freeing them before shooting into the bathroom and locking the door behind me. It's a flimsy as fuck lock, but it's something. Pretty sure it'd be useless if he really tried to break it open, but it makes me feel a little better at least.

I look around the room at the broken tiles, the flickering light, and the window that's been bricked closed. Awesome. Definitely no way out of here except for the door then.

Feeling resigned, I undress, washing as best I can, trying not to look at my reflection in the dirty, grainy mirror. It's impossible to miss the dark purple streaks under my eyes, and my hair is matted and gross.

*How long have I been here?*

I get redressed and splash my face with water, taking a few mouthfuls as I do. The cool, refreshing sips do more for my mood than I expect, so I take a couple more, savoring the small boost of serotonin.

"Are you nearly done, little dove?"

Happy feeling's gone.

He sounds kind, patient even, but I'm not stupid enough to believe him.

One day I'll work all of this out, I just need to survive this very real hell I've been thrust into. Panda never would've raised a finger against me, but I have no idea what this new Evan is capable of.

So I take a deep breath and undo the lock, pushing the door open.

"Feel better?"

I nod, glaring at him as he steps forward with new bindings, handing them to me. "Tie your ankles, and don't make them loose. I don't want to hurt you but I will."

The gun trained on me once more, I take a deep breath and tie my ankles together, not as tight as he had them, but tight enough that I'm not going to be able to slip them without breaking my ankle.

I fucking hate this.

With my ankles bound, he ties my wrists and picks me back up, taking me back down to the basement. He doesn't seem to notice the daggers I'm staring at him. If he does, he doesn't say anything. When we reach the bottom of the stairs, I realize why he'd been so quiet while I was in the bathroom. The table I'd been tied to is gone, and in its place against the back wall is a cot with a thin mattress.

"I thought this might be more comfortable until we're done. I doubt it'll take me long to get you to see the truth and become my phoenix. I'm a determined man. You'll be mine eventually." He drops me onto the cot and I clench my jaw as the water I swallowed threatens to resurface at the jolting movements.

He unties my hands first, binding me to the bed, and then my ankles, before moving to get the IV.

"I think you need to sleep. Everything will be better if you sleep."

"Do not fucking drug me again, Evan," I growl, but he isn't listening to me anymore, he's muttering to himself.

I hiss as he pushes the needle into my arm and tapes it in place before hooking up the tubes.

He brushes my hair behind my ear, and grasps my chin in his thumb and forefinger. "I need to go out, so you need to sleep again."

I whimper as whatever he put in the IV bag burns in my vein and the room fades away.

"Sleep well, little dove. Soon you'll be mine, and there's nothing anyone can do to save you."

The edges of my mind go fuzzy, but in this moment of helplessness, I make myself a promise.

If I survive this, I won't ever be this helpless again.

Ever. Fucking. Again.

# CHAPTER SEVEN

## EAST

Lying in this hospital bed is killing me slowly. I feel like a giant waste of space, unable to help the guys search for V.

That might be what ends me, not the whole, bullet-to-the-heart-with potential-catastrophic-complications thing.

I'm losing my goddamn mind. She's been gone for over a week. A whole eleven fucking days of not knowing who has her, or what's happening to her… of knowing that the others had to ask the Knights for help.

None of it feels right.

Or good.

It's all very much bad, but I'm practically tied to this stupid fucking hospital bed, unable to even walk the length of the fucking hall yet because, apparently, a bullet to the heart will fuck with your ability to do just about anything.

I hide behind a brave face when the boys come to visit because I need them focused on V rather than my shit right now.

The last I heard from Luc was that they thought they had a location. But that was late last night and none of us have heard anything since. The ticking of the clock in this room is so loud that I want to throw it across the damn room, but that would require moving, which technically I'm not allowed to do alone yet.

*Stupid fucking bullet wound.*

I don't regret taking the bullet for Lincoln. I'd take it again a thousand times over if it keeps him safe, but that doesn't mean I have to enjoy the recovery.

It's only ten in the morning. It feels like eons have passed since my meds at seven, but that's the joy of three hours alone in a room with nothing to do and no one to talk to.

As if summoning someone with my very thoughts, the door to my room opens, and a guy I don't recognize stands in the doorway.

"Hello?" It comes out as more of a question, and I grab my phone to dial Luc just in case. Living around the Knights has taught me to be safe rather than sorry, and suspicion is my go-to with people I don't know.

"Easton?" he asks, almost warily as he steps into the room, letting the door close behind him. He looks very at odds with how unsure he seems. His at least five-thousand-dollar suit, shiny shoes, and styled hair scream money, confidence. He looks like a man who is typically sure of himself.

But he says my name like a bomb is about to detonate and my suspicion grows. So I nod, the weird tension in the room growing. There's a pit in my stomach as I take in his appearance, but it doesn't stop me from asking, "Who are you?"

He inches closer to the bed and motions toward the chair. "May I?"

I quirk a brow and say nothing, so he sits down and takes a deep breath. "My name is Chase Armstrong. I received a call from Fiona after she got a message from your brother."

My ears heat and tingle at his words. I can't breathe.

Holy fuck.

This isn't how I expected this to go down.

"You're my father?"

He nods in response and I let out a deep breath. "I haven't heard from your mother in just over twenty years. I never knew…"

The air is thick, and it's like I can't breathe. My chest tightens, like a weight sits on it as I watch him struggle to think of what to say. What excuses to make. Who to blame. I already know the answers to all of that, but it doesn't make any of this feel less stifling.

"You never knew she had your kid," I finish, because he's looking at the floor. Why am I not surprised that Fiona said nothing? Though, it's very likely that was Harrison's doing. He's a giant fucking prick like that.

My stomach churns as he sits in silence, his eyes searching my face as if looking for the answers to the universe. He lets out a sigh and his shoulders drop a little. He takes a deep breath and straightens up again, squaring his shoulders and calling on that confidence I'd expected of him. "Exactly. She only called yesterday, otherwise I'd have been here sooner."

"That sounds about right," I mutter. Of course I nearly die, and she can't be bothered to respond to Linc's message for over a week. Typical Fiona.

I feel awkward as hell sitting across from the man who is essentially my sperm donor. What exactly am I supposed to say here? What does he want from me?

"Why are you here?" I ask, folding my arms across my chest carefully, trying to construct barriers between us. If he thinks he can just walk in here and everything's going to be a love fest, he has another thing coming. He also has that air about him, the one that comes from a lifetime of being tangled up with the Knights, and my hackles are raised.

I am done with being a pawn for those fucking people.

"I don't have any other children, and I'm aware that you are fully grown, your own man, but I'd like to get to know you, if you'd give me a chance." He looks earnest, but the jaded asshole that I am struggles to believe there isn't some ulterior motive here, no matter what he says. Knights always want *something*. "I know you don't know me, where I'm from, the kind of man I am, but if I'd have known about you..."

I shrug, and cut him off. "There is no way Harrison would've let you know the truth, so don't feel too guilty. And if you had, he wouldn't have let you live. Not back then."

"Harrison Saint doesn't scare me." There's a fire in his eyes that makes me question if this guy is a Knight. There *are* three families that sit on the Conclave that I know next to nothing about. "He might be the Regent, but after what Lincoln brought to the table this week, that might not be the case for long."

"So you *are* a Knight." I sigh, rolling my eyes.

Just awesome. Any thoughts of maybe seeing what he wanted just disappeared. I'm not getting any deeper in with the Knights than I am. The idea was to escape, not become one of them.

"I am, only because my family have been since the founding of the Cove. I'm not like the others. I have no need for their particular brand of... ethics. I abhor everything about the organization and if it wasn't for my own initiation, I wouldn't still be with them, but you know as well I do. Blood in, blood out."

I nod. He's not wrong, I know that all too well. He seems earnest, but I don't trust him and he seems to know that. He lets out a deep sigh, and runs a hand down his face.

"I don't expect you to trust me, Easton. Hell, I didn't expect you to let me get this far, I just... I don't know what I wanted, but I needed to explain myself to you. To give you options other than whatever your current situation is." He lets out a deep breath before continuing. "The Knights are the reason I chose never to marry or have children. I didn't want to drag anyone else into the madness. I'd rather see the institution burn to the ground than help it continue. It's why I struggled with coming here to see you and why I helped Stone the way I did when he wanted to leave."

His revelation piques my interest, but I remain guarded, reminding myself that stringing together pretty words, telling you what you want to hear, is what the Knights thrive at. Yet, I still find myself asking him the question on the tip of my tongue. "What do you mean?"

His phone sounds in his pocket. He pulls it out, glances at the screen and silences it before giving me all of his attention once more. He pauses, as if weighing his words, and the air in the room grows thicker.

Fuck this is weird.

I'm not sure if I'd be happier if he never came, or if he'd just say what he came to say. "I mean, that I was the one who helped him craft a way to get Octavia out. I am not your enemy, Easton. And if you'll let me, I could be a very good ally."

My mind spins at all of this new information. This guy is my dad, and he turns up, hating the Knights, offering to help us all. It seems too good to be true. And when something seems that way, it usually is. Yet my heart still races at the possibilities. I'm not about to tell him my every fucking secret, but I might be more willing to hear him out.

I run a hand through my hair, trying to work out what to say, how not to give everything away with just a few words. How desperate I am to find a way to get them all out. Especially when, for all I know, Harrison put him up to this.

I wouldn't put it past him.

"You wouldn't be very good at poker," he laughs. "Your every thought broadcasts clearly. I understand you have no reason to trust me, but I'm going to show you that you can. If you'll let me."

I quirk a brow and fold my arms over my chest, wincing a little at the pressure on my healing incision as I move too quickly. "What do you mean exactly?"

"I mean, that I found your girl, and your brother and his friends are gearing up as we speak to go and get her."

# CHAPTER EIGHT

## OCTAVIA

I've been awake for what feels like hours, but Panda isn't here. It feels like I've been here for days, but I have no idea how long it's been. What I do know is I'm fucking covered in grime and dirt. It's so fucking gross. I've been unbound every time he has let me go to the bathroom, but I haven't been able to escape. He's got the IV in my arm again, but I still haven't eaten and I'm getting even weaker. The dizziness is almost unbearable.

Wherever I am has been dark and silent since I woke up. Not even the lamp in the corner is on. My eyes adjusted a little while ago, but that doesn't help the fact that I really need to fucking pee.

He apparently moved me while I was out. I'm still cuffed, but I have some movement at least. Enough to scratch my nose, thank God, because that was a fucking nightmare earlier.

I keep going over everything in my mind, trying to distract myself from the fact that I need a bathroom, and trying to work through how the hell we ended up here. Panda's behavior is completely out of character for the guy I knew. It's almost as if he's come unraveled. To my knowledge, he doesn't have any history of mental illness, but this sudden and drastic change in him can't be anything else.

It just doesn't make sense.

But the fact that I'm kidnapped and tied to a bed tells me that something obviously happened.

Knowing that he's a Knight explains some things, but he's been a Knight the entire time I've known him. So it doesn't make sense why everything would just change over the last eight or so months.

I can't even remember when all of this started. That's how fucked up my world has been since Dad died. I'm trying not to focus on what P told me about Dad being killed, because well, I've been so angry at him for leaving me, and if he didn't leave me, then the guilt is going to cripple me.

I can't afford to be overwhelmed by that right now.

So I'm focusing on everything else he's told me.

Another thing that doesn't make sense to me is why the Knights sent him to watch me in the first place. He joined the tour about two years in. I can't pinpoint anything that happened around then that would've sparked their interest, but then, I don't know why they killed my dad either.

The creaking of the wooden boards above my head makes my heart race.

Is Panda here? Is it someone else?

As much as I don't want it to be someone else, maybe if it's not P, they'll let me go.

I can hope anyway, right?

I slow my breathing to try and pay attention to the footsteps, kicking myself mentally for not doing more training with Maverick, for not going back to my self-defense lessons, for everything I could've done to not end up here.

The steps move away from me, leaving me to scramble, and as I wave my right hand around, trying to grab the other handcuff, it's like a see-saw effect; the tension on the rope allowing me to move one arm at a time, but only if I sacrifice the motion of the other. If I want to scratch my nose with my right hand, the left one has to be stretched above my head in order to have enough range of motion to reach.

Refusing to get frustrated about how helpless I am, I go still again and close my eyes, focusing on the sounds from upstairs.

It's gone quiet.

Shit. Fuck. Tits. Wank.

Silence has never felt more dangerous.

I try to steady my breathing, but it's all I can hear and that just makes my heart pound harder. It feels like it's too loud amid the quiet, like the beat of a drum. The footsteps start again and I hold my breath, trying to focus on them, when I realize there's more than one person upstairs.

*He's working with someone else!*

The murmur of voices reaches me as the steps grow louder, and it becomes apparent that whoever is here is coming down the stairs. Adrenaline rushes through me, my previously non-existent fight or flight response finally kicking in, but struggle as I might, I can't get free of these stupid fucking cuffs.

I want to cry in anger and frustration.

I hate being this helpless. Weak. Being at someone else's mercy.

It just feels wrong.

The door at the top of the stairs creaks as it opens a moment before the crack of wood echoes around me as one of the stairs breaks, followed by a fuck-ton of cursing.

I pretend to be asleep, but only one set of feet comes down the stairs.

"Little dove?" Panda's voice is loud and direct. The most coherent he's sounded since he's had me here. My eyes flutter open, and I blink a few times, feigning adjusting to the brightness.

"You're awake, good. I need you not to fight me."

He steps toward me and I flinch, jerking my body backward. Not that it gets me anywhere, but he pauses, frowning.

"What does that mean?"

"It means I need you to not fight me," he says, stepping toward me again and pulling a blindfold from his back pocket. "I'm not going to hurt you if you do what I say. I promise."

"Why?" I croak, my eyes wide, my gaze not leaving the blindfold as he advances across the room.

"Because the person who has been helping me wants to make sure you're okay with their own eyes, but they want to remain anonymous."

"But why? If they're helping and you don't want to hurt me, why remain anonymous?"

"That's just how they want it. Once they see you're not hurt. We'll move to the next phase: getting us out of here."

"I can't just leave here, P. Please don't make me." I hate begging, but I can't leave my life here. Panic floods my system and I'm officially too weak to try and fight it off. I hadn't wanted to come back to Echoes Cove at first, but now… now there's too much for me to leave behind.

He shakes his head, anger washing over his features as he closes the last bit of distance between us. "You're still brainwashed. I'll fix that too, don't worry. I'll help you realize the truth of it all."

Before I can respond, his hands dart forward and he wraps the soft material around my head, covering my eyes and plunging my world into darkness. "Panda, please. Don't do this."

My voice is thick with uncried tears. Not being able to see anything makes all of this so much worse. I was not raised to be helpless. "You were supposed to help me. Protect me. But this… this isn't that, P. Please see that."

"I see everything. Far more clearly than you. Just trust me." I feel the warmth of him disappear and choke back a sob. I swore I wouldn't cry, but fuck my life, this is too much. I've managed to survive until now, but this might be the thing that finally breaks me.

"You can come down now!" Panda's voice echoes around the bare room, followed quickly by the creak of the wooden stairs. The smell of peppermint, wood, and spice fills the space. It's so thick it makes my nose itch. "I told you. She's fine. Are you satisfied now?

A beat passes, and Panda says, "Good."

Whoever is standing there keeps their mouth shut as the blindfold soaks up my tears, all while my heart pounds so loud in my chest, I'm sure they can hear it. It feels like eons pass in the silence before the creaking starts again when whoever it is leaves again. At least I assume so. I guess it could've been Panda, but I didn't hear him walk across the room.

When the door slams, my blindfold is ripped away. "We'll be leaving here soon. Our lives are going to be so much better. Just the two of us, far from here, where the Knights can't reach us."

"I will never forgive you for this, P. You're going to have to hold me captive my entire life."

He shakes his head, looking at me like *I'm* the crazy one. "No I won't, not once we de-program you. You'll see." He trails off into a mumble and turns off the lights, flicking on a projector which lights up the wall in front of me, images flickering brightly. I guess this is part of his deprogramming bullshit. I struggle against the restraints as he heads back up the stairs.

I need to find a way out of these fucking bindings, because if he gets me away from here, the only outcomes are that I'm going to end up dead or killing him.

---

I wake up to the flashing of images on the wall in front of me. It's so bright that my eyes water and it takes me a moment to actually see what the images are.

Pictures of my guys, of Indi, of me with them…

I'm strapped back to the table I had been on when I first got here, tilted upright so it's like I'm standing, except there's an extra brace around my neck and forehead so I can't look anywhere but at the images.

Then the pain begins. "They are no good for you. They just want to hurt you," Evan whispers in my ear, and the burning on my forearm intensifies. "They will only bring you pain."

I try not to scream out, try not to play into whatever sick game this is, but it's impossible. I don't think I've ever felt pain like this before. I can't even work out why it hurts so much because I can't see it.

"This isn't going to work, Evan. The only one hurting me is you."

The pain recedes a little before he appears in front of me. "I'm not hurting you. They are!"

He disappears again, the images continuing, and then I hear voices. Their voices. Our conversations playing around the room. I feel the cold sting of metal on the inside of my thigh, before the pain starts again as he slices my skin, blood running down my leg to the sound of Lincoln's voice telling me how useless and pathetic I am.

*I will not let this break me.*

Even if I thought it might. I won't let it. I have too much to live for outside of this hellhole.

The metal around my ankle heats as images of me from Homecoming flash on the screen, and a tear slips down my cheek as I take in the jubilance on my face, dancing with Indi before her guys arrived. The heat grows and I see a flicker of orange out of the corner of my eye.

Flame.

I scream as it licks against my skin, all while trying to hold onto my mental walls. I can survive this. It's just pain.

"Our initiation…" Lincoln's voice starts, and another tear trickles down my face.

"Panda, please," I croak. "Stop."

The heat reduces and he moves to stand in front of me, running a finger down my cheek, wiping away my tears. "We've only just started," he says quietly. "I know it hurts, but this is the only way. I'm doing this for you. Once you're all better, free from their control, then we can stop. Then we can be free."

"I'm already free."

He frowns at me before shaking his head. "You're lying. They made you a liar. I'll bring you back."

He drags his blade from the top of my bicep down to my wrist. "You just need to remember how bad they are for you. All of this is their fault."

I close my eyes and try to shut everything out. The pain, the sounds… that Panda is the one doing this to me.

"Open your eyes!" he yells in my face as the flames lick at my ankle again. I try to clamp down on my lips, to stop the screams that threaten to burst from me at the searing pain. "You need to see that they did this to you. That this is their fault!"

He moves to the other side of the room, returning with a dark pole in his hand. "You need to be reborn in fire, only then will you see the truth. There is no other way."

He uses his knife to cut away part of my tank top, exposing my stomach before placing the tip of the pole against the very bottom of my stomach. It's cold at first, but then electricity rips through my body, and pain like I've never known grips me as I convulse against the table. The voltage comes in bursts as he starts and stops the pain.

Tears run down my face. From the pain, yes, but also for the guy who was once my friend. Whoever this person is, it isn't my Panda. This person is beyond unhinged, and my heart sinks as I wonder just how far this version of him will take all of this.

---

"How long have we been here?" I ask Panda as he walks me back to the basement, my arms bound behind my back and my ankles shackled together. The cuffs rub on the gauze from where he tried to patch me up after his multiple attempts at breaking me. It hurts a bit, but at this point, everything hurts.

I've spent the last day or so—I think—trying to seem more compliant. Hoping I can make him believe I'm coming around to what he wants. After the last time I was taken, my dad and Mac did months of training with me in case I got taken again. Stay calm, don't antagonize, and try to get out. Send up a signal if I can. If only they'd told me how much harder it would be in reality as opposed to my lessons with them. I'm trying now, I just have to hope it isn't too late. If I can get him to trust that I believe him, then maybe he'll unshackle me and I can get the fuck out of here.

That sinister side of him hasn't come back out since his last attempt to 'deprogram' me, and I'm thankful because my entire body still hurts from what he did. It feels like days I've been trying to play on that softer side of him and I think it's working, but I'm still so weak and dizzy that I'm not exactly firing on all cylinders.

"Just over a week," he mumbles as he walks beside me, tapping away on his phone. "We'll be here another few days. The final arrangements are just being made."

I try to look as doe-eyed as I can, all while trying to smother the rage and fear inside of me. "Where are we going?"

He pauses to look at me, almost confused like he expected me to fight him or argue. I can't tell if he's suspicious of my compliance or just shocked. I keep the innocent, doe-eyed look on my face, as if just waiting for the answer while he watches me.

His mouth opens, then closes, like he doesn't know what to say before shaking his head. "We're going far from here. That's all you need to know."

"Okay," I say, shrugging my shoulders and continuing to waddle toward the basement door, looking down at the floor. Being this submissive is not in my nature, it goes against everything I've ever been taught and every part of who I am, but I tried fighting him and it got me nowhere. This is the next option on my list.

I can't wait for someone to save me.

I am not a princess in a tower.

I can save myself.

But first, I need out of these goddamn bindings. He opens the door for me, and I pause at the top step. There is no way I can make it down with my ankles bound, so I wait for him to lift me, the same way I got up here. Inky darkness presses against the windows, the light of the moon the only thing illuminating the kitchen of the dilapidated house.

Thanks to a high fence surrounding the property, I haven't been able to get a sense of our surroundings, so I have no idea if we're even still in the Cove or not.

Panda lifts me bridal style down the stairs yet again, which is more than a little uncomfortable considering my injuries and that my hands are behind my back, but I don't complain. I just use the pain as a reminder of who I am, that I can survive this. That I've survived worse.

*This is not the end of my story.*

I wince as he takes the last step down onto the concrete, jolting me, and he frowns down at me. "What's wrong?"

"My shoulder jarred, it's okay. My wrists are a little raw too. I hurt all over." I keep my eyes down, not looking at him as he places me on my feet.

He pauses, like he's trying to make a decision, but then walks me back over to the cot I've been tied to the last few days. It's better than the table I was on, so I'm not about to complain, but also, I am sick to fucking death of being bound.

"Let me redress your wounds. We don't want them getting infected. I think the deprogramming is working. I don't want to hurt you anymore, but it's for your own good. Just a little more and I think I'll have you back. My little phoenix." My heart races at the thought of going through that again. I barely survived it the first time.

"You don't have to hurt me again. Or have to tie me back up. I won't go anywhere. You're just trying to help me, I see that now," I whimper, and I sound fucking pathetic. I hate it, but it's exactly what I was going for.

"I don't know…" he trails off, turning me back to face him. "You could be trying to trick me."

"I wouldn't do that," I say softly, glancing up to meet his gaze before looking back down. "You're my friend. You're trying to help me. Why would I trick you?"

He looks away, but then shakes his head. "I don't believe you."

"Okay." I sigh and stay compliant as he binds my wrists back to the bed, though he leaves my ankles free, even if they're still tied together. I get to actually sit up, so I'm not going to complain too loudly. It's a step in the right direction.

He moves back to the IV bag and my heart races. I really do hate fucking needles. "Can I have something to eat though? Maybe a drink? I don't like needles. You know that."

He glances at the crate of water bottles in the corner of the room, and I swear my mouth waters. I never thought I'd miss water, but I'd do a lot right now to get my hands on one of those bottles. My stomach grumbles so loudly at the thought of food that it almost startles me. I've only eaten a cheese sandwich and a handful of pretzels twice since being here. It's a wonder I'm not so light-headed that I can't stand. I guess that's the one upside of the IV.

"Please, P," I whimper, one arm clutching at my stomach as much as I can with these stupid fucking cuffs. I'm just glad he seems to be at least hesitating, which means he wants to believe that I'm coming around. He's had that projector flickering images at me for too long at this point. I just close my eyes when he leaves, because some of that shit is horrific.

"Yeah okay, we can do that. I'll give you some painkillers too, just to help." He pushes the IV stand back into the corner, and I let out a deep sigh of relief. One win. I'll take it and clutch onto it with everything I have, because maybe, just maybe, I can do this. I can get myself out of here, and find out what happened to the others.

*God, I hope they're okay.*

They *have* to be.

I won't accept anything else.

P brings me a bottle of water and opens it before passing it to me, along with a couple of pills. I try to sip it down, knowing that if I chug it, I'll probably be sick. The urge to slam it down is almost too strong to resist though. He watches me closely as I swallow the pills and drink the water down, letting me take a few mouthfuls before taking the bottle away. I swear I could scream as he does, but instead I paste a thankful smile onto my face. One advantage to growing up how I did: faking a smile is something I learned how to do real early on.

He seems to accept it and heads back toward the stairs. "I'll go make you a sandwich and then we can talk some more if you like?"

I widen my smile and nod. "That'll be nice."

My eagerness makes him smile and I do a mental fist pump that he seems to believe me. He disappears up the stairs, and I adjust myself to a more comfortable position. Testing the wrist cuffs now that I'm sitting. I still can't bring my hands together, but it's a damn sight closer than it was before.

*You can do this, Octavia. Just a few more steps and he'll free you.*

I take a deep breath, trying to refocus and steel myself to what I have to do. I don't want to kill Panda, but if I have to do it to get free then it becomes do or die. I don't think he'd want to kill me, but if he's backed into a corner… he's still a Knight.

I guess this makes me more my father's daughter than I realized, but right now, I don't give a fuck. The burning anger inside of me is all that keeps me focused. Focused on surviving. I'll deal with everything else when I'm free from here.

If I find out this was the Knights' doing, I'll do whatever I can to burn their entire empire to the ground. Everything I know about them tells me they're rotten to the very core. I'm not one for killing everyone in my path, but if my guys are hurt—if the Knights are responsible—I already know that the darkest parts of who I am will come to the surface, and the part of me that gives a fuck is going to disappear.

Panda reappears with a sandwich on a paper plate. I never thought a slice of cheese between two plain slices of white bread would be so appealing, but here we are. I never thought I'd be tied to a bed in a creepy basement and tortured by one of my closest friends either.

He holds the plate out toward me before seeming to realize that, bound as I am, I'm not going to be able to eat. "Sorry," he says with a shrug before picking up the sandwich and offering me a bite. I take a small one, not wanting to torture my stomach with too much food.

He holds the sandwich until I'm done, then offers me the bottle of water again. "I need to go out for a little bit, but I have the cameras and security up, so you'll be fine here till I get back."

"Where are you going?"

"We need supplies for where we're going, and you'd probably like some fresh clothes… and a shower. I'm going to get what we need, and then we only have another day or two until we start our new lives. Evan and Octavia will die, and we can be whoever we want to be." He sounds so passionate, so rooted in his belief, it's shocking. I just nod and smile.

"A shower would be divine," I gush, smiling wider, not having to fake it this time. Though showering with these bandages is going to be interesting.

He nods before taking back the water. "That's what I thought. I'll be back soon, and then we'll get you sorted. I've missed you, V."

I swallow the bile that rises in my throat as he looks at me like he's loved me a thousand lifetimes, and force out the words I know he wants to hear. "I missed you too, P."

He turns and leaves, shutting off the main lights and leaving me with just the lamp again.

Panic rises at the thought that I only have a day or so to get myself out of this mess. But I have no choice. There is no way I'm being taken away from the people I love.

The only way he's getting me out of here is dead and cold.

---

Evan has been gone for so long that I'm starting to think something happened to him. I can't decide if that's a good or bad thing. The food has perked me up a fair amount and I no longer feel like I'm going to pass out at any given minute, but the burn on my ankle is beyond itchy.

I've been working on trying to slip these cuffs, but I'm at the point where I've realized I'm not getting out of them without dislocating something unless he releases me. My wrists and ankles are already raw from being burned and bound, but the pain is one of the few things keeping me coherent.

He has been softening the closer we get to 'leaving,' and the more submissive to his bullshit I get, the more he seems to let his guard down. I'm just glad he hasn't put me through his deprogramming again yet. Now all I have to do is make him believe I'm entirely on board and with him. I'm not sure how that's going to go, but I am all in and committed to it.

Whatever it takes to get free and get back to my guys.

*If they survived everything.*

I shake away that thought and refocus on my plan. If it means hurting Evan, then that's what it takes. I've come to the realization since he's held me here that survival for me might mean doing shit I'm not happy about, but I'm not letting him win.

Not this time.

I am sick of being on the back foot with everything in my life. Starting now, I'm being proactive rather than reactive. I'm not just going to let shit happen *to* me. I might've had my head in the sand regarding a lot of stuff after my dad's death, and I've tried to be more with it the last few months, but I am done with *trying*.

From here on out, I'm *doing*.

Starting with getting myself out of here. I can't rely on the possibility that someone *might* come save me. My dad taught me better than that, and I'm not about to dishonor his memory by being *that* girl.

The sound of footsteps overhead makes me pause. It's just one set this time, and I'm hoping that means it's just Evan. Something heavy thuds above me and I jump at the sound.

Goddamn being so on edge.

My hands tremble from the exertion of trying to free myself when I have so little energy. I just have to hope he doesn't question it.

I steel myself as the door at the top of the stairs opens and his heavy footsteps clamber down the stairs. "Oh good, you're still awake. It's nearly time for us to go."

I smile softly, biting down on the rage and panic that simmers beneath the surface. "Okay, that sounds good. Can I clean up before we go?"

He watches me closely, as if looking for any sign of deception, but my poker face has always been better than that. "Please don't make me hurt you."

It's all he says as he moves toward me. I eye the gun on his hip, gulping, because if he unties me, this could be my only chance, but the gun puts me at a major disadvantage. If that darker side of him shows itself, I have very little doubt he'll hurt me and convince himself it was to help me.

"I won't," I say, looking down at the ground, but he cups my chin and lifts my gaze to his before kissing me tentatively. My entire body screams at how wrong this is, but I force myself to kiss him back softly. His groans turn my stomach, but I force myself to lean into him.

He pulls back and unties my ankles, then my wrists. I fall forward onto him, and he wraps his arms around me. I pause for a moment, sad for what our friendship has become as I wrap my arms around him, then do what I know I have to.

I wrap my hand around the grip of the gun and pull it from the holster as I step back and dart around him. Pulling the gun up so he's looking down the barrel, adrenaline floods me and I feel like I could do anything.

"Do not make me hurt you," I parrot back at him as his eyes narrow at me. Taking a tentative step backwards toward the stairs, I keep the gun raised, flicking the safety off. "I don't want to hurt you, but I will."

He rushes at me, and in my broken and bruised state I'm not quick enough to get a shot off before I feel the burning pain in my ribs as he tackles me to the ground. I drop the gun, staring at the bloody knife in his hand. He looks shocked and sad as he stares at me.

"Why would you make me hurt you?"

I try not to cry, but the pain is bad. Almost as bad as the burning he put me through, but I can breathe, so I don't think he did any major damage. It just fucking hurts. "Panda, I need—"

My words aren't even fully formed when a loud bang sounds upstairs moments before footsteps clamber down the stairs behind me. I risk a glance at whoever is there and almost cry when I see Lincoln's very pissed off face, with Maverick and Finley right behind him.

Despite them being here, I keep my eyes on a now very angry Evan.

I'm just glad he didn't have time to pick up the gun I dropped, and I use this moment to scurry over and retrieve it.

"You three ruin fucking everything!" he shouts, pulling at his hair. He raises the knife, brandishing it in front of him.

Maverick saunters forward, putting himself between Evan and I, smiling that crazy smirk of his, pulling a blade of his own. "Now you're talking my language," he says, bouncing on the balls of his feet.

Lincoln moves toward me, putting his hand over mine on the gun, taking it from me and passing it to Finn who keeps his own gun trained on Panda. "I got you," he murmurs as he pulls me into his arms. I hiss as I sag against him.

"You're bleeding." His gaze rushes over me, taking in all of the injuries and the bandages before he applies pressure to my ribs. "I got you. You're going to be okay."

"She is supposed to be mine! You don't deserve her!" Evan shouts. "Especially you, after your father killed hers. You're monsters! All of you!"

Lincoln stiffens beneath me at his words as I hold my hand against the wound in my side, but Maverick doesn't respond. Whether he knew, or whether he believes it, I can't tell, he just remains poised to attack should Evan make the wrong move. True or not, I wouldn't hold Maverick responsible for his father's actions. Holding someone accountable for the actions of others is just abhorrent.

“Evan, please.” I sigh, pulling back from Lincoln. “I don’t know how you saw this ending, but it was never going to end the way you wanted it to.”

He looks over at me, almost deflated at my words. “I just wanted to rescue you. That's all I was ever good at.” He raises his blade to his throat and my heart stops. “I failed at even that. I’m sorry. I won’t let them take me too.”

He drags the blade across his throat as a scream tears from me. Lincoln’s arms wrap around me as I dive forward. Maverick and Finn rush to him. Maverick, covered in the spray of blood, presses his hands over the insanely deep wound, blood rushing between his fingers as the artery spurts blood. Evan’s gasping breaths in these moments will haunt me forever. The seconds tick by, lasting eons as Lincoln holds me against him. Evan’s grip of the knife loosens and he stills. Finn shakes his head before looking back at us.

“He’s gone.”

# CHAPTER NINE

## OCTAVIA

I tremble in Linc's arms as the pool of blood spreads on the basement floor.

What the fuck just happened?

Is this it? Is this the moment I break? How the fuck is one person supposed to survive all of this and come out of it in one piece? I might've been ready to kill him to survive, but watching him die like that…

"Octavia," Lincoln murmurs in my ear, while he holds me tight enough to keep me tethered to reality. "We should get you out of here. You need a doctor."

I can't say anything—do anything—but stare at Panda's pale body on the ground. Finn moves toward me, but Maverick just watches me from a distance, not able to meet my gaze.

Finn puts a finger under my chin, taking my focus from the blood so that I'm looking him in the eye. His jaw ticks as he looks me over, spotting the bruising around my wrists, but in a blink it's gone and he looks at me like I'm the most precious thing in the world. "Hey, pretty girl. We've got you, but we need to get you out of here and to a hospital."

I nod, but look back over his shoulder at Maverick who still won't look at me. "Mav?"

"He'll be okay, V. Just let us look after you before you worry about us, okay?" Finn's voice is low and soothing. He could almost convince me everything is going to be okay, but nothing about any of this is okay. "We'll sort this out. Just go with Lincoln, pretty girl."

He strokes his thumb down my cheek as a sob rips from me. Should I cry for the man who stalked and kidnapped me? Probably not, but P was more than that. He deserved better than this.

"He wasn't working alone," I croak as tears run down my face. My mind is running at a million miles a minute with everything. There are so many things I want to ask them that I can't focus properly, so it takes me a second to realize that East isn't here. "Where is East?"

Finn's face barely moves, but his jaw twitches, and I know that something is wrong.

Lincoln turns me in his arms to face him, a murderous calm about him, though I'm pretty sure it's not directed at me right now. "Just come with me, Octavia. Let's get you checked out, and then I'll tell you everything."

I shake my head, ignoring the pain as Lincoln uses one of the spare bandages to wrap my ribs. I don't think he slashed deep enough to do any major damage, it just hurts like a fucker. I wipe the tears from my face as my heart races at the memory of the night I was taken. That image is all I can see. "Where is East?"

"I'll take you to him. Come on." Lincoln's words don't set me at ease, not even a little, but I let him lead me up the stairs and out of the run-down house. It's dark outside, the moon is high in the sky, and I shiver as the cool night air hits me and my sock-covered feet hit the cold ground.

Lincoln curses and opens the back door of the Cayenne. He reappears and pulls his hoodie over my head, which is much better than the now-bloody tank top. My leggings might not be in the best condition, but they are at least warm. He rubs his hands up and down my arms before opening the passenger door and bundling me into the car. Pulling my seatbelt over me, he buckles me in, all without a word.

I open my mouth to say thank you, but the lump in my throat makes it too hard to speak. Trying to process everything is proving too much for right now, so I wipe my mind and focus on getting warm, on the smell of Lincoln on his hoodie, on the soft, supple seat beneath me.

Anything to keep my emotions at bay, because if I let myself feel everything right now, I'm not sure how long it'll take to get myself back from that tsunami.

Lincoln climbs into the car and starts the engine, turning the heaters up to max before pulling away from the house. I have no idea where we are. The house is in the middle of nowhere and there's nothing but flat, open space as far as the eye can see.

"How hurt are you?"

I shrug. "I'm okay," I say, playing down the pain because I know we're already on our way to the hospital. I just need to keep myself conscious until then.

"How did you find me?" I ask, my mind wandering to P and how he even found this place.

His hands clench on the steering wheel, his entire body taut, shoulders stiff as he speeds down the dirt road. "We asked the Conclave for help."

A shiver runs down my spine at his words.

No.

What had they traded for help to find me?

Guilt slams through me at what finding me must have cost them.

"I'm sorry," I choke out. He slams on the brakes and I fly forward, only held in place by the belt he put around me, the sharp pain in my ribs causing my vision to swim.

He turns to look at me, his gray eyes a full thunderstorm. "You don't apologize. Not for anything. None of this is your fault. Do you understand me, Octavia?" A tear slips down my cheek, and he reaches over, wiping it away with his thumb. "There isn't anything in this world any of us wouldn't give for you. We did what was needed, and I'd do it a thousand times over."

I nod at his words, unable to say anything at the angry passion radiating from him. He nods once in return and puts his hand back on the steering wheel, moving us forward again. I pull my knees up to my chest, clinging to them as I make myself smaller in the silence, even though it hurts. It's nothing compared to what I've felt the last however long I was with Panda.

I lose track of time as we drive, it's only once I spot the city in the distance I realize we've been driving for over an hour. I should probably ask how Finn and Mav are going to get out of that house, what we're going to do about Panda, what has happened while I've been gone… but I have nothing right now. It's like I've used every reserve I've ever built up while I've been trapped in that basement.

I know I'm supposed to be strong, at least stronger than this, but I know I'm safe with Lincoln, so I don't have to hold my shit together right now.

We keep driving until I spot buildings I recognize as part of Echoes Cove, and before long we're pulling up to the hospital. Linc pulls the car into a vacant spot and shuts off the engine before looking over at me, scanning me as I sit here shaking.

"Are you okay to walk?" he asks softly, and I don't answer straight away, taking a second to take stock of my body. The trembling isn't something I can control, and all of the adrenaline I felt earlier is long gone. In its wake, I'm just exhausted, dehydrated, in pain, and weak. That being said, I'm pretty sure I can walk into this hospital.

I nod at him and unbuckle myself before opening the car door. Before I've even climbed out, he's out by my side, offering me an arm to lean on, like he knows I'm running on fumes. I'm just glad he doesn't try to take this from me.

I won't let this bring me to my knees. This Royal doesn't crawl.

He walks me into the hospital, and the staff jump to attention, swarming around us like they'd been waiting. Someone appears with a wheelchair and Linc guides me into it, not leaving my side as I'm taken to a private room. One of the male nurses reaches for me and I flinch from his touch. I don't want anyone else touching me right now. The only person in this room I trust is Lincoln, and I'm pretty sure he won't agree to stitch me up.

I look up at Linc, and he must see my unease. He points at the female doctor in the room. "Everyone out of the room but you." His voice gives no room for argument and people scurry at his command. Once they're gone, Linc lifts me from the chair and places me on the bed. "Better?"

I nod, hating how small I feel right now. I'm a fucking mess and I hate it.

"Miss Royal, I just need to run some tests so we can make sure you're okay," the woman says softly. "I need to take some blood and get you some fluids, but if you would like to clean up first…"

She trails off and I nod. "Yes, please."

"Your ribs," Linc interjects. "She was bleeding."

I glare at him, but she moves to me and insists I lift my clothing. She inspects the wound and frowns. "It's not too deep, mostly a flesh wound, but it's going to need some stitches. Once I've done that, you can clean up and we can look at everything else." She glances at the other bandages on my body, and I nod, knowing that between the two of them, I'm not going to win this fight.

I lie on my other side, giving her access to the torn skin, wincing as she cleans the wound, and injects a local anesthetic before stitching me up and dressing it.

"I've covered it in a waterproof seal so you can clean up. Are you sure you don't want me to look at your other injuries first?"

I nod, realizing this must be a Knight hospital. There's no other way Lincoln would be able to overrule the staff the way he had. But I'm going to take the upside, because I really just want to shower. "They'll keep until after I shower."

She looks at Linc, who nods once, and she leaves the room too. I fight the urge to snap at him over pretending like he has the final say in what I do and how I'm treated.

"Did he…?" Linc starts but I cut him off.

"He didn't touch me. Not like that. I'd just really like to shower and get clean." His eyes soften and he steps back.

"Okay, but I'm going to be in there with you. Letting you out of my sight isn't going to happen anytime soon."

I chew on my lip, but relent. I'm not positive I'm going to be all that stable on my feet anyway and I don't have it in me to argue with him. Not when I know his gruffness comes from a place of fear. I take his offered hand and walk to the private bathroom attached to the room; it's not huge, but it has a shower. That's all I need right now.

I twist the handle to turn it on and take off Lincoln's hoodie, shivering instantly at the loss of heat. A wave of self-consciousness washes over me at how gross I am right now, and the fact that his eyes won't leave me. I might've been kidnapped, and I should probably give no fucks, but the way he looks at me is so intense it's hard not to waver.

"You're beautiful, always. Now get undressed and get in the shower before I have to undress you myself." He smirks at me and I feel lighter instantly.

"You're such an ass." I smile, but pull off my tank top and push down my leggings before stepping under the spray of water. I lean against the wall as the hot water cascades over me, letting out a bone-deep sigh as the grime swirls down the drain and the warmth chases away the chill that seems to have taken up residence in my bones. My cuts and burns sting under the water, but the need to be clean outweighs the pain.

"Smithy is bringing you some clothes," Linc says from where he's leaning against the far wall. "Do you want anything in particular?"

"Just some fresh underwear, and something comfortable," I respond, knowing that I'm going to steal his hoodie again once I'm done. If he thinks he's getting that back anytime soon, well, sucks to be him. "Are you going to tell me about East yet?"

"I will, as long as you promise to let the doctor look at the rest of your wounds and run whatever tests she needs when you're done."

A knot forms in the pit of my stomach. "That's not exactly encouraging."

"Promise me, Octavia."

I chew on my lip as I lather myself with the body wash from the pump attached to the wall. I use it to wash my hair too, it might be shit for my hair, but it's matted and gross, so anything is better than nothing.

"I promise," I say finally. He already would've told me if it was anything *really* bad. At least I hope so.

I look over at him, watching as he takes in all of the damage to my body, his jaw ticking as his brow furrows. He doesn't speak again until I shut the water off. He steps toward me, towel in hand, and wraps me up. He grabs a second one and wraps it around my hair before pulling me back into his chest. "I thought I'd lost you again."

The words are almost inaudible, but he's holding me so tight I hear them loud and clear. I don't fight him, letting him take the solace before leading me back to the main room. "There's a robe here for you, or you can put my hoodie back on. It somehow doesn't have any blood on it and it comes down to your knees, so you'll be covered at least."

"Hoodie, please," I say, and he passes it to me. It doesn't take me long to dry off and slip it over my head before he helps me back onto the bed. "Now stop stalling and tell me about East."

He wipes a hand down his face and sits on the bed with me. "He's in the hospital. *This* hospital, down the hall actually. He's okay, all things considered. He was shot, but he had surgery, and he's going to be fine. He just needs a few months of rehab and recovery."

My eyes go wide. "Rehab and recovery? Where was he shot? What sort of rehab?" My mind races through the possibilities, but he's saved from answering as Smithy bursts through the door.

"Oh, Miss Octavia, thank goodness you're okay. I was worried out of my goddamn mind!" I chuckle a little because I don't think I've ever heard him curse before, but lean into the hug he wraps me in. He smells like home and I swear I could cry. He pulls back, looking me over. "I brought clothes for you as requested, along with a few comforts. I've only been allowed back in the house today." He glares at Lincoln for a second, which makes me smirk, before looking back to me. "I hope everything is to your liking. Now, are you really okay? What on earth happened?"

"I'm fine, Smithy. Thank you for the clothes. I'll explain everything shortly, but can I get dressed first?"

"Oh, yes! Of course," he says, flustered. "I'll just step outside. I need to make sure Matthew found his way to your room, I just kind of bolted from the car as he pulled up to the doors."

I raise an eyebrow at him. "Matthew?"

"Get dressed, Miss Octavia. We'll speak in a moment," is all he says before dropping the bag in his hand on the bed and leaving the room. I look at Lincoln who is checking his phone. "Everything okay?"

"Yeah, fine. The others are on their way here now."

"Do I want to know what's happening with Panda?" I ask, and the grim set of his lips tells me I don't. "Okay, I'm just going to get dressed." I point to the bathroom and he rolls his eyes.

"Octavia, I just watched you shower, you can get dressed in front of me."

I'm glad to see that Lincoln is still in there under this softer version of him that's been here since we arrived at the hospital. I open the bag Smithy placed on the bed and pull out a pair of fuzzy socks, some soft leggings, a pair of comfortable undies, and a long sleeved t-shirt. I've said it before and I'll say it again: that man is a godsend.

I wiggle into the underwear and leggings, pulling the socks onto my battered feet before shrugging out of the hoodie to put on the long-sleeved shirt. The hoodie goes back over my head before he can get any ideas about changing his mind and taking it back.

"Better?" he asks. I nod as I snuggle into the neck of the hoodie. "Good, I'll go get the doctor."

"Then I can see East?" I ask, biting my lip. "I just need to see he's okay with my own eyes." Guilt runs through my veins like ice. I *need* to see him.

"Then we can go and see East," he says, seeming to understand that I need to focus on that rather than how shitty I feel, or anything else that's going on. Once I've seen him and I know he's okay, then I'll probably crumble. Until then, I cling to it like it's my last tether to reality.

He steps outside the door and returns with the doctor on his heels. I suffer through the blood tests and another IV being attached to me. I try not to freak out and Linc takes my shaking hands in his, holding my gaze until the doctor is done. She asks me a ton of questions that I answer as best I can. She puts a salve on my burns and cleans and wraps the other cuts on my body. It all passes in a sort of blur.

When she's finished, she turns to Linc. "She needs to rest. She's malnourished, dehydrated, and she's been tortured and drugged. She needs to sleep."

"I need to see East," I say, leaning back against the pillow and murmuring as exhaustion slams into me now that I'm warm and comfortable.

"I've given her a sedative to help her relax. I'm a little worried about her blood pressure, but once she's slept and has some fluids, I'm hopeful it'll right itself. I'd like to keep an eye on her for at least twenty-four hours."

"Understood," Linc responds, as my eyes flutter closed. I hear the door close, and the bed shifts as he climbs in beside me and moves me so I'm lying more on him than the bed. "Sleep, V. I've got you now."

He strokes my hair, and as much as I want to be pissed about the sedative, the beat of his heart under my ear is like a lullaby.

Just this once, I'll forgive him for letting her sedate me.

He saved me. Again. I still don't know what it cost him, but as sleep pulls me under, I promise myself that he won't suffer anymore because of me.

---

I wake up to the sound of hospital machines beeping and I panic for a split second, thinking that me getting out was just a dream, that I'm back in that basement hooked up to the machines Panda had in there.

But then the smell of Lincoln filters into my senses and I feel him wrapped around me. I relax again. The pain drifts around the edges of my consciousness and I groan at the aches in my body.

I open my eyes and find him watching me in the dimly lit room. Leaning down, he kisses me on the top of my head. "Morning."

His voice is scratchy and quiet, like he's not been awake long.

"Hi," I murmur before looking around the room and finding Finley and Maverick asleep in the two chairs that were apparently brought in here while I was sleeping. "What time is it?"

"Early. You should go back to sleep."

I shake my head before snuggling back down on his chest. "When did they get here?"

"About ten minutes after you passed out."

I frown, sad that I missed them. "Is everything okay? What happened with Panda?"

"They dealt with it. Smithy went back to the house to make sure everything is okay for when we head back later on. Though that took more than a little convincing. The old guy is stubborn as hell."

I chuckle softly, nodding. Smithy is a big protective papa bear when he wants to be.

"Is Maverick okay?" I ask, and he frowns.

"Why wouldn't he be?"

"What Panda said about his dad… he wouldn't look at me after."

He glances over at Maverick before looking back at me. "He didn't say anything about that, but we were talking about everything else."

"He can't think I'd blame him for his dad's shit," I say softly. "Whether Panda was lying or not, I'd never blame Mav for that."

"You should tell him that." His voice is low and gravelly, sending a shiver down my spine. Pretty sure that jumping his bones *isn't* what I should be thinking about right now, but I'm wrapped up in him, in bed, and I'm only human.

I shake off the thought, focusing back on all of the other shit we have to deal with. "How is East?"

"Luc swung by after you fell asleep and let me know he's doing okay. He knows you're here though, so when it's not the middle of the night, we'll go see him. Then we can see about getting you discharged so we can go home."

"Your uncle Luc? He's in town? How long was I gone? What else did I miss?"

He winces and that just makes me suspicious. "Yeah, Uncle Luc. And you were gone for nearly two weeks, today is Thursday. As for what else you missed… I'll catch you up later."

I quirk a brow at him and purse my lips. "Why do I get the feeling I'm not going to like this?"

"Because you're not," he says, frowning a little. "Now how are you feeling?"

I let out a deep sigh. Just once I'd like the sand under my feet to stop shifting so I could get some balance. Apparently today is not that day. I take an assessment of my body, the aches and pains still very much apparent, but I'm okay. I'm here, back with them, and I survived.

"Am I sad about how everything ended? Yes, of course, and have I dealt with it all yet? Abso-fucking-lutely not. But it could've ended much worse."

Except… it's not really over yet. Whoever was working with Panda is still out there. I say as much to him, and the frown on his face deepens. "We'll figure it out. Don't change the subject. How are you feeling?"

The guy is like a dog with a bone, but I can't deny anymore that he cares for me. "I'm okay. I swear. It could've been much worse."

"You were stabbed, burned, and have multiple other injuries, Octavia. If he hadn't killed himself, I'd have killed him my damn self."

I cup his cheek with my hand and sigh. "I promise, I'm okay. I'll heal."

He watches me closely, as if looking for a lie. When he doesn't find it, he nods and pulls me back against his chest. "I'm going to wrap you in fucking bubblewrap or something."

I laugh softly. "You could try."

I feel his smirk against the top of my head.

"You two talk too much for this early in the morning," Finn grumbles, and I look over as he stretches while yawning from the chair he slept in. Maverick is still out cold. "Does anyone want coffee?"

"Yes," Lincoln and I say in sync, making Finn chuckle.

"Okay, I'll go get some," he says, looking down at his watch. "I'll grab some food too, then we should be able to go see East before getting the hell out of here. I assume he brought you up to speed?"

He says the last bit just to me and I nod. "He did. Mostly. Thank you. For everything."

Moving across the room until he's standing in front of me, he captures my lips with his while I'm still curled up in Lincoln. "Nothing to thank me for, V. You know I'll always come for you. We all will. I'll be back in a minute."

He turns to leave, and I lean back into Lincoln. I can't help but be surprised at how well they all seem to take sharing me. I can honestly say that sharing any of them would drive me to murder. "We should probably get up."

"In a minute," he says, tightening his hold on me while being mindful of my ribs. So I lie with him until Finn comes back with coffee and food, waking Mav as he turns the light on.

I eat my croissant quietly, sipping at the coffee while they talk quietly about something I'm not in the loop with, but I know they'll tell me later if I ask. We've come a long way since I got back to the Cove and I'm pretty sure they're past keeping stuff from me.

I really freaking hope so anyway.

I finish my breakfast and the doctor comes around to check on me. Once she takes my blood pressure and she's happy enough with it, I'm given the all clear, and we pile out of the room and head toward East's room. I clench my hands to stop them from trembling. I hate that he's here because of me. It occurs to me that

Lincoln never did answer my questions since Smithy interrupted us, so I have little idea of what I'm going to find.

I move a little faster, walking ahead to the room number Linc gave me for East, and push the door open.

My heart about stops when I find him hooked up to a dozen or so machines with a giant gauze bandage down the center of his chest. He smiles at me, but I can't help but gaze back down at his chest.

"He was shot in the heart?" I question before East can say a word as I turn to face Lincoln, who winces again.

"He was, but he's okay. He's getting out of here today too."

I grumble under my breath about stupid boys and only giving half the fucking information, and turn back to East. The man in question is still smiling as I enter his room at last and head straight for the bed. I want to hug him, but he was shot in the fucking chest. I'm not going to hurt him any more by being an idiot.

"Are you okay?" I ask the stupid question because I can't help myself, and he barks out a laugh.

"I've been better, but I'll survive. Are *you* okay?"

"Meh, same." I shrug as I perch on the edge of his bed; the others stay outside giving us some privacy, shutting the door between us. Guilt slams me as I take stock of him. "I'm so sorry."

The words are choked as I speak them, but he takes my hand and squeezes it tight. "V, I'd die to keep you safe. I didn't die, and you have nothing to be sorry about. Besides, I took the bullet for my idiot brother. If anyone should be sorry, it's him for getting in the way of yet another gun." He laughs softly and I roll my eyes.

"Are you seriously making jokes right now?"

"I'm not joking." He shrugs and I shake my head. "They have a lot more power in the world than I do, but that is something I can do. And for you, there's no limit to what I'll do."

I lean forward and kiss him chastely, aware that I don't want to hurt him, but I can't *not* kiss him. Not when he says shit like that.

"I won't break, you know?" He grins as I pull back.

I laugh softly, shaking my head. "You look pretty breakable to me right now."

"This?" he says, waving to his chest. "This is nothing."

"You're an idiot."

"I'm your idiot though." He grins at me, eyes sparkling. He does at least look okay, and he seems perky enough. "Now, can we get the hell out of this place? I've been losing my mind trapped in here."

"Yeah, Linc said he was getting me discharged. I assume he meant you too. I need a bubble bath. A really long bubble bath."

"Want company?" he asks, wagging his brows as the door opens behind us.

"You, Mr. Saint, will not be having bubble baths or any other exertive activities for some weeks." I blush as the woman's stern voice reaches me, turning to see her standing in front of a smirking Lincoln. "We've already been through this. If you won't stick to your care plan, I will *not* be discharging you."

East's eyes go wide and Mav snickers behind Linc. "I'll do as I'm told," he huffs.

"Good, then I have no issues discharging you. We've liaised with the private rehab center your brother set you up with, so they're aware of your rehab schedule. If you have any pain or any of your incisions become infected, you need to come back here immediately. Am I making myself clear?"

He nods, and I fold my arms. "If he gets so much as a slight temperature, he'll be back."

The doctor nods, smiling. "Oh I like her. Hopefully, I won't see you again, Mr. Saint." She nods and turns, leaving the room.

"Is there anything else I don't know yet?" I ask, my glare bouncing between the four of them.

Finn scrubs the back of his neck. "Did you tell her about Indi yet?"

Lincoln groans as I screech, "What about Indi?"

"Guess not. My bad. I'm going to go get the car," Finn says, bouncing out of the room.

"I'll come with you!" Mav shouts and runs after him.

"What the fuck happened to Indi?"

---

After the run down on the drive home of everything I missed while I was with Panda, I swear to storm the fucking gate if Lincoln doesn't get Indi back here by the end of the goddamn day. Otherwise, Alexander Saint is going to answer to me and all of my fury. I'm giving him sixteen hours, and if Indi isn't in my house before the clock strikes midnight, I'll riot.

But for now, I ask Maverick to stay with me while Linc and Finn help get East settled. He's going to need more help than me, and Mav has barely looked at me since Panda announced that Edward killed my dad, let alone spoken to me.

I'm not about to let anything like that come between us.

"Oh, Miss Octavia, you're home!" Smithy greets us as the door closes behind us and he wraps me in a hug so tight my ribs practically creak.

"Smithy, need to breathe and you're going to pop one of my stitches," I push out and he drops me.

"Sorry, I was just so worried." He brushes his hands down my arms as if looking for injury. "Are you really okay?"

"I'm fine, Smithy. I promise. I just need some good food, a bubble bath, and a night of relaxation."

"Food I can do!" he says, almost flustered, before heading back toward the kitchen.

"Don't think I've forgotten about Matthew either!" I shout behind him. He just raises his hand as if to wave me off before disappearing into the kitchen.

I feel restless and I want to talk to Mav, so rather than head upstairs, I take his hand and lead him to the stairs down to the music room. Once we're sealed in the soundproof room, I sit on the piano stool and he sits on the small sofa by the door.

Fluttering my fingers across the smooth ivory, I trill out a couple of quick scale runs. I've missed this, but it isn't why I came down here. Without looking at him, I play a soft melody, pouring some of my pain and anger into it.

"Why won't you talk to me, Mav?" I ask quietly, continuing to play.

He doesn't respond. When I turn to face him his elbows are resting on his knees, hands in his hair, and he's bent forward staring at the floor.

"Mav?"

He glances up at me and the pain on his face breaks my heart. "How can you even look at me after what Evan told you? I'm a monster that comes from a long line of monsters. *That* is my legacy. We're *all* legacies and you deserve better than that."

I move to stand before him and crouch when he still won't look up at me. "I don't care what he said."

He still doesn't look at me and my heart breaks. I need him to know I don't blame him and whatever guilt he's feeling isn't his to feel.

If Edward did kill my father, then that's something he needs to pay for. Not Maverick. Just another line on my list of reasons that all of their dads need to jump off a fucking cliff.

"Look at me," I say, gripping his chin. "You are not your father, and you are not accountable for his sins either. Whether or not what Panda said is the truth, that doesn't fall on you and I will never hold you responsible, do you understand? I love you, Maverick Riley, and nothing and no one is going to change that."

He looks at me with glassy eyes. "No one has ever said that to me before."

I suck in a breath, startled. "Well, then other people are monsters. You are worthy of love, Mav, and I love you. From now until the stars fall."

"I love you too." He captures my lips with his and pulls me onto his lap so I'm straddling him on the sofa. He kisses me like I'm the oxygen he needs to survive.

He pulls back, and that cheeky glint is back in his eye. "I never fucked anyone on a piano before."

I let out a sharp laugh. "Not sure how easy that feat is, buddy. A baby grand isn't a sex toy."

"I do love a challenge." He wags his brows at me and I laugh again.

Before I know what's happening, there's a bang as the piano lid is closed and I'm in the air a moment then find myself sitting on the smooth top of the baby grand, legs spread wide enough to accommodate Mav's body mere seconds after he's pulled off my leggings and panties.

"Princess," he says, sucking in a breath as he sees some of the damage done.

"Don't. I'll heal," I assure him, tamping down the creeping self-consciousness. I refuse to let what Evan did to me interfere with my boys. I can own my battle scars and I know none of them will give a damn about them outside of wishing they could kill him themselves every time they see them.

He runs his hands up from my ankles, following with his lips, tracing every fading line and burn.

"Mav…" I trail off as he moves up my body.

"Yes, princess?"

"What are you doing?" I've never heard my voice sound so damn sexy. All breathy and raspy.

"I'm going to eat your pussy like it's my last meal." If I thought I was wet before, I'm now dripping and aching for him to honor his promise.

"Well, then, don't let me keep you from your dinner."

Propping myself up on my elbows, I watch as he slides his arms under my thighs and grabs my ass so he can access my pussy at the right angle.

Then he's there. His mouth is on me, his tongue lapping up every drop I give him. The sounds he's making are wicked and sinful, like he's forgotten all his manners at the table. I fucking love it. In fact, the sounds and the scent of my arousal are turning me on even more.

Throwing my head back, I let my hair fall to the baby grand as I close my eyes and focus on the feel of his lips. His tongue. His teeth.

With soft kisses and hard bites, Mav expertly works me to orgasm in a manner of moments.

"Fuck, Mav, yes!" My ass is bare and my juices are coating my thighs and now the piano underneath me.

My breaths are coming in faster and when he notices, he looks up at me through hooded eyes and the glint he's fixing me with is made of pure debauchery. He's enjoying this, watching me fall apart at the tip of his tongue.

"Hold on, baby." I don't have time to ask him what for before his teeth latch onto my clit and my orgasm just flies out of me with so much force I think I might lose consciousness for a moment.

My fingers grip onto the smooth wood as my body shakes and quivers from the overload of emotions and sensations.

Then he buries his entire face between my legs and coats my juices all over his mouth, nose, and chin before using his tongue to accompany my orgasm to the apex and back down.

I'm a panting mess, chest heaving and breaths coming in fast and ragged. By the smug look on his face, I'd say Mav is quite proud of himself.

"Time to fuck you, now, princess."

"Here?" I don't know if I even know my name right now, but I do know that fucking on this piano does not sound comfortable.

"Anywhere, but yeah, why not here?" Mav is capable of finding some way to shove his dick in my pussy no matter where we are, but I need a minimum level of comfort.

"I have a better idea." I grin, quickly pulling my panties and leggings back on and leading him up to my bedroom. I head into my closet and pull out the toy box Indi gave me for Christmas. "Want to play?"

I upend the box onto the bed and dozens of sex toys fall from it: restraints, toys, lube, anal beads, and several things I'm not sure I could find my way around if I were given a map. Indi really went the whole nine yards with this box. My heart races at the restraints that fall onto the bed among the vast variety of goodies, but I'm not about to let what happened spoil my fun. Not a chance.

"Oh, princess, you really do love me." He grins wildly as he picks up the restraints. "Trust me?"

I drop the box and move to stand before him, pulling off my hoodie and tank, letting them fall to the ground, leaving me in just my leggings and panties. "With my life."

He drinks me in with his eyes, pausing on my wounds, before savagely grasping my hips, closing the distance between us and kissing me like the beast I know and love.

We're all desperate hands and hungry mouths as we kiss with wild abandon. Picking me up and urging my legs to wrap around his hips, he takes me to the bed and gently lays me down next to the array of sex toys. His body follows mine before he slams his mouth back onto mine once more.

"You taste so fucking good."

His dick is huge behind his jeans, and the need for him runs through me harder and hotter than I ever remember feeling. He pulls back, sweeping most of the toys back into the box on the floor, and looks down at me with so much love, I feel more cherished than I ever have.

"You sure you're good with this? It's not too soon?" he asks, the soft padded cuffs hanging from his finger. My heart races, but I nod. No time like the present to get back on the horse. The bruises on my wrists are still healing and my ribs ache, but if nothing else, this whole ordeal has only reinforced just how short life is.

"Words, princess."

I nod again and say, "Yes, I'm okay. I trust you."

If someone would have told me a few months ago that I'd be here, with him, saying these words, I'd have laughed in their face, but a lot has changed in the last few months.

I raise my arms above my head, a drop of fear and anticipation rushing down my spine as he ties my wrists together, and to the bed frame. "If you need to stop, use your safe word."

"I know, but I won't. I'm okay." I refuse to let fear rule my life anymore. I've let myself be weak enough since they found me, enough is enough. There's too much out there that I have to deal with. In here, with him, with them, I'm not going to be afraid anymore.

He kisses me again, working his way down my body until he pulls my panties and leggings down, throwing them across the room. I shudder under his intense gaze and his eyes darken as he drinks me in. "You're fucking stunning, princess. Words can't do you justice."

I feel a blush creeping up my neck and cheeks as he devours every inch of me with his eyes.

Without looking away from me, he reaches back, pulling off his shirt and throwing it to the side. Biting his bottom lip, my anticipation soars as Mav unbuttons his jeans then pulls his zipper down, his cock springing free. He lets his jeans and boxers fall to the floor, stepping out of them before crawling onto the bed.

"If I'd have lost you…" he trails off and I wish I could touch him. Offer him some comfort.

"You didn't, and you never will."

His eyes burn as he locks his gaze on mine, looking as fierce as I've ever seen him. "Mine," he growls as he grabs the underside of my knees and pulls them up to my chest, his cock pushing inside me in one smooth move that has me arching my back like a wanton, sex-deprived vixen.

Possessing every part of me.

I gasp and Mav moves in to swallow my pleasure with an aggressive kiss that steals my breath. With his hands cradling my head, he thrusts in and out with abandon, making sure his every move rubs up against my clit. Wanting more, I wrap my legs around his waist, using my muscles to pull myself up on every push of his hips. I pull on my handcuffs out of habit, needing to touch him, to hold him, to show him how much he consumes me.

"Mav." I gasp out his name. Not really knowing why, just needing to hear it. Needing him to hear his name—filled with need—falling from my lips. Lips he's kissed and bruised.

"I love you." The words are something like a prayer and he stills, hovering above me, looking down at me like I'm not real.

"Say it again." His voice is little more than a whisper, as his shoulders strain where he holds himself above me.

"I love you, Maverick."

His mouth crashes back onto mine and he devours me without a care in the world. He bites my bottom lip until I bleed. He sucks on my tongue.

"I love you too, princess," he says as he thrusts into me with a vicious force that has my entire body hitching up toward my headboard, but Mav's hands are there to protect me. Always protecting me, like he's promised a thousand times.

He shows me all of him: his fierceness, his wounds, his weaknesses.

As he rubs up against my clit, I feel the first stirrings of another orgasm and I don't even try to fight it. I let it happen, let him consume me.

Mav's mouth moves to my neck and then my shoulder and just when I think I can't hold my climax back, Mav sinks his teeth into the meaty part of my collarbone and my back flies off the bed, pinned by him above me.

Fucking me relentlessly, Mav doesn't slow down as I ride the high of yet another orgasm, letting it rush through my bloodstream. He whispers words of devotion and protection as his orgasm takes over him and he spills inside of me.

Once we fall back down from the intense high, we're both left panting, taking in jagged breaths. Mav reaches for the key and unshackles me, rubbing and kissing my wrists where the already-purple bruising looks angry from the pressure I put on them when I lost control.

"Don't move," he tells me in a quiet voice.

I feel like a cooked noodle and couldn't move if a grizzly were chasing me down.

I watch, sighing at the sight of Mav's painted back and glorious ass walking to the bathroom. I hear the water running and then he's back with a washcloth. Slowly, he spreads my legs and places the warm cloth on my pussy, wiping it down gently. When he's finished caring for me, he wraps himself around me and brings the covers back up.

We're in our own little cocoon, his lips on the crown of my head when he whispers, "I love you, too, Octavia Royal."

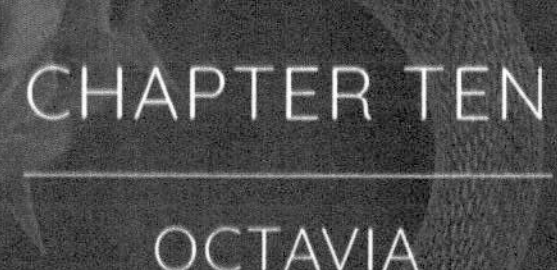

# CHAPTER TEN

## OCTAVIA

Stretching out in bed, my body aches in the best kind of way as I yawn, thankful to be waking up in my own bed wrapped up in Maverick. It is considerably better than how I've woken up the last week and a half.

I check my phone and note how early it is, but the urge to run, to be free, to feel just how alive I am with that burn in my body, runs through me. I bring up my thread with Lincoln and drop him a message.

**Me:**
Want to go for a run?

I bite my lip, waiting for a response as I shimmy from the bed and head to the bathroom, trying not to wake Mav up. When I'm finished and there's still no response from Linc, I realize that I still haven't heard from Indi.

*Son of a bitch.*

I guess I'm not running today.

Today, I'm going to rain down some hell on Alexander Saint. He doesn't get to take my goddamn bestie; I don't give a fuck if it's all tied into the Kings. What is the point of having the power that comes from being associated with the Knights if I can't keep my goddamn friend out of this shit?

While I might not technically *be* a Knight, my guys are and Alexander should know fucking better. I might not have seen Lincoln or the others in the years I was gone from here, but I did see Alexander. He kept in touch with my dad after we left and he'd come visit sometimes.

Hell, I'm pretty sure I knew him better back then than Lincoln did. Though I had no idea about the whole gang, secret society shit. That must be part of why he stayed in touch with Dad.

I might despise everything that the Knights stand for—at least what I know of it—but am I going to use that shit to help Indi right now? You're damn straight I am.

I tiptoe out of my room and downstairs as quiet as I can to where Smithy put my dad's things. I know his journals have to be in here somewhere, so I start going through the boxes as quietly as I can.

I've avoided going through any of this since I came back, but if there's information in here that can help me today, I am absolutely plowing through it. Even if my bruised heart gets a little more battered.

I find what I'm looking for in the fourth box.

*Jackpot.*

I skim through the pages, looking for something, anything, that might help.

I frown a little as I come across a passage about the Knights and Rebels. It brings up memories I'd forgotten about and I remember some of the stuff my dad told me about the Rebels, stuff Alexander would talk about when he visited with us.

My dad might not have told me about the Knights, but sometimes, when he drank too much, he'd get chatty. Hopefully some of what he told me will come in handy today. I'll do what I have to do to get Indi back, but I hope it doesn't come to that.

I keep reading, shocked at how much my dad wrote down in here. There's not much about the Knights, but this is like a memoir of all of the other shady shit that has been going down in and around the Cove. There's stuff on the Rebels, the Kings, and other organizations I've never even heard of.

Alexander might only be a few months older than East, but there's more than a few skeletons in his closet and, apparently, my dad knew a good few of them.

As much as it hurts to realize how much my dad kept from me—hurts to hear his voice in my head as I read his words—I'm thankful that this treasure trove exists… and that I haven't told anyone about it. I grab all of the journals from the boxes, having only managed to get through a fraction of them in the hour I've been down here, and stash them in the vent in the music room. Pretty sure no one is going to look for them in there.

Me:

I assume you didn't hear back from Alexander. I'm getting dressed, and I'll be over in ten. We're getting her back. Today.

Linc:

I'm awake. Making coffee. See you soon.

I jump in the shower, washing off the remnants of the last however long and the evidence of my night with Mav, washing my hair properly, though I'm pretty sure it's a lost cause at this point.

I'm going to need to book an appointment with Gracie.

But that's a luxury for later.

For now, I need to pull on all of that rage that sits in the well inside of me. If Alexander Saint wants a battle, I'll give him one. Battered and bruised or not.

I still can't believe Lincoln's cousin is wrapped up in this bullshit. Do the Saints ever take the easy path? What's wrong with a nice, normal, quiet life?

I swear to God…

Once I'm showered, I find Maverick half awake, but still in bed. "Morning, princess," he mumbles sleepily. "Why are you up already?"

"Indi," is all I say and he yawns, nodding. I head to my dresser and dry my hair roughly, scraping it back into a messy ponytail before getting dressed. Once I'm wearing an outfit that makes me feel like a powerful bitch, I quickly do my face. By the time I'm done, Maverick has showered and redressed.

"I have fresh clothes over at Linc's. Finn's still there from yesterday. You good to go?"

"Yeah, just need shoes," I say, before ducking into my closet and grabbing a pair of boss-ass-bitch stilettos. Is my body in the best condition for this outing? Absolutely not. I'm going regardless. Indi would do the same for me. Ride or die.

I'm more shocked that Ryker hasn't said fuck it and broken her out himself. That's a question for Linc later.

I slip my shoes on and straighten my jacket before following Maverick downstairs. "What do you know about Alexander?"

"Not much," he says with a shrug. "He's run with the Rebels for a long time from what Linc told us. Worked his way up through the ranks, and now he runs the city."

I frown, wondering how much Linc knows of what my dad did. Surely if he knew, he'd have used what he knows? Or maybe he isn't as motivated as I am.

That or he just doesn't want to be an asshole to his cousin.

Either way, Alexander Saint is going to have a bad day if he doesn't hand Indi over willingly.

"Miss Octavia! Good, you're awake," Smithy says as I stride across the living room toward the kitchen, but he frowns when he looks at me properly. "Where, exactly, do you think you're going? You should be resting."

"I have something to take care of. Indi needs my help. I'll rest later."

He purses his lips, glancing over at Mav who shrugs. "Don't look at me, I'm just following her lead."

I roll my eyes, little traitor. He just doesn't want to lose his food privileges.

"I don't think you should be doing anything right now, Miss Octavia. I called the school and told them you wouldn't be back today. I told them you've been ill. I do wish you would stay home and rest."

I sigh, folding my arms over my chest. Arguing with Smithy isn't something I want to do, but he isn't going to stop me right now. "I appreciate that, but I'm helping Indi."

My tone brooks no argument and he shakes his head. "You're too headstrong, just like your father." I level him with a glare and he backs off a little. "Fine, fine. But on Sunday, I'd like us to have dinner with Matthew. Miss Indi is welcome to join if everything is okay with her."

"Thank you, Smithy." I walk over to him and kiss him on the cheek. "I'd love to meet Matthew finally. I'll be fine. Hopefully, I won't be gone all day, but I'll keep you in the loop, okay?"

"That will make me feel better, do you want something to eat before you leave?"

I shake my head, smiling softly. I feel sick even thinking about food. "No, but thank you. My stomach still isn't really feeling up to much, but I promise I'll eat later."

He gives me a quick one arm hug and mutters, "You best."

Once he releases me, I move back to Maverick, taking his hand and heading out the back and through the gate to the Saints'. By the time we enter the kitchen, Lincoln and Finley are already sitting at the kitchen table, coffee in hand.

"I'll just go get changed," Mav says, kissing me quickly before jogging out of the room.

"How is East?" I ask as I pour myself a cup of coffee before joining them at the table.

"Sleeping," Linc says, draining the last of his cup. "He took his painkillers this morning, so I imagine he'll be out for most of the day. Mrs. Potts is keeping an eye on him while we head into the city."

I'm glad Mrs. Potts is here. It means I can focus on Indi without worrying about East. I'd have liked to have seen him this morning, but I'm not about to wake him up just to make myself feel better.

"We doing this?" Mav asks as he strides back into the room in fresh jeans and a long-sleeved black tee and boots. How do they all make such simple things look so goddamn hot?

Lincoln nods and stands while Finn takes my hand and squeezes it. "You sure you're up to this?"

"Wild horses couldn't stop me," I tell him, squeezing his hand back.

"Good," Linc says, grabbing his keys and phone, pulling a gun from behind him and handing it to me. "Then let's get this show on the road shall we?"

---

The drive into the city takes a few hours. Mav and Finn play some stupid game on a hand held console the entire journey, while I spend all my time thinking of nothing but Indi and how the fuck I'm going to make this happen. I still don't exactly have a plan, but I'm not leaving without Indi. And if I have to unearth some secrets, I will. It might piss Linc off, considering it's his cousin, but this is one of those times when the ends justify the means.

Linc's hand rests on my thigh, the same way it has the entire drive. "Do you know why Ryker hasn't just gone in guns blazing and taken her back?"

He shakes his head, the other two going quiet in the back of the Porsche. "I haven't talked to Ryker much since you've been gone, but Indi was taken the day after you were, so I've been a little occupied. I only know that whatever it is that the Rebels want from the Kings, it's not a quick and dry trade. So getting Alexander to give her up isn't going to be easy. I've already tried. Twice."

I look over at him, chewing the inside of my cheek. "I know. I appreciate it, but I can't just quit. There's no way Indi would quit on me, and I can't help but feel responsible. She was out there with you guys looking for me when she was taken." I don't tell him that I'm pretty sure I know what the Rebels want from the Kings, and why the Kings won't just comply.

I also keep the information about Alexander to myself. I don't want to use what I know unless I have to.

We drive the rest of the way in silence, just the songs playing on the radio filling the empty space. It's not long before we're pulling up to what looks like an abandoned warehouse.

"Don't let the appearance fool you," Linc says, taking in the skeptical look on my face. "There are a dozen apartments in there, as well as a warehouse space. Alexander basically made this place a fortress."

Awesome news. Just freaking delightful.

"So how do you propose we get in?" I ask, not wanting to use my hidden advantages just yet. A girl gets to have some secrets, especially with the treasure troves of them this bunch have.

He shuts off the engine and turns to look at me, smirking. "I thought this was your crusade?"

Mav barks out a laugh from the back seat, and I flip him the bird while I glare at Lincoln. "Fine, you stay here. I'll get this shit done myself."

I open the door and climb from the car, slamming the door shut. "V, come on. You know he's just being an asshole. Wait up."

Finn's voice makes me pause, and I turn to face them, brow cocked. "I don't *need* you to help me. I'll get my girl back my damn self."

"We know you don't need us." Lincoln sighs, scrubbing a hand down his face. Something flickers in his eyes that raises red flags, but it's gone as quickly as it appeared. "We are all very aware of that, so maybe just let us help you."

"I asked for your help. You're the one stuck in asshat mode." I turn back around and head toward the door on the side of the building, pounding my hand against it until the small viewing hatch in the door is opened. "I'm here to see Alexander."

"Sorry, lady, you're at the wrong place."

I pull the 9mm Lincoln gave me on the ride here and put the barrel through the hatch before he can slide it shut.

"Shit," Finn curses, and I hear them all move quickly behind me, preparing themselves for war.

"I don't think I am. Now let me repeat myself. My name is Octavia Royal, and I'm here to see Alexander Saint."

The sound of footsteps and shouts sound through the door, but I keep my gun trained on the guy behind the door.

"Do not make me ask again."

"Fuck you, bitch," the guy grunts.

I let off a shot beside his ear.

"That was your last warning," I growl before looking up at the camera by the door. "Get your ass down here, Saint."

My heart pounds in my chest; my bravado is little more than a show right now—I'm just winging it here.

There are more shouts and the sound of metal scraping on metal before I hear

Alex's voice. "Open the door, Benny. She'll shoot you in the nuts and not think twice."

Lincoln looks at me suspiciously, and I shrug. His cousin hasn't come up before now, how was I supposed to know Alex didn't mention that he and my father kept in touch, and by proxy, he'd kept in touch with me?

I holster my pistol as the door opens and a smiling Alex stares down at me. His floppy brown hair falls in his bright amber eyes. I forgot how freaking tall he is, and he definitely buffed up since I saw him last, but he's still the same Saint-looking, sarcastic asshole he's always been. "Baby Royal! It's been a minute."

He wraps me up in his arms and I roll my eyes. "Don't act like we're friends right now, Alex. You have my girl and I want her back."

"Why do I feel like we're missing something here?" Mav says, scratching the back of his head.

"You never did beat around the bush, baby Royal, but that is a request I gotta deny. I already told Lincoln. But don't let this be a wasted trip, come on in. I can show you your girl is in good shape and being treated like a queen."

I look at him skeptically, though I don't miss the glare Lincoln is shooting us both. Alex links his arm through mine and pulls me forward through a web of halls until we reach an open space.

"V?" Indi squeals, running over to me from where she was sitting in a chair under a blanket, squeezing me so tight my ribs ache. "You're okay, thank fucking Christ. What happened? Who had you?"

"Are *you* okay?" I ask, and she nods as she pulls back.

"I could be worse," she says, lifting her casted arm. I glare at Alex. "Pissed off at being here, but Alex isn't the worst, I guess." The guy in question barks out a laugh.

"You're starting to like me. Don't deny it, Indigo."

"What the fuck did you do to her?" I growl at Alex, and he holds his hands up in the air.

"Wasn't me, sweetcheeks. That was my guys. Once I knew she was your girl, I got her looked at and fixed up."

"He's telling the truth," Indi says, glaring at him, but there's something in her eyes…

Does she *like* him?

I shake my head, that is so not relevant right now. I turn back to face Alex, folding my arms across my chest. "What is it going to take to get you to let her go home with me?"

"Come on, Octavia," Alex groans. "Don't make me be a hard ass. You know I don't like it."

"Can one of you fill the rest of us in on just why it is you're so chill?" Maverick pipes up. I glance over at him, he looks about as happy as Lincoln does. Finn has his typical poker face on, but I don't miss the tightening of his jaw.

"Daddy Royal and I were tight while he was on tour. So baby Royal and I hung out a bit while you lot were running around with the Knights," Alex says shrugging, before dropping into one of the comfy-looking chairs across the room.

"I'm taking her home with me, Alex. I don't care what your deal is with the Kings. She's mine."

He leans forward, resting his elbows on his knees, hands clasped. "You don't really have much sway here, V."

I really didn't want to do this. I *tried* to be nice. "Don't make me talk about Colorado."

His eyebrows rise in shock as he blows out a breath. "How do you know about Colorado?"

"What the fuck happened in Colorado?" Lincoln asks, while the others stay quiet, watching with an intense fascination.

"Nothing," Alex says before cursing under his breath. He looks over at Indi and something passes between them. "If you want to go, then go. But, V, Colorado stays buried in the past, you understand?"

I nod. "I was happy to leave it buried. You're the one who told me I didn't have much sway."

"Yeah, well, I didn't realize you knew so much."

"Next time, don't underestimate me."

He shakes his head, before leaning back in his chair. "Well this was fun, but you guys should leave. I need to work out what else the Donovans covet enough to pay their debt."

"You're not going to hurt them, right?" Indi asks him, and he softens.

I have no idea what happened here between them during the last however long, but I get the feeling there is more to this story, too. Trying to block out the waves of rage coming from my guys, I stay focused on Indi and Alex.

He looks almost conflicted. "I'm not going to make promises I can't keep. But maybe talk some sense into Ryker and we can keep the peace."

---

The drive home from the city was pretty quiet other than Indi and I. I caught her up on what happened with Panda and she looked like she was going to cry on my behalf. The guys though… to say that my guys were pissed at me is an understatement. In fact, I've barely heard from them since we got back Friday afternoon.

A day and a half of almost radio silence since then. It sucks, but I get it. I've been pissy enough with them about secrets, and I wouldn't tell them Alex's secret. It isn't something that will help them, and the threat of it was enough to get Indi home. And as I reminded them, it's not like they tell me everything either.

We dropped her off with Ryker, under the promise that I got to see her today. I want to talk to her about what happened while she was gone, but also, I miss my bestie. I feel like we've both been wrapped up in our own chaos lately, that we haven't hung out properly in too long.

At least I got to spend the day with East yesterday, even if the others were MIA. Watching movies in bed with him was awesome, plus I got to make sure he was actually okay. He seemed a little distracted, but other than that, I think he's actually doing okay, all things considered.

I glance over at the clock.

Five thirty on a Sunday morning should be an illegal time to be awake. But here I am. Brain running at a million miles a minute.

I grab my phone and pull up my thread with the four of them.

Me:
Going for a run. Obviously the stalker thing is mostly over, so you don't have to come. Just telling you so no one freaks out at me later.

My phone buzzes almost instantly.

Lincoln:
You don't run alone. Not until we know who Evan was working with. Give me twenty, and I'll come with you.

I smile down at my phone. I guess the silent treatment is over.

Yay me.

Me:
Okay, I'll meet you at the gates in twenty.

Maverick:
You guys are insane. Go the fuck back to sleep.

East:
What he said.

Finley:
Enjoy your run. Crazies. Meet you after for breakfast?

Me:
Sounds good. East, can you come over, or are you still on bed rest?

East:
Pretty sure I can manage it across the yard to yours.

Mav:
I'll be there.

Me:
Perfect. See you all soon.

I throw the covers off and head to the bathroom to brush my teeth and get ready. It doesn't take me long, and I'm down in the kitchen doing my stretches in under ten minutes. Why it takes Lincoln so long is beyond me. I always thought it was easier for guys to get ready than girls.

"Good morning, Miss Octavia." I jump as Smithy appears, letting out a squeak.

"You move so quietly!" I gasp, and he chuckles.

"A man of mystery, that's me. What has you up so early?"

I shrug, grabbing a bottle of water from the fridge. "Couldn't sleep so thought I'd run. I didn't mean to wake you, sorry."

"You didn't, I'm usually up this early. Would you like me to sort you some breakfast for after your run?"

"You're the best. I actually invited the guys over for breakfast, so we can order in if you don't want to cook." The words were worth it for the look of horror on his face.

"I think not! I will arrange breakfast for you all. Order in… Pfft." He mutters to himself as he heads back down the hall to his quarters, and I check my watch. Time to head outside.

I find Lincoln already waiting for me and end up practically drooling. You'd think by now I'd be used to seeing him looking like that, but hot fucking damn. Sweats and a muscle top really are my kryptonite on Lincoln Saint.

"You finished eye fucking me?" He grins, stretching out.

"I'd rather actually fuck you," I mutter as I reach him.

His eyes darken and he gets in my space. "I'm pretty sure that could be arranged."

I suck in a breath, suddenly very fucking warm, and not feeling like running at all. There are much better ways to get sweaty.

Just as I open my mouth to speak, he steps back and puts in his AirPods. "Let's go."

"Tease," I grumble, and put in my own pods before taking off on our normal route. My body is still not where it was, but a few days of running and eating and I'm pretty sure I'll be okay.

We start off slower than usual, but it's not long until I hit my normal pace. I refuse to let myself be beaten. That might make me stupid, but I don't want to be defined by the shit I've gone through lately.

We run in silence the entire way, not making our usual pitstop because I don't feel like I need the break, and I know Lincoln only ever stops for me.

Once we get back to the house, he follows me inside rather than going back to his. We find Smithy, Mav, Finn, and East already in the kitchen, the smell of breakfast making my stomach growl. Linc slides onto the stool next to East while I drop onto the open seat next to Mav.

Everyone seems like they're back to normal. Apparently the silent treatment is officially over.

"Since we're all finally in one place, I have something to tell you guys," East says as Smithy finishes dishing out breakfast.

"What's up?" I ask, taking a bite of my eggs Benedict. Hellooooo hollandaise.

He looks a little nervous, and my stomach twists when he starts and stops speaking a couple times.

"What is it?" Lincoln asks, his concern obvious.

"I had a visitor while I was in the hospital. Chase Armstrong," he says, the name obviously meaning something to the others.

"Who is that?" I ask, and Linc is the one to answer.

"One of the Conclave." He turns back to East, fists clenched. "What did he want?"

"He came to tell me he helped you guys locate V," he says, pausing. Finn nods, as if confirming what he said. East lets out a deep breath and butterflies take flight in my stomach. "He also told me he's my father."

---

After the bombshell East dropped over breakfast, chaos pretty much ensued. It made me realize just how little I know about the Knights and their ranks. The four of them went back to the Saints' to deal with the repercussions of the news once East reassured me he was okay, just reeling.

If I didn't already have plans with Indi and Smithy today, I'd have made them all stay here and keep me in the loop, but apparently the fates like me chasing my tail.

Lincoln and I are overdue for a long talk though. I need to know everything I can if I'm going to survive whatever it is that the Knights want from me.

I don't have time to focus on that as Indi bounds into my room like the ray of sparkling sunshine that she is. "Morning, friend," she sings as she drops onto my bed.

"You're awfully chipper today." I can't help but feel guilt as I take in the cast on her arm again.

She grins at me, blushing a little. "I'm home, I'm happy and healthy. I am loved. What's not to be chipper about?"

I quirk a brow at her. "You had a good homecoming then?"

She giggles, then covers her mouth with her hands, eyes wide. "You could say that. Ryker was very thankful to have me back." She blushes and I smirk. "Though he vowed to break Alex in multiple places when he saw my arm. He also said he owes you one, so tuck that away in your hat. He doesn't hand out favors all too often."

"He doesn't owe me a thing. It was my fault you were out there, that you were taken. How is your arm?" I ask, waving her off, but she shakes her head.

"It wasn't your fault. Alex explained some stuff to me, he'd have come for me another time if I hadn't been vulnerable then. But apparently being around you and the Knights, or with the Kings, makes me a little hard to kidnap usually. And my arm is fine, Ellis took me to an actual hospital, got it looked at; they said it seems to be healing as expected, but I'm going to need the cast on for another few weeks. At least Alex did that bit right I guess." She rolls her eyes and steals a pillow from behind me, hugging it against her chest. "And he wasn't all bad."

"I still want to dropkick the asshole who did that to you. But yeah, Alex is basically a human Labrador most of the time." I snort and she nods enthusiastically.

"Right! I said that exact same thing! He's a human puppy. It's kind of adorable. I don't get the whole terrifying thing everyone else seems to picture him as."

"I mean, you love Ryker. If you don't find him terrifying, pretty sure you're going to look past Alex's brand of scary," I shrug. I haven't seen that side of him, though I'm pretty sure Indi would see the best in a serial killer. "Plus, Alex is a softie under it all really."

"He really is," she says, sighing.

"What was that?"

Her eyes go wide. "What was what?"

"That cutesy little sigh." I quirk a brow at her and she looks down at her hands in her lap, wringing them out.

"He wasn't all bad. I know it makes me a terrible person to think so, all things considered. Considering the issues between him and Ryker… but," she shrugs, looking back up at me. "He was nice."

"Indigo Montoya, what exactly happened while you were with him?"

She lets out a deep sigh. "At first, I was just his prisoner. They broke my arm when they captured me but then Lincoln called and everything changed. He found out I was your friend and all of a sudden I was still his prisoner, but it was like he wanted to be my friend, too. So he brought in a doctor, had my arm put in this cast, and well… he looked after me." She pauses, looking up at me almost afraid.

"What did he do?" I ask, rage bubbling in my stomach. If he hurt her, I swear to Christ, I will burn down his goddamn warehouse and tell everyone all of his goddamn skeletons.

"He kissed me."

"He did fucking what?" I shout.

She chews her lip, and I only just manage to keep a lid on my shit. "He kissed me. I don't think he even meant to. We were messing around, no not like that, but just messing around because there was nothing else I could do, and it just happened. I felt awful about it, he apologized, said he didn't mean to. That he shouldn't have…"

"Did you tell Ryker or the others?"

She shakes her head, and my heart sinks for her a bit. "I don't want to make things worse and they were just so happy I was back, but there's a giant pit of guilt sloshing around inside of me and I feel awful."

"Did you kiss him back? Zero judgment either way, you know that. But he kissed you, you didn't instigate it."

She nods, looking back down at her hands. "I just kind of got lost in the moment. But then I remembered where I was, who he was, everything, and stopped it. Kept my distance. Nothing else happened. I know I should tell them, but they're a little possessive, and well, Alex isn't exactly their favorite person."

I nod, he's not exactly my favorite person right now either, the shit head.

"Do you like him?" I ask softly. There is zero judgment from me, no matter what she says, I just hate that she's hurting so badly.

"I don't think so?" It comes out as more of a question, and she chews on the inside of her lip again. My heart hurts for her.

"Okay, so you need to tell Ryker and the others, but I can be with you when you do. Secrets don't help anyone, especially ones like this. Did Alex tell you what he wants from the Kings?"

"He wants them to join the Rebels. Everyone knows that Diego isn't in the right place to run it anymore, and the Rebels want the territory. But Diego also owes Alex a fuck ton of money. I think that's why Ryker didn't come for me; he didn't have it."

I roll my eyes. "Alex shouldn't need money. He's a Saint."

"He is, and he isn't. Luc and he apparently don't speak much anymore, especially since he got tangled in the whole Rebel thing. He's not a Knight, so he doesn't benefit from the Saint money. At least that's what he told me. He also wouldn't let Lincoln pay him, because he's trying to prove a point. The money needs to come from Ryker and Ellis. It's a street, fear, stupid boy ego thing I think. Who the fuck knows? I'm just worried they're going to get hurt."

"We'll get to the bottom of this," I say, trying to reassure her when there's a knock at my door. It opens and Smithy steps into the room.

"Ladies, dinner will be ready in twenty minutes."

"Thank you for having me over, Smithy."

"Miss Indi, you are always welcome at our table." He smiles at her before turning to me. "Matthew is running a little late but he'll be here before dinner is served. Please be nice."

I mock outrage, clasping at my chest. "Me? I'm always nice."

Indi just laughs. "You are always protective. That doesn't always mean nice. And who the hell is Matthew?"

"I can be nice!" I defend, ignoring her question.

"Please, Miss Octavia. I am rather smitten with him, and you are my family. The two of you getting on would mean the world to me."

"Ohhhhhh." Indi waggles her eyebrows.

I roll my eyes at them both. "I will be nice as freaking pie."

"Thank you," Smithy says before leaving and closing the door behind him.

Indi smiles softly. "He seems nervous and happy. I hope Matthew is a good guy."

"Me too," I say sincerely. "Smithy deserves happiness. He's been alone for far too long. Come on, let's head down and get this party started."

"You can't grill him, you know." She smiles knowingly. "But Smithy didn't ask *me* to be nice."

"You'll lose your milkshake privileges if you start thinking like me too much," I cackle.

The look of horror on her face makes me snort-laugh.

"We didn't talk about you though. You were taken… by *Panda*. How are you holding up?"

I shrug. "Honestly, it's weird. It's like I'm numb to it. I'm sad and I'm angry… but it's like those emotions are removed from me a little. I mean, he told me Mav's dad murdered my dad, but I have no way to know if it's true, and even that just feels… like it all happened to someone else."

She frowns at me. "That doesn't seem healthy."

"Oh I know, and I'm sure when it all catches up to me, when I deal with it, I'm going to feel like I'm drowning. *If* it catches up to me."

"It will," she says, looking overly concerned. "Maybe you should speak to someone? A professional."

"I'm not sure anyone is equipped enough to deal with my shit." I laugh, trying to make light of it.

"V, I'm serious. I'm worried about you."

"I'm okay. But if it will make you feel better, I'm going to try and talk to Lincoln about it all. Or Finn. Maybe all of them; try to work out what's actually true and what's part of this web of lies. Pretty sure once I know for sure what's going on, I'll *feel* more."

"As long as you promise not to just shove it down and put a cork in it. Bottling your emotions up isn't healthy."

"I'll do my best," I say, honestly. "Come on, let's do this."

We head downstairs, but Indi seems to have lost some of her sparkle. "Are you sure you're up for this?"

"If you can survive nearly two weeks of what you did and do this, then I can do this. Alex didn't treat me badly, he just wouldn't let me leave or have any contact with the outside world. Hell, he wouldn't let me see or speak to anyone but him. So yes, I'm up for this. It's just the gross guilty feeling weighing on me."

I nod and take her hand, squeezing it. "We'll get it all worked out."

We head into the kitchen, and find Smithy with a tall man with salt and pepper hair. "Miss Octavia! Good you're here. I'd like to finally introduce you to Matthew." He turns to face Matthew, beaming. "Matthew, this is Octavia and her good friend, Indi."

Matthew smiles at us warmly, but something about him doesn't sit right. I don't know what it is, but my gut is screaming at me. "It is so good to finally meet you both."

He approaches, and takes my hand in his. "I'm glad you're feeling better, Octavia."

"Thank you," I say, painting a smile on my face. "It's nice to meet you too."

He draws me in for a hug, and I try not to stiffen up.

Then the smell hits me.

*Peppermint, wood, and spice.*

# CHAPTER ELEVEN

## OCTAVIA

Linc pulls into the parking lot, and I swear every single student at ECP is here, staring at us.

At me.

None of us have been at school for two weeks, and I have zero doubt that Blair has been reveling in our absence, lying about God only knows what. Knowing her, I'm probably such a slut that I've added Indi to my harem of lovers and we've all run away to an exotic island to get married.

Yep, that sounds like something she'd say.

"Are you ready for this?" Linc asks as he pulls into his spot beside Mav's bike.

No Finn yet.

I look over at him and nod as Mav climbs from his bike and opens the back door. "I'm not about to survive Panda just to be afraid of this place. The only thing I'm worried about is how badly my GPA is going to suffer from being away so much and being so distracted all the damn time."

Here's hoping that Smithy convinced my teachers I was sick enough that they don't have me try to do the work I missed and just give me a pass.

I'm not that lucky, but it would be nice.

At least tomorrow is the start of March, and there are only a few months of school left, only a month and a half until my birthday. If I can just graduate with my required GPA and stay alive long enough to reach 18 then maybe, just maybe, things will start looking up.

I haven't even had much time to worry about it lately with everything going on, but now that I'm here, back in the cold hard light of day—back to real life—it's just one more thing to weigh me down.

Mav jumps onto the back seat and leans forward, kissing my cheek. "Don't worry, princess. We got you. I mean, I don't, but Linc and Finn are boy geniuses.

They'll help you with anything you need, but you're a smart cookie, I doubt you'll even need them."

I laugh softly, turning in my seat to face him. "I like this unrelenting positivity. Maybe some of it will rub off on me."

"I'll rub off on you," he jokes, wagging his eyebrows at me, and I can't help but laugh at him while Linc rolls his eyes.

"I'm sure you would," he mutters. "Where's Finn?"

"Getting coffee," Mav answers before leaning back. "He shouldn't be long."

Indi pulls into her space, waving at me from her Wrangler, so I jump out of the Porsche and head over to her. "Morning, Rainbow Sparkle. How you doing today?"

"Better, how are you? You were weird at dinner yesterday." She frowns as she grabs her bag and climbs out of the car.

"I'm okay, I just felt a bit off. I thought I hid it." I bite my lip, hoping I'd hidden it from Smithy and Matthew at least. I'm sure the smell was a coincidence. I've never met Matthew before, and he's never met me. Probably just some popular brand of cologne. That's the most logical explanation.

None of it makes any sense, and the bags under my eyes are a testament to how little sleep I got last night as I played it out in my head over and over again.

She shrugs, pulling on her backpack. "You probably did, I just know you too well."

"I'll be fine," I say, trying to wave it off. We head over to where Finley is waiting for us with the guys, a tray of coffee in one hand.

"Morning," I say, smiling at him. He hands Indi and I our coffees, and I kiss him chastely. "Thank you, and thank you for including her," I say softly as he tugs me against his side, hugging me.

"She's your person. Of course I'm going to include her." I smile up at him, tuning out Indi and Maverick's bickering until Lincoln's patience runs out.

"Will you two just fucking stop," he growls, and Indi flips Mav the bird.

"I will if asshat does."

Mav scoffs, opening his mouth to say something else, but I move from Finley to between him and Indi before he says something else and puts Linc in a foul mood for the rest of the day.

"Let's just call a timeout, shall we?" I grin, and Mav kisses me.

"I can think of a fun way to spend my time out in the naughty corner."

"You're so cheesy."

"Uhm, guys?" Indi says, stealing my attention. "Incoming."

I turn and find Blair and her bitch squad heading toward us, along with Raleigh, Jackson, and a few of the football team.

This is going to be fun.

"What do you want, Blair?" I sigh as she reaches us, Raleigh at her back. Those two fucking deserve each other.

"I'm not here for you, skank," she says, sneering at me before looking over at Lincoln.

"You don't speak to her like that, Blair. I warned you once already," he says, cutting her off. "Anything you have to say to me, isn't something I want to hear."

"I'm pretty sure you want to know this," she says, smirking. "I ran into Georgia Fontaine over the weekend. We get our hair done at the same place."

I suck in a breath at the name. I hate that girl for zero reason and there is nothing I can do to change it.

"She told me how your father and hers are arranging to announce your engagement at the party your father is hosting on Friday."

Maverick's grip on my hip tightens, keeping me standing as Lincoln takes my hand and squeezes it.

"I guess she must be confused, because I'm not engaged to anyone."

She shrugs, glaring at me, like she knew that too. "I suppose it's possible, but there aren't many other Lincoln Saints in the Cove."

"Was there anything else you wanted, Blair? Or are you just here to stir shit?" Lincoln sighs, like she hasn't just crawled beneath my skin and set my blood on fire.

"Only to offer my best wishes to your brother. Apparently fucking Octavia is a deadly game these days."

Flicking her hair over her shoulder, she turns to walk away from us. She doesn't get very far before Indi darts forward, grabs her by the hair and yanks on it hard enough that Blair tips back on her heels and they both crumble to the ground. Screaming ensues as they attack each other and I move to intervene, but Finley stops me. "I got it."

Maverick holds me in place as I huff, trying to make sense of everything going on inside of my head right now, while Finley lifts a kicking and flailing Indi up off of my cousin who has bloody scratches down her face. Indi has a handful of Blair's hair, which she apparently ripped out, and I bite my lips together to stop from laughing.

Apparently my girl has fire.

"You're going to regret this, you depressive little whore," Blair shrieks at Indi, and Mav finally releases me as I step forward.

"Threaten her again, Blair. I fucking dare you. You might not be afraid of me, but you should be."

"The only thing scary about you is that you're a walking STD," she hisses, touching at the blood dripping down her face. "I'll ruin you both and laugh while I do it."

She storms off, her little band of sycophants trailing behind her, so I turn back to Indi. "Are you okay?"

"I'm fine," she sighs. "She just pisses me off. Walking around here like her shit doesn't stink. Apparently Dylan's bad habits are rubbing off on me."

"That was kind of fierce though." I laugh, trying not to let what Blair said get to me. At least not on the surface.

"It kinda was, huh?" She giggles.

"Come on, killer," Finley says, taking her arm. "Let's go get you sorted, and give those two a minute to talk, shall we?"

She looks at me and I nod, so she goes with Finn and Mav, leaving me alone with Lincoln.

"It's not true," he says, moving toward me, cupping my cheek with his hand. "I would have told you."

"I know you would, but what if your dad didn't mention it to you?" He grinds his teeth together at my words and drops his forehead to mine.

"My father is about to have a whole storm to deal with if he didn't. We need to talk privately about the Knights. About some things we discovered while you were gone." My stomach twists at his words, but I nod and move to wrap my arms around him, resting my head on his chest. "It's going to be okay, Octavia. I won't let them break you. Any of them."

"I know," I say, wondering just how bad the stuff he has to tell me is, but I know I don't need to voice that fear. Not to him.

"I won't let them break you either."

He holds me like I'm made of glass until the bell rings. "Come on, let me walk you to class," he says softly. "We'll talk later."

I pull back from him and he takes my hand, intertwining my fingers with his. Standing next to him like this, I feel like there isn't any battle we couldn't win.

I just hope we can weather the storm that's coming.

---

Today at school fucking sucked, so despite knowing Lincoln and I need to talk, I persuade him to hang out with me and East first. Which is exactly why we're all camped out on East's giant bed, Lincoln in sweats and a muscle top, me in his hoodie and my leggings, watching a cheesy action movie.

Pretty sure East is bored out of his mind, but he sits on the other side of me, and I'm wrapped around the two of them.

Lincoln's phone rings for the eleventy-billionth time since we hit play and he sighs. "I'm going to have to get this," he says, standing and leaving the room. East pauses the movie and looks down at me.

"How are you doing?"

I kiss his cheek softly and smile. "Pretty sure I should be asking you that."

"Well I asked first," he says, his eyes sparkling.

"I'm okay, just worried about him," I say, telling him what Blair said earlier in the day. Lincoln has been distracted ever since. Not that I blame him, but I wish he'd talk to me.

"Harrison is such a fucking asshole. Pretty sure if he didn't think Lincoln would leave, he'd have kicked me out of the house already." I frown at the thought.

"If he does, just come stay with me. I mean, you could just come stay with me anyway. You all could. If I thought it would help, I'd insist on it."

He laughs softly, shaking his head. "I'm sure you would, but unless they can get free of the Knights, there isn't anything that can help them."

"Is there a way to get them free?"

He shakes his head and my heart sinks. "I've been trying to think of a way for years. Ever since Harrison told me I wasn't his heir, that Lincoln would be inducted. I contemplated running away with him, trying to make it on our own, but he was so young, and they inducted him before I had a chance to do anything. The only way out of the Knights, as far as I can see, is death. The only person who is out, without it, is you."

Confusion rushes through me. I didn't think I was free? I mean, I know I haven't been inducted but… none of this makes sense. "Me? But I thought the Knights wanted me? That was the whole point of everything they did to me when I came back here."

"That's part of what I wanted to talk to you about," Lincoln says, as he steps further into the room. I hadn't heard him open the door.

"Sorry man," East says, wincing. "I thought she knew."

"It's fine. I was going to tell her tonight anyway," he says as he moves toward the bed. "Have you had your meds?"

East groans, shaking his head. "No, I wanted to be coherent since you guys were around and they just make me fucking sleep."

"East, you can't miss your meds, you only just got out of the hospital!" I scold, and he frowns. "I want you to get better. If anything else happens to you because of me…"

I trail off and he grabs my face in his hands, making me look at him. "This wasn't your fault." He kisses me, pouring every part of himself into it, and I sigh against him. He pulls back and glances over at Lincoln. "You guys should talk, but I'm here if either of you need a sounding board. Not being a Knight gives me a different perspective sometimes."

I clasp his hand as he releases my cheeks. "Thank you,"

"You don't ever have to thank me, V. I love you. I'd literally burn the world for you if you asked me to. Maybe even if you didn't."

I laugh softly, and Lincoln coughs out something that sounds like "suck up."

"Come on," Linc says, holding his hand out to me. "We should probably get this over with sooner rather than later." He turns to East and quirks a brow. "Take your damn pills. I'll check on you later."

I climb from the bed, kissing the inside of East's wrist as I do. "I love you too. I'll see you tomorrow?"

"I'll be here," he says with an easy smile.

I take Linc's hand and he takes me down the hall to his room. There is something soothing about the room. It could be that it smells like him, or it could just be that this is his inner sanctum and I know that having me in here means something to him.

I move to his bed and climb on top of it, hugging one of his pillows. I get the feeling I'm going to need the comfort for whatever he's about to tell me.

He paces in front of me, running his hand through his hair. "I'm not even sure where to start."

I reach out for him and he moves toward me, sitting on the bed to face me. "Just start from the beginning."

He nods, looking almost sad. "Just don't hate me." He looks so fucking vulnerable, my heart feels like it's going to break in two.

"I couldn't hate you if I tried. And trust me, I tried." I laugh, but it's forced and he doesn't smile.

He takes a deep breath, squeezes my hand, and looks me dead in the eye. "When you were gone, Finley found something. It's how we convinced the Knights to help us find you."

"Okay," I say when he pauses, trying to remain calm as my heart races in my chest. He seems stressed enough having to tell me this, so I do my best not to let my emotions show to keep him from feeling any worse.

"We found the agreement your dad made when he left."

The words hang in the air and I almost don't dare to breathe.

"Your father never really got out. He just kind of stepped down. Stone was the Regent before he took you away from here. He made a deal with Harrison that you would be out free and clear. In return, he would give up his seat as Regent *and* his seat at the table of the Conclave. He would work for Harrison when needed, he would never truly be free, but you would be. And so would any children you were to have in the future."

He scrubs a hand down his face, but confusion clouds my thoughts. "I don't understand. That sounds like a good thing. I'm free?"

He shakes his head. "You *were* free. The contract stated that should any Knight approach or harm you, that you would take your birthright as Regent of the Conclave."

I feel like I can't breathe.

That can't be right.

"Why would my dad put that in there?" I clasp my throat, trying to suck in air.

"My guess is to keep the Conclave from coming after you. It's a pretty good deterrent. No one wants to give up that sort of power, and the Regent's word is law to the sect."

I feel like my entire world just got tipped upside down. "What does this mean now?"

He lets out a deep sigh and squeezes my hand. "I don't know. I've been trying to find that bit out, but unsurprisingly, Harrison is being tight-lipped. What I do know is the senior Conclave has been meeting way more often since I dropped that bomb in their lap."

"But if Harrison made the deal, surely he knew? So why invite me to the gala? Why come after me? Panda—*Evan*—said that he had Edward kill my dad, that they fucked with the will to make sure I came back here. Why would they do that if it meant risking me taking the Regency?"

"I'm working on finding out; it doesn't make sense to me either. Stone must have had something that was worth them risking it. That, or Harrison figured you'd never find out with him being dead. None of the other Conclave members knew about the deal he made, which means it got signed off by one of the Kings of the Prism—the Prism is the tier of Knights that sit above the Conclave. Which also means this goes way higher up than I ever imagined."

"This sounds dangerous," I say, biting my lip, trying not to let fear get the better of me.

"I won't let them hurt you, Octavia. Not while there is breath in my body. No one is ever going to hurt you again."

I kiss him softly and he groans as I pull back. "There's more you need to know."

I wait patiently for him to speak. He's always been someone who weighs his words carefully, and I'm not about to rush him.

"My father… he has made it very clear that he doesn't want me having anything to do with you. He was clear about it before we stormed the Conclave to get you back. He's been even clearer about it since then. He won't have my happiness ruining his plans." He pauses and I open my mouth to curse Harrison out, but he shakes his head. "We need to be smart about this. Harrison isn't an enemy we want, and with this whole Regency thing, keeping him on our side is vital. He's already suspicious. I told him we're nothing more than friends, that you're with Finley, and close with the other two, but that I am keeping my distance as instructed."

"I don't like this." I sigh, my heart sinking.

"Neither do I, but for now, we need to play his game. When we have more leverage, when we know what he wants from you… know more about what Stone did to get you free, then we'll have more wiggle room, but for now—"

"For now we need to pretend that we aren't a thing where your dad is concerned."

"Which means that outside of here, we have to be careful."

"You mean at school."

He rubs a hand down his face and nods. "I mean everywhere but here. I need you to be safe, Octavia, and if that means sneaking around, then that's what I'll do. Sacrificing for you isn't a sacrifice."

# CHAPTER TWELVE

## FINLEY

I sit in the boardroom, twiddling my fucking thumbs, trying not to let my brain seep from my ears in sheer boredom as Harrison drones on about something that I've paid exactly zero attention to. The junior Conclave members are all here, seated with their senior counterpart. Which means I'm wedged between my father and Edward Riley.

Joy of fucking joys.

The six other juniors look as bored as I do, except for Mitchell. Simping little lap dog is about as strong as a wet noodle. If his father had any other children, they'd be here instead. The disdain is obvious every time his father looks at him. But in his father's defense, Mitchell is a sniveling little weasel. I'd trust a venomous snake more than I'd trust him.

The empty chair beside Chase has never felt so ominous before, but the daggers that Harrison continues to glare at him now mean that that chair isn't likely to stay empty for long.

It's either that, or Chase's line will 'mysteriously' end and a new family will be lifted up in rank.

Though as long as it's not Raleigh, I won't get too murderous about it.

"—Octavia Royal."

The sound of her name has my attention back to Harrison, a snarl on my lips that I brush off as quick as it appeared.

"The girl has been recovered and is healing nicely according to Finley." Everyone's gazes swing to me, and I nod once to confirm.

"Obviously the terms of the contract her father made have come to light, so this is something we shall need to deal with. Once she is healed, I will handle it. As we have discovered, there were terms of the agreement that none of us were privy to." Harrison's lips thin and I glance over at Chase. He told East that he helped Stone, but I wonder if even he knew what Stone had agreed to in full. "I have checked the contract over myself and checked it over with the Prism. Only the Regent of the Prism was aware of its existence. It seems it was made with the highest member of the Knights—the somewhat-absent Archon. I know none of us have ever personally met our illustrious leader, but I have had the Prism Regent's assurance that he will check in with Archon to ensure the contract is as ironclad as it seems."

My ears prick up at the mention of the Archon. Stone must have had some sway if the Archon dealt with his deal personally. I didn't think anyone in this sect had ever met the Archon. He's the faceless, nameless leader at the top of the pyramid. I was beginning to think he was nothing more than a myth.

We're all aware that Harrison, as Regent, sits on one of the various Boards. That each board has a King which makes up the Prism who supposedly answers to the Archon, but still… never meeting said person makes them like a bedtime story rather than a reality.

"You mean to say that you will be stepping down for a stumbling girl?" Archer DuPont scoffs from his seat across the table. He's a hapless money bag, but his daughter—Artemis, who sits at his side staring a deathly glare into the side of his skull—is anything but. He might be useless, but her? She is dangerous. Cold and calculating in a similar manner to Lincoln, she reminds me a lot of Blair, and I'm secretly glad that the Board rejected Blair's request to sit in the empty Royal seat. Blair and Artemis together would have been… just no.

"I will take her under my wing, and help her lead if that is what the Archon decrees," Harrison says proudly, but that shadow in his eye tells me it won't be quite so simple. I glance over at Lincoln, seated beside his father, the tic in his jaw bouncing. I guess he believes Harrison about as much as I do.

"What if she doesn't want to take the seat?" Chase challenges, and Maverick snickers on the other side of his father.

"The deal struck was broken, which means the same rule applies for her as for *all* bloodlines." Harrison's words are pointed, but Chase doesn't back down. I'm guessing knowing he has an heir that he wants to keep clear has his back up.

"Then I guess we should all meet with the girl and ensure that she is made aware of *everything.*"

The tension in the room ratchets up, the threat dripping from Chase's words making everyone still, like the calm before the storm. Except Harrison just smiles at Chase. My blood runs cold at the sight of it and it's not even directed at me.

"I will ensure the girl is made aware of everything, but please, Armstrong, feel free to meet with the girl. She will be here with us all, bound by our oaths before long."

I look back over to Artemis, whose face is blank, but her clenched fists give her away. Something is going on with her, and while she's never met V, I'd put money on the fact that that isn't going to last much longer.

"If nobody else has any further questions, we can wrap this up. I have plans for the rest of my evening." Harrison stands as if to dismiss us all, when my father clears his throat.

"We should discuss Rico."

The room sucks in a breath, and it's like you could hear a pin drop. It's as if my father is taunting Harrison, and I don't know why.

"I will deal with Rico, Charles." Harrison glares at my father, and everyone else looks bewildered as to why the Regent of the sect in Cancun is being brought up. "Dismissed."

Harrison strides out of the room, leaving behind a low murmur as people start to make their way from the room. My father turns to me when the room is nearly empty.

His eyes dance with glee and a stone forms in the pit of my stomach. "Play your cards close to the chest, boy. With the Royal girl at your side, there are a myriad of possibilities at hand. Change is coming."

# CHAPTER THIRTEEN

## OCTAVIA

Linc has been treating me like I'm made of glass since our conversation on Monday. This softer side is definitely something I could get used to seeing every now and then, but I almost miss his assholeish ways. I don't want to be looked at like I'm breakable.

It's not who I am.

All it's doing is acting as a reminder of what happened to me, and what could still be waiting.

It could've been worse—so much worse—but I got myself free, and he got me out. We'll find a way around the other stuff. We haven't been able to get a straight answer about this fucking engagement bullshit either, and it has him on edge.

So when I woke up with him in my bed again this morning, I made a decision. If he won't take my words as proof that I'm okay, that we'll be okay, then I'm going to show him with my actions. We haven't taken that step yet, but I'm more than ready.

I pad back into my bedroom and find him half asleep, looking at me in that dazed, still possibly going to fall back to sleep, yet impossibly alert way he has. His shirt is wrapped around me, and when he notices that, his eyes go a little wider and he looks a little more coherent. "You look good with me on you."

I grin at the cheesy line. I love that I get this side of him that no one else sees. It's like we're in a bubble, and I know I'm safe here.

Sashaying over to the bed, I let the shirt drop from my shoulders, and his eyes narrow as he watches me intently. This might be my show, but I'm very aware that my tenuous control of the situation is likely to pass to him when I make my next moves.

The shirt pools at my feet and I stand bare in front of him before climbing onto the bed, slipping beneath the sheets. I move closer to him and capture his lips with mine, running my hands up his bare chest, tangling my fingers in the small patch of hair there. Moving slowly I push him onto his back and move to straddle him as his hands grip my hips.

There might be his thin pair of boxers between us, but it is more than a little apparent that he is on board for what I have in mind.

Maybe I should be more tentative since we haven't done this before, because of everything that's happened between us before now, but I'm tired of denying what he means to me. To him and to myself.

"Octavia," he murmurs as I pull back for breath, his gray eyes dark and stormy as he holds me in place with one hand, another moving to fist my hair. "If we do this, there is no turning back. We already crossed enough lines that I'm never letting go, but this… this means you're mine and there is nothing in this world or any other that will keep me from you. The stars may fall, and the sun may never rise, but you will still be mine."

His words make my heart race, and I nod my head as much as I can in his grasp. His eyes flash and I'm on my back in a heartbeat, his body hovering over me. He leans his forehead against mine, closing his eyes, and takes a breath as my heart pounds against my ribcage. "I've got you, always. Never forget that, Octavia."

He captures my lips again, and I get lost in the feel of him. Every sense heightened by the anticipation of what's to come.

Our tongues move as if in a dance we've been practicing our entire lives and I revel in the feel of his heat. A strong chest hovering above mine—breaths becoming more and more shallow—with arms caging me in while he kisses and licks every inch of me. He tastes like a new morning, like a new beginning, and I can't seem to get enough of him. With my feet planted firmly on the mattress, I push my hips up to meet his crotch but he's keeping his dick away from me on purpose.

My groan and whimper tell him everything he needs to know: I want it, now. He chuckles in my mouth and the lightheartedness of that sound is fuel to my burning fire.

"Linc, gimme!"

"Patience. I want you to beg for it." With that declaration, Linc ends our kiss with a bite of my bottom lip and pulls back, eyes darting all over my face like he's assessing my state of being.

"I'm fine. I keep telling you but you're too stubborn to get it."

"You're fine when I say you're fine." If it weren't for the glint in his steel gaze, I'd be offended by such a declaration. But he's kidding, trying to rile me up, and lucky for him, I'm more than just riled up. I'm near losing my mind with wanting him.

I think I've always wanted him, from the first time we spoke all those years ago. Linc and me? It's been a long time coming.

And hopefully, we'll both be literally coming sooner rather than later.

Wrapping my legs around his waist, I push my heels down on his ass and pull myself up to rub my pussy against his boxer-clad cock. Linc moans and the sound goes straight to my clit, making me shiver with need.

"Linc, please. God, I need you."

"There it is." With a dexterity only he could possess, Linc is completely naked in less time than it takes me to realize it. We're skin to skin—heat to heat—and the feel of him is nothing short of heavenly.

Then he's gone. Completely untangled from my hold, Linc travels down the length of my body, one leisurely kiss at a time. One bite and one suck at a time. His mouth latches onto my nipple—sucking it in almost to the point of pain—and his fingers search out my folds, finding them wet and ready for him. My back arches, aching for more of his touch, more of his mouth. Always more when it comes to him.

With his tongue flicking my hard nub until he tears a long moan from me, he looks up and winks right before his teeth sink down and my entire body springs off the bed.

"What the—" I'm gasping in air, my pussy desperate for more attention as he only rubs my pussy from the outside, leaving me begging for more of him, more of his touch.

"Shh, be good."

I sink my teeth into my lip and squeeze my eyes shut when I feel his hot, wet mouth travel down to my mound, giving it a soft, almost loving kiss. It's so gentle and different from the Linc that I've come to know. Except I'm not a fragile flower and I need more than just soft. I need him to consume me. To bring me to the edge then pull me back to reality.

"Linc, please. I need more. This whole sweet shit isn't going to fly with me."

The fire in his eyes could be from desire or it could be from anger. I'm not quite sure until he shows me exactly what he thinks of my idea.

"You're not the one in control here."

This is when I remember that Linc is not one to take instructions very well. Not from his dad, not from his brother, and apparently not from me either.

"But Linc…"

His teeth sink into my pussy lip before he licks a slow, torturous, path across my flesh. Down one side, up the other. It's like he's playing with my patience and loving every squirm and every whimper I give him.

"Linc, please…"

He doesn't relent. Doesn't even pretend to accelerate his moves to bring me to peak any faster. I'm beginning to think that he's purposefully playing with me like a cat plays with its mouse.

I'm quivering as his tongue circles my clit, around and around, until I can feel my juices spilling over from my overwhelming desire. My uncontrollable want of him.

"Please, Linc. I'm begging you. Please, please, please."

Grabbing me under my thighs, lightning quick, he pulls me into him just as he positions himself on his knees. My back is flat on the mattress and his full frame is towering over me like an ominous yet alluring presence.

"You want the full force of me, V? Are you sure you know what you're asking?" The rawness in his voice and the steel in his eyes make me wetter than I thought possible. His power, his control. His need to dominate turns me on in ways I didn't know were possible. Am I sure?

"Yes. Yes, to both."

"Don't say I didn't warn you."

Grabbing me by my ass cheeks, Linc pulls me up until my knees are over his shoulders and my pussy is level with his hungry mouth. He kisses me like he's a starved man as I try to hold myself as still as possible. At this point, the only part of me still on the bed are my shoulders and head. His tongue is deep inside my channel, licking my walls and biting my folds. His nose is against my mound as his lips suck on every inch of me. When he releases one of my ass cheeks, he slams two fingers inside me—his mouth latching onto my clit—and my entire body shakes with the force of it. I think I cry out but I can't be sure since my brain is only able to register the pleasure he's giving me right now.

Curling his fingers inside me, he presses against the one spot that has me immediately chasing an orgasm.

"Oh fuck!"

My hands are fisting the sheet as he relentlessly rubs against my g-spot before I lose all of my control. My body is no longer mine. It's all his. He's playing it like a fucking violin and I'm okay with it. I surrender completely.

Twisting his fingers inside me, he pulls them out—ignoring my protests like he doesn't give a fuck what I think—and without any preamble, he slides one, then the other, into my ass. He's careful at first, making sure he doesn't hurt me, but when his lips descend on my clit and sucks it in with the force of a hurricane, I lose myself in him. Lose myself as I come harder than I have before. I'm thrashing and crying out while Linc continues to pull the orgasm out of me with precise expertise.

As soon as I come down from my high, Lincoln pulls me down to his cock where he impales me, slowly, inch by inch, like his own personal fuck toy.

Holy fucking shit he feels so good. I am so fucking full and I'm definitely not going to complain about it. I'm not stupid.

His hands move to my ass cheeks as he throws his hips back and forth, fucking me like he's a god and I'm his most treasured possession. My body moves along the mattress as he bottoms out on every thrust; the sounds of slapping skin and wet pussy surround me.

He fucks me like he's desperate for me, like he needs to imprint himself on me, and there's no way for me to stop him even if I wanted to.

He fucks me like a savage until I'm almost at the edge, but stops just this side of Nirvana and I swear I want to throw something at him.

"What are you doing?" I don't even know if he can understand me. My voice is hoarse and my words are spilling together like I'm drunk on him.

"Whatever the fuck I want, V. You should know that about me by now."

In one practiced move, he has me on my stomach, on all fours, as he hitches my ass up just the way he wants it before he slams his hard, thick dick right back inside me. At the same time, he pushes two thick fingers inside my ass and goes back to fucking me with the force of a titan.

I have to clutch the sheets and use every muscle in my body to avoid moving up the bed, even though one of his big hands is holding onto my hip for leverage. In tandem, he fucks my pussy as his fingers bottom out to the last knuckle in my ass. One then the other and my orgasm begins to make itself known. It starts at the bundle of nerves in my clit then radiates throughout my body like electricity traveling through my bloodstream.

"I told you, Octavia. If we did this, you could never get rid of me. Ever. I'm about to come inside your pretty little wet cunt and there's nothing you can ever do to make me walk away. Nothing. You. Can. Do." He punctuates every word with a hard thrust and on the last one, I explode in a flurry of colors and feelings and complete incoherence.

As I try to calm my heart rate, Linc stops everything, takes in a deep, calming breath, and watches me with lust and love engraved in his steel gaze. Every one of his movements is calculated, like he's trying to dominate himself. He didn't come yet so I'm guessing he's testing the boundaries of his control.

It's when he reaches for the lube that everything clicks into place.

The anticipation runs through me and as excited I am to do this, I can't deny that the fear of the pain is real.

"Shh, baby, I'll be careful. Has anyone ever fucked your ass?" I'm loving this caring side of Lincoln Saint just as much as I love the closed-off control freak.

With unwavering care, Linc slowly slides the crown of his head into my ass before I get the chance to answer him, massaging my ass cheeks as he goes, murmuring words of encouragement.

*You're beautiful like this.*

*I love seeing my dick in your ass.*

*I've always loved you, Octavia.*

Finally, he bottoms out, and when he does I let out a sigh of complete bliss. He doesn't move for a bit, just sits there, digging the pads of his fingers into my flesh until I push back, begging for more.

"Linc, please. I need…" He knows exactly what I need, and he gives it to me.

With one hand on my ass cheek, he reaches down with the other to tweak my clit as he pulls almost all the way out before pushing back in. I don't know how he has lasted this long without coming.

"Fuck, the sight of you taking my dick in your ass is more than I can handle, Octavia. I'm not gonna last." I love that I have that effect on him. I love that I am the one who can break him away from his control. It's heady as fuck.

Pinching my clit with one hand, he slaps my ass with the other as he begins to fuck me like I'm all he's ever wanted. Slow at first, easy and careful, making sure he's not ruining it for me. In and out, slap, slap, pinch, until he progressively loses the battle against his primal needs.

With one final thrust that sends me sliding against the headboard, Linc pulls out and the unmistakable sound of him jacking himself off reaches my ears.

He's marking me.

He's coming all over my ass.

I reach down to my clit, even though I know it's a long shot, and try to alleviate the need that I feel at the image of Linc violently stroking himself, about to come all over me.

The first jet of cum hits my sensitive skin, making it come to life like a dormant volcano exploding into the night sky, but when I rub out my clit, the pleasure it produces has me screaming into the mattress.

Linc roars out his orgasm and squeezes my ass as he comes over me. It's hot and it's heady and it makes my head spin, but holy fuck that was hot.

I think I may pass out from pleasure—I feel like Jell-O—but not before I hear the deep timbre of his voice, words dark and ominous yet only making me love him more.

"I'm all over you, Octavia," he declares, panting and deadly. "For-fucking-ever."

We both collapse onto the bed, him on top of me, his dick nestled between my ass cheeks, as he whispers in my ear.

"All mine."

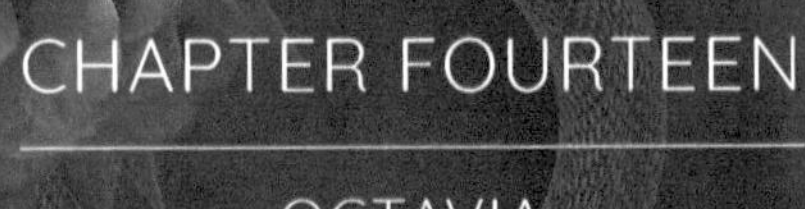

# CHAPTER FOURTEEN

## OCTAVIA

Starting my morning off with a bang—literally—put a definite pep in my step, even if I feel like I've been walking funny all day.

Not that I'm complaining.

Lincoln breaking down that final barrier between us… it's like that final wavering part of myself has found solid ground.

There might be a mass of chaos in my life, but my four guys are here to stay. They'd give anything for me and I'd do the same for them.

The morning at school has passed in a happy blur, so when I sit opposite Indi at the table in the cafeteria, I still have a giant smile on my face.

"I don't know what you had today, but can I have some?" she asks, looking exhausted as she shotguns a can of coke.

It's impossible to stop the laugh that breaks free. "No, no you can't. Pretty sure you and Lincoln wouldn't merge that well. Like, I love you, but no."

She pulls a face, sticking her tongue out. "Yeah no, not my type, but hell yes for you. It's about fucking time you two got down and dirty. Was he a monster dick? Don't answer that. I bet he was. All that big dick energy he has… just damn."

I laugh at her, shaking my head as I take a bite of my burger. "My lips are sealed."

"For now anyway." She giggles.

"What's so funny?" Maverick asks as he drops into the seat beside me. I start laughing uncontrollably. Indi joins in and we laugh till we cry.

"I swear it's not even funny," I say, trying to breathe and stop the laughter.

Mav just quirks his brow at me and steals one of my fries. "If you say so. Girls are weird."

"You love my brand of weird," I tease, and he pulls me into his lap, kissing my neck.

"Yes I do."

Indi shakes her head. "Who would've thought that you could turn Maverick Riley into a cheeseball."

I grin at her, their prodding back and forth is beyond funny.

"Only for her," Maverick says, shrugging. "I can show you my other side if you'd prefer?"

He grins, baring his teeth at her, and I roll my eyes as Linc and Finn join us at the table.

"Oh good, the boss is here," Indi snarks. "Put your leash back on."

"Oh look, they're friends again," Finley snorts as he sits. "I knew you beating Blair the other day would soften him to you."

"Has anything come of that?" I ask, worrying my lip.

Lincoln shakes his head. "I dealt with it. It'll be fine."

I blow him a kiss and the corners of his lips turn up. That might be the best I can get from him in this cesspit of a school, so I'll take it. At least there are only, like, four months left until we're out of this place.

We should probably start thinking about colleges, or at least have that conversation, but with everything else that's been going on, we haven't exactly had time to think about it.

Well *I* haven't.

I had so many plans when I came back last summer: a clear goal and the steps that would get me there.

Now?

Everything has changed.

I can't even say that I'm mad about it, but I definitely need to work some shit out.

"Just so you all know, the party Blair was going on about is happening. Tomorrow evening at the house." He looks directly at me and it's like the rest of the world ceases to exist. "I have spoken to Harrison and he assured me there is no engagement."

"Goddamn right there isn't," Indi huffs. I love her too much. "And if there was, I'm pretty sure between all of the resources at my disposal these days, I could help you make her disappear."

Huh. My little ray of sunshine got *dark.*

I laugh while Lincoln graces her with the rare approving smirk. She doesn't even notice and continues to chow down on her lunch.

"Oh that reminds me!" Indi pipes up. "I got us booked in with Gracie tomorrow. I figured we could use a hair day!"

"That's so perfect! My hair is a mess. Wearing it up all the time does not suit me. Does anyone have plans tonight?"

The boys all look between themselves, before Lincoln answers me. "We have a meeting."

My heart sinks. I almost forgot that they have those. I can't help but flick back to the conversation I had with East, about how they'll never be free, and my chest hurts. What if this whole Regency thing means I could get them free?

I tuck the thought away to ponder over later. "Oh, okay. It's cool."

"We can swing by after?" Finn offers.

I shake my head. "No, it's fine. I was going to say we should start talking about college, but it can wait."

"I'd come over, but Ryker is being a little… possessive right now."

I smile at her, hating how torn she looks, but also hating that this is where we're all at right now. Pulled in a dozen different directions. "Honestly it's fine, I can have a date with my piano. It's been a minute and I kind of miss it. Plus, I can go hang out with East. He's probably going insane."

"Okay," she says, giving me a tight smile.

"You're not wrong though," Linc adds. "He is going stir crazy. Just don't let him exert himself too much."

I smirk at him and shoot him an exaggerated salute. "Yes, sir."

The corners of his lips tip up and his eyes light at my words. Well… apparently he likes that. I'll tuck that away for future reference. Might just get me another morning like today, and well, I'm not about to say no to that.

I turn back to Indi who is grinning shamelessly at me. "What time is the appointment with Gracie?"

"I got her for ten a.m., so I can swing by and grab you if you like?"

"Sounds good."

Maverick kisses my neck softly, stealing my attention. "Eat." I look back at him and he's looking at me, concern pinching the corners of his eyes. "You haven't been eating the same since we got you back, and while I love you no matter what you look like, you need to eat."

I chew the inside of my cheek and pick up my burger. I hadn't noticed, but apparently he has. People—including himself—never give him enough credit. He always says he's not the guy with the plan, not the thinker, more the do-er… but he pays far more attention than anyone realizes.

The bell sounds and I plow down the last bites of the burger before chugging back my bottle of water. Finley stands, grabbing my bag, while Lincoln clears our trays and Mav takes my hand. People stare at us all as Finley kisses me despite Maverick holding my hand, and I couldn't give less fucks if I tried.

They don't have to understand us. We've walked through fire to get here and I'm not about to explain everything we are to small-minded assholes who mean nothing in the long run.

"We'll walk you to class," Linc says as he reappears. I smile at him, nodding as he holds out his hand to me. I falter, thinking back to our conversation. He seems to read my mind and his hand falls to his side, but Finley offers me his instead.

Apparently they all know about the bullshit.

Maverick slaps my ass and releases me as I step up and take Finn's hand. Indi beside me, Linc and Mav behind us. My dad always said that family isn't just about blood, that the family you choose is the best kind of family you can have, and I think I'm finally coming to realize just how right he was.

Blood might be thicker than water, but love is thicker than blood.

After a long day at school of mock exams and the sheer amount of work set for end-of-year assignments to get final grades, my brain aches. Plus the substitute in Gym is an actual beast. I don't remember having ever sweat so bad in a gym class, but this woman is absolutely slaying.

So when I let myself into the Saint house and head up to East's room, I am so excited at the idea of a chill night with him. I texted him after lunch to see if he wanted company tonight and he practically rhapsodized the idea. I guess being cooped up is driving him insane.

I knock on his door and push it open, finding him perched on the edge of his bed in nothing but sweats.

"Are you seriously working out?" I ask, undecided if I should be impressed or yelling at him.

He grins up at me as a bead of sweat runs down his chest. "Rehab is a bitch. Plus, this is nothing, but I refuse to waste away in this room. I have official rehab tomorrow, but my trainer emailed me over some stuff I can be doing at home."

"Should you really be doing this so soon after coming home?"

He nods, running a hand down his chest. "I went and saw the doc today, got the all clear on the incision. It's healed pretty nicely, though the scar is for life. I told her I was losing my mind and she said there wasn't any harm if I was feeling up to it. She also recommended actual therapy. Don't think I've laughed that hard in a while."

I look at the pink, puckered line on his chest, and my heart races with the fact that I could have lost him. We are so freaking lucky that he's still here with us.

"Don't look at me like that, V. I'm not going to break." He looks fierce as fuck as he stands, but I race across the room to stop him. He might say he's okay, but I am so not going to be responsible for him getting hurt again.

"Maybe you won't break, but that doesn't mean you can be Superman just yet either. Sit your ass back down. I thought we had a snuggle date." I grin up at him, trying to make light of the fact that I can feel him trembling beneath my touch. Apparently he already overexerted himself today.

He kisses my forehead before sitting back down on the bed. "Fine, fine."

I don't blame him for being frustrated, I would be if I was cooped up in here all day too, but I need him to look after himself, because I can't lose him.

I can't lose any of them.

I might not have wanted any ties when I came back to Echoes Cove, but a lot has changed since then. I don't even feel like the same person I was last summer.

Once I've helped him get comfortable, I climb over him and snuggle into his side.

"How was your day, anyway? Distract me with your tales of youth," he teases, and I smile at him, kissing his chest. I regale him with the dull nothingness of school, the drama that fills the halls, and when I tell him about Indi and Blair, he laughs so much he snorts and it's cute as fuck.

"It's about time Blair realizes she can't push everyone and not get some pushback," he says as he mindlessly plays with my hair.

"Yeah, but who would've thought Indi would be the one to throw down?"

"Oh I absolutely did. That girl loves you fiercely. She's a little spitfire." He chuckles and I nod. He isn't wrong.

A knock on the door steals my attention and Mrs. Potts appears. "Would you dears like some dinner?"

"That would be amazing, thank you," East says with a smile. "I don't suppose you'll let me have pizza?"

She rolls her eyes at him, and I clamp my lips together to stop from laughing. "You know too well that pizza is off the menu. You boys are incorrigible. How does some lean meat and veggies sound?"

He groans and this time I don't manage to stifle the soft giggle.

"Sounds delicious," I say to her and she grins.

"I knew I liked you, Octavia. I'll be back in a little while with some food for you." She closes the door as East trails his fingers down my ribcage.

"You shouldn't encourage her. It's all lean meats, no processed food… no fun food."

I sigh and move to straddle him so I can look him in the eye properly. "She's just making sure you heal properly."

"Healing is no fun."

"I didn't realize you were so whiny," I tease. "But I can think of some fun we can have."

The doctor said no sex… they didn't say anything about anything else. I lean in to kiss him softly, careful of the fact that he is still healing, but he's not having any of it.

Grabbing me by the back of the head, East curls his fingers into the strands of my hair with overwhelming passion, crashing his mouth to mine like he's a man starved.

Making sure I don't touch him anywhere that could hurt him, I hold myself up on one hand planted next to his head. His hips rise up as his tongue explores every inch of my mouth, my lips, dueling with my tongue.

"I want to make you feel good, East." My words are whispered against his panting mouth.

"You always make me feel good, V. Just being here is everything." He really is a Saint among sinners.

With a wicked glint in my eye, I smile against his lips before giving him a lingering last kiss.

"Where are you going?" His voice is hoarse and if I weren't a sinner I'd feel bad that I'm about to blow his mind while he's trying to heal.

"Making sure you remember I was here." Slowly, I lift one leg and kneel beside him as I push down the front of his sweats until his cock springs free. I'm surprised that he's already hard for me, and when I look back at him he's got a boyish grin on his beautiful face. "What can I say? You just being here makes me so fucking hard, V."

Licking my lips, I kiss the top of his dick, licking along the slit, and revel in the sound of his groan. It's like fuel to my already burning fire.

His hand moves to touch me but I swat it away.

"This is about you, East. It's not about me."

"Don't you know, Octavia? For me, it's always been about you. From the very beginning."

His words make me weak, and matched with the longing on his face, I cave. I slide a little closer to his hand to allow him better access to my skin. I lean in and place my mouth over the head of his cock, sucking softly and caressing him with my tongue.

I lower my mouth until my nose is at his crotch and I'm gagging on his dick. Tears fill my eyes as I take him down before pulling back and wrapping my fingers around his shaft, spreading my saliva with every stroke I give him.

East snakes his hand under my uniform skirt and latches onto my panties, trying to pull me close enough that he can touch me. I give into him because, of course I do, and angle my body just enough for him to be able to touch my wet, aching pussy. His groan as he sinks one finger inside of me, tells me he needed to feel me as much I needed to have him in my mouth.

Harder and harder, I suck him into my mouth, taking him deeper and deeper as I go. East rocks his hips up every time I bottom out, my throat opening up for his cock. The sounds I hear from him only make me want to give him more so I slide my hand down to his balls, rolling them in my hand, eliciting a long, drawn-out moan from him. Every time he reacts to my touch it makes me even wetter and I know he can feel it because he adds another finger, and fuck me, it feels too good.

I should be worried about his wounds but all I can think about is making him feel good, and if making me feel good helps with that, I'm not about to deny either of us that.

I bob my head on his cock faster as he finger fucks me with greater force than before. We're both panting as he tries to bring me to orgasm, and just like that he's taken control of the situation I thought I was commanding. I guess this is what they mean by topping from the bottom.

With my mouth focused only on the head of his cock, I jack him off as I suck and lick and kiss the entire head of him. East's movements become erratic, like he's barely holding back.

"Give it to me, V." I know what he wants and I can't refuse him. Just as he slides the pad of his finger across my clit, I rub myself out on his finger all the while concentrating on using my mouth to bring him to climax. Holding his balls in my hand, I glide down his shaft and let it go as far as it can until I feel his head at the back of my throat, gagging again and not caring about the sounds I'm making.

"Gonna come, V." His words are hoarse and the urgency in his voice is all I need to lose my self-control.

I can't cry out but my entire body moves with the force of the orgasm he gives me just as he spills down my throat, the tangy taste of him coating my tongue.

I swallow every drop—because spitters are quitters—and slowly lick every inch of him clean before I kiss the top of his softening cock and pull his sweats back into place.

Turning to face him, I feel a blush coloring my cheeks when I see the goofy grin that makes him look like the boy I used to know, way back when things were less complicated.

"Best visit ever." He brings his fingers to his mouth and licks them clean before he pops them out from between his lips and winks.

"Best snack ever," I retort. As I'm trying to get off the bed, he shakes his head, grabbing me and pulling me closer to him.

"Don't run away, V. Kiss me, first."

And I do. I kiss him like I love him. With abandon and purity.

---

A night with East was exactly what we both needed. The others joined us after their meeting, but we didn't speak about it. We just hung out like five friends, watching crappy movies and jabbing at the terrible action scenes.

I don't think I've felt that much like a teenager in months. Sometimes it's easy to forget that I'm only seventeen, that I'm supposed to be young and carefree, that life isn't meant to be this much of a mess. This much chaos.

We all ended up crashing at the Saints' overnight, one giant puppy pile on East's bed. It took some maneuvering but we made it work and I can honestly say I've never slept as soundly as I did. Even with the limited space. I woke up with each of them touching me in some way or another and I've never felt safer.

I'd be lying if I said I didn't wake up and think of how much fun we could've all had together, but it was not to be.

Not yet anyway.

Though doing the walk of shame through our yards this morning was more than a little funny. Especially when I noticed our gardener out there a little too late. At least I was dressed, I guess. Even if it was in my school shirt and a pair of Lincoln's sweats.

I looked fucking ridiculous, but it was cute that he offered them to me, even if it was just to walk back home.

The house is quiet since Smithy is spending the weekend with Matthew, so I pad through the house up to my room and take a quick shower, dressing in something comfortable before going down to make myself a bagel with cream cheese for breakfast. I know I can make that without breaking the kitchen, and after Maverick's comment yesterday, I'm trying to remember to eat.

The way Panda used food against me apparently fucked with me more than I had realized. I never thought anything could fuck with my love for food. Apparently I was wrong.

But I'm going to try harder, and that has to count for something. Even if I'm not going to talk it out with anyone. I'd rather work my feelings out with the piano than with another human.

Especially a human I don't know or trust.

Pretty sure any therapist I tried to explain my life to would call me a dramatic bitch that makes shit up since so much of this shit is freaking unbelievable.

Fuck it.

That's what music is for.

My phone buzzes on the counter as I eat my bagel, and Indi's name flashes on the screen.

Indi:
On my way, figured we can grab food and coffee on the way. Breakfast burritos for the win!

Is everyone trying to feed me? Have I really been that out of it? I look at the few bites of bagel I've eaten and wince. They might be right.

Me:
Sounds good, I am here for that burrito.

I wrap the bagel and pop it in the fridge, I can snack on it later. Plus, that burrito sounds too good. My stomach gurgles almost in response and I frown. Maybe I *have* been neglecting myself a little bit without meaning to.

Dashing upstairs, I change into something more suitable for peopling and being outside. I finish pulling on my jeans as Indi buzzes at the gate. That was timing.

I rush down the stairs, pulling on a pair of boots as I shrug into my jacket, my hair in a messy bun on the top of my head. I'm sure the paparazzi would have a field day with how I look if they bothered to stalk me anymore.

Definitely not something I miss about my old life.

Having my life splayed across every tabloid on the planet isn't something I look back on with any kind of fondness.

I reset the alarm and lock up before jogging down the drive and bundling into Indi's waiting car. "Please tell me how you manage to look so put together and flustered all at once? Is there a secret I missed at orientation to being a girl?"

I laugh at her as I buckle in. "Shut up. Like you don't look fabulous as shit for a hair appointment."

She grins at me, sitting there in her leather-look leggings, black tank with skulls, and a long black cardigan. She's a freaking pixie. "Fair point. You ready to go?"

I pat myself down, making sure I have my phone, wallet, and keys, then nod. "As ready as I'm going to be."

"Awesome. Food, coffee, and hair. What else does a girl need?" She grins before pulling away from the curb.

"You sticking with your purple?" I ask casually as she drives, and she shakes her head.

"I'm thinking of going back to blue. I kind of miss it."

I grin at her, 'cause hell yes. "Do it, why the fuck not?"

"You going to let me talk you into adding some color into those luscious locks of yours?"

I bark out a laugh. "Not a chance. I just want to get my length back, maybe once it grows out we can talk about fun colors."

She sticks out her tongue as we pull into the Starbucks drive-thru. "Spoil sport. But fineeeee, I guess."

I cackle as she places our order before we head to the Mexican place. I feel gross still coming here, all things considered, but it's the only Mexican place in the Cove, and I'm not about to let Raleigh and his bullshit stop me from enjoying life.

I head in and grab breakfast for us both before ducking back out to the car. "Let's eat and drive. Gracie will kill me if we're late."

"I'm good with that." I nod before taking a bite of the spicy egg deliciousness.

How could I ever not love food when it tastes like this?

"You're feeling better?" she asks, side-eyeing me as I eat.

"I am." I smile. "I hadn't realized I wasn't eating properly. Mav poked me and apparently becoming aware of it was what I needed."

"Good. I didn't want to say anything while you've been recovering and dealing with all the things, but I was only going to give you another week, tops."

I laugh softly. "I love you too."

"Of course you do, I'm fabulous." She grins as she taps the steering wheel along to the music playing in the background. "How are you feeling about this party tonight?"

"Honestly?" I pause, taking a deep breath. "I've been trying not to think about it. Lincoln says his dad isn't marrying him off so I have to take him at his word. Harrison, that is. There's still so much up in the air about this Regency shit too, I have no idea what's going on, but I've been so focused on trying to get my ducks in a row that I haven't let myself focus on it too much. I know that's probably not the smart thing to do, but I figure the Knights will seek me out when they're ready. I want nothing to do with them, so I'm happy to avoid it all for forever and a day."

"I get that," she nods. "Just let me know if you need anything. I got your back, always."

"I know you do, but if I can keep you off their radar, you better believe I'm going to."

She shrugs as she pulls into the parking lot of the salon. "Don't keep me free and clear if it means you drown. Ride or die, remember? We can drown together."

---

I let out a deep breath as I stare at my reflection in the mirror. Gracie worked miracles with my hair, and I feel better from that alone. We did a whole round of beauty treatments, which made me feel better than I have in weeks, and the shopping trip after helped to remind me that my life isn't just kidnapping, secret societies, and all of the other bullshit I've been dealing with.

I have the best friend I could ask for, four guys who practically worship me, Smithy who rocks my world… I have a lot to be thankful for.

Though my dad hasn't been far from my mind most of the day. I can't help but think what he'd say about how I'm handling everything. If he'd disapprove. If he'd be proud. What words of wisdom he'd give me to help get me through it all.

I didn't know the part of him that was a Knight, so it's not something I'll ever have answers to, but I like to think he'd be proud of the woman I'm becoming. Of the way I'm handling shit… or at least trying to handle it.

That he'd tell me to keep my head held high as I walk into this viper pit tonight.

I've spent most of my day preparing for this stupid party, molding myself into the image of someone who isn't afraid; someone who has survived and come out fighting. Except I don't think I look like me right now.

Imposter syndrome is real.

My dark hair is slicked back, falling down my back in a deadly straight line. My eyes are done in an extreme smokey eye, my lips are pale, glossy. Giant drop earrings in each of my ears make my neck look longer, even wrapped in the gold snake chain that I picked out this afternoon to go with my dress. I even found black stilettos with gold snake clips to match.

It'll all pair perfectly with the little black dress—with a sweetheart neckline and a dipped hem so my ass isn't on show—that is currently hanging on the back of my closet door.

It's going to look amazing; it just feels very… not me, all of a sudden. I feel like I've spent so much time recently dressing up and playing pretend and I'm tired of it already.

But tonight I'm just going to have to suck it up. There's no way I'm leaving the others to deal with the Knights—plus most of the Cove's who's who—on their own. I might not like these things, but I'm not about to abandon my guys.

I grab my phone and shoot Indi a message.

Me:
Be thankful your guys don't have stupid functions like this.

Indi:
Oh I am, but you're going to rock it. Remember, they can smell your fear. You got this.

Me:
I've got something **drunk emoji**

Indi:
Do you need one of my famous pep talks?

I laugh softly at her message.

Me:
No, I'm good. I just really don't wanna.

Indi:
Get through as much as you have to, then sneak away with the four of them hot on your heels. I'm pretty positive none of them are going to complain.

Me:
That's a good idea. Let's just hope Harrison doesn't have other plans.

Indi:
If he tries to marry Lincoln off, we'll cut his brakes.

Me:
You're ruthless and I love it.

Indi:
Only for you. Don't tell Ryker. He still thinks I'm a ball of sunshine.

Me:
You are. You're just as dangerous as a ball of sunshine too.

Indi:

Go, have fun, try not to think about the piranhas circling. Let me know if you need backup… or a distraction.

I drop my phone back on the dresser and move to finish getting dressed.

Ready or not, here I come… I guess.

# CHAPTER FIFTEEN

## OCTAVIA

The Saint house is unrecognizable.

Considering I was just here this morning, it shouldn't look so different, and yet…

I walk up the driveway, which is absolutely *slammed* with cars, psyching myself up for this. Normally I'd just use the side gate, but considering that's hidden and this is an official party, we decided I should use the main entrance. The valet service at the gate looked more than a little horrified when I arrived by foot. For a moment I thought they were going to refuse me entry and did a mental happy dance. Alas, I am Octavia Royal, and his boss recognized me just before he was about to turn me away.

Teetering away on these stilettos as I weave my way toward the house, an icy drop of dread runs down my spine. The steps to the door are lit with fairy lights, the same ones that are woven around the branches of the trees and in the bushes that line the drive. The door opens before I can lift my hand to knock and I come face to face with Dylan.

Indi's Dylan.

In the Saint house.

Opening the door.

In a goddamn tuxedo.

"Ermmm?" is all I manage to say, because I'm pretty sure my brain is broken. He grins down at me and ushers me into the house.

"Looking good, V. I'd take your coat, but I'm pretty sure if I took any layers from you Indi would have my balls and your guys would be next in line."

I look down at the shawl covering my shoulders, held together by my hands that clutch both it and my purse. "Why are you here?"

"Indi wanted you to have some help in this snake hole, and well, the money was good," he says with a shrug. "Hustlers gotta hustle right?"

That twinkle in his eye makes me think there's more to it than that, but I let it go. I am learning that I don't always need to know every single detail. I am not Lincoln Saint, and I don't want to run the world.

I hand Dylan my shawl, considering the temperature in the house I don't think I'm going to need it. "Thanks. Just how insane is the guest list?"

"Not great," he says, pursing his lips. "Most of the Cove's elite are here. The LaFontaines included. Indi's request for me to refuse them entry wasn't exactly easy to uphold."

"It's fine," I say, waving him off, mentally high-fiving my friend. "She doesn't mean anything in the long run, just Daddy Saint waving his dick around like it's made of fairy dust."

He bursts out laughing as he hangs my shawl in the closet. "You and Indi really are too alike sometimes."

"She's the best," I say, looking around with a tight smile. "Don't suppose you want to hide me in that closet too?"

"Nah," he says with a lazy smile. "You've got more backbone than that. I doubt you've ever hidden from a fight in your life."

Doesn't matter that he's right. That closet seems far more welcoming than the rest of this party.

"I guess. Any sightings of my guys?"

"East hasn't come down yet, but the others are out back. I think that's where most of this shindig is happening."

"Thanks," I say with a tight smile. "Better go face the music, I guess."

I head through the house, swiping a glass of bubbles from one of the many roaming servers and throwing it back. Some might call it Dutch courage, but for me it's just a way to tamp down the urge to run.

I don't head toward the smaller kitchen that I usually find the guys in. I have zero doubt Harrison has that part of this floor shut off tonight. God forbid anyone sees the homely parts of this mausoleum of a house. I leave the foyer into the giant living room that leads to the wall of glass at the back. The wall is open, letting people spill down the steps and out into the yard. If you can really call back here a yard. It was definitely created for entertaining. I don't usually pay it any mind, but it seems Harrison had someone in to spruce it up a bit.

Whoever it was apparently has my penchant for fairy lights. They're everywhere and it's beautiful.

"Octavia, there you are." I wince at the sound of Harrison's voice. I should've grabbed more than one glass. I force a smile on my face and turn to face him. He's waving me over to him so I head in that direction, my gaze sweeping the space for my guys, but not finding any of them. "Welcome, it's good to finally see you. I'm sorry I haven't been around much since your return. My condolences about your father."

"Thank you." Suspicion courses through me. What game is he playing? Because doting and caring isn't a façade I'm buying. We spoke at the gala and he was nothing more than a giant asshole. To me and to East.

"Ah, Miss Royal, I haven't had the pleasure. William LaFontaine." The man standing beside Harrison holds his hand out to me, so I shake it because my dad didn't raise me to be rude. Plus, this guy hasn't done anything to me.

I don't think.

"Lovely to meet you," I say with a saccharine smile. "Are you new to the Cove?"

He looks almost flattered by my question, and I don't know whether to be grossed out or not. "We don't live here currently, but I am considering the move from the big city. I understand you recently returned after traveling the world. How would you say it compares to the city?"

My smile tightens as Harrison glares at me. "There's no place quite like home."

"A beautiful sentiment, and too often true," William says with a big smile. My gaze bounces across the room when I see them.

Lincoln with Georgia wrapped around him, her lips at his ear while he smiles like he's never been happier.

*He's just putting on a show.*

At least that's what I try to tell my stupid heart that hurts like it might just break, because I don't know if I've ever seen him look *that* happy before.

Why didn't he warn me he would be here with her? Or that she would be here at all.

I guess I should've known, especially when I saw Harrison with William, but it still didn't click. Stupid me I guess.

Doesn't stop the pain I feel at her hand on his chest, her hold on his arm, caressing him like his lover.

"Ah, here's the couple of the night," Harrison says, grinning down at me. I want to smack that smug-ass smirk right off of his face. Or stab him with my snake stiletto.

Either option might make me feel a little better.

He calls them over, and Linc's eyes go wide momentarily when he sees me before the smile snaps back into place as he brings Georgia over.

"Georgia, Lincoln, how are the happy couple tonight?" William asks, shaking Lincoln's hand when they reach us. "Georgia, have you met Miss Royal yet?"

"I've not had the pleasure," she says, smirking at me, as she gives me one of those, I'm-better-than-you finger waves.

Seeing her, I instantly understand why her and Blair would've gotten along so well: they're cut from the same cloth.

"I'm sure the pleasure is all mine." The words sound like honey as they fall from my lips.

As if summoned like the devil herself, Blair appears with Raleigh beside Linc and Georgia.

*If there is a god out there, please just strike me down dead now.*

"I see you finally met my cousin, G," Blair says, that resting bitch face of hers cracking with a smile like she's one-upped me.

"If you'll please excuse me," I say with a smile, extracting myself from this bitchy pit. Lincoln is obviously a better swimmer than I am, because I feel like I'm drowning surrounded by these people right now.

*Where the fuck are Finley and Maverick, and why the hell didn't anyone tell me about this bullshit parade?*

I head to the downstairs bathroom, glad to find it empty, and lock the door before sitting on the closed toilet lid. Fuck wading through this shit without someone on my side. I can usually handle my shit, put on my public figure face, and pull on all my inner peace bullshit… but after everything that's happened the last few weeks, my quota for dealing with this hell alone is at its limit. I pull my phone from my clutch and open up the group text I have with the guys.

Me:

Other than Linc, who is apparently busy, where the fuck are the rest of you?

I sound more than a little salty, but I don't have it in me to pretend otherwise right now. Logically, I know it's all a game. Emotionally though… emotionally I'm so fucked right now that my heart is very much not listening to my head. Panda's words are still too loud in there.

I close my eyes and rest my forehead on my hands, taking a deep breath. There was me thinking I was a strong independent woman, but apparently dealing with the shock of seeing Lincoln and Georgia together is more than I can take right now. Especially with Harrison watching me with hawk-like intensity. I know that Lincoln said Harrison had told him to break all ties with me, and that he's aware Lincoln is the one who found me, but beyond that, I'm not sure how much he knows. I just know we're not meant to be anything more than acquaintances.

I'm pretty sure after Lincoln busting into the Conclave and demanding they help find me that Harrison isn't fooled, but I don't want to be the reason Lincoln suffers any more than he already has.

"Open the door, pretty girl."

I let out a deep sigh at Finley's voice and reach over to unlock the door. He slinks in, relocking it once he's inside, and crouches in front of me. "How you doing?"

"Oh me? I'm peachy keen, jelly bean," I deadpan, and he smirks at me.

"Glad to see your sense of humor is still intact. We only found out when Georgia arrived that she was even coming. I've been dealing with my dad, who arrived at the same time as William, and Mav is helping East. We didn't have time to warn you what was going on. I'm sorry."

"He's going to announce their engagement isn't he?" I say softly, and the pain in Finley's eyes is the final stab to the heart.

I fucking hate the Knights, what they stand for, everything. How dare he make Lincoln into his whore for his own personal gain.

"You can do this, it's just for show. You're stronger than hiding in this bathroom. You don't need any of us at your side to ride out this storm, but we'll all be there, even if it feels like you're alone. We're never far from you."

I take a deep breath and nod. He's right. I am strong enough to deal with this.

To carry it all. I guess I just needed reminding.

Taking his hand, we stand together and he pulls me into his arms. "Ready to face the sharks?"

"As ready as I'm going to be."

He tucks a lock of hair behind my ear, cupping my cheek, and gazes down at me, his bright blue eyes seeing into the depths of my soul. "Remember, this is all just a show. We know the truth, and we're stronger for it."

I nod. "Let's do this."

He reaches for the door but I stop him. "Wait, where is East? Is he actually coming to this insanity?"

He nods, grimacing. "Harrison insisted. Chase is here too, so East will be with someone we can trust. You just focus on me and playing our parts. Maybe we'll learn some of what we need to and make it out of all of this in one piece."

"Okay," I say softly and open the door, slinking out with his hand in mine as we rejoin the crowd. I steal another two glasses from a waiter as we head out to the yard, offering Finley one, but chugging them both back when he declines.

Blair spots us as we reach the outskirts of the party and heads toward us.

"Incoming," I mutter, and Finley squeezes my hand.

She practically hangs off of Raleigh and my stomach twists.

*Did he rape her? Or does she know about his proclivities and just not care?*

Not the time, Octavia… she doesn't need your bleeding heart.

"Octavia, I see you're hiding away. I guess I would too if my world was about to crumble like yours is."

I roll my eyes at her. "Blair, what do you want? I don't have the time or patience for you and your bullshit riddles."

"I mean, oh cousin dearest," she says with a deadly smile, "that Raleigh and his family are about to be inducted. And I, well…" she trails off and holds up her hand, showing off the giant fucking diamond on her finger.

I bark out a laugh. "You have got to be kidding me?"

Looking over at Finley, he looks as shocked as I feel about the news.

"Who confirmed your induction?" Finn asks Raleigh, an eyebrow quirked.

"Your father," he says with a grin. "I might not be on the Conclave yet, but I hear that some family lines are running out and a seat might just open up."

My stomach twists.

The Armstrongs.

East said his father didn't want to continue his line, that he didn't have children because he didn't want to continue the madness.

There is no way Raleigh could end up in that seat.

"Well I guess you better hope I don't claim my birthright then, huh? " I hiss, and he frowns at me before looking down at Blair. "Oh she didn't tell you? Funny that the queen snake might hide things from you. Be careful who you get into bed with, Raleigh, because she is a black widow in the making."

I walk away from them with Finley at my side. We re-enter the house and he takes my elbow, pulling me toward the main function room, but tucks me into a corner. "Hot as that was, it might not have been a great idea. We don't know how this Regency thing is going to play out."

"Yeah, but they don't know that," I say with a shrug, and he laughs softly.

The sound of a clinking glass draws my attention, so we move to the foyer and find Harrison, William, Lincoln, and Georgia standing on the stairs above us all. Lincoln looks thunderous, but when he catches my gaze I smile at him, trying to pretend that this is all okay. He doesn't need me feeling like shit to add to his plate right now. He doesn't smile back, he doesn't do *anything* as Georgia takes his hand and it's impossible to miss the rock sitting on her finger.

I try not to let it affect me, and Finn squeezes my hand as I look away. I spot my aunt and uncle on the other side of the room, standing with Blair, Raleigh, and his family—all smiles.

"Thank you all for joining us here tonight. It's been a wonderful evening so far. We'd like to share some news and make this night even more special." He pauses like he's building anticipation and I think I'm going to be sick.

"I would like to announce—" He's interrupted by the front doors crashing open and armed FBI agents flooding the room.

"What is the meaning of this?" Harrison roars, storming across the room, coming face-to-face with an agent who waves a piece of paper in his face.

"We're here with a warrant for Nathaniel Royal's arrest," the officer announces as my uncle is torn from my screaming aunt and placed in cuffs.

*What the actual fuck is happening right now?*

---

The party ended swiftly with Nate's arrest and my mind has been spinning since. Finley ushered me back to my place as soon as the FBI agents were done, and pretty much everyone else left at the same time. Way to bring down the mood of a party. Not that I'm complaining; my stomach hasn't stopped rolling since I saw the four of them standing on the steps.

I'm not sure how we stop this.

The Knights are too powerful. They control too much.

I don't even care about myself, I just want my guys to be free to live however they want to.

Finley left me here, with the alarm set, to head back to the madness over at the Saints', with the promise to return with everyone as soon as he could. I hate that I can't help more, that I can't be there for Lincoln—or any of them—right now.

I head upstairs and peel this stupid dress off, scrubbing the makeup from my face, and pull my hair into a messy bun on the top of my head before slipping into Lincoln's hoodie and a pair of leggings with some thick socks.

This charade is over. We need a plan. An *actual* plan, rather than just running in circles and hoping we'll find a path out of the maze that is this society shit. The only thing I can think of is my dad's journals, so I grab my phone and go down to the music room. The alarm is set, no one is getting in the house without me realizing, so I know I can read the journals in peace without worrying about being interrupted.

There have to be some answers in there.

I can't imagine my dad would have left me this helpless against something he wanted me to be free and safe from. It might be putting a lot of trust in him, especially considering he isn't here and he wasn't exactly the most stable at the end, but he was always my dad. He always tried to protect me, even in his darkest moments.

And now there's the rumor that he didn't kill himself. If I let myself believe what Panda said—even if it was fueled by madness—then I have to think he was going to tell me something. His journals might not hold all the answers, but there has to be *something.*

I don't even give myself time to think about why Nate could've been arrested —the possibilities are endless and I'm sure I'll find out eventually. Besides, my family made me very aware that we were not family, that I wasn't their problem, and so, heartless as it may seem, I just don't care enough to worry about it.

I have bigger fish to fry.

Starting with Harrison Saint.

Once I've pulled the journals from the vent, I pore over the pages until my eyes sting. There's so much here, but so little of it is useful information. At least not that I can discern. It's almost like my dad had his own language some of the time and it is frustrating as fuck that I don't understand it.

I guess I really didn't know him as well as I thought.

My phone buzzes and I see Indi's name on the screen, along with the time.

Wow, it got late.

I frown, realizing how long I've been down here and that I still haven't heard from the guys. Finley said they'd come over once the storm died down, but I guess things must have gone off.

I have to trust that they'll tell me when I see them, that me being there would make whatever it is worse, so I swipe my screen and check the message from Indi.

Indi:
I heard you had an insane night. Are you okay?

I pause, a little confused, then remember Dylan was working the party.

Me:
Something like that. I'm fine, just put back in my ivory tower until the world stops burning.

Indi:
That might be a while. **link**

I click the link, beyond curious, and it opens up a local news page

**ROYAL SCANDAL**
**ARRESTED FOR EMBEZZLEMENT AND FRAUD, IS THE ROYAL REIGN REALLY OVER?**

Well fuck.

I skim the rest of the article, reading through theories about my uncle's fall from grace, trying to work out fact from fiction. I guess this could explain the grab he and Aunt Vi made for my money when I got back here. If they really were in a hole, it might have saved them.

Is this what Blair has been chirping on about since I got back? Is this why she hates me?

If it is, why wouldn't they just *say* something, rather than treat me like the scum of their lives?

Shaking my head, I close out the article and put my dad's journals away. It's late and I need to sleep. I haven't learned one damn thing tonight, well, nothing that helps us anyway. Once they're secure, I pad back upstairs, double checking all the doors as I move through the house.

I open my balcony doors, disabling the alarm on them, thankful for the cool air that filters into the room, before climbing into bed. My mind whirrs with the possibilities of what could be happening next door, but the night is dark and silent, so there are no clues there either.

Closing my eyes, I try to shut my brain down and let everything go so I can actually sleep; which is no small feat, but I'm going to be useless to everyone if I don't get some shut eye.

It takes far too long to shut off, but once I'm asleep, my dreams are plagued with visions of my dad, his hands covered in blood. Visions of my mom dead at the bottom of the staircase, lying in a pool of blood.

"Octavia." The calling of my name pulls me from the nightmares, and as my eyes flutter open to the dark of night, I find Lincoln, crouching at the side of my bed, looking as broken as I feel.

"Hi," I whisper into the darkness, the corners of his lips turning upwards. "Are you staying?"

"Can I?" he asks softly.

I smile and lift the sheets. "Always."

He gets undressed and slips beneath the covers, resting his hand on my hip. "We should talk."

Leaning forward, I kiss his lips softly. "We can talk tomorrow."

"Are you sure?" he asks, his thumb tracing across the curve of my hip. I nod and close my eyes as he pulls me onto his chest. "I love you, Octavia. Please never forget that."

"I love you too."

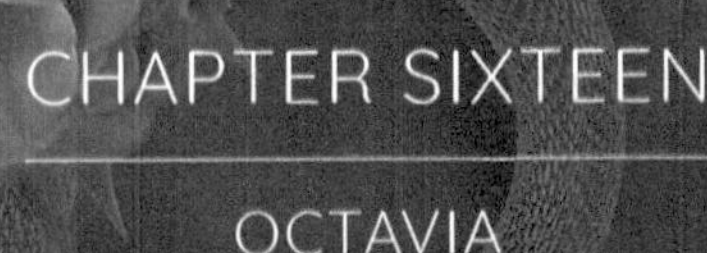

# CHAPTER SIXTEEN

## OCTAVIA

I wake up with Lincoln wrapped around me, and for just a moment, that one between sleep and truly waking, I forget all of the chaos that surrounds us. For just a moment, I am truly happy lying here in his arms.

I cling to those seconds, squeezing all the joy I can from them before reality comes crashing down, and it hits me that Lincoln is engaged.

Engaged to someone who isn't me.

It may not be his choice, and he may not love her, but that doesn't make it any less real. Especially not when I saw the ring on her finger.

"What's wrong?" His sleepy voice breaks through the shadows in my mind, and I turn to face him. His storm-cloud eyes look tired, older than his eighteen years.

I guess a life like his will do that to a person.

"I'm fine," I lie. There's no point in making him feel worse about a situation that is already out of his hands. For a person like Lincoln, who requires control, I can only imagine how this shit with his dad is already making him spin out. "Are you okay?"

He closes his eyes and lets out a deep sigh before leaning forward and kissing my forehead. "I am now, but we should still talk. There's a lot you don't know, and I should be the one to fill in some of the gaps."

I smirk at his choice of words and he rolls his eyes at me, so I shrug. "Hey you're the one picking the words. Not my fault my brain takes me to far off places."

"If we didn't have to talk, I'd show you just how many more gaps I can fill at once," he winks.

Lincoln Saint *winked.* Be still my beating heart.

I laugh softly, shaking my head. "You're terrible."

"I am, but you love it."

I smile at him, running my hand through his hair. "I do. Love you, I mean. We might fight and disagree… a lot. But I do love you."

He twines his fingers through my hair and kisses me with so much passion it makes my toes curl. By the time he pulls back, I'm practically panting. "To be continued. Get your sexy ass out of bed, we need to talk."

He climbs out of bed and pulls on his boxers and jeans. I happily drool over his taut back and peachy ass until he turns back around to face me.

I pout playfully and it's totally worth it to hear his bark of laughter. "Octavia Royal, you are a brat. And if you're not careful, I'll make you pay for it."

I wag my brows at him. "That's kind of the point."

He leans down on the bed and I think he's about to give in, but then he opens his mouth and his low gravelly voice sends a shiver down my spine. "Oh, you'll pay, baby. Just later… when you're least expecting it."

He winks again and kisses my cheek before standing, leaving me wondering who the hell has taken over Lincoln Saint's body. Not that I'm complaining, I am totally on board for this side of him, but I'm definitely pouting for real now… and also excited for whenever later is.

He pulls his t-shirt from the floor and slips it over his head. "I'm going to run and grab a change of clothes, but I'll be back in ten. I'll get some coffee brewing on my way out."

I groan, slumping back down into my pillow as he disappears from the room. As much as I know we need to talk, that I need to know what's going on, I'd much rather have had some fun with him first.

Sometimes his level-headedness is a pain in my ass.

Begrudgingly I climb from the bed and put my hair into a messy bun before jumping into the shower. A brisk wake up is exactly what I need. The cool water shocks me into alert mode and I finish up quickly.

I pull on a long sweater dress and slip on a pair of leggings and some cute socks before heading downstairs where the smell of freshly brewed coffee awaits me.

*Heaven.*

I pour myself a very large mug and slide onto one of the stools at the island before taking a sip.

Ahh, sweet nectar.

I connect my phone to the speakers and put some *Lindsey Stirling* on softly in the background. There's nothing quite like the sound of strings in the morning to hype you up for the day. Goosebumps take over my entire body as I zone out to the enchanting music and lose track of time as I give myself over to the sounds.

I open my eyes as the strings draw to a close and find Lincoln observing me from the doorway. "You are truly breathtaking."

I blush at his words, especially because I know I can look like a total idiot when I get lost in music like that. "What can I say? Music is my higher power."

"Is that what you want to do? After school and college, I mean? Music?" I bite my lip as I realize we've never talked about what we might want for the future. We've spent so much time since I've been back fighting just to *have* a future that we haven't taken the time to talk about what we might want from it.

I nod. "I always wanted to be involved in music. Not like my dad was, but have my own studio. Give artists the freedom to explore who they want to be with the support of a label rather than bog people down with the restrictions most other labels have."

"That sounds like something you'd be good at."

I smile as he grabs a mug of coffee and sits opposite me. "What do you want from the future?"

"My future is already planned out," he says, the light falling from his eyes. "I don't get a say in what I want. It's never mattered."

"Of course it matters."

He shakes his head. "I'll never be free from them, so it doesn't."

"What if you were free?" I ask quietly. "What would you want then?"

He sits quietly in thought before smiling. "Honestly, all I ever wanted was a simple life where I could help people rather than hurt them the way the Knights do. But I've never thought about it much because I know it's an impossible dream. I've never been one to let myself hold on to impossibilities."

I frown, hating that he seems so resigned to his fate.

There has to be a way to get him free.

To get them all free.

Maybe if this Regency thing is real, I can set them free. Even if I don't get to be free with them, they've suffered enough already.

"Octavia." His voice pulls me from my thoughts, his brow furrowed. "We need to talk about last night."

I shrug, not really wanting to, but avoidance has never really been my style. "What part? The whole you're-engaged-when-you-said-you-weren't? Or the part where my uncle was arrested?"

He looks at me, his mouth set in a grim line. "Both."

I let out a sigh and finish my coffee before speaking. "Blair as much as told us about the engagement. We should've known better than to take your father at his word. Self gain at the expense of others is entirely his speed. All I care about is how we stop it."

"I don't know," he says sadly. "But I'm not going through with it. I told him as much. I will play his game and keep up the façade for now, but I will not marry that snake. As for your uncle? There is a lot more to that story."

"Well, I figured he wasn't arrested for being a nice person. I already know he *isn't* nice. What do you know?"

"More than I probably should." He grins, as his phone buzzes on the counter at the same time as mine. "The others are here."

I nod, seeing the messages pop up on my screen.

Our conversation pauses while we wait for them and I refill our mugs. I take my seat again as the front door opens and the three of them filter into the kitchen. East walks gingerly across the room before easing onto the stool beside me, and I kiss his cheek before Mav slips behind me, wrapping his arms around my waist and kissing my neck. "Morning, princess."

"Morning." I smile up at him, kissing him softly before he takes a seat next to

Linc. Finn, who is already sitting beside East, gives me a smile that makes my heart flutter in my chest.

"Where were we?" Linc asks, and I roll my eyes.

"Nate."

Maverick groans and jumps up. "I need a drink for these sorts of conversations."

"All I have right now is water or coffee."

"Coffee it is." He moves to the coffee pot, Finn and East chiming in and asking for a cup too.

"You filled her in on the Georgia situation?" Finn asks, looking at Linc with a raised eyebrow.

Linc's jaw clenches and he nods stiffly. "I did."

"Good, just making sure everything's been covered." Gah, that man. I love that he refuses to keep me in the dark anymore. He's fought Lincoln every time when it comes to telling me things I need to know. At least since he decided I should know about the Knights when Lincoln didn't agree.

It makes my heart swell to know he has my back, even against Linc.

"As I was saying," Lincoln sighs. "Nate was arrested for embezzlement and fraud."

I suck in a breath, eyes wide as that settles in. "Holy shit, so it's true then?"

"Yeah. He's been in a hole for a while, since before Stone died, but you know as well as anyone just how much they didn't get along. Stone wouldn't help him, so the Knights wouldn't either. I discovered last night that Nate was a Knight once upon a time, before Stone married your mother. Stone was always the heir, but as every family is meant to have two votes, Nate stepped into the role when your grandfather passed the mantle. Except Nate fucked up and made a lot of enemies. So he was pushed out of the role when your parents married and your father became likely to produce a legacy."

"I don't understand what this has to do with me?"

"Well, before you came back, we tried to bargain for Nate and Blair to take the Royal seats at the table. Obviously that was declined, though no one told us why. Partly to keep you clear, but partly because Blair came to me for help when she discovered the trouble Nate was in."

Things start to click into place in my mind—things that Blair has said, done—it all starts to make sense.

"You said the deal with her was done. Is this the deal you meant? Helping her out of this mess?"

He nods, taking a sip of his coffee. "There was only so much I could help with once the Knights declined her, but I figured if we could get you out they wouldn't have any choice but to accept her and Nate. But once it became clear that wasn't going to happen, and she stopped keeping her end of the deal, I called it a day."

"What was her end of the deal?" I ask, trying to sate my curiosity.

"At first, help us get you gone. As you can imagine, she was on board with that. But I also needed her to get me some information on her father's fuck-ups. She never did, and then she stopped doing what I asked," Lincoln says, shrugging.

"So how did the FBI get involved?"

Maverick laughs. "That might've been me."

"What did you do?"

He shrugs as he sits back down. "I was sick of her being a bitch, of everything the QB was doing, and them teaming up. So I might've sent some information to a friend of mine."

I pinch the bridge of my nose and let out a sigh. "How bad is this going to get?"

My gaze bounces between all of them and Lincoln shrugs. "We don't know yet, but Harrison is fuming that they raided the party last night."

"Harrison has multiple sticks up his ass currently, one more isn't going to make much of a difference," East snorts. "He'll get over it."

He's interrupted by the buzzer for the gate going off and I check the feed on my phone to see Aunt Vi standing there, pushing the button.

"What in the…" I trail off, showing the four of them the screen.

"Do you want us to stay while you talk to her, or do you want to ignore her?" Finn asks.

This can't be good. "You might as well stay, it'll save me telling you all about it later. Just stay in here, and let me deal with her though."

"I won't make promises I can't keep, princess."

Maverick grins and I roll my eyes as I push the button to open the gate. "This should be fun."

I head to the door and open it, finding my aunt standing there looking like she's bitten into a lemon. "Well are you going to invite me in or leave me standing out here like a commoner, Octavia?"

I bark out a laugh and fold my arms across my chest. "Why on earth should I invite you into my home willingly when you never did the same for me? When there was always a price to pay for your tolerance of my mere existence?"

"You always were dramatic. Just like your father." She rolls her eyes at me, standing there, waiting. I clench my jaw, trying not to snap at her, because she is still family even if I'd happily yeet her off the mezzanine.

"You're making it really easy for me to leave you out here in the cold, ya know?" I quirk a brow at her, and she lets out a high-pitched huff. A laugh escapes me at just how put out she looks.

Her jaw clenches, but she smiles tightly at me. "Will you please allow me in, Octavia?"

I pause a moment, offering her the same level of grace she once offered me before letting her into my home. I close the door behind her then stand, waiting for her to speak. There's no way I'm letting her any further in without knowing what she wants.

"Why are you here?"

She looks around the space, pursing her lips, disdain dripping from her. She seems to think better of saying anything and lets out a sigh. "I need your help."

I bark out a laugh. "You're kidding, right?"

She glares at me, like I'm the one in the wrong right now. "We helped you."

"No you didn't," I snap. "You manipulated me into staying with you, giving you money, and now I apparently know why."

"Well if you know why, then you should help regardless. You're family."

I shake my head. The gall of it all. "We are family, but you get treated the way you treat people. You didn't help me. You weren't even kind to me. My father had died and you treated me like a discarded, dirty burden. Get out of my house and don't ever ask me for help again. You won't get it."

She opens her mouth to say something when Lincoln's voice echoes around the foyer. "She told you to leave. I suggest you listen to her."

My aunt looks like she's going to stomp her foot and throw a tantrum. Must be where Blair gets it from. "You Knights are all the same. Your time will come to fall, and when you do, I shall sit and laugh."

He stands there, hands in his pockets, looking at her like she's the most insignificant creature to exist. I *almost* feel bad for her. "If you still exist, should that happen, you are welcome to. But I wouldn't be so sure of it. A threat to the Knights is usually dealt with swiftly."

Her mouth opens and closes, and I clamp my lips together to stop from laughing then open the door. "You can go now."

"But—" she starts, and I shake my head, cutting her off.

I wave to the door, more than prepared to force her out if I have to. "Karma is a bitch. I'm sure the two of you will be fast friends."

She storms from the house and I watch as she leaves the property. Closing the gate behind her, I let out a sigh, a twinge in my chest as I shut the front door.

"Did I do the right thing?" I ask of nobody in particular. Turning, I find the four of them looking at me like they'd ride into Hell beside me if I asked them to.

Finley steps toward me, taking me into his arms, and I rest my head against his chest. "We will back you, whatever you decide to do."

I sag against him, questioning myself, when I feel someone at my back. "You did the right thing, princess. And if anyone dares to say otherwise, they'll face us."

"Thank you," I say quietly, thankful to have them all on my side.

Lincoln and East move so that I'm surrounded by them. I look between them, and Lincoln grips my chin. "We face the rest of what is to come together. Win or lose. Live or die. Together or not at all."

---

After a stormy weekend, I'm almost glad to be going back to school. For a hint of the mundane, if life at ECP can ever be called that. After a morning of exam prep, and getting the details of our final assignments, my brain is basically Swiss cheese.

Not helped when Miss Celine announces that our final for the year will consist of performing for the school.

I think I'd rather fail.

Stupid fucking 4.0 GPA requirement.

I leave Music and head toward my locker where Indi is waiting for me. "What's up, buttercup?"

I grin at her as I put my stuff in my locker. "Just the thought of performing in front of the whole damn school, no biggie."

"I get to hear you sing again?" she asks, eyes lit up. "You might hate it, and I hate that for you, but I can't be mad about it. You're amazing."

I blush at the compliment and wave her off. "Hardly. You know I'm not exactly a fan of it. But 4.0."

"Yeah, I know. Stupid clause. But, you'll slay it. You always do. Now let's go eat because it's pasta day and I am *starving.*" She rubs her stomach to emphasize her hunger and I laugh. "Did you hear about your aunt and Blair?"

I shake my head. "I don't think so. What happened now?"

"Well, rumor has it, all their assets have been frozen, and they've been kicked out of the house." She loops her arm through mine and pulls me toward the cafeteria. "I also heard that Raleigh dropped her. It's a bad day to be Blair Royal."

"Is she even at school today?" I ask, because I haven't seen her and that's unusual.

"Yeah she's here. Though, she's wandering like a lost lamb. The bitch squad have apparently abandoned her too."

My jaw about hits the floor. Nothing quite like loyalty in the hard times. Fucking hell.

*Am I seriously feeling sorry for her?*

Me and my stupid bleeding heart.

"She deserves nothing else. She's literally shit on everyone to get ahead. It's about time karma bit her in the ass." My bestie sounds fierce as fuck, and I remember that Blair put her through a year of hell before I even got here. Any pity I might have had flits away. She can shit on me and I'll take it, but do *not* fuck with my friends.

"No truer words have ever been said. Fuck the haters and rise above."

She snickers. "Yeah, maybe, but I'm probably going to sit and watch her downfall with popcorn. I can be a petty bitch when I want to."

"Can't we all?" I laugh.

We grab our food, the chicken and spinach cream pasta has me salivating as we sit at our usual table. I finish catching her up on the craziness of the weekend and everything that happened at the Saints' on Saturday night.

"I still can't believe Lincoln is engaged to her. Are you okay?"

I shrug, taking a bite of my pasta. "As okay as you would be if Ryker was engaged to someone because his dad told him he had to be."

"Fair point," she says, looking like she's about to pop off. "Speaking of Lincoln, where are your guys?"

"I have absolutely no idea." I sigh, pulling my phone from my pocket. I drop a message into our group chat asking where they are but get no response.

"Weird," she says, pursing her lips.

Cackling from the bitch squad's table catches my attention, so I look up and see Blair enter the room, trying to ignore the people she used to call her friends as they point and laugh at her.

So much for long live the queen.

Mikayla sure looks comfy with Blair's sycophants crooning to her.

Blair keeps her head held high as she joins the line to get food, but when she's shunned by even the lowest on the totem pole of the school hierarchy, I see her wobble. It's only a moment but it's there.

She grabs her food and glances around the room, locking eyes with me just long enough for me to see the hate and rage she still has for me.

Oh, goodie.

She starts to walk our way, but someone trips her before she can reach us and she eats the floor, her tray flying upward and dumping most of her lunch on her head and back as it comes crashing down.

"You should be more careful where you walk, gutter rat," Mikayla cackles, the room erupting in laughter. Blair pushes up to her knees, and while I feel bad for her, I can't help but think that if it was anyone else, she'd be the one in Mikayla's shoes.

I don't think even going through this will change the way she is.

"Be careful sitting up there on your throne, Mikayla. Secrets only stay secrets if everyone keeps their mouth shut," Blair snaps at her before turning and storming from the room while most people point and laugh.

"I wonder what that means," Indi says, turning back to her food.

I frown, my appetite gone. "It means that war is coming and we better take cover."

Lincoln, Maverick, and Finley appear not long after and slide into the empty chairs at our table. "What did we miss?" Maverick asks before smacking a kiss on my cheek.

"Blair getting what she deserves," Indi grumbles. "Can't even enjoy it, stupid nice person that I am."

I smile at her, glad I'm not alone. "Same. Where were you three? Lunch is nearly over."

"Dealing with politics," Lincoln grumbles.

"What he means," Finn adds, "is that Harrison called and told Lincoln he has a date on Friday."

"You do?" I ask, brows raised.

"This stupid deal of his is pissing me off. But yes. I'm supposed to take Georgia out for dinner to celebrate our engagement," he growls. I hate the sound of the words out loud, but I shove it down and try to remind myself it's all a game.

Finley looks at me with a smile. "Which means, pretty girl, you and I are going on a date too."

"We are?" I ask, shocked. "Why?"

"Well, someone needs to have his back while he's out there in the shark tank, and Mav has an errand to run."

I glance at Maverick who doesn't give anything away, but that makes me worry as much as anything.

"Don't worry about me, princess. It's nothing major. Nothing I haven't done a dozen times before."

"That's hardly reassuring," I deadpan as the bell rings. "This conversation isn't over."

"Course it is," he says, stealing the garlic bread from my plate. "But I look forward to fighting it out with you later."

---

"Are you ready for today?" Indi asks as she pulls into the drive-thru to grab our morning coffee on this sunshiney Wednesday.

Why isn't it the weekend yet?

Though, the weekend comes with its own freaking issues.

Stupid Georgia.

Stupid date.

I let out a deep breath, shaking my head. "I am never ready for the masses of ECP, but with all of the extra press this arrest has been getting, the paparazzi are stalking me again and I'm beyond ready to be done with all of it."

"Yeah it totally sucks about the blow back you're getting. But I kind of meant our presentation in English." She laughs before the robotic voice blares through the speaker.

I lean my head back against the rest, groaning. I don't want to say I forgot about the presentation, but I also can't say that I'm prepared.

"Fuck."

She laughs softly as she pulls forward in the line. "It'll be fine. You've totally got this."

"Here's hoping that my winging it skills are on point today," I groan. "Is it awful that I'm thinking about taking a gap year next year? Just to have a year off and try and settle some of the chaos that is my life?"

"Not even a little," she says, shaking her head. "I thought about doing the same, going traveling, experiencing more of what the world has to offer before I knuckle down and get on with the rest of my life."

"I say we do it. Everyone should travel if they have the option. There is nothing like seeing the world and experiencing everything you can before getting bogged down in plans for the future."

She sighs as we pull up to the window. "Now just to get Ryker, Ellis, Dylan, and my parents on board. Can't be that hard, right?"

I can't help but laugh at the exasperation on her face. "Take the boys with you. Pretty sure they'd like to see the world too."

"God, could you imagine?" She shakes her head, pausing to grab our drinks before handing them over to me as she pulls away from the window, heading toward school.

I put hers in the cup holder before taking a sip of my peppermint mocha and grin. "Actually, I kind of could. I think it would be brilliant. Maybe let's try and persuade them to do a group trip over summer first? Or Spring Break? That could be fun."

"That, my friend, is an excellent plan. And then after Spring Break, we are totally making plans for your birthday."

I roll my eyes as we pull into the school parking lot, finding Lincoln and Maverick waiting for us. "We don't need to do anything for my birthday. I'm happy with tacos and movies."

"After the fuss you made about *my* birthday, you can fuck off. I love you, but no." She grins as she puts the car in park and Maverick bounds over to my door and opens it.

"Morning, princess." He grins, basically scooping me into his arms and out of the car. I squeal as he lifts me, and Lincoln takes my drink before Maverick spins me in a circle.

"Why are you in such a good mood?" I ask, laughing. "And please put me down."

"My dad is going away for three months at the end of next month, my mom is going with him, though fuck knows *why*, but that means my summer is basically free. What isn't good about that?"

He kisses me playfully before putting me on my feet. "That is good news."

Lincoln hands me my drink back and I look around for Finn but don't see his car. "Where's Finley?"

"He's got a project today," Lincoln says, a slight shake of his head telling me that we can't talk about it here.

"Okay," I say as I grab my phone and drop the guy in question a text instead.

Me:
Hey, where are you? Is everything okay?

Finn:
Morning, beautiful. Everything's fine. I've just been looking into who Panda was working with, and hitting dead ends. So I'm spending the day going through everything he had at both houses to see what I can find.

Me:
Do you want help?

Finn:
Not a chance, beautiful. You have your GPA to worry about. I've got this.

Me:
If you're sure.

Finn:

You doubting my skills, pretty girl?

Me:
**shocked face** I would never.

Finn:
Ha! Lies. I'll shout if I find anything or have any questions. How's that?

Me:
Perfect. I still think I'd rather skip school.

Finn:
Don't tell Maverick. He'll whisk you away before you can say boo.

Me:
It's tempting.

Finn:
You got this, V. Go face the masses with your crown on. I'll see you later?

Me:
Okay. Also, since when did you get so good at pep talks?

Finn:
**Wink emoji**

I tuck my phone back away, leaning into Maverick, hating the distance I need to keep from Lincoln in public until this bullshit with Georgia is over. We walk into school; whispers still follow us but it's easy enough to drown them out.

Indi pauses, staring down the hall, and I stop beside her. "What?"

I follow her line of sight and see Blair, crying, at my locker.

"Did hell freeze over?" Indi hisses. "Why the fuck is she waiting for you? For us? And fucking crying? I didn't know she could cry."

"Fuck knows, but I guess we're about to find out," I say as Lincoln's calculating gaze takes in my cousin.

We walk toward her, and she wipes away her tears when she sees us. "Lincoln, I need your help."

Maverick laughs loudly, drawing attention, and I mentally groan.

"Why should I help you, Blair?" Lincoln asks, folding his arms across his chest. I get a little distracted by just how good he looks right now, then turn back to my cousin.

"You have no reason to. None. I'm a bitch, I'm fully aware of it. But I don't have anyone else to ask."

Her voice wobbles and my heart softens. Why am I such a soft touch?

"What do you need, Blair?" I ask.

She looks at me, hatred shining in her eyes. "I don't need anything from you."

"Blair," Lincoln warns, and she flushes.

"Sorry. I just… we need somewhere to stay. They took the house, they took everything until after my dad's trial. My grandparents won't help us, saying they don't want anything to do with Dad's fallout. It's all such a mess. I don't have it in me to try and pretend to be nice."

"At least she's honest," Indi sighs.

I bite my lip, wondering if I shouldn't have been so harsh to my aunt.

"Octavia?" Lincoln says my name, as if making it my decision, so I nod. No one deserves to pay for the actions of others like this. Not even my black-hearted cousin and aunt. "Fine, you can stay in the cottage. It's small, but it's warm. It's on the outskirts of the Cove, so it's close enough for school."

"Thank you," she says to him, even though her smile doesn't quite meet her eyes as she turns to me. She nods, wiping at her tear-stained face before holding her head up high and walking away from us through the masses that call her names and jeer at her.

None of it seems to faze her.

I'll give her one thing: no one wears a mask of indifference quite like Blair Royal.

I just can't help but wonder if it'll do her more harm than good.

# CHAPTER SEVENTEEN

## OCTAVIA

I run my hands down my little black dress, trying to settle my nerves. The thought of watching Georgia paw all over Lincoln tonight doesn't exactly fill me with joy, but he wants us there, so I'm not about to tell him no.

Plus it's a night I get to spend alone with Finn, and it feels like it's been forever since we did that.

The low neckline makes my girls look extra bouncy, and the curls of my hair fall nicely down my back. I've gone for a subdued, natural look for the evening, because the whole idea is not to have any attention on us. Plus, Millers is a super high class place, and I'm pretty sure we only got a table because of the Knights.

Apparently the waitlist is like eight months long. Freaking ridiculous.

My phone buzzes on my dresser and Finley's name lights up the screen.

Finn:
I'll be there in five.

Me:
Sounds good. I'm ready when you are.

I grab my clutch, sliding my phone, keys, and wallet into it and pick up my stilettos before padding down the stairs.

"You look beautiful, Miss Octavia," Smithy gushes as I reach the foyer. He's got his weekend bag packed and his long coat on already.

"Thank you, Smithy. Looking forward to your weekend with Matthew?" My stomach flips at the thought of him. I refuse to believe that Smithy's slice of happy is part of the cause of my misery.

I'm pretty sure that whatever cologne he was wearing is a generic one, which is why I haven't mentioned it to anyone. Unless Finley tells me he's found proof that it's Matthew that was working with Panda, I'm not going to put any weight behind the thought.

"Yes, we're heading to my sister's for the weekend."

"Oh, he's meeting the family, this is a big step." I smile at him as I slip into my heels.

"He already met my family," he says, moving toward me. "And I can't thank you enough for making him feel welcome in our home."

"He makes you happy, Smithy. As long as he keeps doing that, he will be welcome here."

Smithy drops his bag and hugs me tightly. "Thank you, Miss Octavia. I hope you enjoy your dinner date with Master Knight. You have my number if you need anything."

"I do, but I won't use it," I say, squeezing him back. "And hey, it's Spring Break since school got out today; if you extend your trip, I can totally fend for myself."

"So it is!" he exclaims as he pulls back. "I might just keep that in mind."

"Just let me know if you do, or if you need the jet," I say as the buzzer sounds, letting us know Finley is here.

"You're too generous, Miss Octavia. Now have fun. I'll keep in touch and let you know my plans."

"Love you, Smithy."

"I love you too, Miss Octavia."

I wave to him as I leave the house, knowing he'll lock it up securely before he leaves. I sashay down the drive, putting an extra sway in my hips when I see Finn's grin from where he's leaning against the car.

"If Lincoln didn't ask for backup tonight, we wouldn't be going anywhere," he growls, pushing from the car and taking me into his arms. "You look good enough to eat."

I laugh softly. "Pretty sure that's not as filling as where we're going."

"Oh, pretty girl, pretty sure I could fill you up," he winks, and I laugh at him again.

"That was terrible."

"It was, but it made you laugh, so my work here is done."

I kiss him softly. "Thank you, I needed the laugh considering where we're heading."

"You sure you're up for this?"

"Watching my boyfriend being basically molested by the girl he's been forced to get engaged to? Oh yeah, I'm all for it."

He frowns at me, quiet for a minute. "You don't have to come. I can go alone."

"Not a chance. We haven't hung out, just us, for too long. I just need to remind myself that he doesn't *want* to be there."

He cups my cheek, looking down into my eyes. "You have nothing to be jealous about. I guarantee he's going to be the jealous one tonight."

I smile up at him. "Let's get this show on the road, shall we? Don't want to be late, and we need to get there before they do."

"Your carriage awaits." He bows, and I laugh again, moving as he opens the door for me.

"I forgot how freaking low this car is."

He grins at me as he rounds the car, climbing in and setting off to the city at a speed that makes my heart race. He grips my thigh between shifting gears, making my blood heat. We don't speak much on the drive; nerves flutter in my stomach about keeping a lid on my crazy while I watch Lincoln with Georgia tonight, and Finn… well, he's not exactly the talkative type.

I try to distract myself with the songs on the radio, and when we pull up to the valet parking in front of the restaurant, I let out a deep breath.

"Ready?"

I smile over at him and nod. "Let's do this."

He climbs from the car as the valet opens my door. Finn's there a second later, offering me a hand to help me out of the seat, and walks me inside the restaurant. The maître d' smiles widely at us as the door closes behind us. "Mr. Knight, it's a pleasure to see you again. Miss Royal, lovely to have you with us. Please, follow me, your table is ready."

I quirk a brow at Finn who shrugs. Apparently the staff do their research on the clientele. Though I suppose if this is a Knight business, of course they know who Finn is. This 'date' will also help the story Lincoln floated of me being with Finley.

The maître d' pulls out the chair for me and tucks me under the table as Finley sits opposite me. "Would you like something to drink?" he asks as he places a menu before each of us.

"Just water, please," Finley says, and I ask for the same before looking at the menu.

"What the fuck is a mung bean?" I ask incredulously, and he laughs softly across from me.

"Not a fucking clue, but apparently this place loves them."

He isn't wrong. What even is this place?

At least they have steak. Can't go wrong with steak.

Finn stiffens in front of me as he looks over my shoulder and reaches over to take my hand. "Don't look now, she'll see you, but Lincoln saw us already, too."

My back stiffens and I swear I can feel the heat of Linc's gaze even though I keep my eyes on Finley.

A server drops off our water and I focus back on the menu, trying not to look around at where they're sitting.

"I spy with my little eye," Finley says, and I look up to find him smirking at me. "A politician dining with an escort."

My eyes go wide and I look over in the direction he nods.

"This place is discreet about pretty much everything," he adds while I laugh softly.

"How do you know she's an escort?" I ask and instantly regret it.

The laughter in his eyes dims a little. "My father."

"Sorry."

"Don't be," he says, shaking his head. "Did you decide if you're having the mung bean soup, or the tortilla chips with mung bean dip?"

I laugh softly at him. "I need to pop to the bathroom, but I'm thinking the charcuterie board to start and steak for the main course?"

"I was thinking the same." He grins. "I'll order if they come by while you're gone."

He kisses the inside of my wrist before releasing my hand as I stand and work my way across the dimly lit restaurant to the bathroom.

Thankfully, it's empty, and I lean against the door of the stall for a minute just to catch my breath.

I can do this.

Fuck knows I've done worse.

Though tonight is like self-inflicted torture. Even if hanging with Finley is fun.

"Octavia."

I startle at the sound of Lincoln's voice, followed by the sound of the main door to the bathroom locking.

"You shouldn't be in here," I hiss as I open the door and find him standing there, hands in pockets, looking like he gives exactly zero fucks.

"Yeah well," he shrugs. "Want to play a game?"

"A game? Aren't we already playing enough games tonight?"

His eyes sparkle. "Not like this one."

He pulls a hand from his pocket and opens it.

"Is that a vibrating egg?" I squeak.

"Want to play?"

He can't be serious… can he?

"What's the game?" I ask, curious.

"I keep the remote, and you have to try not to come until you leave."

I smirk at him, tempted. "Pretty sure I shouldn't be your focus tonight."

"Fuck her," he growls. "The only person I want to focus on is you. She's snakey enough to not really require my attention. She talks enough for us both. Now do you want to play or not?"

I bite my lip, torn between what I should do and what I want to do.

"Fuck it," I say, holding out my hand.

He shakes his head and kneels, lifting one foot over his shoulder, kissing the inside of my thigh, biting down before moving toward the apex of my thighs. He runs a finger from my clit to my slit and grins up at me. "You're already so wet."

"What can I say? I like games."

He pushes the egg inside of me, kissing my pussy before putting my leg back down and standing up to tower over me. He shows me the small black remote and pushes a button.

Holy shit.

I grip his arms as the vibration rocks through me, a moan slipping from my lips. “I told you I’d make you pay.” He winks and kisses me hard and quick before disappearing from the bathroom.

I might regret the decision to play, but I’m not about to back down.

I just have to work out how to let Finn in on the game.

By the time I get back to the table, there’s a glass of red wine at my setting and Finley is sipping a glass of whiskey. I raise a brow as I slip into my seat, acutely aware of the egg inside of me. “How did this happen?”

“Lincoln sent them over on his way to the bathroom.” He smirks. “I hear we’re playing a game.”

Heat spills across my cheeks as I nod.

“I do love games.” His eyes sparkle. “Especially tag team ones. Now then, where were we?”

---

We fall through the door of the house laughing. Tonight was definitely not what I expected it to be. I feel bad that Lincoln looked so miserable all night, but I’m pretty sure the drink I spilled over his date was the highlight of his evening. Though I did lose our game, much to his and Finn’s delight. Coming as I ate my chocolate torte for dessert was definitely an experience. As was Finley removing the egg in the back of the Uber that brought us home. He had a few drinks, so we decided that was the best plan. We can pick up his car tomorrow.

I kick off my stilettos and shut off the alarm, feeling Finn’s heat against my back before he softly presses his lips against the curve of my neck.

I gasp as a shiver runs down my spine, when his hands flutter down my ribs. Panic hits me that Smithy might find us, but then I remember he’s spending the weekend with Matthew and relax under Finn’s touch.

He spins me around to face him and presses me up against the wall. “I need you, V.”

His words are more of a growl than anything as he kisses me, trailing down my neck, and across my chest until he reaches the sweetheart neckline of my dress. A thought sparks in my mind and I grin. I’ve already been at *their* mercy tonight.

Now it’s my turn.

“Upstairs,” I whisper and he lifts me from my feet, taking off up the stairs at a run. Apparently the whiskey after dinner has him looser than usual, and that works entirely in my favor. He places me on my feet at the end of the bed, turning me from him and unzips my dress, caressing my back with his lips as he drags the zipper down.

“Do you trust me?” I ask, barely more than a whisper, and he stills. I turn to face him, resting my hands on his chest, before moving to unbutton his shirt. He sucks in a breath as my fingers whisper against his bare chest.

“You know I do.” His breath becomes ragged as I move my hands down his chest to the belt of his slacks. I unbuckle him and push them and his boxers down before dropping to my knees in front of him, palming his dick.

When I look up at him, his gaze is on me with an intensity that makes my skin prickle with lust and need. Without taking my eyes off him, I bring the head of his cock to my lips and kiss the top. Engulfing it in my mouth, I suck it like a lollipop, licking it on all sides before darting my tongue in the slit. Finn sucks a breath in through his teeth like he's in pain, but I know better. There's something incredibly sexy about watching the one you love give you pleasure. The visual is part of the erotic fantasy.

One of Finn's hands comes to the top of my head as he tries to take control, but I stop my movements, let go of his cock, and pop a brow at his action.

"No one said you could touch me, Finn. This is my game. Just enjoy the ride." It's Finn's turn to cock a brow, surprised by my audacity. He's always in control and I get it, but tonight? Tonight, I want to be the one working him over. I want him to be able to just let it all go as I make him come.

I didn't think it would work, but I'm thrilled when I feel his hand release my hair and watch as he balls his fists at his sides, eyes like a hawk, watching me with unmistakable desire.

My fingers tighten around his shaft as I bring his cock back into my mouth, licking the underside and circling the head before I pop it back into my mouth, sucking him off as a thrill runs through me, knowing I can bring him to his knees like this.

"Fuck," I hear him mutter, his lips parted and his nostrils flaring. It's fucking hot to see his reaction, this raw need in every one of his muscles. It all just spurs me on.

Speeding up my hand motions, I move closer to him, needing his body heat closer as I place both of my hands on his ass cheeks as leverage as I sink my mouth onto his dick, choking on his girth and not caring that my eyes are watering.

Finn reaches up and with a tender touch and a loving smile on his lips, he uses the pad of his thumb to wipe away a tear from my cheek.

It makes the romantic in me swoon and also makes the slut in me hornier than ever.

"V, I don't want to come in your mouth, baby. Please." Looking back up at him, I give his dick one more suck, using my tongue to swipe at his precum before, once more, kissing the top of his cock and sitting on my haunches as I smile up at Finn like the good girl he loves.

"Fuck, when you look at me like that, I want to—" I cut him off before he gets too carried away. I'm not done playing with my tenuous grasp on control yet.

"Still my turn, Finn. On the bed." He hesitates, his mind warring between his need for control and his desire to meet and exceed my every desire.

"Octavia." One word. It's a warning but also a plea. He's asking me to not take advantage. He's begging me not to take it too far, and I won't.

After a few seconds, I release a breath of relief when Finn steps out of his pants, shucking his shirt, and makes his way to the bed. He's lying down with his arms folded behind his head, his big body on display making my mouth water and brain melt for a second before I spring into action. His posture screams control so I feel I need to bring him down a notch.

Finn watches me intently as I make my way to my secret drawer of toys and come back out with a silk scarf. At first, he's confused and I can see his mind working a mile a second. I know the exact moment he realizes what I'm about to do. His entire body tenses, his eyes narrowing into slits as he stares at the scarf, and I fear I may have gone too far.

"I promise, I will never go too far. If you need to break free, you'll be able to." I wait for him to make a decision and little by little, as his body sinks back down onto the mattress, I send a silent thank you to the universe for giving me a chance.

With my dress completely unzipped, I let it fall off my shoulders and let my bare feet carry me back to the bed, crawling on top of him until I'm straddling his chest.

"Give me your wrists." He only hesitates for a fraction of a second before he presents me with his upturned hands. I place a kiss on the inside of one wrist, then the other, before I place the scarf on them and make two revolutions before bringing them up above his head and to the headboard. I tie the scarf around the wood, making a knot loose enough that he can free himself if things get too intense for him.

I have to respect his limits all the while trying to push them.

"Now what, V? I'm at your mercy. What are you going to do with me?" His voice is pure sex. Dark and honeyed with a hint of danger that makes me so wet I'm sure I'm going to find a wet spot on his chest beneath me.

"Anything I want."

His grin is wolfish, like he's on board but also knows that anything he's not okay with is going to stop and I'm going to pay the price in multiple orgasms. Which, honestly, I'm totally okay with.

I lean in and kiss his forehead, his eyelids, one cheek, then the other. By the time I reach his mouth, he's seeking out my lips, pulling on his restraints trying to get to me.

"Hmm, you're so impatient." I'm trying to use my sexy vixen voice, but it all comes out in a shaky breath because he may be impatient, but I'm not exactly the poster child for patience, either.

What a pair we make.

I kiss him with every fiber of my being, making sure he knows that all of this is a safe space and I would never do anything that isn't built on love and respect.

He gives as good as he gets, our tongues dancing around each other, lips frantic with our kisses. Panting, I back away just enough that he can't reach me before I go back in and kiss his chin, earning a groan from him.

I guess he likes kissing me.

I kiss his neck, slowly making my way back down his chest before I reach the flat disk of his nipple and tease it with my tongue, before doing the same thing to the other.

Backing up, I feel his thick girth sliding between my pussy lips so I move, intentionally coating his shaft with my juices. Back and forth, back and forth, until he's growling at me to just fuck already.

"Tsk, tsk, Finn. No topping from the bottom. I seem to remember that you don't like it when I get sassy with you." I can't deny that I'm loving this.

"Not the same, V." No, I suppose it's not, and yet…

Placing both of my hands on his chest, I let my hair fall all around us as I sink onto his cock, slowly and torturously. As soon as I bottom out, we both sigh in relief.

“Fuck, that feels incredible.”

I agree, it’s been too long and I needed this.

Lifting myself up, I stop just before the head of his cock slides out then push myself back down on him. Once, twice, I do this to get him at the edge of his sanity before I bring my entire body on top of his and kiss his neck as the rest of my body rubs against him, fucking him oh so slowly. I can hear him losing his ever-loving mind, panting his controlled breaths. I’m pretty sure he’s trying to keep his hands bound, trying to show me how much he trusts me, letting me do whatever the fuck I want with his body.

Nibbling his neck, I start getting lost in my own game, actually needing him to touch me, to dig the pads of his fingers into my flesh while I fuck him until we both lose our minds.

We’re both coated in sweat but I know I’m about to lose at my own game. As much as I love the control, I also love when his big hands are all over me.

From below me, Finn thrusts his hips up, making sure he goes as deep as possible, making sure I’m getting the friction I need on my clit. Making sure I feel the utter power of him. Inside and out.

With a quick flick of my wrist, I undo the tie and within seconds, he has me on my back, fucking me into the mattress, his mouth attacking me with desperation and need. I’m his and he’s mine. And this moment, as tender as it began, is now a mass of clenching fingers and entwined legs. A series of moans and groans with hurried kisses and painless bites.

“Fuck, everything about you, V.” His words don’t make sense, but what is missing in his speech is said by his body. He’s hurried, chasing our joint orgasm because he won’t come without me. Never has, never will.

My back arches, my head is thrown back, my eyes closed tight as the fireworks of blues and yellows and pinks and reds explode behind my lids. I think I scream but I’m not quite sure because all I hear is Finn’s roar as his climax takes over his entire body. He’s shaking and jackhammering inside me as I coat his cock with my juices. It’s only when I come back down from that moment that I realize my nails had dug into the skin of his back.

Eyes wide, I search out his gaze, hoping I didn’t go too far, or betray his trust, but he just smirks at me.

“Beautiful, digging your nails into my back while you come all over my dick is more than okay.”

# CHAPTER EIGHTEEN

## OCTAVIA

Maverick arrived in the middle of the night and crawled into bed with Finn and I, so when I wake up sandwiched between them, it takes me a moment to become coherent and remember where we are.

The soft sunlight filters in through my windows, and I try to shimmy down the length of the bed so as not to disturb either of them. It's hard not to laugh at myself as I wriggle like a nutcase until I slink onto the floor, grabbing my robe before heading to the bathroom down the hall. No point in going through that effort if I'm just going to wake them up by using the bathroom.

I pad downstairs once I'm done and set up the coffee pot, staring out as the sun climbs into the sky. I should definitely still be asleep, but apparently my body has other ideas.

Once the pot finishes, I pour a mug and head out into the back yard, sitting on one of the patio chairs, enjoying the early morning sun. I close my eyes and bask in the warm rays, the quiet of the morning so peaceful it's as if the world is standing still.

"Fancy seeing you here so early."

I squeak as I startle, opening my eyes and finding the Saint brothers watching me, almost identical smiles on their faces. It's hard to come to terms with the fact that they have different fathers when they look so alike. I guess they have more of Fiona in them than they realized.

"Why are you both here? What's wrong?" I ask, standing as they approach.

Linc stays beside East, watching him like a hawk as he moves toward me. "Nothing's wrong. I have rehab shortly, Linc is taking me, but I wanted to see you before we go. And he might not say it, but he wanted to see you too."

I smile softly as East reaches me and pulls me into his arms. I close my eyes and sigh as I wrap my arms around him, holding as tight as I dare. "How are you feeling?"

"I could be worse," he murmurs into my hair. "How are *you* feeling?"

I smile against his chest. "I could be worse, too."

"Breakfast?" I ask as I pull back.

East's eyes crinkle at the edges as he looks down at me. "Not if you're cooking."

"Meanie," I tease, laughing a little. "Finley and Maverick are in bed; we all know Finley is the whizz in the kitchen with you out of action. I'll volunteer him as tribute."

"Sounds good. I'm going to go grab a cup of coffee," he says, cupping my cheek and kissing me softly before he leaves me alone with Lincoln.

"Hi," I say with a small wave, feeling almost awkward. Which is a tad ridiculous, but with his date last night hanging between us, even with our game, I'm not sure where to start this morning. Do I ask him if he kissed her? Do I let myself wallow in the misery and jealousy of not knowing?

What are the rules here?

"Morning," he says, his voice low and growly. "Did you have a good evening?"

"It was positively stimulating," I quip. "Did you?"

His eyes narrow, his gaze raking over my very thin robe before he stalks toward me. "I've never been more jealous of Finley in my life."

His low words send goosebumps skittering across my skin as he closes the distance between us, and I can't tell if the heat on my skin is from him or the sun.

"Pretty sure you were still the guy in charge," I say, looking up into his storm-cloud eyes. They seem darker this morning, as if burdened even more than usual. "Was everything okay after we left?"

"You mean after you accidentally knocked into that server and Georgia wore the tray of drinks? Was probably a highlight of the evening." He smirks, before sighing. "Yes, everything was okay after you left."

I bite down on my lower lip, chewing it to stop the questions spilling from my lips. He uses the pad of his thumb to pull my lip from my teeth and leans down to nip it himself. "What do you want to know, Octavia? I'm not going to have secrets between us where she is involved."

His gaze is so intense, I think I might burn up from the inside out. How does he always know the right thing to say? I battle with myself about asking, hating that I sound like *that* girl. Especially when I literally just kissed East in front of him.

"Did you kiss her?"

The corners of his lips tilt upwards, and I clutch at his t-shirt. "I didn't kiss her, and I have zero intention of letting her touch me in any way that is avoidable."

While I feel better that he didn't kiss her, the rest of his sentence doesn't exactly fill me with joy. Avoidable isn't always going to mean no.

He leans down and kisses me softly. "All I could think about the entire night was you. You plague my every waking thought, and my dreams, Octavia. If it was my choice, I would see no one but you for the rest of my existence and be happy."

He kisses me again and I tangle my fingers in the back of his hair, letting his arms take my weight as he holds me flush to him.

"If you're done, Shakespeare, coffee is ready," Maverick's teasing tone breaks our moment before he laughs and I hear the door close.

"He is lucky I love him like a brother," Lincoln grumbles into my neck before releasing me. "Come on, we should go in. I need to catch up with him about last night too. When did he come here?"

"About two in the morning. He grabbed a shower then crawled into bed with Finn and me. Where was he last night?"

"Come on," he says, linking my fingers with his. "We're going to cover it over breakfast anyway."

I nod and let him lead me inside, grabbing my coffee mug from the patio table, finding Mav and East sitting at the counter while Finley is at the stove. "Oh God, that smells so good."

I move over to Finn, putting my mug on the counter before kissing him between the shoulder blades as he flips the sausage on the griddle.

"Morning, beautiful." His voice is still full of sleep, but he looks over his shoulder, smiling down at me. "I figured you'd be hungry after last night."

His eyes twinkle with mischief and I love it. "I'm always hungry," I tease, running my fingertips down his ribs. "But you already know that."

He growls lowly and a shiver of excitement runs through me, making my toes curl. I'm glad he's coming around to my touch, especially when I get to tease him. It's fun prodding them all sometimes.

I kiss his back again before refilling my mug and sitting at the counter. The three of them are already muttering away about something sports related so I tune out and just enjoy this moment of peace. It feels like it's been a hot minute since we were all together and there was nothing urgent hanging above us.

It feels like the first time we've all been together, and in once piece since before I was taken… before East was shot.

I shake off the thought, tuning back into the moment with my guys, and just enjoy the fact that we're all here, alive and somewhat healthy.

Finley dishes up breakfast, kissing my cheek as he sets a plate in front of me before taking the seat next to mine. He looks over at Mav, who is teasing Lincoln about God only knows what, before speaking. "What happened last night?"

They all fall silent, and the light in Mav's eyes dims a little. "What do you mean?"

"I mean, you don't typically crawl into bed with V after a job… so what went wrong?" Finn's voice is soft, but firm at the same time. It'd be hard to miss how much he cares for Mav, even with the forceful tone.

*He's worried.*

Should I be worried?

"Job went okay. That bit was fine," he says, letting out a deep sigh. "It was after, when Harrison cornered me, and told me he wants to see V at the next meeting. That's when shit went sideways."

"He wants what?" I gulp, my appetite disappearing.

Lincoln frowns, but it's East who speaks. "Why would he ask you rather than Lincoln?"

"Because he didn't want to distract me from Georgia," Lincoln says, his jaw clenched.

"What does this mean?" I ask, trying not to sound as on edge as I feel with my heart like a jackhammer against my ribs.

"It means," Lincoln says slowly, "that they've decided to honor the contract."

---

After a tense Saturday of worrying about what Maverick told us over breakfast, then spending yesterday doing some self-defense training with him and Finley in the cage—after Smithy let me know he's taken my advice and is extending his trip—I've decided to try and not worry about it. What will be will be and all that.

It's also like telling water not to be wet, but I'm trying.

Which is exactly why I'm sipping mocktails around my pool with Indi, trying to enjoy the first day of spring break as we soak up some of the early year sun.

"Do you guys have many plans for the week off?" Indi asks before taking a sip of her mango and passionfruit concoction.

"Nothing that I know of yet. To be honest, I'm looking forward to some down time."

She nods. "I get that. I managed to get Ryker to agree to some time away, so we're going for a long weekend from Thursday. Heading back east for a few days. Showing them New York City and some of my old favorite places. I hate that we couldn't all do a group thing, but with my guys still being pissed about the Alex thing..."

She trails off and I wave her off. "Honestly it's fine, and that sounds like fun!" I'm happy for her, truly. She also deserves a break. As if senior year isn't enough of a stressor without everything else we've dealt with on top of it. "I can't wait till summer, we really do need to do a girls trip."

"You know I'm totally on board for that." She grins, and I start making mental plans.

"Just tell me your wishlist, we'll work it out."

She nods, putting her glass back down, and pulls her sunglasses down her nose, peering at me over them. "You going to tell me what's got you so stressed?"

I let out a deep sigh. I thought I'd managed to cover it pretty well, but I should've known better, she reads me like a book every freaking time. "The Conclave wants to see me."

"What the what now?" she exclaims, sitting up.

I run her through everything Lincoln told me about the deal my dad made to get him and me out, and how Panda trying to free me essentially just tied me to them instead.

"That is so fucked up." She runs a hand through her glossy locks and bites her lip. "I realize the answer is probably no, but is there anything I can do?"

I smile at her and shake my head. "No, I'm not even sure what they want. Even if Lincoln thinks they are honoring the contract, I don't see Harrison Saint handing the keys to his kingdom over to me, do you?"

"Not really." She shrugs. "Have you heard anything more about your uncle?"

"Honestly, I haven't really been digging for information. They're family in biology only. He made his bed, and he can lie in it. I know Lincoln is putting Blair and Vi up at the cottage, but I only said yes because I hate the thought of them paying for Nate's major error in judgment."

"They don't deserve any of it. Though I'd do the same. We're too nice."

I smile softly. "I'd rather be too nice than be like most of the other people around here. My conscience is clear at least. I can't say there's no red in my ledger, but I also don't struggle to sleep because I fucked someone over."

"Amen to that," she says, raising her glass. "Do you have anything planned for tomorrow?"

"I don't think so. Smithy said he won't be back until Sunday, and the guys haven't mentioned anything."

"Good." She grins at me, and I almost regret not having plans. She looks positively wicked. "Ryker is giving me my first tattoo and I thought you might want to come."

"Ryker does tattoos?"

She nods, smiling softly. "He's done almost all of Ellis and Dylan's. A few of his own too. He's so freaking talented. He could have his own shop if he let himself see life outside of the Kings."

"Does Ryker know you're inviting me?" I ask, brow quirked.

She smirks. "I like to keep him on his toes. Plus I found these adorable bestie tattoos for us."

I let out a laugh. I've always wanted a tattoo, it's just not something I've ever taken the initiative to set up. Jenna always told me that she was hooked after her first, and I don't need that sort of addiction in my life.

"Sure, why not? I have a design I've always wanted, too."

She lets out a whoop. "Yeah, our bestie design won't be the first one to grace my skin, Ryker wants to paint on me first, but I'm excited! I can't wait to see your guys' faces when you tell them you let Ryker ink you."

I groan at the prospect. "Yeah, I'm probably going to give them a heads up. It won't stop me doing it, but it'll save them from bitching about secrets afterward."

I pick up my phone and pull up the group thread.

Me:

Heads up. I'm getting a tattoo with Indi tomorrow. By Ryker. No you don't get to have input, this is just me telling you.

Maverick:

As if he's the one getting to ink you. I'm coming. If anyone gets to grace your skin with pain, it's me.

I show Indi the screen and she giggles. "Saw that coming. Tell assface he's welcome to come."

Me:
Indi says you're welcome to come, but have you ever even tattooed someone else?

Maverick:
I haven't, but we can both be virgins again. I do like being your first *wink emoji*

East:
Have fun, just be careful. Can't wait to see it.

Finley:
I'm allowed to not want Ryker to see your tits right? *laugh emoji*

I let out a laugh, shaking my head. I mean, I always wanted under my boobs done, that doesn't count, right?

Me:
No tit tattoos happening. You're good.

Lincoln stays suspiciously quiet, but I think he's with Harrison so I don't fixate on it.

"Ryker says it's chill for Maverick to come. He'll even give him a rundown if you do want him to ink you first."

"Sounds good," I say, and reiterate it to Maverick.

Maverick:
Tell me when and I'll be there.

"Well, apparently we have a date." I laugh and she grins.

"Hell yeah we do. This is what I saw for us." She shows me her phone and the two arrow images, similar, but not identical.

They're beautiful.

"Ryker said he can do them easy enough, and they're small enough that we can put them almost anywhere. He also said if you send me a picture of your other design, he can set it up."

"Maybe we should start small, especially if Maverick wants to come and join in too."

"Sounds good. Just let me know, he's so freaking good. Pretty sure if he and Maverick got on better, they'd spend all their time together talking ink. Both of them are covered."

"Mav's is mostly his top half," I say, smiling softly.

"Yeah, Ryker is like, covered. It's fun to trace the lines though." She blushes and takes a sip of her drink. "Anyway, back to more serious talk because I don't want to be gooey and distracted. How is East doing?"

We spend the morning catching up, just hanging out like two teenagers should be able to, and I love the mundaneness of it all. Most people want to be anything but ordinary. Me? I'd do a lot for a chance at normal.

Indi heads home when her mom calls about their dinner date, so we make a date for early tomorrow morning at Ryker's for our ink adventure.

Once she's gone, I get dressed in a pair of cutoffs and a hoodie, plonking myself down on the sofa, attempting to watch TV but failing when my mind constantly wanders.

Maybe this meeting with the Conclave won't be so bad. Maybe they'll just release me and honor my dad's wishes.

If only dreams and wishes were more than air and dust.

They were after me before the Panda thing, which means they knowingly broke the contract, and if I had to bet on it, I'd say they were just hoping I was blissfully ignorant.

My stomach churns at the thought of what it is they could possibly want from me. What would possibly make them risk the terms of my dad's agreement? I wasn't joking earlier, there is no way Harrison wants to hand over his place as Regent, so risking it must mean that whatever they want is huge.

I bite my lip, running over the possibilities, knowing that it's unlikely I'm going to work it out.

All I can do is hope that whatever it is doesn't come at a cost I'm not willing to pay.

---

After spending most of the day spiraling, a text from Bentley—the PI I hired to look into Mom—was out of the blue, but welcome. I'm definitely not pacing in my foyer while I wait for him to arrive.

Nope.

Definitely not.

I jump when the buzzer interrupts my thoughts and find Bentley looking through the camera at the gate. I buzz him in and open the front door.

Not even impatient.

"Miss Royal, it's good to see you," Bentley says politely as he climbs the steps to the house. His casual look is the same as he had when I saw him last time, with his black hair looking like he's mussed his hands through it all day, and his dark, almond-shaped eyes warm as he smiles at me. "Shall we?"

I nod, trying to shut up the butterflies that are hurricaning in my stomach, and step back to let him into the house. His smile might've been to try and help set me at ease, but there's no chance of that happening right now. I lead him through to the kitchen, feeling super awkward. "Drink?"

"Coffee would be great." He smiles warmly before pulling a folder out of the bag in his hand. I pour us both a mug, handing him his, grabbing the sugar and creamer should he want them and putting them on the island before sitting at the counter. "Shall I begin?"

"Sure, why not? That's what I'm paying you for, right?" I laugh nervously. It's not that I'd forgotten about the task I gave him, I've just had a lot of other stuff occupying my mind. My mom hasn't exactly been a major blip on my radar for years. She left us and never looked back. As far as I know anyway. If it wasn't for everything happening with the Knights, I probably never would have searched for her.

But what Panda said about her niggles in the back of my mind, though I'm not sure how trustworthy he truly was at that stage.

"So, I found quite a bit," he starts, opening the folder, and laying out a ton of photos and documents. "In the early years after her separation from your father, she left a frivolous trail. There was no party too exclusive, no shop too expensive."

He hands me credit card records, photos, and clippings from newspapers and magazines.

*How have I never seen any of these photos?*

Something to focus on later.

"But then, around your thirteenth birthday, she seems to have fallen off the face of the earth. I can see where she started trying to wipe her digital print, which isn't easy these days, but if you're good with technology, it's not impossible." He pauses, watching me closely. "But then it all just goes dark. No more parties. No more shopping. No fancy vacations. She fell off the grid entirely, and I have yet to find even a whisper of where she went after that."

I gulp, bringing my coffee cup to my lips even though I don't take a sip. The movement is almost automatic.

"Now I can keep searching, and I'm happy to, but I've spent the last two weeks digging into where she could have gone, and I've come up empty. Unless you have any more details, I'm not sure what luck I'm going to have. I wouldn't want to waste your time or your money."

"I appreciate that," I say quietly. "There's no record of her death either, I assume?"

He shakes his head. "No, nothing at all."

I blow out a deep breath, running a hand through my hair. "Okay, thank you. I don't think continuing to search is going to be of any use if you've already tried and come up empty. You don't seem like the sort of man who chases his tail."

He grins at me and I catch a glimpse of ruthlessness. "I'm not, but I'm also not one to give up so easy either."

I nod, he doesn't seem the type to just quit. "Thank you, I appreciate all of your help."

"If you need anything else at all, you have my number." I stand and shake his offered hand before walking him out.

Once I'm alone, I take everything he brought to me and lay it out over the coffee table, poring over it to see if I can see anything that he hadn't. Any faces that might raise suspicion. Either to confirm or deny what Panda implied.

But there is nothing. I don't recognize any of these people.

I barely recognize my mother.

Letting out a sigh, I put everything back in the folder Bentley brought to me and tuck it away. Maybe she *is* dead, maybe Edward killed her and my dad, just like Panda said, but I still have zero proof of anything.

Giving up I pull out my phone and send a message to Lincoln. Maybe he can get some answers I can't. Or maybe Harrison will tell him the truth of what happened to my father.

I would just like to put my nightmares to rest, even if the truth isn't what I want to hear.

Because when it comes down to choosing whether your dad killing himself or being murdered is a better outcome, life is already all kinds of fucked up.

---

"Are you nervous? I'm nervous. We have nothing to be nervous about right?" Indi's mindless babble as we head to Ryker's in the Wrangler does nothing but make me smile.

"I mean, if assface back there can get a tattoo, I can. Right?"

"Don't you start with me, Pixie Spice." Mav grins and I pinch the bridge of my nose. These two in a small enclosed space might not be the best, even if it is funny watching them bicker like an old married couple.

"Don't call me Pixie Spice, dick for brains."

He grins at me in the rearview. "It's good dick though."

I don't bother containing my snicker.

"So good she laughs about it," Indi snarks with an eye roll before winking at me. I love how far she's come. From cowering to him, to enjoying sniping at him. "We're here."

She pulls the car to the curb and shuts off the engine, bouncing from the car when Ryker appears in the doorway of the house.

"Princess," Maverick says, touching the top of my arm, making me pause. "You sure you're good with this?"

He makes my heart burst, I swear to God.

"I'm good. I won't let what happened hold me back. Plus you're here too. I know you've got me if I need a minute."

He watches me intently before nodding and climbing from the car. I follow suit, taking his hand as I close the door to the Wrangler and head toward where Indi is waiting with Ryker. Dylan appears behind them, all smiles. "Glad to see you two joining the party today."

I wave at him with a soft smile, Mav heading inside with him and Ryker, while Indi holds back, waiting for me. "Ready?"

I grin at her. "Are you?" She pulls me into the house and we head down into the basement, following the guys. Mav looks back, as if making sure I'm still here, as he talks up a storm with Dylan.

"I'm a little nervous, but yes. I asked Dylan to be here, to help keep the peace. Ellis will call Ryker on his shit, but that usually turns into a whole twin thing. Whereas Dylan has zero issues with your guys."

"That's some diplomacy skills at work, my friend."

Ryker pops his head out of one of the three doors that lead to smaller rooms in the basement, gaze searching for Indi. "You ready?"

She takes a deep breath and nods. We head into the well-lit room which looks like a mini tattoo studio.

"Huh, this looks…" I trail off as she grins at me.

"Painting on skin isn't something I fuck around with," Ryker grunts. "It's too easy to get infected or fuck shit up. So this place is all coded and set up the same way any professional shop is. This is just easier, and more fun for me."

The wicked smile that graces his lips practically drips with sin as his eyes dance with mischief.

"Who's going first?"

Indi pops her ass into the chair and wiggles around until she's sitting in it properly. "Me."

"I redrew your arrows, because I'm not putting someone else's design on your skin," he tells her, and she rolls her eyes at him.

"Well, let me see it then," she teases, and he pulls a sketchbook from the counter behind him, handing it to her. She waves me over, and Mav follows closely behind.

This room is not made for this many people.

"That's so good!" I exclaim, trying not to sound as shocked as I feel. I know Indi said that he was talented, but shit. Something so simple, yet so beautiful.

Rather than one arrow, it's two crossed over, an infinity symbol at the crossing, sitting on top of a pink to blue watercolor puddle.

"I figured you could change the colors if you wanted, but this was what I saw in my head."

She grins at me before turning back to him. "I love it. So freaking much. Thank you."

"Okay, well then, let's get started." he says, picking up the tattoo gun on the tray beside the table. "You good with those colors?"

"Yep!" she says, popping her p. "V?"

I nod, leaning back onto Maverick as he wraps his arms around my waist. "I might lose the pink, go more for a green, but otherwise I'm good."

"Where you putting it, princess?"

I chew on my lip, leaning toward the side of my wrist or back of my neck. "What do you think, Indi? Wrist? Neck?"

"I'm thinking foot, though I like the wrist idea. Side of?"

"Ooooo, Pixie Spice is brave," Maverick teases and she flips him the bird.

I shake my head, and focus back on my girl. "Side of the wrist is where I was thinking."

"Decision made then."

Ryker nods. "Okay, well I'm free-handing your other design. We still doing your hip?"

She nods and I take Mav's hand as Ryker glares at us while she unbuttons her jeans. "Come on, let's wait outside."

"You don't have to," Indi says, her gaze flitting back to Ryker's glare.

"It's good." I squeeze her hand. "I'll be just outside."

"You can stay," Mav whispers in my ear. "I'll go play Xbox with Dylan for a bit. Just holler at me before you get in that chair." He kisses my cheek before leaving the room, closing the door behind him.

Ryker nods at me before the buzz of the gun starts up and Indi takes my hand. She hisses as the needles touch her skin, her grip squeezing the life out of my hand.

I watch Ryker work, mesmerized as he draws on her skin. Indi clamps her jaw together, and I think this might be the longest I've been around her with her not talking unless she's asleep.

Once he's finished the first piece, he shows it to her and tears fill her eyes.

It's stunning.

An anchor, lying beside a compass. More watercolor blues behind it, and the words, *'Let your past be your compass, but never your anchor.'*

I get the feeling there is more to that than I know, but I squeeze her hand back, a giant grin on my face. I feel a little better about Ryker's skills having seen it, and my nerves disappear.

"Ready for part two?" he asks her softly.

"Can we pause for a minute? Let Mav do V's first one or something?"

He watches her closely, as if searching for something hidden in her words. "Sure thing."

I open the door and find Mav and Dylan in a heated COD war, grinning as they shoot shit at each other.

"You still want to mark my skin?" I ask, and Dylan lets out a whoop as Maverick gets distracted. He rolls his eyes as he drops the controller, but still grins as he swaggers toward me.

"Princess, I always want to mark your skin." His eyes heat as he reaches me, kissing me until my toes curl.

"Come on, love birds," Dylan teases. "Ink first, fuckery when you're not here."

Indi pads out of the room, her hip wrapped.

"How you feeling, Pix?" Mav asks and she shakes her head, trying not to smile.

"I'm fine, go get your girl ready." She sits gingerly next to Dylan who wraps an arm around her shoulders.

Mav takes my hand and pulls me back into the room with Ryker, who's wiping down the chair.

"You sure you want to let him ink you?" Ryker asks as I take a seat, looking at Maverick skeptically. "It's not as easy as it looks, and it's easy to fuck up."

Mav laughs. "Oh I know. I'm just going to do a tiny line image. You can fancy it up. But I know you get it. Would you have let anyone else tattoo Indi first?"

Ryker's eyes darken. "Fair point."

Maverick shows him the design we picked together, and I tune them out as Ryker walks Maverick through all his shit, way more professional about it than I would've imagined. I guess when something is your art, your passion, you take it seriously. It's no different than my dad and his music. It seems easy from the outside, but the hours, the blood, sweat, and tears, those are the things that people don't see. It's more than just something you do, it's like a living, breathing part of you.

"Ready, princess?" Maverick asks, looking confident as ever.

"I think so."

Ryker prints out the design, and I lift my top, revealing my ribs. "You two sure are gluttons for punishment. Both going for two of the most painful spots for your first time. You sure you want it on your ribs?"

"I'm sure," I say with a firm nod. "The other side still has my stitches, but this side is all good."

He nods and places the paper against my skin, rubbing it over until the purple pen lies on my skin. The birds span across from just under my boob and around my ribs upwards with the words '*Not all those who wander are lost.*'

"Tolkien is a master of words," Ryker says as he pulls away. "Don't attempt the script. Just start with a bird, I'll deal with the rest."

Mav nods and sits on the stool beside the chair, tattoo gun in one hand, the other splayed across my ribs. He looks so intent on getting it right that I relax a little. The buzz starts up and I close my eyes, sucking in a breath as the sting across my ribs starts.

It's a weird kind of pain. Almost not like pain at all.

Maverick hands the gun over to Ryker after a few minutes, moving to the other side of the chair and taking my hand, all while watching Ryker work.

I lose track of time, and when the buzzing stops, I let out a deep breath, admiring the artwork on my skin. "It's beautiful, thank you."

Indi bursts in the door, like she's been not-so-patiently waiting, and grins when she sees my ribs.

"Stunning," she says as she bounces over toward Ryker. "Ready for round two?"

I grin at her, shaking my head. "Why not."

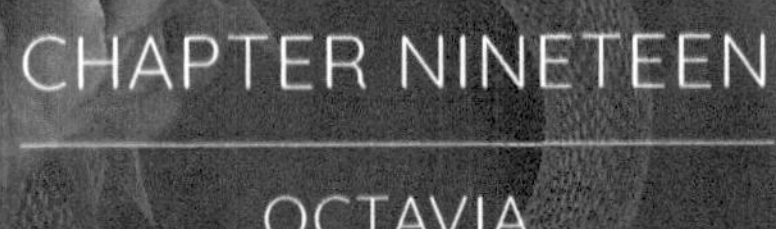

# CHAPTER NINETEEN

## OCTAVIA

"What do you mean you booked us a trip?" I blink at Lincoln across his kitchen table, trying to process everything. "We can't travel; East is still healing."

"I'm staying home," East says softly. "I have rehab and shit to get through, but it's Spring Break, and you all deserve a break."

"We can't go without you."

He takes my hand and kisses the inside of my wrist. "Yes you can. I want you to."

I purse my lips, guilt tugging at my heart, but the idea of a mini break does sound good.

"I mean, it's already booked, we leave this afternoon. You just need to pack," Lincoln says, shrugging as he takes a sip of his coffee. "Surprise?"

I bark out a laugh. "Of course." I sigh and look back over at East. "Are you sure you don't mind being left behind? It feels wrong going without you."

"We've got forever. A few days away isn't going to change that."

"You see," Linc says, "it's agreed. Now go pack."

I quirk a brow at him. "When has ordering me to do anything ever worked for you?"

"I can think of a few times," he says lowly, and a blush spills across my chest.

Asshole.

"Fine. Fine. I need to let Smithy know." I stand, pulling my phone from my pocket as I do. "I might need to go shopping."

"Anything you don't have, we can get when we're there. It's Mexico, not the middle of nowhere," Lincoln says, rolling his eyes at me. "Four nights doesn't require a shopping trip."

East grins at him. "It might."

"Okay, I can totally do this." I paint a smile on my face. I'm awesome at giving gifts, but receiving them… yeah I suck at that.

I kiss them both goodbye and start running through everything I'm going to need in my head. I fire a message off to Smithy to tell him what's happening, sending a similar one to Indi so she doesn't think I've just fallen off the face of the earth.

When I'm home, I drag a small suitcase out of the spare room closet and stare at it.

Can I really go away right now? We have zero answers about who Panda was working with. We don't know what the Knights want from me, and the meeting with them is still hanging over my head. We still don't know if what Panda said about Edward is true… and I didn't get any real answers about my mom.

Wow… when I put it like that, we haven't really achieved much. I know we've had a lot going on, and I'm recovering, all while trying to actually graduate high school, but goddamn we kind of suck at the moment.

I wonder if Linc has put it all together like that.

Who am I kidding? Of course he has. It's blatantly driving him insane, but he's also dealing with his father and the Georgia thing.

Maybe we really do need this break. Just a moment to push pause on the crazy of our lives and come back refreshed so we can actually get shit done.

Letting out a deep breath I drop onto the bed.

Is this really a good idea? Should we go away with everything hanging in the air like this?

"You up there, princess?" Maverick's voice echoes in the foyer, bringing a smile to my lips.

"Yeah, up here," I call out, my smile widening at the sound of his footsteps racing up the stairs.

He bursts into the room, full Superman pose, and I burst out laughing. "Psyched for our trip?"

"Feeling a little guilty about it. Wondering if it's a good time to go away with everything. But other than that… yes?"

His smile drops a bit and he moves to crawl onto the bed, pulling me back against him. "We deserve the break, V. *You* deserve the break. Yes, there's a lot going on, but this is the story of our lives. There is *always* a lot going on."

I snuggle into his chest. "I guess you're right. It just feels weird. I haven't even had my stitches out yet. East is in recovery. Should we be leaving him alone?"

"East will be fine, he's a big boy. Plus Chase has put a layer of protection over him Knight-wise, so he should be good. We'll only be gone a few days." His murmurs make me feel a little better. "Plus, the idea of you on a beach in a bikini for four days is my version of a living wet dream."

"You're incorrigible." I laugh, shaking my head.

"I am, but I'm also supposed to take you to see the doc before we fly, so get a shimmy on with your packing. Personally I'm happy for you to spend the entire trip naked, but I'm pretty sure you aren't going to approve of my plan."

"Definitely not." I scoot out of his arms and throw a few days' worth of stuff in the suitcase, along with an array of bikinis and anything else I might need, because a girl needs options. It doesn't take long to get packed once my decision is made. "I think I'm done."

"Awesome. Let's get you to the doc so Lincoln doesn't tear me a new one, then we'll meet him and Finn on the runway."

"How are we getting there?" I ask. Probably should've done that already.

He grins at me and I can't help but laugh at the devilish look on his face. "Linc spoke to Smithy… we're going in your jet."

"Works for me. I don't mind commercial, but life is so much easier flying private." I shrug. I get why he asked Smithy, he wanted it to be a surprise and we might as well use it. It's already paid for. "Okay, I'm good. Let's go to the doctors and get my ribs checked, shall we?"

"Your chariot awaits." He grins, waving me out of the room, my suitcase in his hand. I lift up on the balls of my feet and kiss his cheek.

Maybe this break is exactly what we need. I, for one, am going to use these four days to indulge in my three favorite F's.

*Food.*

*Fun.*

*Fuckery.*

I let out a sigh. Four days with three of my guys sounds like bliss when I let go of the rest of my baggage.

Here's hoping for smooth sailing.

---

The plane taxis onto the runway, a bumpier landing than I'd like, but vacation mode is fully in place, so I can't find it in me to care too much. The doctor took out my stitches, so I'm left with a faint line on my ribs, my other injuries are healing nicely, and she seemed happy with everything.

So I'm going to try and take advantage of these few days away from reality. Fuck knows I need the brain break. Leaving East at home sucked, but he wasn't cleared to fly, even though I asked at my appointment.

I swallow down the guilt and smile as Maverick grabs my bag. "Ready, princess?"

I look up at him, taking his outstretched hand. "Hell yes I am. Bring on the relaxation."

They usher me off of the plane and into the waiting car.

"You really thought of everything, didn't you?"

Lincoln smirks at me knowingly. "Did you even doubt me?"

Finley tucks me into his side and once everyone's inside, we pull off through the city. It takes about an hour to reach the resort, but the giant buildings make me feel like a kid again. I've traveled to a lot of places, but I don't know the last time I just went on vacation like this.

We climb from the car, and Lincoln heads inside to check us in while the greeter brings us watermelon smoothies that make me want to dance on the spot.

The heat is beautiful and the sun feels so good on my skin. I tilt my head back and close my eyes, just soaking up the rays.

"How you doing?" Finley asks quietly as he wraps his arms around me from behind. Resting my head back on his shoulder, I suck in a deep breath of the fresh air and smile. "Don't just tell me you're fine. These last few weeks have been insane. It hasn't even been a month since you were taken, and we've all been acting like everything is fine, just kept rolling with the punches. But I'm worried about you."

"I'm okay," I tell him honestly. "There's a lot to process, and I should probably journal or something just to get some of it out of my head, but I'm okay. I'm not sure if that means I haven't processed everything fully, or if I'm just repressing shit, but for right now, I just want to be here with you guys and enjoy these few days of bliss."

He kisses my neck, sending a shiver down my spine. "Okay but if you need to talk, I'm here. And if you don't want to speak to any of us, I know a good therapist."

Shock sparks in me, but I'm not about to judge him for talking to someone. "A Knight therapist?"

"She is a Knight, but not like the others. She's aware of the organization, but isn't a part of it. Doctor Patient confidentiality goes a long way."

"I'll think about it, thank you."

Lincoln appears, keycard in hand, looking almost relaxed. "Ready?"

I grin and nod as a golf-cart-style transport appears, the guy taking our bags before we climb in. There are only three other seats, so Maverick pulls me onto his lap, grinning at me as he does. I squeal as it takes off, Maverick laughing at me but tightening his grip anyway. We zoom through the giant resort, weaving through the villas and apartments, our driver pointing out various different pools and restaurants dotted around the place.

We pull up in front of a beach villa and the driver grabs our bags. Lincoln tips him before he zooms off, leaving us with our own little slice of paradise.

"Unpack and then beach?" Mav suggests, and I nod.

I am so ready for a little piece of peace.

---

This hotel room is *everything.* I mean, I have stayed in some very nice places all over the world, but it's like all of my favorite things about traveling have been put in one very sunny location. It helps that everything here is catered to full-scale relaxation, and I feel like we all need this in our lives.

Especially right now.

I still can't get over the fact that the four of them got together and planned this trip for me. I'm sad that East couldn't come, but I fully intend on spending a ton of time with him when we're home to thank him for his part in this.

I shut off the shower and wrap one of the big fluffy towels around me. There is something about a powerful shower after a day on the beach that is just revitalizing. I pad into the bedroom and find the three of them lounging in the room, waiting for me, in various states of undress. Even in Mexico, Finn hides his chest, and it hurts my heart. I hope one day, I can show him that his scars don't define him. That he doesn't have to hide. Until then, I'll just continue to respect his boundaries.

"Shower's free if you guys want it."

Maverick just laughs at me, shaking his head. "Princess, it took less time for each of us to shower in the other bathroom, than it took for you to shower in this one."

"Oh." I grin as a blush spills across my chest. "I'm not even sorry."

"We know." Lincoln smiles as I pad over to the dressing table. They go back to their conversation while I blow out my hair. It's impossible not to feel their heated stares on my skin. When I'm done, I realize they're all watching me silently, so I turn to face them, biting my lip.

Finn tilts his head, leaning forward in his seat, hands clasped. "Want to play?"

My eyes go wide at the three words.

I can't say I haven't thought about playing with all of them, especially after the fun on Maverick's birthday, but it's not something I've pushed. Each of them have their own… quirks. I'm not about to make them play together if they don't want to.

But I'm also not about to say no if it *is* something they're up for.

Standing, I untie my towel and let it fall to the ground. I own my body, curves and scars included, and catch each of their gazes. "Do *you* want to play?"

Lincoln's gaze fixes on the scar that runs across my ribs for a minute before looking back up at me. Everything in his eyes is exactly why I know I don't need to hide from them.

Not anymore.

"You are… there are few words to describe you aptly."

My entire body is on high alert—alive with those words—and judging by the various looks on their faces, mine is a visible reaction.

Lincoln is the first to stand, his lithe body unfurling like a panther, his gaze fixed on his prey.

That's me.

I'm the prey and the feeling of being hunted is, in this instance, exciting, exhilarating.

Finn and Maverick are next, flanking their fearless leader like the trio of danger that they are.

I bite my lower lip, playing coy and enjoying the flare in their eyes as all three pairs zero in on my lips.

I don't dare move because I know this is Lincoln's game. He always calls the shots, the moves, the positions.

Lincoln is the alpha of all alphas.

Finn secures their prey.

Maverick plays with it.

Together, their only focus is to make me come. Repeatedly.

"Get on the couch, Octavia. Legs spread so we can look at you." Lincoln's words are leveled—clear—and as if he's just set a chess game in motion, the others get into position. Finn and Mav take one step forward while Lincoln moves away to give me a wide berth like he's afraid of touching me—following me only with his calculating eyes.

When I reach the couch, I turn, sit, then instantly spread my legs so my pussy is in clear view for all of them.

Hungry eyes stare back at me, hard dicks clearly outlined behind their clothes.

Linc looks over to the guys and without a word, they both come and kneel on either side of me, following his silent command.

Mav's the first to move, wrapping one hand around my wrist and bringing my palm to his cock, rubbing it—harder than I ever would—thrusting his hips into my hold.

Finn mimics Mav's moves after taking my wrist to his lips first—kissing it reverently—before bringing my hand to his impossibly hard dick. I turn to look at one then the other before my gaze lands on Lincoln as he takes one last step closer and drops to his knees, his hands on the inside of my thighs.

I watch in rapt attention as Lincoln licks his thumb then his forefinger, before bringing both to my nipple and tweaking hard enough to make me flinch, but the pain feels so good.

"Fuck," Mav groans, his voice little more than a rumble.

"You should see how wet she is." Lincoln's eyes snap to mine, and he leans in and swipes his tongue through my slit before he lands on my clit and circles it agonizingly slowly.

I'm mesmerized but his steel gaze traps me in his snare. Telling me without a single word that I'm his.

That I'm theirs.

Mav and Finn rub their cocks on my hands, using the fabric of their clothes for friction, and before I understand what's happening, Mav hands my wrist to Finn who places it with my other, trapped together in one unbreakable hold.

In a heartbeat, Mav's lips are on mine, kissing me with an intensity that takes my breath away and just as quickly as he attacks, he's gone.

Finn does the same, swiping his tongue across my mouth—quickly delving inside—before he jumps over the back of the couch and stands behind me, my arms up and above my head.

The position makes my tits push out, my back arch, and my head lean heavily against the headrest.

I'm completely exposed. My thighs are held down, my cunt is being devoured, my arms are trapped above me, and my nipples are primed for the taking.

I practically drool as Maverick and Finn start to undress. Lincoln keeps my legs spread as he leans back and unbuttons his jeans just enough to free his cock through the V of the open zipper.

"How many times have you dreamed of this, Octavia?"

I don't have time to answer Linc's question, because Mav has my throat in a chokehold—fingers pressing down just below my ears with his thumb and middle finger.

"Her pulse is like a freight train. I'm guessing a whole fucking lot." My eyes dart to Mav, blinking to answer him. To tell him that, yes, I regularly dream of having them all at my mercy. That even when I'm not the one calling the shots, I'm still in charge.

Finn bends over my shoulder and takes my free nipple in his mouth, flicking the hard bud with his tongue, fast and erotic. It tears a moan from my lips earning me a chuckle from Linc.

"Fuck, I need to come or else I'm never going to last." Mav leans into my mouth, whispering on my lips. "Time to suck my cock, V. Nice and deep, the way you like it." I whimper at Mav's words, a sound that tells him I really do want to have it in my mouth.

"Such a good girl." Fuck, I love it when Linc calls me that.

My eagerness earns me a finger in my pussy, pushed in nice and deep. Twisting and scissoring like he's preparing me for something. For his cock?

God, I hope so. I'm so fucking ready to get fucked, right now.

Mav licks the seam of my mouth before trapping my bottom lip between his teeth and biting hard enough to hurt.

Then he's gone.

I've got one finger pushing and retreating, turning and twisting inside my pussy while Finn continues to lave my nipples. One, then the other. Electricity runs through my veins. As if my nerve endings are on fire.

"Fuck her mouth, Mav."

I lick my lips and open up for him as requested, anticipation running through me that this is actually going to happen.

Finn grabs me by my upper arms and turns me so I'm lying down on the couch. Linc follows me, finger fucking me without losing a beat.

Contrary to what I'm anticipating, Finn doesn't place my head on a cushion, he lets it hang off the armrest—hair hanging freely toward the floor—face up, mouth still open and ready.

Finn brings my arms to my stomach, his order loud and clear when he squeezes my wrists together. "Don't move."

"Jesus fucking Christ, look at her." Mav is right there at the side of my face, his dick caressing my cheek before he places the head of his cock at my lips and runs it around like he's painting them.

Then he pushes inside. Slowly, until my nose is against his groin, the hair tickling my nose and depriving me of my breath as he grabs my hair and fucks my face for a second too long.

"Give me your tears, V. Fucking give them to me."

Lincoln adds another finger to my pussy, fucking me harder and harder as Mav places his hand on my throat—massaging the column—like he's trying to feel his cock.

Finn steps away and Mav practically straddles my face from behind, his balls heavy on the bridge of my nose, like he wants to fuck my throat, and I love that I make him crazy with need.

Before coming back, Finn takes a belt from somewhere in the room. When he straddles my chest, he takes my hands and uses it to secure them at my forearms, tight enough to give me a bite of pain. My hips leap from the couch, pushing Lincoln deeper into me, harder, in and out.

Finn takes both of my tits in his hands and as he creates a tunnel with them, he places his dick in the valley, lubricating my skin with his precum.

With Linc finger fucking my pussy, Finn fucking my tits, and Mav in my mouth, I'm losing my grasp on reality—my orgasm rising from the depths of my soul.

"The view is fucking fantastic." I hear Mav's words but the adrenaline is rushing through my ears so his voice sounds far away. The only clear sound is me gagging on his cock and loving every second of it. My impending orgasm is so close I can practically taste it along with Mav's precum.

Digging my nails into my palms, I try to fight it off, try to make it last longer, but it's no use.

"She's about to lose it. Pull out, Mav."

He just grins, instead of pulling out, and just fucks me harder, deeper, rather than following orders. He relishes in the saliva that pools at my mouth, the tears falling down and across my temples. He's like a beast, choking me just enough to make the edges of my vision go black but not enough that I lose complete consciousness.

Just when I think I'm going to bite down for air, Mav pulls out and jacks himself off on my lips as I scream out my climax. Ribbons of his cum are jetting across my mouth, my tongue, my cheeks. I'm gasping and trying my best to breathe when Maverick reaches down and possessively spreads his cum over my skin, my chin, my throat as Finn fucks me harder and harder until he, too, loses all control.

Grunting with every jet of cum that hits my tits, my nipples, my cleavage, Finn looks me straight in the eyes as he releases all over me.

"Nice. Took the edge off. Now I can concentrate on you." Mav leans in and kisses my mouth, undoubtedly tasting himself on me but he's Maverick fucking Riley, he doesn't have any fucks to give.

Except, maybe to me. He would give me all of his fucks.

"Enough." Lincoln's voice is deep, like he's using all of his strength to keep himself under tight control. He hasn't come yet. Only using his fingers, he was essential to my orgasm and now… well, now, I think he's going to unleash himself on me.

Fuck, I can't wait.

He disappears and returns with a washcloth, helping me to clean up before dropping a chaste kiss on my lips. "Such a good girl. Ready for some more?"

I nod and he stands, taking the washcloth back to the bathroom.

The three of us are still panting as Finn picks me up and carries me to the bed where Lincoln is shedding the last of his clothing. He and Mav are both naked whereas Finn is still wearing his fucking shirt.

I'm drunk on my orgasm and my mouth opens without any regard to the words that are about to escape.

"I love your scars, Finn. Give them to me."

Finn just leans in and kisses me like I'm giving him life.

Releasing my mouth, Finn places me in the center of the bed like I'm fragile glass.

Maverick is already there with a cheeky smile, kissing me like I'm his queen and he's just a servant, while Finn unbuckles the belt and releases my bound arms. I shake them off but I know better than to think I'm free to touch and do whatever I want. It's not their style.

"Thank you," I manage to whisper, and the mischievous grin Mav throws back to me almost scares me.

"Don't thank me yet, princess."

Oh fuck.

Lincoln kneels on the bed, slowly making his way between my open legs and without any preamble, he pushes his incredibly hard and thick cock inside me as he folds his elbows at the sides of my head, effectively caging me in and holding all his weight on his arms.

Finn and Mav are watching us from either side of the bed, but our position is like a private bubble and here, just the two of us, I can see the side of Lincoln that he only gifts to me. His eyes soften just a fraction as he looks down on me, a small smile etched at the corners of his sensual mouth.

"Octavia Royal, you'll be the death of me but I'll walk willingly into the depths of Hell for a second with you." I don't have time to respond before his mouth is on mine.

Our kiss walks the edge of violence.

He's not just loving me, he's owning me. Fucking my mouth while his dick is a slow piston in and out of my pussy.

Suddenly, I'm turned around, finding myself lying on top of Lincoln. His grin tells me his chess game is going exactly as he planned.

With his hands on my hips, he accelerates his moves, fucking me from below and never losing his rhythm.

That's when I hear the sound of metal on metal. Reluctantly, my gaze lifts and I see them. Finley and Maverick have secured cuffs to the headboard, long chains attached to another set of cuffs for—I'm guessing—my wrists. Thank fuck they look soft with their wool interior and leather straps on the outside.

"Give them your hands, Octavia." Lincoln's order is low and undeniable. His authority isn't something he's practiced. It's a birthright and it fucking turns me on to no end. All the while his dick is leisurely pumping in and out of me, like its only job is to get me worked up.

Once my wrists are secured by soft wool and unyielding metal, I watch as Finn kneels at my side and Mav kneels behind me.

I don't know what's going to happen but I'm sure whatever it is, I'm going to love every second. I trust them enough to know that they won't do anything I won't enjoy.

Finn brings his hand to my cheek and caresses me softly, his lips spreading into a smile that steals my breath. "You're stunning like this: bound and the center of our attention. Always."

My eyes burn with unshed tears at his words.

Fuck, he's amazing.

They all are in their unique way.

My romantic moment is interrupted by my gasp as I feel Mav's tongue licking a hot path up one of my ass cheeks before he bites it, growling like a lust-filled animal. It's erotic and intimidating.

Linc fucks me steadily, a constant rhythm that slowly makes my body hum with vibrant energy. He's building the anticipation and as I turn my gaze back to his steely eyes, I feel centered. I feel secure in the fact that no matter what, he's got me.

Then Mav's mouth is at my ass with a quick swipe before I feel the cold dollop of lube that hits my puckered hole. He rubs it around, pushing a finger inside, and the fullness I feel between Linc's dick and Mav's finger makes me gasp. I instinctively pull at my restraints. I want to reach out and touch them, hold them. Something.

Anything.

Instead, Linc's hand is at my nape—fingers tightening in my hair—calming me, grounding me as Mav adds a second finger.

"Fuck. Oh God."

Finn runs one hand down my spine, up and down, soothing me with his warm touch.

"After tonight, you'll truly be ours," Finn whispers in my ear, and I physically feel my juices coat Linc's dick. He feels it too, judging by the wide grin I get from him.

"You like that, don't you?"

"Yes." It's just one word, but it's a breathy mess of lust.

"Are you ready, princess?" I hear from behind me as Mav scissors his fingers inside my ass. Linc pulls out then pushes in half-way and just when I think I can't get any fuller, Mav presses the head of his cock where his fingers were a moment before. I'm surprised by the stretch. I mean, I knew this would happen but I didn't think it would feel… full. My eyes go wide as my body tenses.

"Shh, baby, relax. Let him in. There's a good girl." Below me, Linc coaxes me to calm down, wills me to listen to him.

"Fuuuuuuck, there it is." Mav slides in the head of his cock and I scream out, pulling on my restraints but not because I want to stop. The bite of pain is there, the fullness, the impossible stretch of my ass and pussy to accommodate them.

But once Mav is in, I only need one thing.

"Fuck me, please. I need to feel… you. Move." I'm gasping, trying to talk with ragged breaths in and out.

"Your command, princess." I don't get the last of the phrase, I lost myself to the feel of them both, reveling in that line between pleasure and pain. Just when I think it can't get any better, Finn kneels at my side and my eyes go straight to his cock where his hand is slowly stroking up and down, almost violently.

The pain subsides, the pleasure taking its place when Finn turns my head and kisses me like life is about to get complicated.

Lincoln reaches up and unlocks the cuffs. I place both hands on his chest, following his instructions as he pushes my head to where Finn's dick is eagerly waiting for me to suck it.

"You are fucking beautiful, Octavia Royal. I love watching you come undone."

I gasp around Finley's cock as both Linc and Mav push deep inside me at the same time. I don't think I'll ever get used to the stretch, the feeling that I may rip in half, but at the same time, the pleasure is so high that I can't imagine stopping either.

"Suck his dick, Octavia. Concentrate on Finn while we focus on you."

"Fuck yeah, this is by far my favorite position." I barely hear Maverick behind me as I sink my mouth onto Finn until my nose is pressed against him, breathing becoming more difficult.

Once I get into the rhythm, I let the pleasure take over my body.

"Come on, V. Suck it. Let me feel your throat swallow me whole." Fuck, I love it when they talk dirty.

"Oh yeah, she's fucking soaked. I can feel her all over my dick."

The more they talk, the more I feel my orgasm creeping up on me.

Linc, who is half-way leaning against the headboard, releases the nape of my hair only for Finn to wrap his fist in it and push my head further down, forcing his cock deeper into my throat. I'm choking, saliva dripping from my mouth as Linc and Mav speed up their movements, alternating their thrusts.

Mav's hand snakes around my waist and the second his fingers circle my clit, I'm done.

I can't scream but my entire body begins to shake, my skin is coated with fire as I dig my nails into Linc's chest.

"Jesus fucking Christ, she's going to squeeze the life out of my cock. Fuck, fuck, fuck!" Mav's chants are like a lifeline as my orgasm threatens to make me pass out.

"You feel amazing, Octavia. Coming all over my cock. Take what you need, beautiful." And I do. I milk them all with my spasms, squeezing both their dicks until I hear Mav roar out his second orgasm.

Linc follows, his fingers so tightly planted in my hips that I know I'll have bruises there later.

"Fuuuuck!" Linc's body rears up, his head pressed against the headboard, and he's never been so fucking gorgeous as when he loses all control.

I don't know how I'm able to continue sucking off Finn but I keep it up until he finally loses himself in my mouth.

Finn throws his head back and grunts his orgasm out, his fingers tightening on my head until he pulls me off of him.

Reverently, he wipes my swollen lips with his thumb and leans in to kiss me, a whispered thank you on his breath.

Pulling out, Mav's heavy breaths echo around the room as he saunters over to the bathroom. When he comes back, Linc has pulled out and the evidence of our orgasms seeps out of my pussy.

A warm cloth on my pussy first, Mav wipes me clean then brings it up to my ass before he kisses my ass cheek again, and I can almost feel his grin.

Fifteen minutes later, we're all four lying on the bed. Half my body is draped over Lincoln, one leg touching Finley with my hand is resting on Mav's chest.

I fall asleep like that.

Cocooned by these boys-turned-men.

Mine.

All mine.

# CHAPTER TWENTY

## EAST

There is nothing quite like being left behind to make a guy mope about like a sap. The fact I helped Linc decide where to go, that I encouraged them to go, doesn't make it suck any less. But being shot will mean missing out on shit.

At least I'm still alive.

At least *she* is still alive.

I have plenty to be thankful for, but staring at the ceiling in my room, in this tomb of a house, isn't something I'm feeling exactly rainbows and unicorns about. It might've been over a month since I was shot, and I feel like I've come leaps and bounds, but my doctor is still cautiously optimistic. I'm healing faster than expected, but I'm not healed.

I grind my teeth together, hating feeling so useless, so I climb from the bed and start some of the exercises my rehab nurse gave me.

It doesn't take long until sweat is rolling down my spine, and I curse myself out for being so weak. I hate feeling as shackled as I so obviously am right now.

I pull off my tank, using it to wipe my face before flinging it in the corner. My stomach growls at me for missing breakfast and lunch, so as much as I need to shower, I decide to venture out into the battlefield of a house to eat. I just hope Harrison isn't here.

The coast is clear as I reach the kitchen, reheating some of the taco pasta Mrs. Potts left in here for me. I check my phone for the umpteenth time, smiling at the picture from V of her on her sun lounger in nothing but a bright red bikini.

Nope, not jealous of those three assholes at all.

The microwave beeps, letting me know my reheated pasta is done, but when footsteps sound down the hall and heading in this direction, my appetite disappears. Harrison sneers at me when he finds me in here, and I take a deep breath, preparing myself for the onslaught I know is coming.

It always does.

"Still here, leech? I'm surprised you didn't run to your coward daddy with your tail between your legs."

Not as bad as I expected. He's either tired, or losing his touch. Little does he know, I've been talking with Chase plenty. It's been weird as fuck getting to know him, and I still don't trust him fully, but he's done nothing but try to help us since he found out that he's my father.

Still feels weird even thinking it.

I roll my eyes as I carefully fold my arms across my chest. He eyes the pink line that runs down it like he wants to cut me back open. I wouldn't put it past this asshole to shove me, just to see if he can put a hole back in my chest. "I told you a long time ago, I won't be leaving without Lincoln."

He laughs at me, like I'm insignificant and absurd. "He will never leave."

"Then I guess you're stuck with me, aren't you?"

His eyes shine, like he has something heinous ready to throw at me, when the doorbell sounds. I hear voices as Mrs. Potts answers the door, and less than a minute later, I spot Chase striding down the hall toward us.

Well, fuck.

"Chase," Harrison snarls. "I don't remember inviting you to my home."

"Good thing I'm not here to see you then." He looks away from Harrison—who bristles at the casual dismissal—to me. "How are you doing?"

I smile at him and Harrison narrows his eyes at me. "I'm healing," I say with a shrug. "Everything okay?"

Being in a room with both of them is awkward as fuck. Mostly because Harrison is looking at me like he'd rather I was bleeding out at his feet than breathing, and we both know he could do it, too. Except now I'm technically an heir and there are rules.

If he wanted me dead, he should've done it long before now.

"Everything is fine, just wanted to check in on you since I know the others are away." He glances at Harrison, who is distracted by his phone ringing.

"Rico?" he says as he strides from the room and takes the tension with him.

Chase eyes him as he leaves, but once he's out of earshot, I relax, grab my pasta, and move to sit at the table with Chase following. "Why are you really here?"

"Exactly what I said. I can't imagine being cooped up here with just that stick up the ass for company is any fun."

I take a bite of the steaming, creamy, spicy pasta and shrug. "I've dealt with it my entire life; I'm used to it."

He frowns at my words, but I'm not going to mind them. He might not have known about me, but I'm not about to change my entire life just because I know who he is now.

"You don't have to—"

I cut him off with a shake of my head. "I will not, under any circumstances, leave Lincoln to deal with that monster alone."

"Understood."

Annndddd now it's awkward again.

"I started looking into the things we spoke about last week," he says quietly. I glance over his shoulder. Harrison isn't anywhere to be seen, but that doesn't mean shit. I'm convinced the walls in here have ears.

I drop my fork, because I want that information, just not here. "Want to go out and grab some food?"

He smiles, looking a little shocked. "I'd like that a lot."

"I'll be two seconds." I dump my pasta in the trash, putting the bowl and fork in the dishwasher, and head upstairs to change out of my sweats.

"You two deserve each other. Cowards, the pair of you." Harrison's vitriol catches me off guard as I open my door.

I sigh, so done with dealing with his bullshit. "Then just fuck off and leave us be I guess. I'm sure nothing would make you happier than never speaking to me again, Harrison."

"You do not speak to me like that in my house," he roars, and I shrug.

I narrow my eyes at him, wondering how far I can push him. "Let Lincoln leave and I'll be out of your hair."

He grins at me. "You'll be out soon enough either way, don't worry."

Without another word he turns on his heels and strides down the hall, turning the corner that leads to his office. I take a deep breath and try to push back the rising anger, remembering Chase is downstairs waiting.

If he has the information I need, then Harrison might not have the power he thinks he does for too much longer.

Change is coming, and I can't wait to watch his downfall.

# CHAPTER TWENTY-ONE

## OCTAVIA

Two days of sheer bliss is all it's taken for me to be able to pretend that this is my new reality. Lying beside the pool shouldn't feel so good. I can do it at home. But what I don't have at home is the three of them walking around, carefree, in just swim shorts, making me drool. The swim-up bar in the pool is a godsend, and somehow we seem to have eight pools—*eight*!—to ourselves.

Definitely *not* complaining.

"You need more lotion, princess?" Mav smirks at me as he steps up beside me, when four men in Hawaiian shirts walk toward us. Maverick stiffens as Lincoln pulls himself from the water and Finley sits up on the lounger beside me, watching their approach with a scowl, moving his body to shield me from view.

The hairs on the back of my neck stand up as the tension increases tenfold around me.

"Why are you here?" Lincoln asks, his voice low and lethal.

"Rico told us where you were staying. Your father offered your… skill set. We're having some problems."

He quirks a brow, looking cold and dangerous, even dripping wet. "No."

I peer over Finley's shoulder as the easy smile falls from the man's face. "It wasn't a request."

"I don't know what to tell you," Lincoln says, shrugging. "My father made an offer he can't uphold. I suggest taking up your issue with him. I'm on vacation. I am not his lapdog."

The second guy steps forward, but the one who spoke stops him. "I am sure we will be seeing you again very soon, Mr. Saint."

They turn and leave, and once they're out of sight Maverick launches a table into the pool. "What the fuck is wrong with your father!"

I sit there, wide-eyed, hating that whatever relaxation we were finally feeling just walked away with whoever that was.

Lincoln grabs a towel and drops down beside me.

"Is that our vacation over?" I ask. They're all so tense. Finley turns to face us, his mouth set in a grim line.

Finley says, "Yes," at the same time Lincoln says, "No."

"Uhm?"

"We're not leaving early because Harrison is an asshole," Lincoln says, placing a hand on my thigh.

"What if they come back?" I ask, my gaze bouncing between the three of them.

"Then we'll handle it," Mav says, moving to stand behind me, rubbing my shoulders.

"Are you sure that's a good idea?" Finn questions, and I hate to side with any of them over the other, but I'm firmly in line with him right now.

"No." Lincoln frowns before turning to me. "If you'd rather we left, we can. I just wanted to do something nice for you, but Harrison is a cunt."

"He is, but I'm not sure I feel all that safe after that. It hadn't occurred to me that they would reach us here. Stupid naïvety I guess." I bite down on my lip, hating how this has all played out, our little slice of paradise marred by shadows.

"The Knights are everywhere, and they can reach you anywhere. There is *no* hiding from them," Finley says quietly. "But we arranged with the Conclave that we wouldn't be called upon this week. It's why they agreed to wait until next week for your meeting. This is bullshit."

"How likely is it that they'll come back?"

"They shouldn't. Rico is more likely to lose his shit at Harrison than send them back here. He's always been pretty reasonable. He likes my father about as much as I do. He was a friend of your dad's."

I blink at Lincoln. It still amazes me that these three know a whole side of my dad that I had no idea existed. I try not to get emotional about all of it, but my bubble has officially burst.

"Maybe we should just help them so we don't have to worry about them coming back? What did he mean *your skill set,* anyway?"

Any traces of warmth drop from Linc's face at my question.

"You don't have to tell me," I say quietly, half wishing I could take the question back. Anytime we end up speaking about what it is they do for the Knights, it's like being plunged into an icy pool.

"There are some parts of me—of us—that we'd rather you never knew existed." He sighs. "But life doesn't work that way."

"She already knows mine," Mav says, shrugging. "My penchant for knives and blood isn't something I've hidden from her, and she barely even blinked. Give her more credit for accepting the monsters that live inside of us."

"You don't have to tell me," I say again. "But you also don't have to hide yourselves from me. I love you. Each of you. Demons and all."

Lincoln's phone rings on the table between mine and Finn's loungers, and he glares as he grabs it and answers. "What?"

He goes quiet, his face turning more thundery with each second he remains silent.

It feels like a lifetime passes as his jaw clenches and his eyes darken. "Fuck you, too," he mutters as he ends the call.

"What was that?" I ask hesitantly, shivering despite the scorching sun.

"That," he growls, "was orders. It seems you're being roped in early."

"She's coming with? Fuck no," Finn says, turning pale.

Lincoln grips his phone so hard, I worry it might crack. "We don't have a choice. Let's head back and get dressed. A car will grab us in an hour."

My stomach churns, and I get a little dizzy. "I thought you said you had an approved reprieve?"

Lincoln stands, turning to look down at me. "Apparently the Regent changed his mind. Long live the King."

---

The car ride has been silent and bumpy. A million thoughts whirr through my mind, but every time I consider opening my mouth, I look at the three of them and reconsider. Lincoln has barely said a word since the call came in, and despite Maverick playfully joining me in the shower, he didn't say a word about any of this either.

They've all officially gone to a place inside of them that I don't have access to. Everyone with trauma has that safe space, and these three have more trauma than anyone else I've ever met. Except for maybe Panda.

I shudder just thinking about the possibilities of it. What they went through.

Though I can't help but wonder just how aware of some of it I'm about to become. While I know *why* Lincoln bows to Harrison's hold, I can't help but wonder if Harrison would actually release the video of Lincoln killing someone. Surely, it would be just as bad for him as it would be for Lincoln.

I keep that thought to myself for now, but it's something to think on. Really, I need to learn more about how the Knights work. I need to pin Lincoln down, or someone, and get answers so I know how to navigate this sinister path I'm on.

I make a mental note to clear a day once I'm home to finish going through my dad's journals, too. I'm not sure what insight they'll give me, but there has to be something.

The car slows, pulling to a stop at a set of gates, the stone wall they're attached to stretches as far as I can see.

"Rico's home away from home," Lincoln says quietly in my ear. "A Knight holding."

The gates open painfully slowly, but once they're open we start moving again. It's a very tense, quiet few minutes as we drive up the cactus-lined drive before we pull up to a huge villa. The white walls and terrace roofing look like something out of a travel brochure.

Except this isn't a place for dreams or paradise.

I get the feeling this is just the shiny front for a place of pain.

The car door opens and the two guys from earlier smirk down at me, offering me a hand, which I take as I climb from the car.

"I see you came around," he says as Lincoln climbs out behind me. "The boss will be pleased. Not so sure about the guy waiting for you though."

"Let's just get this over with, shall we?"

He takes my hand and pulls me into his side as Maverick and Finley walk behind us and we head into the giant villa. The sounds of my footsteps echo in the high-ceilinged room, which is strangely cold.

"Ah, Lincoln, so good of you to come." A man's voice filters down from the mezzanine above us. Rico, I assume. He looks like the cartel bosses you see in films. Tan skin, dark hair slicked back, white pants, white shirt. "I see you brought friends. The more the merrier."

His smile seems warm, genuine almost, as he descends the stairs.

"Oh my," he says as he moves closer, beelining straight for me. Lincoln stiffens at my side as he cups my face in his hands. "Octavia Royal, as I live and breathe, is that really you?"

"Who are you?"

He almost looks taken aback. "You don't remember your Uncle Rico? I suppose the last time I saw you, you were very young."

He takes a step backward. "Martin, take our friends to see our guest. *Si respiran mal, maten a la niña*."

Nothing like being able to understand the people around me. Of course Spanish is one of the languages that I'm more than a little rusty with. The man who spoke as we came in steps forward. "*Si jefe*."

"*Asaca estés cabrones de aqui! Y ponlé in ojo a ellos guys*."

The other guy points a gun at me, and I suck in a breath as Maverick looks like he's about to throw down. "If you'll please go with Martin, he will get you some refreshments."

Mav takes a step forward, but Lincoln barks his name as Finn clamps a hand on his shoulder. Mav's brown eyes are wild as he snarls at Rico, but follows as Martin ushers the two of them into another room to the left of us. "What is going on?"

"Just making sure no one gets any stupid ideas, little Royal." Rico smiles, his eyes darken and his smile turns sinister. "Want to make sure we get what we paid for after all. Now, if you will just follow Jorge."

I look up at Lincoln, whose jaw is clenched so tightly I think his teeth might snap. It would seem Harrison has truly fucked us. "She doesn't need to be there for this."

Rico's eyes sparkle as he laughs at Lincoln's words. "Of course she does. Can't love a monster without seeing its true form."

My heart races in my chest and I grip Lincoln's hand tighter. It doesn't matter what I see, it won't change a thing. Martin moves ahead of us, motioning for us to follow in the opposite direction of where they took Mav and Finn. I glance back, Rico's slimy smirk burned into my brain.

What the fuck is wrong with everyone in this organization? How was my father friends with this guy? I still can't quite correlate the man I knew my father to be with the man who would've been a part of all of this. It's like he was two entirely different beings.

I follow behind Linc as we're taken out back and across a courtyard before we enter what looks like stables. Except, once we're inside it just looks like a torture chamber, confirmed by the guy hanging from one of the beams, his wrists wrapped in chains and a burlap sack over his head.

What in the fuck have we been dragged into?

"What is it you want to know?" Lincoln asks Martin, who smirks at him as he waves his gun at the hanging man.

"There is a rat, he knows who it is. We want a name."

Lincoln nods and rolls up the sleeves of his shirt. "You'll get it. If you'll give us some space, I do my work better without guns in my face. Or hers."

"Not a chance."

Lincoln stiffens, and my eyes go wide. "It wasn't a request. You want the name, you fuck off."

Martin's eyes narrow as he stares at us both and Lincoln maneuvers himself so that he's standing in front of me. While I'm thankful, I also really don't want him to get hurt. I put my hand on the center of his back, feeling him stiffen under my touch.

"Raise that gun in my face again and you'll be wishing you hadn't," Lincoln growls as Martin moves to lift his arm again. He looks a little afraid, and I can't help but wonder exactly what Lincoln has done to instill such fear in these people. To the point that they'd separate the three of them.

"*Chinga te, princessa*," the man growls before turning and leaving the room.

Lincoln stares after him until the door is closed , then relaxes a little. "Octavia, I don't want you to see this either."

He keeps his back to me, his head hung. "I'm not going anywhere. I'm not afraid of you or anything you're capable of, Lincoln. I love you, even the darker parts."

A shudder runs down his spine and I wrap my arms around him from behind. He relaxes further under my touch, covering my linked fingers with his hands.

"Let's get this over with, shall we?"

I pull back from him and move back toward the wall. I'm pretty sure the guy with the gun is just outside the door, so I can't go anywhere anyway, but I'm not about to leave him alone in this. He might not want me here, but I also know he'd rather know where I am.

Leaning against the wall I watch as Lincoln lowers the chains, letting the man sit on the floor, before removing the sack from his head. He leans forward and murmurs something in the man's ear, and the man bursts into tears.

"Please, sir, no. Take pity. I have two daughters and a beautiful wife. I don't know what it is that they want. I tried to tell them." His broken English is hard to understand through his sobs, but I make out enough to get the gist of what he's trying to say. Lincoln offers him a bottle of water, letting him drink as much as he wants before stepping back.

My heart races as Lincoln heads to the table lined with instruments of pain. He picks up a thin blade, no wider than my pinkie nail, and heads back to the man.

"I'm going to ask once more…" Lincoln sighs, swiping the blade on the back of his jeans before pulling on the chains until the man is standing again, his toes just barely reaching the ground. "If you tell me now, we can save you from any more pain. If you don't… it's between your life and hers. I'm going to pick hers."

"Please, sir. No. I don't know anything!" The man screams, and Lincoln shakes his head.

"Don't say I didn't warn you." I don't see what Lincoln does as he stands in front of the man, but the screams that come from the man grow louder, more high-pitched. I don't flinch or look away.

I told him I wouldn't think any different of him, and I meant it. Seeing this side of him doesn't scare me. It probably should, and that likely says more about me than it does about him.

"Name," Lincoln barks as the screams quiet to whimpers. When the man doesn't speak, Lincoln moves forward again; the screams that follow echo around the room.

I lose track of time as the screams turn to sobs. Small flashbacks of my time with Panda flash in my mind as the interrogation continues, but I know Lincoln wouldn't be here if he had a choice. That's the difference.

When the blood letting doesn't work, he uses a towel over the guy's face, pouring the bottles of water over it until he chokes, and even uses the car battery in the corner.

"Thierry," the man whimpers as Lincoln moves back toward him with the jumper cables. "Thierry Montessary."

Lincoln watches him closely before nodding and disconnecting the cables. He uses the sink to wash his hands and arms before coming over to where I'm standing. He doesn't look me in the eye when he speaks. "We can leave now."

He moves to the door and pounds on it. Seconds later, it opens.

"Thierry Montessary," Lincoln says to Martin, who nods and waves us out of the room before taking us back to the main house where Rico is lounging on a couch smoking a cigar. God, it fucking stinks.

"Done already?" Rico says, clapping his hands together as he stands to greet us. "I knew you were the man for the job. Bring his friends out and take them back to their hotel. I'll send my regards to your father."

Lincoln nods and storms out of the main door where we originally entered as Martin disappears to get the other two.

Well… this isn't awkward at all.

"Are you okay?" Maverick asks as he stalks toward me.

"Where is Linc?" Finn asks, searching the room.

I walk toward them, sinking into Mav's open arms. "I'm okay, and he's outside."

Finley watches me closely, but nods before heading outside.

"Come on, princess. Let's go," Mav says, keeping his arm around me as we leave the villa.

Rico's laugh sounds softly behind us as we leave, a shiver runs down my spine as he speaks. "I'll be seeing you again soon, Miss Royal."

The car drops us back off at our little beach cottage, but the sparkle and shine of the place is gone. This was meant to be our slice of paradise. Instead, it turned into just another thing the Knights took from us. The drive back was silent, and Lincoln still hasn't looked at me. He stomped inside the minute the car stopped, face like thunder, before the rest of us had even climbed from the car.

"You should go and speak to him, beautiful. We'll head down to the beach and give you guys a minute," Finley says softly, kissing me before grabbing Mav and dragging him toward the beach. My stomach flips. Facing Lincoln isn't the problem. The problem is making him see that I don't see him any different.

I know what he said to that man was true. It was between my life and his, and he picks me time and again.

I just wish he'd clue in to the fact that I'll pick him too.

No matter what.

I head into the cottage and hear the shower running. I bite my lip before deciding on a plan of action. Kicking off my shoes, I pad into the bathroom and find Lincoln furiously scrubbing at his skin. Any blood was cleaned off back at that villa, but it's like he's trying to scrub the whole thing away. Instead, he's just scrubbing himself raw.

My heart breaks for him, seeing him this fucked up over it all. Especially since I get the feeling that it wouldn't have been this bad if I hadn't been there.

"Lincoln," I start, but he either doesn't hear me or he's ignoring me.

Knowing him, it's the latter, but I'm not about to let him get away with it. Not this time.

I strip out of my clothing, shivering against the chill in the room before stepping toward the shower and opening the giant glass door.

"Lincoln Saint. You don't get to ignore me or hide from me. Not now."

His eyes bounce up, his gaze meeting mine, and my heart cracks at how broken he looks. "I don't want you to see me right now, Octavia. *Please*."

Usually, that please would make me rethink everything. It would make me do whatever he asks. But not today.

"I'm not going anywhere, Linc. I see you, and nothing has changed. I see all of you." I step toward him and place my hands on his chest; a shudder runs through him at the touch. Leaning up on tiptoe, I kiss him softly, trying to show him how much I mean what I say.

It takes a second, but he softens and his arms wrap around me, pulling me flush to him as the hot spray of water washes over us both.

"You have no idea what I'm capable of." His voice is cold as ice. "But I can show you."

He grips my wrists hard enough to bruise. "I'll show you just how much of a monster I am."

I blink back the shock as the temperature between us goes from hot to freezing in the breath of one simple sentence.

"Linc?"

"Shut your fucking mouth, Octavia. For once in your life, just fucking listen." I rear back like he's just slapped me, and suddenly I'm back to the beginning of the year when he treated me like shit on the bottom of his shoe.

"What are you—" I don't have time to finish my thought, Linc transfers both of my wrists to just one hand and with his other, he grips my throat so hard I can almost feel the imminent bruising.

It hurts.

But not as much as his cold, icy stare. The void in his voice. The cruel twist of his lips.

He thinks he'll push me away if he shows me the monster inside him. He thinks I'll run away—cower—at his cruel treatment of me.

It's going to take a fuck load more than his pathetic theatrics to make me run away. Bring it fucking on, Lincoln Saint. I can take it.

The cold, hard tile of the shower slams against my back as Linc pushes me into the wall and levels his glacial glare on me.

I don't even flinch.

"You think you know everything. You think you understand everything. You know fuck all, Octavia. The Lincoln you think you love is a lie. You want to know me? Here the fuck I am."

The smile that spreads across my lips only serves to piss him off more and within seconds, I'm turned and slammed against the tile wall, Linc at my back, kicking apart my legs and positioning himself behind me.

"You want the monster to fuck you, Octavia? You want to know what it's like to have all of me? Well," he brings his mouth to my ear and his dick aligns along my pussy as he finishes his thought, "don't say I didn't fucking warn you."

Without another warning, his cock is slammed inside me. No preamble, no coaxing. No loving strokes.

Letting go of my throat, he grabs onto my now wet and tangled hair and pulls. Hard. Hard enough to make me whimper. Tears spring to my eyes from the bite of pain. I wish I could say that I'm scared—that would be a normal reaction—but I'll never be afraid of him. And he needs to realize it.

Pulling as hard as he can without snapping my neck, Linc keeps his mouth at my ear, grunting like a fucking animal every time he bottoms out.

Fucking me like I'm nothing more than a whore he can use and then throw away.

So I do what I always do. I push back.

"Harder."

My voice is drowned out by the sound of the shower, the water beating down on the tile floor, so I try again, louder this time.

"Harder." I know he hears me this time, his tensing body a clear giveaway.

"You want harder? You want me to break you, little girl?"

Silly man. He thinks I don't know what he's doing.

"That's what I said. What's wrong? Is this all you've got?"

He roars before pummeling my pussy. My entire body slaps against the wet tile every time his dick slams inside me, over and over and over again.

We are reduced to nothing more than grunts and curses, the silence saying so much more than words ever could.

By punishing me, by hurting me, he's punishing and hurting himself.

Except, he can't hurt me. I want this. I want it all. Every single thing he has to offer, because I won't ever get enough of him.

"Don't be a pussy, Lincoln. Fuck me like you mean it. Give it all to me."

Linc roars out his frustration and anger. His hand tightens in my hair, pulling me away from the wall seconds before he releases my wrists, forcing me to brace myself or else fall flat on my face.

Practically at a ninety-degree angle, Linc doesn't miss a beat, fucking me like a ragdoll, fucking me like he doesn't give a shit about me.

Like he's only doing it to wet his dick

Like he's ready to throw me away.

Like he hates me.

Fuck that.

"Harder."

I go to rub my clit out but he's quick to slap my hand away.

"This isn't about you, Octavia. You don't get to come."

Asshole.

My head hits the wall twice before Linc pulls out of my pussy and throws me down on the floor, his dick aimed at my face. Water washes down all over me and I can barely keep my eyes open but I realize what he's doing just as I feel the first jet of his cum on my cheek.

Fucker thinks this will debase me? Degrade me?

Kneeling like a good girl, I open my mouth and greedily try to lick up any of the cum that drips onto my lips and chin.

His stare is cold and unforgiving, but I know he's in there somewhere.

It's only when he turns the water off and steps out of the shower, leaving me there alone, that I realize the extent of his self-sabotage.

Idiot man.

He can't get rid of me that easily.

---

While our time away wasn't what we'd hoped it would be, I can't help but feel closer to Lincoln than I was when we left, even with everything that happened after I saw that side of him. He hasn't apologized, but I don't need him to. I told him I love him, dark parts and all, and I meant it. At least we did get a bit of a break… even if it wasn't as peaceful as we'd have liked.

Lincoln pulls the Porsche into his driveway, stopping by the garage. "Do you want to come in?"

I grin at him and nod. "Yes. I want to see East, too. It's been strange being away from him, even if it was only a few days."

He nods, putting his hand on my thigh as I unbuckle. "Octavia… what happened in Mexico…"

"It's already done and dealt with. We're good."

He smiles tightly at me. "I know, but maybe, let's just not mention it to East just yet. I don't want him to freak out. His heart… I know he's making progress in therapy, but it's only been six weeks. He still has a way to go. I don't want anything to delay his progress."

"I won't lie to him, but I won't offer the information either," I say grimly, not exactly happy he's putting me in this situation, but at the same time, I get it. He watches me closely before nodding and releasing me. I shake it off and climb from the car, excited to go and see East when the front door opens and Harrison stands in the doorway.

"Go home, Octavia. Lincoln and I have some things to discuss."

I look over at Lincoln, fully prepared to stand my ground and tell Harrison to fuck off, but Linc rubs a hand down his face before nodding at me. "It's okay, we'll call you later."

I guess with the whole, we're-not-supposed-to-be-in-a-relationship thing, and everything that happened in Mexico, we should've been expecting this, but fuck.

I grab my bag from Linc's trunk and start making my way down the drive. An icy drop of dread runs down my spine, and I can feel the heat of their eyes on me when I hear Harrison's voice. "I'll be seeing you soon, Miss Royal. Make sure not to be late."

# CHAPTER TWENTY-TWO

## LINCOLN

These last few days didn't exactly go to plan, and the message from Harrison on my phone before we boarded the plane home isn't exactly filling me with joy either. I tap my fingers on the steering wheel, counting it out to try and calm myself down as I pull up beside the garage. I look over at the girl who I've come to realize owns me entirely, but who I know I don't get to keep.

Harrison has made that all too clear, so until I can figure out a way to extract myself from the claws he has in me, I'm fucked.

Regardless, I'm going to enjoy every fucking second with her that I can. At least for now, I can enjoy this moment with her. "Do you want to come in?"

She smiles at me and the tight knot in my chest loosens a little. Ever since she saw my monster, she's accepted all of the poison I've spat at her and still looks at me like that. I don't understand it, any of it, but I'll accept it like the selfish bastard I am. "Yes. I want to see East, too. It's been strange being away from him, even if it was only a few days."

I put my hand on her thigh, unable to keep myself from touching her. I think I'm starting to lose myself a little, but losing myself in her is basically all I've ever wanted. Though I already know what I'm about to ask of her is going to piss her off. Not that that means I won't ask it. I don't have a choice. "Octavia... what happened in Mexico..."

"It's already done and dealt with. We're good."

She thinks I mean what happened after, but I don't. Rico was not part of the plan when I took her away, and East is going to freak the fuck out when he finds out. I just want to know his heart is going to be okay before we tell him something that's going to stress him out. The smile on my face is tight before I let out a deep breath. "I know, but maybe, let's just not mention it to East just yet. I don't want him to freak out. His heart... I know he's making progress in therapy, but it's only been six weeks. He still has a way to go. I don't want anything to delay his progress."

"I won't lie to him, but I won't offer the information either." Yep, there's the fire I expected. I watch her closely, because I can't look at her without wanting to see all of her. Except this time I can see as the anger dances in her eyes before the reluctant acknowledgement that she knows I'm right settles on her.

She climbs from the car, my cold heart beating like a traitor as I watch her ass shimmy out. I know her smiles are for East, not for me. Especially right now, but I'm going to drink them in regardless.

I run a hand down my face, wondering exactly when I became such a sappy asshole, but since it's only her that will ever truly know it, I don't mind so much.

Climbing from the car, I slam the door shut when Harrison's voice fills the space. I clench my jaw at his arrival. Of course he couldn't give me just another day.

He stands in the doorway, glaring at the girl who owns my heart. I told him she's with Finn, but I'm positive he doesn't believe me.

"Go home, Octavia. Lincoln and I have some things to discuss."

She looks over at me, that fire in her eyes that's enough to make my heart beat, but this isn't something I want her mixed up in if I can help it. I rub a hand down my face, wishing that Harrison would just drop dead on the spot, but knowing how unsatisfying that would be after all of my fantasies of ending him.

I nod at her and sigh. "It's okay, we'll call you later."

She looks pissed, but I'm hoping she understands. She might be okay with my monster, but if Harrison ever had reason to put his hands on her… I clench my jaw just at the thought. No fucking chance in Hell.

She grabs her bag from my trunk and walks away from us. I refuse to follow her movements, because while Harrison might not believe that I'm not with her, I don't want to give him anything to use against me if I can help it. I grab my own bag when his voice rings out around us. "I'll be seeing you soon, Miss Royal. Make sure not to be late."

Asshole.

I shoulder my bag and move toward him. "You wanted to speak to me?"

He puts his hands in his pockets and stares at me like he's trying to read my thoughts. He fucking wishes he had that power. Paranoid asshole that he is.

He turns and walks into the house, and I grit my teeth at his expectation that I'll just follow. Except I do because I have very little choice about much of anything. I follow him up to his study. East pops his head out of his door, smiling, but I shake my head in response and his smile drops. He notices me following Harrison, then looks as pissed as I feel, but closes the door and retreats.

I need to find out what happened here while I was gone. But first, I need to get Harrison off my back. Even if the reprieve is temporary.

Walking into his office, I close the door behind me, dropping my bag beside it as he stands on the other side of his desk.

I fucking hate this room. Memories assault me every time I step foot in here, no matter how much I want them to stay buried. I might not wear scars on my skin like Mav or Finn, but that's only because mine are buried deeper. Harrison made sure of it.

"You disappointed me." He clicks his tongue as he waves to the chair in front of his desk, the silent command ringing between us.

My feet feel like lead as I pick them up to make my way across the room. I fucking hate it in here, and he knows it. I take a few deep breaths, trying to stave off the weakness that rolls through me, the panic and dread that sits on my chest like an unwelcome visitor.

"You disappointed me in Mexico, Lincoln." His gaze is unwavering as he watches me, and I try not to buckle beneath the weight of it.

I clench my jaw, trying to keep my shit in check as I answer him. "I was promised a reprieve. It was agreed upon by the Conclave."

"Well I changed my fucking mind," he roars, throwing the glass in his hand across the room. The smash as it shatters against the wall makes my jaw tic, but I try to stay calm. He wants a reaction from me, and while I can't do much against him—for now anyway—this I can control.

"Apparently. I did what Rico asked, so I don't see what the problem is." I lean back in the chair, slipping into that cold, aloof mask, trying to cover the writhing panic that this room evokes. I'm not the same kid I was back then. I have no reason to fear this fucking room.

He glares at me, his hands shaking with his rage. Apparently he's drunk too much today. Usually he's better at keeping a lid on his shit. "You and the Royal need to be over."

"I'm not with the Royal."

He takes a deep breath, realizing that I'm not going to lose control like he has, and I watch as that cold mask slips over his skin, too. He takes a seat opposite me and watches me silently.

This is when you should be afraid of Harrison Saint. The loud, ballsy bullshit isn't anything terrifying. But the quiet calm… that's when he's dangerous.

"You will stop seeing the Royal and focus on Georgia or I will have her throat slit and make you watch as she bleeds out on the ground. I don't care what agreements her pathetic father made, if she continues to be a problem, she will be dealt with."

I remain as still as I can, despite my heart feeling like it's going to beat out of my chest. I grip the arms of the chair, and he smiles.

I'll slit his fucking throat and laugh as he bleeds.

"I told you, there is nothing between me and her." The words come out clipped, and his grin grows.

"Then there won't be a problem with you finally securing your engagement with Georgia, will there? And I'm sure you'll have no objections to sharing a room with her after the party I'm throwing next week. Where your engagement *will* be officially announced. If one more Royal gets in my way, I will watch them all burn."

"The Royals won't be a problem. I already told you I won't fuck the girl, but I'll play the rest of your game."

His eyes darken as he leans forward on the desk. "You will do whatever you have to, even if that means fucking her. Because if she doesn't believe the engagement is real, she will tell me, and your precious fucking bitch will reap the consequences."

He pauses, making sure I understand everything he isn't saying, then dismisses me like I'm nothing to him.

I stand and leave, knowing that all it would take is one phone call to fuck with his plans, but I won't risk Octavia like that.

Except that she's probably going to hate me for what I have to do to keep her safe anyway. But I'd rather she was breathing and hate me than love me and wind up dead.

# CHAPTER TWENTY-THREE

## OCTAVIA

Sliding into my dad's Range Rover, I hook up my phone and let out a deep breath. The first day back to school after break always sucks, but knowing that my guys are going to be MIA today as a result of whatever the fuck happened with Harrison after he dismissed me yesterday makes it suck even harder.

But, for a change, I'm picking my girl up for coffee and breakfast before school. After Finley inspected my car at ass o'clock this morning while Lincoln and I went on our morning run. Apparently they're still not taking any chances. Not that I can be mad about it.

My phone buzzes as I start the engine and I smile when I see Smithy's name.

Smithy:
Good Morning, Miss Octavia. We shall be flying home this evening, so I will likely make it back to the house sometime tomorrow. I hope you had a wonderful break. Make sure to eat breakfast, and have a good day at school.

Me:
Morning! Totally fine, take your time and enjoy yourself **heart emoji** Heading for breakfast now. See, I can adult!

Smithy:
Yes, if you say so. **raised eyebrow emoji** See you soon.

I laugh as I place my phone back on its holder, putting on my morning playlist before pulling out of the drive. The trip to Indi's doesn't take very long, and I drop her a message to let her know I'm outside.

She emerges from the house, practically skipping toward the car and I can't help but grin at her. She is an enigma wrapped in a conundrum. She's such a bad early morning person, but get her ready for the day and she has so much pep, it makes you sick.

She bounces into the car, her blue fishtail braid swinging free, and hugs me like she hasn't seen me in four months, not four days.

"Morning!" she practically sings as she squeezes me. "How was Mexico?

"It was good. Maybe a little too… exciting at times, but good."

"Oh no. What did those assholes do now?" She frowns as she pulls her seatbelt on, and I pull away from the curb.

"Not them. The Knights. It's nothing, but they won't be at school today."

"I did wonder why I got you back for the morning. I'm not sad about it, but is everything okay?"

I shrug as I stop at the light, waiting for the green. "I have no idea. I think so. Lincoln didn't give much away this morning—shock, horror—but I like to think if it was really bad, then he'd tell me."

"How is he doing? Juggling the whole Georgia thing?"

"Honestly, he doesn't say much about her. Which I guess is a good sign, but I don't really know. He doesn't want to upset me by talking about her, so he doesn't say much. I know he's ready for the charade to be over and that's about it."

"I don't blame him, poor guy." She frowns as she taps away on her screen. "But I'm glad you had a decent break, even if it did come with a little excitement. Now back to the drama of ECP. You heard anything from Blair?"

I bark out a laugh as we pull into the Starbucks drive-thru. "Never in a million years is the answer to that question going to be a yes. Why, what did you hear?"

"That your uncle is in deep shit. Like, royally fucked. Oh, look, I'm punny." She giggles before dropping the smile and getting all stern again. "But for reals, I think it's going to get bad. We might get another paparazzi swarm here."

I groan as we pull up to the mic. "Just what I need. You want your usual?"

"Course." She grins.

I order our usual drinks before pulling around to the next window, wondering how the fuck I'm going to deal with another influx of paparazzi if it happens. With everything that's going on with the Knights, the last thing I need is people watching my every move and trying to capture it on camera. I've just finally gotten used to not having to hide everything I do.

What a pile of ass.

I grab our drinks and toasted sandwiches, handing them to Indi before I head toward the school. "Have they announced official charges yet?"

"Not that I've read. I've been following it online as much as I can. They're playing it close to the vest, but I think they are going to be out a lot of money when all the details come out. There is going to be a lot of hate thrown in his direction. Blair and Vivianne might not be able to stay in the Cove if it gets too bad."

"What a shame," I deadpan, rolling my eyes. "Like I feel for them, but also, they can get fucked."

We pull into the parking lot and I park in Lincoln's usual spot. It's weird not seeing their cars here. "Let's do this shall we?"

"At least Ms. Summers won't be too crazy this morning. We handed in our assignment already. Pretty sure it's just going to be exam prep between now and the end of the year," she says cheerily as she hands me my drink before climbing from the car. I follow suit, grabbing my bag from behind her chair and making sure to double check that I've locked the doors. I don't exactly have a great track record with cars, so I'm trying to make sure I look after Dad's car. Even if it is technically mine now, I guess.

We head inside, dropping our stuff off at our lockers before heading to the library, slipping into our usual early morning study spot. I munch on my toasted sandwich while I read through my Business textbook, trying to make sure I'm up to date with the reading before today's class.

We're sitting quietly, reading and prepping for the day, when a shadow descends over the table. I sigh when I look up and find Blair staring down at us. "What do you want, Blair?"

She still looks haughty as fuck, looking down her nose at me like I'm beneath her. If she wants my help, she needs to sort out her resting bitch face.

"All of our assets have been frozen, and we need to sort Dad's legal fees." Her face twists, like I just stabbed her. "Mom asked if you would help us. We're trying to make it go away quietly, and to do that we need a Knight lawyer."

"What exactly do you want me to do, Blair?"

She sighs dramatically, like I'm the one asking her for a favor. Jesus fucking Christ, this girl needs to get a grip. "I need you to speak to Chase Armstrong. He's a lawyer, the best in town. He's a Conclave member. We need him."

Indi's eyes go wide at the mention of East's dad. Pretty sure *that* isn't public news yet, so I shake my head subtly. "I'll see what I can do."

She nods, looking like she's sucked on a lemon. "Thank you."

She doesn't say another word before turning on her heel and storming away, head held high like she's still the queen bee around here. I have a feeling even with everything going on, she's going to come out on top.

"Do you think she knows?" Indi asks quietly.

I shake my head. "I don't know how she could. No one outside of you, me, Harrison, and the guys knows. Pretty sure they haven't even mentioned it to the Conclave. Harrison wouldn't like that sort of embarrassment," I say rolling my eyes. "I'll speak to the others about it when I see them next."

The bell rings and we're packing our stuff up when she asks, "Are you going to speak to Chase?"

"I said I would," I say with a shrug. "I doubt it'll make much of a difference, but it can't hurt right? Plus, if it can be kept quiet-ish, and I avoid my house being swarmed again, then I'm all for it."

I let out a deep sigh as I pick up my books and drop my trash in the can beside the table. Here's hoping this goes the way I want it to. I am not feeling any more chaos in my life than already exists.

---

Today is kicking my ass.

If I thought school without the guys was bad yesterday, it's nothing compared to today. Mikayla and the bitch squad have ramped up their torture of the freshmen threefold, and I've about had enough of it. I don't want to be queen, and Blair might have been an asshole, but even she seemed to have some limits.

Mikayla is ruthless and needs kicking down a peg or two. It's only lunchtime, and I've already seen more girls crying in the last two days than I have in my entire year here so far. I leave class and head toward my locker so I can meet Indi, and another girl runs past me toward the bathroom, tears staining her cheeks.

I find a vibrating Indi, clenching her fists at my locker.

"What's wrong?" I ask, wide-eyed. It takes a lot to make my sunshine friend this angry. I pop my stuff in my locker and give her my full attention.

"Mikayla," she growls. "She went full tyrant in our last class, then terrorized a group of freshmen that were waiting in the hall afterward. She needs to be stopped. I'd take Blair over this bitch."

"Funny, I was just thinking the same thing. I'm just not sure how." I frown, wishing I had a better idea. Bringing down empires is definitely more Blair's thing. She's by far the more cold and calculating one of us. Sometimes I wish I had a bit more of that in me, but cold and calculating just isn't who I am.

Angry and vengeful? Sometimes, yes.

But I definitely didn't get the traits from the family tree that would handle this situation best.

I look up and spot Blair walking past us, and figure fuck it. "Blair, hold up."

She pauses, turning to look at us, eyebrow raised. "What?"

"How does getting your crown back and knocking Mikayla down a few steps sound?" The enemy of my enemy and all that.

She heads toward us, obviously interested, but more than a little wary. "Why would you help me?"

"I'm not helping you. I'm helping the freshmen. You might be a bitch, but she's a tyrant." I shrug as she barks out a laugh. "Do you want to help or not?"

"I'm in, what did you have in mind?" she asks, folding her arms over her chest.

I grin wide. This mini truce might just work, and I can feel good about having done something positive with my time here. Even if it's not *that* great. "Well you see… that's where you come in."

"What does that mean?"

"It means," Indi says sarcastically, "that we need your evil genius brain."

Blair walks with us to the cafeteria as Indi explains what we want from her. "Sounds good, I've already got an idea but let me sit on it and we'll talk tomorrow. Now if you'll excuse me, I'd rather not walk in there with you both."

She flicks her blonde hair over her shoulder and heads inside, leaving me slack-jawed.

"That girl has got some fucking nerve," Indi growls under her breath.

I laugh, shaking my head. "I think I'd be more shocked if she did anything else. Come on, let's head inside. The guys will be here soon and I'd rather eat something before Mav arrives and tries to steal half my lunch."

She grins at me, all thoughts of Blair gone. "I get the feeling he'd rather eat something else."

I laugh at her as we head toward the line. "You're as bad as he is."

We walk in, finding the guy in question already in line. He turns as we enter and grins at me. When we reach him, he pulls me into his side and smacks a kiss on my cheek. The big dork.

"You're in a good mood," Indi snarks at him, and I clamp my lips together.

"What's wrong, Pixie Spice? You not getting enough good D? You should really speak to those Kings, shouldn't hold out on a girl." I elbow him in the side, rewarded with an *ooph* and a smile from Indi.

She skips past him and picks up a tray. "Keep talking about my kitty cat and see how much Ryker likes it." She winks before grabbing her food.

"I'd rather focus on *your* pussy," he growls into my ear, and heat spills across my chest. "Sleepover tonight?"

"I'm going to see East after school, but sure, why not?" I grin and he slaps my ass.

"That's my girl. Now, let's get some grub. You're going to need the energy for later."

---

Lincoln pulls into his garage, turning off the car before he looks over at me. He has barely spoken to me since Harrison dismissed me on Sunday, and I've had about enough of it.

"Are you going to tell me what happened?" My words come out snappier than I wanted, but I'm sick of the silent treatment. Going backward isn't what I want. We've played this game before, I'll be fucked if we go back.

"There's nothing to tell. Harrison doesn't want me spending time with you. He wants me to focus on Georgia. My *fiancée*. This isn't news," he snaps right back before climbing from the car and slamming the door.

"Why are you being such a dickhead?" I yell at him as I climb from the car. He spins on the spot and his eyes dance with fire before he narrows them at me.

"This is just who I am, Octavia. Take it or fucking leave it. I'm not changing. Not for you. Not for anyone."

I stand there, speechless, as he storms away from me.

What the fuck is going on with him? There has to be more to it than he's telling me. He doesn't usually just snap at me like that.

I'm obviously not going to find out what it is right now, not when he's in whatever mood it is that he's in, so I paint a smile on my face and head into the house tentatively.

I find East in the hall, about to head upstairs.

"Hey, you."

"Hey, yourself. Come to keep the bedridden company?" He grins so I know he isn't as forlorn as his words make him out to be, so I slip over to him and he kisses me like I'm oxygen and he's struggling to breathe.

When I pull back to find air, he grins down at me. He looks happy. "How was your appointment today?"

"It was really good. Doc said my age and health are on my side. Incision is still looking good, bloodwork was good, no signs of infection. Sternum and muscle healing is basically done, likely thanks to my age. Things are looking real good. Apparently I'm very lucky."

"Really? That's freaking amazing news!" I hug him gently and my heart soars that he's doing so well. The severity of his injuries have been weighing on me a lot. It was my fault he got shot. My fault he nearly died—that he technically *did* die.

"Yeah I'm not sad about it, and my day is even better now you're here."

I laugh softly at him. "You're such a cheeseball. So do you even need to still be cooped up in your room?"

"No, not really, but Harrison is on the warpath, so I'm staying out of his way. Plus, I was hoping you'd swing by tonight, too. Because I got some other good news today. Since I'm basically all healed up…"

Quirking a brow at him, I wait for him to continue.

"Oh no, sweetheart. I'm going to show you rather than tell you. It's more fun that way."

"Where are we going?" I laugh as he takes my hand. This playful side of him is fun, I've kind of missed it among all of the crazy we've been juggling.

"Show, not tell, remember." He grins, wagging his brows at me.

"Then by all means, show away."

He tugs me up the stairs, pulling me into his bedroom and closes the door behind us before pinning me against the door. "Fuck, I missed you."

His words are breathy before he kisses me like a starving man and I'm his favorite meal. I tangle my hands in his hair as he presses against me, his dick very much making itself known.

"I thought you weren't allowed to exert yourself," I pant as he pulls away. He just grins.

"Good news, remember?"

"Oh," I say, eyes wide. "Are you sure?"

He grins at me, devilishly. "Doc said yes, I'm not about to question it."

My smile matches his as I run my nails down his chest, careful of the scar I know is beneath his t-shirt. "Who are we to question medical advice?"

"My thoughts exactly." He smirks before kissing me again.

We are all tongues and lips and lost breaths as he cages my face in the palm of his hands like I'm the one who's fragile.

It doesn't matter though, because the way he holds me so reverently makes me feel like I'm everything. Like I'm his whole world.

One of his thighs pushes between my legs, just below my skirt that I can feel riding up my thighs. Reaching down, I unbutton my blazer and throw it blindly to the side, hoping it doesn't break anything. Without missing a beat, I kick off my shoes, my concentration still very much on East and his talented mouth.

The harder he kisses me, the more his hands roam, the more turned on I get. I don't have to touch myself to know my panties are getting soaked with how much I need him.

"Touch me, V. Don't hold back." In the back of my mind, I know I shouldn't get carried away, I know I need to be mindful of his injury, even if he says he's okay, but at his words my fingers curl around the fabric of his shirt until I'm fisting it with an urgency that we can both feel.

"That's it. Fuck me, you're so wet."

My pussy on his thigh, I ride him—chasing my pleasure—as his mouth slams back onto mine.

I don't know how long he kisses me but I relish every second of it. Sometimes, a kiss is just a kiss. But sometimes? It's a fucking volcano. Explosive, hot, destructive.

Letting go of my face, East runs his hands down my arms until he reaches the hem of my shirt before unbuttoning and ripping it off then throwing it into the depths of the room, pausing our kiss for the briefest of seconds.

Our tongues are once again fighting for control, caressing until we have to break apart for breath.

East rests his forehead on mine and, with his eyes closed, he stays there for a few seconds, his chest heaving.

"Are you okay?" I ask, alarmed that maybe he's not up to this yet.

"I'm good, V. Just trying to decide what to do to you first." When he opens his eyes, his gaze is full of heat, a spark of something that makes my heart rate skyrocket. If I thought I was wet before, I'm fucking soaked now.

He kisses me once more, abrupt and hurried, then pulls away again, his teeth trapping my bottom lip as he slowly releases it.

When his gaze travels to my chest, the swell of my breasts peeking out from beneath my bra, I rely on the door to keep me upright. East is attentive and loving, but I can't forget that he's a Saint at heart and his dominant side is never far from the surface.

Hands at the cups of my bra, East glances up at me, a mischievous glint telling me he's about to do something that might piss me off.

The sound of ripping fabric confirms that, yes, he's going to get an earful but… not now. Right now, I just can't bring myself to give a shit.

"That's better," he says right before his mouth is on my nipple, sucking and pulling until I'm a mess of hormones running wild in my blood.

Too soon, his mouth is gone. When I open my eyes, he's on his knees pulling my skirt and panties off before placing his mouth on my pussy, licking up every drop that I give him.

My head bangs against the door as my hips push into his mouth. I need more, so I plant my hand on his head and without questioning my actions, I hold him steady as I basically try to fuck his face, searching out the friction on my clit and chasing my orgasm.

Until his mouth is gone.

My lids fly open. My eyes, wild with lust, search him out and when I find him, he's sitting on his haunches watching me.

"Who's in charge, V?"

*What?*

I must voice my question aloud because he asks again.

"Who's in fucking charge, V?"

"You?"

"Is that a question?"

"No?"

Taking my hand, he places it on his head then warns, "I fuck your pussy, V. I'm in charge." Without actually saying the words, I understand that me taking control of the situation is not in the cards.

I suppose after what happened, he deserves to feel a little control in his life.

I get it. That's why I let him call the shots. Also, because it's fucking hot.

With his mouth back on my pussy, East works his magic and no more than a minute later, I'm coming all over his tongue and chin and it's the hottest fucking thing in the world. My entire body shakes with the aftermath of the orgasm, my legs barely able to keep me upright.

When East pulls back, he looks straight into my eyes—wiping his mouth with the back of his hand—and smiles like a man crazed.

"I love eating your pussy."

Once he stands, I don't have time to catch my breath as I'm thrown over his shoulder in a fireman's hold. East carries me across the room and carefully places me on the bed while he stays on the side, watching me.

"You might be okay, but you probably shouldn't be carrying me," I say, frowning up at him, unable to stop the worry that floods me.

"Don't freak out, V. Everything is fine."

East reaches back and pulls the collar of his shirt up and over his head, flinging it to the side before he pushes his gray sweats down and simply steps out of them before he joins me in bed.

I gasp at the sight of his scar but I try to remember that if the doc said it's good, who the fuck am I to argue?

When East joins me in the bed, he pulls the covers up above our heads as we come together, face-to-face—chest to chest—with our legs intertwined and my pussy riding his thigh.

Then he brings our mouths into another heated kiss where I can taste myself on his lips. It should probably be weird how erotic that is, but I'm not about to question it.

Positioning us just perfectly so, East takes the back of my thigh and hikes it up his waist as his cock finds itself inside me in one smooth, invigorating slide. We're both breathless again. The fullness of him, the intimate position in our man-made cocoon of sheets and covers, makes it feel like the outside world doesn't exist. The only important thing is him and me.

His hips piston back and forth, my clit searching out the friction of his groin as he takes his time fucking me, almost painfully slowly. Deliberately.

I can feel every delicious inch of him as he glides out, the sounds of my wet pussy and our accelerating breaths all we can hear.

We don't talk, our bodies are speaking loudly and clearly. We aren't fucking, really. He's making long and intense love to me, and that slow burn is working its magic on me. But he's not immune to it, either.

East shifts just a little so that he's at a better angle, giving me access to his back with my nails. This way, he can thrust harder, fuck me deeper, and with every slam inside me, my nails dig deeper, my groans grow longer. My grunts a little louder.

"I need you to come all over my dick, V. Give it all to me."

With his mouth at my neck, my hands on his back, his finger searches out my clit and the moment he circles it just once, I'm coming like I haven't climaxed in a lifetime.

I gulp down air as the tsunami that is my orgasm grips me in my lower belly before traveling up my chest and into my throat, turning into a desperate scream.

East groans, his own climax fueled by mine.

Seconds later, we are both trying to come down from the intensity of our lovemaking when he kisses my lips once more and repeats his words from earlier.

"Fuck, I missed you."

# CHAPTER TWENTY-FOUR

## OCTAVIA

After my evening with East, and Maverick staying over last night, I feel like a hussy. A very satisfied hussy, but a hussy nonetheless. Which makes my run with Lincoln even more frustrating. He met me at my gate, like he does every morning, but I feel like we've gone backward about four months. He's barely spoken to me, and when he has, I wouldn't call it talking so much as I'd call it snapping.

I wish he'd just let me in. That he'd share whatever the hell is eating at him. But I've tried to ask him half a dozen times what's wrong and nearly lost my head, so I don't see that happening any time soon.

He runs two paces in front of me, the same way we've been doing since everything happened with Panda, but today, he takes a different turn after we pass the pier.

"Where are we going?"

He doesn't answer and I want to throw my fucking sneaker at the back of his head, but rather than let him win and see how pissed I am, I push through his punishing pace so I can keep up with him. There's no way I'm giving him the satisfaction. Especially not when he's in this mood.

We head up the hill, and I swear my lungs feel like they're going to explode between his pace and this fucking incline.

"Lincoln!" I half shout, half huff, because fuck.

He doesn't pause, he just keeps going. Whatever demons are riding him that he's trying to exorcize this morning must be insane, because even in asshole mode, he never ignored me.

Not since I learned the truth of everything.

Not like this.

I call his name again, and he finally slows. Glancing back, he finds me in the middle of the road, bent in two, sucking in air.

"What are you doing?" he barks, while running in place. "We don't have time to slow. You need to be faster. If you're not in pristine shape, you're going to get yourself killed."

And then it dawns on me.

The demon riding him is me.

My meeting with the Conclave.

Lincoln Saint is *afraid* and it's driving him insane.

I stand up straight and walk toward him. "Is that what's wrong? The last few days? Is that what this has all been about?"

He stops all movement, staring at me before tugging on his hair. "Everything I've ever tried to do is about keeping you alive. Keeping you safe. And now the Conclave wants to meet with you, but Harrison won't tell me a goddamn thing about you. He wants me focused on Georgia and sealing his deal. You should not be on my radar as far as he's concerned, but he doesn't see that you are *everything.*"

I place my hand on his chest, his racing heart pounds beneath it as he looks at me with wild eyes.

"It seems like people have been coming for me my entire life, Lincoln. I've survived this long. We just need to play their game, find out what it is they want, and then we can make a plan."

"You don't understand. The contract Stone made… that potentially jeopardizes everything Harrison holds dear. If he sees you as a threat to his seat—his power—he'll kill you without a second thought if he thinks he can get away with it. The only thing keeping him from it right now is the fact that everyone knows about the deal. It would be obvious it was him. There might not be a ton of rules in the Knights, but killing other members, especially Conclave members…"

He trails off and it occurs to me that if that's the line, then it's possible they've already crossed it. If Panda is to be believed anyway.

"Is that why no one knows if Edward killed my dad? Because it's against the rules to kill another Conclave member?"

"Yes and no." He sighs. "Technically, Stone wasn't a member of the Conclave anymore. The seat was just empty. The reason I can't get a straight answer about your dad is because *if* that's what happened, it's likely it was just between Harrison and Edward, and neither of them is going to say a goddamn thing."

"That makes sense," I muse. "When am I supposed to be meeting with the Conclave? I haven't heard anything. I assume I'm going to be summoned?"

He nods, pulling us out of the road to stand on the pavement. "Yes, you'll be summoned, but again, I don't know when and it's driving me fucking insane. I can't keep you safe if I don't know the plan, and that's probably Harrison's fucking idea."

His phone buzzes and his mouth twists. "Finn has news about who was working with Evan."

My eyes go wide. It's not like I'd forgotten about it, but I was beginning to think we'd never know since P killed himself. "What did he say?"

"Nothing but that. It's safer not to say anything in a message."

Well I mean, duh, Octavia.

"Okay," I say, trying not to be disappointed. I know Finley won't keep me on tenterhooks for too long. That's Lincoln's game.

"So the Conclave?" I ask as we start jogging up the hill.

He glances over at me, frowning again. "I'll try and get some information from Chase, but considering his known stance on everything, I'm not sure how much use he'll be either."

Shit. "I need to speak to Chase anyway, so maybe I could ask him."

"What the fuck do you need to speak to him about?"

We reach the crest of the hill and I could almost do a happy dance realizing the rest of the way home is downhill. "Blair came to speak to me. Nate needs a lawyer and funds for said lawyer. She asked me if I'd speak to him."

"Does she know about him and East?"

"I doubt it, but who knows? This place is full of the worst kept secrets. She didn't make out like she knew, so I'm assuming not." He stays quiet for the rest of the run home and doesn't say another word until I key in the code on my gate.

"Leave Chase to me. I'll speak to him for Blair too. The less you have to do with the Knights, the better."

He turns and stalks off up his drive without another word, leaving me staring at his back as he walks away from me. Just when I thought he was slipping out of asshole mode, he whips it straight back out.

One day I'll understand Lincoln Saint, but today is not that day.

---

I end up not having any time to speak to Finley about what he learned about Panda's accomplice, because my morning turned into a whirlwind of Indi having a meltdown over Alexander showing up in the Cove last night and being spotted by the Kings.

So when Blair accosts me at my locker, I know my day likely isn't going to get any better. "Did you speak to Chase yet?"

"No, Blair. I haven't spoken to Chase yet. Lincoln is going to speak to him, since he actually knows him." I close the door to my locker and turn to face her.

She rolls her eyes at me and it takes all of my strength of will not to just slap the condescending look off her face. "You'll never survive their world if you let them do everything for you."

I let out a sigh and fold my arms across my chest. "If I want your advice, Blair, I'll ask for it. Was there anything else?"

"I have an idea of how to bring Mikayla down, but you're not going to like it."

"Of course I'm not, you came up with it. But that was the whole idea. What's the plan?"

She grins, and I swear my blood turns to ice. "It involves Raleigh."

"Blair—" I start but she cuts me off.

"I know, he's a monster. But he's a monster I have on a leash, even if everyone thinks I don't."

I quirk a brow and lean against my locker. "I'm listening."

She tells me her diabolical plan as we walk toward the library where I said I'd meet Indi to study over lunch.

"You're twisted, you know that?"

"Thanks," she grins. "So I won't ask if you approve, but are you okay to do your part?"

I bite the inside of my cheek, just as a girl appears from the bathroom, still crying, clutching her blazer to her chest, her shirt in ribbons.

"I'm in," is all I say before I approach the girl.

"Do you need a shirt?" I ask her, and she looks up at me, wide-eyed. Like she's afraid of me.

"N…n…no," she stammers, eyes darting around us like she thinks it's an ambush.

I open the bathroom door and wave her in. "In."

She scampers back into the bathroom, and I call in after her. "I'll just be two minutes."

I haul ass into the library, finding Indi at our usual table. "Do you have a spare shirt?"

"I always have spares. Why what happened?" she asks, looking me over, confused.

"Girl in the bathroom down the hall, shirt in shreds."

She frowns harder. "I swear to God, we need to deal with Mikayla. If I wasn't so opposed to just outright killing people…"

"I mean, fair, she's the devil incarnate."

"I never thought I'd miss Blair being the Queen Bitch. You wait here, I'll grab the shirt and help the girl. You're a little more intimidating than I am."

My jaw drops and she laughs as she bounces away from me. While I'm glad she's helping the girl, I hate the thought that the girl was scared of me.

I'm not intimidating.

I'm the nice Royal.

Or so I thought.

*Shit.*

I chew on it, while I unpack my stuff onto the table. It's only a few minutes before she flounces back in, all smiles. "All sorted, and Florence is all smiles again. She's a sophomore, never had any issues, even tried out for the cheer squad and did okay. But apparently she looked at Mikayla wrong today."

She drops into her seat opposite me and opens her text book.

"I'm not intimidating… am I?"

She bursts out laughing, literally holding her stomach as she cries with laughter. "V, I love and adore you. I know you're like, the nicest human, but yeah, you come off as intimidating. And having those three at your side most of the time doesn't help. You're the girl who overcame and rose above. If anyone was going to be able to take the throne from Blair, it would've been you, but you don't want it, so it fell to the she-devil."

I shake my head, that's so twisted.

"You have a very humble way of viewing who you are, and those around you, but from the outside, yeah you're still Octavia Royal, The Nation's Princess." She shrugs and pulls a soda from her bag.

"I guess I thought everyone just kinda forgot about all of that. I'm just me."

The doors to the library swing open, and the three dark knights in question enter like the three horsemen of the apocalypse—which feels oddly fitting for them.

*Halloween idea next year!*

Mav rubs his hand on the top of Indi's hair before dropping to the chair next to her. She punches his arm and ends up shaking out her hand like it hurt.

We really need to teach that girl to fight properly.

Lincoln takes the seat between Indi and I and Finn sits on my other side. They both seem tense as fuck and my stomach knots.

What the fuck did Finley find in his search?

"Just tell me, I can't take any more tension today. A girl my age should not live through this sort of stress." I sigh, looking at Finn.

"Wait, what did I miss?" Indi asks, looking around the table.

"Finley found a lead on who was helping Evan when he took Octavia. He's been tracing the Dranas lead, and with Luc's help, we finally got some answers." Lincoln's voice is solemn and my heart pounds against my chest.

"Will someone please just tell me what the hell you think you've found?"

Finley looks down at the desk before looking back up at me and the pain in his eyes breaks me. I almost don't want to know. The words nearly fall out of my mouth, but I shove the weaker parts of me down and stay strong, even when I don't want to.

"I found out the name of the person who booked the team with Dranas. V, I…"

He trails off, looking at Lincoln, like he doesn't want to have to tell me. So I drag my gaze to Lincoln, who looks like he wants to tell me about as much as he'd like to cut off his right hand. But he nods at Finn and turns to me anyway. "The name of the person who booked the team was James Smith."

---

"How many more stores do you want to hit?" I groan as Indi drags me into another boutique. We've been shopping for an hour and I'm dragging already. Today's Professional Development Day means we have a free Friday, which gave us chance to shop for the stupid Knight ball Finley dropped on me late last night.

He's still looking into the Dranas thing, because I flat out *refuse* to believe Smithy had anything to do with it. I don't care if the money trail magically lines up, that shit can be faked. Also, who would be stupid enough to book something like that in their own name.

And I don't care that Lincoln said it would be genius to do exactly that, *because* no one would believe it.

It's so stupid. I can barely focus on a fun day with Indi because I'm tripping over everything else going on.

"Earth to V," Indi says, shaking me to get my attention.

"Sorry, I spaced."

"Oh, I noticed. You okay?"

I shake my head. "Not really. There's too much going on. It's hard to work out which way is up sometimes. I can't help but wonder what it would be like to be a normal seventeen-year-old. Just focused on boys and college and thinking that was literally the end of the world."

She frowns at me, tugging me deeper into the store, away from the ears of the three girls behind the counter. "Do you want me to come tonight?"

"I love you, but fuck no. I don't want you in their crosshairs. Plus there is no way Ryker is going to *not* kill me if I lead you into that viper's nest."

She snorts. "That's true, but he also doesn't rule my life. If you want me there, I'm so there."

I chew the inside of my cheek. It would be awesome to have her with me, she'd be the perfect wing woman, but I also never want her in danger ever again because of me.

"Thank you. Let me talk to Lincoln and Finley, make sure there's no reason to not bring you—anything that could get you killed. But let's get you a dress just in case."

"Hell fucking yes. Let's do this!"

I drop a message in the group chat, asking the question, then put my phone away to continue with our penis-free day.

We spend the next hour trying on dozens of dresses, having a full-on 90's *Clueless* fashion show between us in the changing rooms, snapping way more selfies than any person needs, but it's so much fun that I forget about the chaos of my life for a blip of time and actually enjoy myself.

"Did you decide on a dress?" Indi asks as she comes out of the changing room, redressed with a dress back over her arm.

"Yeah, I like the sapphire one."

"Ooh! I love that. And it'll look amazing next to my red one." She winks. "I'm going to get Gracie to do my hair tomorrow, I'm thinking new extensions, all black, crazy long and curled. It'll look amazing with this dress."

"You always look amazing. Do you think Gracie can squeeze me in too?"

"I have zero doubt that she can." She grins at me as we head to the counter. "Do we need shoes?"

"Of course we need shoes." I grin at her. It's fun being able to treat her. I feel like we haven't done enough of this lately and it fucking sucks. I'm hoping this impending doom of a meeting with the Knights will straighten shit out so I can at least start to plan my life out again. I'm past thinking I can just escape it. I know too much to be stupid enough to think that.

But rather than drown under the wave, I'm going to follow the current and try to push back to the surface.

That has to be the better idea, right?

Indi grabs a pair of kitten heels, which I add to the counter, deciding on wearing a pair I already have because my Choos are comfy as fuck. I check out our stuff and we make our way back to the car. My phone buzzes in my pocket and I see Sir Grumpalot's name on the screen.

Lincoln:
No reason why not.

To the point as ever. I wish he'd pull his head out of his ass. I know he has a lot on his mind, we all do, but using me as his emotional punching bag is a shitty thing to do.

"Looks like we're good to go to this thing together," I tell her as we slide into the Range Rover.

"Woop. I'll tell the boys the plan once I'm there. You okay taking my dress back to your place? I figured Gracie can come there, do our hair, and we can just get ready without making the extra stops. It'll be like Homecoming, just better."

"Sounds good," I say, nodding. Smithy went out of town with Matthew this morning and while I'm so happy he's happy, I miss the old guy. Hopefully when life calms down, I'll get to spend some more time with him, too.

Another reason there is no way he was the one working with Panda. He's too busy with his new beau to be meddling in the chaos of my life.

I pull away from the curb, focusing back on the road, when Indi puts *Girls Need Girls* by Sophia Scott on the playlist. "This song, right here. I'm declaring this our song."

I laugh as I listen along to the lyrics. "Hell yeah it is. This is our *jam!*"

---

I lie back on my sofa with a groan. Between running, shopping, and just this week in general, I need a spa day. I love Indi, but she shops like a freaking beast. But at least we have outfits for tomorrow.

It was just a morning of shopping, but I'm beat, and I am *not* looking forward to this Knight party. Not even a little. Being the show pony at a Knight event isn't on my fun time list, but since my presence was requested by Harrison, I'm hoping I get some answers about what it is they want from me.

That this isn't just another dick measuring contest like last time.

Though Lincoln and Finley don't seem as optimistic as I'm trying to be about it all.

My phone buzzes in my pocket, pulling me from the thoughts that have stopped me sleeping properly the last few nights, and I smile when I see the guys' names on my screen. I pull up the group chat thread and try not to laugh.

Maverick:
Princess… what ya doinnnnn?

Finley:
You're such a sap, Mav. But yeah, what are you doing?

Lincoln:
What they mean is, come over here.

Oh look, he seems to have put asshole mode on the back burner. Well kind of.

East:
What my brother means, is please **eye roll**

Lincoln:
She knew what I meant.

Maverick:
Stop being an asshole otherwise she won't come and play.

Me:
Play? What are we playing?

Maverick:
**Wags brows** come and find out.

I give in and laugh, because he's ridiculous, but curiosity is definitely going to kill this cat.

Me:
As long as I get a foot rub out of this, I'm down. I am so not ready for tomorrow night.

I stand up and stretch, glad I'm still feeling kinda cute in my denim skirt and bralette. I tie the plaid shirt in a knot at my stomach and slip my Converse back on before heading next door.

Lincoln:
We're in the basement.

Different. I slip in the back door and head down to the basement. The sounds of *Closer* by Nine Inch Nails blast through the speakers, the bass vibrating through my body as I skip down the stairs. I pause when I reach the bottom of the steps, Finley and Maverick are in the boxing ring while Lincoln runs on a treadmill and East lounges on one of the benches.

"You assholes think this is playing?" I fold my arms over my chest, because this wasn't the sort of play I had in mind. Though watching the four of them get sweaty isn't exactly my idea of a bad time either.

Maverick grins at me from the ring. "What's up, princess? Don't want to get sweaty?"

I bark out a laugh and head toward the ring. "More self-defense today?"

"No, we thought there were more fun ways to get sweaty with you. Did you bring a swimsuit?"

"No one said I needed one."

"You don't. Swimsuits aren't required in my hot tub," Lincoln adds from where he runs on the treadmill.

I swear I'm getting whiplash from his emotional back and forth. When the others are around, he's this version, but the second we're truly alone, he turns back into asshole mode.

I don't say anything because I don't want to provoke the asshole side of him, and the nympho side of me is down for being around all of them sans clothing. Maybe this is how I'll reach him. I peel off my shirt and kick off my shoes, practically skipping toward the door where I know the hot tub and pool are down here. "Last one in loses."

"What do we lose, princess?" Mav jumps over the ropes, his muscles tensing with the effort, and it makes my mouth water. Finn, just shakes his head at Mav's antics—bending enough to exit the ring like a normal person.

"You don't get your dick sucked, asshole," Linc calls out from the treadmill, slowing his run to a walk and then a stop before he turns off the machine completely.

Looking over my shoulder as I reach the door to the hot tub, I see East hot on my heels.

Mav is right behind him and Finn is following with his long strides that make it seem like he's bored.

But I know better.

He's focused. Totally different thing. Focused, I'll enjoy.

At the tub, I push my skirt down and kick it to the nearest wooden bench and turn to see East right there, inches from me.

"I never get tired of seeing your naked body, V." Threading his fingers through my hair, he curls them around the strands and brings our mouths together in a kiss so passionate I feel my juices pooling onto my panties. We're all lips and tongues and teeth, my hands grabbing onto his forearms as he grips his free hand to my hip and obliterates the offensive space between our bodies.

My hips automatically search out some kind of friction when I feel the heat at my back. It's Mav. His scent is unmistakable. While East is devouring my mouth, Mav brings a finger around and circles my clit through my panties, using the lace to add a pinch of rough to the experience.

I barely register the sound of water when East pulls back, taking my bottom lip with his teeth—his eyes glinting with fire—and Mav places an open-mouthed kiss on my shoulder before he's gone.

"Come on, babe. Let's get in." East's words are whispered against my mouth and just as he finishes his last word, Linc walks through the double doors and every atom in the room charges with an electricity only he can conjure.

Suddenly, the space is filled with barely sustained anticipation. We're ready; it's time to be the center of these men's lives.

Time to see if they really are ready to share.

All of them.

"Get in the tub, East." Without even a hint of a scowl, the big brother obeys the younger one. It's still fascinating to me how Linc takes control of any room he enters.

Without so much as a glance at East, Linc walks up to me and palms my jaw—his fingers squeezing hard enough to make my mouth pop open.

"Today, we own you, Octavia."

I nod, as much as I can in this position, before Lincoln's mouth is on mine, his tongue demanding entrance and not waiting for permission. He explores every last inch, licking and biting, sucking and caressing, as his other hand traces down my body.

Apparently he's still in asshole mode, but pretty sure I can get on board with this version of asshole.

Linc's finger pushes my panties inside me until he's breached the lace. Nothing stands between my pussy and the pad of his finger. Pulling at the hole he's just created, he brings me closer, widening the hole as he does.

"Fuck, that's hot," I hear Finn say from the tub, Mav agreeing with his signature grunt.

Linc's hold on my jaw tightens just enough for me to feel the difference, his lips pulling away until he speaks into my mouth.

"Get in the tub and sit on East's lap." I go to move, but Linc stops me with his finger still fucking me through my panties.

"But Octavia? Your first and last orgasms belong to me, so don't you dare come before I allow it." He smiles at my body's reaction to his words. It's no secret that his controlling qualities in the bedroom turn me the fuck on. I'm not too proud to admit it and there's no way I could hide it even if I was.

"Go." Simultaneously letting my jaw and pussy go, I shimmy out of my destroyed lingerie, reaching back and lifting my bralette over my head before stepping into the hot water and heading straight to East.

Flanking him, Mav and Finn have eyes only for me. Linc is right behind me but instead of sitting next to one of the guys, he plants himself across from us—arms resting along the back of the wood, legs spread and chin high. He looks like a king and acts like a god, and we are his subjects to rule over.

East reaches out, turning me around before pulling me onto his lap where his heavy, very hard, cock rests against the crack of my ass. I'm facing Linc, because of course I am. He's got a front row view of us and is in the perfect position to orchestrate our every move.

"Use your fingers, East. Get her cunt nice and ready for us." Linc's words are harsh, which only makes my heart race faster.

My eyes are solely on Linc, watching him watch me is addictive as fuck.

Linc's words come back to me and I whimper as East pushes two fingers inside me without preamble. He just thrusts them in up to the second knuckle and curls them just enough to earn him a gasp.

I can't come.

It seemed so easy to obey before the reality of it was here. The second Lincoln notices my wide eyes, a slow, primal grin spreads across his beautiful lips, and in that moment I see the devil inside of him that I love.

The one that gets off on this control. Knowing he's wielding his power over me. Over all of us.

From across the tub, his eyes are like molten steel, taking in each movement from East. Each reaction from me. He can't possibly see what he's doing—it's all under water—but his imagination is likely as potent as the reality.

"Tell me how she feels."

"Like home." East's words hit me in the chest, making my head lean back onto his shoulder where I feel his mouth come down to my neck, nuzzling, licking, kissing me like I'm his favorite toy and taking care of me is his life's mission.

That's when I feel two mouths on my nipples and without even looking, I reach out to grab Mav and Finn's cocks but I'm stopped before I can reach what I want.

"Octavia." Lincoln's voice is sharp, and I want to challenge him in spite of it, consequences be damned, but then Mav bites down on my nipple and all thoughts of stopping this disappear. I'll listen for now, but later, he's going to deal with it.

I'm a greedy bitch and I want them all.

That's when I feel him at my mouth, whispering like danger.

"Octavia." His tone could cut glass.

"I'm sorry." I breathe out trying not to sound too petulant. "I'm just so…" Lincoln grabs my hair, pulls back and forces me to look into his steely gaze.

"Tell me." Searching my face, Linc looks over my features before he leans in and licks an erotic path across the seam of my lips.

"Tell me," he repeats, his tone softer, more controlled.

"I want to please you. All of you."

"Oh, Octavia. Don't you know? Every part of you pleases us." I can't help the smile that spreads across my mouth until he pulls my head back, sharply.

"But this is my kingdom, my rules. My fucking call, Octavia."

"Okay," I tell him, pouting despite my pussy getting fucked even harder by East as I feel my juices coating his fingers with every word that comes out of Linc's sullen mouth. As if none of this is happening, Finn and Mav just keep licking and sucking on my tits. Jesus, I can't believe I'm trying to have a conversation with Linc all the while getting delightfully handled by the other three.

Linc goes back to his perch, his seat right across the water from us, and resumes his voyeuristic position.

East continues his magic touches, alternating between sliding his fingers in and out and flicking my clit for what feels like an eternity. My body rises quickly to its first orgasm and no matter how hard I try, having two mouths exploring my body and two or three fingers fucking it is really hard to ignore.

"Hold on, Octavia." I try to think of anything but the feel of tongues and fingers all over my skin, inside and out. I try to think about the homework I should have done. About the fucking shootings and hospitals and sects that are trying to ruin us all.

I try really fucking hard not to come but they are seriously pushing all of my buttons.

"Come sit on my face, Octavia." Oh God. He's being crude on purpose. Linc knows his dirty talk is like a flame to a moth.

Asshole.

East takes his fingers out of me, turning my face to the side so he can kiss me like he needs it to breathe.

Every nerve ending is on fire as I walk across the space between us and I'm on the edge of losing my fucking sanity when I see the devious grin on Linc's face. I refuse to give him the satisfaction of punishing me for coming before I'm allowed.

"Ha! See? I can control myself, too." The words fall from my mouth and as I clamp my mouth with my hand, Lincoln's smile turns devilish. Like my outburst is the best thing he's ever heard.

"Is that so?"

*Fuck, fuck, fuck.*

My mouth gets me into way too much trouble sometimes.

"Mav, Finn. You hungry?" Linc doesn't even look at them as he speaks, his eyes are solely on me, taking in my small gasp, the widening of my eyes, the tensing in my shoulders.

There's no fucking way I can keep myself from coming if both of them are eating me out.

This is fucking torture. A sweet torture, but still…

"You wouldn't!"

"Oh baby, not only would I, but I was hoping."

Asshole switch is fully in the on mode.

In the moments that follow, I find myself lifted until I'm sitting on the ledge of the tub, my feet planted firmly on the wooden seat, legs spread, pussy open and on show for all four of them.

"Fuck, she's beautiful." Mav's words hit my ears a millisecond before I feel his tongue part my lips and his mouth sucking on my clit. Then he's gone and Finn takes his place, his tongue fucking my pussy as he searches out my juices and drinks them up.

Back and forth, they take turns eating my pussy, making me squirm, taking pleasure in watching me lose my ever-loving mind.

As I'm leaning back on my elbows, I let my head fall back and stare at the ceiling, wanting to think about anything other than the fact that their mouths will be the death of me.

My hips search out their touch, wanting more and less all at the same time. The battle between body and mind is a raging war, and I'm not sure it's one I'm going to win.

It's while I'm trying really hard not to come all over their faces that I feel the heat on either side of me.

Drunk on them, I turn to one side then the other and through my lust-filled gaze, I see my favorite brothers looking at me like it's Christmas and I'm the fucking feast laid out for them.

East kisses me, deep and soulful, then he retreats leaving me to Linc who—contrary to the oldest Saint—kisses me like he's invading the enemy territory on his way to save the love of his life.

Both kisses are passionate in their own way and I love that they are so different.

I've got four mouths on me and if I die right now, I'd be okay with that.

"My turn." As Linc's words echo throughout the room, everyone stops moving and I feel cold, but not for long.

Looking down the length of my body, Lincoln makes himself comfortable between my legs, kissing one nipple then the other before giving me that smile of his that's just for me.

"Such a good girl. And good girls get rewarded."

My heart flutters and I fill with warmth at his words.

My head falls back once more just as Linc brings his mouth to my pussy and eats me out like a savage. Alternating strokes with his tongue and his fingers, he uses his entire body to fuck me with his face. East, Mav, and Finn take turns sucking on my mouth and nipples and neck. Anywhere they can touch me, they do. It's when I hear Linc say, "Give it to me, Octavia," that my entire body abandons the fight and lets go completely.

I hold my breath, my entire body convulsing, my gasps swallowed by East as he continues kissing me.

I don't know how long my orgasm lasts but I can feel it surge through my veins, the blood rushing, my lungs working overtime.

All the while, Linc continues to eat me out, taking every single drop that I give him.

First and last. Those are his.

As the fog starts to dissipate from the intensity of my orgasm, I open my eyes—my breathing labored—and see a look pass between Linc and Mav, who is running the back of his fingers over the smooth plane of my stomach.

I miss his touch immediately but when it's replaced by Finn's mouth and the kisses he rains down on my skin I feel better.

"Catch." I blink and my gaze goes to Linc just as he catches a packet of something.

They all see my questioning look and Finn whispers across my skin.

"Lube."

Images of all of them inside me at once run through my head and I almost panic.

But then two fingers slide into my pussy, scissoring and preparing me for… what?

"Relax, beautiful. We'd never ask for more than you can give." I trust them but my imagination is pretty fucking healthy and dirty as fuck, so I'm not sure they've considered all of the possibilities I have.

Though looking at the way they watch me, maybe they have.

Still, I nod, not wanting this to end.

East's fingers are gone and seconds later, Linc's dick is inside me thrusting once, twice, a couple more times and then he's out.

"You're so fucking wet, Octavia. We're going to have so much fun tonight." His words would be ominous if I didn't know him better.

Next thing I know, Finn is carrying me—my arms wrapped around his neck—and I spy the other three over his shoulder, whispering in hushed tones with calculating looks all over their faces. It's when I turn back to see where we're going that Finn whispers in my ear. "Say the word and everything stops. Same rules as always."

"Never." My word is final and I can't imagine a reason why I would ever stop what is about to happen.

In the corner of the space, between the hot tub and the sauna, they've set up a quaint little space with a huge mattress and pillows all over. It's all black, red, and white. It's so fucking romantic with all the candles and shit that I almost laugh at the contrast. There's nothing romantic about getting gangbanged by the four men you love equally.

Fuck, maybe there is.

Finn gently places me on the mattress and grabs his cock like he just needs to relieve the pressure or else he'll lose his mind. I like the idea of me causing him to lose it.

Soon, I'm the center of four pairs of eyes all showing different levels of lust and need.

"East, you lie down. We'll be doing all the work tonight. You can just enjoy the ride." Lincoln smirks at his own words. I guess I'm the ride East is about to get. Joining me on the bed, East lavishes me with his warm kisses before he taps me on the hip—silently telling me to get on top of him.

I don't make him wait. Straddling his hips, I brace myself against the wall and let my hair fall in a curtain of black strands over his chest.

"Fuck, her ass…" Mav, ever the modern-day Shakespeare.

Finn positions himself behind me just as I align myself up and over East's dick. We both breathe in through our teeth, making similar sounds as I reach the hilt. He's so deep like this, filling me so perfectly.

Our gazes meet and all I see is love through his long lashes. He's reverent, always has been, but I can see he hates that he's not one hundred percent healed. It doesn't matter though. We'll have other opportunities.

Looking over my shoulder, I watch as Finn coats his cock with the lube, stroking himself like he's trying to calm himself first.

"Finn, I think our girl wants to stroke it for you."

*I really fucking do.*

And since we never do things simple, I'm greeted with two dicks—one for each hand—as East lets me fuck him slowly, deeply.

Finn and Mav are so fucking hard it's like handling steel.

"Hold her back, East." I have no idea what that means until Linc grabs my chin from behind and pulls my head back until I'm facing the ceiling, my throat taut with the effort.

Standing, Linc steps close and places his balls on my lips. "Suck." I open my mouth and use my tongue to lick his ball sack up and down, then around one then the other.

"Fuck, that's hot." Mav is getting even harder at the sight of me sucking on Linc's balls while I jack them off, all the while getting fucked harder by East.

Linc places both of his hands on the nape of my neck, arching my back as far as possible until his dick is sliding inside my mouth. Hearing Linc grunt as he pushes down my throat hits me like an aphrodisiac.

"Fuck, I don't know what you just did, but she's soaking my cock right now." I hear East's words, but I'm too focused on Linc's dick sliding down my throat to pay it any attention. I've even stopped stroking Finn and Mav so they each cover my hand and help me, squeezing my fingers as tightly as they need.

I gag on Linc, tears following with the pull of gravity and running into my hairline while he softly coos words of encouragement. He tells me that I'm perfect. That I'm beautiful swallowing up his entire length. That I'm a queen for giving them so much.

Too soon, Linc glides his dick back out of my mouth and gently straightens me back up. I'm light-headed, the blood having gone to my head, my vision glassy and blurry. When I can see again, it's East's face that greets me. He slides his hands in the strands of my hair and pulls me in, resting his forehead against mine and murmuring.

"So fucking beautiful." His breathing is labored; he's stopped thrusting up into me, like he's trying to catch his breath and avoid losing his load inside me.

While I'm sharing this intimate moment with East, Finn and Mav let go and my hands fall on the wall behind East. I get a soft kiss from Finn on my shoulder while Mav sinks his teeth on the fleshy part of my collarbone.

Fuck, those two are so similar for two men who are complete opposites.

"On all fours, Octavia."

My heart thumps in my chest. This is it. And yet, I have no idea what they are planning.

My body hums with anticipation and no matter what they have planned, I'm ready. So fucking ready.

East pulls out of my pussy as I reposition myself on all fours, my upper body resting on my forearms. He brings himself up to a sitting position, my face now between his legs and his dick still hard and angry looking.

"This may hurt, baby, but just say the word and we'll stop." Finn's words as he slides beneath me, swiping his tongue across my pussy as he passes by, make me suck in a breath, but I'm not stopping. No fucking way. I want this too much. I've been dreaming about this.

He stops when his eyes are level with mine, East's cock looming between our faces, and his gaze on me is filled with heat so intense I'm afraid he'll set me on fire. Mav draws my attention with a slap to my ass and I tear my gaze from Finn's to look over my shoulder. He swings a leg over Finn's knees, straddling him and positioning himself behind me, then he winks at me like he's got the best plan in the world before he pushes his thick cock inside me in one long, hard thrust. I gasp and brace myself. East and Finn hold me steady by the nape of my neck and my hips, their fingers digging in.

It's only once Mav slides in and out of me a couple times that the cool silk of the lube coats my pussy allowing him to glide easily in and out.

Finn slides one huge hand from my hip to my lower back and uses the other to slowly guide the head of his cock to my already-full pussy.

"Shh, you're okay, babe. It's going to sting a little and it might burn a little but you'll get all the pleasure after," East is cooing, his thumb caressing the side of my neck in a soothing rhythm.

Then he's in. The bulbous part of his head rips a cry from me but as quickly as it burns it's gone and the fullness is amazing.

Both Finn and Mav are inside me.

I look up at East and his smile is infectious.

"That's a good girl," Linc tells me, suddenly at my side, kneeling and stroking himself as he watches me getting fucked by his two best friends.

Reaching out with his free hand, he pinches the closest nipple to him and Mav groans, telling him it's making me wetter and wetter which only encourages Linc to continue.

Then East pushes my head down and his cock is pushing into my mouth, achingly slow.

I don't know how they do it. How they orchestrate the dance of it without losing the synchronicity of it all.

I'm sucking a dick while two others are fucking my pussy and my nipple is getting a good fucking work out.

Linc bends down and whispers.

"My turn."

I swear to fuck, those words almost make me come but I hold back.

Linc is gone and the faint sound of lube is back.

The cool gel of it hits the crack of my ass.

One finger slides in and I swear I see stars.

Did I think I couldn't get any fuller?

Fuck, was I wrong.

Two fingers. Two cocks. Holy shit.

Panting around East's cock, I try to keep my rhythm but really, East is coordinating it all. My mind cannot comprehend what is happening.

Linc scissors his fingers in, turning, thrusting, curling and widening my hole.

"Lean back, Mav." His fingers are gone and I feel the angle of the two cocks inside of me shift, drawing a moan from somewhere deep inside of me that has East hissing and his cock twitching in my throat.

I feel the makeshift bed jostle, and a moment later Linc has lined himself up with my ass, my entire world falling into place with a crystal clarity I've never experienced.

They are everything. I'm the center and they are the slaves to my orgasm.

I moan around East's cock again as Linc slowly pushes inside my ass and for a brief moment I think it might be too much. For a brief moment, I think I might tap out.

But the moment passes and there is only ecstasy left behind.

"Fucking hell. Yeah, that's it, V. Fuck yeah." East is pushing my head further and further down as I get thoroughly fucked from behind.

It's too much.

It's everything.

And I love every single moment of it.

I'm the first to come when Mav reaches around and stimulates my clit faster and faster until everything explodes behind my lids.

This prompts East, who pushes my head down until I'm choking and swallowing his cum. I don't care that I'm a mess. I lick up everything that's escaped my mouth while behind me, Mav roars his own climax and Finn follows right behind him. They both pull out and once they're gone, Linc fucks me like his entire life depends on this one, final orgasm.

Skin slapping skin, nails sinking into the flesh of my ass cheeks as Linc fucks my ass with fierce abandon.

It's when I hear the guttural cry he releases that I look over my shoulder, watching in rapt attention as he throws his head back and holds my body close to his as he empties himself out inside me.

Seconds pass as he lets everything go and when he does, his eyes search me out and in that one moment—when our gazes lock—I know everything he's feeling. Because I feel it too.

Once Linc pulls out, I drop down on top of Finn, and I've never felt more deliciously used than I do right now.

East, Finn, and Mav shuffle me to the center of the makeshift bed while Lincoln walks off, naked, to the bathroom and comes back with four warm cloths and for the next fifteen minutes, I'm cared for, coddled and loved until I pass out from the most incredible evening of my life.

# CHAPTER TWENTY-FIVE

## OCTAVIA

This night is not going how I expected it to. Starting with Lincoln not arriving with Maverick and Finley to pick us up. East is sitting tonight out. Advice from Chase apparently, and I'm not opposed to it. If he can stay free and clear of the Knights and all of their bullshit, then awesome. I've been second-guessing bringing Indi with me all freaking day.

But Maverick's reassurance that he wouldn't leave her side made me feel a little better since Finn and I have to play the happy couple tonight.

The Lincoln thing is driving me nuts. I haven't heard from him all day. His father called him this morning and we haven't seen him since. Finley showed me the message he got from him, telling him he wouldn't be coming with us tonight, but that was literally all it said.

Goddamn Saint is frustrating as fuck.

I just want to know what the fuck is going on with him

As the town car pulls up to the same Saint mansion that we'd gone to for the charity ball, Indi lets out a low whistle. "Wow, these guys sure do love their swanky manors, huh?"

I laugh softly as Finley smiles at her.

"Better get used to it tonight, Pixie Spice. This place is full of pretentious bozos in fancy, shiny shit to try and hide who they really are. All of this is just a shiny exterior so no one looks too hard for the truth."

"I just meant it looks nice," she says, rolling her eyes.

I shake my head and lean forward. "You two need to play nice tonight. It'll only take one of these assholes to hear you arguing to decide that they want to use it against us."

Finn lifts my hand and kisses the inside of my wrist. "Relax, pretty girl. We aren't going to let anything happen to her. Or to you. This is just another ridiculous event for the bigwigs from the city and the Knights to show everyone how rich they are. I doubt they'll even try to speak to you tonight, but you not attending would have been a snub—especially since Chase helped us find you—and that is the last thing we want."

The car rolls to a stop and the valet opens the door. The boys climb out first, then help Indi and I out. The steps are lined with spiral-cut trees decorated in twinkle lights, and people of all ages are ascending them into the mansion.

Music plays softly, servers walk around in their black shirt and tie uniforms, far less obscure than the ones they wore the last time I was here.

This all looks almost, dare I say, normal.

"I don't know what you were so worried about," Indi murmurs as she slides up beside me as we enter the main room. "This just looks like a stuffy party."

Maybe she and Finn are right. Tonight is nothing more than a party for the rich and pretentious.

"Let's get a drink, shall we?" Mav says, clapping his hands together before holding out his arm, which Indi takes, even if she does pull a face at him as she does.

Finn grips my hand tighter and leans in closer, "How long till you think they end up killing each other?"

"I give it about twenty minutes. We probably shouldn't leave them alone too much."

"You're probably right," he murmurs, the warmth of his breath sending a shiver down my spine. "If I didn't tell you how stunning you look tonight, I should definitely be fired as one of your boyfriends." He pulls back and smiles down at me, before glancing around the room.

A tall, waif-like blonde approaches us, resting bitch face in place.

"Fuck," Finley mutters and entwines my fingers with his.

She stops in front of us, her gaze roaming over me, as if sizing me up.

Finley smiles tightly at her as he pulls me closer into his side. "Artemis, I'm surprised you bothered to come."

She looks a little older than us, but I don't recognise her. If she's here though, and she knows Finn, she must have something to do with the Knights.

"I thought I'd come and meet the infamous Octavia Royal, considering all of the fuss that's been made about her lately."

I quirk a brow at her as her heated gaze sweeps over me again, and her mouth tugs up in the corners. "I guess I can see why you've been tripping over yourself."

Finley chuckles as he kisses my hair. "Octavia, this is Artemis DuPoint. She sits on the Conclave, too."

"Nice to meet you," I say, offering her my hand, even though it feels awkward as shit.

She takes my hand and kisses it, making Finn laugh hard. "Pleasure was mine. I'll be seeing you."

She winks at me before walking away, and I just gawp after her wondering what just happened.

"I think she likes you," he teases before kissing me softly. He pulls back, gaze darting around the room when his smile drops. I follow his line of sight and I see why.

Descending the staircase is Georgia, her red hair piled up on her head and her creamy skin highlighted by the scarlet dress that's basically painted onto her. Her arm is looped through Lincoln's, whose smile is so bright it almost hurts my eyes.

*It's just for show.*

I repeat the line in my head like a mantra. *I know his real smile, that one he has just for me.*

"Come on, pretty girl. Let's get a drink," Finley says softly, stealing my attention from the two of them. I smile up at him, swallowing down the rising jealousy. I have no reason to be jealous.

I know who he really is. I know he loves me.

He already told me he wouldn't touch her, I just have to remember that.

Finn takes my hand and leads me to the bar, where Indi and Maverick are bickering over cocktails.

"Appletinis are not a girl's drink," Maverick growls. "They taste fucking delightful."

"If you say so." Indi laughs before turning to face me.

I know the instant she sees Georgia and Lincoln over my shoulder, because traces of amusement leave her face and her eyes shine with anger. "Imma claw that bitch's eyes out."

"Calm down, Kujo. Lincoln knows how to play the game. Too well. He's about as willing to be with her as any of us would be," Maverick murmurs to her, placing his hand on her shoulder to make sure she stays in place.

"It's fine," I say, waving it off.

*Fake it till we make it, right?*

I don't even turn around to look at them, even though I feel eyes on my back. It'd be a lot easier to swallow if Lincoln hadn't been a giant asshole lately. But this is obviously what had him so stressed.

Indi sucks in a breath, her eyes widening as she looks behind me. I already know what's happening before I look.

I step closer to Finn, who puts his arm around my waist and pulls me even closer. "You've got this. Just rise above."

"Octavia, it's so lovely to see you again!" Georgia's lilting voice makes me want to wince, but instead I paint a smile on my face and look over to the redhead hanging off of Lincoln's arm, catching a glimpse of Maverick moving Indi closer to him. I'm not sure if it's to protect him or to make sure he can stop her lunging at the bitch beside me.

"Georgia, you too. How have you been?"

She laughs, and it's so twinkly and ladylike, I want to punch her in the throat just to stop it.

"Oh, I'm great. I hear you had a bit of a rough time lately. Poor Lincoln told me about your rehab in Mexico. I hope everything is okay now." Her smile is wicked, her eyes glinting like she knows something I don't. I know rehab from the kidnapping was what Lincoln explained to Harrison, but I get the feeling Georgia knows more than she's letting on.

I glance at Lincoln who just looks indifferent. He barely even acknowledges me. It stings, but I just keep reminding myself this is the game.

"I need to go powder my nose, sweetheart," she says, leaning over and kissing Lincoln's cheek. "I'll be back. Octavia, join me?"

"Of course," I say, softly shaking my head at Indi before extracting myself from Finley. Lincoln's eyes go wide, a hint of panic filling them before he controls his reaction.

Weird.

I follow Georgia across the room and back up the stairs she just came down. "There's a private bathroom up on the mezzanine, though I imagine you already know that."

I just nod, not saying a word as I follow. I only agreed to this little jaunt to find out what it is that she wants. Maybe she's not as bad or as conniving as I think. Maybe she doesn't want this engagement any more than Lincoln does. Maybe I should've asked him, but he won't speak about her to me.

We head into the bathroom, and she moves straight to the mirror, opening the clutch that hangs from her wrist. "I'm surprised you let him go so easily, you know."

"I'm sorry?" I keep my confusion from my face as best as I can.

"Lincoln. I'm not an idiot, Octavia, and Blair filled me in on the little whore ring you had going on. But knowing you let Lincoln go so he could be truly happy… it surprises me. Especially with a cock like that. Can't have been easy to give up."

I swallow the writhing jealousy—because how the fuck does she know about his dick—and smile at her in the mirror as I reapply my lip gloss.

"I have Finley, that's all I need." I shrug, hoping my nonchalance is believable.

She puts her lipstick away, the same shade on her lips as her dress, and turns to face me. "Well, I mean, I can understand that. He definitely isn't hard on the eyes. But that thing Lincoln does with his tongue… I'm not sure I could give that up."

"I didn't realize you two were so close."

"We weren't until you got back from your trip. I was as surprised as you are, but when he came to me, who am I to say no to the man I'm going to marry? I was a little resistant to the marriage at first, but after sampling his dick, and knowing his net worth… who am I to fight it when he seems to want it, want *me*, so much? I have to say, those dimples on his back are just adorable though. The freckles that almost make up the Big Dipper just above them, too. Who would've thought a man like Lincoln would have such adorable features underneath that steely exterior."

My blood runs cold at her words.

How the fuck does she know any of that?

"Well, I don't need to tell you, you know all of this. You ready to head back?"

I force a smile, hoping it reaches my eyes. "Sure, let's go party shall we?"

"Let's."

---

I pull the pins from my hair, trying not to hulk out. How I managed to contain myself all evening and night with the two of them all night is beyond me. Iron strength of fucking will is all I can figure.

"Are you going to tell me what happened?" Indi asks as she appears from my bathroom in her pj's. She flops onto the bed, staring at me as I try to calm myself.

"Georgia was just enjoying telling me intimate details of Lincoln's body and expressing how much she enjoys his tongue and dick. That's all."

Her jaw drops, and she blinks at me, as if computing, then screeches, "I'm sorry, fucking what?"

"It has to be a lie, right?" I say as I step out of the sapphire gown, not caring about the garment as I try to contain the whirlwind inside of me. "He wouldn't fuck her. And he wouldn't hide it from me if he did."

She sits, quietly raging on the bed, her fists clenched. "What did she say, exactly?"

Much as I really don't want to revisit the conversation, I tell her everything and by the time I'm done, she's practically vibrating. "I assume the dimples and dipper are real?"

I nod as I pull on my pj's and put my hair in a messy bun on top of my head. "They are."

"Could she have known the details from Blair?"

I shrug. "It's possible, but Lincoln hasn't fucked Blair. It doesn't mean she didn't find out from someone else, but Lincoln doesn't exactly whore himself out."

"Yeah, I'm not sure he's even fucked anyone but you at ECP," she says, twisting her lips. "That doesn't mean he hasn't though."

I drop back onto the bed, throwing myself backward so I can stare at the ceiling.

"It's not fair for me to be this jealous, right? I have all four of them. How can I justifiably stop him fucking someone else and not be a hypocrite?"

"Oh, hell no. One, they said they only wanted you, that they were happy to share, and you told them outright you wouldn't share them. They agreed to that shit, so you can absolutely be angry and jealous. Two, we don't know for certain he fucked her. You need to find that out before you do anything."

"You're right. I should just ask him." I get up and grab my phone, dialing his number before putting it against my ear.

It goes straight to voicemail.

Awesome.

"Try again, he was probably peeing or something," Indi encourages. I hate to be *that* girl, but I hit his number again anyway.

The line rings, and rings. Just when I'm about to give up, it answers and I hear her voice. "Hello?"

"Georgia," I say, trying not to growl at her answering his phone. "I just needed to ask Lincoln a question, is he there?"

"Oh of course, silly me. Sorry, we have the same phone, I didn't even notice I grabbed his. Let me grab him, he was just heading for a shower."

I clench my fists as she calls out his name, while Indi sits silently, watching me intently.

The sound of running water filters through the speaker and the sound of muffled voices reaches my ear before he speaks. "Hello?"

"Lincoln," I say, trying to remain calm. "I had some questions for you, but I see you're busy."

"What do you want, Octavia?" he snaps, and I feel my eyes fill with tears.

"Did you fuck her?"

"Octavia," he starts, sighing. I can almost picture him running his hand through his hair with frustration.

"Yes or no, Lincoln. It's a simple question."

"Nothing's ever that simple."

"Is that how she knew about the Big Dipper on your back?"

"Octavia, let me explain." He sounds angry that I even asked the question, but he doesn't deny it.

"That wasn't a no. Have a good night, Lincoln." I drop the call and fall to the ground as sobs rack my body.

"I'm going to sever his dick from his body," Indi growls as she rushes across the room and wraps me in her arms.

I can't speak. I can't do anything but cry as my heart aches in my chest.

I really thought we could survive all of this. His dad, Georgia, all of it.

But apparently I was wrong.

More fool me.

---

After spending the night tossing and turning in bed, Indi made me come and hang out with her and the Kings today. I left my phone at home after letting East know where I was going—she has hers if I really need to speak to anyone, but I don't see that happening any time soon.

We've been in the basement at Ryker's all morning while Dylan and Ellis play Xbox and Ryker… well he does whatever it is he does to keep his empire running.

Indi has been locked with him in his office for the last half hour, and I'm glad she's so happy, but being here, as a part of her happy bubble, is just making me see how fucked mine is.

"What's wrong, Princess Peaches?" Dylan asks as Ellis disappears into Ryker's office. "Indi wouldn't tell us anything, just said you had a shitty night and needed to chill."

"Would it be too dramatic of me to just say everything?" I sigh and he bursts out laughing.

"Honestly, probably not, knowing some of the shit you've been dealing with. Is there anything we can do?"

"Put out a hit on Harrison? Help me bring down the empire of the Knights? Storm the castle with me and help me save the princes? Maybe put out a hit on the redheaded snake sucking the life from me too?"

He raises his eyebrows and just blinks at me. "I mean, we probably could, but…"

I shake my head and bark out a dry, humorless laugh, "But why would you? It's fine. I'm just being a dramatic little bitch. Just need to lick my wounds then act like nothing's wrong. Story of my life."

"Want to go shoot shit? That always makes me feel better."

I start to shake my head and stop. "Ya know what, fuck it. Let's go shoot shit."

"That's my girl! I knew I liked you!"

"Should we tell them where we're headed?" I say, nodding toward the door.

He grins and walks over, banging on it with the side of his fist so loud I jump even though I knew he was going to do it. Indi squeals and Ryker swings open the door, eyes wild.

"V and I are going shooting. Thought we should let you fuckers know." He tries not to laugh as Ryker lunges at him and they end up wrestling on the floor. I lift my feet from the ground up onto the sofa with me, not sure whether to laugh or cry as they beat the crap out of each other, but since Indi appears in the doorway and just groans, I go with laughter.

"Ellis, will you help?"

Ellis appears, takes in the two titans rolling around the room, and shakes his head. "Not a chance I'm getting in there."

"Wuss," she teases him, sticking her tongue out at him. She takes a deep breath and shouts, "If the two of you don't stop, I'm not sucking *any* dick for two weeks."

She blushes when I laugh, but the ruckus on the ground stops almost immediately.

"Aww, but short stack, you suck dick so good." Dylan's groaning makes me laugh harder and Ryker pushes the big guy off of him as he climbs to his feet.

"No need to mope, asshole. We stopped. You're lucky she made us stop too."

"I could've taken you." Dylan grins back at him.

"Boys," Indi warns, and they both grin at her. "Now then, who are we shooting?"

"And that, short stack, is why you're my favorite." Dylan whoops and picks her up, tipping her over his shoulder. "We're shooting things, not people."

"Dammit, I thought for sure we were going to deal with that hopped up rich bitch," Indi groans. "Now put me down, ya giant."

I can't help but giggle as he slaps her ass before planting her on the sofa beside me. "You feeling okay?" she asks softly.

I nod, "Yeah, Dylan is a great distraction, and shooting should be fun."

"It's a shame we're not killing the redhead. I'd happily watch her bleed."

I shrug, pulling the sleeves of my hoodie down over my hands. "Maybe another day. Or maybe Lincoln truly is happy and I've been lying to myself. Or maybe he didn't fuck her and it's all one big misunderstanding. But he isn't talking to me, so I don't know what else to do but keep marching on."

She side hugs me as the boys get their shit together. "Come on, let's go shoot some shit, maybe sledge hammer some stuff, get out all the rage. You'll love it.

Then after, Smithy should be home, so we can go back to your place, milkshake up, and snuggle on the sofa with a horror movie."

"You, Indigo Montoya, might just be my one true love."

She giggles at me. "Same, just don't tell *them* that. They might sulk." She nods over to the guys who are watching us both closely.

"Come on, boys," she says, slapping her hands against her thighs before standing up. "Let's go break stuff."

# CHAPTER TWENTY-SIX

## LINCOLN

### THREE DAYS AGO

Listening to my brother with my girl is a fucked-up thing. It's not like I intended on it, but she isn't exactly quiet. A grin tugs at my lips at the thought of her crying out beneath me. Soon enough, I'll have her to myself again.

First, I have to get through the rest of this week and the party on Saturday. If I can survive that, then I can start planning a way to make Georgia think she was the one to decide against this farce of an engagement. I clench my fists just thinking about the corner Harrison has me backed into.

I've been trying to fight off my demons all night, and despite the hell I put my body through tonight, nothing, not even my exhaustion can keep them away.

Even in my sleep they haunt me.

Octavia might say she's understanding of what I'm having to do, but if I saw her with anyone who wasn't part of our group, I'd burn down the fucking world, so I know there is no way in hell she's actually handling it as well as she's trying to pretend she is.

Or maybe she's less of a jealous asshole than I am.

I turn on the shower in my bathroom and hit play on my playlist so the room fills with music that matches my mood. When *Bring Me The Horizon* screams through the speakers, I strip out of my workout gear while I wait for the water to heat.

Stepping beneath the scalding water does nothing to distract me from the bullshit I've got to try and work my way through, but it does at least help loosen some of the tension in my shoulders. I lose myself to the music and the beat of the water as it assaults my skin.

I lean my head forward, resting my forehead against the cold tile, the clash in temperature sending a shiver down my spine.

The thought of Octavia writhing beneath my brother down the hall plays in my mind, and while it shouldn't be hot to think of her with the others, it is. Especially when I know there are some noises she makes that are just for me.

The caveman inside of me likes that a lot.

I freeze at the feel of fingertips on my spine. "Happy to see me, I see."

My jaw clenches at the sound of her voice. "Why are you in my shower, Georgia?"

I don't turn to face her, because Harrison's words ring out in my head, my hard on officially disappearing.

"Your dad gave me a key to this place. I thought I'd come surprise you, show you just how good we can be together. I know all about the other girl, but I can make you forget all about her."

She presses her chest to my back and a growl escapes me.

She seems to mistake it for encouragement and traces her fingers around my ribs to my chest. "I knew you'd forget her when you felt me pressed against you."

I have never felt more violated in my entire fucking life—and that's no small feat—and I remain still, trying to work out how to get her the fuck out of my shower without putting Octavia at risk. If Harrison gave her a key, I'm sure he encouraged all of this, and I'm also sure that she'll run back to him if I flat out reject her.

I'm going to be fucking sick.

She palms my limp dick and giggles. "I'm sure I can change his mind about me too."

"Let go of my dick, Georgia." I clench my fists, but she squeezes rather than letting go with another laugh.

Fuck this.

I grab her wrist, squeezing hard enough that she gets the message, and she releases me. I spin, keeping my hold on her wrist, and face her. I keep my eyes on hers, not bothered about whatever her body looks like, because she's not Octavia.

"Harrison may have invited you into my house, but I sure as fuck didn't invite you into my shower. I don't know who the fuck you think you are, but when it comes to my dick, I make the rules."

Her nostrils flare as I push her back against the tile, keeping a distance between us.

"I know you want me, Lincoln." She glances down at my dick and smiles maliciously. "You can try to fight it, but you won't win."

Her eyes glint as I let go of her, hating the feel of her skin against mine, and storm from the shower, wrapping a towel around my waist before leaving the room.

Fuck this shit. Fuck it all to hell.

I wonder if I can get Octavia out of the country and out of my father's reach. I'm positive she'll fight me on leaving—she fights me on everything—but maybe if I try to explain it to her…

Georgia strides into my room, still fully naked, dripping onto my carpet. She stalks toward me and fingers my towel where I've knotted it. "I'm fairly certain you don't want your father to know you're rejecting me. I'll let it pass for now, but make no mistake, Lincoln. I get what I want. Always."

She picks up a slip of black material I hadn't noticed by my door and pulls the dress over her head until she's covered. "I'll see you on Friday, fiancé."

Waving her fingers at me, she leaves the room with a smile, closing the door behind her.

What the fuck am I going to do?

# CHAPTER TWENTY-SEVEN

## OCTAVIA

It's been two weeks since that stupid Knight party and Lincoln has barely looked at me, let alone spoken to me. Finn and Mav haven't talked to him either, and East said he's about as much fun to live with as a bear with a thorn in its paw.

But no one can get any answers from him about what the actual fuck is going on with him because he won't speak to anyone.

Frustrated and devastated doesn't even begin to cover how I feel.

But more than anything, I'm just sad and angry.

What's worse? I haven't heard from Harrison either, so I still have this bullshit with the Knights hanging over my head. I don't want to think that it's all wrapped up in the Lincoln stuff, but at this point, I have no idea what to think anymore.

I roll over in bed, grabbing my phone from the nightstand.

Eleven at night on a Friday and here I am, living the rockstar life of pining over a boy.

I pull up my private thread with him. His last message stares at me from weeks ago…

Tears prick my eyes. Nope, doesn't hurt at all.

Me:
Are you ever going to explain?

My thumb hovers over send for a few seconds before I hit it and stare at the screen like a crazy person. I know I should be content. I have the other three, and it's not like I love them less, or I love him more… I just don't understand.

The message shows as delivered.

Then read.

And then nothing.

I bury my face in the pillow and let out a scream so as not to alert Smithy. The one weekend he doesn't stay at Matthew's and I have a minor breakdown. Though it could be the sheer volume of tears, ice cream, and murder shows I've worked through the last two weeks that made him stay home this weekend.

It's the first night I've been alone since that night. Between Indi and the guys, someone has been here, but I told everyone I was okay. That I wanted a night alone.

I really don't want to be *that* girl.

But here I am, staring at my phone like a crazy person.

Three dots appear on the screen, and I hate myself for the way my heart skips a beat.

I practically hold my breath waiting for the message, but they just disappear.

Of course they fucking do. I pull up an audiobook, hoping that the sound of voices will lull me to sleep, but then my phone buzzes and I drop it, slapping myself in the face.

Might just be the highlight of my night.

Fuck my life.

I pick up my phone and see his name on the screen.

Lincoln:
You seem to have already decided you know everything. What's left to explain?

Fuck my life. Why is he such a pain in the ass?

Me:
You didn't deny it.

Lincoln:
I didn't think I'd have to.

I bite my lip, guilt slamming through me. Is this all my fault? Did I overreact?

Me:

She knew things, Linc. Things she shouldn't know unless she's been naked with you.

Lincoln:
You want the truth?

Me:
Always.

Lincoln:
I was naked with her.

Lincoln:
But I didn't fuck her.

Lincoln:
I also didn't choose to be naked with her. She accosted me in the shower. So I guess that's how she knew whatever she told you.

Lincoln:
But it fucking sucks that you don't trust me… trust us… enough to already know that I wouldn't touch her. I told you I wouldn't. And you still believed her.

A lump fills my throat.

He's right.

I fucked this up. I didn't trust him. I did believe her.

God, I'm such a fucking idiot.

Anger simmers under the surface at what she did, and I add her to my list of people that are going to burn when I find a way. How fucking dare she do that to him?

Me:
I'm sorry.

Lincoln:
You have nothing to be sorry for. When you called, I was with her. I was in a shower and I didn't explain. Harrison forced me to share the suite with her that night and she was right there. I didn't know what to do. What to say. I didn't come to you after. But Harrison… It doesn't matter what the excuses are. None of this is your fault.

Me:
I'm still sorry.

Me:
I miss you.

Lincoln:
I miss you too.

I drop my phone onto my chest and just stare at the ceiling. This might've explained some stuff, but there still feels like there's this giant chasm between us. I don't know how we get back from this. Will there even be an us while Harrison rules over him? While the *acting* Regent of the fucking Conclave insists that Georgia is in his life?

If I looked better in orange, I'd be tempted just to take her out purely for what she did to Lincoln. Pretty sure that Harrison would make sure I was locked up for it though, and he'd throw away the damn key.

I toss and turn in bed, waiting for sleep to take me, but it doesn't come. When I check my phone again, it's two a.m.

Awesome.

A rustling outside my balcony door has me sitting up in bed, reaching for the gun Maverick insisted I keep in the drawer beside my bed. But when I see Lincoln open the balcony door, I stop, my heart hammering in my chest.

Why is he here?

And why do I feel so awkward that he is.

"You know you don't have to keep coming in that way, right?" I quirk a brow as Lincoln crosses my room toward my bed. This push and pull between us is getting to a point where we either need to fix things, or I need to put more distance between us until we can sort out the web of lies we're trapped in. I hate this limbo.

He clenches his jaw and shrugs as he slips out of his jacket. He drops his phone and God knows what else onto the bedside table, stripping down to his boxers before climbing into bed and lying down beside me in silence.

I open my mouth to speak but nothing comes out, so I close it again, wishing things weren't like this with us.

I know I'm probably overreacting, that this isn't his fault, but my stupid heart can't make sense of it all. All I have is pain and jealousy, no matter how unreasonable it is.

He rolls over to face me and lets out a deep sigh before pulling his phone from the bedside table. He taps the screen a few times before turning back to me and slipping an AirPod I hadn't noticed him grab into my ear. "I never thought I'd be the one you couldn't talk to. That we'd be here. That I wouldn't have the right words to fix this. So I'm hoping that this will say what I can't."

He goes quiet as the track starts playing in my ear. I close my eyes and listen to the lyrics, breaking a little inside—in the best way—over the fact that he chose to reach me with the one medium he knows speaks to the deepest, darkest parts of me.

*So, can we close the space between us now?*
*It's the distance we don't need.*
*You're everything I love about the things I hate in me.*

"What song is this?" My voice is croaky as waves of emotion wash over me. He shows me the screen as the song starts to play again.

*Favorite Place* by All Time Low.

My heart shatters in my chest, but not in the painful way I've been dealing with lately. I break in a way that I think I might be able to rebuild from. With him.

With all of them.

I just need a way to free them. To free us all.

I make a promise to myself that as soon as there is a way, I'll save them. All of them. No matter the cost.

As I roll over, the song still playing, he curls around me from behind, and that's how I fall asleep.

---

I wake up to the feel of Linc's lips fluttering down my neck, the press of his dick against my ass. I can't say that I haven't missed this.

Missed him.

I know I should be over what happened, that it's all for show, but that doesn't make my heart hurt any less. Not when I know I'm going to have to keep seeing him with her. That there's nothing I can do to stop it.

*We said we'd do everything together.*

But this… he didn't tell me. Didn't warn me. Again.

And then I fell for her lies.

We both fucked up. Time and time again.

"Linc." His name is breathy as it falls from my lips, a shiver running down my body as his teeth graze against my shoulder.

"Linc, stop." He freezes at my words, pulling back from me as I turn to face him. I know I already asked him last night, but I need to see his face when he answers. "Did you fuck her?"

I hate how vulnerable I feel right now. How pathetic I feel.

How much I want to believe him no matter what Georgia said, but I know he won't be able to lie to me. Not to my face.

He grips my chin, a fire in his eyes. "I already told you I didn't. I swear to you, I've never touched her. She was there when you called, so I couldn't exactly explain. She knows Harrison has me by the balls… and the threats he made. Octavia, I will never risk you. Never. She knew what she was doing. She's a fucking snake."

He lets out a sigh, shaking his head. "All I can tell you is my truth. Do you really not believe me?"

I look into his eyes and I know he isn't lying. Some might call it me wanting to believe him, being naïve, others might recognize it as blind faith. But I know him, and despite my stupid warring emotions, deep down, I know he wouldn't do that to me.

"I believe you," I say softly. "Doesn't make any of it hurt any less, but I believe you."

"I'm sorry it hurt you, Octavia. Truly. I'd do anything to take that pain from you." The sincerity in his eyes weakens my heart a little, so I lean forward and kiss him softly.

He pulls me against his chest and buries his hands in my hair, holding me so tight it feels like he might never let go. "I missed you so fucking bad," he breathes.

He kisses me again, setting my entire world on fire.

"I'm going to make sure you never forget it."

Our legs intertwined, our mouths sealed, and our tongues searching, we make out like the teenagers we are. Rubbing against each other, Linc's hand tightens even more at the nape of my neck, my hair trapped between his fingers. That little bite of pain keeps me alert and needy, just the way he likes me.

"Clothes off." I stop everything, my lips pressed against his and look up into his intense gray eyes.

"You're the one groveling. You should be the one undressing me." I laugh, making sure to add a little sass to my voice because there's nothing sexier than Lincoln trying his best to rein in his frustration. And nothing frustrates him more than me mouthing off.

Payback is hell.

"Octavia. I will grovel with my dick inside your cunt. And I will make sure you come so many times you forget all of this. But," he pulls back on my hair and traps my bottom lip with his teeth, biting down hard enough for the sting to get my attention before releasing it and pinning me with a serious glare. "I still call the shots. Always."

I shrug like it's no big deal, but I wouldn't have it any other way. Still, playing with him is so much fun.

"Fine." I make a whole show of it and don't miss the arched brow he gives me, like he's about to show me where my attitude is going to get me.

Which is nowhere.

Absolutely nowhere.

I scramble up and in a flash, I'm completely naked and beyond ready to have his hands all over me.

"Good girl. Now, undress me." I have to seriously check myself to make sure I don't roll my eyes at his order. I mean, he could have taken off his own boxers and saved us some time, but of course he wants me to do it.

Linc rolls onto his back and arches that fucking brow at me again, and I'm equal parts annoyed and turned on by his brass attitude.

Grovel, my ass. He's loving this.

I bite my lip as I get on my hands and knees, shaking my ass as I straddle his chest—backwards, because fuck him. I can follow orders and have my fun all at the same time. The growl that rumbles out of him as I run my hands down his hips and slide my fingers under the hem of his boxers, pushing myself down his body with them in tow, tells me that I might actually get away with it. I throw them off to the side once they're off and smile over my shoulder at him, finding his Cheshire grin well in place as I sit up on my haunches and turn to position myself between his legs.

"Now what?" I ask, certain he already has a plan.

"Now, Octavia, you lie down on your back and let me worship every inch of you before I fuck you within an inch of your life." I grin like he's just told me it's Christmas morning and all my gifts are under the tree.

Eagerly, I jump up and position myself in the dead center of the bed as Linc vacates his space. As soon as I'm laid out for him, he covers my body with his and starts at my lips. Kissing and biting, sucking on my tongue and lips, Linc spends a long time paying attention to my mouth before he moves to my chin and my neck.

He holds himself up on his forearms, hands cradling my head as he leaves open-mouthed kisses on my neck. When he spends a little too much time on one spot, I smile knowing he's leaving a mark. Fucking barbarian.

Sliding down the length of my body, he reaches one nipple, laving it with his tongue before moving to the other and showing it the same attention.

My back arches, my chest chasing his mouth, wanting more, needing him to give me a little pain with my pleasure. So, of course, I tell him.

"Linc, please, m—"

"Do not fucking finish that phrase, Octavia, or I will stop right the fuck now and go back to my place."

He's lying through his teeth.

Right?

He has to be.

I mean, he wouldn't dare leave me like this.

Would he?

That's the thing with Lincoln Saint. He's capable of pretty much anything to prove a point and I'm not ready for this to stop.

Snapping my mouth shut, I let him go at his pace and reel in my frustration for the greater good.

"Good girl." He winks at me. Winks. Like he's won. Spoiler alert—having an orgasm means I win.

Once he finishes teasing my tits, he trails a hot path of kisses down my stomach, and when he reaches my pussy, he kisses my clit then rises up on his knees.

"On all fours. Now."

I don't even hesitate. I position myself on my forearms, my ass nice and high for him, unable to hide just how much I want him.

"Fuck, you're so goddamn gorgeous like this. All ready and shaking with need for my fucking cock. Mine." He places both of his big hands on my ass cheeks and pulls me into him as he nudges the entrance of my pussy with the head of his cock. I feel it there, just waiting and teasing. Sliding up and down my slit like he's teasing himself—teasing me—before giving me what he knows I want.

I'm about to sink onto him when I realize what he's doing. He's testing me. He wants to see how long I'll last before I act out.

Asshole.

As tempted as I am, I clench my fists and resist the urge.

Looking over my shoulder, I give him my best innocent look and bat my lashes at him—my only act of rebellion.

Linc smiles and it's a mixture of pride and danger right before he pulls my hips back into him and slams inside me to the hilt.

I grunt as he groans out his pleasure and freezes. His head hangs back, the pleasure of being squeezed by my pussy written all over his face.

Fuck, he's beautiful.

He slowly glides in and out of my pussy, thrusting in and out a couple of times, before he reaches up and wraps the strands of my hair around his palm, pulling me back up to kneeling, my back flush against his chest.

His mouth comes to my ear as he whispers, "Do you feel that?"

I nod because the fullness of him in this position robs me of words.

"You are mine, as much as I am yours, Octavia. Don't *ever* fucking forget that."

Letting go of my hair, he slides his hand to my throat—his thumb and middle fingers on my pulse points—squeezing until my head falls back on his shoulder as he fucks me.

He's in total and complete control as he times his thrusts perfectly. Evenly. Dragging out every fucking moment and driving me insane.

I love when he gets like this. When he uses that calculating side of himself in the best of ways.

When his free hand finds its way to my clit, and he pushes up with his cock as he circles with his finger, I about lose my mind. I moan as the combined stimulation awakens every nerve ending in my body.

With every snap of his hips, he grunts in my ear like he can't stop himself.

His control is slipping, little by little.

It's my favorite part of us. Feeling the moment his walls come crumbling down, and for a moment, he's a mere mortal like the rest of us.

"Fuck, Octavia. Come all over my cock, beautiful." And I do. I let it all go because I want to and because he needs me to.

Reaching back, I dig my nails into the back of his neck as my breathing is constricted by his tightening hold on my throat. It's such a fucking high, the intensity of my orgasm is overwhelming.

"That's it, give it to me." Linc doesn't relent, he fucks me like he's losing his mind. Fucks me like he's not ever giving me up.

I try to scream, but it's in vain—his hold is too strong.

That's when he turns my head, lets go of my throat, and crushes his mouth to mine, swallowing my cries as he comes deep inside me.

I've never felt more possessed in my entire life and I fucking love it.

---

Lincoln left before breakfast, with some excuse I was too boneless to hear coherently, so I've been lounging around for most of the morning. Smithy went to the Farmer's Market with Matthew, so I decide to do something productive.

I'm going to read some more of my dad's journals and finally try to work out some of the insanity around me. Now that everything else is tucked away, things are a little less manic in my mind and I can actually focus.

I shower and get dressed, thinking that dressing like I'm going somewhere will make me more productive, before making my way back downstairs.

Just as I head toward the basement, the buzzer for the gate goes off, stopping me in my tracks. I head to the control box and see a black car sitting outside the gate.

"Hello?"

I wait for a response. The window rolls down, but I don't recognize the man looking at the camera. "Car for Miss Royal. I was sent by Harrison to collect you for your meeting."

Wait, that's now?

Why the fuck did nobody tell me?

What if this is a trick?

"I'm sorry, I wasn't aware of a meeting today," I say back into the mic. Seconds later, my phone buzzes in my pocket.

It's an unknown number, but I answer it anyway—because, weird timing.

"Miss Royal, get in the car," Harrison all but barks down the line. "Do not keep me waiting.'

The line disconnects, and I clench the fist not holding my phone.

Tripped up asshole.

I let out a deep breath, trying to calm myself and push the buzzer again. "I'll be a few minutes."

Without waiting for a response, I rush back upstairs, grabbing a black blazer to shrug over my band tee, and grab a pair of bad bitch heels to make me feel a little better. Paired with my skinny jeans, I look the part of heiress.

Now I just need to believe I can play the part of Queen. Anything less and Harrison Saint will eat me alive.

I pull up my phone and drop a message into the group chat. I assume they already know, but better safe than sorry.

Me:
I've been summoned by Harrison. If I don't see you there, I'll let you know what happens.

Finley:
Had no idea. Keep your phone on, I'll track you. If we don't hear from you in an hour, we're coming for you.

I smile at the phone as I lock up the house and walk down the drive to the waiting car, sending Smithy a message to let him know where I've gone, too.

Can't be too cautious when it comes to Harrison.

The driver climbs from the car and opens the door to the back for me, closing it once I'm settled on the cream leather seats.

It feels like the drive lasts forever, but that could just be my nerves. I stare up at what looks like an office building—a really fucking tall office building. The car pulls to a stop by the front doors and the doorman opens the car with a smile. "Miss Royal, we've been expecting you. If you'll follow me please."

"Uhm, sure?" I climb from the car, trying to look more confident and put together than I feel, and follow him into the building.

No one pays any attention as we walk through the lobby to the bank of elevators. He pulls a card from his pocket and waves it over the black box on the wall before pushing the button. "Private elevator," he says, like that explains everything.

It only takes a few seconds until it *bings* and the doors open. We enter the car and make the ride up to the forty-fifth floor—which I only know because of the single lit button inside with the number forty-five on it—in silence.

The car *bings* again before the doors slide open. "Have a nice evening, Miss Royal. Mr. Saint is waiting for you."

I step tentatively out of the elevator, looking back as the doors close behind me.

Nope, this doesn't seem ominous at all. Taking a deep breath, I try to calm myself, to build some walls to hide all of my inadequacies that are very much on show before entering the small lobby up here.

My heels click on the marble floor, echoing in the quiet space.

"Good of you to finally join me." Harrison's voice catches me off guard as he appears in a shadowed doorway to the right. "I don't have all night."

He disappears inside the room, so I make my way down the hall, hoping I'm not walking to my death.

I enter the room, closing the door behind me, shocked to discover it's just the two of us.

My phone buzzes in my pocket, but I ignore it. I get the feeling Harrison isn't the type to be ignored because I have a text.

"How can I help you?" I ask as I slide into the chair in front of the desk he's put himself behind. He steeples his fingers, resting his chin on them as he examines me.

"We need to discuss the contract I made with your father."

I nod once, crossing one leg over the other as I lean back in the chair. "What is there to discuss? I was approached by the Knights, on *several* occasions, before I was kidnapped and tortured by one. I'm pretty sure the terms of the contract are clear as to the next steps."

God, I sound way more ballsy than I feel. And if the tic in his jaw is anything to go by, he's pissed. But considering everything he's done since my arrival in Echoes Cove, the shit he's done to Lincoln his entire life, I'm taking the small win.

His nostrils flare as he folds his arms across his chest. "So you wish to take your seat as Regent?"

"I didn't realize there was a choice."

"There is always a choice, Miss Royal." He grins, and my stomach flip flops. "If you can acquire for me the thing I approached you for when you first arrived in the Cove, I'm sure I could arrange to uphold the freedom your father bartered for."

"What is it that you want?"

I hold my breath as he watches me silently, assessing me. It makes me feel fucking dirty the way he watches me so intently.

"Your father was a very powerful man, with access to a lot of information, and a lot of friends in high places. Some in very low places as well. It would seem that as a backup plan, a failsafe as it were, he collected information. On me, our sect, on the Knights as a whole. Information that would be… damning, should it fall into the wrong hands. I want that information, Miss Royal. I want every trace of it returned to me, so that it can be kept… *safe*."

My heart hammers in my chest. "Is that why you had him killed? You hoped Edward would find the information after killing him?"

He smiles, it's so cold that a shiver runs down my spine. "My, my. You are astute, aren't you? I wonder which of your little lap dogs worked it out and told you."

My heart stops at his confirmation.

He killed my dad.

He'd probably have killed me if he could get the information without me.

My mind races, when a single thought screams in my mind.

"What if I have a different deal I want to make?"

He leans back, eyebrow raised, hands clasped in his lap. "And what sort of deal is that?"

"The information, but not just for my freedom. For Lincoln's. For Finley's. For Maverick's. Forever. There is no arranged marriage, no whoring out of your son. All ties are cut, but they are still afforded the same protections I am."

"No deal. I will not lose all four of you."

I shake my head and grit my teeth. Clenching my hands against the arms of the chair so he doesn't see them shake as I push myself to standing. "Then no deal. And now I know the information exists. When I find it, do not think I won't use it."

"Sit down, Miss Royal!" His voice booms around the room, turning my blood to ice in my veins. "The information for their freedom then. But not yours. I wonder, will you sacrifice for them, the way they have for you?"

"If I agree to this, I want their trust funds released instantly. With zero strings. No way for you to take back what is granted."

"You're stronger than I thought you'd be. If we bring you back into the fold, if I agree to your terms, you understand you will become my heir for Regent. You cannot take the seat until your eighteenth birthday."

I nod. "I understand."

He picks up the phone and makes a call, putting it on loudspeaker so I can hear as he speaks to Edward and Charles. As he tells them the deal. They're beyond pissed, but they do not argue.

Next he calls his lawyer, and I wait as he releases the trusts for all three boys. He signs the document emailed to him while we wait on the line, and his lawyer confirms it is done.

"It was nice doing business with you, Miss Royal. You have two weeks to find me the documents your father had or I will pull those three back in so fast their heads will spin, and none of you will ever find another way out."

"I won't fail," I say through gritted teeth. There is no way I'm going to let them down.

He stands, offering me his hand. "Then I accept your deal, Miss Royal."

My legs shake as I rise to my feet. I take his hand, an icy drop of dread running down my spine.

I just sold my soul to the devil, and I'd do it all over again in a heartbeat.

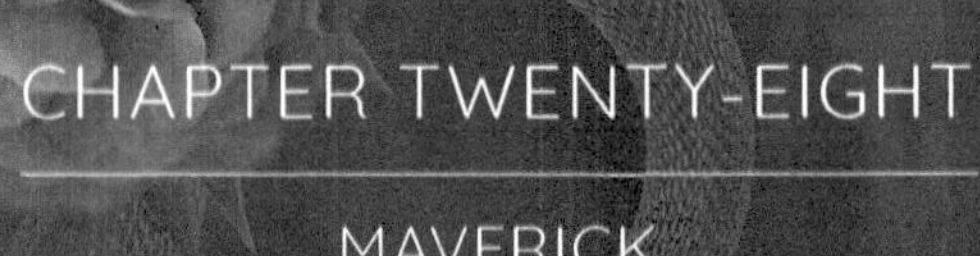

# CHAPTER TWENTY-EIGHT

## MAVERICK

My knuckles split as I hit the bag again and again. I don't feel the pain. All I feel is the trickle of wet down my fingers and that the bag gets a little slippery. Everyone says not to hit these things with bare knuckles, but how else do you prepare yourself for a real fight?

Real life is a lot more painful. There aren't gloves or wraps to protect you. All you have is yourself and your ability to block out the pain for longer than your opponent.

I've had a lot of practice at blocking out pain. I almost thought I'd become immune to it. Living my life in a numb state.

I thought I had no weaknesses left.

Until Octavia Royal blew back into my life.

I was a fool to think I had conquered pain and fear. Because now I realize that I was just living a half life. A life where I had just become used to the pain because that's all I had left.

But now that she's back, she's buried herself under my skin, and for the first time I can remember, I'm afraid.

Truly afraid.

Because if my dad did kill hers, I think I might lose her. And without her, the only future I have is either turning into my dad or being buried.

I almost don't want to know the truth, it's why I haven't looked at it too hard, but I can't keep hiding from it. The guilt is eating me alive. She might say she doesn't blame me for the actions of my father, but there is no way that she'll look at me the same if it's true.

If I was her, I wouldn't be able to look at me at all. I'm basically his mirror image. I hate it about myself, but there is fuck all I can do about it.

I stop hitting the bag when the slick becomes too much to land a decent hit and lean back against the wall. All day I've tried to distract myself from the fact that

I'm here. I've tried to spend as little time at home as I could since my dad nearly killed me, but leaving my mom here alone with him permanently just isn't an option.

If we could be rid of him, life would be much simpler.

I leave my gym and grab a quick shower to wash off the blood and sweat. Mom asked me to be home today and I can't say no to her. She might be just as bad as he is, but she's still my mom. I've never been able to hate her the way I do him. Maybe that makes me weak, Dad sure thinks it does, but it's not something I can change.

I pad downstairs and grab a bowl of cereal, glad for the quiet in the house. It's rarely quiet. They're usually either screaming at each other or my dad is in the basement so my mom blasts music to drown *that* mess out. It doesn't matter that the basement is soundproofed, it's impossible to ignore what happens down there.

Most of the time I'm just thankful it's not my mom or Octavia down there. I'm aware that it makes me a terrible person to ignore it, but I've suffered too much to die at the hands of my father.

I have too much to live for now.

Unless he did kill Stone. If that's the case… well, I don't know what happens then.

Octavia is a better person than I am, a thousand times over, she probably wouldn't hold it against me. But I'd hold it against myself.

She's already too good for me, but I'm too selfish to let that be a reason to give her up… but this, I don't think I'd ever recover if it's true.

I finish eating, and rinse out my bowl, putting it on the draining rack by the sink when I hear my dad on the phone. He sounds pissed.

He walks into the kitchen, eyes dancing with rage as he slams his phone down on the counter. "You."

The single word makes my blood run cold. "What did I do now?"

I try to sound unaffected, bored almost, but his sadistic grin tells me I failed. I grab a bottle of water from the fridge, turning my back to him, which I know is stupid, but I hate that he makes me feel like a scared little boy.

I am not as weak as he'd like to believe.

I hear his footsteps as he strides across the kitchen, and shout when he grabs my hair in his fist, dragging me out of the room toward the basement door.

"Stupid fucking children! None of you know what you've gotten yourselves into. It's time for you to learn."

"What the fuck are you talking about?" I shout as the door slams closed behind me, my hands gripping his, trying to release his hold as he drags me down the steps.

The click of the light switch is all I hear before the pitch black room flickers as the overhead lights come on, bathing the room in an awful yellow light. He throws me to the ground, the crunch of my knees hitting the concrete echoes in the space. I groan at the pain, though it's only a shadow of the pain I've endured at his hands, before I look around the room.

*I think I'm going to be sick.*

The walls are lined with cages. Some of them occupied, some of them empty. I don't let myself linger on them as I take in the metal table in the middle of the room, lined with more instruments of torture and blood letting than I think I've ever seen in one space.

"What the fuck?"

Edward grins down at me, moving toward the table in the middle of the room. He pulls a gun and points it at my head. "You were a waste of fucking spunk, kid. I should've done this a long time ago."

A whimper behind him steals my attention and I glance over his shoulder.

*No.*

I look back at him, eyes wide. "I wondered how long till you spotted her. My prized pet. I nearly had the whole collection—her in my cage, his blood on my knife—and the princess would've joined her mom, but then you fucking idiots got in my way. You *keep* getting in the way. I've had enough."

"Emily?"

"Oh she won't answer you, kid, she wants to be here. That Royal knows who her master is. Pity you didn't learn the same lesson."

It takes a second for it all to fall into place in my head. He has her mom, he killed her dad, and he wants her down here too.

Blood rushes through my ears, the roaring all I can hear as I let out a guttural cry, pushing up from the ground, pulling a knife from the table and charging at him.

I knock him backwards, and he laughs as I slash at his forearms.

"Only you would be stupid enough to bring a knife to a gun fight, kid."

I roar again, attacking him with everything I've got, trying to wrestle the gun away from him. The knife clatters on the ground when it falls from my hand, distraction enough for my dad to get the upper hand.

He knocks me to the ground, but I end up pulling him down with me. The pop of the gun going off between our bodies is deafening as we hit the ground, pain tearing through me.

*I'm sorry, Octavia.*

# ACKNOWLEDGMENTS

I swear writing this part of the book is harder than writing the rest of the book.

First, thank you to my besties, my sprint team, my cheerleaders. This series would absolutely not have made the light of day if it wasn't for you guys.

David, you sparkly unicorn you, thank you for everything, including the hilarious laughs when you should 100% be asleep! Thank you for loving these guys, and calling me out when it's needed. For making the words shine and well, for being my social butterfly bitch aha.

Eva, thank you for always being there when I need to gripe, and for well, all the things. If I listed it all I'd be here all damn day ahaha.

To my alpha & beta teams, you guys are freaking rockstars. Lisa, Zoe, Megan, Kiera, Jeni, Liberty, Kyla, Sam, Jessi & Nicole. Thank you for your priceless feedback, and for loving these characters as much as I do.

Thank you to Sarah and Sam for making sure the words shine by the time I'm done fucking around with them, and for letting me corrupt you aha.

Finally, to you the reader, thank you. For taking a chance on an author you've probably never heard of. For picking up a new book. For running the gauntlet with us. Just thank you.

Book 4 won't be long, so I guess I better go dive back into the book cave.

Peace out

xoxo

# 29

## BONUS SCENE

### LINC

Her screams haunt me night after night but for some reason, tonight, it's like each scream is a fresh tear of my already shredded soul. I always know when she's fallen asleep because her screams reach me the minute she succumbs.

How Smithy deals with it is beyond me because I'm not as close as he is, and to me, they seem *so fucking loud.*

But then, I've always been in tune with each and every part of her.

Maybe that's why this wrecks me so bad. Doing all of this to her, knowing that it's for her own good… it doesn't make it any easier.

After over half an hour of her screams, they finally stop and I know she's woken herself up. I clench my fists as I try to stop myself from moving, but I already know I'm going to cave.

I've managed to resist this long, but tonight… Tonight is my undoing.

Call it a culmination of everything until now, or call it me finally giving in to what I actually want to do—no *need* to do—but I find myself pulling on a pair of sweatpants and pocketing my phone.

It might be two in the morning, but I barely sleep these days anyway.

I pad barefoot through the house and across the lawn onto her property. It should probably feel weird, but it doesn't.

After a moment of contemplating overriding the alarm to the kitchen doors, or climbing the trellises, I decide the climb is the easier option. She has the balcony door which she never fucking locks and this way I can be in and out without anyone else knowing.

Because God forbid anyone know that Lincoln Saint has actual feelings.

Thanks to the insane training I've endured my entire life, even barefooted, the climb takes no more than thirty seconds. I reach for the balcony door and find it unlocked.

Fucking Octavia Royal.

I shove down the caveman urge to yell at her and open the door as quietly as I can but it still creaks. She rolls over in bed, sitting up and facing me, a look of disbelief on her face. The bags under her eyes, and her bed head of hair make me both want to smile and break things. But I resist the urge as she opens that sassy fucking mouth of hers.

"What the fuck are you doing here?"

I don't say a word as I glare at her, keeping the mask in place that I know she needs right now. Because even though I'm here, calling a truce for a night, she still needs to hate me.

Without a word, I pull back the sheets and climb into the bed beside her, trying not to remember just how many times I've done this before.

I live and breathe for the girl glaring at me, and she has no fucking idea.

"What are you doing?" she screeches as she grabs the sheets, trying to stop me. It's half-hearted, because really, I know she knows why I'm here.

Instead of fighting her, I lie down, grabbing the sheets myself. "I can hear you screaming from my room. Now lie down and sleep, I'm not going anywhere."

She scoffs at me, but as I pull her toward me, I feel her melt beneath my touch. She might hate me, but this right here… She's always been safe in this bubble with me.

Even now with everything, she knows it even if she doesn't want to believe it. She glares at me for a second, before turning her back to me as she lies down.

I consider leaving the distance between us, but fuck it. I'm here now, might as well just cave entirely for one night. I pull her back toward me and tuck her against my chest, draping a protective arm over her.

She whimpers softly as sleep starts to reclaim her already, but I can feel how stiff she still is. I close my eyes, hoping that she gives in and whisper to her. "You don't need to cry anymore. I'm here now."

She slips into sleep and relaxes against me entirely. I already know I'm not getting any sleep tonight, but at least she can, so instead I lie and listen to her breaths even out, holding her tighter when she starts to whimper, but she doesn't scream.

Not once.

When the sun finally comes up, and I know that she's going to be okay, I slip from her room like I was never there.

No one needs to know I was because I was only weak for just one night.

And that's all it can ever be.

One night.

THE KNIGHTS OF ECHOES COVE

LILY WILDHART

*I read of a man who stood to speak*
*At the funeral of a friend*
*He referred to the dates on the tombstone*
*From the beginning...to the end*
*He noted that first came the date of birth*
*And spoke the following date with tears,*
*But he said what mattered most of all*
*Was the dash between those years*
*For that dash represents all the time*
*That they spent alive on earth.*
*And now only those who loved them*
*Know what that little line is worth*
*For it matters not, how much we own,*
*The cars...the house...the cash.*
*What matters is how we live and love*
*And how we spend our dash.*

LINDA ELLIS

# CHAPTER ONE

## OCTAVIA

## TWO YEARS AGO

*"Come on, kiddo. Time to get up," Dad calls out, and I groan into my pillow. We've been on the road for seven weeks, and after leaving Dallas late last night after his show, all I want to do is stay in bed and forget the world.*

*"Dad, I'm tired. Just let me sleep a little longer."*

*"We did that already," he says, and I can hear the smile in his words as I pull the duvet up over my head. "In fact, we did that three times already this morning. Come on, we're stopping soon. I thought we might have a day, just us. Like old times."*

*Guilt and excitement weave together inside my chest. I really would like to stay in bed, but it's been forever since I just hung out with Dad. Not that that's entirely my fault. He's been so busy prepping for this tour, and then actually being on stage and performing... not that I'm complaining; I love our life. I love our friends and family, love doing home schooling and actually learning about real life shit as I interact with people so different from those I grew up with.*

*I just miss him.*

*Fuck it.*

*I kick the sheets off as I roll over and climb from the bed. "Where are we? And where are we going?"*

*He grins wide at my question as I reach for my duffel and pull out a pair of jeans and a t-shirt. "We're in Nashville. You slept for a long time, Bug, we arrived early this morning—the first time I came to get you..." he teases. "I was thinking a walk by the river and then we could go for ice cream?"*

*"Let me grab a shower, and that sounds great, Dad."*

*If possible, he smiles wider as he claps his hands together. "Perfect. I'll let Mac know. Panda is fixing you a late breakfast."*

*"Thanks, Dad," I call out over my shoulder as I head out of the tiny bedroom at the back of the tour bus and make my way to the even smaller bathroom.*

I can't fucking wait for a hotel stop, just for a decent shower.

*I jump under the tepid stream, trying to scrub away the exhaustion that still clings to me. We've been living like this, on the road, for the last four years. It feels like forever since we were in Echoes Cove, but other than my friends, I can't say I miss it. Even between tours we never go back. We spend the time going to our favorite places around the world.*

*I love the down time. Even though security comes with us like, everywhere, it's still better than touring. Though, watching women throw themselves at my dad is just plain gross. Admittedly, not as gross as watching the panties thrown on stage being cleared up after the show.*

*No sixteen year old girl should have to experience that.*

*I finish up my quick shower, toweling off as fast as I can—because rule number one of using the one bathroom on a tour bus is never be a bathroom hog—and get dressed in my ripped jeans and faded Nirvana t-shirt before heading out to the sitting area up front. The smell of bacon and eggs wafts throughout the bus, and my stomach growls so loud that a flush works its way across my cheeks.*

*"Morning, V." Panda smiles at me as I grab a mug of coffee before sliding into the booth we use as a dining table, and he drops a plate of bacon, eggs, and toast in front of me.*

*"Morning, P." I fall on the plate of food like I've been starved for days and basically inhale it while Panda, Dad, and Mac talk about the security for our little trip—because even if Dad goes full Hannah Montana, there's no way Mac's letting us go out alone.*

Spoilsport.

*It's the only thing about tour life that I don't like. The fact that I can't go anywhere alone. It definitely made getting my first period* heaps *of fun. Especially since most of the team are guys.*

*I shudder at the memory.*

*Maybe one day I can go back to being anonymous. Once I'm not on tour with Dad and I open my own studio, the hype around being 'The King's' daughter should die down. I can dream anyway. Normal life seems so far away from this world.*

*I glance up at my dad as I hear my name whispered among them but shrug it off and finish my breakfast. I check my phone, noticing the time. Maybe I should call this lunch instead. I laugh under my breath to myself, because I'm just that ridiculous, and drop a message to Jenna.*

*Me:*
*We're in Nashville. Doesn't your tour cross over with us this week?"*

*Jenna:*
*It sure does, Summertime Starlight. We're opening for your dad tomorrow and Friday, then we headline from Sunday. Wanna hang when we get there tomorrow?*

*I laugh at the nickname she has for me, which just happens to be the title of the song they're about to drop this weekend.*

## CHAPTER ONE

*Me:*
*Hell yes. I miss you guys!*

*Jenna:*
*Perfect. Tacos and chill for us.*

*Me:*
*It's a date. Let me know when you guys get in.*

*I smile at the picture she sends me of her and the rest of the Midnight Blue girls pulling faces at me. They toured with my dad a few years back and we've been tight ever since. Even more so since they blew up, because unfortunately, these days it's hard to tell friend from frenemy.*

*Rinsing off my dishes before I put them in the small dishwasher, I try to dawdle until Dad is ready. Thankfully, he doesn't take much longer, so I just flick through the news app on my phone. Only world news though, because the gossip rags usually make me gag, and social media isn't any better, which is why I ignore its existence. I don't care if Dad's PR manager moans at me every single day about it, it is so not happening.*

*"Ready, Bug?" Dad calls out, drawing my attention from the headlines of a corporate scandal in New York with Winchester, Duke & Patterson LLC. Some fancy law firm in hot water for something or other. I slip my phone into the front pocket of my jeans and slip my feet into my Chucks.*

*"Ready." My smile matches his as he waves me to the exit of the bus. Mac heads out first, while Panda hangs behind looking a little pissed. Guess he's not coming. Though, he's not security so that makes sense. Even if he is around most of the time. I grab my leather jacket and aviators from the back of the chair I dropped them on last night and slip them on before skipping down the stairs of the bus.*

*Damn, it's bright out here. I'm glad for the aves as my long hair blows about in the breeze. Nashville in the height of summer is fucking* hot. *I keep my jacket on though, because I burned way too easily when we were here last year.*

*My dad drops onto the pavement behind me, draping his arm over my shoulder. "Come on, kiddo, the ice cream is calling my name."*

*I look around, noticing the chain-link fence running alongside the bus, and realize we're parked at the stadium. As we step clear of the bus, the screams erupt from every direction as fans begin crushing each other to get closer. I groan as Dad chuckles beside me. "We're not going to get time alone are we?"*

*"'Course we are, that's what Mac and I were discussing while you ate." He squeezes me in closer and I roll my eyes at him.*

*"Good. Watching women throw themselves at your feet during the shows is enough, thanks." I stick my tongue out at him and he laughs.*

*"Don't hate the player, hate the game."*

*I groan at his cheesiness while he continues to laugh at me as we approach the convoy of blacked out Range Rovers. Dad opens the back door for me, taking just a moment to wave to the screaming women before turning his attention back to me. "After you, Bug."*

*I climb in and he shuts the door, so I buckle up while he walks around to the other side and Mac climbs in the front.*

*The convoy takes off, then splits up, each car taking a different direction. I look over at Dad, who smirks. "Told you we'd be fine. It's just us today, Bug. Well, and Mac, but we both know he hides in the shadows better than anyone."*

*I look up and catch Mac grinning at me in the rearview mirror.*

*"Good." I smile and relax into the soft leather seats as we head through the city. It doesn't take long until Mac pulls the car to a stop in front of an ice cream parlor.*

*I return my gaze to Dad, raising my eyebrow. "I really wanted that ice cream," he says, laughing. I join him, shaking my head; he's nothing but a big kid sometimes. "Ice cream, then the walk?"*

*"Sounds good." I smile as I unbuckle and climb from the car, ignoring Mac's grumbling. There's no way he didn't scope the place out as we pulled up. I close the door behind me, looking around and realizing I'm right. The street is almost dead, as is the parlor. Just a few people sitting at the tables in there, and no more than a handful of people walking the streets. When I reach the sidewalk, my dad is climbing from the car, and Mac is already inside.*

*We head in, and I take in the giant wall board of a menu. "Holy crap," I utter. How the hell is a girl supposed to make a decision when there are like eleventy billion flavors available?*

*Dad rubs his flat stomach, sighing. "I'm going to regret this later when I have to hit the gym, but screw it. What's catching your eye, Bug?"*

*I blink at him before turning back to the menu. "Cherry ice cream scoop, with a dark chocolate scoop, whipped cream, chocolate syrup, and hazelnuts. I think." I pause, glancing at the myriad options, but decide to go for my favorite. Why not? It's not like I eat ice cream all that often anyway.*

*Dad waits a second until I nod, letting him know I've made my final decision, and he gives my order to the somewhat starstruck girl behind the counter.*

*"I'll bring those over for you in a minute, Mr. Royal," she stutters before grabbing three sundae glasses. I head to sit at one of the high tables at the back of the store, because sitting up front just isn't a real option, and Dad hops up onto one of the stools while Mac situates himself at the table one over from ours. He sits with his back to us to give us the illusion of privacy while he watches the main entrance of the store.*

*"I was thinking this might be our last tour for a little while, Bug," Dad says, shocking the hell out of me.*

*"Really?"*

*He shrugs as the girl brings over our order, and he waits until she's gone before he speaks again. "We've been on the road for a long time, I thought you might want to settle for a little while. Senior year is coming up soon and I thought you might want some of those typical teenage experiences."*

*"You want to go back to Echoes Cove?"*

*"Oh, hell no." He scowls just hearing the town name. "We can go anywhere in the world, why would we go back there?"*

*I shrug and take a bite of my sundae, groaning as the cherry and dark chocolate bursts on my tongue. So freaking good.*

*"While there is breath in my body, kid, we'll stay far away from there. Too many memories." He scrubs a hand over his face before looking at me again. "Unless* you *want to go back?"*

*"I dunno, but I like our life. I like traveling around, experiencing everything the world has to offer. But if you want to stop touring, that's okay too."*

*He shakes his head as he swallows down a mouthful. "No way, kiddo. I love doing this. The music grounds my soul. I just figured I should be a parent first, but if you're truly happy, then on tour we'll stay."*

*I grin at him before taking another bite, feeling relieved. Tour life might be sucky sometimes, but the thought of not living like this… just nope.*

*Life is only going to get better from here. I can feel it.*

---

*ONE YEAR LATER*

*"Where is she?" Dad yells, and I wince as I hear him stumbling around his dressing room. I really thought he'd keep his promise this time. That he'd manage a day without drinking.*

*It feels like forever since Dad managed to stay sober for a whole day, in reality it's probably only been six months, but watching his descent into this, watching him slowly kill himself… well, it's killing me.*

*I don't know what happened when we were in Los Angeles for New Years Eve—I didn't want to go to the swanky party he went to—but whatever it was, it fucked him up and he won't tell me what happened or what's wrong.*

*I've asked him a dozen times, and he just rambles on about protecting me, and ignorance being bliss. I just wish I knew what was wrong with him. He never used to be like this, but it's like he's running from something and using the bottle as his hiding place. It guts me every time I see him stumbling around after one of his shows, but there's nothing I can do about it. Every time I bring it up, he just denies it all and tells me he's the parent.*

*I miss the man he used to be.*

*Mac's voice bellows down the corridor before I hear the opening and slamming of a door, knowing he's in my dad's changing room. The amount of coffee and fuck knows what else Mac pours into him before a show so he's able to perform is eye watering, but even that might not cut it tonight.*

*Erin, Dad's PR manager, might have to dream up a freaking miracle to keep all of this under wraps. I have no idea how she's managed to keep it quiet for this long, but I guess that's why she gets paid the big money from Dad's label.*

*I should feel bad, hiding from my dad, pretending that none of this is happening, but I can't stomach seeing him like this anymore. I need to wait for his show to be over and catch him while he's coherent. Plead with him to stop drinking. Try to make him see what he's doing to himself. To me.*

*We can't keep on going like this.* He *can't keep going like this. He's going to kill himself, and I can't let that happen.*

*The sound of the support band wraps up, and I pray Mac managed to calm dad down enough to get him ready for the show.*

*We only have two weeks left and then the tour is done. Maybe Mac will help me get him into rehab somewhere. Or maybe we need to actually take a break from life on the road. Give him time to settle his soul and get back to* writing *music instead of performing all the time.*

*A knock on my door has me groaning internally as Panda appears in the doorway. He looks like he's seen a ghost, but he's never really liked seeing my dad this messed up. "Mac needs you," is all he says before he disappears back down the hall.*

*Way to be an emotional support right now, P.*

*I let out a sigh and slip my feet into my Chucks. Should've known I wouldn't be able to hide from this forever. I head down the hall to where Mac is arguing with my dad, who very obviously hasn't sobered up. "Octavia, thank God. He's refusing to drink any of the coffee or anything without talking to you. Can you please just listen to his ramblings for a minute so we don't have to cancel the show? I'm going to get the support act back out for a long encore to give us some time."*

*"Sure," I sigh, smiling sadly. He squeezes my shoulder and heads toward the main stage to sort out the stall tactic while I take a deep breath and prepare to face my drunk-off-his-ass dad.*

*Entering the room, I find him slumped on the couch, his head in his hands. He looks up when the door closes behind me. "There's my princess. I need to talk to you."*

*"You've got a show, Dad, we should talk later." I pour him a mug of coffee from the pot that Mac had brewing. "You should drink the coffee. Eat the food Mac brought down here for you."*

*"I don't want the damn coffee!" He stands, stumbling as he does, and my heart breaks a little more. I love my dad, but this version of him isn't my dad. "I need you to listen to me. The Knights are looking for us. You're going to be queen if they don't stop, but I don't want that. You're my princess."*

*I shake my head at his ramblings. He gets like this when he's drunk. Some of the things he says are beyond insane. It's easier to just smile and nod sometimes.*

*"I'm not going to be queen of anything, Dad. I'll always be your princess. Just like you're the king. Please, just drink the coffee."*

*"Fine," he grumbles. "Just never become king. Even if James says it's safe. It will never be safe."*

*Who the hell is James?*

*My heart cracks some more at his ramblings.*

*"I won't become king, Dad. I can't be a king. I'm a princess."*

*"You better be," he sighs as he starts gulping down the lukewarm coffee and eating the pastries Mac bought for him.*

*"I'm going to go find Mac," I tell him softly, patting his shoulder. "Promise me you'll eat the food. All of it."*

*"I promise," he groans, rolling his eyes at me. "I'm sorry, princess."*

*I close my eyes to stop the tears that prick at them. "It's okay, Dad. We'll talk more later, okay?"*

*"Okay."*

*I leave the room, taking a deep breath as I lean my back against the closed door in an effort to compose myself before heading off to find Mac. I need to get my dad some help.*

*Just two more weeks.*

*That's what I need to remember.*

*Two weeks, and then I can get him better help.*

# CHAPTER TWO

## OCTAVIA

Everything since leaving my meeting with Harrison has been a blur.

*I really just sold my soul to the devil.*

Taking a deep breath, I hold it to try and calm my racing heart. I might have sold my soul, but I saved them; that's all I've wanted since I realized they were shackled. At least now they can be free.

*I'm* only temporarily restrained.

*I hope.*

What I'm not too stupid to realize is that I'm going to need some help, so I drop a message to Bentley, the PI I hired to look into my mom. If anyone can hunt down this information, it's likely going to be him.

The part that doesn't sit well with me—that's had my stomach churning since I left that office and slid into the back of this town car—is that I need to keep all of this a secret from the guys. I've yelled at them so often about keeping things from me when they thought they were protecting me, and this makes me such a fucking hypocrite, but it was one of Harrison's terms, so as much as I hate it, I'm not going to ruin the chance I have to free them over something so stupid as my guilty conscience.

The car pulls up to my house and I find Smithy home, collecting the mail.

"Miss Octavia, where have you been?" he asks, eyeing the black car as it drives away.

I try to smile, but it falls flat. He frowns in response and wraps an arm around my shoulders. "How about I fix us some milkshakes and you tell me all about it?"

Pausing, I question whether that's a good idea, but I need to tell *someone*, and Smithy knows about the Knights—he knew my dad—maybe he'll know how to find whatever my dad had buried away that Harrison wants.

I stretch up on tiptoes and peck his cheek. "That sounds perfect, thank you."

He squeezes my shoulders tight before leading me inside and pushing me onto one of the stools at the island counter. The cold granite countertop helps me ground myself and slow my racing thoughts as I try to filter through everything I need to say in order to explain this properly.

Smithy flits around the kitchen, and it's soothing to be back here, just the two of us. It's almost like a flashback to before I realized what a fucking mess my life was. Before secret societies and death threats and stalkers were a part of everyday life. When a school bully was my biggest problem.

And to think I thought I had issues then.

I start to laugh, and Smithy looks at me like I've lost it. Hell, maybe I have, because I laugh until my stomach hurts and tears roll down my face. Each time I try to calm myself by sucking in a breath, I just look up at him and the laughter starts again.

This isn't funny, and that only makes it funnier.

Fuck my actual life.

He makes the chocolatiest shakes I've ever seen; with syrup, whipped cream, chocolate curls, and God knows what else, before sitting down opposite me and sliding one of them over. Once my laughter subsides, I take a sip, sighing at the happy memories the flavor evokes while he watches me.

He lets me procrastinate for a minute while I sip down the thick shake before quirking a brow at me.

I let out a sigh, running a hand through my hair before telling him everything about Panda; what he said while I was gone, having Bentley look into Mom, freaking *everything*. I know he knew some of it already, but I can't tell him the next part without him having the whole picture. Once he's up to date on all of the fucking insanity—and not exactly looking pleased about some of the information I've omitted up to this point—I tell him the part I've been working up to with my ramblings. "I made a deal with Harrison Saint."

He sucks in a breath, frowning at me, but motions for me to continue while he takes a pull on his shake.

"I got the boys free from the Knights. No more strings, no repercussions. Instant access to their trust funds with no stipulations."

"And how, Miss Octavia, did you manage such a feat?"

I pick at the skin by my thumb nail, not exactly enjoying the way he watches me like I'm a naughty toddler. But I suck it up and press on. "Dad set up a contract when he left the Knights. It stipulated that I was free of the Knights, but protected by them. That would be true for me and the rest of my line unless I, or anyone in the future, chooses to join them. It also stated that should I be approached, hurt by, or initiated into the Knights, I instantly take the Regency."

He opens his mouth but I continue, because if I don't get this out now, I never will. "I met with Harrison today, and he gave me the option to stay free." I pause and take a sip of my shake, like the sugar will give me the boost I need to tell him everything. "I could be free if I gave him information Dad has collected on him and the rest of his Sect… or the Knights as a whole, I'm not sure. So I tried to barter the information for everyone's freedom, but he shot me down."

"And then what?" he asks, and I can't read him. His voice is low, like he's pushing down a simmering anger, but I try not to focus on that. Enough people are going to be pissed at me when they realize what I've done, at least to start with.

"Then I told him no deal, that I'd just find the information and release it, so he was fucked either way."

Smithy barks out a laugh and reaches across the counter, taking my hand and squeezing it. "That's my girl."

"Then he offered me their freedom in place of mine. That I would become the Regent heir until my birthday. He gave me two weeks to find the information, which just happens to fall in line with two weeks before my birthday. He also said I couldn't tell the guys of our deal until the deal is done and he has the information."

"Convenient," he huffs, and I smirk at him before continuing.

"Then he admitted to having Dad killed for the information. That Edward Riley was responsible for it. He didn't say outright that I would suffer the same fate if I didn't comply, but it was implied."

His face turns a mottled red as his anger bubbles up to the surface and he takes a few breaths, muttering incoherently under his breath.

"I had suspected as much. Evan said something along those lines when he held me captive, and he had no reason to lie about it. Not really. I just wish Dad would have told me about all of this when I was younger. There might've been something I could have done to save him."

"Absolutely not," Smithy shouts before taking a deep breath. "Miss Octavia, anything your father kept from you was to keep *you* safe. I am positive that he wouldn't have wanted you wrapped up in all of this darkness, and kept it from you as his way to ensure that stayed the case."

"If that was the case, then why would his will require that I come back here? Why not keep me away?"

The corners of Smithy's mouth turn up as he thinks over my question. "I think *that*, my beautiful girl, is likely because of me. Your father knew I was here and alone; I can only assume that he thought if you and I were both alone, better that we be alone together."

I squeeze his hand back, hating to think of him being lonely. It's one of the few reasons I'm glad my dad sent me back here. The thought of not having Smithy in my life now isn't one I want to dwell on.

"Regardless of the why, this is where we are now, and we need to work out how to make the best of it. I do wish you'd come to me before you made a deal with that scoundrel, but if there is anything I can do to assist with your search, please let me know. As for what you did for the boys… while I'm sure they won't be pleased about your sacrifice, in time I'm sure they'll come to see it for what it was."

"Thank you, Smithy." I finish my milkshake, nervous energy gripping my muscles. "At least now we know I'm somewhat safe. The Knights want something from me, so they kind of need me alive; my stalker situation is done with, so I can breathe a little easier; there are still threats, but I know what they are now. That has to be a bonus."

"Hmmmm." He raises an eyebrow at me, his skepticism noted. "We can hope at least."

"Exactly," I say, smiling wide as I jump from my seat. "I need to run, so I'm going to go and get changed, then head out for an hour or so."

"Okay, I'll ensure dinner is ready for you upon your return."

I move around the island and hug him tight. "Thank you, Smithy. For everything."

With a peck on the cheek, I dart upstairs and get changed out of the stuffy clothing I had on for the meeting and change into my leggings, sports bra, and pull a tank over the top.

Definitely wasn't how I pictured my Saturday going, but I can't help but smile.

I bought their freedom, and even if they hate me for it, at least I'll know they're free.

---

After running until my legs turned to jelly—because running from my problems is obviously how I'm going to get things done—and Smithy making me taco boats, because he loves me just that much, I stare at Bentley's name on my phone.

I haven't reached out to any of my guys all day, and I haven't heard from them either, but I know I need to get the ball rolling on this shit that Harrison wants before I chicken out. The only way to get their freedom, and make sure I don't end up buried next to my dad, is to find the information.

I dial Bentley's number and the ringing seems to go on forever, but when he finally answers the phone, his surprise is audible. "Miss Royal? Is everything okay?"

I can't help but smile. I only met him twice, but he almost sounds concerned. "Hey, Bentley. Yeah, everything is okay. I just wondered if you had some time for me this week? I have some more work for you."

The sound of rustling papers and the closing of a drawer sound through the line before he answers. "I absolutely can. In fact, I'm free this evening if you don't mind a late one? I'm about half an hour away from Echoes Cove."

"That's perfect, thank you. I'll drop you my address if you're okay coming to the house?"

"No need, I still have it. But yes, coming to the house is fine. I'll see you soon." The line drops, and I bite the inside of my lip.

At least I'm getting this out of the way sooner rather than later.

I pad back into the kitchen and find Smithy making himself a cup of Earl Grey. "Miss Octavia, is everything okay?"

"Yeah." I smile at him as I grab a bottle of water from the refrigerator before jumping onto the counter, the cold from the stone surface penetrating my leggings. "My private investigator is heading over; I figure he's going to be a good bet to help me with finding the info Harrison wants."

He looks at me skeptically. "Are you sure you can trust this man?"

I nod at him and smile. "I'm sure. He was recommended by a friend, and he helped me look into Mom to see if we could find her. He's discreet, and I trust him to be professional."

"Who is he?"

"His name is Bentley… that's actually all I know about him," I say, laughing while I shake my head. "Should probably know more, but my gut tells me I can trust him."

"You're a good judge of character, so I'll take your word for it, but how about we get to know him a little if he's coming over this evening?" Smithy's suggestion isn't wildly out there, so I nod my agreement.

"Can't hurt anything."

We talk through the possibilities of where my dad would've hidden something he'd deemed so important, making a list on my phone, and it occurs to me that I should probably speak to Mac too. Nobody on the tour has reached out about Panda, so I have no idea if they know about the stalking or even that he's dead.

Too much has been falling through the cracks lately, but I vow to be a better friend now that some of the chaos in my life should start to settle. Not just to those who were basically my family the last few years, but to everyone around me. Speaking of which…

"How are things with you and Matthew?" I ask Smithy, and he smiles in that lovey dovey way that you just can't help when you're head over heels.

"We are doing just fine. Thank you, Miss Octavia."

I grin at him, my heart soaring that he's so happy. "I'd like to get to know him better, if you'd like that? I know we did dinner, but you might've noticed I've been a little distracted lately."

He barks out a laugh, nearly choking on his tea. "No, it had escaped my notice."

I stick my tongue out at him, and his smile grows. "Well, hopefully things should quiet down a little, so if you're both open to it, we should do something. Even if it's just another dinner. You're family, so if he's important to you, then he's important to me."

"I would like that very much." His smile is contagious and warms my heart.

"Perfect. Well, work out when is best for you guys and I'll make myself free. I know I've got finals and stuff coming, but I'm sure we'll pin down some time."

"Are you ready for your exams? Are your grades where you need them to be?" His fatherly tone isn't lost on me, but instead of coming off as condescending, it just makes me feel loved.

"My grades are fine, I'm just about scraping by, and a few teachers have given me extra credit assignments since I missed those few weeks, but I think it's going to be okay." He pats my shoulder reassuringly just as the buzzer to the gate sounds. I check my phone and see Bentley's smiling face on the screen. I hit the entry button as Smithy strides out of the kitchen to get the door.

It doesn't take long for Smithy to reappear with Bentley, the two of them talking as they enter the room. "Glad to see you guys are fast friends." I laugh as Bentley grins at me.

"You certainly surround yourself with some interesting characters, Miss Royal."

"Please, just call me Octavia," I say, waving for him to sit. "Coffee?"

He nods as he sits. "I'd love some."

I move to make it, but Smithy tuts as he bustles around the kitchen to fix the drink before he places the steaming mug in front of our visitor and takes a seat beside me.

"So, what can I do for you, Octavia?" Bentley asks before taking a sip of the coffee. His eyebrows rise as he sips it. "This is possibly the best coffee I've ever had."

"Miss Octavia is something of a coffee snob," Smithy snorts. "Only the best here."

Bentley grins, his eyes crinkling at the edge as I try to look put out, but I know it misses the mark because I can't help but laugh. He isn't wrong. I love coffee.

"A girl needs the good things in life," I say with a shrug. "As for what I need you for, it's… a little sensitive."

His forehead furrows as he nods. "Ruin people sensitive or get me dead sensitive?"

"Both?" The word comes out as more of a question than a statement as a blanket of tension settles over us all.

"What exactly are you mixed up in?" Bentley asks skeptically. I open my mouth to answer, but Smithy interrupts me.

"Before we tell you that, why don't you tell us a little about you?"

Bentley seems taken back by Smithy's question but composes himself quickly. "My name is Bentley Kensington. I grew up on the East Coast, living among the rich and famous, where I learned that secrets are as good a currency as money itself. My older brother took over the family business, which I was glad for, because it had never interested me, and I joined the Marine Corps. I can't tell you much about my time with the forces because it's classified, but if you have the access I assume you do, it shouldn't be too hard for you to uncover if you want to look." He pauses, taking another sip as I process everything he's saying. "When I decided enough was enough with ops, I came home and realized I had a skillset that I could mix with what I had learned about secrets when I was younger. I've been doing this for about six years now, and the connections my family has meant I've had some very upscale and high risk clients. Which is exactly how Octavia found me."

Smithy nods, like he believes every word. Not that we have any reason not to, and my instincts still tell me I can trust him.

"Kensington as in Kensington Enterprises?" Bentley smiles at Smithy's question and nods.

"The one and the same."

Smithy stands and pats my shoulder. "Ice cream anyone? I think the rest of this conversation is going to require comfort food."

Bentley looks a little shocked, but nods. "Glad I passed the test."

Smithy chuckles while I nod, agreeing to ice cream, because I'm not an idiot. "You start filling in our friend, Miss Octavia, while I sort the snacks."

I grin at him before turning back to Bentley. "This might take a while, so buckle in."

After Bentley leaves, I feel a lot better than I did after I finished my meeting with Harrison. To say he was a little taken aback by everything I told him would be an understatement of epic proportions. I gave him the option to back out after I laid all my cards on the table, but he laughed at me and told me he's faced scarier people than rich white guys.

He left about an hour ago, and I've been staring up at my ceiling for the last forty minutes, trying to will sleep to come to me. I texted the guys in our group chat, but no one responded. Not that I'm all that shocked, it's nearly one in the morning and most people are sleeping. If they're sane, anyway. And while my guys might not always fall into that category, they're not exactly party animals either.

I'm just hoping Harrison has kept his word and doesn't have them out doing something for him.

I toss and turn, wishing for sleep, and after another twenty minutes, give up.

Late night swim it is. Maybe I just need more exhaustion to shut my brain down.

I kick off the covers and stomp to my closet, slipping out of my pj's and pulling on my swimsuit, wrapping my robe around myself before heading downstairs.

I hit the button to uncover the pool, steam rising from the surface of the water into the cold night air as I flick the lights on so I can actually see.

Dropping the robe onto one of the patio chairs, I break into a run as the cold air hits my skin and dive into the heated water. I push to swim under the surface until my lungs burn and surface to finish my lap before pushing and doing laps until my muscles quiver.

When a shrill ring cuts through the silence of the night, I pull myself from the water and sprint to my phone.

Dread slams through me when I see Finn's name on the screen.

I quickly dry my hands on the robe before answering. "What's wrong?"

My heart pounds in my ears, so loud I almost don't hear him through my panic. "It's Mav. You need to get to the hospital. Now."

# CHAPTER THREE

## MAVERICK

"Mav!" The shouts of my name stir me, but I feel like I've been hit by a fucking truck and my eyes feel like they've had sand poured into them as they open. Everything is blurry.

I blink a few times to clear my vision as the memory of what happened comes back to me, just as pain roars in my lower back. That's what I get for dropping the knife I guess, my own fucking knife in the back.

Fuck me.

My dad's dead weight is crushing and my head pounds as I try to bring my arms up to push him off of me. The weakness from the blood loss makes it a lot fucking harder than it should be. The girls in the cages just stare at me with wide eyes, silently. It's not like they can help me; they're literally locked away.

"Down here," I try to shout, but it doesn't feel loud enough, so I try again, barely able to breathe under the dead weight above me, too weak to roll him off.

Please, fuck, don't let me die like this.

I take a few breaths to try and replenish the energy I don't have. I'm covered in fucking blood and I don't know how much of it is mine, but the fact that I can barely focus isn't good. I've been trained for this situation, so I don't freak out, I just need to get some help.

I hear them calling my name above me and realize the door must have been left open a little. That's when I feel my phone start to ring in my pocket. It's set to loud and the ring is so fucking shrill that I can only hope the boys hear it all the way down here.

The sound of the door slamming open followed by footsteps banging down the stairs brings me so much Marie-fucking-Kondo-level joy.

I am not ready to die. I have too many things I want to do with my girl before I die.

"Fuck, Mav!" Finn's voice sounds more panicked than I'd like.

"Help me," I groan as he and Linc pull my dad's dead body off of me. "Knife… in my back."

Lincoln hisses as he rolls me over. "Go grab a towel or three so we can secure this," he barks at Finn, who nods and disappears.

"We've got you, man. Just hold on." He scrubs a hand down his face and I nod, letting my eyes flutter closed.

Fuck it's cold on the stone ground.

"Is that…?" Linc asks, and I look up at him and nod. "Fuck."

Finn reappears and I bite down as they wrap the knife with the towels to make sure it doesn't move before lifting me from the ground.

"We need to get you to the hospital. We'll come back and deal with… whatever all of this is once you're there," Linc says before they drag me up the stairs and through the house. Finn opens the back door of the Cayenne and they lay me down face-first on the back seat before climbing up front.

The Porsche grumbles to life, and I let my eyes close again.

"Wake up, man." Finn's words just about rouse me as he pulls me from the car. Linc strides toward us, a team of doctors and nurses behind him with a stretcher.

The voices all merge together as my knees give out and the world fades to black again.

---

The sounds of voices and beeping greet me as I wake, wondering exactly why it is I feel like I took the worst beating of my life. It takes way too much energy to open my eyes, but I find Finn sitting in the chair beside my bed, asleep, and Lincoln murmuring in the doorway with what looks like a nurse.

"S'up, boys," I croak, trying to smile as Finn's eyes open and Linc turns to face me. The relief that washes over them both is palpable.

"Oh good, you're awake." The woman I recognize as Dr. Stanton from when Easton was in here pushes past Lincoln as she approaches me. "I've seen too much of your friends lately, Mr. Riley. I suggest no more run-ins with knives."

I grin at her, trying not to look as lousy as I feel. "Come on Dr. Stanton, you know I can't make promises like that."

I look back toward the door, looking for my girl, but don't want to say anything until the doc is gone.

"Indeed, Mr. Riley." She quirks a brow at me before letting out a sigh. "You are extremely lucky. Other than blood loss, your injury was fairly minimal. By that, I mean the blade didn't hit anything too vital. But it did go fairly deep, so you're going to be sore and healing for a few weeks. We had to repair your kidney, which was damaged by the blade, but not so bad that it had to be removed. Your CT scan showed no brain bleed, but it's likely you have a concussion. We've stitched you up, and you're going to need to take it easy, but no major damage. You'll be out of here in a day or two as long as you remain stable and feel well enough."

"Doc, it almost sounds like you care."

She twists her lips as she rolls her eyes. "I'd just really rather not see you boys again. Now there's a Foley catheter in place to measure your urine output due to your injury. I'll have someone come and remove it now you're awake."

"There's a tube in my dick?" I ask, and now the discomfort makes sense.

"Yes, Mr. Riley, there is a tube in your penis. Please try to refrain from playing with it until the nurse arrives."

Finn barks out a laugh as I groan before the doc turns and leaves the room. That's some bedside manner she has. I turn to face Linc once the door is closed and drop the bravado about how much I fucking hurt. "My dad?"

"The house is locked down, but we haven't been back there to deal with it yet." He looks at Finn then back at me. "Was that Emily Royal in the corner?"

"Yeah, apparently she's my dad's favorite pet. *Was* my dad's favorite pet." I run a hand down my face, trying to think of how the fuck we're going to break this to my girl. "Where is V?"

"We called her, and she was here, but you were in surgery for a while, so I made East take her home, despite her arguments to stay. I'll call her in a minute now that you're awake." I nod at Linc's answer, I bet that argument wasn't fun.

"Did you tell her?"

Finn shakes his head. "No, we didn't get a good look at her so we didn't want to say anything until we spoke to you. Did your mom know?"

"No fucking clue, but I doubt it. Dad didn't let her anywhere near the basement. What the fuck are we going to tell the Conclave?"

Linc quirks a brow at me. "You don't think Harrison knew she was down there?"

"Oh no, I have no doubt he did. I meant about the fact that my dad is dead." I let out a deep sigh. I'm fucking exhausted, but I want to see my girl before I go back to sleep.

"We'll deal with that later. First, let me call V and get her here. Then Finn and I will head to the house and deal with the clean up. And the girls down there."

I nod, leaning back and closing my eyes when he finishes speaking. "Get my girl here."

Finn laughs softly. "I'm on it." He stands and grabs his jacket from the back of the chair, leaving without another word, while Linc pulls his phone from his pocket.

"We're going to need some help with your dad and this bullshit."

"Who are you calling?"

He glances up at me before speaking. "East first. I figure Chase is as good a guy as any to have on our side right now as well. Then I'm going to call Alex and see if Luc is back in the country."

"Wait, what?"

"Yeah, that's why he disappeared on us. Classified something or other. So I'll ask if Alex knows anything." He puts the phone to his ear and paces the room. Fuck me, this getting stabbed shit is draining. I've been stabbed before, but never lost as much blood as I did this time. I guess that'll teach me.

Some people might find it weird that I have absolutely zero regret or remorse for killing my dad, but I don't. I won't dwell on it. He tried to kill me, and the one thing he taught me is that you don't need to be the strongest to survive this world. Just the deadliest.

I'm also not worried about the repercussions, because one, I have my boys, and two, there's no way the Knights will let my dad's proclivities get out. Which means they'll cover it up, even if we don't.

My biggest worry is what this means for me regarding the fucking business bullshit. I am not made for that shit. Also, I am so not ready to be declared a fucking responsible adult. But it's not like my mom is in any better shape than I am. She's been away, sunning it up on a beach since she got out of the hospital a few weeks ago to try and sort her own mental state out.

Fuck my life.

Edward being gone is definitely an advantage, but it's also a total pain in the dick.

Lincoln circles back to the bed and drops into the chair Finn vacated. "Luc is not back, but Finn just picked up V and East is on his way to get Chase. You should probably rest until they get here."

I snort a laugh. "Yeah, 'cause with the way Finn drives, I'll manage to get my eyes closed for all of five minutes."

"I made him take her to get food." Linc smirks. "We both know she won't have eaten, and she's still not eating properly after the bullshit with Evan."

I frown, mulling over his words. It's not like I hadn't noticed, but I thought she was getting better.

A nurse enters the room, interrupting me as I open my mouth to respond. "Mr. Riley, I'm here to remove your catheter."

I wince, and Linc stands pretty quickly. "I'll be outside," he says with a smirk before dashing out of the door.

I groan as I lie back. "Let's get this over with. And if I get a hard on, it's not my fault. My dick has a mind of its own."

# CHAPTER FOUR

## OCTAVIA

My heart has been like a hummingbird since Finn called me in the middle of the night. Seeing Maverick hooked up to all those machines just gave me flashbacks of East.

Too many of us have been in the hospital lately, and I'm sick of it.

I'm furious that Edward tried to kill him, that Harrison obviously fucked up somewhere because why else would he try to kill him other than Harrison releasing him from the Knights. Guilt is eating me alive. I can't tell them about it either, so it's stewing inside of me, threatening to make me vomit with every breath I take.

When Linc ordered East to bring me home after we knew Mav would be okay, I was pissed, but I was also relieved. I was exhausted, and being in the hospital just brings back stuff I don't want to relive any time soon.

That being said, I'm on my way back there with Finn now, and my hands won't stop fucking shaking.

"He's okay," Finn says softly, gripping my hand in his. "I saw him, awake, joking around. Typical Mav. Probably wasn't even really that hurt. Just fucking around with us."

I smile at him, appreciating the reassurance, but until I speak to him myself, the worry is going to gnaw at me. I'm not sure the guilt will ever disappear.

Especially while I'm keeping secrets.

I just have to hope they forgive me eventually.

We pull up at the hospital, and I drop East a message to let him know we got here. He said he was going to see Chase, and I didn't question it. There's so much going on right now, and with Edward being dead, we're going to need a Conclave member on our side.

Maybe more than one.

But that's a future me problem. Right now, I want to focus on Maverick and make sure he's actually okay, and not just pretending to be, because… well, trauma.

I climb from Lincoln's Porsche that Finley picked me up in and round the SUV to where he's waiting for me, his arm outstretched. I take the offered hand and let him lead me back into the hospital. An emergency follows us through the doors, so it's chaos. Finn pulls me back against him and presses us against a wall as the paramedics wheel someone past us, one of them on top of the stretcher doing CPR as they rush past.

I stay pressed up against Finn until the swarm of people have moved past, hoping whoever it is is okay, then turn my focus back to Maverick. Stepping forward as soon as Finn's hold loosens a little, I lead him to Mav's room, finding Lincoln sitting in the chair beside the bed, the two of them laughing quietly as I open the door.

Mav's eyes find me the minute I step through the doorway, and something inside of me settles. He's really okay. My eyes flit over him, trying to make sure that what my mind is saying is real.

"I'm okay, princess," Mav says, patting the bed beside him. It breaks me from my trance and I move toward him, taking his hand and kissing him gently when I reach him. He tugs me down onto the bed and I let out a small squeal before he deepens the kiss. "I've been wanting to do that since I woke up."

I press my forehead against his, smiling to myself. I school my smile and pull back, looking down at him. "You scared me, Maverick Riley."

"Sorry, princess. I won't promise not to do it again because, well, occupational hazard, but know I'll always try to come home to you." He looks so serious, and despite wanting to swoon at the last part of his sentence, I can't help but frown.

I wish I could tell him he's not tied to that life anymore.

Just a couple more weeks.

"You should sit," he says, moving a little on the bed, and I scoff.

"I am not getting into that bed with you. I'll hurt you."

His eyes narrow and he tugs on my hand, pulling me against him, laughing at my squeak as I fall. "Wasn't a request. I need to tell you something, and I need you close while I do."

My heart hammers in my chest. "What is it?"

East and Chase enter the room as I finish my question.

"That's timing. Saves me saying this twice," Mav says, letting out a deep breath. I look across the room and find Linc and Finn watching us. I can't make out what's wrong as both of them have their cold masks in place. That on its own tells me I'm not going to like whatever I'm about to hear.

"Good to see you awake, man," East says, before sitting on the uncomfortable looking couch to the right of the room. Chase follows him.

"What else do we need to know?" Chase asks, looking from Maverick to Lincoln.

Mav shudders beside me, and my stomach twists. Not much fazes him, so this must be bad.

"I'm just going to start at the beginning, because some stuff still doesn't make complete sense to me," he says, and my stomach twists. Guilt burns the back of my throat, but I stay silent. I can't be the reason that he doesn't get free. "Tonight, my dad was in a rage, which isn't new. Not sure what pissed him off, but he said something about 'us kids not knowing our place' or some bullshit like that. Then he did something he's never done. He said he was going to teach me a lesson and dragged me into his basement."

He takes a deep breath, but the whole room stays quiet. He grips my hand in his and squeezes tightly. "I've never been into the basement of my house. I've heard the screams, the cries, but going up against my dad was never an option. He told us to stay away, so I did. I had no idea…"

He trails off so I squeeze his hand back, trying to be the support he needs. "There were cages lining the walls. Girls in those cages. His pets, he called them. Octavia…" he pauses and my blood turns cold. He never calls me Octavia. "He had your mom down there. He said she was his favorite pet. It's why he agreed to kill your father. He wanted you down there, too, so he could have the collection."

I think I'm going to be sick.

I sit up and turn to face him, but he won't meet my eyes. "My mom is in your dad's basement?"

"Octavia," Linc says, stepping forward. I glance at him, then Finley, then East.

"You all knew?"

"Only from when Mav woke up while you weren't here. East had no idea," Finn says. The anger inside of me wants to rip at them for keeping secrets. I have my own that I'm keeping and I'm trying not to be a spoiled fucking bitch, but holy shit this is… I have no words.

I turn back to Maverick, wanting to know the whole story. "Then what happened?"

"Then my dad pulled a gun. He told me there was no point in looking to any of his pets for help, because they were loyal to him. We struggled, fell, I landed on the fucking knife I dropped, and the gun went off as I banged my head on the ground. The next thing I remember was these two showing up."

I let out a breath, leaning back on the bed, trying to let it all sink in without overreacting. I can't tell if I'm numb, or just in shock.

My mom was in his dad's basement. I wonder for how long? "Are the girls still down there?"

"Yes, that's why we asked East to bring Chase. We're going to need some help sorting this out," Linc answers as Mav holds me tightly, as if he's scared I'm going to run away.

I have zero intention of running anywhere.

"I want to see my mom."

"Maybe we should assess what sort of state she's in first. If she's been down there a while… well, Edward isn't—wasn't—the nicest guy. They're all very likely going to need some professional help," Chase says softly.

Finn nods. "The Knights facility that my mom's in. We could move the girls there. Get them help, treatment, and then once she's assessed, I can take you to see her."

Lincoln nods, glancing at Mav who hasn't said anything. "Should we move your mom there too? I know she's been away for a few weeks, but you said she was fragile. This might just tip her over."

"Probably for the best," Mav says with a nod.

The door opens, and Dr. Stanton enters, frowning at me when she sees me on the bed. I try to move, but Mav's hold doesn't relent. "Sorry to break up this party, but visiting hours are over for this ward for a few hours and Mr. Riley needs some rest. You can come back this afternoon if you wish."

"Doc—" Mav starts, but she shakes her head, cutting him off.

"Rest, Mr. Riley, is the only way you're getting out of here." She looks pointedly at him, and he rolls his eyes.

"Fine," he says before kissing the top of my head. "Come back and see me tomorrow?"

"You know I will," I murmur before jumping from the bed, watching as Linc, Finn, East, and Chase talk quietly.

East moves to me and smiles sadly. "Come on, I'll take you home while they deal with everything else."

I nod, taking his hand. "Okay."

He looks a little shocked, I assume at my lack of fight, but I really just need to process. I thought my mom left me, that she *chose* not to come back. But I could've been wrong. Maybe she *couldn't* come back, and that is a whole new mindfuck for me to try and work through.

---

The drive home is quiet. East lets me lose myself in my head and I'm grateful. The emotions are like a tsunami fighting a hurricane. The guilt at what happened to Maverick, knowing that this is almost definitely linked to the deal I made with Harrison, the shock of discovering my mom was being kept by Edward—Harrison already told me he had killed my dad—it's all a lot to process.

That on top of the deal I made, the fact that I'm still working through what that means for us all from here… I hate keeping secrets, especially from the four of them, but I know I have to if I want them to be free.

Harrison seems like the kind of snake who will get free of anything if there's even the slightest possibility that he can. I'm not going to give him the chance. The guys deserve to be free, I just hadn't considered that Harrison didn't promise they'd be *alive* and free.

Fucking loopholes.

We pull up to the gates, East tapping in the code before we head up the drive and pull to a stop in front of the garages. "Are you okay?"

I look up at him, trying to work out how to answer him without outright lying. Leaning my head back against the seat, I close my eyes for a minute, hoping the pounding in my head might subside. "I will be. I'm just so sick of the shit those three have to put up with."

"I am too. I've been trying for years to find a way to get them out the way Stone got you out. I know Chase helped with the details of your dad's contract, him being a lawyer and all, but he's a little sketchy about the details. Considering I'm not technically a Knight, I get it. Maybe he'll give you more details?"

My heart skips a beat and I try to lock down my reaction. "I'm not a Knight."

"Not officially, but the contract your dad made means it's probably going to happen at some point." He shrugs before unbuckling and climbing from the car.

Keeping this secret is going to be harder than I thought. I need to work on my poker face.

I climb from the car and follow him inside, finding Smithy and Matthew in the kitchen. "Miss Octavia, Master East. How is Master Riley?"

He pulls out one of the stools for me, motioning for me to sit down, and East sits beside me, watching Matthew closely.

"Where are my manners?" Smithy says, flustered. "Master East, I'd like you to officially meet Matthew. Matthew, this is Easton Saint. One of Octavia's suitors."

"Nice to meet you." East eyes Matthew warily, and I subtly nudge him with my elbow.

Matthew laughs, so I guess it wasn't that subtle. "Likewise. I've heard so much about you all, I feel like I already know you."

"Funny, because I haven't heard anything about you."

"East!" I hiss. "You sound like Lincoln. Stop it."

He looks at me and has the decency to look sheepish before turning back to Matthew. "Sorry, it's been a long few days."

"I get it," Matthew says, waving him off. "How about we have breakfast together, then you can learn I'm not some nefarious monster in the dark."

I press my lips together, trying not to laugh. If only Matthew knew the monsters we usually play with. I can't help but wonder if Smithy has told him about the Knights. I glance over at him and he's busy cooking, not paying any attention to us.

"Sounds good." East smiles, and I leave them to it, listening in as Matthew tells East about his work—something to do with hedge funds. I tune out when they start talking numbers—not my strongest suit. Maverick in the hospital plays on my mind, and I try to think of a way to confront Harrison about it without getting Maverick in deep shit. I have no idea how the Knights will handle this, but my deal called for them to have the same protections as the Knights. I just hope it's enough.

I tune back into East and Matthew talking about a trip Matthew and Smithy took skiing. The conversation drives me over to Smithy at the stove.

"Hey, is there anything I can do to help?" I ask, needing the distraction, even if just to get out of my own head.

Smithy looks down at me, smirking. "Nothing needs burning, Miss Octavia, but if you'd like to pour everyone a drink, I'm sure it would be welcome."

I laugh softly, shaking my head. "I can do that. Maybe you should give me some cooking lessons. If I get to go away to college, I'm going to need to learn how to survive."

"Indeed," he says, frowning. "Or I can just relocate with you."

I haven't given much thought to college lately. I remember when my goals were so set, but this year has been a minefield. It strikes me that none of the guys have talked about college either, not really. I wonder if they'll go now that they're free?

My future is uncertain, I don't even know if college is still in the cards for me thanks to the deal with Harrison, but that isn't for me to worry about right now. "Sounds perfect," I respond to him, smiling. "Though, you might want to settle down with Matthew rather than coming wherever I go."

"Oh, Miss Octavia, I might be fairly certain I'm in love with him," he says quietly, glancing at Matthew and East behind us. "But if you need me, you are, and will always be, my first priority."

I reach up on my tiptoes and kiss his cheek. "I love you, Smithy."

"And I you. Now pour everyone a drink, breakfast is almost ready."

I've never been more glad that I told him my secret. I only said I wouldn't tell the boys, and I'm certain Smithy will hold the information in confidence. The last thing I want to do is jeopardize anything, but I also needed *someone* to know.

Heading to the coffee pot, I pour everyone a mug, distributing them on the counter before sitting back down next to East, leaning into his side when he drops an arm around my shoulders.

"So, are you two an official couple?" Matthew asks, and I press my lips together, trying not to laugh.

"Something like that," I say, sitting back up straight as Smithy dishes up the bacon, eggs, and biscuits.

"All four of them are her boyfriends," Smithy offers, and my cheeks flame.

Matthew looks at me, eyebrows raised. "How very unconventional."

"And perfect," East adds, squeezing my hand.

"Each of them offers something that I couldn't live without," I tell Matthew, taking a deep breath and catching the scent of peppermint and spice again. I sneeze as the memory of it assaults me. "That's some cologne, Matthew. What is it?"

"It's a Versace cologne that my daughter buys me every year." He smiles fondly.

"I didn't realize you had a daughter."

"Yes, well, being a gay man in my youth wasn't something I admitted to. It wasn't until ten years ago that I told my family the truth about it all. I am very lucky that my children are as open-minded as they are. I was not so lucky as James to find love early in life, but I have it now, and I'm thankful for it every day." He gazes at Smithy with so much love in his eyes, there's no doubt that whatever they have between them is real.

"I'm glad you found each other," I say, before digging into breakfast.

"So what is the word on Master Riley?" Smithy asks, turning the conversation away from him and Matthew, and I leave East to answer while I eat, watching Matthew closely. I don't want to believe he was the one in that basement, but I can see how much Smithy cares for him and I can't risk his heart on this. I think it's time I get in touch with Bentley again.

# CHAPTER FIVE

## LINCOLN

I enter the Riley basement for the second time in my life, again with Finley beside me, cursing out Edward. Descending the steps fills me with dread, but this needs to be done. Chase follows behind us, already on the phone to the facility where Finley's mom is a resident, preparing them for new arrivals.

We're just not sure how many yet.

The light is still on from where we dragged Maverick out of here earlier, but it's freaking eerily silent. Edward obviously trained them to be quiet. Just the thought makes me feel sick.

When I reach the bottom of the stairs, I look around the white, sterile room, actually paying attention to detail this time. The walls are lined with cages, stacked two high. Not all of them contain women, but the ones that do are more than enough. On the far right wall is a bigger cage, and sitting in the back corner is Emily Royal.

She looks broken. They all do; pale skin, ratty hair, dirty, covered in cuts, bruises, and dried blood. The smells make my stomach turn, dried blood, urine, and God only knows what else.

Fuck only knows what Edward put them through.

Edward's dead body is pallid, open eyes staring up at the ceiling, as disgusting in death as he was in life, lying in a pool of his and Maverick's blood. It's not dry yet. I guess that much blood takes a while to dry.

"I've got him," Finn almost whispers, nodding toward Edward. "You guys deal with the girls. I'll put him in the trunk of your sedan, Chase. We can take him to the crematorium before we head out to the facility."

I'm not surprised he chose to deal with Edward. He's seen the mess the man has made more often than I have. Him and Mav have always been closer, so Mav usually calls him first. I know Finn has faced off with Edward more than once, but it's always easier facing someone else's monster.

He bends down, lifting the dead weight like it's nothing, and hoists the body over his shoulder before heading back upstairs.

"There are seven girls here," Chase utters, disbelief clear on his face. "Plus Emily."

I look at him, trying to take his measure. "Surely, being on the Conclave, you knew about most of their extra curriculars?"

"I tried to keep my distance," he says, shaking his head. "I never wanted to be a Knight. So once I was on the Conclave, I did what I had to but no more. My family's businesses are all above board, I don't let the Knights touch them, and I tried to not ask about their extras. I've used my legal skills to help them when it has been demanded, but this… this is—"

"This is nothing compared to what some of them do," I snap at him. "How do you expect to be of any use to us, to East, when you have no idea what's really been happening around you? They kidnap kids, sell them, fuck them, turn them into murderers. That's just scratching the surface. These girls are just more of the helpless fucks the Knights got their claws into. I'm sure there are mass graves of others just like them."

He blinks at me, like he's only just considering what I'm saying.

I don't have time for this. "Get back on the phone, tell the facility how many are coming, then start getting them out. I'll go grab some clothes from upstairs so they're actually fucking dressed. Leave Emily for me."

He nods and I jog back up the stairs, heading to the laundry room through the kitchen. There's a ton of Mav's shit here, and I'm sure he won't mind me using it. I grab as many hoodies and sweatpants as I can find before heading back downstairs. Finn reappears seconds later and takes the clothes from me, moving to help Chase.

I really hope he has more up his sleeve if he intends to help us.

Running a hand over my face and taking a breath, I steel myself before moving to the larger cage that holds a woman who could be Octavia's twin.

"Emily," I say as softly as I can as I reach the door, undoing the bolt that holds it closed. She could've easily reached through the bars to undo this. I guess that was part of Edward's mind fuckery; giving them the illusion of being able to escape, making them believe they chose to stay here.

I open the door, and she scurries backward, pressing against the wall. "Get out, I don't want to go with you. I want Edward."

"Edward is gone." She shakes her head, panicked.

"He can't be gone. She's the one who's gone. He promised…" she continues to ramble under her breath unintelligibly, shaking her head as she wraps her arms around herself. I'm just glad that she's actually clothed.

I have to assume the *she* that she's rambling about is Octavia. "Octavia is safe. She's at home. Edward won't hurt her. Come on, let's get you out of here so you can be safe too."

Offering her my hand, I wait patiently. She has to be the one to take my hand. She smiles wickedly at me, her entire demeanor changing, and my blood turns to ice. In a blink it's gone and she takes my hand, letting me pull her from the cage.

I don't know what the fuck that was, but there is no way in hell I'm letting Octavia anywhere near her until I work it out.

Glancing back, I notice Finn and Chase have the other cages empty and Finn is the only one left waiting for me. He raises his eyebrows, and I realize he saw it too. I shake my head subtly, passing her over to him and letting him walk her upstairs without another word.

There are too many secrets hidden in this room, and I'm going to find every last one of them.

---

It took a few hours to get the girls and Emily situated, and they're all now on a 72-hour lock down while the doctors assess them. After checking back in on Maverick, Finn and I came back to the basement of the Riley house to try and work out its secrets while Chase went to collect Mrs. Riley.

After spending the last few days scrubbing the room clean and dismantling the cages, today we started rifling through the rest of the shit in here. So far, we've found nothing.

"We have to be missing something." Finn tugs on his hair as he stares at the blank white walls. "This place has to be more than a torture chamber."

"Maybe, but maybe not," I offer. "Edward was like a cannon. Harrison would point him in a direction and he'd cause destruction. Maybe he didn't keep anything important. Harrison isn't the type to trust anyone with his secrets but himself."

"Yeah, I guess. Fuck, this is frustrating as hell. I was hoping we'd find something that might work as leverage."

"You and me both." I let out a sigh, trying not to let disappointment flood me. I usually try to dispel any hope, but the thought of Edward being dead, and what that could mean for us… it's too big to completely quash.

Except now that hope is like an icy cold grip on my heart as I try to shove it away.

I check my phone and curse. "We should clean up then head to the hospital. It's nearly time to get Mav."

"Are we bringing him back here?" Finn asks.

"That's up to him. I'd rather he stayed with one of us, but the house is empty, and his biggest reason for avoiding this place is dead now." I pull on the strands of my hair, the sting helping to focus. "We should probably check in with Octavia. None of us have spoken to her for a few days."

"Does she even know Mav is getting out of the hospital today?"

I shake my head. "I haven't said anything, so unless he has, I'm going to go with no."

"We really don't deserve her," he mutters, running a hand over his jeans, dusting himself off. "When I spoke to her the other day, she asked for some space to process the Emily thing, but we always end up so wrapped up in Knight bullshit, then days pass…"

"I get it. I do. I don't disagree with you either, but I'm not letting her go. Not now, not ever. She'll have to pull herself from my cold, dead grasp."

He smirks at me, shaking his eyes. "You've got a weird way with words, man."

I bark out a laugh. "We're all a little bit twisted, but you can't tell me you feel any differently."

"Never said I did."

I softly laugh again, sending Alex another message to see if he has any information on Luc's whereabouts. Fucker ignored my last message. Pretty sure he enjoys messing with me. "Come on, let's get this over with."

We climb from the basement, locking it—and the ghosts of its horrors—away, and head upstairs to clean off. After we both shower and redress, I drive us to the hospital where Maverick is already being wheeled toward us. "It's home time! Where's my girl?"

He looks behind us, his smile dropping.

"You can see her later," I tell him, the nurse frowning at me as I do so.

Finn follows her to get his meds and discharge details sorted as I take him out to the car. "Why isn't she here?"

"She asked for a few days after finding out about her mom. I'm sure we'll see her soon enough."

"Fuck that. Where's my phone?" he swears as he pats himself down, pulling it from his pocket. "She's not going to ignore me. Just take me to her place."

I shake my head, almost jealous of his lack of fucks when it comes to smothering her. "Are you going to be staying with her then?"

He frowns, shaking his head. "No, I don't want to be a burden, not if she's dealing with her mom." He scrubs a hand down his face. "Fuck, this whole being considerate thing is bullshit."

I bark out a laugh. "Yes, yes it is. So where are you staying? Home? With me? Finn?"

"I'll stay with you if the offer's open. Keeps me close to her, and Mrs. Potts will make sure I don't starve."

I nod at him as I help him into the car. "Sounds good. I'm going to try to get Finn to relocate to my place, too. Then we're all close. There's too much going on right now, and leaving her alone feels fucking wrong."

I grab my phone and text East to see if he's heard from Octavia, closing the door to the car once Mav's inside, before heading around to the driver's seat. Finn appears moments later, jumping in the back.

"You're moving in with me for a bit," I tell him, and he nods.

"I figured I would be if Mav was staying there, too. Makes sense."

I don't say another word before pulling away from the hospital. I'll get them settled in, then I'm going to hunt down our girl.

# CHAPTER SIX

## OCTAVIA

After being a zombie at school these last few days, I'm kind of glad that Indi was away with her parents this week. I've been in a state of shock since I learned about my mom, and I'm just not ready to talk to her about it yet. It's like I'm numb and nothing but anger can touch me right now. I hate it.

I want to feel something else. *Anything* else.

But with the guys dealing with the fallout of everything that's been going on the last few days, and Mav being in the hospital, I've been stumbling around in the dark on my own a little.

I still haven't heard anything about my mom, and I haven't pressed it because I'm not even sure if I want to see her. Plus, I'm the one who asked for space.

It's not like I'd know what the fuck to say anyway.

Do I just jump in with a "why the fuck did you leave us?" Or do I start with, "how did you end up locked in a basement?" Apparently, I have some resentment toward her bubbling under the surface, and now that I know she's not dead, it's all coming to the forefront of my mind… which isn't exactly the greatest way to go meet my mom when I haven't seen her for basically half my life.

Which is exactly how I find myself in the Saints' basement.

Their gym setup is decidedly better than the makeshift one I've got at home, and even if I just feel exhaustion when I'm done, maybe that will kickstart everything else inside of me and rid me of this rage I can feel building so I can work out how the fuck to deal with all the things I've been ignoring.

Maybe I can figure out a way to confront Harrison. But that would also mean acknowledging that Edward is dead, and since I have barely seen the guys, I'm not sure where we even are with that. Since I haven't heard from Harrison, I can only assume our deal is still in place as I can't exactly ask the guys about it.

I fucking hate secrets.

I start on the treadmill. My pace is punishing and sweat runs down my back, the blue sports crop top and matching leggings giving me room to breathe. I increase my speed anyway.

When my legs feel like jelly, I move to the free weights Lincoln has set up, going through every curl, lift, and fuck knows what else I have stored in my memory until my muscles quiver with exhaustion.

But it doesn't seem to change a thing. It's still like there's a barrier between me and the rest of the world. I can't see it, but it's definitely there.

I drop down onto the mats, fisting my hands in my hair, the sting a welcome relief.

"V? What are you doing here? I thought you were with Lincoln." East's voice wraps around me, and finally, I feel something. I need him.

I look up at him and I don't know what he sees on my face, but his smile drops as he strides toward me.

"What's wrong?"

I open my mouth to speak, not knowing which words to string together that will explain the chaos running through my mind.

His eyes darken the longer I stay quiet. I know he knows what happened, but he doesn't know the constant commentary going on in my head. He's the one person I know won't see me as weak if I break in front of him. He's always been my white knight.

He puts one arm beneath my curled knees and another around my shoulders, lifting me so I'm leaning on his chest, and carries me back upstairs to his room. He heads straight for his bathroom and turns the shower on, stepping beneath it with us both fully dressed.

The cold water sends pebbles skittering across my skin before it starts to warm, and I break a little. I've tried to just push it down, stay strong, be who everyone expects me to be.

"You guys have got to stop nearly dying on me," I croak.

He places me on my feet, putting his finger beneath my chin so I'm looking up at him. "We're not going anywhere, V. Not one of us. Did something else happen that I don't know about?" he asks, and I shake my head. "Then why do you look like your world is ending?"

A shiver runs through me again, and he slowly peels off my wet workout gear before stripping out of his own clothes and holding me against his chest. The fading pink line of the scar over his heart is beneath my ear. I listen for that heartbeat like it's the only sound I'll ever hear again and it soothes me a little.

"My mom." The words are little more than a whisper, but he tenses beneath me so I know he heard. "She was in Edward's basement. She saw what happened with Maverick and Edward. She's been down there for years, kept in a cage… and I don't know if I even want to see her. What would I even say to her?"

I trail off and his arms tighten around me. He doesn't say anything, but I get it. What is there to say to that?

Tears stream down my cheeks, masked by the falling stream of water from the shower. "I can't feel anything."

He pulls back from me, his gaze searching my face before leaning down and kissing me softly. I cling to him like he's the oxygen I need as want pierces through me.

"Let me look after you," he murmurs. His lips move down my neck, caressing my skin, leaving a trail of heat as he moves down my chest.

I gasp as he takes my nipple into his mouth, licking, sucking and biting, and my slick grows between my legs.

"More," I gasp, plunging my fingers into his dark hair.

He looks at me, a mischievous grin on his face, his steel eyes molten as he curls my hair around his fist and tugs so I'm looking up at him. "You don't have to beg, Octavia. I'll give you everything until you can't take any more."

Heat rips through me at the unspoken promise of his words. "Yes," is the only word I can find as he releases me before gripping the back of my thighs and lifting me against him, his hard dick pressing against my stomach as he shuts off the shower and walks me back into his room, gently placing me down onto the bed. His heated gaze walks a path of fire starting at my feet and clawing its way up my body until his eyes meet mine.

"Every inch of you…" the words trail off as he sinks his teeth onto his bottom lip, his entire body primed for the taking, his gaze wild with need, "is mine."

A whimper escapes me, but I nod.

"There isn't anything I wouldn't do for you, Octavia. You know that, right?"

"Yes," I breathe.

With one thigh between my legs, East cages me in against the mattress; eyes like liquid desire stare down at me as his forearms are planted on either side of my head. For what feels like hours, I wait for him to move, to talk, to do *something.* Instead, he simply studies me like I'm the only thing that exists in his universe. At first, I'm not sure what to do with myself. Am I supposed to touch him? Should I be kissing him?

It's only when my entire body begins to tremble with the need for him that I understand his intentions.

He's taking the power and control I am oh-so-happy to hand over right now, taking all the responsibility I just cannot handle and making it his. East wants my attention on him and only him, and from the look in his eyes, he is ready to make me feel every single thing I need to.

Slowly, he rubs his thigh up and down on my pussy with just the slightest pressure, just enough to make me push up against him, eliciting a mewl from deep inside me.

I close my eyes and East immediately stops.

My lids fly open and I'm greeted with his sexy-as-sin half smile. "Look at me, Octavia. Look at us."

Our gazes lock and East brings his mouth to my forehead, pressing his lips there for a chaste kiss before he moves to one eyelid then the other. Next, he gifts me with soft kisses across my cheek and down the column of my neck. When he reaches the hollow of my throat, he pushes his thigh a little harder against my core and I can't stop myself from grinding against him, desperate for more.

The tip of his tongue flicks at the indent of my collarbone and is gone just as quickly as it appeared, tracing a hot path down between my breasts. His eyes dart up, meeting my hungry gaze as he takes one nipple in his mouth and sucks before nipping, then gives my other nipple the same attention.

I can't stop myself from crying out, pleading for more. I try to rub my thighs together to gain some added friction but his thigh between prevents me from having to do anything at all. I know East, he doesn't want me to work for it. He wants to do the work for me. He wants—no, *needs*—to fix it all for me, whatever it is.

The hint of a smile at the corner of his mouth tells me he knows exactly how much he's torturing me, even if it is the sweetest torture I've experienced in a while. He buries his fingers in my hair, tightening his hold on me, and that edge of pain makes everything else feel so much fucking better.

"Stay with me," he demands, not waiting for a response.

Releasing me, he drags his body down the length of mine until he reaches my navel, his lips leisurely dragging down my skin and lighting up every one of my nerve endings as he goes. Yet, with all his good intentions, his slow descent down my body is nothing short of excruciating.

He merely skims his breath over my pussy as he continues mapping out my curves with devilish open-mouthed kisses, going straight for my thigh, behind my knee, my calf, the arch of my foot, before he mimics the same path on my other leg and finally completing the circuit at my core.

I'm panting; every breath ragged from the torment of his slow burning foreplay.

"What do you need, beautiful?"

He pauses, not taking his eyes from mine, but when I don't speak, he flicks his tongue over my clit for a fraction of a second. "This?"

I growl from the deepest parts of my desire, but he chuckles softly, like he knows how impatient I am.

"What about this?" The pad of his finger runs up my slit and it feels so fucking good I almost shed real fucking tears.

"Yes!" I watch him as he throws me a wicked smile filled with dirty promises.

"Hmm, I had a feeling you might."

In one single move, his mouth latches onto my clit—sucking it hard into his mouth—as two fingers plunge into my pussy, curled exactly right and striking that perfect place deep inside me. I cry out from the perfection of it.

My orgasm is right there. I can feel it building in my core and just when I think I can't possibly wait another second, he changes the angle of his fingers and my entire body detonates like a nuclear weapon.

"Oh my God. Fuck!" I'm gasping out every word as East continues to draw out my orgasm with every lick of his tongue and caress of his fingers.

When I can finally breathe without feeling the burn in my lungs from my screams, I look up at East, my gaze still hungry as I take in his beautifully sculpted body. On his haunches, he takes his cock in hand and begins stroking himself, unhurried and calm. Teasing. Taunting. He looks so fucking hot, my need comes crashing back inside me as though I haven't just had a fucking orgasm. How does he do this to me?

"You taste so fucking sweet, V. Like honey. I could lick you up all fucking day long and never tire of it."

He brings a finger back up to my pussy, coating it with my wetness.

I whimper at the touch, the sound of my need echoing off the walls. It's so intense my legs shake with desperation. I look down at him and see he's driving himself just as crazy as I feel. I know what he's doing. This man won't let himself come until he's wrung out every single orgasm he can from me first.

With both of his big hands at the back of my thighs, East pushes my legs back so that I'm balanced on my shoulders and head, my legs folding over his shoulders as his mouth goes straight for my pussy.

I swear to fuck I see stars, full constellations, and the goddamn heavens open up from just the feel of his tongue as it teases my clit before he pushes two fingers back inside of me to the knuckle.

Oh shit.

My body tightens at the intrusion, and his moans as I clamp down around him almost push me over the edge. The fingers on his other hand tighten against my thigh just hard enough that the bite keeps me from falling off the cliff.

I can't catch my breath as my eyes water when another orgasm threatens to take me away again. It's at the base of my spine, tingling up the nerve endings, and just when I fear it's too early to come a second time, East sucks my clit and I lose all control over my body.

I don't have an ounce of control over anything.

"Oh my God, East, it's too much." I'm going to lose my mind.

"It's never too much, V. Let it all go, I promise I'll catch you."

I don't doubt him on this because I know for a fact, he will always be my safe space.

"Well, I don't doubt you'll always catch me but I just don't want to die of orgasm overload." He smiles at my sass, but the devilish glint in his eyes makes me fall in love with him just a little bit more.

I'm so lost in my dreamy post-orgasmic haze that it takes me a second to realize what's happening. East takes me by the hips and flips me over so I'm pressed face down into the pillow. Lifting my hips so that my ass is in the air at the perfect angle for him to plunge his tongue back inside my pussy, eating me like he's starved.

Holy fuck, that's so hot. The cool air from the open window breezes around us, but I barely feel it, my every thought consumed by his touch. When his soaked fingers reach forward for my clit, I have to bite the pillow below me to avoid squirming from the pleasure pain he's causing. My clit is hyper-sensitive to his touch, but my body is still hungry for more.

His free hand reaches up and tweaks my nipple, and I swear to fuck there's no way he can coax another fucking orgasm out of me. It's physically impossible, right?

He must feel it, sense that I'm doubting his prowess, because for the briefest of seconds, his mouth releases me and he flashes a cocksure grin that makes my entire body react in an instant. "I know your body better than you think, Octavia."

His words unleash the tightened coil inside of me and my orgasm rips through me, my throat ravaged as I scream, and I'm gone. Fucking obliterated by this climax that takes my breath away, right along with my ability to speak or move.

I'm frozen, my fingers burning from how hard I'm gripping the sheets, my lower body spasming while East continues to devour my pussy, dragging out my orgasm almost to the point of pain.

Long after the aftershocks fade away, East continues to lick every inch of me until he's lying beside me, kissing my lips for the first time and sharing my taste with me.

"I think you broke my brain." My words are barely a whisper.

"Then my job here is done." He gives me his sexy grin and my world feels right—at least in this moment. "For now at least."

"Maybe I should distract myself from being so broken, and break you too." A smile teases my lips as I swing my leg over him until I'm straddling him, lying forward so my chest is pressed to him. "Then we can be broken together."

"I'll be anything you need me to be," he groans as I rub myself on his still very hard cock. I gasp at the feel of him sliding between my folds, ready to be tortured by him all over again.

---

After my afternoon lounging in bed with East, we came down to forage for food. Halfway through making the biggest sandwiches I've ever seen in my life, the front door crashes open and in strolls Lincoln, with Mav behind him and Finn bringing up the rear.

Lincoln pauses when he sees me wearing nothing but East's button down, and the man himself standing behind me in just a pair of boxers. "I see you've both been enjoying yourself."

"Damn, man, I might be jealous," Mav groans as he steps past Linc. I rush toward him and wrap my arms around him, pressing my head against his chest, enjoying the sound of his beating heart. "Hey, princess," he murmurs, drawing my attention back to his face. "Miss me?"

"You know I did," I breathe before stretching up on the tips of my toes and kissing him, showing him just how much I missed him; how worried I've been.

"If that's your welcome home, I might get stabbed more often."

I pull back from him, my hands on my hips. "Maverick Riley, don't you fucking dare."

"Damn, you're hot when you're bossy."

Finn nods his agreement before kissing my cheek and heading toward the counter, and I turn to find Linc already sitting at the table. Mav's hands grip my hips and he pulls me back against him. "I'm looking forward to being fully healed, princess."

His low growl in my ear sends a shiver down my spine and I press against him, leaning up to whisper in his ear, "Me too."

His eyes go wide as I smile playfully before sashaying over to the table, making sure to sway my ass extra because I know he's watching. My day with East has helped a little, but I'm still torn up about everything.

For right now though, I'm going to focus on what I have and be thankful for it. These four are here, and they're all alive, despite too many close calls lately.

I slip onto the empty chair between Lincoln and Finn, and East brings my sandwich over. "So, what have I missed the last few days?"

My question hangs in the air as I take a bite, my long, wavy hair falling over one shoulder as I look up at them. All eyes are on me, and I fight the smile that threatens. Apparently, we all need a distraction at the moment. "My eyes are up here, boys."

"Not much," Lincoln says, his gaze meeting mine. "Your mom has settled into the facility along with the others, and everyone seems as okay as can be expected. We've been blessed with a reprieve, in that Edward was supposed to be away for a few weeks, so no one has been asking questions as to his whereabouts. But when he doesn't check in with Harrison, he's likely to start asking questions."

"How much trouble are you in?" I ask Maverick, who scratches the back of his neck.

"Not sure. Usually killing a Conclave member is really bad, but he was trying to kill me, and I'm also Conclave. It seems to be a bit of a gray area."

"So you should be okay?" I ask and he nods, a small weight lifting from my shoulders. I'm not sure how my deal with Harrison is going to affect him here, and worry pools in my gut. "What about my mom and the other girls?"

"As long as they're in the Knights' facility, they'll be fine. The doctors will work with them, make sure that they're okay, but also make sure that they don't say anything once they're ready for release. I'm getting weekly updates on all patients so I can keep track of them too."

I let out a deep breath as I lean back in my chair. "So, we're really okay?"

"It seems that way," Finn says before reaching over and stealing a quarter of my sandwich.

Relief that they'll be okay fills me. That I'll be okay.

Though I still need to speak to Harrison.

My phone buzzes on the counter, so I push back from the table and go to grab it. Bentley's name lights up my screen.

Bentley: I might have something for you. Coffee?

Me: Sure, I'll be home tonight if that works for you?

Bentley: Can't do tonight, but I can do tomorrow. Be there around 9pm.

Me: Sounds good.

I lock the phone, looking up to find all of them watching me closely.

"Who was that?" Linc asks, and I quirk a brow at him.

"Jealous?"

"Don't answer a question with a question, Octavia," Lincoln grumbles.

I fold my arms over my chest, not wanting to lie to him, but I can't tell him about Bentley either. "You do not own me, Lincoln Saint. You don't get to know all my secrets. A girl has to have *some* mystery."

# CHAPTER SEVEN

## OCTAVIA

My stomach churns as I drive to school. Indi is back today, and she's my bestest bitch, so she's going to know something's wrong. I'm not even sure where to begin when she asks me what's up, because I know she will.

It's why I chose to come in alone today. I needed some time to clear my mind, prepare myself to talk about my mom. I can't tell her about the deal I made… but I really need to tell someone other than Smithy, because I'm not sure that keeping it just between us is the best idea. With so much going on around us, if something happens to me, I need someone else to know the truth. Especially when making a deal with the devil feels like a surefire way to end up on the wrong side of alive.

I pull into my usual parking space and take a deep breath as Indi pulls into the space beside me, smiling widely as she shuts off the car. I grab the coffees I picked up on the way in from the cup holders and climb from the car to meet her.

Coffee is always a good distraction.

"Bitch, I missed you!" she squeals, taking the coffee and hugging me. "Never let my parents keep me hostage again. Upside: I'm down from cast to splint so I can finally drive again!"

"I am happy for you, my friend." I smile, looping her splinted arm through mine before taking a sip of my coffee. "How was your trip back east?"

"It was sucky, and wet. I never thought I'd prefer the west coast, but apparently the sunshine grew on me. Could also have something to do with my parents trying to set me up with their friend's kid. Like, I might have a thing for twins, but I'm taken."

"They did *what*?" I screech as we enter the school. "How did the guys take that?"

She looks at me, wincing. "About as well as you'd imagine. Apparently my parents don't approve of my current relationships." She rolls her eyes as we head to my locker. "But fuck them. Like I told them, Sawyer St.Vincent is lovely, he's a little older, cute in a labrador puppy kind of way, but he's not for me. I'm in love and I'm happy. Plus, I'm pretty sure he has a girlfriend and his mom just hates her."

"Ouch. I'm sorry, dude. That sucks." Dropping her arm, I grab my books for class before heading to her locker.

"It's all good. What did I miss?" she asks as she sorts herself out. "Shit, I forgot to grab a book from the library. Detour there before class?"

"Sure," I say, smiling tightly. She seems to forget her question and tells me all about the people she met back home, including Sawyer, his twin Asher, and his other friends. I smile and nod, *oohing* and *aahing* where expected, trying to ignore the churning in my stomach as we approach the library. At least it's quiet and mostly deserted. I can answer her questions without having to deep dive into everything.

We glide past the librarian as we enter, and she pays us no attention as Indi drags me to wherever it is she can find the book she needs. Once we're in the back of the stacks, she asks again. "So what did I miss? And don't tell me 'nothing'. I saw how your face dropped when I asked before."

Goddamn, she's perceptive.

The warning bell sounds, saving me a little. "Short version?"

"For now," she nods, grabbing a book from the back wall.

"Mav's dad tried to kill him. Mav won, but ended up in the hospital. And my mom was in a cage in their basement."

She looks at me wide-eyed. "What the actual fuck? Stupid bell! Stupid school! Stupid short version! I'm coming over tonight and you're telling me the long version. Don't bother trying to stop me."

I nod, hurrying us back to the main desk so she can check out her book. We make it to class just as the final bell rings. Miss Summers raises a brow at us as we slide into our desks but doesn't say anything further.

Today is no different than the rest of this week. I go through it in a fog, glad I downloaded the dictation app on my phone for class after seeing a tip online about it, because I'm going to need all of the notes when it comes to trying to catch up.

My classes pass in a blur so by the time I leave music and head toward the cafeteria, not paying much attention to my surroundings, I find Blair at my locker.

Fuck my life. I'd forgotten about the shit I started with her. I'd forgotten about pretty much everything outside of my deal with Harrison, and my mom.

I really need to get my shit together.

"We need to talk," she hisses as I throw my stuff in my locker.

"What do you want, Blair?" I sigh. I know this was my idea, but I don't have the brain space for her right now.

"Not here," she says, rolling her eyes. "I'll come by the house after school."

"Sounds good," I say, nodding, and she flicks her icy blonde hair over her shoulder and struts away from me.

Awesome, another thing to try and remember.

That's when I remember Indi mentioning coming over tonight to discuss what I dropped on her this morning.

I head to the cafeteria and realize I haven't seen any of my guys today. Not that shocking with Mav, he's still healing, but I thought I'd have seen Linc or Finn, so I drop a message in the group chat to ask where they are. East's replacement as Coach was taken on full-time when his injury was as bad as it was, which sucks. It *does* mean we don't have to hide our relationship anymore, but it also means I have fewer places of sanctuary in this hellscape.

Mav: In bed, could do with some company ;)

Finn: Mav, fuck off. We're just wrapping some of the shit up with Chase, pretty girl. Sorry we didn't let you know.

East: I thought someone else was supposed to tell you *glares at Linc*

Linc: So sue me, I knew she'd try and join us and she has her GPA to worry about.

I smile at that before messaging them back

Me: As long as you're okay. I'll head to lunch, if you need me let me know

Mav: I need you. In my bed. On my dick.

I burst out laughing, because of course.

Me: Maybe later ;)

I pocket my phone and take a deep breath before walking through the doors to the cafeteria, my jaw dropping when I take in the sight before me.

What in the actual fuck?

---

After avoiding the chaos in the cafeteria with the weird as fuck beat down between the football team and the hockey team, I was glad to escape the wave of insanity that seems to have crashed over ECP this afternoon.

When I get home, I let out a deep breath and climb from the car, preparing myself to speak to Indi about everything that's been going on. I'm just glad Smithy is already in the know. Bentley is heading over tonight anyway, so if I'm looping people in, this is probably the best way to do it. I feel sick to my stomach at not telling my guys about it.

For some reason, I feel the most guilt about not telling Finn. Probably because he's fought so hard to be transparent with me, but if it buys their freedom, their happiness, I'm just going to have to suck it up.

I'm half hoping that Indi or Smithy will tell me I'm doing the right thing, because doubt fills me every time I let myself think about it. Making a deal with Harrison Saint is the equivalent to selling my soul, but surely one soul for the good of the many is worth it. Especially when it's not forever.

Right?

I rest my forehead on the steering wheel hoping for some sort of sign that I'm doing the right thing. When I sat in that room with Harrison, it was the obvious answer. It was the solution to all of their problems. To their suffering. To giving them the chances and opportunities they deserved. They didn't deserve to live a life of writhing pain and darkness. They'd done enough.

My sacrifice was the least I could do.

It's not the sacrifice I'm second-guessing. I would never.

It's the secrets I have to keep until my birthday. The thought of telling them they're free brings me so much fucking joy, but I know none of them are going to take it very well.

Least of all Linc.

Especially after all of my bitching about secrets being kept 'for the best.' I'm such a fucking hypocrite, but I can finally see why they keep a piece of themselves back. Well, except for East. He's been all in since the beginning.

If I thought he wouldn't tell Lincoln, I'd tell him in a heartbeat, but those two keep very little from each other, and getting them free is more important than alleviating my guilt.

I climb from the car and trudge into the house, smiling when I hear Smithy singing from the kitchen. I'm definitely going to need comfort food for the conversations I need to have tonight.

I round the corner, startling him, but still he smiles at me. "Oh, Miss Octavia. I didn't hear you get home. How was your day?"

"It was a weird one, Smithy," I say as I grab a bottle of water from the refrigerator and climb onto one of the stools at the center island. "Indi is coming over later, as is Bentley."

He raises his eyebrows at me, looking shocked. "Both of them? That's an interesting combination."

"It gets more interesting. Blair is heading over *before* they get here."

He sneers at the mention of my cousin and the corners of my lips tip upward. "What on earth could she want?"

"Bitchy high school queen bee take down plots if I had to guess." He looks at me, thoroughly bewildered. "I know, I know. But Mikayla took her throne after everything that happened with Nate, and she is even fucking worse than Blair was. While I dislike Blair for the most part, she was better than Mikayla is, and better the devil you know, you know?"

I shrug my shoulders as he pushes up from where he's leaning against the counter. "Well, I've never been one to second guess your judgment, so if you think this is the right path, then I'll follow you down it. Do you need anything from me this evening?"

I rake my teeth against my bottom lip, contemplating my answer. "Not with Indi or Blair, but if you could be here when Bentley comes. Not that I don't trust him or anything, just, I'm not sure what he's going to tell me, and some support might be nice."

"Of course, Miss Octavia," he says, coming to my side and giving me a one-armed hug. "Anything you need, all you need to do is ask."

"Thanks, Smithy."

"Always, Miss Octavia. Now, if your cousin is coming over, I'm going to make you some taco boats. You're going to need some happy food."

I grin widely at him. "You're the best, Smithy."

He winks at me and I bark out a laugh. "I try, Miss Octavia. My only request is you keep Blair in the lounge area. I don't need that negativity in my kitchen."

I nod at him and jump down from my stool as the buzzer for the gate sounds. "Of course. That'll be her now. "

I open the gate from the app on my phone and move to the front door to let her in, dropping Indi a message to tell her to get her ass here so I'm not alone with the she-devil for too long. Sometimes I miss how close I used to be with Blair, and others… others I remember the shit she did to me when I got back here—how she ruined all of my dad's shit—and those times I couldn't give a fuck.

But this is for the greater good. So I suck up my inner 'I don't wanna' and paste a smile on my face as Blair approaches.

"Good, you're here. Let's get this sorted shall we? Where is your sidekick?" She breezes past me, like the child of privilege that she is, and barely even looks at me as she does. Grinding my teeth together, I close the door, remembering that Blair isn't the big bad in my story.

Even if she does manage to push every single fucking button I have.

"Sure, come on in, Blair. I'm great, thanks. You? Oh, that's awesome. I'm so glad I helped you find legal defense for your dad. Yeah, of course, make yourself at home."

She narrows her eyes at me before rolling them and flicking her blonde hair over her shoulder. "Don't be such a dramatic bitch, Octavia. You came to me, remember? I don't need to be here."

"And I don't need to keep encouraging Chase to help Nate," I counter, and she sighs before dropping onto the couch.

"Fine, fine. Do you want to hear what I have planned or not?"

I move to the couch, sitting on the opposite end and turning to face her. "That depends, do you need my help for any of it?"

"Of course not," she scoffs, looking at me like I'm insane. "I do need the guys' help though. No one can cut a bitch to size in a second quite like they can."

I let out a dry laugh, cause she isn't wrong. "I'll speak to them once you tell me what you have planned."

The buzzer for the gate sounds again and I check my phone. Seeing the Wrangler out there, I let Indi in. "Indi is here."

"Of course she is," Blair huffs as my bestie bounces into the house with a smile on her face. The smile drops when she sees Blair's icy look, and she rolls her eyes as she drops next to me.

"Don't pause on my account. We've all got shit to do."

So Blair tells us her plan to dethrone Mikayla using her boyfriend, who isn't actually her boyfriend. How she'll need the boys there to cut her to pieces in front of everyone, because despite them not being as involved in school politics as they once were, they're still the true kings of the school.

*My kings.*

"It could be worse," Indi says with a shrug, and I nod.

"I'll talk to the guys."

Blair stands, and brushes down her skirt. "Perfect. I'll get out of here. Just don't let me down."

"Have I ever?" I ask with a raised eyebrow, and after a second she looks a little sheepish.

"I guess not. I'll let myself out. See you at school." She breezes out of the house as quickly as she appeared, and I let out a deep breath.

One hard conversation down, and an even harder one to go.

"That was surprisingly painless." I look over at my bestie, who seems much less relaxed now that Blair is gone, which I didn't expect. "But you and I still need to have some words, bestie."

"I know," I say before running a hand through my hair. "I wanted to go and see Mav tonight, but there's so much going on, and you only know half of it. But I need you to promise me that what I'm about to tell you goes no further than here. Some of this stuff, only you and Smithy will know."

Her eyes go wide, and she opens her mouth to ask a question, but I shake my head and interrupt. "It'll make sense when you know."

I move to make a start when Smithy appears. "Milkshakes! I figured these would be needed." He drops the drinks onto the coffee table and presses a kiss into my hair before bustling back to the kitchen.

"Damn this must be bad," Indi mutters as she picks up her milkshake and sucks on the straw. "Okay, now I'm ready."

If only I were.

I pick up my drink and take a mouthful, letting the chocolate distract me while I pull myself together, then I tell her everything. What happened with Mav, about my mom, about Edward, and finally, my deal with Harrison.

By the time I'm done, she's just staring at me slack-jawed.

I give her a minute to process, taking another sip of my milkshake. She closes her mouth, then reopens it like she's going to speak before closing it again.

I think I might have broken her.

It takes another full minute before she explodes. "Are you fucking insane? Harrison Saint is the epitome of evil incarnate. He's like the real life Dolores Umbridge. Why in the ever loving fuck would you sign yourself over to him?"

I look over at her, hoping she understands, because I'm going to need my bestie's support to survive this. "To free them."

The answer is as simple as that. I've seen the lengths my kings are willing to go through for me, so now, I'm willing to step up to the plate and sacrifice for them. Like any queen should.

Understanding flitters across her face and she deflates. "I don't like it, but I get it. And now I see why the secrets. They're going to lose their fucking shit when they find out what you did."

"I know," I say, sounding as small as I feel. "But it's worth it."

"I hope you know what you're doing, but you know I'll be at your side no matter what. Ride or die."

I lean forward and wrap my arms around her, squeezing her tight. “Ride or die.”

“So how do we get this information the dick supreme wants?”

I pull back, and clasp my hands in my lap. “I have a plan. I’ve hired a PI—he’ll be here later on if you want to stick around—but I’m also going through all of my dad’s old stuff. What Harrison wants isn’t something that he’d have just left lying around, so I have to assume it’s here or in the personal belongings that were shipped back from the tour.”

“I’d love to stick around, but I have to check in with Ryker. He had a major blow out with Ellis earlier. It was really fucking bad. Dylan called me after school and well…” She blows out a breath and shrugs. “I don’t even know how the fuck to fix it, but I have to try.”

“I get it. I’ll let you know what Bentley found, even if it’s nothing. And thank you for being here for me.”

“Always, bitch. Always.”

# CHAPTER EIGHT

## OCTAVIA

After a weekend of going through my dad's shit and still barely seeing my guys, I'm almost desperate for some time with them. Which is why instead of heading to my garage, I'm hauling ass next door. I know Finn and Mav are staying with the Saints on a somewhat-permanent basis now, so I know everyone will be here, and dammit, I need some time with them.

I push open the back door to the kitchen and find the four of them at the table: East in his t-shirt and sweats, the other three in their school uniforms. Linc looks like perfection, his tie straight, blazer pressed, and hair done. Finn looks a little rumpled, but still put together, and Mav… well, his shirt is half undone with the sleeves rolled up, his ink on display, his tie is loose around his neck, and he has total bed hair.

Yet every single one of them makes my thighs clench and my mouth drool.

Hell fucking yes.

"Morning." The word is more of a purr than an actual word as they all drink me in with their eyes. East is the first one to his feet, and he strides toward me, pulling me into his arms. He doesn't even say a word before he presses his lips to mine and kisses me until I'm breathless. My fingers grip his t-shirt like I'm holding on for dear life. Hell, at this point, I might be doing just that.

"Fuck, I missed you," he murmurs against my lips before pulling me back against him, his arms locked around me tight. It's been almost a week since I saw him, and it's too fucking long. On the one hand, I was grateful, because not seeing him meant not lying to him, but damn I missed him. I tell him as much as he releases me, and I find the other three smirking at me.

Maverick stands and swaggers over to me, capturing my hips in his hand before pressing up against my back, his hard dick pressing into my ass. "Did you miss me too, princess?"

I groan as I lean my head back on his chest, and he peppers kisses down the sensitive skin on my neck. "You know I did."

"Good," he breathes in my ear. "I'm going to find you later, and I'm going to bury my dick so far inside of you that you're going to feel me for days."

I whimper at his words as his hand dips from my hip, under my skirt, and into my panties. His growl in response to how wet I already am makes my knees weak. "Fuck me, she's soaked," he tells the others, whose heated stares are all on me.

Lincoln is the first to break the spell as he stands. "We should get to school." He acts unaffected but the outline of his hard cock in his slacks is blatantly obvious. I grin at him as he looks at me with a promise in his eyes.

I might have missed them, but it's obvious they all missed me too. I don't know if this will last forever, especially because I know they're not going to take the news of my deal with Harrison well, but I push that to the back of my mind for now.

I want to enjoy this—them—while I can.

"Yeah, school," I murmur as Maverick grinds into my ass before pulling back, as if reminding me of his earlier promise.

Finley stands, moving toward Linc, but I look to East. "What are you doing today?"

"I'm doing some more physio. Need to get back in tip top shape so I can make sure I can keep up with you." He winks at me and I laugh softly.

"I'm sure you're already keeping up plenty," I tease, and he grins back at me.

Finley grabs my hand and pulls me along with him through the house, following Linc, with Mav behind us. "You're riding with us today."

I glance up at Finley, who seems as tightly wound as I feel after my welcome from Mav and East already this morning. Just under a week with zero orgasms from them and I'm a wanton mess. Sometimes I don't even recognize the girl I've become, but I'm not sorry about it. Not when the four of them are everything I ever wanted.

Lincoln climbs into the driver's seat, and Mav hops in the front with him, calling shotgun.

"Guess that means I've got you to myself for the ride," Finley growls in my ear, opening the back passenger door for me. He grabs my waist and lifts me into the seat, buckling me in before moving around the car and climbing in himself. He moves to grab his seatbelt before looking over at me. "On second thought…"

He trails off before reaching over and unbuckling me. I squeak as he pulls me across the backseat and situates me on his lap. "Much better."

"Knew I should've sat in the back," Mav grumbles as Linc starts the car. He catches my eye in the rearview mirror now that I'm sitting on Finn's lap behind him, and the heat in that look is enough to leave me scorched.

"You like how he watches you, pretty girl?" Finn's words are no more than a whisper in my ear as he trails his fingers along the inside of my thigh, making me squirm in his lap. His fingers never move to where I want them and he uses his other hand to clamp me in place so I can't grind down on him either. "Patience is a virtue."

His breath against my neck sends shivers skittering over my skin, and I only realize the journey is over when Lincoln climbs out of the car.

Holy fuck, if this is how they're starting my day, I know I'm going to combust before it's over. And how beautiful it'll be to burn.

---

The bell rings for lunch, but this day just feels bizarre. We're trying to get back to what should be 'normal' for the God-knows-which-number time this year and it still feels weird. Like, how the hell am I supposed to just keep going with the mundane of everyday with everything else I've got going on.

That's on top of how the guys have spent every opportunity today riling me up. Touches here, glances there, kissing me until my lips are swollen between classes. I knew they were going to tease me today, but I'm not sure how much more I can take.

A door opens to my right as I pass by and Maverick's grinning face fills my vision before he drags me into the empty classroom. He locks the door behind him and pushes me up against the wall.

"I've missed you, princess." He claims my lips like they were made for no one but him and kisses me until my lungs burn.

When he releases me, I let out a soft laugh. "I missed you too. How is your back? Are you healing okay?"

His eyes narrow as he watches me. "I've been fine for days, but you've been avoiding me. All of us. We don't run from each other."

"I wasn't…" I trail off and stop because I don't want to lie to him. I spent most of the weekend with Indi or holed up at home looking for answers for Harrison, and I haven't paid much attention to my phone. "I didn't mean to. I've just been trying to give you space to heal."

"I never need space from you." His words are fierce, but the flicker in his eyes tells me that he's hurting.

"Is that why you've all been driving me insane today? Because I've been avoiding you?"

He smirks at me. "That's one reason."

It's not hard to read between the lines: he's been avoiding me too. He was only next door, but I know this whole thing with Edward and my mom has been eating at him. It's written all over his face. I reach up and cup his cheek in my hand. "You know none of this is your fault, right?"

His eyes flash and I know, without a doubt, he's blaming himself entirely.

"None of this is your fault, Maverick Riley," I say, bringing his hand to my heart.

He takes his hand from my chest and runs it through his overgrown hair. "Then why are you avoiding me?"

"I'm not avoiding you."

"Yes, you were," he bites. "Now I'm going to show you what happens to bad girls when they avoid me."

He spins me around and pushes me against the wall, my wrists clamped in one of his hands at the small of my back while he uses the other to pull down my panties. He taps my ankle and I lift each foot so he can take them off. "These are mine."

I look over my shoulder at him and his wolfish smile as he pockets them. I open my mouth to object but he kisses me again, reaching around with one hand and teasing my clit.

"What if someone comes in?" My eyes dart to the door, and I'm grateful that he had the wherewithal to lock it.

"Someone will come in, princess." His words are at my ear, a whispered sin that lights me up every time. "I'm going to come in your pretty, tight, fucking voodoo pussy."

"Well, that's not much of a punishment." My sass will get me into a fuckload of trouble one day, but getting into trouble with them is too much fun for me to worry.

Mav doesn't answer and with no time to analyze the devious mind that belongs to Maverick Riley, I gasp as he plunges two fingers inside me and bites down on my earlobe.

"Fuck." We both curse at the same time, me from the feel of him inside of me after a day of teasing, and him at how ready for him I am.

"I love how wet you get. Your body is always primed for me."

He's not wrong. And right now, I'm not beneath begging for him to satiate the need that's been building in me all day.

Taking his fingers out of my pussy, he coats my lips with my juices, painting them on like lipstick as he lines up the head of his cock at my entrance.

The anticipation is killing me, reminding me of how much I've missed him.

Just as I open my mouth to suck on his fingers, he thrusts both in my mouth and his dick deep inside my pussy.

He freezes once he's buried as deep as he can get, the fullness that is Maverick Riley making my insides burn with need, and my arms scream with pain as he holds them tight behind me. "Fuck, I needed this. I needed to feel you, princess. You don't get to hide from me ever again."

Shoving his fingers practically down my throat, he fucks me against that wall like a man possessed. I've never been so willing to hand myself over to him.

Once his fingers are sucked clean, he places his hand at my throat and uses that pressure to hold me in place as he fucks me so hard that I see stars. He did promise I'd feel him for days, and holy fuck is he delivering. The only thing that keeps me from screaming is the knowledge that anyone could open that door if they hear us.

"Think anyone will notice if I leave my fingerprints on your throat? Think they'll walk away from you knowing that you belong to me?" His movements are erratic, his thrusts desperate and hard, his voice rough around the edges, his fear of losing me clear in each of his words.

He shows me just how much I belong to him, mixing my pleasure with pain as he bites down on my shoulder when I don't answer him. His brand of pain never felt so good.

"I'm yours, Mav. With or without your mark, I'm yours."

"Damn fucking straight you are. *Mine.*" He continues to slam me against the wall until his fingers tighten on my throat and he orders, "Rub your clit, princess. Do it fast because Mrs. Banks will be coming back to this classroom in about three minutes."

*Fuck.*

He releases my trapped wrists, moving his hand to my hip while keeping his other at my throat, and I make quick work of placing two fingers on my clit and rubbing furiously as he pounds into me.

Once. Twice. On the third drive against the wall, I bite down on my lip—the taste of copper exploding on my tongue—to avoid screaming and letting the entire school know I'm being fucked within an inch of my life in the middle of the fucking day.

"That's right, fuck yeah!" Squeezing his cock with my pussy as he squeezes my throat, my orgasm seizes my entire body, making me clamp down on him harder and push him over the edge. I revel in the feel of him unraveling, knowing that it's all because of me.

"Fuck, I needed that." His words make me feel alive as I suck in air when he releases his hold on my neck.

"Me too, Mav, but seriously, I still don't know how that's a punishment."

Turning me around, he takes my wet fingers, pushes them between my legs, and coats them with us both before guiding them back in my mouth where I suck them dry.

That's when he kisses me, tasting us both on my tongue.

"Good luck avoiding me now, princess." And then he's gone.

He took my panties.

As if on cue, his cum trickles down my thigh, leaving a sticky mess behind.

That's my punishment: spending the rest of the day without panties and sticky from him.

Asshole.

I haul ass out of the room after him and dive into the nearest bathroom to clean myself up as best I can. Thank fuck my next class is music. Miss Celine isn't such a stickler for time keeping. Once I'm no longer sticky, and I put myself back together as best I can, I rush through the halls, darting into class just as the final bell rings.

My phone buzzes in my pocket and I risk a glance at it since Miss Celine isn't here yet.

I regret it instantly.

# CHAPTER NINE

## EAST

I wait until the four of them have left for school—half wishing I was still teaching, just so I could be with them, but not hiding my relationship with Octavia is a definite upside that I'm not willing to give up—before I head down to the gym in the basement.

As much as I try not to feel removed from the unit that we all make up, it's harder, being older than them. Especially when my injury has sidelined me so much the last few months. But I'm finally getting back to fighting fit and I intend on being able to keep up with her, with all of them, for a long time.

I've spent most of my life being miserable, trying to find a way to defeat Harrison, and while that's still definitely a focus of mine, it's no longer the only thing I'm living for.

Now, I have her.

She lights up my world and shines on all of the darkest parts of it, bringing me back to life. I never really let anyone see the darkest parts of me; I wasn't a Knight, and I knew the boys had much harder shit to deal with, so I tried to be the light and breezy one.

That didn't mean that I wasn't my own version of broken. Harrison saw to that. With every dig, every bruise, the cracks inside of me grew. And now Octavia is helping me see that being broken can be a good thing. That I don't need to hide those parts of myself.

At least not from her.

Or from them.

It's because of her that I've been so willing to try and get to know Chase.

I peel off my t-shirt as I climb onto the treadmill and start my warm-up. My heart is healed, but the scar on my body is a reminder of how close I came to losing everything. Those moments of pain, when the bullet entered my body and ripped through me as I dove in front of Lincoln, it was like all I saw was her.

The happiness that I'd finally had the chance to love her, and the devastation that our time was over, that I couldn't regret saving Linc. But sacrificing any more time with her would be something that would cling to me in my final moments.

As I push my body past its limits, running until my lungs scream and my muscles burn, I focus on that feeling. It's what keeps me going, fighting for a better outcome for us all.

When my heart feels like it's going to explode in my chest, I slow the treadmill before starting on the free weights. I don't have a job anymore, so this is how I've been focusing on not losing my mind with everything that's been going on.

After punishing my body for a few hours, I decide to get ready to meet with Chase. I need to speak to him about this whole Edward thing and check in on how things are going with Uncle Nate. While we were all happy for Nate to rot after what he'd done—not only to those he'd stolen from, but to Octavia—I was reluctant to ask Chase to help him, but it turns out I can't deny her anything. Not that I'm going to admit that to *her*.

Well, maybe.

I pull on a shirt and a pair of jeans after my shower then step into my favorite sneakers. Smart but casual, and where we're going isn't exclusive enough to require any more than that. I check the time on my Breitling watch before pocketing my phone and grabbing the keys to my Mustang. We agreed to meet at Tucci's in the city. His work keeps him there a lot, and it's not like I have anything pressing to stop me making the drive.

I hook up my phone, putting on the playlist Octavia shared with me, the corners of my lips tipping up when *Carry On* by Falling In Reverse blasts through the speakers. I'm pretty sure music is her love language, so her playlists always make me feel closer to her—even if the music isn't what I'd typically listen to. Thankfully, my taste in music is pretty eclectic.

I put the car in gear and pull out of the garage, the car gliding through the gate and opening up as I leave Echoes Cove.

The drive is reasonably long, but it affords me time to think over what I want to cover with Chase today. While I know he'd like a relationship that is more than just helping us deal with the Knights, it's not all that easy to bridge the gap from where we are to where I know he'd like us to be.

He's proven himself to be an ally, that we can trust him—to a point anyway. Outside of the five of us, we don't trust very easily. Though lately we haven't had much choice but to reach beyond the limitations of our group. There's been too much shit going on.

I also want to speak to Chase about what he thinks is going to happen with Octavia now that the contract Stone made has been uncovered. None of the Knights have approached her again as of yet, and I can see how much it's weighing on everyone. Hell, I can feel it hovering in the background of every day, like we're all just waiting for the ax to fall.

Once I've pulled up to the front of Tucci's, I hand the valet my keys and head inside.

"East!" I look to the back of the room when I hear my name called and find

Chase already seated. I smile at the hostess and make my way past her toward where Chase is waiting. He stands as I approach, offering me his hand paired with a big smile when I reach him. "Glad you could make it."

I take my seat, and the server brings me a glass of amber liquid to match the one already in front of Chase. "Could I get a water as well?"

She looks shocked, but nods and rushes away, leaving me to turn my attention back to Chase.

"This still just as awkward for you as it is for me?" he asks and I laugh, nodding. "Oh good, at least we're both in the same boat, I guess. After the tongue lashing I got from Lincoln at the Riley place, I didn't know that I'd hear from you again anytime soon. It would appear that keeping myself as removed as possible from the Knights puts me at a disadvantage."

I shake my head, mentally rolling my eyes at Lincoln. "Don't take it personally; that's just Lincoln's way. He's cold, calculating, and absolutely the guy to get shit done. He also doesn't have much tolerance for people who don't operate the way the three of them do."

"Oh, I noticed," he says before taking a sip of his drink. "I can't imagine what it was like for the two of you growing up with Harrison, knowing about the Knights. My father was an asshole, but Harrison makes him look like a fucking angel."

"Harrison is so far beyond an asshole," I say with a shrug. "But we've survived him thus far, and we'll continue to do so to the best of our ability. Speaking of… does you finding out that I'm your son mean I'm going to have to go through induction? I know you never brought in a second because you didn't have anyone else, and I know how the Knights work."

He frowns as he leans forward. "No one has said anything yet, but I'm sure Harrison is biding his time. As much as he hates that I didn't have an heir, I think he was looking forward to my line being over so he could replace me with someone he deemed more worthy. But I'd expect the nod, better that than not being prepared."

My heart sinks. I knew it was a possibility now that we know the truth of my bloodline, but I was still hoping it would be different. I've been trying to find a way to get Lincoln out, not end up in myself.

The server reappears with my water and takes our order. I go with steak without even glancing at the menu. Steak is good everywhere, and I'm not really here for the food. Once she disappears we make small talk, learning things about each other, like how he got into Law because his father forced him, but as soon as he was able, he changed his style of practice and started to work as a prosecutor rather than defense attorney, and only helps the Knights when absolutely necessary. He's still the best in the state though, which is no small accolade. I learn about the family I should have had, though they don't sound much better than the Saints.

Once the food is brought out to us, we eat in a somewhat comfortable silence, but there are still answers I need, and as amenable as this has been, my family—my real family—comes first. "Is there any news about what's going to happen to Octavia since she was attacked by a Knight?"

Chase's eyes flare as my question sinks in, and he wipes at his mouth with the napkin before he answers. "Not yet. Though there have been several heated debates within the Conclave about it. I helped draw up the contract for Stone, but I was never privy to who it was that got it pushed through. Now that we know it was the Archon, people are hesitant to try and bring her back into the fold. Except for Harrison. He seems almost eager to bring her back. Of course, Edward and Charles were on his side, but now that Edward is no longer a player, he's going to have issues forcing the matter if it isn't something she wants."

"That surprises me." I lean back, letting all of that process. "The agreement stated that she would become Regent, I can't imagine Harrison agreeing to just step down."

"Neither can I. He obviously has something in mind, but he's not sharing it. I know he met with her, but as far as we were told, it was just the two of them discussing the contract Stone put in place. No offers have been made in either respect."

I frown at his words. Harrison never does anything without being four steps ahead. Chase's words mirror what V told us about her summons to him, but something still doesn't feel right.

"You should also know I'm doing what I can for Nate, but without the Knights officially greasing the wheels on his behalf, the case against him is pretty solid. The only thing I've been able to ensure is that Blair's trust, and the apartment that was in her name in the city, is still hers and completely untouchable by the IRS."

I nod, letting it all sink in. What a fucking shit show this has all become. "Thank you for helping with him. I'll give Octavia the update, though I'm not sure how well that'll go down either."

He watches me closely, leaning forward before asking, "Are you happy?"

I startle at the question and he must see it, because he continues. "With her, I mean. It's no secret that she is involved with the four of you. I'm not a jealous man, but even *I* can't imagine sharing her."

"Then you've obviously never loved someone the way we love her," I tell him with a shrug. "She needs each of us. There are so many different sides to her that no one of us could meet every single need she has. This way, we can. And as long as she's happy, so are we."

His eyes sparkle at my answer and he takes another bite of his meal. "I can't say I'd ever thought of it that way, but as long as you are happy, then I'll do my best to ensure that no one interferes with it. My reach is limited, despite being on the Conclave, because I've kept myself so removed, but I will do what I can."

---

After my meeting with Chase, I'm glad to be home. When Lincoln got back from school, I suggested watching the football game together, and to my surprise, he agreed.

"Oh come on!" I yell at the TV, while Linc groans beside me. It's been forever since we just sat and watched a game. It might be a game we missed from last season, but fuck it. This year has been a lot and we haven't exactly had time to just sit and chill the fuck out.

We've had a heavy few months, but I think there might finally be some light at the end of the tunnel.

A knock at the door draws my attention and I turn to find V standing there, looking almost unsure as she enters the room.

"What's wrong?" I ask, because she looks like something's on her mind, but then she grins, and I swear, it goes straight to my fucking dick.

"Octavia?" Lincoln says her name as more of a question when she locks the door behind her.

"I thought we could blow off some steam," she says to me before glancing at Lincoln. "I didn't know you'd be here, but you can join us if you want to…"

I glance at him, wondering what she has in mind when she starts to unbutton her coat. I groan as her bare skin peeks through until she drops it to the floor, standing before us in just a black lace and silk bra and thong, with black stilettos a mile high.

"Holy shit," I mutter as my dick stands to full fucking attention and I drink her in.

Glancing over at Lincoln, I can tell he's as enchanted by her as I am.

"So, want to play?" she says, her laugh twinkling as she stands with her hands on her hips.

I jump over the back of the couch, glancing at my bed. "Hell fucking yes."

As I stride toward her, she giggles, and once I capture her, she whimpers in my arms as I steal her breath with my lips. She tastes like cherries and fucking sunshine.

If there's one thing I know about my brother, it's that his entire life revolves around control. Especially during sex, which is why I turn to him, a smirk firmly planted on my lips, and raise a questioning eyebrow.

With a subtle tilt of his chin, he tells me to lie down and have her straddle me. But it's only when I see him sitting on the oversized chair facing the bed that I realize he wants to watch first.

So, watch he will.

I take V to my bed—propping myself up against the headboard—then capture her mouth once again, reveling in the feel of her melting beneath my touch. Our tongues dance as she straddles me and lets her hair fall around us in a silky curtain. There are no sounds—Linc having turned off the television as soon as we realized exactly what game V wanted to play.

I'm pulled from drowning in her by the sound of a zipper sliding down. Realization dawns on me that my brother is enjoying the show as much as I am. Though, as much as he loves V's luscious ass, I'm guessing he's jonesing to see her pussy—open wide and wet for us. Not just wet, she's fucking soaked. I can feel her need as she rubs herself on me, her heat destroying the barrier of my sweatpants.

Reluctantly, I break our kiss and turn her around. She's still straddling me, but now she's facing Lincoln. If the dark pupils that have obliterated his gray irises tell me anything, it's that he's so fucking turned on he might not let me play with her alone for long. Not that I mind sharing, but I'm going to revel in having her to myself while I can.

V places the palms of her hands between my legs and starts rubbing her panty-clad pussy on my rock-hard cock—it almost hurts, it feels so good—giving Linc a fantastic view of her rack, which gives me a prime view of her ass. Fuck, I love her body.

She's getting herself off, teasing us both as she moves slowly and seductively, and it's hot as fuck.

With my back to the headboard, I watch—ensnared in her sexy little private show—as Linc's intense stare moves from her eyes to her mouth to her tits to her pussy and then back again. Over and over, his eyes scan her body as if trying to decide which part of her he's going to mark first.

I know he's reeling himself in, trying to drag all of this out as long as possible. To anyone watching, he looks almost bored. But I know better and so does V. The too-tight hold on his now exposed cock. The tic in his jaw like he can't wait to bite the softness of her flesh. The intensity of his stare, the way his attention is focused solely on her. They're all signs that what he really wants is to be buried deep inside her and fucking her within an inch of her sanity.

As his older brother, it is my duty to push him to his own limits, so I do what I must.

Raising one hand, I snap off her bra and let the soft fabric fall on the mattress between her spread legs. Linc's eyes follow the bra down and slowly trace their way back to her tits—all swollen and plump with desire. And just to fuck with him, I place my right hand on her tit and pinch her nipple, eliciting a mewling sound that I can feel straight in my balls. With my other hand, I reach up and wrap her long, silky hair around my fist and pull her head back enough to expose her slender neck.

Then I lick her exposed skin and watch my brother as his restraint tumbles away every time my tongue teases her flesh.

"Touch yourself, V. Show us just how fucking wet you are." My voice is low but we can all hear my words, and by the slight jolt of Linc's cock, I know he's going to kick my ass later for pushing his control, but I don't care. This is what V loves—driving us fucking crazy—and I will always do whatever she wants.

V slides her hand inside her panties and begins fucking herself slowly, rubbing up and down my cock, all the while teasing her own clit.

I'm torturing myself as well as my brother. This feeling of almost being inside her is one of Dante's circles of Hell, I'm sure of it.

"Look at him while you get yourself off. He's so fucking hard for you, V. What he really wants to do right now is come over here and take complete control. He wants to mark you. Bruise you. Come all over you." With every one of my words, V's hand picks up speed, rubbing herself into orgasm while Linc tightens his hold at the root of his dick to keep himself in check.

"Enough." One word and we both freeze.

Rising to his full height, his cock exposed through the zipper of his jeans, he brings his hands to his shirt and takes his fucking time unbuttoning every one of his buttons before letting it fall off his arms. Without looking, he throws it on his recently vacated chair—his eyes only on V.

"Rise up, Octavia. Show me your cunt."

She obeys without a second's hesitation, forcing me to let her go—my hands falling to her waist.

Linc's right hand returns to his cock, leisurely stroking himself like he has all the time in the world when, in truth, he's probably seconds away from ripping shit up like a savage.

Kneeling in front of her, he reaches up with his free hand and places one of hers on his cock, silently telling her to continue what he's started. Meanwhile, he latches onto the thin straps of her panties and with one flick of his wrists, the material snaps—her panties falling between her legs on top of her discarded bra.

"Much better," he praises, his mouth now just an inch from her lips. Her body is vibrating beneath my fingers, her anticipation of Linc's next move palpable.

"If I had my way, you'd be naked for me all day and all night."

I couldn't agree more.

Clutching the back of her head, Linc takes possession of her mouth, kissing her hard and fast like he just can't help himself—the need for her too strong to resist. His fingers are inside her, fucking her with abandon.

Leaning in, I pepper soft kisses to her neck and back, reveling in the goosebumps that pop up along her skin.

*We* do this to her. *We* make her body react like this. It's heady and I never want it to end.

V's sudden cry shakes me from my kissing trance—her body freezing, her breath caught in her lungs—as Linc pushes two fingers inside her pussy again, his eyes flashing with the feel of her. Or maybe because of her reaction to his touch. It's addicting the way she responds to us.

Bringing her to her first orgasm, her cries are swallowed up by his mouth, her body convulsing in my hands. I can't help myself as I lick a path across her shoulder blades, from one side to the other, as she shakes and moans for us.

"Now, be a good girl, Octavia, and turn around so I can fuck your ass while East destroys your pussy." She whimpers in response, and my cock jumps in my sweats.

Turning around, she looks up at me, her drunken gaze taking a stroll down my chest and I know instantly that she doesn't approve of my still-clothed body. Reaching behind me, I fist my shirt and immediately rip it off, exposing my naked chest for her.

Linc makes his way to the drawer of toys where he digs around for the lube. I take this as my cue to push my sweats and boxers off, all without displacing my girl. Her hands are splayed across my chest, her mouth following them, her lips sucking on one nipple before making her way to the other—her wet, naked pussy rubbing along my hard shaft. It's torture. Beautiful, magnificent torture.

My gaze flicks to Linc where he's lubing up his cock, his breathing running wild yet controlled. Only he could make those things happen at the same time.

"Up, Octavia," he commands, and she moves instinctively. Rising on her haunches, she aligns my cock with her entrance and slowly—oh-so-fucking-slowly—the little vixen sinks down, engulfing my entire dick deep inside her tight little pussy.

A groan falls from my lips at the feel of her sheath around me, and I don't care to control it. I kiss her with abandon as she moves on my dick.

I won't ever get tired of this.

Of her.

She pulls back from me, glancing over her shoulder to watch Linc, and I can't help but follow suit.

His jaw tics with anticipation as he watches her ride my dick before he moves in behind her. He grabs onto her hair, pulling her head back and claiming her mouth like a fucking beast, before he leaves a hot trail of open mouth kisses down the nape of her neck. Her moans are breathy as I move my hand to cup her cheek, bringing her lips back to mine while Linc feasts on her.

She devours me, moaning every time she feels Linc's touch as he rubs the lube across her tight little ass.

I can't fuck her hard or I'll never last, so I keep her rhythm slow with my hand on her hip as she rises and falls on my dick. She gasps as one of Linc's fingers, maybe two, plunges into her ass. I can feel it along my shaft through the thin layer between her holes. The noises she makes are like gasoline to the fire already stoked within me, and I have to hold her still on top of me for a moment while Linc opens her up.

Behind her, Linc fucks her harder and harder with his fingers, the movement pushing her more and more onto me—her kisses becoming more and more aggressive as I feel him reach around her with his other hand and stroke her clit. She clamps down, coming apart all over my cock, and it takes all of my restraint not to fuck her through it.

My hands are all over her—her tits, her waist, her face—until she comes back down and grins at me. I end up digging my fingers into her wild mane and start to fuck her again, pushing my cock deeper and deeper inside her as Linc withdraws.

"Stop."

I do as he commands, which earns me a bite on my bottom lip. My impatient little vixen is not happy about having to wait, despite the fact that she's already come once.

"Fuck," she breathes, gripping my shoulders as Linc pushes inside of her. He curses as I feel him enter her, and V's closed eyes and open-mouthed expression show me just how good she feels.

"Breathe, baby. Relax and let Linc in." Biting her bottom lip, V exhales slowly, allowing him to push in deeper. It takes him a minute to settle in but once he does, her pussy gets so damn tight I struggle to keep myself under control.

We're both inside her, her mouth on me again briefly before Linc wraps his fist around her hair and pulls her head back so he, too, can kiss her already swollen lips.

We get into rhythm, him pulling out every time I bottom out. Me sucking her nipple, biting at her exposed skin while he ravages her neck and jaw and lips.

We push her past her limits, burying ourselves in her, working to a rhythm that means she's full of one of us at all times. We take turns burying our cocks inside her until Linc's gaze flicks to mine in a silent order to make her come again.

My mouth latches onto her nipple and my fingers seek out her clit as I expertly ravage her body, loving the way she responds to me. To us.

Her cries get louder and louder as I increase my strokes across her clit while we pound into her. Between us, she's losing her fucking mind and I love every second of her falling apart in our arms.

"Fuck! Yes, God, yes, please." She's barely coherent as I fuck into her pussy, Linc setting the speed and me just keeping up.

At this pace, we won't last much longer.

No sooner does the thought come to me before V begins to move erratically, her orgasm building again right in front of my eyes. I watch as it takes over her entire body and when her cries erupt between us, we all freeze for the briefest of seconds as she clamps down around us both.

It's all too much for me.

The tingling at the base of my cock is my only warning that I'm about to explode inside her.

Linc nods, and at the same exact time, we bury ourselves inside her all at once, coming together as she rides out her orgasm.

I pant as I come back down to earth, her forehead resting on my shoulder while she shivers as Linc withdraws from her.

Fucking hell.

Best impromptu visit ever.

I lift her from me, tucking her against my side when Linc disappears into my bathroom and returns with a washcloth to help clean her up. I take care of her before cleaning myself up, leaving her tucked into my side.

Lincoln climbs up behind her as she practically purrs between us, one hand on my chest, and the other on his thigh as he wraps himself around her.

We might have to fight to keep this bliss we've found, but I already know we'll all fight with everything we have to ensure she is the one that remains happy.

No fucking matter what.

# CHAPTER TEN

## OCTAVIA

Having made Indi my alibi for the night, I check the message from earlier as I climb into my car. I hate to do it, and I'm lucky she loves me, but there's no avoiding tonight.

Harrison: Your training starts Wednesday evening. Do not be late. 8pm sharp.
<Pin drop>

I double check the address as I put it into my maps, trying not to freak out that I'm being taken out into the middle of nowhere. I wasn't stupid enough to follow Harrison's directions without telling Smithy where I was going, and Indi knows as much she needs to know to cover for me, but I don't want to drag her into this any more than needed.

It's enough that I'm tangling myself up in this; I don't need to drag her down with me.

I take a deep breath and start the car. *Going Ghost* by Jeris Johnson blasts through the speakers, helping to calm my frayed nerves. I have no idea what training consists of, but I took Smithy's advice and wore something ultra comfortable just in case. So I have black leggings, combat boots with thick socks, a crop top, and hoodie on. My leather jacket is along for the ride, just in case.

I look way more badass than I feel. My heart pounds wildly as I pull out of the driveway and make my way toward wherever the fuck it is that Harrison's leading me to. I try not to think about what could be waiting for me in the middle of nowhere, or what the Knights' version of "training" could consist of. With what I know about them, it could be anything.

I guess I should be thankful Harrison didn't mention an initiation. The thought of having to kill someone, just because, doesn't sit right with me. Not that I judge my guys for doing what they had to in order to survive—I'm all for fighting to survive—but I made this deal, and the thought that I may have agreed to just kill someone makes me want to vomit.

If someone came at my family and they needed to die in order for them to stop, then I'm all for it, but just because a jumped-up guy in a suit says so? Yeah, no.

I leave Echoes Cove in my rearview with *blink-182&u* by Cali Rodi as my theme song. I sing along with her at the top of my lungs, trying to pump myself up for whatever is going to happen tonight.

My phone buzzes in its holder, and Linc's name pops up on my screen.

Linc: You sure you can't hang out with us tonight?

I tap my apple watch and speak my response into it.

Me: I can't, girl time is required. Tomorrow?

I wait, hating that I'm lying to him, as those three dots bop up and down as he types his response.

Linc: That's too far away. Come and climb in my bed when you're done. Doesn't matter what time.

Me: Are you okay?

Linc: I will be when you're here in my arms.

God he makes my heart hurt sometimes. If tonight wasn't part of holding up my end of the deal, then I'd turn this goddamn car around and head straight back to him. Something is obviously wrong, but I also know he hates talking about shit over text.

I chew on the inside of my lip, wondering if he's found out the truth somehow. If Harrison told him as a fuck you, but I shake that thought off. If he knew, he'd be less wanting to hold me and far more shouty.

I have between now and my deadline to work out how to break the news to him. Thankfully, I still have about a week until then. It doesn't seem like that much time when I think I still have to find the information Harrison wants, to learn as much as I can to take my seat as Regent and lose a part of myself so that they can be free.

I've totally got this.

At least I fucking hope so.

The map directs me off the main road, and the night grows darker as I approach my destination. My stomach churns when I notice that the screen says I'm only ten minutes away from where I'm heading. I drive through what looks and feels like a ghost town, my phone directing me to weave through the streets, bringing me to an abandoned warehouse. Well, warehouses. I'm in the middle of an abandoned industrial park.

Totally not creepy. Nope. Not at all.

I shut off the car and take a deep breath before pocketing my phone and climbing out.

"I wondered how long till you arrived." I spin on my heel at the voice, trying not to scream. When the figure steps from the shadows, relief floods me. "Good to see you again, Octavia."

"Alex? What are you doing here?"

He barks out a laugh as he steps toward me, hands in his pockets. "It seems the deal you made with my Uncle left some holes. So I've been dragged in."

My jaw drops as my heart sinks. That was never meant to happen. That wasn't what I arranged. I didn't think I needed to protect Alex too.

Fuck.

"Alex—" I start, but he cuts me off.

"Nothing to be sorry about, baby Royal. This was a seat I wanted anyway, there was just no way in for me. Now there is. But don't worry, your secret is safe with me. That being said, *you* need to keep this secret too." His eyes narrow as he watches me. It takes me a second to understand, but then it clicks.

I nod, not having any other choice. "Okay. I can do that."

"Good, that means you pass the first test. Now come on, Dad's waiting for us inside. It seems the Knights want to assess our skills before we start our training." He rolls his eyes as he steps toward me and puts his arm over his shoulder. As much as I shouldn't be, I'm relieved I'm not going through this alone.

"Wait, your dad? Luc is the one training us?"

"I am," Luc's voice cuts through the night, just as light spills from an open door. "Now get in here. We don't have all night."

Alex squeezes my shoulder and leads me inside.

Whatever happens from here, I can't regret it. Not when I know what this means.

Not when it's for them.

---

"Good to see you again, Octavia."

I startle as my name echoes in the giant empty room. Looking around, shock floods me when I see the blonde on the opposite side of the room. "Artemis?"

"The one and only. You're looking beautiful as ever." Her grin is wide as she sashays toward me, and Alex laughs beside me. She wraps me up in a quick hug, kissing both my cheeks, leaving me beyond shocked. I jolt back to reality and hug her back before she pulls away.

"What, no love for me?" Alex grins at her, and she snarls at him. "I guess not."

"Enough fucking chit-chat. Let's get this show on the road shall we? Power off your phones and get your shit together." Luc's orders make me stand straighter as he storms across the room. I do as he asks, quickly pocketing my phone once it's off, waiting for whatever's coming next. The lights go down in the room, and green neons illuminate the space.

Artemis hands both Alex and me a gun. "Let's see what you've got, shall we?"

She walks away from us as Alex steps up beside me, excitement rolling from him. “It’s like extreme laser tag.”

I roll my eyes at him and look over the gun. I expel the clip and check the ammunition. Blank rounds.

What the actual fuck?

“Well, that’s no fun.” Alex pouts, but then grins again. “Good luck, baby Royal. Let the hunt begin.”

Smoke starts to fill the room, making it even harder to see, and Alex disappears around one of the temporary walls.

I guess I better get started. Becoming the hunted doesn’t sound like much fun at all. The only problem is I have no idea what my target even is.

Stupid fucking disadvantages. Knowledge really is power.

I duck in the opposite direction to where Alex went, trying to focus on the sounds around me since the visual space in here is basically zero. And then music starts up, along with strobe lights.

Is this a fucking rave?

A rave with firearms. How the fuck is this training?

I move through the space, pistol raised, trying to clear the space. I don’t even know what I’m looking for and I feel fucking ridiculous.

The next thing I know my feet are being swept out from underneath me. I fall backward, my back slamming onto the concrete, and the breath whooshes out of my body.

Mother of fuck.

Artemis’ face appears above me and she blows me a kiss. “No hard feelings, but do better.” Then she flits away, disappearing into the smoke.

Okay, so goal one: don’t get knocked on my ass again.

I groan as I push myself to my feet and pull my hair up into a ponytail. I need it out of my face if I’m going to get through this. Especially if I don't want to get my ass handed to me again.

Dusting myself off, I crouch down and try to get my bearings.

Knowing that Artemis is the hunter, it’s probably safe to assume Luc is as well. Which means Alex and I are the hunted.

At least now I have a semblance of an idea of the game.

Taking a deep breath, I head in the direction Artemis went when I hear a cackle of laughter that has me spinning around.

There’s no one there.

Fuck these Jedi mind tricks.

I blow a loose tendril of hair out of my face and spin back around, trying to get my bearings. This is the weirdest fucking training I’ve ever experienced. I hear a yelp followed by a crash somewhere in the distance.

I guess someone got Alex.

At least if they did we’re one for one. Petty as it is, that makes me feel better.

Just as I get my head on straight, the music cuts out, the lights stop flashing, and the fluorescent lights above me flicker on.

“That was pathetic!” Luc roars, I can’t see him, but that doesn’t stop me wincing at the dressing down. He stomps into view, motioning for me to follow him, and I pick up the pace to make sure I don't lose him. He comes to a stop where Alex is face down with Artemis sitting on his back. It takes everything in me not to laugh as I clamp my lips together.

Her eyes dance with laughter when she sees me and jumps to her feet, letting a grumbling Alex up. I'm a little surprised she bested him, considering who he is and where he's risen to, but apparently there is more to Artemis than I realized. Maybe she does live up to her namesake.

Luc shakes his head at Alex. "Let's see how you do working in pairs, shall we?"

He stalks away and Artemis gives me a delicate finger wave before rushing off behind him. I turn to Alex, who looks pissed, and shrug when he raises his eyebrow. I'm guessing because of the giant smile still on my face. "I'm glad I'm not the only one she took down."

"Yeah well, she's fucking psycho."

"All the best girls are," I tell him with a wink.

"Uh-huh. There's nothing quite like being beaten to make me work harder though. You ready for this? Now that I have an idea of the rules, I refuse to be the prey in their game of cat and mouse."

"I'm ready. What did you have in mind?"

---

After a few hours of being assessed and then reamed for everything we did wrong, Luc dismissed us, muttering to himself about unskilled wannabes. I didn't bother to correct him because tonight showed me that I have a lot to fucking learn if I want to survive this world. My dad might have given me a fuck ton of skills, but he never intended for me to end up in this cesspit. So while they might help me in the life of a 'normal' person, I'm barely treading water over here.

"Hey, Octavia! Wait up!" I pause at Artemis' request, waving to Alex as he heads back to his car, exhaustion painted all over his face. I get it. I'm looking forward to curling up next to Lincoln just as soon as I'm back.

Artemis reaches my side just as Alex climbs into his car, and a yawn rips through me that I have to stifle. "What's up?"

"You did good tonight," she starts, and I snort a laugh, looking at her sideways. She just shrugs. "Okay, well maybe not good, but okay. There's definitely potential. It's harder, as a woman, to do what these guys do with such ease. Typically, anyway. Luc is going to be handling most of your tactical training, but I wanted to offer myself up to help you too, if you'd like. I've had to learn a lot of shit the hard way."

I watch her closely, trying to work out why she's being so nice, and she must read it all over me because the corners of her lips tilt upward. "No ulterior motives here, Octavia. Just a helping hand. I've seen what your guys are capable of and I'm not about to cross them if I don't have to. Plus, I like you." She shrugs, her gaze raking over me again.

It could be a really bad idea, but fuck it. "Sure, that'd be good, thank you."

"Perfect. I know you run with Lincoln every morning, but try and hit some free weights to work on your upper body strength. That shit will help. Luc will have you training with him three out of seven nights, I'll claim two others, then you've got two for other shit. We'll have you turned into a lean, mean killing machine in no time."

I bark out a laugh at her. "Sounds totally reassuring."

"Better to kill than be killed." Her voice has lost any lightness from before, and I nod solemnly as we reach my car. "I'll be in touch. Night, Octavia."

I climb into my car, aware that she's watching me. She stays there, watching, as I drive away, blurring into a shadowy figure in my rearview.

I groan when I see the time. Maybe climbing into bed with Lincoln right now isn't a good idea. I can't decide if he'll ask more questions about the time or if I just don't go to him at all. When I leave the ghost town, I let the car idle as I power my phone back up. It buzzes in my hand as a few messages come through.

Indi: Hope everything went okay. Please let me know you're alive. I don't want your guys to skin me if you're not.

I laugh at her and drop her one back.

Me: I'm alive, a little bruised, but alive. I'll catch you up tomorrow.

Then I check the other.

Lincoln: I don't know what you two are up to, but come home. I'm in your bed. I didn't want to be without you tonight.

I guess that answers that question. I put the phone on the holder, hitting play on my playlist and turning the volume down as *Crash and Burn* by Maggie Lindemann starts playing. The drive back doesn't take as long, mostly because of how late it is, but my lead foot might've played a part in it, too.

I'm so ready for bed.

When I get home, I park the car in the garage and head inside. It's so freaking dark, so I use the flashlight on my phone as I tiptoe up the stairs to my room. I open the door as quietly as I can and find a sleeping Lincoln Saint in my bed, the sheets just barely covering him, bunched at his hips.

Damn he's so freaking beautiful. It's rare that he looks so peaceful, but when he sleeps, it's the only way to describe him. He murmurs softly as I close the door and I head into my bathroom. I need to rinse the night off of me, so I strip out of my clothes and grab the fastest shower of my life before drying off and slipping into shorts and a tank. I sneak back into the room, finding him still asleep. Which is surprising, considering he's usually so guarded.

He must be exhausted.

Slipping between the sheets, his heat calls to me, but I don't want to disturb him.

"Octavia," he murmurs as I settle, his eyes fluttering open, still blurry with sleep. "Good."

He doesn't say anything more, just pulls me into his arms so I'm splayed against his chest, wrapped up in his warmth. I press my lips softly to his shoulder, and he purrs softly, already asleep again, so I close my eyes and lose myself in his warmth.

I could get used to coming home to him.

# CHAPTER ELEVEN

## OCTAVIA

Waking wrapped in the heat of Lincoln and the smell that is just so thoroughly him brings a smile to my face. It feels like too long since I've had any alone time with him. With any of them—except for East.

My smirk grows thinking about the last time I was alone with East, and Lincoln stirs as his alarm goes off on my bedside table. I run my hands up his bare chest, enjoying how he squirms beneath my touch as goosebumps rise on my skin. "Keep teasing me and see where it gets you."

His voice is gravelly and full of sleep, yet the promise in his words zips straight between my legs. "That doesn't really sound like a deterrent."

His hands reach down and circle my hips, pulling me on top of him, and I groan at the feel of his hard dick pressed against me.

Goddamn clothing in the way. He arches up to grind against me, pulling another gasp from my lips. I look down at him, my hands on his chest, and he looks like some sort of dark god. His dark hair messy and bed mussed, his gray irises so light that they almost shine like silver. His eyes narrow as I grind down on him again and I whimper at the feel of him beneath me.

Going on top isn't something that we've done just the two of us. He's more prone to domination when it comes to me. Not that I'm complaining, but the thought of bringing someone as powerful as Lincoln Saint to his knees beneath me is heady as fuck.

I lean forward, pressing my lips against his and his arms clamp around me, crushing my chest to his as he devours me, rolling us without breaking our kiss until I'm caged beneath him. He pulls back just as my lungs start to burn and lifts my tank. I arch my back and raise my arms to help him remove it before he throws it across the room.

He sits back, perched between my legs, and stares at me. Using the pad of his thumb, he pulls my lip from between my teeth, then drags his hand down my throat, between my breasts, across my navel and to the hem of my shorts.

My entire body tingles in anticipation of him as my eyes rake over his bare chest and the outline of his huge cock in his boxers. I lick my lips, pressing them together as I feast on the sight of him. He pulls my shorts down and I lift my hips, impatient to feel him.

When he throws them behind him, he slides backward and lowers himself to my core. "Linc," I gasp when his hands press down on my thighs as he drinks in the sight of me. I writhe with anticipation, his breath dancing erotically across the lips of my pussy.

"Please."

I have no issues begging him if that's what it takes.

"Quiet, Octavia." His rumbled words send shivers down my spine, and I grasp at the sheets to stop from tangling my fingers in his hair and riding his goddamn face. His tongue flat against my clit earns him a guttural cry just before he pulls back, the cool air caressing my pussy where his hot touch used to be. "I said *quiet*."

Holy fuck. I can't do quiet. But the way he's looking up at me from between my thighs makes me want to do whatever he asks.

I press my lips together, desperate to feel him.

"Eyes on me, Octavia."

I swallow the whimper at his command, but do as I'm told, watching as he moves back to my pussy and swipes his tongue, slowly, up my slit to my aching clit then back down again.

Mother of fucking God, yes.

He teases me lazily, taking his sweet-ass time, his gaze on me as I drink him in. I'm enraptured by him, by his every fucking move. Every touch and every word sends a bolt of electric energy straight to my clit.

My back arches off the bed as he sucks my clit between his teeth. It's getting harder and harder to keep my eyes on him, the need to close them nearly impossible to ignore. Around and around, his tongue circles my bud of nerves, driving me to the point of insanity. All I want to do is latch on to his hair and keep his mouth at my pussy for hours. Or forever.

I crawl closer to the edge, my toes tingling as he licks and sucks every last inch of my soaked lips, his hands splayed across my thighs, fingers indenting my flesh with the force of his need.

Just when I think I'm about to fall into oblivion, he pulls back, eyes sparkling. It takes everything I have not to scream at him for stopping. He told me to be quiet, so that's what I'm going to do.

"Such a good girl," he purrs before thrusting two fingers deep inside me. I clamp down around him. "Be a good girl, Octavia, and come all over my fingers."

The digits slide almost all the way out before plunging back inside me, curling as they hit that perfect spot before he teases my clit again with his tongue. He adds a third finger just when I think I can't take any more, and that extra bit of sensation is all it takes to push me over the edge. My body screams in the way my voice wants to as it loses all control to the ministrations of his mouth, his fingers, his fucking talent at making me come like a savage. All the while he keeps on finger fucking me until I lose my fucking mind.

"You come so pretty for me." He sits up, his fingers still inside me, leisurely fucking me, in and out like he's got all the fucking time in the world. I preen under his words, wanting to please him further. Pushing up, I rub my hand over his still covered dick, desperate to have him in my greedy little mouth.

Our gazes crash and there's no doubt he knows exactly what I want. In seconds, he brings his fingers from my pussy and pushes them into my mouth, making me taste myself. "Suck."

I lick and suck them clean, the way I want to suck on him. He pushes them further in, making me gag, his eyes widening a little as I do. "Kneel."

Scrambling from the bed, I do as he asks, sitting back on my haunches, waiting for his next command.

"I do like it when you're this pliant." I glance up at him, and his gaze screams power. It sends a jolt through me, and I know that right now, I'd do pretty much anything he asked of me. He approaches me slowly, as if he's stalking prey, pushing down his boxers when he reaches me, and I gulp as his dick bobs freely in front of my face.

Licking my lips, I cast my eyes up to his as he grips his cock at the base, stealing my attention with each stroke of his palm. "Open your mouth and stick out your tongue. Keep your hands on your thighs."

My heart races with his every command, feeling strangely empowered when I follow his instructions. Hands on my thighs and mouth open like his dirty little toy. With my tongue waiting for him, he rubs the tip of his cock against it, groaning as he smears the bead of precum all over it. I dig my nails into my thighs as the need to wrap my lips around him, to drive him as insane as he makes me feel, grows, but when he calls me his good girl it stirs something deep within me and that keeps me planted where I am.

Two fingers grip my chin, tipping my head back until our gazes meet, and he pushes his dick in further, slowly, until I gag around the tip of him, saliva pooling at the back of my throat as he holds his dick there.

Tears slide down my cheeks, his eyes glinting as he watches them fall. Pushing his dick as far down my throat as he can, he pulls out just before I'm at my limit and tilts my head further so he can start the process all over again. I groan around his cock, making sure to keep my mouth wide open and tongue out as he instructed.

His hand leaves my chin, fingers curling around the long strands of my hair before he pulls down hard, the lick of pain making my eyes water. "I'm going to fuck this pretty little mouth, Octavia, and you're going to take it without complaint. And the next time I tell you to be quiet, remember my favorite way to make that happen."

I whimper around his dick, my heart racing as he pulls out again, his hand in my hair keeping my head where he wants it before he does as he promised. Drool runs down my chin and onto my bare chest as he fucks my face with abandon; my wetness pooling between my thighs tells me just how much I don't hate it.

"Fuck, Octavia. You feel so fucking good." His groans make my pussy pulse and I desperately want to touch myself, get myself off while he uses me to do the same.

He pulls out, my throat raw from taking him as roughly as it did, and he pulls me to my feet by my hair. I scramble to stand at his will. “Bend over and hold your ankles.”

I reach forward when he releases me, wrapping my hands around my ankles, my thighs burning at the pull. He glides his fingers through my wetness from behind, pulling a moan from me as he gathers my juices and stretches me open again. “So ready for me.” I barely feel the head of his dick against my entrance before he takes me in one hard, powerful thrust. “Use that filthy mouth of yours to tell me how good this feels."

Thank fuck.

He grips my hips and drills into me, eliciting cries from deep within me with each and every thrust. I was already so close from being his toy, but the thick feel of him dominating every inch of me threatens to push me over the edge of sanity.

“Please,” I beg, and he responds by running two of his fingers over my painfully engorged clit, gathering ample amounts of my slick before moving them to my asshole. Cries fall from my lips as he coaxes me open with the pad of his finger while increasing the tempo of his thrusts. In and out, he alternates his rhythm. Fucking my pussy with his dick while his fingers fill my ass. I am so fucking full, and it’s delicious. Linc is everywhere, everything. All over me and inside me. The dual sensation makes me lose my fucking my mind. I gasp and I moan, sounds coming from somewhere inside me I didn't even know existed. He changes up his speed, alternating between filling me with his dick and his fingers, and I feel like his ragdoll. Taking everything that he’s willing to give as I hurtle toward my orgasm.

“Come for me, Octavia.”

With his permission, I come savagely all over his dick, my breath hitching with the force of it. His hand at my hip keeps me upright as my knees go weak. He thrusts into me one final time with a roar, his body shaking with the power of his climax as his dick pulses inside of me.

Holy fuck.

Pulling out of me slowly, he uses the hand that was on my ass to keep me steady as the other moves to my pussy, pushing his cum back into me.

Fuck, that’s hotter than it should be.

“You can let go of your ankles now, Octavia,” he says before wrapping his arm beneath me and lifting me, bridal style, into the bathroom. “Let’s get you cleaned up, shall we?”

He sits me on the counter before turning on the shower. Once the water is heating, he comes back and cleans me up with a washcloth, and I’m thankful he’s taking charge once again because he fucked me boneless. When steam starts to build in the room, he takes my hand, pulling me from the counter into his arms, and walks me into the shower.

“I love you,” he whispers, capturing my lips with his as we move under the water. “And I’ll do whatever it takes to keep you.”

After a draining day of school and exam prep, my brain is fucking mush. It might have something to do with the mind-blowing way I started my day, but I am not about to complain about that.

Upside, I haven't had a moment to worry about my fuck fest of a training session last night, even if it felt like more of a test than training.

My head rests on my folded arms atop the counter, where I've been sitting for the last hour trying to understand the sample exam question that the business substitute gave us and failing. My phone buzzes beside me, and the voice in my head that begs for sleep tells me to ignore it, but it could be Indi or one of the guys, so I lift my heavy head and glance at it.

Fuck my actual life, should've just gone to sleep.

Harrison: Conclave Meeting in two hours. Do not be late, Miss Royal. <Pin drop>

Ughhh!

Just what I need. As if last night wasn't enough. My phone buzzes again and I want to bang my head on the counter.

Luc: Training's rescheduled. See you Saturday, kid.

Then I notice an earlier message from Alex sitting in my inbox

Alex: Did you get summons this morning, Baby Royal. I'm still in EC. Grab me on your way?

Me: Got it just now. But sure, I'll text you when I leave.

Since Luc's message requires no response, I close the message threads just as Smithy enters the kitchen. "Why so glum, Miss Octavia?"

"I'm tired, and I just got summoned to my first Conclave meeting. I'm sure Harrison did it on purpose so I don't have my wits about me, but that doesn't exactly make me feel any better."

His lips twist as his frow burrows. "That man… well… I won't speak my true thoughts in front of you, Miss Royal. Now then, why don't you run and grab a shower, it might perk you up. I'll sort out a light dinner for you and make an extra strong coffee to help too."

I slide from the stool and wrap my arms around him. "You're the best, Smithy. Thank you for everything. I don't know what I'd do without you."

"Well, let's hope you don't have to find out for quite some time." He quickly squeezes me back, and when he releases me, I grab my textbooks from the counter and drag them up to my room with me. I rush through a cold shower, the icy chill of the water doing what I hoped it would and waking me up a bit. I dress in skinny jeans, a pair of red-bottomed heels, a white shirt, and a blush blazer before running my fingers through my wavy hair.

It's not the best, but it's a major improvement on how I looked before. Once I'm back in the kitchen, I rush through my food and chug down the coffee, realizing I have to leave if I'm going to grab Alex and get to this fucking meeting on time.

"I'll see you later, Smithy!" I call out as I dial Alex's number and put the phone to my ear, grabbing my keys and heading to the garage.

Alex picks up as I slam the car door closed. "S'up Baby Royal?"

"Your ass better be ready, Alex. Where am I picking you up?" I ask, hitting the speaker as I put the phone in its holder and start the car. I reverse out of the garage as he laughs.

"Look behind you, Baby Royal."

I glance up at the gates and hit the brakes. I open them and Alex strides toward the car as I end the call and set up the map to the pin drop Harrison sent me. Once he's in, I pull away as quickly as I can. The last thing I need is one of my guys spotting us together. Not that I've heard from them since school, but that isn't the point. If they saw me driving off with Alex, they'd ask questions I can't answer.

Escaping their notice, all of their notice, is the first downside I've discovered to being with all of them. Go figure.

We drive in silence for a while until Alex's bouncing leg starts to grind on me as much as his tapping on the dash. "Will you stop?"

He grins sheepishly at me, running a hand through his blond hair. "Sorry, Baby Royal. It's the first time I'm coming face to face with the big, bad Masters of the Universe. Has me full of nervous energy."

I scoff at him, rolling my eyes. "They're not Masters of the Universe. Just jumped up assholes with more power than anyone should have."

"Exactly. Which is precisely why you made your deal with them. You knew it was the only way *because* they're Masters of the Universe, or at least our sect. They command the way the world works, even for those who have no idea of their existence. *That* is power. Being the puppet master."

"They're not even the top of the food chain," I sigh, tucking my hair behind my ear. "They just think they're the puppet masters, but even they answer to someone."

"You mean the Prism?" he asks, and I nod.

"Them, and then the Archon. He's the one that made the deal with my dad, which is how I ended up here."

"Yeah, I heard."

I side-eye him, wondering how exactly he heard about that, but that's not really important. Especially since he's joining the Conclave.

My eyes go wide as one thing occurs to me. "Do you think the guys have any idea *why* they're not at this meeting tonight?"

"They haven't been told there's a meeting. Juniors don't have to go to *every* meeting." I glance over at him, eyebrows raised in question. "I met with Harrison this morning and asked the same question."

I grumble under my breath about fucking secrets, feeling like a hypocrite, when he sighs. "It's that building ahead."

I look up at the behemoth building that I met Harrison in before and take a deep breath.

Time to face the music and see just what my deal with the devil looks like.

---

I slide into a seat one down from the right of the head of the table, giving the Mitchell pair a quick once over as I do. They might be as useless as Artemis said they were if I'm going on sight alone. They really don't seem like they want to be here, like they're so disinterested they might just fall asleep, so I wonder why, or even how they managed to keep their positions in the conclave. Pretty sure that Harrison isn't one to tolerate incompetence.

Artemis grins coyly at me across the table, a subtle nod of hello before her bitch mask falls into place. I let my own slide over my features, waiting for the rest of the Conclave to enter the room.

Chase enters next; he pauses when he sees me, but it's so brief that it would've been hard to notice if I hadn't been watching so closely. He sits next to Artemis, whose dad enters moments later, followed by Alex who sits between me and what I'm sure is Harrison's seat. He salutes me with a cocky grin on his face, and I can't help the upwards tug at the corners of my mouth.

Finally, Harrison and Charles enter the room, meaning that everyone is here and my first Conclave meeting is about to begin.

This doesn't seem as terrifying as everyone makes it out to be. It feels more like a dick measuring contest about who can do what, but what do I know? We haven't even started yet.

Charles takes his seat opposite me, his distasteful sneer growing as his gaze roams over me before Harrison takes his seat beside me.

He glances at me before turning his attention to the rest of the room, and an icy drop of dread runs down my spine.

Yeah, this isn't going to be fun.

I try to pay attention as he makes a quick introduction of Alex and I to the rest of the Conclave, then jumps into talking about business that I have no fucking idea about. I slip my hand into my pocket, hitting the record button, so I can at least try to decipher some of this later with Smithy and hopefully have it make more sense.

"We have another pressing issue. The Kings are pushing back against our previous agreement. I need someone to take care of that." My head spins toward Harrison, gaining my attention instantly. "Alex, I think with your position within the Rebels, you are the best suited to deal with the Donovans. Do not disappoint me."

Alex nods once, squeezing my thigh reassuringly under the table. I don't dare show my panic on my face, or my palpable relief knowing that Alex won't hurt Indi's guys.

Harrison turns his gaze to me, pinning me with his unrelenting stare. "As for you, Octavia, you are already aware of what we need from you. The clock is ticking."

I dip my chin, acknowledging the thinly veiled threat for what it is. Artemis raises a brow at me, but I don't react.

"If that is all, I have to head to the Pit. We have some new recruits ready for initiation. This is one of my favorite parts. Helping mold our new members into who, or shall I say *what*, we need them to be."

No one says a word, though the look of disdain on Chase's face is unmissable. After a beat of silence, Harrison claps his hands once and stands. "Good. I'll see you all in a week. Alex, if you'll walk out with me, I'll run you through the King issue."

Alex stands and leaves with Harrison, Charles filtering out quickly after them. The Mitchells leave next with Artemis' dad, leaving me with Chase and Artemis in the room.

"I assume that East does not know about this… latest development." Chase frowns at me like I've committed the worst sin possible, and maybe I have, but fuck him. He doesn't get to judge me.

I quirk a brow, giving him my best ice bitch glare. "He does not. None of them do. And it's going to remain that way, as per my agreement with the Regent."

He just looks disappointed as he shakes his head. "Be careful playing with fire, Octavia. You will get burned."

Without waiting for a response, he stands and exits the room, leaving me alone with Artemis, who just smiles at me salaciously from across the table. "And then there were two."

# CHAPTER TWELVE

## OCTAVIA

This week is kicking my fucking ass. Between the 'assessment,' running with Linc, the start of prepping for finals, and dealing with Harrison, I'm about at my limit. Which is why my text reminder from Luc at four this morning was grossly unappreciated.

Luckily, Maverick slept straight through me leaving, and he'll likely still be asleep when I'm done here.

"Octavia, your stances are just fucking sloppy," Luc barks again, and I lose my shit.

"Maybe if I wasn't woken up at four in the fucking morning and dragged here by half-past, I'd be a little more coherent. But it's now barely five, I've had no coffee, and I'm fucking tired."

His eyes narrow at me before he drops his stance and stalks toward me. "You think the Knights are going to make sure you're in tip top form everytime they send you out? You think the ones who will come for you once they know who and what you are now will care if you're half asleep when they attack you? You need to be prepared for *anything*."

I deflate at his words. He's right. I know he is. He softens when he realizes his blows hit their mark. "I'm trying to prepare you, Octavia. Trust me, I'd much rather none of us be in this mess, but we don't have the luxury of being able to go through life with rose-colored glasses on. Now, let's go again."

I tighten my ponytail and drop into the stance he's showing me. Thankfully, my somewhat casual training with Maverick, and the training my dad and Mac put me through on tour, gave me a peek into what I need to know, but my time with Luc, albeit short, has shown me I am woefully unprepared for the hellscape I've stepped into.

My bruises are going to have bruises.

He comes at me again, attacking me, quick as fuck and deadly as a viper. I know he's pulling his punches, but not so much that they won't leave marks.

Hiding those is going to be fun.

We spar for the next hour until I'm panting and broken. "You did good, kid. We'll get you to where you need to be, just try to stay alive in the meantime. We'll go again Monday. Hoping to have you fighting with blades by the end of next week. Make sure to hit the gym daily to help your conditioning. And eat right, none of that starving yourself to be thin bullshit. Give your body what it needs."

I stare at him slack-jawed as he throws me a towel, and I drop back onto the mats of the gym we're in. Though "gym" is me being generous. I don't recognize the place and Luc assured me the guys wouldn't find me here.

That's all the reassurance I needed.

I suck in air, groaning as I lie back and close my eyes. He just said fighting with blades. I am not Maverick, and as much as his blades fascinate me, the thought of using them… nope. Give me a gun over a blade any day. Though I get the feeling my preference isn't going to make any fucking difference to Luc. He's following orders as much as I am, so my opinion on it is worth fuck all.

Pulling myself back up, I move to the side of the room, grab my keys, phone, and water bottle and hightail it out of there back to my car. Thankfully this place isn't far from home and Maverick should hopefully still be fast asleep.

I make the drive home quickly, stashing the car away in the garage before rushing upstairs. Maverick is still very much asleep, and I loosen the breath in my chest, the weight that's been sitting there since I woke up lifting a little.

I need to shower. I'm fucking gross right now.

Moving into my bathroom, I turn on the water and undress while it heats. We have no plans today, and I'm kind of looking forward to having a chill weekend. We've all been full speed ahead with everything lately and I feel like none of us have had any time to breathe.

I've also barely seen Indi, and that's pissing me off too. Once upon a time, I didn't have anyone, but I also had no one dictating my actions to me. Of course, now that I have people I want to spend time with, someone is trying to pull me away from it all.

I'm not sure what I did in a past life to deserve all this, but apparently karma is a bitch and she's enjoying herself.

I start showering, groaning as my fingers run over the soreness of my body, when I hear movement in the room. I open my eyes and find Maverick's eyes on me, devouring me as his heated gaze takes in every inch of me.

"Now this is a wake up call." He grins salaciously as he stalks toward me—obviously ignoring my bruised skin, not that I'm complaining—pushing his boxers down as he does. "And I could get very used to having you as my breakfast every morning."

---

Sitting next to Finley in the Lamborghini, my anxiety is skyrocketing as we hurtle down the highway toward the facility where my mom is being looked after. After the insanity of training with Luc this morning, and then my second wakeup call with Mav, when Finn asked if I wanted to spend some time with him, I jumped at it. His calm usually helps to center me. But when I got in the car and he told me where we were heading… well, I've felt sick ever since.

I could have said no, told him I didn't want to, but I've also vowed to try to stop running from my problems. It hasn't gotten me anywhere, but I'm trying. Having made my deal with Harrison, while it's got me tied up in knots, I don't feel as shitty as I should about it because it was *my* choice. Not a reaction to something happening to me.

There's something freeing about it.

So… here I am, shitting my pants about facing the woman who birthed me. Sure, we had some good memories before she left, and of course now I understand her fear and why she wanted to leave, but I still don't forgive her for leaving Dad and me behind. Who knows what we could have survived together?

Finn reaches over and twines his fingers with mine, squeezing my hand once. He doesn't say anything, because we both know he doesn't have to. There isn't anything *to* say.

He's going to check up on the others who were prisoners of Edward's, ensuring that the staff are giving Linc all of the information on them. As for me… well… I'm going to try and not vomit before I see my mom.

I still have exactly zero idea of what the fuck it is I'm supposed to say to her. I don't know, and could likely never understand what she's been through at Edward's hands, but she doesn't know me either. I don't know if she even *wants* to know me.

And that, right there, are where my mommy issues come to a head. All I ever wanted was for her to love and want me. But she left. Dad was amazing up until he wasn't, but at least he was always there. And I can't help but blame her, at least a little, for how he ended up. If she hadn't left, things might have been different. He might have been able to stand the pressure and bullshit that came with his fame along with the demands of being a Knight.

But now we'll never know. All because she wasn't strong enough to stick it out.

There's also the chance I'm wrong, and that she didn't want to leave. She just wasn't brave enough to stay. While I can understand that, it makes me sick. It doesn't matter how afraid I was, if I had a child, I would never leave them behind.

Never.

"Your thoughts are so loud, pretty girl. Is there anything I can do?"

I glance over at the blond, tortured god beside me, both loving and hating that he sees the darkness in me but doesn't shy from it because he has the same darkness in him. His might run deeper than mine, but we're all a little broken, and that's why we fit together.

"No, I'm just nervous. And angry. And conflicted about being angry. I'm a mess." I let out a breath, blowing a few strands of hair off of my face, wishing I could make sense of everything in my head.

"I'm sure your mom is just as nervous."

"Does she know I'm coming?" I hadn't even considered that. Chewing the inside of my lip, the butterflies in my stomach start freaking raving, even as he shakes his head. "No, I asked them not to tell her, in case you weren't ready. But she has to know you'll be coming to see her sooner or later. Though, considering how long she's been with Edward, she might not have thought about it at all."

I don't know how to feel about that. What if she doesn't want to see me? She did leave after all. Even if she ended up ensnared by Edward, I know she was free for a few years before he took her. Though I still don't know *why* he took her and probably never will.

I focus on the passing scenery as we finish the journey in a comfortable silence while I get lost in my head again. When we pull up to the entrance of the facility, I'm shocked by what I see.

The beach in the background, the sleek, white, modern building that almost looks like a hotel. It emits a feeling of calm that I hadn't expected. Apparently Ocean Falls Wellness center is nothing like I imagined, even though I had no idea what to expect. Finley pulls the car into the parking lot, not moving once he kills the engine.

He gives me a minute to try and settle the nerves inside of me, but I'm not sure they're going anywhere. This is fully going to be a 'fake it till you make it' moment.

I squeeze his hand before releasing it, unbuckling myself and climbing from the crazy low car. I'm glad I wore jeans, 'cause climbing from this thing in a skirt is asking for me to flash my panties. I straighten my leather jacket and smooth down my hair, nerves getting the best of me before Finn rounds the car and pulls me into his arms.

"If you're not ready, we can just head home." He squeezes me against him, and I swear the storm-ridden waves inside of me calm as his heartbeat fills my mind. I take a few deep breaths, matching my breathing to his as I sink into him.

He stands there with me for a few minutes, just holding me, giving me the space to be anything and everything I need to be, while he fills the role of life jacket. With a final squeeze, I pull back from him. He doesn't release me right away, his gaze on mine, watching me intently as he brings his hand to cup my nape, a thumb swiping over my cheek. "You are all that matters to me, if you don't want to do this, you don't have to."

I shake my head as my heart swells. "I need to do this. I need some answers that only she has. But thank you." Stretching up on my tiptoes, I softly press my lips to his, and he kisses me like I'm the only thing he'll ever need.

"Whatever you need, I've got you."

"Then let's do this." He watches as my resolve takes over my expression and nods, taking my hand back in his.

"Let's do this."

He leads me inside and I follow willingly, despite my erratic heart beating wildly in my chest. He speaks to a woman at the front desk like he's known her forever. Considering when he put his mom in here, he probably has.

"If you'll just wait here, I'll go and see if they're ready for visitors," the older woman says to Finn with a kind smile, and he leads me over to the couches in the bright space.

"This is a Knights place?" I ask him quietly and he nods. I have so much to learn, and I wish they could help me, but I'm pretty sure if I ask too many questions, they'll start to wonder why.

"The franchise is owned by Aretmis' dad. The sects across the country use them when needed. There are dozens across the Americas. Not really surprising that they're required with what the Knights are responsible for, but they're also open to the general population. The whole world is fucked up." I clamp my lips together and nod. He isn't wrong, the world is fucked, but I'm glad that this place is open to everyone. The Knights would only have the best of the best here, and people deserve access to that.

I can't help but wonder if they target people, vulnerable people, that come here. It seems like something Harrison would do. Though it occurs to me I don't even know how far this sect reaches. That's probably something I should learn if I'm going to take my mantle as Regent.

I need to start writing questions down in a notebook or something.

The woman from the front desk reappears, looking a little frazzled. "I'm very sorry, Finley, but Mrs. Royal has denied visitor access."

My heart sinks at her words, but it also pisses me off.

"It's fine," I say, reining in my anger, because it's not her fault and there's no point in shooting the messenger, though Finn's frown looks anything but fine. I turn to him and squeeze his thigh. "You do what you need to do, I'll wait here for you."

I try not to let him see the churning waves inside of me picking up force once again. I'm not sure why I'm surprised she doesn't want to see me. She left. She didn't want me, want us. It makes more sense that she wouldn't want to see me.

So I swallow down the disappointment that I hadn't expected and keep my head held high.

This is just a bump in the road, and I'll get the answers I want some other way. It might just take a little longer than I thought. With that in mind, and my deadline with Harrison imminent, I pull out my phone, and ask the devil for an extension on our deal. I need more time, there's been so much going on, I've barely had time to start searching for what he wants.

He doesn't keep me waiting for long. And while I get what I want, it doesn't make me feel any better.

Harrison: Two more weeks, Miss Royal. I'm being overly generous here, it won't happen again. Ensure I have those documents by your birthday, otherwise our deal is done. The boys will stay exactly as they are, and you… well, you will be right alongside them with no hand to play.

---

I let out a deep sigh as I step into the hot tub. This day has been draining as fuck, so when Finn suggested chilling out in the Saints' hot tub, I was not about to pass it up. Especially when he offered up a back massage too. Those hands of his are big and strong; they're too fucking good against my skin.

I close my eyes and rest my head back against the rest, waiting for him to join me as the hot water starts to loosen my muscles. I'm exhausted, mentally more than physically, and I really need some down time.

*I wonder if Indi is up for a girls' weekend.*

Not that I don't have enough shit to be juggling right now, but escaping sounds like fun, and after the storms in the East, I know the slopes are thick with snow and calling my name.

God, I miss not having any ties to my time or destination.

I hear footsteps approach, and a smile plays on my lips at the thought of Finley unwinding with me. Fuck knows he needs it too.

They still don't know my secrets, and it's killing me to keep it from them, but knowing that their suffering is nearly over brings so much joy to my heart that I can handle the fact that they're going to be mad as fuck when they do find out.

"How you feeling, pretty girl?" I open my eyes at Finley's low, smooth voice and lean on his shoulder. "Better now?"

"Much," I sigh as I hear a second set of footsteps before Lincoln comes into view and climbs into the tub with us. His eyes are hooded as he watches us. "I didn't realize you were home."

"You didn't ask," he says, his voice so low that shivers break out over my skin. I'll never know how I got so lucky as to have all four of these guys look at me and love me the way they do, but I'm not about to question it.

"Come here," Finn says, pulling on my hand until I'm sitting in his lap. His hands move to my shoulders where his strong fingers start to massage at the knots in my muscles there.

My eyes drift closed as I let out a moan. "Fuck, that feels good."

His lips feather against the skin where my neck meets my shoulder, but his hands continue to work me, making me boneless beneath his touch.

Behind me, the unmistakable hardening of Finn's cock doesn't escape my notice. Knowing that I do this to him makes me immediately wet for him. For them. Reaching back, I gather my hair to one side and bow my head as Finn massages a particularly hard knot.

The slight splashing of water gets my immediate attention—I'm hyper aware of Lincoln's every move—prompting me to open my eyes. My gaze lands directly on his hand wrapped around his rock-hard cock, making my tongue dart out and lick a wet path across my lips.

Anticipation skitters over my skin like lightning, my mouth watering for the taste of him as he rises from his seat and makes his way to me in less than three steps.

Finn's hands never falter as Linc buries his fingers in my hair at my temple, dragging them down until his entire hand is cradling my nape, pulling my head back until I'm forced to look at his stormy, gray stare.

"Think you can suck my cock while Finn pummels your pussy?" His words are crude but his eyes—those deep slate-colored eyes—are heated.

I don't answer right away, licking my lips provocatively just to fuck with him a little, but watch him as he follows the deliberate stroke of my tongue.

"You know I can."

He smirks at me as his hand tightens against me. "Yeah, I do. Open your mouth."

I don't hesitate. My mouth drops open and behind me Finn grips my hips hard enough to position me right over his rock-solid cock—my knees now straddling Finn's thighs as I kneel on the bench. My eyes fix on Linc as I wait for Finn to pull me down over his dick, but he doesn't. He just rubs the head of his cock through my slit, gathering my juices as they mix with the water in the hot tub.

Linc smirks and I swear just the power of him makes me shake with anticipation.

"Eager little vixen, aren't you, Octavia?" His words are soft, the head of his cock gliding over my top lip, then my bottom, tracing the "o" of my open mouth.

Slowly, he pushes his cock inside my mouth as Finn teases my clit with the head of his cock. Around and around, he teases, earning them a moan around the length of Linc's dick as it slides all the way to the back of my throat.

"Such a good girl. Swallow, let me feel it." I do. I work the muscles of my throat and my reward is the curse that escapes Linc's delicious lips.

Finn applies more pressure on my clit, making me squirm in his arms. Afraid to fall forward, I latch onto Finn's forearms, taking advantage of the move to try and slide down his cock

Linc *tsks* at me, but I can't speak, my mouth being full of his cock, yet I feel so much.

Finn's entire length gliding, slipping inside of me briefly but pulling right back out makes me whimper.

Linc's grip on my hair tightens as he begins to fuck my mouth until tears stream down my face. Pushing in and out at a steady rhythm, my gaze never leaving his. Linc bites his bottom lip as he tells me everything he never says with a look alone.

"Take it." His order is full of lust, desire so strong I can taste it in the pearl of precum that coats the back of my throat.

I do as he commands, preening at his string of curses as I do.

His gaze flicks behind me to Finn and not a second later, I'm full of cock. My pussy and my mouth both full to the hilt. I'm choking on Linc, my eyes watering deliciously with the force of his thrusts. When he pulls out, Finn stays buried inside me, cursing and telling me how tight I feel. How warm I feel. His mouth at my ear, he tells me he loves me. How he wants his dick buried in my pussy all fucking day. All the fucking time.

I don't have time to register everything Finn says because in the following second, he's pulling out as Linc is pushing his cock back inside my mouth.

"Play with your clit, Octavia. Make yourself come while we fuck you." God, his dirty mouth will be the death of me. I used to think there was something deeply wrong with me because I loved this so much, but now? Fuck it. It's who I am.

Reaching down, I bring two fingers to my clit and rub in time with their thrusts. One in, the other out and on and on they fuck me. Deep, hard, precise plunges inside me. It's like they've been practicing their moves. Or maybe we're just made to be together like this.

"Such a filthy girl, Octavia. Sucking my cock and fucking Finn in this hot tub. Such a good girl."

His words ignite my orgasm like a small ember that starts at the base of my stomach and explodes into a million licks of fire throughout my entire body. I can't even continue rubbing myself, afraid I'll fall into the water. Linc holds my head hostage as he slams his dick in and out of my mouth—coating himself with my dripping saliva.

"That's right, V. Fuck, you feel so fucking good all over my dick." Finn fucks me almost punishingly, when Linc pulls out and comes all over my mouth, my lips, my chin. His grunts and moans are fuel to my fire as my orgasm continues to ravage my body.

Finn roars as he comes inside me, pumping quick hard thrusts to the hilt right before he freezes and groans in my ear.

A shiver courses over my body as he empties inside of me, and I lick Linc's cum from my lips and chin, his eyes heating again as I do. His control snaps and he kisses me, tasting himself on me as my pussy quivers around Finn's dick.

"Fuck," he groans from behind me as his fingers dance up my spine.

The door to the room slams open, startling us all, and Linc spins to face whoever is coming toward us, hiding me from them. I peek around him when his shoulders relax and see Maverick striding toward us as he reaches behind him and pulls off his t-shirt. Pretty sure he shouldn't look so fucking hot doing that one action but, fuck, he does.

"Looks like I missed the fun. Guess I'll just have to tap in now."

# CHAPTER THIRTEEN

## LINCOLN

These last few weeks have been more bleak than light, but I am desperately fighting against the waves that keep threatening to suck me under and drown me. My father might think he's a God, but Poseidon he isn't, so these murky waters are not going to steal me and the things I love.

I fucking refuse.

Trying to keep V happy while dancing around the minefield my father has dropped me in the middle of is proving more work than I ever expected, but for her, I'd happily do the dance a thousand lifetimes over.

What I'd rather not do, is deal with the red-headed succubus that supposedly wears a ring that is meant to bind us together.

Over my dead and cold body.

I just need to find an alternate way to keep Harrison happy so that he doesn't follow through on his threats to rip Octavia away from me if I don't do what he asks. I knew when she came back here that if I let myself fall for her, claimed her as my own, she would become my weakness. I knew it would hurt her—hurt us both—and yet, I was her captive the minute her hazel eyes met mine her first day back.

Even if I fought it, I knew we were inevitable. I knew that once I gave in, I'd never let her go, no matter what.

Unfortunately, Harrison seems to have his own fucking plans for my life, but like I've told him before, I'm not a whore, and it's my fucking dick. If he wants the union so bad, he can fuck her. It's not like he's opposed to younger women or devoted to monogamy. God knows he's cheated on my mom their entire marriage, even if he does demean her for doing the same damn thing.

I finish my reps on the chest press, dropping the lift with a thunk before grabbing my towel and swiping it over my face. I've been in the gym all morning trying to clear my mind of the bullshit so I can focus on this afternoon.

Date day with my girl.

I haven't been able to snag much alone time with her lately and it's pissing me off. Between the Knights bullshit, dealing with the guys and everything else we have going on, and keeping that succubus away from me, I've barely had time to breathe, let alone spend time with Octavia. I mean, I got quality time with her yesterday, but I still had to share her. While sharing with my brothers isn't a hardship, I just want to be selfish for a night. Which is why I made her promise me her afternoon today.

I am going to distract her from all of the darkness around us, even if it kills me.

She shone so bright when she first got back, and it's impossible not to see how being around us has started to dim that light. Not that there's anything wrong with her being dark, but we never meant to break her.

Fuck me, my head is a mess.

I jump in the shower, freshening up before drying off and shucking into a pair of jeans and a t-shirt, running my hands through my damp hair. What I have planned for today doesn't require anything but comfort.

Once I make it back to the kitchen, Mrs. Potts is already waiting for me. "Oh, Lincoln, dear. Good, you're here before I take off. Are you sure you're ready to make this on your own?"

Her smile is warm and loving, the surrogate mother who basically raised me, and I feel nothing but kindness for her. Even if she is doubting me.

"We've been practicing this meal in pieces for years. I can do this." I grin wide at her, and she rolls her eyes.

"Well, it's true you've always been able to do anything you set your mind to." She huffs out a breath and finishes wiping down the already-spotless counters. "Just remember to clean as you cook so you don't destroy the kitchen, and do not open the oven until the souffles are fully risen. I've stocked everything, it's either in the refrigerator or the pantry, so you should have everything you need."

She saunters over to me and presses her hands against my cheeks. "And if you break my kitchen, I will make you repair it by hand. None of this hiring someone else to fix your mess bother."

Winking at me, she releases me and I laugh softly. "I promise not to break anything, though if I do, you'll never know because it will be repaired before you can find out."

"A woman always knows, Lincoln Saint. You'd be wise to remember that."

I shake my head with a smile as she leaves. She might be the only adult in my life that has always treated me as a human, with love and kindness, rather than wondering what it is I can do for her.

Once she's gone, I hook my phone up to the speakers, putting on *Fall to Pieces* by Pale Waves

, and get started on the prep work for my plans with Octavia.

I intend to take her on a sensory rollercoaster that she'll never want to get off of. I start by melting the chocolate before dipping the strawberries and putting them in the fridge to set. Could I buy them? Of course, I could buy every single thing I have planned, but that's too easy, and I'm not about taking the easy way out.

Not when it comes to her.

I pick up my phone and pull up my thread with her.

Me: T-minus two hours.

Octavia: I'm both excited and afraid. Are you sure you won't tell me what you have planned?

Me: Oh I am absolutely sure I won't. Just come comfortable ;)

Octavia: Hmmmm, if you say so. The anticipation is killing me.

Me: That's the best part.

I grin as I pocket my phone again and deep-dive into this prep. I'm looking forward to this date afternoon more than I'm willing to admit.

Losing myself to the prep, the time flies by, and by the time the back door is opening, I'm just wiping down the last of the counters from my clean up. She breezes into the room, her long hair cascading down her back in waves, in no more than a pair of cutoffs and a crop top.

"Goddamn you are beautiful," I groan. This girl makes me fucking weak, and I'm useless to stop it.

A blush spreads across her cheeks as she smiles bashfully at me while she toes off her Converse by the back door before skipping over to me and wrapping her arms around my neck. "You look pretty fucking edible yourself."

Oh, she's going to be eating me… she just doesn't know it yet. I smile down at her as I grasp her hips. She stands on her tiptoes, fingers intertwined behind my neck, so I lift her to sit on the counter. She squeaks as her feet leave the ground and the sound goes straight to my fucking dick.

Once she's perched and I stand between her legs, I capture her rosy lips and take from her. She nips at my lip, stirring a growl within me, and I tighten my hold on her. When I pull back, her chest rises and falls as she pants, eyes closed, before fluttering her lashes open to look at me. "I could get used to that kind of hello."

I grin coyly at her. If she had any idea the things I'd happily do to her, as a hello or anything else, that blush of hers would spread. I've only just barely skimmed the surface of the things I want to do with her, but I figure we have forever, so why rush? Long gone are the notions that I'll ever give her up.

"So, what exactly do you have planned for this date of ours?" she asks, trying to look innocent. But I know better than most that there is nothing innocent about Octavia Royal.

Not anymore.

I feather my fingertips across the bare skin of her waist, moving down until I grip her thighs. "It's a surprise."

She pouts at me and I let out a soft laugh before pulling down on her lip with my thumb. She nips the pad of it, and my eyes go wide as my heart picks up its pace. "You're playing with fire, Octavia."

"Maybe." She shrugs before sucking my thumb into her mouth. "But maybe I want to get burned."

---

Having my girl tied, blindfolded, and naked is fucking exquisite. Watching the way her body writhes in anticipation, especially now that her eyes are covered, is enough to push me to rush, but there is no way in hell I'm rushing through this time with her. There is something freeing about being bound, giving up the control and responsibilities of anything and everything. I love that I can give this to her—the freedom in my control—and so much more.

"Lincoln." She calls my name, almost breathless, tugging at her bindings. "I thought this was supposed to be us hanging out."

"Are you complaining?"

She bites her lip at my question before shaking her head.

"Good girl. Now, be patient and you will be rewarded for it." She whimpers as she tries to rub her thighs together, the anticipation making her fucking wet already. Little does she know, I intend on dragging this out all fucking day.

She is mine to feast on, but half the fun is in the build up. I've toyed with edging and denial with her a little, but I haven't dragged it out like this. Not that I intend on denying her anything, just letting her think that I am.

I adjust myself in my jeans, my dick rock fucking solid already, and I haven't even started.

Leaving her tied to my bed, I leave the room, making sure the door is locked, and head downstairs to get everything I prepared for today. Everyone else is out, with strict instructions to stay the fuck gone until later.

This is my time with her, and I intend to enjoy it.

Grabbing everything I need, I put it in the basket Mrs. Potts tucked away for me and head back upstairs. I open my door quietly, padding into the room, barefoot on the carpet. "Are you there?"

Her voice is quiet, but already dripping with need. She is enough to test any man's patience.

"I'm here," I call out as I close the door, before slowly making my way over to where she's bound. I open the basket and lay out the sensory feast I prepared earlier, before heading to my closet and grabbing a few other goodies I'm going to need. I watch her from the bottom of the bed, spread open for me, and swallow a groan. This is about her. Everything she doesn't even realize she wants. But the way she reacts when I call her a good girl tells me everything I need to know about how much she's going to enjoy all of this. "Open your mouth for me."

Her tongue swipes across her lips before she parts them, her hands clasping at the ropes that tie her to the bed frame. Moving closer, I grab one of the chocolate-covered strawberries and press it between her lips, her breath hitching as she tastes the sweetness. "Bite."

A moan reverberates through her as she does as she's told, and a smile plays on my lips. She follows orders so fucking well. I can't wait to test her limits.

Once she swallows, she smiles softly. "That was… unexpected. And delicious."

Leaning forward, my lips brush against her ear, "I like unexpected." A shiver runs through her, dragging my smile wider as goosebumps appear on her skin when I press my lips against the sensitive skin on the column of her throat. "Want to keep playing?"

She nods, and I clasp her throat, giving just the right amount of pressure for her to feel like she's being deprived of air, without actually taking anything from her. "Words, Octavia."

"Yes," she pants, and my cock twitches again.

"Better."

I pull an ice cube from the bag in the basket and move to place it against her ankle. She squeals at the cold, trying to pull her leg away as I trace the cube up her calf, tracing it with my tongue before moving it up her thigh to the apex of her legs. She whimpers when I run it across the lips of her pussy, and I feel my inner caveman beating on my chest.

Mine.

All fucking mine.

To do with what I please.

I pick up the feather from the floor and trace it down the other side of her neck, moving to the curve of her breast, trailing between them and down to her navel as she mewls at the light touch.

"Please."

Her pleas as she writhes beneath me make me shake my head, even though she can't see. "Soon."

The slam of a door shakes the foundations of the house, and I whip my head toward the sound, even though I can't see anything.

"Lincoln!" I wince at the roar of my name.

Fuck my life.

The one person I couldn't control coming and ruining this did exactly fucking that.

"Lincoln?" She says my name like it's a question, and I let out a sigh as I lift her blindfold.

"Sorry, baby, the monster calls. I'm going to untie your hands, then run down to see what the fuck he wants. Get dressed. The last thing I want is you vulnerable up here while he's this pissed."

She nods her head and I kiss her, putting every fucking flame inside of me into it before I untie her.

"Hopefully, I won't be long."

She nods at me, a frown marring those beautiful lips as she looks up at me with her big doe eyes.

I could fucking kill Harrison right now.

Maybe I will.

---

I clench my hands as I fold my arms over my chest. After being yelled at about fuck knows what for an hour, I texted Octavia and told her she should probably head home because I had no idea how long Harrison was going to go at it.

She texted me back to let me know she'd snuck out the back. Thankfully, she didn't have to pass Harrison's office.

He's been sitting, seething quietly with a glass of scotch, for the last half hour. I tried to leave before texting Octavia again, but he threw a glass at my head, so I ground my teeth together and put my phone away. I've been waiting here for Harrison to actually let me know what the fuck it is he wants since, but my patience is running thin.

I thin my lips, and he raises an eyebrow at me, like he's waiting for me to lose my shit. Luckily, I'd dropped a message to the boys to let them know to avoid the house until I gave them the all clear. I'm half hoping they're over at Octavia's, because the thought of her there alone when Harrison is in this mood is enough to put my teeth on edge.

"So, when were you and your little friends going to tell me about Edward?"

I keep my face straight, maintain my posture and give absolutely nothing away. Just like the monster himself taught me. I don't know what he knows, but I knew this was coming. My biggest worry is what this means for Maverick.

He leans forward, his elbows on his knees, glass cradled in his hands, eyes never leaving me. I know what he's waiting for, but unfortunately for him, he trained me himself to not bend. I don't bend, I don't break; not for him, not for anyone.

After watching me for two full minutes, he smirks. "Well, at least I trained you right." He pauses, finishing his glass before he stands. "I already know what happened, and I understand why you didn't say anything. It's being dealt with, but this leaves a hole. Maverick will have to step up."

I keep still, refusing to give away just how much his words piss me off.

"As long as he does that, he can remain a solo chair, like Chase has done up until now. I'm sure you'll be glad your brother will finally be a brother-in-arms. I assume he's told you all about that?" His smirk grows as my jaw tics. "Oh dear, I guess not all is well in your little circle like you thought. No matter. You don't need them. You're the Regent Heir. Your path is already forged. Speaking of…"

He trails off, moving to pour himself another drink as I take a deep breath, trying to reinforce my walls against him. No one else has the power to cut me down like he does, and I fucking hate it.

"You have a date with Georgia the weekend after next." He turns to face me and I grind my teeth. It's Octavia's birthday that weekend and he fucking knows it. Despite my denial of being with her, I'm not stupid enough to think he doesn't know. "Seal the fucking deal already. I told you, if you don't secure this, it will be your little girlfriend who pays. Keep her on the side once you're married, I don't give a fuck. But you will secure this alliance for me. Otherwise your girlfriend will suffer the same way her mother did."

My stomach drops. There are more than enough Knights with proclivities similar to Edward's. He might've been one of the worst, but there are always other monsters lurking in the shadows waiting for their time to strike. The thought of Octavia, captive to one of them…

"Or I could just be done with her once and for all. Not like there isn't enough Royal blood on my hands already."

"Fuck you," I growl, hating myself for the slip. It'll be worse for us all in the long run, but I have heard too many threats toward her fall from his fucking lips. I'm at my limit. "You leave her the fuck alone, otherwise you'll regret carving me into everything you wished you could be."

He barks out a laugh. "There's the little monster I created. Good to see you're still in there, that she hasn't turned you soft. But do not push me, boy. Marry the redhead, fuck the Royal, I don't give a shit, but do what I told you to do, otherwise I'll show you what a *real* monster looks like and *she* will pay the price."

# CHAPTER FOURTEEN

## OCTAVIA

I smile as I bounce down the stairs; Maverick's laughter as he trails behind me is intoxicating. After my morning run with him and Linc, then my afternoon that was cut way too short with Lincoln, Mav has been in a playful but competitive mood since he came over when I got back—even if I was a cranky bitch at first because well… all revved up with nowhere to go. That being said, I love afternoons like this, where we get to just be teenagers. They're few and far between.

Soon, he'll have this every day and I can't wait. I'm excited for him.

"Penny for your thoughts?" he asks as he jumps off the bottom step and lifts me from behind. I let out a squeal as his arms clamp around my waist.

I laugh as he spins me around and when he comes to a stop, I lean my head back on his shoulder so I can look up at him. "Just that I like this. Seeing you like this. It's nice."

"Oh, I can be more than nice," he jokes, wagging his brows at me.

"I'm very aware, now put me down, you brute."

He spins me in his hold and I wrap my arms around his neck and my legs around his waist. "Looks to me like you like where you are."

"Maybe I do," I tease as he strides across the room toward the kitchen.

He puts me down on the counter so he's standing between my legs, a devious grin on his face. "How do you feel about keeping up my joyful spirits?"

I quirk a brow at him, trying not to laugh. "What did you have in mind?"

"A bet."

"A bet?" I ask and he nods, his smile growing.

"A bet," he says, wagging his brows at me again. I laugh loudly as he nuzzles my neck, tickling me until I squirm in his hold.

"What's the bet?"

"I bet that you can't stay quiet enough for me to eat you out right here, right now, without someone finding us."

My heart races in my chest. Smithy and Matthew are here this weekend, I have no idea where but they didn't tell me they were going out. Regardless, I can't deny that the thought of getting caught is both terrifying and exciting all at once. My skin prickles at the thought, and I lick my lips as I consider it, especially since I'm still coming down from my time tied to Lincoln's bed. "Okay, so if I win, then what?"

His grin is breathtaking as he stands between my legs, his fingers toying with the bare flesh of my thighs. "If I lose, you get to ride my bike with me sitting in the bitch seat."

I gasp quietly. He doesn't let anyone play with his baby. Hell, he fucking adores that bike. I've been itching to play on his pretty, and his territorial hold on it just makes me want it more.

"And if I lose?"

"Well, if you lose," he pauses as my breath hitches, his pupils blowing as he watches me like the predator he is. "If you lose, you choke on my dick, and be my little fuck toy until I can't go anymore."

Knowing how many times he's capable of performing, that's a little daunting, but my pussy clenches as he brushes his fingers up my thigh, under my skirt, and against my panties.

"I don't know," I murmur, worrying about Smithy finding me splayed out on the counter if he is home.

Maverick pushes his fingers past the lace of my panties and pushes through to my clit, making me groan as I tip my head back. "That wasn't very quiet, princess. I guess I can understand you not wanting to lose."

I bring my head back down to glare at him. "I won't lose."

"Does that mean the bet is on?" he asks, his lips whispering against mine as his fingers gently tease my pussy before sliding inside of me. I gasp at the intrusion and bite down to stop my groan spilling from my lips.

"Yes." The word falls from my lips and he kisses me with so much heat, I'm sure they'll bruise.

"Good girl," he whispers when he pulls back. My eyes go wide as he pulls a switchblade from his back pocket. "You like this don't you, princess?"

My eyes stay on the glinting metal as he glides it down my chest, cutting away my crop top, which falls down my arms, and I try not to breathe a sound as the blade slices my skin a little. The cut walking the line of too much as he undoes my shorts and teases my clit through the lace of my panties.

"Tell me you like it," he demands, eyes darting to the thin line of blood that trickles down my chest before bending down and licking it up, kissing the broken skin when he's done.

I groan as the pleasure mixes with the pain in a way that Maverick seems to have perfected. "I like it."

He growls as he rips the knife away. "Hips up," is all the notice I get as he rips my shorts down before dropping to his knees.

Splaying his large hands over my thighs, Mav pushes as far as they'll go and pulls me to the edge of the island.

Bracing myself with one hand behind me and the other on Mav's dark head of hair, I audibly gasp as he takes my panties in his teeth and rips them apart like the savage he is.

Fuck, that's hot.

The look he gives me—a smirk firmly planted on his lips—tells me he knows exactly what he's doing. The whole time he'll be eating me out, he'll do it with the sole purpose of making me scream.

I may have gotten myself into a mess, but I'd walk across burning coals before admitting that to Maverick fucking Riley.

My knuckles ache with the force of my grip in his hair as his mouth kisses my pussy lips and his tongue plunges inside me, licking one side then the other, his fingers digging into my flesh with every move of his mouth.

I moan, the sound stifled by my self-control. Just barely.

Mav looks back up at me, his eyes crinkling with amusement and determination. He knows he's only seconds—maybe a minute or two if I'm lucky—away from winning his ridiculous bet. Actually, what's ridiculous is that I would subject myself to this torture.

Who the fuck am I kidding?

Staying quiet with any of them is so freaking hard. I just tried this game with Lincoln and failed miserably. No idea why I think I'm going to win this time, but I'm not one to back down from a challenge.

My breaths are coming in fast and gaining in fervor with every lick and suck and bite that he offers my greedy little cunt. I'm riding his face when he plunges two fingers inside me, his mouth closing around my clit and his tongue flicking it with laser sharp precision.

I don't even realize I'm screaming until his mouth is on mine—capturing my screams—sharing my taste with me as our tongues battle in a kiss so hot it makes my orgasm prolong around his fingers still fucking me. Hard. Fast.

"I love winning my bets almost as much as I love hearing you scream my name."

Had I screamed his name?

"Oh yeah, princess. Loud and fucking clear." His answer tells me he's able to read my confused expression. "And now, I'm collecting my winnings."

Goddammit. I knew I wouldn't be able to win this.

Barely aware of my surroundings, I grab Mav by his hair and stare at him with—I'm guessing—horror written all over my features.

"Did Smithy and Matthew hear me?" Oh, fucking hell, I would never be able to look them in the eyes ever again.

Mav's laughter roars out like a dark storm over the ocean. God, I love seeing him freed like this. Happy. Carefree, even.

"No one's home, princess. I made fucking sure of it before I brought you down here."

My eyes narrow on him and I suddenly feel feral. "You fucker!"

"I sure am, princess. But first, you're going to suck my cock just the way I like it." The next thing I know, Mav carries me in a fireman's hold over to the couch and lays me down with my head hanging over the armrest.

Yeah, his favorite way to get sucked is with my head hanging and his access to the back of my throat, so he can grasp my neck in his hands and feel himself as he fucks me.

I love it like this too, but I'm definitely not telling him that or else he'll find some other depraved way of making me come.

Once I'm settled, my mouth eager to taste him, his jeans are down around his ankles and his cock is already in his hand, rock hard as he strokes it, gripping it tightly. He almost looks angry.

When our gazes meet, he looks at me like I'm the center of the Universe, the softness in his eyes so endearing, so honest, it makes me fall in love with him all over again.

"Open that gorgeous mouth of yours, V. Take all of me in." Bracing himself on the back of the couch, he leans in and angles his cock into my mouth, slowly, until he's all the way in the back of my throat. He moans, the sound so fucking sexy it makes me wet and achy all over again.

"Fuck, your mouth is heaven."

Once his groin is pushed against my face, his free hand comes to my throat, squeezing hard enough to make my eyes water and saliva pool at the corners of my mouth.

"Goddamn, you're stunning with my dick buried so deep in your throat I can feel it against my fingers."

I can't answer him, obviously, but I can acknowledge his words. As filthy as they are, for Mav, they are as romantic as can be.

I use my throat muscles to squeeze the head of his dick and revel in the beauty of him throwing his head back and moaning.

Because I do this to him.

He pulls out, looking down at me and when our eyes meet again, determination is written in the depth of his gaze.

His determination to fuck the breath out of me.

Just by the tautness in his shoulders, I can tell he's going to fuck me after this and it's going to be glorious.

Without a word he moves back, tugging me down so I'm on my knees and he grasps my chin, opening my mouth wide. He barely gives me time to suck in a breath before he shoves back inside, his fingers pressing against the sides of my throat.

In and out. Pushing through my gag reflex, using my nose to breathe, I allow him to fuck my face like the animal he thinks he is.

He's my lion. Feral, protective, and dominant to his last breath.

"Fuck, I love your fucking mouth. Play with your clit, princess. Make yourself come for me." His order sends a bolt of lightning up my spine, and I cave to his demands.

My fingers reach down to my clit, two of them rubbing over my hard, swollen nub while I try to concentrate on his accelerating rhythm. Faster, he fucks me with precision, never giving me too much, always careful not to hurt me. Too much.

It takes me less than thirty seconds to get my orgasm building again, my eyes trained on Maverick's beautiful face. He's enraptured as he watches me play with myself, his hand wrapped around my throat as he feels his cock sliding in and out of my mouth. He licks his lips—slowly and deliberately—like he misses tasting me even though it's been no more than minutes since he last had his tongue inside my pussy.

His gaze comes back to mine and I hear his silent words. His silent demand. He wants me to come.

My hips buck up and my fingers quickly gather my juices from my slit and bring them up to my clit where I rub circles—almost frantically—all the while trying not to choke to death on Mav's cock.

He knows exactly when I'm seconds from coming because he buries his cock inside my mouth and grinds down against my face, making my orgasm explode from deep inside me. I can't breathe and that fact makes my climax all the more powerful.

"Holy fucking hell, princess. You've never looked more beautiful than you do right now."

I must look a mess. My eyes watering. My mouth coated with my dripping saliva. My pussy soaked with my second orgasm, yet he calls me beautiful. He might be a monster, but he's my monster.

Mav, who still hasn't come, pulls out of my mouth and adjusts my position, pushing me back onto the couch before burying his cock inside my pussy, my legs hanging over his shoulders as he kneels.

He's not gentle. All semblance of control seems to have left him as he pummels me like he hasn't fucked me in years. The smell of sex and the sounds of skin slapping on skin are all around me. Trying to keep up with his frantic fucking rhythm, one hand clutches the back of the couch while the other grabs the armrest behind my head as I watch him plunge in and out of my hungry pussy—his eyes darting from where our bodies meet to my eyes and back again.

He's like a man possessed, his need for me overwhelming and beautiful.

Mav is a lot of things, but more than anything, he's in love with me and fucking me like this is the best way he knows how to show me.

With his intensity.

His commitment to bringing me pleasure.

And fucking hell, does he ever bring me pleasure.

"Your pussy is so desperate for my cock, princess. It's soaked, your cum is coating my cock like a fucking waterfall." He's close. So fucking close I can feel him growing inside me. Then he stills—his dick so deep inside me I can practically feel him in my belly.

I catch my breath as one of his hands comes to my clit—his thumb working my sensitive nub into another orgasm. How does he do that? "Come for me again, princess."

I am captive to his hold on me. He looks at me and every one of his feelings are written in his eyes. I am powerless to his demands and I come once more, clamping down on his dick, dragging him over the edge with me.

He rests his forehead on mine, his heaving breaths in perfect time with my own as he rests while I try to pick up my broken psyche from the ground around me. It's useless. I am his, and I have zero regrets about that.

"Holy fuck, princess." His words are little more than a murmur as he kisses me once more, his dick hardening again without having even left me.

He pulls back, rocking his hips and making me gasp as I meet his gaze, his eyes sparkling. "Oh, I'm not done with you yet, princess."

---

After the rollercoaster of the weekend, I'm almost glad it's Monday morning and that I'm pulling on my uniform for school. My workout with Luc this morning was fucking brutal, followed by my run with Linc, and I swear I could sleep for four days. Pretty sure Lincoln could tell I was flagging, but there's nothing I can do about it other than push harder.

Which is exactly what I intend to do.

My phone buzzes on the dressing table, Artemis' name flashing on the screen.

Artemis:
Don't forget that you're with me tomorrow, girlie. See you bright and early, sweet cheeks. And yes I mean your ass ;)

I laugh out loud, dropping her a message to say I haven't forgotten. It should probably be weird that she kind of hits on me every time we talk, but it's not. I'm all about accepting people for who they are, and this is apparently who she is. Plus, she makes it funny every time, so I know she's harmless. It might be nice to have a friend who understands this crazy world. At least she knows my secret, and has zero judgment for me handling my shit.

Blowing out a breath, I run a hand through the waves of my hair before grabbing my bag and going downstairs.

When I reach the kitchen, I find Smithy and Matthew dancing to the music filtering through the speakers. They look so freaking happy, so I keep my mouth shut and just let them be until the music stops and Smithy notices me leaning against the wall. "Oh, Miss Octavia. You're awake."

It's cute how flustered he still gets when I catch him with Matthew.

"I am, I've been up and out already. Just wanted to grab a protein bar before I go get Indi."

"Protein bars are not breakfast," he huffs, rolling his eyes.

"James, leave the poor girl alone. We can't all eat organic, GMO-free foods all day." Matthew winks at me as he teases Smithy. It's still weird to hear him called James. I don't think I've ever heard anyone else call him James.

"At least take a tumbler of the smoothie I made this morning." He doesn't wait for me to say anything before he grabs my matte black cup and straw and starts pouring the pink smoothie into it. I shake my head, smiling, and take it from him once I grab a protein bar from the cupboard.

"Thank you." I peck his cheek as I take the cup. "I'm going to be out tonight, so don't worry about dinner."

"You say that like he won't just leave leftovers out for you," Matthew teases, his eyes crinkling at the sides.

This, all of this right here, is how I know the cologne from the basement wasn't his. He freaking adores Smithy, and while I might not always be the best judge of character, now that I have gotten the chance to know him, he just gives off good vibes. I'm sure that he wouldn't hurt Smithy, and hurting me would hurt the old man.

"Well, if you do, I'll make sure not to blow up the kitchen when I heat them." I stick my tongue out at Smithy as he flicks a tea towel at me.

"Get on with you. You'll be late to school if you don't leave soon."

I check the time and realize he's right. "I'll see you later!"

"Drive safe!" he calls out as I run to the garage. Once I'm on the road, I relax a little. At least there's only another two weeks until my birthday, and then there won't be any more secrets.

I just have to hope that they're not so pissed at me that they don't just bank it and drop me anyway. Not that I think they will, but the possibility is still there.

Pulling up in front of Indi's house, I beep my horn twice and slam down the protein bar, taking a sip of the fruity smoothie Smithy gave me. My little ray of sunshine bounces up the sidewalk before diving into the passenger seat of my car, all smiles. "Morning!"

Her grin is infectious as she pulls on her seatbelt then swipes my smoothie. "Oohhhh this is good! Smithy is a freaking God. I'm going to steal him. Or better yet, let's go to the same college, and we can room with him."

She looks so hopeful at the prospect that I can't help but laugh. "Maybe. I really need to send in my applications. I'm so fucking behind."

"Pfft, you'll be fine. You're Octavia freaking Royal. Even if you weren't richer than God, I'm pretty sure the Knights could pull whatever strings needed to get you into whatever school your heart desires." I glance at her as I pull away from the curb, and there's not an ounce of resentment on her face. She's just speaking the truth as she sees it.

"Yeah, maybe. Though I'd rather not use the Knights. I just need to get my shit together. Too much has fallen by the wayside lately. Speaking of which, we need some girl time before exam season kicks in. Spa weekend again soon?"

She slurps down the last of my smoothie before nodding. "I am so down for that. I loved our last weekend away. Have you thought much about prom? 'Cause we're going to need to start shopping and preparing for that soon too."

I clench my hands on the steering wheel. I haven't thought about any of it. My senior year has not gone how I thought it would. Stalkers and secret societies will do that to you. "I don't even know if we're going."

"You have to go! It's our prom! And after homecoming, we deserve a good fucking prom. Please?" She turns her big puppy dog eyes on me, and I already know I'm not going to be able to say no.

Letting out a breath, I nod. "Sure, I'll try and talk the guys into it if yours are coming…"

"Yes!" she exclaims with a fist pump. "They're coming, but if yours won't, then we can just go together. Pretty sure Ryker would rather rip off his fingernails than go to another dance at ECP, but he has a problem saying no to me when it comes to stuff like that."

Her salacious grin makes me chuckle. "Oh, I bet he does."

We pull into the school lot, finding the boys standing around Lincoln's Porsche, and I maneuver the Range Rover into the space beside it. I know I said I should get another car, but there's something about driving my dad's that just makes me feel close to him when I'm in here. It's weird, but I'm not about to question it. There's enough crazy in my life that I've stopped questioning the things that bring me some semblance of comfort.

Indi bounces out of the car and I follow suit, moving over to where my guys are standing, their conversation stopping once we reach them. I raise an eyebrow at them. Not suspicious at all. "Everything okay?"

Maverick swaggers over to me, all showy, and wraps himself around me before planting his lips on mine. "Better now that you're here."

Indi rolls her eyes, and I smirk as he sees. "Don't be jealous, Pixie Spice, just cause there's no D here for you."

"I've got plenty of dick, thanks," she snaps at him playfully. "At least mine don't paw all over me like barbarians every time we're in public.

"Sounds like you're jealous to me, Pix."

"You're such an ass," she hisses at him while Finn rolls his eyes. I look over to Lincoln, whom I haven't heard from since escaping his house yesterday thanks to Harrison's interruptions. I ask him with my eyes if he's okay, and he nods subtly. Doesn't exactly fill me with hope, but until I can get him alone, it'll have to be enough.

The bell rings, jolting me from my thoughts, and putting a stop to Indi and Mav's bickering. "Come on, let's head in. We don't want to be late."

I loop my arm through Indi's and wink at Mav as I do before sashaying away from them, feeling their heated stares on my back. A girl could get used to this sort of attention on a permanent basis.

Now I just have to hope that they won't hate me once they have their freedom.

The morning has been a blur of exam prep, final assignments being set, and of course, Miss Celine reminding us all of our performance in front of the entire damn school for music—something that had entirely slipped my mind. Originally I'd been paired with Raleigh. Obviously, that isn't the case anymore, so now I need to compose my own piece to perform.

The thought of singing in front of the school makes me want to be a little sick, so I'm thinking maybe a piano piece, but I'm not sure that Miss Celine is going to let me get away with that.

I'm so lost in my thoughts that I'm not paying any attention to my surroundings until I walk into something hard and end up sprawled on my ass on the floor.

Fuck me, that's going to bruise.

I look up and find Raleigh glaring down at me, like I summoned him with my thoughts. "If you wanted another run at me, Octavia, all you had to do was ask."

"Suck my dick, Raleigh," I hiss as I push myself up, grabbing my backpack once I've brushed myself off.

He barks out a laugh, running a hand down his face. "I knew there was a reason I was so drawn to you when you came here. I also know I fucked up, a lot. Any chance you're ever going to forgive me?"

"Maybe when it snows in hell." I shrug, folding my arms across my chest. "Is there any reason you were in my path, or did you want to shove me down again?"

"I wanted to talk. Privately." He looks hopeful as he watches me, but fool me once and all that.

"Raleigh, there isn't anything left to say between us."

I make a move to step around him, but he moves back into my path. "Come on, Octavia. We're going to be family soon. I'm a Knight now, even if I'm not sitting on the Conclave yet, it's going to happen. We'd be better as friends."

"What do you want, Raleigh?" I sigh, realizing he's not going to let this go until he says whatever it is he wants to say.

He glances around, face paling a little as he does. "Not here. I'll text you."

He turns on his heel and strides away from me, leaving me slack-jawed. Fucking Raleigh. I glance around to see what or who could have made him react like that, but I don't see anyone. Pretty sure everyone else is already outside on the quad enjoying the sun or in the cafeteria.

Weird.

I head to my locker and put my bag inside along with my books, just keeping a hold of my card purse and my phone before heading to the cafeteria. Pushing through the doors, I walk in and suck in a gasp as the cheers and shouts echo around the room. Mikayla is sprawled on the ground at Blair's feet, shrieking, while Blair glowers down at her.

I guess the plan she had in place either didn't work, or she had enough of Mikayla's bullshit. Glancing over to our usual table, I see my guys, sitting with Indi, watching everything unfold. I nod at Lincoln, because while this isn't what we discussed, he can play his part now. He grins before his icy mask drops into place and he stands, strolling over to the two disgraced queens, who are now engaged in a silent standoff, with his hands in his pockets.

The cafeteria grows quiet as the king approaches and the crowd parts as he reaches them. "This is over. Mikayla, you've had your fun, but you're obviously not fit to wear a crown if you can't keep it." He glances over at me and I suck in a breath.

*Don't you fucking do it, Lincoln Saint.*

I glare at him, but the slight tipping up at the corner of his lips is all I need to know that he's going to fucking do it anyway.

"Neither of you are fit to be queen. The only true queen here is the Royal herself. My queen." He tips his head in my direction and everyone's gaze swivels to me.

*Fuck you, Lincoln. I never wanted the goddamn crown.*

There isn't anything I can do here but nod, undermining his power isn't going to look great, but Blair is going to fucking kill me. If the blazing look in her eyes is anything to go by, she's already picturing me writhing on the ground in pain.

*Just awesome.*

"So be it," is all Lincoln says before moving to stand beside me and claiming my lips in front of everyone. My mind goes fuzzy from the intensity of his kiss, and I clasp the lapel of his blazer in my fingers as the rest of the room fades to nothing.

Goddamn can he kiss. He pulls back, that secret smirk he has just for me on his face disappearing quickly before he leads me back to our table. So much for keeping our relationship under wraps.

The crowd disperses now that he's spoken, murmurs and glances follow us as we sit down and Indi's eyes dance with delight as I slide into the chair beside her.

"Long live the Queen."

# CHAPTER FIFTEEN

## OCTAVIA

I drop onto the couch and turn on the TV. Smithy left me a note to say he and Matthew are going away for a few days to see Matthew's family, so I have the place to myself. I can't help but smile, happy for him, because if anyone on the planet deserves some happy, it's Smithy.

After Lincoln's declaration at lunch today, everyone seemed to decide that being my friend was top of their to-do list. My cheeks ache from the fake smile I've had plastered on for most of the day. Indi thought it was a riot and gave me all the shit about it the entire drive home. I swear, if she calls me queen one more time, I'mma lose my goddamn mind.

Once I dropped her off, Mav and Finn took me to the fighting gym again, helping me work through some self-defense techniques with them. Picturing Lincoln's face on the punching bag as they walked me through combinations during my warmup helped deal with some issues, especially since he disappeared to God only knows where after school.

I know the guys saw my bruises from my Knights training, but neither of them questioned it. And I'm eternally thankful for that because between self-defense with them, training with Luc, and running with Linc, I'm freaking exhausted. That's on top of the fanfare at school.

Mav strolls in from the kitchen, bowl of popcorn in his hands, before he drops down beside me. He grins at me and shoves a handful of popcorn in his mouth like an animal. I chuckle at him, shaking my head as I put on one of the crime documentaries I have on my watch list. "You good with this?"

"princess, as long as I'm with you, I'm good with whatever." He passes me the bowl of popcorn and pulls my feet into his lap. I groan as he rubs circles into them with his thumbs and starts the show. It feels so freaking normal, and just, good.

I try to focus on the TV, but I get lost to the rhythm of his touch and drift off to sleep. I only realize I've dropped off when I wake as he lifts me into his arms, tucking me against his chest. "Sleep, princess. I've got you."

I nuzzle into his neck as he holds me in his strong arms, enjoying the warmth of him, but a pang of guilt wakes me further. "We were supposed to hang out."

"We did, and now we're going to go and sleep. I'm just going to have to make sure you have a good breakfast since you missed dinner. But you're obviously tired. It's been a heavy few months, we're all tired."

"Should you even be carrying me? How are your stitches healing? You probably shouldn't be carrying me." My thoughts aren't exactly coherent, but he just laughs.

"There is nothing in the world that's going to make me put you down right now. My wound is practically healed; I've had worse. Trust me, carrying you isn't exactly a hardship." He kisses the top of my head and I trust that he'd tell me if he was in pain, so I snuggle back into him as he starts up the stairs.

He sits me on the end of the bed once we reach my room. "Arms up." I follow his instructions and he peels my hoodie and t-shirt off of me, leaving me in my bralette. He taps my hips and I push up, letting him drag my leggings down.

"Goddamn you're beautiful," he breathes, his gaze raking over me. He lifts me again and pulls back the sheets, sliding me onto the bed once he has, and tucks me in. He strips down quickly after and dives in on the other side, pulling me onto his chest. "Sleep, princess. I got you."

"Not going to check for monsters under the bed?" I tease as I roll toward him, throwing my leg over his hip and snuggling in.

"There's no monsters in here but me," he murmurs as he wraps an arm around my waist, holding me tight against his chest. "Even if there were, we both know I'd be the bigger monster."

"You're not a monster," I murmur as my eyes flutter closed, pressing my lips against the warm skin of his chest. "But even if you were, you'd be my monster."

His monster is just part of who he is, but I know he wouldn't hurt me. Not again. He wants to keep me safe, but he wouldn't cage me or break me. "I'll be whatever you want me to be, princess."

"I love you, Mav." The words are little more than a whisper, but I feel him relax beneath me as I say them. He runs his hand down my hair, twisting it around his fingers.

"I love you too, princess. Now sleep."

Like his words command me, I drift off, wrapped in his warmth, feeling safer and more content than I remember feeling in a while.

---

"Again!" Artemis shouts as she comes at me once more and I try to fight her off. Goddamn she is quick. Fucking lethal, too. She grabs my arms, twists and pulls, using my momentum against me, and the next thing I know, I'm on my back, winded, with her above me. "You really need to focus."

She climbs off of me and offers me a hand, pulling me up from the ground once I manage to pull air back into my lungs. "I'm trying," I wheeze. "You are just wicked fast."

She nods. "The men in our world underestimate women. They see us as feeble, weak, slow. Not someone to be feared. You can use all of that to your advantage. We are smaller, typically weaker, but with the right knowledge, you can use it against them. We can be faster, because we're smaller. You can use their momentum and strength against them. You just need to know how to do it. You've got some instincts, and it's obvious you've been trained, but it's been sloppy. That, or you've forgotten most of it, gotten complacent."

I can't deny that. Other than my occasional sessions with Maverick, I haven't done anything to keep my self-defense skills up since Dad died. I probably should have, but it's not like I've not been busy. "Complacency is my weakness."

"It's the downfall of most. But not on my watch, girlie. Tonight, you, me, and Luc. I'll fight him, you can watch, and then I'll walk you through how I beat his ass."

I bark out a laugh. "You think you can take him?"

"Oh, I know I can." She grins as she sashays away from me, grabbing two bottles of water and throwing one to me. "I also know I can teach you how too—if you'll pay attention. Now hydrate, and show me what you've really got."

I roll my eyes at the mirth on her face and drink the water. We've already been here for forty-five minutes, and I need to be going soon if I'm going to make it back in time to run with Linc. I hope Mav didn't wake up while I was gone, cause I have no idea how I'd explain to him why I wasn't there.

Maybe I should stop letting them sleep over.

*Nope, don't like that.*

"Let's go!" I flinch at her bark, swallowing down the last of the water, and try to remember everything I've learned about fighting. Stamina isn't a problem, my issues are all down to technique, so that's what I need to focus on. Maybe watching her and Luc later will help.

She runs me through a few test throws, showing me how to use her speed against her, the same way I would a guy. To use their momentum to incapacitate them. "With the Knights, if you need these skills, your options will be fight or kill. Ensuring they're on the ground is the easiest way to do either. Throat, eyes, knees, and balls are your go-to zones. Soft, fleshy, and easy to damage. The knee is harder, but if you can kick at the right angle, with enough force, you can make it so they can't chase you if you need to run."

I nod, trying to soak it all up. I check my watch and balk. "I need to go."

She nods once and wipes her brow. "Go, just be back here later. I'll text you a time once I've spoken to Luc. No excuses."

"I wouldn't dream of it." I smile at her playfully and she swats my ass with her towel, causing me to let out a yelp.

Her responding grin is almost feral. "Make sure you don't."

---

The masseuse rubs at the knots in my shoulders while Indi groans from the table beside mine. "Enjoying yourself?"

Her eyes flutter open as she turns her head to face me. "We should do this more often. Like, I am totally down to be your wingman when you are stressed and need this as an outlet. As your best friend, I'll sacrifice to help you. Especially when it means missing class."

I cackle at her as the guy rubbing her back smirks. "I'm so glad you're so willing to be on hand for me."

She closes her eyes and sticks her tongue out at me. "What can I say, I'm selfless as fuck."

"Oh yeah, totally," I murmur as I drop my head back down onto the rest as my masseuse moves to my head. "Hot tub after this?"

"Whatever you want, bestie. Selfless, remember?" I snort a laugh and she flips me the bird, making me laugh harder.

The soft music spills out over the quiet of the room, the scented oils filling my senses; every possible trick and toy to help trick the body into utter relaxation. I'm glad for it, because I really need this. After Gracie refitted our extensions and colored her hair, we decided a spa evening was the best way to continue our day.

Obviously.

The soft chimes ring out, signaling the end of our session, and I let out a deep breath. I've basically melted into the bed, become one with it, and I don't want to reject it by getting up, but I also know that there's someone booked in here after us.

Indi groans beside me, obviously feeling the same way I do. "Come on, oh selfless one. Let's go dip in the hot tub before our facials."

"Fine," she sighs as I push myself up and swing my legs around. My masseuse hands me my robe and I slip it on, Indi doing the same before they leave us to redress. Once the door is closed, I drop my robe and pull on my bikini top, my panties still in place under the towel. Once it's on, I pull the robe back on, noticing Indi is already done and waiting for me.

"All joking aside, thank you for this. I know you're dealing with a ton of stuff at the moment; I know you're busy."

I quirk a brow at her, then frown. "What's wrong?"

"It's nothing." she says, looking down at her feet.

"I know I've been busy and wrapped up in my own drama, but that doesn't mean I don't have time for you. Now, spill it, sunshine."

She sucks in a deep breath and shudders as she expels it. "Alex… he kissed me. Again."

My eyes go wide as I reach for the door handle. "I'm sorry, what? You've seen Alex again?" Wow, I really have been a shitty friend lately if I didn't even know that. I open the door and she hurries through it. I follow her out then loop my arm through hers, pulling her through the spa to where the hot tub and pool area is. Since it's mid-week, the place is a ghost town, so I encourage her into the tub, following closely behind.

"Okay, spill it," I say once we're both seated in the hot water and the jets are going.

She bites at her lip and I stay quiet, letting her start in her own time. "He came by the house to talk to Ryker. About whatever issue it is that they have. I answered the door, and he looked shocked to see me, but I didn't think anything of it. After he was finished with Ryker, I was heading home, so I walked him out and he kissed me. Again. Dylan saw."

Her last words are little more than a whisper, but holy shit. "What did he say?"

She shrugs, and wrings her hands out. I could kill Alex for making her feel like this. Fucking asshole. "Dylan is… Dylan enjoys watching me with others. Usually just the twins, but well, he didn't seem to have an issue with Alex. But you know how he is. Dylan would raze the world if it made me happy. He said he saw how I kissed Alex back, and if I wanted him too, then he was good with that."

"And do you? Want Alex like that, I mean?"

She looks up at me through her lashes, obviously torn up about it. "I don't know. Sometimes I think I do, but the thought of speaking those words to Ryker or Ellis… I don't know if I can do that. Surely that means I don't want him. Not enough. And it's greedy, right? To want someone else as well."

"I think if it's what you want, and you're already in a poly relationship, then these things evolve and adding to it could be as natural as breathing." She nods at my words. "But the real question is, what do you think you want? Once you have the answer to that, the rest should fall into place. Especially if Dylan is on board. If you want Alex too, I'm sure he and Dylan will help you when it comes to the twins."

"Yeah, maybe." She drops her gaze, tucking a strand of her hair behind her ear. "Could you imagine telling Lincoln or Maverick that?"

"No," I answer honestly, "but I also can't imagine wanting anyone but the four of them. But you are not me, my friend."

"This is insane, right?"

I take her hand and squeeze it. "The matters of the heart usually are, but my dad always said the heart will never lead you wrong, so walk down that path, no matter how dark it gets. Because there is always light in darkness."

---

"You are such a bed hog," Indi groans as I rip the sheets from her. "Why do you hate me?"

I can't help but laugh at her. My sunshine friend is all sparkles, except when she very first opens her eyes for the day. "I've been up for hours, been training with Luc and been for my run with Linc. I was barely in the bed to hog it."

I leave out how I was also training with Alex, and that I chewed his ass out about kissing her again. She doesn't know about his training with the Saints, which I also chewed him out about, especially if he's making moves on her. She deserves to know. I gave him until my birthday to decide if he wants this thing with her and if he does then to tell her, otherwise I'm going to tell her myself. It shouldn't come from me, but I'm not going to leave her in the dark.

"Yuh-huh." I shake my head at her grumbling and finish pulling on my uniform. "Smithy is back and making breakfast, so if you want a shower before school, you're going to need to get up now."

"Fine, fine!" She sighs as she dramatically throws herself from the bed, flicking her newly blue hair over her shoulder as she pads to the bathroom. I stifle the laughter that rises and grab my blazer before heading downstairs.

"That smells delicious." I practically drool as I enter the kitchen. "I didn't realize you'd be back already."

He turns and smiles at me, waving for me to sit at the counter. "With everything going on around here at the minute, I didn't want to be gone longer than necessary. Matthew had some business to deal with, so we went to see his family too, but his trip got extended and I decided to come back."

"You didn't need to do that." I frown at his back, hating that he's putting his life on hold for me. He's done that enough for my family over the years.

"Nonsense, Miss Octavia. I like being here with you. It's not exactly a hardship. Not like I could assist Matthew with his business anyway, whereas here I'm helpful. Useful. And I worry about you when I'm gone. Especially right now. This way, I can try and make sure you're at least safe." He looks at me, and I can see his worry and love reflected back at me.

"As long as being here, with me, isn't a burden to you." I wring out my hands, hating feeling like I'm keeping him from living properly, but I'm also clueless as to how I'd survive without him.

"You could never be a burden, Miss Octavia. You are like the daughter I never got to have. It is my pleasure to be here for you, to help you when I can."

I jump from the stool and wrap my arms around his waist. "You're my family too, Smithy. I don't think I'd have made it through the last year without you."

He wraps one arm around me and squeezes. "You'd have made it through. You're stronger than you give yourself credit for." He pauses, kissing the top of my head before patting my arm. "Now sit back down. These breakfast burritos are nearly done."

"Did you say breakfast burrito? Smithy, my man, you are a GOD." Indi bounces into the room all smiles and heads straight for the coffee pot. "Want some?"

"Is water wet?" I deadpan and she laughs, grabbing two cups from the shelf and pouring us both a drink.

I hop back into my seat as Indi brings the coffee over and Smithy serves up our breakfast burritos.

"So, how is your training going? Have you had any luck finding the information Harrison wants? Your deadline is soon, right?" Indi's chatter stops me as I lift my burrito to my lips, and I let out a sigh as I drop it back on my plate.

"Training is fine. Getting my ass kicked every damn day, but it's fine. As for the information, honestly, I haven't had a chance to really start looking between training, school, and sleeping. I have Bentley digging around, and I'm meeting him on Saturday to discuss what he's found so far, but yeah my deadline is next Saturday. My birthday."

"Happy freaking birthday to you." Indi sighs. "We need to do something to celebrate."

"I'm good with something low-key." I groan and take a bite of my burrito. "Holy shit this is good."

"How about a dinner here? Just family and friends," Smithy suggests like he didn't hear me.

Indi's eyes light up. "Yes! We could totally do that. As like, a prelude. Dinner, a night with the boys, and then girls' weekend. Just like we did at the start of the year."

"Oh yes! We could book something, all of the bells and whistles. Especially now you're both eighteen, it opens up places for us too."

They both get excited, carried away with details, and I let them. I'll let them down gently later about how I have exactly zero intentions of celebrating my birthday.

It's why I haven't focused on it much beyond it being the date of my deadline with Harrison. Birthdays were about cherry chocolate sundaes and movies with my dad. This will be my first birthday without him, and I'm not exactly looking forward to it. But I'm not about to rain on their parade right now.

I check my phone, eyes wide. "We need to go, otherwise we're going to be late."

"Crap," Indi gasps, and Smithy jumps to his feet.

"Let me wrap those and you can eat on the way in."

He rushes around, taking our plates and wrapping the burritos in foil as we grab our bags, taking the burritos before rushing out to her Wrangler.

"If I'm late, my mom is going to kill me," Indi groans as she starts the car.

"We won't be late if you put your foot down." I grin, pulling my seatbelt on as she tears past the gate and out of the drive.

I laugh wildly as she breaks every speed limit through the Cove, tires screeching as we pull into the school lot. "Go, go, go!"

Eyes wide, she scrambles from the car, and if it wasn't for her panic, I'd just laugh the entire way in. The sound of the bell rings as we're rushing up the steps. We don't bother hitting our lockers, sliding into our seats in class just as the final bell sounds.

"That shit was close," she gasps, chest heaving. "Man, I need to work out more."

"I can think of a few guys who wouldn't mind helping you." I wink at her, and she rolls her eyes.

"Do not give them ideas. Have you seen them? Ellis is the least active of them all and he's still lean as fuck. They'd kill me off. Nope. No thanks."

"Better than the training I'm doing." I sigh as Miss Summers walks into the room, closing the door behind her.

She turns to face us, the look on her face making me sit up a little straighter. Her gaze roams over the room, settling on me, and something inside of me sinks. "This is it. The start of the end."

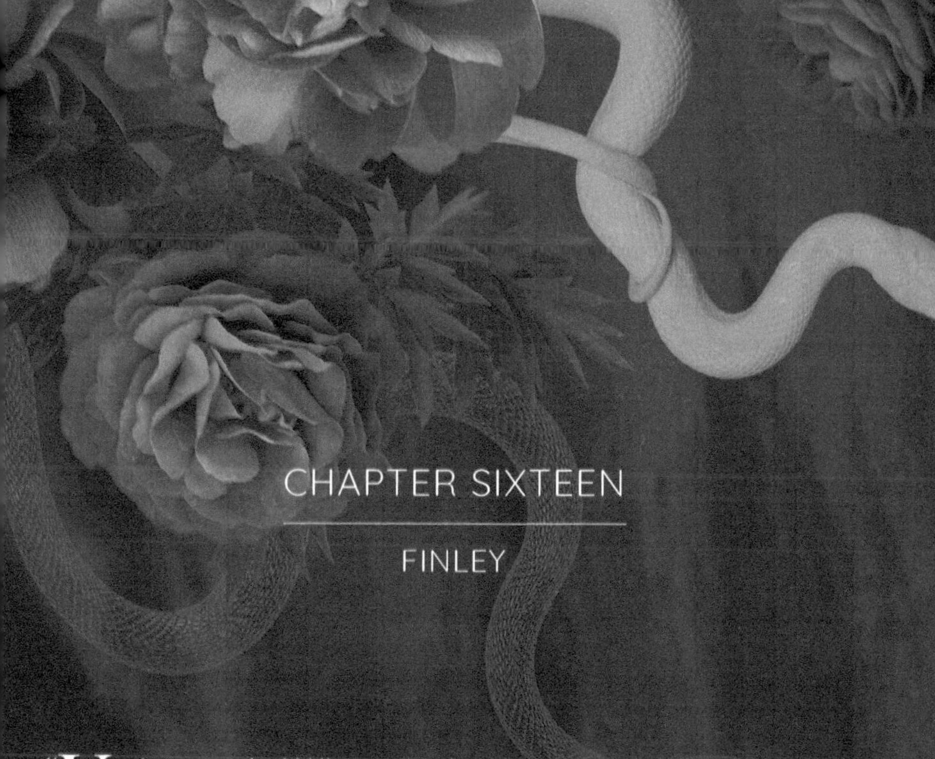

# CHAPTER SIXTEEN

## FINLEY

"You've got to be kidding me." I sit with my spoon halfway to my mouth, balking at my dad. "Running for mayor? Why the fuck would you do that?"

"The mayor's term is up at the next election, and he's going to be announcing that he's stepping up into the big leagues. He's going to run for governor. Which leaves it open. The Conclave decided it would be best to have one of us in the position, one less person to manipulate. So I'm going to run. He'll stay in our pocket and having him in that position is good for us. I could go for that, but he has the political capital I don't, and, honestly, I have my hands full anyway."

Coming home this morning at my parents' request wasn't something I was looking forward to, but I definitely wasn't expecting this. I glance at my mom who is beaming from ear to ear.

There is no way these monsters should be put in office, but it's not like I can say that out loud. "Why are you telling me? You never run this stuff past me."

My father quirks a brow at me as he finishes his mouthful, pointing his knife at me. "I'll need you to be around for the campaign. We're going to be getting started soon."

"What does that mean, exactly?" My gaze bounces between the two of them. I'm still not quite over the fact that she's even here, and my dad grips his knife tighter.

"Oh, Charles." My mom sighs, patting his arm. "Of course he has questions. Just answer him. I'm sure Finley will do what is needed. Isn't that right, dear?"

Her gaze turns back to me, but I'm not foolish. I know my mom is just as fucked up as my dad—maybe more so—so I say nothing and just stare at my father, waiting for him to answer me. The election is November, and I'm hoping to be far, far the fuck away from here for college by then.

"We don't need you for much. Just don't fuck up between now and then and be around for photo ops. If I need you for anything else, I expect you to come running." He grins maliciously at me, tilting his head, and my stomach drops in anticipation. "That also means distancing yourself from the Royal girl. Can't have my son seen to be fucking the town whore."

I grind my teeth together, dropping my spoon into my bowl and clenching my fists. "Fuck you. She isn't a whore, and I'm not distancing myself from her for you or anyone."

"What else do you call a bitch who gets on her back for the four of you? You're not fooling anyone by pretending otherwise. And you either distance yourself by choice, or we will arrange it for you."

"Do not threaten me, Father."

"I don't make threats, Finley. You know that." The twist of his lips makes my heart beat erratically. I'm fully aware of just how much my father doesn't bluff about this shit. Fuck.

I push my chair back and stand. "I've suddenly lost my appetite. I'll just grab some of my things, and then I'll be gone."

"Finley—" my mom calls, but I'm already storming from the dining room toward my bedroom. I grab a duffel from the bottom of my closet and throw most of the contents of my closet into it. If he thinks I'm coming back here after that, he has another thing coming.

We need eyes on Octavia.

Permanently.

We've all basically been living next door to her the last few weeks, and Mav has wrangled a few overnighters at her place, but I'm thinking we need to try and stay with her.

Once the duffel is bursting at the seams, I glance around the room. I should probably feel something about leaving this room, hopefully for the last time, but this place was tainted a long time ago. The whole fucking house, for that matter.

There is nothing but relief rolling around in my chest at the thought of never coming back here. Because even if my father does actually run for mayor, I'm not coming back. I was already set on it, but this… this confirmed it for me.

I might not be able to free myself from the Knights yet, but I can escape this toxicity. Until we find a way out that doesn't equal death for us all, this will have to be enough.

Closing the door to my childhood room, a weight lifts from my shoulders. It's not like I'm leaving the horrors behind, those are etched into both my mind and my flesh, but I don't have to see them, be ruled by them anymore.

Octavia taught me that much.

I stride out of the house, ignoring the shouts from my parents, feeling freer than I ever have in my life.

I might still be chained to the Knights, but the demons that kept me captive in this house… they're not going to hunt me anymore.

I climb into my car, reveling in the power beneath me as it purrs to life.

Today might just be the start of a new chapter, now I just need to work out where I go from here.

Mr. Collins, my AP Computer Science teacher, drones on at the front of the room, and I tune him out. Everything he's prattling on about is shit I taught myself years ago. I took this class because I knew it would be an easy win for me, and I'll need it for my degree access.

All of my college applications were submitted months ago. Even before I knew if I'd survive the year. Lincoln, Mav, and I all applied to the exact same schools. It wasn't necessary, we all know that the Knights can pull strings and put us in any school they or we want, but we wanted to do something normal.

I'm not sure if Octavia submitted any, what with everything she had going on, but submission deadlines aren't really a problem when you have money. Sounds crass, but it's true.

The bell finally rings, and I massage my temples before grabbing my shit and heading to my locker. I didn't get to see my girl before class this morning, but she dropped us a message to let us know her and Indi were just running late.

After the conversation with my parents, I need to see her, just to prove to myself that she's okay, that my father hasn't already fucked with her. Not seeing her this morning had us all on high alert, especially after I told the boys about what my dad had said.

I hate how they use her against us, but I wouldn't give her up for anything.

By the time I'm striding into the cafeteria, my nerves are on fucking edge. I grab a burger and fries with a soda and sit at our usual table. No one else is here yet, so I play with my foot, knee bouncing.

I don't breathe easy until she breezes into the room, Indi at her side, laughing about something. It's like a weight is lifted from my chest, and I can take in a full breath again.

Lincoln and Mav enter the room seconds later, but rather than joining the line, they head straight toward me.

"What's wrong?" I ask as they sit. Lincoln is stiff as a board. He glances over his shoulder at Octavia before leaning forward.

"Our fathers need to fucking die."

"What did Harrison do now?" Mav asks, sighing.

"He called me at the end of class. More threats about Georgia, but apparently East is pissing him off. Something about him snubbing the Conclave seat, but he told me if I don't secure the deal with Georgia, either East or Octavia will pay the price, and I'll get to pick which."

I grind my teeth together, pushing away the tray in front of me. I get why he didn't get food now. It's like a lead weight in my stomach. Mav steals the tray; him and his thing with food is well known between us, so I don't say a word about it.

"He wants you to actually marry her? Is he fucking insane?" I hiss, glancing back up at our girl laughing with her best friend like she has no cares in the world.

If only she knew the danger she was in now. "What about Stone's contract? Her taking the regency? It's like he's just forgotten about it."

"There is no way Harrison will give her that seat. I know they spoke, he said that he offered to uphold the contract of her being out if that's what she wanted, and she agreed. I don't trust him, but she said the same thing, so I guess she's out. Just under constant threat because she's attached to us."

"Maybe since I now sit on the actual Conclave, I can keep her safe?" Mav interjects. I open my mouth to refute it, but then close it. Wives aren't always necessarily safe, but as long as they toe the line, they're usually left alone.

Much as I want to be the one who claims her like that, her being married to Mav might make her a little safer than she is right now.

"I hate to say that's a good idea—" I start, and Lincoln nods.

"I know. Same."

"She's coming," Maverick says before taking a bite of my burger, and we shut the fuck up. A silent agreement to come back to this later.

I smile as she slides into the seat beside me and kisses my cheek. "Hey, pretty girl. Good morning?"

"Not really, but I remain hopeful for the day. You guys okay? You all look so serious."

"Just Knight bullshit," Lincoln says, dismissing it. "Nothing major."

She watches him closely, but whatever she sees seems to convince her and she shrugs. "If you say so."

"Have you guys started getting your college acceptance letters yet?" Indi asks, and I grin.

"Acceptances?" Octavia gasps. "I haven't even applied yet."

"You've got time," I say to her, squeezing her thigh. "Where are you looking to apply?"

"Honestly, I haven't even decided. I might just apply to a dozen and go from there."

Mav grins at her from across the table. "That's what we did, but between your money and our connections, you can go wherever you want, princess. Don't sweat it."

"You say the sweetest things," Indi deadpans at him.

"Don't hate the player, Pixie. Hate the game." He winks at her, and I groan. Sometimes it's funny to watch these two battle it out, but my head already hurts with all of the bullshit from my dad and Harrison.

"Maybe I'll do both," she snarks at him. "But rather than talk about college, we have more important things to discuss. V's birthday."

"I told you, I don't want to celebrate," my girl says, glaring at Indi. "So let's not."

"Of course we're going to celebrate," Mav counters, and Lincoln barks out a laugh.

"Did you just agree with Indi?" he asks, and Mav's eyes go wide.

"I would never," he declares before smiling. "Or maybe just this once. What did you have in mind, Pixie?"

# CHAPTER SEVENTEEN

## OCTAVIA

"I hear you have tomorrow off school," Luc barks from across the sand ring he's been training me in. A shout from across the room as Artemis takes down Alex distracts me and I end up on my back, winded, seeing stars. "Pay attention, Octavia. You'll end up dead if you get distracted."

I groan as I sit up, bringing my knees up and resting my elbows on them while I catch my breath. "Yeah, yeah. I know. I'm trying."

"Try harder," he growls as he takes my hand and pulls me up to my feet. "How is your scavenger hunt coming along?"

I raise my eyebrows, surprised he's aware of what Harrison asked of me. "Harrison?"

He nods once, and I'm torn. He's close with Lincoln, but he's obviously under Harrison's thumb. "I'm working on it."

He looks disappointed, but that's not my problem. What *is* my problem is finding time to look through Dad's stuff. Which is exactly why I'm glad I don't have school tomorrow. I asked Smithy to get all of his boxes put up in the spare room. If I have to spend the whole weekend searching, it's what I'll do, because I can't let the guys down.

Not that I'm about to tell Luc that.

"Again," he barks and comes at me. These few days of training with him and Artemis have helped more than I thought they would. I dodge his fist before spinning a roundhouse kick at him, using his movement against him. He stumbles and I kick out again, planting my foot on his chest, making him fall backward.

As much as I want to do a happy dance, I pull the blade from my boot and pounce. But I'm too slow. He's already off the ground and grabs my wrist, sending a fist into my ribs while trying to disarm me. He tightens his grip and twists, causing me to cry out and drop the knife. He pushes on my shoulder while sweeping my ankle and I drop to the ground. Pissed and panting, I wrench myself away from him, rolling up into a crouch, flicking my hair back out of my face.

He smirks at me, and it stokes my anger.

I let it burn, but take on his advice from earlier. A parroting of my dad's from when he used to train me.

*Let the anger fuel you, not rule you.*

I take a deep breath and lunge for him again, except this time, I go full bitch. I fake a swing at his jaw, but bring my knee up to connect with his dick. As he gasps, I thread my fingers in his hair and lift my knee again, feeling the crunch of his nose before I fling him to the ground. I grab the blade from my other boot and dive onto him, bringing the blade to his throat. I feel a pinch in my side and hiss, looking down to see my blade from earlier pointed at my ribs.

"Better, but not good enough. Not yet." I roll off of him and he climbs to his feet, wiping at the blood running from his nose. "We're getting there though. Training with Artemis too is obviously working for you, so I'm going to leave her to deal with your hand-to-hand. I'm going to work on your shooting with you. Not tonight, you've been here long enough, but Saturday. Take tomorrow off, be fresh for Saturday, because that is going to test you."

I swallow the lump in my throat from the implication in his voice but nod. "Saturday, here?"

"I'll grab you in the morning. Be ready by six."

I blow out a breath. Don't these assholes understand the need for sleep? Goddamn. "Sure thing."

I start walking away from him, grabbing my phone, keys, and water bottle from the edge of the room where I left them, hearing Luc yell at Alex about being done, but I don't wait around to listen to them bitch. I haul ass out of the warehouse and to my car.

Checking my phone on the way out, I notice a message from Indi.

Indi: <image> I'm holed up in your media room, it's such a hardship being your bestie and alibi. I'll be here when you get back.

I grin at the screen and let her know I'm heading back now before peeling away from the warehouse. I can't tell if it's because of my speed, or just because I'm getting used to the drive, but the journey home passes in a blink.

By the time I'm strolling into the media room, I'm hungry, in need of caffeine, and ready to drop.

"Wow, you look like shit."

I roll my eyes as I drop onto the couch next to her. "Thanks, sunshine. You're so good to me."

"That's what besties are for." She sticks her tongue out at me and I laugh, rubbing a hand down my face. "Long night?"

"Just exhausting. All of this is just so tiring. The secrets, the training, trying to keep up with the guys, school, not losing touch with my freaking life. I still haven't started looking for my dad's stash for Harrison, and I have no idea what I'm even looking for."

"Dude you need a break. Or to tell the guys what you did."

"I can't." I sigh. "That was part of the deal, remember? Plus, if they find out before it's a done deal, they'll find a way to undo it. They've done enough for me. It's my turn to do something to save them."

"I get the feeling they're going to try and find a way to reverse it regardless once they find out."

Pinching the bridge of my nose, I take a deep breath. She's not wrong. They're going to be angry. Especially Lincoln, even though he's the most likely to understand it. Probably *because* he'll understand.

"Maybe. But first, I need to find what Harrison wants. He already gave me one extension, I doubt I'll get another."

She nods, pulling her blanket tighter around her. "Truth. Do you need my help?"

"I wouldn't ask that of you."

She quirks a brow at me and I can't help but smirk. "Then I guess it's a good thing the question was just a formality. I'm helping."

---

"Would you girls like some refreshments?" Smithy asks as he climbs to his feet. We've been in the spare room going through all of my dad's boxes all freaking morning. So far, we've found sweet fuck all, but I refuse to give up. My guys' freedom rides on whatever my dad had hidden, and it has to be here *somewhere*.

"I'd kill for an iced coffee," Indi exclaims, wiping her brow. "All I've found so far that might lead to something are some random keys and a receipt for a locker in New York. Not sure what use that'll be."

"It's more than I've found. Come on, let's go get some java, have some lunch, and then we can dive back in after."

"Sounds perfect. Come, ladies. Let's fuel up, shall we?"

Smithy turns and heads out of the room, and I glance over at Indi. "You don't have to stick around for this."

"Shut up, bitch. I've got nothing else to do with my Saturday, so I'm here for as long as you need me. Even with the three of us, we've only made it through a quarter of the boxes in here, and we don't even know if what you're after is in here."

I scrape my hair into a messy bun on top of my head and nod. "I know, it's like looking for a needle in a stack of needles, with no idea what the needle looks like. Couldn't be as simple as a USB drive with a label saying 'Knight Shit,' could it?"

She laughs as she climbs to her feet, shaking her head. "If only life was that simple."

I watch as she worries her lip, and concern floods me. "What's wrong?"

"Alex." She starts and I curse him out in my head.

"What did the fuckwit do now?"

"He texted me, says he wants to talk."

Oh… I guess he took my advice. "You going to meet him?"

"I mean… I think so, but I was wondering if I could have him come here. That way the guys don't see him around my place, and it's like neutral ground. Plus, I could use you in my corner."

"You know I got you. Mi Casa es su casa. and all that shit. Whatever you need, and if that means me kicking his ass, I can do that too." I grin as I stand, but worry that she's going to be pissed at me for not telling her about training with him. I'm sure she'll understand, but I hate that it'll be a thing between us.

"I love you."

"I love you too, now let's go eat before we come back to this mess."

We spend an hour or so eating, caffeinating, and just gossiping. Indi texts Alex to say she'd talk with him here, and he said he'd come over this afternoon, so at least their talk will be done. Once everything is agreed, we dive back into my dad's boxes.

We find a few extra random keys that I have no idea what they belong to, a few notes in one of his journals, but fuck all else.

"This was such a bust." I droop against the wall, feeling a little beaten. This is all of my dad's shit. Other than the locker in New York we found the receipt for, I have no idea where else he might have hidden something. I don't even know if he still has the locker, for fuck sake.

"We still have a week until your birthday, right? Maybe we'll find something else before then? Or we can fly up to New York tomorrow afternoon and see what this locker is." Indi's optimism isn't as catching as I'd like, but that could be from the overwhelming urge to throw up.

"It's worth a try."

Her phone rings, and her eyes go wide when she looks at the screen. "Alex."

"Well, answer the phone."

The line goes dead, followed by mine starting to ring. I see his name on the screen and answer, putting it on speaker. "Baby Royal, I'm outside, as per my summons. Now, be a doll and buzz me in."

"Alexander, where are your manners?" I tease and Indi rolls her eyes.

"Saving them for the demon. Now, can I come in? Please?"

I look over at Indi who looks like she's going to vomit, but nods. I might need to find this information for Harrison, but considering we're getting nowhere on that front, I am here for this distraction.

"Opening the gate now." I end the call and open my app to unlock the gate. "I guess we should head back downstairs. Do you want to speak to him alone?"

"Yes, but no. Maybe wait outside the room or something? So you're not too far away?"

"Are you afraid of him?" I ask, surprise flooding me.

She shakes her head vehemently. "No, I'm afraid of this conversation though.'

"Well, I've got you. I'll do whatever you ask."

She takes my hand and squeezes it. "Then let's go face the music, shall we?"

---

You ever have one of those moments, where you'd just like to curl up in a ball and escape reality? Yeah, that's me right now. After a morning of being absolutely *schooled* by Luc in just how shit I am with a firearm—which I'm totally not, he's just a fucking jedi master or some shit—I'm waiting for Bentley to arrive and my guys keep messaging me.

I get it, I've been MIA, I've had to be with all this fucking training. But I just have one week left till my birthday. Next Saturday, I turn eighteen. My deal with Harrison will be complete—if I find these fucking documents—and they will be free. I can come clean with them and we can work out where we go from here. My biggest worry right now is East because he doesn't win with my deal. He's already out… and I don't want him to think that I didn't think of him when I made this deal, but I did. All I thought of was them.

The four of them will finally be able to exist outside of Harrison's reach, and *that* is what I get to gift to East. While I hope they don't hate me over it, I'm big enough to wear the consequences of my actions. So I'll shoulder whatever happens, even if it breaks me.

The upside to the long weekend so far is that Indi didn't hold the whole Alex thing against me. Though her shock at him becoming a Knight was… painful. I'm not sure how they'll make it work, but they seem to want to. In fact, they're flying off to New York this afternoon to look into the locker for me at Smithy's suggestion, and since she's from there, there was no real need for an excuse like I would've had to have. I trust Indi with my life and I trust Alex to not fuck me. He gets what he wants if Lincoln is released from the Knights, so it works in his favor not to screw me over.

Indi said she'd call me as soon as they found anything, so now it's a waiting game on her, and on Bentley to arrive. I'm hoping Bentley has good news, because fuck do I need some. I know he said he'd found something, but Lord only knows what that means.

So yes, curling up in a ball and escaping reality sounds really fun right now. But life isn't that simple, and running from my problems hasn't gotten me anywhere. So I'm taking control of what I can and dealing with the rest, even if running away sounds better.

My phone buzzes again, and I smile at the group text.

Mav: Princess, stop ignoring us. Don't make me beg. We're trying to be good and give you space to catch up on your school work, but my dick misses you.

East: Oh yeah, Romeo. That's really the way to woo her. Such sweet words you speak.

Mav: Better than letting her think I've forgotten about her, ass sack.

East: She knows I haven't forgotten about her. I've been busy with Chase.

East: You know I've not forgotten about you, right Octavia?

Lincoln: You lot keep simping like this, and the only dick she'll ride will be mine.

Finn: Wouldn't be so sure about that, Linc.

East: Octavia?

Mav: Come on, princess. Come and play.

Linc: Let the girl study. Jesus christ. I'd have muted your asses too.

Mav: *pouts* You haven't muted us, right princess?

Finn: Silence is pretty telling Mav. Come and work out with me. It will distract you.

Mav: Fine, fine. I'm on my way.

Linc: Thank you, maybe now I can focus too.

I cackle as I close out the message. I need to keep up my façade of school work, at least until Bentley is gone. Once I know what he knows, then I can reassess. I know they're all planning something for next weekend for my birthday, despite my protests, but I miss them. I know I've seen them, but still. This is the most closed off I've been from them since we decided to make this work.

I don't hold East's absence against him. I have no idea what he's doing, but I'm trying not to pry like a hypocrite. If anything, whatever is keeping him busy is working in my favor. It's one less person to dodge and lie to. Though, barely seeing him the last two weeks hasn't been exactly fun either. I see the others at school, even with everything else we have going on, we have that.

I don't even have that with East. I just have to hope he doesn't hold that against me, too.

Blowing out a breath, I check the time again, wondering what is keeping Bentley when I see his car pull up in front of the gates. I hit the button in the app to allow his entry without waiting for him to buzz in.

"He's here," I call out to Smithy, who appears from the hall off the kitchen.

"It's about time. I've been looking into Kensington. He seems like someone we can trust. Whoever recommended him to you did a stellar job." He squeezes my shoulder as he moves past me to open the front door. I hear the murmur of their voices as Smithy lets him in, but can't make out their conversation. Probably Smithy being over-protective again.

I smile to myself as I turn on the coffee pot, and they enter the room. "Octavia, good to see you."

"You too. Coffee?" He nods as he sits at the counter while Smithy watches over him. I pour two mugs, knowing better than to offer Smithy any, and take a seat. "So what did you find?"

"Your dad is a pack rat. He has hidey holes all over the world," he starts, and I let out a sigh. That doesn't sound promising. "But I did find this."

He pulls an envelope from inside his jacket and upends it on the counter. A black USB drive falls from it and I raise an eyebrow at him. "What is it?"

"Whatever it is, it needs an encryption key. I've been scouring the hidey holes along the west coast searching for something that could help, but all I've found so far are stashes of newspaper clippings, a journal, some jewels, and some bearer bonds. I've got them here for you too." He motions toward the bag at his feet and my heart sinks.

"Thank you. I guess it was too much to hope this would be easy."

"I think that that USB file will be crucial, you just need to work out how to open it. I have a hacker friend, but I figured you wouldn't want anyone else looking at it. Your friend is a hacker right?"

I gulp and nod. He means Finn. "Yeah, but I don't want to involve him if I can help it either."

"I wouldn't blame you. I've learned a lot of things about your Knights while working for you, and I have to say, I'm not comfortable helping you join their ranks. They're just as likely to kill you off when you hand this over as they are to welcome you." He glances back at Smithy who is nodding. "I'll keep searching if you want, but some of these hidey holes are on the other side of the world. London, Paris, Sydney…"

He trails off but I hear what he's not saying. There isn't enough time to search them all. I take a deep breath and mull it over. "Keep searching, as much as you can. Cost isn't a problem. We have until Friday, so we need to do what we can before then."

"Okay. I can do that." He stands, grabbing his case and opening it for me. "This is for you."

I glance inside, wondering why my dad hid all of this. Maybe it was just a way to disguise whatever he was hiding in one of the others. "Smithy, would you mind?"

"Of course, Miss Octavia." He takes the case, closing it, before disappearing into his quarters. I know he'll arrange for it to be put where it should be. I wouldn't even know what to do with most of that stuff.

"Walk me out?" Bentley says, watching Smithy disappear.

"Umm, sure." I jump from the stool, noticing he didn't touch his coffee. We walk outside in silence, but when we reach his car, he takes hold of my arm, watching over my shoulder at the front door.

"Be careful who you trust, Miss Royal. The Knights reach might be wider than you think. I would suggest if you find what you're looking for, make a copy and keep it somewhere safe. Somewhere that isn't linked to you. These are dangerous waters you're playing in."

"I know," I say with a nod. "Can I really trust you?"

He smirks at me. "I would suggest trusting no one, but yes, I have nothing to do with your Knights. I have managed to stay unaffiliated, by some miracle, my entire life. Even from my own brother's reach. If you want me to keep a hold of the information you seek once we find it, just let me know."

"I'll think about it," I say, just as the front door opens behind me and Bentley takes a step back.

He puts his friendly mask back on and glances over my shoulder at Smithy, his brow furrowing so minutely I wonder if I imagined it. Weird. He looks back to me and warmth fills his eyes again as he opens the driver's side door to the car. "I'll let you know if I find anything else."

# CHAPTER EIGHTEEN

## OCTAVIA

"If you don't focus, he's going to pin you again," Finn barks, and I huff at how right he is. I might not have told these guys the truth of why I wanted to train with them, but they are kicking my ass for real.

"I'm trying." My words are sharp and terse. I thought hanging out with the guys would've taken the edge off of my meeting with Bentley earlier, but I'm still wound up so fucking tight. Add that to everything else I have going on and its not a surprise I'm a fucking mess.

I was hoping my training with Luc and Artemis would've helped me a bit more, but Maverick really is just a fucking lethal machine and I am useless compared to him.

*Woe is fucking you, Octavia. This isn't the time for a tiny violin, buck the fuck up.*

"Again." Finley's voice snaps my focus back to reality in time for me to see Maverick barreling toward me in the Octagon. I try to brace myself but I'm too slow as he slams into me, tackling me to the floor. I grapple with him, trying to bring my legs up to kick him off of me or flip him onto his back, but he smiles at me as his hands cage my wrists and uses his hips to pin me to the floor.

"I'm definitely not opposed to this position, princess," he growls as he grinds his dick against my core and I whimper beneath him at the touch.

Maybe that is exactly what I need to get rid of this humming beneath my skin.

So I lift up and press my lips to his, knowing that Finley is watching, hoping they both get the fucking hint.

"Hey, Finn, looks like our little fighter here is itching to get fucked." Mav's grin takes up half his face as he grinds his half-hard cock against my already-wet pussy.

Finn's heavy steps end behind my head, his eyes landing on me from above—the filthy glint in his eyes unmistakable.

"Looks like it." Cocking his head to the side, he adds, "Who are we to deny her?"

"Indeed." It's the only word Mav throws at me before I'm suddenly turned onto my hands and knees, my leggings gone right along with my panties.

Finn disappears for a heartbeat before he's back—a good length of rope in his hands—settling in front of me.

The scent of sweat quickly gives way to sex as he places the silky material around my throat, sliding it back and forth at the nape of my neck. All the while, Mav feasts on my pussy from behind, moaning and grunting as he goes deeper and deeper.

Crossing the ends of the rope at the base of my neck, Finn looks me straight in the eyes and grins.

"You look beautiful all tied up."

His words and Mav's expert tongue wreak havoc on my body, my nerve endings blazing with my rising need to come.

"She's almost there, Mav." Finn's gaze never leaves mine as he speaks.

"I know, she's fucking dripping wet."

Closing my eyes, I revel in the feel of Mav's tongue, now joined by his fingers, as he traces circles around my swollen clit. It's all exacerbated by the silky feel of the rope sliding over the skin of my neck—back and forth.

Mav pushes two fingers inside my pussy as his tongue slides over to my puckered hole, pushing and prodding, moaning his pleasure as he fucks both of my holes. I can't help it, the sensation is too much and my orgasm overtakes me without warning. The heat of it spreads throughout my body is almost overwhelming.

"Don't be a greedy bastard, Mav."

He curls his fingers inside me, ripping a cry from my throat with the pleasure of it. Gasping, I try to catch my breath but Finn tightens my ropes and the slight deprivation of air just makes my orgasm that much more potent.

"That's our good girl." Finn's words heat me from the inside but I don't have time to think about this newfound praise kink I may or may not have, because the next thing I know, I'm kneeling on the octagon—straddling Mav's cock as it juts up and teases my swollen lips. Pushing into me, he groans in my ear as Finn's rope is pulled taut around my neck, dragging my head down toward Finn's now-exposed cock. He slides it into my mouth and we both moan at the feel.

Two large hands push up my sports bra, exposing my already hard nipples to the air. Using his grip on me, Maverick fucks me slowly, deliberately, his fingers pinching my nipples every time he bottoms out. Alternating their movements, Mav pulls out just as Finn drives his cock deep inside my throat.

Mav thrusts once more, then twice, and on the third push he pulls me off and turns me around as if I weigh nothing.

With one hand in my hair, Mav presses my mouth onto his dick, deciding the speed and force with which I suck his dick. Behind me, Finn is impaling his cock inside me without any preamble. One hand on my hip the other on the rope that he uses as a leash.

It's demeaning—degrading even—and I love it.

"How do you taste on my cock, princess?"

I don't answer, obviously, but I moan and it's answer enough for him.

"Fucking delicious, aren't we?"

I moan again as he fucks my face, Finn behind me fucking my pussy with determined thrusts.

Again, Mav pulls out of my mouth, this time pulling my head up to his mouth and kissing me hard and fast, his tongue licking a hot path across my lips before his teeth bite into my bottom lip hard enough to break the skin. The tip of his tongue flicks over the drop of blood that pebbles where he broke skin.

"Like I said: fucking delicious."

I'm spun around once again, my mouth on Finn's dick, my pussy getting rammed by a very horny Maverick, whose curses and grunts echo throughout the gym.

This time I'm on my hands and knees, Mav's hands on my hips controlling the speed of his fucking, mindful that I'm also sucking off Finn and biting would be frowned upon.

I spend more time in this position, licking and sucking on Finn's dick, I taste myself all over his shaft, licking it all up right up to the slit sitting on top of his swollen head. Finn's control is slipping, his moans rivaling Mav's. Typically, he's more reserved, but even Finn has his limits.

He tightens the rope, pulling me closer just as I swallow him down at the back of my throat.

Mav reaches around and plays with my clit as he continues thrusting inside me, hard and fast.

"Fuck, Mav, I'm not going to last much longer."

I hollow my cheeks on his next thrust and I swear I feel him grow inside my mouth. Finn pushes my head down an extra inch with the rope tight around my neck, his girth feels restricted in my throat making us both tremble with how good it feels.

"Fuck!" Finn cries out as he pulls out quickly, his fingers squeezing the base of his cock. I was sure he was going to come.

Behind me, Mav drives into me once more before he pulls out and turns me on my back where he begins to eat me again—licking my slit and sucking on my clit. I look up at Finn, his eyes dark with lust and love as he bends over me and kisses my mouth deeply—lovingly.

It's weird how they can be so animalistic and caring all at the same time.

Finn's hands trail down to my tits where he places them both, big and warm, over them and massages hard enough to make the walls of my pussy spasm against Mav's prodding tongue.

"She's so wet, Finn. So fucking wet."

Finn inches around me, his mouth never leaving my skin as he peppers me with tender kisses on my jaw, my neck, my tit, and his hands never leaving my flesh as he slides them along my sides. His mouth settles on my nipple, his tongue flicking the hard peak before he sucks it deep into his mouth as his thumbs press against my hip bones.

Giving my other nipple the same attention, his tongue circles over and over again before he nips at the tender flesh, making me gasp from the pleasure and pain.

Finn's finger is now on my clit as he pulls me up to a sitting position, forcing Mav to lick me up one more time before he stops and they're both looking at me with lust written all over their features.

Without speaking, Mav moves away from my pussy and straddles my chest taking Finn's rope and wrapping the silk around the palm of his hand until I'm forced to take his cock in my mouth. Just as Mav bottoms out, Finn's cock spears my pussy with a force that almost causes damage to Maverick's beautiful cock.

"Watch it, Finn. I need my cock attached to my body."

Finn doesn't respond, only grunts as he grabs my thighs and tilts me back. Mav's hand is at the back of my head as he lowers us back down, never missing a beat.

One hand on the octagon, Mav holds his weight as the other wraps around my throat. He doesn't care about ropes or anything else. I know from experience that all he wants is to feel his cock as I swallow him whole.

Finn's thrusts are getting harder, faster as I suck Mav's cock with more and more gusto. A thumb grazes my clit and I swear I'm about to lose my mind all over again. I'm trying really fucking hard to keep up with their frenzied fucking—my hands fly up to Mav's naked chest, fingers digging into his hard abs, nails leaving a mark—as my climax erupts inside me. They leave me no choice but to take Mav's dick out of my mouth so I can scream out the ecstasy of it all.

The first spurt of Mav's cum lands on my chin, the next on my lips. The rest of his orgasm is in my mouth. I swallow just as Finn roars out his own climax, causing aftershocks to tremor through my body. I take it all inside me. Filled with their cum, I heave a deep breath, willing my heart to slow down.

"If this is how you train, princess, no wonder you need to practice."

---

Waking up in a puppy pile of my guys might be my favorite way to start the day. After my training fuckery with Mav and Finn yesterday, we came back home, and Linc and East joined us for a movie marathon before crashing here. It was a much needed night with them, and I could see it on them as well as feel it in myself. East still seemed a little distant, but that's probably just me projecting.

Mav is wrapped around me from behind, his face nuzzled in my neck; East has an arm draped over us both, his hand resting on my hip; Lincoln is in front of me, his legs intertwined with mine, my head on his chest; and Finn is on the other side of him, as if watching over us all.

I don't want to move, I'd happily stay here all day, but my bladder is about to burst.

Slipping out from the entanglement of limbs without waking anyone feels impossible, but I do my best and slip into the bathroom. I freshen myself up once I'm done, wiping away the raccoon eyes that look back at me in the mirror, and run a brush through my hair.

"You okay?" Finn asks as he pops his head around the door. When he sees me standing in front of the mirror in my tank and boy shorts, he enters the room and shuts the door. I try not to drool over him as he stretches in front of me and he yawns, wearing even less than me. He pads sleeplly over to me and pulls me against his chest. "I miss you," he breathes the words into my hair as I wrap my arms around him.

"I miss you, too," I say before pressing my lips to one of the scars that adorn his chest.

"We going to talk about these bruises of yours anytime soon?" he asks quietly, and I stiffen in his arms. "You don't have to tell me, the others might not have noticed, Mav is usually too distracted by you being half naked, and I'm guessing you've told the others they're from sparring with Maverick and me… but I see them, Octavia. Just tell me you're not in trouble."

I gulp down, blinking back tears from how reasonable he's being and how much of a bitch I feel. "I'm not in trouble. I'll explain soon, just… just give me some time?"

He pulls back and clasps my chin in his finger and thumb. "I can do that, and I won't mention it to the others either, but whatever is going on, we're with you. You can let us in."

"I will," I murmur, his eyes fixed on my lips as I run my tongue over them. "I promise."

"That's all I ask." He captures my lips with his and I give myself over to his kiss. Letting him take everything he wants from me without question.

When he pulls back, letting me suck in some much needed oxygen, he holds me against his chest again. "I'm going back to Ocean Falls today to see my mom, if you want to try and see yours again?"

A shudder runs through me. I'm still waiting to hear back from Indi and Bentley, but maybe my mom might have an idea of where Dad might have hidden something. Assuming she'll see me this time anyway.

"Sure, maybe this time will be better."

"Let's hope so. Come on, I said I'd be there early." He takes my hand and pulls me from the bathroom. We find the others awake already, half dressed and sleepy eyed. "Breakfast, then Octavia and I are driving out to Ocean Falls."

Linc looks at me, as if checking that I'm okay, and I nod. It seems to appease him, cause he nods back.

We head downstairs and Smithy fusses around us all, sorting breakfast, and once we're fed, Finn ushers me next door to his car, and we make our way to Ocean Falls.

He keeps my hand clasped in his the entire way, leaving me to my thoughts in the way that he always does. It's why coming here with him is probably the least daunting it could be. I know he won't make me talk about everything that's swirling around in my head if I don't want to, but I also know he'd listen to me talk about it if I needed to.

His presence is enough to stop me falling in the well of anxiety though, even if I am teetering on the edge.

I'm not even sure if I want her to agree to see me, or if it'd be easier for her to just keep rejecting me. Rejecting me means I don't have to deal with the reality of her, of what happened to her, but that feels like running away from my problems. Again.

Except if she does want to see me, I still haven't figured out what the fuck I would even say to her.

We pull up out front again and the butterflies in my stomach start a riot.

"You've got this, pretty girl. Come on." Finn squeezes my hand before releasing me and climbing from the car. I take a deep breath and follow suit, rounding the car to join him at the door. He takes us to the receptionist, who smiles widely at him just like last time we were here.

"Mr. Knight, lovely to see you. Your mom checked back in last night, I assume you're here for her?"

"I am," he confirms to her, squeezing my hand again. "And Mrs. Royal."

Her smile drops a little. "I will see what I can do."

She disappears and we take a seat, waiting for her to return.

"It will be okay, whatever happens." Finn's reassurances barely break the surface of everything going on inside of me, but I lean into him and accept the comfort nonetheless. It's not until the receptionist reappears, looking wary.

"Your mom is waiting for you Mr. Knight."

"And Mrs. Royal?" he asks as I hold my breath.

"She agreed to see her daughter, albeit briefly. Though I must say, I don't know that this is a good idea." My heart pounds as her words sink in. I guess this is it, bad idea or not.

"Thank you Annie, we'll be fine I'm sure." Finn stands, pulling me up with him, and leads me through the frosted glass door we didn't make it through last time I was here. We walk down a sterile white hall in near-silence before he asks, "Do you want me to stay with you while you see your mom?"

"No, it's fine," I say, shaking my head. "It's probably better that I see her alone and you need to see your mom anyway, right?"

"I do, I need to talk to her about some stuff going on with Dad. I'll catch you up on that later, but even so, if you need me, I won't leave your side."

We pause in the hall outside of a door that says Emily Royal on the attached whiteboard. "I know, and I love you for it, but this is something I should do alone. Go, see your mom, do what you need to. I'll meet you at the car when we're done."

"Okay, but I have my phone if you need me."

I reach up and kiss him chastely before pushing him down the hall. "Go, I've got this." I smile at him, feeling like I look more confident than I actually feel. Once he turns the corner with a wave, I take a breath and knock on the door to my mom's room.

"Come in," her voice is quiet through the door, but clear enough to make out. Pushing on the door, I head inside, trying not to let her see how much my hands shake. I find her sitting on her bed, knees pulled up against her chest. Her dark hair is pulled back in a tight bun, she's wearing jeans and a white sweater, but they seem to hang from her thin frame. The glow I remember her having, the light in her eyes… none of that is present anymore. It's not surprising, but for some reason, I can't not see it. The woman looking back at me is a shadow of a human and less than a shadow of the woman I knew as my mother.

"What do you want, Octavia?" Her words are little more than a hiss as she sneers at me from across the room.

I pause in the middle of the room, not sure what to say. I clasp my hands in front of me, wringing them out, feeling like that little girl she left behind so long ago

"I said, what the fuck do you want, Octavia? Haven't you already done enough? Daddy's little princess ruining my life, three times over now. Have you come to fuck with me some more, demon spawn of mine? I don't know what I did to deserve a child like you, but if I could go back, I'd fucking abort you."

I suck in a breath at her tirade as tears spring in my eyes. "I didn't do anything to you! I thought you left us!"

She rolls her eyes at me and grabs a pack of cigarettes on the nightstand, lighting one up and sucking down the nicotine before turning back to me. "I did leave, because your daddy loved you more than me. We were in danger, but he always put you first. Everything he ever did was for you. I left, and I was finally happy. Free. Free of you, the shit that followed him around… and then you came of age and he decided once again you were more important than the rest of us."

"I don't understand…" I trail off, clenching my fists at my sides. I might not have had much idea what coming here would be like, but I definitely didn't expect this.

"Of course you don't," she says, blowing out another lungful of smoke. "Lose one to save one. I don't know how many fucking times I heard that stupid ultimatum. Do you know what it means, Octavia?" Her sneer makes me take a step back as I shake my head. "It means that to keep you, I had to be lost. To buy your freedom, your dad sold mine. To that monster. I was caged, trapped, tortured, raped, all so you could escape the life your daddy originally had you for. Fucking bullshit. And now you stand there, looking at me like a lost fucking puppy, like I have the answers to save you. Well, fuck you, Octavia. I'm not saving you ever again. Stop coming here. I don't want to see you. You died to me a long time ago, just like I did for you. Let's keep it that way."

She takes another drag on her cigarette before glaring at me once more. "Get the fuck out of here, little girl, before I really make you regret your existence."

I gulp, blinking back the tears in my eyes, and leave without another word.

My dad sacrificed her to save me. Just another person lost so I wouldn't have to be a Knight. Am I really doing the right thing with this deal with Harrison? Going against everything they sacrificed for me?

I guess it's too late now. I don't look at anyone as I leave Ocean Falls, but once I'm outside I slide down the side of the car and pull my knees up to my chest, letting the tears fall as the wounds my mother just ripped open bleed out.

I guess I really am an orphan after all.

# CHAPTER NINETEEN

## OCTAVIA

"So there was nothing?" My heart drops as Indi tells me the bad news.

"Sorry, V. We looked. The locker was a bust. If there was anything in it, it's not there anymore. Your dad only had the locker for two weeks. That was eighteen months ago." She grabs our coffee order from the drive-thru window, handing them to me before pulling off toward school.

"It's fine. We knew it was a long shot. Was everything okay with you and Alex?"

She glances at me as we drive through the center of the cove, biting her lip. "Yeah, we talked through everything again on the flight, and now I need to talk to Ryker. I already spoke to Dylan, he's chill, but before I do anything with Alex, the twins need to know. I'm not sure what it is between us, but there's something there… something about him that calls to a part of me that I didn't even know was there."

I nod, knowing exactly how she feels.

"How was visiting with your mom? Did she have any ideas about your dad's hidey holes?"

My stomach flips at the question, wishing I could just scrub that part of my weekend from my mind. "It was horrific."

She looks at me wide-eyed as we pull into school, and I give her the quick version of what happened, watching as she grows angrier on my behalf.

"Goddamn, what a bitch! Like, I know she's been through a lot, but it's hardly your fault. She's blaming you for the fuck ups of the people in your life. What an asshole."

I shrug as I unbuckle myself. "It is what it is, I guess. She doesn't want to see me, and I'm not going to make her. Finley said she'll likely live out the rest of her life in that place. She knows too much to be let out, for one, but also, due to her trauma, it won't be good for her to go back out in the real world. Not for a long time anyway. I'm sad she's suffered, but I have family now and if she doesn't want to be part of it, then that's her choice. She left me a long time ago."

The words taste like ash on my tongue. It's not a lie, but it's also not something I've fully accepted, despite what I'm saying. I thought she left me, but the possibility that we could've had a relationship has been skirting around the outside of my mind since the guys told me she was alive. That's no more than dust now and there's nothing that I can do about it.

I need to focus on what I can control.

Which is finding these fucking documents and unlocking this USB without asking Finn for help. I will if I have to, but I'd really rather not. I know he'll be pissed about everything and he'll try to stop me from doing what I'm determined to do.

"You and me, tonight. Girls night. Smithy can make us margs. Who gives a fuck that it's Monday? Media room, margs, and karaoke. That is what we need, my friend. Let's blow off some steam. It won't be the first time someone's gone to school with a hangover."

I match her grin and nod, "That sounds like perfection. But first, we must survive the day."

We climb from the car and find my guys, minus East, waiting for us. I try to shake off the sadness from thinking about my mom, and lose myself to the bickering of Mav and Indi and the predictability of school.

The day passes in a blur, and before I know it, Indi is bundling me back into her Wrangler after pulling me away from Linc—who told me we need to talk, not ominous at all—to get ready for girls night.

Being around Indi is like being around a whirlwind of energy. Her excitement is contagious and it's impossible not to get pulled in by her joy.

I officially have the best bestie in existence.

Once we're home, I follow her as she bounces inside, and I hear her squealing and laughing with Smithy as I take off my shoes and drop my bag.

"You're the best, Smithy!" she exclaims as she bounces back toward me. "Come on, you!" Grabbing my arm, she drags me toward the media room and I can't help but laugh at her.

"So what is the plan, oh sensei of joy?"

"There is no plan, *that* is the fun of it. Smithy is on pizza and marg duty. We may not be legal, but he's a big softie. As long as we keep it to three. That was the deal. And we just have some fun."

She pulls out the karaoke machine I'd forgotten was even in here and hooks it up to the big screen, "First, we need something cathartic. How about we go old school?"

She turns to the screen, flicking through the options, then glances at me over her shoulder, waging her brows at me. "Found it!"

The opening bars of *My Happy Ending* by Avril Lavigne start playing and I laugh at her. It is kind of perfect. She lifts one of the mics to her lips and starts singing as the lyrics appear on the screen, making a drama show of her performance, waving for me to join her. It takes me nearly a minute before I decide fuck it.

By the time Smithy appears with two margaritas and the biggest pepperoni pizza I've ever seen, my throat is scratchy from screaming at the top of my lungs, the old school pop-punk tunes being absolutely slayed, and not always in a good way.

I fall onto the couch, pulling a slice of the cheesy goodness, I take a bite while Indi finishes up *Bring Me to Life* by Evanescence.

"I might not be Amy Lee, but damn I love singing that song." Indi grins at me as she drops beside me, taking a sip of the icy drink, as *The Black Parade* starts playing in the background. "Goddamn that is good. Weak, but tasty regardless."

"Honestly, I'm surprised he put any alcohol in them at all." I shrug and grab another slice. Smithy makes the best damn pizza.

"Smithy is aware that teens are going to drink. He's a chill old guy. Any adult that thinks their kid doesn't drink is either stupid or delusional. Even the straight-A students kick back sometimes. I think he'd rather us drink here, where it's safe, than anywhere else."

I smirk at her, "God, could you imagine if someone like Mikayla's mom saw what I did on tour? She'd have a freaking conniption."

Indi bursts out laughing. "Oh my God, yes. I'd pay to see her face backstage at a show. Hell, just *at* a show. Did you see her when she came in to speak to Principal Evans after the whole, you-were-crowned-queen thing? Someone was *not* happy."

"No! Why on earth was she there about that?"

"Apparently, Mikayla was being bullied by you and Blair." She cackles before taking a slice of pizza. "Unfortunately for Mikayla, enough people had witnessed her bullshit and came forward before it even got that far, and now she's been outcast as a snitch."

"Holy shit," I giggle. "Can you imagine if *that* was the worst part of our year? Being dethroned?"

"I think Mikayla would've perished at the first obstacle you faced, my friend." She raises her glass in a toast before taking a sip as *Face Down* by The Red Jumpsuit Apparatus starts playing. "Oh my God, I love this song!"

She drops the glass and her slice and starts dancing around the media room, not giving a fuck as I laugh at her antics. "Come on! Dance it off, shake it out! Meredith Grey says this shit is the best way to shake off a funk. If her and Swifty say it, it must be true."

I shake my head but stand with her, dancing as the playlist changes to *Miss Murder* by AFI. Now this is a fucking classic.

We sing at the top of our lungs once more and I thank God for my best friend. This night is exactly what I needed.

My phone buzzes on the couch, so I prance over and grab it, my smile dropping when I see the message on the screen.

Harrison: Your time is nearly up, Miss Royal, which means our deal is about to expire. I already gave you one extension. Do not disappoint me. You might find it's the last thing you do.

---

After being dropped back to reality by Harrison's message last night, girls night turned somber, and Indi headed over to see the twins to try and talk to them about the whole Alex thing. She offered to stay with me, but there was no point.

Harrison effectively dropped a bomb on us and killed the mood.

So I decided to skip school today—after I messaged the guys in a group chat to let them know I was okay but wouldn't be around—and have spent the best part of my day reading through all of my dad's journals that I'd stashed down in the music room. I hadn't gone through them with Indi the other day, we had enough stuff, and older journals.

These journals are from more recently, so I'm hoping theres something in them that will help with this fucking USB drive. I don't even know if what I need is on the fucking drive, but it's all I've got, dammit. I even tried to open it on my laptop, but just like Bentley said, it asked for an encryption key.

"More coffee, Miss Octavia?" I look up and find Smithy hovering in the doorway of the music room, while I'm in the middle of a dozen open journals. I bet I don't even look crazy.

He already has a steaming mug in his hands, because he's freaking awesome like that. "You're a God, Smithy. Thank you."

"I wish I could be more help—"

"It's fine. This is something I need to do myself. Plus, I don't know that I'd feel okay with anyone else reading this stuff. It feels like an invasion of Dad's privacy enough, me reading them. At least I was there for a lot of this, even if this is like a window into his mind. But so far, there's just ramblings. Though," I pause, finding the journal I was reading earlier. "I've noticed these symbols reoccurring throughout the journals. Do you have any idea what they might be?"

He takes the journal, flicking through the pages at the lines and dots that make no sense to me. It's almost like a code, or shorthand, that I don't have the cypher for.

"I'm sorry, I don't know. I could keep looking if you like, but even as well as I knew your father, he always did like to play things close to the vest. They could be something, but they could be nothing but drunken scribbles."

"Don't I know it," I huff. "Thank you anyway. I texted Bentley earlier, so I'm hoping I hear from him soon. He flew out to Sydney after he left here on Saturday, then he was going to go from there to Prague, then Rome, Paris, and London. The last few he thought he could do in a day with how quick the flights are. So I'm just hoping he comes up with something."

He offers me the mug and sits down on the couch opposite me. "Would it be the worst thing if he didn't?"

I look at him wide eyed. "How can you—"

He cuts me off with a wave of his hand. "The Knights are no joke, Miss Octavia. You are free, and I can't imagine Harrison wants to give up his power to you. If you don't find the documents, you remain free, yes? I know that means that the boys wouldn't be, but this is a life they are used to. Maybe it would be for the best. Anything that Harrison wants this badly… I can't imagine it would be good to give it to him."

I chew on my lip, because I know he's right about that last bit, I've thought about it a dozen times since I made the damn deal. "I know, but I can't leave them tied to the Knights. They've been through so much, and they've saved me time and again. They deserve to be free, to pick their own futures."

"I know they do, Miss Octavia, but sacrificing your own future probably isn't the best way to buy theirs. Along with whatever else is on those documents that Harrison wants."

I frown, feeling hopeless again. "I thought you were on board with my plan? You didn't say anything before."

"I will always support you, Miss Octavia. But I can't deny that I'm worried. I didn't want to be overbearing, you're nearly eighteen. It's not my place to try and tell you what to do. I just want to make sure that you've thought about all of the outcomes here."

"I have," I say, chewing the inside of my lip. "But when I asked Harrison for an extension, he said that if I don't find the documents… well, I might not be free anyway."

His brow furrows when I tell him what I've been holding back for the last week. "Show me."

I pull up the message from Harrison and show him my phone. His face turns a deep shade of red as he reads the message. "That man—" he blows out a breath, like he's too angry to keep speaking. "—Well, I suggest you keep looking, and I'll try to work out a plan for just in case you don't find them. Maybe one for if you do."

He stands and leaves me sitting among the pages of the journals, coffee in hand, wondering if I've managed to disappoint everyone in my life with this deal I've made.

I keep reading, and find nothing but the weird code that might not be anything anyway. Regardless, I copy it from the pages to my notebook, in date order, in the hope that something makes sense or I find the cypher for it.

My phone buzzes, pulling me from my trance, and my stomach rumbles as I start paying attention to the world around me again.

Linc: I'm heading over. You weren't at school and we still need to talk.

Me: Okay, see you in a few.

I stand up, dusting down my leggings, straightening my sweater that falls off one shoulder, and make my way upstairs, running a hand through my hair as I go so I don't look a total freaking mess. Not that Lincoln would care, but I do.

I reach the kitchen just as Linc appears at the back door. He's still partially in his uniform, the arms of his shirt rolled up to his elbows, the top few buttons undone, and his hair looks like he's run his hands through it all day.

"Where were you?" He asks once he closes the door and moves toward me. He leans against the counter, arms folded, and I quirk a brow at him.

"Hi Linc. Yeah, I'm okay. Thanks for asking. How was your day? Oh, dull? I'm sorry to hear that." I deadpan, but he doesn't move an inch. I let out a sigh, running a hand through my hair again. "I was home all day. I just needed some alone time."

He continues to watch me as if looking for the lie. It wasn't one, not entirely, so he won't find it. My stomach churns once more at keeping stuff from him, but he nods once and then visibly loosens up.

"Sorry, I worry. And you never go MIA." I push myself up to sit on the edge of the counter, and he moves to stand between my legs. "I meant it yesterday when I said we needed to talk."

"I really hate that sentence," I tell him and he kisses me softly, like he's trying to make up for whatever it is he's going to say already.

When he pulls back, I already know I'm going to hate whatever falls out of his mouth next. He clamps his lips together when I sigh. "Just tell me."

"I have a date with Georgia at Harrison's insistence."

"I thought that shit was over with." I am going to give Harrison fucking *hell* about this. Lincoln is supposed to be free of that skank. He still looks like he's holding something back, something that I don't want to know. "When?"

"Friday," he tells me and I clench my fists. "It was supposed to be Saturday, but I refused. That's your day. Friday was the compromise."

I grind my teeth together, trying to keep a lid on my shit, because this is not Lincoln's fault. Fighting Harrison is like trying to ride a surfboard in a tsunami. Especially when he has to live with him. *This* is exactly why I made that fucking deal in the first place. Lincoln shouldn't be subjected to this bullshit.

Especially not by his fucking father.

"It's fine," I grind out and his shoulders stiffen under my fingers. "And yes I'm pissed, but not at you."

"Octavia—"

"You don't have to apologize, Linc. This isn't your fault. Am I furious? Of course I am, imagine if the roles were reversed and I was being forced to date, be engaged to, and fuck knows what else to someone."

His eyes darken to thunder clouds at my words. "I know, I'm working on getting out of it, it's just—"

"That your dad is a fucking psychopath? Yeah I know." I let out a deep breath, running my hands through the end of his hair. "We'll figure something out."

"I love you," he says, resting his forehead against mine. "One day we'll be free, and when that day comes—"

I briefly press my lips to his then pull back. "Don't make promises, Lincoln. The Knights are unpredictable assholes. But we *will* deal with Georgia. Even if I have to do it my damn self."

# CHAPTER TWENTY

"He found something?" Indi squeaks as I close my locker and pull my bag up on my shoulder. "Do you know what it is?"

"No, Bentley is all kinds of weird about talking over the phone. He reminds me of my dad a bit like that. Though, with everything I know now, my dad's aversion to technology is kind of understandable." I pull out my keys as we make our way out of school. "But he flew back this morning. He's coming straight to the house when he lands, so I need to haul ass home."

"Okay, call me when you know what it is, if it's what you need. And if it's not, we'll work out an emergency plan. I might not exactly be on board with you being a Knight, but I know doing this for the guys is important to you, so I'll support you no matter what."

"And that is why you're my best bitch." She grins before hugging me quickly then darting around to her Wrangler.

"Call me! Gotta go deal with Ryker fallout from yesterday!" She jumps in her Wrangler and I laugh as I slide into the Range Rover, waiting for her to reverse before I even start the car. I catch sight of my guys coming out of the door, and pull out of my space before they can question what I'm doing.

Just two more days until I can stop hiding shit from them.

I have no idea how they did it. Keeping secrets is fucking exhausting. Especially ones like this. All I want is to tell them the truth, but I'm also aware of the consequences of that.

I try not to think about it and turn up my sound system as *Street Lightning* by The Summer Set starts playing. Losing myself to music is always the answer when the voices in my head get too loud. And right now, there is so much going on that I've pushed aside to deal with later that the voices are more like a stadium full of angry fans.

It's *loud.*

Just not for much longer, I hope.

I come to a stop at the gate and see Bentley's car coming down the street, so I wait for him to pull up behind me before I tap the code in. I drive into the garage, darting into the house and opening the front door for him just as he's about to knock.

"Miss Royal," he says with a smile.

"Come in," I utter, waving him in the house and closing the door. "Do you want coffee?"

He nods, yawning at me. "Yes, please. The coffee on the flight from London was abysmal."

We head into the kitchen, finding Smithy already pouring coffee. That guy really is a saint.

"Miss Octavia, I have dinner in the oven warming already. You're welcome to join us, Mr. Kensington."

"Thank you, but after we're done here, I'm going home to sleep for three days."

Smithy nods as he slides a mug of coffee in front of us both. "Of course."

"Thank you." Bentley pulls a laptop out of his bag and boots it up as he reaches back down. "I found this in Sydney," he says, pushing a notebook across to me, and an envelope with my name on it. "Then I found this in Prague, and this in London." He produces another USB and what looks like a children's coding toy.

"What is all of this?"

"I didn't read the letter, that was obviously for you. But the journal is what seems like a log of someone's movements, maybe a few people. Part of it reads like a ledger. The USB I think is the encryption key, and the cypher… well I'm not sure what that's for yet, but let's have a look, shall we? Do you have the other USB I gave you?"

"I have it, let me go and retrieve it." Smithy heads off into his quarters, while I stare at the envelope with my name like it's trying to kill me.

I don't know what it says, but I'm fairly certain that whatever it is, I'm not ready to read it. I might make out like I've moved past my dad's death, but I'm very aware that I still haven't fully dealt with my grief. I've shoved it down since I got back to Echoes Cove and locked it in a box, put it on a shelf, and shut the door on the room I stored it in. Reading that letter is going to rip away all of the chains I locked around that door. My focus has been purely on dealing with everything that's been going on, and graduation.

Grief hasn't really factored into the last nine months.

I can't believe it's been nine months since he was taken from me.

I choke down that realization as Smithy reappears, USB in hand. "Here you are," he says, handing it over to Bentley. He puts the two drives into the slots on his laptop then hands it over to me.

"You should be the one to open the files," he says as I look at the screen. He reaches over and taps a few buttons and the screen whirrs to life, the encryption box popping up again. Then he clicks something else, the screen flashes, and a folder opens.

The top file, a video file, is titled 'Octavia', so I click on it, my heart in my mouth.

A window opens, and a small cry works up my throat as the screen comes to life and I see my dad's face staring back at me. He's fiddling with the camera before taking a seat on the chair placed in front of it.

"Octavia," he starts, a sad smile on his face. "If you're watching this, I imagine that you're confused, pissed off, and probably crying." I hiccup a laugh as a tear runs down my cheek. Hearing his voice again rips me in two, but seeing his face… I hadn't realized that I'd forgotten his smile a little until now. "There's a lot I should have told you, but I wanted to keep you away from the darkness that has haunted our family for decades. If I'm dead, chances are you know about the Knights. I'm sure they've tried to reclaim you, I just hope that I did enough to prepare you for them. I tried everything I could think of to keep you out of their grasp, but I am just one man. Just remember that even within the pits of darkness, light is easily found. You, Bug, were that light for me. I hope that my death hasn't dimmed that light too much.

"I've spent years collecting the information on this drive, it's everything you need to ensure Harrison comes to heel. I don't know what will have transpired for you to find this, but trust your gut. You always had the best judgment. If you've ended up a part of them, I understand. If you found your mom, I'm sorry. I made the only decision I had at the time.

"I hope the boys have helped bring you into the loop, and always trust Smithy. He will lead you right while I can't. I trust him with your life, so even if you take no other advice from me, take that part. Trust him. Implicitly. I don't have much time, just know that I love you, Bug, whether I'm there with you or not, I'll never really leave you. I'm just sorry our time was cut short.

"And if you need help working out my codes, just remember raindrops."

He looks off screen, and I hear Mac's voice calling him for rehearsal, "I have to go, Bug. I love you. Always. Trust yourself, trust your friends, those boys will always look out for you, and trust Smithy. I hope everything I collected is enough to help."

The screen flickers to black as tears silently travel down my face as I stare at the black screen. I didn't expect that. Not at all. I thought the letter would be bad, but seeing his face…

I take a deep breath and shove it down to deal with later as I swipe the tears from my cheeks. "Let's look at these files shall we?" I don't look at either of them as I close the video window. If I see the pity or sadness on their faces, I'll break, and we don't have time for that.

I start opening the other files, and there is all sorts of information in here: videos, voice recordings, copies of emails, Shit that would bury Harrison, Charles, and God knows how many other Knights. There are names of senators and people in just about any other position of power there is in here. "Holy shit."

"Something like that," Bentley agrees. "This is definitely what he wants from you. What do you want to do with it?"

I chew on my lip and look at Smithy, remembering our conversation from the other day. "We should make a copy of it, in case Harrison reneges on his side of the deal. Or if anything should happen to me, because he's a dick like that."

Smithy nods, almost looking like he's proud.

"Will you hold the copy for me?" I ask Bentley. "No one around here knows you, or that you're linked to me."

"I'd be happy to." He smiles, glancing at Smithy. "And if something should happen, then what?"

"Then we release the documents to the press." I grin wickedly. "Burn them all to the fucking ground."

---

The car pulls up in front of the building where I met Harrison the last time he called on me. I take a deep breath and open the car door as it comes to a stop, making sure that the USB is in my pocket. Looking up at the building, a feeling of foreboding settles over me.

If Harrison works out I made copies, he'll kill me. Bentley assured me he wouldn't know, that he masked the copy, but my stomach still flips at the possibility.

The guys all knew something was off with me at school today, I told them I just didn't feel well, and they left me to myself, but I could tell they weren't fully buying it. They stopped questioning me though. I'm just glad that after this is final, I can tell them.

As of Saturday, I'm eighteen, I'll be the regent heir, and I get to tell them what's been going on. I'm both looking forward to it, and dreading it. I'll just be glad that there will be no more secrets. I'm so tired of secrets.

I make my way through the lobby to the private elevator in the back, hitting the button for the top floor. When the doors close, I relax a little, knowing that once they reopen, I'm going to have to be on edge the entire meeting, and probably for the entire time I'm associated with the Knights. Likely after too, but who knows what the hell life is going to look like then?

The number above the door ascends, and when the 'P' shows for the top floor, the *bing* sounds to tell me the doors are opening. I straighten my shoulders and find Harrison standing outside the elevator waiting for me.

"Nothing like sailing close to the wind, Miss Royal." He looks down at me, arms folded over his chest, and it takes all of my willpower to not roll my eyes at him.

"It wasn't the easiest of tasks. But I have what you want."

He purses his lips and looks me over. "Well, let's go check that shall we?"

He turns and heads toward the office we met in previously, expecting me to follow. The audacity of this guy. I follow, because I have no other option. He enters the office, leaving the door open for me, and I take the seat I occupied previously.

"Let me see the documents."

"First," I say, pulling an envelope from my bag. "I had a contract drawn up. To confirm everything we agreed to when we spoke last, including the freedom of

Lincoln, Maverick, and Finley. I added Easton considering his newly discovered bloodline. Considering your unwillingness to stick to our agreement the last few weeks, and yes I am talking about Lincoln and Georgia, you haven't exactly instilled confidence in me that you'll keep your word." He scowls at me as I slide the papers across the desk at him. "Once you have signed, I'll show you what I found."

He grinds his teeth as he picks up the contract that Smithy and Chase helped me put together last night, and I try not to smile at his obvious anger.

"You'll note that I haven't amended any terms, just what we originally agreed to, including my limited time as a Knight. The only additions I made are that I get to tell the guys on Saturday, my birthday, myself. That if you break this deal, you give up your seat as Regent, effective immediately, but the four of them remain free regardless."

"I can see," he grinds out, flicking through the pages of the contract. He grabs a pen, and signs the document before slamming his pen on the desk.

I take the contract from him, tucking it back away, before I pull the USB drive from my pocket. "This is what you asked me to get." I say, sliding it across the desk. I deleted the video from my dad, Bentley ensured it wasn't retrievable, because that was for me, and Harrison can suck a dick.

Anyone would think I'd just pushed dog shit across the desk from the look on his face. "What is that?"

"I just told you. It's what you asked for." He sneers at the drive before swiping it into the top drawer on his desk. "You don't want to check it?"

"I signed your contract, I know how much you want this deal, Miss Royal. I trust that what I wanted is on there. I'll go through it in my own time."

Well, that wasn't what I expected at all. "Very well, if that is all…" I trail off.

"Not quite. Lincoln will still need to go on his evening with Georgia tomorrow. I require it to finalize my deal with her father, but after that, he will be free from any responsibilities to me and the Knights."

"That wasn't our agreement." I clench my fists in my lap as he grins at me.

"No it wasn't but I have the drive now, Miss Royal. It's just one small term. And then you get what you wanted." I should've known he'd pull something. He didn't expect the contract, so this is his power play.

Asshole.

"Fine, but anything after this I will consider a breach of our contract, and I will go above you if needed." I push the chair back and stand, smoothing out my blazer as I do. "I'll see you on Saturday."

He grins at me as he relaxes back in his chair. "Yes, yes you will."

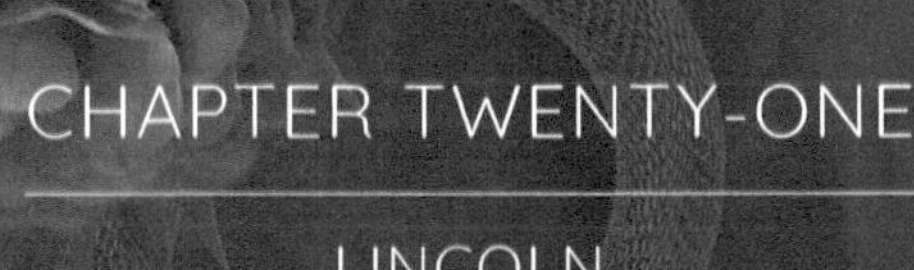

# CHAPTER TWENTY-ONE

## LINCOLN

The tension in this car is fucking insane. So much has been going on that I haven't had much time to spend with Octavia, but since I told her about my so called date tonight, she's been pissed. I get it. Tomorrow is her birthday, we were supposed to be hanging out tonight, but my hands are tied. Harrison's threats against her have been ramping up, and I feel fucking sick.

The thought of breathing the same air as Georgia makes me want to suffocate.

My knuckles are white on the steering wheel from my vice grip on it. I'm trying not to be pissed that she's hung up on the Georgia thing again, but every time it comes up, it's like she doesn't trust me and *that* pisses me off.

I know the waves of tension aren't coming from just me.

Even yesterday, she said she felt sick, but I'm sure it was more than that. She's been so distant lately, and I know she's hiding something, but I can't work out what. She's never hidden stuff from us before which makes me terrified… but for some reason, with her, it comes out as anger.

"Are we going to talk about this?" she asks, the bite of her words not as bad as they were earlier.

I glance over at her, trying not to let my rage shine through. "What is there to talk about?"

"Don't give me your bullshit." She snaps. "I'm tired of this Lincoln, can we just get this night over with and deal with everything else tomorrow?"

That is fucking it. I swerve the car off the main road, pulling onto the dirt before turning and glaring at her. "My bullshit? You're the one who's angry. I thought this whole Georgia thing was clear between us!"

"So did I! You're the one who's been walking around like this is my fault all morning!" she yells before climbing out of my Cayenne and slamming the door.

*Fuck me.*

I am so sick of everything to do with Georgia, especially when it affects

Octavia like this, but I'm pissed too. She leans back against the car and I climb out, slamming my door as well as I walk around the car toward her.

"This is fucking ridiculous. You're hiding something, and you're acting like you're pissed about Georgia to hide it. I know you, Octavia. You know I don't give a fuck about her, I fucking love *you.*" The words fall from my lips so easily. The truth isn't always that easy for me, but telling her that is simple. I grab her blazer and pull her toward me a few steps, her hands pressing on my chest as my lips fall on hers, and I devour her. I walk her backward until she's pressed up against the car, trapped between me and it, not relinquishing the control I have over her breath. The power I have over her body.

When I pull back, she pants as I lean my forehead against hers.

"I love you too," she whispers as she closes her eyes. If my heart wasn't already like a stampede of wild horses, it sure as fuck is now.

Maybe I need to show her just how serious I am about the fact that she is it for me.

"When will you understand that there is no one else for me?" My fingers trail up the soft, supple skin of her thigh and slip under her skirt, teasing along the edges of her lace panties.

My dick twitches at the wet heat. Fuck I love when she's ready for me. I swear the fighting turns her on. "Maybe you need a quick reminder that you are mine."

"Maybe, I do."

I don't hesitate. My fingers are inside her before she finishes her last syllable, the word ending on a moan as I push deep into her wet heat.

Stepping fully between her parted legs, I rub my already hardened cock over her naked thigh. "Feel that? You do this to me. You. *Only* fucking you." I punctuate my words with the curling of my fingers and revel in her gasp.

Her fucking mouth will be the death of me. Not able or willing to resist her plump lips, I'm on her in a heartbeat. My lips devouring, my tongue searching, my breath mingling with hers. I'm not being gentle. Fuck that. I'm fucking her mouth with the same determination my fingers are fucking her pussy.

"You're so fucking wet, Octavia. You like this, don't you? Making me fucking insane. You like to push me?" Her eyes flash as my fingers curl around her long tresses, angling her face so the only thing she can see is me. My lust, my need. My fucking love for her.

Retreating my fingers, I don't blink as I pull down the zipper of my slacks and pop off the button until my engorged dick is out and begging for her wet hole.

I push Octavia onto the hood of my car—my hips nestled between her legs—and admire the art that is her body. Fucking hell, she's perfect.

"Be careful, Octavia. Don't fuck up the paint job on my Porsche." I don't give two fucks about my car. I can buy ten more like it. But what I do like is giving her ultimatums. Giving her limits. Inevitably, she'll push the line and just the thought makes me harder than fucking steel.

"If you cared so much, you'd fuck me against that tree over there." Smart girl.

I'm done playing, though. I need to be inside her.

Flipping her uniform skirt over her hips, I scan her half naked form before zeroing in on the wet spot she's left on her panties. I can't help the smirk that creeps up the corners of my lips. I flick my gaze to hers and she just shrugs. She knows exactly what I'm looking at.

"You make me wet, Linc. Even when we fight. *Especially* when we fight. That shouldn't be a surprise to you." It's not, but I won't lie, it turns me the fuck on.

My hand lands on her panties and without preamble, I push them to the side—my other hand on my dick—and I sink inside her wet, hot, pussy.

I sigh at the feel of her walls squeezing my cock. I almost don't want to move, but the need to fuck her rules above all else.

Octavia's entire body bows at my intrusion. Her chest reaching for the sky while I push down on her hips and thrust twice inside her, hard enough to make her jolt.

"You know what I'm going to do?"

"I think you're already doing it." I can barely hear her words, they're so breathy.

"Not yet, but I'm about to." I plunge back inside her so hard, I think the actual fucking car may have moved an inch.

Again, I'm not gentle. I pull out slowly and then slam back into her, stealing her breath on every plunge.

"I'm going to…" grabbing the back of her thighs, I push them against her chest, giving me deeper access, "… make it crystal fucking clear…" I pull out, waiting for her whimper before I slam my dick back inside her again. "… that my cock is. Only. Yours." Every word is punctuated with a thrust so deep, I'm certain she can feel me inside her fucking soul. "Do. You. Fucking. Under. Stand?"

I don't realize I'm practically screaming until the silence falls all around and all I can hear is the sound of my dick plunging in and out of Octavia's hungry pussy. She doesn't answer—out of stubbornness or because her voice is caught in our rhythm, I have no fucking clue. It doesn't matter.

I bring my face close to hers so the only thing she can see is the truth in my eyes. Slowing down my thrusts, I place two fingers on her clit and torture her with slow circles while my dick leisurely fucks her, in and out. I want to see her come—watch as she completely falls apart in my arms—and then I want to destroy every doubt she's ever had about my love for her. My devotion to her.

"Feel that, Octavia?" My free hand tweaks one of her nipples beneath her button-down all the while keeping my rhythm on her clit. "Do you feel what you do to me?" She nods, her mouth open and breaths coming in small hiccups. I know that sound. It's my cue she's about to fucking come all over my dick.

Fuck, I love her.

Lifting my thumb to her mouth, I push it in. "Suck." No hesitation, she wraps her pretty little lips around my digit and sucks like a fucking pro.

"Good girl."

And then I make her come with that same thumb on her swollen clit.

I don't slow as her torso lifts from the hood. In fact, I fuck her even harder. I go even deeper. Seeking out that place inside her that makes her scream my name.

Octavia's arms search out something—anything—to grab onto, but all she's got is her own clothes. I watch as her fingers reach for her shirt and in half a second, she's pulling—the buttons flying and bouncing off my new paint job. Fucking hell.

My name is spilling from her open mouth as my dick continues to fuck her, helping her come down from her very vocal orgasm. Her cum is coating my cock with every plunge inside her, testing my control.

When she finally settles back down, I decide to make it last just a little longer.

Pulling her back onto her feet, I slip out just the few seconds it takes me to turn her around and place her hands on the hood. Her panties are in my way again and instead of being a gentleman, I rip that shit right off before I slam back in from behind—my mouth at the shell of her ear.

"You're mine, Octavia."

I've got both hands on her tits and I'm fucking her raw, animal-like, grunting and growling every time I bottom out. I can't help the pride I feel when her breaths whoosh out of her lungs.

"But more importantly…" I slam one final time inside her and freeze as my entire body shudders—my legs trembling—with pure, unadulterated pleasure. My cum is filling her tight little pussy, coating her walls with my mark. My very existence.

"More importantly, I'm yours."

Reaching up, I place the palm of my hand on her jaw and turn her beautiful, satiated face toward me. I kiss her with every tender fiber in my soul. Mouths searching, tongues dancing, we seal this angry fuck into a promise.

"I'm yours, Octavia. Always."

---

Pacing the kitchen waiting for Harrison to deign me with his presence has me on edge. It's Octavia's birthday and I wanted to be over at her place already. Maverick and Finley are already out picking up the cake and dozen cupcakes we ordered for her. East is grabbing the gift from the jewelers, because the last part wasn't finished until last night.

All of it has me on edge.

I'm telling Harrison I'm done. I've tried to tell him a dozen times, but this time, I'm going to make him listen. I don't care what he threatens, or what manipulations he has tucked away, I am *done.*

I turn to pace back across the kitchen as Harrison walks down the hall toward me. Pausing, I wonder if the apocalypse is coming, because… Harrison is *smiling.*

"Good morning, son." He claps my shoulder as he strides past me and pours himself a cup of coffee.

*What in the name of the pod people is this?*

"You seem like you're in a good mood," I pry, moving to lean against the table as he sips on his drink.

"It's a beautiful morning, and my plans are finally coming to fruition. What's not to be happy about?"

This is weird as fuck. I run a hand through my hair, and figure if he's in a good mood, this is as good a time as any to broach the subject of Georgia. "Speaking of plans, I wanted to speak to you about Georgia."

"Yes, indeed. I set the wedding date with her father last night. Let the planning begin."

I fold my arms across my chest, mentally preparing myself for battle. "No."

"Oh?" He raises his brows at me, still smiling, and it's creepy as fuck. "You've decided you're done fighting for the Royal girl's life? If you don't care about hers, maybe I'll go after your bastard brother's? I'm sure you care for him. Which of them will it be? The girl or the brother? One of them will die should you chose to disobey me."

"Why are you so fucking twisted?" I hiss, my battle-ready walls crumbling.

He waves me off as he takes another mouthful of his coffee. "Oh, don't get so worked up, Lincoln. Your little girlfriend already went to war for you. The wedding is off. I spent last night finalizing the deal so you can scurry away with your dick fully owned by the Royal bitch."

I try to disguise my shock. "What do you mean?"

"It's good to see she's a woman of her word. The Royal girl came to me a month ago, bartering once that contract of Stone's came to light, and we reached an… agreement."

My stomach drops at the glee on his face. What the fuck did she do?

"What agreement?" I ask, my jaw clenched. Fucking Octavia, why would she hide this from us? From me?

"She bought your freedom. Yours and your friends'. As of today, you are free from the Knights. Your trust funds were released without condition on the day we made the agreement. You will benefit from everything, as you would've as a member, but you are free from us."

My stomach twists, because there's no way he'd let me go. Let us all go. What the fuck did Octavia offer him?

"What was the rest?"

His eyes sparkle with glee as he finishes his drink and places his mug down on the counter. "She offered up herself. Along with some other things of Stone's that I was after. She will be my heir apparent, and now… she's mine."

Without another word he strides past me, grinning from ear to ear.

This doesn't make sense. She wouldn't.

Except she would.

Fucking woman is infuriating. She has no idea what the fuck she's done. Harrison doesn't stick to deals he makes unless they're entirely beneficial to him. Ever.

Rage pools in my stomach. She lied to us, kept secrets, after berating us, me, for doing that to her when she came back here.

Why wouldn't she speak to us first? We would have come up with another way.

Fuck.

I grip my hair, willing the pain to tug me back to reality, but anger rolls over me, creating a red haze over everything. Grabbing my keys, I storm from the house, going to the front gate without even really thinking.

Before I realize it, I'm standing in front of her gate, anger boiling over, when I see her appear in her front door. She waves at me and moves toward her car. The door opens and I lose sight of her as the engine starts.

That's when I feel the heat on my face, my ears ringing as I watch the flames engulf the black metal, the explosion knocking me to my knees as smoke billows into the sky. I blink, hoping, praying she wasn't in the car, or even near it, but I saw her open the door. She was right there. I tap in the code to the gate and my feet are moving before I can stop myself, but I'm stopped by a tackle from the side.

I try to fight them off, I need to get to her. I need to get to my girl. The world around me blurs in on itself, my focus solely on helping her.

"Master Saint." Smithy holds me down as I scream and struggle to get to the girl who holds my heart.

"Master Saint, you can't." His voice is firmer this time, and I turn to look at him, seeing the truth in his glassy eyes.

"Smithy, she… I…" The words just won't come out, everything good about the world has just… I can't even think it… I can't concentrate. My world is crumbling around me and I struggle to breathe. "She…"

His head hangs as he finally loosens his hold, sirens blaring in the distance. "I know, Master Saint. I know."

*Octavia.*

# CHAPTER TWENTY-TWO

## MAVERICK

I smile at the girl in the bakery, flirting in the hopes that she moves a little faster so we can get back to our girl quicker. I wouldn't have agreed to this stupid little errand if V hadn't asked for the morning to herself. I've been wanting to go to her since midnight to wish her a happy birthday. Birthdays have always been her thing and I refuse to let this year be any different, even with the shit show we find ourselves in.

Sirens blare outside, followed by a fire truck, ambulance, and police cars flying down Main Street.

"What the fuck was that?"

Finn rolls his eyes at me as the woman behind the counter appears with our order. "I'm sure it's nothing. Come on, we need to get back. I want to see Octavia."

He pays for the cakes while I grab the boxes and we head outside to Linc's SUV. My Ducati and his Lamborghini were not suitable for the sheer amount of cake that Indi told us to order. I'm not sure how any of us are going to eat this much cake.

I lay the cakes out in the trunk and hop in the passenger seat, my knee bouncing with excitement as we head back toward Linc's place.

When we turn onto their road, the car rolls to a stop, a line of traffic halting us in place. "What the…?"

I see the smoke first and something inside me tells me to get the fuck out of the car.

"Mav?"

I ignore Finn as I bail. Panic has me in a choke hold and I start running up the road, through the traffic, not wanting to believe what I can see in front of me. The barrier around the Saint and Royal houses from the first responders aren't enough to keep me out.

Finn reaches me, and I realize he bailed too. I push through the crazed masses and find Lincoln standing with Smithy and East. The looks on their faces… I can't…

*No, no, no.*

"Where is she?" I ask as I run toward them. Lincoln doesn't even look my way, he's just looking through the gate to Octavia's house.

"Mav—" Finn starts, but I don't pay attention.

I move closer, looking in the direction of Linc's gaze and see the dying blaze, the burnt out car, and part of the Royal place is damaged, the smoke a light gray, but I still don't see her. My heart pounds, while my stomach twists.

"Where is she?!" My words are more of a bellow as I turn back to face them.

"Master Riley…"

I fall to my knees, my legs not able to keep me standing as something inside of me breaks.

---

Since Smithy moved us all away from the scene in front of the Royal house, I've been hammering on the punching bag in Lincoln's basement. My knuckles are split, my blood runs rivulets to the ground, but I feel nothing.

Nothing but rage.

She can't be gone.

I can't accept that.

Music blares through the speakers, blocking everyone out. I don't want to see any of them. They're too busy pretending they don't feel, too, looking into how this could have happened.

After Lincoln explained what happened, I left the table. Smithy is working with the morgue, or so he said when he came down to speak to me, but I wasn't in a talking mood.

I'm still not.

The only thing that is going to make this better is it not happening. Or bleeding out whoever is responsible. Slowly. Oh so slowly.

Until then, I'll make myself bleed for not being able to save her.

The music cuts out, and I turn to scream at whoever is trying to fuck with me. I find Indi standing at the bottom of the stairs. Her face is stained with tears, but I still don't let myself feel anything.

"What the fuck are you doing down here?"

"Don't start with me, Pixie."

I turn back to the bag and beat on it. I don't know who is responsible, but when I find out…

"Fuck you! You don't get to hide away and be an asshole right now."

"Indi," I growl. "I don't want to be an asshole to you right now, but asshole is all I've got, so back the fuck off."

"What is wrong with you?!" she screams at me, putting herself between me and the bag, pushing on my chest. "How can you just stand there, like she isn't gone? Like this wasn't so obviously Harrison? How are you not burning the entire fucking world down?"

She hits me, pushes me, and I let her. I deserve it. I should have protected her harder. I should have worked harder to make her leave. If she hadn't stayed, she wouldn't be…

Tears run down Indi's face as she whales on me, and I take every hit without a word until she falls against me, sobs wracking though her. Only then do tears threaten to fall down my face.

I fight them, because I know if they fall, if I let myself feel, there won't be any coming back.

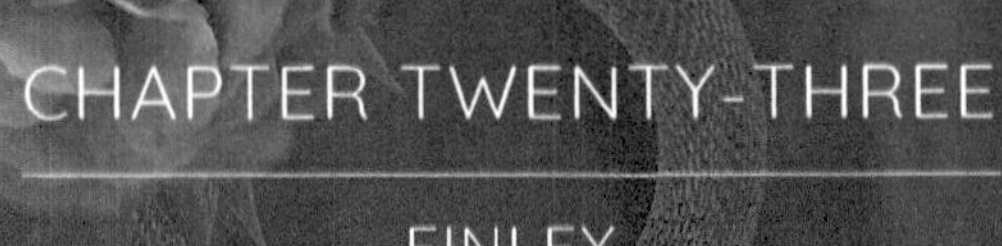

# CHAPTER TWENTY-THREE

## FINLEY

It's been three days. Three days since our world was torn apart, and I've barely been able to function since then. Lincoln hasn't slept; he's been looking at every single possible lead as to who could have done this.

The list isn't that long—the Knights are our main focus, namely Harrison. After everything on Saturday… Lincoln told us about the deal she made with him. To free us. Apparently, Harrison is upholding his part of the deal even in her death. That alone is suspicious enough, but his joy at his son's devastation is sickening.

East… he's basically disappeared. He's been gone the last few weeks, so I don't know why I'm surprised, but it's also suspicious. He was the first of us to be on Team V, so why the fuck did he disappear, and why isn't he here now when we need him most? When Linc needs him most.

And Mav… well he's basically living at the fight club. I tried dragging him back here, but after Indi's visit… I'm not sure how to pull him out of the hole he's gone into. Especially when I'm in one of my own.

The body in the car was charred beyond recognition. If it hadn't been for Lincoln seeing her approach and unlock the car, I'd question if it was even her. But she has no reason to disappear. No reason to leave us behind. I get that she was keeping secrets, keeping her arrangement with Harrison from us, but I understand that.

Something like this… I just can't see her hiding from us.

Nothing about this makes sense. Harrison isn't really the blow-them-up kind of guy. He's usually more subtle, so as much as Lincoln is convinced that his father is behind this, I can't stop thinking about the guy who came to visit her while Evan had her held hostage.

Which is exactly why I've started trawling through Evan's past. My father didn't know how Evan came to be a Knight, and none of us know either. Just that he was one. My problem is that Evan doesn't seem to have existed until six months before the tour.

I'm not sure how no one noticed this before. I haven't looked into Evan before now, and admittedly without paying a lot of attention, it's not something you'd find, but still… the Knights are more thorough than that.

Unless the Knights gave him the new identity.

But that doesn't make sense either, and losing myself down this rabbit hole is exactly how I'm going to distract myself from the endless pit of despair that is calling my name.

I finish hacking into the local P.D. system and find the file on Octavia's case. There isn't much to go on other than a pipe bomb, triggered by a suspected pressure plate. But that doesn't line up with what Lincoln said… he said the engine started and then it blew. That suggests a trigger rather than pressure, unless it went off as she sat down.

I need to look at the car.

I slam my laptop closed and grab my keys. I'm going to find out what the fuck is going on. Between Evan's mysterious past, and East just being gone… nothing is adding up.

Grabbing my jacket, I head downstairs. The sound of bass from the basement means Maverick is likely back down there, beating himself up. I can't remember a time when a distance like this existed among us all.

"Where are you going?" I turn at Linc's words and find him leaning against the wall, hands in his pockets, looking a fucking mess. He's coming apart at the seams, and it's showing.

"I'm going to look at Octavia's car."

"What's the point? We know how she died. You should be helping me look at Harrison."

I take a deep breath, trying not to let his snappy bullshit get to me, but I am walking the end of my rope. "I'm sure you've got it covered, so I'm following my own suspicions."

"This is bullshit. Why do none of you give a fuck what happened to her? East is gone, Mav is out beating the fuck out of anything that moves rather than helping, and you're not even looking in the right direction."

"Fuck you, Linc," I snap. "Just because you think you're looking at the right thing, doesn't mean you are. Mav is coping in his own way. As for East, I don't have a clue what's going on with him, but he's probably working through his grief in his own way, too. Just like you are."

"Of course you'd stick up for him," he scoffs, rolling his eyes. "Just run along on your little scavenger hunt while I do the real work. Like always."

I clench my fist around my keys, the pain of the metal digging into me grounding me and stopping me from lashing out at him. I watch him deflate in front of me, not what I expected. I thought he'd fight back, get angry, something Linc like, but he just crumbles before my eyes, and that hurts almost as much as the wound of losing Octavia. He's hurting, we're all fucking hurting, so I swallow the words on the tip of my tongue that want him to fight back, to show him that there is more than anger, and instead I turn on my heel and leave the house.

I've got shit to do, and if I want to not fall into the darkness inside of myself, especially now I'm free, I need to find out the truth. Otherwise, everything Octavia arranged for us will be for nothing. I refuse to let her sacrifice mean nothing.

# CHAPTER TWENTY-FOUR

## EAST

I never thought I'd regret my choices of the last two weeks… but here I am, faced with the reality of where those decisions have led.

Octavia is gone. It doesn't matter that it's been four days, I'm still in shock. I'm in denial.

She can't be dead.

I can't have given up that last bit of time I should've been with her willingly.

If only I'd made a different decision, maybe she'd still be here.

I haven't been back to the Saint house since Saturday morning. I can't be there. Not when every nook and cranny of that place reminds me of her. Not when I can look out my window and see on to her property.

See the scorch marks on the ground.

I just can't.

The problem is, I'm letting them down—letting *her* down—by hiding away. I've spent most of the last few weeks here at Chase's, so it made sense that I'd escape here. Though I've barely left the room I've been staying in since I got back Saturday morning.

I can't get the sight of that charred SUV out of my mind.

I hit replay on the playlist she shared with me a few weeks ago, yet again. Wallowing in the thing she held closest is about all I've managed to do for four days. It's pathetic, yet I can't seem to make myself do anything else.

I should be there for Linc, for Mav, for Finn. I've always been the chill one… but I can't find it in myself to do much of anything.

A knock at the door has me lifting my head off of the pillow as Chase's face appears through the gap. "Morning, I'm getting ready to head down to the police station. I wondered if you wanted to come with me? I'm going to go and see Smithy too. Offer my condolences."

"I don't know if I can." God I'm such a woe is me asshole.

Chase sighs and enters the room fully. "I haven't been around for much of your life, Easton, but I get the feeling that you've never been one to run from your problems. Do you think Octavia would want you to start now?"

"Octavia is dead." My voice sounds as hollow as I've been trying to feel.

"She is, but that doesn't mean that you died too. You need to keep living. Your brother, your friends, they all need you. I'm doing everything I can to ensure that her case is investigated properly, but I can't do that *and* worry that I'm going to find you dead when I come home. I'm not trying to be an insensitive dick, and I'm obviously not great at this parenting thing, but you need to be around the people who are hurting just as much as you are."

"Are you kicking me out?"

"Never," he sighs, running a hand down his face. "You always have a place here. I meant it when I said that, just like I meant it when I said I wouldn't officially claim you so you'd never be subject to the Knights' bullshit, but you need your brother, your friends. Hell, maybe even Smithy. These are the people who have always been there for you when you've fallen down. They'll be there for you now too, and they'll need you. Losing someone is never easy, but being around others who are grieving them as well can help."

I consider what he's saying. I'm not sure there's any way I can feel worse or any more guilty. Maybe being around the others, talking about her, will be good for me. For them.

Letting out a deep sigh, I sit up. "Fine, I'll just pull on some clothes and I'll head over to see them."

He smiles tightly, nodding once. "Okay, good. I'll check in with you later."

"Thank you," I say quietly and he strides across the room, putting a hand on my shoulder.

"Always, Easton. I missed enough, I don't intend on not being there for you ever again." He turns and leaves me alone with the sounds of *Lately* by Future Palace playing on my phone from her playlist.

He's right. She wouldn't want this. She dealt with all of the loss in her life like a fucking warrior. I'm not about to dishonor her by doing anything less.

---

I make my way home the long way round, purely so I don't have to pass her gate to get to ours. Pain rips through me as I enter the driveway, knowing that she should be just next door, but that she won't be there ever again.

Taking a few deep breaths, I pull myself together before shutting off the car and heading inside. It's quiet. Creepily so.

"Hello? Anyone here?" The deafening silence is all that greets me. It doesn't seem like even Mrs. Potts is here. Well this is a shit pile.

I head upstairs and change into sweats and a muscle top before going down to the basement, which is where I find Lincoln running on a treadmill, headphones in, like he's running from all of the demons that chase him.

He glares at me when he sees me, sneering as I approach. "So the prodigal son returns. Good of you to finally show your face."

"Fuck off, Linc. I've been dealing with all of this too."

He scoffs as he slams his hand down on the screen of the treadmill, bringing it to a stop. "Dealing? What the fuck have you ever dealt with in your life? You've never been the one with the weight of the world put on you. You got to fuck around with zero responsibilities, and the first time something happens that we actually need you for, you fucking disappear. You've barely been around for weeks, even before this. We all noticed. *She* noticed. So don't come back here like you're here to save the day. You're not the white knight here, brother."

Apparently he's hurting more than I could've imagined. That or he really has always been this much of a fucking asshole.

"Don't get all holier than thou, *brother,*" I sneer. "You're the one that was an asshole to her when she arrived. You tried to make her leave. You lost that time with her. A few weeks is nothing compared to that."

He charges at me, knocking me to the ground and winding me before bringing his fist down on my cheek. I fight back, and while I might not have the training he does, I'm not exactly a green eyed wonder.

I manage to pin him and get in a few shots of my own before he bests me once more. He rains down blows on my face and chest, before I hear shouts and he's ripped off of me.

"What the fuck is wrong with you two?" Finley roars as he holds Lincoln back. He struggles against his blond haired friend, but Finley has more bulk than Lincoln and holds him with relative ease as I try to suck in a breath.

"She's gone." Linc's voice is so quiet I almost miss it before his knees give way and he crumples to the ground. He looks up at me with glassy eyes, and the devastation reflecting back at me breaks another part of me. "She's really fucking gone."

He chokes on a sob as his pain rips through me worse than any of the blows he just landed. I don't think I've ever heard him so broken. So small. He's always been strong, stronger than any of us. I know how much he loved Octavia, but I'm not sure he's going to come back from losing her.

Finn drops down beside him, like they're propping each other up, and I watch my little brother break beside his best friend who breaks right along with him. Sobs wrack Linc's body, and something inside of me breaks with them.

I don't think I've ever seen Lincoln cry.

Groaning, I pull myself up and move to sit on his other side, supporting him in the only way I know he'll let me right now, and let my own tears spill down my cheeks.

She's really gone, and there's nothing any of us can do about it.

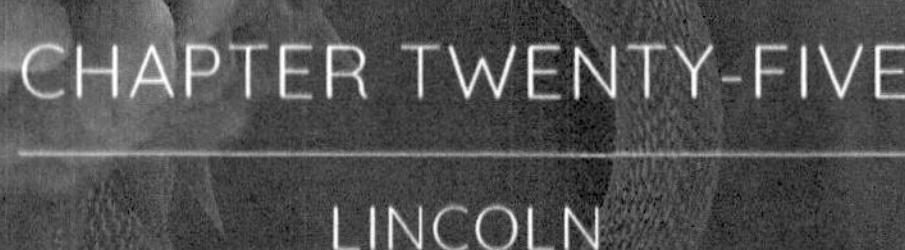

# CHAPTER TWENTY-FIVE

## LINCOLN

After an emotional day yesterday, I called it quits on even attempting to keep up the pretense that I'm okay. I find myself sitting alone at the table in a baggy t-shirt and sweats. It's not that I've stopped giving a fuck, it's just that I've run into wall after wall trying to figure out what the fuck happened to Octavia, and there are only so many walls I can crash into before I admit that I need some help. That I admit I'm not coping and accept that she isn't coming back.

We got a message from Smithy last night to tell us that her funeral will be held in two days. Just something small. She didn't have many people left, so we wanted it to be the people she would've wanted there.

Acceptance seems like all I have left.

Except for revenge.

I'm still convinced it was Harrison. He made too many threats. Even that morning when he told me the deal he'd made with her, he was too fucking happy about it. I might not know everything, but I know Harrison. I know there is no way he'd be happy about being cornered into a deal with her. Releasing the three of us.

I just wish I knew what she gave him. Maybe then this would make more sense. It might give me a lead on what happened to her.

I'm not going to give up. Even if it takes my entire life, I will find out the truth.

I've already called in a dozen favors, having the Range and the remains of the device used for the explosion moved to a federal facility to have it looked over privately. My, well, I wouldn't call him a friend… but my contact there owes me a few times over, so he's looking over it himself.

The problem with fire that burns that hot is that it destroys everything in its path. There isn't much to go on, so it's more about looking at the components of the explosive, how it was built, to try and get a lead.

I've already been through all of the security feeds from here and Octavia's place, but they were scrubbed remotely. I have another contact trying to see if they can recover anything, but I've still heard jack shit.

Antsy isn't a good look on me, but neither is helpless.

I've been speaking to Artemis. After hearing about the explosion, she reached out to offer her condolences, told me about her training with Octavia, and offered her help. She knows people in some fucking seriously low places, so she's put out feelers too, to see if we can find if a contract was put out. If so, who took it up, and who the fuck hired them.

The problem with grief is that I know I'm missing something, but my brain is so fucking tripped up that I can't work out what it is. It doesn't help that I'm not sleeping. Every time I close my eyes, I see her smile before she got in that car. Then I feel the heat on my face again. In my nightmares I hear her screams, but I'm sure the only screams I heard that day were my own.

A buzz on the intercom has me glancing at my phone. Who the fuck could be here now?

"Hello?" I say into my phone, speaking to whoever is at the gate.

"Mr. Saint? This is Special Agent Carter. Can we come in?" I flick the app over to video and see the badge of the guy who's speaking, seeing another three agents with him.

"What is this about?"

"I'd rather discuss it once we're inside." I hit the button to open the gates and drop a message in the group chat for the guys to get their asses down here.

They all clamber down the stairs as I move to the front door.

"Feds are here," I say, their faces ranging from suspicion to surprise.

"At six in the morning? What the fuck?" Mav rubs at his eyes. This isn't exactly his favorite time of day.

"I guess we're about to find out," I say as a knock sounds on the door.

I step forward and open it, finding the four of them standing on the steps. "Mr. Saint?"

"Yes," I answer with a nod, wishing like fuck I was dressed like I was going to court instead of the gym. Something about being dressed like this makes me feel like I'm going in without my armor.

"We're looking for your father, is he home?" the agent asks as he glances over my shoulder and sees the others.

"I don't think he's left for the day yet," I tell them, still suspicious as fuck.

Agent Carter pushes past me, and him plus two of the others spread out throughout the house. "What the fuck is going on?"

The last agent stands at the door. "If the four of you will step outside. We have a warrant for Harrison Saint's arrest, and to search this property."

I look at him, slack jawed, seeing the other agents waiting at the gate. What the fuck is going on?

I take the warrant from the agent, scanning over it, when Finn curses behind me. He hands me his phone, open on his news app.

*"Documents were leaked late last night regarding the involvement of several*

*prominent members of our community, involved in everything from fraud and money laundering to human and drug trafficking."*

Oh shit.

A picture of my father, Edward, Charles, and a few of the other Knights flashes on the screen as the guys watch over my shoulder.

We move outside at the insistence of the agent as Harrison is dragged down the stairs, half dressed, handcuffed, and shouting blue fucking murder.

They pull him past us as he struggles against them, and for the first time in five days, a smile tugs at the edges of my lips.

Maybe this time, the king will actually fall.

---

After the arrests this morning and the news reports all day, an emergency Conclave meeting was called by Chase. Apparently the fact that we've been released from the Knights skipped the memo, so we've been summoned. Chase even called in East, since he's linked to all of the stuff that's going down.

We sit around the board room, everyone on edge as we wait for Chase to reappear. He's the most senior Knight left on the Conclave currently, which is kind of hilarious, but it is what it is.

"Do you have any idea what this is about?" Artemis hisses at me from across the table.

I shrug and pull down the sleeves of my shirt. "Considering everything else that happened today? We're probably about to get read the riot act and then be told to keep our mouths shut until we're told otherwise."

"This is such bullshit. How did your dad even let that sort of information leak out into the world?"

"Fucked if I know, maybe he really pissed someone off."

She eyes me, watching me like she's trying to see inside of me. "Did you do this?"

"Me? No, though I wish I had. You should've seen his face this morning."

She smirks at me, before her eyes turn sad. "You still think he's behind what happened to our favorite Royal?"

The whole room sucks in a breath at her question, and I nod once. "I do. And if he did, well he already had this coming, but he can go to hell for all I care. He made his bed."

She nods as the door opens and Chase strides into the room, moving toward his normal seat rather than taking the one my father usually occupies. "Thank you all for coming. This emergency meeting was called by the Archon, who will be here momentarily."

The room is blanketed in a heavy silence as I look at the others wide-eyed. Artemis sits a little taller, while her father looks like he's about to shit his pants.

"Keep your mouths shut, and do not speak unless spoken to, do you understand?" His gaze bounces between us all as we agree.

"Why is the Archon here?" I ask him, and the corners of his lips tilt up.

"You'll see. He won't be long."

We sit in a tense silence, voices approaching slowly up the hall. This is fucking ridiculous. I know we're supposed to be afraid of the Archon, he's the head of the entire fucking society, but still. Recent events have me feeling a little reckless. Maybe if I push his buttons, he'll punish Harrison some more.

I watch the clock, the second hand seeming to take way too long to tick over, but the voices outside get louder, though they're muffled by the closed door. After a few more seconds, the voices go quiet.

The door opens, and East pales as an older man enters the room. "Matthew?"

The man glances at my brother and nods, but the person who follows behind him is the one who makes me sit a little straighter.

"You have got to be fucking kidding me?" Anger and relief war inside of me. How is this possible? Did he betray her? Did she know all along?

Is he the reason that she's dead?

Smithy looks sadly at me before clearing his face to the cold mask all of us know how to wear. He walks to the front of the room, his presence commanding attention in a way I've never seen him do before and sits in Harrison's usual seat.

"Thank you all for coming tonight. I called this meeting because of recent events that I know you are all aware of. I'm sure my presence is something of a shock to some of you, but all of that will be explained in due course."

What the fuck is happening right now?

Smithy is the Archon?

*What the fuck?*

# CHAPTER TWENTY-SIX

## STONE

*I have been pacing up and down this office so much the carpet is starting to wear. I have done a lot of things in my life that I'd take back if I could, but one thing I will never regret is keeping my daughter safe. I might not be a good man, but I've made damn sure that I'm a good dad.*

*Even after Emily left and I lost my shit for a bit, I tried to be there for her as much as I could stand. Lying to my little girl isn't something I wanted to do, but I learned a long time ago that sometimes lying is the kinder path.*

*One day, I'll have to tell her the truth, but for now, she's too young. She's lost too much. This new opportunity I've been handed is the perfect excuse to get me away from here, from the legacy my great-great grandfather passed down to us ...*

*The Knights are not what they once were. Once they were loyal, working to help strengthen the power of each family. Keep our people safe.*

*But now? Now it has become something dark and twisted. Something so far from what it was intended to be, but once you're in, there's almost no way out other than death.*

*I refuse to accept that fate for her. My Octavia. She has been the ray of light in my life since the minute she came screaming into the world. There isn't anything I won't do to protect her. Even sacrificing her mother.*

*The deal I agreed to with Harrison was such fucking shit, but it's my only way out. I know the only reason he was willing to let me go is because he'll take over my seat as Regent.*

*If only it were so simple as filling the power vacuum. Making a deal with Harrison Saint is like making a deal with the devil himself. Especially when Fiona let him believe that she was fucking me instead of my pool guy. Nothing like that to add to the tension between us and make saving my daughter a little harder.*

*Each time I try to think of another way around this, stopping her initiation without giving up my seat, I see the impossibility. I don't want the seat—I don't want Harrison in it either—but my wants versus Octavia's needs are not an even match.*

*"Master Stone, there you are." I look up and find Smithy smiling at me. "Still debating if this is the right idea?"*

*I shake my head, running a hand through my hair. "I know it's the right decision, I just wish there was someone else."*

*"You and I both know that Harrison is the only one stupid enough to make the deal you want. He won't see past what it will do for him."*

*I drop onto the couch in my home office and he sits opposite me in the leather chair. "I know. I just wish I could save the boys too. We both know that taking her from them..."*

*"They will survive. I will make sure of it. They will suffer, the way we all have, but I cannot save them the same way I can save our Octavia. Their parents do not see the darkness that has taken over the organization, or if they do, they thrive in it. Between you and I, we will find a way to restore the Knights back to what they once were."*

*"You really think this will work?" This one part of our plan has plagued me since we came up with the idea of how to get what we both want with one action. What if I can't find what we need? What if it hurts him? Hurts Octavia?*

*None of it will be worth it if it hurts her. That's the one thing we agreed on.*

*"I do," he says, seeming far more confident than I feel right now. "I will keep residence at the house, ensure that you are kept apprised of everything that happens here, while looking out for the boys as much as I can. If I could stop the initiation, you know I would. Those boys already struggle. Master Lincoln the least, but the Knight boy... it's impossible not to see that he is already haunted. We're not doing this just for us, we're doing it for all of them. The Knights cannot continue the way they have been. The other sects aren't exactly sunshine and roses, but this sect... under your father, too much changed. I know it wasn't all on him, but after everything... we need to fix what was broken."*

*I drop my head into my hands, trying not to think too much about my father and his bullshit. "Is it even possible? I know that you're the Archon. Is there no way that you can just stop all of this?"*

*"The Knights have evolved past that. It's something of a hydra. Even if everyone fears the supposed mythical person at the top of the ladder, they only do so because of lies and stories. I am but one man."*

*"So am I."*

*"But together, we can do this, Master Stone. I know that how we came to be aware of each other was not exactly the best start to a relationship, but your father, God rest his soul... well, he was a complex man beneath it all. With his illness—"*

*"His illness didn't make him a monster to me. He was that long before. And Emily's parents are going to be a fucking nightmare about me taking Octavia away from here. They've done nothing but argue with me since Emily left. They still blame me for her disappearance. They can never find out the truth."*

*Smithy lets out a sigh, giving me a sad smile. "Your father loved you, even if he struggled to show it. He was never the type to show emotion easily. Look at how he was with your mother before she passed."*

*My father was a shit to me, but he was worse to my mom. I think the only person he ever truly loved was the man sitting in front of me. "He showed you."*

*"Yes, but only in private, and hidden beneath enough secrets to break the world. And once his illness claimed him... well, I don't need to tell you about that."*

*No he doesn't. My father was a monster long before his illness, but with the loss of his mind, he became even worse. I refuse to become him or be the kind of father he was.*

*"This has to work," I say, swallowing my resolve. "For her. This cannot be her future. I won't allow it."*

*His smile grows and he nods. "Then let's get to work, Master Stone, because this deal... this is just the beginning."*

# CHAPTER TWENTY-SEVEN

## OCTAVIA

### SIX DAYS AGO

*I am exhausted. Between school, training, finding everything that Harrison wanted, and finally handing it over, I am fucked. The thought that in less than twenty four hours, I can tell the guys everything that has happened... that alone has me all kinds of giddy, but I know I still need to get through tonight without losing my shit over Lincoln having his final date with Georgia.*

*I can deal with just one more. Because then he is mine. They all are. As long as they don't hate me for signing myself over to the Knights. It's not forever, but I'm aware that what the Knights can make you do are things that will haunt you.*

*Panda was living proof of that. The things he did, that he witnessed, were enough to push him over the edge.*

*I'm aware that this probably wasn't my brightest idea, but I will not regret sacrificing for them. I know what I'm getting myself into. They had no choice. Now they do.*

*First, I just need to last until Saturday without spilling my guts.*

*I already told the guys they couldn't stay tonight, because I don't know how to keep seeing them and not tell them, so I told them I wanted tonight with Smithy, and first thing tomorrow I'm going to swing by and see Indi real quick before I lose myself in the four of them for the whole weekend.*

*A knock at the door disturbs me from just staring at the ceiling counting down the minutes until I know Lincoln leaves to be with her. I sit up and find Smithy already striding toward the door.*

*Weird. I didn't hear the buzzer.*

*"Smithy, good, you're here too." I blink at the sound of Luc's voice, turning to find him and Smithy heading toward me. "Octavia. We need to talk."*

*I sit up straight as he strides around the couch to stand in front of the TV, while Smithy stands to my side. "That sounds terrifying. What's wrong?"*

*"My fucking brother," he growls. "He contacted me tonight with a new task."*

*"For me?"*

*He grinds his teeth together. I don't know what Harrison did, but I know that Luc is pissed. "Not exactly." He looks over to Smithy before glancing back to me. "I assume he knows everything?"*

*"He does," I say with a nod. "Someone that would give a fuck had to know in case I disappeared. My deal only stated the guys couldn't know."*

*Luc nods, running a hand through his hair, tugging on the strands. "Fuck, this is so fucked."*

*"Why don't you sit? I'll get us all a drink and you can explain what exactly Harrison has done now."*

*Worry churns in my stomach while Luc paces in front of me. I don't think I've ever seen him so off-kilter. He's done a lot of things, so whatever Harrison has asked him to do must be fucking crazy to have him react like this.*

*"Should I be worried?" I ask as Smithy appears with a bottle of whiskey and two glasses, plus a steaming mug of coffee. He hands me the coffee and pours two fingers for Luc, who shoots the drink back in one go.*

*"Yes." Luc finally answers my question, and I put my mug of coffee on the table. "He wants me to kill you."*

*"I'm sorry, he what now?" I blink in shock up at Luc, trying to process what the fuck he just said.*

*"He wants me to kill you."*

*Smithy stands, hand gripping his whiskey glass so tight it looks like it might shatter. "Luc, sit down. There are some things we need to discuss."*

*"Smi—"*

*"Sit down, Lucas." My eyes go wide at Smithy's tone. It's like he became an entirely different person before my eyes. Luc shifts quickly to sit in the leather chair to my left while we wait for Smithy to speak. "There are some things that you need to know. Both of you. Some of this is going to seem outrageous, some of it ridiculous, but know, Miss Octavia, that I never wanted anything but your happiness. Some secrets had to be kept for everyone's safety, including my own."*

*I open my mouth to speak, but Smithy shakes his head, so I keep my comments to myself. Probably not helpful right now since I'm just low-key freaking out about the whole 'Harrison wants me dead' thing. It's not that surprising, but fuck me, it's different knowing it's a reality. I try to turn my focus back on Smithy because he looks deadly fucking serious.*

*"Something I learned very early on in life, one of the first things my father taught me... there are two parts of this world: one that most people don't see—where those with power revel—and they will do anything,* anything *to keep it. The other part lives in an ignorant kind of bliss. Walking through their lives without even a hint of the darkness that lurks around them. But that darkness..." He pauses, turning to face me again. "It is why who I am has always been guarded."*

*"You're talking in riddles, old man," Luc grumbles, and Smithy shoots him a glare.*

*"How's this for a riddle? I am the Archon."*

*Luc's eyes go wide, and I rack my mind for why that sounds familiar to me. "Oh shit, wait—"*

## CHAPTER TWENTY-SEVEN

*"Yes, Miss Octavia. I am the one who arranged the contract with your father for your freedom."*

*Luc stands, moving behind the chair, before bracing himself on it. "If you're the Archon, how the fuck are you here as a house manager?"*

*"That is a long story." Smithy sighs, motioning for Luc to take a seat as he sits in the leather chair to my right. I haven't said much yet, because holy shit, this is a lot to process. First, Harrison wants me dead, and second, Smithy is the head of the Knights.*

*Mind blown doesn't quite cover how I feel right now.*

*"Well, we have time, considering we need to come up with a way to save not just Octavia's life, but mine and Alex's too. If Harrison finds out I'm here, or if she doesn't die tomorrow morning, we're fucked."*

*I blow out a deep breath and lean forward. Holy shit this is a lot. "He wants me to die tomorrow? He really never intended on keeping his part in the deal, did he?"*

*"We will find an answer to all of this, Miss Octavia. But first, let me tell you about how I ended up here, and how I worked with your father. Then I think we should call Mr. Kensington."*

*Right. Bentley. He has my copy of the documents I gave to Harrison.*

*"Okay," I say with a nod, trying to process, knowing that there's still so much more to come.*

*Smithy leans forward and pats my knee. "Well, I guess I should start with how I ended up working for your family. That all started with your grandfather… that man was the love of my life."*

---

*Happy freaking birthday to me…*

*Today is the day I die. I've barely slept, even after I was up until the fucking ass crack of dawn with Smithy, Luc, and Bentley, I couldn't sleep once I finally crawled into bed.*

*Is this really my life now? I survived so much for this to be the way everything ends? We came up with a plan, but I'm not sure it will work. It's not that I don't trust Luc, I mean, he didn't have to come here. He put a lot at risk by coming here and speaking to us, but there are so many things that could go wrong.*

*The only upside to last night was that I was definitely distracted from Lincoln's date with Georgia and the fact that Dad won't be here for my birthday. Can't say Indi's sunshine disposition isn't rubbing off on me if I can find an upside to someone trying to kill me.*

*Again.*

*I shower once my alarm goes off, preparing for my day, wherever it's going to lead me. I take extra time doing my hair and makeup, snapping a picture and sending it to the group chat I have with the guys with the caption, Happy Birthday to Me.*

*If I'm going to die, at least they got to see me smile.*

*I pull on a pair of leggings and a hoodie, because birthdays are for comfort, before heading downstairs. There's no sign of Luc, but Bentley is sitting at the kitchen counter, sipping on a mug of coffee, while Smithy stands at the stove. He turns to face me with a tight smile before striding toward me and wrapping me up in a hug. "Happy Birthday, Miss Octavia."*

*I hug him back so tight that my arms almost ache. It was definitely a shock hearing his truths last night, but I've learned recently that secrets are the currency of Knights. I'm past holding it against anyone. Especially with the secrets I hold myself.*

*"Are you ready for today?" Bentley asks as Smithy releases me and pushes me onto a stool at the counter opposite him.*

*"Not even a little." I grimace. "But I guess I better just put on my big girl pants right?"*

*"Indeed," he says, the corners of his lips tilting up. "Trust me, Miss Royal, this isn't my first rodeo. We will get out of here in one piece as long as you follow my instruction."*

*I let out another deep breath, shaking my arms out. "Okay, so run me through it once more. You know, so I don't actually end up dead by accident."*

*He smiles at me while Smithy scoffs at the stove. "I can do that. Let's get some caffeine in you so you're alert. Even one misstep could mess with everything. I need you to stay focused."*

*I nod, the seriousness of all of this very much apparent.*

*"I mean it, Miss Royal. It will only take one distraction on your part for this all to go to hell."*

# CHAPTER TWENTY-EIGHT

## LINCOLN

James Smith is the Archon.

Harrison and Charles are in jail.

Octavia is dead.

My world has officially blown the fuck up, and I'm not sure I give a fuck anymore. About anything. The only upside to any of this is that my trust fund is free and clear from Harrison's bullshit. So I don't *have* to care. I can get the hell away from here and never look back.

There isn't much of anything here for me anymore. The guys are all hurting just as bad as I am, and they're the only reason I'd stay. Pretty sure they'd be more than willing to leave. If she was still here, I'd probably be pissed beyond recognition about the fact that she sacrificed her freedom for ours, but she's not. So I just have to swallow that anger.

Our freedom cost her life, and that's something we'll have to carry for the rest of our lives, but I won't waste what she gave me. No matter how much I want to climb into a hole and never resurface.

I wait in the lobby of the Knights' meeting place as per Smithy's request before the end of the meeting. Not sure why he wants to see me on my own, but despite my freedom, I know how much he meant to her, so I stay.

After much persuasion, Finn, Mav, and East went home. We each have our own devices for coping right now, focusing on anything that isn't Octavia being gone is mine.

I put my headphones in while I wait for them and torture myself some more with the playlist she made for me, putting on *As You Leave* by Canaan Cox. The lyrics rip me apart, shredding me into little pieces, but the hurt is better than the numb feeling that's been threatening to swallow me whole.

Smithy has placed Matthew as temporary Regent while he sorts out the mess that is happening around us. He's made it very apparent that he intends on changing things up, including freeing anyone that wants out. I'm glad that he's making changes, apparently bringing the Knights back to what the Knights were meant to be, but I'm not foolish enough to think everything is going to change.

Change like this takes time.

It took time to corrupt the Knights, bringing them back from the pits of hell isn't going to be any quicker. If anything, it's going to take longer.

I've been trying to focus on all of this, and who killed Octavia, to try and stave off the reality that she isn't coming back. I'm not ready to accept it yet.

I'm not sure I ever will be. They say time heals everything, but whoever the fuck they are never had Octavia Royal in their life.

Movement brings me back to reality, and I tug out my AirPods, putting them away as Smithy approaches. He motions for me to follow him into the office Harrison used to keep and turns, not waiting for me. I let loose a deep breath and stand, following him without a word.

Closing the door behind me, I take a seat on the opposite side of the desk, and wait for him to speak.

"This must be quite a shock for you, Master Lincoln." I look up at him, trying to reconcile the man I thought I knew with the myth I've always heard about. Smithy being the Archon wasn't something I ever expected, but I have questions. So many fucking questions.

"Did you orchestrate Octavia's kidnapping?" He leans back in the chair, watching me closely.

"Not what I expected your first question to be."

"Your name was on the trail for who paid Dranas. We figured it was a set up, because you would never hurt her. But it seems like maybe we didn't know you after all."

He takes a deep breath, fiddling with the cufflinks on his shirt before answering me. "Yes, I was aware of it. Evan is… was, Matthew's son. We didn't realize just how unhinged he'd become. He did not follow the plan we had set out. Once we found him, Matthew went in to ensure she was okay. Once we knew what had happened, I was working on an extraction, but then you found her instead."

Anger flares in me at his confession, even if I had suspected once I saw him tonight. Evan being Matthew's son barely registers on my radar because of the surprises being thrown around tonight. "East nearly died."

"I'm aware. I ensured he had the best possible care once I was made aware. As I said, Evan went off script. No one was meant to get hurt. Not your brother, and certainly not Miss Octavia."

"Are you the reason she is dead?"

He shakes his head, resting his chin on steepled fingers. "No, that bombing lies at Harrison's feet. It's why I have pulled any and all support from him, and if I discover anyone helping him… well, I am the Archon after all." His smile is darker than I've ever seen, but despite everything, I know he loved Octavia like a daughter.

"Good."

I wait for him to continue, knowing that he didn't pull me in here just to talk about Evan and my father.

"As I said in the meeting before, I am going to honor the deal Octavia made. You boys are free of any binds that have been placed on you. I am just sorry I couldn't prevent everything you have been through up to this point." He pauses, as if waiting for a response, but I don't have one for him. "I have made the arrangements for the funeral, it will take place in two days. If there is anything any of you boys need, please, just ask. I know you didn't know who I truly was, but I still care for you all very much."

I try to swallow around the lump in my throat at the thought of her funeral. I can't cope with all of this. Smithy was always the warm father figure, even if we didn't see him often. He always made cake for our birthdays, helped us bandage ourselves up, or just allowed us to stay at the Royal place if we needed to escape. Reconciling that version of him with this one is just… it's fucking hard.

"Thank you," I croak as I stand. "Was there anything else?"

He pauses as he examines me, and I know he can see how raw I am. I hurt too much to hide it. "No, nothing. You can go."

He smiles sadly as I turn to leave, one thought piercing my mind as I do. Turning back to him as I open the door, I smile cruelly. "I want my father dead."

---

Finding out that Harrison truly is responsible for Octavia's death has lit a fire in me that burns so hot that I should probably be worried that I'll emerge from the ashes a different person, but losing her has already changed me irrevocably.

"I still can't believe Smithy is the Archon," Finn says, rubbing at his temples. The four of us are sitting around my kitchen table, talking through everything we found out last night. "And somehow, I'm less surprised that Harrison is behind everything else."

Maverick snorts, shaking his head, while East sits clenching his fists.

"I knew it was him, I just couldn't find out the details." I take a drink from my bottle of water, my skin feeling too fucking tight. I need to punch something or make someone bleed.

I'm turning into fucking Maverick.

"I want him dead. I told Smithy as much, and he didn't dissuade me. Just told me to speak to Luc," I tell them, having already filled them in on the rest of the conversation I had last night.

"That's weird… why would you speak to Luc?" East asks, looking as confused as I feel about that little bit.

"I'm guessing he has contacts that can get the job done. It's not like there's any love lost between the two of them." I shrug, leaning back in my chair. "I asked him to come over later anyway."

I push the chair back and stand, needing to get out some of this tightness in my chest. "I'm heading to the basement. I've got someone watching Harrison's movements, but he's not the guy to end him. Right now, I just need to not think."

They all stand up and follow me down into the basement. Apparently I'm not the only one who needed to not think.

I crank up the speakers, *Hell and Back* by Self Deception blares through as I make my way to the treadmill. East heads straight for the free weights while Finn and Mav move to the mats in the middle of the room to spar.

I run until sweat streams down my spine in thick rivulets, trying not to think about how I won't be doing my morning runs with Octavia anymore. I push myself so far past when I should stop that by the time I get off the machine, my legs are shaking.

"I figured if I followed the music, I'd find you boys." Looking up, I find Luc approaching me. "You asked me to come over, how are you holding up, kid?"

He wraps me in a hug and I lean on him for a minute. His hugs make me remember that I'm only eighteen and my life shouldn't be this fucking complicated and broken. I let myself take solace just for a moment before I break the hug. The music shuts off and the others join us, each of them saying hello before I move on to why I asked him to head over.

"I figure you've heard the news about Smithy?" A trace of something shadows his eyes before it disappears again.

"Yeah, the Knights might be a secret organization, but fuck me do these people gossip worse than a bunch of women in the salon."

"Yeah, though I'm sure Smithy will put a stop to that soon enough. Anyway, I met with him last night, and he told me to get in touch with you about how to deal with Harrison." A bolt of hatred spears me just thinking of my sperm donor and everything he's done to fuck with my life.

"What do you mean, deal with him?" He eyes me closely, but I know he already knows.

"I mean, he killed Octavia. I want him dead. I wanted him dead before and there wasn't anything I could do about it. With everything that's happened, now there is. I'd rather do it myself, but Smithy seemed to think that was a bad idea."

I'm still not sure why he was so opposed to it. Even if I got caught, it's not really a problem anymore. Not for me anyway.

"And he told you to call me?" Luc asks and I nod, even when he frowns.

"I guess he figured you'd know a way to get it done without us getting caught. I have someone watching him already, I just don't have anyone I trust to do the job. But I have money."

His frown deepens, but I push past him and head back upstairs. Everyone follows, just like they always have. It's how I know Luc will get this done. It's why I know that the others might not agree, but they won't stop me.

I grab another bottle of water from the fridge and lean against the counter as they make their way into the room. Looking at Luc, I see when he notices my resolve. He might not want to help me, but that doesn't mean I won't get it done. I have resources, so even if I don't know someone in prison, it doesn't mean I won't find someone. The Knights deal with enough people that I'll find someone. Hell, Ryker probably knows someone, and considering his issues with Harrison, I know he won't say no. Even if he did, all it would take is a word to Indi about Harrison being responsible and he'd be on board. I should've just gone to them first. Luc is family, but that's probably a reason not to involve him this time.

"You're sure about this?" Luc asks, and I nod.

"I am, and if you don't want to help, it's fine. I just came up with another option."

He shakes his head, scrubbing a hand down his face. "No way, kid. Your dad has been an ass my entire life, I'm not giving that kill to anyone else. It might just take a minute."

I nod before finishing the rest of the bottle. "Just make sure it doesn't take too long."

My phone buzzes in my pocket, and I grind my teeth when I see the message. "It'll be easier now anyway."

"What do you mean?" Finn asks from across the room.

I look up at them all, trying to tamper down my rage. "I mean, Harrison apparently had a federal judge in his pocket because he just made bail."

# CHAPTER TWENTY-NINE

## MAVERICK

I can't believe this day is here. I've spent the last week in denial, trying to break everything around me, bleeding people out, fighting at the club every night, but nothing has made the hole in my chest feel any smaller.

I'm at the point where I'm so broken, I don't even want to break anything anymore. I just want to fall into the abyss over the edge of the cliff where I've been living since I saw the smoke rising into the sky on the day she was taken from us.

Today feels like nothing more than going through the motions. I'm not ready to say goodbye to her. I'd rather join her than let her go. I'm only going to the funeral because I know that the others won't understand.

They've never understood the knife edge I've lived on. She was my safety net, the light in the never-ending darkness. My dad made me a monster, but she loved the monster inside of me. She liked to play with it, and I loved her so fucking much for it. She was the only place I've ever called home, and now that's gone.

I've spent a week trying to break everything else, just to try and feel *something*. Anything.

It didn't work.

I'm not sure it ever will again.

I step out of the shower, my dark hair dripping wet, the purple rings under my eyes an obvious sign that I've barely slept since that day. Every time I sleep, I dream of her, and waking without her hurts too fucking much to keep torturing myself like that.

I towel off, pulling on the black shirt and trousers that Mrs. Potts laid out for me. She's officially tried to take over as our live-in-mom since we all moved in here, and while she's been good about giving us all space this week, she's been hovering around the edges of existence, trying to make sure that we don't lose ourselves to the anger we all feel.

The only one dealing with our loss in a somewhat normal way is East, I think. But then again, he was always the least broken of us. I'm almost jealous of how he's dealing with it. Don't get me wrong, he seems like he's hurting, but on the outside at least, he doesn't look like he'd rather die than live without her.

Which means he's already doing better than I am.

Once I have the shirt and slacks on, I put the tie around my neck before throwing it back on the bed. Fuck a tie. I'm not that guy, and Octavia would never ask me to pretend to be anything that I'm not.

Fuck, I miss her.

So fucking bad.

The pain claws through my chest and I crouch down, trying to suck in breath. Being without her is literally like trying to survive without oxygen.

It's fucking impossible.

I struggle to breathe, pain tearing my insides to ribbons as I try to fight off the tears that threaten to overwhelm me. Images of her flash through my mind, her smile, hair a mess, dressed in my t-shirt; flicking to me having her pinned against the wall at school, my knife pressing into her skin, the smile on her face before she kissed me, even when she was angry at me. Especially when she was angry at me. The soft smile she'd give me when she first woke up. The feel of her in my arms as we'd fall asleep.

Fuck.

I'm not going to survive this.

Maybe I'll kill Harrison my fucking self. It sounds like a worthy way to die.

"Mav," Finn calls out, knocking at my locked door. I open my mouth to answer him, but nothing comes out. He knocks again, trying the handle, and I wrestle every fucking emotion in me back down, knowing that I can't break.

Not yet.

Not until Harrison is dead.

My resolve in place, I take a breath and stand, grabbing my suit jacket and yanking the bedroom door open. "I'm ready."

My voice is laced with venom, thoughts of ending Harrison before joining my girl are all that's on my mind.

I follow him downstairs, finding Linc and East waiting for us. We're all matching in our black shirts, pants, shoes, and jackets. Without a word, Linc heads outside and down the drive to where the car is waiting for us outside of the gates.

We've barely reached the car when I spot Smithy approaching us. "Boys, before you go. We need to talk."

Pausing at his words, the gate to the Royal house opens and we head back up the drive. I stuff my hands in my pockets wanting this day to be fucking over with.

We meet him at the front door, and he looks about as shitty as I feel.

"What is it?" Lincoln asks, his patience apparently as thin as mine.

Smithy smiles sadly at us, and opens the door to the house. "I need you all to come inside for a moment."

# CHAPTER THIRTY

## OCTAVIA

I hold my breath, waiting for one of them to speak. To move. Just do anything. I know they must be angry, shocked, hurt.

I never wanted to hurt them, but there's a lot that's happened the last three weeks.

They all stand there, dressed for the funeral they no longer have to attend. They look like something out of a magazine shoot. All in black suits, black shirts, and skinny black ties, except for Mav who never wears a tie. It's enough to make a girl's mouth water.

Also makes me wish I was dressed in something more than jeans, a crop top, and a shirt hanging over my shoulders.

Lincoln steps toward me and then pauses, emotions running over his face, but he locks it down quickly, his cold mask slipping back into place, and I stand, captured in his gray eyes that look like ice cold metal.

"Fuck this," Maverick says, rushing toward me and wrapping me up in his arms, lifting me off the ground. "Don't think I'm not happy to see you, princess, but what the fuck?"

He places me back down on my feet, and East steps in, taking his place. He holds me like he can't believe I'm here.

I get it. I didn't want to keep everything from them, and God knows there's still a lot to say between us, but when Maverick grips my chin and pulls my attention back to him, all thoughts of words disappear. He pulls me from East's arms and presses his lips against mine as East presses against my back.

He kisses me until I struggle to breathe and as I pull back, he grips my hair so tight, my scalp stings. "I'm not letting you out of my sight again, princess."

I smile up at him, a hand on his chest as I lean back onto East. "Understood, but I think we should talk first."

I glance over to where Lincoln and Finley haven't moved. I can't tell if they're more pissed or hurt, but I do know that Finn is likely to soften first. Extracting myself from East and Mav, I move toward them, brushing my hand against Linc's as I put my hand on Finn's chest. Linc stiffens but doesn't move. I knew he'd be the biggest hurdle. The one who would find it hardest to forgive me. We said no secrets, and then I held back more than a few truths.

"I'm sorry."

Finn's blue eyes look down at me and I can feel his heart race beneath my palm. "We thought—"

"I know. I wanted to tell you guys, but until it was done, I had no choice."

"You could have trusted us," Linc hisses, drawing my attention back to him. "You could have trusted me." I wince at his roar and try to find the words, though I know none will erase what they've been through this last week.

"There's so much that you still don't know," I sigh, exhausted from my earlier conversation with Smithy, my mind still reeling from everything I've learned this last week, but I need to do this with them now. Make them see.

"Then tell us." Linc's demand makes my spine stiffen, his cold, detached bark reminding me of the way things were a year ago.

"Lincoln, don't be such an asshole." Mav mutters as he and East crowd around me.

Linc glares at him. "We thought she was dead! Fucking *dead!*"

"But she's not," Finn says softly, his eyes roaming over me like he thinks I might disappear at any moment.

"I'm not going anywhere. Not ever again," I say, looking at Lincoln, but I'm talking to them all.

Lincoln's growl reverberates through me as he steps forward and claims me with a bruising kiss. When I feel heat at my back, arms wrapping around my waist, I pull back to take a breath, leaning my head back and looking up into Finley's eyes. I press my lips to his as Lincoln kisses down my throat. "I thought we lost you," he whispers against my lips. "There was so much darkness."

My heart clenches at the pain in his voice. I hate that I put it there. The others give us a little space, and I realize that for whatever reason, my being gone is going to haunt him the longest. I reach up and cup his cheek with my hand. "I won't leave. Ever again. I promise.

He closes his eyes and rests his forehead against mine, just holding me, breathing me in, as if convincing himself this is real. My eyes flutter closed, and I squeak when he bends and lifts me against his chest. He strides up the stairs to my room, the other three close behind us.

Once we're all in the room, East closes the door and flicks the lock. I guess no one wants any interruptions. Finn puts me on my feet and steps back, the four of them standing before me with my bed at my back.

"I missed you. All of you. I'm sorry I didn't reach out, but there was too much at stake. I hate that I hurt you—"

"Later," Mav growls, as he strides forward and grips my throat. "First, we're going to punish you for leaving."

"Then we're going to reward you for taking it so well," East adds.

"Then you get to explain everything,." Lincoln finishes. I glance over to Finn who just nods. My four kings stand before me, waiting for me to say something, anything. Instead, I drop to my knees, and look up at them.

“I am yours to do with as you wish.”

My gaze travels to all four of the guys, pausing at each of them like we're having our own little conversations. Like I'm begging for forgiveness with just one long, apologetic look.

They all grunt at my immediate submission, and a tremor runs through me at the sound, making me wet within seconds.

Four gorgeous, lethal, hurting men standing in front of me and I have no idea who to go to first.

True to his character, Mav steps forward first, one hand already making quick work of his belt while the other holds my throat at the perfect angle for his taking.

"You're lucky I'm more thankful than seething right now, or I'd make you bleed for what you did." He scoffs at himself and then adds, "Hell, I still might."

His words are deathly quiet, like he's speaking only to me. The enormity of the moment isn't lost on me. He wants my blood. As a punishment or to release some of his pent-up pain? Either way, I won’t deny him what he needs. I hold out my arms and tell him, "I'm yours. Do what you must, Maverick."

The pressure at my throat increases under the pads of his fingers and the look on his face darkens. "I'll decide when and where you bleed, you’ve made enough decisions about us lately.”

My breath catches at his words and by the tiny smile that creeps up one corner of his mouth, I'm guessing he felt that at the tips of his fingers. I bet he's hard as a rock behind that zipper.

I give a longing look at the bulge that's right in front of my face and then raise my gaze to find his hard stare. I already know it's going to take time to earn their forgiveness, but I’m willing to work at it. I'll make it up to them. Eventually.

In my periphery, I see Lincoln languidly make his way over to my small couch where he makes himself at home.

"Get up." Mav gives me the order, bringing my focus back to him but he doesn't wait for me to rise on my own. His forearm bulges as he pulls me up by my throat until I'm face to face with him. Our mouths are so close I can feel his breath on my lips, his heat on my skin—the anger that's simmering just below the surface of his touch.

This is my atonement—and I happily accept it—which is why I don't even flinch when he pushes me back onto the bed. I accept it because the look in his eyes tells me an entirely different story. His relief at me being here with him is stronger than any anger or deep-rooted agony he may have felt thinking I was dead. I can't imagine having to survive the death of any of them, and the guilt has weighed on me heavily this last week, but there really was no other way.

"Clothes off." I don't hesitate, and before I get the chance to slide my panties off, Mav curls his fingers around the soft fabric and rips them off of me, letting them drop at his feet.

Four pairs of eyes are roaming different parts of my body and never in my life have I felt more alive, and more on edge, than this very moment.

"When I think how you made us believe that we'd lost you. Lost this… angry doesn't even begin to cover it, princess." My teeth sink into the flesh of my bottom lip as I try my best not to justify my actions.

Mav kneels at the foot of the bed and, with his big hands on my thighs, pulls me to the very edge of the mattress, a millisecond before his mouth is on my pussy. Licking, sucking, and biting every inch of the skin between my legs. The cries fall from between my lips, but Finn kneels behind me, resting my head on his thighs and slaps his hand over my mouth.

"This isn't about you, V." His words are harsh, but his finger caressing the underside of my chin tells me a whole different story. It's punishment, no doubt, but it's also so much more.

Mav hits a magic spot that makes my hips spring from the mattress, the pleasure taking over my body without warning.

"He feels good, doesn't he?" Finn whispers from above, the pressure against my mouth increasing and the bulge of his hardening cock pressing against my temple.

Movement has my gaze swing over to East, then Linc. They are both sitting on their own ends of the couch, flies open, hands stroking their cocks, hungry eyes on us.

I lick my lips as the scene before me sinks in. Here I am, getting my pussy thoroughly fucked by Mav's tongue while Finn effectively shuts me up and the Saint brothers jack off to the sight of it.

My thoughts are brought back to the bed as Mav tweaks my nipple and Finn snaps, "Focus, pretty girl."

I almost narrow my eyes at them both but the reminder of my penance is in his eyes, so I take everything they have like the sinner that I am.

Two fingers sink inside my pussy while Mav continues to worship my clit.

"Fuck," I hear Finn above me. Raising my gaze to his, I see his hard exterior melt into red-hot lust. It's heady and Mav licks up my reaction to it.

"Goddamn, she's fucking delicious," he groans as grunts sound all around.

My hips buck when Mav pushes in two fingers again, curling them just right and making my entire body shake.

Finn replaces his hand with his mouth, his lips almost imitating Mav's as he bends over me. I'm so hyper aware of them that it's difficult to keep any sort of rhythm going. I'm bucking at Mav and moaning into Finn's mouth as his tongue sweeps in and out from between my lips.

My hands are at my sides, my fingers curling around the sheets beneath me as I get devoured from either end. I know better than to touch either of them without permission.

It doesn't take long to bring me to orgasm again, the stimulation is almost overwhelming. When it does come, though, I'm a quivering mess. Finn doesn't let up, his mouth is hot on mine. Lips gliding over lips. We swallow each other's moans while Mav fucks my pussy with two, maybe three fingers, pummeling the same spot over and over again. It's when he squeezes my clit with his teeth that I lose my fucking mind. My hands reach out, trying to grab at anything, begging to be tethered to something, but Finn holds me down, his fingers cuffing my wrists and pushing me down against the mattress without once lifting his mouth from mine.

The orgasm flies through my body like a tornado, wreaking havoc with my nerve endings.

And still, they won't let me touch them.

Heaving and fighting for every breath, Finn licks a path at the seam of my mouth before he releases me and Mav comes into my line of vision. "I think Finn needs to sink into your pussy."

My tongue darts out, licking my swollen lips at the suggestion. I'm aware that while they love me, right now, I'm their toy, and I'll take the position willingly.

They trade places and as I'm looking up at the evil glint in Maverick's eyes, I smile up at him. He may be a psychopath but he's *my* psychopath, and I wouldn't want him any other way.

I gasp when Finn kneels on the mattress between my legs and, without warning, plunges inside me to the fucking hilt. The burn from the stretch of him is enough to make my eyes water. When I open my eyes, Mav's glint turns into a blinding grin that takes my breath away.

"Finn was right. This isn't about you, princess. This is for us." He rises on his knees and straddles my face, his balls dancing over my lips.

I get it. They need to let go of the images of my death in their minds. I'm being punished in the most delicious of ways and I'm okay with that.

"Lick."

My mouth opens at Mav's command and my tongue searches out the fragile ball sack as he slowly jacks himself off above my face. But my attention is on Finn as he grunts with every thrust. His fingers press hard into my thighs, the jerk of his cock brutal on my core. Mav moans at the feel of my tongue when I flutter the tip over the seam between his two balls.

"That's it, princess, make me come all over your face." What does it say about me that his words make me even wetter than I am?

"Do it," Lincoln commands from across the space between us, the deep rumble of his lust-filled voice makes my hips buck just as Finn takes my hand and places it on my clit.

"Play with yourself," Finn orders and I don't hesitate, not even for a second. Being back with them has me all kinds of needy.

My senses are on full alert with the sounds of Mav stroking himself harder and faster as Finn's thrusts inside of me increase in tempo. Bottoming out with every plunge to the hilt. My fingers are soaked as I stroke myself.

"That's it, V. Yeah, fuck, I'm gonna come." Finn's movements become less controlled and wild like the man himself as his stare pierces me, his intentions clear.

*See my hurt.*

*See my pain.*

*See the shell you would have left had you really been dead.*

My chest aches at the truth of his what he says to me wordlessly, his walls completely broken down as he pulls my thighs into him and buries his dick so deep inside me I swear to fuck I can feel him in every molecule of my being.

Finn roars out his orgasm, his pain echoing against the four walls of my room before it hits me with its force and I come all over his cock.

"Fuuuuuuck!" Mav moves so quickly I barely have time to understand what he's doing.

On instinct, I open my mouth and while my own orgasm is still rushing through me, I swallow every drop of Mav's cum as he spurts down my throat.

"Good girl. Now, go suck Linc's dick before he embarrasses himself." Mav wipes a drop of his cum from the corner of my mouth, pushing his finger between my lips before helping me up.

Finn drops a kiss on my navel, his eyes on me and his words clear in my head as though he's saying them out loud.

*Thank you for coming home.*

If only he knew…

On shaky legs, I stand, but Linc is having none of it.

"Crawl to me, Octavia."

Oh yeah, he's pissed off. There's no doubt about that. But I do as he commands, dropping to my hands and knees.

Without taking my eyes off his hard stare, I slowly make my way to him, watching in fascination as he slides his pants off and lets them drop to his ankles before kicking them—and his dress shoes—to the side. Despite the anger that's rolling off of him in turbulent waves, his dick is hard and thick lying proudly against his lower abs. He's magnificent at any time of day, but when he exudes power and control… he's simply breathtaking.

I dare a look at East, who's been quiet this whole time, probably ruminating in his own head, wondering where he went wrong. Possibly even blaming himself somehow for not being able to protect me, even if from myself and my decisions.

Like his brother, East has placed his mask on, making it impossible for me to read him.

Once I reach Lincoln, I kneel in front of him and wait, palms flat on my naked thighs, for my next instruction.

And I wait.

What feels like endless seconds turn to minutes before Lincoln wraps his palm around his cock and begins to stroke himself in front of me. His hard stare is penetrating, irises cold as steel, plump lips drawn in a straight, unforgiving line.

I'm almost afraid as I look at him that he may never forgive me. Of the four, Lincoln was the biggest gamble, but it doesn't matter. I stand behind my actions, even if I have to live without one of the men I love. Knowing they are all safe is enough for me.

It has to be.

"Suck." He strokes his cock twice more before adding, "my." Twice more with a swift glide of his thumb across the tip. "Cock."

He lets go of his dick and sits on the couch like a king on a throne—arms resting on the back, eyes sending daggers that pierce my heart with every glare.

And still, I don't hesitate. I move to grab onto his shaft but I don't have time to before I'm flying in the air, an arm banded around my stomach.

I gasp when I find myself kneeling between Linc and East, my mouth on Linc's cock and my ass ready for the taking by East.

I have no idea how I ended up like this but I'm pretty sure East didn't feel like watching this time.

Linc doesn't touch me, but East runs a large hand over the globes of my naked ass. Fingers probing my pussy, circling my clit then sliding back up to my ass before starting the process over and over again.

I think I feel his lips on my flesh, but I'm concentrating on Linc's thick cock and trying my best not to choke on it.

Apparently, I'm not sucking hard enough because Linc finally touches me with one hand in my hair—pulling tight against my scalp—as he takes control of the blowjob and starts to fuck my face.

He pushes my head down until he can feel me choking, my saliva dripping freely all over his dick. I might be humiliated if I wasn't so fucking turned on.

"Jesus Christ, she's soaked. Her pussy lips and her thighs are dripping." East's groan does nothing but make me needier.

"You like sucking on my cock, Octavia? Huh? You like knowing you're about to make me come when you don't get to?" I try to reply, but Linc doesn't let me and I realize he's not seeking out an answer. He's pissed off and feeling betrayed to the depths of his soul, and making me gag on his cock is his way of proving I'm still here.

Alive.

East shifts behind me and just as I'm pulled almost off Linc's cock, East thumbs my clit and thrusts his tongue inside my pussy, fucking it the way Lincoln fucks my mouth.

I feel him eating every inch of me, licking one side then the other, and it's fucking with my rhythm on Linc's cock.

If I weren't so afraid they'd stop, I'd tell him to stop distracting me.

I'm not that stupid though. I give them the upper hand, the control they lost this last week. It's the least I owe them after how they've been suffering.

Linc's dick swells under my tongue as I feel an orgasm wash over me, the telling tremors running through my entire body.

"Goddammit!" One word and Linc screams it out like he's angry that I've made him come in my mouth.

But I lick it all up, swallowing every drop. Trying to ignore my own orgasm, I take everything he has to give all while East feasts on me like he's been deprived of food for weeks.

All too soon, I'm pulled away from Linc's cock and I think he'll discard me when, instead, he roughly takes my mouth, no doubt tasting himself on my lips.

His kiss is hard and unforgiving. It's angry and devoid of tenderness.

But that's okay. The fact that he's kissing me gives me hope, and right now, I'll take it.

I know the exact moment that Linc is done with me. His lust-filled eyes turn to ice, his walls firmly back in place, as he hands me over to his brother.

I feel the loss of his heat but don't have time to linger on my hurt before I'm straddling East, his forehead resting against mine, my soaked pussy gliding easily down his waiting cock.

We both sigh once I'm fully seated on him and he begins to whisper. His breath bathes my lips with every "Thank God you're here" that falls from his mouth. I revel in the heat of his body, in the hardness of his chest and the welcome in his embrace. I'm thankful too, so I tell him as much.

"I love you, East. So much." Large hands travel from my thighs to my waist and up and around to my shoulder blades where he tightens his hold on me. Finally, our lips meet, our mouths crashing together with a clash of teeth and hurried tongues. Frantically, I begin fucking him, rolling my hips, trying to show him just how much I mean everything I've said, all the while our kiss lingers.

He's giving me as good as I'm giving him, meeting me halfway with his thrusts from below—his palms on the balls of my shoulders as he controls the rhythm. It almost hurts, this pace, this frantic need we have to feel each other.

"Come again, V. I need to feel you all over my dick." He's practically begging, but we're hidden behind a curtain of my hair, in our own little world where he doesn't have to hate me and I don't have to beg for forgiveness.

"I can't, East. I c—"

"You will. You'll fucking come for me, V." I concentrate on the friction of his groin against my aching clit. On the intensity of his kiss. I visualize every movement, every dirty thing he's doing to me, and just when I think it's just not possible, I explode.

My head falls back and as quickly as it comes it fades away, but I don't care because East is filling me, giving me everything he's got.

When we both catch our breaths, East kisses me again before he takes my hips and rises from the couch like I weigh next to nothing.

Slowly, he walks me to the bed where he reverently places me on top of the comforter, legs spread, chest heaving, and looks at me in awe.

They're all there, standing around me. Watching me, each of them painted with a different emotion. But I know them, and I know we'll be okay once they've forgiven me.

Mav, as always, is the first to move. Placing his hand on my chin, he kisses me hard and fast before turning me back on my stomach and hitching up my ass so he can, unceremoniously, thrust inside me from behind.

I gasp and so do the other three men standing around watching as Mav fucks his anger out on me.

I know it all will be okay when his hands land on my tits and he flicks at my nipples before leaning down and biting my shoulder as he begins a punishing rhythm that rips every breath out of my lungs when he plunges to the hilt.

Mav is often the volatile one of the group, but right now he's calculated and in control, which means I'll have hell to pay later.

It doesn't take him long to slam into me and hold me in place as he empties himself inside of me, his cries filling the large space of my bedroom.

"Fuck yeah!"

Gasping for air, my breaths erratic and short, I let myself fall onto the mattress once more and smile when I realize they've all fucked me except for Linc.

He can't refuse or else they'll have something he doesn't and he's never going to let that happen.

With the ace up my proverbial sleeve, I use every ounce of strength I have left to heft myself up and turn around to face him.

"Show me your cunt, Octavia." With a grin that feels like it might rip my face open, I spread my legs and show him just how battered I am and still… I'm ready for more. For him.

"Christ, she's fucking beautiful." That's East, who is now settling behind me as Finn and Mav lie down on either side of me—hands and mouths roaming across my skin.

"Fuck." That's Lincoln's resigned sigh, because we are all bonded and there's no fucking way he can walk away from me.

At least I fucking hope not.

The bed sinks under his weight as he lifts my ass up and sinks deep inside me. I gasp into East's mouth as Mav licks at my nipple and Finn leaves tiny bites across my other tit. I've got four pairs of hands on me, three mouths worshipping, and one huge fucking dick pounding me into my next existence.

Even if it's the last time, it's fucking worth it.

Lincoln doesn't take long before he pulls out and comes all over my stomach, his cum falling in spurts of white thick liquid, marking me as visibly as Finn and Mav's bite marks.

Holy fuck.

I suck in a breath, trying to make my lungs work properly again.

Linc looks down at me, the warmth that flickers in his eyes disappears again as quick as it appeared. "Now, you need to tell us what the fuck happened."

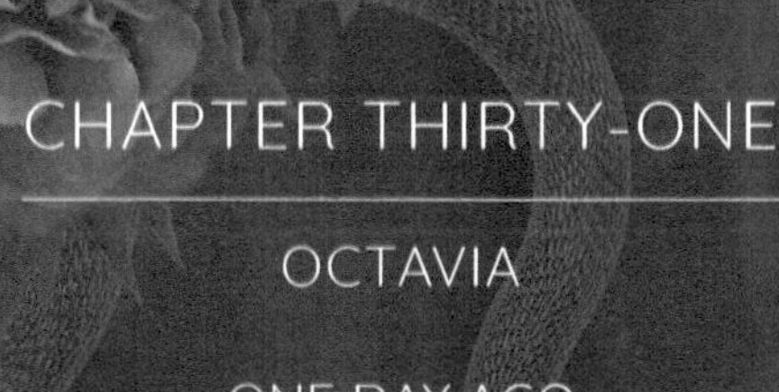

# CHAPTER THIRTY-ONE

## OCTAVIA

### ONE DAY AGO

*One part of me feels guilty about the breaking of the worlds that's happening in the media right now. The secrets that are coming out, especially for the innocent parties that are being swept up in the tidal wave, but I'm not sure that anyone associated with the Knights is truly innocent.*

*There might be some children affected by parents being caught up in the storm, but while this might suck for them, I guarantee it's better than a future with the Knights. Even if they won't see it that way. Some stains on the soul are impossible to get rid of.*

*I pace around the safe house that Bentley holed me away in after rushing me from the inferno of my dad's Range. I don't have all the details as to how he, Smithy, and Luc faked my death, all I know is it was really fucking good. All I have to do is put on the news to see that.*

*My biggest regret is that the guys and Indi don't know I'm alive, but Smithy and Luc hammered home the importance of no one knowing the truth until Smithy had things in line on his end. My head hurt as he tried to explain the many moving parts of his chessboard, but I trust that he'll get what needs to be done, done quickly so I can go home.*

*He and Bentley told me the risks of coming back, the fact that I would be in danger purely because of who I am, because of the people I was going to hurt by releasing some of the documents Dad had stashed away, but there's too much in the Cove for me to disappear under a new identity.*

*That was their original plan. Then the boys would be free, because Smithy would ensure it, but so would I. I could live anywhere, do anything, be anyone I wanted to be, but as I told them… I wouldn't get to be the me I want to be without the people in my life that I hold dearest.*

*A knock at the door has me readying my gun before I check the peephole. I let out a breath when I see Luc's face. I didn't know he knew I was here, but I guess it makes sense that he would. He is one of the four people who know I'm still alive after all. I unlock the million locks Bentley had me engage when he left this morning, and let Luc in, keeping the safety off my gun until he's inside and the locks are back in place.*

*"Good to see you in one piece," Luc says with a tight smile, checking out the windows of the remote cabin I'm stashed in. "Keeping yourself sane?"*

*"As sane as I can be, having been on my own for a week while everyone I love thinks I'm dead. How are they?" I can't help but ask, I know he'll have seen them, and by the twist of his lips, I already know it's not good.*

*"They're in a bad way. East is just about holding it together, but Linc… he's even colder than normal, frantically chasing down every lead for your killer. Mav is beating the shit out of everything that moves—and some things that don't… and Finn. Well, he's gone inward again. Like he did when you left."*

*I nod, swallowing down the rising emotions. I knew it would be bad, it's why I wanted to tell them what was really going on, but they had to think I was dead for Harrison and the others to buy it. If those four weren't so raw, then people would be suspicious. Just because I see the merit in it, doesn't mean I agree with it.*

*"How much longer do I have to stay here?"*

*"Not my decision," he responds and my heart sinks. I knew it would be his answer, it's exactly what Bentley said, but fuck my life. "I'm here because Linc has put a hit out on Harrison."*

*"Shit," I sigh, running a hand through my hair. I knew it was a possibility that he'd work it out and do something like this. It's Linc. If anything I'm surprised it took this long.*

*"Something like that. As much as I'd like to see my brother dead for everything he's done, I don't want it on Linc. He might feel like there's no redemption for himself, but some things you can't come back from."*

*I nod, because I thought something very similar myself already. "What are we going to do?"*

*"He asked me to take care of it, but I have a feeling if I don't do it, he has a back up plan."*

*I bark out a laugh. "Of course he does. He's Lincoln Saint."*

*There's another knock on the door, which has us both on high alert and me reaching for my gun again. Luc motions for me to stay hidden as he answers the door. Bentley strides in, nodding to Luc as he does before turning his gaze to me.*

*He drops a passport on the table before folding his arms. "It's decision time. That there is your ticket to a whole new life. I've arranged access to money, and there is no way for you to be traced back to this one. It would be the much safer option."*

*I stare at the passport on the table like it might burn me, before turning my gaze to Bentley. "Safe doesn't mean happy. Nothing worth doing comes without risk."*

---

# CHAPTER THIRTY-ONE

This day has been exhausting. Amazing, but exhausting. And it's not over yet. Having explained everything to the guys after taking my punishment, and then taking it all over again, my body is sore in the best of ways. I ache every time I move, but my day isn't over yet.

There's one more person I need to see, and I'm kind of terrified about it.

My bestie might be sunshine and puppies embodied in a human, but she's a spitfire, and she's going to kick my ass.

I'm not sure what Smithy said to ensure she wasn't at the funeral earlier, all he said was that he had invited her this evening, which is why I'm sitting curled up in a ball on the couch, waiting anxiously for her to arrive.

We haven't announced that I'm not dead yet, Smithy is handling all of that, but it means not using my phone, so I can't even text her and tell her to hurry her ass up. My knee bounces as my nerves get the better of me.

Somehow, facing Indi is scarier than the guys. She was there for me from the second I stepped into the Cove. She is my ride or die. It's very probable that she is going to be the angriest of anyone because I didn't tell her.

Smithy strides into the room from the kitchen, patting my shoulder as he moves to the front door, and my heart races as he opens it.

"Hey, Smithy," she says quietly, hugging him as he greets her. "What did you want me to come over for? Are you okay?"

It hurts me so bad that her sparkle is dulled right now. I can't see her, she's hidden behind Smithy, but I can hear it in her voice. I get up quietly, moving to the other side of the couch, feeling nervous as fuck.

"Yes, Miss Indi. I have something I need to tell you." He moves to one side and my gaze lands on my best friend who screams and then crumbles to the floor, sobbing.

My heart breaks as I rush across the room, dropping to the floor and hugging the walking rainbow that I hurt so much. "I'm so sorry, Indi."

She holds me tight while she cries. Smithy leaves us while I cry for the bestie I broke so badly.

"I can't believe you're really here," she whispers shakily. "What happened? When Maverick called me… I thought he was fucking around. But then I saw the news, I saw Maverick… You were dead."

"I know," I sigh, running a hand through my hair to try and ground myself a little. "So much happened, and it all happened so freaking quickly. There wasn't time, and it wasn't safe for anyone to know the truth."

"But it's okay now?" she asks and then her eyes go wide. "Oh shit, it was you wasn't it? That leaked all of that information! It can't be safe for you to be here already, surely?"

"Smithy says I'll be fine. I was hidden at first, but he's been working tirelessly this week to ensure that I'm protected better than the freaking president. Plus, after this, I doubt the guys are going to leave my side much."

She laughs, then gazes around the room. "Where are they?"

"Smithy forced them to go next door while I spoke to you. There was a lot of angry testosterone up in here about an hour ago, my friend."

"Yeah I bet." She tucks her hair behind her ear, looking at me like she has more questions.

"What?" I ask, worried that the relief of me being alive is running out, and that the anger I left is going to rear its head any minute.

"I get why you didn't tell me, didn't tell anyone, but I want more details on how this all came about and where the hell you've been. And I'm still kinda pissed you didn't tell me. It's unreasonable, but I never said I made any sense."

"It's not unreasonable," I sigh. "I'd be pissed too." I stand up, offering her a hand, and we go and curl up on the couch in the media room while I tell her everything. About Luc coming here that night, and everything that happened since then. I can't answer every question, because I have some questions myself, but I tell her everything I know.

Even some things I probably shouldn't, but the same way I didn't keep secrets from the guys, I won't keep them from her either. I've had enough secrets to last a fucking lifetime.

"Does Blair know you're not dead?" she asks, shocking me.

"No, why?"

She presses her lips together and then shrugs. "I can't believe I'm even saying these words, but she was pretty torn up when the news broke. You should probably tell her."

Well shit, I definitely wasn't expecting that. I nod, taking it on board. "Okay, I'll reach out to her tomorrow. Today has been a long ass day."

"Yeah I get that, so what happens next?"

"Honestly?" I blow out a breath, trying to loosen the tightness in my chest. "I have no fucking idea."

---

When Indi leaves, I'm exhausted, so I pad back to the kitchen to say goodnight to Smithy and find him on the phone. Now that I know who he is, the fact that he only stayed here for me, even though he could've been living life very differently, it's weird.

On the one hand, I can't help but wonder why he stuck around here, but on the other, it makes me feel loved.

But whatever he's talking about can't be good, not by the look on his face. He holds up a finger, signaling he'll just be a minute, waving at me to sit down, so I grab a bottle of water from the refrigerator and take a seat, waiting for him to finish his call.

"I don't care what you need to do, just fix it," he growls and ends the call. "I swear, people that require micromanagement shouldn't be involved in complex matters. Sorry, I just wanted to get that sorted, but there's something we need to discuss."

Butterflies take flight in my stomach at his words. "That doesn't sound ominous at all."

He smirks at me as he makes a cup of tea before sitting down with me. "It's not too ominous, we just need to talk about the Knights, and about Harrison."

"Yeah, not ominous at all, old man," I tease and he scoffs at me, making me laugh.

"I'm not sure if Lincoln or the others mentioned that Harrison managed to weasel his way out of prison?"

I shake my head, chewing on the inside of my lip.

"Well, that makes sense, I imagine that they were more focused on you being alive. Well, this has caused a slight hiccup, in that he has to reside at home. So I've invited the boys to move in here until we can deal with Harrison."

I just blink at him, processing that little nugget.

"This means that I don't really want you back at school yet. I won't stop you going back to your life. It might just mean I put extra security on you when you're away from the house. I've already arranged for extra security here. They will stay out of the way, but they will be here before you wake up tomorrow."

"Okay. That's a lot, but okay. I appreciate the security, but I really do just want to get life back to normal. I can deal with the extra security if I get my life back."

He nods, smiling as he takes a sip of his tea. "I'm glad you're being rational about it. Though I must say, I had a whole speech prepared to persuade you why it was necessary."

I stick my tongue out at him. "I can be an adult ya know. Sometimes."

"Oh, I know, Miss Octavia. The way you have handled all of this… I couldn't be more proud of you." He reaches over and pats my hand, squeezing it tight. "Now, for the next thing I need to speak to you about. The Knights and your Regency."

He pauses and I just kind of stare at him. I am way too tired for him to keep dropping these bombs. It has been a day, but I promised myself while I was gone that I was going to try and not just react to stuff, that I'd try and think it out before I do anything. So I take a deep breath and center myself.

"What about it?"

He interlinks his fingers on the counter as he watches me, myriad emotions flit across his face so quickly that I can't really catch what he's feeling.

"Well, technically the Regency is yours, what I need to know is if you still want it."

I open my mouth to respond with a resounding hell no, but he cuts me off before I can start. "Let me finish. I do not want the Knights to be what they are. That isn't the legacy I want, and it's going to take time, and people I trust to get to where I want it to be. Some things can't be left to chance, it's why the Knights were created in the first place, but I don't want the guns or the drugs. The flesh trading. The use of children. All of that just turns my stomach.

"Other sects don't do any of these things, and that's exactly why I stayed here when I discovered the truth of this place. It's why your father agreed to collect the information for me, he was in a better position, he had an 'in' with all the people we needed to connect with that I didn't. It didn't play out how I wanted, and for that I am truly sorry, but I think between the two of us, we can make this sect what it was meant to be."

"That is… Wow."

He smiles sadly at me. "I know, and I don't expect you to answer right away. I just wanted you to know what I'm thinking, but if you say no, I will understand."

We sit and talk for another hour about what me taking the Regency would mean, the reality of what that would mean for my life, and it's a lot to take on board.

"Just think on it. Please. It's getting late, so sleep on it, and if you have any questions, please don't hesitate to ask." He gets up, moving around the counter and kisses the top of my head. "I'm going to retire to my rooms, but I'll introduce you to the security team in the morning. Goodnight, Miss Octavia."

I blow out a breath and watch him walk away, trying to process everything. "Night, Smithy."

# CHAPTER THIRTY-TWO

## OCTAVIA

"I still can't believe you're really here," Linc murmurs, kissing me softly before tucking my hair behind my ear. He snuck in here a few minutes ago after I finally decided to crash. Turns out Harrison fled the country after his release, so the guys didn't have to move here, but it has me a little on edge that no one can find him.

The last week since I've been back in the Cove, and come back to life… well, if I said it had been insane, that would be an understatement. I still haven't given an answer to Smithy about the Regency, because I have no idea what to do. There have been many heated conversations between me and the guys about it.

Linc pulls me against his chest, kissing the top of my head. To say he's been mercurial since everything happened is an understatement. Sometimes he looks at me like he wants to kill me himself, and others… he looks at me like this.

I hate how much I hurt him—hurt them all. It's going to take a long time to make it up to them, I'm acutely aware of that, but I'm willing to do whatever it takes.

"I'm here, and I'm not going anywhere. Ever again," I murmur, my lips brushing against his.

His hand moves from my cheek to my throat, and he wraps his fingers around it, squeezing until it feels like I can't breathe. "If you ever…" he growls and my heart races, my pulse fluttering under his fingertips.

He releases me, pushing me away from him, making me stumble. "Strip."

There is no tenderness in the word. None in his face, or in the rigid set of his shoulders. "Linc—"

"I told you to strip, Octavia. Do not make me tell you again."

A shiver runs down my spine as his eyes narrow at me, his heated stare burning my skin. His is a fire I will happily burn in until the end of time.

I step back as he moves to sit on the end of my bed, his eyes never leaving me.

I grasp the bottom of my sweater, lifting it over my head, my nipples pebbling against the lace of my red bra.

"Now your jeans," he orders and a shiver runs down my spine. I love Linc when he's like this. Not that I haven't enjoyed the softer side of him, but this… well hot damn.

I unbutton my jeans, pulling the zipper down slowly, pushing them down my legs, turning so my ass is in his face as I do, before kicking them off, glancing back at him over my shoulder. In a blink, he's standing behind me, his chest pressed to my back, and he pushes me up against the wall. "I might have punished you once already, but I don't think you've been punished enough."

I bite down on my lip, eyes on his as I nod. This might be punishment to him, but I'm definitely not complaining.

I'm trapped between the cold surface of the wall and the burning heat of Linc's chest pressed against my bare back. They say the opposite of love is indifference and from the steel rod peeking between the open flaps of his zipper, there is nothing indifferent about Linc. I imagine he's still struggling with what happened so when he pushes his pants down just enough to free his cock completely, and when he bends just slightly at the knees to align his head with my soaked pussy, I ache with the need for him.

When he sinks his teeth into the fleshy part of my collarbone as he slowly buries his cock inside my pussy, I moan for him.

When he grunts my name as soon as his cock is completely enveloped by my heat, I tell him I love him.

I know he hears me because those three little words awaken the beast in him. The angry force inside him that hasn't quite forgiven me for causing him more pain than he ever thought he could handle.

He pulls out and spins me around before pushing me back up against the wall. He wraps his long fingers around my outer thighs and grips me like he's afraid I'll disappear. I wonder how long it'll take for him to realize that I'll never leave him again.

I barely finish that thought when I feel the first punishing thrust as my back and head slam against the wall. It feels fucking amazing, but it's how he punctuates each thrust with his feelings that make me melt into him.

"I am so fucking angry."

He thrusts again, this time his mouth latches onto the flesh just below my jaw before he reveals a little more.

"You hurt me."

Slowly, he pulls out and plunges right back in before I can get my next breath causing, me to rasp out a soundless "Yes!"

"I was dead inside." The pain in his voice makes my throat thick with emotion as tears prick my eyes. I slam my own head against the wall, the desperation pouring from him making my heart cry out. "I'm so sorry."

With his cock completely sheathed by the walls of my pussy, he secures his hold on me and carries me back to the bed, before kneeling then gently placing me on the soft covers.

The look in his eyes is pure and unshielded. He's completely open, vulnerable once again, telling me his truth as best he can. As much as I love it, because he never does that, I know this is going to hurt.

"You didn't trust me enough to tell me your plan."

He sounds like the boy who needed to control his entire world and like it or not, I've been his entire world since we were kids. And then I broke him because I left. Again.

"Linc–"

His gaze shutters and I don't have time to utter another word before he's fucking me like he's punishing me all over again. I can feel every hard ridge of his abs as he slides up and down my body with every unyielding thrust of his hips. We're both quiet now, but our bodies are saying everything we don't. The chaotic sound of skin against skin, our sweat mingling and creating more heat between us.

My breathing becomes harder to control as Linc continues to fuck me without mercy.

I lose myself in him as my hands glide up his back, the glean of sweat making it harder to latch onto him until I dig my nails into his shoulders and push him harder into me, the heels of my feet locking him in place, begging him for more.

And he doesn't disappoint.

With every deliberate plunge inside me, we both grunt out our pleasure. He gives me everything he's got, and I lay myself bare to him, letting him take whatever he needs.

I'm dizzy with it, loving every fucking second of it, but nothing compares to the moment he roars out my name and slams his mouth onto mine on the last syllable, just as he grinds against my aching clit.

My orgasm is swift and all-consuming. It shatters me into a million pieces as I feel it bloom in the base of my stomach and run a fiery course throughout my bloodstream and every nerve ending in my entire body.

It's electric and I know Linc feels it too.

Our kiss is messy—all tongues and teeth and slipping lips—but it's real. It's everything we are and will ever be.

As Linc spills inside of me and kisses the life right back into me, I know we'll be okay. At least I hope so, because I can't give him up.

Even if it leads to my demise.

---

I curl into East on the couch in the media room while Maverick has my feet in his lap. Finn and Linc are on the couch behind us, the lights turned down as the movie credits start rolling. This entire day has been so relaxing, exactly what I needed after the whirlwind of the last week.

Coming back to life is exhausting.

But this day with the four of them is exactly what I needed before we head back to the chaos of school tomorrow. Prom is coming, exams are coming, decisions about our future are coming, and it all feels really overwhelming.

We've barely had room to breathe this year, and I'm so ready for summer.

We haven't talked about what everyone's plans are, especially now that they're free, but this last week has been more about me being alive than what the future holds.

But we need to talk, especially since I haven't told them about Smithy's proposal yet.

"You okay?" East murmurs into my hair, his arms squeezing me tightly against his hard chest, making me feel all kinds of safe and loved.

I clear my throat before grabbing the tablet that controls the room to stop the movie and turn the lights up. "I'm good, there's just something I need to tell you guys."

Linc and Finn move instantly, standing before me. I pull myself up to sitting, taking my feet from Mav's lap and planting them on the floor. Linc looks stoney already, and I haven't even told him what's going on. Not that I'm surprised. He's the unpredictable one of the group. "What is it?"

He folds his arms over his chest, the black sweater hugging every chiseled inch of him. My gaze slides to Finn, who looks about as happy as Linc right now, and I let out a sigh. "Smithy wants me to take the Regency seat."

Surprisingly, East is the first to speak. "Are you fucking kidding me?" He springs up from the couch and starts pacing. "I thought after all of this you'd be free and clear."

I look to Mav, who is somehow the calmest one of the four.

Have I stepped into the Twilight Zone?

"What are you thinking?" Finn asks quietly. So I tell them everything Smithy said to me last week, giving them all of the information I have because this isn't a decision I should make on my own. If we're going to work, we need to start working as a unit. My time away gave me a lot of alone time to think and reflect. I came to the stark realization that I need to change my mindset if this thing between us is going to work.

I don't have to do everything alone.

"So he really wants change?" East asks skeptically.

"It makes sense," Linc adds. "Smithy is a good man. In his position, that sort of power can corrupt people, but it hasn't with him. That much is obvious in just how he has looked after us all."

"You think she should do it, don't you?" Finn asks him.

Linc's gaze slides to mine and he nods.

"I do. But I think if you're Regent, then we should take our seats too."

"Nothing like keeping it in the family," Maverick laughs.

"Do you think Smithy would be open to that?" East asks me, and I nod.

"I do. Plus, I'll be Regent, so I'd get that say anyway. I want to keep Artemis too, she's a force to be reckoned with, but I think the Mitchell kid needs to go. He isn't the brightest bulb in the box from what I can make out."

"I second that," Linc scoffs. "He's about as useful as a knitted condom."

Maverick snorts a laugh beside me before pulling me onto his lap. "What we're basically saying, is we support whatever choice you want to make and we'll be by your side every step of the way."

I kiss his cheek and smile. "Thank you." I turn to the others too. "I mean it, thank you for always being there. But if we do this, what does this mean for college?"

"We can cross that bridge when we get there. We should speak to Smithy, see what he thinks about it all," East says, squeezing my hand. "But wherever you are, we'll be there too."

"I love you guys," I say wistfully. I really don't know what I'd do without them.

"We love you too, pretty girl," Finn says with a smile.

I check my watch, noticing the time. "Shit, Blair is supposed to be coming over in twenty minutes. I'd totally forgotten."

"What does she want?" Linc asks, eyebrows raised.

I shrug. "She just wanted to come and talk. I'm guessing about Nate. I haven't really paid attention to everything that's been going on with them, but Indi told me that Blair was pretty broken up while I was gone, and this last week, she's actually been nice."

"Yeah, I noticed," Finn smirks. "It's weird as fuck."

"She's only nice to you though, she's still a bitch to everyone else," Mav adds.

"Blair is who she is. She's unapologetic about it, and I'm kind of starting to love that about her."

"Of course you are," Linc responds, rolling his eyes. "Well if she's heading over, we'll go home. I'm waiting on a call about Harrison anyway, so hopefully we'll have some answers about his whereabouts by tomorrow."

"That will be good, I hate feeling like he's out there unchecked."

"We won't let him hurt you," Maverick says, squeezing me tightly before kissing me. "Never again."

They leave after an extended goodbye, and I barely shut the door when the buzzer to the gate sounds. *That'll be Blair.*

I blow out a deep breath, trying to psych myself up for this. I know Indi said she'd turned a corner when I was 'dead,' but still…I have flashbacks to when I first came back to the Cove, and just how shit she was to me. It's hard to reconcile that version of her with this new one, but I want to give her the benefit of the doubt, and not just assume that she's playing me.

She didn't know I wasn't dead, and I trust Indi when she says that there was a change. I mean, I've seen glimpses of it, but at school, she's still Blair.

I open the front door, finding my blonde cousin standing there waiting for me, looking almost nervous. "Hey."

I smile at her before stepping back to let her in the house, but she launches herself at me and hugs me. I freeze, shocked for a second before I hug her back. "You okay, Blair?"

"Shut up, let me just be happy you're not dead." I can't help but chuckle at the very Blair thing that falls from her lips before she releases me. "I know I've still been a bit of a bitch at school, but if those assholes sense even a millimeter of weakness, the sharks will circle. I really was devastated when I thought you died."

She tucks her hair behind her ear and I close the door before leading her to the couches. "Thank you?" I say, a little unsure. We had a weird truce before my 'death' but that doesn't make this feel any less weird.

"Don't be weird," she says, flicking her hair over her shoulder as she sits down. " I just wanted to talk about everything that happened before. You being 'dead' made me look at myself in a way I never have before. I felt responsible, even though I didn't do it. Like, what if something I had done or said sent you down the path that led to that moment. I hated myself for what I did to you."

"Blair—" I start, not sure what to say but she cuts me off.

"No, don't. I just wanted to come and clear the air. Properly. I know we had a sort of truce before, but I don't want our entire relationship to be some sort of weird alliance. You're family, and God knows we don't have much of that left. I want you to know I'm sorry, and if you'll give me another chance, I'll show you that I'm more than a raging, jealous bitch."

She stands, brushing down her skirt, while I sit there trying to find words.

"I don't expect you to forgive me instantly, but I'm willing to show you that I've changed."

I smile at her, everything she's saying slowly registering. "I'd like for us to try to be friends, Blair."

"Good," she says with a nod. "I've got to go, Mom is meeting with Chase, and I want to be there, but I'll text you later."

Without another word, she breezes from the house like she didn't just rock my world. I sit there in shock, trying to process the new version of Blair I just witnessed, hoping that it's not just a blip.

---

After Blair's visit, I head back to the kitchen and find Smithy making supper. "You need any help?"

"Miss Octavia, you know better than trying to mess with my kitchen," he teases.

"I'm going to need to learn to cook one day, ya know."

He waves the wooden spoon in his hand at me. "That is very true, but today is not that day, and not in my kitchen."

"Fine, fine. What are you making?" I ask, grabbing a can of soda from the fridge before sitting on the counter.

"Chicken Alfredo with garlic bread."

"Yes," I groan, my stomach rumbling at the thought. "You're too good to me, Smithy."

"Hardly, Miss Octavia. I love you like my daughter, and I like seeing you happy. Food makes you happy, and I love to cook."

He turns back to the stove and I bite the inside of my lip, trying to think of how to start the conversation I know I need to have with him. Except, there isn't really a guidebook for weird conversations with your surrogate dad.

"I spoke to the guys about the Regency thing," I blurt out, because well, in for a penny, in for a pound.

"Oh? Have you come to a decision?" he asks as he starts plating the meal. I jump down from the counter and take the plates from him as he pulls the garlic bread from the oven.

"I have," I respond as he sits opposite me. "We have some questions about what the future will look like, but I want to accept the chair. I think it's what Dad would've want. I know he was a Knight, and that he obviously wanted more—his deal with you shows as much—but I want to be a part of the change."

He beams a smile at me, clapping his hands together once. "Oh, Miss Octavia. I'm so glad. This will be great for us both. It's rare to be able to trust people as much as I trust you."

"I agree, but the guys would like their seats on the Conclave back too. East included."

His eyes go wide momentarily as he takes in my words. I pick up my fork and take a mouthful of the creamy deliciousness on my plate, not wanting to rush him.

"I think that is a great idea. Your Conclave should be comprised of people you can trust. What about the other current members?"

"I'd like to keep Artemis if she wants to stay, but the Mitchell kid can go."

He nods as he swallows his mouthful. "Very good decision."

"I was also thinking…" I pause, hoping this is a good idea, but it just feels right. "I know we all need a second chair. I figure Alex and Linc can take the Saint seats, Mav and Finn we can work on, Chase and East will have theirs, but for my second seat… I was thinking of inviting Blair into the fold. I know Aunt Vi and Uncle Nate have always been pretty awful to me, but Blair and I have grown closer since Nate's arrest."

He quirks a brow at me, his surprise obvious. "Now that, I was not expecting. You really think that's a good idea?"

"Blair is cold and calculating, but she's also very good at looking at the big picture. How to break things down and build them up. She's all kinds of ruthless. I think she'll be a good second, and it's not like we won't keep her in check. Plus, it evens out the male-female number a little better. Artemis and I are a little outnumbered currently."

He chuckles softly as he takes a sip from his glass of water. "You're not wrong there, Miss Octavia. It is entirely your decision who you have as your second, and I will support you regardless. You're a good judge of character, always have been."

"Thank you."

"What about Miss Indi?" he asks, and I twist my lips.

"I had thought of her, but I didn't know if we could offer her a seat, or if she'd even want it. Especially with Ryker and the boys being part of the Kings."

He smiles at me and winks. "There are always new partnerships to be made, Miss Octavia. But I think Indi and her gentlemen would be a good addition, as long as they're open to our new ways."

I nod, mulling it over. I guess I have a lot to consider before I make any decisions.

"What would this mean for college?"

"You would still be going, Miss Octavia. Your education is of the utmost importance to me, your career path can be whatever you want it to be, you will just have extra responsibilities on top of college parties and your studies."

I laugh softly. “Okay, that’s good to know. I’ll have a think on it all and let you know.”

“That sounds perfect. Have you thought about your college options? I know you haven’t applied to any, but your status gives you an advantage where that isn’t really a problem. We should probably still get it sorted for you quickly.”

I smile at him, thankful to have him in my life. “I have a few ideas…”

# CHAPTER THIRTY-THREE

## OCTAVIA

"I can't believe we're actually here," Indi grins at me from the mirror across the room. "We made it to the end of the year, prom is tomorrow, exams are about to begin, and college is calling our names. Freedom, my friend. I can almost taste it."

I laugh at her. She's been so excited the last two weeks since I rose from the dead. Everything has been about prom, summer trip planning, and college. Though I still don't know if I'm going straight to college. I have to graduate first, and if I called this last year rocky, it'd be the understatement of the century.

"Well, we'll be going to prom if we ever decide on dresses," I giggle and she glares at me.

"You can't rush perfection." She sticks her tongue out at me and twists and turns to take in the sight of the floor-length midnight-blue dress she's wearing. It's unlike anything I've ever seen her wear, but it's perfection.

It looks like the night sky, the sewn-in beads and gems like a blanket of stars on the inky material. Her newly dyed hair is black, making her pale skin glow even more than usual. The dress adds to it, but my compliments have fallen on deaf ears.

"You really think this is the one?"

"Indi, you've tried on thirty two dresses in three hours. You've put this one back on four times. It's stunning. So I think you already know the answer to that."

She sticks her tongue out at me before looking back at the dress. "Not all of us decide as quickly as you did."

I laugh because she's not wrong. When I put my dress on this morning, it was the first one I picked, but the way Maverick's eyes lit up when I walked out of the dressing room sold me on it instantly.

The blood-red number made me look so vampy, and the halter neck did all sorts of things to my girls. I was sold. He snapped a picture, and then ducked out when he knew it was the one I was getting to go to his tux fitting with the guys.

Even East is coming to prom, and I'm so excited to be able to experience it with all of them. It's the next step to the rest of our lives.

I still need to talk to Indi about the Knights, and if that's something that she'd want. I've been meaning to bring it up all week, but I haven't worked out how yet. Especially since Ryker is still well and truly pissed at me.

Making his girl cry put me on his shit list, and I get it. Alex hasn't exactly been sunshine and rainbows with me either, though Ellis and Dylan were a little more understanding. No real surprises there. I was more shocked to find Alex there with the rest of them when I went to get Indi this morning.

Apparently my death brought them together, so it's not all a bad thing. Even if I am still sorry about it all.

"Okay, I'm buying the dress!" Indi announces, and I beam at her.

"Good! Let's get this thing paid for and then I demand lunch. I'm starving over here."

"Oh yeah, you're absolutely wasting away," she deadpans, and I bark out a laugh.

"Fuck you. Come on, you know you want a big cheesy slice from Tony's." I grin wider as she looks like she's about to drool all over her dress.

"Fine, yes, you know I can't say no to cheese. Unzip me?"

I stand and help her out of the dress, then head to the checkout while she dresses. I buy her the matching drop earrings too, and wait for the woman to box it up. "Are you okay to deliver it?"

"Yes, Miss Royal. Absolutely," the girl behind the counter responds, a little flustered. She was the same way when we came in at first too, and Indi and Mav teased me about it. Apparently she was a big Stone Royal fan. I give her Indi's address since her guys are all going with her to this dance

"You didn't have to do that, you know." Indi sighs as she finds me at the counter, motioning to the box.

"I know, but I wanted to. Gift giving is my love language, just let me love you."

"Fine," she grins, rolling her eyes at me. "But lunch is on me."

"If you say so," I tease, looping my arm through hers. We exit the store and head two blocks over to the new pizza place, which has been jam packed since it opened a week ago. We enter, finding Scout at the hostess station.

"Hey you guys!" She waves at us excitedly. "Just the two of you?"

"Yes, please," I say with a smile. She looks so much like Ryker and Ellis, she could easily be their triplet. "Busy morning?"

"Yeah, who would've thought so many people wanted pizza for breakfast?" She laughs as she grabs the menus. She hugs Indi quickly before leading us to an empty booth in the back of the place.

"Drinks?" Scout asks as she hands us our menus.

"I'll take a coke please," I say, and Indi has the same. Scout skips off behind the serving counter to grab our drinks.

"How are the guys dealing with her working here?" I ask Indi, smirking. 'Cause I'd put money on them stressing the fuck out.

"They're not," she giggles, pointing to a guy sitting at the far end of the counter. "That's one of Ryker's guys. The argument about her having a babysitter was earsplitting, but obviously, Ryker is a stubborn asshole. So she's been messing with Karl all week."

I take the guy in. He's tall, even curled over the counter the way he is, it's impossible to miss. So are the tattoos that cover every visible inch of his skin. The seat beside him is empty, and I can't tell if that's due to Scout or the sheer menacing aura he's projected. His eyes never leave Scout as she flits around the place, and there's a reverence in the way he looks at her that makes me smirk. "I think Ryker might have more trouble on his hands than he thought he would."

Indi cackles, nodding. "You saw that too, huh? The boys are oblivious to it, and I'm not about to say anything. I'm not sure how she feels about him, but I'm not about to rain on her parade."

I high five her across the table. "We should invite her on our girls weekend."

"Yes!" she exclaims, her eyes shining. "That'd be amazing."

"What would?" Scout asks as she appears with our drinks.

"V was just saying you should join us on our girls trip the weekend after prom." Scout turns to me, eyes wide.

"Really? I'd love that!"

"Then consider it done. We'll grab you after school on Friday," I tell her, making a mental note to adjust the booking I made yesterday when Indi and I decided on a belated birthday trip. The guys weren't exactly happy about me going away without them, but I reminded them that we have all summer, and the road trip we have planned is all kinds of epic. It quieted them down for the time being at least.

"You guys rock! Thank you! And since I'm with you guys, I can ditch the babysitter!"

"Only if you want to," I wink at her, and she smirks at me, flicking her dark hair over her shoulder.

"I think it'll be good for him to realize I don't need him." Her eyes sparkle with mischief and I can't help but laugh. I haven't spent much time with Scout, but I know she's good people from what Indi has said about her, and that's all I need to know.

I grin at her, nodding. "Got to keep them guessing."

---

Prom is finally here. I've spent all day primping and preening. Gracie came over and removed my extensions, cut my hair since it's mostly grown back now, and put it up for me. Butterflies flutter in my stomach at the thought of the dance. I know things have changed dramatically since homecoming, but illogical fears are just that.

The limo collected us from the house about ten minutes ago, and we're heading to the hotel the ECP prom committee picked for this year's prom. The theme is red carpet, so I'm sure it's going to be all kinds of glam, but I can't really think much past the guys right now.

They look good enough to fucking eat. You'd think with the amount of fucking we've been doing since I got back that my appetite would be satiated, yet… apparently I'm a greedy bitch, because I want more. All of them in their black-on-black suits is fucking mouthwatering.

"Hungry, pretty girl?" Finn murmurs in my ear, his fingers playing with the bare skin on my back. The material of the back only just covers the top of my ass, and the thigh-high splits in the skirt make this dress possibly the most risqué I've ever worn, but when I saw Mav's face in the store, I knew this was the dress to have.

I glance at him, nodding, and he pats his lap.

The other three are talking, not paying too much attention to the two of us. Even as I glance at them, I can tell that whatever they're debating has them distracted for the moment. Not a surprise with everything we have going on now that everyone's back on board with the Knights, and we had our first Conclave meeting this week about how to fix the sect, but that's for later. Right now, Finn has my attention on him, and I'm debating if I'm going to do as he asked.

Fuck it.

I climb into Finley's lap, thankful for the thigh slits as I straddle him. His hands clasp my hips as I lean forward, kissing him and rolling my hips against him.

"Looks like our princess is putting on a show," Maverick calls out from behind me. "I am always here for that."

Fucking Mav. Such a voyeur. Not going to lie that it makes me hotter though.

Finn moves one hand from my hip and through the slit of my skirt, hissing when he realizes I have no panties on. He runs one finger through my slick and groans. "She's fucking soaking."

I whimper at his touch as he gently teases me, trying to roll my hips again as I search for more friction.

"Fuck our girl, Finn. Give her what she wants." Linc's words are like a sharp sting across my back as Finley plunges two fingers inside of me.

"Can't deny her anything," he murmurs as I move to unzip his pants. I palm his already hard dick, loving his groans as I work my hand over the tip of him. Lifting up, I move my dress aside and line him up with my pussy as he withdraws his fingers. He pushes them into my mouth as I slide down onto him, tasting myself on his fingers as I burn at the stretch of him.

As soon as he's buried to the hilt, my head falls back with pure ecstasy and satisfaction at being this full. Finn's large palm is right between my shoulder blades, holding me steady as the limo takes us to our final destination.

"Fuck, she looks fucking delicious." Mav's words are dancing in my ears, but it's Linc's command that sends shivers down my spine.

"East, I think our girl is hungry. Feed her your cock, keep her quiet." With my eyes closed, I moan out my approval.

East gets into a kneeling position and, careful of my hair, curls his fingers around the nape of my neck and pushes my mouth down onto his steel-hard dick.

Behind me, I hear the shifting of fabric and the thought that Mav and Linc are both jacking themselves off as they watch me fuck and suck in the back of this limo amps up my growing need. I'm flustered and horny and my body is aching for more.

Finn places a hand at the small of my back with his other firmly on my thigh as he fucks me like he's trying to ruin me—I've never been more willing to be ruined—all while East fucks my mouth until I'm gagging on the head every time he slams it to the back of my throat.

"Fucking hell."

Linc's groan makes me feel like a filthy princess as my pussy and mouth get a hard pounding.

"We're almost there." Finn's words are my undoing. I moan around the thick flesh of East's dick as he fucks my face with abandon just as my orgasm builds up from the friction on my clit. Finn grunts, my name falling from between his lips as he spills inside of me.

East lets out a roar as he buries my nose in his groin and feeds me his cum right down my throat before pulling out and kissing me with panting breaths.

I'm a fucking mess as the limo pulls up to the curb and the engine shuts off.

"I don't know whether to let you step out looking like a hot mess who's just been fucked to within an inch of her life, or allow you fix your filthy mouth." Linc grins like he already knows the answer.

Fucker.

He hands me my clutch that was lost in my fuckery and I take a minute to sort my face. Thank God for unsmearable lip stain! I retouch my eyeliner, my hair has barely moved despite everything, so it only takes about thirty seconds for me to put myself back together.

"Perfection," Finn utters as he turns my head back to him, kissing me gently. "Ready, pretty girl?"

A flash of what happened at homecoming sears my mind, but I push it away. I'm not that girl anymore. "Let's do this."

---

I sway in East's arms as *I'll Be* by Edwin McCain plays over the sound system. I grin over at Indi who is slow dancing next to us with Alex. As the song finishes, I extract myself from East, kissing him softly before moving over to Indi.

"Can I steal my girl?" I ask, but not really asking as I take her hand as *Shivers* by Ed Sheeran starts playing. I'm not sure who chose the DJ, but I'm here for it. He's been laying down some absolute jams tonight.

We laugh as we dance to the beat like loons, loving that we don't take ourselves too seriously. We dance through the next four songs, laughing as we do, our guys all huddled around one table. Apparently my 'death' brought a lot of people together.

Maybe asking Indi and the guys to join the Knights is a good idea. Sunday, when Indi and I go out to lunch, I'm going to ask. It's decided.

"Ladies and gentlemen, it's time to declare our prom king and queen!" Blair's voice sounds across the room. She's standing on the raised platform where the DJ booth is in a shimmering, spaghetti strap silver dress that hugs every inch of her. She looks amazing.

Everyone turns to face her as Indi drags me from the dance floor to where our guys are sitting, waiting for us.

"And our prom king is… Maverick Riley!" My jaw drops at the announcement of Mav's name, who looks as shocked as I am that Blair just called his name. The spotlight moves to our table as cheers and applause fill the room.

"I don't know which of you fuckers did this, but revenge will be sweet," he threatens as he stands and heads toward the stage. Blair places the crown on his head and he stares menacingly out at the school body. My giggles erupt as he glares at me across the room.

"And our prom queen is…" Blair pauses for effect, winking at me before she opens her mouth. "Indigo Montoya!"

"What the fuck?" Indi groans and I laugh.

"Not so nice getting the crown, is it?" I tease. Feels all the sweeter after the shit she gave me about homecoming. "Now go rock the shit out of that crown."

"You're always a queen to me, Sunshine," Ryker says to her, kissing her before pushing her toward the stage. The cheers and applause greet her too as Blair gives her the sash and crown.

"Now for the Royal Dance!"

I burst out laughing, and Finley snickers next to me. "Those two dancing is going to be hilarious."

While Indi and Mav have come pretty far the last few weeks, they still bicker like siblings, but he takes her hand and leads her to the dance floor.

"If he touches her ass…" Ryker starts, but Ellis punches his arm.

"Don't be a dick, it's Mav. He's not going to do a damn thing."

I smile at Ellis. It's so nice that everyone is finally getting along. It's the start of something promising. While I hate what we had to go through to get here, I'll never regret the outcome of it. The photographer for the night snaps shots of them as they dance like fools to *Stay* by Justin Bieber and The Kid Laroi. They wave for us all to join them, so I coax the rest of the table up, and once we're all there dancing, everyone else joins in too.

This night is everything I wanted it to be. The cheese of prom and one of the better memories from our senior year. We all deserved a night like tonight, just something fun after the craziness of this year.

I dance and laugh with each of my guys, with Alex and Indi, and lose myself to the laughter of it all. A year ago I thought I wanted nothing less than to come back to Echoes Cove. That there was nothing here for me… and despite the reasons for my return, my new found family are more than I could've ever hoped for.

# CHAPTER THIRTY-FOUR

## OCTAVIA

I walk into the back yard, heading for the pool. The sun is finally hot enough for a day on the sun loungers, and while I intend to swim some too, I am overdue a day of lying by the pool and reading, so that's exactly my plan. I have the house to myself after practically shoving Smithy out the door with Matthew this morning, making Matthew promise to make Smithy have a good weekend.

He deserves some rest. I'm not the only one who's been through the wringer lately. Plus, my feet still hurt from dancing all night last night, so a day of chill is exactly what the doctor ordered.

Sitting on the lounger, I pop my Kindle and phone on the table before rubbing in my lotion, aviators in place so I can actually see for the time being. Once I've finished my lotion, I grab my Kindle and move to lie back when my phone buzzes.

Mav: Remember the conversation we had about your punishment? And your safe word?

I suck in a breath and bite my lip, instantly fucking wet just from that message.

Me: Yes.

Mav: Run.

Holy fuck.

I glance around, not seeing him, but I feel his eyes on me. My breath hitches in anticipation as I scramble to my feet. Movement in my peripheral makes me run toward the back door. I know I agreed to this, I just didn't think it would be so fucking hot, while being so fucking terrifying.

Being hunted by my very own psychopath, knowing he intends on ruining me and making me bleed shouldn't make me this hot. Yet, I almost don't want to run.

But that's half of the game.

Bringing the predator out in him.

When I reach out for the door handle, it doesn't turn all the way. It's fucking locked. I don't remember locking it.

Shit.

Flattening my back against the wood, I frantically look right then left and try to think of another path to take, another entrance into the house.

The garage.

I don't see him anywhere, but I know he's here, his presence is palpable along every hair on my body.

Just as I'm about to make a run for the other side of the house, I stop dead in my tracks at the sound of whistling coming from the far end of the property. Close enough to hear, far away enough that I can't make out where, exactly.

A few weeks before my fake death, Mav and I binged on the Kill Bill movies and, like a fucking idiot, I told him the whistle they used was creepy and made my entire body shiver with fear.

The motherfucker is whistling that exact song right now and I've never been surer of his psychotic tendencies than at this very moment.

"You're evil," I mutter the words but I wouldn't be surprised if he heard them.

There's no time to figure out where he is, I need to run if I want any hope of winning this game. This very sinister and fucked up game that's making me wetter by the second.

Maybe I've got some psychopathic tendencies, too.

I make a run for it, heading straight for the side door to the garage and I'm a little wary that it's not locked. Then again, he couldn't have planned this, right? He hasn't been anywhere around here today.

Grateful, I rush inside, closing and locking the door behind me. With a panicked three-sixty I try to find a good hiding spot just in case this is a set-up. The garage is big and he can't just read my mind.

Then it hits me.

The panic room.

Dad built it to look like the continuation of the wall, said it would be my secret hiding place if ever I needed to feel safe.

I turn to the side and run on the balls of my feet to avoid making too much noise. The coast is clear, the hand drawn flower on the wall my clue to where the opening would be.

The thought of going into a small, confined space of my own accord makes my skin crawl as panic begins to rise, but I remind myself that this is my punishment and no matter what, I'm safe.

I'm always safe with Mav, even if the fear spike makes my heart race.

Breathing heavily, I open the door by pushing in the mechanism and quickly shut myself inside, fighting the urge to double over and hyperventilate.

Except, I don't have time to react because I don't bump into a wall.

Not even close.

"Getting brave, aren't we?"

I gasp so loudly at the low and dark tone of his voice that I nearly pee myself a little.

I'm about to tell him he scared the fuck out of me when his hand clamps down on my mouth and pulls me back against his chest. His dick is so hard, I'm not sure what I'm most afraid of right now. The dark or his huge cock.

How did he get here before me? He was out there whistling like a fucking maniac when I ran in here.

I want to ask him a million questions but they all die on my hitched breaths when I feel the cold, hard steel of what I'm pretty fucking sure is a blade pressing against my flesh.

Needless to say, this is not ideal. Trapped in a small space in complete and utter darkness, at the mercy of a man who has serious blurred vision about the line between what is right and wrong. Who is currently sliding a knife up the inside of my thigh.

It should be a huge fucking red flag. And yet…

On instinct, I fight him. I try to get myself free of him, crying into the palm of his hand as he clamps down harder and puts more pressure on the knife that has almost reached my pussy.

My wet as fuck and treacherous pussy.

"You should know by now, princess, that you can run…" he slides the knife to the small piece of fabric that holds my bathing suit together and slices it right off. "But you can never fucking hide from me."

I freeze as the lines between fantasy and real life fucking fear blur in my mind. The darkness is making things fuzzy, almost giving me the feeling that this is all in my head. That it's a dream or a nightmare, despite all of my senses being on high alert.

He moves the knife upward, slicing off the strings of my top and I'm suddenly completely naked in this fucking black hole.

Panic spikes in me again when I hear his breathy voice at my ear, the sultry sound running through my nerve endings like a small electric pulse.

"When I release your mouth, the only sounds I want to hear from you are your grunts while I fuck you hard enough to bruise your pretty little skin."

I shake my head no but what I really want to say is "Yes! God yes!"

But telling him no, fighting him, is like a red flag to a bull. So of course, I do whatever it takes to make him slam his dick inside my empty, wanting pussy.

I shake my head in a show of no consent, pretending to fight him and smile when he moans his approval.

"Tough fucking shit, princess. I said yes."

When I try to bite down on his hand, I clench my thighs at the filthy curses that pass through his lips, the breath landing on the column of my neck. I am so fucking turned on right now. I know we discussed playing out this whole non-consent thing, but fuck me it's hotter than I thought it would be.

When I start to fight him harder, turning and twisting and trying to grab at him on one side and the other, I almost sigh in relief when he grabs my forearms and pins them at the small of my back.

That's when he releases my mouth and pushes the side of my face against the wall.

I scream, my lungs filling with air and then releasing a screech like my life depends on it.

"Fuck, I love the way you cry." At first I'm confused when I hear him, but when he buries his fingers in my hair—holding me tight against the wall—and he licks a path up my cheek, taking his time to go from my jaw to my eye, I realize tears are falling freely and he's licking them up like they're his favorite meal.

I can't see him and he can't see me, but somehow he knows I'm crying before even I do.

With my hands secured behind me, and my legs kicked apart enough for his big body to nudge in between my thighs, he plunges inside me in one hard, quick move.

We both groan at the feel of us joined once more. At the fight that led us here. At the fantasy that he made a reality.

"This pussy will always be mine. Day, night, any hour. When I want it, when I crave it."

He's probably right.

But agreeing with him is not part of the fantasy.

Fighting him off? Yeah, that's what it's all about.

I push my ass toward him and try to free my hands, but almost weep when his dick slides out of me.

The next thing I know, my wrists are tied with whatever it is he'd had on hand.

"I thought you might disagree, so I made sure to be prepared."

*Fucker.*

I think that's all he's going to do but that was my first mistake.

Never underestimate a man with no limits.

Mav turns me around and in one smooth move, he's got my arms up over my head, the rope secured somewhere above me.

Fucking hell, how did he do that?

I'm guessing he put a lot of thought into this and for that alone, I want to kiss him. Hard and long.

Hiking my thighs up with his hands, he slams back inside me, but this time, he shuts me up with his tongue.

His kiss is demanding and invading. We're all lips and tongues and curses as he fucks with the force of a tsunami on the shores of an island. He's the power of the waves and I'm the sand that submits to his will.

"You think you can lead this dance, princess?"

"Fuck you." I spit the words out and cringe at the thought that I may have actually spit on his mouth.

"Hmm, is that your way of begging me for more?"

God, I love this man.

There are no words that I could say that would be as filthy and dubious as I want, so I say nothing as he pummels my pussy without a care in the world.

Our sweat mingles and our muscles are tight as he pistons in and out of me, making sure to grind against my clit every time he's at the hilt.

“Get off me!” I scream at him, feeding the fantasy, and I feel him grin as he bites down on my shoulder, making me cry out again.

*I'm so close.*

So fucking close but I don't dare say anything to him.

"Do it, princess. Come all over my dick."

He thrusts in once more, then again, and by the time he's slammed in the third time, I go off like a fucking volcano.

I scream again, this time his name falling from my mouth like a prayer. I repeat it over and over again as the shaking subsides and the warmth of my climax washes over me.

Blinking my euphoria away, I whimper as he continues to pound into me. He hasn't come yet.

"Mav?"

My arms are suddenly freed and his hand in my hair pushes me down to my knees as he slides out of my pussy.

"Open your mouth."

Fuck yes.

I do as I'm told and without waiting for a command or permission, I take his balls into my hand and swallow his cock all the way to the back of my throat.

He tastes like me and him together and it makes me fucking hot all over again.

"Fuck yes. That's it, princess. Take my cock down your throat. Suck on it like a good girl."

God, his filthy mouth does things to me.

Placing both of his hands on the sides of my face, he rears back and fucks my face without abandon.

"I'm going to come so fucking hard down your throat. Come with me, princess. Play with your clit and come with me."

I move quickly at his demand and in the time it takes him to thrust three or four more times inside my mouth, we both let go.

Of every fucking thing.

I come all over my thighs and he jets his cum straight down my throat and I swallow every fucking drop he has to give me.

He roars in the small space before pulling out of my mouth. I fall back from my knees to sit back on my legs, spent and exhausted.

Mav picks me up and cradles me in his arms as he opens the door and leads me straight to my bathroom where there’s already a steaming bubble bath waiting for me. He sits me on the counter while he strips out of his clothes, then picks me up again and carries me into the tub, sitting us down, shifting me so I can lie back against him.

“I love you, princess,” he murmurs, his hands rubbing circles on my thighs.

I let out a contented sigh and lean my head back so I can look up at him. “I love you too, Mav.”

---

“Surprise!”

I startle at the shouts as I walk into the private room of the restaurant with Indi, grinning from ear to ear as I take in everyone here. Smithy and Matthew, my guys, Bentley and Luc. Indi's guys. Jenna and the Midnight Blue girls, plus Mac and some of the others from the tour.

"Happy belated birthday, V," Indi says, squeezing me. "And while I'd like to take all the credit for this, Smithy and the guys did most of the hard work. I have plans for next weekend though" She wags her brows at me and I laugh, hugging her back before making my way around the room, saying hello to everyone here.

Even Ryker hugs me, which shocks the shit out of me.

I sit down at the head of the table, Lincoln to my left, Indi to my right, and I try not to cry at just how happy I am to have everyone I love in one room. Seeing my past and present collide is kind of overwhelming in the best of ways.

I take a deep breath, trying to wrangle the emotions flooding me as I grin at Smithy, who is sitting opposite me at the end of the table, tucked between Matthew and Luc. I never thought I'd have a huge family, but I've learned family isn't blood. It's the people that show up for you, even when you don't ask them to.

These people right here are my family.

Smithy looks to me, then glances at Indi and back, and I can see the question in his gaze. Did I ask her yet? I shake my head, letting him know I didn't, and he gives me a quick nod. He knows I was going to ask her today, but I was going to ask her over food.

I wasn't expecting any of this, so I haven't had the chance.

"Thank you for all of this," I murmur to Lincoln, who takes my hand and squeezes it.

"Anything for you, Octavia. We had plans for your birthday before Harrison ruined them. This is just the start of what we have planned." He winks at me and I swear to God my pussy flutters at the sight of it.

*Down girl.*

"Any news on Harrison?" I ask, and he shakes his head.

"No, we know he's back in the States, but he's been very fucking clever about disguising his movements. We will find him though, and he will be dealt with." His eyes darken with rage, before he shakes it off. "But we can worry about that tomorrow, let's just enjoy today."

He kisses me quickly before my attention is pulled across the room to where Jenna and East are mid laughing fit. All I hear is the word tequila sunrise and I groan. "Jenna, whyyyyyyy?"

"Oh come on, Summertime Starlight. You know it's a good story." I flip her the finger, and she tells the story about my first ever drunken episode on tour. The dancing on table tops, thinking I was living my best *Coyote Ugly* life, singing at the top of my lungs like I was Mariah freaking Carey.

The whole room is just love and laughter, and I feel so blessed.

The servers filter into the room to get everyone's drink orders. Once they move further down the table, East pulls me to one side, where there's a gift table, and pulls a small jewelry box from his back pocket.

"Happy Birthday, V."

I smile up at him, taking the box from his outstretched hand. "You totally didn't have to get me anything."

"Shh," he says, putting a finger over my mouth. "Just open the damn box."

I roll my eyes at him and remove his hand. I look down at the sparkly infinity charm, lined with black crystals. "East—"

"Forever. That's what I want with you, Octavia. That's what this is. I don't know where life is going to take us, but I am going be at your side for all of it." He cups my cheeks in his hands, looking at me like I'm the center of his universe, before he kisses me. He pours so much love into the action that my heart feels like it's going to explode.

"I love you," I whisper against his lips.

"I love you too." He pulls back, lifting my hand, and undoing my bracelet before slipping the new charm on and reattaching it to my wrist.

"Come on you two, it's time to order!" Mav hollers and my stomach gurgles as if in response. East chuckles at me as he leads me back to the table.

Hours pass in a blur of laughter, drinking, and food. I wasn't sure how we were being served alcohol until Matthew mentions that he owns this place. A few more things made sense after that.

I try to stifle a yawn, but Finn catches me, smirking at me as he moves to my chair. He stands me up, sits in my seat then puts me back in his lap. "Tired, pretty girl."

"Yeah," I nod, "but I also don't want to leave."

He kisses down my neck and shoulder, making me gasp as my eyes flutter closed.

"Well, isn't this just cozy?" The entire place goes silent as my eyes fly open and I see Harrison standing across the room, a gun raised, pointed in my direction. "I should've known I'd find your little whore in the arms of another man, Lincoln."

"Harrison," Lincoln starts, as Smithy stands facing off with the mad man holding a gun.

"What the fuck are you playing at, Harrison?" he hisses, and quicker than anyone can react, Harrison brings up his arm and smashes the gun into Smithy's temple. He drops to the ground like nothing, and I let out a scream. Matthew dives for him, but I can already see he's unconscious.

"Who would've thought the little Royal slut could cause so much damage? I should've killed you along with your daddy," he snarls at me. Finn is up and out of our chair, standing in front of me in a second, as Harrison moves toward us, one gun trained on me before pulling a second and keeping it on the rest of the room.

Lincoln stands, coming to stand in front of Finn, blocking Harrison's way. "Get out of my way, Lincoln. I don't want to kill you, but I will. She's ruined enough lives. I am here to put things back to rights."

"I don't fucking think so," Maverick yells, charging at Harrison with East. They tackle him and I scream, as the entire room bursts into movement. The gun pops three times, and screams erupt from in here and in the restaurant. I freeze, trying to look for my guys, when I hear Harrison's voice, and find him face to face with Lincoln, guns trained on him and on Mav. Finn holds me in place as I struggle against him, trying to get to East who is bleeding on the ground. I know he's not the only one hurt, the whimpers in the room from Indi and Matthew fill my ears.

"I told you not so long ago you'd have to pick between your brother and your slut. I guess you made your choice."

My ears ring at the next pop, a scream pierces the air as my knees go weak and the world goes dark.

# EPILOGUE

## FINLEY

ONE YEAR LATER

I sit in the sand, watching the lights from the pier illuminate the night sky. The sounds of the waves fill my ears, calming me despite the hubbub of voices and rides from the pier. It's weird being back in The Cove after being away for so long.

I've never been away from my home town for this long, and it was almost impossible to come back.

So much has changed in the last year. It's hard to wrap my head around it all. There was so much pain, so much anger, that we all got a little lost for a while after Octavia's surprise party. Blame was passed around from pillar to post, but that didn't get us anywhere.

The last time I was here, in this spot, I was comforting Octavia as she cried.

Fuck me, that feels like a few lifetimes ago.

"Finley, is that you?" I look up and find Indi hand-in-hand with Ryker, Ellis and Alex not far behind them.

"Hey, Indi. You got here early."

"Yeah, I wanted to walk the beach before we did this. Remember the good times, ya know?"

I nod as she smiles wistfully at me. "Yeah I know, it's why I came out here on my own too. The others shouldn't be long though."

"Yeah, Dylan is meeting us here, he had to help his dad finish up in the garage before he could head over." The other three say hello as they sit in the sand with me, filling me in on what's happened to them since we all left here at the start of last summer.

About twenty minutes later, Dylan lopes up on the beach, a giant grin on his face. "Look who I found in the parking lot!"

Octavia laughs from her perch on his back before squealing as he drops to sit with her still attached to him, her arms around his neck, and legs around his waist. "You're such an ass, Dylan!"

I press my lips together, trying not to laugh too hard at her fake outrage. It's so good to see her smile. There was a minute back there when I wondered if she'd ever smile again.

She's been through so much, but my girl is a fighter, and she's made it through the darkness that tried to take her from me.

Indi leaps on her once she detaches herself from Dylan and the two of them laugh, catching up like they didn't FaceTime on the flight home earlier. I sit quietly, listening to their conversation as they talk like they don't talk to each other every single day.

I know it's not the same since we're on opposite sides of the country from her bestie now, but you'd never know there was a day that they'd been apart to look at them.

Thick as thieves.

Have been since day one.

It makes me so fucking happy that she had a friend like that through everything that happened senior year. After everything we went through, I think it would take the armies of Hell to separate those two, and even then, my bet's on the girls.

A figure drops down beside me, and I turn to find Mav sitting there, East dropping beside him in the next second. "Took you long enough."

Mav pushes me with his shoulder, making me rock into our girl who slides onto my lap. "Hey, pretty girl."

She leans in to kiss me, then moves to Mav and East, doing the same with them.

"Are we doing this thing?" Ryker asks, impatient as ever. Some things will never change.

"Let me just grab my bag. I put my stuff in there, since the gorilla man carried me down the beach," V smiles, moving back to where Indi is sitting next to her back pack.

She pulls out the box we put together earlier today while Mav and Ellis go and gather wood to start the fire.

"You sure you're ready for this?" I ask her, and she nods.

"Yeah, it's time. I'll never fully let him go, but I need to be able to move forward, and this seems like the best way to do that."

Indi smiles sadly at her, taking her hand and squeezing it. As much as I know Octavia loves us, and needs us, I'm not sure she'd have survived the last two years without her walking rainbow of a friend.

It doesn't take long for Dylan to get the bonfire lit, the flames crawling higher into the sky as the heat increases.

"Getting started without us?" I turn and smile as Lincoln, Smithy, and

Matthew find us. V runs to them, wrapping each of them in a hug, leaving Linc for last. He scoops her into his arms and kisses her before joining the rest of us.

After Harrison was shot in the restaurant last year, a lot of things fell apart. Lincoln lost himself a little to a black hole, despite his hatred for his dad, it was still his dad, and he was covered in brain matter from the police officer's shot.

The fact that we nearly lost East and Smithy at his hands after losing so many others, including Stone… Linc took on the full force of guilt for his father's actions. It took our entire summer road trip before he fully came back to himself.

Thankfully, spending our freshman year together at Saints U in New York has been a breath of fresh air. I never thought I'd like the cold of the East Coast, and despite missing the sunshine of California, we all loved it there in our shared house.

V moves forward, pulling her dad's journals from the box and moves toward the fire. "I miss you, Dad, each and every day, but I know you wouldn't want me to keep looking back. So I'm doing this for you, as well as for me."

She holds the journals in shaking hands, so I move to stand at her back, my hands enclosing hers. "It's okay, pretty girl. You can do this." I help her as she drops the journals into the fire, purging the bad memories along with the words she's read endlessly the last year as she clung to his memory once her personal nightmare was over.

Each person steps forward, casting the memories they want to let go of into the fire too, taking a seat in the sand once they're done.

There is a peace as I let go of the last pieces of my parents, a weight lifting from me as I drop their pictures into the fire. The house that they ruined me in burned down last summer, by Maverick's swift hand, and that was how we got the idea for our little burn party. A way to cleanse the shadows on our souls.

Octavia drops back into my lap, leaning her head back on my shoulder. "It feels good to be home," she murmurs before turning her attention to Indi, and I smile as I press a kiss into her hair.

I never thought I'd agree with her, but she's right.

It is good to be home, and my home is wherever she is.

The End

# ACKNOWLEDGMENTS

I can't believe we here, at the end of this book, the close of the series. It has been the wildest ride and there are so many people I need to thank.

First, thank you to KC for getting me past the finish line on this one. It was a hard bloody slog at the end there, but we made it!

Rose, you know you're my wifey, thank you for the FaceTimes at all times of day to keep my mental health on track so I could get to this point.

Nikki, for keeping my shit in line while I've been squirreling really freaking hard with this book. I appreciate the hell out of you, thank you so much for everything you do.

David, you sparkly unicorn you, thank you for everything, including the hilarious laughs when you should 100% be asleep! Thank you for loving these guys, and calling me out when it's needed. For making the words shine and well, for being my social butterfly bitch aha.

Eva, thank you for always being there when I need to gripe, and for well, all the things. If I listed it all I'd be here all damn day ahaha.

To my alpha & beta teams, you guys are freaking rockstars. Lisa, Zoe, Megan, Kiera, Jeni, Liberty, Kyla, Sam, Jessi & Nicole. Thank you for your priceless feedback, and for loving these characters as much as I do.

Thank you to Sarah and Sam for making sure the words shine by the time I'm done fucking around with them, and for letting me corrupt you aha.

Finally, to you the reader, thank you. For taking a chance on an author you've probably never heard of. For picking up a new book. For running the gauntlet with us. Just thank you.

Here's looking forward what comes next!

Peace out

xoxo

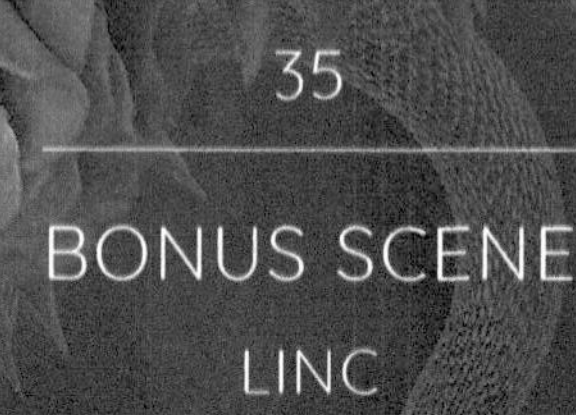

# 35

# BONUS SCENE

## LINC

Her screams haunt me night after night but for some reason, tonight, it's like each scream is a fresh tear of my already shredded soul. I always know when she's fallen asleep because her screams reach me the minute she succumbs.

How Smithy deals with it is beyond me because I'm not as close as he is, and to me, they seem *so fucking loud.*

But then, I've always been in tune with each and every part of her.

Maybe that's why this wrecks me so bad. Doing all of this to her, knowing that it's for her own good… it doesn't make it any easier.

After over half an hour of her screams, they finally stop and I know she's woken herself up. I clench my fists as I try to stop myself from moving, but I already know I'm going to cave.

I've managed to resist this long, but tonight… Tonight is my undoing.

Call it a culmination of everything until now, or call it me finally giving in to what I actually want to do—no *need* to do—but I find myself pulling on a pair of sweatpants and pocketing my phone.

It might be two in the morning, but I barely sleep these days anyway.

I pad barefoot through the house and across the lawn onto her property. It should probably feel weird, but it doesn't.

After a moment of contemplating overriding the alarm to the kitchen doors, or climbing the trellises, I decide the climb is the easier option. She has the balcony door which she never fucking locks and this way I can be in and out without anyone else knowing.

Because God forbid anyone know that Lincoln Saint has actual feelings.

Thanks to the insane training I've endured my entire life, even barefooted, the climb takes no more than thirty seconds. I reach for the balcony door and find it unlocked.

Fucking Octavia Royal.

I shove down the caveman urge to yell at her and open the door as quietly as I can but it still creaks. She rolls over in bed, sitting up and facing me, a look of disbelief on her face. The bags under her eyes, and her bed head of hair make me both want to smile and break things. But I resist the urge as she opens that sassy fucking mouth of hers.

"What the fuck are you doing here?"

I don't say a word as I glare at her, keeping the mask in place that I know she needs right now. Because even though I'm here, calling a truce for a night, she still needs to hate me.

Without a word, I pull back the sheets and climb into the bed beside her, trying not to remember just how many times I've done this before.

I live and breathe for the girl glaring at me, and she has no fucking idea.

"What are you doing?" she screeches as she grabs the sheets, trying to stop me. It's half-hearted, because really, I know she knows why I'm here.

Instead of fighting her, I lie down, grabbing the sheets myself. "I can hear you screaming from my room. Now lie down and sleep, I'm not going anywhere."

She scoffs at me, but as I pull her toward me, I feel her melt beneath my touch. She might hate me, but this right here… She's always been safe in this bubble with me.

Even now with everything, she knows it even if she doesn't want to believe it. She glares at me for a second, before turning her back to me as she lies down.

I consider leaving the distance between us, but fuck it. I'm here now, might as well just cave entirely for one night. I pull her back toward me and tuck her against my chest, draping a protective arm over her.

She whimpers softly as sleep starts to reclaim her already, but I can feel how stiff she still is. I close my eyes, hoping that she gives in and whisper to her. "You don't need to cry anymore. I'm here now."

She slips into sleep and relaxes against me entirely. I already know I'm not getting any sleep tonight, but at least she can, so instead I lie and listen to her breaths even out, holding her tighter when she starts to whimper, but she doesn't scream.

Not once.

When the sun finally comes up, and I know that she's going to be okay, I slip from her room like I was never there.

No one needs to know I was because I was only weak for just one night.

And that's all it can ever be.

One night.

# REBEL HEART

THE KINGS OF THE COVE

LILY WILDHART

*Rebel Hart*
The Kings of the Cove


Editor: Encompass Press, LLC
Proofreader: Sassi's Editing Services

# CHAPTER ONE

"You're kidding, right?" My mom rolls her eyes at me as we head into the suburbs my parents have dragged me to after zero notice that they were upending my entire life.

"Come on, Indi. This move is great for your dad. I know this isn't the city, but give it a chance."

I grumble as I put my AirPods back in, wishing I was back in New York, sad that I'm going to miss the Stone Royal gig I had tickets for tomorrow night.

I miss the city already.

Usually I'm all about the bright side of things, finding every silver lining, but I'm not sure what the bright side of this is. Though that could also be because we've been on the road since three am after spending last night in a hotel.

I mean, I didn't exactly have a ton of friends back home, but the city was my playground. The music scene, the alt scene, the tattoo bar where I worked on weekends was amazing, and well… this place is a far cry from the city.

There, it didn't matter that I don't always people well—they tend to find me a little odd, and that's fine, because I am. But it makes moving to a new place kind of suck extra balls.

I gawk as we pass the mega-mansions, half praying that we're not moving to this side of town. My folks aren't exactly short on money, but those places scream old money and rich bitches. It's bad enough that school starts in two weeks and I'm being enrolled in a prep school. I can't deal with having those people as my neighbors too.

We drive through the streets of Echoes Cove and some of my previous reservations lift. It doesn't seem as small as I first feared. My grin widens as we pass a Mexican place, the Starbucks drive thru, and a ton of other stores and restaurants.

Okay, well at least I don't have to give up my whipped, blended, chocolatey goodness start to each day.

Some things are vital to being my normal peppy self, and that is absolutely one of them.

Now here's hoping there are some actual normal people in this town. Because from what I've seen so far, it's a bunch of Ken and Barbie dolls.

*Jeebus save me.*

I push play on my iPad, hoping to finish the latest episode of *Adams Ever After,* a guilty pleasure of mine that I'm not guilty about even in the slightest, pulling my focus away from the sights around me.

Usually I'd try to be upbeat about moving. Hell, I'm usually upbeat about everything, but my parents gave me zero notice, so being peppy about this is going to take a minute. I think my sullen response has my parents fully thrown because, well, I don't think I've ever not been their sunshine and rainbows child.

But jeez, give a girl some warning. Some time to process.

When my episode finishes, I glance back out the window and notice we're in what I'd call the normal part of town. The houses aren't exactly small, but they're not the McMansions from before either.

We pull into the driveway of a white house with a blue door, the U-Haul van my dad is driving pulls in behind us, and my mom claps her hands together. "Day one of the rest of our lives, Indi girl. Smiles on."

I swallow the tart response on my tongue and try to remember that my parents are actually super excited about this move. So instead, I paste a smile on my face, pull down my heart-shaped sunnies and tuck my blue hair behind my ears.

"That's my girl." Mom beams before climbing from the car and practically skipping to my dad.

God, they make me nauseous sometimes with how in love they are. Mostly, it's jealousy because I'm not convinced that type of love finds everyone, but still, positive thoughts only.

That's my normal motto anyway.

Let's hope this weird-ass town doesn't fuck with me and my motto too bad.

I climb from the car just as another truck pulls up. "Indi! We have a surprise for you!" my dad calls, waving me over. "I know this was all a bit of a shock, but I thought that this might take the sting away a little."

A crunch of metal from the truck reveals a dusty blue Jeep Wrangler.

Holy shit.

"You got me Stiles' truck?" The question is more a screech as excitement races through my veins.

"I don't know what a Stiles is, but this is the right one, right? The one on your vision board?" my dad asks hesitantly, but smiles when I scream and leap on him with a hug.

"Thank you! This is the best gift ever!"

He holds me tight before putting me down so my feet touch the ground again. "There's my sunshine girl. I've missed your smile."

"I'd say I'm sorry, but I'm too excited!" I beam, bouncing on the spot. The guy who delivered my truck, and apparently my parents' new cars, walks over and hands my dad the keys.

"Once we've unpacked the U-Haul, I'll give you the keys. Deal?"

Even the thought of having to unpack doesn't dim my excitement. Some people might think it's ridiculous to be this excited about a car, but those people don't understand my love for Stiles Stilinski.

"Deal!" I agree, nodding at him.

Maybe this move won't be the worst thing in the world after all.

We spend the rest of the morning unpacking the moving truck, and I'm just glad that Dad had someone come in already and deal with the big furniture. All I had to do was move my new room around to how I wanted it and unpack my clothes.

"Indi, come grab some lunch!"

I grin when my mom yells, feeling a little more like myself after the few cups of coffee I had while I sorted through my stuff. Skipping downstairs to the chaos of the rest of the house, I try to ignore the disarray and clutter.

Just no.

I wouldn't call myself a neat freak as such, but this is kinda gross.

I find my mom in the kitchen with a bowl of what smells like pea soup.

"Eat up," she says, grinning at me as I slide into one of the chairs at the table. I take a sip of the soup and wince.

Yep. Pea soup.

Gag me.

"Mom, I think I'm going to explore this place and find some edible food out in the real world."

She frowns at me and takes a mouthful of my soup, wincing when it hits her tongue. "Okay, yeah, that's disgusting. You've got your credit card?"

I nod and tap my pocket. "Wallet and phone are never far from me."

"Fine, okay." She digs in her pocket and fishes out a set of keys. "Please drive safely. I know you've had your license a while, but you didn't drive much back home."

I grin at her, trying not to bounce on the spot. "I'll be fine, Mom. Thank you!"

"Let me know if you get lost."

"Mom, my phone has GPS," I deadpan. "Getting lost isn't really an issue anymore."

"Yeah, yeah. You kids and your tech. Go on. Just don't be home late. I daresay your room isn't finished yet."

"Art takes time," I tease with a wink before grabbing the keys and skipping from the house.

I slide into the Wrangler, rubbing the leather of the steering wheel. This shit is beautiful. Holy crap.

I can't believe this car is mine.

I squeal again as I notice the sound system has been upgraded. I connect my phone to the Bluetooth, setting up my 'Most Played' list, and start the engine.

Ugh, she even sounds beautiful. This might be Stiles' truck, but mine definitely runs better than his ever did. No duct tape here!

I head in the opposite direction than we arrived from, and after a few minutes, my grin falters.

Of course I ended up on the bad side of town.

Though, this place feels more familiar to me. Like the streets of the city.

Maybe this is exactly where I'm meant to be.

My smile returns and I drive until I find a little diner, my stomach rumbling at the thought of a greasy burger and fries.

Oh, and a milkshake.

Absolutely yes.

I need it.

I pull into a space, taking a minute to check my eyeliner before I climb from the car. I should probably worry about standing out like a sore thumb in my tutu skirt, ripped tights, Docs, and band tee, but… well, I've always stood out.

This won't be anything new.

Taking a deep breath, I climb down from the Wrangler, more aware of my short stature than usual thanks to the car, and lock it before striding up to the doors of the diner.

I enter the place like I've been coming here my entire life and take a seat in one of the booths to my right. I do love a good window seat.

I grab the menu, like I don't already know what I want, and ignore the people staring. With a quick glance around the room, it's obvious that I don't belong here. This diner looks like it's full of freaking gang members and juvie convicts… but dammit, I'm hungry and it smells so good.

A girl who looks more like a model than a waitress struts over to me in a pair of jeans, crop top, and more attitude than anyone I've run into in the city. If it wasn't for the name tag and the notebook in her hand, I'd have no idea she worked here.

She looks me up and down before beaming a smile at me. "What can I get you?"

"Bacon cheeseburger with fries and a chocolate milkshake."

"You're new around here, aren't you? Or are you just lost from the other side of town."

I look her over to try and tell if she's being a bitch, or if she's lining me up for something. I can't tell, but I do notice how it got real quiet in here since she started talking.

"I'm new, and definitely not from that side of town."

"Good to know. I'll get Benny on your order now. Just flag me down if you want anything else."

She struts off back to the kitchen, flicking her hair over her shoulder, and I try to ignore the feeling of eyes on me. Instead, I smile wider and grab my phone to check in on my socials.

Before I know it, the girl is back with my milkshake. Instead of just dropping it off, she has a second one in her hand and slides into the opposite side of my booth. "I'm Scout."

"Indi," I respond with a smile, trying not to be as hesitant as I usually am with new people.

"So, new huh? Where you from?"

"Yeah, drove in this morning. New York, originally. I found out about the move two days ago."

She takes a sip of her shake, so I do the same, and holy fucking chocolate gods. "That explains the accent, New York. Sucks about two days though. What landed you in this shit hole?"

"My dad's job. I don't really know all of the details." I shrug and suck down some more of the shake.

A guy wanders over, scowling at Scout who flips him the finger as he drops our burgers and fries onto the table before heading back to the kitchen.

"Such a good smile you've got there, Benny!" she shouts at his back. He just flips her the bird before ducking back into the kitchen. Apparently these people use finger signs as shows of affection. "So, since you're new to town, and you seem like good people, you should come with me to the beach party tomorrow night."

I stare at her, open mouthed, with my burger halfway to my lips, before dropping it back to the plate. "Party?"

"Yeah, there are only two weeks until school starts back up, so we're throwing a party. You should come. Unless you don't party?" She quirks a brow at me before eating one of her fries.

"I party," I lie. I absolutely do not party. I don't drink either, but I get the feeling saying no to this girl is akin to social suicide. "Count me in."

Her smile widens as she picks up another fry. "Good. You and I are going to be good friends, Indi. I just know it."

---

After an interesting welcome to Echoes Cove, these last few days have actually been okay. Scout even managed to get me a job at the diner with her so I can earn some extra money. My parents weren't too thrilled about it, but they've been harping on about me being independent, so they don't really have a leg to stand on.

Plus, I don't start school for over week, so it's not like I don't have time to adjust to the Cove before jumping in with both feet.

Which is exactly how I find myself walking toward the beach, trying not to freak out about coming to a party with a girl I just met a few days ago.

Yeah, I know, big bad New Yorkers aren't supposed to be afraid of anything, but one… I'm not a big bad anything; I definitely fit in the category of sparkly marshmallow. And two… well, new people are terrifying, and if Scout's crowd is anything like the one from the diner, then I'm pretty sure I should be at least a little afraid.

Scout introduced me to a few of her friends the last few days, but she also said something about not having real friends because everyone was scared of her brothers, but that I'd be fine, because I'm an outsider.

She really has a way of filling a girl with hope, that one.

The sound of the bass reaches me before I even reach the sand. Apparently these guys know how to party. Not that I have much experience with parties—I wasn't exactly party girl central back home—but God knows I've seen enough tv to know a rager when I see one.

There are people everywhere, some with red cups, but this seems to be more of a whole-bottles-of-hard-liquor kind of crowd. The music isn't exactly to my taste, but I can appreciate anything. If the half-naked people dancing around the bonfire is anything to go on, it makes total sense.

"Indiiiiiii!"

Scout comes running at me, squealing my name with a huge smile on her face.

*Apparently someone started partying early.*

She jumps at me, looping her arms around my neck and clinging. I wrap my arms around her, mostly to stop her momentum from landing me on my ass.

"You came," she coos as she pulls back.

"Of course I came," I say with a smile.

She sways on the spot, and I can't tell if it's due to the alcohol or if she's dancing. I press my lips together so as not to laugh. "You have to come and dance with me! And you need a drink."

She takes me by the hand, spinning around in the sand as if to pull me back in the direction she came from, when three guys emerge from the shadows.

My eyes go wide as I drink them in. My mouth suddenly feels like the Sahara inhabits it and I freeze.

"Scout, who is your new friend?" the smiling behemoth on the right asks, while the other two—who, holy freaking hell, are twins—remain silent as they all pause on the sand. Scout sighs and stomps toward them, dragging me with her.

"Sorry about this," she mumbles just before we reach them. Oh yeah, this girl is all about giving me hope. "Buzz kills one through three, meet Indi. She's new to the Cove and I like her, so be nice."

She wags her finger at the three of them like they're bad puppies, which just makes me want to laugh again. A small squeak escapes me as the middle one, with eyes like honey and skin painted like a color by numbers, scowls at me harder than he already was.

Awesome.

I lift my arm and wave the most awkward wave of my life, trying to smile. "Hi."

The middle one rolls his eyes, while the slimmer and slightly-less-tattooed twin glances over at me, his eyes slowly raking up and down my body. When his eyes reach mine, he smiles as I squirm. "You're new to the Cove?"

"Yep," I answer, popping my P, and the first guy laughs as the middle guy stomps away in the direction they came from. "Got in from New York a few days ago."

"I'm Ellis," the slimmer twin says, his eyebrow rising as I meet his stare, even though standing under his gaze makes me want to turn into sand and disappear. He points a thumb over his shoulder before continuing. "Grumpy over there is Ryker, and this is Dylan."

I smile wide, trying to seem as non-threatening as possible, because I get the feeling this is not the crowd I want to threaten. Also, I'm about as threatening as a Labrador wanting treats. "Nice to meet you all."

Ellis turns and follows Ryker while Dylan stands in a stare off with Scout. "Why must you provoke them?" he asks. She just shrugs.

"It's fun. Plus, I just brought a friend. Who knew they'd freak?"

"You don't have friends, Scout. You knew they'd freak, and you know exactly why." He frowns, glancing at me, before setting his gaze back on her. "Just be careful."

"Yes, sir," she says with a mock salute. He sighs, running a hand down his face before turning and heading toward the twins.

"Who was that?" I ask once they're out of earshot.

"The twins are my big brothers and the other one is their ride or die, Dylan. He's pretty cool, and basically another big brother. Just what I need." She rolls her eyes and sighs. "They've totally killed my happy. Do you wanna go grab some food?"

I smile wide, because parties really aren't my thing, and nod. "Sure, food sounds good. I brought my car."

"Epic, then you can drive 'cause I definitely am not."

She links her hand through mine and pulls me away from her brothers. A tingle on the back of my neck makes me feel like we're being watched, but I put it down to paranoia. I can't help a backward glance as we walk away, and find Ryker's eyes on me. His stare feels like a death ray aimed right at my soul.

*Awesome. So freaking awesome.*

# CHAPTER TWO

To say my first week in Echoes Cove has been unexpected would be an understatement. I spent most of the weekend with Scout at her place, which was a little awkward with her brothers and Dylan around. Especially since Ryker just glared at me all weekend. But I've decided that whatever his problem is, it's fully a him problem.

I don't need that sort of thunderstorm raining on my sunshine parade.

Which is why I'm trying not to be filled with dread about heading back there this morning. The sun is shining, I've got my two-piece on under my tank and shorts, and I'm ready to swim, since Scout said a pool day was needed before she goes to work later.

I bop along to Concrete Castles in the Jeep, smiling wide as I soak up the early sunshine, not missing the city as much as I thought I would. Turns out, having a friend makes moving a lot easier.

I'm still a little unsure about the start of the school year next week, but despite my pleas to Mom and Dad about attending the same school as Scout, I'm still heading to the prep school. Joy of joys.

I pull up at the house, jamming out to *Shapeshifting* by Taylor Acorn, singing terribly at the top of my lungs as I shut off the engine, dancing away in my seat. The song finishes and I look up, realizing I've had an audience for God only knows how long.

My cheeks heat, but I straighten my shoulders and smile at Ellis, who stands on the front step, leaning up against the door jamb as he watches me. I climb down from the Wrangler, trying to push away the rising embarrassment, and run my fingers through my hair before adjusting my sunnies.

"You're here early," he calls out with a playful smile as I approach.

I shrug as I put my fingertips in my pockets, my keys taking up too much space to hide an entire hand. "Scout demanded an early start and I rise with the sun."

He mutters something under his breath that I miss, but stands up straight and pins me with a stare before I can ask what he said. "She shouldn't have invited you today, but since you're here, just keep your head down. I'll try to keep Ryker off your case."

My eyes go wide, not fully understanding the whiplash of his words. "Thank you? I think?"

He just laughs quietly and nods inside. "Scout's in the kitchen. Go straight there." I nod and try to move past him, but that requires rubbing up against him since he's filling up the doorway. "Oh, and Indi? Do not go down to the basement today. That would be bad, you understand?"

"I understand," I say, keeping the *weirdo* I tag on in my head. The Donovans are kinda nuts. That is what I have learned in the last week, but Scout is good people, so I can ignore the fact that her brothers are beyond bizarre.

I follow the sound of Scout's voice and find her in their kitchen at the back of the house. "Bitch, yes! Thank God you're here. I am sick of the constant sausage fest this house is."

I laugh at her outburst as I enter the room. Ryker grumbles something and she flips him the finger as she gets up from the table. "Glad I could help even out the numbers."

"Oh, they're never even. The amount of dicks in this house is obscene on the best of days. But today is all about the end of summer sunshine. Let's go to my room first, then we'll go out to the pool. I already made some iced tea. It's in the fridge."

I nod as she takes my hand and drags me down the hall and into her room. It's everything I expected it to be. Turns out, Scout and I really are alike. The metal and pop-punk band posters on the wall, the gig ticket stubs on her cork board along with a ton of photos—mostly of her with the twins.

The room is a sea of black with small hints of blue. Which is funny, considering that's literally my entire aesthetic. She puts on her music and The Maine starts blasting through the speakers. She quickly turns it down before flopping onto her bed, front first, facing me.

She gasps when she notices my shoes. "Where did you get your Converse? I need some!" I squirm at the attention, because well, it's never been my happy place.

"They were just plain black, I jazzed them up a bit," I say, talking about the electric-blue hoops and laces, plus the blue hearts up the side. "I get creative when I'm bored sometimes."

She bolts off of the bed and squeezes my biceps. "You have to do mine, but with red. I'm definitely moving into a red phase."

I nod, feeling a little uncomfortable. But this is what friends do. "Sure, just get me the Cons and I'll take care of the rest."

"You rock, Indi. Right, I'm just gonna grab my suit. You got sunscreen?" she asks, and I shake my head. "Top right drawer of my dresser. Help yourself!"

She opens her closet, grabs a red swimsuit, and heads into her bathroom. I grab the lotion from the dresser and drop onto the bed, lathering up my shoulders, chest, arms and legs. I'll have to ask Scout to do my back when she's done.

When she comes back, my jaw drops. "Your brothers are going to have a fit."

She grins, modeling the barely-there red two-piece she has on. "Right? But one of the guys I like will be at the house today, so fuck it."

Considering she's a year younger than me, goddamn does she have some curves. She's all golden skin, dark hair, and just freaking stunning. Yeah, I don't feel self-conscious at all. Nope. Not one bit.

Fuck my life.

"Plus, pretty sure with you around, my brothers won't be paying me any attention." She winks at me and my cheeks heat, but I wave her off, dismissing her words. "Come on, let's get out in the sun before it's too hot. I intend to bake slowly."

---

We end up spending most of the morning bouncing between the sun chair and the pool. Thankfully, the boys have left us the hell alone, so I haven't had to feel weird about being around them. Especially when Ryker just stares and glares every time I'm in the same room with him.

We've just entered the kitchen to grab some food when the front door slams open. I jump, letting out a squeak, and Scout looks at me wide-eyed. "Bedroom. Now."

"What?" I screech, but she grabs my hand and drags me back down the hall.

She puts a finger against her lips and my panic grows. What the actual fuck is going on?

Closing her door quietly behind her, she points to her bathroom, and I head inside, my hands shaking so much I can barely turn the handle. The shouting is so loud that even with two closed doors between us, it's impossible not to know that something is very, very wrong.

"It'll be okay, this is just a usual day at the Donovan household. Diego won't let anything happen to us."

Who the fuck is Diego?

My thoughts must flash on my face, because she sighs. "My oldest brother. I told you my brothers were shady, but I might have played down just *how* shady they are. I'll explain later, I swear, but we need to stay quiet."

I nod, clasping my hands together to try and stop them from shaking.

Everything goes quiet and I hold my breath as I crouch behind the bathroom door next to Scout. My ears ring when the *pop* of gunfire starts and I freeze. Scout's lips are moving, but it sounds like I'm underwater. Everything is muffled.

In an instant, the sounds refocus and Scout is shouting at me to move. Gunfire seems to continue as she drags me into the tub with her. I curl up in a ball, my hands over my head as I tuck it into my lap.

"We are never hanging out here again," I whisper-shout at her, and she winces but nods.

"Agreed."

"This can't be a casual everyday thing," I hiss.

"It's not," she answers, shaking her head, her voice wobbling as she does. "I swear it's not. There's almost never shots fired, just a lot of shouting and posturing."

The sounds outside the room go quiet and we shut up. The crack of a door slamming shut is all I hear until the door to Scout's bathroom opens and Ryker storms in, his ebony eyes ablaze, like he's ready to set the world on fire.

"Are you okay?" he asks before turning his gaze to me. I open my mouth to speak but nothing comes out. Between the gunfire and the look on his face, I'm fucking paralyzed. "Speak!"

"We're physically fine, asshole!" Scout manages as she stands, offering me a hand. "Fuck you for barging in here and shouting at us."

They yell back and forth for a minute before Ellis arrives. "Woah, woah! Calm the fuck down. Ryker, go help Diego downstairs." His command silences his twin and they stare at each other, obviously engaged in a power struggle, before Ryker finally leaves, presumably to do as he was told. Ellis approaches the tub slowly and crouches down in front of me. "Are you okay?"

He takes my hands for a moment before releasing them and grabbing me by the hips and lifting me from the tub, pulling me into his arms while he speaks quietly to Scout.

He pulls back and I'm still frozen stupid, just letting him manhandle me while I try to calm my racing mind.

"You're going to be okay." He sounds so calm, so soothing, that I almost believe him. Despite living in the city, I've been lucky enough to avoid any run-in with guns up to this point in my life. Who would've thought that I'd end up mixed up in this shit in the fucking suburbs?

He leads me back through to Scout's room, where she glances at me with a sad smile before leaving me alone with her brother.

"And here I was thinking that keeping you out of the basement was the biggest challenge of the day," he sighs as he sits me on the bed. "I'm sorry you were here when all of this happened, and I know it's not fair, but I need you to not mention this to anyone."

I blink at him, still riding the wave of fear that came with the first gun shot.

"And none of this is Scout's fault. Please don't hold it against her."

His words trigger me and something inside of me snaps. "Why the hell would I hold your shady shit against your sister? She was with me in that tub, fucking terrified. I try not to judge people, but how the fuck can you guys be so protective about her having a friend, to the point that Ryker looks at me like I'm shit on his shoe, yet allow people with guns to come into your *home* and risk her life? You guys are fucking insane."

I drop onto the bed, the small burst of adrenaline leaving my body, and exhaustion washes over me. He doesn't say anything, and when I look up I get the feeling I haven't said anything he hasn't told himself before.

"I should go home," I say with a sigh. "I'mma go get my shit from the yard and just go."

He doesn't say a word, just nods and leaves the room, leaving me realizing I'm half naked and so freaking tired.

I lie back on the bed and close my eyes, just trying to calm my heart back to normal.

Though I'm not sure I even know what normal is anymore.

# CHAPTER THREE

Have I hidden in my room for two days, faking being sick? Absolutely. Am I confident Scout knows I'm bullshitting? One hundred percent. But today I'm supposed to start working at the diner, and she got me the job, so I can't keep pretending.

I check my reflection for the hundredth time, trying to make sure that I look cute, but I'm still not going to be able to be on my feet for the next eight hours without absolutely dying. I have my trusty knee-high Cons on my feet, denim cut-off shorts, and a long-sleeved cold-shoulder tee that loops over my thumbs.

It might be the worst idea ever to start this job, especially when it's not like I *need* the money, but it'll be nice to not use my parents' money for stuff I want. I'm aware that I'm lucky, that not everyone gets to be as comfortable as we are, but I think I should still earn my own way.

I pull my long blue tresses into a ponytail, touch up my eyeliner, and finish the look with an old-school tattoo choker.

Perfect.

Now if only the butterflies in my stomach would calm the fuck down. I already decided breakfast is going to be a java chip frappe because food isn't going to happen this morning. My phone pings on my bed, drawing my attention, and I see Scout's name on the screen.

**Scout:**
*Ready to stop pretending you're sick yet? You working today?*

Well shit. I mean, I called it, but still.

**Me:**
*Yeah I'm working, just getting ready to leave now.*

**Scout:**
*Awesome. Swing by and grab me on your way?*

I blow out a deep breath, my nerves buzzing at the thought of going back to that house. The gunfire and gang bullshit is bad enough, but Ellis being nice to me was just as weird. Especially after Ryker being so… well, Ryker.

**Me:**
*Sure thing. I'm leaving now.*

I grab my keys and bag, yelling to Mom to let her know I'm heading to work. There have been more than a few arguments about my job this week, but they caved because independence is something they have beaten into me since I was a little kid. How important it is not to rely on others and to forge your own path.

Did I use that against them? Yes. Does that seem stupid considering everything that happened at the beginning of the week? Probably, but I'm not about to tell them that now. Instead, I breeze out of the house like nothing's wrong and hop in my Wrangler, putting on my early morning playlist, hoping that screaming some Taylor Acorn at the top of my lungs will help me feel better.

I swing by Starbucks to pick up my frappe before heading to Scout's, and by the time the caffeine starts to hit my systems, I'm already full of pep with my butterflies behind me. I might not be a bad ass bitch, but I can do this. I can work this job and *not* get involved with the shady shit the Donovans are obviously mixed up in.

Even if Scout's brothers are hotter than fucking hell. God, even with them hating me, I'd still lick them both up and down like a lollipop on a hot day.

Not that I'm ever admitting that to Scout.

Nope. That little nugget is staying in the vault.

By the time I pull up at her house, Scout is already waiting for me outside, Dylan standing guard over her. She flips him the bird and hops in the car. I give him a little finger wave and he leans against the car door, putting his head through the open window. "You drive careful, Short Stack. City girls tend to drive like crazy people."

"I'm not a crazy person," I respond drily, even when his grin widens. "And I'm not that short."

"Sure you're not, Short Stack. See you girls later." He bangs his hand against the inside of the car door before walking back into the house.

"He's a bit of a jerk," I sigh as Scout puts on her seatbelt.

"He's actually one of the nicest guys I know, just protective."

I glance at her, eyebrows raised. "Oh, wait, are you—"

"Gods no!" she exclaims. "He values his dick too much, but he's also just like another brother to me. Plus, he wasn't hanging out here to see me," she says with a wink, making me blush. "Anyway, you could definitely do worse."

I shake my head and pull away from the house, "*So* not my focus right now."

She grins at me and I try to ignore it. "We'll see how long that lasts."

"Stop," I insist, and we spend the rest of the journey singing along to my playlist. I pull up out front and Scout curses before pulling out her phone. "What's wrong?"

"What's wrong is that's Lincoln Saint, and if he's here, nothing good is coming from this day."

---

Despite Scout's theory that today would suck, it's actually been okay. Danny and Carla, who run the diner, have been lovely. Even when I dropped a dozen things on my very few orders. Dylan arrived about ten minutes after Scout texted her brothers. He spoke to the dark-haired angry god that she called Lincoln Saint, who left after delivering whatever message he passed on, but neither of them looked particularly happy after the exchange.

"You counted out?" Scout asks as she grabs her bag from under the counter.

I nod as I grab my own. "Just finished."

"Not a bad start. You want to come over for dinner? I hate cooking for one and the boys always just want freaking pizza. I feel like something a little more complex. Call me extra, but I love cooking."

I bite my lip, wondering if going to her house is a good idea after last time, and she sees my hesitation, which isn't really a shock. I've always been an open book and I don't exactly have a poker face.

"Come on, no gun fights tonight. Plus no one got hurt on Monday, it was just a scare tactic. The Rebels are assholes."

"Well, the scare tactic worked, but who are the Rebels?" I ask, hating how curious I am.

Scout grins wickedly at me. "Come have dinner and I'll tell you."

"You girls ready?" Dylan asks as we round the counter.

"Yep, but Indi's coming back to the house, so you don't need to babysit me anymore," Scout answers, patting his chest as she brushes past him like a princess dismissing her staff.

He looks at me like he feels the same way about it as I do. "You sure that's a good idea?"

I shake my head. "Not at all, but apparently it's what's happening. You try arguing with her." I shrug and he barks out a laugh.

"All four of them are the same. Arguing with them is like yelling at a wall. Come on, Short Stack, just keep your head down and you should be fine."

"You can't keep calling me that," I sigh as I leave the diner.

"Sure I can, I like it."

"I don't," I grumble, and he smiles wider.

"Oh, I know, and that's why I like it. Did Scout invite you to Friday yet?"

I shake my head and he smiles sadly. "She will, just say yes. She needs someone like you in her life, Short Stack."

I flip him the finger for my new apparent nickname and hop into the Wrangler while Scout smirks at me. "Yeah, yeah, I'm coming for dinner. Now spill."

"Okay, so the Rebels are a gang from a town not far from here. They've been in a war with the Kings, which Diego heads up here in the Cove, for as long as I can remember. But the real overlords are far worse. Which is why Lincoln Saint being here was a problem, but that's a whole different world and an entirely different conversation. The Rebels and the Kings fight over turf mostly, but Ryker beat the crap out of one of the Rebel lieutenants last week, which is why they showed up with dicks out on Monday. Like I said, scare tactics."

"Wait," I say, trying not to hyperventilate. "Your brothers *run* a fucking *gang*?"

She shrugs and puts her hair up in a ponytail. "Yeah, kinda."

"Holy fucking shit, Scout. No wonder your brothers hate me being at the house."

She smirks at me before pulling down the visor and checking her makeup. "Oh, they don't hate you. Not at all."

My cheeks heat again and she laughs when she notices.

"Don't sweat it, you're hot. If I was into girls I'd totally dig on you too, but I am strictly about the dick."

I burst out laughing at her blasé attitude about not just her brothers, but sex in general. I mean, I'm not a virgin and people might judge me for that, considering my age, but fuck them and their hypocritical views, 'cause I'd bet they didn't wait till they were eighteen either.

Still, if I had brothers, I doubt I'd be so chill about them and their fuckery.

"So just chill. Ryker just needs to unbunch his panties. Maybe getting laid will chill him out."

"I am not fucking your brother, Scout," I deadpan, and she smiles again.

"We'll see."

Deciding to change the subject to something less likely to have me wanting the floor to open up and swallow me, I ask, "So what's for dinner?"

---

I groan as I take a bite of the chicken and shrimp Alfredo. "Damn, Scout, you can cook!"

"Thanks," she beams from across the table. That's about when the sound of approaching footsteps reaches us.

"What smells so good?" Ellis asks, not even looking over at the table as he heads to the stove.

"Alfredo," Scout answers, making him look over. He pauses when he sees me, then glances behind me. I already know from the prickling on the back of my neck that Ryker is there and glaring at me. Pretty sure Scout is wrong.

He definitely seems to hate me.

"Scout—" Ellis starts, but she waves him off.

"I'm allowed to have friends. You dicks said I was safe here, so my friend is here. If Diego can't get his shit in line enough for that to be allowed, then I'll start going out more."

A growl from behind me has me turning to see Ryker entering the room. "Do not provoke me, Scout. Not today."

She pales a little at that, and I can't help but wonder the significance of today, but keep my mouth firmly closed.

"There is plenty of pasta, I cooked too much like always, so help yourselves," she says quietly, and the two of them each grab a bowl.

They move to leave, but Ryker stops at the table before they make it through the door. "You know the rules, Scout."

"I do," she says with a nod, and he glares at me once more before leaving the kitchen. Ellis smiles apologetically and takes off after his twin, but doesn't say anything else.

"Sorry about that," she says and I shake my head, finally chewing the piece of pasta in my mouth.

"Don't. It's fine. Ryker hates me, I'm aware. I can just leave, I don't want to make your life harder."

Dylan enters the room, groaning and rubbing his stomach, interrupting our conversation. "Damn Scout, you gotta warn a man when you're cooking the good stuff. Those assholes didn't even bring me any."

"Help yourself, D." She smiles at him, traces of the sad girl all gone.

"She invite you yet?" he asks me before grabbing himself a bowl of the pasta.

Scout looks guilty as she smiles at me. "He invited you to my party?"

"No, he didn't even say it was a party, just asked if you'd invited me to Friday."

"It's my birthday. The boys are throwing me a party, but it's not really for me. I'm going to use it as an excuse to let loose and have fun though. I just wasn't sure you'd want to come."

"It's your birthday?" I ask, and when she doesn't correct me, I make a decision despite her brothers. "Then of course I'm going to be there. What sort of friend wouldn't party with you on your birthday?"

Dylan smiles at me before quietly leaving, and his words from earlier ring through my head.

We finish eating while Scout fills me in on Friday, then I help her clean up, despite the argument that guests don't tidy even though she was the one that cooked.

Dylan was right about that too. Stubborn as a mule.

"Where's your bathroom?" I ask, once I put away the last of the dishes.

"Just down the hall. Ice cream?"

I let out a sigh of disbelief, "Like I'm going to say no to ice cream."

"Girl after my own heart. I'll serve it up and take it to my room."

"Sounds good. I'll be up in just a minute." I leave the kitchen, hoping that I pick the right door, considering there are three and I have no idea which is the bathroom.

I open the first one and find the living room before moving to the next and coming across a staircase that goes down. The voices that float up are enough to tell me I'm in the wrong place so I close the door, but when I turn around, I come face to face with Ryker.

"Who sent you?" he growls as he cages me in against the closed door.

My mouth goes dry and I try to answer him. "Wh-wha? No one… I was looking for the bathroom."

My heart races like a hummingbird's wings as I try not to shrink under his stare, but he looks like he'd kill me without a second thought if I was a threat to his family.

"I'm watching you. Stay the fuck out of the basement. Even better, stay the hell away from my sister. From my whole family. You don't belong here."

He remains a breath away from my face as he threatens me, and I think I might be sick. He stays there for what feels like forever before pulling back from me. "Get the fuck out of my house."

I squeak at the command and haul ass back to the kitchen, finding Scout with a tub of ice cream in her hand. "I need to go."

"What happened?"

"No-nothing. My mom texted and I need to head back."

The smile drops from her face, but she nods. "Okay, I'll see you for the party tomorrow though, right?"

I pause, trying to stop my hands from shaking, and throwing on a fake smile. Ryker might terrify me, but I meant what I said earlier. "Of course, it's your birthday. I'll be there no matter what."

# CHAPTER FOUR

Dancing with Scout has me all kinds of happy, especially with the slight buzz I've got from the whiskey she plied me with earlier. Nothing too major, just enough that I've stopped worrying about the daggers Ryker has been throwing at me all night.

His warning to stay the fuck away from his sister was still ringing in my ears when I got ready for the party and might be part of the reason I decided on a corset with a tutu skirt and my Docs. I look hot as fuck, and if he's going to be staring at me all night, why not look hot while I suffer the intimidation?

That was my thinking anyway. Now, with the guy I don't know behind me who keeps pawing at my ass, I'm regretting it just a little.

"I need water!" I shout at Scout, hoping she hears me over the music. She nods and gives me a thumbs up, so I make my way across the dark warehouse. The strobe lights are not exactly making it easy to navigate on top of the whiskey, but I know the bottles of water are near the twins, so I just follow the heated stare that's made my skin tingle all night.

As I approach them, Ellis straightens, even as Ryker continues to just glare at me like I'm the shittiest human on earth. I stumble a little and someone behind me catches me. I turn to find the guy from the dance floor and smile a thank you, despite feeling a little weirded out that he followed me. I was raised with manners, and I'm not about to lose them just because he's a little creepy.

I head to the cooler full of ice and bottles of water that's placed pretty close to Dylan, and offer him a wave before I open the water and chug it down.

Sweet baby jeebus, that is so freaking good.

I finish the first and take a second. They're only baby bottles, so I don't feel too bad. Dylan smiles at me and nods as I wave again and turn to find the bathrooms. Water was needed, but unfortunately that means I now need to pee apparently.

I work my way around the edges of the warehouse to where Scout pointed out the bathrooms earlier, clinging to the shadows to avoid all of the people in here. I finally see the red light showing the way when I feel hands grab my waist and I'm tugged back. My head bounces off the wall as I'm shoved against it. I groan, blinking against the water filling my eyes, trying to orient myself when the guy from the dance floor presses himself against me.

No.

Absolutely not.

I push against him, dodging as he tries to press his lips against mine. I succeed, but barely and he kisses my neck, despite my struggles. "Get off of me!" I shout, but against the music, I'm not sure anyone can hear, especially hidden back here.

I struggle, maneuvering my hands to press against his chest and push, causing him to fly backward. I blink in shock, but quickly realize it wasn't me that made him move.

Ryker looks like a bull about to charge as he stares down at the guy who is now lying on the floor, while Ellis comes to my side. "Are you okay?"

"Not really, but I will be."

He nods like he understands, and the guy who just assaulted me moves to all fours as if he's going to stand. Ryker steps forward and kicks the guy in the gut, then swings down with a punch to the jaw, causing the guy to end up flat down on the floor groaning. I wince at the violence, but also, fuck him.

Ryker crouches down and grabs the back of the guy's head and says something, but I can't hear what. All I see is the guy look over at me, fear shining in his wide eyes, before he nods. Ryker smashes his face against the floor before releasing him and standing again. He strides over to us, his heated stare back on me.

"Let's go," he commands when he reaches us, and I realize Ellis hasn't let go of me the entire time. He tucks me against his side, and I realize just how small I am compared to these two giants. Guys this age shouldn't look this good or be this tall. Fact.

I also probably shouldn't be thinking about just how good Ellis smells as he leads me through the warehouse. Ryker says something to Dylan, who nods and heads to the dance floor. Ellis doesn't break stride and just continues to follow Ryker outside.

"We're leaving?" I ask quietly, and Ellis nods.

"Yeah, Blue. We're heading home. Dylan will make sure Scout is okay, and he'll bring her back in your Jeep."

"Oh, okay," I say as he opens the door to the front passenger side of their truck. Ryker is already sitting in the driver's seat. I pause, gulping as Ellis lifts me into the seat, and I feel even smaller than normal. "I'm sorry I cut your night short."

Ryker glares at me again, his bloody fists clenching the steering wheel, but Ellis grabs my chin and turns me to face him. "You have fucking nothing to apologize for. You understand?"

I nod, and he smirks at me. "Words, Blue."

"I understand," I say quietly. He reaches over me and buckles me in before jumping in the back of the truck. It rumbles to life, and the vibrations run through me. The ride back is so tense, that when we pull up to their house, I don't even think to object to not being home before I do a weird awkward struggle to escape from my seatbelt and jump out of the truck.

Ellis is already there waiting for me and tucks me back under his arm before leading me inside. Ryker stomps in behind us, but Ellis takes me upstairs, where I've never been before, and into one of the bedrooms. It's dimly lit by a lamp, decorated in all dark blues and whites, and for some reason I feel instantly at ease.

"This is your room?" I ask when the scent of him reaches me, and he nods.

"Yeah, you can stay here tonight." He moves me further into the room, flicking on another lamp as I try to take in the surroundings some more.

"I can't kick you out of your room, I can just go home," I offer, but less than a moment later, Ryker is in the doorway, glaring at me again.

"You're not going anywhere. Whenever I can't see you, you end up in trouble." His words are low as he fills the doorway, his arms resting against the top of it.

I open my mouth to object when Ellis presses up behind me, his arms wrapping around my waist. "You don't have to kick me out, you know."

His breath tickles against my ear and a shiver runs down my spine.

This is a bad idea.

"We could both stay with you," he says quietly. "Keep you safe." He presses his lips against my neck while my eyes never leave Ryker's.

This might be a bad idea, but I can't say I'm exactly pushing him away. They might terrify me sometimes, but I'd be lying if I said they also didn't excite me or turn me the hell on. They're walking sex on a stick.

"Okay," I gasp as Ellis bites down on my shoulder, and Ryker moves toward me as if that single word unleashed him. He presses against my front and all of a sudden I'm drowning in them, one hand behind me on Ellis's abs, the other pressed against Ryker's chest.

On instinct, my eyes follow the path to Ryker's heated stare just as he wraps his long, thick fingers around my wrist and brings it to this mouth. I think he's going to kiss me, but find myself flinching when his teeth sink into my flesh instead, followed by a long, sensual lick. It's like he's punishing me before we even begin, and from the shiver that runs down my spine, I know I'm definitely okay with it.

Behind me, the warm path from Ellis' tongue over the side of my neck has another shiver traveling from the bottom of my spine up to my nape.

"We've been watching you, Blue." In any other context, Ellis' words would be creepy, but right now, it's making me wet. My thighs clench, my clit throbbing with my need for him… for them.

"I know."

I let out a sudden gasp as my head is pulled to the side by the strands of my loose hair, which are now tightly clamped in Ryker's unrelenting hold.

"It's a good thing, too. Putting yourself in danger like that was fucking stupid." My first instinct is to lash out but I don't have time. His mouth is on mine, all sliding lips and nipping teeth as his tongue demands entrance. I allow it, giving him the access he seeks and trying not to moan into his mouth. It's when his free hand wraps around my throat that I realize there's nothing I won't let these two do to me.

Shock at him touching me like this floods me, but it feels so good, I don't give myself permission to question it. Even if I get them for just one night, I'm going to enjoy the hell out of it.

"Do you like that, Blue? My brother devouring you, fucking your mouth like he owns you?" I can feel Ellis' dick getting impossibly harder as he presses against my ass, making me grind for more.

I can't answer but I moan, knowing the sound will get lost in Ryker's expert mouth. Something about that makes me needier. Like knowing he's swallowing my reaction makes this whole thing more intimate.

"Do you know what's going to happen next?" I shake my head at his words and I don't even know how I can follow his conversation with Ryker consuming my mouth like I'm his last meal.

Ellis doesn't answer but I don't have to wait long to find out what he meant.

One minute my lace panties are securely covering my pussy, the next, they're gone. They're ripped right off my body and handed over to Ellis, whose face is right next to mine. Bringing the panties to his nose, he inhales, deep, like he's savoring a bouquet of roses, before Ryker turns my head and relinquishes my mouth to his brother.

Their kisses are different. One is rough and demanding, the other is languorous and deep. Just as Ellis' tongue is battling mine, Ryker slams two or three—fuck, I have no idea—fingers inside me. I gasp, and Ellis takes advantage of my wide open mouth to devour me, use me, and bite me before licking the seam between my lips.

When he lets go, I can barely breathe. My chest is rising and falling to the beat of Ryker's fingers fucking my swollen and throbbing pussy.

"Is she wet?"

"She's fucking begging for it."

Blinking my heavy-lidded eyes open, I forget to blush at his crude words when I feel the sudden emptiness between my legs, only to realize Ryker's fingers are now at my mouth, pressing none-too-gently against my lips until I open wide and suck myself from his skin.

"That's right, baby. Lick it all up. See how much you want us? You're fucking soaked, almost ready for our dicks."

Pulling his fingers out of my mouth, Ryker then puts them in his own mouth and grins like a fucking predator. "Delicious."

The next thing I know, I'm flung onto the bed with two pairs of dark eyes watching my every move. They're like hunters sizing up their next meal, and I'm the prey they're about to destroy.

"Spread your legs, let me see how much your pussy needs us." Lifting myself up on my elbows, I spread my thighs as I bring my heels up on the edge of the bed. My tutu skirt is so short it leaves me completely open to them. There's no way I can hide anything, and I don't think I'd want to even if I could.

"Fuck," Ellis groans. He's definitely the talkative one. The one who uses his words to get me riled up, whereas Ryker is the one who shows me what he wants. As if he's going to make me come with his body while Ellis makes me come with his words. The perfect combo.

Ryker turns to Ellis and without a single word, they look like they're having an entire conversation. Then, their attention is back on me as Ellis kneels at the edge of the bed and buries his face between my legs, his tongue licking a long, slow path between my lips until he reaches my clit and sucks it in deep enough to sting.

"You're right, she's fucking amazing." As though I weigh nothing, Ellis picks me up by the waist and climbs up on the bed, positioning himself so he's lying underneath me with my pussy directly over his face. I thought I was exposed before but now there's no escaping him.

I'm afraid of actually sitting on him. What if I suffocate him?

My musings are interrupted by the disappearing act of my skirt. One second it's on me, covering half of Ellis' face, and the next it's just gone, giving me an unhindered view of Ellis' tongue traveling along my inner thigh before he grabs onto my ass cheeks and buries his face in my pussy.

"Nice." Ryker is kneeling behind his twin's head, looking at where we are joined and letting his gaze slowly travel up my corset, lingering on my cleavage before he reaches my mouth. I'm mesmerized by his tongue as it darts out to lick his bottom lip, dragging his teeth along the plump flesh before reaching out to bury his fingers in my hair. My breathing is erratic, not just from Ellis' tongue doing ridiculous things to my pussy, but from the way Ryker is looking at me. Like I'm fresh water after a marathon.

"Time to put those fuckable lips to good use." Holding me steady with one hand, he deftly unbuttons his jeans and releases his long, thick cock. His eyes are on my mouth when I realize I'm licking my own lips as I enjoy the view in front of me.

Pulling me toward him, he brings me close to his mouth, the anticipation of kissing him again is making me shake with want.

Except that's not his plan.

"Suck." Just as he throws that one-word order, his brother slaps my ass, eliciting a gasp from me and giving Ryker the perfect opportunity to fill my mouth with his hard dick. Ellis digs his fingers into my flesh, sounds of my wet pussy being eaten with abandon echoing throughout the room.

"Fuck." Ryker doesn't speak in complete phrases, and for some reason it makes me hot every time he does say something. Like every one of his orders or expressions are rare and priceless.

I'm on all fours now, my pussy on Ellis' mouth and Ryker's dick in mine. Trying not to use my teeth, I lick and suck until Ryker pulls my hair and slams his cock inside, pushing right down my throat.

"Breathe through your nose. And if you choke on my dick, that's okay, too."

Beneath me, I feel more than hear, Ellis chuckle at Ryker's words, and I wonder if it's because those words made me press my pussy harder against his devouring mouth.

"Goddamn, that's good." He pulls my head back, the sting at my scalp only making me wetter. “Look at me, baby. Let me see your pretty little tears.” I didn’t even know I was crying until he said that. The trail of tears is a warm river of lust from the give and take between the two brothers.

That’s when he pushes my head down and holds me there, his dick deep down my throat, my breathing nonexistent as Ellis licks up my slit and sinks his teeth into my clit.

I lose it.

I'm not even sure where my orgasm comes from. All I know is that my entire body is seizing, my heart beating like a drum behind my ribcage as Ellis sucks every drop of my cum into his mouth and Ryker revels in the sound of my gags as he fucks my mouth with his impossibly big dick.

My first non-solo orgasm, and hot damn. Can we do that again?

Just when I think I can’t go on without taking a deep breath, I’m released from them both and placed on the bed.

“Orgasms look good on her, Brother.” Ellis is talking to his brother but looking straight at me as I lie there boneless, yet still so fucking turned on. “We should give her more.” Ryker just smirks as he gets down from the bed and walks over to the dresser.

“Second drawer.”

”I know where you keep your shit, E.” Ryker’s growl is almost cute if it weren’t fucking scary.

“Now, let’s get this off you. I want to bury my face between your tits.” As Ryker rummages through the drawer, Ellis makes quick work of my corset, groaning as my breasts fall free.

“Jesus Christ, Blue. You’re fucking gorgeous.” I can feel the blush erupt across my chest and throat, the heat of it reaching my cheeks and making me feel shy all of a sudden. I don’t understand it, since only moments ago I was sitting on his face while sucking off his brother. Yet this is what makes me blush? A compliment?

“Got it.” At Ryker’s words, I look over to find he’s got a bottle of lube in his hand and a devilish grin on his face.

Yup, this is happening.

Ellis takes my mouth in a scorching kiss and all thoughts of lube and ass-poundings go right out the window. We’re all lips and teeth and sliding tongues when I feel the cool gel on my ass. I don’t hesitate, just spread my legs to give Ryker more room as Ellis distracts me with his deep, luscious kisses.

Then he’s gone.

A little dizzy and a whole fucking lot turned on, I blink away my lust and direct my hazy gaze to the guys who are now shedding their clothing.

Fuck, they’re so freaking beautiful. Ellis is long and lean, muscles defined and hard, skin the color of deep gold. Ryker is bigger, broader, but no less defined. Both of them painted in shades of black and color from their ink.

They’re fucking magnificent and I can't wait to feel them inside me. Both of them. At the same fucking time.

I know I should be nervous, but I don’t even feel a hint of apprehension.

I want this.

I want them.

Naked now, Ellis returns to kissing me, taking my mouth before trailing his tongue down my neck, my collarbone, and my chest while taking his sweet time with my tits. He sucks and bites my nipples, almost to the point of pain, all while Ryker is prepping the tight ring of my ass with his fingers, lubing up all around and slowly applying pressure before breaching the tight ring of muscle.

I gasp, my back arching, my chest bowing, giving Ellis even better access. We all moan at that one move, which is when Ryker decides to push his finger in all the way.

Holy fuck.

It's not necessarily painful and it's only uncomfortable for a brief moment, but it is fucking hot as sin.

And I want more, so I tell him as much.

"Please. More. Oh, God, please."

"Hmm, sounds like begging to me." Ellis speaks around my other nipple, and Ryker pulls his finger out before adding more lube and pushing two fingers in this time.

"Yes, yes!"

One hand grabs onto the comforter while the other latches onto Ellis' hair, curling my fingers around the messy strands.

Ryker's fingers pump in and out, scissoring and molding my hole to ready me for the sheer size of him.

I know it'll eventually fit, and fucking hell, I'm going to need all the fucking lube in that bottle.

I'm so distracted by all the kissing and the prepping that I don't realize Ellis' hand is traveling down my stomach until it reaches my pussy and, without preamble, he pushes two fingers inside me, making me tense at the fullness I suddenly feel.

"That's it, Blue, just relax and let us get you nice and wet." Their fingers are fucking both of my holes, in and out in a practiced rhythm. Clearly, this isn't their first rodeo and I'm thankful for their experience, because all I feel right now is pure ecstacy.

"Fuck, she's so tight." Ellis' words are soft but the crease between his brows and the hard line of his mouth tell a whole different story.

"Come look, E."

I'm completely exposed, my ass and pussy at their mercy, and although I should probably feel self conscious, right now all I feel is wanted.

"Fucking hell, I think she's ready for us." Ellis turns his mischievous eyes on me before adding another finger to the two already buried inside me and curls them just right, adding the perfect friction exactly where I need it.

My entire body goes rigid, another orgasm threatening to overtake me.

"Look at her, she's so fucking primed. I bet she'll come at least twice more before we spill our load inside her." Ryker's voice is even, calm. But the hint of a growl says he's losing the tight control I've noticed he likes to have.

And I am so here for it.

"Fuck this, let's do it. I'm not waiting any longer. I need to fuck."

In a whirlwind, we're all naked and I'm suddenly on my hands and knees, Ellis lying back under me, his hands on my tits, squeezing and pinching my nipples. That little bite of pain is a direct line to my clit.

I've never felt so much.

Everywhere.

And I still haven't had actual sex yet.

Sliding down my stomach and across my hips, Ellis' hands grab onto both of my ass cheeks, pulling them far apart as he pushes me down onto his cock, sliding my slick pussy up and down his dick, my cum lubricating him from root to tip.

"Fuck, the sight of this," Ryker groans. I'm too far gone to care about what he's seeing. Essentially, my ass is wide open for him. And I don't fucking care. Not even a little bit.

"Now."

I suck in a breath as Ryker pushes his cock into my ass, slowly, diligently, just as Ellis guides my pussy onto his rock hard dick. Inch by deliciously painful inch, the twins own my body. I'm lost to the sensation of them, the groans coming from me are all the proof I need that I'm a fucking horny mess.

"Fuck yeah. So goddamn tight." Ellis' eyes close as my pussy engulfs his entire length and my ass takes in the last inches of Ryker's cock.

"Oh my God. So full. So, so full." I can barely speak full sentences with the sensations of everything. The guys aren't moving, letting my body adjust to their sizes, but when Ellis lets go of my ass cheek to bring his thumb to my clit, my body instinctively begins to beg for more.

"She's ready," he says with his eyes only on me. He takes my nipple in his mouth, sucking hard and biting. Distracting me from the retreat of Ryker's cock before he slides right back inside me. Filling me so completely, it's like they're invading every inch of my body.

It's then that it all happens.

Ryker pushes inside as Ellis pulls me off his cock. Ryker sliding out of my ass as Ellis pulls me down on his ram-rod shaft. Hard. Demanding. With incredible precision.

Faster and faster, the twins fuck me into oblivion. With a thumb keeping the rhythm on my clit, they take me like their own fuck doll, except I'm very much alive, very much feeling every inch of their big dicks fucking me like they own me.

My mouth drops open as my orgasm builds higher and higher—more and more—until the tsunami overwhelms to the point of incoherence.

I scream, I pray, I beg and beg some more. All the while their thrusts are harder and faster, their moans more significant, their grunts more animalistic.

I've never, in my life, been so used yet felt so revered as I do right now.

But when Ryker grabs the hair at my nape and pulls my head back enough to angle my body exactly the way he wants it, he whispers in my ear, "You're ours now, baby."

The entire universe, with us in it, explodes into a million pieces of lust. Ryker comes in my ass with a grunt that I feel in every nerve ending. Ellis pinches my clit as he spills his cum deep inside my pussy. And I lose my goddamn mind. The orgasm is like nothing I've ever felt before. It's smooth and fiery. Painful from the intensity of the pleasure.

It's everything.

Ryker slowly retreats from me, making his way to the bathroom while I lie a shattered mess on Ellis' chest. When he returns, he cleans me up before pulling me from Ellis and finishing up. Ellis heads to the bathroom while Ryker climbs back onto the bed, curling me up in a ball before lying behind me.

Ellis returns and crawls in on my other side, moving me so I'm lying with my head on his chest, but Ryker's arm is draped over my waist.

"Sleep, Blue. We've got you. No one will hurt you now."

Ellis' words are like a balm to my soul and my eyes drift closed. The murmurings of them speaking lull me closer to sleep, and even though I know this means nothing, a little seed of hope blooms in my chest.

# CHAPTER FIVE

I wake up cold and alone, a little disoriented, but it doesn't take long for the memories of last night to hit me.

Oh, fuck my life. I cannot believe I fucked the twins.

This isn't going to be awkward at all. Nope.

I groan into Ellis' pillow, half regretting my choice, especially now that I'm waking up alone. But only half. Because holy sex on a stick, I was right, those two are just fucking fire.

I throw the sheets off of me, tiptoeing around the room looking for my clothes and phone, but the room is spotless.

What the actual fuck?

I find my phone on the dresser and send Scout an S.O.S.

Seconds later, there's a soft knock at the door and I squeak as I dive my naked ass back into bed seconds before it opens. Scout's grinning face pops through the gap before she shimmies in. "Ohhai, bestie. Have a fun night?"

"Shut up, Scout. You don't want to hear about your brothers' dicks."

She gags as she closes the door and I take the slight, wiping the smug look off her face. "No, I absolutely don't. Ellis is a bit of a neat freak, so your stuff is already in the washer. I brought you a pair of cutoffs and one of Ryker's t-shirts. Should be fine till your stuff is dry."

"Thank you," I sigh, going full grabby hands on her as she throws the clothes at me.

"Are you okay though? For reals? D told me what happened last night." Her eyes fill with concern and her brow furrows as she sits on the end of the bed.

I let out another sigh, but try to play it down. "I'm fine. Guy obviously had too much to drink and got grabby. It could've been worse if the twins hadn't stepped in, but they did. Honestly, I'm just trying not to think about it and move the fuck on."

"Some might say you found the best kind of distraction," she teases, and I wallop her with one of the pillows. "Fine, fine. I'm going to go start breakfast. Get dressed and come down. None of this hide away bullshit, you're a bad ass bitch and we don't hide from boys."

I have no idea how she knew exactly what was running through my head, but I nod, agreeing. She bounces from the bed before skipping from the room.

Man, I thought I was the peppy morning person. I climb from the bed and slip into the clothes she gave me, hating that I have no underwear. Ryker's t-shirt is fucking huge on me, it literally comes down to my knees, you'd never even know I had the shorts on. I consider tying a knot in it, but decide against it. I don't want to face his wrath if I fuck up his t-shirt.

I'm under no illusions that last night was anything more than just fuckery. Though I am still fully dickmatized, I'd happily just lay in bed all damn day, but that isn't what is in the cards. I need to eat and get home, because facing the twins is going to suck enough.

One night stands aren't usually my thing, and I'm not sure I can go back to seeing them hate on me after last night. At least not right away.

I run my fingers through my hair so it doesn't look like a total bird's nest, take a deep breath, then make my way downstairs to the kitchen. I find Scout cooking, with the twins and Dylan already at the table.

Yep, definitely wanting the ground to open up and swallow me whole.

"Morning, Short Stack," Dylan says with a grin, and I keep my eyes trained on him, trying to not look at the twins, because how the fuck am I supposed to navigate this?

I push down the swirling vortex of nerves inside of me and move further into the room. "Coffee?"

"Just finished the pot," Scout says. "All the crap is in there for a new one," she finishes, pointing at a cupboard.

Relief floods through me at having something to do rather than just sitting down at the table. I barely look at the twins while I wait, just scrolling through my phone instead, listening to the three of them talk about something that makes zero sense to me.

Scout is in a world of her own while she cooks, I learned that much the other night, so I leave her to it while I wait. She puts plates of eggs and bacon in front of the boys and with a chorus of thank you's, they dig in as she heads back to the stove.

"Just getting ours on now," she says and I nod, staying quiet so as not to draw attention to myself.

Once it's ready, I make myself a cup of coffee, sighing after my first sip of the joyous black liquid.

"See you later," Dylan announces, drawing my attention back to the boys. The three of them are standing, plates empty. They leave the room without a word or glance in my direction, and I don't know if that pisses me off or fills me with relief.

I'm erring toward being pissed off, because like, I was awkward and not saying hello, but like, at least look at me dammit.

"You okay?" Scout asks as I clear the table of their plates.

I shrug as I drop into one of the chairs. "Sure, it was just sex. I didn't exactly expect a one-eighty from them because we fucked."

"If you say so," she throws back as she sits opposite me, sliding a plate of food across the table.

We eat, talking about her plans for the weekend and the fact that school starts next week.

"Tuesday is going to suck," I sigh. I really am not looking forward to starting Echoes Cove Prep even a little.

"What's the worst that could happen? And if you really hate it, you can always transfer."

I groan, dropping my head onto my arms on the table, because whenever someone asks me that question, things always go to shit. "You just had to ask, didn't you."

---

After a fully awkward morning, I came home and went back to sleep, face down in my sheets because why the fuck not? My parents are away—shock, horror—and won't be back till next weekend, so there's no one to tell me not to.

It kind of sucks that they dropped me here in a new town with a new school I don't want to go to and just fucked off, but my parents can be a little flighty. I'm also not stupid enough to think this move was just about Dad's job. After everything that happened over winter break in the city… well, yeah, it makes sense that they'd want me far away from that place.

Doesn't mean I have to like it though. I was doing just fine after everything.

I bounce out of bed, opening my curtains to dispel that particularly twisty train of thought, and my phone pings.

**Sex God:**
*Want to come out to play ;)*

I blink down at my screen, trying not to laugh.

**Me:**
*Erm, who is this?*

**Sex God:**
*I think you know ;)*

**Me:**
*Apparently you're wrong. So bye.*

**Sex God:**
*I'm never wrong, Blue. Come open your door.*

Ellis? I burst out laughing at the thought of him putting himself in my phone under Sex God and rush to my closet. I pull on underwear, a pair of my own cutoffs, a Stone Royal tee that's all torn to shreds, and slip on my Cons before I bounce my way down the stairs.

I open the door with a smirk on my face and find Ellis Donovan standing in my doorway. "Sex God, huh?"

"Not wrong," he says cockily. "So, you want to come out and play?"

He wags his brows at me and I burst out laughing. This is not the Ellis Donovan I'm used to.

"Don't you have responsibilities that include ignoring my existence and pandering to your brothers?" I retort, and the smile drops from his face.

"Ryker is an ass, and when you came down this morning, you didn't seem like you wanted me to talk to you, so I left you alone. But then you left without saying goodbye and I decided I didn't like that. So I'm here."

I mull over his words. I *was* pretty icy this morning. Was he really just reading my cues and going with them?

Ugh, boys are so confusing.

"So, want to hang out?"

I take all of a second to consider it and decide, fuck it. "Sure, why not."

"Way to sound enthusiastic, Blue." He reaches out and tucks a strand of my blue hair behind my ear. Never in my life have I been called anything but Indi… yet, when he calls me Blue, it makes my heart flip-flop.

I roll my eyes at him. "You really want me to bounce on the spot with pompoms? Do I seem like the cheerleader type?"

His gaze runs over me and I squirm under it. "Not exactly, but damn… the thought of you in that tiny skirt."

I turn away from him and grab my bag and keys. "So where are we going?"

"Well that would be telling, now wouldn't it?"

I jump in his car and his music starts playing. State Champs' version of *Chicago Is So Two Years Ago* makes me smile and I sing along as he starts to drive. He takes my hand, placing it on the gearstick and intertwining his fingers with mine.

My heart goes all squishy again, and I try to tamp down the emotions that being around him elicits, but there is something about him that calls to me. I've never been so comfortable around a guy that I'm so attracted to. Nothing about him makes me nervous, the connection between us is just so… well, it seems too good to be true, and a part of me is terrified by the fact that he could shatter me.

That much I already know.

But I try to push the negative thoughts away. He's driving, oblivious to the twisty thoughts racing through my head, so I take a deep breath and he glances over at me. His smile could melt my freaking panties. "Come on, Blue. Let's go on an adventure."

---

“Caves? You want me to walk through caves?” I screech when he finishes dragging me through the forest, which I’d only entered with great reluctance. “I’m still not convinced that you’re not dragging me out here to murder me.”

He laughs again, which I guess if I was a serial killer, I’d laugh too. “I’m not going to murder you. I just wanted to show you my spot. There’s a reason this place is called Echoes Cove, now come on, Blue. Just trust me.”

“Said the spider to the fly,” I grumble, taking his hand and letting him lead me into the dark cavern. The temperature drops almost as soon as we enter and a shiver runs down my spine.

Yeah doesn’t seem ominous at all.

I lose track of how long it takes us to walk through, and we do so in almost complete silence while I focus on not slipping and falling, making an absolute ass of myself.

The sound of the ocean grows louder as the light starts to increase, but at this point, I’m so turned around, I wouldn’t be able to get back on my own if I tried.

“Nearly there,” Ellis says, making me jump at the break in the silence. He chuckles lowly at me, shaking his head. “Anyone would think you didn’t trust me, Blue.”

“Can you blame me?”

He pauses and turns to face me, half his face hidden in the shadows of the cave, and he looks every bit the dark avenging god I know he was last night. “I would never hurt you.”

I swear my tongue about doubles in size and I can’t speak. I can’t swallow. I can’t breathe.

He cups my jaw in his hand, stroking my cheek with his thumb. “That much you can trust, Blue.”

I nod because it’s about all I can do while trapped in his stare. He releases my chin and reclaims my hand. “Just a little further.”

Following him, still stunned stupid, I stay quiet and focus on the uneven terrain again. It’s only when the brightness grows that I look up and gasp.

“Welcome to my little piece of paradise.”

We’re in a little cove somewhere on the beach. The water is stunning and the cliffs go out so far on both sides that there’s no way in here but via the water or the cave we just walked through, and it’s so freaking peaceful.

“Ellis, this place is…” I trail off and he squeezes my hand.

“I know, I had a feeling you’d like it too. Come on,” he says, taking off his shoes. I follow suit and he leads me across the sand before dropping his backpack. He pulls out a blanket and lays it down, motioning for me to sit. He pulls out sandwiches, strawberries, a few bottles of mocha cold brew, and some chips.

I swear my heart squeezes in my chest. He must’ve pumped Scout for info, because even the sandwiches are my favorite: chicken and bacon ranch salad.

“Thank you,” I say quietly when he hands me a sandwich.

He grins over at me and winks. “This is just the start, Blue. Just wait and see.”

# CHAPTER SIX

After spending a dreamy day with Ellis at the beach yesterday, swimming in just our underwear, talking, and eating, I'm feeling good about tonight. The big end of summer blowout at the Donovans'. I'm a little nervous about Ryker, because well… he's Ryker, but I'm excited too.

I don't know what to expect, but I've been texting back and forth with Scout all day. She seems pretty excited too, so I'm taking my cues from her. Apparently a lot of the Kings will be there, but so will a ton of people from her school.

Doesn't help me come Tuesday, I'm still going to know absolutely no one over at prep, but I'm already embracing it. I don't *need* people at school. I didn't have them before. I've always been the outcast. Besides, now I have Scout.

Things are looking up.

I do another glance in the mirror, making sure my dress fits perfectly in all the right places. It's black with buckles, chains, and a pentagram for a neckline, but it's fucking stunning and entirely me.

I pair it with my favorite Docs, my bright blue hair redone this afternoon by a new stylist I found. Gracie might just be one of my new favorite people. Especially with the extensions she put in my hair. My locks now come down to my waist and I look like some sort of pop-punk princess.

Definitely a look I can live with.

I put in my skull drop earrings, slide on the matching ring, and nod. My eyeliner is on point, my lips are a dark purple, and I look hot as shit, if I do say so myself.

Grabbing my skull clutch bag that looks like it has brass knuckles for a handle, I slip in my lipstick, eyeliner, keys, and phone before heading out to the Wrangler.

Upside of the parentals having abandoned me is that I don't have to tell them where I'm going.

My speakers blare with Magnolia Park's *Feel Something* as I put the car in drive and head across town to the Donovans'. Scout told me to get there early, which I'm glad about because walking into a room full of people I don't know isn't exactly my idea of a good time.

Except when I get there at ten-thirty, there's already music playing and people everywhere.

I take a deep breath, trying not to curse Scout out for the heads up, but dammit. She said nobody would start arriving until like eleven.

I end up parking two streets away thanks to the sheer amount of cars, but I'm thankful for the cool night air as I head toward the house. The bodies spill through the front door and onto the lawn, but I ignore the looks and shouts, heading inside to find Scout instead.

I make my way straight to her room, but the door is locked, which makes total sense, so I text her instead.

**Me:**
*Where are you?*

**Scout:**
*Sorry! Meant to text, shit got crazy. I'm in the kitchen.*

I sigh and put my phone back in my bag. I could text Ellis, but he'll be with Ryker, so I figure sticking with Scout is the safer bet to start with.

I push through the masses of people to the kitchen and find Scout with Diego. I haven't seen much of her oldest brother, but there's no denying they're related. She's basically a smaller, prettier version of him.

To be fair, all four of them are so similar, what with the tan skin, dark hair, and dark eyes. They don't look like anyone else in town and it makes me wonder if they're actually from here. I already know their parents are gone, Scout told me as much, though she skirted the details, and I'm not about to pry with something that's obviously painful.

"Hey!" I shout when I reach them, the music isn't as loud in here, but it's not exactly quiet either. She wraps her arms around me in a hug.

"Sorry! I'm so glad you're here. Everything kind of started early with the boys inviting way more people than we expected."

Diego watches me closely, a weird smile on his face. "So you're the new friend. Nice to officially meet you."

"You too," I say with a nod.

"Come with me," he says, motioning with his head for me to follow him. I look to Scout, who looks as confused as I feel, but I shrug and follow him anyway.

He glances back to make sure I'm coming and leads me toward the basement.

I already know it's a bad idea, but he moves me to walk in front of him, his hands on my shoulders as we descend the stairs. At least I'll get to see Ellis.

We reach the bottom of the stairs and I'm kind of shocked. It just looks like a boys' game room; a pool table, huge tv with a few consoles set up, sofas. A few doors that go God only knows where, but it's not the gang leaders headquarters I envisioned.

Apparently I've watched too many movies.

Diego keeps his hands on my shoulders and turns me to face the far side of the room where I see the twins and Dylan. I move to step forward, but falter.

Dylan catches my eye and looks instantly apologetic. He looks over my shoulder and his face hardens again.

I turn to look at the twins and find both of them with tall, leggy girls in their laps. They're everything I'm not and the twins don't exactly look like they're having a bad time.

Ryker, I expected. He made it clear we were just a fuck. But Ellis… the girl is running her hand underneath his black tee, kissing his neck, and his head is tilted back, eyes closed.

"My brothers don't need a distraction like you," Diego says in my ear. "As you can see, they already have plenty of distractions. Superior ones. I suggest you get the hell out of this house before I make you regret having ever stepped inside Echoes Cove."

I blink, still shocked, wondering why this hurts so much. Ryker moves, and his gaze catches mine. He's as stony as normal until he glances behind me and sees his brother. A smile graces his face, but his eyes look like he's holding the rage of a thousand wildfires. He taps Ellis' leg and motions to me, but I don't want to wait and see his reaction to me seeing him.

It shouldn't hurt this bad.

We fucked

Had one date.

I'm obviously nothing to them.

So I step away from Diego and get the hell out of the basement, out of the house, and retreat back home.

The Donovans are nothing but trouble, and Diego is right.

They don't need me in their lives, and I sure as hell deserve better than this.

---

If I said I didn't cry myself to sleep last night I'd be lying. Usually I identify as a sparkly marshmallow, but today is not that day. I look like a puffy sad bear. I shut my phone off when I left the party last night, and I've spent the morning in my PJs moping, eating everything in sight, and wallowing.

Turns out I was right. Living in Echoes Cove is going to suck.

I flick through my watchlist for the hundredth time and settle on *How to Get Away with Murder*. It kinda suits my mood, and the drama is enough of a distraction from the image of Ellis last night.

For some reason, seeing Ryker didn't hurt so bad, but he never pretended I was anything to him. Ellis… well, I guess I read it wrong.

So much for never hurting me.

Fuck him. I don't need boys.

I certainly don't need ones wrapped up in as much chaos as they seem to be. Mostly, I'm sad that Scout probably just thinks I ditched her, but she's never allowed to be without a guard if she's out of the house, and I don't want to be anywhere near the boys.

Knowing what I know about Diego—which is admittedly very little—I have no doubt he could follow through on his threats with ease.

Banging at my front door makes me jump, moreso when my name starts being yelled too. Christ, the neighbors will call my parents and they'll never leave me alone again if I let this go on.

I haul ass to the door and yank it open, dodging Scout's fist as she tries to hammer the door again, not realizing my face is there instead.

"Oh. You answered. Hi." She looks sheepish while I look at her in disbelief. "You weren't answering your phone and you disappeared last night."

"Yeah, no shit. Diego made sure of it."

Her eyes go wide in shock. "Sorry, what?"

I let out a deep sigh and wave her into the house, closing the door behind her before padding back to the fort I made myself in the living room.

She sits in the recliner chair and glances around the room while I bury myself in my blanket pile. I give zero fucks about how pathetic I look. I'm allowed to wallow. I'm allowed to be sad and feel my feelings and fuck anyone who wants to judge it.

"So, what happened?" she asks, and I fill her in on what happened when Diego led me from the kitchen. She remains quiet while I tell her the saga, including my day with Ellis just to rub salt in my wounds, but it's the only way to make sure she gets it.

"God, my brothers are dicks. Like, we all know Ryker is, he doesn't ever try to be anything but the asshole we know he is. He owns that shit. But Diego was out of line. And Ellis… I'mma ram his balls down his throat."

I shake my head, redoing my ponytail. "There's no point. It's nothing. We were nothing. One date and a night of fuckery does not a commitment make. I'm just being butthurt. I'll deal."

She looks at me skeptically but doesn't contradict me.

"So, what's the plan? Diego warned you off the boys, does that mean you're ditching me too?" She tries her best not to look or sound hurt, but I catch it.

"No," I respond. "If I was ditching you I wouldn't have let you in. I just can't be at your house, and we're not going to the same school. I'm not sure how we'll hang out without your brothers tagging along."

She lets out a sigh and runs a hand through her hair. "D… Dylan. He's outside in the car. That's how. They trust him like he's a Donovan, and he won't snitch either. God, Diego is a jumped up asshole. I know he started all of this to protect us, to keep a roof over our heads… but damn. He can't keep dictating our lives."

"Does Dylan want to come in?" I ask, glancing out the window and seeing the guy in question leaning against their car. "It's hot as balls out there."

"Probably."

I nod and decide fuck it. I might have to avoid the twins, but Dylan seems nice enough. Even if he is annoying. "You go get him, I'll get ice cream."

She grins at me and jumps to her feet.

"Sounds like the perfect day before diving into the hell of sophomore year."

"Wait, you're a sophomore?" I ask, shocked.

"Yeah, me and the twins were all held back a year when our parents died. They're going into junior year when they should be seniors," she says before dipping out the front door to get Dylan.

Well, I guess every day is a school day.

---

Yesterday was much needed and it turns out Dylan really is hilarious. He even let Scout shave his hair into a mohawk and we dyed it blue to match mine. It was the most fun I've had in a while. They kept me distracted all day, which, considering how nervous I feel this morning, is much appreciated.

I think I'm going to vomit.

I keep glancing at my reflection in the mirror, hoping it changes. This uniform is fucking horrendous.

The skirt is black and white plaid, which comes with thigh-high socks and a starched white shirt. Along with them is a black and white neck scarf thing and a fitted black blazer, both embroidered with the school crest, which has accents of a teal green.

I look like a fucking pod person, and this skirt is criminally short.

I slip on the shoes that arrived by courier with it this morning, courtesy of my mom, and I feel gross. Freaking Mary Janes.

I've never felt less like myself in my entire life.

Stripping off the shirt, I put on my Nirvana tee underneath it and grab my messenger bag covered in band pins and patches. This, along with my blue hair, will have to be enough for me not to feel like a lizard person is invading my skin.

The moping continues as I make my way downstairs and grab a granola bar.

Today I need Starbucks and my floofie coffee. Nothing else is going to turn me back into the sparkly unicorn I know I am.

I scarf down the bar before heading out. God knows I have enough time to actually *enjoy* my breakfast, but it sits in my stomach like a lead weight.

Starting a new school fucking sucks.

I head to Starbucks and get my java chip, doing a small happy dance with the first sip before putting the school in the maps app on my phone.

It even looks pretentious on the map, but I try to reserve judgment and put the car in drive.

Before I know it, I'm pulling into the lot, and holy shit, I do not belong here. The parking lot screams money, and that's before I even take in the building. I pull the Jeep into an empty space and gawk at the school.

It looks like the type of school you see on TV, with the pale stone arch over the large main entry doors. The year the school was founded along with the school crest—a shield with a horse and swords, topped with a crown, surrounded by flora—is engraved at the apex of the arch. The red brick exterior is covered with ivy, and it screams money. It might only be a three-story building, but it's so fucking imposing.

Yeah, I really don't belong here.

Everyone I see looks like a fucking supermodel.

That's when I notice the dark god that is Lincoln Saint standing on the steps, along with two other guys and a bunch of girls. They look like they're holding court, and their minions hang onto their every word. Though all three of the guys look bored as fuck.

I grab my bag and jump out of the car, swinging the handle over my head, and clutch it like it's my fucking life line.

Avoiding those eight wannabe royals is absolutely top of my list. Every school has that clique, and I'm not stupid enough to think I fit with them.

I am not a main character. I barely manage sidekick.

Outcast is my place. I just need to find the others like me, and I'll be fine.

Lord fucking help me.

I almost manage to skirt around them without notice when I hear, "Blue!" called out and I freeze. I turn and find Lincoln's eyes on me. "Yeah, you, Punk Princess. Are you lost?"

Fuck my life.

"Nope, just heading to school."

His eyebrows rise as he looks me over. "You're coming here instead of public?"

"Looks like it," I snark back, and instantly regret it when what looks like the queen bee steps forward.

She's all platinum hair, giant boobs, and legs. She looks exactly like she belongs here, like she thrives on it. Her blue eyes are cold as they stare daggers at me.

"Who the fuck do you think you're talking to, reject?"

My mouth opens and then closes. I glance at Lincoln and he smirks, but walks away, leaving me to deal with Queen Barbie and her band of merry clones.

Awesome.

"You don't get to speak to me, whore. You don't belong here. You won't last the semester. I'll be surprised if you last the week."

I jut out my chin, hating the rising tide inside of me because I know I'm going to regret this encounter, but fuck it. Dad always said take out the top dog and less people will fuck with you.

"You have no idea who I am, or what I'm capable of. Maybe you should be more careful who the fuck you're talking to." The words come out sounding fiercer than I ever have, and I try to keep my face in check so the shock isn't so obvious.

She steps closer to me, so we're almost nose-to-nose, and my stomach twists. This was such a bad idea. Her cold, calculating smile sends a shiver down my spine, and when she laughs, my blood turns to ice in my veins.

"Welcome to Echoes Cove, reject. Let the games begin."

# ABOUT THE AUTHOR

Lily is a writer, dreamer, fur mom and serial killer, crime documentary addict.

She loves to write dark, reverse harem romance and characters who will shatter your heart. Characters who enjoy stomping on the pieces and then laugh before putting you back together again. And she definitely doesn't enjoy readers tears. Nope. Not even a little.

Visit her online:
www.lilywildhart.com

For exclusive content, freebies and giveaways every month.
www.lilywildhart.com/subscribe

# ALSO BY LILY WILDHART

**THE KNIGHTS OF ECHOES COVE**

*(Dark, Bully, High School RH Romance)*

Tormented Royal

Lost Royal

Caged Royal

Forever Royal

**

**THE SAINTS OF SERENITY FALLS**

*(Dark, Bully, Step Brother, College RH Romance)*

A Burn so Deep

A Revenge so Sweet

A Taste of Forever

**

**STANDALONES**

Rebel Heart - Coming 2023

*(Dark, Bully, High School RH Romance)*

The Secrets We Keep

(*Dark, Mafia, RH Romance*)

# ALSO BY SLOANE MURPHY

Lily Wildhart also writes dark, reverse harem, paranormal romance under the pen Sloane Murphy.

**THE SEVEN REALMS SAGA**

**THE SHADOW WALKERS SAGA**

*(Reverse Harem Paranormal Romance)*

A Crown of Blood and Bone

A Crown of Smoke and Ash

A Crown of Shadows and Secrets

A Crown of Thorns and Lies

A Crown of Fire and Wrath

A Crown of Pride and Ruin

**THE SHADOW WEAVERS SERIES**

*(Menage Paranormal Romance)*

Witch's Curse

Hunter's Heart

Demon's Blessing

**THE SHADOW QUEEN SERIES**

*(Reverse Harem Paranormal Romance)*

The Shadow Queen

**THE SHADOW LEGACIES I SERIES**

*(MF Rejected Mates Romance)*

Luna Rising

Alpha Bound

Alpha Born

***

**THE DARK FAE DUET**

*(Paranormal Romance. Dark Fantasy)*

Summer Princess

Winter King

***

**THE IMMORTAL CHRONICLES**

*(YA Paranormal Romance. Complete Series)*

Descent

Crash

Soar

Rapture